THE DRAGONRIDER HERITAGE

BOX SET

BOOKS 5-8

N
W
E
S
GAVRAL TUNDRA
WHITE WASTES
ETHALAN
ICEDRIFT SEA
WESTERN OCEAN
WHITECROWN MOUNTAINS
VORDEGA
HALONAR
DAM
VAAR

AVORA
FORRAN PLAINS
TIBRUS
HOLVRADIX
VOCRAN OCEAN
BRASKOL
NOLTHAM
ELONDIA
LUNTHARDA
MALDOBAR
ELONDRAN OCEAN
UTHERN SEA
RIENKA
NAR'HALEEN

Title and cover design by Covered by Nicole

Interior and Cover Illustrations by Kiki Moch Rizki

THE PANTHEON OF MALDOBAR

THE FOREGODS

God of Was: Itanus
God of Is: Enais
God of Still to Come: Milontos

THE OLD GODS

God of Earth: Giaus
Goddess of the Sky: Astaris
The Fates: Viepol

THE LESSER GODS

God of Life & Nature: Paligno
Goddess of Death & Decay: Clysiros
Goddess of the Sea: Undae
Goddess of the Moon: Adiana
Goddess of Mischief: Iskoli
God of War: Proleus
Goddess of Love: Eno
God of Luck: Tykeron
God of Mercy: Ishaleon

SOJOURNER

THE DRAGONRIDER HERITAGE
BOOK FIVE

PROLOGUE

"Bad. So bad. This is a *really* bad idea, Zuri," the boy whimpered. With a frame as tall, thin, and knobby as an oak sapling, he followed along behind a much shorter girl and gripped the back of her robes so he didn't lose track of her in the gloom. His teeth chattered as his hasty, panicked breaths made the wide, round lenses of his spectacles fog up in the cool cavern air.

Ahead, the light from the candle made the shadows on the crudely cut halls dance and waver as they shuffled along. "We shouldn't be here. It's not allowed. The High Inquisitor is going to—"

"Oh, come on, Clarke. It'll be fine! You'll see," the young girl urged as she forged ahead, navigating the twisting stone tunnel by candlelight. "You're still having those nightmares, aren't you?"

Clarke swallowed thickly, his head swimming a bit at the thought. "Y-Yes," he confessed weakly.

"Then it's time to get answers! High Inquisitor Bellavora still won't tell you anything, right? But she definitely knows *something*. That means she's keeping it a secret on purpose, and I'd bet that whatever these dreams are about has something to do with what's in that book. We're going to find it. You're going to read it. And then maybe we will finally get to the bottom of what's really going on with you."

Clarke nodded as he staggered along behind her, unable to match the confident grin Zuri cast him over her shoulder. She'd always been far surer of herself than he had ever been—something Clarke privately envied. It was embarrassing, honestly. Where he was a lanky sixteen-year-old, she was only nine, half his size, and yet she never faltered in the face of anything mysterious or dangerous.

Clarke was ... not like that. He didn't remember when, exactly, he'd become such a coward, though. Maybe after he'd accidentally memorized the entire History of the Divine Arcanum texts when he was six years old? Hmm. Probably. After all, that was when he had first realized two very important things. First, that divine magic was incredibly dangerous to mortals like them. Second, that no matter what he did, he couldn't seem to forget a single word from any of those massive old tomes, even though some of them were written in ancient Avoran—a language he hadn't even realized he understood.

A language that, according to High Inquisitor Bellavora, no one had spoken in Damaria or Nar'Haleen in thousands of years.

After that, no one in the Compendium Library had treated him the same. The scholars and archivists regarded him with a hushed reverence that felt cold and distant, as though they saw him as a rare artifact that they both admired and feared. The other wardlings of the library, orphaned or unwanted children like him who had been abandoned at the library to be raised by its keepers, kept their distance, too. But their hushed whispers and prickly glares were more jealous than afraid, almost as though they thought he was just doing these things to suck up and get into the good graces of the scholars.

Well, all except for Zuri. She had arrived at the library in much the same way all the other wardlings had before her. A mysterious robed figure dropped her off as a wailing toddler, leaving her to the care of the Compendium's many scholars. She had taken a liking to him right away, and Clarke had to admit that it was nice to, once again, have someone who actually wanted to be around him—even if she was still in diapers and drooling like a baby goblin at the time. Now, thankfully, she had grown out of all that.

Too bad Clarke hadn't grown out of his own ... problem. A problem that had started out so small and innocent, but now had grown into a strange and terrifying habit of memorizing *everything* he read, even if he didn't mean to. If anything, it had only grown worse over the years. Now, it wasn't just words he could recall with perfect accuracy. Maps, diagrams, images, constellations, and even conversations he had heard all seemed to burn themselves into his brain before he could stop them. With every month, it seemed to intensify. And at the same time, it made his head throb like his skull was a basket being filled with stones until it threatened to rip apart. Even his dreams had been invaded by echoing voices and whispers that seemed to come from the vast collection of books, scrolls, and texts stored within the library's countless caverns that spanned through and deep into the cliff-side like an anthill. It was as though the pages called out to him, pleading for his attention.

And one tome in particular was loudest of all ...

Honestly, Clarke wasn't sure how much more his brain could take. It felt like one more word might make his head explode. And while High Inquisitor Bellavora wouldn't admit it, he could read the deep, worried lines in her expression as plainly as he could the lines of ancient texts he sometimes deciphered for her. She seemed to know that there was something powerfully wrong with him. But if she understood what it was, or had any ideas about why he'd come upon this strange ability, the High Inquisitor had not dared to breathe a single word of it. She warned him to be careful. To find time to rest. To nurture his mind with joyful, normal things that couldn't be found in the pages of books.

Easier said than done when the books spoke to him even in his sleep.

He trundled along after Zuri, still gripping her cloak and hunching over as the cavern's ceiling sloped lower and lower. His thick mop of unruly white hair stuck to the sweat beading on his brow, neck, and cheeks as he glanced around, flinching away from every strange whisper that hissed from the shadows—things he knew Zuri couldn't hear. No one else heard the tomes speak the way he did.

"There!" Zuri whispered excitedly, pointing ahead to a place where the tunnel opened up to a small chamber.

The ceiling was a bit higher inside, but Clarke stayed bent and scuttled along behind his much younger companion as she stepped inside. She quickly lit the torches resting in iron sconces around the circular room, offering a view of the heaps of books, papers, and dusty scrolls littering the floor. The shifting light of the flames made the shadows dance and waver as Clarke eyed each pile, a hard knot forming in the pit of his stomach. He couldn't help but search, listening for the source of that particular whisper. The tome that had been so loud in his dreams.

The one that had been calling him here for months.

"Is it any of these?" Zuri asked, leaving him standing alone in the center of the room as she went to peruse a few of the crumbling wooden bookshelves that had been shoved into various corners of the chamber. Most of them were so loaded down with texts that they looked like they might buckle and collapse into a pile of splinters at any moment.

Clarke shook his head, making his shock-white hair swish over his brow.

"But you're sure the voice was coming from this direction?" she pressed, her cherubic features scrunched with worry as she turned back to stare at him.

"I-I ... I think so, yes." He scratched at the back of his neck, shifting his weight as his eyes darted around the chamber.

Lock and Key ... The gate shall hold ...

Clarke froze, his gaze fixed upon one of the crooked, sagging bookshelves on the far side of the chamber as the whisper filled his mind like a cold spike. His hands shook at his sides, and his mouth hung open as he gasped in fast, shallow breaths. That voice curled and flexed in his mind like a serpent in a net, straining and trying to burst free.

"There," he managed to wheeze hoarsely as he raised a trembling finger to the shelf. "It's there."

Zuri glanced between him and the shelf, confused. "Are you sure? Clarke, that shelf is nothing but maps. I checked it already."

"NO!" he shouted, surging for it so suddenly it made Zuri stagger back with a yelp of alarm. "It's there! I can hear it! It's right there—it has to be!"

He hit the shelf like a charging bull, grabbing fistfuls of ancient maps and delicate scrolls and ripping them out of the way. He cleared one shelf at a time, raking the contents of the bookshelf onto the floor in a frenzy as his heart hammered like a booming war drum.

The boundary of Fates ... And Souls ...

Closer. He was getting closer. He had to be. It was so much louder now.

"Clarke," Zuri whimpered from behind him. "What's going on?"

He saw it. Hidden at the back of the middle shelf, tucked behind all that clutter, a small, silver symbol was leafed into the old wood. The shape of an eye with a vertical pupil.

The Dragon's Eye.

The Eye of the Fates.

Clarke's vision swam, seeming to spiral in and out of focus as though the room were spinning around him ... save for that one mark. It never moved. Never wavered. His heartbeat skipped as he reached out to brush his fingers over it, and the symbol sparked to life. It glowed and pulsed with light, seeming to match the racing rhythm of his pulse.

Click!

The bookcase flinched, shifted, and slowly swung inward on creaking ancient hinges.

Zuri let out a gasp, and he could barely feel her hand close around his as she curled against his side like she wanted to hide. "What is that?" she whispered shakily.

Straight ahead, Clarke's gaze focused with that same unfaltering intensity on the only object sitting in the small, darkened room beyond the bookcase. A large book was held aloft by a black iron pedestal shaped like a tangle of thorny briar vines. The silver Dragon's

Eye leafed onto the black leather cover shone in the light of Zuri's torch like it had been painted in pure starlight.

Clarke moved forward—closer to it, leaving Zuri hesitating in the doorway. His pulse stirred with every step. A dribble of something warm oozed from his nose and dripped down his chin. Blood?

"Um, Clarke, I ... I think we should go," Zuri called out suddenly, her tone hushed and panicked. "I hear something! I-I think someone's coming this way!"

He didn't stop. Another step. Then another. With each one, the voice became louder. Clearer. Stronger.

Blood and blade ... And twisting spark ...

"Clarke! Something's wrong! I-I think something's happening in the archives!" Zuri grabbed his shoulder as though trying to break his focus. "Someone is screaming! What are you doing? We have to run!"

His hand stretched forward, reaching for the mark upon the black leather cover as everything else around him seemed to grow distant. Every sound a dull, muffled rumble, like he'd stuffed his ears full of cotton.

A smell like smoke hit his nose and made him hesitate just as his fingertips brushed the surface of the book. Warm. It was warm and thrumming with something like a pulse of energy.

As though it were alive.

Before he could even consider it, his body moved as though pulled by some unseen force. He slid his spectacles down his nose, just far enough that he could gaze over the lenses and down at the book. Immediately, the rush of the whisper became louder as though he'd stepped out from behind a magical barrier. It set his mind ablaze. Pain surged through his head, searing along his scalp and making him choke out and gasp for air.

Too much—it was too much!

He had to make it stop!

"CLARKE!!"

Everything dimmed, growing dark and distant around him—all except for that symbol. That tome. The thorny metal pedestal seemed to writhe, as though it were coming to life just to relinquish the book to him. The weight settled into his hands like the bulk of an anchor. His knees buckled, and the dark rushed in like a roaring ocean tide.

Down—Oh, Gods! He was falling deeper, sinking down so far. Too far. The depths were endless nothing, smothering and complete.

Save for that whisper.

To fracture ... Break ... And rend apart.

PART ONE

REIGH

I

CHAPTER ONE

"Get pressure on that wound! He has to be fully stabilized for transport!" I shouted over the ambient rattle, clash, and roar of combat that filled the jungle around us. Sweat ran down the sides of my face, seeping into the already damp padding of my helmet. My chest heaved for deep, ragged breaths that made the glass eye-slit on my helmet fog up in the thick, humid air. My body burned, every muscle set ablaze by a rush of adrenaline.

Before me, three other dragonriders huddled around the form of one of our own—a rider already shot down and badly wounded. He lay motionless on the jungle floor, his bronze armor smudged with crimson in various places. Not moving. Not making a sound.

"Hurry it up! They're on approach, coming in for pickup!" I roared as I stood back, my twin curved kafki blades gripped tight in my hands. My gaze cut skyward, beyond the nearly interwoven arms of the massive trees to the patches of blue sky beyond. Two massive, dark shapes blurred by, momentarily blotting out the shafts of light that fell around us like beams of radiant gold mist. Curse it—they were early. We had to get this done.

"He's stabilized," one of the riders attending to our downed comrade shouted. One of *my* students. She looked up, her eyes wide but focused through her own helmet's eye-slit. "We're ready! Bring them down!"

Another of our group darted back, pulling a cylindrical glass vial filled with a thick red liquid from her belt and smashing it against the ground. Immediately, scarlet smoke boiled up from the shattered vial, billowing upward into the air and giving away our location. She turned to give the rest of us a few hurried signs in the dragonrider hand-code, letting us know to brace for our transport's landing.

Like the rest of us in this small group, her helmet, pauldrons, and breastplate had been painted with the design of a red eagle—Maldobar's eagle—with its wings spread wide against a white circular background. That symbol was ours, the insignia for our small band, and it was unique from any other flight in the entire dragonrider service. We were Red Flight, and we had only one purpose on the battlefield: to rescue and evacuate as many injured dragonriders and soldiers as possible, moving them to a safe location where medics could hopefully implement life-saving treatments.

Hopefully being the key word there.

We were smaller than the other dragonrider flights, with only six members in all, and we didn't wear the traditional blue dragonrider cloaks trimmed in white fox fur that the rest of our brothers-at-arms did. Well, not in battle, anyway. Our cloaks were also white, bearing that same red eagle on the back, with a blue trim around the border. It made us easier for our own ranks to spot, which was sort of the whole point. We weren't made for stealth or tactical assault maneuvers. We were meant to be the white banner of mercy on a field of hellfire and blood.

And today, that mission was being put to the test. Gods and Fates, I just hoped we didn't screw this up big time.

Our plume of smoke drifted upward, seeping past the canopy of trees and into the sky. So far, so good. A little off schedule, but still within range to be effective. We were going to pull this off. I guess the Fates were smiling on us today.

"Inbound!" I shouted, quickly sheathing my blades and throwing my arms wide in a gesture for the rest of my company to fan out and clear the area. I backed up as the trees around us began to groan under the forceful wind bursting off of powerful wings.

SMASH!

A huge, scaly body dove through the limbs, snapping them like dry reeds. A muscular yellow and blue dragoness touched down, snapping her jaws and snarling around at us with jagged fangs dripping with crackling, smoldering venom. She crouched low, ears slicked back as the knight in full battle armor sitting astride her saddle gave her cues. He wore the same ensemble, the marks of Red Flight emblazoned on his armor and rippling white cloak, and motioned to the rest of us to begin the process of loading our patient onto his much larger, specially-designed saddle. It wasn't sleek and streamlined for aerial combat maneuvers. Instead, it had been crafted to make carrying additional passengers—*wounded* ones, in particular—as easy and safe as possible. It fit much farther down the dragon's back, with a small frame built in where we could secure the medical stretcher with a series of thick straps and metal clips.

"Go, go, go!" I shouted after the three riders around me, urging them on as they picked up our patient and carried him on the stretcher toward the dragon. The device clicked into place flawlessly, and it took less than five seconds for them to have him tied down and ready for departure.

My eyes instinctively darted over the patient, criticizing their work. They'd done a good job of immobilizing him, stabilizing his head, neck, and back to minimize further trauma. But would it be enough? Would taking off through those trees be too dangerous? Too late to consider that now. We had no other alternative for a departure point.

"Stand clear!" I stood back, seizing one of the other riders by the back of his cloak and dragging him along as I stepped a little farther away. We gave the dragoness as much space as the jungle would allow as she rose up, unfurled her powerful wings, and prepared to take flight.

The rider on her back gave me one final hand-signal. *"Ready for departure."*

"Go safely," I signaled back.

With a few powerful strokes of those mighty wings, her claws digging through the wooden trunks of the trees, and a booming roar, the dragoness kicked off from the trees and launched skyward. I watched, scrutinizing every wing beat until she disappeared above the treetops.

Decent.

Relief washed through my brain, making it easier for me to suck in one deep breath. But that was it. No time to celebrate. This wasn't over yet.

And we couldn't stand around here for one more second and wait on someone else to notice our red smoke bomb. It was a good signal to call in our aerial comrades, yes, but it also made us a big juicy target.

"Pack it up, we have to move! Right now, people!" I barked sharply.

It didn't take them ten seconds to have all our gear packed away into bags again. All four of us formed up, taking positions with me at the lead of the group. I led the way back into the fray, onward into denser jungle ahead. Just the feel of my feet squishing into the moist earth made every one of my senses draw as tight as harp strings. I picked my way easily through the familiar shapes of massive ferns and snaking vines as thick around as my leg, immediately drawn back into that mentality that Kiran had hammered into my brain when he trained me to be a scout in Luntharda.

Everything about this place—the smell of the rich, loamy soil and the feel of the moss-covered tree trunks under my palms—reminded me of that jungle where I'd grown up. My old home.

Sometimes, it felt like it had been my only home.

Ugh. No. I couldn't get carried away in those thoughts. Not now. Not after years of work, planning, and training that had all boiled down to this.

Forward. I had to keep my focus, my will, pointed ahead. Don't look back. Don't think about what was. Push it down, lock it away, and don't touch it again. The past was a poison I wouldn't allow myself to sip on today.

The here and now—that's where I had to stay.

"Lieutenant Reigh, look!" One of the riders following along at my side drew his bow back, assuming a flawless aiming stance into the thickets ahead. The flash of a thousand mirror-like scales zipping soundlessly through the lush, green undergrowth made my body lock up.

A shrike.

This far inland, it was probably wild. Wild, hungry, curious about all the chaos we were stirring up, and undoubtedly not hunting alone. Shrikes always preferred to move in packs.

Not a good combination, even on a good day when I wasn't surrounded by a group of jumpy avians trying to make it through their final battle scenario exam.

I bared my teeth as my hands darted to the hilts of my blades. "Spore-tipped arrows only," I ordered quietly as I took a careful, smooth step forward. "Remember your training. Hold your fire until my signal, then ... give it everything you've got."

SEVEN LONG, SWEATY, AND FRANTIC HOURS LATER, I SLID OFF MY DRAGON'S BACK AND hit the ground back safely within the boundary of Blybrig Academy. Finally. Another year over, another batch of candidates for my Red Flight program now approved to carry out their duty in real combat. And this mission's success was even more substantial, because it now meant we had enough graduates to send to each of the four watches, so that a Red Flight could be fully staffed at each one.

I should have been relieved. Satisfied, even. That was the culmination of basically my entire career as a dragonrider, so far. But my body burned and ached, tender around a few places where old scars still didn't like the constant pressure of my gear and armor. My back was especially tender after a full day of lugging around all the emergency treatment supplies. Maybe I could see about adding some additional padding there for next year.

Ugh. Just the thought of it—another *year* of this—made my head throb under my sweat-filled helmet, and my arms and shoulders feel like battered blocks of lead.

To be fair, it had been *fourteen* years since I had first set foot in the dragonrider academy. That was fourteen years of living primarily out of a canvas bag, wearing heavy armor every day, and having to hide from students just to get to eat a meal in peace. They were relentless, and followed me around or lurked outside my room or office, ready to hound me for last-minute test answers or stories from the glory days of the Tibran War.

Because that's exactly what I wanted to do in my downtime—relive some of the most horrifying moments of my entire life in front of a bunch of eighteen-year-old students. They didn't understand that, of course. How could they? These students were growing up in a peaceful world that I and many other dragonriders had fought and bled to give to them. In their minds, war had now become a faraway and historical thing you could read about or play training games to prepare for. But did they really *get* what kind of blood-soaked pandemonium we were preparing them to potentially survive in? Hard to say sometimes.

My sleek green dragoness, Vexi, craned her neck as I walked around to her other side. She chirped musically, her blue eyes watching my every move as she bumped me with her snout. "Good work today, girl," I sighed and gave her strong, sloping neck a few pats.

She snuffled through my sweaty clothes and filthy armor as though she were assessing me for damage. Or searching me for treats. Probably a bit of both.

"You kept all those young drakes in line pretty well, didn't you?" I chuckled as I unbuckled all my bags of gear from her saddle. Each one hit the sandy earth with a *thunk*.

Vexi gave a blasting snort of approval and stretched out on her belly, beginning to preen the scales on her wing arms while I worked at unfastening her saddle. We had a little time off now that the battle scenario was over. Might as well give her a break from her gear, too.

"You both did," a deep, familiar voice spoke up from behind me.

I rolled my eyes and smirked to myself. I didn't even have to turn around to tell who it was. "Don't you have a debrief with Jaevid to get to?"

"Don't you?" Murdoc countered. He came to stand next to me, his sharp eyes silently appraising me like a wolf on the hunt. I'd gotten used to it over the years, though. It wasn't personal. He looked at everyone like that—as though he were mentally calculating how fast he could disarm and kill them, if he had to. Chalk that up to being raised and trained for most of his life by the world's most dangerous league of secret assassins. Honestly, as long as he kept using that look to scare the crap out of his fledgling and avian students during combat training, I'd never complain.

"And here I was hoping he'd postpone that until after the holiday," I groaned as I slid Vexi's saddle off her back. She murred and grumbled happily, rubbing her head against my back to mark me with her scent like an overgrown, fire-breathing housecat. She stood up and stretched, shaking herself and beginning to sniff the night air—probably looking for her favorite nesting buddies to settle in with for the night.

I guess of the two of us, she was much more content here.

"I don't know about you, but I'm not prepared to sit through anyone's critique of my work until I've had a bath and at least three ales," I said.

"As if the esteemed Academy Commander would ever allow such laziness," Murdoc laughed darkly.

"He was a lot more fun before he had kids." I clicked my tongue thoughtfully. "Come to think of it, so was Jenna. And now I'm trying to imagine just how obnoxious you'll be after Phoebe has this baby. Gods preserve me. I need to change careers now, before it's too late. Maybe I could try being a baker ... or a pig herder. Wrangling fledglings seems like it would be good experience for that line of work."

Murdoc's expression was about as consoling as watching a viper smile. We had all aged some. Grown up, I guess. But his features had only become sharper and more intense. He wore a short, dark beard and kept his black hair cut up neat and short. Being out in the light of the blistering desert sun had tanned his skin to a much darker hue and put deep lines in the corners of his smoldering hazel eyes. "You honestly think Jaevid would let you walk away from this?" he said.

No, I absolutely did not think that. Not even for a second. But that didn't mean a guy couldn't dream, right? I'd been lukewarm about this dragonrider path from the start. I did love being with Vexi, flying with her, and keeping my hands deftly tuned to the hilt of a blade. That was a perishable skill, after all, and I was discovering daily that being in my early thirties was the point at which my already tired and battle-torn body looked for any excuse to be sore and stiff. Fantastic.

But once again, I felt like I was settling into a rhythm that wasn't my own. I hadn't fit into the harmony of life in Lunthardа as a scout and healer at Kiran's clinic, or at the castle with my royal family playing the part of the dutiful youngest prince. Now I didn't know if I should even keep trying to find that right fit. Maybe there wasn't one for me, and I should just be content right where I was. I, Reigh Farrow, would always be that jagged, unruly piece that didn't quite fit.

"Phoebe wanted me to ask if there were any more adjustments you needed for the evacuation saddle," Murdoc muttered, as though he could sense my general frustration. Or he'd just given up on me giving him an answer.

I shook my head. "Nope. This model is working perfectly. The students seem to be able to work with it much more easily than before, and I didn't see any malfunctions on takeoff. I haven't gone to assess the damage to it afterward, though. That's my next stop, I guess." I sighed and finally pulled off my helmet, tossing it onto the mounds of discarded gear at my feet.

The rush of cool, late evening air to my sweat-drenched hair made me take in another deep, reclaiming breath. I raked my fingers through my bangs, pushing them out of my face so I could massage my forehead and temples. It had grown out some, almost reaching my shoulders. I'd have to cut it back soon, if only to get it off my neck.

Murdoc bent down and began helping me gather up all my stuff. "Good. Now she'll want me to ask if that's really true or if you're just saying that because you don't want to make a pregnant woman work."

I snorted and flicked him a teasing glance as I threw two of my bags over my shoulders and steadied the weight. "Then you're my witness. Come on. Last time those avians couldn't get Thatcher out of the stretcher and he wound up lying there for two hours until I came in to check and see how they were doing."

"He volunteered to be one of your rescue victims again?" Murdoc arched a brow curiously.

"I think he just didn't want to have to go stomping around through the Canrack jungle again. Last time he got into a patch of snarethistle and I was pulling briars out of his face and hair until past midnight."

"Sounds about right," he laughed again. "Well, at least it wasn't greevwood spores again."

"I'd have preferred that over the briars, honestly. He's a grown man and he still cringes like a little kid." I led the way toward the massive, multistory barn where all the dragons and our bags of gear were kept within the boundary of the academy. It wasn't nearly as big and luxurious as the one that stood on the castle grounds in the royal city of Halfax, but it functioned well and the students were in charge of keeping everything clean and orderly. That meant all I had to do was dump my stuff in the door and yell at a fledgling to take care of it. Easy.

"Some things never change," Murdoc murmured, letting his arm bump against mine in what was probably his attempt at a passive, friendly gesture. I guess he was still working at all that normal friendship stuff, even this far out from his time among the Ulfrangar. Thatcher had helped him along, considerably. Those two were still inseparable. Er, well, most of the time.

Murdoc being married to Phoebe now had changed things up some, but only when we were away from Blybrig Academy. As long as we were within these walls, those two kept up their same old antics. And for whatever reason, they still insisted on dragging me along, too. Murdoc the former assassin of the notorious Ulfrangar, Thatcher the Godling of Mercy, and me—the wayward prince who couldn't seem to get his life figured out. The recipe for chaos no one had asked for ... just waiting for the next world-ending disaster.

I just hadn't expected to find it standing outside the barn's entrance, dressed in a long traveling cloak, with glittering scarlet eyes and a cattish grin of amusement peeking out from under the hood.

2

CHAPTER TWO

My heart hit the pit of my stomach like I had swallowed a cold river rock. All the feeling seemed to seep away from my extremities as I watched her step forward from the shadows to meet us. Gods and Fates, how long had it been? Ten years? More? Why—why would she come here now? What could that man possibly want from us?!

"Now, now. Don't look so excited, Your Highness," Violet cooed as she stared me down. "Someone might accidentally assume you're happy to see me."

For the record, I was *not* happy to see her—or any of Arlan the Kinslayer's agents—roaming the grounds of Blybrig Academy. Not even a little.

As soon as she spoke up, Murdoc and I froze and exchanged a meaningful, silent sideways look. Neither one of us had to say it out loud. There wasn't a single good reason why she would sneak her way into this place. This meant trouble.

And she was one false move away from being pinned between our blades. Violet was extremely skilled as a fighter, true. But so were we. And we had her outnumbered on home turf.

"You've got about three seconds to explain yourself," I growled through my teeth, my heartbeat kicking like a bucking mule in my chest.

"I'll only need two," she quipped, brushing back her hood to reveal her beautiful, heart-shaped face. Her hair fell in long, smooth bolts of pale blonde down to her waist that shone silver in the failing light. "*He* would like a private audience with you, Jaevid, and the godling boy at the holiday ball in Halfax to discuss ... urgent matters."

I arched an eyebrow. *Urgent matters?* What the heck was that supposed to mean? I glanced to Murdoc again, hoping he had some clue as to what she was talking about, but his gaze had gone all squinty and suspicious. Hmm. Apparently not.

"What matters?" I demanded. "What is this about?"

"I'm not at liberty to say," she replied coolly, her scarlet eyes darting over me from head to foot as though she were studying me carefully. Then another taunting, coy smile spread over her lips. "And besides, it would take longer than three seconds to explain."

I bit back a curse and reached for the hilt of my blade, but she clicked her tongue and waggled a finger disapprovingly.

"Honestly, when have I ever given you cause for that?" She frowned and slowly shook her head. "Behave yourself, little prince. Now isn't the time to choose enemies carelessly."

"Go, then. You've done your duty and delivered the message. Consider it noted. But you know Jaevid Broadfeather won't tolerate Kinslayer's meddling in this place," Murdoc warned, somehow managing to sound a lot more cool, composed, and supremely admonishing than I did. Ugh. I had to work my delivery.

And my temper, I guess. I still had issues with that ...

"Take care what you say and to whom," She cast him a quick, reproachful glare before nodding and stepping toward us. "No one must know of this meeting, so I trust you'll be discreet. That goes for your direct family members as well. For your safety and that of everyone, there must be no evidence at all that anything is amiss. Surely you reckless lot can manage that much?"

The lengths of her long, black silken cloak brushed at my leg as she cruised past, moving with all the effortless grace of a shark twisting through the shallows. Violet pulled her hood up as she went by, and I could have sworn I saw her wink in my direction.

I didn't react. Nope. Not even going there. She'd always enjoyed toying with me, for whatever reason, and even if she was alarmingly attractive ... I knew better than to take a bite out of greevwood fruit or try petting beautiful vipers. Reciprocating that little flirty game with her was basically the same thing. Dangerous. Probably deadly.

And I was in no state to go chasing that kind of trouble.

I didn't turn to watch her leave. I didn't want to know how she'd managed to slip past the dragonriders who were supposed to be keeping watch over the fortress walls. Figuring it out would probably only make me furious, and I'd spent enough time yelling at people today. She would leave without hurting anyone—I felt reasonably sure about that. Violet was slippery and dangerous, but she wasn't stupid. She hadn't come here to kick the proverbial hornet's nest, and I doubted her boss would approve of her causing that kind of a spectacle. It would be lousy for his "secret criminal lord" image.

Murdoc must have known that as well, because he didn't move to watch her go, either. He just bowed his head and gave a deep, resigned sigh. "Go ahead and see if you can get Jaevid to excuse everyone else so we can talk. I'll go get Thatcher and meet you there."

"You know what he's going to say as well as I do," I murmured.

Murdoc's tone was as empty as it was exhausted. "Yeah. I do. But it's not like we have a choice now, right?"

I nodded to myself. One way or another, I'd be repacking my bags and heading for Halfax soon. So much for a bath and a drink. "Try to put on a happy face, if you can manage it. We don't want the students getting suspicious," I reminded him as I started for the administration building on the far side of the compound. Jaevid would almost certainly be there, poring over paperwork or holding meetings with some of the other instructors in his office as usual. Poor guy still didn't know how to take a break and relax.

And I was about to wreck his entire day.

"YOU KNOW WHAT THIS MEANS, REIGH," JAEVID SAID QUIETLY. SITTING BEHIND HIS broad wooden desk, leaning forward with his elbows resting on the stacks of papers piled onto its surface, he stared at me with his sharp, half-elven features drawn into a look of controlled horror. Like it was taking everything he had not to have a complete meltdown and start throwing things. Or sobbing. Not that I'd ever known Jaevid to be the crying sort, but this situation was enough to make even a hardened soldier buckle.

Just the thought of dealing with Arlan the Kinslayer again, getting caught back up into his web of criminal dealings, made my stomach turn. I swallowed back the urge to gag as I bobbed my head once. "Yeah, Jae. I do. But what choice do we have? It's been quiet for, what, ten years now? We knew, sooner or later, he'd come to call. We owe him a favor, and he's not the kind of person who just lets that go. He's going to want to collect."

Jaevid put his face in his hands. "The question is ... how? What could he possibly want from us?" He groaned something under his breath, but his voice was muffled by his hands so I couldn't make it out. Probably had some elven swears tossed in, though. "What am I supposed to tell Beckah? She's less than two months from her due date, and the midwife insists it is twins this time."

In spite of the awfulness, I couldn't hold back a sly grin. "You guys must really hate sleeping at night."

He shot me a weary glare from between his fingers. "Believe it or not, it's not the little ones that have us losing sleep these days."

I leaned back, getting more comfortable in the chair across from his desk and crossing my arms. "Maylea is still giving you all forms of grief, eh?"

His eyes disappeared behind his fingers again. "She doesn't listen to a word either of us say. She's headstrong and clever, exactly like her mother. And needlessly reckless like her father. I keep expecting to look up and find you or Murdoc dragging her in here by her collar after discovering she's snuck her way into the ranks of fledglings."

"I didn't think she had a dragon of her own, yet." Last I'd heard, Jae was insisting on keeping her away from all this until she was older.

Heh. As if he actually had any control over that.

"No, but I'm not an idiot, Reigh," he groaned quietly. "She's got two accomplished dragonriders for parents, and Thatcher—curse him—keeps bringing hatchlings over from the Cromwell estate when he visits. Sometimes I think he's actually conspiring to make sure she's chosen. Regardless, it's only a matter of time."

"So? What's wrong with letting her find a dragon and attend?" I reasoned. "She's plenty skilled enough as a fighter. You, Jace, Murdoc, and I have been teaching her to duel practically since she could walk. Beckah has taught her how to use a bow as well as any Lunthardan scout I've ever seen. She could probably best any seasoned lieutenant in our ranks."

"Because she is *fourteen* years old, Reigh. She has no idea what the real world is like. Everything she's been taught about fighting and combat has been from behind the safety of dueling people who don't actually want to hurt her. Don't pretend that doesn't make a difference," he argued, using that fatherly voice that made him seem a lot older—even if he barely had two years on me. "For her, swordplay is still a game. She's never witnessed real violence or death. I know she could manage well here. I'm acutely aware of her skill. But more than that, I know her innocence when it comes to the true evils of the world. When she is old enough to decide for herself if this is the path she truly wants, then I'll be more than happy to have her attend. But right now, the monsters from our bedtime stories are the only ones she has ever known."

"If Kinslayer is moving pawns again, that could all change very quickly." I flinched as Murdoc suddenly spoke up from the doorway. He had a way of doing that—of slipping around without making a sound. It still gave me a little thrill of panic sometimes. Creepy former-assassin stuff.

"I know," Jaevid admitted. Sitting straight again, he motioned for everyone to gather in closer to his desk. "Lock the door, would you?"

Murdoc strode in with Thatcher right on his heels, still wearing that crimson-smeared bronze armor from our battle scenario training. He flashed me a crooked, roguish smile and ruffled his hand through his now shorter styled, but still corn silk-colored hair. Granted, the roots of it were getting a little darker, and it fell around his lightly stubble-flecked jaw rather than being tied back in a little ponytail anymore. But of the four of us, he seemed to be the only one who had grown *up* without growing old.

Towering at well over six feet now, puberty had eventually caught up with Thatcher Renley shortly after he'd survived our years in the dragonrider academy as students. He'd shot up, filled out, and lost that mushy, baby face that had made him look like a little kid. Now, his features were much more squared and sturdy, and his frame was stockier than mine or Murdoc's—which I found personally unfair considering how much more time I'd spent behind a blade.

Ugh. Stupid baby-faced kid. It didn't matter how tall or muscular he got, he was still an airhead who'd happily walk off the edge of a cliff while chasing a butterfly.

"We have to play this carefully," Murdoc advised as he took a seat next to me. "Whatever Kinslayer is plotting, we have to assume we are only a small part of it. The fact that he is reaching out now, after so long in silence, means there must already be something else happening—something we aren't even aware of. That agent he sent was adamant that we maintain utmost secrecy."

"All the more reason to send word to Jace," Jaevid muttered. "Perhaps his network has noticed something."

"Too bad Judan is still in the wind." Thatcher stayed standing, his arms crossed over his broad breastplate as he stared down at the floor with a thoughtful frown. "He always did have a nose for this sort of thing. Jace still won't talk about it? There had to have been a falling out or something to make him just vanish like this without telling anyone."

"No. And believe me, I've pressured him. Jace is better than most at keeping secrets. Even Phoebe has tried to contact him several times, but he never responds. It's been about six years since we last heard anything from him. I'm not confident he's even in Maldobar anymore at all," Murdoc said quietly.

"We can't count on him to be of any help in this," Jaevid resolved, lacing his fingers together and staring between us with his pale eyes sharp and his jaw set in determination. "What we can count on is each other. Whatever happens next, we need to close ranks. We'll grant Arlan's wish and keep this quiet to everyone outside this room, even friends and family. But we must not withhold anything from one another. We don't know what Arlan is going to want from us, but if he intends to ask about it personally at the holiday ball, then it must be serious. We only have a few days to prepare. So, gentlemen, let's make this time count."

3

CHAPTER THREE

"Oh no. No, no, no! I can't find my—crap—has anyone seen my socks?!" I briefly caught a glimpse of a panicked Thatcher-shaped blur in the mirror as he darted behind me.

"No one's been wearing your clothes but you," Murdoc grumbled from where he reclined casually on a velvet sofa, legs crossed and eyes closed. He was already fully dressed in his ceremonial dragonrider armor, complete with a long royal blue cloak trimmed in white fox fur at the collar. Of the three of us, he was the only one ready to walk out the door.

But I wasn't far behind.

"You better not make us late," I sighed as I leaned in closer, scrutinizing my reflection and checking one last time for any smudges on my ornamental breastplate. Finally. Not a hair out of place. I had achieved the perfect veneer of I've-got-my-life-figured-out princeliness. Now maybe my sister, Queen Jenna of Maldobar, wouldn't give me the stink eye when she spotted me in the ballrooms tonight. This was her biggest celebration of the year, after all. This was the holiday to mark the official end of the Tibran War and Maldobar's great victory over Argonox. She wouldn't stand for anyone to mess it up. She also knew I hated these kinds of parties. But such was the struggle of noble life—a revolving circus of ridiculous fancy parties, military meetings, political visits, tactical dinners with foreign ambassadors, and swimming in a sea of curious glances and hushed whispers from the commonfolk every time I left the castle.

Completely exhausting on every level imaginable.

I couldn't deny that had been a huge motivating force behind devoting nearly all of my life to the dragonrider academy. It gave me a safe place to hide from all that. But I couldn't stay there indefinitely. And now, standing on the eve of a meeting with one of my least favorite people in the world, I had no choice but to come out of hiding.

"He won't make us late. He's had days to make sure he had the right socks for this," Murdoc retorted. "He can go sock-less."

"No, I can't," Thatcher growled back as he made another frantic pass through the common lounge room that connected our three suites. "I'll have blisters the size of dinner plates by the end of the night. I won't be able to walk right for weeks."

"Well, pain is the only way you learn anything, so ..." Murdoc finally opened his eyes and lifted his head when I walked by to grab my own cloak and buckle it onto my shoulder pauldrons. For this occasion, I'd decided to go with the traditional dragonrider blue one, rather than the white one I used for my service as a member of Red Flight. I wasn't up to fielding questions about that tonight—not with other, more important things to worry about. "You look sulkier than usual. Something got you worried? Apart from the obvious, of course."

"No. Just ready to get this over with," I muttered. "I hate this—this calm before the storm."

Murdoc arched an eyebrow, clearly not buying that. He didn't push it, though, thank the gods.

I turned around and almost crashed right into Thatcher, who despite now standing several inches taller than me, still managed to look like a pouting little kid as he looked down at me mournfully. He had grown a lot, sure. I had to admit, he was somewhat less pathetic now, but his personality hadn't changed much.

He was still about as aggressive as a freshly picked tulip, even as an officially oathed in dragonrider.

"Can I borrow a pair of your socks?" he started to beg. "Please, Reigh! I must have left them in my other boots, and I can't go the entire ball without—"

"Fiiine," I groaned. "You're an idiot, you know that?"

"Yes, yes, you've all told me a thousand times," he called as he darted off for my bedchamber where he would undoubtedly wreck all my neatly folded gear and clothing while looking for a single pair of socks.

Ugggh.

"I'm gonna head down there," I said, giving Murdoc a sideways glance. "In case my sister wants a word beforehand."

He nodded, but that dubious expression that made one of his eyebrows lift and his mouth set in a hard line didn't budge. "Try not to let anything slip to her. The last thing we need is a bunch of royal guards fumbling around and making things complicated."

I flicked him a glare and didn't answer. All this time, and he still talked down to me like that as though I had no idea how to handle myself.

I left the spacious suite in the wing of the castle that Aubren and I still shared. Uh, well, sort of. We might have shared it, if either of us spent much time here now. I was usually away at Blybrig, and my elder brother kept himself very busy with the infantry and running around to various foreign kingdoms as my sister's trusted ambassador.

Now, this place felt more like a visit to someone else's home than a return to my own. I didn't keep my personal belongings in my chambers anymore. I usually carried that sort of stuff with me. I didn't have any pets that would miss me. No ladies to write to. No friends apart from this batch of idiots I'd been zooming around the kingdom with for so long.

There wasn't much at all that tethered me here, so it was easy to feel like a visitor or a stranger as I started down to the grand hall of the royal castle. I'd gotten used to the typical layout of massive noble estates around the kingdom. They weren't that different from one to another, even if each family boasted theirs was the grandest or the most unique of all. The elements seemed to all be similar. Big rooms. Massive halls with polished marble floors and lofty painted ceilings. Mahogany paneling on walls lined with oil portraits in gilded frames. Nothing out of the ordinary here, either. This was the royal castle, yes, but it was still built in the same style. The Maldobarian style, that is.

I made my way alone, passing courtyards, ballrooms, and halls that were all richly adorned in wreaths of flowers, flickering candles, and drapes of gold and royal blue. I ducked past crowds of guests already gathering to join in lively conversations and debates. I didn't have time or patience for pleasantries tonight. That was half the reason I'd chosen to leave alone, ahead of the others. I was less likely to draw attention if I moved around on my own instead of with a bunch of extremely well-known war heroes and officers.

The other half of the reason was ... exhausting, frankly.

In keeping with Maldobar's tradition, all the prominent officers from the infantry and dragonrider ranks had come to attend this grand, celebratory ball. It was meant to be a night full of wine, music, conversation, and dancing as we mingled with the nobility and our comrades and told our battle stories to a captive audience. And for most people, that's exactly what it was.

But *I* wasn't most people.

I was a dragonrider, yes. I'd graduated from Blybrig Academy alongside Murdoc and Thatcher years ago. Unlike them, however, I was also a Prince of Maldobar. More dangerously, I was an *unattached* Prince of Maldobar. I didn't have a wife. No fiancée. No one on my arm at all. And for a guy like me, that was about the most precarious position someone could be in. Just the thought made me shudder.

I knew I'd spend the evening dodging noble mothers who insisted on shoving their appropriately mortified daughters into my path so I would notice them. I'd have to stand there and force a smile while they gave me a not-so-subtle salesman's pitch about why their daughter would make the perfect addition to my powerful royal family. It was about as much fun as being set loose into a pen filled with ravenous wolves with a big fat steak tied around my neck.

Most of the time, I could duck away with an excuse. But that didn't work every time—especially if Jenna was anywhere nearby. She'd give me that smoldering glare of warning from across the ballroom. I was supposed to behave myself. Be courteous. Act appropriate. After all, if this was some kind of elaborate social performance, we were the stars. We had to put on a good show.

Even if it was excruciating in every way imaginable. I couldn't afford to be a spectacle tonight. I had to keep my head down. I had to wait for our cue, and fortify my mind in every way possible for what came next.

After all, a meeting with Arlan the Kinslayer wasn't something you just waltzed into unprepared. We didn't know what he wanted, and all Jae's efforts to discreetly ferret out a sense of what had brought this on had proven useless. Now, our only option was to keep on our toes. Guard up. Eyes open. Braced for anything.

Prepared for the worst.

Standing on the edge of the ballroom, I tucked myself back into a corner behind a particularly large sculpture as far possible. Hidden? No, not exactly. But maybe if I was very still, they'd mistake me for a sculpture, too.

A guy could hope, anyway.

After several hours, the holiday ball was in full swing, and I had managed to dodge all but two invitations to dance. Not that I disliked dancing. If anything I was indifferent to it. But knowing it came with an obligatory conversation from a partner I didn't know and who definitely wanted to marry me because I was royalty was ... uncomfortable.

Apart from that, everything seemed to be going swimmingly. Wine was flowing, couples were dancing, and the air was filled with that all-too-familiar roar of excited conversation, laughter, and music. Everywhere I looked, ladies in glittering ball gowns hung on the arms of infantry officers and dragonriders in gleaming ceremonial armor. Servants passed with silver trays adorned with glasses of wine and spirits. Food was served on long tables at the far corner of the room. Nothing out of the ordinary for an event like this.

No sign of any shady activity, at all.

Until someone nudged me with an elbow.

I glanced over, gaping silently as my father stood casually beside me with that signature half-smirk of his that some accused me of replicating from time to time. They all said I looked a lot like him. Well, except for the hair.

"You look a heartbeat away from throwing yourself out a window," he mused, scratching at his thick white beard as he turned his gaze back out to the ballroom before us. He wore the years a lot more harshly now that he was in his early seventies. Sometimes, it was hard to picture him standing next to Jaevid when they were the same age, dueling monstrous evils and bargaining with gods. Then again, I'd done my fair share of that, as well. Getting tangled up in the affairs of the gods always left a mark, even if it wasn't obvious. Jaevid had endured a forty-year divine slumber, so he hadn't aged like my father.

Mentally, though, I doubted anyone could slip anything past the great Felix Farrow. "Now, I happen to know for a fact that they throw even grander parties than this in Luntharda, so you can't tell me it's because you're not used to it," he laughed hoarsely.

"No," I admitted. "It's just at those kinds of events, people usually aren't stalking me like a band of trophy hunters tracking a faundra stag."

He laughed louder and clapped a large hand onto my back so hard it made me stumble. Even if he was aging, looking more and more like a bent old man with each passing month, he still had a strength to him I had to admire. Chalk that up to his past as a dragonrider, as well. It was one thing we did have in common, even if the rest of our relationship had always been ... well, awkward at best.

I didn't have any hard feelings toward my father. Felix Farrow, the former King of Maldobar, Duke of Solhelm, and lifelong best friend of Jaevid Broadfeather, was a figure anyone would've been fortunate to call their dad. But growing up separated from the rest of my blood relatives, hidden away in Luntharda thanks to my birthright as the Harbinger of Clysiros, had thrown things into chaos the second I was born. It'd taken a brutal war, some backhanded deals with gods, and no shortage of divine miracles to rectify all that.

And through it all, I'd wanted nothing more than to find my biological family again. Not that I'd suffered for being raised in Luntharda, but I guess I'd sort of hoped that reuniting with them would give me a sense of identity I'd craved all my life—a purpose and place in life that was undeniably mine.

Yeah. Well, it hadn't quite worked out that way. On the surface, I knew I had everything I'd ever said I wanted. A family. A home. A purpose within the academy, equipping a future generation of dragonriders to be better than we had ever been. A place that my bloodline was tied to. So why did I still feel so ... lost? Drifting. Empty. Directionless.

I didn't know, and saying that out loud to anyone felt even worse. Like I was just some whiny little kid who wasn't happy with every gift he'd just gotten on his birthday. My soul wanted—*needed*—more. Of what, I didn't know, but I couldn't shake that hunger no matter what I did or where I went.

Something inside me was still broken. Maybe it always would be.

"If you're in need of another dance partner, I'm sure I can arrange something," my father suggested, grinning wolfishly.

I sighed loud enough he would definitely hear it. "Why are you even here for this? Aren't you retired?"

His grin widened. "From parties? Never."

I crossed my arms, assuming what was probably a very similar stance to his as I watched another group of finely dressed guests assemble on the ballroom floor before us just as a new song began. "Oh, but saving the kingdom, fighting monsters, bartering with gods—that's all no longer your problem, right?"

"Exactly."

I rolled my eyes. Typical. I didn't have much of a relationship with my father—mostly because every encounter we had felt stranger than the one before it. But I knew him well enough now to identify his quirks. And avoiding work had become one of his finer skills in his old age. Not that I expected him to take up a blade, but he could've made more of an effort, right? Ugggh. Whatever.

I grumbled under my breath and looked away. "Yeah, well Jaevid did his share, you know. Jace, too, and he's older than you ..."

My father gave a dismissing flap of his hand. "I *do* know, actually. But unlike Jaevid, I didn't get to just pop out of a magical forty-year-long nap still as sprightly as a teenager. Some of us have bad knees and mysterious intermittent back pains now."

"And Jace?"

He snorted like that should have been obvious. "I think we can all agree he runs on pure spite and stubbornness ... neither of which I have."

Hmm. Fair point.

"You seem to be well on your way to achieving both, however," he added. His expression was a bit sharper as he flashed me another sideways glance. "Don't think I haven't noticed my youngest child's indifference to the absolute joy of being a hero twice-over in a room full of lovely admirers and comrades."

I looked away. "It's not indifference."

"Then what is it? Still nursing some heartbreak over that little elven woman? That was quite a while ago. Maybe it's time you finally let that go, son."

Wow. Well, he didn't mince words, I had to grant him that.

My mouth scrunched as a little ember of anger sparked to life deep in my chest at the thought of her. "Enyo had her reasons for ending things. I'm well past it."

My father gave another deep chuckle. "Fates, I hope that the future of our world never hangs on your ability to lie, boy."

Okay. Fine. I wasn't *completely* over it. But that didn't mean he had to sling it in my face right here in the middle of the ball. If this was his way of chasing me out of this corner so I'd go dance and fraternize, he'd only been partially successful.

"I need a drink," I growled through my teeth as I stepped away and made for the nearest balcony offset from the grand central ballroom. It was only a half-fib, though. I did need a drink—but I wanted some fresh air to go with it.

Snatching a goblet of wine off a passing servant's tray on my way out, I downed the glass in one swallow on my way to the long, sheer drapes that separated the broad marble balcony from the rest of the ballroom. I couldn't help but cringe as the warm, thick, somewhat bitter drink burned down my throat all the way to my stomach. It left my face feeling hot as I stepped out into the cool night wind, replaying my father's words in my head over and over again.

Of course, I still had feelings about how things had ended with Enyo all those years. What did he expect? She and I had only been together for, what, close to a year? And even so, all indications had pointed to me eventually proposing and making her a Princess of Maldobar. My princess.

But I'd apparently misread something crucial along the way.

Now I was here, just like everyone wanted.

I just couldn't understand ... why.

As I stepped outside, the moonlight washed over the figure of a woman already standing out on the balcony before me, her back turned and her sweeping gown draped over her lithely muscular frame like a sheet of blood red silk. Now there was a style you didn't see often outside Luntharda. Maldobarian fashions were much more modest. A gown like that, clinging so close at her hips and thighs before flaring out to pool on the ground behind her, made for interesting shadows around her form—things I probably shouldn't spend too long staring at.

Prince or not, that was a great way to get slapped.

I stopped cold and the woman slowly turned around, her eyes shimmering in the same vibrant, scarlet hue as her gown when she smiled. My stomach gave a frantic lurch. Crap. I'd know that cunning grin anywhere.

4

CHAPTER FOUR

Violet wore a smile like a rose wore thorns. Something about it was always sharp and potentially lethal. Great. This couldn't be a good sign if she was here already. Was she singling me out? Was this it—the time to go and meet Arlan?

Cocking her hips to one side, Violet crossed her arms and clicked her tongue disapprovingly. "*Tsk tsk*. If it isn't my favorite little prince. Slinking away from a ball in the middle of the festivities, are we? How scandalous."

I sank into my heels. No point in leaving now. She'd probably follow just out of spite. So instead, I trudged past her, wandering over to lean against the stone railing. "I'm not slinking anywhere," I muttered. "It's too loud in there."

"Clearly. I must be imagining that look of wary dread in your eyes, then," she laughed. Her black glass heels clicked over the marble as she followed and sidled up to the railing right next to me. With her back to the rail, she tossed her long white-blonde hair away from her shoulders and sighed. "Don't worry. He isn't here yet. I'll let you know when it's time."

Right. Sure, she would. I worked my jaw to one side and angled my face away.

She didn't let it go, though, and leaned around to keep staring at me. "What's the matter? Don't tell me you're not enjoying this lavish affair. Do fancy cakes, expensive wine, and giggles of admiring young ladies not agree with you?"

"Not really, no." I gave her a once-over glance out of the corner of my eye. Not to admire her or anything—sweet Fates, no—but I was curious just how many weapons she'd managed to sneak past the guards manning the doors in a dress like that. Hmmm. Not to mention, how had she gotten an invitation in the first place? Unless Kinslayer had pulled some strings ...

Who was I kidding—of course he had. That was practically his sole mission in life.

"Are you here with someone?" The question slipped out before I could stop it. Fates, curse it. That sounded totally—

"Why? Jealous?" Her smirk was incorrigible.

"*No*," I snapped quickly. Too quickly, maybe, because she giggled and flapped a hand at me.

"A grown man, a prince, and a dragonrider and yet you're so easily ruffled. It's adorable." Violet's smile faded and she picked at her nails. "Rest easy, little prince. I came alone. I am merely here to take note of a few things until it's time to send you all on your way. Nothing more."

I narrowed my eyes. *Take note?* What did that even mean? I opened my mouth to ask but she spoke up first.

"I'm surprised to find you here unattached. Seems you go everywhere with the esteemed ambassador of Nar'Haleen these days." Her tone had the faintest traces of a suggestive edge. "Did you not invite her to be your date this evening?"

Great. Not this again.

I sagged against the railing and hung my head. "Isandri and I are *friends*. We've always been friends. That's it," I muttered. "Why does everyone always assume we're together?"

"Because you usually are," Violet snickered.

"Yeah, well, she's also a priestess—a holy woman. She's not allowed to marry or ... anything like that," I explained for what must have been the ten-thousandth time. Why did everyone automatically assume we were a couple? She was my good friend, yes. I trusted her before nearly everyone else. But we had never been like *that*. I didn't keep track of her movements. Yes, she wrote to me fairly often. I tried to write back when I could. But that was about the limit of our interactions these days.

"Is she, though? Technically, she's a goddess, right? And I assume a goddess can do whatever she pleases," Violet countered. "Maybe it's just that the *closeness* of someone else frightens you."

I frowned down at the gardens that stretched out below the balcony. No point in arguing. She just wanted to get under my skin. Or in my head, I guess. Either way, I couldn't let her get to me.

"I understand, though. It's important to have those people in your life you know you can always rely on." Violet's expression softened as she looked away, the wind catching in her long platinum hair. "Truth be told, I'm quite impressed by her. She's adapted well to life in the court and gives good counsel on interactions with the nobility of Nar'Haleen. Their social structure is so different from Maldobar's ... I'm glad Her Majesty is so open-minded to learn."

No kidding. In the past, Maldobar had been a lot less involved in international affairs. Our trade market had been good, sure, but Maldobar had always preferred to focus inward—more specifically, on fortifying its military strength. That had always been the pride of the kingdom, since we were the only place in the world with wild dragons.

But we couldn't afford to continue on with that mindset.

"After what happened with the Tibran Empire, Jenna's on a mission to make sure communication stays open between all the kingdoms," I said.

"And what of the Tibrans?" Violet asked, looking convincingly distracted with her nails again. "Have they still sent no word to your sister? No ambassadors? No mysterious messengers from afar?"

Ahh. There it was. The real reason she was needling me like this. She wanted to know if my sister had divulged anything secret and useful to me.

"I'm guessing that's what you're here to 'take notes' about, eh?" I snorted and shook my head. "Sorry, but you're fresh out of luck. I don't get invited to *those* kinds of meetings anymore, and it's not something anyone talks about around the family dinner table—on the rare occasion I'm actually here to sit at it."

She flashed me a look, blinking quickly like she was shocked. "I didn't come here to question you, Reigh. Honestly, it was just a bit of personal curiosity. I'm certain my employer already knows those things. Gathering the information flowing through the royal court isn't my area of expertise."

I crossed my arms and faced her. "What is, then?"

She hesitated, her ruby-colored eyes holding my gaze for a quick, reluctant moment. "My eyes are ordered to stay watchful over a few divinely-touched individuals. One in particular, tonight."

My heart gave a little jolt. Wow. She was ... actually telling me the truth? Why? "You're talking about Thatcher, right?"

Her lips pursed sourly. "Not very discreet, are you?"

"Not at all." I smirked. "But then again, I'm not the one working as a slimy little snitch for a crime lord."

She tossed more of her hair over her slender shoulder and turned away, tilting her chin up stubbornly. "Well, then. So much for trying to be friendly. Enjoy your evening, I'll be in touch when my employer is ready to speak with you."

Ugggh. Why? Why did it always go like this? No matter who I tried to talk to, nothing seemed to come out right. I never knew what to say. And what I did say was usually taken the wrong way, or much more seriously than I intended. Somehow, I wound up looking like the same mouthy jerk I'd always been.

I didn't like her, sure, but I didn't ... you know, despise her. I didn't have a specific reason to other than her job, which I knew almost nothing about when it came to specifics. But in the little I'd interacted with her before this, she had been a lot more forthcoming and helpful than I expected from someone who worked for the most notorious crime lord in the world.

I at least owed her a small amount of civility.

As Violet sidestepped around me to leave the balcony, I reached out and grasped her arm. Tugging her gently to a halt, I tried to give her an earnest look so maybe she'd know I wasn't trying to insult her or pick a fight. "H-Hey, uh. Look, I ... I crossed a line. Sorry."

She lifted a brow, looking wholly unimpressed. "You might consider working on that princely apology of yours. It's a tad clunky." Her gaze flickered between my face and where I still lightly grasped her arm right above her elbow.

Oops. Maybe I should step back and—

"Dance with me, then," she said as though it were some kind of challenge.

"Dance?" Why the heck would she want to dance with me? Wasn't that a little risky for someone who was supposed to be an undercover agent?

One corner of her mouth curled into that annoying little smug grin again. "That would be a much more appropriate gesture of apology. You do know how, don't you? I know you were raised as a commoner in Luntharda, so please don't be embarrassed if it's still a bit ... beyond your ability."

Um. What?

No. No way was I going to stand there and take that kind of abuse. I tightened my grip on her arm and tugged her in a little closer as I leaned down to whisper, "I guess you'll find out, won't you?"

No one would ever accuse me of being a fantastic dancer. I knew how, of course. Well, sort of. I could get by without completely humiliating myself, though. Good enough.

Violet didn't seem to care about my actual dancing abilities whatsoever as we moved fluidly around the ballroom, spinning and swaying in sync with the other couples around us. Every now and then I caught a fleeting glimpse of a group of nobles gaping at us as we passed. They whispered and stared, probably wondering who Violet was. That revealing red gown of hers was going to get us both in trouble at this rate.

Somehow, the smug little grin on her lips made me wonder if that hadn't been her plan all along—to scandalize my reputation and stir up the nobility with whispers of some mystery affair with an unknown foreign woman so my sister gave me a good tongue lashing later?

Yep. Sounded about right. Well played.

"It's customary to make conversation while dancing, you know," she teased as she leaned in to rest her wrist lazily on my shoulder. Ugh. Yet another subtle, familiar gesture that would get the nobles talking. They'd be stirred up like pigeons around a freshly thrown bread crust.

"I guess I'm not too skilled when it comes to casual conversation," I sighed and flicked my gaze away, barely catching sight of Jaevid standing with Thatcher and Murdoc at the buffet table. He nearly dropped his wine goblet when he saw me.

Well, at least I had his attention.

"Clearly," Violet jabbed and gave my ear a flick, like someone scolding a naughty child. "It's been a while since we spoke at all, hasn't it? Since that little errand with your nephew, I believe. So, how goes that project you've been working on? Starting a medical group within the dragonrider ranks, I believe it was?"

"Yeah. It's going as well as it can, I guess," I said, not really sure why she cared about any of that at all. Maybe she didn't and she was just patronizing me—but, hey, she was the one who insisted on talking at all. "We've sent the newest batch of graduates on their way, and I've already gotten a dozen more applications from the upcoming avian ranks to begin their intensive healer's training with Kiran. Not all of the ones who volunteer are actually cut out for it, though. Kiran puts them through some intense disqualifying challenges to see who can really stomach dealing with serious injuries when they evacuate wounded riders off the battlefield. Every dragonrider gets a little basic medical instruction already—mostly self-rescue stuff in case you're injured in battle. That's been a part of the curriculum for decades. But this training takes them far beyond that, making members capable of stabilizing the gravely injured and getting them to safety."

"Interesting," she tilted her head to the side, watching me closely with those eerie scarlet eyes. Strange. I wonder how that had happened, exactly. I'd never seen anyone with eyes like that before, and it'd never seemed like a good time to ask her about it.

"Why?" I held her gaze for as long as I could manage it, trying to detect any signs of deception as I asked, "Is this something Arlan has an interest in?"

Her lips pursed unhappily, like I was spoiling the whole moment. "No, but *I* do."

I frowned. What? She was interested in ...? No. Nope. This was some sort of ploy. Yet another mind game.

No way was she just casually interested in *my* life. Like a friend or something. Heh. Yeah, right. I must finally be losing my mind. I had met her only a handful of times. Four—maybe five—at the most, over the course of the last ten-or-so years. I'd first met her when Arlan helped my sister with my nephew, Ronan. He had a particular and deeply troubling condition that, unfortunately, I could relate to. After that, I'd caught glimpses of her moving through events like this. The annual officer's ball. Gatherings at court. She came and went like a midnight shadow, and sometimes approached to taunt me a little. That did not make us buddies.

Acquaintances, yes.

Friends, absolutely not.

"It's a surprisingly noble cause you've chosen to pursue. And I hear you've invested a lot of your time and energy into it. I just wondered if it's all come together the way you'd hoped," she continued, her tone casual as she stared up at me. She didn't seem to care much that I didn't look back at her, though.

Not that she was, you know, bad to look at. But eye contact had become sort of difficult for me after all these years. I didn't really even understand why. It just was. It felt like trust, somehow. And trust hadn't gotten any easier for me, even with people like Isandri or Jaevid, who I counted as my closest friends.

"It's rarer than you realize, Your Highness," she mused with a knowing grin. "Being drawn to a cause that requires so much from you but gives nothing in return. Especially amongst those members of society who are provided more opportunities than the rest of us."

Hmm. That almost sounded like the truth. But it probably wasn't. Spies weren't exactly renowned for their honesty, right? I couldn't afford to let my guard down.

"Fine. Fair enough. I wouldn't call it noble, though. It was an obvious need. And I'm in a unique position to provide a solution." I swallowed, trying to shake off that stiff discomfort in the back of my throat. "As long as we're discussing work, did you really come here just to check in on Thatcher? Godling status aside, he's still got Murdoc glowering over his shoulder most of the time. Er, well, under his shoulder, I suppose. Regardless, I don't think there's a soul alive in Maldobar brave enough to try to do anything to him at this point."

"I do hope you're correct." Her smile was thin and never quite reached her eyes. "I've been in my current line of work for twenty years now. I know my employer well. Or, at least, I thought I did. But he's been more ..." she hesitated, as though struggling to find the right word.

"Anxious?" I asked. "Paranoid?"

Violet didn't answer aloud, but her lips thinned into a tense little frown as she looked away, out across the ballroom, almost like she was checking to see if anyone suspicious was watching us.

Ahh. Okay. So she was here on orders from Arlan to keep an eye on Thatcher because something—Gods only knew what—had him on edge.

Well now, I didn't like the sound of that one single, tiny, minuscule bit. Arlan was by far the most powerful and well-connected sorcerer I had ever seen. He held power I hadn't even imagined was possible. I wasn't sure if that was because of his powerful Avoran Elf blood or not, but if something or someone had Arlan the Kinslayer nervous, then I shuddered to think what that might mean for the rest of us.

Bad things, to say the very least.

As our dance slowly came to an end, I stood back and offered Violet the usual formal bow, as was expected in courtly dances. At least, according to my sister, anyway. Instead of returning it with the customary curtsy, however, Violet stepped in and grasped the back of my neck, pulling me down closer. Her entire expression had gone cool and calculating, almost like her mind had suddenly swapped over to a different personality altogether. She stood up on her toes long enough to press her lips against my cheek right next to my ear.

My whole head went hot like someone had just doused my hair in dragon venom and lit it on fire. What the heck was she doing?!

She held me there, her grip on my neck firm and relentless, and whispered quickly, "Jaevid and the others are watching us. Signal to them to follow from a distance. It's time."

Oh ... Oh, crap. It was time to go and meet Arlan? I must have missed something—some cue she'd been waiting for.

"Now," she said through her teeth as she stepped back and offered me a painfully forced smile. "Take my hand and guide me off the dance floor. Walk me to the main hall. Take the stairs to the second floor."

I moved in, fixing her with a hard stare as I took her hand and guided it into the crook of my elbow. "And where are we going exactly?"

She didn't even look my way, somehow managing to speak without even moving her lips as she kept on smiling widely out across the ballroom. "To your chambers. He's waiting. Hurry now, we don't have much time. And, if you can manage, try to look a little less miserable, would you? We don't want to make the general public suspicious now, do we?"

PART TWO

MAYLEA

5

CHAPTER FIVE

Whew. Okay. This was it. Fourteen years of training had all boiled down to tonight. Fine, so maybe not all fourteen, but most of them. I'd had a blade or a bow in my hands practically since birth. So, really, how could anyone be surprised that I—Maylea Broadfeather, daughter of the famous lapiloque and Seraph—was not content to sit here in this room with a bunch of little kids and rot while everyone else got to have a good time. Who saw that coming, right?

Besides, I had a mission. Somewhere in this huge castle, my very best childhood friend was probably locked away somewhere. That's the only reason I could come up with that I hadn't seen him in six years. Tonight, though, I was going to find him—even if that meant I had to sneak out and search room by room.

I slipped out of bed, easing my feet onto the cool marble floor. Carefully ... carefully. No noise. No wrong steps. I couldn't afford to mess this up now. Otherwise, I'd wind up spending the whole night watching the maids chase my two little brothers around like someone trying to catch a pair of wild cats.

No way. Not again.

Not that it wasn't hilarious to watch, but I had already seen that particular performance many times. Daily, in fact, since my parents spent a lot of time doing the same thing at home. Our housekeeper, Navalie, usually helped out as much as she could—but we weren't anywhere near our family estate tonight.

For the next few days, we were staying at the royal castle for what was always the biggest celebration in the entire kingdom. It was the party everyone talked about and looked forward to all year, even more than the solstice or midwinter holidays. Every spring, my parents dressed in their finest clothes, packed up our family into our nicest carriage, and made the journey from our home outside Solhelm all the way down to the royal city of Halfax to join in the festivities.

But more importantly, it was my one chance all year to look for *him*. It had been so long, I wasn't sure Ronan would even remember me if he saw me now. Hopefully. Otherwise, this was going to be seriously awkward—because there was absolutely *no way* I was going to spend yet another year caged up in this room with the little kids. I had a plan. I had the skills to finally pull it off. I just needed this chance to get out there and search.

I cringed, holding my breath as I carried my boots and made a dash across my room. I leaned against the wall right next to the bedroom door and stopped, holding my breath to listen. As far as my parents knew, I was determined to stay locked up in here sulking for the rest of the night. I'd put on a pretty good performance for them earlier—teary eyes, shouting about not getting to dance, the whole childish show. Acting wasn't one of my finer skills, but I was pretty sure it had been enough to convince them I wouldn't be setting foot outside this room for the rest of the evening. Er, well, maybe.

Fates, I hoped so.

I set my jaw as I crouched down, moving as slowly and carefully as possible. Beyond the door, the voices of my parents still echoed in the main room. But they wouldn't stick around for much longer. It was well past sunset, and the ball downstairs was sure to be underway by now.

I held my breath as I peered through the keyhole, checking to see if they were leaving yet.

Beyond my bedroom door, I spotted my father's tall frame standing before my mother's much shorter figure while she adjusted the fur collar of his cloak and smoothed down a few locks of his hair. He stared down at her, admiration in every corner of the gentle smile that made the long scar over one of his eyes crinkle at his cheek.

"You look so beautiful," he murmured.

She laughed quietly and shook her head. "So would you, if you bothered to brush your hair a bit more. Look at these knots. Honestly, Jae. Did you even try?"

"Oh, you know, I was going for that windblown, rugged look."

"What you achieved was the 'I ran out of time and forgot to brush my hair' look." She flicked the end of his nose. "It's much less fashionable."

He chuckled and shrugged. "I'll keep that in mind."

They both paused, seeming to share in a moment of tense, uncomfortable silence before my mother finally cleared her throat. "You should go and talk to her before we go, Jae. You know she has always had better ears for the things you say," she urged, her tone soothing and gentle as she put a hand on my father's arm. "I know she's becoming every bit the stubborn young woman I was—and Gods rest my father's spirit for putting up with me—but she wants *your* approval."

He stared down at her, so tall and stoic in his shining ensemble of dragonrider armor. With his sweeping cloak of regal blue rippling at the heels of his polished boots, and his ashy, silver-colored hair pulled partly back to expose his pointed ears, he looked like a knight straight from the old stories of heroes and gods.

Because ... he was.

I had been told those tales for as long as I could remember. But it wasn't until recently that I had really started to understand what those stories actually meant, and that one of the most famous heroes from them was standing right out there, taking my mother's hand and smiling reassuringly.

"Alright, I'll see what I can do. Wait for me?" He bent down to kiss her cheek and run an affectionate hand over her round belly.

She patted his back and smiled. "Always, my love."

His eyes followed her as she turned to leave, waddling a bit thanks to being so pregnant. She didn't have much longer to go, and the midwife had told us it might even be twins this time. Probably boys again, with the way my luck usually went. Yay ... *more* little brothers. So fun.

Not.

I leaned back, ducking away from the door quickly as my father turned and started walking back toward my room. Oh no! He'd catch me for sure.

Hide. I had to hide. Now!

Dropping my boots, I dashed back to my bed and dove under the mountain of downy-stuffed blankets. I pulled them up to hide the fact that I was, in fact, not dressed at all for going to bed or spending the night inside. The opposite, actually. I wore my favorite long, dark green tunic and broad leather waist-belt that Uncle Reigh had given me. He'd said they were the same style that Gray elven scouts wore in the jungles of Luntharda—not that I'd ever been there myself. Along with a pair of black leggings and my resin-soled boots, I was ready to blend into the shadows like a phantom, just like Uncle Murdoc had taught me. He knew the most about being sneaky and moving around without anyone knowing.

And tonight, that was the name of the game.

"Maylea?" My father called as the door cracked open.

I rolled over onto my side, giving him my back. I had to play this just right or he might get suspicious.

His heavy footfalls approached and stopped right at my bedside. Then his hand brushed my hair, giving one of my slightly pointed ears a playful tug. "Come on, little flower. Listen, I know you think I'm being unfair. But give your old man a chance to explain himself, would you?"

Ugh. Seriously? Not fair. He had called me that since I was a baby, and it worked every time. I couldn't even pretend to stay angry, especially when he gave my cheek a teasing poke.

Urrrggh. Fine.

I rolled over and gave him a sad attempt at a withering glare.

"I know you want to go down to the ball," he said as he petted my hair again. "And this is the last year I'll have to tell you no. Next year, you'll be fifteen, and I'll have no choice but to buy you the fanciest dress in all of Maldobar, with all the jewelry and whatnot that goes with it, and stand back and glower at all the lieutenants who dare to try asking you for a dance. I'll have to keep a list of all their names and make sure to punish them severely. Dragon dung-shoveling duty for months."

"Not funny, Dah." I pursed my lips and narrowed my eyes, retaliating with that elven name I knew would soften him up. "You wouldn't dare."

He grinned broadly and winked. "It's in my contract as your father. Sorry. I'm obligated."

"That's ridiculous."

"I agree," he said. "But you'll have to take it up with my commanding officer."

I arched a brow. "And who is that, exactly?"

"Your mother."

I rolled my eyes and looked away. Why did he always have to do that? Try to joke and make light of it? It wasn't funny—not to me.

"Come on, little flower. Don't be angry," he said, the smile gone from his tone. "Is this just about going to the ball?"

"No!" I snapped, flipping back over to turn my back to him. "I'm so sick of you guys treating me like I'm still a little kid. I'm not a baby anymore. It's not just about going to the ball, Dah. There's a whole castle out there, and every time we come here, I get lectured about how I can't go off by myself. I have to wait until one of you old people is willing to follow me around. And what for? What's so dangerous about this place? It's the *royal castle* —what could possibly go wrong here?"

For almost a minute, my father didn't answer. He stood at the edge of my bed, not making a sound. At last, the bed flinched and I stole a look back to find him sitting right next to me, his elbows on his knees and his head bowed some. "I know it doesn't seem fair, Maylea." His dark brows drew together, his forehead rumpling as his lips pressed into a thin, uncomfortable line. I could see a thousand thoughts flickering in his eyes like crackling dark flames. "It's not this place that's dangerous. Not really. But there are things that happen in this world, sometimes within these walls, that are ... beyond even my understanding. There are powers that lurk in the shadows of the world, just waiting for a chance to emerge and hurt anyone who wanders too close. They only want to snare another soul to their cause. And that is what I worry about most of all."

I sat up a little, risking him spotting my scout's tunic just so I could lean around and study his expression more closely. I'd never heard him talk about things like this before. Not to me, anyway. He sometimes whispered about them with Mother, or even Uncle Reigh. They murmured about the things they'd done, hissing names I didn't recognize into the candlelight. But only when he thought no one else would overhear.

Good thing I was extra-good at being sneaky, right?

Something about his tone, the faraway look in his eyes, and the tremor in his voice made my heart twist deep in my chest. I just wasn't sure what he meant by all that. Dark powers lurking in the shadows? Was he talking about the gods? Or terrible people like Argonox?

Hadn't he and the dragonriders gotten rid of everyone like that? Bad people who wanted to hurt others?

Before I could ask, he reached over to put a hand on my head and brush his fingers through my hair. "One last time, Maylea, promise me you'll stay here—where I know you are safe. I know it seems like a lot to ask. I know it feels unfair. But I need you to do this, especially tonight. I need to know that you will be somewhere out of reach if something should ... go wrong."

Uhh, what? Go wrong? What was that supposed to mean? What was he talking about? Was something else happening here tonight? Something other than just a celebratory ball?

My stomach clenched, seeming to tangle up into a cold knot as I watched him stand up and bend over long enough to kiss the top of my head. "Stay here, in this suite, as I've asked. Watch over your brothers. Wait for your mother and I to come back. Do this for me, little flower. And next year, you'll have free run of the ballrooms and dance until dawn without a word from me."

I DIDN'T PROMISE. NOT OUT LOUD. ALL I COULD MANAGE WAS A HALF-HEARTED NOD because at least that didn't feel quite as much like a lie. I hated lying to him. It stung at my heart like a swarm of angry hornets.

Now it felt like I didn't really have another choice, though.

If there was something happening in this castle tonight, something dangerous, then I needed to find Ronan. I needed to know he was okay. I needed to apologize for suddenly disappearing. I wasn't sure why my parents had decided we couldn't see each other or play together anymore when we were little, but it had eaten a hole away in my chest like a rotten spot on an apple for all this time. He probably thought I was the reason why. He probably assumed I didn't want anything to do with him anymore. And none of that was true.

I sat up in my bed, waiting while my parents finished shuffling around in the main room beyond my door. Then everything went quiet. They were gone. And for a few, fleeting minutes ... I had the room to myself.

Immediately, my thoughts raced in that heavy silence. I stared around at all my belongings scattered on the bed and dresser. The ivory brushes and combs my mother used to braid my hair. The little bottle of perfume father had brought me from Luntharda. Something cold and prickly squeezed at my chest, making me shudder as I stared at the tall door that led out into the main room.

It wasn't safe out there tonight. Something was making my father nervous about being here tonight. And I was about to do exactly what he'd made me promise not to.

My father, Jaevid Broadfeather, was the greatest hero to ever live. Hmm well, in Maldobar, anyway. I'd barely been anywhere beyond our family's estate, so I couldn't be completely sure about the rest of the world. But here, he wasn't just the Academy Commander over the school for dragonriders. He had saved hundreds of thousands of people when he ended the Gray War by wielding the power of Paligno, the God of Life. Then he'd come back from a divine sleep and fought alongside Uncle Reigh against the brutal tyrant, Lord Argonox, and led the way to defeating the Tibran Empire.

Basically, there was nothing that should have frightened my father. Not gods. Not tyrants. Not enemy empires or magical powers. He'd faced all that and been victorious.

And yet ... tonight was the very first time I'd seen him look scared. Like there was something out there that had shaken him to the core.

I swallowed hard against the rising stiffness in my throat. It was one thing to sneak out to explore the castle in search of my long-ago best friend. It was another to go poking around in a situation that had rekindled dark memories in my father's eyes.

I needed to know why—why he'd said those things. What was happening? What wasn't he telling me? Did Mother even know? What if he needed help?

I frowned hard at the toes of my socks. I swallowed hard. Now wasn't the time to second-guess myself or get scared. I wouldn't get another chance. This was it—now or never.

The maids in charge of watching us were busy wrangling my little brothers into the baths. Not an easy job. Sile was ten, and might've been the only person who stood a chance at being as stealthy as I was. If those maids turned their backs for even a second, he'd be gone without a trace, like a puff of smoke. Calem, on the other hand, was only seven, and he had a knack for finding the most dangerous, wild, noisy thing to do and heading straight for it like a furious wolverine. He also hated getting his hair washed. So, yeah, those poor maids had their evening more than occupied. They would have no idea that I'd even left.

Which was why I had to go right this second.

I took in a deep, slow breath and shut my eyes tightly, focusing on my frantic pulse for a moment. I let my racing, worried thoughts trickle down like raindrops and slowly go quiet. Then I looked up at the door again and squeezed my hands into fists.

Time to be brave.

Bounding for the door, I seized my boots and quickly slipped them on. It only took a few seconds to lace them up to my knees before I dashed out into the main room without making a single sound.

⸙ 6 ⸙

CHAPTER SIX

I didn't waste a second.

Crossing through the main room of the large suite my family was sharing for the duration of our stay, I ignored the frantic spinning and flipping of my stomach and seized the knob on the door that led out into the rest of the castle. It clicked softly in my grasp, and I pushed it open just a little—barely enough to peek my head out and glance both ways.

The hallway in either direction was empty and eerily quiet. Not a soul in sight—maid or otherwise. No guards on patrol. No other guests making their way down to join the festivities. Just the shadows and me, exactly the way I liked it.

I couldn't resist a grin as I stepped out into the hall and carefully closed the door behind me. The air flowed gently along the cool, polished marble floors, smelling faintly of flowers and the distant aroma of banquet tables. With any luck, maybe I'd find my way to the kitchen and be able to swipe a little of the treats being handed out to all the party guests. I could bring some to Ronan, if he wasn't at the party already.

Hmm. I'd have to check on that first. Then I could start my search through the rest of the castle wing by wing. I just had to be fast and careful.

The massive chandeliers hanging far overhead on thick iron chains had all been doused for the night. Only the occasional gilded candelabra on a tall stand or a lone candle flickering in a glass sconce lit the hallway ahead. Drapes of rich, heavy velvet were drawn over the towering windows, and most of the doors I passed were closed. Oil paintings of battle scenes, dragonriders sitting astride their gleaming scaly mounts, and various royal family members or noblemen and women hung in massive, intricate golden frames. Huge painted porcelain pots sat in corners, filled with exotic-looking flowering trees or plants that had probably come from Luntharda.

I darted from corner to corner, speeding along as fast as a firefly's flicker. I kept close to the walls and paused every so often to listen for the sound of any voices or footsteps—just the way Uncle Murdoc had taught me. Swift and light. Senses on high alert. Leave no trace. Keep to the balls of your feet and mind your breathing. My mind blurred through everything he'd ever told me about how to move with perfect stealth. Part of me had to wonder if he'd be proud, or at the very least, satisfied with how I was doing. His lessons had always been the hardest, but the most rewarding. He knew things no one else did about how to read the environment—even inside. He'd spent hours showing me how to read people's movements, expressions, body language, and how to follow their trails even if they were trying to be sneaky, too.

Like a tigrex on the hunt in the wild jungles, I prowled the halls of the castle and made my way to the grand staircase. The cascade of white polished stone steps and fine red carpet spilled down into a cavernous atrium, flanked with engraved railings in the shapes of hundreds of dragons. Here, the distant rumble and rush of the celebration reached my ears like the rhythm of the ocean. People talking and laughing. Music from the small orchestra. Footsteps. The clatter of dish ware.

If I went down those steps, I had a pretty good idea that I'd wind up on the same halls as the ballrooms. Not ideal. Someone might spot me and get suspicious. Like a guard.

Or worse—my father.

I'd have to find a better place to watch the festivities and see if there was any sign of Ronan. A hidden vantage point where I could look through all the ballrooms and halls. Glancing up, I studied the only partially lit chandelier hanging far overhead against a ceiling adorned in engraved beams and painted scenes of dragons soaring in a field of clouds. One section of the ceiling right next to the huge chain that held up the fixture made me pause ... and a smirk curled up my lips.

Perfect.

Whirling around, I dashed back down the hall a short distance, searching along the intricate white paneling that adorned the walls until I found it: a small doorway nearly completely hidden in the design. There was no knob or handle, but all I had to do was press against it and the door swung inward, revealing a narrow corridor that led off into the dark.

I hesitated. The servants' passages were harder to navigate. They usually weren't well lit, and snaked around the perimeters of each room, leading from floor to floor all over the castle like the hidden tunnels in an anthill. It made things easier on servants who had to carry food or laundry, giving more direct routes to the various ends of the estate and leading to places that most guests and nobility had no need or interest in going. More importantly, it also had the added benefit of being completely out of sight to almost everyone.

I'd have to figure this out on the move.

I slipped into the gloom and let the door fall closed at my back. Excellent. Now all I had to do was make my way closer to the ballrooms, and then I would find the passage that led up to the ceiling—the same one the servants would use to raise and lower the chandeliers so they could be lit or doused as needed. Talk about the best seat in the house, I would be able to see everything from up there. And best of all, no one would be able to see *me*.

Perfect.

I started slow, letting my eyes adjust to the near dark before I picked up speed. I breezed along the narrow passages, stopping only when I came to a split where the corridor led off in different directions. Lucky for me, there were arrows painted on the walls that labeled each turn, so getting lost wasn't an issue.

I'd get there in record time.

Taking a sharp left and rushing down a flight of steps, I couldn't fight the smile that spread over my face. From somewhere close by, right outside the secret passage, I could hear the dull thump of the music and roar of conversation growing louder. My heart pounded faster, and energy tingled in all my fingers and toes. I was getting closer. Just a bit farther, and then—

CRASH!

I darted around a tight corner and immediately slammed straight into the big figure of a servant heading in the opposite direction. We bounced off one another like a pair of clashing cymbals, and the big platter of dishes he'd been carrying went smashing to the floor.

"Watch it! Wait, who are you? What are you doing here?" he shouted.

Oh no. Bad. This was bad. I had to run—right now!

Scrambling up, I ducked around him as fast as a cat and bolted down the passage.

"Hey! Come back here, kid!" The servant kept yelling.

I stole a glance over my shoulder just in time to see him take up the chase, waving his arms and commanding me to stop. Not a chance, buddy. Zooming through the passages, I dashed around corners and darted through intersections. A couple of servant girls carrying more used glassware screamed and leaned out of the way as I ran between them. They joined in pursuit as the guy I'd crashed into barreled by, and now I had three angry servants on my tail like hunting hounds.

Uh oh. Okay, now it was worse. Time for a different plan.

Hide. I needed to hide.

But where?

I skidded to a halt as I almost dashed right past a trickle of light from an exit door. There! Pushing it open, I scrambled out into another darkened hallway somewhere in the castle. I couldn't tell what wing I'd gone to or even if I was anywhere close to the ballrooms, but now wasn't the time to stand around and figure it out. I sprinted down the hall, my footsteps completely silent on the long red rug that stretched along the white marble floors. I darted past open doorways and whirled around corners. All the while, the voices of the servants still shouted at my back. Gods, now it sounded like there were *more* of them.

I nearly tripped as I scrambled to a sudden stop in the middle of a four-way intersection where two of the massive hallways met. Giant pots filled with the exotic flowering trees and broad-leafed ferns stood against the walls, and a beautiful alabaster sculpture of a dragon stood in the center. Spinning in a circle, I tried to figure out which way to go. What was the right way? Where could I go to hide? The last thing I wanted to do was dash right into the middle of a crowded ballroom or parlor where the guests could see me.

Think—I had to think.

No, I had to hide!

Charging for the nearest cluster of pots, I scrambled back behind the biggest one and mashed myself as far into the shadows of the corner as I could. My heart pounded in my ears, beating so fast I thought it might fly right out of my chest. Sweat ran down the sides of my face, and my hands shook as I tried to hold perfectly still.

Nothing.

An eerily calm silence filled the area as I fought not to wheeze or pant for breaths out loud. Had I lost them? I couldn't hear any shouts or footsteps. Maybe I'd lost them at that last turn?

Time to check it out.

Keeping low, I gathered my feet back under me and prepared to carefully and quietly leave my hiding place—just for a quick peek. I steeled my nerves and clenched my teeth, coiling my legs to stand.

Out of nowhere, a big hand smacked over my mouth and an arm wrapped around me, dragging me back into the dark behind the pots before I could even get a good enough breath to scream.

I SQUIRMED BUT THE ARM HOLDING ME IN PLACE WAS STRONG. IT HELD FAST, PINNING my arms at my sides so I couldn't get free. The large hand clamped over my mouth did, too.

Panic poured over me like someone had filled my veins with icy slush. Every muscle in my body locked up at once. I couldn't think. Gods—what should I do?! Who was this? What did they want? Was I being abducted? Was this the evil lurking in the shadows my father was talking about?

I didn't know. And it was as though every self-defense lesson anyone had ever taught me had been completely wiped from my mind. Fear squeezed all the breath from my lungs as tears blurred my vision.

I shut my eyes tightly, breathing frantically through my nose. *Focus, Maylea. Get ahold of yourself. Don't get scared. Think!*

I ... I could do this. I had been trained for this. All I had to do was side step, gut check with my elbow, and sweep his—

"Shhh. I'm not going to hurt you. Be still, or they'll find us both," a young, masculine voice whispered right against my ear.

Huh? Wait a second—who was this guy? He was hiding, too? Why?

Heavy footsteps and the clunking of armor approached down the hall, moving fast and coming closer. Deep voices shouted to one another, giving out orders to search the nearby parlors and storage rooms. Castle guards? Were they looking for me, too?

I froze, holding perfectly still as two large men in golden-toned armor jogged passed the nook where we were tucked up tight into the shadows, using a massive potted fern for cover. The guy behind me held perfectly still, as well, although he lifted his hand ever so slightly away from my mouth.

I had half a mind to bite him just for spite. But I didn't dare to even blink as the guards ran past, followed not far behind by a group of servants. I recognized one of them right away as the one I had crashed into earlier. His face was flushed bright red and he yelled ahead to the guards, telling them what I'd looked like.

Oops. Not good.

I shrank back father into the shadows, unable to fight the instinct to hide—even if it meant I pressed my back closer into the chest of the guy hiding with me. Whatever. He'd just saved me from getting caught, so he couldn't be that bad, right?

Uggggh my father was going to kill me.

Seconds dragged and I counted my thudding, frantic heartbeats until, at last, everything became quiet. The noise of the guards and servants faded down the hallway. It seemed clear.

I dared to let out a deep, shaking breath. I felt the guy behind me do the same, his breath puffing against my hair and his chest still pressed against my back. His arm around me relaxed some as he whispered, "That was a little too close for comfort."

Yeah. Tell me about it. I pulled away and spun, facing him in a crouch. He jerked back at the same instant, throwing his hands up in surrender and staring at me with strange eyes of vivid yellow. Yellow ... and with vertical pupils, sort of like a cat's.

Wait a second—what the heck was this guy?

I hesitated with my fist already cocked back to strike, staring at him in silent awe. I'd never seen anyone with skin that shade of soft emerald green before. Or pointed ears that long—much longer than a regular elf's. He looked like he might be a little older than me, but not by much. Maybe sixteen at most. Or maybe it was just that his sharp, angular features made him seem that way. His chin was narrow and his nose was long, but not too pointy. He had long black hair wound into a thick braid that hung over his shoulder and all the way to his waist, and I could have sworn I spotted little stubby green horns peeking out of his wispy bangs just above his ears.

"Wh-Who ... are you?" I asked before I could stop myself.

He lowered his hands and tilted his head to the side, blinking a few times. "I am called Lukani," he answered simply, although his voice was tinged with an accent I didn't recognize. Weird.

"Lukani," I repeated, trying to get the inflection right.

He grinned broadly and nodded. "Yes! And you are Maylea."

I frowned. "Wait—how do you know my name?"

His long ears swiveled, seeming to droop somewhat as he looked sheepishly away. "I'm not supposed to be talking to you or anyone else here. I'm sorry. I forgot."

"Why?" I asked, glancing him over again from head to foot. With his lean frame still crouched in the corner, it was hard to tell much else about him. Well, except that his legs seemed really long and he wasn't wearing any shoes. "Are you an assassin or something? Is that why you're sneaking around and hiding from the guards?"

His mouth scrunched like he'd bitten into something bitter as he met my gaze again. "No. But I'm sure that a real assassin wouldn't just admit to it if someone asked."

Hmm. Fair point. "What *are* you doing here, then?"

Lukani didn't answer except to shake his head and look away again.

Fine. Whatever. I didn't have time for this. "Well, look, thanks for helping me ditch those guys, but I can't stick around to chat." I glanced back into the hall, checking both ways to make sure no other guards or servants were in sight. So far, it was still clear.

"What are you doing outside your chambers?" he asked, still keeping his voice hushed. "I thought you and the other children weren't meant to be out in the castle unchaperoned."

I whirled back, rage making my face burn all the way to the tips of my only somewhat pointed ears. One of my eyes twitched as I stared him down. "Did you seriously just call *me* a child?" I hissed. "I am *not* a child. I'm fourteen, for your information, and I don't need a chaperone or anyone else breathing down my neck like a nanny."

"Oh." He blinked, as though completely surprised. "Then why were you being kept in the same room with them?"

Hit him—I was gonna hit him. So. Hard. Probably right in that too-straight nose of his. "Because my father is a stuffy, overprotective old worrywart, that's why. He thinks everything is out to get us, and that I can't handle myself. But he's wrong."

"I see," Lukani said, still looking thoughtful. "I ... didn't realize. Arlan is that way about me. He doesn't like it when I go off on my own. But he isn't my father. He will be angry when he finds out I've left again. But tonight, I had to keep watch."

I frowned harder. Nothing he said made any sense. What was he? Some sort of forest spirit? Or a different kind of elf? And who was Arlan?

"Keep watch over who?" I finally asked.

"You." He fixed me with a worried stare that made my face feel even hotter and my collar a little too tight.

My heartbeat skipped. *Me?* But why? We didn't even know each other. I knew, without a doubt, that I had never met this guy before in my life. You didn't generally forget people with green skin. So why did he care what happened to me? And what was there to watch out for anyway?

I opened my mouth to ask, but he spoke first. "You should go back to your chambers, Maylea. It isn't safe out here. Not tonight."

There it was again—that same warning. It made my throat jump as I drew back slightly. "Why not?"

He shook his head a little. "I can't say. He'll be angry if I tell you too much."

"Arlan?" I guessed.

Lukani's mouth rumpled again. "Please go back."

I sank into my heels, sighing as I looked him over more closely. He had such long legs. He'd probably tower over me if we stood side-by-side. But his frame wasn't heavy or brawny. His clothes fit him loosely, almost like the billowy robes the Gray elves wore. Although his didn't have sleeves, and they were made of a coppery-colored fabric that shimmered whenever he moved. His black pants were baggy and gathered at the ankles, and he wasn't wearing any shoes. Everything about him was strange, although not in a way I'd ever seen before.

And that was saying something because I'd grown up with a *lot* of strange people coming and going from our house.

"I can't do that," I answered at last. "There's someone in this castle I have to find. Until I see him, I can't go back to my chambers."

Lukani's expression brightened as he looked up, long ears perking some. "I can help you, then. It will go much faster because I know this castle."

My heart gave another fluttering skip. "You're ... you're serious? You are really willing to help me instead of ratting me out?"

He smiled warmly and leaned in closer, offering one of his big hands for me to take. "Yes, of course. I know this castle very well. I'm sure I can show you the way. Now, who you are trying to find?"

7

CHAPTER SEVEN

I stared at Lukani's much larger hand and hesitated. I probably should have been more wary of a complete stranger who knew my name and claimed that he was keeping a watchful eye on me. Buuut then again, I had my suspicions that my father probably had something to do with it. Putting a secret, weird-looking guard out to make sure I didn't sneak away? Yeah. He'd totally do something like that. Maybe that's why Lukani didn't want to say who had given him the order to watch me. Or, if it was that Arlan guy, maybe he was someone who worked for my father.

Either way, this had Dah being overprotective again written all over it.

All the more reason for me to continue on. If Lukani really did know this castle as well as he claimed, then he was my best shot at finding Ronan in record time.

"His name is Ronan," I said, keeping my voice hushed as I seized his hand and let him guide me out of our hiding place. "He's my age—fourteen. But I don't know where he is, exactly, only that he used to live here. My memory is a little hazy about some of the details, honestly. But I remember what he looks like, or what he looked like six years ago, anyway. I was going to try searching the ballrooms first. He might be there with all the other guests."

Lukani nodded and squared his shoulders, his grip firm as he tugged me to my feet and then prowled ahead. That's when I noticed another one of his, um, interesting features.

A tail.

He had an actual *tail*.

It sort of resembled a lion's, with a wispy tuft of dark hair on the end. It swished when he walked, and I could barely contain the urge to ... you know ... touch it. I mean, how often do you see someone with a tail? Never, right? At least, not in Maldobar. It might have been common wherever this guy came from, but there weren't any people walking around my hometown with tails, that's for sure.

We sped along the halls, taking sharp turns and stopping at intersections to flatten against the wall. We listened, silent and perfectly still, until we were certain it was clear, then we continued on. I had to admit, Lukani did seem to know these halls a lot better than I did. He seemed to have the timing of the patrolling castle guards memorized, as well, which was a little unnerving. He knew exactly when and where to hide to avoid them, and how long we had until the next group came by.

I decided not to dwell on that too much since, er, it was a little assassin-y. Nope. Not even going to consider that I might be helping an assassin abduct me.

Happy thoughts only.

The farther we went, the more the ambient trill and rush of music thrummed in the air, making the floor beneath my boots vibrate. The dull roar of conversation, excited squeals, and laughter from hundreds of people filled the air almost as richly as the smells of perfume, fine foods, and wreaths of flowers strung along the ceiling and framing every doorway. We were getting close now.

My heart hit the back of my throat when I spotted the voluminous skirts of two ladies peeking around one of the corners. Thankfully, Lukani saw it, too, and we immediately turned into an adjacent parlor, ducking through a darkened room, and exiting on the other side to avoid them.

Whew. Okay, that was a little *too* close.

I tried not to let my relief show too much when he finally brought me to another hidden door in a tiny alcove. Just a short distance down the wide, cavernous hall, I could see radiant golden light spilling from beyond a turn. That must have been where the ballrooms were. I stood frozen for a second, marveling at the golden light glittering off the polished floors and the sounds—rich and full—so close by I could feel them prickling over my skin like an invisible current.

Next year, I'd be able to go and find my place in that light. No more skulking around in the shadows. And with any luck, Ronan would be there with me. That tiny flicker of hope made me smile as I turned to follow Lukani through the small, hidden door.

Inside, it was so short and narrow I couldn't stand up straight. Lukani was practically squatting as he crawled ahead of me, stopping every now and then to look back like he was making sure I hadn't gotten lost. His eerie yellow eyes caught in the weak light like a cat's, giving me a little chill up the back of my neck.

"Watch your step," he whispered, and once again I felt one of his hands close around mine. He guided me up a narrow, extremely steep set of stairs, twisting and winding into the darkness overhead.

The steps ended abruptly, dumping us out into a room with a low ceiling of bare wooden beams. I gasped and held still, watching Lukani prowl ahead still in a squat with his long tail swishing and his ears perked. It almost looked like an attic, albeit an extremely huge one, with gaps in the wooden floor planks in certain places that let in beams of that same brilliant golden light. There were three spots in the center, spaced out across the massive room, where the chains holding up those enormous chandeliers fed up and were attached to big metal gears and cranks.

This was it—the place where the servants could raise and lower them so they could be doused or lit for events like this. The hole cut for the chains wasn't huge, maybe only a foot across, but it was enough.

My heart beat in rhythm with the music far below as I made my way across the floor toward the nearest of the three chandelier chains. Lukani watched me and kept close, as fast as a cat on his bare feet. He joined me in crouching down next to that opening, peeking over the edge to the staggering drop below. Gods and Fates, we must have been fifty feet up. From there, we could see every corner of the ballroom below spread out like a glittering carpet of ladies ballgowns, men in polished armor, shining golden stone floors, and towering white alabaster pillars. Buffet tables were set against the walls, stacked high with shining glasses of wine and plates of roasted boar, lamb, vegetables, fruits, pastries, and cake.

So. Much. Cake.

My stomach twisted up at those savory aromas, reminding me that I hadn't eaten my dinner as part of the theatrical tantrum I'd thrown for my parents. Ughhh. What I wouldn't give for just one bite.

"Do you see him?" Lukani asked, scooting in a little closer to my side as he peered down at the ocean of grandeur spread out below.

Oh. Right. I was looking for Ronan. Gah! I had to focus.

I began to search the room, scanning figures along the walls and making my way across the entire ballroom. There were hundreds of guests, and it seemed like none of them stood still for long. Couples twirled on the dance floor by the dozens, moving in sync with the music like figures in a music box. My breath caught when I spotted my father standing near one of the doorways that led out onto a large balcony. I ducked down lower, just in case he happened to look up. Okay, fine, so he probably couldn't see me at all from this distance. But it still sent a jolt of fear through me like cold lightning.

I watched him pace, scowling and looking back into the ballroom. Almost like he was ... waiting for someone. Strange. But who?

He straightened, his expression going stony and focused as he nodded to the figures of three other men in armor who emerged from the crowds to join him. One of them stopped and glanced back, giving me a clear view of his face framed by loose, pale blond bangs.

Thatcher?

My mouth opened as I studied the other two. The mop of shaggy red hair paired with dragonrider armor was a dead giveaway. One of them was definitely Uncle Reigh. And that last one—tall, dark hair trimmed short, and moving with that distinctive precision in every step. That had to be Uncle Murdoc.

They grouped up at the doorway, standing close together and seeming to exchange a quick conversation with tense, frowning expressions. Then they all moved swiftly out of the ballroom and continued out onto the balcony together.

Okay. That was definitely bizarre.

I sat back on my heels and chewed at the inside of my cheek. Where would all four of them be going together? Wherever it was, it hadn't looked like any of them were thrilled about it. No smiles. No laughing or joking around—which was strange for that lot. They always teased one another.

My stomach gave an aching, throbbing lurch and I curled my toes up inside my boots. Something tickled at the back of my mind, like an itch I couldn't scratch. Why would they all go off together like that? Was something happening? Is this what Dah had been referring to before? Were they heading off to fight someone?

I had to know.

"Where does that balcony lead?" I whispered to Lukani, nodding to the direction where they had all disappeared outside.

"To the Garden of Heroes," he answered.

"And what's out there?" I pressed. "Do people usually go out there during these parties?"

He shook his head, making his lengthy black hair swish against his cheeks and forehead. "I don't think so. The garden isn't closed, but it's usually just a pathway to take people to the Deck, where the dragons are housed, or to the stables. Some might stroll among the statues or visit the fountain, but other than the queen's private solarium, there isn't—"

"Is the solarium open?" I interrupted suddenly.

His face paled some, turning a lighter shade of green as he looked down, away, up—basically anywhere except back at me. "I-I, uh, well, no ... not tonight. B-But, it's probably not a good idea to poke around there."

I narrowed my eyes at him dangerously. "Because that's where my father is going, isn't it?"

"N-No." His throat jumped as he swallowed hard. His cheeks flushed deep red and his mouth scrunched to one side.

Wow. He might have been the worst liar I had ever seen. Definitely not a spy, then. Or at least, not a very good one.

"Lukani," I growled his name like a warning. "Tell me the truth. I just saw my father and some of our closest family friends go that way. Are they going out there to do something dangerous?"

His long ears drooped and he stared down at his bare toes. "Yes," he mumbled softly. "But nothing *too* risky. Not yet."

Not *yet?* What the heck did that even mean?

Argh! No time to sort it out now. I seized him by one of his ears and dragged him backward, away from the light of that chandelier chain-hole, so he had to look me in the eye. "You've got to take me there right now. I'm not kidding. If my father is in trouble, I'm going to be there to help. Got it?"

He bobbed his head once, wincing at where I still had a hold on his ear. "O-Okay. I'm sorry! I just ... it's supposed to be a secret. He said it must be the most secret anything has ever been. He has to ask them, has to convince them to help, but no one else can know."

"What?" I demanded. "Who is asking them? You're not making any sense."

His mouth screwed up, brow drawing into a look of fretful despair as he finally stared back at me eye-to-bright-yellow-eye. "Arlan the Kinslayer," he whispered shakily. "He must convince them to stop the end of the world."

PART THREE

CLARKE

❧ 8 ❧

CHAPTER EIGHT

Everything hurt.

My arms. My legs. My chest every time I took a breath. But my head was the worst. Every thump of my heart made my brain throb like it might burst. I-I couldn't move. I couldn't even think. I was floating. Drifting. Dying?

Something poked my cheek.

My eyelids fluttered, giving me a glimpse of bright light. The sun? Was I outside? No. Not possible. I'd been in the library, down so far into those caverns. Unless someone had carried me out, there was no way I'd ever—

It poked me again, harder this time.

Wait a second, was that ... a stick?

"I saw him move!" a small voice whispered excitedly.

"No you didn't. He's obviously dead. Look how pale he is," another one muttered.

"I think that's just his normal skin color."

"Ew! No way. Not possible. Only corpses look like that."

"Well, look at his hair. It's basically white, isn't it? So maybe all of him is just sickishly pale?"

"What about how skinny he is? Nothing but bones. He's probably been dead a few days," the second voice snorted dubiously. "Maybe from a shipwreck and he just washed up."

"Don't be stupid. You know bodies that wash up get all puffy. Then they sink," the first one argued. "What are those things on his face?"

What was almost certainly a stick moved, scraping up my cheek to poke at my glasses.

"They're so shiny," the first voice gasped in awe.

"Want them?" The second one, who must have been manning the stick, gave a chuckle. "They look ridiculous."

"What are you two doing?" A much louder, more mature, but definitely feminine voice demanded. "I can't leave you boys alone for five minutes before you start slacking off.

You're supposed to be taking in the nets, not—holy gods!" She gave a sharp, panicked scream. "What is that?!"

"A dead guy," one of the younger voices announced proudly. "We found him."

"I told you, he's not dead!" the second one protested again.

The two, childish-sounding voices went back to bickering as all three of them seemed to come closer. Footsteps crunched and sloshed like they were walking through water.

Something cold and wet spattered over my face and into the corners of my mouth. Salty. Was that ... ocean water?

A hoarse, broken groan leaked through my teeth as I tried to force my eyes to open. Up. I had to get up. To move. I-I wasn't going to die. My eyelids fluttered sluggishly. But that was enough. The sudden rush of sunlight flooding my vision made my head throb harder—right up until a trio of heads eclipsed it. One of them leaned down over me, their face too blurred for me to see any detail. Something soft brushed my neck. Hair?

"He's alive! Go and get Noa!" the older voice commanded. "Now! Hurry!"

The younger voices giggled excitedly as they retreated with quick, sloshing steps. Then there was silence. No, wait. Not silence. I could hear it now—the low rumble and whoosh of the surf. The lonely calls of seagulls. The stirring of the warm wind. The musical clatter of the water shifting the little pebbles and stones around me.

I-I wasn't dead. I was lying on my back, my legs and arms floating while the rest of me lay beached on a rocky shore. My heavy robes were drenched and clinging to my skin, and my throat burned when I tried to swallow.

"Just hold on. You're going to be okay. I've got you," the older female voice cooed. Strong arms looped under my shoulders and began to drag me away from the water, out onto the pebbly beach. My head lolled and my legs dragged like two useless, overcooked noodles.

As the young woman laid me out on the sun-warmed stones, I finally managed to open my eyes and blink. My vision cleared, and the pulse of pain still scorching through my head seemed to subside. Then again, maybe I was just adjusting to it. Headaches weren't exactly uncommon for me.

Water dotted the thick lenses of my glasses, making it hard to see at first. But then I saw her leaning over me, her sun-kissed skin a deep, golden bronze hue. Pointed elven ears peeked through her long black hair, and her sharp, turquoise-colored eyes looked me over with a tense, worried frown.

But I didn't recognize her. Obviously, she was a Rienkan elf. But that didn't exactly narrow it down. It didn't matter right then, anyway.

"Goddess, where did you come from?" she whispered, seeming to be talking to herself instead of me.

Her eyes went wide and she flinched back some when I managed to rasp, "C-Com ... pen ... dium ..."

Her full lips parted, slender brows knitting together as she leaned down closer to me again. "Compendium? You mean the library?"

I couldn't force out any more words, my throat seizing in scorching pain whenever I tried to make a sound. Water. I needed water.

"Kaili!" A new, much deeper voice called out suddenly. A man?

I squinted up through the glare of the sun and the spots of water on my glasses to see a new face peering down at me. He seemed to be a good bit older than the others, maybe in his mid-twenties, but he had the same wild, windblown black hair, pointed ears, and vivid turquoise eyes that stared down at me with quick, evaluating precision. His skin was a deeper brown, and I could barely pick out the darker lines of swirling, runic tattoos around one of his eyes and along his cheek all the way to his jaw.

"He's alive," the young woman, Kaili, said quietly.

"Has he said anything?" The man was already bending over to scoop me up off the ground.

Kaili followed along as they hurried away from the shore, lugging me along like a sack of waterlogged flour. "Compendium," she answered so softly I barely heard her. "But that's impossible, isn't it? How could anyone have escaped?"

My heart kicked with a sudden, desperate thud in my chest that made my eyes open wider. *Escaped?* What? What did that mean? I-I couldn't remember ... anything. How I'd gotten here. What had happened. Everything was so blurred—tangled up in my head like an endless ball of knotted twine. Flashes of memory hit my brain like white-hot spikes.

The smell of smoke. Burning pages floating in the air. The flash of fire. The taste of ash. Screams in the dark.

I whimpered and my head rolled back. I barely caught a glimpse of Kaili's worried expression before my eyes rolled closed and the darkness dragged me back under. I was lost. Tossed endlessly through the flickering, crackling, smoldering flames of those twisted memories.

Days or hours passed—I honestly wasn't sure. But when I finally opened my eyes again, I stared up at a reed-thatched ceiling in a small, unfamiliar room. The rough wooden walls had been painted in brightly colored designs of fish, waves, and hippocampi. The strong smell of sea salt hung thick in the cool air, and the flavor of something sweet and soothing still lingered in my mouth. Medicine? Whatever it was, it must have worked. I could swallow and cough without pain.

Clenching my teeth against that old, familiar pain that still throbbed in my temples, I raised my head to get a better look around. There was one other wooden, low bed just like the one where I lay on the other side of the room, and a pair of small hammocks made of woven strips of colorful fabric hung from a ceiling beam in the far corner. Rugs of woven grasses were spread out on the floor, and a few tall chests stood against the walls.

But everything was quiet and still. Peaceful.

I spotted my glasses resting on a small bedside table, and immediately sat up. The bed creaked as I reached for them. I cringed. Had anyone heard that? Or was there anyone even around?

Fumbling with my glasses, I let out a deep, shaking breath of relief as I slid them back on. They didn't make much difference when it came to my actual vision. I could see rather well either way. But the relief to my pounding, aching head was immediate. It dulled that droning, constant pain back to something a lot more tolerable. I could actually hear myself think, again.

And there was a *lot* to consider.

Like the fact that I wasn't wearing any clothes apart from some very unfamiliar smallclothes. Oh, gods. Was I borrowing someone's underwear?

Well. This was, by far, a personal low. Nowhere to go but up, right?

Gods, I hoped so.

Pulling the blanket off the bed, I wrapped myself up in it as best I could before I even dared to waddle across the room. A curtain of sea glass beads and tiny shells had been hung over the only door. It rattled and clinked musically as I carefully pulled a few of the strands aside—just enough that I could peek through into the next room.

"HE'S AWAKE!" A little boy shouted suddenly, going off like an alarm bell and jabbing a finger in my direction.

I stood, paralyzed in shock, as the other three figures in the room looked up at me. Or, uh, the tiny part of my head that was sticking through that curtain.

Oh ... oh no.

"Finn and Malik, you two stay put and keep working," the man scolded as he stood from where he'd been sitting with them, weaving something out of a network of dried grasses.

Both of the boys, who looked like they might be about seven or eight, groaned and whined, flailing their arms in dismay. They must have been the ones who had been poking me with that stick earlier. His kids? No, that couldn't be it. He didn't look old enough to have kids that age.

Siblings, then? It was impossible to tell just by looking at them. Apart from all being Rienkan elves, they all had different face shapes, varying tones of deep bronze, coppery tanned, or nearly ebony skin.

Even the young woman, Kaili, didn't look like she was related. Her features were much sharper, with high cheekbones and deeply set eyes that studied me intently from where she sat, legs crossed under her, while she tended a small stone fire pit in the middle of the room. Her full lips parted some, her expression still tinged with worry as she got up and followed the man on his way toward me.

I floundered back, nearly tripping over the blanket I was wrapped in. The bed gave a sharp creak of protest as I collapsed back onto it and scrambled to cover myself as much as possible. By the time they both came into the room, only my head was poking out of the blanket like a swaddled-up infant.

Okay. Probably not the most dignified look. But it was all I could do at that point other than sit there nearly naked.

"It's all right. We found you on the shore and brought you here. This is our home. You're safe here," the man explained, dipping his head and raising his hands some in a gesture of peace. "My name is Noa, and this is Kaili. The young ones are Finn and Malik."

It took a second to process all of that. I, uh, didn't have a lot of experience when it came to meeting new people. The only strangers who came to the library were there to do some sort of research through the archives ... or drop off another orphan for the scholars to raise.

The same way I had been.

"Who are you?" Kaili pressed, stepping around Noa to get a better look at me. Or, rather, what little of me was peering out of the blanket. Basically just my face. "What is your name?"

"It's ... it's, uh, Clarke," I managed to wheeze.

"And you came from the Compendium Library?" Noa asked, rubbing at his chin thoughtfully.

My voice caught as I stared between the two of them. "I-I, um, yes. I did."

"But the elders said there were no survivors," Kaili gasped. "They searched for three days and found nothing but bones. How did he manage to escape?"

Wait—what? No survivors? My pulse quickened as a cold shiver rushed up my spine. My hands shook as I gripped the blanket harder. "What ... what do you mean? No survivors of what?"

Noa didn't answer right away. He took a careful step toward me, his expression becoming stern and ominous. "We found you nearly dead, washed up on the beach with your clothes badly burned. You really have no memory of what happened in that library?"

"It's all blurred." I shook my head slowly. "There was a fire ... I think. Something must have happened, or a spell went wrong, or ..." My voice died in my throat as another memory flashed through my mind.

A book. *The* book. I'd been so close to it. Had I touched it? Read it? I couldn't remember.

And I *always* remembered. Everything. Everything about everything. That was my whole problem in life, honestly. The one thing that kept me from fitting in with all the other kids who had been raised in the library. The reason my head always felt like it might suddenly burst, and why I had to wear these glasses to try to give my mind a break from the constant onslaught of information.

I could not forget anything—ever—for as long as I could remember.

Until now.

"Clarke?" Kaili took a cautious step closer, leaning down as though she were trying to read my expression.

"What happened to the library?" I managed to rasp weakly.

Noa and Kaili swapped a wary, sideways glance. She shifted uncomfortably, and Noa rubbed at the back of his neck, but neither of them said anything.

"Tell me," I begged, my voice quaking as tears welled in my eyes.

"We don't know, exactly," Noa replied in a soft, consoling tone as he came over to squat down in front of me so that we were eye-to-eye. "But several days ago, a group of our foragers who harvest food along the shoreline noticed black smoke rising from the Opal Cliffs. They saw it coming from the place where the library's entrance is hidden, high along the jagged paths. We sent a few warriors and trackers to investigate, but they were too late. The library had been destroyed. Burned from the inside out. They ... did not find any survivors. I am sorry, Clarke."

My ears rang as I sat in numb silence, staring at him but not really seeing him. Someone had burned the library? And killed everyone in it? But ... why? The library was a peaceful place. It didn't align with Nar'Haleen, Damaria, or any of the other tribes and factions caught up in the civil war. It had always been neutral. A place of learning. The cradle of knowledge where all the greatest historical documents and archives were kept.

Why would anyone want to destroy it?

My throat seized and I bowed my head. The blanket slid off my head to fall around my waist as I buried my face in my hands. I couldn't hide it, though. My body shook as I sobbed. Zuri. High Inquisitor Bellavora. The other orphans who had basically been my siblings, and the scholars who had raised me since I was just a baby. They were all gone.

And I was ... alone.

9

CHAPTER NINE

Noa and Kaili didn't push me for any more information. I guess they could sense that I really wasn't up to a full-blown interrogation right then. After a few minutes. Kaili slipped out of the room and Noa came over to put a hand on my shoulder.

"You can stay here with us as long as you want," he offered. "We do not have much, but we are happy to share."

"Th-Thanks," I sniffled as I wiped my eyes on the back of my hands.

"Your old clothes were ruined. Kaili tried mending them, but too much had been burned," he went on, stepping over to begin rummaging through one of the chests along the wall. He sifted through the folded stacks of clothing tucked inside until he found the pieces he wanted—a loose purple tunic with no sleeves, made of a thin, silky linen, and a pair of baggy, black sirwal-styled pants. "These will probably be too big, but they'll do."

I swallowed against the thick knot of emotion that still hung in my throat as I took the clothes and nodded. I knew I should thank him again. These people had saved me. They'd taken care of me and now were letting me stay with them. But it hurt to even try to speak, and I didn't want to start crying again. I had to pull myself together, at least for now.

Noa stepped out long enough for me to get dressed. He was right, though. The clothes hung off me like a half-stuffed scarecrow. My face burned with embarrassment when he came back in, took one look at me, and sighed loudly. Obviously, these clothes were his, and they didn't even come close to fitting me properly. He was older, yes, but he also had a much more athletic, lean, and efficiently muscled build. I doubted I'd ever look even remotely like that.

Noa didn't say anything about it, though. He didn't tease or taunt me about being a pale, scrawny, heap of bones. Instead, he showed me how to tie up the lower part of the pants so they were tight against my calves, and used the tip of a dagger to punch new holes into a broad leather belt that went over my tunic from my ribs to my hips. Then he stood back, mouth scrunched to one side, and scrutinized my attire again.

"Better," he surmised with a nod, and gestured for me to follow him. "We'll see about getting you some sandals later. Come on. Dinner is ready."

I could have cried again with relief as I sat down at the low table with Kaili, Finn, Malik, and Noa. The savory smells wafting up from the spread of food arranged on clay and carved shell plates made my insides cramp up and my mouth water. Grilled fish sprinkled with herbs. Stir-fried vegetables. A spicy rice porridge, and freshly baked flat bread.

I couldn't decide what to try first.

The two younger boys stared at me with similar awed expressions while we ate. They whispered to one another without taking an eye off me, then broke into a fit of hushed giggling. Finally, one of them dared to point his spoon at my face and ask, "What are those things?"

I blinked. Huh? Oh. Right. I tapped the metal frames of my glasses and managed a half-hearted smile. "These? They're called spectacles. Or some people call them glasses. Some people wear them to help them see better. But mine are a little different."

"Different how?" Now even Kaili looked interested.

"They, um, they're for ... not-reading, I guess." I wasn't sure how to describe how magical devices like my glasses worked. Even I didn't understand it all that well. Not in practice, anyway. I'd read enough on the theory and method to grasp the mechanics, but the actual practice still seemed bizarre. "They have a bit of magic in them to protect me from, uh, reading too much."

"Reading *too* much?" one of the boys cackled. "That's dumb."

"We never read at all," the other chimed in. "It's boring."

Kaili rolled her eyes and went back to eating, seeming to lose interest as Finn and Malik went on asking those teasing questions. They wanted to know why my hair was white if I wasn't old and why I'd never ridden on a hippocampus before.

I didn't have good answers to a lot of their questions, and eventually Noa must have gotten tired of listening to me struggle. He swatted the closest boy over the back of his head and growled at him. "Hush and eat. You've got work to do before sunset."

Finn and Malik's sulking didn't last for long before they were back to asking me about the library, how many books I'd seen in my life, and why I didn't have real parents. They decided that my parents hadn't liked my glasses, or my weird white hair, and that was why they had dropped me off at the library when I was a baby. It was just teasing. I knew that. But I couldn't deny a tiny sting of pain at the suggestion. Or maybe that was just the fear that, to some degree, they were probably right. I'd considered the possibility before that my birth parents had probably picked up on my ... strangeness early on. High Inquisitor Bellavora had never told me anything about them, or why they'd brought me to the Compendium, but I could only assume that's why they hadn't wanted me.

Dinner ended in awkward silence with Noa, Kaili, and me still sitting at the table while the boys bounded outside like two wild hound pups. They whooped and shoved one another, taking playful swings back and forth until they disappeared through the front door and out into the warm afternoon light. Then it was just us.

"I am so sorry about them," Kaili murmured as she swirled her spoon in what was left of her porridge.

I forced another smile and a thin, cracking laugh that probably wasn't very convincing. "Don't be. I got that kind of treatment at the library, too. I guess I'm strange no matter where I go."

"I grew up hearing that the library had a reputation for taking in orphans," Noa said. "Especially ones who were in need of special care. You're the first one I've ever met, though. I'm sure you know that those scholars rarely left the caverns. What we know about the way they lived and things they did is little more than myth and legend."

I leaned back some, trying to focus on the warm, delightfully stuffed sensation in my belly instead of the splitting pain of memory pricking at my chest. "I wouldn't call it anything that grand. The scholars are—er, um, *were*—reclusive. But most of them were just regular people. There isn't anything mythological about caring for ancient scrolls and dusty books. It was just their way of life, and they devoted all their attention to it. The Compendium was our home. We wanted to take care of it."

"And you truly don't remember what happened? Or know of anyone who would want to attack it?" Kaili stared at me, her expression earnest.

I tried to think. To remember. To call back anything distinctive from before everything had gone dark. But there was only fire.

And the book.

I didn't want to mention that. I couldn't. It would be pointless, wouldn't it? No way these people had any idea what a book like that might be. Besides, that symbol on the cover—The Dragon's Eye—was one that hadn't been used in thousands of years. I had only recognized it because of accidentally memorizing the History of the Divine Arcanum. It was the symbol associated specifically with the Fates, who were said to be the gatekeepers to the realm of the gods. They'd been worshipped throughout history, held in high esteem in cultures all around the world. More recently, though, as the younger gods arose, the Fates had lost some of their relevancy. Now, people referred to them a lot, but very few even understood what they were.

So, really, there was no point in even bringing it up. I'd seen it on the cover of that book, yes. That didn't mean anything, though. Ancient divine symbol or not, it was still just a book.

What harm ever came from reading a book?

"Perhaps it had nothing to do with the contents or people in the library," Noa spoke up when I didn't answer. "The war is growing worse. Now that the Tibran Empire has been removed from power, the powers of Nar'Haleen have mustered to resume their campaign to unify the southern kingdoms. They march on Damaria's border cities already. I've heard a few of our fishermen say they've glimpsed their warships embarking to Rienka, as well. This might have simply been a matter of eliminating a place where they feared their enemies might try to hide."

Hmm. True. The library had always been neutral to wars, dynasties, and crowns. But that didn't mean the heads wearing those crowns might not try to control it, or remove it as a potential sympathizing party. If Noa was right and the war was reaching its climax, there might not be any room left for neutrality anywhere.

Which meant there would be no safe places left for anyone.

SITTING ON THE END OF A LONG, RICKETY PIER MADE OF PATCHED-TOGETHER driftwood and rope tied to floating pontoons, I let my bare feet dangle into the clear ocean water. The swell of the surf made the whole pier ripple and the warm waters race between my toes. Schools of tiny silver fish darted through the shallows, zipping over the rocky bottom and disappearing into the tall reeds that grew right along some of the bank.

The library itself was hidden away on a remote part of the coast that was more rural and too treacherous for large ships to even try getting close. It was meant to be the sort of place you didn't just stumble upon. You had to know where to look, and then you had to manage to get there. All the better for remaining ambiguous and neutral in a land that had been locked in a civil war for six hundred years.

Here, though, the war felt like a faraway thing. A "somewhere out there" problem. Here, life looked as simple and carefree as you could ever hope for. Or at least, that's how it seemed from where I was sitting.

Before me, Kaili and Noa's village was tucked into a small, sheltered cove amidst the craggy shoreline, nearly out of sight from any vessels moving through the deeper waters along the coast. As far as I could tell, it didn't have a specific name or title. Maybe it was too small, or too new, to have earned a proper name. But I liked it nonetheless.

As the sun sank low to the west, the sky turned a brilliant gradient of scarlet to violet—something I'd only read about before now. I'd seen the outside a few times, sure. Mostly through windows or doors. But I'd never seen it, the world, like this. Every sound of people laughing and seagulls cawing, the rumble and rush of the waves, the smell of the briny wind, and the rippling heat of the setting sun on my face, saturated my senses.

But I guess there were some things you just couldn't adequately describe in those books. This felt so much richer, vibrant, and more intense than I'd expected. And the more I drank it all in, the more I realized ... I liked it. This village was small, sure. But it felt bigger than anywhere I'd ever been.

I watched older men and women wading in the shallows, wearing baskets they used to harvest oysters, or using long spears to hunt giant crabs. Other kids about my age, or even some who looked a bit younger, blitzed past me on the backs of hippocampi. The horse-like creatures cruised through the warm water like tongues of silvery lightning, their scales flashing and the long fins on their necks and legs flared. Their tails lashed as they let out sharp shrieks, diving, jumping, and riding the swells like dolphins—only much faster.

I floundered back along the pier and pulled my legs out of the water as one of the hippocampi darted close and zoomed right up to where I'd been sitting. Merciful gods, it was much bigger than I expected up close. It must have been twelve feet from head to tail, and every inch of it made of solid, scale-clad muscle. The young female rider seated on its back laughed as she pulled a pair of makeshift goggles away from her eyes.

"Don't be scared, Clarke," Kaili giggled. She used two long leather straps fixed to a bit and bridle in the creature's mouth to steer it around closer. "Do you want to try riding?"

No. No, I absolutely did not. "I-I'm fine, thanks."

Kaili shrugged and tossed some of her long black hair over her shoulder. Then, sliding her goggles back down over her eyes, she gave a whistle to her mount and they turned, surging back out to the water to catch up to the rest of the racing herd still skimming the curling waves farther from shore.

It ... did look fun. Sort of. But I wasn't dumb enough to assume I'd be any good at it. I'd never ridden a regular horse, let alone something like that. I didn't even know if I could swim. I'd never been in water over my head before. Now did not seem like a good time to admit that, though. Not when I'd only just met these people.

Better to space that kind of disappointment out as far as possible, right?

Still, watching her race away with the sun glowing over her light brown skin and the sea wind blowing through her hair made me smile a little. She seemed like she was close to my age, maybe a little older, and there was no denying how beautiful she was.

Not that I stood a chance at ever catching the eye of a girl like that.

Or any girl, probably.

Maybe that was for the best. Given my situation, I wasn't in a position to think about anything except what to do with my life next. Where was I supposed to go? Was I meant to stay here? Here seemed pretty incredible, and so far, everyone had been kind and welcoming. After a while, it might start feeling like home. And after even longer, I might work up the nerve to go back to the library and see if anything—books, some of my belongings, or anything at all—had survived.

I wasn't ready for that yet, though.

Right now, I just wanted to make it to sunrise. To try to remember. To put the pieces back together.

"We aren't so different from you, you know." I recognized Noa's voice before he even sat down next to me.

I stared at him, trying to figure out if he meant that literally or metaphorically. His hard, sharp expression as he stared at the far horizon was impossible to read. "O-Oh? I, um, what do you mean?"

"Kaili and I were from a larger port city much farther down the coast, closer to Rienka. It was attacked when the Tibran armies came and mostly destroyed. We both lost our families, but found each other in the ashes. We stuck together and managed to avoid being abducted into the Tibran ranks, worked when we could to make enough coin to stay fed," he explained. "We found Finn nearly dead from exposure in a hollowed-out canoe that his parents had likely set him adrift in when their village was attacked later on. He was little, barely more than a baby, but we took him in. Then, a few months later, we rescued Malik from a band of Damarian slavers. We moved around a lot over several years, then eventually settled here. That was, gods, five years ago now. We aren't exactly a family, but we are as close as any of us will ever get now. Sort of like your life in the library, I think."

I nodded. It did sound similar. "I guess so." Shifting in my seat, I made a point not to look at him as I asked. "So, um, does that mean you and Kaili are ... you know ... *together?*"

He snorted and cast me a sideways glance. "No. And I doubt very much we would ever consider one another that way."

"Why not?"

"She is more like a sister to me. I looked after her when we were younger. She was barely three when I found her. I was only ten or so, myself. We've been together longer than we were with our real families," he continued as he fiddled with a bone-carved ring he wore on his thumb. "To be honest, I don't remember much about mine. I'm not sure Kaili does, either."

"You miss them, though, right?" I dared to ask.

His expression closed, seeming to become grim as he bowed his head some. "Can you miss someone you can't remember?"

I had to think about that. "Yeah," I decided at last. "Because they still leave an empty place behind in your heart."

Noa's mouth mashed into a pensive, puckered frown as he seemed to mull that over for a moment. "I suppose you're right."

We sat for a few minutes, letting the crash of the surf fill the silence between us. It did feel awkward, though. Noa had a quiet tranquility about him I had to admire. He looked sort of wild with beads and bits of shell braided into some of his hair, and tattoos that wound around his eye, down the side of his neck, all the way to his chest and forearm. Or at least, he did compared to the robed scholars I'd grown up with. But he was a lot friendlier and more patient than a lot of them had been.

"We should go and set out the crab traps for the night. Want to help me?" With a huff and a grunt, Noa got back to his feet and offered a hand down to drag me up alongside him.

"You'll have to show me how." I grinned and took it, unable to stifle a yelp as he hauled me up with one firm yank. Good grief. He was a lot stronger than I thought.

"I can do that," he muttered as he turned away and started down the pier. "And, hey, I know I said it before, but I want you to know you really are welcome to stay with us, if you want. We know what it means to have to start life over from scratch and rubble, and we're willing to help you. Don't feel like you have to decide now, though. Just know that the offer is there if you want it."

I jogged after him. "Thank you, Noa."

He just shrugged. "Don't thank me, yet. We've got twenty traps to set, and I hope you're not squeamish about fish guts."

10

CHAPTER TEN

I was, in fact, squeamish about fish guts. But only at first.

After two weeks of living with Noa and the others, I began to fall into the rhythm of their lifestyle in the small fishing village. Mornings were spent taking in crab traps left to soak overnight, then cleaning the traps and repairing any that had seen damage. I watched from a safe distance while Kaili took care of her hippocampus, and dodged her every attempt to get me to try riding it. Nope. Not ready for that leap of faith just yet.

Noa figured out pretty quickly that I had basically no swimming experience. Thankfully, he did not advertise this to Kaili or the younger boys, which almost certainly would have gotten me laughed at again. Instead, he took me out to the shallows and began teaching me. After a few days, I could paddle around pretty well. Diving was still a challenge, and I had to fight the urge to pinch my nose closed, but wearing those large, glass-made goggles over my eyes helped. I noticed that Noa didn't wear anything like that, though. In fact, he seemed every bit as comfortable in the ocean as he was on land, and could hold his breath for over five minutes.

Kaili showed me how to shell oysters, prepare crab, and debone fish to be cooked for meals. Her small hands were nimble and fast, and she always seemed to find the oysters that had a pearl or two hidden away inside. Those she carefully set aside, explaining that they could be traded for other things when we sent people to one of the larger nearby villages for supplies like grain, cloth, and anything metalwork. Noa sometimes went on those ventures, but Kaili explained he didn't like being around lots of people. It made him tense and anxious. I guess, given his last experience in cities when it came to losing his family, I could understand why.

The two boys, Finn and Malik, pretty much roamed like jackals most of the time. Noa forced them to help with some of the chores, and they were in charge of mending the big, weighted fishing nets that Noa took out in his small canoe on some afternoons. Overall, though, it seemed like those two had dodging all forms of work down to a refined art. They did, however, miraculously materialize whenever Noa decided to offer a grappling lesson on the sandy part of the beach to some of the other young men. He seemed to have a pretty good handle on hand-to-hand combat—not that I was any kind of expert. But he was fast and strong, able to take on more than one of them at a time and still win every round.

To his credit, Noa did invite me to join in. But I decided that nearly drowning during our swimming practice earlier that morning was more than enough humiliation for one day. No need to overdo it and lose all of his respect at once. Besides, I had absolutely no illusions of ever being good at combat in any form.

The evenings were spent in their small cottage, eating dinner and sitting together around the fire pit. Kaili kept herself busy threading pearls, shells, and bits of sea glass onto strings she either meant to sell, or hang around her own neck, while Noa told stories about things like mighty pirate ships that came alive whenever the ancient sea dragon stirred, and mystical Rajinna sorcerers who could shapeshift and cast fiery spells. I'd heard similar stories. Or rather, I'd read them in books. But somehow, hearing them told out loud was so much better. Noa acted them out and made sound effects that had both of the boys on edge. Okay, fine, so he made me jump a few times with his sea dragon roar, too. But it was really convincing.

By the end of the second week, I noticed I'd begun to get a little bit of a tan from spending so much time out by the ocean. Even Malik told me I looked "a lot less dead" than before. I decided that must've been his attempt at a compliment.

"At least we won't have to worry so much about you burning," Kaili giggled as she waded through the waist-deep water, fiddling with the leather saddle strapped to her hippocampus's back. The beast didn't seem to mind and nibbled lazily from a basket of kelp she'd brought along to distract him.

With a crest of vibrant purple fins and a silvery body adorned in bright green stripes, I couldn't deny the urge to reach out and touch his long, horse-like snout. Just once—to see if his scales were as smooth as they looked. But every time I hedged even a little closer, the creature's head would lift and his slender, finlike ears would perk forward, and I suffered a small panic attack.

"He won't hurt you," Kaili said, keeping her face angled away like she didn't want me to know she'd been watching the whole time. "Pasha is very tame."

Yeah. Easy for her to say. She'd been the one lugging along the basket of kelp-treats, so of course he liked her. "I'm not sure I'm a horse-guy."

She shot me a glare over her shoulder. "Good thing he's not a horse, then. Come here. Stop being such a baby. I'll ride with you."

A baby? Okay, that was just uncalled for. I was taller than her. Probably not stronger, but hey, that might just be temporary if Noa kept having me lug full crab traps up and down the beach every day.

Scowling back at her, I shuffled a few feet closer and tried my best not to wince as I stretched out a hand toward the hippocampus's neck. Once again, the beast lifted its head and stared at me, still chewing away on a mouthful of kelp as it flicked its ears forward and gave a snort. Somehow, that felt like disapproval. Or maybe a warning.

Oh, gods, what was I doing?

I cringed as I stood there with my hand out, only inches away from its neck.

"Ugh. You're ridiculous, you know that?" Kaili grumbled, suddenly grabbing my hand and dragging me the distance. She put my hand against the beast's strong neck, showing me how to run my fingers along the slick, glassy surface of his silver scales. "Always stroke with the scales, never against them. They're very sensitive to touch."

Her hand drifted away from mine as I went on petting the hippocampus, running my hand along its head down to its muzzle. It gave another blasting snort and turned away, going back to its kelp-snack with a dismissive swish of its long, powerful tail. The deep V-shape of its tail fin was definitely meant for speed, and it reminded me a little of a marlin or a swordfish. As my fingers drifted along its powerful shoulder, I couldn't help but wonder what that kind of speed would feel like. Terrifying, sure, but maybe a little ... good? Fun, even?

"Well?" Kaili asked, grinning as though she could read my mind. "Want to try it?" She patted the seat of her saddle.

"Is there, uh, really room for two?" It didn't look like it. Even if I wasn't an especially beefy guy, that seat was small.

"If I sit in your lap, sure," she said ... like it was nothing.

Oh. Oh gods. Her sitting in *my* lap? Th-That was just—I-I mean, I'd never had a girl do ... you know, that. Not that it meant anything, really. It was just kind of, er, intimate. Very close friends-y. Maybe even slightly flirty.

"You know, just in case you panic and fall off, I can still hold on," she added.

I tried not to whimper as my ego deflated like an empty waterskin. Well. So much for flirting.

"NOW, SWING YOUR LEG OVER. THAT'S IT," KAILI COAXED AS SHE TRIED TEACHING ME how to mount up on the hippocampus's back. Easier said than done when everything I tried to hold onto was wet and slippery.

With a grunt, I managed to haul myself over into the saddle, scooting into place with my legs dangling down either side of its lean, powerful body. "How do you know so much about this, anyway?" I asked as I grabbed onto the two long leather straps she used for reins. Each one was tied to a different side of the bridle, giving us some ability to steer—or so I assumed.

"Mostly on my own. I bought Pasha with coin I had earned collecting pearls and other things to sell at the market. Then I had to learn on my own. A few of the others here rode, and they did help me some. But every hippocampus is different. They have minds and personalities just like people, so what works for one doesn't always work for the next when it comes to training." While she talked, Kaili sprang fluidly onto the creature's back, settling into place right in front of me ... in my lap.

I tried not to dwell on that as she adjusted my hold on the reins and gave Pasha's neck a reassuring pat. "Now, then, you must ask him first. A little nudge of your feet to get his attention. Once he starts moving, hold on tight with your legs. Use the reins to guide him, but be gentle. Like I said, he is very sensitive. He can feel even the smallest gesture you give him."

I looked down on either side, noting where my feet hung along his ribs. Every breath he took flexed against the insides of my legs, and every swish of his tail sent a ripple of strong muscle down his sides. Oh boy. This wasn't a good idea. I didn't know what I was doing. I was going to fall off, or drown, or—

"You must lean into his speed. It will make it smoother," she added, then gave a tap of her toes to Pasha's scaly sides. "Now, hang on!"

That was it. That was the only warning I got as the hippocampus shot forward in the water with alarming speed. One mighty swat of his tail and we were off, forging toward the open water so fast I could barely see thanks to the ocean spray. Well, that explained why she wore the goggles.

We raced along the curling waves, springing over them and diving briefly to skim the ocean floor ten feet below. At first, it took everything I had just to cling onto the reins for dear life. The longer we rode, however, the more I began to feel it—the rhythm to the beast's movements. The motion of its powerful tail. The steering of its finned front legs. The position of its head to make us dive or rise in the water. We conquered the depths with speed to rival any dolphin or swordfish, racing the breaking waves with a flash of bright scales and shrieking cry from our mount.

Slowly but surely, a grin stretched across my face from one ear to the other. I ... I loved it. The salty spray on my tongue. The sun on my face and the wind in my hair. The raw, primal speed as he zoomed out of the cove toward the open ocean. I'd never felt anything like it. I had spent sixteen years, all my life, in the library, but this—today—was the first time I'd really felt alive.

And it was all thanks to these people. Kaili, Noa, and ... maybe even a little bit, Finn and Malik.

Pulling on the reins, I tried to guide Pasha out farther from the cove beyond the shallows to where the deeper water turned a much darker shade of blue. There, the waves swelled much larger, throwing up foam around big white rock formations that jutted up from the foaming depths. Some of those sea stacks connected, making arches where flocks of seagulls and pelicans roosted.

With powerful swishes of his tail, Pasha jumped and soared over the surface of the water. He sailed more than ten feet with each leap before diving back beneath the depths. Each time, I was thankful Noa had been teaching me how to swim. I could hold my breath and look around, and every time we broke the surface, Kaili gave a loud shriek of delight and giggled. She threw her arms out wide, the wind catching through her long hair as she tilted her head back so that it nearly rested against my chest.

I, uh, tried not read too much into that.

As we turned wide, cresting around another towering sea stack, the horizon spread out before us as far as I could see. The sun dipped low, nearly touching the ocean and seeming to set the waters afire in hues of crimson, purple, pink, and deep gold. Wreathed in a thick veil of scarlet clouds, I marveled at the massive rippling red orb. Somehow, before I'd come here, seeing the sun had always felt like something forbidden. Like being outside was the same thing as being vulnerable or exposed. Now, I drank in that radiant heat and closed my eyes, soaking in the feel of the wind and salty spray as Pasha skimmed the waves.

Maybe this was where I was meant to be all along?

Kaili's hands suddenly seized mine, practically wrenching the reins from my grasp as she brought Pasha around in a tight turn and pulled him to a halt.

Huh? What was that about?

When I opened my eyes again, I found her staring off to the east, back along the coast, with her eyes wide and mouth open in silent terror. I looked, following her line of sight, to a trio of large, ominous dark shapes on the horizon. Ships.

War ships.

I knew their make by outline alone—I'd seen many diagrams of them in books about Nar'Haleen's military history. Tall and slender, with two decks, rows of portholes for cannons, three huge masts, and purple sails flaring out on each side like the fins on a lionfish, the ships traveled in a V-formation straight toward us.

Had they spotted us? What were they doing? Heading for Rienka to join the war? Would they even care if they spotted us out in the water like this?

I knew that the people of Nar'Haleen had no love for Rienkan elves or Damarians. But it's not like we were soldiers. We weren't a threat to them. They'd have no reason to come after us ... right?

"Go, Pasha!" Kaili urged, her voice shaking as she gave the hippocampus a firm tap with her toes. He gave a shrill cry in response and sped off, hurtling back toward the cover of our cove in an instant.

I gripped her waist, struggling just to stay in the saddle and lean into Pasha's speed as he made longer bounds, deeper dives, and zoomed so fast it nearly stripped the goggles right off my face.

Then I heard it—the low, resounding call of a horn like the distant bellow of a mighty beast. I looked back, through my tangled locks of drenched hair and the rising wake from Pasha, just in time to see the closest of the three ships lowering five smaller longboats into the water. Each one was big enough for about thirty armed men, and it didn't take them five seconds to deploy their pop-out sails and turn straight for us.

O-Oh, gods, they had definitely seen us.

I couldn't even breathe as panic surged through my body like a wild current. Faster—we had to go faster! We had to hide. To warn the others in the village. To run away. Something!

When she noticed them taking up pursuit, Kaili hissed a curse through her teeth as she leaned down closer against Pasha's neck, her expression twisted in pure horror. "We cannot let them follow us back to the village! Hold on!"

I did. Or at least, I tried to. Wrapping my arms around her waist, I stayed as close to her as I could as we veered down the coastline, riding the shallower waters and tracking west as fast as we possibly could.

"Why are they chasing us?" I called up to her, not sure if she could even hear me over the rush of the surf.

"Because they are Nar'Haleenan and we are not—they need no other reason. That is war," she seethed bitterly, steering Pasha sharply through a gap between two towering sea stacks and giving him a stern nudge with her heels. It made him lower his head, scaly ears slicking back as he gave a mighty sweep of his tail that sent us bolting into another arcing leap over a ridge of exposed reef.

Surely those boats wouldn't chase us through an area like this. Even if they were smaller than the war ships, they couldn't hope to get through without running aground.

I glanced back again, just in time to see a few figures scrambling around on the longboats. They stood up, assuming a wide stance and drawing back bowstrings to take aim. Arrows zipped through the air, pinging off the rocks or hitting the water around us. Pasha gave a piercing cry of pain and faltered, floundering for a moment before he dove back beneath the safety of the water's surface.

I held my breath, clinging hard to Kaili as we descended. My head throbbed from the pressure until I remembered to hold my nose and blow, forcing my ears to clear just like Noa had taught me. Then I looked upward. Sunlight rippled beyond the surface ten or fifteen feet overhead. We couldn't go any deeper, though. And we couldn't stay underwater forever. Even Pasha had to come up for air eventually.

Kaili thrust a hand forward suddenly, pointing ahead to a dark chasm before us. Nestled into the coral beds and nearly hidden by a patch of wavering green kelp, the entrance to a submerged cave opened like a giant maw before us.

Every instinct in my already terrified brain screamed in protest as we zoomed straight for that dark abyss. No! What was she thinking?! We couldn't go in there! What if there was something even worse sleeping in that darkness—or worse—what if we got stuck in there and drowned?

I tugged at her arm, sending her pleading looks and shaking my head in protest. We couldn't do this. I wasn't going to make it. I needed one more breath, at least! But Kaili shrugged me off, keeping her determined scowl focused squarely on that sea cave ahead.

As my vision went blurry and my lungs spasmed and ached for even the tiniest bit of air, we plunged headlong into the darkness ... and disappeared into the cave far below.

PART FOUR

REIGH

CHAPTER ELEVEN

Moonlight poured through the glass domed ceiling of the solarium. Standing alone amidst the flickering light of torches and small candles in colored-glass lamps, the building was meant to be something of a sanctuary for Jenna. She sometimes had private teas there for her special guests—usually Beckah, Isandri, and Phoebe.

Tonight, however, my sister was more than occupied with her guests inside the castle. We had this place to ourselves, you know, since it was supposed to be locked, guarded, and off limits to party guests. Hah. As if a few locked doors had ever stopped Arlan the Kinslayer before. Not likely.

As we slipped inside, making our way along the pristine stone paths that wound through the towering mini-jungle, I spotted him already waiting. Arlan stood with his back to the room, gazing out the broad glass wall to the garden beyond. There, statues of all the past heroes of Maldobar stood in rows, immortalized in stone and bathed in golden torch-light. I sort of doubted any of those figures held much significance to him, though. With his arms folded and his long golden hair hanging down his back in a loose ponytail, I couldn't help but notice that he wasn't dressed in any fancy party attire. Hmm. Strange. This sort of event was big and public, yes, but I also happened to know that he liked to rub shoulders with nobility whenever he could. Hiding in plain sight had worked out pretty well for him so far. So why wasn't he dressed for an evening of wine sipping and schmoozing?

He didn't carry a blade, either. Not that he needed one, necessarily. He was, without a doubt, the most powerful sorcerer Maldobar had ever seen. Maybe even the world. He could've roasted us all alive on the spot and been gone before anyone could even start patting out the flames.

He didn't move or make a sound as we entered and gathered around the lavish little sitting area right in the center of the solarium. Unsettling? Oh yeah. Tense, anxious energy hung in the air like smog as I quietly shut the door behind us. From this distance, I could barely make out Arlan's eyes glowing in the reflection of the solarium's glass walls like two bright golden spots against the gloom of the night. Even more unsettling. Creepy, even.

Without a word, Jaevid, Thatcher, Murdoc, and I sat down and waited. We had all played this game before. Several times, actually. Rushing things or getting anxious wouldn't do anything to help our case. Arlan had come here because he had something to say—something worth a long journey in the middle of the night, all the way to a very well guarded castle packed full of the kingdom's finest soldiers and knights. Not a small gesture for a man in his line of work. Whatever he wanted to say, it was important. And that fact made my heart pump like mad as I sat next to Thatcher on a plush sofa and waited.

On my other side, Violet stepped from the shadows of the giant potted ferns, exotic palms, and flowering ornamental trees like a shrike materializing from thin air. I clenched my jaw, determined not to let her see me flinch. Sweet Fates, I hadn't even noticed her there. She was a lot stealthier than I'd ever given her credit for.

She cruised over, heels clicking over the stone floor, and stood by the end of the sofa with her arms crossed and her expression far more tense than I'd ever seen before. Her ruby red lips were pressed together firmly and her jaw worked back and forth as she seemed to study her employer like she was attempting to read his thoughts. Not a good sign. I'd never seen her be so ... incomposed.

It made my hands curl into sweaty fists on my knees as I waited.

Something big and probably terrible had to be going on.

"I trust you've all had a pleasant evening thus far." Arlan's smooth voice came softly, but it was every bit as cold and concise as I remembered. He didn't turn around or make a move as he continued, "I do apologize for the interruption, but I'm afraid this matter could not wait."

"And what matter would that be?" Jaevid demanded. I could tell by that angry little crease right in the middle of his eyebrows he had no intention of making pleasantries. Not this time, anyway.

Arlan turned slowly, facing us with his hands clasped at his back. I really shouldn't have been surprised that, even in fourteen years, he hadn't aged a single day. He still looked exactly the same as the last day we'd spoken, all crowded into his private office in Osbran. No wrinkles anywhere. No gray hairs mixed into his deep golden hair. Not even a sign of any stubble on his pointed chin.

"One that we are able to discuss only briefly now, as time is of the essence. Violet, my dear, if you don't mind, our new guests are currently entering via the balcony of the east wing. Be a dear and greet them for me."

I didn't know Violet all that well. I'd only met her a handful of times. Danced with her once. And tonight had probably been our longest actual conversation to date. But I knew in a single glance there was murder on her mind as her scarlet eyes narrowed and one corner of her lip curled in a half snarl.

Thatcher blushed ten shades of red as she reached her hand down the front of her evening gown and produced a very ... tactically hidden dagger.

"Absolutely, my lord," she hissed as she spun it through her fingers with incredible speed as she strode briskly away and disappeared into the manicured jungle-garden once again.

"What's going on here?" Jaevid demanded with an ominous growl. He was already getting to his feet, rage fresh on his sharp features as he stared Arlan down. "Someone is sneaking into the castle? Who is it? What do they want? We must alert the guard—"

"Remain calm, please," Arlan interrupted, his demeanor completely unfazed. "It's nothing my agents can't handle. I doubt anyone beyond this room will even be aware of it. And furthermore ..." His tone took a hard edge as his gaze went steely. "They have not come here for you or any of the other esteemed guests gathered for the ball. Your family is quite safe, Commander, I assure you."

Murdoc sat up straighter, his hands already clenched in fists. "Ulfrangar?" He snarled the word like a curse.

A little chill of panic tingled through my chest at the thought.

"Of course not. The individuals in question are an issue unrelated to any of your previous ventures, in most regards. They seek what I am about to give you." Arlan stepped closer, pausing to look over our group with a pensive frown. His gleaming golden gaze halted when he got to Jaevid, studying him for a few silent seconds. "Information of the highest value. I trust you haven't forgotten that *you* still owe me a favor?"

Jae's brows rose some, recognition dawning over his features. His arms went slack at his sides as he slowly sank back down into his seat. "I-I ... have not forgotten."

"Good," Arlan replied, seeming satisfied.

"But I thought we repaid you already," Thatcher spoke up suddenly. "We helped you retrieve that magical mirror in Northwatch tower."

"Indeed, you did, but that was an exchange for the information regarding how to deal with Iksoli," Arlan clarified. "The favor I'm referring to was the payment agreed upon for my assistance in reclaiming the now King Phillip."

"Ohhh." Thatcher's mouth scrunched up unhappily as he glanced between Murdoc and me. I guess he'd forgotten all about that encounter. Typical.

"Name it, then." Jae cut straight to the chase. I guess he didn't like all this dancing around details any more than I did.

Whatever or whoever this was about, Arlan was playing things unusually carefully by refusing to drop any names. I had to wonder if that was because he thought someone else might be listening in on us. Or maybe he thought one of us might betray him. Either way, I was beyond ready for him to get to the point. Especially since it sounded like we might have some extra company soon—if Violet couldn't handle it herself, that is.

Arlan gave a deep, resigned sigh. "What I would require of you is not so simple, I'm afraid. I had hoped it might not come to this, but I find myself without another viable option. Take care and listen, as I won't repeat any of what you are about to hear. It is risky enough to voice it aloud knowing those who would misuse this information are close by, but I find myself without another alternative." He paused, seeming to collect himself for a moment before he fixed Jae with a somber, unblinking stare. "There is an artifact, of sorts, that must be retrieved from Nar'Haleen immediately. It must be done with extreme caution and complete secrecy. Even now, it is already in great jeopardy of falling into the wrong hands. I had placed it somewhere I believed it would be secure for the foreseeable future, but there has been a recent ... drastic change in the sort of power Nar'Haleen has at its disposal."

"What sort of change?" I asked, already bracing myself for the worst.

I'd heard Jenna and her advisors discussing the balance of power in the southern kingdoms a lot, in the past. We had known for a long time that the situation in the southern kingdoms was tense, at best. Downright genocidal, at worst. As best I could grasp it, there had been a rift between them long ago that had split the once-massive dynasty of Nar'Haleen in two. On his death bed, their last all-sovereign emperor had split the kingdom between his two sons, rather than choosing one over the other as a successor. Naturally, that had caused a lot more problems than it solved, and the kingdom now called Damaria was born. There were many who disapproved and believed this split weakened the dynasty. Succeeding emperors sought to reclaim Damaria in order to reunify their lands. But Damaria, apparently enjoyed being its own kingdom, and their king refused to give up his seat of power. Thus began a long, brutal, and bloody civil war that had raged on for centuries.

Then there was Rienka—its own little ball of problems.

Until right before the Tibran War, Rienka had been the royal city of Damaria. It was apparently the jewel of their entire kingdom, a flourishing, large port city that was the main thoroughfare for trade in and out of all the southern kingdoms. So, naturally, it had rocked a lot of very full merchant boats when they suddenly declared themselves an independent nation, stripping Damaria of its mighty navy that had operated out of the same ports there. Now, both Damaria and Nar'Haleen were on a mission to retake it, while Rienka defied them both with a superior fleet of ships that could outmaneuver anything else on those waters.

A mess? Oh yeah. I did not envy anyone with royal blood living in that part of the world. You were either a part of the problem ... or a walking target. Both, in some respects.

So, no, the idea of going there for any reason did not fill me with happy, warm, and fuzzy feelings. Maldobar had a tentative agreement with Rienka just to keep trade routes open and commerce flowing, but that was only going to last as long as they could keep themselves free of Damarian or Nar'Haleenan domination. It was the political equivalent of a dung-filled tornado down there, and I was not eager to join in the fun.

Judging by the look of controlled exasperation on Arlan's eerie, ageless features, neither was he. "The divine sort, I'm afraid."

Oh. Wonderful. This again.

"You want us to sail to Nar'Haleen to get some secret divine trinket?" Murdoc arched an eyebrow. "Why can't your agents do this for you? We have no experience in maneuvering through that part of the world."

Arlan's stare was as exacting as it was ominous. It sent a little chill up my spine and made every hair on the back of my neck prickle. "Not merely a trinket. An ancient codex containing vast amounts of divine power and precious knowledge that must not be allowed to fall into the wrong hands."

"Hands like those currently sneaking into the castle?" Jae guessed.

Arlan nodded. "Precisely."

I shifted in my seat, my stomach churning at the thought as that word—divine—kept echoing through my brain. *More* divine magic? Fates curse it all, not this, not again. Whenever we got mixed up with the dealings of anything divine, it never went well. Someone always got hurt.

Usually me.

"Be clear, then, who are these people? What do they have to do with the change in Nar'Haleen's power? And why do they want this codex?" Murdoc pressed, obviously nearing the end of his patience. His left eye always got a little twitchy when he was about to lose his cool. "If we are going to be of any use at all in this, then we need to know what we're up against."

Arlan's expression darkened, his jawline going rigid as his glowing eyes panned away, staring off into the shadows of the solarium as though he were trying to compose himself before he said it out loud. "They call themselves the Hands of Fate, but what they are is ... unfathomable. They are a powerful group of individuals who have been instructed in the ways of Avoran magic, gifted with our empowered weapons, and sent to claim this codex and the secrets it contains so that they may crack open the very gate of the divine realm."

12

CHAPTER TWELVE

You could have heard a mouse sneeze in the silence that hung in the dim, cool night air of the solarium. I let out a breath that hung in my throat, almost choking me. Jaevid's face had gone completely pale, as though he'd died on the spot and was just propped up like a mannequin in fancy armor. And Thatcher, well, he looked about a second away from throwing up.

Only Murdoc managed to keep his composure as he kept his piercing stare on Arlan. "Is that even possible?"

Bowing his head slightly, Arlan's eyes closed and he turned his face away. "When aided by a high-ranking Avoran sorceress with specific knowledge of divine magic ... yes, it very well might be. Such things were not beyond the sorcerers of old, long before the War of the Stones. Now, new talent thirsts for that ancient knowledge."

"New talent like your sister," I guessed before I could even stop to think about what I was suggesting. "Her name is Sadeera, right? This is her doing, isn't it? Another one of her aspects? Like the one that had infiltrated the Ulfrangar?"

He nodded once. "I believe so. In fact, I'm almost certain her aspect is in Nar'Haleen at this very moment, acting as advisor to the emperor and encouraging his campaign to find the codex first."

"Gods and Fates," Thatcher gasped as he sank lower into his seat and combed a hand through his messy, light blond hair. "Why, though? Why does she want to tear down the gate to the divine realm?"

"To conquer it," Arlan replied simply. "To learn its secrets and have the power of the gods for herself. You see, if a mortal manages to slay a god ... they become the inheritor of its power. While we Avoran elves live for centuries, far beyond lowlanders like yourselves, we are still mortal. We can still be killed in a very mortal sense. But a god cannot truly die. At least, not in the normal sense. Its essence—its power—must go somewhere. With the proper rituals and knowledge, one might aspire to make themselves an vessel for such power."

"You're saying she's trying to make herself an all-powerful goddess?" Jaevid asked, his tone low and hushed.

"I believe so," Arlan replied. "But she is a long way from that goal. This codex is only one of many things she needs in order to even access the divine realm that way. The more of these required ingredients we can snatch from her grasp, the greater our chance of both destroying another of her aspects and thwarting her plan entirely. But first, we must ensure that the codex is beyond her grasp. That is the first and most important step if we are to thwart her plans."

"I don't understand. These people, the ones who call themselves the Hands of Fate, are currently attempting to infiltrate this castle because they think *you* have this codex already?" Jae pressed.

"No. But they know that I am responsible for hiding it away two hundred years ago, and they seek to ... extract its exact location from me." Arlan moved as smoothly as a jungle cat as he walked over and stood in our midst, his glowing gaze panning over every single one of us. "I can provide more details, specifics of its location, before your departure, but such information must be carefully guarded and I will not risk divulging it here. Tonight, you will return to your festivities and act as though nothing is amiss. Then you will leave here first thing in the morning and go to Southwatch. One of my agents will meet you at the Speckled Sow—a tavern on the eastern end of the docks. She will give you further instructions. You must tell no one of your movements and plans, not even your family members. My sister is already aware of all of you. She knows we have been involved in the past, and likely suspects I would call upon you if I had the need. But with her focus now on Nar'Haleen, I am counting on her reliance upon her agents in the Hands of Fate to give you as much of a head start as possible. I intend to draw them off, to behave as though you have rejected my plea for help, and depart here in despair. That should give you ample opportunity to depart and be out of the kingdom before they catch on."

Another awkward pause made the squeaking of the metal springs in the sofa cushions painfully obvious, like rusty little screams, as Thatcher squirmed in his seat.

"Nar'Haleen is a long way from here," Murdoc pointed out. He rubbed the short beard and rough stubble along his jaw as he stared ahead, deep in thought. "Four or five days at sea, and that's if the winds are favorable and we don't get accosted by pirates or warships. Then the mission itself will take time. None of us have any experience moving in Rienkan, Damarian, or Nar'Haleenan culture. We're going to stick out like warts on an extra toe. Not to mention I'm the only one who even speaks the Sokraal language they use down in that part of the world. Then there's the journey home. That's a lot of room for risk. And time-wise it could take up to a month."

Thatcher cast him a sympathetic glance, like he already knew why Murdoc was so concerned about the time this little errand would take. Not that it was all that hard to sort out. Murdoc was working at Blybrig Academy now, teaching combat fundamentals to fledgling and avians nearly year-round. He couldn't just disappear. Not without someone noticing and getting too curious for comfort, namely his family—and very pregnant wife. They would be worried. They'd start asking questions, and rightfully so. Phoebe would be ready to tear the whole kingdom apart looking for him.

After all, the last time Murdoc had gone missing, he had been captured by murderous assassins and basically held prisoner in their ranks for eighteen years.

And Jae? Well, people would definitely notice if the Academy Commander himself just vanished without an explanation. Nothing secretive or discreet about that. And then there was his family ... he had a wife and three young kids. Not to mention more on the way.

This little errand had all the earmarks of being dangerous and potentially deadly. He shouldn't even be asked to put himself in danger like this again.

Sooo ... that really only left one option. But, man, did it ever suck.

"I'll do it," I muttered.

All of a sudden, I felt every eye in the room focus squarely on me. Even Arlan seemed taken aback and blinked hard, like he thought he might be hallucinating.

"Isandri has been teaching me some Sokraal. Enough to get by. And of all of us, I'm one of the only ones no one is going to panic over if I happen to disappear for a month or two. Jae can cover for me at Blybrig and to my sister. So, I'll do it. But only if Jae stays here. Got it?" I added quickly. "And I get to pick who tags along with me."

Arlan's eyes narrowed some, but I couldn't tell if it was from irritation or amusement. "*You* were not the one who made the deal, Your Highness."

I glared back at him. "Maybe not. But you never specified that he was the only one who could pay this debt. Jaevid has a lot more to lose than I do. Or, rather, he's got more people who can't afford to lose him. So, consider him officially out of the game. I'll go to Nar'Haleen and play fetch for you."

"I'm sitting right here, you know," Jaevid grumbled under his breath.

"Just shut up, look surprised, and be grateful, would you?" I shot him a warning glare. "Going over the Southern Sea all the way to Nar'Haleen isn't like skipping across the border to Luntharda. There won't be any hasty retreats to safe territory. No cavalry to call in if things get shaky. This is a lot more dangerous than anything we've tried before, Jae. It's literally a warzone down there. We might get killed in a battle we have nothing to do with before we even find this codex."

"He's right," Murdoc agreed. "You'll be going into extremely hostile foreign territory. The kingdoms of Rienka, Damaria, and Nar'Haleen have been locked in civil war for nearly six hundred years, and none of them are overly friendly with Maldobar. I'm sure they appreciated the help with the Tibran Empire, but I wouldn't expect them to roll out the welcome wagon."

I sputtered, nearly choking on my own shock. Murdoc had practically made a sport out of contradicting me every chance he got. If he was agreeing with me about this ... then it must really be as bad as it seemed. Crap.

Jaevid didn't give up so easily, though. He wore that signature pinched up scowl that made his nostrils flare a little as he growled, "I can't just simply sit back and let you take all the risk when—"

"*Let* me?" I interrupted. "Come on, Jae. Don't make this awkward. You may be a two-time war hero, savior of the world, and the Academy Commander ... but *I'm* a Prince of Maldobar. I will pull rank on this if I have to." I motioned to Arlan, hoping to get the point across. "My choices were what got us mixed up with these kinds of slippery, stab-you-in-the-back, shady criminal types in the first place—no offense."

Arlan arched an eyebrow, but didn't object.

"All of it was my responsibility," I continued. "Jenna gave that mission to me. And this is a loose end I've got to tie up."

Defeat settled over his features like snow over a smoldering battlefield. His head bowed slightly and his lips pressed into a tense line. But he didn't argue.

"Very well," Arlan relented, his tone still tight and edged with bitterness. "I will accept your offer to repay this favor, Your Highness. But I would advise that you choose your companions with great care. I will also send along one of my own agents who is more affluent in the local culture and who knows how to safely interact with and transport the relic."

"Garnett?" Thatcher looked up, his face as bright and hopeful as a spring daisy.

"No," Arlan deadpanned. I guess their gooey relationship didn't interest him whatsoever. "I will provide more information once you've arrived in Southwatch. Take close care what you say once you leave this room, and do not tarry too long before departing tomorrow. Time is of the essence now, and I assure you, everything you do and say is being carefully noted." He turned away again, waving a hand to dismiss us. "Now, go. I will do what I can to draw all attention away from you, but I cannot promise success. Be on your guard and tread carefully, for there are vipers hidden in your path you may not detect until it is far too late."

"THIS IS ABSURD," JAEVID SNARLED THROUGH HIS TEETH AS HE STORMED AHEAD OF US through the castle halls. His shoulders hunched and fists clenched, his pale eyes flashed with wrath as he glared sideways at me. "You do realize you just agreed to go to Nar'Haleen on your own, don't you? How do you intend to explain this to your sister?"

I shrugged. "I don't know. Haven't thought that far ahead yet. But I'm willing to bet it'll be easier than if you had to explain to your wife why you had to go."

His jaw clenched so hard a vein stood out against the side of his neck and he looked away.

I guess the truth stung. Oops.

"Look, I know I don't have the best reputation when it comes to thinking things through, but this is different. I'm the best, most logical choice for it. And it's not like I *want* to go, but ... I ... well, I'm really the only option, aren't I? The only one that makes sense, anyway. If it makes you feel better, I'll take Thatcher along. He's ... sort of useful. Moreso than last time, anyway."

Jaevid glanced my way again, looking significantly less furious. Progress? His eyebrows rose and he studied me as his pace slowed and his shoulders dropped. "I just wish there was something I could do to help you with this."

"Maybe there is," Murdoc offered suddenly, appearing at my side like a phantom.

I bit back the urge to cringe away and curse. Fates, I had completely forgotten those guys were following behind us. Murdoc had been away from the assassins of the Ulfrangar for a while now, but he still had a way of slinking around as quietly as a cat.

"You're going to need significant backup for this. Specifically, from people who can keep a low profile," he continued. "And most importantly, you're going to need them *fast*. He wants you leaving for the port tomorrow? That means we basically have twenty-four hours. Maybe less. The good news is a lot of the people we know who might be able to help are here tonight."

Hmm, true. I hadn't considered that. "Got any suggestions?"

"I'll go," Thatcher volunteered. "I'm not much good when it comes to knowledge of foreign cultures, but you said yourself I can handle myself in a fight now."

"Well that makes one. But we need someone who actually speaks the language." I rubbed at the back of my neck.

"Reigh, you know who we have to ask—" Jaevid began, using that soft, fatherly voice he'd gotten so good at lately.

Too bad it didn't work on me the same way it did his growing brood of kids.

"I'm *not* asking her," I cut him off. "Isandri isn't ... she ... she doesn't need to get involved in this mess. Her relationship with her homeland isn't what you're thinking. She doesn't *want* to go back. She's told me that a thousand times. It's a pit of painful memories for her, and I won't ask her to go through that on my account." I quirked my mouth and looked down. "Not to mention, I already dragged her through that mess with Iksoli. I can't ask her for this, too."

"Technically, she joined that particular mess on her own," Murdoc countered. "She followed us across the kingdom for it, if you recall."

Ugh. He didn't get it. I shook my head and cast him a glare of warning.

It wasn't like I didn't want her to go. If I had my way, I'd have her planning this entire mission. There were times when it felt like she was the last person in the world I could trust completely. My secrets stayed with her, and I didn't doubt that for a single second. I owed her that same sort of loyalty and nothing less. And one of those secrets, I knew, was how she felt about going back to Nar'Haleen or any of the southern kingdoms. Isandri hadn't been a powerful noble or public figure there. Her family had basically dumped her on the front steps of a temple and told the priestesses "Figure this problem out for us." Then she had never seen or heard from either of her parents again.

Then there was her actual life in the temple. She'd been isolated from the other kids—apart from Devana, who was another special case, but even their interactions had been strictly monitored and eventually forbidden. She'd been forced to train in combat and lectured endlessly on religious lore. They'd barely treated her like a human being at all. To them, she was a blunt instrument they had to hone into a weapon that would fight for their cause. They'd never allowed her to be a regular kid.

And after all this time, Isa had not forgotten that. Even now, she struggled with getting close to people because she'd never been allowed that kind of thing before. I knew I had proven myself and won a special place in her mind as a friend. I wasn't about to screw that up.

"Reigh," Murdoc's tone was grim and heavy with warning. "If you go and don't tell her about it, how do you imagine she will react? You really think she will be fine with you suddenly sailing off into the sunset to do something incredibly dangerous on her old home turf without saying anything beforehand?"

Weeeell, when he put it that way, yeah. She would probably chase down our ship and hang me over the bow by my toenails.

"Besides, even if she doesn't want to go, maybe she has some suggestions for how we can pull this off as fast as possible," Thatcher chimed in. "You know, like safe places we can stay or what to do if we need to ask for local help. What the customs are and all that."

"A good point. I know a few of them, but only in theory," Murdoc agreed. "You need an insider's perspective on the local social customs if you're going to make this happen without blundering your way into getting arrested for saying or doing the wrong thing."

I let out a long, heavy sigh that left my chest feeling hollow. "Fiiine. I'll ... send her a letter. I can have it mailed out tomorrow. It'll take us a day to get to Southwatch. Depending on what Arlan's agent there has for us, we may even get an extra day there to prepare ourselves for the journey. I have to figure out what I'm going to do with our dragons. Somehow, I suspect convincing a ship captain to haul two adult, fire-breathing dragons into the middle of the ocean on a ship made out of wood is going to be a challenge all its own."

Jaevid gave a bemused snort as he stopped ahead of us, hesitating on the threshold of the wide, sloping steps that led up into the balcony just off the grand ballroom. "Arlan wanted dragonriders for this job, so I can only assume he's taken that into consideration. I wouldn't go anywhere without Mavrik at my side—not while knowing there are hostile enemies on my tail. We will just have to see what he has planned, and hope for the best."

"Hope is about all I've got at this point," I groaned as I moved past him, beginning my climb up the stairs toward the ambient light and rumble of the crowd inside. "Hope, a dragon, and what I'm starting to suspect is the beginning of a stomach ulcer. You know, I'm a little annoyed that no one warned me that becoming friends with the great Jaevid Broadfeather would also mean sentencing me to a lifetime of stress, sleepless nights, and near-death experiences. I sort of feel like someone should have given me a head's up on that."

"That just goes with the hero lifestyle, Reigh," Jae chuckled as he fell in step right beside me, giving me a familiar punch to my arm. "Next time, read the fine print."

13

CHAPTER THIRTEEN

After a long, restless night of poring over pieces of parchment, only to crunch them up in disgust halfway through and start over, I handed off a very long, sealed letter to one of the royal couriers first thing the next morning. Ughh. I was no good at this—writing down my thoughts or feelings. I could talk to Isandri face-to-face about this sort of thing easily. But writing it down without sounding like an idiot? Not my strong suit.

Hopefully, somewhere in all my panicked rambling, she'd get the basics of what I was trying to say. I was going to the southern kingdoms to run an errand for a certain individual to whom I still owed a favor, and I did not expect her to come because I knew what that place had done to her in the past. Also, if I didn't come back in about six months, maybe she should tell my sister what had happened, because at that point ... I probably died somehow.

That was it. I didn't expect her to come rushing to my aid, or to even offer any advice. The others obviously had their own ideas about that, but I knew better. Isa was probably only going to offer us two words of advice when it came to this mission: don't go.

It would take a few days for the letter to reach her, even via a royal courier on a shrike. She had been hard at work in Luntharda, assisting with a very recently discovered ancient temple deep in the jungle north of Aular. Since she'd received such an extensive education in all things divine, she had volunteered to offer her expertise as the temple ruins were excavated. It was probably hard for them to get mail in and out of a remote place like that, especially in Luntharda where just about everything that lived in the wild jungle wanted to eat you. By the time Isandri got my letter, I'd already be long gone.

Throwing my bags over my shoulder, I started for the Deck just as the first few rays of sunlight broke over the horizon. This early, there wouldn't be anyone except servants and castle staff moving around. Any guests who had been staying the night here would likely be sleeping off the previous night's festivities. The cooks would be just beginning breakfast preparations. Some of the groundskeepers were already out, cleaning up and preening the gardens as I made my way out through the open courtyard to the massive, round complex where the dragons were housed.

Thatcher, Murdoc, Jae and I had gone over our plan several times the night before. Jaevid was to stay put with his butt planted firmly in bed and sleep until noon. If anyone was keeping an eye on possible movements for world-saving efforts, we were all willing to bet good coin he was the one they'd be watching the closest. He'd liked that about as much as you can imagine. I guess getting told to sit this one out was harder on him than I'd anticipated. I'd never seen him pout that much. We couldn't risk any undue attention from prying eyes, though, and he was basically a giant walking bullseye for every spy and assassin who might even think about interfering with us.

Beyond that, our plan was actually sort of simple. Thatcher, Murdoc, and I would all arrive at the Deck at different times, so as not to arouse any suspicions from anyone who might be watching us. We'd depart one at a time, with Murdoc and Thatcher heading west before arcing down toward the southern coast—just to throw off any further suspicions. Murdoc had insisted on going with us at least to Southwatch. I guess he didn't like letting Thatcher out of his weirdly overprotective sight. There wasn't much he could do about it, though. He'd be hanging up his babysitter status for a while, like it or not. Or, rather, trading one baby for another.

By nightfall, we would all meet up in Southwatch at the Speckled Sow Tavern, just as Arlan had instructed. There, we'd hopefully rendezvous with his agent and get the rest of the information we needed about how we were going to make the journey across the Southern Sea all the way to Rienka. How that was going to work, exactly, I still didn't know. Thatcher and I both had dragons, and I had absolutely no intention of leaving Vexi sitting on the docks—not if I was about to sail straight into the teeth of a brutal civil war where we were definitely not welcome.

I didn't know much about ships, but I did know they were made primarily of things that burned easily. Wood. Cloth sails. Ropes. That would likely pose a problem to any captain who might let us onboard. Oh well. That was a problem for Arlan to solve. If he wanted this done, he'd have to take into consideration that I was a package deal with a reasonably large green dragoness.

A dragoness who chirped and crowed excitedly as soon as I rolled open her stall door and stepped inside. Unfurling from her bed of fresh hay, she shook herself and lumbered forward. Vexi rubbed her head against me and purred, nosing through my hair as I carried my bags over and sat them down next to her.

"Hey there, beautiful," I crooned and gave her chin a scratch that made her smack her lips and close her large, sky-blue eyes. "Sleep well? I hope so, 'cause we've got a long flight today."

With her smooth green scales shimmering like a jungle snake, and her plated underbelly a citrine yellow, Vexi had grown out of most of her babyish behavior. Her lithe body had thickened up with muscle, and her neck, wing arms, and back now had faint stripes of a much darker green. The slender spines along her back were now tipped in that same bright yellow hue, and she had more pronounced curls on the ends of the two long, sweeping horns on her head.

She puffed a snort in my face as I stepped around her again, searching me for any sign of a treat—a bad habit I'd started by giving her hunks of smoked salmon every now and then when we had an especially hard day of training at Blybrig. Now she wanted one every time I came around. Ah well. She was my queen. I'd give her whatever she wanted.

Leaving her to stretch and preen her scales, I walked fast on my way back down to the tack room where the saddles were kept. Most were dragon saddles, but there were a few odd, much smaller ones made for shrikes, as well. Grabbing Vexi's off a stand by the door, I hesitated. Something rustled in the corner of the room. Was there someone else here this early? Or had stable staff already come in to start their daily chores?

When I turned to look, I didn't see anyone. Just me and a room full of finely oiled leather saddles. The little hairs on the back of my neck and along my arms stood on end. Hmmm. I hadn't imagined that sound. Almost like rustling. Movement. A footstep.

I shut my eyes and shook my head. Gods and Fates, I had to calm down. We hadn't even left yet and this whole mission already had me on edge, thinking I was hearing assassins in the shadows. I had to get it together. Now was not the time to get paranoid—not when I had work to do.

With a sigh, I slung my saddle over my back and started back for Vexi's stall. She squirmed excitedly at the sight of it, and immediately flattened herself down against the floor for me to begin tacking her up for the journey. It wasn't all that far from here to Southwatch, so long as the weather stayed fair. We could probably manage it in six hours. Maybe less, if the winds favored us.

But knowing we weren't coming back here, to Halfax, or maybe to Maldobar in general once we set sail, made me want to double-check every buckle and strap. I'd taken the time in my chambers last night to make sure I had anything personal packed away in my saddlebags. Letters. A few changes of my clothes—both Maldobarian and Lunthardan. My favorite small hunting knife that Kiran had given me for a birthday a few years ago. A really nice haversack made from faundra hide that Isandri had bought for me last year. I'd never had a chance to use it before now, and part of me cringed at the thought of it getting dirty or damaged.

Then there was the necklace—the one Phoebe had given each of us as part of an enchanted set. I didn't wear mine as faithfully as Murdoc and Thatcher did, but I still kept it around. Years ago, she had made these as a way for us all to stay connected in case one of us needed help. We had been a lot more spread out then, and Phoebe had told us how to activate the tiny crystal embedded in the small round pendant in order to send a signal to anyone else wearing one of these necklaces.

Having it around my neck again somehow felt like slipping into a suit of old armor that didn't quite fit. Strange. Uncomfortable. Yet oddly familiar. Like most of my personal belongings, the memories attached to it made it seem heavier. I didn't have a lot of sentimental things, but these were ... the few belongings I had that were important to me. The only things I couldn't stand to leave behind.

I'd squirreled away some other supplies, of course. A few candles, some rope, a waterskin, rolls of clean parchment, an inkwell and quill, and two full emergency medical kits that were stocked with everything from surgical supplies to medicinal salves. I really didn't know what we would be up against when we arrived in Nar'Haleen, but I was expecting the absolute worst.

Hey, I'd either be right, or pleasantly surprised. And after our last little runaround with Arlan's people—traipsing through Northwatch tower while insane mercenaries rained arrows down on my head—I had a feeling I'd be stitching up more of my friends this time, too.

Maybe even myself, if past adventures were any indication. I never walked away from these things clean. This was bound to be yet another scar, bad memory, and thing I'd lose sleep over for years to come.

With everything in place and my bags tied down to the back of Vexi's saddle, I went to roll open the rear door of the stall that looked out across the broad, circular courtyard in the middle of the Deck. The entire complex was built like a colosseum, only with stalls around the outside rather than seats. Most of them had their exterior doors already ajar, making the area surrounding that wide courtyard look like a massive honeycomb.

I glanced skyward, noting the gathering clouds on the dawn horizon before I slid on my helmet and went to mount up. Storms from the east might slow us down, but if I was fast, maybe we could get most of the way there before the bad weather hit.

Slipping my legs down into the boot-shaped pockets on either side of my saddle, I leaned down against Vexi's strong back and gave her neck a pat. She shifted excitedly beneath me, her sides swelling against the form-fitted leather saddle with every breath. Her wing arms flexed, muscle rolling under vibrant green scales as she crawled forward and sprang from the safety and gloom of her stall to the open air of the courtyard. She flared her wings, wind catching in their leather membranes, and with a few graceful wingbeats, we were gone. Soaring high and fast, catching the cool morning breeze and arcing a path straight southward.

My stomach flipped and swirled, hands shaking and unsteady as I gripped the saddle handles and stole a glance at the city of Halfax slipping away far below. I could have sworn I saw another shape flying not far behind like a blurring silver streak. Probably a shrike.

It flew a similar path for about an hour before finally veering down, landing somewhere in the farmland outside of Halfax. Then we were alone in the air, gliding through the updrafts and cresting the edges of the occasional cloud. Halfax's sprawling mass of rooftops, crowded streets, and guarding outer walls faded behind us, lost to the rolling hills, grassy floodplains, and deep forests of the south. And for a few fleeting hours, Vexi and I bathed in morning sunlight, free to chase the wind as fast as we pleased.

Cold rain and gusting wind greeted us when Vexi and I finally touched down outside of Southwatch. Ugh. Typical. This time of year, in the late summer, storms were frequent right along the coast.

Thunder rumbled like a deep, hungry growl and tongues of lightning popped from cloud to cloud. It was more than enough encouragement to land and find shelter as soon as the city came into view. Amidst the driving rain and heavy clouds that had choked out the sun, the port city sat amidst brackish bogs where the rivers from the everglades stretched all the way to the ocean. It was surrounded by tall grass and wild cane, and masses of floating water plants slowly drifted along deeper canals. The people here had built up a unique way of life that was much different from the rest of Maldobar. They navigated the glades with rafts or shallow canoes and long steering poles. They fished and farmed crustaceans, edible sea grasses, gathered shellfish, and grew rice in neat rows inside specially-dug, flooded fields.

I'd never spent much time here, and the only thing that was even remotely familiar was the shape of a tall dark tower rising up from the middle of the city like a black iron spike. That was the dragonrider tower, where the southern forces were housed.

I could have stayed there, of course. They probably had the best accommodations for dragons in the area, and no one would ask too many questions about why I'd come. The downside, unfortunately, was that they would recognize me instantly. Rumors would fly like cows in a hurricane about what a prince was doing here unannounced. Word would spread, and if I was really being watched as closely as Arlan suggested, then someone foul would take notice.

I'd have to find other lodging for Vexi if this dragged on for more than a day or two.

She could fend for herself for a short time. She had been born in the wild, after all, and I had always let her roam whenever we had spare time. Not to mention, she really enjoyed digging and rolling around in the sand, so I wasn't about to deny her that chance. The weather didn't bother her nearly as much as it did me, not when she'd been hatched and raised along the jagged and often stormy Breaker's Cliffs. There, the wild dragons conquered the raging stormfronts, coasting those wild winds and seemingly unconcerned by the occasional snap of lightning.

With my being dressed out in *metal* armor, I was extremely concerned about it, though. Time to find this tavern—the Speckled Sow—and dry off.

"Just stay close, and keep an eye out for Fornax, okay?" I said as I slid off Vexi's back. My boots hit the muddy, sparsely paved road with a *squish*.

She gave a worried, low murring sound and bumped her snout against me as I unfastened my haversack and saddlebag with all my weaponry. Her hot breath stirred in my hair as she puffed a disapproving snort right against the back of my head.

I gave one of her scaly ears a tug. "I'll be fine. Just going to find a dry place to spend the night. Not everyone likes slogging around in the rain, you know."

She smacked her jaws defiantly, giving the back of my cloak a nip and tug that nearly yanked me off my feet as I began walking away. It made me smile to myself as I staggered, collected myself, and kept going. Vexi had never liked it when we had to be separated. Not that I enjoyed it either, but there had been a lot of times in the past when she couldn't be right there, puffing her smelly dragon breath right down the back of my neck like she wanted.

Usually for her own safety.

Fates, I just prayed this mission wasn't going to be another one of those times.

❧ 14 ❧

CHAPTER FOURTEEN

Two long, rain-soaked hours later, I finally stepped under the eaves of the Speckled Sow Tavern and Inn. Perched right on the old, creaking boardwalk facing the docks, the place looked like it might be one strong gust of wind away from caving in. The wooden shingled roof sagged in the middle like an old mattress, and smoke curled up from its three crooked stone chimneys. Warm light burned in the old, wavered glass windows, and a sign cut in the shape of a pig hung on a pole from the front porch. It creaked back and forth on rusted chains in the stormy winds, the painted lettering almost completely flaked away.

Under the eaves of the front porch, I took a moment to throw back the hood of my cloak and try shaking some of the water out of my hair. Setting down my bags, I tried doing the same thing with my cloak ... not that it helped much. Everything I wore was drenched, and there wasn't much I could do about the fact that my boots were sloshing and caked with mud. Oh well.

Ducking inside, the smell of stale ale, simmering stew, sweat, and stagnant sea air engulfed me immediately. Rusted iron fixtures holding flickering oil lamps hung from the bare wooden beams overhead, casting a weak light through the three connected rooms. The first, where I stood, was the largest and boasted a bar that stretched from one end of the room to the other over the entire far wall. Glasses, mugs, ale horns, and goblets were arranged on floor-to-ceiling shelves behind the bar, alongside dozens of bottles of different wines and liquors. Casks were stacked on one wall in a wooden frame, and a narrow doorway on the other must have led into the kitchen.

All around the space, tables were crowded with men and women exchanging hushed words, focusing on card games, or telling drunken tales. It filled the room with the constant rumble of conversation. No one seemed too interested in me as I basically left a slime trail through the front door of the tavern all the way to the tall bar top where a stocky woman in a tightly-synched corset and voluminous skirt wiped at the inside of an ale horn.

I put down my bags before the bar and gave the bartender a gesture to call her over. She ambled my way, her wild yellow curls pulled into a bun on top of her head in a way that sort of resembled a too-big party bow or a springy golden shrub. She smiled, revealing that one of her front teeth was ... uh, missing. "Aye, love, welcome to the sow. Don't you look a proper mess! What can I do for you?"

"You've got rooms here, right?" I asked, trying my very best not to stare at the gaping hole in her smile.

"Aye, yes, we do." She gave a hearty chuckle, but I noticed her keen eyes giving me that once-over, appraising look—as though she were trying to figure out who I was.

"I'll take one, then. Just for the night, till the weather passes. And a meal with a strong drink." I fished a few coins out of my pocket and slid them over to her.

A hand clapped down over my little stack of silver pieces before the bartender could even reach for them, raking them back my way and replacing them with a trio of golden ones.

A shorter, petite female figure stepped in close beside me, nudging me away from the bar with her shoulder. I caught the flash of scarlet eyes an instant before I recognized her voice. "He's with me, Agatha. We'll be upstairs."

Violet. Yet again. Was she following me? Or had Arlan set her on me like some kind of nanny?

I was about to ask, but then she reached down to take my arm and lean into my side some. I saw her expression seize for an instant, that veneer of a cunning smile cracking with a pale, shuddering look of pain. She stumbled some, sucked in a sharp, steadying breath, and then went ahead of me toward a narrow flight of stairs just inside the next room. No one seemed to pay us any mind as we stomped up to the second floor, me still dripping wet and dragging all my luggage, and her holding onto my arm like she might collapse at any second.

In the faint glow of the lantern-light, I spotted a dark splotch around a puncture on her black leather leggings, about halfway down her thigh. Fates, was that ... a stab wound?

If it was, based purely on the size of the possible bloodstain and how it had begun to run down her leg all the way to the top of her boots, she'd been walking around on it for a while. Not good.

"G-Good of you to come early," Violet whispered, almost as though she were clenching her teeth, as we topped the stairs and turned into the first room on the right. "Where are your friends?"

"Coming," I said, turning back to shut the door behind us.

She staggered again, harder this time.

I whirled around just in time to see her legs buckle.

"Violet?!" I dropped all my bags and rushed forward. I grunted as I stooped low and caught her before she hit the floor, dragging her back upright just long enough to sweep an arm under her knees to carry her. "I knew it. You're hurt, aren't you?"

"I-It's ... not so bad," she slurred as her head lolled to the side and came to rest on my shoulder.

Not so bad? I wasn't sure what she considered "bad," but in my modest, professional medical opinion, that amount of blood running like a spring river down her leg was definitely not a good thing.

I carried her over to the nearest rickety bed and guided her down into it. Her eyes rolled back some as though she were fighting to stay conscious. Not good.

"You're losing too much blood," I growled under my breath as I hurried to unfasten her belt and snatch down her leather leggings far enough to see the wound better.

Her scarlet eyes popped open suddenly, and she flashed me a frantic, enraged glare as she seized one of my wrists with surprising strength.

I glared back at her. "You know I'm a healer. It's this or I cut them to access the wound. Your choice."

She stared at me blearily, her anger seeming to fizzle just as quickly. She fell back on the bed again, muttering something in a language I didn't recognize. Probably some profanity with my name tossed in.

Seemed like as much of a "yes" as I was going to get. I continued working her pants—*just* her pants, not, you know, everything else—down far enough that I could see the deep stab wound on her upper thigh. Three inches long, clean entry, and that much blood? Definitely from a dagger. For her sake, I hoped it hadn't been a poisoned one like the Ulfrangar assassins were so fond of using. Otherwise, stopping the bleeding was about to be the least of our problems.

"It might have nicked your artery. I've got to make sure that's not what's behind all this bleeding. This is gonna hurt. Just stay with me, okay?" I took her belt and quickly wrapped it around her leg above the wound, bearing down hard and tying it off.

Violet let out a whimpering cry, but held steady.

There. It wasn't a true tourniquet, but it would do.

"You're ... enjoying this ... aren't you?" She seethed through gritted teeth as I dug through my bag and pulled out one of my emergency surgery kits.

"What? Being wrist-deep in your blood when I'm supposed to be having a nice warm ale downstairs? Of course. Loving it. So much fun." I scowled, wiping my hands off on a sterile piece of cloth before I took out a curved needle and spool of fine thread wrapped up in a spool of gauze and a small vial of sterilizing ointment.

"I mean ... p-playing the hero again," she huffed and winced. Her teeth chattered as she lay still.

Normally, I'd have insisted on a chaser root potion to knock her out a little so she didn't move around while I was trying to stitch her up. Unfortunately, there wasn't time. I didn't know how long she'd been bleeding like this, but every second counted with a wound like that.

I had to give Violet some credit, though. She held still even when I began fishing through the wound and probing it with my finger. My heartbeat skipped when my fingertip struck something solid that wasn't supposed to be there. Curse it. The tip of the dagger must have broken off inside.

"Bite down on this," I instructed, handing her a thin piece of wood I kept in there for, well, just this sort of occasion.

She took it and stiffened, whimpering as I used a long pair of metal tweezers Phoebe had designed and crafted especially for this kind of situation to reach down and begin working the broken-off dagger tip out of the wound. Blood ran out of her leg even with my tourniquet slowing the flow substantially, and I went through nearly all my gauze and rags trying to keep the area clear enough to see what I was doing.

I couldn't mess this up. I'd trained for this very thing with Kiran probably a hundred times. Surgeries weren't my strong suit, however. Especially not with minimal supplies and no time to prepare.

Whether Violet realized it or not, she was flirting with death tonight.

A few minutes later, and I might have been too late.

Now, I just had to be sure I did my job well ... or it might not matter whether she found me or not.

THE COPPERY SMELL OF BLOOD HUNG THICK IN THE AIR AS I WORKED, RAINWATER STILL dripping off my bangs and into my eyes or running down the bridge of my nose. But I found her femoral artery whole and undamaged, which was good news. A smaller vein had been severed, which was what had caused so much bleeding, and did my best to repair that situation. Then I sterilized the wound as best I could to stitch it closed. She wouldn't be running any sprints or breaking any land speed records for the next week, at least. She would live, though.

Now, for the next problem.

"You've lost a lot of blood. Walking around with that dagger tip doing more damage every time you took a step didn't help, either. This healing salve I'm applying to the wound will help accelerate the healing process, but it would be good for you to ingest some, as well. It tends to be more potent that way, especially when treating blood loss," I explained as I propped her upright with a stack of lumpy pillows on the bed. "Tastes like crap, though. I can dilute it in some ale, if you want."

"Aren't you just the doting doctor," she chuckled weakly, her eyes still seeming foggy as she blinked owlishly at me. "Do you hand out candies, as well?"

I snorted. I guess she must have felt better—she was back to her regular level of snarkiness. "Only to well-behaved patients."

"Was I not well-behaved?"

"Depends on whether or not you sit here and wait for me to come back with something you can wash this salve down with. Trust me, you'll want it." I shot her a glare of warning as I finished wrapping up her leg in a tight layer of gauze and cotton bandaging. There wasn't much else I could do for her in these conditions, and without my full medical kit. But she would live.

Yay.

Packing up my now mostly-expended emergency medical kit, I sighed and raked some of my soggy hair away from my face. "For the love of all the gods, don't try running off or walking on it, yet. I need to be sure that stitching is going to hold. The bandage will help, but give that salve at least a few hours to start working."

She gave me a mock-salute. "As you wish, Your Highness."

Ughh. Why did I get the feeling she had absolutely no intention of following my orders? *Doctor's* orders?

Because patients almost never did, that's why. Especially the stubborn, fighter-sort.

My soggy socks squished and slurped in my boots all the way down the stairs. I found Agatha at the bar and ordered two ales—one for myself and the other to mix that salve into. Back upstairs, I could have fainted from shock as I pushed the door open and found Violet still sitting on the edge of the bed. Wow. Okay, then. Maybe she did take me a *little* bit seriously?

Naaah.

She sat, dressed in her leggings again, and scowling despairingly at the fresh hole in them from the stab wound. Her mouth scrunched from one side to the other, as though silently wondering if she could fix them somehow.

"I don't guess you're going to tell me how long you've been walking around with a gaping hole in your leg?" I asked as I sat down at the narrow, sparse room's tiny table. I stirred in some of that salve into one of the mugs before I handed it off to her. "Or maybe who put it there?"

"I didn't stop to ask his name," she quipped. "Seeing as how he was rather set on killing me at the moment."

I rolled my eyes and handed her the mug. "Fine. Keep your secrets, then."

I must've sounded more upset than I intended, because she hesitated before taking it, her scarlet eyes flicking between my face and the mug. Her lips pursed slightly, and she puffed a heavy sigh before finally taking it. "The Hands of Fate were waiting for us in the castle. Originally, I assumed it was just as Arlan said—that they had come there to try to capture and interrogate him. But ..." Her voice faded, falling to silence as she stared down into the murky depths of her drink.

"But what?" I pressed. Something in her tone, that tinge of unease, made my pulse quicken.

"I found them in the Upper East Wing, and it didn't seem like they were interested at all in that area," she said, keeping her tone so hushed I could barely hear her.

My chest seized with a sudden rush of panic. Wait—Upper East? Those were Ronan's quarters, weren't they?

"They were looking for my nephew?" I demanded.

"I-I think so." Violet made a face, cringing and wincing as she took her first good gulp of my ale-and-healing-salve concoction. "Ack! Merciful gods, that is *terrible*. What on earth is in that stuff?"

I couldn't answer. Not with my brain still circling that horrible realization that this obscure, fanatical secret organization was looking for Ronan. My only nephew. "Why would the Hands of Fate be looking for him? Ronan isn't even in Maldobar. He hadn't been for several years now. That boss of yours promised my sister years ago to put him somewhere safe, where he could learn to control his curse."

"True," she conceded. "I don't think they realized that. Or maybe they were trying to find some evidence of where he might have gone. To be perfectly honest, I'm not sure how they realized he even existed at all. Your sister has been very wise in keeping him from the public eye until he's ready. You know as well as I do that there's much more complicating his young life than merely his curse. The very nature of his existence is ... sure to ruffle quite a few feathers, once it gets out." Her expression softened, something sad settling over her features as she spoke. Sympathy. Understanding, even. "Fortunately, Arlan has kept all that information very secure. He told only a select few of us where Ronan was being kept. I don't know if your sister was even given the precise location. I can assure you, however, that it is a good place. A place where he will be welcomed, cared for, and educated to the highest degree. If anyone can guide him down the tricky paths to his future, it is the people residing there. And it is better for everyone involved if as few people as possible are aware of his presence there."

"But you know where that is, don't you?" I guessed. The way she talked about it almost made it sound like she had firsthand experience with that place—wherever it was.

Violet bobbed her head once. "Which, I can only assume, is the reason those agents for the Hands of Fate didn't kill me outright. Perhaps they wanted to interrogate me, instead. A lot of good it would've done them, even if they had tried it." She made a sarcastic, chuckling sound in her throat, as though the idea of being interrogated was a bad joke.

I could relate.

"Who else knows? Garnett?" I asked.

She made another sarcastic sound. "Hah! With her still fawning all over that godling boy like a lovesick puppy? Not a chance. She's gotten especially bad at keeping secrets from you lot. Sympathizing, softhearted dear that she is, it's begun to make her quite unreliable as an agent."

"I'll bet," I muttered as I took a long sip from my own mug. Maybe it'd help soothe my now thoroughly frazzled nerves. The Hands of Fate were looking for Ronan? That couldn't be good. Power like his was something I'd only played at when I served Clysiros as the Harbinger. Whatever they wanted from him, I doubted it was of a world-helping variety.

More like world-destroying.

"Your nephew is safe, as far as I know," Violet murmured quietly, almost like an apology. Maybe she felt guilty for not being able to tell me anything more than that. "And those that did manage to escape me and leave the castle last night did so empty-handed."

"And then you came all the way here? With a gaping hole in your leg?" I arched an eyebrow. Hmm. Maybe that shrike I'd seen on my way here, darting low and moving in the same direction, was hers?

"Well, I couldn't exactly patch it up myself, could I?" She laughed and downed the last of her ale, making another wincing face and smacking her lips sourly. "Good thing I knew a very experienced healer would be here, hm?"

"And what if I'd been late?"

She flapped a hand dismissively. "Oh, gods, no. You're *far* too stubborn for that."

Sinking back in that rickety chair, I folded my arms over my chest and rubbed at the stubble beginning to grow in on my chin and jaw. "You think you know me so well, eh?"

She cast me a meaningful sideways glance and grinned.

Great. What was that supposed to mean? That she had been spying on me enough that she thought she knew what I was thinking? Yeah. Right.

And creepy.

Putting her mug aside, Violet held onto the bed to balance herself as she stood. She wobbled at first, and I sat forward a little—just in case she took another nosedive toward the floor. After a few seconds, she straightened and took a deep, steadying breath. Fates. I couldn't imagine it didn't hurt to be putting weight on her leg like that. Not to mention, she was risking ripping out my stitches.

I tried to communicate all that to her with one, solid, disapproving scowl.

She grinned wider and hobbled past me, her gait awkward as she tried to walk without limping. No way was that going to happen. Not today. "Oh, calm down, Your Highness. I'm very accustomed to pain."

"Reigh," I corrected in a growl.

She hesitated by the door, turning just enough to cast me a much less patronizing stare over one of her slender shoulders. Her scarlet eyes flickered over me, as though silently trying to read my intentions.

"It's not very discreet to go around calling me that. Not if we're trying to be stealthy about this departure," I amended with a shrug. "And I've never cared for that title. I'm a dragonrider first, and a prince when I have to be."

"And I thought you would enjoy the flattery." Her tone was coy, but not nearly as much as before. If anything, it sounded forced.

"No. Flattery is for the insecure. I don't need any ego stroking, thanks."

Her lips pursed slightly, brows knitting together as though she had to ponder on that for a moment before turning back to the door. "Very well, then, Lieutenant. We can't linger here. The rest of your companions will be arriving any moment, and there is much work to be done tonight."

I got up with a groan and went to retrieve my things before following her out the door. "Fantastic," I muttered. "Can't wait."

PART FIVE

MAYLEA

15

CHAPTER FIFTEEN

My father was going to be *furious*.

No. Not furious. Explosive. Volcanic, even.

After sneaking into his secret meeting with that strange, glowing-eyed man ... I didn't have much of a choice. Dah wasn't going with them, but it was clear based on everything I'd heard, that Uncle Reigh needed more help. Thatcher was a good fighter, sure, but he was just one person. Uncle Murdoc wasn't going for the same reason my father couldn't. Auntie Pheebs was about to have a baby, too. They needed to be close by in case anything went wrong, and to help out with the babies.

That really only left me with one, obvious choice.

I'd have to go in my father's place.

He would never allow it, of course. He would come up with a thousand reasons why it was too dangerous, I was too young, and I wouldn't be able to handle myself in a place like Nar'Haleen. All a bunch of fodder, of course. He and Mother had been about my age when they set off on their first adventures to rescue Grandpa Sile. They'd fought monsters, slavers, and faced down a king drake.

So, why couldn't I? I'd had loads more training than either of them had back then. I'd practically been born holding a bow and dagger. I was much more competent.

I was meant for this.

Finding Ronan, well, it would just have to wait for now.

The only person I needed to convince about this was walking next to me, shaking like a leaf in autumn, as we hurried into the Deck early the next morning. Lukani hadn't left my side, even if he seemed to be getting more and more nervous about what we were about to do. He walked with his shoulders hunched, head dipped low, and long ears slicked back as we crept along the rows of dragon stalls.

I knew better than to follow Uncle Reigh too closely. He was a former scout, trained in Luntharda, so he'd pick up on anyone tracking him if we were too careless. We had to hold back, observe from a distance, and plan accordingly.

We also needed one key thing. Probably the hardest thing in the entire kingdom to get.

A dragon.

Mavrik would let me ride him. But I seriously doubted that grouchy old beast would listen to me if I asked him to take me all the way to Southwatch without my father being along for the ride. Thatcher's big orange and black drake, Fornax, might listen to me if I was wearing those goggles that helped him see. Unfortunately, Thatcher always carried those with him, either around his neck or in his pocket. Phevos belonged to Auntie Jenna, and he'd do just about anything for fresh salmon ... which I didn't have.

That pretty much just left one option.

"We've got to get Blite's saddle," I whispered to Lukani as we ducked into the tack room where all the saddles were stored. It was packed full, thanks to so many dragonriders coming to the ball, but I had ridden Blite enough times to remember which one was his.

I zipped through all the wooden stands arranged in long rows, each one holding a large, polished leather saddle. The rich smell of the soaps and oils used to clean all that fine leather filled the dim air, sending warm shivers of delight all through my body. I had always *loved* that smell.

Blite's saddle was the only solid black one with bright red stitching and golden-plated buckles. Fancy. And also stocked with a few of the weapons I'd need for this. Uncle Murdoc didn't use a bow, but he did keep some backup daggers tucked in a sheath on either side of the seat—just in case.

I took them and tucked them into the sides of my boots, then went to lift the saddle off the stand.

"Someone's coming!" Lukani gasped suddenly, practically pouncing on me and crushing me to the floor just as the door swung open and light poured in. I froze and held my breath, lying halfway under Lukani's much larger body. Footsteps approached. Someone sighed, muttering under their breath as they made their way down the rows of saddles.

Was it Uncle Reigh? It had to be. At this hour, there was no one else dallying around out here yet. Oh gods, if he found us ... I'd spend the next twenty-four hours getting the lecture of a lifetime from my father instead of setting off to Nar'Haleen.

I shut my eyes tightly and tried not to move or even breathe.

Something rustled behind us.

I flinched.

The man—probably Uncle Reigh—stopped and held still.

Oh. Oh, gods, no!

Slowly turning my head, I locked gazes with Lukani. He was gripping the end of his tail and staring back at me with wide, horrified eyes. Seriously?! His tail had bumped something? Didn't he have any control over that thing?

A second passed. Then another.

No one moved. No one made a sound.

At last, Uncle Reigh began rummaging around again, gathering his saddle off one of the stands, and left. As soon as his footsteps retreated and faded in the distance, I wriggled free of Lukani's grasp and shot him a scathing glare.

"Seriously? You almost blew our cover!" I hissed quietly.

He flushed scarlet around his cheeks and nose and dipped his head even lower. "S-Sorry. My tail gets twitchy when I'm nervous."

Yeah. Obviously. "Come on, we don't have a lot of time. He's going to get too far ahead of us, and then we'll never find him. I've never flown that far on my own. I don't know how to get to Southwatch, let alone that Speckled Sow place, unless I follow him there ..."

I stopped, noticing a sudden and all too familiar shift in my new companion's body language—avoiding my eyes and chewing on the inside of his cheek. Shifting his weight. That tail flicking quickly back and forth. Like there was something important he knew but didn't want to talk about.

I narrowed my eyes. "You know where it is, don't you?"

He didn't answer and still wouldn't look my way.

"Lukani," I warned and scooted closer to grab the front of his silky shirt. "Do you know how to get to Southwatch? Do you know where the Speckled Sow is? You better tell me, or—"

"Yes! Yes, I do but ... it's very far," he whined as he rubbed the back of his neck.

"I know. That's why we need a dragon to take us there. I think I can convince Blite to do it. He's basically a big puppy, once you get to know him. Well, aside from breathing fire and having a lot of teeth. And really big claws." I let go of his shirt and sat back, watching his twitchy demeanor intensify. "What's wrong? Haven't you ever ridden a dragon before?"

He bobbed his head. "I have. But, um, I would prefer not to take one from Murdoc. He can be sort of scary. I don't think taking anything from him is a good idea."

Good point.

I leaned back on my hands and frowned. "Well, do you have a different idea?"

He grimaced and sucked his bottom lip into his mouth, chewing on it fiercely for a moment before he managed a small, reluctant, "Yes."

My eyebrows rose. "Oh?"

His strange yellow eyes shone with flecks of electric green and glistening gold as he finally met my gaze again. His broad shoulders flexed and relaxed with a heavy, defeated sigh. "Yes, I do. But I cannot do it here. And you must promise to do your very best ... not to scream."

I TRIED. I REALLY DID.

But as soon as we stepped out into the corridor outside, checking both ways to make sure there was no one else in sight, Lukani clenched his hands into fists and shut his eyes. His tall form wavered and shifted, changing like a mirage in the weak light of the dawn. I floundered back against the wall with my heart pumping wildly. I gaped at him, unable to keep in a tiny yelp of alarm as his form swelled and changed. He sprouted another set of limbs, long iridescent wings, and his skin grew thousands of mirror-like scales. In a matter of seconds, he wasn't the tall, greenish-hued boy I'd met. He looked like a real, actual shrike!

A shrike with vibrant yellow eyes that considered me almost reluctantly before fluttering his wings and swishing his tail.

Whoa. That was ... incredible!

"You're a shapeshifter," I gasped as I pushed away from the wall. Stepping closer, I held out a hand toward his now bony snout.

He made a low, chittering sound and pushed his nose into my hand, then nodded toward his back.

Oh. Right. I ... I could ride on him now. I'd never ridden a shrike before, but surely it couldn't be all that different from a dragon, right?

Grabbing one of the shrike saddles off a stand in the tack room, I scrambled around him to fasten it on. Thankfully, it didn't fit too differently from a dragon's saddle, even if it was much smaller and lighter. Once I was pretty sure I'd gotten it fastened to his back correctly, I swallowed hard, and made my way around to his side. My sweaty hands slipped on the freshly oiled leather and slick surface of his scales as I climbed up onto his back. It took a few seconds to figure how I could sit between his six powerful legs, translucent wings, and rolling shoulder muscles, especially since the shrike saddle didn't have those handy pockets on the sides for my feet.

Finally, when I felt decently secure, I gave his neck a pat. He hissed and coiled those six strong legs, springing forward to dash down the corridor back to the entrance of the Deck.

From somewhere nearby, I heard the trumpeting roar of a dragon taking off into the growing light of the dawn. Reigh was leaving. And we wouldn't be far behind. Now, we just had to get to Southwatch, figure out which ship he was leaving on, and sneak onboard without anyone noticing—before my father figured out where I was.

Yeah. I could totally pull this off.

Lukani bounded forward, going faster and faster, until he flared those almost dragonfly-like wings and leapt into the sky. With a piercing cry and the hum of the wind vibrating from his rapid wingbeats, we blurred forward and kept low to the ground as we followed the much larger shape of Uncle Reigh and Vexi.

The wind snagged in my hair and the warmth of the sun kissed my face as we dipped and dodged along the rooftops of the royal city, zipping through the sky like a gleaming silver arrow. I grinned and leaned down into his speed. Fates, he was so much *faster* than a dragon. His flight was smoother, more agile, and he could corner on a knife's edge.

I'd have to figure out some way to thank him for this. I knew full well he didn't want to take me to Southwatch. He was disobeying orders from that Arlan guy—the same one my father and the others had met with last night. I had to admit, something about that man was definitely creepy. Otherworldly, almost. He didn't seem like the sort of person you wanted to cross.

But Lukani was doing this to help me. Why, I still didn't understand, but I could figure that out later.

Right now, I kept my gaze trained forward to the approaching trees of the forest and rolling marshlands beyond. Somewhere ahead of us, Southwatch waited. And once we got there, the real challenge would begin. I needed to find a proper longbow, a quiver with some arrows, and any other supplies I might be able to get my hands on before we boarded that ship.

I wouldn't be able to hide from Uncle Reigh forever. I knew that. All I needed to do was make sure he didn't find me until it was way too late to send me back home.

Glancing down at Lukani's big, yellow shrike eyes, I had to wonder if he would want to follow me onboard the ship, too. Probably not, right? Why would he? He had been instructed to watch me, but I sort of doubted that agreement extended to me deciding to leave the kingdom altogether. He had to stay here with Arlan.

Besides, it's not like I would be alone. Uncle Reigh and Thatcher would be there to back me up. Or, rather, I'd be there to back them up. Lukani wouldn't need to keep babysitting me like this. I could handle the rest myself.

I *would* handle it.

Because I was a Broadfeather. And just like my parents, if there was a call for help, I would answer—no matter the danger.

Or potential risk of being grounded for the rest of my natural life.

16

CHAPTER SIXTEEN

There was absolutely nothing fun at all about crouching in a filthy alleyway, in the pouring rain, just so we could watch the front door of the Speckled Sow Tavern in case Uncle Reigh and the others came out.

But that's what Lukani and I did ... for three long, miserable hours.

Even in the rain, the smell of the food coming from the tavern made my head swim. My stomach growled and squirmed, reminding me that I hadn't stopped to eat anything all day. I had almost made up my mind to send Lukani inside to swipe some bread or anything he thought he could get his hands on, when the door opened and four hooded figures hurried out into the downpour. I recognized the saddlebags three of them carried—Uncle Reigh, Uncle Murdoc, and Thatcher—as they followed behind one much smaller figure. A glimpse of silky-smooth white hair from under the figure's hood was a dead giveaway, though. That must be that pretty woman who'd been in the meeting with Arlan.

The one who kept making sad eyes at Uncle Reigh whenever he wasn't paying attention.

"Look! They're on the move!" I whispered and gave Lukani a little nudge with my elbow.

Back in his regular form, he huddled next to me looking every bit as soggy and miserable as I felt. He looked up, ears perking some as they passed by and made their way down the boardwalk. "They're going toward the docks," he whispered back.

"Then we have to follow," I urged.

He hesitated, his lips thinning as he stared after them for a moment. Then he nodded. "Okay. But it's hard to hide out there. And ... Miss Violet is very clever. She knows me, too. We will have to be very careful now."

Oh. Good to know.

We moved as fast and quiet as shadows, taking cover behind crates, barrels, and giant spools of mooring rope as we followed from a safe distance. In the pouring rain, it wasn't easy to keep track of where they'd gone from that far away. They moved down the boardwalk and crossed out onto the network of docks that led between the massive dark shapes of the ships docked at the port. There were dozens of them of all shapes and sizes, rocking and dipping at their moorings, with their sails wrapped up tight and their decks cleared to weather the storm.

The smell of stagnant salt water stung my nose as we moved farther and farther down the docks, leaving the larger three- and four-masted ships behind, and arriving at last before one of the smaller, more sleek ones near the end of the port. Only one mast stretched up from its deck, and the shape of a beautiful horse-like creature with the long tail of a fish was engraved on the very front. The, um, bow, I guess. I didn't know many ship or sailing terms. I'd never even seen the Southern Seas before now.

On the back of the ship, painted in shimmering golden letters against the black-stained wood, the name *Fog Dancer* shone in the light of two big iron lanterns hanging off either end. I guess that was so no one crashed into them from behind. More light glowed from the few porthole windows on the back, below deck, where there must have been crew or cargo quarters.

Someone was home.

We ducked behind a stack of old crates and a mound of tangled fishing nets, watching as Uncle Reigh and the others walked up the wooden gangplank that led up onto the deck. Someone with a lantern stood waiting for them, but from this far away, I couldn't tell who it was.

"We have to get on that ship." I turned to Lukani, hoping he would have some idea.

One look at his drenched, miserable expression, and I knew I wasn't going to get much more out of him tonight. That long flight had taken a lot of strength, and we had to stop several times on the way so he could rest before he could change shape again. Now, his greenish complexion had seemed paler, like maybe using that much of his magical power wasn't something he had ever done before. Not like that, anyway.

Guilt swam in the pit of my stomach like a bunch of eels in a bucket. So far, he'd been working so hard and using his shape-changing magic to fly me all the way here. He'd nearly exhausted himself doing it. Expecting him to go even one step farther with me was reckless. I didn't know him very well, and even if he'd been put in charge of watching over me in the castle, this was far beyond the limits of that responsibility. He didn't owe me anything, and I had no right to ask for any more of his help.

"Okay, listen," I said and grabbed his hand, giving it a jostle so he would look me in the eye. "You've been so amazing, Lukani. I can never thank you enough for all your help. But I know you're worried about getting in trouble for helping me, and I don't expect you to come with me on that ship, or even one more step. So ... I guess what I'm saying is ... if this is as far as you are willing to go, I understand completely."

His brows drew up, expression crinkling into a look of panicked concern. "You don't want me to go with you anymore?"

"No! No, that's not it at all," I objected. "I'd love for you to come. But I don't want you to feel like you have to just because you're watching out for me, or—"

He put a finger against my lips as a sad, crooked grin curled over his features. His rain-drenched black hair stuck to his cheeks and forehead as he tilted his head to the side a little. "Where you go, I go. Okay?"

My cheeks got strangely hot and tingly as he pulled his finger away. I-I didn't know what to say. He really wanted to keep following me? Knowing I was probably headed for Nar'Haleen? That was a long way to go on a whim, and we'd only just met. And what about that Arlan man? Wouldn't he be angry when he found out Lukani had snuck off that far?

Not that my situation was going to be much better when Dah figured out where I'd gone. I shuddered at the thought. He'd be hurt. Furious. Worried. Mother would be, too.

But I didn't have a choice.

"Okay," I said quietly. "We do this together, then."

"Together," he agreed.

I took a steadying breath and peered back up at the looming, dark shape of the ship. Lightning popped in the clouds overhead, flashing bright and creating an eerie silhouette of the vessel's many ropes and lines stemming from that central mass like a spider's web.

I was going to have to come up with one heck of an idea for how to get onboard without anyone noticing. And once we did, we had to be extra careful. That ship wasn't very big compared to some of the others we'd passed—maybe sixty feet from end to end. It would be difficult to find a place to hide where no one would find us before they departed.

This was going to be riskier than I'd hoped.

"The trick is going to be getting up to that window," I thought aloud, glancing back up at it. Yep. That was probably twenty-or-so feet straight up to climb from the water to that window. Then there was the matter of opening it—if it even opened at all.

Still risky, but doable. And currently our best bet to get onboard without being seen.

Grabbing Lukani's hand again, I tugged him along after me toward the very edge of the dock. We ducked behind another cluster of barrels and crouched down. Gods, from this close, the ship seemed much bigger. Scarier, even. I had never been on a ship before. I didn't know what might be waiting for us beyond that window.

Reaching down into the sides of my boots, my hands closed tightly around the hilt of the daggers I'd borrowed from Uncle Murdoc's saddle. He'd taught me to do this years ago. I could manage it ... even in the rain. At night. On a ship.

Yeah. No problem.

I shut my eyes for a moment and took another deep breath. Whew. Okay, time to—

Something poked me in the shoulder.

I turned around, looking directly into the many, massive blinking yellow eyes of the biggest spider I had ever seen in my life. I stumbled back, hitting the wooden dock on my rear end as all the air rushed out of my lungs at once. I couldn't think. I couldn't scream. It was, Gods and Fates, it was as big as a nightmare! With silky black hairs everywhere and little wiggling mandibles.

The spider crawled toward me, the curled black hooks on the ends of its legs clicking over the wood. Then it stopped, dipping low, and raising two of those legs to point at its back.

Wait a second—*Lukani?!* He could change into a spider, too?

"H-H-How did you?" I squeaked and stammered, my legs still shaking as I got back to my feet.

I guess spiders couldn't talk or make as many sounds as shrikes, because he just kept pointing at the bulbous part of his back and then up to the window. Oh. Right. Spiders might not have been able to talk, but they could climb.

And climbing was what we needed.

Tucking the blades back into the sides of my boots, I tried not to cringe or gag as I climbed onto his back and stayed low. In this shape, the glossy dark hairs all over his body were coarse and prickly, but pitch black and surely harder to see in the gloom of the stormy night. We might just stand a chance at pulling this off without being spotted if we moved quickly.

After all, spiders could climb a lot better than I could.

Lukani skittered back a few feet, hunkering down and giving a little butt-wiggle before he dashed across the dock, staying low and moving as fast as a shadow. He climbed onto one of the big mooring ropes that tethered the ship to the docks and climbed, fast and silent, all the way to the back of the ship.

And I, well, all I could do was hang on for dear life as the barnacle-encrusted back of the ship drew closer and closer through the pouring rain.

My knees shook some as I stood on Lukani's spider-form side like a step, roughly twenty feet from the foaming, rough ocean below, with the wind and rain in my face. Before me, the dark porthole window was locked, but I wasn't giving in yet. I hunkered against the side of the ship and fished one of the daggers from the side of my boot. I slipped it between my teeth long enough to position myself just right, and then slid its thin point between the glass pane and the latch to begin working it open. A nudge, twist, and click later, the window swung in with a soft creak.

Without a sound, I stuck my head in for a quick look around, and let out a trembling sigh of relief to see nothing but stacked crates, boxes, and barrels. The cargo hold. No wonder this window wasn't lit.

I scrambled through the window, and dropped to the floor in a crouch with a soft thud. My clothes and hair immediately dripped a puddle onto the floor, and I scooted over so Lukani could follow. He crawled through, looking like his normal self again as he hit the floor next to me on the balls of his feet like a cat on the hunt. His tail flicked as he blinked and squinted around the dark space. The earthy smell of potatoes, sharp aroma of ale and fragrance of wine filled my nose with every breath. Food. They had food here.

My stomach growled and cramped, making my eyes water. There wasn't time right now, though. I had to find out where Uncle Reigh and the others were. I needed to know what was happening, if this really was the ship they were planning on taking all the way to Nar'Haleen, and when they were planning on setting sail.

Now I just had one problem.

And he was crouching next to me with rainwater dripping off his nose, chin, and from the tips of his long, pointed ears. Lukani obviously had a lot going for him. He could shapeshift and climb or fly. But we had already established in that saddle room back at the Deck that being stealthy was ... maybe not his strong suit.

Time for me to take over.

"Can you change into something smaller?" I leaned over to whisper into one of his long ears. "Like pocket-sized?"

His mouth scrunched thoughtfully, then he nodded. Shutting his eyes tightly, his face contorted as though he were in pain as his form began to waver again, shifting and warping as he shrank down smaller and smaller.

A small, white, yellow-eyed rat blinked up at me and wriggled its tiny whiskered nose. I had to contain a squeal of delight as he sat up on his hind legs, his tiny front paws so pink and cute. Scooping him up, I put him on my shoulder and smirked. Perfect. Now, at least, I wouldn't have to worry about him blowing our cover. Time to find the others.

Creeping quietly through the cargo hold, I kept one dagger still gripped firmly in hand as I darted from shadow to shadow, not making a single sound. At the far end of the room, a set of double doors led up to another open area with a set of stairs leading up—probably to the deck. Flashes of lightning lit my path as I moved carefully, keeping my eyes peeled for anyone else lurking in the dark. But there was no one. No sign of sailors or members of the crew. Nothing.

Strange. Shouldn't someone be here, even if they were at port? Like a guard or something? Unless, the captain or whoever owned the ship had invited his crew to leave while this secret meeting was going down.

Whatever the case, it made sneaking around a lot easier. I made my way back up on deck without a hitch, and braved the rain again to slip to the back of the ship where the large, luxurious-looking main cabin was positioned right behind the ship's wheel, or helm, that must have been used to steer it at sea. The colored glass windows of that cabin were lit warmly, and I could see shapes of people moving around inside, sometimes eclipsing the light.

Found them.

Now, how to get inside without any of them noticing.

Keeping low, I made my way over to one of the windows and stole a glance inside, just a quick look around to see the layout of the room. It was difficult to see clearly through the dark red glass pane, but I could pick out the outlines of six people silhouetted against the tall glass windows at the very back. Five of them stood around, while the sixth sat at what looked like a large desk. I couldn't make out what they said over the howling wind, rain, and thunder—but it didn't sound good. Not happy talking, at least. I recognized Uncle Reigh's voice shouting over the others. It sent a bolt of panic through my body, making my teeth chatter and my toes curl inside my boots. I'd never heard him sound so furious. What was happening in there?

Footsteps approached the doors right next to where we were listening in. Oh no. Were they done with their meeting already? Lukani let out a squeak of alarm before he burrowed into my hair to hide. I glanced at the doors, noting the placement of the hinges, like Uncle Murdoc had taught me. They would swing outward. Perfect.

I dashed over to stand right outside them with my back to the wall. The lock clunked and the old salt-rusted hinges groaned as the door swung out in front of me, covering my hiding place just in time. I had to turn my head to the side so my nose didn't get smashed. Still—I had to stay perfectly still. No sudden moves. No loud breathing.

"Jenna is going to be furious," Uncle Reigh seethed as he stormed past. "How could he let this happen? Right under his watch! Gods curse it straight to the abyss. And now we just trust that he's going to somehow track down Ronan in a foreign land where we have basically no allies? And that's assuming those madmen haven't killed him already!"

My heart gave a wild, desperate thump and seemed to stop altogether. Ronan? Did he mean the one I'd played with when we were little? The same one who had been my best friend? The one who had disappeared?

I swallowed hard as every muscle drew tight. I bit down against the urge to move, to rush out and demand to know who he was talking about. It couldn't be the same Ronan, could it?

Then again ... the Ronan I'd played with lived in the castle. Uncle Reigh was a Prince of Maldobar. I'd suspected Ronan might be related to them somehow, but no one had ever said it outright. Maybe Ronan really was a member of the royal family. But why would they keep it a secret? Why would they hide him away?

And what had happened to him now?

"She'll be furious *and* heartbroken," Uncle Murdoc added as he followed them out. "Maybe he's right and it's best not to tell her yet. She wouldn't be able to resist that instinct to start sending armed forces to the area to try and retrieve him, and that might spark an international incident. That's exactly the kind of attention we don't need over there. I don't like it, but I have to admit Arlan is right about this. We need a precise, discreet rescue and extraction plan. And before that, we need outfitting. So, let's get that done, get back here to the ship, and work on planning our next step."

I caught a glimpse of Thatcher clapping a reassuring hand onto Uncle Reigh's shoulder as they headed for the gangplank to leave the ship. "One problem at a time, Reigh. We've got your back. One way or another, we *will* get Ronan back, safe and sound."

PART SIX

CLARKE

17

CHAPTER SEVENTEEN

Pasha broke the surface in total darkness.

As soon as my head broke the surface of the water, I gasped in frantically, and gulped down as much air as possible. I clung to Kaili's waist, feeling her tensing as she coughed and sputtered, too.

We were alive. Alive and ... maybe safe? It was hard to tell. For a moment, we just hung there in the dark water, gripping Pasha and catching our breath. Every splash and gasp echoed off the cavern walls somewhere overhead. But all I could do was blink and stare around blindly, unable to see even my own hand in front of my face.

Pasha must have been able to see better than we could, though, because when Kaili gave him a little nudge and gentle whisper, he swam along the surface without hesitation. We slowed and stopped again, and Kaili slid off his back and out of my grasp.

"H-Hey! Wait! Where are you—?" Before I could finish, light suddenly sparked and bloomed in the dark.

Kaili stood on a bank right next to where Pasha was still treading water and carrying me. She held up a freshly-lit torch that filled the small chamber with a wavering glow. The sea cave wasn't very big, maybe twenty feet long at the most, and the low ceiling was crusted with barnacles and shells. Beyond it, the roar of the surf sounded like thunder, and the only place to stand on dry land was a little rock shelf that was scarcely big enough for Kaili and I to sit down on side-by-side.

"Come on," she urged as she held out her hand.

I seized it and swam away from Pasha's back. Somehow, wading through that churning water felt far more dangerous in the dark. I couldn't even see the bottom to know if there was something terrible lurking down there. Scrambling onto the bank, I sat down next to her and pulled the goggles down off my face. My thoughts raced as I tried to catch my breath again. Were those ships still pursuing us? Would they know where we'd gone to hide? How long could we stay here? Was there a way back to the surface other than the way we'd come in?

Kaili's expression had gone stony and distant as she crouched down by the water and held out her hand. She clucked and called to Pasha, then grabbed his bridle to hold him steady while she looked over his body by the light of her torch. Her brow snapped into a desperate look of fear when she stopped along his tail. There, an arrow bolt stuck out from between his scales.

"Hold this for me, Clarke," she commanded.

I immediately sat up and scooted closer, taking the torch and keeping it angled so she had enough light to see. Her hands shook, smeared with blood as she began gentle probing at the area around the arrow. Pasha's nostrils flared and he snorted, shifting and tensing at the contact.

"I have to pull it out," she murmured, her voice catching as she stole a glance over at me.

I nodded.

Her jawline went tense as she gripped the arrow's shaft close against his side. Then she shut her eyes tightly and gave one stern, swift yank. Pasha shrieked and floundered. He pitched wildly in the water and broke free of her hold on his halter.

Falling onto her rear beside me, Kaili stared at him in teary-eyed fear as her hippocampus paddled away from us and tossed his head. I could faintly see the trail of his blood swirling in the water. Slowly, her gaze tracked from him to the blood-soaked arrow in her hand. She grimaced and snarled, taking it in both hands and snapping it in half before she threw the pieces back into the ocean.

"Will he be okay?" I asked quietly.

Her chin trembled as she stared at Pasha, his dark eyes and scales glittering in the dark as he swam just beyond the torchlight. "Yes. But he cannot carry us any farther. I-I ... I am so sorry, Clarke. I didn't realize he had been this badly wounded."

My mind started to whirl as my body flushed hot with worry. What was she trying to say? That we were stranded down here now?

Kaili turned away some, as though trying to hide her face from my view. "This was the only place I could think of where we would be able to hide. And we cannot stay here for long. This cave will flood when the tide returns."

Oh. Oh, sweet gods. That wasn't good. I could swim decently now, sure, but I didn't believe for a single second I'd be able to find my way out of this cave in the dark while holding my breath.

"What can we do? Are we stranded?" I asked, unable to keep my own voice from shaking.

"I don't know," she admitted. "The only thing I can think of is trying to send a message to Noa and the others somehow ..." Kaili's voice trailed away to silence as she went on staring at her mount.

After a few minutes, Pasha paddled back over and made a soft, worried rumbling sound. She took his snout in her hands and rubbed along his long muzzle and around the fins that crested his head and down his neck. That look of resignation on her face hit me like a knife to the heart. It ached like a deep rot and brought back every painful word Noa had said to me about how they'd come to live here in the first place. The war between Nar'Haleen and the neighboring kingdoms had already cost her so much. Now it was threatening to strip away this happiness she had finally found here.

I had to do something. I had to think of something. Right now.

Fortunately, thinking was what I did best.

Standing up, I stared around at the cave by the light of our single torch. There were a few other things tied to Pasha's saddle, and I spotted an old, barnacle encrusted chest on the far side of the small shelf where we sat. It was already open, and inside, I could see more wooden sticks with ends wrapped in dense cloth for torches, a piece of flintstone, and a handful of other basic tools that all looked like they'd spent a lot of time underwater.

Ahh. So that's where she'd gotten this light from.

"Did you put this here?" I asked.

Kaili nodded. "Noa and I found this cave a while ago. We stashed a few things here, just in case."

I held up a blade made of a solid piece of sharpened white bone, the hilt wrapped in leather strapping that had been oiled so that the water wouldn't destroy it as quickly. "Is Noa the only other person who knows about it?"

She shrugged. "He might have told some of the other villagers, in case they needed to hide here like we are."

I gripped the dagger and started back toward her. "Good."

"What are you doing?" she demanded with a disapproving frown as I began tying the dagger to one end of Pasha's reins. I tripled the knot, making extra-sure it would hold even if Pasha swam at top speed.

Then I stood back, my chest heaving with heavy, anxious breaths. "Sending a message. He can't carry us, but he can still swim, right?"

"I-I, um, yes. He can," she confirmed.

"Then send him back to the village right now. Someone had to notice us riding out of the bay earlier, or at least heard that horn blasting from the ships. If Pasha can return with that knife and Noa or one of the other villagers finds it, they might guess where we are." I turned back to face her—

Just in time for Kaili to grab the front of my shirt and jerk me down to her height so she could plant a kiss right on my cheek.

"Yes!" She let me go just as fast and rushed away to Pasha. "That's brilliant, Clarke!'

I staggered and nearly tripped over my own feet. B-Brilliant? No, it wasn't, er, *that* brilliant. Was it? No. It was just, you know, common sense. Right? Anyone could have figured that out.

My face burned as I touched my cheek where she'd kissed it, watching her mutter quietly to Pasha before she gave his head a final stroke. Then she barked a command, a word in the Rienkan elven tongue, and swatted him on the neck.

"DOMU!"

The word for "home."

KAILI AND I SAT ALONE IN THE DARK FOR WHAT FELT LIKE AN ETERNITY, THE ROAR AND rush of the surf seeming to grow more intense with each passing minute. I tried not to let my mind wander too far into that, or think about what it might feel like to drown in the dark like this. If someone had told me back when I was at the library that I would someday die by drowning in an underwater sea cave with a pretty girl after being chased by Nar'Haleenan warships, I probably would have laughed.

Laughed ... and then passed out.

I fidgeted with my goggles where they hung around my neck, then wiped at the thick lenses of my glasses, which I'd carried along stowed safely in the chest pocket inside my tunic. If I held them just right in the torchlight, I could just make out the shapes of tiny runes etched into the glass right around the outermost sides of the lenses. The spellwork that helped keep my head under control.

"You know I used to get teased about these all the time at the library?" I thought aloud, laughing a little under my breath at the memory.

Kaili sat close beside me, and looked over when I started to speak. "Why? You said you need them, don't you? To keep you from reading too much?" Her tone made it all too obvious that she still didn't quite understand that.

I didn't blame her, though. I still didn't understand it, either.

"Just because you need something in order to live or be healthy like everyone else doesn't mean people won't make fun of you for it," I sighed as I slid them back up the bridge of my nose. "Without them, I get bad headaches, and I ... remember things."

She tipped her head to the side slightly, her expression creased with a thoughtful frown. "What things?"

"*Everything*," I whispered. "Something has been wrong with my head ever since I was little. Anything I read or see, I can't forget it. Ever. It's like it becomes a part of me, and I can't do anything to stop it. It was overwhelming, so they made these for me. It helps hold things back, to keep me from remembering."

"You weren't wearing them while we were riding earlier," she seemed to realize aloud.

My cheeks grew hot again and I looked away. "I know. It's okay. I ... want to remember that."

I could hear the smile in her voice as she laughed quietly. "You are a little strange, Clarke. But I like you. I'm glad you decided to stay with us."

"Yeah," I murmured. "Me too."

"Was there anyone else at the library who had strange abilities like yours?" she asked.

The question hit me like someone had just lobbed a rock and hit me right between the eyes. I sat rigid and still, my mind already blurring back to the days I'd spent in tutoring with the scholars, watching the ones who tampered with arcane magics studying or creating runes. They didn't take in a lot of wards, or go out looking for them in orphanages just because they needed help or wanted companionship. While I lived there, I had only known of twelve others.

Until the day there were thirteen.

He had arrived late one night, flanked by guards in shimmering silver armor and draped in heavy blue cloaks with their necks lined in white fox fur. They'd carried swords and spoke in strange accents as they exchanged hushed words with High Inquisitor Bellavora. Then, they had left him behind and departed just as quickly.

I'd only gotten a few glimpses of him, and I realized right away that he wasn't like the other wards the scholars had in their care. For one thing, he was a lot older than their usual adoptees. Instead of being a baby or toddler, he was probably somewhere around eight—a little younger than I was at the time. He had dark hair and big, frightened blue eyes.

And there was a strange mark on the top of one hand. It wasn't a rune I had ever seen the scholar's use before—and I certainly would have remembered if they had. It was a symbol I'd only seen that once, and never again after ... just like the boy.

I didn't know where in the deep, winding caverns of the Compendium they had taken him, but after that night, I had never seen him again. The library was as vast as it was ancient, and there were areas I knew I'd never been to before, places the High Inquisitor didn't want us to go—like the place I'd found that book.

I had to wonder if they'd taken him somewhere like that. Somewhere to a vault all his own. Maybe he had been like me. Different. Strange. But whatever was off about him, it must have been dangerous somehow. Why else would they keep him isolated? Why else would the scholars pretend he didn't exist at all when I asked about him later?

Whoever or whatever that boy was, he had been a secret. Another mystery of the library I'd nearly forgotten about.

"I don't know," I answered at last. "It's possible, I guess. There were a lot of strange things in the Compendium. It was the kind of place you go to find answers no one else can, or store secrets you don't want anyone else to find."

"What does that make you?" she asked, giving my arm a playful little nudge. "An answer or a secret?"

I had to think about that. Honestly, I'd never really considered it. "Neither," I resolved at last, and gave her a mischievous grin of my own. "I'm a problem no one knows how to solve."

18

CHAPTER EIGHTEEN

The roaring of the surf outside our cave was so loud I could barely hear it when Kaili shouted my name.

Scooting closer together, we interlocked our arms and watched as the water steadily began to rise. First an inch. Then three. Then a foot.

The tide was coming in.

In a matter of minutes, this cave would be fully submerged—and so would we. No air. No light. No way out.

"How far is it to try to swim out?" I yelled, looking desperately at the only exit that led back out to the ocean.

"A thousand yards at least!" Kaili cried, her eyes wide and terrified. "But it is not a straight swim. The tunnel winds and I cannot navigate it in the dark!"

Great. I didn't know if I could swim that far even if I was able to breathe the whole time. Sweet merciful gods. We weren't going to make it. Even if we tried.

But what other choice was there?

"We have to try!" I shouted and took off my glasses. I crammed them back into my pocket and pulled my goggles up, then seized her hand to start tugging her toward the shallower water. Already, the shelf where we'd been sitting was under a foot of water. "When the chamber fills, there's a chance there will still be an air pocket at the top. We'll wait and see. If not, then we have to try to swim for it!"

Kaili nodded, gripping my hand so tight I lost the circulation to my fingers. "O-Okay."

We waited in the rising water as it swelled to our legs, then our waists. Then our shoulders. Kaili was shorter, so she had to start treading water first. I held onto her to let her rest as long as possible before I lost contact with the bottom, too.

I couldn't grip her hand and the torch, but I wasn't willing to let go of her. The torch sank to the depths, and then we were both paddling furiously in the dark. My legs and arms ached. My lungs burned. I couldn't keep this up forever.

My head hit the ceiling as the water rose, and finally seemed to stop. O-Oh gods! I had stopped! I had to swim with my head tilted back to breathe, but there was just enough of an air bubble left that I could suck in desperate gulps.

"Clarke," Kaili whimpered.

"We're okay! We're going to make it. There's enough air. We can hold on till the tide goes out, and then ..." I stopped. And then what? We sat here for another cycle only to paddle for our lives again when the tide came back in? We weren't going to last long like this. No food. No fresh water to drink.

It made drowning quickly seem like a mercy.

Then something strong grabbed my ankle.

I screamed and kicked, fighting to throw it off as it began to pull me down. I was yanked under, tossed in the dark water. Gods, what was happening? Was it a monster? Something trying to eat me? Was this the lair of some carnivorous sea creature?

One desperate flail and I managed to break free, clawing my way back to the surface again and gasping in a choking, sputtering breath. "Th-There's s-something under th-the water!" I panicked.

But Kaili was gone. No answer. No splashing. Nothing.

"Kaili?" I yelled and looked around, feeling around blindly through the water. Even with my goggles on, I couldn't see anythi—

Light bloomed in the water below me. I stared, half in horror and half in awe, as a bluish light glowed from the depths and rose. It came closer and closer, and finally broke the surface of the water right in front of me.

I paddled backward, trying to put some distance between myself and whatever it was. Visions of horrible deep-ocean angler fish with glowing lures and toothy maws flashed through my mind.

But it wasn't one. It was a man. A man wearing something that glowed vibrant blue wrapped around his head like a crown. Vines? Or some sort of sea plant?

"Clarke! Hold onto me!" Noa shouted as he grabbed my wrist and dragged me in closer.

I could've hugged him like a scared baby squirrel right then, but instead I grabbed onto his forearm and took in one last, deep breath. Then I followed him down into the churning dark water far below.

Noa led the way deeper, all the way down to the bottom of the chamber where a single hippocampus waited. Not Pasha, though. This one was bright orange and white, with longer fin-frills on its front legs and tail.

Noa basically shoved me down onto the saddle in front of him before he mounted up and seized the reins. He gave the beast a meaningful nudge and we rocketed forward, shooting forward through the dark tunnel like we'd been launched from a crossbow. The hippocampus darted up and down, taking sharp corners, and navigating the twisting tunnel without any hesitation. I guess they could see very well in the total darkness. Lucky.

Just as my lungs began to twist and ache, feeling like they were shriveling up in my chest, silver light appeared dead ahead. Moonlight shining through the water. Gods, how long had we been down there?

I didn't even want to think about it.

Noa urged the hippocampus upward, and with a mighty flick of its tail, we zoomed to the surface. My head broke the surface, and I sucked in a sputtering, wheezing gasp. Behind me, Noa did the same. It made me feel a little less pathetic by comparison.

"Where's Kaili?" I demanded, looking back at him for an explanation.

I bit back a scream as another hippocampus carrying two passengers suddenly broke the surface next to us. It gave a shriek and tossed its head, then paddled over to swim alongside us. Clinging to its back, her eyes wide and face pale in terror, Kaili stared straight at me. I guess she was still in shock, though, because she didn't say anything.

"Hold on," Noa warned as he gave our mount another bump of his heels. "You're all right now."

It wasn't until we were surging over the surface of the water, jumping the waves and making our way back down the coast, that I could really wrap my mind around what had just happened. My plan had worked. Pasha had made it back to the village, and someone had found him. They'd figured out where we were, and Noa had come for us.

I couldn't decide if I wanted to laugh, cry, or throw up. All three would have felt right at that moment, but I just didn't have the energy. Slumping against the hippocampus's neck, I decided to just focus on the taste of the sweet, free air instead. Almost right beside us, Kaili was clinging to the back of the other beast, and still looking a little catatonic. Fortunately, the young man sitting behind her, guiding the creature, was on high alert ... and injured.

Until then, I hadn't really stopped to consider him. It wasn't anyone I knew personally, but the crude bandaging wrapped around his head and chest were stained with blood. What? Had he been attacked by the warships, too?

I glanced back at Noa, who was pushing our mount harder as we neared the cove where our village was tucked back against the shores. He had a deep gash along one of his cheeks, and more superficial cuts and slashes on his arms. Worst of all, there were dark red splotches across his chest, like a severe burn. More of those splotches were on his forearms and hands, some a lot worse than others.

Oh no.

The realization hit me an instant before I saw it—the entrance to the cove where our village was. It glowed in the night, the grass rooftops of every hut burning like bonfires. Dark shapes floated in the shallow waters, not moving and bristling with arrows. Overturned canoes licked with flames. Hippocampi streaked away, fleeing in panicked groups like they weren't sure where to go now that their home was ablaze.

And no warships or longboats in sight.

Tears welled in my eyes. Gods, no. No!

I looked back, blinking against the ocean spray, and caught another glimpse of Kaili. The distant glow of the flames lit her face and sparkled off the tears streaming down her cheeks. I tried to speak, to say something, anything, but no sound would leave my throat. There were no words for this.

No one in that village had anything to do with the war. They weren't soldiers or spies. They were just simple fishermen. Good people, who had taken me in out of the kindness of their hearts when I had nothing to offer in return. Nar'Haleen had no valid reason to attack people like that.

But it was just like Kaili said.

This was war—and that was the only reason they needed to justify cold-blooded murder.

I STOOD, NUMB AND SILENT, AS WE LEFT OUR MOUNTS IN A TINY LAGOON TUCKED behind a tree-covered outcropping. It gave enough cover that we could move around without worrying about being spotted, and I noticed that there were several other hippocampi resting in those still waters.

Kaili let out a sobbing scream when she saw Pasha and ran to him, wrapping her arms around his neck and burying her face against him. My shoulders dropped and I let out a breath of relief I hadn't even realized I was still holding in. At least he had been saved. That was something.

"We need to move inland," Noa muttered as he walked past me through the knee-deep water. He'd taken that weird, bioluminescent crown of vines off his head and left it with his own mount, and begun limping for the shore. A deep slash across his calf made his gait halt and stagger with every step. It left a trail of blood across the sand as he trudged onward a few more paces before finally stopping, turning back, and whistling to call us along.

Kaili gave Pasha one last kiss on the nose before she left him and followed.

I followed, too, still unable to say a word. What could I possibly say? They—we—had just lost everything. Where could we go? What would we do for food and shelter?

I knew those questions must also be running through Noa's mind as he led the way through the dense foliage beyond the beach. Ahead, a few spots of light winked through the trees and undergrowth. The closer we got, the more I heard sounds echoing through the night. Crying. Wailing. Grieving.

Out of the entire village, only twenty or so people crowded around three small campfires on the jungle floor. Men, women, and a few children with haunted expressions and singed, blood-spattered clothes. Some of them were injured, and it didn't look like anyone had proper medical supplies to work with for bandaging, so they had torn off strips of their own clothes, instead.

I searched every face around each of the campfires, looking for the boys. Where were they?

"Where are Finn and Malik?" Kaili demanded suddenly, seeming to notice their absence at the same moment.

Noa didn't answer.

My heart hit the soles of my bare feet. My chest seized, and once again, it felt like I was trapped in that dark cave, gasping for air. No. Gods, no, they couldn't be ...

"NOA?!" Kaili screamed as she rushed over to grab his shoulders and force him to stop. "Look at me, Noa! Where are they? Where are our boys?!"

He stared back at her, his expression utterly empty of everything except anguish.

He didn't have to say it.

They were gone.

Kaili fell into him, weeping so hard her whole body shook against his chest. He wrapped his arms around her, still looking dejectedly away from the fires and into the dark of the jungle. He never said a word.

Sometimes, there just aren't any.

The night slipped on, eerily indifferent to our tiny group huddled around the firelight. Noa had managed to save a few things from their hut before it was set ablaze, and he handed Kaili a bag of her pearls and a quilt to wrap up in. She clung to them like anchors in a storm as she sat, staring silently into the flames.

I offered back my goggles, which were his anyway, and sat down beside Noa on the other side of the campfire. After a few minutes, I couldn't take it anymore. I had to know. I needed to ask, "Was this our fault? Did they attack because they saw us outside the cove?"

Noa's head turned and he cast me a strange, sideways scowl. "No. Why would you think that?"

"Because they spotted us first, didn't they? They tried to chase us down in longboats. We barely made it into that cave," I answered quietly.

Noa stared back at the fire, his sharp features seeming much older in the wavering light of the flames. "They would have found our village either way, Clarke. It is rare for Nar'Haleenan warships to cruise so close to the shoreline because of the rocks. But when they do, they often attack villages as a show of force. We who have ancestral ties back to Rienka are not welcome in their lands anymore."

"That's what Kaili said." I couldn't decide if that made me feel better or worse. About the same, I guess. "Where are we going to go now?"

"I've spoken with the few elders who survived. They want to take everyone to the city of Uru'Nai. It isn't far on foot, and there is supposedly still a censure district there for people born of Rienkan or Damarian descent." Noa kept his voice hushed, but it didn't matter. Kaili heard him.

Her face flushed with anger all the way to the tips of her pointed ears. "I will not be confined to some squalid, glorified prison camp! I'd rather live in the wilds, here, and take my chances."

"You can, if you wish," Noa countered, his tone sharp and admonishing. "But there are others here who don't have the luxury of a choice. There are elderly, injured, mothers with young infants. And we have nothing for them—not even weapons to defend ourselves."

Her mouth snapped shut and scrunched bitterly, tears welling in her turquoise eyes again as she lowered her head and looked away.

I didn't know all that much about censure districts. Not really, anyway. I'd read about them, sure. They'd been opened long ago, after Damaria first rebelled. At first, Nar'Haleen had forced only the humans with Damarian ties to go there. Then, they'd become one of the few places in the kingdom where even a Rienkan elf didn't have to live in fear of what had just happened to us. But conditions were said to be cramped and filthy. Supplies were minimal, and desperation plentiful. A dangerous mix, especially in wartime. Based on what I had read, it didn't seem to take long for places like that to become incredibly dangerous. There, people were kept under strict guard by a kingdom that didn't want them there to begin with, to turn into makeshift prisons.

And bloodshed inevitably followed.

"We can't go anywhere tonight." Noa sighed and leaned forward to rest his elbows on his knees. "Tomorrow morning, a few of us will go back to the village and see what else we can salvage. Then, we can make a choice about where to go next."

"And what if *he* is still there?" another young man, the one who had carried Kaili back on his hippocampus, spoke up.

"Who?" I asked. Had they seen someone specific during the attack? A general or a captain?

"There was a young man with them when they came ashore. They guarded him well, but I don't know why. He didn't need any extra protection," Noa spat, his expression seething. "Not when he could make the flames dance at his command."

Huh? A young man who could *control fire?* Seriously? Was that even possible? I had read stacks upon stacks of ancient tomes about the arcane and divine magic. But I'd never heard of anything like that before. Not even from the lore of the godstones.

I glanced at Noa, trying to figure out if he was being serious or this was just an over-embellishment of some magical weapon the guy had carried. "You mean he had an artifact of some kind, right? Some object he used to make fire?" I'd read about things like that, too.

Noa shook his head. "He used only his hand—a hand branded with a strange black marking."

⸙ 19 ⸙

CHAPTER NINETEEN

I almost fell off the log where I sat next to Noa. A young man ... with a black marking ... on his hand? No. It couldn't be. Not possible. It couldn't be the same person.

Unless ...

Oh, gods, what if it was? What if that was the reason he'd been brought to the library? What if he did have something bizarre and powerful about him, as well?

"You, uh, you didn't get a good look at him, did you?" I asked, my voice cracking a little.

Noa cast me another scrutinizing sideways look. Almost like he suspected I was holding something back. "I did not. I only glimpsed him through the flames. I think his hair was dark, but not long. He didn't seem to be an elf. Apart from that, I can't say."

I suddenly wished I could crawl back into that sea cave and hide. It couldn't be the same boy I had seen come to the library all those years ago. He would have died in whatever attack destroyed it, if he was even still there at all. I had no way of knowing how long he'd been staying at the library.

My head spun and throbbed, even with my glasses on. It kept replaying the memory of seeing him arrive that night. It was only by chance that I'd even seen it at all. I was up late, reading of course, and I needed a fresh candle because mine was about to go out.

"Why? Is this someone you know?" Now even Noa's voice had a slightly accusing edge.

"No. I-I don't think so, anyway. I saw someone once with a tattoo on their hand, but it was a long time ago," I answered quickly. "And it wasn't someone I knew personally."

His vibrant turquoise eyes narrowed some, and his dark eyebrows scrunched together, like he wasn't sure if he believed me or not. That look made all the swirling dark tattoos around his right eye wrinkle, too.

I winced and looked away. It wasn't a lie, though. That was all I had known about that boy. Our paths had never crossed again after that night, and the High Inquisitor never spoke about him. Whoever he was, he hadn't come to the Compendium to be another ward like the rest of us.

My head kept whirling like a top all night, circling that memory and all the questions it stirred up. One by one, the other surviving members in our group began to use whatever they could—blankets, cloaks, or big fern fronds—to make beds around the firelight. Some stayed awake to keep watch, but most found ways to lie down and rest.

Kaili curled up in her quilt, still not saying anything. Although, every now and then, I could see her shaking and hear her sobbing quietly. I wished there was something I could say. Something to reassure her. But I didn't want to make it worse by saying the wrong thing. It was probably better to just give her some space for now.

I laid down on a makeshift bed of broad leaves and part of a half-singed blanket. But I couldn't sleep. Not yet. Not with my thoughts still whipping around like a palm tree in a typhoon. I'd never spent much time trying to picture what life was like outside of the library, but I never would have been able to imagine anything like this.

Lying on my back, I could see a tapestry of a million glittering stars between the palm fronds overhead. Beautiful, but cold and indifferent. Some of the lore I had read said the stars were gateways to the realm of the gods. Others believed they were an eternal burning prison for those cursed by the Fates in the afterlife. There were a lot of theories, and I wasn't sure which was true. Maybe none of them. But staring at those stars, scattered like diamonds across a field of endless darkness and soft silver moonlight, finally made my eyelids grow heavy.

I had almost drifted off, lulled into a sense of calm by the crackling and warmth of the fire, when a soft thud on the ground next to me made my eyes pop open again—just in time to see Kaili curl up right beside me. She draped the quilt over both of us and lay down on her side, her back against my chest, and her knees drawn up to her chest. I guess she thought I was already asleep, because she didn't say anything as she pulled the quilt up to her chin and went still again.

Something strange and tense stirred in my chest. A feeling I didn't have a name for. She was scared, that much was obvious. And she had every reason to be. Finn and Malik were gone. The village was, too. And we were faced with a terrible choice when it came to going to one of those censure districts. If that is where they chose to go, I didn't even know if I'd be allowed to go with them into a place like that. I wasn't ... well, anything. Not that I knew of. I didn't have Damarian golden eyes and golden skin. I didn't have the pointed ears and turquoise eyes of a Rienkan elf. I didn't have the ebony complexion and muscular build of a Nar'Haleenan.

I was tall, scrawny, and awkward. My hair had grown out in a strange, grayish-white color and was wavy and fluffed up whenever it was the least bit humid. Oddly enough, my eyebrows and eyelashes were still a dark brown color. My skin was a lot fairer than most of the people from this region—and not just because I'd spent most of my life indoors. Although, I guess that hadn't helped much.

Even stranger, I had light blue eyes, which was a rare color in this part of the world, and much more squared, hard features with a wide jaw and rounded, human ears. Whatever I was or wherever I'd come from, it obviously wasn't anywhere in the southern kingdoms. Someone had likely traveled a long way to bring me to the Compendium. I just wish I knew why.

And if they ever meant to come back for me.

I drifted off again, relaxing into the makeshift bedroll and letting the sounds of the fire and the distant calls of night birds carry me away. Before my eyes finally rolled closed, my gaze settled back on where Noa still sat on a log next to the fire, the glow of the flames dancing in his eyes. His mouth was set in that grim, focused frown. I'd never noticed until then that the tattoos on the right side of his face extended all the way down to his neck, shoulder, bicep, and right pectoral. Something about them struck a chord in my mind. A shape I must have recognized from something I had read. Something about ... pirates, maybe? Or maybe thieves. But right then, I was too tired to focus on it.

MORNING CAME EARLY, WITH NONE OF THE COMFORTS ANY OF US WERE USED TO. NO clean clothes or baths to start the day. No smells of breakfast cooking, or taking up the day's chores, readying fishing nets, or taking in crab traps.

Noa gathered a couple of other young men, armed with spears and swords they must have taken off dead Nar'Haleenan soldiers during the fray yesterday. They spoke quietly around one of the smoldering campfires, then all glanced my way at the same time.

Noa curled a finger at me, calling me over to join them.

My stomach sank to the soles of my bare feet as I sat, poking the ashes and adding little dried twigs to try to kindle the fire back to life. Uh oh. What was going on? What were they talking about? Was this about last night, when I asked about that guy with the mark on his hand?

I swallowed hard and got up, dusting off the seat of my pants before I made my way over to join in the conversation. I was probably a good five years younger than all of them, but I guess by comparison, I was one of the only able-bodied, uninjured people left in our group.

Still, if they were about to ask me to join them in spearfishing or hunting, this was doomed to be a disaster.

"A few of us are returning to the village to see if there's anything more that can be salvaged," Noa explained as he gestured to the rest of the group. "I don't want Kaili or any of the others coming. They don't need to see it."

"O-Oh," I stammered.

"But we need as many hands as possible in case we find any more survivors or things we can use," Noa went on. Then he handed me a spear. "You're coming with us."

I fumbled and almost dropped it. "R-Right. Yeah. Okay, I can, uh, I can do that."

He nodded firmly, his gaze sharp and steady as he looked me over. "We saw the ships depart, so we don't have any reason to believe there will be more soldiers still lingering around the village. But we must be careful. We don't know if any of them might have survived and been left behind, as well."

"And, uh, if there are?" I shouldn't have asked. Part of me already knew the answer even before Noa said it aloud.

"Then we deliver them to the gods without hesitation."

Right. Sooo more murder. I-I could ... I could totally do that. Stab someone with a spear while they begged for their life. No problem.

Oh, gods, I was going to throw up.

"Um, Noa? I've never actually fought anyone before. Ever. I don't even know how to fight or, you know, use a spear," I admitted quietly, hoping the other guys wouldn't overhear.

One of them rolled their eyes. Yep. They definitely heard.

Noa put a hand on my shoulder and began guiding me out of our pathetic little makeshift camp with him. "I know. And I don't intend for you to begin today. But if you need to protect yourself, you now have the option to try."

His hand slid away as he forged on ahead, carving a path through the dense jungle along the coast. Watching him stride so confidently forward, with his head high and his shoulders thrown back in determination, made me feel about two inches tall. I'd never been that confident about, well, anything. I couldn't help but envy him. Whether Noa realized it or not, everyone else in the camp of remaining villagers all looked at him when he spoke. They watched him for cues. They moved when he moved.

He was a leader, even if he didn't know it.

It was only a couple of miles to what remained of the village. The closer we got, the more careful we were about the path we picked through the dense foliage. The smell of smoke drifted through the jungle, faint but growing stronger with each step we took. Then, through the trees, I saw it. The first of the homes left in charred shambles. The roof had been entirely burned away, and all that was left was a charred wooden frame and heaps of black ash.

My stomach twisted and spun, and my heart pounded in my ears like booming war drums as I kept close behind Noa. He crouched just inside the tree line and watched, keen eyes scanning the beach and cove with a deep scowl of extreme focus. After almost five minutes, he held up a hand and gave a signal to the others. All clear.

The other young men fanned out, choosing to keep to the trees until they reached a place where they wanted to investigate or check the debris. Noa, on the other hand, led the way out onto the beach with his spear gripped firmly in hand. The morning sea air teased through his long black hair as he looked around, gaze panning over all the charred, cindery remains of homes, docks, smoke houses where they'd cooked fish, and canoes. A few twisted figures caught my eye as we passed, making my heartbeat skip and stall. They were definitely people—but were so severely burned I couldn't tell anything about who they were.

"Wait here," Noa commanded when we reached the place where our home had once stood. There wasn't much left now. Broken, scorched logs and remnants of framework with the front door still there, hanging partway off its hinges.

I nodded and stood outside as he went ahead inside. Tears welled in my eyes, and after a few minutes, I had to turn my back. Seeing it like that hurt too much, and I couldn't bear the fear of seeing more scorched bones or bodies in the wreckage. I didn't want that memory to be locked away in my brain, where I could never forget it.

Holding my spear tightly in both hands, I wandered a short distance down the beach toward the water. More canoes bobbed, most overturned and charred. A body of a hippocampus that had been shot full of arrows lay limp in the surf.

I stopped suddenly, my footsteps crunching strangely, almost like I'd stepped on something brittle but solid.

Was that glass?

I frowned and bent down to look, running my fingertips over the surface of the sand. No, not sand. Not anymore. It had all been *melted.* Turned to glass by intense heat.

Looking out over the beach, patterns of glass rippled in V-shaped patterns all over the place. Sweet gods. That was impossible, wasn't it? It took more than just mere flame to do something like that. Melting sand to glass took incredibly intense heat. Something you'd find only in forges or lightning strikes.

How had this happened? How had this glass gotten here? What had produced that kind of heat? Was it from some sort of weapon that the Nar'Haleenan soldiers carried?

I needed to know. I *needed* to understand.

A startling chill spread over my scalp and raced down my spine, suddenly making me shudder hard. My breath caught and I stood up straight again, trying to shake off the strange numbness that tingled in my fingers. What was that?

I blinked. My head, it ... it felt strange. Lighter somehow. I blinked harder a few more times before I finally realized what was off—gods, my head didn't hurt at all. I'd gotten so used to that constant ache, that I'd forgotten what it felt like to not be in pain.

What the heck was happening to me?

Looking up, my gaze caught on a figure far across the beach, heading toward me, right along the water's edge. My heartbeat skipped. Who was that? Someone from our group? It had to be, right? The shape seemed masculine, even from that distance, and it wavered and rippled almost like a mirage.

A dream? Was I imagining this?

No. No—wait.

My pulse stammered to a halt and my hands shook as I slowly slid off my glasses. Immediately, the figure cleared and seemed to become solid.

It was definitely a man. I winced as the morning sunlight glinted off a breastplate and greaves of black flawless metal. A long dark cloak blew at his back, fluttering in the ocean wind like a licking dark flame. A soldier? No. It couldn't be. The closer he got, the more I could pick out the details. A stern face with a long, sharp jaw, deeply-set eyes of cobalt blue, and thin frowning mouth stared at me through lengthy locks of black hair. Even with those features, I could tell he was young. Maybe even younger than me by a year or two.

Just a boy.

A boy I had seen only once before, many years ago.

I stumbled back, nearly dropping my spear again as he stared straight at me and came closer, purpose in every step. Something like wrath crackled in his hauntingly focused gaze—a blind fury that made my blood run like ice water in my veins. And all that rage was focused squarely on me.

I took another step and my heel slipped on the glass.

CRACK!

I fell, hitting the ground on my back and sending out a web of splintered breaks all around.

But he didn't stop, or even seem to notice. Who was this guy? What was he still doing here when the ships had gone? Had they left him behind or ...?

He stopped abruptly, less than ten yards away, and stared me down. His lip curled, twitching into a half-snarl as he began to lift his hand toward me—a hand emblazoned with a strange, tattooed mark. That symbol. A three-pointed star with three off-shooting rays at each opening, breaking beyond a surrounding circular boundary. Each ray ended with an arrow point, and around the circle was an intricate series of interlocking rings all made from patterns of runes. I'd only glimpsed it once before, but now I recognized it.

That was the mark of Enais, god of all that is present.

Why would he be branded with a mark like that?

He stretched that hand out toward me, brows drawing inward into a furious snarl that made his chin twitch. The blue irises of his eyes flashed, turning a smoldering red, as the palm of his hand began to glow. It turned as red as molten metal, glowing brighter and brighter until I had to look away.

I dropped my spear threw up my hands to shield my face and turned away.

"Clarke? What's wrong?"

I looked up. Noa stood over me with a look of puzzled concern.

Wh-What?

I looked back at where the armored guy had been. There was nothing. Not even footprints in the sand. Almost like ... none of it had been real. Just an illusion.

Or a memory.

I tensed as that old, familiar throbbing pain rushed back through my head, and I floundered to cram my glasses back onto my face. The relief was instant, but not complete. Not like before when there hadn't been any pain at all. Now it was just bearable.

"Are you all right?" Noa asked again. He bent down to study me more closely. "Did you see something?"

I couldn't speak. Not at first. Staring at the empty place in the sand where that guy in black armor had been, everything tangled in my brain. The words hung, caught in my throat like crabs in a trap, clawing to get free but unable to find a way out. I let out a shaking, deep breath and looked back up at Noa.

"I-I, uh ... I tripped. There's ... glass everywhere," I managed to rasp weakly.

He nodded and offered a hand to help me back up. "Yes. The man who commanded the fire did it. The flames were so hot they burned white. The first people they hit were incinerated on the spot. There was nothing but ash left behind. It turned the sand to glass."

Fear burrowed in deep, writhing and twisting in my gut like a worm into an apple. It was the same boy who had come to the library that night. I was sure of it. And now, I understood why he'd come. He really was like me—different.

But far, far more dangerous.

20

CHAPTER TWENTY

I still couldn't get my hands to stop shaking when we arrived back at the camp. We hadn't found all that much to bring with us. A few more blankets that weren't completely burned, some tools and weapons, and a couple of small sacks of dried fruit that had been buried in barrels. We had found enough salvageable pieces of wood and lengths of rope to make a couple of rickety rafts to transport some of the young and injured who couldn't manage the journey on their own without help. It wasn't much, honestly. But right then, we needed any victory we could get.

While Noa and the others worked on getting our small group ready to move and begin the journey toward the city of Uru'Nai, I went with Kaili back to the lagoon where the hippocampi were still paddling around. Most of them shied back, making anxious, high-pitched calls and keeping well out of arm's reach. They were still wary of people after what they'd been through the day before.

But not Pasha.

As soon as he spotted us, he dove and swam the distance to where Kaili and I stood on the bank. He stuck his head up and pushed his snout against her hand as she waded out into the water to meet him. I stayed on the shore, giving her some space, and watching as she ran her hands over his smooth scaly sides and along his back.

"I can never thank you enough. You saved us," she whispered as she leaned down to let her forehead rest against his. "I know you would follow me anywhere if I asked. But I cannot let you come to Uru'Nai. They would take you from me. They would force you to work, hauling ferries, barges, and ships. You would work hard and die young. I won't let that happen to you."

Her hands slipped around his neck to slide the leather bridle away from his face. Then she did the same with the saddle. Loosening the straps made the leather seat slip away and float nearby. I couldn't see her face, but I could hear the tears in her words as she stroked his head one last time. Then, step by step, she backed out of the water and stood on the shore beside me. The sun lit her deep bronze skin, and the breeze tangled her long black hair.

Once again, there was nothing I could say. So, instead, I just took her hand and held it tightly. It was the right thing to do—letting him go. But I knew for her, it was also the hardest.

"We should go help the others," I suggested quietly.

She gave my hand a small squeeze. "Okay."

"Kaili?"

She looked up at me, fresh tears still rimming her beautiful, ocean-colored eyes. "Yes?"

I *almost* told her. I almost confessed everything that had really happened while I was with Noa and the others at the ruins of our village. About that vision and the boy with the mark on his hand. I probably should have.

What if that guy showed up again? Or what if he was in the city when we got there? What if he recognized the members of our group and sought to finish what he'd started? Or what if he recognized me from the library?

I wanted to tell her. At the last second, though, the words stuck in my throat like a fistful of thorns. I just couldn't do it. What if this was somehow my fault? What if it had something to do with what had happened at the library? If he had been there, too, then wasn't it possible he was the one who had destroyed it?

Gods, what if he had brought those warships and followed me here?

Not that I had a single clue as to why he would do that. We hadn't known one another, even if we had crossed paths that one time. We'd never even said a word to each other that night. I didn't even know his name. Why would he want to track me down?

No, there had to be something else. A detail I was missing. A reason.

I just hadn't figured it out yet.

"Are you okay?" Kaili asked. She must've thought it was weird for me to call her name like that and then never say anything.

I looked down at my toes, now mostly buried in the sand as the waves lapped gently around my ankles. "I don't know," I confessed. "I guess none of us are, really."

"No," she agreed. "We aren't."

"For the record, I'm worried about going to Uru'Nai, too. I'm afraid they won't allow me to go into that censure district with you because I'm not Rienkan or Damarian. I'm afraid we'll be separated, and I won't be able to find you or Noa again."

Her hold on my hand tightened again. "We won't let that happen, Clarke. We'll find a way to stay together. I promise."

I wanted to believe that. She believed it—I could hear it in her voice. But the truth was as bitter and cold as the deepest depths of the sea. We didn't have any control over what might happen to us in that city. I'd never set foot in a place like that, and even I knew how dangerous they could be. Port cities were sprawling, busy, and rife with crime and treachery. Not to mention, Nar'Haleen was hostile to anyone they thought might be affiliated with the other two southern kingdoms. For people like us, there wouldn't be a warm welcome there.

But with nothing to our names but a few fire-scorched odds and ends, and so many who were wounded and needing real medical help, our choices were limited. There was safety in numbers, even in censure districts, and that was the one hope we had to cling to for now.

"If they will not let you into the censure district, I will stay with you. I won't follow the others inside," she said firmly, as though daring me to argue.

I wasn't about to try that, though.

"I don't know where I'll go. Or what I'll do. I don't know anyone outside the library except for you and Noa," I told her.

"Maybe we can find out if anyone else from your library survived or managed to flee. Anyone who did might have also come to the city," she suggested.

Ahh. Now there was an idea. She might be right about that. If anyone else, especially one of the scholars or even the High Inquisitor, had managed a daring escape, that is probably where they would go. I could ask around. Search markets and inns. Maybe I would get lucky.

Hope kindled like a tiny spark in my heart, and I managed a faint smile. "Now *that* sounds like a plan."

ANOTHER MEMBER OF OUR GROUP HAD PASSED AWAY IN THE NIGHT, AND WE TOOK A moment to bury the elderly woman at the base of a tree near our camp before we started to move out. No one spoke or shed a single tear as we covered her with soil and walked away from that place. The grief was heavy, constant, and exhausting. It would take time to feel anything else again.

It took the rest of the morning for us to get two decently-stable rafts built and taken down to the lagoon. My hands and back ached as I helped Noa lash all the wooden pieces together with the lengths of rope. We had to be sure nothing came undone, or we would risk losing precious cargo to the ocean depths. Sweat ran down my face and into my eyes as we tied a pair of the hippocampi to the front of each one. It took several of us to help load our meager supplies, the surviving children, mothers with infants, and four injured onboard.

By the time we were finally ready to depart, it was past noon, and Noa's tone had become sharp and anxious. He seemed more than ready to put some distance between ourselves and this place.

I couldn't help but agree.

My heart seemed to drag behind me with the weight of an iron anchor as I trudged over the sand back to the shore of the lagoon. The cool embrace of the water gave some relief, but it was only temporary. With the rest of us doubling up on three more hippocampi, Kaili and I worked at releasing the remaining mounts as we all headed back out to the open sea.

I sat behind her again as we prepared to leave, but not on Pasha this time.

A bigger, stronger hippocampus carried us alongside one of the rafts, giving Kaili a little trouble at the reins when Noa sent off the rest of the herd to the wild open waves. She hissed commands through her teeth and squeezed with her knees, frustration and anguish fresh on her face until we were well away from the lagoon and the hippocampus calmed.

Then, in unison, Kaili and I looked back.

Together, we watched Pasha swim away farther down the coast toward the shallow reefs and sea stacks where he'd grown up. Kaili didn't cry, though. Not this time.

Instead, her sea-green eyes stared out across the ocean and tracked Pasha's movements without ever saying anything or making a sound. Her expression had gone empty, as though she had been drained of all emotion. Her eyes caught the light of the sun gleaming off the ocean as she watched Pasha leap from wave to wave and finally disappear into the distance.

It must have felt like her own happiness was doing the same thing—leaving her behind in an empty ocean of uncertainty and fear.

I felt it, too.

The library was gone. Now this place was gone, as well. What would come next? I had a horizon full of questions ... and no answers.

No path but the one that lay before us, somewhere beyond the rolling waves.

PART SEVEN

REIGH

21

CHAPTER TWENTY-ONE

Ever since I had first met Jaevid Broadfeather all those years ago in Luntharda, I had experienced several "I can't believe I'm about to do this" moments in my lifetime. Instances of deep, personal reflection where I briefly contemplated what I was doing with my life. They usually preceded us doing something impossibly dangerous that was basically guaranteed to get someone maimed or killed.

As I stepped out onto the gangplank to board what was supposedly our ride to Nar'Haleen, I realized far too late that this felt *a lot* like one of those times.

Great. Good times coming, then.

I stole a glance back through the pouring rain to swap a wary eye with Murdoc. He wore that signature, cold-eyed assassin stare I'd come to treasure when we were about to deal with dangerous people. It was the same look a wolf gave through cage bars, just waiting for someone to get stupid and poke their hand inside.

Only, this time, we were the ones doing the poking in this situation.

By ship standards, the sloop where we stood wasn't very big. I didn't count myself as any sort of sailing expert, but I'd seen enough ships cruising around the oceans offshore now to be able to pick out a few of them on sight. Haldor loved to give lengthy, over-embellished descriptions of them whenever he even suspected someone was interested. His family owned a merchant company, after all. I guess they probably had a lot of ships with their house name emblazoned on the side.

The name of this one, however, read *Fog Dancer* in fancy golden letters. Not a name I'd ever heard of before, but I knew a sloop like this one was fast, nimble on the water compared to the bigger merchant galleons, and shallow enough on the draft that it could scoot along just off the reefs without getting stuck. Haldor had regarded ships like this with a wrinkled nose and curled lip. Apparently, they were often the preferred vessel of choice for pirates.

I probably should have mentioned that before a burly deck hand with a beard like an overused scrubbing brush and a nasty-looking scar over his forehead led us to the captain's quarters. If we were about to deal with pirates in any capacity, I desperately needed

Thatcher to keep his mouth shut. But before I got the chance, the deck hand opened the door and let us in to a dimly lit room. The wall at the very back was covered in floor-to-ceiling windows, and more round porthole ones made with panes of colored glass lined the walls down either side. None of them gave any light to the cramped interior, though.

The only source of light came from a collection of golden, teardrop-shaped glass lanterns that hung from the beams down the center of the room. They swayed like pendulums with the motion of the ship and cast eerie shadows over a space that was packed tight with gaudy furniture. The red velvet and gold, claw-footed chairs, massive mahogany desk with golden trim, canopy bed with heavy purple drapery, and gilded frames looked like they should have been in the home of a very self-important count. Even the woven wool rugs on the floor and locked bookcases filled with trinkets, scrolls, and statuettes struck me as an odd choice.

Then again, this was my first time on what I suspected was definitely a pirate ship. Maybe this was standard fare for them?

With my cloak and bags dripping puddles on the floor, I shambled ahead of the rest of our group into the room and stood there awkwardly. Staring around, I squinted into the gloom for any signs of life.

Then I saw her.

Sitting behind that massive desk, her legs crossed and heels resting on the top, a woman reclined with her face mostly obscured by a broad-brimmed black hat. A single golden feather stuck from one side of it, swishing some as she slowly raised her head to grin up at us with her teal green eyes aglow in the dim light. Her hands were folded over her waist, an assortment of glittering rings sparkling over her interlaced fingers, and the lengths of her long, dark purple frock coat spilled over the arms of the chair to brush the floor.

Her smile widened, revealing a flash of white teeth, and her eyes narrowed slightly as her gaze fixed squarely on me. "You're late. It's rude to keep a lady waiting, you know," she purred in a strong Rienkan accent. That and her long, pointed ears were a dead giveaway. She was not from anywhere near here. "Well, now. Don't you lot look like a soggy heap of poor life choices."

Gods and Fates, she had *no* idea.

Her gaze panned smoothly to the side, landing on the shape of a man who stood so still I might've mistaken him for a statue if not for those familiar glowing eyes. "Arlan, darling, you didn't tell me I'd be ferrying *royalty*." The way she said that—royalty—almost sounded sarcastic. Patronizing, even. "And to think, I might've freshened up a bit. Put on a clean shirt. Or curtsied when you came in."

I brushed back the hood of my cloak and forced a returning smile. "And you are?"

"Captain Malina Skyhart," Arlan spoke up as he stepped forward. "She has agreed to take you to Nar'Haleen at dawn."

Her smile faded like mist at sunrise, and she cut a prickly sideways glance at him. "Yes. I've agreed to ferry you scraggly lot into the maw of the beast, as it were. But *not* anything with scales, wings, and fiery venom. There will be no dragons aboard my ship."

"Now, Malina, I can assure you—" Arlan began, as though they'd already been having this argument before we walked in.

She didn't let him finish. "You can assure me that the beasts that breathe a spray of highly combustible venom, which can't be doused by water alone, are safe to have aboard my wooden ship that also happens to be stockpiled with powder kegs? Hm? Is that what you were going to say, darling?" She arched one eyebrow at him, her full lips puckered in distaste. "You can promise me not a single dragon belch? Not one sneeze the entire journey?"

Arlan tilted his head back some, briefly looking skyward as though silently praying for patience in that moment. "If you'd allow me to finish, I was going to say that I can assure you I can offer a solution to make the transport of *one* dragon far less dangerous."

Wait—*one* dragon?

Thatcher and I exchanged a look. Did this mean only one of us was going to be able to take our dragon on this little mission?

Oh, this just kept getting better and better.

"That's still one dragon too many." Malina's eyes shone like firelit embers in the gloom as she stared him down.

Murdoc let out a growling sigh as he crossed his arms. "I agree. This will never work. Honestly, you're sending them in a Rienkan pirate vessel? Tell me you're joking. This ship is tiny. It won't survive the first real storm."

BANG!

Thatcher nearly jumped out of his boots when Malina slammed an open hand down onto her desk, making all the stacks of papers, bags of coins, and little decorative statues rattle. "What the *Fog Dancer* lacks in size it more than makes up for in other ways, boy," she snapped. "We are the fastest vessel this side of Elondia. I've outrun Nar'Haleenan warships against the wind."

"And yet, I'd still prefer a solid Damarian frigate," Murdoc muttered, refusing to meet her gaze as he picked his fingernails. "Perhaps Haldor could loan us something from the his fleet. The Kal'Sheems have plenty of fine vessels, and he owes me after marrying my sister."

"No," Malina seethed through her teeth. "I know what you're doing. It won't work."

"Then I will double the pay," Arlan spoke up suddenly.

All eyes turned to him.

No one said a word for a few grueling, awkward seconds.

"Triple," Malina countered, her expression now all but glittering with interest. Or, maybe that was just greed. I guess with her, coin spoke louder than pride ... or general safety of her crew. Good to know.

"Done," Arlan replied so quickly it made her sit back and blink in shock, almost like she hadn't expected him to agree.

"One dragon," she clarified, holding up a single finger. "And you'll keep your word to make it as manageable as possible?"

He nodded.

Malina sank back in her chair with a sulky frown and folded her hands back over her hips, just over her wide golden-buckled belt. "Fine, then. Have it your way. Bunch of crazies, you are. Wanting to sail to that hell-pit of a place in wartime with dragons and whatnot," she muttered under her breath before finally giving us a wave-off. "Out, then. Say your little prayers to whatever gods you like, and make ready. We sail at dawn."

"Wait a moment," Arlan interrupted before any of us could even take a step.

Malina made an unhappy, grumbling, blowing sound and sank lower in her chair like an angry cat.

"There's a matter I need to address before we depart. I had hoped we might discuss it at one of my secure locations within the city, but I'm no longer satisfied that those places are not being watched." Arlan stepped forward, his hands clasped at his back "It has come to my attention, after leaving you all in Halfax, that in the throes of searching my history and the movements of my agents, the Hands of Fate have made an unforeseen strike against a place I had believed to be of the highest security and secrecy. Now, I must tell you that the Compendium Library has been attacked and likely destroyed. I received a distress call from a longtime ally there."

Beside me, Violet sucked in a sudden, sharp gasp. Her eyes went wide and her mouth opened slightly. "You mean ...?"

"I don't believe they obtained the codex, as their efforts to search my various safe-houses have not lessened in the slightest, but that is not to say this attack was ... fruitless for them." His tone tightened, becoming reluctant in a way that froze the blood in my veins.

I had dealt with Arlan the Kinslayer several times now. I knew his guarded, emotionally controlled way of speaking all too well. He never moved, never said anything, without that air of precise confidence. Not tonight, though. Something about this had him rattled.

And that was enough to put every nerve in my body on edge.

"Ronan was being housed at the Compendium Library," he said quietly. "He, and several others of peculiar and powerful origin were receiving special training to harness and control their abilities from some of the highly educated scholars there. I had no reason to believe it would ever come under attack. The Compendium has been a safe and secret haven for people in similar situations before. It is, by ancient law, considered politically neutral. And when your sister and I came to the agreement to have him secretly educated there for several years, I had absolutely no reason to believe that would change."

I couldn't move. The words pinged off my mind like hailstones as I stood there, barely able to keep my knees from buckling, and stared at him. The Hands of Fate had my little nephew? *WHAT?!*

Arlan bowed his head slightly, pinching the bridge of his nose between his eyes. "I have spent the duration of the day attempting to ascertain who has been lost and to what end with a scrying glass. It is not a simple or precise magic, but what I have been able to glimpse has left more questions than I feel comfortable with. I strongly suspect that my sister has taken custody of your nephew and now hopes to utilize him in her own agenda. He is alive and unharmed, as best I could tell, but I don't know what she intends to do with him."

Rage like a roaring inferno blazed through my body. I dropped my bags and started for him, my hands clenched into shaking fists which I had every intention of using to beat his skull in. "How could you let this happen under *your* watch?! You put that codex and my nephew in the same place?!" I yelled. "What did you think would happen?! You *IDIOT!*"

Strong hands caught me on both sides and held me back. I fought and twisted, trying to get free as Thatcher and Murdoc struggled to keep me back.

"You are correct, Your Highness. I was careless and brazen in thinking I could place more than one precious item in that place and it would not be tampered with. But I had no idea that my sister would move her hand so quickly after I destroyed her aspect puppet near Osbran. I had assumed she would recoil, regroup, and take some time before making her next move. Now, I see I was gravely mistaken. And for that, I take responsibility."

"YOU BETTER!" I roared again, finally managing to jerk away from Thatcher's grasp to thrust an accusing finger at him. "You did this. You have to fix it. Get him back!"

"I am attempting to," he snapped and took a step forward to meet me, the golden glowing light of his eyes seeming to intensify. "That is why I am sending you and your dragon there as soon as can possibly be managed. I've alerted every agent I can in that area to be on the lookout for any strange movements from Nar'Haleen, since my sister is undoubtedly manipulating their royal court now. I've also insisted they seek out any survivors of the attack that might have been able to flee to safety. I intend to use no small amount of my magical power to ensure this is a successful retrieval of both your nephew and the codex because in her hands, both are disastrous—but should she have control of both simultaneously, it will be the dawning of a divine war unlike anything our world has ever seen." The more he spoke, the faster and sharper his words became until, at last, he stared me down from an inch or two away.

I could feel the anger wafting off him like heat from a forge—but it wasn't directed at me. Not really. His sister had outmaneuvered him again. And for Arlan, I suppose that was the greatest possible slight to his criminal ego. He didn't just want Ronan back and the codex secured, he wanted revenge.

And I was ready to hand it to him if it meant bringing Ronan home safely.

"Be advised that I have not told your sister, Queen Jenna, of this situation. Her Majesty knows nothing about Ronan's capture or the attack on the library. Since that reckless temper of yours tends to be a strongly carried family trait, I would urge you to exercise discretion and not report it to her, lest we incite a war between Maldobar and Nar'Haleen." Arlan took a few steps back and turned away, as though trying to collect himself. "We will fix this, Your Highness. But it will require you to do exactly as I say and leave nothing to chance or impulse. By way of this ship, I will see that you all reach the city of Uru'Nai in Nar'Haleen as quickly as possible. That is the place where, should there be any survivors of the attack, those individuals might seek brief refuge. But they will likely not be safe there for long. Time is quickly turning against us. Now, if you are able to compose yourself, go and take rest at the tavern while you can. I will have preparations completed to handle your dragon in the morning."

22

CHAPTER TWENTY-TWO

I knew I probably wasn't going to find the answers to any of my problems at the bottom of an ale horn or wine bottle at the Speckled Sow Tavern. But just for good measure and absolute certainty, I tried.

Sitting around a table close to the tavern's roaring hearth with Thatcher, Murdoc, and Violet, I sat my second empty wine bottle on the table and stared at the reflection of the flames dancing in the green glass. My head swam and buzzed with a delirious heat that made all my thoughts sluggish and hazy. It didn't do much to take my mind off Ronan or my sister, though. Gods and Fates, curse it all, how was I ever going to explain this to her? Even if we pulled it off, got Ronan back, and brought him safely home—I still had to tell her everything. I still had to justify not telling her in the first place. I'd break that trust bond with her forever. And what then? I'd be alienated from the only family I had.

Once again.

"I can't take Fornax on this ship," Thatcher spoke up suddenly, as though he were finally voicing his own inner struggle. "If we can only take one dragon, it has to be Vexi. Fornax won't let anyone else ride him, and if we got separated and he didn't have another dragon there to help guide him ... it would be too risky. He could get hurt. Or lost. Or even killed."

Murdoc put a hand on his shoulder. "I'll look after him. Don't worry. I can even take him up to the Cromwells, if you'd like."

"I know," Thatcher mumbled. "I just hate leaving him behind like this. It's bad enough to be so far from Garnett all the time. But going that far away without my dragon is just as bad. Maybe even worse, because he doesn't do well if I'm not around."

"How long has it been since you saw dear Garny?" Violet asked from over the rim of her still mostly-full wine glass.

"A few months, I guess. We came directly from the last part of the dragonrider academy's academic year, and normally this is the break where she and I get to spend some time together," Thatcher lamented as he took up his mug of ale and stared down into it sadly. "I guess she probably already knows what I'm doing instead, though."

Violet's lips pressed into an uncomfortable line and she didn't reply.

"In the interest of drawing attention off you guys, I think I'm going to take Fornax and Blite and head out tonight once the weather starts to lift," Murdoc said. "The more we keep moving, the more our enemy will struggle to split their focus and monitor us all."

"I do so admire that Ulfrangar practicality." Violet cast him a tired smile and took a sip from her glass before setting it back on the table.

"I take it you'll be joining us on the ship tomorrow?" Thatcher asked, his own forced smile doing nothing to hide the obvious disdain in his tone.

Violet leaned back in her chair, stretching her arms over her head before letting them rest in her lap again. "Oh, of course. My employer wants his best and brightest helming this operation. Why he chose Malina to be the one to get us there is beyond me. I suppose, in a broader view of the situation, she is one of the least likely to side with the Hands of Fate. But she does have her own little constellation of issues. Hopefully none of that interferes."

"She really is a pirate, isn't she?" I asked, doing my very best not to slur. Or drool on myself. It was getting hard enough just to sit upright, so I crossed my arms on the tabletop and slumped forward, resting my chin on my forearms.

"I believe the term smuggler would be more appropriate, as she doesn't do much actual stealing these days. The Skyhart family was once quite notorious in the southern seas. But that was many years ago, and they've since fallen from that power and infamy." She studied me out of the corner of one of those sparkling scarlet eyes.

Strange. I'd never asked her why she had eyes that color. Maybe I should. Yes, that was a good idea. Brilliant. Best one I'd had all day.

I opened my mouth to ask, but what came out was, "I saw a white squirrel with red eyes once."

Well, crap.

Thatcher made a choking, snorting sound down into his cup that might have been a laugh.

Murdoc did that lip-pursing thing like he was trying not to smile.

Violet just arched an eyebrow. "Is that your drunken way of asking whether or not I'm albino?"

"Well, you're not a squirrel," I slurred again, like a complete moron.

"Good of you to notice." She frowned a little, almost disapprovingly. "I'm not albino, either. Now be a good boy and pass out, would you? It's getting late, and I promise, dawn will come early."

I obliged. Or rather, I nodded off when Murdoc and Thatcher started talking about training at the academy. With my head resting on my arms and my mouth open so I could drool a nice puddle onto the tabletop, I must have slept that way for an hour or two before Thatcher finally hoisted me up and looped my arm over his shoulders to help me up the stairs.

"You really overdid it this time, huh?" Thatcher grunted as he helped me stagger and wobble up the steps to the second floor. "I know you're upset about Ronan, but you've got to pull yourself together. Otherwise, it's me leading this mission, and I think we can all agree that would be a disaster. Or, well, I guess Violet could do it. But I'm still not sure who's side she's really on."

"S'long as it's the Get-Ronan-Back-And-Stab-Anyone-Who-Tries-To-Stop-Us side, I don't care," I grumbled.

He basically poured me off his shoulder and into an all too familiar narrow bed on the far wall. I heard him muttering as he found the leftovers of my emergency medical treatment on Violet still drying on the floor. "Is that blood? Ugh. Seriously? Did someone bleed out in here? This place is just foul. Why would Arlan want us to stay here?"

I tried to answer that, but it just came out as a long series of sad, moaning whale noises. I couldn't remember much after that. My face met the soft, mildewy-smelling pillow and everything else faded to a pleasing, spinning haze. I lay, clothes and hair still damp from the rain, and my body aching from flying so far all day. Everything hurt—my body, my head, my heart. Nothing felt right.

And somehow, I had a feeling this was only the beginning.

"Good morning, Lieutenant! Rise and shine!" A feminine, sing-song voice chimed right in my ear.

I yelled and snapped upright in bed, still dressed from the day before—right down to my boots. Sweet Fates, where was I? What happened? And why by all the Fates was Violet sitting on the bed beside me?

Unless—no.

Nope.

Not even in my wildest, most terrible drunken nightmares was *that* ever going to be a thing.

Sitting on the edge of the bed, I rubbed my temples and tried to force my mind to clear. I couldn't remember the last time I had managed to sleep through the whole night without waking soaked in sweat and shaking from a nightmare. Fifteen years?

Although, waking up to Violet standing beside my bed, whistling and tapping her foot on the floor impatiently, was its own kind of nightmare.

"It'll be dawn soon. We should get going," Violet huffed. "Don't tell me you're still drunk?"

"No, unfortunately," I groaned as I stood and cast her a withering glare. "Where are Thatcher and Murdoc?"

"Murdoc took the other two dragons, Fornax and Blite, and departed in the night. He asked me very specifically to tell you 'don't screw this up or get yourself killed'—which I can only assume is his way of wishing you luck." There was an annoyed crinkle between her two slender brows as she looked me up and down, stopping on my hair for a moment. I guess it was standing on end. I might have combed it down with my fingers, but knowing it exasperated her somehow made me want to leave it alone.

"Yeah. Something like that. Curse it—we gotta get moving. Why didn't you wake me earlier? I still have to find an apothecary or alchemist for more supplies. And then somewhere that will sell me some cloth for medical bandages, and—"

"No need." She dangled a rolled-up leather pouch in front of my face proudly, a smug little grin playing over her lips. It was wrapped up sort of like a thick scroll, and tied closed with a leather cord. "Thatcher and I took care of it while you were asleep."

I narrowed my eyes at her suspiciously as I unwrapped the rolled-up kit. Inside, arranged in a series of pouches and sleeves, a fine set of surgical tools, needles, knives, cauterizing implements, proper tourniquets, spools of thread, and bandaging were all arranged above a series of vials containing an assortment of herbal remedies and potions.

Wow. This was ... a lot nicer than anything I had on hand. I'd never bothered to buy myself a real surgical kit. I'd never needed it, honestly.

"Where did you get this?" I asked as I took out one of the slender sets of long steel tweezers.

"That's an odd way of saying thank you," she scolded gently, her voice still brimming with excitement. "In all seriousness, though, I bought it when we went out for the rest of the supplies we'll need for the trip. I owed you after that grand display of medical heroism yesterday."

I snorted and barely held back a chuckle. "Riiight. If that's what you want to call it. How's the leg? You don't seem to be limping today."

"Much better. I hope you don't mind, but I reapplied some of that fine healing salve of yours. Excellent stuff, isn't it?" She fluttered around me like a proud sparrow while I tucked the new kit into my haversack. I guess Murdoc had taken my saddlebags already when he left. All of my essential gear and personal items were now compacted neatly into the haversack. If it had been anyone else doing it, I might've been furious. But out of everyone, Murdoc was the least likely to go through my letters and personal effects.

He absolutely did *not* care about that kind of thing. Not when it was someone else's business. Thank the gods.

"Right, then. I'm guessing Thatcher is already at the ship, then? Guess we should go meet up with him and that crazy pirate captain. I wonder if she's still willing to haul my dragon across the Southern Sea, or if she came to her senses after we left." I went to the door and held it open so Violet could go out first.

She stared at me, the open door, and back at me. Almost like she thought this was the setup for some sort of trap. Her brows rose and she glanced me over again. "You do realize your hair is sticking up everywhere. You look like a lit matchstick," she quipped on her way out the door.

I rolled my eyes. "Flattery will get you nowhere."

THE DAWN LIGHT BREAKING OVER THE OCEAN HIT MY EYES AND PRACTICALLY SET THEM on fire. My head throbbed as I squinted around, trying to get used to it before I took another step beyond the tavern's front door.

Ugggh. I'd never drink wine again.

The clatter of footsteps and wagon wheels over the boardwalk, shouts of dock hands and sailors working around the ships, and shrill calls of seagulls all mixed with the ambient rush of the surf. An occasional horn blared, signaling when a vessel was ready to be towed from its place in the crowded docks to the bay. Even this early in the morning, with barely enough daylight to see by, the fishermen were already setting out to lay their nets. Merchant ships were preparing to embark. Wagons full of crates and barrels, stocked with goods, were rolled up and down the gangplanks.

At first, it seemed chaotic. But the longer I stood there, the more I noticed a particular rhythm to it. There was almost a mechanical predictability to the way the wagons rolled by, forming lines and stopping at their respective ships. They emptied one boat, then rolled down to begin taking fresh cargo off another. Back and forth, all while the sailors whistled and called to one another, climbing ropes and masts like tiny mice. They adjusted sails and scrubbed decks, and some sang tunes to keep themselves on pace.

"Not a lot of port cities in Luntharda, I take it," Violet mused as she stood beside me.

"No, there aren't. At least, not where I grew up." I said, and stepped off onto the boardwalk to join the flow of traffic moving down the docks.

"You get used to the noise … and everyone smelling like sweat and fish." She kept pace, falling in step right at my side. I hadn't realized until that point how much smaller she was than me. Not that I was a huge guy. Average, I guess. Barely six feet. But even in those fancy, heeled leather boots she barely came to my shoulder.

Hmm. What was she? Red eyes, white-blonde hair, extremely fair skin, round ears, and small stature. I couldn't figure out where in the world she'd come from. She seemed human enough in most of her features, I guess. But it felt weird to ask.

"So, what did you do to piss Arlan off bad enough that he sent you on this mission with us?" I decided to ask instead.

She gave a dark little giggle and smirked up at me. "It's not enough that I just enjoy your company?"

"To sail to Nar'Haleen, an extremely hostile kingdom locked in a civil war, to try to track down my nephew and some ancient divine artifact lost in the middle of the gods-forsaken desert, probably being held in the clutches of Arlan's insane and alarmingly powerful sister? No. That's definitely not enough," I laughed.

"But you're willing to do it for Jaevid," she pointed out, her tone a bit softer and more cautious.

"Well, yeah. He's my friend. And he's got a lot more to lose if this goes badly." I turned my face away, not wanting her to use that probing stare to try and read me again. Even if I was pretty sure it didn't work, I wasn't willing to risk it. "Besides, now that I know Ronan is involved, I have no choice. I have to go. I won't leave my only little nephew to fend for himself in this mess."

Violet frowned. "I … wanted to apologize for that. For his entanglement, that is. I was aware he'd been taken to the library for proper instruction about his power, but I don't think any of us foresaw him being in any danger there. Certainly not Arlan. I know he can come off as rather detached and cold, but he is not without sympathy—especially for people like your nephew."

"You've known him a while, eh?" I asked, trying not to sound too interested. She might clam up if she thought I was probing her for information about her enigmatic crime lord of a boss.

"Since I was very young," she verified. "I've seen him change through the years, too. Or rather, the world has changed him. This pursuit of his sister is more than just a personal vendetta for him. It's an obsession. He won't rest until he has humiliated and dispensed with her, and it won't be enough unless he is the one standing over her when she draws her last breath. I don't know what happened between them, exactly. But I do know that it is what drove him from Avora."

"You mean he didn't leave voluntarily?" I'd just assumed he had left that shining, near-mythical land of floating, mist-laden cities for a life of crime on his own.

Violet's lips pursed and she looked down, as though she'd realized she might be telling me too much. I guess that didn't stop her, though. She sighed, her shoulders rising and falling, and then looked up at me again. "No. He was exiled, many centuries ago. And for an Avoran elf, that is a punishment worse than death …"

23

CHAPTER TWENTY-THREE

I had to let my brain chew on that new information the rest of the way to where the *Fog Dancer* was moored at the far end of the docks. Already buzzing with motion and activity, I spotted crewmen filing up and down the ship's gangplank. More of them hoisted ropes, readied the deck, and loaded cargo.

It was easy to pick out Arlan, Thatcher, and especially Captain Malina in all that chaos—mostly because of her enormous feathered hat. The captain stood behind the helm, her hand resting on the wheel while she barked orders to her crew. Thatcher and Arlan stood behind her, but began to move as soon as they saw us approaching.

We waited on the docks while the pair of them made their way down to meet us. I guess despite whatever Arlan planned to do in order to make transporting Vexi less of a hazard, Malina still wasn't going to let my dragon put a single toe onto her ship until it was done. Fair enough. Based on the number of black powder kegs those sailors were lugging below deck, I was good with as little fire as possible.

For now, anyway.

There was a good reason Maldobar had never utilized those sorts of weapons, and it had claws, fangs, wings, and more than enough burning venom to make that an extremely unreliable and dangerous weapon option. It was also currently making zooming passes back and forth along the mouth of the port, green scales flashing in the morning sun like polished emerald. Vexi swooped low around a few of the fishing vessels, nipping at the seagulls that were swarming their decks and following them out to sea. She knew better than to get too close to the boats, though. When we had come to port cities previously, Mavrik, Jaevid's king drake, had warned a lot of the younger dragons off getting too close to ships and keeping to the beach areas instead.

Thanks to having Southwatch and all its dragonriders so close by, seeing dragons soaring over the ocean in this area wasn't out of the ordinary. I doubted the sailors or crew on any of the ships would even stop to take note of her. But a dragon climbing down into the belly of one of the ships? Yeah. That might raise a few eyebrows.

We had to figure out some way to pull it off, though.

I smiled. Vexi didn't like to go far from me, even when I tried insisting. Bad things had happened in the past when we weren't together, and I guess she hadn't forgotten about that.

As soon as Arlan reached the spot where we stood at the base of the gangplank, he kept walking and motioned for us to follow. I guess he didn't want to do any grand feats of magical power right here in the open. Smart move. This was supposed to be a secret-ish mission, after all.

Falling in behind him, Violet, Thatcher, and I made our way to the very end of the dock, just on the other side of Malina's ship. There, we were more out of sight from the general traffic moving along the boardwalk. The rickety wooden walkway gave way to the sand of a narrow beach, and we stomped along for a few dozen yards before Arlan finally stopped and turned around. His severe, molten gaze settled onto me, and I could have sworn I saw slightly dark circles under his eyes. Maybe he hadn't fared as well when it came to resting last night?

"Very well. This will have to do. We must do this as quickly as possible. If you don't mind, Your Highness, summon the dragon." His command was quiet and not nearly as forceful as usual.

Something sure had sucked the wind out of his sails.

Or rattled him to the core. Either way, it put all my nerves on edge right away. Violet's words still thrummed like harp strings in my head. This situation with his sister was bigger than we knew. It was older than any of us. I had seen firsthand the sort of magic they could fling at one another in a fight—and it was beyond anything I could even begin to understand.

Arlan and his sister played with the weapons and powers of the gods like children's toys.

Giving Thatcher a wary, sideways glance, I stepped away from the group and stared out across the bay ahead. The shape of my dragon's silhouette against the rising sun, her wings as graceful as a falcon's as she dove and skimmed the waves, put a deep ache in my chest. Whatever happened next—whatever Arlan did—he better not hurt her.

I put my fingers in my mouth and gave a shrill whistle. Immediately, she wheeled toward me and beat her dark green wings harder. The sunlight glinted off her horns as she gave an answering roar like a distant clap of thunder.

WHOOM WHOOM WHOOM—BOOM!

Vexi soared in low, letting her hind legs drag the surface of the water before she finally made a landing on the sand before us. I threw a hand up to shield my face and eyes from the flying sand. It didn't help much. I got a shower of itchy grains all over me, down my tunic, and into my boots. Great. Well, she got me good with that one.

I laughed as I sputtered and spat, trying to get the grit out of my mouth. "Think you could try that a little closer next time? I don't think you got any up my nose."

Vexi lowered her head and rubbed her cheek against me. She purred and nosed through my hair before looking behind me to where the others were waiting. As Arlan stepped forward, she withdrew her head back, ears perked forward and nostrils puffing in deep to get his scent. Her spines bristled warily as she studied him, then glanced back at me as though trying to get an indication of whether or not he was friend or foe.

"He's fine, girl," I assured her and ran a hand down her neck. "But he's gonna have to, uh, take a closer look at you. We're going on a little trip. And in order for you to come, we have to—" I stopped and stared at Arlan. "What are you going to do to her, exactly?"

"Something I've not tried on a beast her size," Arlan answered vaguely. "But I can assure you it is not painful, and will not be permanent. She should suffer no ill effects apart from a drastic diminishment in stature."

Wait, what? Did that mean he was going to—?

Before I could finish that thought, Arlan got to work. He pulled a slender, carved wooden stick from the sleeve of his robes and began drawing a series of circles and geometrical shapes, lines, and runes into the sand around her. With Vexi at the very center, he took a step back and crouched down at the edge of the outermost circle and held the point of that wand-like stick to his lips. He puffed a slow, steady breath against it. His already gleaming eyes glowed brighter until they shone like two stars in the early dawn. Likewise, the tip of that stick glowed to life, wavering and flickering as though it were on fire—but not with any sort of flame I'd ever seen before. This one was greenish blue, and as soon as he touched the tip of the stick to the circle, it lit up with that same vibrant light. Each ring, line, and rune ignited one right after another, surrounding Vexi.

She gave a growl and lowered her head, tucking her wings in tight and curling her tail around her legs. Her ears pinned back and she stared at me through the growing brilliance of those shining marks. They shone brighter and brighter, giving off a thrumming heat that tingled over my skin with a strange, crackling energy.

I drew back, wincing and shielding my eyes again as a blinding flash lit up the beach around us.

VOOOOM!

A low, concussive sound rattled my teeth and hit my chest like a heavy weight.

"Vexi!" I shouted, forcing myself to squint back through the glaring light just as it began to wane.

But there was nothing there.

GONE.

My dragon—she was gone.

My heart dropped to the soles of my boots and I took a staggering step toward that spot in the sand where she had been only seconds before. Where was she? Where was my dragon?!

Arlan staggered back, wheezing hard and almost falling backward onto the sand. When his legs buckled, Thatcher and Violet rushed forward, catching him by each of his arms, and holding him upright. Arlan sagged into them with his head lolling and his face ashen, still gasping in tight, wheezing breaths. That was the only thing that kept me from lunging to grab the front of his tunic and punching him across the jaw. What had he done to Vexi?!

I ran forward, dashing over the marks he'd drawn in the sand. They had all vanished, too. Now there was nothing—nothing except ...

Something stirred in the sand, right in the center of where all those circles and runes had surrounded Vexi.

I staggered to a halt.

My mouth fell open.

Vexi squirmed out of the sand and shook herself, hissing angrily and snapping her jaws. She swished her tail and snarled at Arlan, then flared her wings and zoomed over to land ... on my *shoulder*.

Gods and Fates. She ... she was barely the size of a squirrel!

He had shrunken her!

Vexi's now tiny claws gripped the leather of my jerkin and left little pinprick holes as she crawled in close to perch right next to my neck. Her growling sounded more like angry chittering, and she curled her tail under my arm like a monkey gripping a tree limb for balance.

"H-How did you?" My voice cracked and halted as I slowly turned to face the rest of our group. "Is she going to stay like this forever?"

Now sitting on the sand, his face ashen and his lips blue, Arlan glared up at me between desperate, rattling breaths. "N-Not ... per-permanently. The sp-spell will last o-only ... fourteen d-days."

Two weeks? She'd be tiny like this for two full weeks?

Whoa. My mouth hung open and I couldn't do anything to hide my amazement. He was just full of handy tricks lately.

But it didn't look like any of them came easily to him.

"You going to be all right?" I asked as I came closer. My medically-trained brain couldn't ignore the way he was still gasping and clutching at his chest. That was typically not a good sign for anyone.

"He's used too much power," Violet said, her tone sharp and guarded as she flicked me a look of warning. "Give him a moment."

Ah. What was this, then? Was she a bit protective of him?

"I can try to help," I offered, raising my hands in a gesture of surrender.

"I-It is n-not ... something y-your talents c-can assist ... wi-with, I'm a-afraid," he rasped weakly as he closed his eyes and leaned forward, resting his forehead in one of his palms. "P-Please, just give m-me a moment."

We all stood around, watching him fight for breath for nearly five minutes before Violet finally helped him shamble back up to his feet. He wobbled at first, leaning into her and whispering something to her in a language I didn't understand. Avoran? Probably.

Violet nodded like she understood, but the look on her face was fretful and uncertain as she let him go and took a step back.

"Malina should have n-no further objections," Arlan said. He winced as he forced himself to stand tall again, shoulders back and those dusky circles under his eyes much darker than before. "Now, then. The last order of b-business."

Reaching into his robes again, Arlan pulled out a milky white glass sphere roughly the size of a tangerine. He held it out to Thatcher with a meaningful look.

"What is it for?" Thatcher asked as he held it up, peering at its opaque surface curiously.

"It is a binding stone, and one of only two in the world, so see th-that you don't break it," Arlan warned. "A bit of your divine magic sh-should activate it. Then you must throw it toward one being and it will be contained within it until you use the same power again t-to release it. It w-will not work on large beasts, like your dragon, however."

"But it would on your sister?" Thatcher guessed. "Or, uh, on her aspect, I guess."

He nodded once.

Right. Well, that was certainly handy. But something about the look on Arlan's face made me wonder if that's really who he intended it to be used on. It put a deep, aching pain in my chest as I turned around, too afraid someone—namely Violet—would notice my expression.

I had never spoken to anyone about the affliction that Ronan had been suffering with his whole life. It wasn't the sort of thing you shared around a dinner table. And even now, knowing we would be searching for him, I wasn't sure how to tell Thatcher. Violet knew about it, of course. She had been there on the night when Arlan first tried to help my nephew.

That was a long time ago, though. And things with Ronan's condition hadn't gotten any better.

They had gotten a whole lot worse.

"I will be watching as often as I can through my scrying glass," Arlan said as we slowly made our way back along the beach toward Malina's ship. "But should anything go wrong, there will be very little I can do to help from that distance."

"You've done more than I expected already," I murmured as I gave Vexi's thumb-sized head a little scratch. She still growled like an angry lapdog in his direction, all her little spines bristled down her back and her tiny teeth bared.

"There are dangers and wonders in the southern kingdoms the likes of which you have only begun to comprehend," he murmured quietly, his voice still halting and breathless as we climbed back onto the boardwalk and headed for the dock. "Take care what you say and how you say it. I would warn you against using your real names, as word of great heroes does travel far—even unto those lands—but your presence there may not win you allies. Likewise, tell no one you are of Maldobar's royal line, and should you find yourself in need of allies, look for the mark of a crescent moon with a sword. That is the emblem of the Zenith's Call. They are familiar with my name, as we have had many successful dealings over the years. Mention my name, and they may smile upon you, as well."

"Zenith's Call?" I repeated, probably butchering the pronunciation. "And that's a criminal organization, I'm guessing? Or assassins? Or both? It's both, right?"

Arlan didn't answer. But the sour, exasperated frown on his face made me think I'd assumed right. Not that I was about to turn down potential allies in a foreign land. The idea of approaching a bunch of criminals for help wasn't exactly appealing, though.

I'd save that for desperate times and last resorts.

⸙ 24 ⸙

CHAPTER TWENTY-FOUR

"Weigh anchor! Hoist that main sail! You better shake the lead out, boys, we're burning daylight!" Captain Malina Skyhart shouted as she stood at the helm, still grasping the ship's wheel and cutting a scrutinizing eye over all the sailors scrambling around on the deck.

With Vexi still perched on my shoulder, hunkered low against my neck and hissing at anyone who came too close, I stood at the bow and watched as *Fog Dancer's* single, large sail unfurled to the morning wind. It swelled and filled, sending us forward with a sudden burst of speed that sent waves curling off the hull. I watched, adrenaline pumping as wild as lightning through my veins, as we cut a path through the rising sea straight out from the bay.

Before us, the entire ocean spread out before us as vast and daunting as the horizon. Eternal. Unpredictable. Boundless and free. My heart pounded as I climbed forward, leaning over to watch the dolphins leaping and drafting off our wake all the way until we reached the deeper, bluer, foreboding ocean. There, the wild waves were painted rich scarlet in the dawn's first light. We raced past other, larger but far slower ships, some with three or four masts all flying broad sails.

And, Gods and Fates, I couldn't stop smiling.

The blast of briny wind filling my lungs and whipping my hair back. The taste of the sea spray coating my lips. The power of that speed, surging fast and true with the sun to the east rising higher like a massive orange disc. The shriek of the seagulls following us out, their wings catching the same free air that drove us on.

Next to me, Thatcher had climbed up onto the very edge of the bow and was leaning out over the bowsprit with his arms spread wide and his head thrown back. "Look, Reigh! I'm king of—"

"—Absolutely nothing, so get down, you idiot!" Violet yelled suddenly. She'd come out to join us standing on the deck, and caught him like a mother scolding a naughty child.

That dummy. Last thing we needed was him falling overboard before we were even a mile away from shore. Although, if he did, then we could just leave him with the peace of mind knowing he might be able to swim all the way back.

Hah. Murdoc would definitely kill me for that.

On my shoulder, my now tiny dragoness had finally stopped hissing and growling. She unfurled to stand on her hind legs, eyes closed and sniffing the air. Her spines all smoothed down and her ears flapped like two little flags, her wings still tucked tight to her sides. Maybe she didn't like being travel-sized. It was probably a blow to her usually very healthy ego. But she seemed to enjoy the smell of the open ocean.

We pressed on hard, taking no breaks and riding the strong winds for miles. Looking back, I watched the coast of Maldobar fade behind us like a mountainous green wall. Somehow, it seemed so much smaller now—especially compared to the seemingly endless sea around us. My mind swirled with questions, things I'd never learned about sailing or how to live on the ocean like this. How were we going to be sure we were heading in the right direction? I knew about using the stars at night, of course. But what about during the day? What happened if we hit a storm? Or encountered another vessel?

It didn't take long for my curiosity to drive me back to the helm where Malina still shouted orders occasionally. The wind blew through her long, loose black curls and rustled in that golden feather pinned to her hat as Captain Malina stood proud and sure, her frock coat billowing behind her and her sea-green eyes fixed ahead. She didn't even look my way as I came to stand off to the side. All business, I guess.

Good. That's the kind of focus we needed.

After several hours, though, everything seemed to settle into a rhythm. The crew, roughly sixty-five sailors in all, moved in perfect synchronicity about the ship. Each one had a job, a shift, and enough sense to know not to slack off or cross their captain. Most of them were human, but there were several Gray elves and even a few Damarians in her ranks. One especially large, burly man must have come from somewhere farther to the west, and his body was covered in heavy tattooed images of sea life, constellation charts, and script in a language I couldn't understand.

Most of Malina's crew seemed to regard us with absolute indifference. They didn't offer conversation, good or bad, and seemed to prefer to keep to their own business. I had to wonder if that was their captain's doing—if she had insisted they not pay us any attention or talk to us since we were *special* passengers. They were smugglers, right? So they were probably accustomed to the mentality that the less they knew, the better.

I did catch a few of them eyeing my squirrel-sized dragon, though. Not that I blamed them. That was bound to be a first for, well, just about everyone.

As the sun began to sink, the work pace on the ship changed. So did the crew, who changed out shifts at some of the duties and took time below deck to eat, drink, and rest.

Malina left her first mate, a Gray elven man with all his long, white hair shaved off one side of his head, at the wheel and disappeared back into her quarters. Hmm. I guess she wasn't feeling too chatty, either. That might have been policy for her, too, though. I didn't know how much Arlan had told her about us, but she hadn't seemed enamored with the idea of having us on her ship in the first place. We were definitely high-risk cargo for her.

I guess that was why she had elected to keep her distance, as well.

"I keep thinking if I look hard enough, I'll see Maldobar back there. A tiny speck or something," Thatcher sighed as he came to stand next to where I was leaning against the railing on the poop deck at the rear of the ship. "I know it's impossible, though. We must be a hundred miles from there, now."

"I have no idea," I confessed with a laugh. "I never spent much time studying the maps of the Southern Kingdoms. But the sun's about set that way, so we must be pointed south-east still. That's the direction of Nar'Haleen, so I guess that means we're at least going in the right direction."

Thatcher laughed, too. "I remember thinking that Dayrise was the farthest from home I'd ever been. Gods, my father never would have believed any of this. His lazy son turned out to be a dragonrider, and now I'm sailing to Nar'Haleen on a smuggler's ship."

"Don't forget you're a godling, too," I added.

Thatcher's expression fell some. His mouth flattened into an uncertain, uncomfortable line and he bobbed his head. "Yeah," he agreed quietly. "As hard as I try, I can't seem to forget about that, too."

"Not enjoying the notoriety of being a future god?" It sounded weird even as the words left my lips.

His mouth twisted to one side and he gave a shrug. "No, to be honest. It's hard to think about. And quite frankly, it scares me. I don't know what my future is going to be like, or if I'm going to change as time goes on. Will I always be like this—myself—or will continuing to use my power make me turn into something or someone else? And if I do, will I even remember anything that's happened to me? Or will I forget all of you? Forget who I am?"

Hmm. Now I had to ask. "Is that why you've kept things so ... non-committal with Garnett?"

He blinked in shock like I'd just smacked him across the face. "No. I-I mean, yes, it's hard to get serious when we are both still committed to our work, but she's never treated me any differently because of the Ishaleon thing." He smiled to himself, almost secretively, as he looked back out across the water. "I think that's one of the things I like best about her. I can be myself, unapologetically, when she's around. And she doesn't want or expect anything else."

Envy twisted in my heart like a coiled, venomous viper. I remembered that feeling, of that kind of love, all too well. And in the end, it had bitten me—hard enough to leave a mark and a memory I could never forget.

Enough to make me feel like a part of me had died.

"So you'll marry her eventually?" I mumbled, only half-interested now. Tales of his relationship bliss were a little bit more than I could stand to stomach. It was hard enough being around Phoebe and Murdoc together, and my sister and Phillip, Jaevid and Beckah, Kiran and Lin Broadfeather, and ... well, basically everyone else in the entire world.

Ughhh.

Thatcher just shrugged again. "If she wants to, eventually, sure. But we're not putting a time limit on it or anything like that. We're just ... enjoying being together."

"Good for you," I sighed and pushed away from the railing. "I'm going to bed."

"Hey, Reigh?" he called before I got even ten steps away.

I paused. "What?"

"Do you, um, do you think we're going to be getting tangled up with a lot of divine magic this time, too?" His voice had gone quiet, and he looked fretfully at the ground as he shifted his weight some and rubbed at the back of his neck. "It's just that, you know, my powers are pretty limited still. And I don't really know how that sort of thing might affect me."

"I don't know, Thatcher. But I think that if there was a chance it might impact you negatively, Arlan would have said something," I said. "You saw him. This situation has rattled his cage in a big way. He's taking no chances and pulling no punches. I don't think he would have agreed for you to be a part of this mission if he thought for a second you'd wind up being a liability."

Thatcher's mop of shaggy, light blond hair swished as he nodded. He flicked his gaze up to meet mine for a moment, somehow managing to still look like a bashful kid rather than a man who was now taller than I was. "I've got your back. You know that, right?"

I nodded back and forced a half-hearted smile. "Yeah. I do."

"Good. If you want, I'll stay up and keep an eye on things. We can swap out in the morning?"

"Sounds good." Plucking Vexi off my shoulder, I passed her over to him and gave her small head a little rub. "Keep on him, alright, girl?"

She made an unhappy chattering sound but settled down onto his shoulder with her tail wrapped around his neck. Good enough for me.

"She's kinda cute like this, yeah?" Thatcher grinned as he stroked her back as though she were a small, scaly cat.

"In a might-bite-your-finger-off kind of way, sure," I grinned back. "Keep a sharp eye out. So far, this Captain Malina seems to be pretty professional. But I'd be a dumb sap if I took a pirate at her word."

"Smuggler," Thatcher corrected as I turned to walk away.

I wafted a hand dismissively. "Apples or oranges—it doesn't matter. It's all just fruit in the end, Thatch."

THREE DAYS INTO OUR JOURNEY, I DID SOMETHING REALLY STUPID.

I started to hope.

Nothing had gone wrong. No one had tried to throw us overboard, kill us in our sleep, sink our ship, or even poison our food. The time passed in quiet monotony, with only one small storm to break up the usual routine aboard the ship. But even that small bump wasn't anything to write home about. Captain Malina reacted fast to the rising clouds and managed to guide us on an alternate course so that we skirted the worst of it.

And I dared to dream this would go as planned.

Stupid, stupid, stupid.

"We're making good time," Malina announced as we sat around her desk late that evening, enjoying a bottle of her wine and swapping a few pleasantries. Nothing too personal, of course. She didn't seem interested at all in who we were or what we intended to do once she had delivered us to the port city of Uru'Nai in Nar'Haleen.

"You think we'll spot any warships once we get closer to the coast?" Violet asked over the rim of her glass.

Malina gave a groaning sigh and downed the last of her own goblet before dropping it unceremoniously back on her desk. "Probably. But I'd love to see those tail-draggers try to catch us. Loaded down with cannons and men, they can't do much more than crawl. So they drop longboats packed with soldiers to try and run down easy prey. But we're too fast for 'em. Nothing to worry about. They may try a few shots off the bow as we breeze by, but we can wave at them as we pass."

"Why would they attack us at all?" Thatcher asked.

"Because they're out to push muscle on anyone they can. It's a game of dominance, you see. If they can drag foreign ships in, rough up the crew, take anything they want, and leave us empty-handed with a ship full of holes, they get to feel extra big in their boots when they go home," Malina scoffed and poured herself another goblet of the rich red wine.

"That's how it is with the richies, though, isn't it? They do so love to punch down. Makes 'em feel nice and safe in their big cozy beds at night."

"Sounds like you side with Damaria," I murmured.

She puffed a little snort and tossed some of her long black hair over her shoulder. "I'm on no one's side, little prince. Sides are for people too stupid to know when they're being shuffled across the board like little pawns in a game. They don't notice they're the ones doing all the stabbing and dying, while the richies are happy to give them nothing but a nice little pat on the head—a little petting just to keep them dying for the right cause. Can't have them waking up and realizing it's all just been a sham and they've given up everything for a cause they don't even understand, let alone believe in." She laughed and swirled her glass proudly before taking another sip. "Sides are for fools, darling. Remember that."

A low blast of a horn made everyone sitting around her desk go quiet. Malina slowly lowered her glass, staring past us to the door where the dark shapes of crewmen ran by the windows. Shouts echoed from the deck beyond. Her jawline went rigid and she downed the whole glass in one long swig before slamming it down on the desktop. "Well, now. We've got company. Look alive, you lot. And pray it's just a warship. Else we might be in for a wild night."

25

CHAPTER TWENTY-FIVE

It wasn't a warship.

As we rushed out of Malina's private quarters and onto the deck, we stepped into absolute chaos. Sailors rushed in every direction, shouting and carrying weaponry and bits of armor, and her first mate ran up to give a full report. They'd spotted a pair of ships off to the west, approaching fast. No banners or flags. And one of them, apparently, was a large galleon.

Pirates.

Malina hissed what I could only assume were Rienkan curses through her teeth as she threaded a broad, black and gold leather belt low around her hips. It was weighed down with several objects I didn't recognize—strange L-shaped devices made of richly oiled wood and polished metal. One was larger than the others, with a bell-shaped opening at one end. It glistened with inlays of onyx and mother of pearl into black stained wood, and was about the length of my entire forearm. The two others she had were considerably smaller and buckled to either side of her hips. They looked identical, with dark brown wood covered in shining filigree of silver.

I had no name for whatever those were, but the way she handled them made me suspect they must be some sort of handheld weapon. I'd heard that the Damarians were especially clever when it came to black powder and using it in warfare—something Maldobar had never invested in. But I had never actually seen weapons like that in action. And when Malina pulled the largest one out to load the front, bell-shaped opening with a pouch of black powder and a thumb-sized ball of iron, I took a biiig step back.

Yep. Definitely a weapon—most likely of the exploding variety.

"Should I bring us broadside and load the cannons?" the first mate panicked, handing over a long spyglass as he watched Malina, waiting on edge for any indication of what to do.

She snapped it out to its full length and raised it, but not before flicking him an irritated glare. "Hah! Already? We've only just met. Let's dance with them first, shall we?" Malina snickered as she held the glass up to her eye and angled it at the two tiny dark shapes approaching from the western horizon against the setting sun. "I want full-sail and push her hard, let's make 'em work for it!"

A chorus of answering shouts went up from the crew as they scrambled to work. Some climbed up the network of rope-rigging, called shrouds, that hung sort of like massive webs from the masts to the deck. They dropped more sails from the front of the ship, calling to one another and securing them. Other sailors began passing out short swords, crossbows, and daggers. Strangely, they didn't offer us any.

We didn't need handouts, though.

I dashed below deck with Thatcher right on my heels and Vexi clinging to my back like a scared baby lemur. She squawked and flapped unhappily, chattering at me like an angry wren. Flinging open the small chest at the foot of the cot I'd been given for the trip, I seized my belt and kafki blades and buckled them to my waist. Thatcher grabbed his much larger, Ulfrangar-styled crossbow that could automatically reload between shots due to the large, circular canister of bolts that fit into the front. We both strapped on our breastplates and bracers—but full armor was out of the question when we might inadvertently take a swim at some point.

There was real envy glittering in Malina's turquoise eyes when she saw Thatcher with the large black and silver crossbow, striding over the deck to stand at her side again. "Aye, boy, where on this sweet earth did you get that little beauty?"

He winked and smirked from ear to ear as he cocked it, and the mechanism spun into place to load a fresh bolt. "You wouldn't believe me if I told you."

"Hah! You're a touch mad, aren't you? I like that in a man." Malina laughed and tossed the spyglass back to her first mate. Then she drew her own curved scimitar, giving it a spin over her hand as she took the wheel in the other. "Now then, turn with the wind, lads! We're in for a chase. I want updates on the minute!"

It only took four to tell we were in real trouble.

The first one to spot that the other two ships—the big galleon and a much smaller schooner were chasing us down. As soon as we took off over the waves, they dropped all their sails as well and took up the chase. While the larger ship seemed to fall behind quickly, unable to match our speed, the opposing sloop was a man-o-war, and had two masts to our one, so it was already gaining fast.

"A striker," Malina growled. "They're going to try to intercept and cripple us so big brother can catch up and end us."

Curse it all. Why did I feel like this was going to end in a bloodbath?

The second minute, a small half-elven boy called down from the crow's nest that both ships had dropped colors. Now our enemy had a name, or at the very least, a symbol. A rippling flag of pitch black shone against the light of the failing sun, bearing the insignia of a pair of intertwined, finned serpents connected at the tail.

All the emotion seemed to drain from Malina's face as her first mate gave the report. Then her gaze went steely. Her jaw worked from one side to the other as though she were grinding her teeth, and the sunset flickered in her eyes like green flames as she stared at that other, larger ship's silhouette.

"It's her," she seethed quietly.

"You're sure, Captain?" the Gray elven man faltered, his hands shaking as he lowered his spyglass and stared at her with his own features going paler.

"Yes. I know those sails. I know her like a mother knows her own baby." Malina gave the wheel a spin, spinning it to a sudden halt and bringing our ship around to face the oncoming attack. "Load the chase gun and run a shot across the bow. He wants to bring me in, so be it. But we don't go down without a fight."

"I'm sorry—*WHAT?!*" I spun on her, hoping I was somehow hearing this wrong. "You know who that is?"

Her eyes narrowed on the larger of the two approaching ships. The galleon already had her gun ports opening down either side to reveal thirty-two cannons, sixteen down either side. Oh, dear sweet gods. They had twice as many as we did, and probably longer-range, too.

"Aye, most who sail these waters know that flag. That's the *Squall Queen*, but the man at her helm is no captain worthy of the title. Ship-stealing scum—he is. He deserves iron in his throat and a grave in the depths." Her voice cut sharp with absolute hatred as she spun the wheel in fast, jerking motions.

Standing beside me, Violet looked equally thrown as her hands brushed two of the six daggers she had belted down the sides of her legs. "You must be joking. I thought you were the fastest ship in the southern seas? We're going to *fight* them? We're outnumbered! We don't stand a chance in a head-on fight!"

"Speak for yourself, Pitathi girl," she growled and spat on the ground at my feet. "You lot may know dragons and castle battles, but I know the sea and I know my ship. Now, go and make yourself useful. Arlan said you'd be good in a fight. I guess we'll see, won't we?"

"SHE'S INSANE!" I SHOUTED AS I RAN WITH VIOLET AND THATCHER TO THE MIDDLE OF the ship. "We'll be outnumbered ten to one. Even on land, I'd hate these odds, but she wants to do it in the open ocean?"

"It's a matter of pride now," Violet grumbled as she tied her silvery-blonde hair back into a long ponytail and drew two of her daggers to spin them artfully through her fingers. "We've no choice now. Try to stay together. One way or another, we must survive and find a way to Nar'Haleen—even if that means bartering with a different captain to do it."

BOOOM!

The deck flinched under our boots and the ship rocked as a huge explosion shattered through the air. A massive iron cannon mounted on the front of the ship belched black smoke and sent a ball of iron as big across as a dinner plate hurtling toward the smaller of the two ships. It sailed just a few feet off to the left—er, no, I guess it was their *port*—bow. Ship terms. I'd have to get used to that.

I waited, gripping the wooden railing with Violet and Thatcher on either side of me. Together, we watched in mute horror as the two ships approached, growing larger by the second. Fates, they were closing in fast. We had maybe five minutes before they would be upon us. And then?

Then it would be chaos and cannon fire.

BOOOM!

The smaller, faster schooner returned fire with a warning shot of its own that sailed wide and hit the water with a splash only a hundred yards shy of our side. The spray of cold ocean water peppered my face and made the ship rock slightly.

Gods and Fates. What was that? A demand to surrender?

I took a step back, watching Malina who had an expression like a rabid, feral raccoon as she shouted down to her men, demanding they load the cannons and ready the boarding hooks.

"Give them a volley as soon as they're within range! No warnings this time, boys. It's for blood or breath!" she shouted as she jabbed the point of her scimitar toward the approaching enemy. "Once they hit us, I want someone down there burning fuses! Send them to the drakkon with iron in their bellies, boys!"

A chorus of fierce shouts went up from her crew, and I bit down hard against the rising tide of cold fear that swelled in my gut. This was about to get nasty. And I had no idea what kind of a fight we were truly in for. I could guess, of course. With her crew readying those massive, black powder-fed cannons and gods only knew what else, we were already out of our depth in more ways than one.

Now, I had to wonder if we would even survive to reach Nar'Haleen at all.

Never in my strangest or wildest fantasies had I imagined that I might wind up on the deck of a ship, fighting a small army of angry pirates alongside Thatcher and Violet.

But here I was.

I whirled and ducked, dropping low as a muscle-bound pirate brandishing a huge, curved cutlass blade took a swing for my head. He bellowed like a furious bear as the blade howled right over my head, missing by inches. I practically felt the wind off it rustle my hair as it passed. Close one.

Blood rushed in my veins, hot and frenzied, as I bared my teeth and kicked forward. I surged in, making a tactical upward parry as he swung down at me again. I locked our blades with a *clang*, and spun to disarm him. His blade clattered away across the deck, and I immediately knocked him off balance with an elbow check to the gut.

Whipping around to face him again, I drove the point of my sickle-shaped kafki blade deep into his chest and ripped it free, finishing him off with a kick that sent him sprawling backward and over the side of the ship.

SPLASH!

He hit the ocean somewhere below.

Great. One down, about a hundred and forty-nine more to go.

If we were lucky.

And let's face it, we *never* were.

"INCOMING!" Thatcher shouted suddenly as he landed next to me seemingly out of nowhere, crossbow in hand. He spun to put his back to mine, blood trickling down the side of his face from a fresh wound on his forehead.

I looked toward the enemy schooner, which had come alongside us and was preparing to open up a round of crossbow fire right over the side of our ship. I snarled a Gray elven curse and gripped my blades tightly. "VIOLET! GET YOUR BUTT OVER HERE!"

Through the fray, I couldn't see her anymore. But she was only lightly armored compared to us, and brandishing daggers. I had never seen her fight, so I wasn't altogether sure how well she would manage. Maybe she wouldn't. After all, this wasn't exactly the kind of conflict someone with a sneak-and-stab fighting style would be—

Someone on the enemy ship's deck shouted—giving the command to fire. Immediately, all the crossbows fired at once, their strings slapping with one loud *TWANG!* Our comrades ran for cover, diving behind anything they could as the cloud of bolts hailed down toward our deck.

"Do it!" she screamed, practically appearing at my side like she'd materialized there.

She only had one set of her daggers left, gripped firmly in hand, as she crouched low and cut her gaze across to the enemy ship.

Thatcher stretched a hand upward to the sky, his eyes flashing with a brilliant, radiant golden light as his outstretched palm and fingertips shone like forge-heated metal. A shield of rippling golden light dropped around us like a shimmering bubble, hitting the deck of the ship with a low *VOOOM!*

The bolts pinged off it like pebbles off a dragon's hide, harmlessly hitting the deck or hanging suspended in the force field.

Thatcher snapped his fist closed, letting out a sharp, primal shout as the golden bubble burst with a *POW*—and all those stuck bolts went flying outward and back toward our enemy.

"If we can cripple or sink the smaller ship, the bigger one won't be able to catch us. We can make a run for it!" Violet shouted as she darted back into combat, intercepting another enemy pirate who had climbed aboard our ship with a sword clenched in his teeth.

Sweet Fates, how did they keep getting on here?

I leaned over the side just long enough to see a whole group of them, at least twenty, gathered around the side of our ship. They were riding on something—animals I didn't recognize at all. They almost looked like horses, but instead of having hooves or hind legs, they had tails like a fish and a crest of fins down their backs. Fitted with saddles, each one could carry a pair of riders at speed over the waves. They came racing through the water, as fast as dolphins, in groups of five and ten. I tracked their path all the way back to the much larger galleon. Gods. That was it! They were all coming from that big ship.

Violet was right. We had to end this or we'd be overwhelmed in minutes. Fleeing was our best option—as soon as that striker ship was taken out.

"Thatch, cover me!" I yelled over the noise as I sheathed my kafki and grabbed Vexi, prying her, squawking and hissing, off my shoulder and dropping her onto his. I slipped a dagger free from the back of my belt and put it between my teeth, pirate-style.

"On it!" he called back, unloading a round of bolts from his crossbow down the side of the ship at the host of pirates still trying to climb aboard like ants up a cupboard.

I sprang onto the ship's railing and took one look over the edge to the water far below. Twenty feet, maybe? No problem.

"REIGH! What are you doing?!" Violet screamed, seeming to suddenly realize what I was about to do.

I gave her one last glance and a parting wink, then dove headlong off the side of the ship—streaking like a spear all the way to the roiling, cold ocean waves.

26

CHAPTER TWENTY-SIX

Water shot up my nose and blurred my vision as I dove beneath the surface. But instead of coming back up, I paddled forward underwater, squinting through the stinging of the saltwater in my eyes. Dead ahead, I spotted one of those bizarre, horse-like creatures with an empty saddle swimming in a panicked circle, tossing its head and lashing its tail as though in panic. I guess its rider had left it to try boarding our ship. Or been shot down. Either way, that seat was now empty—and as far as I was concerned, it was mine.

I had to time this just right.

Swimming forward with all my strength, my lungs ached for want of air as I stretched out a hand just as the creature blurred past. My hand closed around the long leather straps tied to either side of its bridle like reins, and I was immediately jerked along its wild, speeding path.

Pitching wildly through the water, I flailed for a second or two before I finally managed to flip over onto my stomach and curl my body inward. I wrapped my legs around the beast's back and dragged myself in against the rush of the water until I was sitting in the saddle. Then I grabbed the other rein-strap and pulled, willing the creature to a stop.

Holy gods. It ... it really was like some kind of horse. Suspended underwater, the beast tossed its head and gave a high-pitched shriek like the call of a dolphin or whale, then turned to look back at me with one big, panicked yellow eye.

Whew. Okay. I could do this. I'd ridden faundra and horses more times than I could count. How hard could this be? It was bound to be similar, right? Right. I totally had this.

Fates, what was I doing?

I gave a stern kick and leaned down, bracing myself for the alarming burst of underwater speed as we surged upward to where the sunlight rippled beyond the surface.

We broke into the sky with a leap, and I tossed my soggy hair out of my eyes as we charged forward. With my dagger still clenched between my teeth, I leaned into the beast's impressive speed as we bounded over waves and zoomed across the surface of the water straight for the opposite side of the enemy sloop. All their focus was on us as they came broadside and began hurling grappling hooks across our deck, attempting to lash us together so we couldn't escape.

Only... that wasn't going to work for long. Not if I had anything to say about it, anyway.

I had a plan—and it was so utterly insane, even Jaevid might have been nervous.

Hah. Yeah, right.

I brought the sea-horse-thing around to the side and cut my gaze upward, noting that no one seemed to even be watching this side of the boat. They weren't expecting any surprised attackers with all the focus on the other side. Excellent.

I climbed off the beast's back and started upward, using my dagger to give me extra leverage on the steep climb up the side. The sharp edges of the barnacles encrusting the first five or six feet cut up my palms, but I didn't let go. I made it to the top and peered just over the edge. There, enemy pirates scrambled around in the same sort of chaos I'd just left on our boat. Some lay dead from our crossbow fire. Others were working on readying boarding lines and flinging more grappling hooks. Up at the helm, the sight of a young man with deep ebony skin and pointed ears holding the ship's wheel made my heart jolt for a moment. A Lunostri elf? I'd never seen another one except for Isandri. And the instant thought of her put a sting in my heart.

I shut my eyes tightly and looked away, down toward the middle of the deck to the hatch that led into the ship's underbelly. That's where they kept the cannons and all their black powder. And that's exactly where I had to go.

I waited, coiling my legs beneath me, and preparing to spring at the first instant I saw a clear path. With any luck, no one would notice me thanks to all the ambient chaos on deck.

Wait for it ... wait for it ...

NOW!

My pulse kicked in rhythm with the cannon fire as I sprang up onto the deck, over the railing, and ran headlong for that open hatch. I stayed low, moving like a blur across the deck and skidding to a halt at the top of the stairs that plunged down into the belly of the ship. Darkness and the smell of burning powder made my stomach turn.

And something else. A sound. Not the normal, expected shouts of men giving orders or working at the cannons to load and fire. No—this was something else.

Wait a second was that ... panicked screaming? Um. Yeah. That definitely sounded like the desperate dying screams of sailors coming from *below* deck.

What the heck was going on down there?

Well, now wasn't the time to hesitate. I had a mission and a very short time before that big galleon, the *Squall Queen,* was upon us. Then there would be no escape.

Drawing my kafki, I descended the stairs into the gloom below deck. The smell of blood and powder hung thick in the air, and I nearly stepped on a few fallen sailors that lay in bloody heaps on the floor—almost like they'd been trying to flee back up to the deck. A cold chill spread through my chest as I prowled forward, every nerve drawn as tight as bowstrings. Ready to snap and react at any moment. I followed the trail of bodies and blood deeper into the ship, growing closer to the sound of the cannon fire. Dead ahead, a broad opening led to a long room where that sound and the acrid smell of burning black powder was the strongest. That must be the gun deck, where the rows of cannons were lashed down next to rows of portholes, and could easily be loaded again and again by the crew within the protection of the ship's hull.

Flashes of flame lit up the near dark as some of the cannons fired, making the floor beneath my boots flinch and the ship rock slightly. Then everything went still. Quiet. No screams of men. No rustling of reloading. No more cannon fire.

Sucking in a deep breath, I prepared myself for the worst. Something had obviously gone wrong down here. Now, I had to face it in order to continue with my plan of, well, basically simultaneously igniting all the powder left on the ship to blow it all the way to the gods' doorstep. One hit, one solution.

My sweaty palms squeaked on the leather grips of my blades as I gave them a preparatory spin over my hands and stepped into the doorway. Whatever was in there, man or beast, I'd send it back to the gods right along with the ship. My pulse throbbed in my fingertips as I stood there, scanning the shadows of the gun deck for any thing—any movement, reflection, or something that seemed even remotely out of place.

Something cold and sharp pricked at the side of my neck suddenly.

I froze, every muscle locking up solid at once. I knew that feeling.

The point of a dagger.

"I wouldn't move if I were you," a female voice hissed in the dark. "Now, be a good boy, and drop those blades."

I licked my teeth behind my lips. Curse it all straight to the deepest pit of the abyss. How?! How had someone gotten the slip on me?

"I don't surrender," I growled back. "You'll have to kill me."

The blade slid, lightly scraping my skin as a small, feminine figure stepped out from where she had been hiding just inside the doorway. The light from above the deck spilled over her face, and our gazes locked.

My heart stopped. My mouth fell open. My blades nearly slid right out of my grasp.

Oh. My. Gods.

She stared up at me with a similar expression of utter shock all over her beautiful, albeit extremely young face. A face I knew all too well.

"MAYLEA?!" I yelled, half in fury—half in total horror. What, by all the Gods, Fates, and anything divine, was *she* doing here?!

"H-Hi ... Uncle Reigh. Guess we ... had the same idea. Pretty neat, huh? What are the odds of that, I wonder?" Her nervous little chuckle cracked and seemed to die in her throat as she withdrew her blade from my neck and gave me a cringing little smile.

No.

This wasn't happening. It couldn't be. I was hallucinating. Or dead. Or this was some cruel trick one of the gods was playing on me. I could not be here, hundreds of miles away from Maldobar, in the throes of a pirate battle in the middle of the ocean, staring at the Broadfeathers' oldest daughter. The very one I had helped train practically since she was able to walk.

H-How ...? When ...? And for the love of all things divine ... *WHY?!*

Then it hit me. The worst part of all.

My blood ran as cold as arctic water as I stared past her, into the dark, and found my doom somewhere in the yawning maw of the truth:

"Oh. Oh, gods. Jaevid is going to kill me."

FOR A FEW SECONDS, ALL I COULD DO WAS MAKE FRANTIC, DISAPPROVING CHOKING sounds. Then it all burst out of me at once. "YOU! Gods and Fates, girl, do you have any idea how close to death you just came? What are you doing here? Why would you—no.

No, it doesn't matter. Get yourself back on the other ship right now! I mean it! Your father is going to rip me in half with his bare hands when he figures out you snuck onboard!" I thundered as I pointed one of my blades back behind me, to the hatch.

She scowled and did that excellent, although distinctly much more feminine impression of her father's challenging glare. "Through the frenzied crowd of enemies? Sure. Sounds like an excellent plan. I got here first. I killed all the men firing the cannons. This is my plan, so let me finish it!"

Uggggghhh. Teenagers.

She did have a point, though. I couldn't very well send her up there on her own. If anything happened to her, Jaevid would beat me to death. Then he'd probably negotiate a deal with some god to bring me back to life so he could kill me again.

"You know what—forget it. You stay right here where I can watch you and make sure no one comes through that door. This isn't a negotiation!" I fumed as I stormed past her.

"Just so you know, you have to intertwine all the fuse lines," she chimed proudly at my back, a sly little grin playing over her lips. "Oh, and the powder kegs are over there."

Unbelievable. That attitude—now *that* had to have come from Beckah. Jaevid was a lot of things, but he'd never been smug. Not about something like this, anyway.

I clenched my teeth, tasting blood and every angry word I wanted to shout as I sheathed my blades and got to work. It didn't take long for me to tie up every last barrel in their stores to a long fuse line and unwind it all the way to the doorway where Maylea still waited, arms crossed and hips cocked to one side.

"See?" She grinned wolfishly as I stormed past. That grin faded, though, when I grabbed the back of her tunic and dragged her out with me like a naughty puppy.

"Once it's lit, we've got about three minutes to get as far away from here as possible. Got me? So you run. No hesitating. No coming back for me if I'm not behind you. RUN. Understand?" I growled through my teeth as I bent down. Pulling my flint stone from my belt, I used the edge of one of my blades to strike a shower of sparks right over the fuse line. It caught and lit, beginning to burn steadily toward my makeshift death charge. If that didn't sink this ship, nothing would.

"GO!" I bellowed and ran for the stairs that led up to the hatch.

Maylea dashed ahead of me, as fast as a shadow with her dagger still in hand. We rounded the base of the steps and started up, me right behind her. I looked up, able to see open sky beyond the sails and rigging of the ship. Almost there. Almost out. Just had to make it over the side of the ship and then swim for dear life. We could do it. We would make it.

We had to.

SLAM!

A solid iron grate fell over the top of the steps, blocking the entire passage out of the ship's hold. A few leering faces of pirates laughed and jeered down at us, spitting and taunting as they brandished a single heavy lock that clamped down to keep the hatch closed tight.

"NO!" Maylea shouted as she gripped the iron bars and tried shaking them.

It was no use. They'd trapped us below deck ... with only minutes, maybe seconds, before my death charge exploded.

My mind raced, blurring between options. There wasn't one. Not a good one. Either I ran back in and tried to cut the fuse before it went off, and then we would be taken captive, tortured, and killed slowly by a bunch of pirates, or we went down with the ship.

No. There had to be something else, something I could—

An idea struck me so suddenly, I flinched back. It was stupid. Reckless. Unlikely to succeed.

But it was the best I had.

Grabbing Maylea by the arm, I dragged her after me, back down the stairs, and ran headlong for the other end of the ship. Behind the forward bulkhead, I ducked down and pulled her in against my chest, wrapping my arms around her to try and shield her. This ship was going down because I'd set it up to blow a massive hole right in the keel. It would fill quickly and sink.

But the massive hole that would be left behind might be our only way out now.

I shut my eyes tightly and braced, listening and holding my breath.

Then it came like the pounding fist of a vengeful god.

BOOOM!

☙ 27 ❧

CHAPTER TWENTY-SEVEN

The whole ship shuddered hard. Wood cracked, splintered, and flew. The hull gave an ominous groan as the ground beneath us began to shift. Barrels, boxes, and crates slid as the ship began to go down by the stern. Above us, footsteps scrambled over the deck. Men shouted and cried out in panic. Horns blared.

We were sinking—fast.

"Come on," I shouted as I skidded and stumbled over the steeply angled floor. Opening the door to the main hold, the rush of water greeted us in a roaring swell.

"Uncle Reigh?" Maylea whimpered as she gripped my hand. Her teal green eyes had gone wide and teary in panic. I guess this little plan of hers wasn't going the way she'd hoped.

That made two of us.

"There's only one way out now. Hold your breath and follow me!" I jumped in feet first and immediately took in a deep breath, swimming with all my strength through the collapsing debris and drifting bodies of dead pirates, crates, ropes, and fragments of wood all the way to the gun deck. The doorway had been blown apart, and I had to squirm through what was only a narrow opening between a few cracked wooden planks. Maylea was smaller, so she made it through much more easily.

We swam down, deeper into the remains of the ship as the water churned and whirled around us. The light gave way to a growing dark, and panic gripped me like a fist to the throat. Oh, gods, what if we didn't find a way out before we sank too far? What if the pressure killed us? What if we drowned?

Then I saw it—light from the surface pouring through the massive hole in the keel of the ship. I swam for it with all my strength, only pausing to look back and make sure Maylea was right behind me. With her cheeks puffed full of air and her eyes wide and frantic, she paddled for it right alongside me.

Against the rush of the water surging into the ship, I managed to drag myself out from its demolished interior. I immediately clung to the opening and reached back in to seize Maylea's hand, helping her scramble out.

Free. Gods and Fates, we had made it out! And in one piece!

I dared to hope as we swam like mad back up toward the surface, dodging a shower of more debris and sailors diving off to make a break for it before their ship went all the way down.

VOOOOOM ...

A sound, deep and concussive, sent out a shockwave through the water around us and made my heartbeat stall and stop for a moment. What the heck was that? Something about it made my skin tingle strangely. It felt like ... well, sort of like standing too close to one of Arlan's magical spell circle when he'd shrunken Vexi.

But surely there wasn't an Avoran elf or anything that powerful onboard that galleon. No. It couldn't be. Malina would have mentioned that. She would have warned us ... right?

Maylea and I broke the surface with a gasp, looking around as nothing but the very tip of the enemy schooner's mainmast was left above water now. Beyond it, though, that galleon was encroaching fast. It lurked so near, I could see the figures moving around on its massive deck.

One individual stood separate from all the others, positioned on the grand ship's raised platform that held the helm. It was hard to tell from that distance, but it looked like a man. A tall man with dark hair.

Was that the captain Malina had mentioned?

He moved, grasping onto something right next to the ship's wheel. A lever or ... some sort of handle. I couldn't tell. But when he raised it and slammed it down, it sent out another shockwave just like the first.

VOOOOM!

"What is that?" Maylea cried out as she treaded water next to me.

I didn't now. Not at first. I wasn't acquainted with most of the things pirates used on their ships—not beyond a purely hypothetical or academic sense. But somehow, this felt different. Ominous.

Dangerous.

As the rush of that shockwave spread out over the ship, it sent a strange ripple along the big galleon's hull. A shimmer of light like an aurora that rippled over the wood with an eerie blue-green glow.

It was magic. But what kind? What did it mean?

Then, I got my answer.

Or, rather, the ship did.

From somewhere far below, an answering wave of energy boiled upward and made the surface of the sea vibrate and ripple like someone bumping a table underneath a cup of water. It was much louder. Bigger. Stronger.

Taking in a breath, I plunged under the surface to try and figure out what had caused that—just in time to see a massive eye open directly below us. The eye alone must have been seven feet across, with a round pupil focusing right on us. A gargantuan scaly head turned, the eye blinking and focusing past us to the ships bobbing in the water. There was something broad and distinctly snakelike about its head, with long jaws and an upturned mouth covered in long whiskers like catfish. Only, this was no catfish.

I couldn't gauge the true size of the monster—only that it was bigger than anything I'd ever seen. The head alone was the size of a ship, and I caught a glimmer of something like scales in rich colors of blue and yellow as it turned away to disappear back into the dark endless ocean beneath us.

As best I could tell, its body was long and serpentine in the water, with a ridge of red and yellow fins that grew longer toward its tail like an arapaima—only far longer. Gods, it must have been four hundred feet at least.

And whatever it was, it was answering the *Squall Queen* with a similar burst of that magic.

Run. We had to run—no—swim. Swim away quickly.

Right now.

"Ship! Go back to the ship!" I shouted at Maylea. "NOW!"

She didn't hesitate and took off swimming for the *Fog Dancer*. I followed, paddling like mad with my heart in my throat. I wasn't afraid of being eaten outright. No, that creature probably considered me a tiny appetizer, like a pumpkin seed. But if it decided to gnaw on our ship? Well, we couldn't do much to stop it. Sure, we could try cannons or maybe even harpoons. I had a feeling nothing would pierce the scales I'd seen, though. Nothing manmade, anyway. We had no choice. No backup plan.

Other than try to get away, and pray it didn't chase us down.

"MAYLEA?" THATCHER WHEEZED IN SHOCKED DISMAY AS HE HELPED DRAG US BOTH OVER the side and back onto the deck of our ship.

"Yes, she's here. Yes, it's bad. We'll address it later," I grumbled as I raked my soaked hair out of my eyes and looked out across the *Fog Dancer*.

Captain Malina was back to shouting orders, and her crew was frantically trying to patch the sails enough to get underway and fend off what remained of the enemy pirates who had still managed to get onboard.

I guess we were making a run for it, after all.

"Gods and Fates, what is that thing?" Thatcher gasped as he stood, his expression slack and pale in horror, watching the massive serpentine body of that sea beast arc around the *Squall Queen*. It breached like a whale, and then dove back down, seeming to keep close to the ship as though protecting it.

"A drakkon." Violet's voice was so hushed, I barely heard it above the noise. "Sea serpents of ancient magic and power. Some called them leviathans. There can only be two at a time, and should they meet, they will fight to the death."

"Why is it protecting that ship?" Maylea asked, still standing close at my side.

"Because the hull was not made from wood alone," she answered, her gaze panning slowly from the *Squall Queen* to where Malina still stood up at the helm. "It is said that when these beasts hatch in the deepest parts of the ocean, if you can manage to retrieve their egg shells, you can crush them into a fine powder. That powder, when merged with the wood of a ship's hull, instills it with great power. It is a massive undertaking—a thing of pure legend—and requires an incredible amount of magic to accomplish. But doing it binds the drakkon to the ship forever. It sees the ship as a part of itself, and will protect it fiercely ... and follow its captain's commands."

"How do you know all this?" I had to ask—mostly because I didn't like that strange look she was giving Malina. Not one tiny bit. Something was up. Something they hadn't told us.

"Because there is only one other drakkon ship sailing the ocean in the entire world." Violet backed away from the ship's railing. Her scarlet eyes met mine for an instant and sent a jolt of raw terror through me as she murmured, "And it sails as the flagship for Nar'Haleen—the crown jewel of the dynasty's navy."

"And this one? Who does it sail for?" Thatcher pressed with a determined scowl.

Violet shook her head slightly and looked away. "Once? It belonged to a long family line of notorious and powerful pirates known as the Skyharts. Now, it only obeys one master. The *Squall Queen* and her drakkon are under the command of the pirate king," she replied. "A man known only ... as Fiendheart."

PATHFINDER

THE DRAGONRIDER HERITAGE
BOOK SIX

PART ONE

MAYLEA

❦ I ❦

CHAPTER ONE

You never swim faster than when a giant sea monster and a ship full of angry pirates are chasing you.

That was just one of many important lessons I had learned since I'd left my parents and Maldobar behind to very discreetly join Uncle Reigh's special mission. He, um, weeell ... he hadn't exactly been *aware* of my decision to come along until recently. Very recently, to be precise. And until that moment, when I recognized his fiery-red hair and twitchy scowl looming over me in the gloom of that enemy pirate ship, I hadn't considered how I would eventually break that news to him. I mean, obviously I was going to have to do it sooner or later. But I'd sort of been counting on having a few more days at sea to work out what I would actually say. Surprise, maybe? Mmmm. Maybe not.

Now, I was going to have to figure it out in record time.

I staggered to my feet on the deck of the *Fog Dancer*, my boots sloshing with seawater and my drenched clothes and hair clinging to my skin. My heart pounded and my lungs ached with every gasping breath as I caught myself against the railing of the ship. I'd never had to swim this much in my life—but now wasn't the time to let anyone see me get rattled and winded.

Especially not Uncle Reigh.

He didn't want me here. So now it was up to me to prove to him that I should be. An uphill battle if there ever was one.

Uncle Reigh stood close beside me, just as soaked as I was from our daring watery escape. He kept a strong hand planted firmly on my shoulder. Not in a comforting way, though. More like he was trying to make sure I didn't go slinking off back into the shadows to join the fight again.

A valid concern, really. I had bigger things to worry about than getting his approval about my presence here.

I still had to find Lukani.

My new, green-skinned friend had shapeshifted into one of those swimming horse creatures long enough to carry me to the enemy ship, but I hadn't caught a glimpse of him after that. He had to be somewhere on our ship, right? Gods, I hoped so.

Watching the monstrosity of a beast swimming around beneath our ship, circling and coiling like a colossal serpent, a cold knot of dread lodged in the back of my throat. I had to believe that Lukani was somewhere safe. He was fast, strong, and clever. He could take care of himself.

I just hadn't found him yet.

"We can't fight that thing," Uncle Reigh growled through his teeth like an angry guard dog as his light amber eyes focused into the distance. There, the enemy galleon lurked like a massive dark fortress, the ocean waves foaming around its hull and its sides bristling with twice as many cannons as we had.

We were faster. I'd figured out that much when we initially tried to make our escape. But that ship—the one they kept calling the *Squall Queen*—had been the one to summon that massive leviathan. Somehow, I doubted they'd called that beast here just to give it a chin scratch and send it back on its way. This wasn't an empty threat.

It was a last chance for us. A huge, scaly ultimatum—surrender or die.

My heart pounded hard in my throat with every flash of the sea beast's vibrant scales above the water. My hands shook as my mind raced, searching desperately for an alternative solution. A way out of this. An angle no one else had thought of yet. I couldn't even begin to fathom how we were going to make any kind of escape. Our ship was faster, yes, but it was heavily damaged now, too. We had taken a lot of cannon fire from the other, smaller pirate vessel that Uncle Reigh and I had just successfully sunk.

Well, mostly me. He'd just shown up after *I* had already done all the heavy lifting. Ugh. Typical.

Even damaged, we might be able to limp away faster than the galleon could pursue, but then they might just send that drakkon-monster to play fetch. There wasn't much we could do to contend with a monster that size. I sort of doubted we had the cannon-power to do much to it other than make it incredibly angry.

So, either way, we were in a bad spot.

Fleeing was pointless. Fighting was futile. That pretty much only left one option ...

"We're going to have to parley," Uncle Reigh muttered like a curse. I guess he was thinking the same thing I was. We would have to try to negotiate our way out of this.

Thatcher flashed us a look of panic and sputtered, "With the pirate king? We just sank one of his ships! You think he's going to listen to anything we say now?"

Hmmm. Yeah, that might be a problem.

"What other choice do we have?" Reigh snapped bitterly. "I didn't come this far to get blown to bits or eaten alive thanks to some guy calling himself the pirate king. I've got work to do, and he's in my way."

Uh oh. I knew the crazy look that sparked and crackled in the depths of his cognac eyes like the kindling of a wildfire. Not good. I'd never met anyone else who had a temper worse than Uncle Reigh's. Not even my Dah could match him in that department.

"We don't have much to bargain with," Thatcher panted as he came over to stand at Reigh's side, occasionally flicking a worried glance down at me. I guess he was concerned that I might get caught up in the fray if it all went bad.

Naturally, I had every intention of getting caught up in it--especially if this was about to turn back to flames and blades. I couldn't exactly advertise that, though. Looking sheepish and slightly terrified was safer ... for now.

"I don't suppose Arlan has any connection to this Fiendheart person?" Reigh asked, turning his attention to the petite, slender woman with eyes that shone like rubies and skin as pale as fresh cream.

It was hard to look at her without feeling a little twinge of jealousy. Not because of how pretty she was, though. She was lovely, sure, but I'd seen her fighting with her pair of daggers before Lukani and I snuck off the ship. What I wouldn't give for reflexes like that ...

She shook her head, making her long white hair swish around her waist. "Not for lack of trying, of course. But this fellow has proven very skillful in eluding our agents. We've only caught glimpses of him from afar, and no one has been able to identify who he really is ... or discover where he might have come from. What we do know is that he is clever and utterly ruthless, so I would not expect much in the way of mercy. Any deal we make with him will likely come at a high price."

"Great," Reigh snarled under his breath. Flicking a sideways glare down at me again, he licked his teeth behind his lips—as though he could already taste the venom of every angry word he wanted to yell at me.

It sent a little flutter of panic up my spine and I winced. Oooh yeah. I was in for it this time. No doubt about that.

"Thatcher, take her below. Find someplace safe and make sure she *stays* there. Understood?" Uncle Reigh said as he gave me a nudge and another glare of silent warning.

Yikes.

"Violet, you're with me. Let's see if the good captain can be reasoned with before we're all dragged down to a watery grave." Reigh stormed away, heading for the quarterdeck with Violet right behind him.

For an instant, her scarlet gaze locked with mine, and a furrow of concern crinkled her fair brow. Almost like she was worried about something. Me? No, surely not. I didn't even know her.

Why would she be concerned about me?

"Come on. Let's go." Thatcher urged and put a much gentler hand on my shoulder. His smile was painfully forced, though, and I didn't see any traces of the playful light I could usually find in his light green eyes. If anything, he seemed worried. Maybe even a little bit sad. It made my stomach twist and turn, tangling itself into knots as I walked with him.

Out of all the powerful figures, dragonriders and assassins-turned-heroes, that had been frequent guests in my family's home for as long as I could remember, Thatcher had always treated me more like a little sister. He had spent a lot more time playing with me—normal kid games instead of showing me how to throw knives or escape wrestling choke holds at record speed. He was more like a big brother ... and the thought that I'd done something to upset or disappoint him put a painful, prickling feeling in my stomach like I'd swallowed a fistful of needles.

He guided me onward, ducking through the chaos that still raged all across the ship around us. The crew scrambled to put out fires, pry off the enemy's boarding hooks, and repair the sails. Only a few of the enemy pirates still fought on, cornered and outnumbered by our own men. They wouldn't last long.

"Where have you been hiding out until now?" Thatcher asked as we stepped below deck and into the near-dark of the ship's sublevels. "Must be a pretty good spot since no one found you until now."

I swallowed hard and kept my head down. "The back of the cargo hold. No one goes down there much, and it's easy to hide."

He didn't answer and followed close behind me all the way down the steps to the base level of the ship. We walked in awkward silence to the very back of the large cargo hold, making our way through stacks of wooden crates and barrels. They were all lashed together with ropes so they didn't shift or slide around with the motion of the ship, and I'd found a perfect little corner amidst some sacks of grain and crates packed with wine bottles all nestled into hay. There, on a ratty blanket I'd swiped from the crew's quarters when no one was looking, was where Lukani and I had spent the last few days in hiding.

Comfortable? No. Definitely not. But it was out of sight, and many of the supply crates had food stocked in them so we didn't go hungry.

Looking over my meager hideout, Thatcher sighed heavily and ran a hand through his shaggy, light blond hair to rake it away from his eyes. His broad shoulders drooped and he flicked me another disappointed sideways look that made my soul want to shrivel up like a sun-dried fig.

I cringed and quickly looked back down at the toes of my boots.

"I can't help you, Maylea. You know that, don't you?" he said quietly. "Reigh is beyond furious and I'm not sure anything I say is going to convince him that it's okay for you to be here."

I wiggled my toes around inside my boots. "Yeah ... I know."

"Not that I don't get why. Fates, anyone could tell you were destined for this kind of thing when you can fight the way you do. But sneaking off?" He clicked his tongue and shook his head slowly. "You chose to run away from your parents—to come aboard this ship—without anyone knowing. I have to believe that you knew this wouldn't end well for you. How did you think Reigh was going to react? And your parents? You do realize they are probably losing their minds right now, right?"

I grimaced and turned my face away. Chewing on the inside of my cheek was the only thing that kept my mouth from screwing up at the thought. I knew it was bad. I knew I'd be in huge trouble when everyone found out. But what other choice was there? Ronan—my *friend*—was in trouble. He needed help. And my father couldn't be the one to give it this time. Was I just supposed to shrug and walk away? Did everyone expect me to turn my back on Ronan like all the time we'd spent together meant nothing at all?

Hot, angry tears welled in my eyes as I bit down even harder on my lip to keep my chin from trembling.

Thatcher seemed to be able to sense that I was barely holding it in. I guess he'd gotten pretty good at reading my expressions over the years. He sighed again and patted the top of my head. "Look, we will talk about this later. I'm not promising anything, but I'll try to talk Reigh down to at least mid-level rage. You've got to stay here where it's safe, okay? I don't know what's going to happen with the pirates, but he's got that crazy look in his eyes now, so it probably won't be anything good. Lay low and try not to let anyone see you, okay?"

His hand slid off my head and his heavy footsteps began to retreat back into the dark maze of crates and barrels.

"Thatcher?" I whirled around and called after him.

He stopped. "Yeah?"

"Thank you ... for understanding. I mean, I know it was wrong. But I did have good reasons for coming. And I knew Dah and Uncle Reigh would never allow it. But I couldn't let it go." I hesitated. Should I tell him why? Would he even care? I didn't know. I had always been able to trust Thatcher before. I guess now wasn't the time to start second-guessing him. "I overheard you guys talking about Ronan. I heard you say he was in danger. And after that, I-I ... walking away—not going—it just felt so *wrong*. I can't explain it, and I know that doesn't make any sense, but it felt like I didn't have any other choice. It felt like I was meant to come with you."

Thatcher didn't say a word. Not at first. He stood there for what felt like hours before, finally, he turned back to face me. That sad look in his eyes was gone, but he wasn't smiling, either. I didn't recognize that strange, almost distant expression that made the light in his green eyes seem misty, clouded, and strangely gentle. He walked back over and stopped in front of me, looking me over from head to foot as though he were searching for something.

Then he reached under his shirt and took something—a necklace—off. Sliding the cord over his head, he held it out to me in his open palm.

I stared, my mouth open in awe, at the white, bone-carved pendant that rested in his outstretched hand. I knew that necklace, even if I'd never even touched it before. It was the one my father had worn many years ago in the Gray War against Luntharda. I had seen it countless times in paintings and statues of him from that time. He had passed it on to Thatcher before I was born, a gesture I'd never stopped to think about until right this second.

"I was a little older than you when your father gave this to me. But I'll never forget what he said when he did," Thatcher murmured softly. "I won't pretend to be as articulate as he is, but ... you need to understand that this is something very special that was passed down in your family. Your father wore it. Your grandmother wore it. And before them, many powerful lapiloques of the Gray Elves wore it. Generations of your ancestors believed this represented great power and responsibility. It has hung around the neck of people who changed the world for the better." He reached for my hand and pressed the pendant into it, closing my fingers around it with a firm squeeze. "Now, I believe it's time for it to be returned to your family. I think your father would want you to have it. And more than that, I think you're going to need its strength just like I did."

My mouth stayed open, but nothing would come out. No sound. Not even a panicked squeak of surprise. He was passing this to me? Now? But why? I-I wasn't like that—a world-changer like the others. I certainly wasn't a lapiloque like my father and grandmother, or a godling like Thatcher. Why in the world did he think I was ready to wear something like this?

"Thatcher I-I ... I don't know if—" I began to protest.

He cut me off by giving my hand another, reassuring squeeze. His smile stretched from one cheek to the other, shining with more certainty than I'd ever seen before as he interrupted, "I know. I wasn't either. But right now, we're outnumbered. There's an enemy ship and a huge monster right outside, waiting to destroy us all. And more importantly, there are people that need our help. People we love. So, my question for you is ... what are *you* going to do about it?"

2

CHAPTER TWO

I stood motionless, staring at the necklace in my hand long after Thatcher had left to return to the deck. My heart beat like a war drum in my slightly pointed ears, so loud it felt like my whole head throbbed along with it. Each thump made every inch of my brain seem to come alive at once. My thoughts raced like shooting stars, blitzing in a storm with me caught right in the eye. My jaw locked tight as each breath made a strange, wild heat rise in my chest.

And all the while, Thatcher's words echoed in my head over and over.

What was I going to do about it?

Exactly what I'd come here for in the first place.

I was Maylea Broadfeather, and I hadn't made it this far to be put in timeout like a child. I was here. I had a blade and a purpose.

I didn't need anything else—least of all anyone else's approval.

Slipping the necklace around my neck, I started out of the cargo hold and made my way back to the deck above. I had to be careful. Discreet. If Uncle Reigh or any of the others spotted me, they'd undoubtedly send me back down. They might even try locking me up in the brig this time. I'd have to call upon every ounce of training I'd ever had to pull this off.

Peering out from the stairwell that led below, I narrowed my eyes upon the raised section of the ship's deck where the captain stood at the helm, gripping the wheel as she swapped angry shouts with Uncle Reigh. I guess their attempts at coming up with a good plan for how to get out of this situation weren't going so well. No surprise there.

Fortunately, I already had a plan of my own. Uncle Murdoc had taught me how to think in situations like this. We were outmatched. Outgunned. Outnumbered. Taking the drakkon or the enemy galleon would be impossible, and any attempts to negotiate would certainly be at a disadvantage because we didn't really have anything to leverage. That meant we had to change targets. If we were going to come out of this on top, then I had to make a precision strike and eliminate the heart of the threat.

I had to kill Fiendheart, the pirate king.

Waiting for the perfect moment, I quickly scanned the deck before me. There was still enough ambient chaos that I felt reasonably sure I could move around without catching anyone's eye—so long as I timed it right, anyway. I waited for a crowd of our deck hands to rush by and immediately sprang out to move with them, staying low and keeping my face turned away from where Uncle Reigh and the others stood on the quarterdeck.

Swift as a fox in the night, I dipped to snag a small, light crossbow off the body of a fallen pirate and sling it over my back by its long leather strap. I did the same with a grappling hook and a spool of rope, and dashed the rest of the way to the very front of the ship. The wind snagged in my still-damp hair as I stared out from the bow at the enemy galleon, its sails puffed and colors flying as it eased toward us on a cautious course to intercept. I guess they were still waiting to see if we were dumb enough to try making a break for it.

That answer came as a series of shouts and whistles went up from the crew still racing around me, calling attention to the single white flag being hoisted high on the mainmast. A flag of surrender? Well, I guess that meant Uncle Reigh had talked our captain into trying to negotiate, after all.

I scowled back at the galleon. No doubt they were all feeling pretty smug over there. I'd fix that quickly, though.

Using the far side of the ship that faced away from our enemies, I tied my grappling hook to the spool of rope I'd found and looped it across my shoulders. Then I climbed over the railing and down to the wooden figurehead that was engraved into the very front. It had been cut to resemble one of those fishlike horses—the same sort that Lukani had shifted into in order to carry me onto the last pirate vessel.

My mind tangled at the thought of him, lost somewhere in the chaos all around. What I wouldn't give to have his help right now. Gods and Fates, I hoped he was somewhere safe. I shut my eyes tightly, muttering a prayer under my breath as I wedged myself in against the filigree and cutout details of the figurehead. Once again, my resin-soled scout's boots helped me get the traction I needed even with the hull slick from salty spray. I could wait here until that ship got close enough. I just had to hope no one noticed me before then.

My heart hit the back of my throat as our ship suddenly flinched, jerking violently as though it had run aground. It hadn't of course. Not in the middle of the open ocean. No, something had hit us.

The drakkon.

I watched its immense body slide by only feet beneath the surface of the waves, each scale as wide as a knight's shield and probably five times as thick. I let out a slow, shaking breath. Keep it together—I had to keep it together. No panicking. No getting scared. Not now.

Second by second, the enemy galleon drew closer. I could spot the faces of men in each of their sixteen gun ports that ran down either side. More sailors stood on the deck, jeering and shouting at us, swinging blades in the air as they whooped in victory. I guess they thought they had this fight in the bag already.

Hah. We'd just have to see about that.

Closing in the last few yards of distance, the *Squall Queen*'s crew threw dozens of grappling hooks and lowered boarding planks, preparing to take us and our crew as prisoners. With their ship now sidled up right alongside ours, I waited until I heard the shouts and barking of commands on the deck above me before I took my own grappling hook firmly in hand. I glared across the distance from our figurehead to theirs, which happened to be cut in a design eerily similar to that of the monstrous sea dragon still circling around us like a massive python. From this close up, it was easy to tell that the *Squall Queen* was a much older ship than ours. It had scars from previous battles mottling the hull, and even the wood had been worn by the wind and sea until it shone a strange shade of deep, almost bluish color. A thick armor of barnacles clung to the sides, and painted golden filigree around the cannon portholes and windows had been scratched, battered, and worn completely off in some places. It dwarfed our much smaller vessel like a black swan sidling up next to a frazzled little duck in a pond, and my heartbeat skipped and raced as I eyed my target.

I gripped the grappling hook tighter, biting down hard against the rising flare of panic that made my throat want to close up. I had to do this fast. Any delay meant I might get spotted.

Sucking in a deep breath, I set my gaze upon the *Squall Queen*'s much bigger figurehead, and began swinging my grappling hook in a small circle.

Once just to get a feel for the weight.

Faster the second time, readying my aim.

A third time, watching for the perfect moment.

Wait for it—wait for it—

—Fourth swing ... and I threw it with all my strength.

MY GRAPPLING HOOK SAILED THROUGH THE OPEN AIR BETWEEN THE TWO SHIPS, crossing the distance in less than a second. As soon as I saw it wrap around the lowest curl of the drakkon figurehead's tail, I gave a sudden yank on the rope and wound it up tight. The hook slid, scraped, and caught firmly into the wood. My rope went taut.

No time to think or hesitate.

I sprang out, clinging to the rope and swinging from our ship, the *Fog Dancer,* over to the enemy galleon. I hit the bow and immediately began to climb the rope with my ankles interlocked and my hands burning with every movement. Faster. Silent. I'd only have seconds. I couldn't afford to slip and screw this up now.

A gasping grunt leaked through my clenched teeth as my palms hit the wood of the drakkon figurehead. With one final stretch of my legs, thighs shaking and sweat running down the sides of my face, my grip clamped down solidly on the tail of the wooden drakkon.

I hung, far over the foaming ocean below, and let my rope fall away as I executed a flawless pull up and immediately drew my legs in to my chest. From where I hung, I could see a length of rope that went from the tip of the ship's frontmost mast, the bowsprit, to just above the figurehead itself. It must have been used to tie down the smaller sail at the front, but I didn't know enough about ships to really be sure. All I did know was it was close, tied down securely, and just what I needed to make my way up onto the deck.

Arching my back, I angled my body into a swinging motion, using the weight of my legs to get momentum and finally hoist myself up the rest of the way. My legs caught the rope on the first try and for a moment, I hung upside down with my ankles locked around that rope and my hands still gripping the figurehead like an acrobat on a high wire. Every muscle in my body burned as I let go of the wooden drakkon and curled my body in again to grab hold of the rope with my hands, too.

It didn't take me thirty seconds to scale the rope all the way to the frontmost deck and heave myself over the railing. I landed in a crouch, keeping low and kicking into an immediate roll to duck behind a stack of crates.

Perfect.

I gave it to the count of three, holding perfectly still and listening for any sounds nearby or indication that someone had spotted me, before I finally dared to let out another shuddering breath. No shouts of alarm. No one running in my direction. So far, so good.

Peering out from behind the crates, I quickly surveyed the broad deck of the *Squall Queen*. Currently, all focus was on the crowd of crew members gathered on the main deck. They had begun boarding the *Fog Dancer* and were hauling our crew members over, one by one, with their mouths gagged and their wrists bound like prisoners. The pirate crew taunted and spat at them, poking their sides with the tips of scimitars and shortswords as they were marched over and lined up right in the middle of the *Squall Queen*'s main deck.

My soul nearly jumped straight out of my body as I spotted Uncle Reigh's unmistakable mop of red hair and Thatcher's tall, wide-shouldered frame among the people being forced to their knees. The enemy pirate crew held blades to their backs and chortled in victory, obviously enjoying themselves.

Oh gods. I-I ... I had to hurry before this got out of hand.

Searching the crowd of pirates—men, elves, and other races I didn't even have a name for—I looked for anyone who seemed like they might be in charge. Any guy calling himself a pirate king was bound to be easy to spot. But scouring the vagrants all gathered around my friends, I didn't see anyone who looked that important. Just a bunch of bloodthirsty thugs.

So where was he?

Hmmm.

I'd have to get closer.

Staying low, I moved along the edge of the ship like a shadow. I darted from one pile of crates, to a cluster of barrels, then behind some big spooled up piles of rope, and kept my movements as swift and silent as possible. It was easy when all focus seemed to be on the middle of the main deck. None of the pirates seemed to be worried with anything else that might be happening on their deck.

Their mistake.

And my advantage.

I kept my head down as I skirted right behind the crowd, a blade already prepped in my hand in case anyone decided to take a second glance in my direction. Adrenaline made every muscle burn and shake, and my sweaty fingers slid on the leather hilt of the dagger as I took gradual steps toward the back of the ship.

A sudden roar of excitement from the enemy crew made me look up just in time to see our captain, Malina Skyhart, get dragged onboard. They had her bound up tighter than the others, and shoved her to the ground at the front of the group. She cursed and seethed despite the gag they'd tied over her mouth, glaring out at them and fighting against her bonds. It was no use, though.

One of the pirates stomped a foot right in the middle of her back, sending her crashing onto the deck face-first, and another chorus of delighted whoops went up from the crowd.

I cringed and looked away. Hurry—I had to hurry.

Scurrying to the base of the stairway that led up to the quarterdeck, I stole a glimpse at the helm to see if the so-called pirate king was there watching everything. But the man holding the ship's wheel didn't look like king material. He was older, yes. And he wore a frayed white beard and weather-beaten long coat. But none of the other crew members seemed to pay him much attention.

A first mate, then? Or just some crewmember who had been put in charge of watching the wheel? Either way, not the man I'd come for.

Time to look below deck.

Murdoc's words practically tolled in my head like cathedral bells as I stood straighter and squared my shoulders. *If you want to hide in plain sight, then you can't hesitate. Move with purpose and confidence. Find a menial task and do it like you've been doing it all your life. People on edge will always notice someone who seems lost, reluctant, anxious, or like they're searching for a reason for being there.*

Right. I needed to be confident. No hesitating—like I belonged here.

I picked up a small crate and balanced it onto my shoulder in one smooth motion, then walked tall and proud on my way by the crowd. Nothing to see here, just another pirate following orders and delivering something to the captain.

I kept the crate angled so no one could see my face, and moved with intent straight for the tall pair of double doors that led down into the quarters below deck. If the layout of our ship was any clue, I knew that was where I'd find the officers' quarters and, more importantly, the captain's.

No one stopped me or even looked my way as I opened one of those large, heavy wooden doors and ducked inside. It shut with a soft thud at my back, and immediately the roar of the commotion outside became much quieter. I set the crate down carefully and ducked to the side, hiding in the shadows right beside the door as I slipped my second dagger from my belt.

Before me, another smaller stairwell led down to the right. Directly ahead, another grand set of doors inlaid with silver designs in the shapes of ocean waves and the arching back of the drakkon made my pulse kick hard against my ribs. That had to be it. Green glass lanterns hung on either side of them, giving off a faint flickering light. But there was no one else in sight. No movement. No sound except for what was happening right outside.

A bolt of panic shot up my spine as the door beside me suddenly swung in.

I froze in place. Oh—oh no. Not now!

One of the pirates from outside, a burly man in a ragged ensemble of old silken robes, rushed by and rapped his knuckles on those gilded doors. "Cap'n! We've got 'em all lined up for ye, as ordered! Neat as a line of caught tuna—an' ye'll never guess who was at the wheel o'that one! A mighty prize indeed. Yer kingship's gonna be right pleased, I guarantee it!"

Silence.

Seconds ticked by with my heart still pounding in my throat, silently praying to every god that might be listening that the thug didn't turn around and spot me there.

At last, a deep, smooth voice called back through the door. "I'll be out in a moment. No one puts a finger on them until I give the order, understood?"

"Aye, Captain. As you say," the thug barked, seemingly almost disappointed at that command.

Then he turned, about to go back to the doors.

Oh Fates. This was it. He would definitely see me now.

I had no choice. I had to strike first—now. Before he spotted me and raised the alarm.

This was my only chance.

My hands slipped down to the blades—Uncle Murdoc's twin daggers—still belted to my hips. My pulse slowed as every one of my senses seemed to sharpen and focus. My mind went silent except for that little whispering voice. Their voices, all fused together as one.

Everyone who had trained me from the time I was old enough to walk.

My eyes narrowed.

Now ... strike!

❧ 3 ❧

CHAPTER THREE

The pirate thug was much bigger. But I had the element of surprise.

And that was all I needed.

I sprang like a striking viper, my blades spinning in a silvery blur over my hands, and hit him. Fast and efficient. No hesitation. No holding back. Two precise slashes to the neck. He staggered. With a ducking sidestep, I whirled around behind him and caught him under the arms as he began to fall. My knees shook under his weight as I slowly eased him to the ground so he didn't make a sound. He lay still, without so much as a cough or wheeze, and didn't move.

Dead.

It was over—but my mind was still ablaze with adrenaline that roared through my veins with all the heat and fury of dragon fire.

Now for the captain.

I touched a hand to the floor, feeling for the impact of footsteps vibrating the old wooden boards just on the other side. As soon as I felt them approach and pause, I braced for it. The gilded knob turned, clicking open, and I sprang again.

I launched into a flying kick with all my force and sent the door slamming inwards—right into the face of whoever was directly on the other side of it.

The captain, I could only assume.

He let out a sharp curse of pain and alarm as the door cracked off his head. I took that opportunity to slip inside and slam it closed again, sealing us both within. In the gloom of the dimly lit chamber, I sprang to my feet and immediately dove at him with a feinting strike—not completely unlike the one I'd just used to dispatch his big henchman outside.

CLANG!

My daggers met with sudden resistance, clashing against the crossguard of a larger weapon—a curved scimitar. Curse it, he was quick.

But I was quicker.

I immediately dropped back, whirling out of the way as a second scimitar slashed in from the side. Ah, so he had a secondary weapon? His off-hand, most likely. His strikes from that side would be weaker and slower. Easier to use against him.

Uncle Murdoc's voice still echoed in my memory. *His weapons are larger, so you've got to stay in close. Make it difficult for him to match your speed. Use the terrain. Don't get sloppy. Look for an opening. Don't stop moving. Keep him on the defensive.*

I bared my teeth and dodged in again, my movements like the flicker of a shadow in the candlelight. Flawless. Exact. As fast as a lightning strike.

I went in low and fast, keeping the fight too close for his comfort, and dipped easily around the howling swings of his scimitars. I had to give him credit—he moved pretty fast, too. But I was smaller. Lighter. Far more flexible. As he lunged in with both weapons to make a series of whirling slashes, I threw myself into a full backbend, flipping and landing in a crouch. Then I instantly kicked forward, launching at him at full speed.

I hit the grimy wooden floor on my knees and slid right between his legs, slashing at both his calves on my way by. The points of my daggers tore through the fabric of his pants and leather of his boots, and sparked and scraped off the metal greaves he was apparently wearing underneath. Curse it! *Hidden* armor?

Okay. Fine. This guy was a bit smarter than I'd anticipated.

I sprang to my feet and spun to face him, dodging sideways as he whipped around and made another swing at my head. Dropping low beneath another one of his strikes, I kicked into an evasive backward roll and stopped in a crouch, daggers still clenched in a reverse grip in each hand as I glared up at him. I'd have to find his weakness. Something I could exploit to get the upper hand.

"Slippery, aren't you?" he growled through his teeth as he turned the rest of the way around to face off with me. And that's when I finally got my first good look at my opponent.

The pirate captain who apparently called himself Fiendheart.

He stood tall and lean, his clothes a mixture of dark silks, braided leather belts, a fine black and red jerkin, and a long frock coat that brushed the heels of his knee-high boots. His light brown hair hung down past his shoulders in ratty, wind-tousled locks, parting only for his pointed ears that were pierced through in different places on either side with rings of gold, studs of silver, or sparkling gems. He was a half-elf? Like me?

Er, well, sort of. I was more like a fourth-elf, I guess.

"What fool would dare go to the Ulfrangar and put a contract on my life?" A crooked, bemused smirk put deep lines in the corners of his dark green eyes as he studied me. It was hard to tell in the weak light, but he looked like he might be about my father's age. Maybe even a little older.

Strange, though. I ... could have sworn I'd seen that smirk somewhere before.

But where?

"I'm not an Ulfrangar," I seethed through my teeth as I slowly stood and spun my daggers over my hands again in a flourish of strength and speed.

His dark eyebrows snapped together, and that roguish grin faded. For an instant, I could have sworn he almost looked confused.

And I took that opportunity to strike again.

Shock and awe, Uncle Reigh's words echoed through my head as I dove in for a straightforward, full-force assault. *You're small and light, so most enemies are going to expect you to avoid immediate confrontation. Being able to get up in their face and demonstrate your strength will throw them off balance. Use that to your advantage.*

Fiendheart gave a surprised bark of a laugh as I bore in hard and interlocked my daggers with his scimitars, swatting them out to the side and going in for a full-force head-butt straight to his chin. My skull met his nose with a satisfying crack, and I jumped up, drawing my legs in close to my chest. I landed with a whirling kick to his chest that sent him staggering back.

He caught himself on the edge of the desk, sending an avalanche of papers and empty wine bottles clattering to the floor.

"A Lunthardan scout, then?" he guessed as he pushed away from the desk and faced me once more, blood now running from his lip and nose. He wiped it onto the sleeve of his coat and looked back at me, smiling broadly now. Almost ... proudly. Like he thought this was fun.

I mean, it sort of *was* fun. But still.

What the heck was wrong with this guy? Was he just toying with me? Letting me hit him like that?

"No," I snapped again.

"And yet you use both styles of combat," he countered. "Interesting ... and something I've only seen a few other times in my life."

"And this time will be the last." I spat on the ground and paced, looking for my next chance to end this before he tried to talk me to death. Uggggh. Why did bad guys always feel the need to monologue? I'd just assumed that was something they exaggerated in the tales of my father and his companions. Nope. Apparently not.

Fiendheart's eyes narrowed, and something menacing sparkled in the depths of that cattish grin. "We'll see, won't we? I've a few tricks of my own, little girl."

I heard it—faintly, but still there. An accent I recognized, too. He sounded almost Lunthardan. Kiran and even Uncle Reigh talked that way sometimes. Strange. How had someone from Luntharda—a half-elf—wound up captaining a notorious pirate ship like this?

The thought was distracting. It made me hesitate.

And that almost cost me everything.

FIENDHEART HIT LIKE A HAMMER, SWINGING DOWN IN A MIGHTY STRIKE THAT I ONLY barely managed to deflect. His scimitar scraped off my daggers, sparking and making my ears ring and my muscles ache from the impact. Gods and Fates, he was strong. The impact made my teeth rattle, but I didn't back off. He'd closed the gap. And a hit like that meant he had committed a lot of momentum to it.

I kept my blades locked with his and whipped around, stepping in and using every bit of leverage I could muster for a disarming maneuver my father had taught me years ago. My form was flawless. My speed was by far my greatest strength. I could do this. Without his weapon, he'd be at my mercy.

CA-THUNK.

Nothing.

I pulled with all my strength, but the blade didn't even budge in his grasp.

N-No. Not possible. That couldn't be. I'd done this move a thousand times on Uncle Murdoc, Thatcher, and even Gran-dah Felix. It should have worked! It always worked!

I yanked again, harder this time, but the blade still wouldn't so much as slide in his grasp. Gods and Fates, it was almost as though that blade was fused to his arm.

I dared to look, allowing myself a single, solitary second of complete shock to stare at the place where his hand gripped the hilt of that scimitar.

Only, there was no hand.

There was only the hilt ... and some sort of odd metallic bracer-vambrace-gauntlet-thing made of shiny golden metal and gears. Somehow, his weapon was affixed into it like an extension of his arm where his hand should have been.

What the—?

"And that would be a dragonrider tactic," Fiendheart chuckled suddenly, seeming to cherish my horror as he used his other hand to hit me across the face with the pommel of his other scimitar.

My head snapped to the side. Everything went starry and I staggered back, barely catching myself against a bookshelf. I'd bitten my tongue so hard the flavor of warm copper filled my mouth.

I looked up, wincing and spitting blood, and glared at him with every shred of nerve I had. He'd gotten lucky with that shot. It wouldn't happen again. Maybe I couldn't disarm him with that sword attached to his arm like that, but I wasn't giving up. I had to take this guy down before his crew came down to investigate. The lives of all my friends depended on it.

"Now I'm certain of it," he said, his deep voice thrumming with that heavy accent as his footfalls approached slowly. "There's only one place in all the world where someone might find all three of those fighting styles merging. You've been sent here by—"

He stopped cold.

By the wavering light of a big iron chandelier right above our heads, I guess Fiendheart finally got his first good look at me. Immediately, his face went pale. His dark green eyes grew wide and his lips parted, recognition etched into every sharply angled feature.

"N ... No," he breathed quietly, his gaze darting down to the pendant that hung around my neck. "It's not ... it's not possible. It can't be."

Then his mouth snapped shut and skewed up bitterly. His long nose wrinkled, nostrils flaring as he suddenly threw down his scimitar—the one that wasn't locked into the metal gauntlet on his forearm. He took another threatening step toward me and leveled the point of that remaining blade right at my chest. "What is your name, girl? Who sent you here? Answer me!"

I glowered back at him, determined not to let him see my confusion. Why did he care who I was? I'd been thoroughly warned never to give away my identity to my enemies if they didn't know who I was already. Surely this man wouldn't know me. We were on a pirate ship in the middle of the ocean. My father had never gone this far from Maldobar. I was certain about that. So, there was no way Fiendheart could know me or my family's name.

But the way he still stared at the pendant hanging around my neck ... and that accent ... and the fact that he'd recognized every single one of my fighting styles.

I couldn't help myself.

I stood straighter, still gripping my daggers firmly as I held his gaze with a defiant frown. "I am Maylea Broadfeather," I growled bitterly. "No one sent me. I came on my own to end you for the sake of my friends onboard that ship you just took captive. Let them go right now, Fiendheart, or rest assured ... I'll spend my very last breath making sure we both go to meet the Fates together."

PART TWO

REIGH

4

CHAPTER FOUR

I was no stranger to impossible odds. Working alongside Jaevid Broadfeather for so many years—it sort of came with the territory. After a while, you get used to constantly staring your own mortality in the face while executing some bizarre, last second, slapped-together plan and praying it worked.

But the monstrosity of a beast swimming around beneath our ships was beyond any horror I'd ever seen before—and that's saying something. It made that underbeast I'd slashed my way out of when we were trapped in the tunnels beneath Northwatch look like a real shrimp.

Unfortunately, at the moment, the massive leviathan wasn't my biggest problem. Or, I guess, if we were only talking about actual size, it still was ...

Eh, anyway, it wasn't the most pressing issue.

Having my hands tied behind my back and a gag over my mouth, while also being led at sword-point onto the main deck of the enemy's ship, however? Yeah. That had just become my primary concern. Needless to say, negotiations with the bloodthirsty pirates were not going well.

Shocking, I know.

I had expected a strategy, an outlandish plot, or *something* from our captain other than a wild-eyed glare and orders for all of us to lay down arms. That command hit me like she'd just smacked me across the face.

What the—? We were just giving up without a fight? After I'd nearly gotten myself blown up and drowned taking down that other enemy ship?

Granted, we would almost certainly lose a battle with that much larger and more heavily armed galleon, even if it weren't being guarded by a massive sea monster. But still—it went against the grain of my many years of dragonrider training to just throw down my weapons and drop to my knees in surrender to a bunch of vagrants and thieves. Surrender wasn't in the dragonrider vocabulary.

The crazed look of wrath still smoldering in Captain Malina's turquoise eyes as she surrendered her weapons made me wonder if she wasn't up to something. Did she have some secret plan she didn't feel like sharing with the rest of us? Or maybe she was just attempting to be noble and do what she could to spare as many of her crew members as possible?

Either way, it wasn't looking good for any of us now.

I set my jaw, biting down hard against the urge to fight back as I dropped my dual kafki blades and slowly raised my hands. The pinprick of tiny claws digging into my shoulder and the side of my neck made me wince as Vexi, still miniaturized from Arlan's spell, flapped over and landed on me like an angry, scaly green parrot. She growled and hissed at the pirates who tied me up. They laughed and jeered, taunting her and trying to swat her away ... right up until a spray of burning dragon venom set one of their hands on fire. The pirate howled in pain and tried wiping it off, which—of course—didn't help at all. Most everyone knew that dragon venom was extremely combustible and ignited whenever it came into contact with air, but unless they had actually dealt with it before, the average person probably wasn't aware that it was also incredibly acidic, sticky, and couldn't be doused with water.

I smirked behind my gag as I watched this particular pirate thug figure that out for himself.

Heh. Idiot. Served him right.

"What's the meaning of this? Can't you numbskulls do even one simple thing right?" A deep, booming voice thundered over the crowd of brigands that were trying to deal with their still-burning friend while also getting the rest of us lined up and chained together like a string of sausages.

Thunk—thunk—thunk.

Heavy footfalls approached, and the crowd parted before us as a towering figure emerged to glare down at us from a full two feet taller than anyone else on the ship. My eyes slowly panned up and my mouth fell open at the sheer size of, um, whatever he was. Enormous, elf-like, mountain of muscle. With skin of deep sun-tanned bronze, a mane of thick, wild, and bushy black hair that hung down his back, the second I saw him my whole body locked up with a flash of fear.

Holy. Gods.

The mammoth of a guy was almost as broad as he was tall—at least in the upper body, anyway. He had bulging arms that looked like he could've popped my head clean off my shoulders with one chokehold. His broad, barrel chest was striped with a mixture of old scars and faded tattoos of strange runic marks. He glared down at us, his light brown eyes as keen as a wolf's and his long, crooked nose wrinkled in a half-snarl.

That's when it hit me—I had seen someone like him before. Well, sort of. I'd met another individual of similar stature and appearance. Jondar Broadfeather, Jaevid's nephew who lived in Dayrise, bore a striking resemblance to this man. Or, at least, similar enough to make me do a double-take. I had never met Jondar's father myself. He had died in battle years ago. But we all knew that he had been a giant of a man. Specifically, a Holvradix elf from the far north.

Seeing this guy gave me a brand-new appreciation for how dangerous Jondar might become if he ever decided to take up a blade. The giant elf's twisted scowl panned over us from a solid seven feet tall, like an angry bear considering a bunch of kittens running around him.

Then his gaze stopped on Malina.

His heavy dark brows rose and his scowl gave way to a look that I could have sworn almost seemed like ... disappointment. Sorrow, even. Like a father who'd just caught his kid in the middle of disobeying. A look that, from my younger and more unruly days, I'd become well acquainted with.

She stared back at him, now gagged and bound like the rest of us, with angry tears rimming her turquoise eyes. If looks could have killed, that fury in her glare would have left that monstrous man nothing but a towering pillar of ash.

A second passed as they stared at one another, and then his brawny shoulders rose and fell with a deep, rumbling. The man shook his head and turned away, shoving the nearest one of the much smaller pirates so hard it sent the guy flying back a good five feet. Yikes.

"Take them to the ship. The captain will want to address this personally." His voice rumbled low and ominous. "Then search the rest of the ship. No one slips through our fingers. Now!"

That last word cracked in the air like a peal of thunder. It sent the rest of the pirates scattering like scared mice. They immediately scurried off to follow his orders and get us moving, chained together single-file, onto the *Squall Queen.*

One of the thugs, a younger guy with a long ponytail, snuck up brandishing a sheet of canvas that had probably been cut from a sail and threw it over Vexi. He cursed as he essentially balled her up inside it like an angry cat. My tiny dragon yowled and fought as sections of the canvas started to smoke and turn black—right up until he swung that makeshift bag and slammed it up against the side of the mast.

VEXI!

I pitched, fighting my bonds as he held up the bag of cloth again, wincing and seeming to wait for further signs of her still struggling inside.

I didn't get a chance to see if she was still moving or not. Our captors shoved me onward, across the narrow plank that led from our ship to the *Squall Queen.* With Thatcher tied up in front of me, and Violet not far behind, I bit down hard against the gag in my mouth as my entire body shook with wrath. They were hurting her. *My* dragon.

And by all the gods, they would pay dearly for it if it was the last thing I ever did.

THE SECOND MY BOOTS HIT THE DECK OF THE *SQUALL QUEEN*, I BEGAN TAKING inventory of anything I could use to make a daring escape. Slipping these bonds would be easy enough. I'd had more than enough training and practice at that. But I didn't have my kafki, and I needed to find out what they'd done with my dragon. Gods, if they'd killed her ... I'd paint this whole ship red with their blood.

There was plenty of taunting and jeering as we were marched to the middle of the main deck and made to get down on our knees. That is—right up until Captain Malina took her place at the front of all of us. Every ragged scoundrel on the ship went quiet as she stood, shoulders back and head still up in proud defiance even with a gag in her mouth. They'd bound her up separately, apparently taking a bit more care in her bonds and fixing her hands at her back with iron shackles. I guess they expected more resistance from her. The enemy crew all gathered around and stared at her, something haunted and slightly terrified in their expressions.

Strange ... but, then again, Violet had said something about the Skyhart family owning this ship before. Was Malina Skyhart a part of that family? That would certainly explain why that massive Holvradix elf seemed to recognize her, and now why every soggy pirate on this ship was gawking at her like they'd seen a ghost.

Now wasn't the time to try putting all those pieces together, though. Right now, I had to work on getting us out of here alive.

Thatcher and I exchanged a look and a slow, meaningful nod from down the line of our captured crew. Years of interrogation training had ultimately prepared us for a situation exactly like this one. We had to coordinate our moves at just the right moment.

Standing nearby, I spotted a pirate with a longsword strung sloppily through a loose leather belt around his hips. I could take it easily enough. Then, I—

BAM!

The door of the captain's quarters at the front of the main deck suddenly flew open wide. I stiffened, bracing myself as my gaze settled on the imposing figure of a man in a dark green frock coat, broad hat with a plume of black feathers at the back, and very freshly broken nose that still dribbled blood down his chin.

My heart stopped with one frantic, hard thump.

Gods and Fates.

No. It ... it wasn't possible. This was a trick of foul magic. It had to be.

Because there was absolutely *no* logical reason whatsoever for him to be standing before us, dressed the part of a scruffy pirate captain right down to that ridiculous hat, and gripping Maylea by the arm as though to keep her from running off.

"JUDAN?!" Thatcher shouted from down the line. I guess he had already worked his gag out of his mouth.

Judan, son of King Jace Rordin of Luntharda, glared across our company with an expression I couldn't quite place. Crazed confusion? Wrathful bewilderment? Eh, it was something in that territory, and it made his eye twitch as he slowly shook his head and sucked his front teeth—like he was actively fighting the urge to start shouting and throwing things.

Then his gaze landed on Malina. Judan and Malina stared one another down for what felt like a frosty eternity without so much as blinking. Judging by the angry little vein standing out against his forehead, he must have known her, as well.

Oooh boy. I could smell the drama from ten miles away.

Malina's furious, teary-eyed glare followed Judan as he stepped around her and dragged Maylea over to where I was still on my knees with the rest of the crew. He stopped before me and let out a long, deep, growling sigh.

"Blowing up one of my ships, sending Jaevid's daughter to try and assassinate me, and partnering with that Skyhart woman," he muttered bitterly, biting each word through his teeth like a curse. "I might have known this was your handiwork, Reigh Farrow."

"Uh, well, actually ... she was sort of a stowaway," Thatcher answered for me, since I still had a gag in my mouth.

"Is that so?" Judan's evergreen gaze never left mine as his brows rose, taking in that new information. "And yet she seems to be the only one among you with any tactical sense. If I were anyone else, she'd probably have my head on a pike by now."

Still forced to stand at his side, Maylea's cheeks flushed and she avoided looking my way. Great. Well, so much for trying to put her somewhere safe so she wouldn't get caught up in this mess. That girl didn't listen to a word anyone else said.

I would definitely have to deal with that sneaky, conniving little *problem* later.

Providing we all survived the next few minutes, anyway.

"What should we do with them, Captain?" the towering elf asked as he made his way to the front of the crowd of pirates still thronging around us.

Judan pursed his lips thoughtfully, looking over our company before he finally gave another, much more resigned sigh. He stood straighter and raised his left arm to gesture to all of us with the shining golden gauntlet that replaced his missing hand.

An old injury I was all too familiar with.

"Cut them loose and send the crew back to begin repairs on that ship. Adavar, I want you overseeing their progress. No one sets a toe out of line or else they can take a swim with the drakkon," he ordered. Then his gaze settled back on Malina with a steely, distrustful squint. "Except for *her*. She goes to the brig. I want three guards posted at all times, and make sure you search her thoroughly."

"Aye, Captain." The massive elf, Adavar, gave a nod and turned to begin barking orders to the sailors gathered around.

"As for you lot," Judan added as he beckoned to Maylea, Thatcher, Violet, and me. "Regather your wares and come with me. I want an explanation—and it better be a *good* one. You've cost me a ship and many good men today. That rickety little bucket you've been floating around in won't come close to matching the speed of my interceptor. So, for your sake, I hope you have quite the story to tell."

Thatcher's head hung some and he cast me another meaningful sideways glance. "Oh, trust me," he muttered somberly, "we do."

❧ 5 ❧

CHAPTER FIVE

It took me a few minutes to find the pirate who had tied my tiny dragon up in a makeshift bag and smacked her up against a mast. But when I spotted him standing amidst the crowd, still holding that sack, I didn't waste a single second.

Now free of my bonds, I stormed straight for him and gave a shout to get his attention. "HEY! You! Yeah, you!"

He turned to face me, seeming utterly bewildered as to why I was calling him out—right up until the moment I reared back and punched him across the face with all my strength. Maximum fury straight to his nose.

He dropped like a newborn calf and hit the deck with a *thud* and didn't move.

Unconscious in one hit. Hmm. That might've been a first for me. A personal best. And, man, did it feel good.

I grabbed the sack out of his limp hand and opened it, reaching in to collect the tiny scaled creature from inside. Vexi blinked up at me, her hide shivering some and one of her legs tucked up close to her body as though it were injured. Great. How was I going to find anyone that could help her? I ... I was a healer, yes. But I didn't know much about giving medical care to dragons. Especially not miniaturized ones.

"Easy, girl. I've got you. You're okay," I cooed as I carefully placed her back up on my shoulder. She had to hang on with the clawed tips of her wing arms to stay balanced, but she still managed to tuck herself up against the side of my neck. Her small body vibrated with a growl as we walked past the crew to rejoin the others that now stood waiting with Judan.

"You didn't kill him, did you?" Violet asked with a bemused snort.

I glanced back over my shoulder to where some of the other pirate crew members were dragging their unconscious friend away by the ankles. "I don't know. I didn't check for a pulse."

A coy smirk curled over her lips as she arched an eyebrow. "Tsk tsk. You naughty healer, you."

Something about her playful tone made me smile in spite of myself. Too bad it didn't last long. As we fell in step behind Judan, making our way toward the captain's chambers below the quarterdeck, a ruckus made everyone stop and watch as the sailors charged with moving Malina down to the brig struggled to hold her at bay. She twisted and fought with every step, managing to work the gag out of her mouth and down to her chin in the process. She screamed and cursed at them with her voice broken and face flushed deep red, as though she were fighting back sobs.

She froze when she noticed Judan and the rest of us watching her. Malina's chin trembled as a look of pure, unbridled hatred smoldered in her eyes like heat rising from an active volcano. Like she wanted nothing more than to drive a blade into his heart and twist it—just for good measure. Interesting.

It seemed like Judan had a story of his own he needed to share.

He stared back at her just like he had before, nothing but a glint of cold indifference in his eyes, as though she was nothing but useless trash to him.

Hmmm. That couldn't be a good sign.

I'd never known Judan to be cruel or ruthless. He could be a little impulsive, sure, but he usually kept a level head about things and tried to go about his dealings fairly. King Jace had taught him to be an effective fighter, and Judan had been the primary driving force behind forming Luntharda's own network of spy agents that now spanned several kingdoms. No small feat, especially for a prince who constantly had to hide his royal reputation from potential adversaries.

But captaining a stolen pirate ship and calling himself Fiendheart? Well, that's not something I ever would have expected from him. And I had absolutely no doubt that his parents, the King and Queen of Luntharda, had no clue what he'd been up to, either.

As far as any of us had known, Judan had been missing for a while—or, as we assumed, deep undercover running his spy network. Or in some foreign land establishing more branches of it. Bartering secrets. Monitoring the Ulfrangar's movements under the new Zuer. Basically anything but, well, whatever this mess was. Running away to play pirate?

I would have to make sure I wasn't standing anywhere close by when Jace and Araxie found out.

"Make sure she is well secured. She has a history of being rather ... slippery," Judan mumbled as he gave his men a parting nod and turned away, seeming to dismiss the entire situation in the blink of an eye.

No one dared to say a word as we followed him below to the privacy of his captain's quarters. There, behind closed doors, we watched in awkward silence as he lurched around the grand cabin space. The captain's cabin of the *Squall Queen* was far larger and more luxurious than what we had seen on the *Fog Dancer*. The ceiling was higher, adorned in engraved wooden paneling, and the tall colored glass windows depicted scenes of a drakkon's massive form arcing through spiraling waves. Silver chandeliers swayed on chains overhead, and a series of glass-fronted cabinets and tall bookshelves on either side of the room held countless artifacts, tomes, and ornate glass wine bottles.

Judan made his way to the back of the room, stopping only to pick up some papers and empty bottles that had fallen into a heap on the floor. He muttered under his breath as he shuffled around behind a large, claw-footed desk that spanned nearly the entire width of the room. Beyond it, a long dining table was already set with fine china and silver candelabras, and another set of doors that must have led into the bedchamber.

"I see you've made some interesting allies," Judan observed coolly as he settled into the plush, high-backed velvet chair behind the desk. His gaze flicked toward Violet but didn't linger. He went digging through his pockets until he found a handkerchief, then started gingerly wiping at his extremely broken nose.

"So have you," I countered as I stepped forward to sit down in the chair on the opposite side of his sprawling desk. "You want to tell me what's going on, Judan? What are you even doing out here? And why are you calling yourself Fiendheart?"

"I could ask you the same—and I intend to." He shrugged and grinned, still carefully wiping at the blood on his chin and nose. Maybe he thought I wouldn't be able to tell he was in pain. He definitely needed to get that looked at.

Judan avoided my gaze as he shoved his handkerchief back into his pocket and opened one of the desk drawers, taking out a long smoking pipe and a tiny platinum box filled with fragrant dried leaves. "As for the name, I thought it sounded ominous, and pirates are a superstitious lot. You give yourself a scary name or title, and suddenly you become notorious."

"It's that easy, huh?" I wasn't buying an inch of that excuse.

He must've been able to tell, because that wolfish grin of his widened.

"You know Phoebe is worried sick about you," Thatcher muttered angrily as he crossed his arms. "She wanted to check on your gauntlet and make sure it was still working properly. You know if anything happened to you, she would blame herself for not making something good enough."

Judan's smirk faded and he paused where he'd been stuffing some of those dried leaves into the pipe. "Whatever happens to me will be my own doing. She has no reason to blame herself for anything,"

"I agree. But what are you doing out here, Judan?" I pressed. No point in skirting around the obvious. "I know losing your hand was difficult, but this—"

"It has *nothing* to do with my hand," he cut me off sharply. A little too sharply, actually. Enough to make me pretty certain that was exactly what all this was about. "I think the more important question is what are you doing out here, so far from Maldobar, and with a crew of cutthroats and thieves? Likely not running another suicide mission for Jaevid. Not with *her* tagging along." He tipped his chin toward Maylea.

She shifted and stared down at the toes of her boots again, but didn't say a word. Smart choice.

"I doubt the esteemed Commander Jaevid Broadfeather would send his young daughter across the sea, even if she does fight better than most accomplished Lunthardan scouts more than twice her age. Almost got the best of me. If I had been any other captain, she would have walked out of here victorious. But it seems we've had a similar upbringing when it comes to our unique combat training." Judan chuckled and leaned forward in his seat, his deep green eyes sparkling with interest. "So, what are you doing out here, Reigh?"

What were we doing out here? There was no good way to answer that question. Not without giving absolutely everything away at once. And quite frankly, I wasn't so sure I should be revealing all my cards to him now. Not after he'd, you know, basically tried to kill us.

But what choice did I have?

I hesitated, my heartbeat skipping as that question settled over me like a lead collar. It made every part of my soul go numb, like I was slowly turning to stone from the inside out. Going cold, becoming stone, was the only way I'd been able to withstand these kinds of adventures in the past.

Once, I had relied on Judan as an ally. I'd trusted him completely. He'd been there for us when we dealt with Iksoli—a fight that had nearly killed several of us, Judan included.

Right then, with him smirking at me as he lit his pipe and blew some smoke rings over the desk while we all sat onboard his *pirate* ship ... I wasn't even sure I knew him at all anymore. I couldn't tell if he was still someone I should be trusting or not.

And right then, I knew I didn't have a choice. Judan had our ship, our crew, and our captain. We had a short deadline and a fleeting opportunity to head off a divine war that might destroy the entire world. There wasn't time to play mind games. Either Judan was going to be someone we could count on for help ... or not.

"It's bad, Judan. Worse than before," I said, my thoughts still a frantic, racing blur as I tried to figure out what to say. Not easy to do on the spot. "Jaevid didn't send us here. Arlan the Kinslayer did."

JUDAN WASN'T SMILING ANYMORE.

He sat back in his tall velvet chair, drawing in deep puffs from his pipe as his brow furrowed and his keen gaze darted around at all of us again, then finally paused squarely on Violet.

For the briefest instant, I saw it. That familiar light shone in his eyes like a spark of vigorous energy revealed by the glow of the ashes in his long wooden pipe. He'd been a real force in Maldobar and Luntharda. As sharp and cunning as a fox. Always thinking two, maybe three steps ahead.

Too good to be playing whatever this game was, now.

"Remember that little deal we made with him in order to get information on Phillip's whereabouts? Well, Arlan called that in. And this mess he's asking us to clean up is, well, it's bad. World-ending bad. Worse than anything we've seen before. Arlan is rattled. He's pulling out all the stops. Calling in all the debts," I explained, trying to keep my tone quiet and calm. Anything too loud might draw the attention of his crew outside, and this wasn't information that needed to leave this room. "Rather than letting Jaevid leave his very pregnant wife and young children behind to deal with this, I insisted on taking this on without him. He didn't like it, of course. You know how he can be. Always likes to be on the side of justice, blade in hand, whenever destiny comes knocking. But that entire mission with Iksoli and Devana was my responsibility from the start. Contacting Arlan and making that deal was ultimately my call, so this is my bill to pay."

"Fine words," he mused, holding the thin mouth of the pipe between his teeth as he studied me from under the brim of that wide, feathered hat. "But you've left out the most important details. What is it Kinslayer has tasked you with, exactly? This world-ending problem, as you call it."

"It's his sister. The one who calls herself Sadeera," Violet replied quickly, her expression earnest. "She's back, and the strings she's pulling this time are far more dangerous than before, Your Highness. She has made her way into Nar'Haleen's royal court, and has already orchestrated the destruction of the Compendium Library."

Judan's eyebrows rose some. "I did hear something about that. Word came along that the library had been burned and sacked. Supposedly there were no survivors."

My stomach turned, clenching so hard it felt like a ball of iron in my gut. No survivors? That couldn't be true. I wouldn't believe that. Not until I saw the ashes and bones myself.

I wouldn't accept that Ronan was ... gone.

"As I understand it, the library was supposed to be a neutral place. An ancient archive that has always stayed out of the long-standing conflicts of the southern kingdoms. Why would anyone want to destroy it?" Judan asked as he glanced between us again.

"Because of something that had been hidden there," Thatcher answered, looking somberly my way as he hesitated to go on. I guess he didn't know how much he should tell Judan, either. This must have been his way of asking if he should mention Ronan, at all. "Sadeera is trying to track down a sacred artifact—a codex—to crack the kingdom of the gods open. She wants a war, but not with Maldobar, Rienka, or Damaria. She wants a war with the gods."

Judan stopped puffing on his pipe. His jaw went a little slack as his brow slowly creased with a frown. "Did she ... obtain this codex?"

"We don't know." My voice wouldn't come out as much more than a hoarse, forced whisper. "That's why we have to get to Nar'Haleen as soon as possible—why Arlan put us on that ship with Malina. We can't waste any more time. We need our ship. We need our captain back. And we need to get to the Compendium and figure out just how bad this really is."

He didn't reply. Seconds passed, and I finally managed to stand up straighter to level a no-nonsense glare on him. Maybe he wouldn't be able to read the agony I was swallowing down like poison—the constant pain of not knowing where my nephew was or if he was even still alive.

But the longer we sat there, the more I saw Judan's expression smolder and cool to someone I didn't recognize. That tiny glimpse of familiar light I'd seen before was completely gone from his eyes when he spoke again. Whoever this was, I didn't know him.

It made dread spread over my body like a cold rain.

"I'm afraid I can't do that, Reigh. As much as I might like to, you sank my interceptor. I need a ship to replace it," he said, smug confidence dripping from every word. "You also brought me the one person in the world I'd hoped I would never see again, so now I have to deal with her, as well. It's an unpleasant business, pirating. But it's profitable. And here, on this ship, *I* am king."

"What are you saying?" I growled through my teeth. "You're going to kill us?"

"Oh, gods, no. Nothing like that. Don't be so dramatic," he scoffed and waved a hand at me like *I* was the one being borderline insane about this. "Put yourself in my shoes for a moment. I've heard these grandiose speeches, warnings of doom, and promise of heroic destiny many times before. All my life, in fact. And I played that game. I followed all the rules, like a good little soldier. And what did it get me, hm? What was my hero's reward?"

Judan held up his left forearm, the weak light gleaming off the tarnished golden surface of the gauntlet he wore. Phoebe had made several fixtures that could be interchanged, and the one he wore now was crafted in the shape of a metallic hand that fit into a complex bracer all the way up his forearm. "My reward was having my hand cut off thanks to a switchbeast's bite while I tried to save the life of the man who stole the only woman I'd ever loved from me. My reward was having my father dismiss me from the spy agency I helped build for over a decade. My entire life's work—gone with a single word."

What? Jace had dismissed him from his spy network? When? And why? No one had said anything about that to me. Surely Jenna would have mentioned it if she knew, right? We'd all been wondering what happened to Judan and why he hadn't been around at least to touch base with Phoebe to do repairs or modifications to his gauntlet.

Judan's deep green-toned eyes narrowed slightly, as though he could read my confusion. Maybe he'd assumed we all knew that already. "Given all that, I hope you'll forgive me if I am less than sympathetic to your current crisis. I won't be playing that game again. If you had any sense, you wouldn't either. What has playing hero gotten you, Reigh? Where is your wife? Your children? Your happily-ever-after? Do you really think the ending will be so different this time? You think destiny will finally give you the reward you've been seeking all your life?" He slowly shook his head, clicking his tongue sympathetically as he took another long pull on that pipe. "Take your chances again, if you wish. I certainly won't try to stop you. But don't expect me to leap at the chance to join you on another fool's errand. I'll take you all as far as Rienka, for old time's sake. But not an inch farther. What you do from there is none of my concern."

"You're making a mistake." My voice rumbled with a deep growl as I fought to keep my temper in check. "You think I haven't paid with flesh and blood in every cause we've fought for? You think I don't know what it feels like to lose someone I care about? I've walked in the Vale and stood alongside the Fates. I've seen what lies beyond the divine gate through the eyes of death itself. You have *no idea* what will happen if we don't get that codex before Sadeera does."

"You're right. I don't know," he quipped and sank back further into his seat, crossing his arms over his chest. "And this time, I don't care to."

6

CHAPTER SIX

I was ... speechless. Gods and Fates, there were no words. I must have stood there for three whole minutes just gaping at Judan, half-expecting him to suddenly burst out laughing because he was just joking.

But this wasn't a joke.

And no one was laughing.

I only had a few cards left to play now. I didn't want to use either of them. Not like I had a choice now, though.

With a nod to Thatcher and Violet, I led the way to the door and let them leave ahead of me. Then I stopped and leveled one last meaningful glare at that imposter wearing Judan's face. I had to believe that somewhere beneath that ridiculous hat and wolfish grin, the man I knew was still in there.

"She has Ronan, by the way," I murmured and looked away. "He was staying in the Compendium Library, receiving instruction and treatment for his condition, when Sadeera sent forces to attack it. Now, we can only guess what she'll do to him, if he's even still alive."

Judan didn't make a sound.

"Enjoy your new life, Judan. I hope it's one you can still be proud of when the world is burning down around you." I let the door slam behind me on my way out, leaving him to sit alone in that gaudy room. The little kingdom he'd chosen over everything else.

He could rot in it for all I cared.

My heart pounded so hard it made my vision swerve as the anger took me like a roaring inferno. Curse him and that stupid feathered hat straight to the deepest pit in the abyss. He'd *take* us to Rienka? Like that was any kind of favor? Rienka was hundreds of miles away from where we needed to go—nearly on the opposite end of the continent. He might as well have left us in the middle of the ocean on a rowboat for how helpful that was.

The sounds of shouts and commotion jarred me from my internal fit of wrath. I looked up just in time to see Thatcher come bursting in through the exterior doors, his expression pale and panicked.

"Reigh! Y-You need to come see this!" he gasped.

I hurried him back out onto the main deck, stepping into absolute chaos as about a dozen members of Judan's crew scrambled around a net with something fighting and pitching around inside it. It took four grown men all struggling at once to hold the creature down inside that net, while the others crowded around with swords already in hand.

At first, I only caught glimpses of the greenish, human-sized thing as it writhed against the net, trying to tear itself free. What the heck was going on?

"Filthy little rat! We found him hiding away in the belly of that ship!" One of the pirates standing nearby chuckled. "What a price he'll fetch in Kua'Tar!"

Wait—*he?* That was a person?

I started to move, to step in and put an end to this. No way would this sloppy, salt-reeking lot be selling anyone on my watch. Before I could even take a step, a small figure darted past, out ahead of me, with a shrill scream of panic.

"LUKANI!" Maylea cried out as she seized the arm of one of the pirates and tried to pull him away from the net. "Stop it! Let him go!"

What? Lukani was here, too?!

The thug immediately flung her off, sending her stumbling backward. She practically bounced off my chest as I walked up behind her, and I held her shoulders to keep her from falling.

Maylea blinked up at me, her light green eyes rimmed with tears and a smudge of dried blood around her mouth. Sweet Fates. What a mess.

Honestly, how did Jaevid even keep track of this girl at all?

"You have to help him," she begged. "They'll hurt him and he's already—"

"Go with Thatcher back to our ship," I ordered, keeping my tone as firm and calm as I could manage. I had to hold it together, even if it felt like I wanted to run a blade through the next pirate or thug who dared to look at me wrong.

"B-But—" Maylea started to protest.

"I'll take care of it. Go. *Now.*" I let my tone carry a hint of wrath with that last word. Enough to let her know I was very quickly approaching the end of my sanity today.

I guess she got the message.

Maylea scampered away to stand at Thatcher's side, holding onto his arm and staring at the spot where Lukani was still fighting around inside that net.

One problem at a time.

"HEY! BACK OFF!" I shouted over the noise of the crew still wrestling and taunting their captured prey. "He's with us!"

"You?" One of them balked and wrinkled his nose. "You're traveling with this little piece of Rajinna scum? Hah! We don't—AUGH!!"

The guy let out a squeal like a caught piglet as he was suddenly lifted off the ground, held by the back of the neck by a huge, powerful hand. I watched, mouth hanging open, as the towering Holvradix elf held his mouthy comrade off the ground. His face twitched with anger as he leaned in and growled right in the man's face. "They said the boy belongs with them. Let him go, or I'll let you go for a swim with the drakkon."

A hush fell over the deck as the man kicked and fought, trying to escape Adavar's grasp. It didn't work. He finally managed a breathless, garbled sound of agreement.

Adavar immediately dropped him into a heap on the ground and panned his glare across the rest of the pirates on the deck. "Cut the boy loose. Now. Captain said we can't lay a hand on these folk. If the boy is one of them, then that applies to him, too."

For a few seconds, no one moved. Even Lukani lay still, and I could barely make out his face through that net, staring up at Adavar with wide, terrified eyes. Maylea was right. It really was him. I hadn't seen that shapeshifting little trickster in years. At least, not that I'd been aware of. Maybe he'd snuck by me and I'd never realized it was him. That was completely plausible for someone with his particular skill set. Still, if he was here on this ship ... and only Maylea knew about it ... that explained a *lot* about how she'd managed to sneak onboard in the first place.

Yeah. She had quite a bit of explaining to do.

First things first, though.

I approached the net, realizing only once I'd stooped down to start pulling the net off Lukani, that Violet was right on my heels. She muttered and cursed under her breath as she helped me untangle him, her brow locked into a ferocious scowl. Once we had the net off, Violet looped her arms under his shoulders and helped Lukani get back on his feet.

He immediately swooned and almost collapsed, sinking into her and almost knocking her over, too.

"Easy, easy," I coaxed as I looped one of his arms over my shoulder and took his weight instead. "You're all right."

"Gods, curse it. He's used too much power," Violet seethed quietly, her scarlet eyes flashing with a mixture of worry and frustration. "He needs to rest."

"I take it Arlan didn't intend for him to come tagging along on this little adventure?" I asked, already confident I knew the answer.

"Of course not! Lukani might be powerful, but he's still just a child. Arlan would never risk putting him in this kind of danger," she snapped.

"Let's get him to the ship. Watch my back. I don't trust these guys not to try to pull something nasty when Judan isn't looking," I muttered as I started helping Lukani hobble away.

"What about Malina? She's still in the brig," Violet whispered.

Right. I hadn't forgotten about our captain. Currently, however, I had a pair of kids to look after, and that took priority. "We'll have to handle that later."

"You think Judan will kill her?" Violet whispered again, almost as though she were fretting out loud to herself. "I don't understand it—how did he come to be captain of the *Squall Queen* instead of her? Did he take the ship from her somehow? Or was it a mutiny of the whole crew?"

I didn't know. Clearly something had gone horribly wrong. But before we could even begin trying to unravel that mess, we had to make sure our own lives were secured. And I still had to deal with Maylea even being here at all.

Maybe it was a good thing I'd never had any kids of my own. I couldn't even manage Jaevid's.

Although, in my defense, neither could he. Otherwise, she wouldn't be sitting in the belly of our ship right now, waiting for me to give her the lecture of a lifetime about why sneaking aboard pirate ships headed for the most dangerous place on the planet was a *bad* idea.

Fates preserve me.

WE MADE OUR WAY BACK ABOARD THE *FOG DANCER*, DUCKING CREW WHO WERE rushing around, working desperately to make repairs even long after sunset. In the cramped navigation room where Violet, Thatcher, and I had been staying for the duration of our trip, I helped Lukani lie down on one of the bed rolls spread across the floor. Violet lit a few small lanterns that hung on hooks overhead, then came swiftly over to help me get Lukani settled.

There wasn't much I could do for him, honestly. Physically, he only had a few small cuts and bruises, and while his responses were sluggish and slurred, he was still in his right mind. He knew all of us, could tell us his name, and had feeling in his extremities. All good signs. But his skin seemed more ashen than usual, and his breathing was shallow and rapid. He shivered as a cold sweat beaded on his skin, and immediately curled up on his side when we spread a blanket over him.

"I-Is he going to be okay?" Maylea's voice shook as she petted Lukani's hand.

"He'll be fine," Violet assured, keeping her tone soothing and soft. "He has used far too much power, though. Arlan has always been careful with him when it comes to his magic, not allowing him to push himself too far too soon. I know he doesn't look it, but Lukani is very young for a Rajinna. And at this stage, his power can be unpredictable. He can hurt himself just as easily as someone else. And as you've seen, he has a very gentle heart. He cares immensely for others. Fighting, violence, and even defending himself goes against his nature."

"That's how I met him. He was ... looking out for me in the castle. Watching over me when I left my room. He helped me every step of the way, and never asked for anything in return. I lost him in the fight right before we sank that ship. I thought he was following me, but I turned around and he was gone. I-I was so afraid he was dead. And it would be all my fault." Maylea whispered, wiping her cheeks on her forearm. She winced as she tried wiping her mouth, too.

Hmmm. From where I was standing, I couldn't see any evidence that she was still bleeding. But I also couldn't tell if someone had knocked her teeth out.

"Come here," I said, trying my best to keep my temper from sharpening my tone. According to Thatcher, I had a bad habit of venting on anyone standing too close when I was angry. Patience. Calm. I needed both of those.

She eyed me warily, like a fawn that might dash away into the trees at any sudden wrong move.

I sighed and waved a hand, beckoning her to get up and follow. "Maybe you're not aware, but you've got blood all over your face. I need to see how bad it is. And we need to talk."

Maylea Broadfeather seemed to shrink a good five inches on her way across the room to stand before me. With her big aquamarine-colored eyes already brimming with tears and her shoulders shaking, it took everything I had not to just throw my hands up and surrender any effort I'd been saving for scolding speeches. After all, I'd watched this girl grow up from a drooling baby. I had helped teach her to fight, to protect herself with the same Lunthardan scout techniques Kiran had taught me.

Yeah, she had screwed up big time. She had stepped off the edge into the ruthless furnace of the world after we had all told her for years she would get burned. But what was done was done. She was here, even if she was just a kid.

And once upon a time, I had done the exact same thing when I wasn't much older than she was. I had run away from home—from Kiran—the only adult who had loved and raised me like a son my whole life. Back then, I had thought that I needed more. I'd been an impulsive, selfish, short-sighted brat with a few sword skills and far too much confidence. And it was only because of Jaevid and Kiran that I'd survived, not just that once, but several times over.

Now, it was hard not to see myself when Maylea came to stand in front of me, cringing up like she was waiting for me to start yelling.

"Follow me. I need to take a look at what happened to your face," I said, gesturing for her to walk ahead of me to the other side of the room where I had tossed down my bedroll and bags of medical supplies.

She went without a word, dragging her feet past Thatcher, who stared at us with a look of obvious worry creasing his brow like I was marching her off to be beheaded or something. I gave him a small, reassuring nod, just to let him know I had this. I was angry, yeah. But I wasn't unreasonable. Certainly not on the verge of beheading anyone.

Yet.

Dropping my belt and kafki blades next to the bedroll I'd been using for the last several days, I sat down onto my rear end with a grunt. So many nights on the floor of a creaking, swaying ship wasn't exactly the formula for a good night's sleep. Follow that up with fighting, swimming, and dealing with pirates and unruly teenagers? Yeah. I was really looking forward to sleeping in an actual bed again. I'd even take a cot at a dragonrider tower at this point. It wasn't like my back was getting any better with age.

"Have a seat," I sighed and reached for my bag to start digging out the new medical kit Violet had given me. Time to break it in. "Are you hurt anywhere else other than your mouth?"

Maylea sank down and sat in front of me cross-legged with her arms folded in her lap. "No," she answered so quietly I barely heard her. "I just bit my tongue. It's fine."

I arched an eyebrow. "Really?" She'd dueled with Judan and walked away with just a pop to the mouth? Impressive. "I'll be the judge of that."

She winced as she tried to mash her mouth closed, eyes still welling with fresh tears. She looked up, down, and pretty much everywhere else except for back at me. "I was really careful, Uncle Reigh."

"Not careful enough," I muttered as I leaned in closer and grasped her chin and tilted her head back to get a closer look. "Open up. Let's see how bad it is."

Thankfully, it wasn't. She'd taken a solid hit to the face and bitten her tongue, but no teeth were loose or missing. Her jaw would be sore, but it wasn't fractured or broken. I couldn't hide my relief as I sank back with a sigh.

Maybe Jaevid would only maim me, instead of killing me outright.

Ehhh, probably not.

"I'll mix up some tea that'll help with the pain and keep it from getting infected. You'll have to drink it tonight and tomorrow. After that, you should be fine." Closing up my medical kit, I hesitated for a few seconds as I tried to collect my thoughts for what I had to do next.

Parenting.

Ugggh.

"Uncle Reigh?"

I turned back to find her finally staring at me, her whole face twitching like she was barely holding it together. Gods. What was I supposed to do? I didn't know how to handle this. She was just a kid.

And I was just the idiot trying to keep her alive.

"I-I didn't mean for ... I sh-should have ..." she started to cry and buried her face in her hands. "I'm so sorry. I know I messed up. I-I just wanted to help. I just wanted to ... prove that I can handle myself. That I can be like him."

"Like your dad?" I guessed.

She bobbed her head.

"Well, listen, unfortunately no one can be like him. Take that from someone else who's already tried and failed many times over." I rubbed at the rough, short stubble on my chin as I tried to piece together the right words—what she needed to hear right now. What I needed to hear when I'd done the same thing, all those years ago. "Yeah, you messed up, kid. There's no question about it. No sugaring it up. You snuck away from Halfax. You followed us to Southwatch and somehow managed to stow away on this ship. You engaged in combat on your own. And all without saying a single word to your parents about where you were going. They'll probably blame me for all of this, so thank you for that. But most importantly, they're probably going out of their minds trying to find you right now. You do realize that, don't you? They probably think you've been abducted or killed. Your dad will tear the kingdom apart to find you, and I have no way of contacting him to let him know where you are."

Maylea sniffled some, wiping at her eyes as she went back to avoiding my glare of disapproval. "I-I know ..."

"Do you? *Really?* Cause I seem to remember pretty vividly how all of us have warned you about how dangerous the world can be, and how important it is for you to wait until you're ready to choose your path out into it," I said, still managing to keep my tone controlled and firm. Trying to channel my inner Kiran wasn't as easy as I'd hoped, though.

"And what if I am ready?" she countered, and I saw a hint of that familiar Broadfeather stubbornness in her eyes as she flashed me a quick, challenging glance.

"You better be," I countered quickly. "Because ready or not, you're in this now. I can't send you back to Maldobar. Not by yourself. And should, by some miracle, we all get out of this alive and make it back home—you better be thinking of the world's greatest apology to give to your parents. Better be a long one, too, because that's when I intend to make a run for it and I need as much of a head start as I can get."

She snorted and quirked her mouth to one side, going back to avoiding my eyes as she fidgeted with the hem of her tunic. "All I wanted was to help Dah. At least, that was the reason in the beginning. I saw you all talking to that man, Arlan, at the castle. Dah was so upset. So worried. He wanted to go and fight, but he wouldn't because of mother and the little ones. Then I heard you talking about Ronan, too. I've wanted to find him for so long. You keep saying he's in trouble, that this Sadeera person is going to do something terrible to him—and I want to stop her. I need to. He's my very best friend, Uncle Reigh. I can't just turn my back on him now. Not if there's a chance that I can help bring him home safe. I know everyone thinks I'm too young, or that I'm just being reckless and naïve. But I know I can do this. I can't explain it. It's like there's this ... string tied around my heart. It pulls me. It's what pulled me here."

"I don't know if anyone can help Ronan now, Maylea." I hung my head some and turned away to start prepping a small metal tea steeper. Anything to keep my hands busy. "But I intend to try. There's a lot going on with him no one outside our family even knows about—secrets Queen Jenna doesn't want shared with anyone." I paused, my hands shaking some as I tried to pack dried medicinal leaves into the steeper.

I set my jaw and shut my eyes for a moment, trying to calm my nerves. Maylea wasn't the only one worried about that boy. My nephew was in more danger than anyone else understood right now. Well, except for Arlan. If Ronan was still alive, then it was a safe bet that he was in the fight of his life. Not against Sadeera, though. Against himself ... and the curse he'd been born with.

The one that would eventually consume him, body and soul.

"Get Thatcher to bring you some hot water and drink this," I commanded as I handed her the tea-steeper. "Then get some rest."

Maylea stood, taking the steeper, and still poking gingerly at her jaw and cheek as she started away. She stopped after only a few steps and glanced back, her expression now riddled with worry. "What about our captain? Her name is Malina, isn't it? Are we just going to leave her behind when we get to Rienka?"

I leaned forward to rest my elbows on my knees, my gaze instinctively drawn across the small room to where Violet was still tending to Lukani. She wasn't looking at either of us, or even saying anything, but I could tell she'd been listening the whole time. Something about that little crease right between her eyebrows when she frowned gave it away.

"No," I answered at last. "I don't intend to leave her behind."

"Then we're breaking her out?" Maylea did a horrible job of hiding her excitement at that idea.

I flicked her a solemn, weary-eyed glare of warning. "*We* aren't doing anything. *I* will take care of it tomorrow. Right now, everyone in this room needs to sleep. Sleep—and say a good, long, heartfelt prayer that Judan doesn't lose the rest of his mind before dawn and decide to toss us all overboard."

⁂ 7 ⁂

CHAPTER SEVEN

A few hours after sunset, things finally began to get quiet and still on both ships. All crew members, both from our vessel and from the *Squall Queen*, had retired for the night. Only the occasional individual who'd been charged with night watch duty strolled by as I made my way out of the cramped navigation room up to the poop deck at the back of the ship. A little air, a little time to think—that was all I needed. Tomorrow, I would have to start solving some of the new problems that were currently making my head pound like someone was beating on it with a blacksmithing hammer.

Like what to do with Jaevid's daughter. And Malina. And Judan.

Gods help me.

Leaning against the railing and watching the waves slowly ripple by, sparkling under the light of a silver crescent moon, I let out a heavy sigh. And like always, my thoughts ran away and scattered to the soft, salty winds that blew through my hair. Back to a little farmhouse near Dayrise where Kiran had begun living with Ms. Lin Broadfeather and all her children. Back to a little healer's shop in Luntharda that was probably being run by one of Kiran's apprentices now. Back to the academy where Murdoc probably hadn't slept a single night through since we left. Back to Halfax where my siblings, Jenna and Aubren, were likely wondering where I had disappeared to this time.

Back to the Broadfeathers' home in Solhelm ... where Jaevid was undoubtedly ripping fistfuls of his hair out wondering where his little girl was.

"There you are," a soft, feminine voice laughed from behind me. "Thinking of taking another dive overboard?"

Hah. Tempting.

I turned to find Violet striding toward me with one hand on her hip and that knowing grin curled over her red-painted lips. And for the briefest, tiniest instant, I caught myself thinking she looked ... beautiful, especially with her long, nearly-white hair shining under the sterling moonlight.

I froze and blinked hard, shaking my head to try and clear those thoughts right away.

No. Nope. Definitely not going there. I was just tired. Yeah, that had to be it. Because she was bad news in high-heeled boots, and I was *never* going down that road again.

"With a drakkon swimming around somewhere down there?" I snorted and shook my head.

She stopped beside me, staring out across the horizon and giving a little sigh of her own. "Well, that certainly made for an interesting day. Garnett was right—never a dull moment with you lot." Her eyes flickered over me, catching the moonlight like two brilliant rubies as she studied my face. "Are you all right?"

I gaped stupidly like she'd just slapped me across the cheek. Me? She was asking about *me*? Gods and Fates, why?

"Worried I'm having second thoughts about all this?" I asked, trying to make it sound teasing. It came out hoarser and more panicked than anything, though. Ugh.

"Mmm ... no. More worried that you're beginning to split at the seams while you try to hold everyone else together," she clarified. "I'm not stupid, Lieutenant. I know what that man, Judan, means to you. He was a close friend, wasn't he? Someone you counted on?"

I snapped my mouth shut. Even trying to speak felt like trying to swallow a big rock. Awkward. Uncomfortable. And somehow ... humiliating.

"That happens a lot, doesn't it? You finally let those prickly walls down and start to depend on people, to trust them, and then they disappear or betray you." She leaned against the railing next to me, tossing some of her long white hair over her slender shoulder.

"I don't have prickly walls," I grumbled as I looked away.

Violet just giggled softly and grinned. "For the record, I thought you handled the girl very well. I admit, I was a little impressed."

"Don't be. I've known her since she was in diapers. I've also spent the last ten-or-so years training pampered noble brats to be dragonriders." I rubbed the back of my neck. "I've had lots of practice with naïve kids who think they're ready to be soldiers. Granted, she's leagues ahead of most of the fledglings I teach. But I hope that today was a wake-up call for her. This isn't a game or a training duel in her family's garden. These are real dangers. Every fight she decides to get involved in could be one she doesn't walk away from. I'm pretty sure today was the first time she's ever taken a life. Once the adrenaline wears off, she's going to crash hard. Thatcher is better at that part, though. He's always treated her more like a little sister. Played games with her. Let her tie ribbons all in his hair and draw on his face with paints."

Violet clicked her tongue thoughtfully. "I see. So, then, who does that for you? Puts you back together when the adrenaline wears off and you crash hard?"

I chanced a speedy, sideways look at her. "You do realize I'm a grown man. I've done this kind of thing before. Several times, in fact. Diving overboard and blowing up a ship full of enemy thugs doesn't even make the top ten of the most dangerous things I've done."

"Oh?" She arched one of her dark eyebrows. "What's first on that list, then?"

I had to think about that—mostly because I wasn't sure I wanted to share that kind of thing with her. Besides, she worked for Arlan the Kinslayer. Didn't that mean she already knew pretty much everything I'd ever done? Was this some kind of test, then? A way for her to get in my head?

Fine, then. Two could play this game.

"I don't swap stories unless it's mutual," I warned. " If you want to know about the scariest thing I've ever done, then you have to tell what *pitathi* means. That's what Malina called you earlier, right? I've never heard that word before."

Her lips pursed unhappily and she looked down, picking at her fingernails as she murmured. "You won't like that story, Lieutenant."

"They say it's all in the delivery," I coaxed, keeping my tone as neutral as possible. I didn't want to put too much pressure there. Not when I had no idea how she might react. I'd never pushed her for anything personal before. "And would you just call me Reigh, already?"

Her head rolled to the side, nearly resting her cheek on her shoulder as she gave me an exasperated look. "Pitathi is what I am. Or was. Rather, it's a very crude word, not what my people call ourselves. It means something akin to 'dirty snake' in Rienkan."

Okay. Now she had my full attention. That explained why she'd gotten upset the last time I, uh, mouthed off about her current career choices. I'd called her a slimy little snitch, and that had apparently struck a very sensitive nerve. Now it made a little more sense.

"And why would anyone call you that?" I dared to ask.

"Oh, I assure you, it's well-earned. As a people, my ancestors don't have the most sterling of reputations," she explained, her tone softening some as she went on picking at her fingernails. "It's quite a long tale, actually. But suffice to say that not every race of people were made by gods with benevolent intentions. Elves were created out of a pursuit of perfection and enlightenment, humans out of an admiration for bravery and hardiness, and Viperi ... were made out of jealousy and a thirst for revenge. It's all most of us ever know."

"And that's what you are? Viperi?"

She nodded. "Albeit, not a very good one. Not by the standards of my kin, anyway. I've yet to manipulate and murder a single one of you, after all." She gave a weak, humorless chuckle—a pathetic attempt at masking the pain in her voice.

"And where do they live? The rest of your people, I mean." I pushed a little further. I couldn't help but wonder how she had found her way to Maldobar and Arlan.

Violet's jaw worked from one side to the other, almost like she knew the answer would sting and she was working herself up for it. Bracing for impact. With another sideways glance from those strange, vibrant red eyes she turned to face me and crossed her arms. "That was not a part of our bargain, Lieutenant. I've told you what pitathi means. Now, if you'd be so kind—it's your turn."

I narrowed my eyes. Really? She was throwing up walls now? What difference did it make where in the world they came from? "And you really want to know what the scariest thing I've ever done is?"

She nodded again.

I paused, thinking it over. Dealing with gods was always terrifying, and I'd done plenty of that in the past. I'd also been held prisoner and tortured by an insane tyrant, swallowed whole by an underbeast, and had to be Murdoc's sparring partner in dragonrider training. All very unsettling experiences.

But there was one that loomed over them all like a smothering dark shadow.

"I murdered my father," I admitted at last.

Violet frowned, her brows knitting together as she seemed to ponder that. "You ... you're talking about the Gray elven man? Kiran?"

I held her gaze like my life depended on it. My toes curled up inside my boots as that familiar, aching tightness seized in my chest. I couldn't think about it—couldn't even say it out loud—without that feeling returning. Panic. Dread. Regret. It took hold of me so quickly I could hardly breathe, and it took everything I had not to let it show.

I didn't want her to know how much it still terrified me, even after all these years.

"He's the only real father I've ever known," I managed quietly, not trusting my voice to hold steady if I spoke above a whisper. "And before you say it—yes, it was an accident. I was just a kid. I couldn't control my power as the chosen one of Clysiros. I didn't mean for him or anyone else to get hurt that day. But that doesn't take away the fact that I stared right into his eyes while he died at my own hands. So, yeah. That's the scariest thing I've ever done."

Violet's boot-heels clunked over the wooden floorboards of the ship's deck as she stepped closer. One of her small hands came to rest on my chest. But it was still all I could do just to look her in the eye.

"You need to forgive him," she said. "That scared little boy who did such a terrible thing. He's worthy of forgiveness, isn't he? I think so. I also think that's why you tend to cling so desperately to things. Why punish yourself for every small failure? So think on it, would you?" Her smile was sad as she reached up and patted my cheek a few times, then stepped aside and began walking away. "And get some rest. I'll keep watch. Trust me, Lieutenant, *nothing* gets past a Viperi."

PART THREE
MAYLEA

8

CHAPTER EIGHT

The tea Uncle Reigh gave me tasted absolutely awful. But it did help to numb the throbbing pain in my mouth and jaw. Too bad it didn't do anything about the weird, tingling frenzy that seemed to buzz in my chest. It was a nervous, frantic energy I didn't understand. A quiet panic. And it wasn't until I sat back down next to Lukani, holding his hand as I watched him still struggle for breaths, that I fully, truly felt it.

All of Uncle Reigh's words replayed in my head, hung in an endless loop that only made that feeling more intense. My parents were upset. I'd hurt them. I'd almost gotten Lukani killed. I'd put my life in danger without a single thought about how it would impact anyone else. If Lukani and I had died before Uncle Reigh found out I was here, no one would have ever even known what happened to us. What if I hadn't been able to hold my own against that Judan guy? What if I had gotten blown up in that ship?

What if I never saw my parents or my siblings again?

Tears welled in my eyes again and I put a hand over my mouth, not wanting anyone else around to hear me sniffle as I tried to calm down. Breathe. I just had to breathe. I was okay now. I was safe. Uncle Reigh and Thatcher were here. I would be safe with them.

So why did I still feel so ... small? Terrified? Empty? Confused?

"M-Maylea?" Lukani rasped suddenly.

I flinched, my heart skipping a beat. I looked down to find him staring up at me with a bleary, delirious smile as though he were relieved. His hand squeezed mine slightly.

"Y-You're ... okay," he said hoarsely. "I was ... s-so worried."

I squeezed his hand back gently. "Lukani, Gods and Fates, I am so sorry about this. I didn't know it would hurt you to use so much of your power. I never meant for you to be in danger like this. I should have never—"

He smiled weakly, cutting me off before I could finish. "W-We're friends," he insisted. "I-I told you ... I will keep watch over you."

My heart sank. That's the same thing he had told me when I first met him in the castle. He had been watching over me then, and had immediately jumped to my aid without question. I didn't know why in the world he was so devoted to helping me, but I'd been so selfish to just assume he would keep doing it.

My eyes closed and I bowed my head some, letting out a shaking breath as I tried to steady myself. "I need you to start looking out for you, too, Lukani. This can't happen again. You're right—we are friends. And I don't want to lose you," I whispered, unable to keep my voice from shaking some. "I really messed up. I thought I had all these good reasons for coming here. Now, it's like I can't remember any of them clearly."

"P-Please ... don't doubt yourself. You've come s-so far," he managed to wheeze as the corners of his mouth tugged at a faint smile. "We'll be okay. We will find Ronan together."

I wanted to believe that—so badly. More than anything. I'd come here for a lot of little reasons, but that was the biggest one. The most important thing. Everything went blurry as my eyes welled. All I could do was nod. Closing my eyes, I could still picture how Ronan had looked the last time we played together. We were almost the same age, right down to the day. And being with him had instantly felt like I'd found another piece of myself that had been missing. His deep blue eyes always caught the light like the darkest of sapphires. His smile was so bright, and he always knew how to make me laugh. He saw things I couldn't, was braver than I'd ever been.

Or, at least, he had been—right up until that last time.

On that final day Ronan and I spent together, he seemed so sad and quiet. He didn't want to play any of our usual games. But he wouldn't say why. Instead, we had gone to the Deck to peek at the dragons. We had found an empty dragon stall and sat on the very edge of the open doorway, watching the dragonriders take off and land while the sun began to set. And that was when he told me he was sorry. I didn't understand why. He wouldn't explain it. Maybe he wasn't allowed to. Or maybe he had known that was the last time we would see each other. None of it made any sense. I was left without answers, without my best friend, and without any hope that I would ever see him again.

"The memory used to be so blurry, but lately ... it's all I've been able to think about," I murmured. I didn't really expect him to understand. Somehow, though, it just felt better to say it out loud. It felt more real. "It's like there's this hole in my soul where Ronan used to be. Like he's out there somewhere, crying out for help. Wanting to be found. Wanting to come back. I know it doesn't make any sense."

Lukani blinked up at me from where he lay, still shivering as he blinked slowly. His brow crinkled with worry, as though he were trying his hardest to understand.

But that was the whole problem. No one did. Not my parents. Not Uncle Reigh. Not even me.

Settling onto the small bedroll beside him, I curled up on my side and closed my eyes. The rolling motion of the ship still swaying in the waves felt like I was slowly being rocked. The groaning of the hull, the faint sound of the sea outside, Lukani breathing steadily as he slept, and Thatcher snoring on his back across the room, gradually made my thoughts go hazy. I hadn't slept all that well since we got on this ship. The floor was too hard without a proper bedroll, and I had been constantly worried about being discovered.

Now, I finally felt a tiny trickle of security being with the others. Lukani and I weren't on our own anymore. We would be okay now. We could do this. We could find Ronan together now that we had help, right? We had to. I had to bring him back home safe somehow. I *would* find a way.

Or so I prayed ... with all my heart.

Something soft tickled the end of my nose. Some of my hair? I twitched, wriggling my nose back and forth to try to get it off. It didn't work. I tried moving my head, turning away. Shaking my head. No luck.

Ugh. What was going on? Was someone messing with me while I was trying to sleep?

I cracked an eye open.

Immediately, warm light shone in my eyes. I blinked and squinted, putting a hand up to shield my face for a moment while my eyes slowly adjusted. Then I saw it. My mouth fell open as I stared around at the forest where I stood. Golden sunlight winked through the limbs and leaves far overhead. But all around me, trunks of massive trees covered in lush green moss stood like columns in an ancient temple. The faint calls of birds echoed like distant melodies. The air savored strongly of that deep, earthy musk of moist soil and flourishing plant life.

My pulse fluttered with apprehension as I slowly turned in a circle. Everywhere I looked, there was only endless forest for as far as I could see.

Where ... Where was I? What happened to the ship? Where were Lukani and the others?

"Hello?" I called out. "Is anyone there?"

No answer. Just a warm, gentle breeze slipping by and stirring in my hair.

The soft, mossy ground sank a little under my boots as I stumbled forward, moving carefully and quietly past tiny flowers, mushrooms in vivid colors, and tall ferns. I couldn't be sure I really was alone here, and I had visited Luntharda enough times to know that not everything in the wild places of the world meant me no harm.

Suddenly, ahead, I spotted movement. A ripple of something like fabric moving through the trees ahead.

Every muscle in my body locked up solid. I froze in place, not even daring to breathe, as I slowly panned my gaze back and forth. But there was nothing. No crunch or squish of footsteps. No animal calls. Not a single sign of movement.

I swallowed hard. My stomach flipped and fluttered, spinning erratically as I stood perfectly still. Should I turn back? Run the other way? I-I didn't know. I had no idea where I was or what I should—

"Well, hello there, little sprout. I've been waiting for you," a rich, smooth, and intensely deep voice seemed to whisper from right behind me.

Every single tiny hair on my body stood on end. My heart beat skipped with a lurch. I whipped around, expecting to find someone standing there.

Nothing. Just my own footsteps still pressed into the mossy earth.

Oh no. This couldn't be good. Was I hallucinating? Or was this some trick of magic?

"Come along now. We haven't much time," the voice chuckled smoothly.

I let out a yelp of alarm as something suddenly flitted down from above, zooming past my head, and landing on a lichen-covered stump nearby. Was that ... a bird?

The tiny creature was no bigger than a sparrow, with feathers of blue, purple, and brilliant yellow. It rustled its wings and hopped, turning its head quickly from side to side while it looked at me.

Seriously? A *bird* was talking to me?

Just what the heck was going on here? I had to be dreaming. Birds didn't talk. And I couldn't remember how I'd even gotten here in the first place.

Definitely a dream, right?

I took a step closer, stretching out a hand toward the tiny, colorful creature. The bird fluttered farther away, landing on a large fern front and looking back as though it were expecting me to follow.

Oookay. I guess the bird really was talking to me.

"Who are you? Where are you taking me?" I asked as I followed, never managing to get within more than a few feet of the bird before it flew off farther ahead. Each time, it waited for me to catch up, always watching to make sure I was coming.

The bird didn't answer. And the farther we went through the forest, the more the landscape seemed to change. The trees grew closer together, so closely crowded that their interwoven branches blotted out the sunlight from above. The air grew dim and heavy, carrying more of the scent of decaying leaves and rotting wood. A thick fog curled around my legs, and I had to walk faster and faster as the bird began to fly ahead much more quickly.

Curse it—didn't he want me to follow? How could I keep up like this? I'd lose him in the dark unless he slowed down.

"Hey! Wait a second!" I called after him as I began to run through the gloom. Sweat trickled down the sides of my face. My heart hammered in my chest. I could barely see him at all now. Just the occasional glint of colorful feathers darting this way and that through the tree trunks.

Then I saw it.

In the distance, a glint of golden light broke through the canopy and shone like a spotlight to the forest floor below. Was that the way out? I set my jaw and started for it, keeping my gaze focused on that one bright spot. I pumped my legs as fast as they would go. My thoughts and heartbeat raced wildly. What was I doing? Where was I going? Should I even be following strange birds like this? What if I was stuck here? What if this was some sort of trap?

I came to a sudden, flailing halt at the edge of a small clearing where that shaft of golden light poured down from overhead. There, right in the center of it, a figure sat on an old, moss-covered log.

It seemed human in shape, although I couldn't see a face at all thanks to the heavy, emerald green cloak that basically swallowed its entire frame. With the hood pulled down low, head bowed, arms crossed, and wide shoulders slumped forward, the figure didn't move at all as the little bird landed on its shoulder. It twittered and chirped musically for a moment before fluttering away into the forest again.

Then, slowly, their head began to lift. Most of the figure's face was still shrouded in darkness thanks to that oversized hood, but I could see a narrow, pointed chin and a wide, smiling mouth peeking out from underneath.

"There you are," that same beautifully deep voice seemed to come from everywhere at once, even if the lips on that figure didn't move at all.

I sucked in a sharp breath. Who was this? Was I in danger? I reached down to my hips where my blades should have been buckled but there was nothing there. Oh, Fates. I had no weapons at all!

"You don't have to be afraid," the voice said as the figure's head tilted to one side slightly. *"Come closer."*

Riiight. Cause that's exactly what a dangerous stranger would want me to do, right?

I narrowed my eyes and took a small step back instead. "Who are you?"

"Who? Why not what? Or when? Or how and why?" the voice chuckled. *"All are interesting questions. But you already know the answer. Your blood has known me from the very beginning."*

I frowned. What? None of that even made sense! How could I already know who this was when I—

Oh.

My eyes went wide and my stomach dropped down to the soles of my boots. A new, prickling sense of fear climbed my spine one inch at a time, leaving me totally numb as I stared back at the figure. This figure—*he*—was right. I did know who he was.

"Paligno," the name slipped past my lips like a whimpering gasp.

His smile widened.

I-I ... was seeing Paligno. The god of all living things. But why? I'd heard the stories of my father's interactions with this entity countless times, and as best I could understand, the connection between him and our family had been severed at the end of the Tibran War. Dah had broken the stones that connected the "essences" of the ancient gods to the mortal world. That meant they no longer needed to possess mortal people in order to carry out their acts of power. Now, they were free to roam and meddle in the mortal realm like they had thousands of years ago, before the War of the Stones—which was a completely different subject I knew basically nothing about. Something to do with a bunch of gods warring against one another over who got to control the mortal world?

Ugggh. Now I really wished I had been paying more attention while Dah and Grandma Araxie rambled about that stuff. It had all seemed so trivial and pointless at the time. I mean, what difference did it make what happened in wars that had happened ages ago, before anyone I knew was even born?

A lot, I guess.

Crap.

⚜ 9 ⚜

CHAPTER NINE

"Do you think I've come to harm you?" he asked.

I swallowed hard against the panic that still made my throat feel numb. "No. Dah said you are one of the good gods."

He laughed again. *"Good. Bad. I suppose that all depends on whose side you're on, doesn't it? I do so love how my dear children enjoy drawing their little lines in the sand."*

"I-I, um, I thought there weren't going to be any more lapiloques?" I asked, my voice shaking as I took a faltering step closer to him.

"Is that what you believe I've come to ask of you?"

"I ... guess?" I took a few more hesitant steps, studying him much more closely now. I still couldn't see the rest of his face beneath that heavy hood.

My gaze traveled over his wide-shouldered form, soaking in every detail I could. That cloak wasn't nearly as grand as I'd expected when it came to things that a god might wear. It looked ragged, threadbare, and faded—more like a cloak that had been hung out on a laundry line and forgotten for years. The hem was covered in colorful splotches of moss and lichen that came all the way up to his knees, and there were twigs and leaves tangled in it. The mud caked on one of the shoulders had a few tiny mushrooms sprouting in it, and I had to blink a few times to make sure I wasn't hallucinating the beetles that crawled along the other one. Their shiny green and blue shells caught in the light as they went along, making their way down his arm to the log as though this were a typical part of their day.

"I didn't come to ask anything of you, little sprout. I came because of what you asked of me," the old god said, his tone still as calm and even as a lazy forest stream.

What? But I had never even thought about ask—oh. Oh, sweet Fates. I *had* asked him. I had prayed for help. For a way to bring Ronan home.

I just ... had never dreamed anyone would actually hear me.

"Did you assume I would not hear? Or that I do not care for the pleas of my children?" he asked.

"I-I, well, I never, um," I choked and stammered as my face started to burn with embarrassment.

His smile widened again. Paligno moved, the folds of that strange cloak shifting as he slowly stretched out a hand toward me as though he meant for me to take it. It looked normal enough, like any other person's hand. A wide palm with five long fingers. But as soon as I dared to touch it, warmth spread through me like I was wrapped up in my father's loving embrace. Safe. Loved. Cherished.

"I can give you what you want, little sprout," he murmured, his tone now much more somber. *"But such things carry a price that cannot be avoided. What you wish for are the means to save your friend. What you need is the power to pry him free from those who now hold him. That I can give. But you must understand that this road will take you to his battlefield. There, you will have to fight, just as your ancestors did. The pain will be great. The scars will be many."*

"You mean I'll have to fight in a war? Like Dah and mother did?" I tried to understand, but the way he said it somehow seemed bigger than all that. Bigger than kings, crowns, and kingdoms.

His voice came like the whisper of first frost over a withering wood. Foreboding in a way that made my whole body shudder at once. *"If you choose this path, little sprout, then your eyes will see a war that will crack the very heavens. That is where your friend is going, and the only place he can be set free."*

I couldn't speak. I couldn't even think beyond the shock. He was offering me what I needed—a way to help Ronan. But accepting this would mean getting tangled up in the affairs of gods and spirits with powers I couldn't even comprehend. Somehow, it felt like everything my father had ever warned me about all piled up into one big heap. I knew what he would want me to say. Uncle Reigh and the others would probably agree.

I should walk away from this. I should let someone else worry about saving Ronan.

But in that moment, all I could think about was the fact that my best friend was already caught up in this coming disaster and he'd never even been given a choice about it. He'd been taken from that library where he was supposed to be safe. And I had no idea what was happening to him now, although I couldn't imagine it was anything good. He must have felt so hopeless. So alone and afraid.

Could I really just walk away? Could I turn my back and let him suffer—maybe even die—just because I was afraid to get involved?

No. I couldn't.

Because just like my father and mother before me, I didn't back down from a fight. I didn't let my friends suffer. I didn't fear gods and spirits.

I was a Broadfeather, and I fought for what was right until my very last breath.

Before I even spoke out loud to give him my answer, that smile had spread across the ancient god's lips again. His head tilted back slightly, and in the pitch-black shadows of that oversized hood, I caught a glimpse of two brilliant, light green spots of light. Eyes that shone like peridot stars stared back at me from a place far beyond my own understanding. His much larger hand closed around mine a bit tighter, but still so gentle and warm.

"Take heart and do not lose courage. There will be great sorrow, but also great joy," he said, his voice seeming to fill up that emptiness in my soul that had ached so badly. He reached out with his other hand, extending a finger to touch the pendant that hung around my neck. The same one my father and grandmother had worn. The one supposedly made from his own bone. *"For even as the days grow dark and the faithful stumble in their fear, the world will learn your name. My power will be yours to wield, and they will call you the pathfinder who guides all back from the brink. You shall be my greatest champion. My paladin."*

I AWOKE WITH MY HEART STILL POUNDING LIKE WAR DRUMS AND MY MUSCLES quivering, lying in the dark belly of the *Fog Dancer*. Every inch of me seemed to thrum with energy, like lightning sizzled under my skin and I could hardly hold still. My hand shook as I touched the pendant around my neck. I hissed a curse and quickly pulled my hand away. The pendant—it was *hot*. The smooth surface of it felt like it had been baked in an oven.

Wow. Was that because Paligno had touched it? Had he infused some of his power into it?

I didn't know for sure. Honestly, I wasn't even sure what being a paladin or a pathfinder even meant, but I didn't doubt for a single second that he would keep his word. Paligno had helped my father save the world twice-over. He had brought my mother back from the dead. He had always kept his promises to my family.

Why wouldn't he do the same for me? I just had to have faith.

Easy, right?

I sat up, still catching my breath as I stared around the small navigation room where I lay on the bedroll. Lukani, Thatcher, and the others were gone. Nothing but walls with shelves stuffed with maps and a few neatly arranged piles of gear.

Strange ... Had I just overslept?

A yelp tore past my lips as the ship suddenly gave a shudder. It slung me and all the gear to one side of the small room as the whole vessel seemed to list dangerously and then slowly rock back and right itself.

Oh no. That couldn't be a good sign.

Something rolled right past me, smacking into the side of my leg. I reached for it, closing my hand around what seemed to be a smooth sphere made of milky white glass. It was only about the size of a kiwi, but wherever my fingers touched it, the surface of the ball glowed with a strange greenish light. Weird. What was this thing? Had it come out of someone else's bag? Or was it stashed away on one of the shelves in here?

No time to figure it out now.

Springing up, I crammed the trinket into my pocket and bolted out the door and back out onto the deck—right into the teeth of pure chaos.

Fierce gusting wind snagged in my hair and cold rain hit my face like a thousand tiny needles. I squinted, trying to shield my eyes and see through the mayhem. Before me, crew members scrambled like mad across the decks, fighting with lines and sails. Lightning snapped overhead, so loud it made my eardrums throb. Thunder rumbled in the deep, sending a pang of fresh dread through me.

Directly ahead, the stormfront approached like a wall of boiling, churning, towering darkness.

Oh gods. We were about to get caught in that ...

"Cut the lines and draw back the planks!" A sailor shouted over the howling wind. "We gotta break off or we'll both be visiting the drakkon tonight!"

In an instant, I saw it. Our chance. We could get away. We could set this right. I just had to act—right now.

Cutting my gaze quickly over the deck before me, I searched for the familiar features of my friends. Uncle Reigh's red hair was easy to spot. So was that woman, Violet, thanks to her long silvery white hair. But I didn't see Thatcher or Lukani anywhere. Curse it. Where were they?

Darting down onto the main deck, I shoved and ducked past the scrambling pirate crew as they worked frantically to separate the two ships. I guess heading into a storm tied together like that was basically a death sentence.

I staggered as another monstrous wave rolled our ship to the side, making the hull bash against the *Squall Queen's* with a harrowing *CRACK*.

Bad. Definitely a bad sound. Faster—must go faster.

I surged forward again, barely making it a few steps before the deck began to shift as the ship rolled back in the other direction. I stumbled and lost my balance, catching the edge of a barrel and landing face-first against something much bigger and solid. It knocked the wind out of me and I drew back, seeing stars as I tried to keep my balance.

A pair of big hands suddenly grabbed my arms and held me upright. "Maylea?" A familiar voice shouted over the wind.

I squinted up, realizing now that I'd crashed right into a person. "Thatcher!" I gasped in relief.

"What are you doing up here?" he demanded with a scowl, all his shaggy golden hair now soaked with rain and sticking to his face and neck.

"Where is Lukani?" I shouted back.

Thatcher just stared down at me for a second or two, wild-eyed and frantic. I couldn't even tell if he had actually heard me or not. Then he snagged an arm around my waist and dragged me in against his chest again, flinging his other arm out to catch the mainmast and hold on. The ship rolled dangerously, so steep that crates and barrels slid past us like boulders. Sailors went flying, their screams lost to the raging wind.

CRAAAACK!

The hulls of our ships smashed together again.

We ... we weren't going to make it if they couldn't get the ships cut apart. We would both sink in this storm.

"Get back inside!" Thatcher yelled again and began to let me go. He gave me a shove back in the direction of the main cabin.

"I have to find Lukani first! If we can get Malina out of the brig, this might be our chance to escape! Lukani might be able to—" I didn't get to finish.

A thud and low roar echoed behind me. Thatcher's eyes went wide. I turned to see the lithe, shimmering shape of a shrike standing on the deck with its head bowed and yellow eyes focused squarely on me.

I grinned. Found him. Or, um, *he* found me.

And I guess he agreed with my plan.

Rushing for him, I climbed onto the back of Lukani's shrike-form and hunkered down. Thatcher shouted in protest, waving his arms as he ran after me. But it was no good. He was fast—but no one was faster than a shrike. I turned my focus to the deck of the larger galleon that rocked and bobbed in the stormy waves right beside our ship. The crew had almost managed to sever the ties that bound the two vessels together. Excellent. We could do this. We had to. Losing the *Squall Queen* in the storm might be our only shot to get back on track so we could rescue Ronan. I couldn't waste this chance.

We just had to pull off a little jailbreak, first.

❧ 10 ❧

CHAPTER TEN

As the final rope was cut, the two ships veered apart in the roiling, churning dark ocean as more tongues of lightning split the sky like cracks in the floor of the heavens. The sails unfurled to receive the powerful gales, and I knew we didn't have much time. We had to do this quickly—before anyone onboard the *Squall Queen* could even guess what we were up to.

I leaned down into Lukani's speed, trying to keep as flush against his back as possible, as he zipped ahead through the pouring rain. Below, the rising ocean swells foamed and rippled, so large they washed over the decks of both ships and threatened to send them rolling sideways. My stomach flipped and spun as we spiraled toward the deck, dodging the swinging ropes, sails, and top yard beams that spanned out from the main masts.

For an instant, I caught a glimpse of that man, Judan, at the helm of the ship. He shouted orders to the men scrambling all around him, fighting the storm to get everything on deck secured while he steered the ship straight into the waves. Our eyes locked through the wind and rain, and his brow snapped into a fierce, snarling frown.

I smirked back.

Sure, he might be onto me. He could probably guess why I was here, up to no good again, but Mr. Pirate King had his hands full right now. Too bad.

Catch me if you can, old man.

Lukani landed hard, digging his claws into the wood and holding on long enough for me to scramble off his back. He shifted back into his normal human-like form before I could even blink, and I seized his hand and started for the hatch that led down into the ship. We had to find the brig, release our captain, and get everyone back to our ship as quickly as possible. Preferably before anyone tried to stop us. But just in case, I kept a keen eye on every pirate and sailor that rushed past.

For now, they all seemed thoroughly distracted.

So far, so good.

Lukani and I dove into the dark of the Squall Queen's sublevels, ducking through the gun deck, and rushing through the cargo hold. The ship pitched violently, bouncing in the stormy sea, and sending us skidding and sliding as the rain seeped from every tiny crack above the deck and dripped around us. It was like trying to navigate through a damp barrel while someone rolled it down a hillside. If not for the rush of adrenaline that had every corner of my mind blazing with focus and desperate energy, I might have been sick.

But there was no time for that.

We found the brig at the very stern of the ship, so far below deck it felt like we might as well be at the bottom of the ocean. There, the familiar form of a massive, brawny elven man loomed before the metal door like a colossus. Adavar was his name, wasn't it? Ugh. Great. How were we supposed to get past this guy? I could've stood on Lukani's shoulders and he still would have been taller.

Luckily, with his back turned and his focus on keeping his balance as the ship continued to rock, it didn't seem like he had even noticed us yet. We only had seconds, though. Plan—I needed a plan. I couldn't possibly fight this guy with any hope of winning.

What to do ... what to do ...

On pure instinct, my hand slipped down into my pocket and took out that shiny, milky glass orb. Lukani's eyes went wide at the sight of it, as though he had seen it before and knew exactly what it was.

"My power will not activate it," he whispered frantically. "Only divine power will—"

He stopped short. I stumbled to a halt right next to him, just in time for the big elf to slowly turn around and glare down at us. I-I guess he heard that. Oops.

My gaze flashed between the giant of a man and the orb. Divine power? I didn't know if I had that. But Paligno had said I would be his paladin. Maybe that meant I did?

No time to overthink it!

The giant elf reached for the sword belted at his hip, scowling at us and opening his mouth like he was about to try to warn us off.

But I rushed straight for him. With the sphere gripped tightly, I held it out at arm's length. I shut my eyes tightly, reaching for something—anything—that felt like divine power anywhere inside me. I needed it, and the only memory that seemed even remotely close that I could cling to was that sensation when I'd first touched Paligno's hand. That warmth that had filled my soul like fresh spring water.

And I found it.

I gasped in deep as it hit me like a rushing avalanche. That feeling, Palgino's power, but so much stronger than before. Wild. Pure. Overwhelming.

I could see the brilliant flash of radiant green light even with my eyes closed.

My pulse fluttered and skipped. My skin tingled and all my toes curled as my breath caught. I dared to force my eyes open just in time to glimpse his towering form vanishing like a wisp of golden, shimmering mist that was instantly pulled into the glass sphere in my hand. Trapped within that small clear ball, the gold mist spun and whirled like a tiny tornado trapped inside it.

Whoa.

I-I ... I had done it.

Slowly, I turned to face Lukani with the orb still in my hand.

He stared back at me, eyes as big as dinner plates and his mouth hanging open. For a moment, we just stared at one another in complete shock. H-How? How had I done that? And what exactly had happened? Had I just killed that man? Or was he inside this glass ball now? How was that even possible? Was he trapped in there forever now?

Gods and Fates, where had this thing even come from?!

"We must hurry," Lukani managed to wheeze hoarsely and nodded ahead, to where the metal door that led into the brig was still closed. Probably locked, too.

Pfft. As if that had ever stopped me before.

I pocketed the glass ball and got to work, pulling a few pins from my belt and picking the lock in a matter of seconds. Hah. Child's play. Auntie Garnett had taught me how to pick locks when I was only four. Not that my parents knew anything about that, of course. I couldn't let them in on all my secrets. Otherwise, they would start putting more sophisticated locks on the things they didn't want me messing with.

Like the trunks where they stored all the weaponry.

The mechanism in the iron door surrendered to my prowess with a low *clunk* and it immediately swung inward, revealing a nearly-dark room lined with three cells. The metal bars were rusty, and the only light came from a single lantern hanging by the door that creaked back and forth with the violent rocking of the ship.

In the very middle cell, with her wrists still bound in shackles, I recognized Captain Malina right away. They'd taken her fancy long frock coat and hat, but she didn't seem to be injured. She stood up and blinked hard, almost like she thought she might be seeing things, as Lukani and I rushed in.

"Who, by all the stars, are you?" she demanded, still staring between us in total bewilderment.

"The rescue team," I said as I got to work unlocking her cell, too. "There's a storm outside. They had to cut us loose from the *Squall Queen*. This is our chance to get away."

A broad, cunning grin curved over her lips as I popped the second lock in a matter of seconds and her cell door swung open. "You're a clever one, I see."

I winked and tipped my head back to where Lukani was still standing guard in the doorway. "Yeah. I guess *we* are. Now, come on! There isn't much time. Judan definitely spotted us up on deck, and I'd bet anything he's—

"—GOING TO BE FURIOUS ABOUT YOU SPRINGING MY PRISONER?!"

I froze.

Uh oh ... I definitely recognized *that* voice.

JUDAN WAS HEADED STRAIGHT FOR US, STORMING DOWN THROUGH THE CARGO HOLD like an angry dragon. He was practically snorting steam as he ran, sword already in, er, well not his hand. Sort of his hand? Whatever. He'd affixed that metal gauntlet with the bladed attachment again, and there was murder in his eyes as he came straight at us.

Time to go!

"You're not taking her or my ship anywhere!" Judan snarled as he rushed in.

Lukani answered with a piercing, shrieking roar like the yowl of a jungle cat. Judan staggered to a halt, his face going pale as Lukani planted himself between us defiantly. His form shifted and unfurled into the shape of a monstrous feline beast with six legs, a gaunt sinewy body, and a long whipping tail. He sank low and bared teeth like a hundred slender needles. There was terror and recognition all over Judan's face as he hesitated, looking like he might suddenly turn and bolt.

And that was the only opportunity I needed.

Digging my hand into my pocket, I seized the glass orb and clenched it hard, reaching down again for more of that power. It wasn't as difficult the second time. The rush of Paligno's power seemed to leap up like oil poured over flames. The glass ball glowed in my hand like a caught star, and I threw it at Judan with all my strength.

Blinding light burst through the gloom again.

THUD!

CRAASH!

"AUGH!" Judan let out a guttural cry of surprise as something massive smashed into him. No, wait. Not something—someone.

It was Adavar! He came flying out of the orb, still looking shocked and furious, and hit Judan like a boulder being fired from a catapult. They both crashed into a stack of barrels and crates, sending sawdust and splinters flying everywhere.

"Run!" I yelled and took off for the exit.

In the near-dark of the rocking ship, with flashes of light, bursts of golden mist, Judan yowling like an angry stray cat, and crates and barrels smashing—it was absolute chaos. The perfect cover.

And maybe our only chance.

I dove ahead, seizing Lukani by his long, whipping tail and giving him a yank to follow me. I didn't even have to call to Malina. She fell in step right behind us and we ran like mad for the other exit that led from the cargo hold to the gun deck of the ship. Our only way out.

My heartbeat boomed in my ears as I ran, not daring to look back to see if Judan and that giant elf guy were following us. A sharp cry tore past my lips as the ship suddenly pitched upward, sending us all sliding backward like eggs rolling down a wooden plank. I flailed, crashing hard into Lukani—who must have reverted forms again because he caught me by the waist with his strong human hands and held me in place.

Gods and Fates, even if we got out of here, would our ship be able to survive a storm like this? Unlike the *Squall Queen*, the *Fog Dancer* had taken some significant damage in our skirmish. It might just break apart and leave us all clinging to scraps of wood like a bunch of drowning rats.

I tried not to focus on that as I pushed off of Lukani and tried to start forward again. So close—we were so close! The open doorway that led upward toward the main deck was right there.

My boots slid on the now wet floor as I tried to get my balance. I guess one of those broken barrels had something liquid inside. Wine, maybe? Ugh. It certainly stank like it. Great. I'd never get that smell out of my boots.

Gritting my teeth, I hoisted myself forward along the steep incline as the ship rolled upward again, probably taking on another wave. I got a rush of confidence and hope as my hand hit the doorframe, using it as leverage to scramble the rest of the way up.

We were going to make it!

A strange and incredibly strong metal hand suddenly grabbed my wrist.

What the—?!

I looked up—right into Judan's furious face. His whole head had nearly turned purple with rage as he pried my hand off the frame with one, furious yank. My thoughts scrambled. Hadn't he been using a blade affixed to that weird metal gauntlet-thing? And now he had ... a metal hand there? How was that even possible?

Then he held up the shimmering glass orb. One of his eyes twitched as he snarled, "What is this?! You thought you were just going to slip away from me?"

My breath caught. For a single second, I glanced between him, the glass orb that was no longer filled with shimmering golden mist, and the doorway ahead of me. A terrible idea sprung up in my mind, and my body moved before I could stop it.

We had to get out. We had to get back to the *Fog Dancer*. This ... this was the only way.

"YES!" I yelled and slammed my other hand down onto the orb, forcing another burst of power into it. Another radiant burst of light bloomed through the ship. Lukani cried out in surprise just as he began reaching for me again, almost like he was going to try to get Judan away from me.

But I didn't need his help this time.

Judan's towering, wrathful form vaporized instantly. He became nothing more than a plume of that glimmering, swirling golden mist that quickly filled the orb.

I barely managed to snag it out of the air as it fell, no longer held in his grasp. Close one. Fates, I did not want to imagine what might happen if it broke while someone was, er, trapped inside it.

Somehow, I doubted that would be a good thing. But, hey, tonight was my first time using magical artifact-y things. Who knew, right?

I stood up shakily, holding the orb as my pulse raced like mad and my mind whirled between shock and bewilderment.

I flinched as the giant elf, Adavar, suddenly appeared again. Panic shot through my body as sharp and cold as the bite of an icy whip. I drew back, hands shaking, as I gripped the orb tightly. If he wanted his captain back, he'd have to pry it from my cold, dead—

My jaw dropped suddenly when I noticed Adavar wasn't alone. He was standing with an arm around Malina's waist, holding her upright similar to the way Lukani had been helping me. His desperate gaze was focused on her, with emotion crinkling his features I didn't understand. Regret, maybe? Anguish? Sorrow?

She stared back at him with tears welling in her turquoise eyes. And somehow ... I just knew. It was as though I could feel it in the air between them. They loved each other. But it didn't seem like a romantic love. Not like Dah and my mother. It was more like the way Dah looked at me, honestly.

Did that mean ... he had raised her? Was he her father? Surely not, right? Other than the long, pointed ears, they didn't look anything alike.

"Go," Malina commanded suddenly, and at first, I thought she was talking to Adavar.

Then her gaze snapped over to Lukani and me, fresh tears making the kohl around her eyes run down her cheeks. "You must go—now!"

"Wh-what?" I stammered in shock. We had just broken her out of the brig. Didn't she want to get out of here?

A strange, sad smile dimpled her cheeks as she put a hand on Adavar's arm and glanced back up at him. "This is my family's ship. This is where I belong. If the crew will see me back at the helm, then I want to stay here."

Adavar bowed his head slightly. "We will, Captain."

"Then you two have to go—go back to the *Fog Dancer* immediately. Take that cursed fiend with you and make for Rienka," she urged, her tone sharp as she curled her lip down at where I'd tucked that glass sphere into my pocket.

I stared at her, struggling for words. I couldn't do this, could I? Captain Malina wanted us to just leave her here? Alone? Well, I mean, I guess Adavar was here. And he did seem happy, or maybe even relieved, to see her. But was this really going to be okay?

"You will ... be all right here?" Lukani asked worriedly.

She nodded. "I was born on this ship, boy. Its planks have known my family's blood for a dozen generations. Now that I have her back, I won't let anyone take her from me again. That man, Judan, stole her from me once. Tricked me into believing he cared for me, and led a mutiny built on nothing but lies. But now I have her back, and I'm no fool. I know I have you lot to thank for it." Malina turned and stretched out a hand toward me, offering to shake. "A Skyhart always pays their debts. If you ever need my help again, you have only to ask. Send word through the Zenith's Call. I swear to you now, I will answer."

I swallowed hard. I guess this was something I'd just have to take on faith. There wasn't much other choice. It didn't seem like she was going to change her mind, and we couldn't exactly force her, could we?

Reluctantly, I seized her hand and shook it. "Thank you."

Her grin was roguish as she nodded ahead, gripping onto Adavar hard as the ship pitched around us again. "The storm's growing worse. Hurry, or you might lose the *Fog Dancer* in it. Your first mate should still be able to get you to Rienka. On your lives, now, go! And may the sea god favor you!"

11

CHAPTER ELEVEN

My head whirled, torn between what I had just agreed to, and what I knew we still had to accomplish. I didn't know if leaving Malina behind on the ship was the right choice or not. Sure, I had overheard Violet say something about the Skyhart family owning this ship before. But I didn't know how Malina had managed to lose control of it to Judan in the first place. I wasn't sure if it was something done forcefully, or if she had given it up voluntarily. Judging by their interactions, I sort of doubted the latter had been the case.

I did know she was the one that Arlan's man had chosen to take us to Nar'Haleen safely. That meant she must have a deep understanding of how to get around these foreign seas. Would our first mate actually be able to take on that task now? Or was leaving her behind a huge mistake?

I didn't know. There was no one around to ask. And right now, I only had one clear objective: get back to the *Fog Dancer* as soon as possible.

With Judan still trapped in that magical glass orb, all I could do was hope that no one would be angry that I hadn't come back with the same captain we'd left Maldobar with. We could still make it to Nar'Haleen without her, right? We just needed a ship and someone with some sense of how to sail it. Malina had suggested the first mate, so that must mean she had confidence that he could handle it.

And that would have to be enough.

Gripping Lukani's hand tightly, we ran together for the main deck of the ship. The storm practically swallowed us whole as we forged forward, trying to reach the railing. My boots slid on the soaked wooden planks, and the wind yanked at my hair and clothes. Thunder clashed and boomed so loud it sent a jolt of raw terror through me. Before us, the swells of stormy waves rose up like dark, foaming mountainsides, and my stomach dropped to the soles of my boots.

H-How were we going to get through this? What if we sank? I couldn't even see the *Fog Dancer* anywhere now.

CRACK!

I let out a shriek as a tongue of lightning popped off one of the ship's masts, sending a shower of sparks and cries of alarm through the crew members still struggling to keep the ship on course. Lukani grabbed me again and pulled me closer against him, shuffling along low and fast toward the main mast.

With his taller form shielding me from the wind somewhat, I scoured the toiling sea for any sign of the *Fog Dancer* amidst the roiling waves and churning black clouds. My pulse skipped every time a lightning bolt popped nearby, giving off a brilliant flash that lit up the night for an instant.

Then I saw it—far in the distance. A few tiny specks of light coming from the lanterns hanging on the front and back of the ship peeked out above the swelling waves. Hope and adrenaline surged through me, and I tugged on Lukani's arm. "There! I see it!" I pointed frantically to where the lights were beginning to disappear as it sailed down the opposite side of the wave.

He must have seen it, too.

It was so far. The winds were so strong. Even if he changed into a shrike, he might not be strong enough in flight to make it there without getting tossed by the stormy gales.

Lukani's jawline went rigid. His eyes narrowed with sharp focus as his brows furrowed deeply. He wrapped his other arm around the mast and held on, squinting through the pouring rain. His brow furrowed and his jaw set an instant before I felt his arm around me go tense. He blinked hard and I saw his pupils go narrow like a cat's.

Or ... something else. Something familiar.

I recognized it only a second before his features began to warp and change, his body swelling as his skin and clothes gave way to a burst of golden scales. The arm gripping me around my waist grew large, with fingers tipped in curled black claws. Two massive leathery wings burst from his back as he ran forward, snatching me off my feet and carrying me along. I screamed as he kicked off the deck of the ship out into the open air—and immediately the wind was snatched from my lungs.

Lukani took to the air in the shape of a large golden dragon, his powerful wings fighting the gusting winds. He surged toward the *Fog* Dancer, still holding me against his plated chest in two massive, clawed hands. A low snarl rumbled in his throat as we skimmed the surface of the swells. Ahead, I only caught glimpses of the faint and flickering point of light winking atop the massive waves. Gods and Fates, it was getting too far away. What if we lost both ships in the storm?

Fear gripped my heart as though it were being squeezed in an icy fist. I held onto Lukani's massive scaly toes and tried to think—to concentrate. We would make it. Lukani was strong. He was powerful. He could get us through this. I believed that.

Every muscle in my body locked up solid as a bolt of lightning snapped off the water beside us. Lukani snarled and beat his wings faster, swerving and dodging as he surged for the *Fog Dancer*. Below, I finally caught a clear glimpse of the ship. Its sails were puffed and its bow angled straight into the oncoming waves, taking on each one while the crew held fast to the lines. They shouted when they saw us, probably assuming we were something else terrible that had come to destroy them.

Except for one person.

His red hair caught my eye immediately, and I knew it had to be Uncle Reigh standing out there on the center of the deck, waving his arms like he was trying to signal us in. Lukani spotted him, too, and began to dive downward, growling at the wind that stung our faces and gusted against his wings. His powerful shoulders flexed with every forceful wingbeat, as though the storm were trying to hold us back from ever reaching the ship.

Closer ... closer ... Almost there!

As we dropped in low for the final approach, pushing full-force against the raging winds, I realized we had a problem. A big one. Lukani was too large in this form to land on the deck. He might capsize it with the impact of his landing, or get tangled up in the sails and lines. Oh, Gods. What were we going to do?!

Only an instant before impact, Lukani suddenly curled himself into a ball. He held me close, as though trying to shield me. And then I felt his massive form begin to shrink. His scales faded back into soft, warm, greenish skin. His wings disappeared.

We howled through the air the last few yards like a comet, slamming into the deck at full dragon speed.

THUD!

Something popped as we hit, and white-hot pain rushed through my shoulders. I bit down hard and kept my face hidden against his chest as we rolled and finally skidded to a stop in the middle of the rain-soaked main deck of the *Fog Dancer*. I wound up lying on top of Lukani, breathless and limp as the world spun around me and my vision went gray. Beneath me, Lukani's chest rose and fell with rapid, gasping breaths. He shakily lifted his head to stare down at me, as though checking to make sure I was okay.

All I could manage was a wheezing cough and a hazy smile.

W-We made it. We were alive.

For now.

"HAVE YOU ABSOLUTELY LOST YOUR MIND?!" UNCLE REIGH ROARED EVEN louder than the storm. He appeared over us like a tower of wrath and grabbed me by the arm to hoist me up. I shrieked as pain shot through my arm and shoulder and flailed away, cradling it against my chest as I sat up on my knees.

Gods, what had I done? Why did my whole arm feel so strange? It tingled and burned, hurting in a way I couldn't even describe.

Uncle Reigh's expression of pure rage instantly went slack. His eyebrows shot up and his face paled a little. He didn't waste a second. Scooping me up into his arms, he carried me quickly toward the captain's quarters and shouted, "Thatch, help the boy and follow me! Violet, get the door—and someone go get my medical kit! She's hurt!"

Thatcher rushed for Lukani, quickly hefting him to his feet and keeping a hand on his shoulder to guide him along after us. I couldn't see clearly enough to tell if Lukani had been hurt by our crash-landing, too. Gods, I hoped not.

"What happened? Were they just flying around in this weather?" Violet's tone was sharp with disapproval as she rushed forward to hold the door open for us. She didn't stick around to hear an answer, though. As soon as we were safely inside, Violet dashed back out into the storm.

The door shut behind her, sealing us off from the raw chaos of the storm outside. The violent clash and snap of the thunder and lightning became muffled, rumbling thuds. I could finally hear myself gasping for breath. My teeth chattered. Fates, why did I feel so cold? Was it just because my clothes were soaked? Everyone else was drenched, too, but none of them seemed to be shivering like I was.

I whimpered through my teeth as Uncle Reigh sat me down on the desk at the far back of the room. Just that small movement made pain shoot through my shoulder again. Was it broken? Gods and Fates, what if it was? What would I do? Curse it all, that was my good arm! The one I used to hold a bow! Not that I had one to use right now—but still.

With his soggy hair sticking to his face and neck, and rainwater dripping from the end of his nose, Uncle Reigh looked me over frantically. His hands shook some as he carefully took my injured arm into his hand. Our gazes locked, and I could see the worry in his light cognac-colored eyes, even as he murmured gently, "It'll be okay, Maylea. Let me take a look."

My mouth screwed up and I looked away, trying my best not to wince or whimper as he slowly moved my arm and felt of the muscles along my shoulder and collarbone. He probed along my wrist and forearm all the way to my shoulder, scowling fiercely the entire time.

Then he sank into his heels and let out a deep, relieved sigh. His eyes rolled back for a moment and he shook his head. "You dislocated it. Nothing's broken. Thank the gods for that."

"C-Can you fix it?" I asked, hating how small and scared my voice sounded right then.

"Yeah. It'll be sore for a little while, but it should be fine," he replied quietly and flashed me a quick look of disapproval. "Do you have any idea how lucky you are to even be in one piece right now? Sweet Fates, what were you thinking?"

I would have shrugged, but even thinking about it hurt. So, instead, I looked away and tried not to think about how he was already positioning himself with my arm and shoulder in his grasp to pop it back into place. It would hurt, wouldn't it? Probably. Ughh. Now was not the time to get squeamish. I had to get it together and stop messing up like thi—

POP!

Uncle Reigh applied a sudden burst of force and I felt that sensation again, like something had snapped in my upper arm. Instantly, the tingling in my arm and fingers ceased. I could move it normally again. And while there was still a little dull, aching pain, it wasn't anything like before.

I sank back some, wiggling my fingers and flexing my hand for a moment before I reached back into my pocket and took out the milky glass orb that still glowed with golden mist. "I was thinking that we need a captain," I answered at last.

Uncle Reigh's eyes went wide. His mouth opened slightly and he began to reach for it. "You ... put Malina in this? How?"

"I'm not sure," I confessed as I handed over the shining little sphere. "I think Paligno may have helped me."

"That's what Arlan said when he gave it to me," Thatcher interrupted. He helped Lukani sit down in the big, fancy chair behind the captain's desk, then wandered over closer to see what we were talking about. There was a wide, smug grin on his lips as he gave me a wink. "It takes divine power to activate it."

"Divine power," Uncle Reigh echoed, his tone quavering some. He held the sphere up, his eyes narrowing as though he were trying to spot anything solid floating around inside it. "And Malina is in here?"

"Well, I-I, er, no. Not ... exactly." Oh boy. I had no idea how they were going to respond to this—the snap-decision I had made about who to carry off that ship. Would it be more fury? Or satisfaction?

Somehow, I doubted it would be the latter.

Thatcher's smirk faded some as he reached out to take the orb and inspect it, as well. "Then who—"

A flash of golden light lit up the room suddenly, making us all cringe back. Lukani let out a panicked growl and Violet screamed from the doorway as she ducked back in from the storm. An angry and all-too-familiar voice cursed and spat as a large, drenched shape of a man landed in a heap on the floor right in front of us.

I immediately slid off the desk and went to stand beside Uncle Reigh. Lukani jumped to his feet with his fang-like teeth bared and tail swishing. We exchanged a quick, wide-eyed look of panic. After all, the last time we had seen this guy, he had been charging for us with a blade.

Judan scrambled to his feet, staring around at all of us with a wildly confused snarl like a cornered animal. His hazel eyes flashed with panic as he seemed to realize he was no longer in the belly of the *Squall Queen*. Oops. Surprise, I guess.

"I gave it back to her. The ship, I mean." I looked toward Violet with a hopeful smile as I tried to explain. "You said it belonged to her family, right? But he took it from her somehow. So, I gave it back, and—"

Judan lunged for me, barely managing to stagger to his feet as he tripped over his own soggy coat. "YOU! You wretched little menace! Once I get my hands on you, I swear I'll—"

Uncle Reigh didn't let him finish. He stepped in front of me, seized the front of Judan's frilly-collared tunic, and gave him a violent shove backward. "You'll what? You better think long and hard before you finish that thought!" He snarled, cocking a fist back as though daring Judan to take another step. "Whatever I do to you will be *nothing* compared to what Jaevid does if he finds out you laid a hand on his daughter. You really want to pick *that* fight?"

Judan stumbled back and nearly fell, barely managing to catch himself on the edge of the desk. He glared at Reigh, both eyes twitching as his face flushed deep scarlet. "You had no right—no right to mess with my life any further!"

"Yeah? The way you were going to mess with ours when you shot our ship full of holes? We didn't drag you into this—you invited yourself when you gave that order to fire," Reigh snapped. "All I'm doing now is making sure you don't try slinking off before seeing this through to the end."

"You think you can hold me here? Force me to do what you say?" Judan bit angrily at every word as he brought up his blade-tipped arm in an unspoken threat.

Thatcher stepped forward, holding up the glass orb again in a similar, ominous gesture of warning. "Yeah. Actually, I'm pretty sure we can."

But Reigh just sighed heavily and put his hands on his hips, striking a pose that reminded me of my dah when he was about to dive headlong into another lecture about acceptable behavior. "Look, Judan, I'm not interested in taking a hostage, but we need a captain to sail this ship to Rienka. You know the position I'm in. You said in this ship's current state, getting to Nar'Haleen isn't an option, so I'm willing to make a deal with you—that is, if you can manage to pull your head out of your butt long enough to actually hear me out."

Judan's mouth twisted to one side, his broad chest still heaving with angry breaths as he glanced Reigh up and down as though he were sizing him up. "I'm listening," he finally muttered bitterly.

"The way I see it, you've only got two choices," Reigh said with a grim frown. "Either you help us get to Rienka, and maybe I let you keep this ship afterward so you can go about your pirating business—if that's what you really want to do with your life now—or we put you back in the bad attitude time-out ball and I deliver you back to your parents personally after all this is over. The last one is, of course, dependent on us actually surviving and managing to stop an all-out war with the gods, but frankly the idea of dropping you at your father's feet while you're wearing that ridiculous hat is almost too good to pass up."

Judan continued to stare him down like a snarling wolf, and for a few extremely uncomfortable seconds, no one said a word. No one even dared to cough or sniff.

Uncle Reigh's light amber eyes narrowed dangerously. One corner of his mouth twitched some. But he didn't say another word.

Finally, Judan licked his teeth behind his lips and looked down. "You are truly willing to let me have this ship? Just like that?"

"Just like that," Uncle Reigh confirmed. "Not like I can actually do anything with it, given my circumstances. I'd ask you to stick around and maybe ferry us back to Maldobar when all this is over, but I know better than to expect that kind of hospitality out of you now."

Judan arched an eyebrow like he wasn't quite buying that story. "You do realize you could make a small fortune selling it at the harbor. Enough to fund your little venture to Nar'Haleen twice over."

"Yeah. But I also know I didn't come here to make money as a ship-broker. We've got connections through Arlan to get us where we need to go. Right?" Reigh glanced over at Violet.

She nodded slightly, her expression as cool and guarded as the surface of the moon. I guess she wasn't ready to trust Judan quite yet, not that I blamed her.

I didn't like that prickly bite to his tone, or the way he kept eyeing Uncle Reigh as though he were searching for a weakness. He definitely didn't seem like the kind of guy I wanted in my blind spot.

Uncle Reigh seemed willing to give him a chance, though. He stepped forward and stretched out a hand for him to shake. "Can we make a deal then? You stop being a huge jerk long enough to get us to Rienka, and you get to keep this ship and sail off into the sunset?"

Judan hesitated. His keen gaze darted between Uncle Reigh's outstretched hand and the rest of us, as though he were trying to assess whether or not the rest of us were onboard for this truce. If Violet's distrustful scowl and Thatcher's foreboding frown were any indication, that answer was a hard no.

Judan gave an exaggerated, groaning sigh as he shook Uncle Reigh's hand once. "So be it."

"Excellent. So glad to be back on the same side," Uncle Reigh mumbled sourly. He rubbed the back of his neck and jaw, muttered something under his breath, and then started for the door. "Keep an eye on our new *ally*, would you? I'm going to have a word with the first mate."

Uncle Reigh didn't even look my way as he walked by. I had always thought there was something sad about him, like a foggy dimness in his eyes that never seemed to go away. And looking at him now, I could tell the dark circles under his eyes were heavier than ever. It was as though that dimness was spreading and becoming more intense.

Was that ... my fault? Because I'd snuck onboard this mission? Or was it from dealing with Judan? They had been real friends before, hadn't they? Maybe the betrayal was taking a toll.

I didn't know, but there was a distinct sense of anguish in the way he trudged for the door and left without another word. From across the room, I noticed I wasn't the only one keeping an eye on him. Violet's gaze tracked him, too, and her smooth, porcelain-perfect brow crinkled slightly. Her lips pressed together, and it almost seemed like she might follow him.

Then our eyes met.

Instantly, that worried look faded like dew at sunrise. She swallowed hard, quickly turning away to go check on Lukani.

Hmmm.

I might be just a kid in the eyes of all these other, admittedly more battle-seasoned people, but I knew that look. I'd seen it many times before, ever since I was a child. And I knew exactly what it meant.

Because that was the same look my mother gave my father when he was having nightmares about his time in the wars.

PART FOUR

CLARKE

12

CHAPTER TWELVE

"Clarke! Clarke, it's time to wake up now!"

My eyes flew open and my whole body jolted. I sat up, the old wooden bed creaking under my weight. A sound I knew all too well—just like the distant sounds of laughter and footsteps echoing through the cavernous halls. I-I knew the smells of fresh ink, old parchment, freshly brewed chamomile tea, and the soothing aroma of burning incense. The small room was crowded with two other beds like mine, a bookshelf loaded down with tomes and papers on the far wall, and a small writing desk piled high with more texts.

This was my room.

I-I ... I was home.

Chills swept over me, tingling from the top of my head all the way down my spine to my toes. How was this possible? Where were Noa, Kaili, and the others?

Had it all just been a dream?

No. No, that couldn't be. I had been with them, traveling to—

"Clarke? Are you coming?" A cheery feminine voice called again.

My heart gave a desperate, wrenching lurch in my chest. Oh, Fates. Was that Zuri? I hadn't seen her in so long, not since ...

Emotion like a white-hot ball of steel lodged in my throat and made my eyes well. It was her. It had to be. She was here. She was okay. Her voice sounded so close, as though she were right outside in the hallway.

And I had to see her.

"Zuri!" I called out as I threw the blankets off me and seized my glasses off the big stack of books right next to my bed. "W-Wait up! I'm coming!"

I didn't even bother putting on my shoes as I dashed for the open doorway. I skidded to a halt, looking both ways down the narrow, twisting hall. But there was no one there. Not a soul in sight.

"Zuri? Where are you? Is this some kind of a joke? You better not jump out and scare me! I mean it!" I called out as I slowly made my way forward.

No one answered. Somewhere in the distance I heard voices again. The giggles and laughs of other wards like me. They were all coming from the direction of the nearest intersection where four halls all met.

I walked faster, dashing around more stacks of books that stood in piles like stalagmites on the floor and against the walls. Nothing out of the ordinary there. In fact, everything about this place was exactly the way I remembered it. The faux windows made of colorful glass were enchanted with dwarven runes that glowed to give the effect of daylight. The stone walls were all hand cut from the heart of the sea cliffs, and I knew where every little flaw, hidden seashell, or tiny fossil was.

My pace slowed and I stopped right in the middle of the common room where all the halls that led to the ward dormitories met. Toys and blocks were scattered across the many wool rugs spread out over the floor. A fire smoldered low in the small hearth.

And my heart ... ached. It was as though everyone had just vanished right where they sat. Cups of hot tea on the low tables still steamed. Books were spread open alongside ledgers for practicing writing. But the other wards, my brothers and sisters, were all gone.

I swallowed hard, eyes watering as I slowly turned around to search every darkened corner. "Zuri?" I rasped. "Are you there?"

Another chorus of giggles, nearly ghostly and faint, echoed from the larger hall that led off into the rest of the library. That cold chill raced down my spine again. My heartbeat skipped.

Slowly and cautiously, I stepped toward that hall. My hands shook, every nerve drawn tight, as I stared down the darkened depths of that path. The rune-lit windows were all dark that way. I couldn't see more than about ten feet or so. Something wasn't right. Every shred of common sense screamed in my head, warning bells telling me this was wrong. I shouldn't go any closer. Something terrible was waiting for me down there.

But ... what about Zuri? What if she was down there? What if she needed my help?

I took another step. Then another. My heart pounded, and I stared straight ahead, not even daring to blink. Sweat ran down my brow as I paused at the threshold. I sucked in a deep breath, and prepared to take a step into that hall.

Thunk!

My head cracked off something solid in front of me and I stumbled backward. What the—? Was that glass?

I hedged forward again, arms outstretched to feel for whatever invisible forcefield I'd just crashed headlong into. My fingertips brushed something cool, solid, and crystal-clear blocking the entire passage into that hall. It really was glass, almost like a window, but so clear I couldn't even see it unless I pushed my hands against it.

Where had this come from? I had never seen it there before. Was this some sort of magic, or ...?

Light flickered and flashed behind me suddenly, catching my eye in the reflection of that glass pane that blocked the only way out. A wave of heat rippled across my back and I whirled around to find it all—the dormitory halls and common room—engulfed in flames. The fire rose, crackling and snapping with a blistering heat that made me cringe back against the glass. Oh, gods! What had happened?!

Out! I had to get out!

I beat my hands on the glass and yelled for help. But it didn't so much as splinter or flinch under my fists. Black smoke began to choke the room and I coughed, eyes stinging as I looked around for something I could use to break the glass. A chair or maybe an iron poker from the fireplace.

"Hello?" A feminine voice called out suddenly.

I turned back, beating my hands on the glass again as I squinted through the curling smoke. There ... there was someone. A figure stood on the other side of the glass only a few feet away. Small and slender, I could barely make out the features of a girl with long hair and pointed ears. Kaili? No ... she seemed to be wearing armor of some sort. She was shorter than Kaili, too. And even though I couldn't see any of the details of her face, the shape was different.

Whoever this was, I didn't know them.

But somehow I just knew she was my only chance. My last hope.

"Help! Please, you have to get me out of here!" I yelled as I hit the glass again.

"Hello? Is someone there?" The girl's head tilted to one side curiously. Almost like she couldn't quite see me. She moved closer, a hand outstretched like she was going to touch the other side of that glass pane.

"I-I'm here! Please! I can't get out!" I yelled.

She hesitated, and for the briefest instant, I caught a glimpse of something hanging around her neck by the light of the flames that roared at my back. A pendant no bigger than the size of my thumb hung right in the center of her chest, and it glowed as brightly as a star in the dark. She reached for it, closing her hand around it as she kept staring straight in my direction.

But it was as though she couldn't see me at all.

"I don't understand," she called out. "Where am I? What's going on? What does this mean?"

"I'm right here! Please—you have to do something! I can't get through!" I screamed as the flames suddenly caught the back of my tunic and I fell against that crystalline barrier, beating my fists against it until they went bloody. Every hit left crimson smears on the glass. "HELP ME!"

And then, with a flash of flame and surge of agony, it was too late.

"CLARKE!"

Someone smacked me hard across the cheek and I gasped, eyes flying open to the cool and calm of a familiar waterside campsite. Noa and Kaili stared down at me, their expressions riddled with concern.

O-Oh. Oh no. I had to ... oh, gods.

My whole body shook as I floundered to sit up and crawl a few feet away from my bedroll. I barely managed to stagger to my feet before I threw up.

"Clarke, it's okay. It was just a nightmare," Kaili whispered gently as she hurried over and stood beside me, rubbing a hand on my back while I retched. "You were tossing and turning, screaming in your sleep. But we couldn't get you to wake up. It's okay now. You're safe here."

I stood hunched over with my hands on my knees, still spitting to try to get the awful taste out of my mouth as I shivered. My clothes and shaggy white hair were absolutely drenched with sweat. Every muscle in my body ached like I'd spent the whole day helping Noa haul timber around.

"Here. Rinse your mouth." Noa appeared on my other side with a waterskin, offering for me to take a drink.

I did. And after a few turns of swishing and spitting, I finally gulped down some of the water. It soothed the scorching pain in my throat and made my pulse gradually start to slow.

Kaili was right. It was just a dream. A nightmare. It hadn't been real.

But, spirits divine, it certainly felt that way.

"Kaili, see if you can find him a dry shirt. I'll keep an eye on him," Noa insisted, and I could hear the unspoken, guarded concern in his tone. He just wanted her to go so he could talk to me alone.

I guess Kaili figured that out pretty quickly, too, because she shot him a stubborn glare before storming silently away.

Biting down hard, I managed to hold it together until she was well out of earshot. Then I bent over and retched again. All my insides seemed to twist and bind up at once, like someone wringing out a washcloth. I whimpered and coughed, spitting until Noa handed me the waterskin again so I could rinse my mouth.

"You've been acting strangely since we returned to the village," he pointed out, fixing me with one of his piercing, super-intense stares, as though he were reading my mind.

Had I? We had only been traveling for a couple of days, and in that time, I had tried not to let it show. To keep my head down and share in the work as much as possible. But that vision of the boy from the Compendium, clad in black armor and wearing the symbol of Enais branded on his hand, had been replaying in my head almost constantly. I didn't understand what it meant, or why I was even seeing it in the first place.

And now ... this. A new nightmare. More questions. No answers.

I took another drink from the waterskin before handing it back to Noa and wiping my mouth. "I'm sorry. I'm fine."

I could hear the disbelief in his tone, even if I was too embarrassed to look him in the eye. "Is that so?"

For a few painfully awkward seconds, neither of us spoke. Then, at last, Noa let out a deep breath of resignation. He slung the waterskin's leather strap over his shoulder and put his hands on his hips. He stared down at me with what I could only interpret as parental-ish disapproval. Some of the scholars at the library had looked at me that way, as well—usually when I had done something wrong or clumsy again.

"I'm not going to force you to be honest with me, but I can't do anything to help you unless you are." He cut straight to the chase. "I'm not a fool. I know trauma when I see it. I've survived my fair share of it, as well. I can assure you that holding it in and refusing to deal with it will not make things any easier. It will consume you, overwhelm you, and may even destroy you."

I sank back on my heels, still avoiding his probing stare. Swallowing hurt, but it was all I could do to keep the emotion from breaking through.

"Is it because you're afraid we will tell you to leave?" he asked.

Every muscle in my body locked up solid. Slowly, my gaze lifted to stare up at him. I'd never felt so small. So pathetic. So helpless. All I could do was nod once, slowly and shakily.

Noa's mouth mashed into a dissatisfied line. "That won't happen. You are one of us now. Your problems are ours."

I cringed. He sounded so sure about that. So steady and certain. I couldn't imagine Noa ever saying anything he didn't mean. He wasn't one to say much of anything unless it was absolutely necessary. But this was ... dangerous. I hadn't been completely truthful with him or Kaili from the beginning. Even if my memory of what had happened at the library was spotty, I had never told them what I could remember.

And now he would know why.

I clenched my teeth as Noa took a step closer and put a hand on my shoulder, as though trying to reassure me. It only made me feel even more childish and pitiful for not being honest with them. They had been nothing but kind and accepting. And I was holding back.

"I-I think ... I might have something to do with what happened to the library," I heard myself confess, my voice scraping and shaking over every bitter word. "I don't remember what happened, or who attacked it, or how I ended up in the water. And it scares me so badly, Noa. Because I always remember. *Always*. All I can recall is fire, screams, and a book I wasn't supposed to touch. I can't even remember what it said, but I know I went too far. I ... I think I read it."

"What kind of book was it?" he asked quietly.

I shook my head. "I-I'm not even sure. It had a symbol on the front, like an eye. The scholars called it the Dragon's Eye. But they wouldn't tell me what was written in it, or why it seemed to ... call to me."

Noa's eyebrows rose. "*Call* to you?"

"I know it sounds crazy," I blurted, unable to keep all the frantic words from spilling out now that I'd started. "I didn't even say anything to the scholars for the longest time because I thought it was just all in my head. I do have a lot of things in there—in my head, that is—so it's not unimaginable that I'd hear things now and again. Sort of like echoes of stuff I'd read, or seen, or heard. But this was different because it felt like it was calling to me. It even happened when I was asleep. I couldn't think about anything else, and it felt like I was losing myself to it. I shouldn't have gone down there to find it, but I—"

Noa held up a hand to stop me suddenly. "Is this what has been troubling you again? This book?"

I hesitated, sucking in a few panicked breaths before I realized I'd been rambling. "No. I guess not. At least, I don't think so. But when we were at the village, I saw something else. It gave me that same feeling like when I saw that book for the first time."

His thin mouth locked into a frown as he set his steely gaze upon me intensely. "What did you see?"

I tried to take a few more breaths, to calm down, before I let my mind flash back to those few, fleeting seconds on the shore. "I saw someone from the library. I think he was another ward like me, but the scholars didn't put him with the rest of us. They kept him separated. I'm not sure why. But he was there, on the beach, walking toward me in black armor. It wasn't a dream, though. More like a vision. It was like seeing him there in the moment, like I'd gone back in time. It almost seemed like he could see me, too. I think he was the one that did it—the one who burned everything."

Noa licked his lips and drew back some, his expression a strange mixture of shock and thoughtfulness, as though he were trying to figure all this out on the spot. Good luck with that. I'd been mulling it over for days now and I still couldn't figure out why I had seen that boy.

"Did you see him? A boy in black armor on the beach that day when the warship attacked?" I asked, almost not wanting to know the answer.

Unfortunately, I saw it in Noa's eyes before he ever said a word. A sense of knowing ... and fear. "Yes."

Gods and Fates. That meant it really was a vision. I had seen him, even though I wasn't there when it happened. I'd somehow read the history of that place.

How?

And why?

The sudden rush of confusion, of a million questions, all hitting my brain at once made me stagger and my vision go starry. Noa caught me by the arm and held me steady as I struggled to breathe. Real—it had all been real. I'd seen an actual vision of the past.

"I take it you have never had something like this happen before?" he asked, keeping his voice much quieter now.

All I could do was wheeze and shake my head again.

Noa stood with me in silence, but I could practically feel his emotions shifting as he processed all of this information. "And tonight, you dreamt of him again? You were crying out for help in your sleep."

"N-No," I managed to rasp. "It wasn't him. It was something different, but it still felt so real. I was back in the Compendium, in the rooms where I lived with all the other wards. I couldn't find any of them, even though I kept hearing their voices. It's like they were invisible, or just ghosts. Then it all started to burn. I couldn't escape. There was this barrier over the way out. I could see past it, but I couldn't break through." I hesitated, my voice catching at the thought of that girl beyond the glass. The gleaming pendant around her neck. Should I mention that, too? That part had felt different from the rest of the nightmare. Almost like she was outside my mind somehow, and was peering into it like someone peeking through a window. It didn't make any sense at all.

"Perhaps it was only a normal nightmare, then," Noa said, that sense of calm and certainty back in his voice. "It's perfectly reasonable for you to have them, given what you've been through."

"Y-Yeah." I rubbed at my temples and eyes under the frame of my glasses. Maybe he was right. I was just having nightmares about the fire. It was normal. Nothing to worry about. That girl was probably just my mind trying to rationalize what had happened to Zuri and that's why I'd heard her voice, at first.

"I need to ask you not to speak of the boy in armor to Kaili or the others. Those of us who saw him during the attack have discussed what can be done if he returns, but there is no need to frighten anyone else." Noa patted my shoulder and tipped his head back toward the camp.

"Right. Okay," I agreed.

"If this individual really was a ward at the Compendium Library like you, then it is possible he may recognize you if we do cross paths with him again. But I don't think what happened was your fault, Clarke. I don't believe he followed you to us. Nar'Haleen's military forces have become far more aggressive lately, and they are always on the lookout for anyone they can use to further their cause. Their soldiers and warships attack and murder without any cause." Noa went on explaining as he followed me back toward the camp. "We may finally be approaching a boiling point when Nar'Haleen attempts to retake Damaria and Rienka. But that is no one's fault—especially not yours."

I knew he was right. I had no proof that the attack on the village had anything to do with me at all. It was just a feeling, the haunting sense that someone somewhere was watching me. Like a silent phantom peering over my shoulder, observing everything I did and said.

I just had no idea who.

Or why.

Or if that feeling would ever go away.

13

CHAPTER THIRTEEN

The days passed with grueling exhaustion and constant anxiety as we made our way along the coastline to the west. Every tiny speck or disturbance on the horizon immediately drove us inland to hide and wait while Noa and a few of the other warriors watched from the cover of the trees. The idea of another warship coming after us put dread like an open sore in my gut. The constant terror made my muscles feel cold and achy, like I had some sort of fever. We wouldn't survive another attack like that. We would have to run and hide, praying the soldiers didn't find us. And I honestly didn't know if we would stand any chance of getting away or not.

If the solemn look of focused anger and steely determination on Noa's face was any indication, though, the chances probably weren't good.

After three full days of traveling that way, we came to a place where the mouth of a canal fed out into the ocean. We turned and followed along it, leaving the ocean's broad, rippling surface far behind. After that, the stress and silent anxiety in our group seemed to ease a little. The canal was deep enough for the hippocampus to continue carrying our small, makeshift barges along, but it was far too shallow for a warship to follow us.

And I started to hope.

Maybe we stood a chance, after all. If we could follow this canal all the way to where the massive port city of Uru'Nai was located just a little farther south, then we might not have to worry about any more of the royal military forces coming after us at all. Er, well, as far as I could tell, anyway. My understanding was limited to the things I'd read and maps I had seen in the library. But I had a pretty good idea of where we were now, and Uru'Nai should only be another day or two ahead of us. We could make it. We just had to keep being careful.

The mood had definitely grown lighter and more optimistic as we all gathered around small evening campfires on the bank of the canal. A few people had volunteered to collect food for the night, and were fishing from the banks with nets or diving for shellfish in the shallower waters. Kaili was busy tending to the hippocampi, making sure they had plenty of kelp to eat and checking them over for signs that their saddles and harnesses might be chafing anywhere.

I had gotten used to helping unload the bedrolls, cooking tools, and blankets from our wagon-barges, but Noa gave my arm a nudge as he walked by and muttered, "Let's get more firewood."

"Right. Okay," I agreed and fell in step behind him as he left the narrow, stony beach and started into the jungle.

With a spear slung over his back with a simple leather strap, Noa picked a careful route ahead through the trees. The forest floor squished under my feet, carpeted with layers of wet fallen leaves and thick moss. The late evening sun barely managed to break the dense canopy overhead, and we wouldn't have long until night fell. Even the eerie calls of the jungle birds were beginning to fall silent, giving way to the melodious chirps of hundreds of tiny frogs.

These sounds and smells were still so alien to me—so different from the home I'd known in the library. It felt like I had stepped off the edge of the world into a different universe altogether. One where I still didn't quite fit in. I couldn't move as silently as Noa, who practically made no sound at all as he moved through the undergrowth. He stopped every now and then to pick up a fallen branch or small log, and handed it off to me.

"Any more bad dreams?" he asked quietly, keeping his back turned as he prowled ahead.

"No," I answered, and hesitated for a moment. "But, uh, there is something I wanted to ask you about."

He turned and arched an eyebrow at me expectantly. "Yes?"

I shifted the weight of the pile of wood in my arms and stammered, "I-I, um, I wondered if, when we get to the city, if you knew of a way I could find out if anyone else from the library survived. Other than me, I mean. I know you said there were no survivors found inside the library, but I just thought maybe someone else washed up like I did—only, you know, somewhere else. Or maybe they escaped during the attack and fled to the city."

His lips pursed thoughtfully. "I suppose we can try to find out. The city praetor may have some knowledge, or at the very least, may want to speak with you about what happened."

"O-Oh. Yeah, you're probably right." I shifted uncomfortably and looked away. I hadn't considered that, but Noa did have a very good point. If no other survivor of the attack on the Compendium Library had come forward to tell any government officials about what happened, then I might be the only word they had to go on. I might be the only one who had lived to give any testimony about it.

Of course ... that might not be a good thing, either. If it was Nar'Haleen's own military forces who attacked it in the first place, then going to a city official might just paint a big target on my back as the only evidence of foul play.

Saying nothing didn't feel like the right thing to do, though. I frowned down at the big pile of sticks and branches in my arms. Even if it was dangerous, I wanted to know if anyone else had survived. The other wards, scholars, and even High Inquisitor Bellavora—I needed to know if any of my former family was still alive.

Noa continued on, gathering more sticks and tucking them under his own arm now that mine were full, and I stumbled along at a distance, my thoughts still a whirlwind of worry and doubt. We wound through the tree trunks, working silently and swiftly, as the daylight began to fade. Noa spotted a large, downed branch and immediately set to work hacking it up into smaller, easier to carry pieces with a hatchet he had brought along.

I stayed close, inspecting some of the large, moss-covered boulders that stood nearby.

Their smooth, black surfaces had almost been swallowed up completely by moss and ferns. But I could barely make out the faint, weathered designs of something that seemed to be engraved into them. Were those ... faces? Strange. Was this part of some ancient relic?

I turned back toward Noa so I could ask.

He stood only a few yards away, his face completely pale and his eyes as wide as two moons. "Clarke," he whispered so quietly I could hardly hear him. "Do. Not. Move."

I froze in place, not even daring to blink or take in a breath. My heart hammered against my ribs. I stared at Noa, watching beads of sweat form on his brow as he slowly moved toward me, taking one extremely slow step at a time. With his eyes trained on the ground around my feet, he squeezed the handle of his hatchet so tightly it made his knuckles blanch white and veins stand out against the skin of his forearms. His nostrils flared as he sucked in slow, deep breaths—as though he were steeling himself for something awful.

Like a fight.

At first, I didn't see it. Then, as a light breeze stirred in the tree branches overhead, allowing a shaft of the fleeting sunlight through the jungle canopy. It sparkled off the damp leaves around my feet, and off a thin silver wire laid out in a loop and partially covered by the dead foliage. I spotted a second set about two paces to my left. Then a third placed farther out on the right. And another ... and another.

Oh ... oh gods.

My legs began to go numb and my knees trembled as I slowly looked back up at Noa. There must have been dozens of them. Were these ... traps? Like for animals? Sweet Fates, how had I managed to get this far into them without stepping on one?

"I can't get to you. There are too many in the way," Noa whispered again, his jawline locked in a tense look of earnest. "On my count, you are going to run to your right as fast as you can. Do you understand?"

I nodded shakily.

"Are you ready?" he held up three fingers like he was going to start counting.

Oh, sweet holy gods above, no. I was absolutely not ready. I shut my eyes tightly and tried to take in a deep breath. Don't think. Just do.

I nodded again.

"One ... two ... thr—"

A single, small stick fell from the stack in my arms. I watched it fall as though the whole universe had begun moving in slow motion. My body immediately jerked in response, trying to catch it before it hit the ground and touched any of those wires.

TWANG!

A desperate yell tore from my throat and I pawed at the air, searching for anything to grab onto as I was snatched upward. Leaves and sticks flew everywhere. My arms and legs flailed and my glasses flew off the end of my nose as the world suddenly spun out of control and I sailed through the air like a rag doll.

"CLARKE!" Noa shouted.

I only caught fleeting glimpses of his panicked face as I dangled like a strung-up chicken, swinging slowly back and forth ... upside down. But one quick look was all it took.

I spotted a flash of movement right behind Noa an instant before his expression went slack. *CRACK!* A sound, like metal meeting bone, made my blood go cold. Noa let out a low gurgle of pain an instant before his knees buckled and he dropped to the ground, limp and completely still.

Gods—NO!

Had someone just killed Noa?! I-I couldn't even stop myself from spinning long enough to be sure. What the heck was happening?!

I screamed out again, wriggling and flailing against the wire that bound both my ankles together. I had to get free. I had to help Noa. I tried curling up to get my hands on the wires, anything to try prying myself free. But it was no good. I had nothing, no weapon to even try cutting through the metal wire. It was wrapped so tightly around my legs my feet were already going numb.

Trapped. I was trapped.

"No! Stop! Leave him alone!" I shouted as the dark shape stood over Noa. The slim, small figure of a person holding some sort of weapon crouched over his motionless body and made a low, hissing sound. It clutched something like a club in one hand, and grabbed a fistful of Noa's hair with the other.

I couldn't tell much else as I hung, still swinging and slowly spinning back and forth several feet off the ground. Then I felt it—pain like a sharp bite exploded through the back of my head.

CRACK!

My whole body went slack. My arms dangled, and I could feel something warm and wet running down the back of my head. I barely managed another rasping, slurred cry before everything began to grow dim. I was drifting, fading, slipping far away. And then it was too late.

I was lost in the dark ... again.

MY EYELIDS FLUTTERED AS SOMETHING COLD AND WET TOUCHED MY BARE FOOT. I gasped suddenly, jerking awake and lifting my head to stare out into ... nothing.

I sat, staring out into complete darkness all around me. Darkness—and the stench of something absolutely terrible. Like old soured, sweaty laundry. Or like that time Zuri tripped over our chamber pot and it spilled all over the bedroom floor.

I shuddered, and immediately bit down hard against the flare of pain that thrummed through me all the way to the tips of my bare toes. My head ... auuuugh, it was absolutely killing me. Not that I wasn't used to headaches, but this was enough to make my stomach wrench. Every heartbeat seemed to make my brain throb against my skull, like my whole head might explode at any moment.

Up—I had to get up. Right now. I had to find Noa and—

I tried to move, to stand up, but I couldn't even wiggle my arms. Oh no ... I-I was tied up.

No. No, no, no. This wasn't happening. I could get out. I had to! I twisted and struggled, trying to move, but someone had bound my wrists behind my back around something like a wooden beam or pole. The ropes wrapped around my ankles were so tight my feet had gone tingly and numb.

Think. I had to think. There had to be a way out of this—wherever it was.

"Noa?" I whispered. Maybe he was somewhere close by, tied up like I was.

No answer.

I took a few shaking breaths. Then I called out again, a little louder. "Noa!"

Something moved in the dark. A scuffling sound like fabric against stone. Then a low, hoarse voice whispered, "Keep it down, kid. You don't want them coming back in here any sooner, trust me."

I sat, frozen and bewildered, and stared in the direction of the voice. I couldn't see who it was, but it sounded masculine. Or maybe that was just because it was deep and a little scratchy.

"Wh-Who ...?" I tried to ask, but my voice kept shaking. I shut my eyes tightly. Sometimes that helped to get my eyes adjusted to night vision. It didn't help this time, though. Wherever we were, there was absolutely no light.

"Who am I?" The voice guessed, their words twanged with a thick accent I had never heard before. "I'm a prisoner, like you. Or a meal, depending on how you look at it."

A ... *meal?* What the heck was that supposed to mean?

"I don't understand," I whispered back, forcing the words through chattering teeth. "Where are we? What's happening?"

There was a long, tense pause before the voice replied, speaking much more quietly than before, "I hate to be the one to tell you this, but we're, uh, we're in a goblin cave. As for what's happening—I guess you could say we're in temporary storage. That's just my best guess, though. They come and go to fetch a few people out at a time. No one they take ever comes back."

My breath caught and I flinched against my bonds. *Goblins?* Gods and Fates. I had only read about them a little, but it was enough to make my pulse kick into overdrive. The few myths I had read referred to them like mischievous little monsters born of ancient foul magic, long before the War of the Stones. Supposedly, they were reclusive and ruthlessly evil, preferring to live in smelly caves and hunt right at sunset so they could feed all through the night ... usually on naughty children who were out when they weren't supposed to be. But in all those texts, goblins had seemed more like a fairy tale than anything real. Like a scary story meant to keep kids from wandering off at night. Some of the legends said they stalked the canyons and dark places of the southern kingdoms, never caring what went on with the rest of the world. They only lived to hunt, feed, and squat in their caves.

And I was now on the menu.

My throat closed up as I struggled to breathe. Calm. I had to stay calm. And think. There had to be a way out. Something—anything—we could do to get away. Noa. I had to find Noa. He would have a plan. He always did.

The voice spoke up again, sounding a bit more earnest. "Listen, kid, I don't know you, but this might be the last chance either one of us has to ever see daylight again. If we're gonna make it out of here, we gotta work together, yeah?"

"First of all, I'm not a kid," I muttered.

"You look like one to me."

I frowned. "Well, I'm not, and how can I trust that you're—wait a second, you can *see* me?"

The voice gave a faint, proud chuckle. "Sure can. A little dark's no match for dwarven eyes. We were made for caves."

It was ... a dwarf? My mind tangled with that new information like a kitten wrestling in a ball of string. Of course, like most things, I had read about them. But dwarves weren't exactly common in the southern kingdoms. They came from the deep mountain halls much farther to the west, and supposedly they didn't often leave.

So, what was this one—he, I guess—doing here?

"Are you tied up, too?" I asked, trying to writhe my hands in my own bonds. It was no use, though. The ropes had been knotted tightly.

"Aye. It's not a big room, but there's wooden poles about five feet apart going up to the ceiling. That's where they've been tying folks. You're about two poles down from me, and it looks like they used regular ropes on you. Lucky," the dwarf explained. "Guess they knew I might just snap those buggers right off, so they tied me with metal chains."

Hope surged through me and I sat up a little straighter, my back braced against the pole. "Is there anyone else here with us? I was traveling with someone—an elven man with dark hair and tattoos on his face. Do you see him? Did they bring him here, too?"

"Aye, I saw him. But he's not here now," the dwarf confirmed, his tone becoming stiff and reluctant. "They, uh, they took him out not long ago."

Oh no. The goblins had taken Noa already? Where? Why? Oh gods, were they going to eat him?!

I struggled harder, jerking against the bonds around my wrists. I had to get out—I had to help him!

"Easy there, you'll hurt yourself. Or worse, you'll make a racket that'll bring them in here," the dwarf warned.

"I have to get out of here," I panted, staring out into the dark void for something—anything—I could see. But there was nothing.

Just that voice in the blackness.

"I agree. We both do. And if you're willing, I think we can help one another out. I've an idea that might get us out." He made another grunting sound, like he was shifting around, too. "What do you say? Shall we give it a go?"

I took in a few more heaving breaths, bowing my head. There was no other choice. I didn't know this guy. I didn't know if I could trust him, or if I was just trading one trap for another. But I didn't have a choice.

I set my jaw, summoning every shred of nerve I had left.

"Okay," I agreed. "Tell me what to do."

14

CHAPTER FOURTEEN

"Okay, this is gonna sound a bit nutty," the dwarf said, still keeping his voice hushed. "But since they bound you up in ropes, I've got a little trick that can get you out. Once you're loose, you can let me go. Then we're off."

I swallowed against the stiff, bitter flavor of dread in my throat. "Uh, okay. What do I do?"

"Nothing yet. Just hold still. He's a bit jumpy around people he doesn't know. He might nip at you some, but it's nothing to worry about," he assured me.

Wait—what? Nip at me? What the heck was he talking about?

Before I could ask anything else, I heard the dwarf guy begin making soft, *pspsps* sounds. Sort of like the noise you made to call a cat. "Aye, there you are. Go on, then. Give those ropes a little nibble, would you? That's a good boy," he chuckled with approval.

Nothing answered. No animal chattering. No mewing. No barking. Nothing. Not even a squeak.

Great. So I was trapped down here with a dwarf who had lost his mind. Somehow, given my past run of luck, that didn't surprise me at all.

But the feeling of soft tugging on the ropes that bound my hands? That almost sent me into a full-on screaming fit of panic. I cringed away as far as my bonds would let me, biting down hard to keep from screaming. The feel of tiny whiskers, fur, and nibbling teeth made my whole body cringe up.

I guess the dwarven guy could tell I was a breath away from freaking out, because he whispered frantically, "Easy there, kid. He won't hurt you. Calm thoughts. Deep breaths."

"Wh-Wh-What is that?" I rasped in hushed terror.

"Just 'ole Trick. He's a good boy," he answered. "Very smart, too. Aren't you, Tricksy?"

Trick? That was a name? When he said it before, I just thought he meant something magic, or maybe a—

The ropes around my wrists suddenly went slack. Something like tiny little feet scurried up my back, across my shoulder, and jumped down into my lap. A tail. I definitely felt a tail. Not a fluffy, soft one, either. It was cold and bare. Oddly skin-like. Almost as though it were ...

"Holy Gods, is that a *rat?!*" I wheeze-whisper-screamed and flailed away, launching the tiny creature somewhere into the dark. It let out a dismayed squeak of alarm and I shuddered, brushing off my legs as I felt down to the ropes that tied my ankles.

"Hey now! You be nice to my Trick. He's just got you loose, hasn't he?" the dwarf fussed quietly. "Now hurry it up, boy. You'll have a trickier time undoing my bonds with those half-useless human eyes of yours."

He wasn't wrong about that. It took me several minutes to untie my own legs, and I couldn't resist a sigh of relief as I felt the rush of blood and feeling return to them. No time to celebrate, though. On my hands and knees, I crawled forward over the ground while the dwarf gave me directions to where he was bound up. The stone was cold under my palms, and I could feel an occasional object or wet spot along the way.

"A little farther. More to the left now. Oops—that's a bone, don't worry about it. Now more to the left," he coaxed.

Then my hand struck something warm and very much alive. A large, hairy, bare foot.

"Got me," the dwarf's whisper came with a sigh of relief. "Now, come around here to my hands. You gotta look for the link that's a clasp. It'll feel a bit different than the rest. Go on. And hurry it up!"

I tried. But fumbling around in the total dark like that, feeling along a long length of chain for one link that was supposed to be different from the rest, wasn't easy. My hands shook, adrenaline surging through my system as my frustration grew. Curse it, why couldn't I find it?

Suddenly, my whole body locked up solid. The dwarf's encouraging whispers stopped. My heartbeat thudded to a halt.

Voices. There were more voices. High-pitched, scratchy ones. I couldn't understand anything they said, not from this far away, but I could tell they were coming closer. Oh gods, were those the goblins? Were they coming for us now?

"You gotta find it," the dwarf whispered frantically. "Right now, boy. Find it!"

"I-I'm trying." I searched faster, feeling along each link in the chain until my fingertips brushed over something. A flaw in the metal? No—a hinge!

I pressed it, and the chain popped loose.

"Good! You got it! Now stand up, we haven't got much time." The dwarf stirred, probably working at unlocking his feet himself now that his hands were free.

I shambled up, as well. But with no special awareness of anything around me, and my feet still a bit numb from being tied so tightly, I wobbled and staggered. Then a rough, much stronger hand grabbed my wrist and held me steady.

"Easy does it, human. Come with me," he urged and basically dragged me forward into the dark.

I could tell by the angle that he was, in fact, a lot shorter than I was. But he was also considerably stronger, and managed to fling me up against a bare stone wall and hold me there with one arm.

"You stay right here. Don't move. Don't make a sound," he warned. "We've got company."

He was right. The scratchy, shrill voices were much closer now. They squabbled and bickered like two angry birds, and I could finally make out some of what they said.

"Fools! We has warned you many times! No setting the traps too close to the big water! Now the

food will know we are here! They will suspect. Come looking. Find your paths and hunt you here! The big'uns will be angry and eat us instead!" one of them squawked.

"No!" A second voice objected in a squealing whine. *"We was careful! So careful! Covered our tracks extra good."*

Okay, I was no expert in the many diverse races of the known world. I'd done a lot of reading, sure, but my first-hand experience was minimal at best. Even so, I was willing to bet my life that whatever was talking was not even close to human. Or elf. Or even dwarf, for that matter.

And whatever they were, goblin or otherwise, they were getting closer by the second.

We didn't have weapons. I couldn't see. And the only objects in the room were some ropes, chains, and apparently a few bones.

Not good.

My sort-of friend spat a dwarven word I recognized ... because it was a curse. All the kids at the library liked using dwarven curses, I guess because they sounded a lot cruder than the elven or common ones. "Okay. I got this. You stay put, yeah?" he growled quietly.

I nodded, hoping he would see it. You know, since apparently the pitch-black down here wasn't an issue for him.

I guess it worked because the next thing I knew, that group of squabbling voices erupted into a chorus of angry hissing and dismayed yelps of pain. Scuffling, thuds, cracks, and yowls sounded all around me, and I didn't dare to move a single muscle. Gods and Fates, what was happening? Were we winning? Or ...?

Silence.

Then a few footsteps and a scraping, dragging sound went all the way past me before stopping with another thud.

"Blasted goblin scum," the dwarf muttered angrily. "Didn't even have a decent weapon on 'em."

"It really was goblins?" I sputtered in horror. "B-But I thought ... I thought they were just made up."

"Obviously not. World's a strange, twisty place, isn't it? These gobbies must have a little more sense than the others, though. They knew right where to put their snares and not get caught. Explains why we've not seen any sign of them in the area."

We? Was he part of a larger group, too? I was about to ask when I felt him grab onto my wrist again and force something into my hand. It felt suspiciously like a wooden club. Oh dear.

"I'm not so good with weapons," I tried to warn him ahead of time.

He barked a gruff laugh. "I figured as much. It's a club. You hit stuff with it as hard as you can. Not much technique needed there, human. If a goblin can figure it out, surely you can."

"Actually, uh, my name is Clarke."

He paused, and I could practically feel his gaze on me like an invisible force, sizing me up from head to foot. "I'm Traegan," he finally sighed. "We got a long way to go to get out of here. But I got an idea for that too. You can't see spit in your own eye down here, so I'm gonna tie a rope around your waist, yeah? Drag you along after me so you don't go staggering off into the abyss. Sound good?"

I bobbed my head. "Yeah. Thank you. But, um, I-I can't just leave."

"And why not? You like it down here in gobbie-filth?" he balked.

"No! No, it's just ... I can't leave my friend. Please, we have to find him. We have to get him out of here, too," I begged. "He saved my life not long ago. I can't just walk away from him now."

More silence. At last, Traegan let out another deep, grumbly sigh. He muttered a few more dwarven curses as he roughly tied something—a rope—around my waist. "Fine. We can go on for a bit and see if we can find him, but I'm telling you now, it's not likely we will. At least, not still livin' anyway."

My heart sank. I knew he was right. I had no idea how long we had been down here, or how long ago the goblins had taken Noa away to be fed to, well, presumably the other goblins.

But I knew Noa. He was stronger than anyone I'd ever met before. If anyone could survive down here, even at these odds, it was him.

And I owed it to him to try to help any way I could.

Traegan moved fast for someone who, based on what little I could tell in the dark, must have been about half my size. He was also totally silent when he walked, and the only way I could keep any track of him at all was thanks to the rope he'd tied around me like a dog leash. Not the most dignified way to get around, but since he was right about my inability to see anything down in this gods-forsaken cave, I didn't have much of a choice.

Truth be told, I didn't know if I could trust this guy at all. Yes, he had helped me escape. And yes, he had taken care of the goblins who seemed to be the ones that had abducted us in the first place. However, I had no way of knowing if he actually intended to help me find Noa, or if he was just saying that so I'd go along with him willingly.

I was taking this entirely on faith.

"How did you get captured?" I asked, still keeping my voice down as we made our way farther into the dark.

"Eh, well, I'm not really supposed to say. But seein' as how we might die, I guess it doesn't matter. I was running a secret-y sort of mission, observation of enemy forces up and down the coast and in and out of the local ports," he explained.

"You mean you were spying on the Nar'Haleenan military?" I couldn't disguise my surprise.

He made a scoffing sound. "You could say that, but believe it or not, they're not the worst thing slinking around these parts. Anyway, we had a little skirmish with these gobbies along one of our routes. I guess they'd figured out someone was using the old jungle roads and set up traps. They nabbed quite a few of us, but we didn't go down quietly. Took a lot of them out, too." He went silent for a moment, then cleared his throat a little. "How, uh, how did you get caught, eh?"

My insides bound up, tangling into a thousand aching knots at the thought. It sounded like he was being pretty straightforward. Maybe I should reciprocate. Besides, he might be right. If we died down here, what would it matter? "I was traveling with a group of people, as well. Our village was attacked by a Nar'Haleenan warship a few days ago, so we had to flee. We were trying to get to Uru'Nai."

He gave a snort of disbelief. "No offense, but you don't strike me as the villager-sort."

My ears burned a little. "I know. I'm not ... or I wasn't originally. They took me in."

"Where'd you come from originally, then?" Traegan pressed, not seeming to notice or care how uncomfortable this conversation had gotten for me.

"The Compendium Library." I looked away and chewed on the inside of my cheek, wondering far too late if I should have told him that.

"The library?" he sounded surprised. "Oh boy, well, if we do happen to make it out of here in one piece, I got some questions for ya. Word's beginning to spread about what happened there. We were supposed to investigate. Obviously, we didn't quite make it there, though."

"Someone sent you to investigate what happened to the library?" I couldn't hide my own shock, either. I had just assumed no one would really care all that much. The library hadn't been a token of any political power, after all. Generally, the crowns of the world seemed to only spare concern for things that could further their agendas and prosperity. A library that refused to take political sides wasn't going to be of much interest to them.

Or so I had assumed.

So who was it this guy worked for who actually cared? Someone in the Nar'Haleen royal court? Or from Damaria? Or maybe even Rienka?

"Aye," Traegan said. "But we can talk about it later. Keep your voice down. Smell that awful reek? Like someone's left rotting meat to stew in old vomit? That means we're getting close to the gobbies' nest."

15

CHAPTER FIFTEEN

Oh. I *definitely* smelled it. You couldn't miss a stench like that. It made my eyes tear up and my throat lurch. It took everything I had not to gag as I stumbled onward.

Granted, I still couldn't see anything. Not the walls I occasionally brushed against, or the rubble on the floor I kept tripping over, or even my own hand in front of my face. All I could do to orient was hang on to the rope tied around my waist that was connected to Traegan with one hand. In the other, I still held onto the club he'd given me. It made me feel slightly better to have it. But I sort of doubted I'd be much use with it when it came to a fight—especially since I was basically blind down here.

I had to try, though. Noa was counting on me.

The cold air in the cave made my skin prickle and the bottoms of my bare feet go numb. The farther we went, the stronger the smell became until I had to focus on breathing through my mouth just to get some relief. Even Traegan let out a few choking, gagging sounds whenever an air current sent a gust of it our way. Whatever that stench was coming from, I did not want to see it.

I tripped again, my toe catching on a pile of old bones that looked like the remains of some sort of animal. A deer, maybe?

I stopped, making the rope go taut between Traegan and I. Wait a second ... I could *see* again! I glanced all around, trying to figure out where the source of the light was coming from. Maybe there was a passage nearby that led to the surface, or torches we could grab, or—

A primal shout from straight ahead made me look up. In front of me, my much-shorter companion was still staring down the narrow tunnel ahead. We both stood, staring in shock, as a brilliant golden light seemed to be coming closer and closer. It was headed straight for us. At the center of it, I could see a figure running. A spirit coming to rescue us? Or a god?

Nope.

My mouth fell open as I recognized Noa running straight for us, his eyes wide and expression twisted in a look of pure terror. There were trails of fresh blood running from his neck and arms, and he had a curved sword clenched in one hand and a lit torch in the other. He waved it at us like a madman as he sprinted headlong in our direction.

What the—? Where did he—? How?!

"RUN!" Noa shouted about half a second before I noticed the dozen or so figures chasing after him down the tunnel.

Oh, sweet holy gods.

I gaped, paralyzed in horror at the small hoard of monsters storming straight at us. Some were short, stumpy, and frog-like with pudgy, round bodies and gangly legs. Goblins. But the others were taller, bulkier, and loped on their massive knuckles and feet like huge, slimy green gorillas. They thundered after Noa, yellow eyes gleaming in the torchlight and tusk-like teeth bared as they bellowed.

"TROLLS!" Traegan yelled in panic as he took off in the opposite direction.

Yep. Definitely time to run.

A jolt of terror put a surge of frantic energy through my body and I whirled around, my heart already in my throat. The rope between us went taut again, dragging me a few steps before I finally got my footing and dashed after him back into the dark. That tether was all I had to steer by until Noa caught up with us, torch in hand, and I got my first good look at the path ahead.

The cave twisted and turned, growing narrow and dipping up and down. We ducked around sparkling stalactites that dripped from the ceiling, and slid down steep inclines where the floor was wet and slippery. But we didn't dare stop or even look back.

The thundering cries of the trolls grew louder, shaking the tunnel as they pounded their fists against the ground and shoulder-checked the walls. It sent showers of dirt, rubble, and dust down over us. I let out a scream of alarm as something suddenly whizzed past my head, narrowly missing me and clattering off the stone floor ahead. An arrow? Were the goblins shooting at us?!

"There! Dead ahead! Take a left!" Traegan yelled.

I barely saw it in time to skid sideways and make a sharp left turn down an off-shooting passage. It was much smaller than the others—maybe too small for the trolls to chase us. A guy could hope, right?

With Noa still right on my heels, we darted along the twisting, snaking path. We squeezed between areas where debris had fallen in, nearly blocking the passage entirely. My eyes caught on fleeting details as we ran like mad, picking up on what I could have sworn looked like patterned engravings on the walls. And on the floors, too. We blurred by what almost looked like a cracked, crumbling archway. But that couldn't be it. It must be the shadows playing tricks on my already exhausted and overstressed brain.

The very second I had told myself I was just imagining things, the truth hit me like a wall to the face—literally.

I didn't notice that Traegan had stopped suddenly right in front of me, and I barreled right past him and smacked right off a massive, smooth stone wall that blocked the entire passage ahead. I bounced back and landed on my rear end in a cloud of dust. Sitting up, I heaved for every hysterical breath as I stared up at the wall. A dead end?

Oh no ...

Noa stopped right beside me, seizing me under a shoulder and hauling me back up onto my feet. He stood panting next to me, staring at the solid stone slab blocking our path with a pasty look of bewilderment. It really was a dead end. We were cornered. Trapped.

And behind us, the sounds of yipping, hissing, and snarling echoed down the tunnel. The goblins were still coming.

"STONES CURSE IT, YOU'VE GOT TO BE KIDDING ME!" TRAEGAN GROWLED AS HE GAVE THE wall a crack with the end of the large femur bone he was carrying like a weapon. It didn't do much but leave a little white mark on the surface of the stone.

"There has to be another way," Noa reasoned, still gasping for breath as he spun and began searching the tunnel nearby by the light of his torch.

"Aye, there *was*. Now it's blocked. And the only way out is back where we came—back through all those gobbies and trolls!" Traegan fumed.

By the flickering light of Noa's torch, I got my first real look at my new dwarven friend. He seemed a lot younger than I'd been expecting. After all, dwarves had much longer lifespans than most. Certainly a lot longer than humans, anyway. But besides being literally half my size, his features were smooth, youthful, and extremely squared. He had a broad nose and forehead, a head full of thick black hair that fell around his big ears, and only the short, stubbly beginnings of a black beard on his wide jaw.

I took a wary step back as the shoulder of his tunic moved strangely. What the heck was that? The fist-sized lump traveled along underneath the fabric all the way to his neck. Then a small, furry head popped out of Traegan's shirt collar with a squeak.

I blinked hard, just in case I was hallucinating, as a big, black and white rat crawled out of his shirt and perched on his shoulder. It wiggled pink ears and sniffed in my direction, its tiny dark eyes glinting in the torchlight.

Was that the same rat that had chewed through my ropes? Trick, right? I didn't get a chance to ask.

Traegan glared my way with eyes of a dark, faded purple hue and spat another dwarven curse. "We'll have to make a stand somewhere. Might as well be here. At least the trolls can't get to us. It's far too narrow for them to squeeze through."

Noa didn't seem so sure about those odds. His expression had gone distant and grim as he stared up at the wall blocking our path. "There must have been more than twenty chasing me. They took my spear and hatchet. I found this blade, but it is very old and brittle. I am not confident it would hold up for long in a fight."

"We've got a bit of rope. Maybe we can set a snare of our own, eh?" Traegan was already untying it from around his own waist.

I stared at the wall of solid stone before us while I did the same. Something tickled at the back of my mind. An itchy, tingling feeling like someone was teasing the back of my brain with a feather. It made my stomach flip. My heartbeat skipped and my breath caught as a shimmer along the edge of the stone caught my eye.

Was that ... a symbol?

My stomach dropped instantly and I staggered some, staring up at the slab as my head throbbed with a sudden flare of pain. I winced, grabbing the sides of my head. What was happening to me?

Then it was gone. Like a burst of pent-up energy, the pain vanished and cool relief rushed in. I stared at the surface of the stone wall, unable to breathe or make a sound, as lines of light rippled across it. No—not light. Symbols. Runes written upon the dark stone as though they had been painted there in pure starlight. They glowed along the edges of the walls, spanning out like rays from a single, large symbol at the very center. The shape of a sun with an eye at the center.

A voice filled my mind like I'd stuck my head into a tower bell while someone banged on the outside with a hammer. It rattled my teeth and shook my bones down to the marrow. I whimpered, gripping the sides of my head harder as I shut my eyes.

But there was no escaping it. No ignoring it. No blocking it out.

AWAKEN.

"Clarke?" Noa rushed over, dropping his torch and grabbing me by the shoulders. "What's wrong?"

"I-I ... Augh!" I cried out, slumping against him as my eyes flew open. It was as though my gaze were stuck on that symbol, locked onto it and I couldn't look away. I couldn't hide from it. It invaded my mind and filled my thoughts like a swarm of a million wasps, all stinging and buzzing and crawling inside my head.

Something warm ran from my eyes and nose. My body shook out of control.

T-Touch. I had to touch it. It wanted me to. Right now.

I stretched out a hand toward the symbol.

Noa grabbed my wrist to stop me. He held me out at arm's length and gave me a violent shake, as though trying to rattle me. "Clarke, what's going on? Is it happening again? Snap out of it! Listen to me, Clarke! You have to fight it!"

I couldn't. Not without my glasses. My mind was blown open like a window smashed in a hurricane.

That's when I knew. It wasn't a wall. It was ... something else.

My fingers brushed the stone, and immediately that familiar, cold chill raced down my spine. Relief poured through me like cool stream waters. My muscles relaxed. My pulse slowed. The raging storm in my head went completely silent.

Under my fingertips, the stone flinched. The runes flickered with a rippling flash. Then, one by one, they seemed to melt away. And before me, the massive slab of stone swung inward like a door.

My knees buckled. I fell, unable to move my arms and legs to even try to catch myself.

Noa caught me barely an inch before I hit the ground. With a grunt, he swept his arms under my knees and back and lifted me up. I could faintly hear him muttering under his breath as he carried me, following Traegan through that open door.

"You wanna tell me what by all the stacked stones of the elders just happened, elf?" Traegan demanded as he led the way, holding up the torch to light our way.

With my head lolled against his shoulder, I couldn't see Noa's face. But I knew the sound of that disapproving, smoldering frown in his voice. "I don't know."

"You don't know? Seems like you did while he was having a fit just now," Traegan argued. "Is that how it's gonna be?"

Noa's chest heaved with a sigh. "I mean it, dwarf. I don't know what he did. This has happened to him before, but we don't understand why," he muttered. "Come, we can discuss it later. Find me a place to put him down. We need to push that door closed again before the goblins can see it open. With any luck, they'll be as stumped by it as we were."

16

CHAPTER SIXTEEN

It must have worked.

Lying on my back on the cold stone floor, I still couldn't move my arms or legs. I couldn't even roll over or lift my head. But I also couldn't hear the sounds of angry goblins. I decided that was a good sign.

Minutes passed. Or maybe hours. I couldn't tell. But when I finally began to get the feeling back in my fingers and toes, I heard Noa and Traegan talking nearby. The glow of the torch moved around, as though they were exploring our new surroundings. At least it didn't sound like they were arguing anymore. Another good sign.

I bit down hard and groaned through my teeth as I forced myself to sit up on my elbows. My head pounded with a dull, throbbing pain in rhythm with my pulse. It ached all the way down to my neck and shoulders. Fates, what had happened to my glasses? I-I couldn't do this—I couldn't go on without them. They kept the pain at bay because they kept this power, whatever it was, under control. I couldn't manage it on my own.

"Clarke?" Noa called out. I guess he had noticed I was up and moving again. Er, well, sort of.

I pushed myself into a sitting position with my elbows on my knees. "I'm okay," I managed weakly.

His scowling expression seemed completely unconvinced. "You had blood running from your eyes and nose. That hardly counts as okay."

"What happened?" I rasped.

"You tell us, kid," Traegan interjected, standing beside Noa with his brawny arms crossed and his pet rat nibbling at his shirt collar. "You went all batty and touched that wall. It made all manner of weird markings appear on it, then it just swung in like a vault. Your eyes were glowin' like two harvest moons, and you had a glowing symbol right in the middle of your forehead."

I stared at him. What ...? Was that true? I felt my face, probing along my forehead, but nothing seemed out of the ordinary.

"We managed to get the door closed again. For a while, we could even hear the goblins scratching around on the other side, but they didn't make it through." Noa said and nodded back to where the rectangular shape of the closed door stood only a few yards away.

From this side, it was very obvious that it was a door. There was an engraved frame around it, and even markings carved on the surface of the door itself. But from the other side, the one I'd apparently activated somehow, it had just looked like a plain block of stone.

Whoa.

"You're either lucky, cursed, or mad," Traegan surmised. "Either way, we're safe for now. But I've got no idea where we are. Best the elf and I can tell, this seems to be the remains of an old temple."

"A very, *very* old temple," Noa amended, flicking Traegan a frown.

We were in an underground temple? Or ... maybe it hadn't always been underground. There were countless ancient places in the southern kingdoms. This, after all, was where society was supposedly first created by the gods thousands of years ago. In all that time, it was possible that entire cities had been buried and forgotten long ago.

But something about this place felt strange and ominous. It put a twinge of unease in the pit of my stomach as I stood. That feeling of being watched, like someone was peering over my shoulder from the shadows, made the tiny hairs on the back of my neck stand on end.

I didn't like it here one bit.

"If there's a door in, there must be a door out," Traegan said as he panned his gaze around the open cavern around us. "And going by the significant lack of goblin-filth and bones, I don't think we'll have to worry about running into them again."

"I hope you're correct," Noa mumbled as he picked up the club I'd been carrying and motioned for me to follow. "This way. We found another passage leading off from this room, but we didn't go far."

I nodded and followed. The meager light from the torch was enough to keep us oriented, but it only revealed ghostly outlines of the massive structure around us. Even so, it was pretty obvious right away that this place wasn't a natural cave. The floors and walls were smooth and polished, cut from the black stone and refined to shine like obsidian. Granted, it didn't seem like anyone had been down here in a long time. We left trails of footprints in the fine layer of dust on the floor as we made our way past towering columns. Our voices echoed off the lofty ceilings, all cut with buttresses in intricate, angular designs.

I stared up in awe as we approached a sweeping staircase, eyeing the passage ahead that was flanked on either side by two colossal statues of dragons. The creatures sat up on their hind legs, necks arched and jaws open, their snouts facing inward to the open hall ahead. Their eyes were set with fist-sized rubies that seemed to flicker with the reflection of the flame from our torch.

"It's strange," Noa observed as we stepped carefully onward. "There are no signs of life here at all. No remains of people, goblins, or otherwise. It's as though this place was completely abandoned."

I had to agree. I still couldn't shake that feeling—a prickle of unease on the back of my neck—that we were being watched. It must have been my already exhausted brain playing tricks on me, though, because there was no other evidence that anyone had been here. No other tracks in the dust. No lights. No smells other than something like stagnant, old air and the lingering hint of incense. No sounds apart from our own voices and footsteps.

If anything, this place reminded me more of a tomb than a temple.

"It's like a labyrinth," Traegan groaned, clearly not as mystified as we were. "We'll starve to death wandering around trying to find a way out."

He did have a point. Maybe the reason there were no other remains of anyone or anything down here was because we had stumbled across the only door. That idea made my stomach turn and my head pound with another sharp pain.

"Look there!" Traegan called suddenly. Trick let out a squeak of dismay as his master bolted forward and pointed to where the weak light of our torch sparkled off something.

Noa and I followed, jogging fast and exchanging a meaningful look. We stopped at a T-intersection where the hall abruptly ended, shooting off in opposite directions. The passages on either side were equally as inviting—dark, ominous, and empty.

But the wall straight in front of us made Noa, Traegan, and me stop and stand in silent awe. An intricate mosaic was crafted into the dark stone, set with jewels and round tiles of gold and silver. It spanned from floor to ceiling, about twenty feet, and depicted three beings with their arms interlocked. They looked mostly humanoid in shape, apart from each having a pair of sleek bat-like wings. They wore sweeping robes of black, dark blue, and silver, and had slender pointed ears and long white hair. I couldn't tell if they were male or female, but the figure in the center had eyes set with what looked suspiciously like diamonds. That wasn't what made me choke out loud, though.

That figure in the center ... had a symbol in the middle of its forehead exactly like the one I had seen on the door.

The other two figures, standing on either side, had symbols on their foreheads, too. And suddenly, it was as though the earth itself shifted under my feet. Seeing them all together like that, wreathed in tiny tiles made of glass, silver, and gold to mimic a night sky and radiant light beams—it all made sense.

They were the foregods. The ancient ones. The weavers of the universe.

Itanus, God of Past.

Enais, God of Present.

And right in the center, with diamond eyes seeming to stare straight through to my very soul, was Milontos, God of All Future.

I sucked in a sharp, shaking breath. My pulse raced. So little was known about these figures. Many of the writings about them had been lost, and what could be found at the Compendium was vague, at best. They were supposedly all-seeing, all-knowing, and all-powerful. They had hung the stars and walked the surface of a dead world, seeing all that was, had been, and would be. They had brought forth the first living things—the old gods—to serve them. From those gods, more life had come. Creatures and peoples of all shapes and sizes filled the earth.

And then, naturally, it had all gone wrong.

That's generally where the texts I'd read began to have different accounts. Different perspectives coming from different cultures and races throughout the world. Some of the themes were similar. There had been a great, all-consuming war that involved both mortals and the gods. It had nearly destroyed the entire world. And because of that conflict, there had been a lasting split between the realm of the gods and the mortal beings.

I had to wonder if this place predated all that, or maybe was created sometime during the War of the Stones. Regardless, it didn't exactly fill me with warm, fuzzy feelings. The foregods weren't known for their love, compassion, and mercy. Not nowadays, anyway.

"We should move on," Noa warned as he faced down the hall to the left, then turned to consider the right. "This torch won't burn forever, and I'd rather not wind up lost in the dark."

"Dark for you, maybe," Traegan chuckled. "Which way, then?" He seemed to be doing the same—considering both paths and trying to tell which one we should take.

"I would think a dwarf would be able to navigate well underground," Noa muttered, his eyes narrowing distrustfully on our new friend.

Uh oh. This didn't seem to be going anywhere pleasant, and now was not the time to argue. If we were going to survive and find some way out of here, we had to keep working together.

"I-I, um, I have an idea." I raised my hand to get their attention.

It was hard not to be offended by the way they both stared at me like I'd just sprouted a second head. Right. Maybe I wasn't the most battle-hardened guy, but I did have a lot of experience living in caves ... considering that's exactly what the Compendium Library was. A network of very old caves.

"Let me see the torch for a second." I held out a hand expectantly.

Noa's squinty-eyed look of suspicion intensified as he passed it over, but he didn't object.

Walking to the wall at the base of the mosaic, I carefully placed the torch on the ground, lying on its side, right at the base of the center figure. Then I backed away, motioning for them to do the same. Standing back, I watched as the flame flickered and danced, wavering straight up.

Then, for the briefest moment, it gusted slightly to the left.

I held my breath, trying my best to ignore the dubious looks I was getting from Noa and Traegan. Just a little more, then I would be certain.

A minute passed, and the flame wavered again, blowing slightly to the left just like before.

I let out a shaking sigh of relief and pointed down the hall to the right. "There's an exit that way."

"And how, by all the stones, do you know that?" Traegan crossed his arms and sank into his heels some.

"There's an air current flowing in from that way. It's making the flame move," I tried to explain.

"Aye, and how do you know it's not wind blowing out of the cave?" he argued. "No offense, but you don't exactly have the look of someone who's spent a lot of time outdoors, in caves or otherwise."

I couldn't decide how, exactly, I wasn't supposed to be offended. I mean, yes, he was sort of right. I was not the rugged, sword-hefting person they probably wished I was. But I was certain about this. "It's got to do with the air pressure. It moves from hot places to cold. It's hot outside, and cold in here, so that must mean that the air is flowing in from the outside in that direction."

Traegan flapped one of his big, hairy hands dismissively. "Pfft, sounds like a bunch of made-up fodder. How would you know anything about air currents and caves?"

I snatched the torch up and marched past him straight down the tunnel on the right. "Because I read, you stubborn dolt. You should try it sometime."

WORDS COULDN'T DESCRIBE MY SILENT, SMUG-FACED GLEE WHEN THE TUNNEL TO THE right ended at a large atrium with a massive, circular hole cut in the domed roof like a skylight. Granted, it was about thirty feet in the air, but silvery moonlight poured through the veil of foliage that grew over it. Vines hung down to dangle like tendrils from a chandelier, and moss, ferns, and lichen covered the stone floor.

"I don't suppose either of you can fly?" Traegan grumbled as we made our way to the middle of the room, passing through a circle of moss-covered statues of human-like figures that stood directly below the opening far above. Each one was fairly tall, but so obscured with plantlife it was hard to tell who they might be.

"I've got a bit of rope," Traegan said as he unwound the same length of rope that we had used to tether us together earlier from across his brawny shoulders. "It's not going to be enough, though, even if we had a good grappling hook."

"What if we climbed on top of the statues and tried throwing it from there?" I suggested.

"Hmm. Might work. Still need a hook, though," Traegan mused, rubbing at his stubbly chin. "Any ideas, elf?"

Noa sighed and looked despairingly at the torch I still held. "Only one. And it isn't a good one."

Oh no. The torch in question was small and throw-able. It was even made of a sturdy wood, which might be enough to hold our weight. But ... throwing it would also mean dousing it. Or potentially losing it altogether.

"What about the club?" I suggested.

"I don't know if I can throw it that far," Traegan admitted, running his hand through his shaggy, wavy black hair.

"It's not worth the risk." Noa mumbled as he paced around the statues, staring up at the opening far overhead, and frowning thoughtfully. "We don't have much to start with, and we would be climbing out into an unknown area of the jungles without so much as shoes on our feet. We need to find a different way."

"And what if there isn't one?" Traegan argued. "I see sky right there, elf. But you want us to go back into the dark unknown?"

"No," Noa's tone went frosty again. "But I'd rather not lose one of the few tools we have and still be stuck here, or worse, one of us get injured or killed trying to make that climb."

Now seemed like a good time for me to point out a, uh, somewhat embarrassing fact. My face burned and I looked down at my filthy bare toes. "I, um ... I don't think I can climb a rope that far."

I could feel both of them staring at me again. It made my shoulders shrink up to my ears and I kept my gaze down. Great. Well, so much for redeeming myself a little with my air current knowledge.

"Why am I not surprised?" Traegan sighed loudly.

Noa didn't sound quite as exasperated, thankfully. "That settles it, then. We must press on."

"Let's look around some." Traegan suddenly slapped one of his big, meaty hands on my shoulder like he was trying to reassure me. "Who knows, maybe you'll stumble across another one of your air current ideas."

Right. Well, that wasn't exactly going to work in here. Not with a giant hole in the ceiling. It was impossible to read air currents now.

We spread out through the room, using the ambient silver moonlight that poured through the ceiling to scout around the atrium. Other than a dried-up fountain, more mosaics, and a handful of toppled braziers, there wasn't much to be found. Four much smaller passages led off from each corner of the chamber, but we couldn't tell any difference in where they might go. This place was practically a maze.

And we might very well be lost in it forever.

I tried not to think about that as I searched around the statues in the middle of the atrium. All three were identical—well, apart from the varying growths of moss and ferns all over them. The white stone features of crowned, winged beings looked a lot like the mosaic of the foregods we had seen before. These, however, were all standing with their arms raised upward to the open hole in the ceiling above. Their smooth, somewhat elven-looking features peeked through the greenery, as though they were wearing living drapes of green.

But their heads were all bowed, looking down instead of up.

Strange ...

Walking through them, I stopped right in the center of all three statues. Being right there, right in the center, almost made it feel like those ghostly white stone beings were staring down at me. Or, wait, not me—something else. Something that was supposed to be right where I was.

I looked down to the thick patch of moss and lichen growing over the stone floor under my bare feet. I couldn't see anything right away. There was too much dirt and plant life in the way. But maybe underneath ...

I bent down and began peeling back the carpet of moss and sweeping away the dirt with my hands, exposing more of the mosaic underneath. Little by little, an image came into view. Every handful of dirt revealed scales made of pearly white shells, wings of tiny golden tiles, and horns of glass. My heart raced as I pulled back another hunk of moss, revealing a pair of brilliant blue eyes made of what looked like pure sapphires.

I sat back on my heels, gaping in awe as I recognized the symbol set in gold right in the middle of the creature's forehead. A symbol I knew well, even if I had only seen it a few times before—including one, fairly recent instance on the cover of a certain book.

A book that had been calling out to me in my mind for months.

That symbol was the Dragon's Eye.

So this creature must be ...

"Avgior," the word slipped past my lips as a hushed, frantic gasp.

"And what is that?" I flailed back as Traegan's voice suddenly barked right over my shoulder. Gods, he was quiet!

"It's, uh, it's a mosaic. I think it's supposed to show an entity called Avgior, but I've never seen any depictions of him like this before. There isn't much written about him." I bent down again, brushing my fingers over the golden symbol on the dragon's forehead. "He was supposedly the first hand of fate. The predecessor to the Fates as we know them. The legend was that Avgior was killed in the War of the Stones, felled by a mortal man, but because gods themselves can't truly be killed, his essence was split and scattered across the world. That supposedly gave rise to the two Fates that now preside over the final destinies of all mortal souls."

"Learn all that from books, did you?" Traegan arched one of his thick, dark eyebrows.

My mouth scrunched up as heat crept over my cheeks again. "I, um, well, yes. Mostly."

I could practically feel his breath puffing on my face as our new dwarven friend leaned down to stare at me more closely, his eyes narrowed suspiciously. "Really, now? Because a few minutes ago, you were cracking open ancient doors like walnuts with your eyes glowing." He jabbed a thick finger down at the golden symbol. "And *that* same mark shining right in the middle of your forehead."

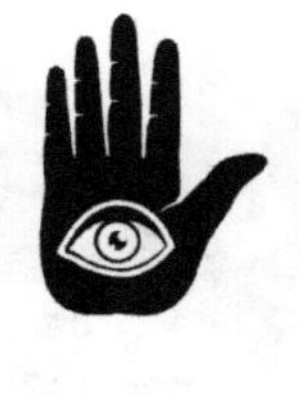

PART FIVE

EDARIX

❧ 17 ❧

CHAPTER SEVENTEEN

"You have disappointed me yet again." The emperor's sharp tone filled the chamber like the crack of a whip on a cold winter morning. Sharp. Biting.

It made my body jolt with the instinct to reach for a weapon. But I didn't dare to make any suspicious or threatening moves here. Not when ten heavily armed royal guards lined either side of the room, their eyes trained upon us from beneath their polished bronze helms, ever watchful for any sign of foul play.

Patience was more than a virtue here. It was all that might keep me alive. The imperial throne room of Nar'Haleen was no playground for the foolish or faint of heart. And while, as a younger and more reckless man, I had flourished in acts of daring and pride—I now had a much greater appreciation for my own insignificance. The background was a far safer place to be when heads began to roll.

"First, you fail to retrieve this so-called codex from the Compendium, and now I find that you've gone and burnt the place practically to the ground. Murdered scholars. Destroyed ancient texts. All for nothing. You've nothing to show for it apart from this human brat, who you claim will be of great service to the empire!" The emperor fumed from his lofty, white marble throne. His hands clenched on the wide armrests as he leaned forward, narrowing dark eyes upon us. "Do you have any idea what the political fallout will be if it ever comes to light that I had any sort of involvement in that disaster? The empire already hangs by a thread. And now I've come to hear that you have been wasting military resources attacking fishing villages on our own shores? Do me a favor, Auguress Riva, and provide me with a single good reason why I shouldn't have all three of you burned as heretics in the city square!"

I stole a sideways glance to the thin, white-haired woman standing beside me. Dressed in dark purple and red ceremonial robes that fell over her willowy frame like sheets of velvet over a scarecrow, her mouth pinched up and her nose wrinkled slightly. There was defiant wrath in her gaze to rival even the emperor's, but I guess she knew better than to make eye contact with him. That sort of insubordination was bound to get us flayed alive.

"I acknowledge and am filled with the greatest of regret that such measures were taken, but I humbly beg your consideration. I had strong evidence to compel those actions, Your Eminence. We were able to discern the location of the codex within that village, but by the time we arrived, it had already been taken elsewhere. You have commanded that I plead to the gods for a path to the reunification of all the southern kingdoms, with you as their sovereign leader, and this is the path I was shown." She kept her voice as smooth and even as a mother gently cooing to a fussy baby. I guess the dynamic wasn't so different.

The emperor wasn't buying it, though. Not today. The jewel-encrusted rings and bangles on his hand sparkled as he thrust an accusing, bony finger down at the third member of our party—a young teenage boy who stared vacantly at the floor as though, mentally, he was a thousand miles from here.

I guess, in a way, he was.

"It is becoming increasingly apparent that you have no control whatsoever over that *thing* you took from the Compendium. That—or you have a desperate need of shortening his leash," the emperor snapped. His lip curled as he stared our young ward down, considering him like someone who had found a dead mouse on their doorstep. "I don't care what god or goddess has marked him with power. He is a risk I refuse to tolerate. Either you bring him to heel and produce swift results, or I'll have his head first, and yours to follow."

"Of course, Your Majesty," Auguress Riva murmured, her tone now tinged with bitterness as she gave a low, sweeping bow.

I did the same, and waited until she and the boy had begun walking away, down the length of the throne room's immense and heavily shadowed hall, before I turned on a heel to follow. The open halls of the palace loomed before us with massive arches and solid alabaster pillars more than fifty feet tall. Lengths of rich deep purple silks hung down against walls made of jade, white marble, and flawless onyx. Details of gold sparkled in the intricate mosaics that covered the floors, depicting scenes of great battles and victories past. The faint smells of fine incense hung in the air, sweet and alluring.

But I'd grown numb to the glittering veneer of grandeur, power, and wisdom this place displayed from every nook and cranny long ago. The towering statues of the gods standing in line on either side of the vestibule, bathed in the midday sunlight that spilled from the rows of amber glass windows far above, might as well have been made of mud for all the reverence they received. The bickering crowns of the southern kingdoms had forgotten the forces that first put the lands and seas under their command. They blessed the gods in the morning, and cursed them in the evening. They only kept the rituals that they thought would bring about fortune and favor, but neglected all other rites and traditions. They pled to the gods for favor, but when their plans and machinations succeeded, they claimed it was by their own strength, not because their prayers had been heard.

Blasphemy to everything I had ever been taught.

But calling an emperor a blasphemous heretic was an excellent way to be found guilty of treason and burned in the city square. I had seen many other priests go that way, screaming with their dying breaths that Nar'Haleen had betrayed itself. My mentors. My elders. My friends.

First, the Tibrans had come and burned our temples, enslaving any who would submit, and slaughtering those who resisted. The temple where I had grown up and served was, as far as I had heard, nothing but cold cinders now. But I couldn't grieve that loss. Not when the emperor I now served was all but mad with lust to become the sovereign ruler of all the southern kingdoms. He hid that desire behind the claim that he only wanted to reunify the land—the same excuse many emperors had used before him. His efforts had proven far more desperate, though. Desperate ... and violent. He was willing to entertain any method, no matter how dark or dangerous.

And any who dared to defy him, or speak out against his methods, were declared traitors and heretics.

With that sort of constant threat looming over our heads, the days had grown dark. Rumors were as lethal as poison-tipped arrows. Accusations of treason to the crown were enough to get a person executed—even without evidence that it might be true.

The emperor was growing more paranoid by the day. The fear of failure closed in slowly like the teeth of a vice. Sooner or later, it would surely be the death of us all.

Even now, there were only a few of us left to tend to the divine temples in the Hall of Holies, and we had learned to be cautious. We had to be quiet, choose our words carefully, and guard our true feelings.

Well, most of us.

I watched Auguress Riva stride ahead, paying no mind to the divine images around us as the lengths of her long robes dragged behind her. With her head held high and arms folded into the long, bell sleeves of her gown, her mouth stayed pinched tight and her gaze focused straight ahead. She didn't say a word until we had passed out of the royal palace, through the Solistirium Courtyard, and into the Hall of Holies where the high priests, like us, were housed. Behind the gilded doors of that sacred ground, she finally lost it.

"That blathering, ignorant, old fool!" Riva seethed through her teeth as she stormed forward, walking faster toward the archives room. "Who does he think he is? How *dare* he question me? I've given him every powerful weapon he has! His navy now boasts a drakkon in its ranks because of me—*my* work! Did I not promise him sovereign rule over all the southern kingdoms? Have I not given him agents on foreign soil that bring back all manner of their secrets? That ungrateful cur. I stand at the threshold of the divine and will soon rend those gates wide open, and he would dare spit in my face!"

"We have promised him much," I reminded her solemnly. "That we could restore the unity of all three of the southern kingdoms, that the gods would bless it, and that he would do it all with a weapon crafted by the very gods themselves."

To be honest, I was shocked the emperor had even believed those claims in the first place. Riva spun a good tale, yes. She had a way with words that twisted in people's minds like a worm in an apple. But still—I'd assumed the emperor had more sense than this.

I had been wrong about that and a great many other things, lately, though.

Auguress Riva flung the doors open to a broad, circular chamber lit by one, central skylight above. There, shelves crowded the curved walls, many holding ancient texts, tomes, and scrolls. Others stored stone tablets, bottles and vials. Ancient artifacts and relics from thousands of years ago were crammed into any available space and left to gather dust. Several long tables crowded the room with chairs where, once, young priests like myself had spent their days studying the histories and rituals of their faiths.

Now ... I was one of the only ones left.

I turned to shut the door behind us, bowing my head some as I tried to gather my thoughts. Calm my nerves. Think. "The emperor is growing impatient, yes. But it is not unexpected. He has gathered his armies down to the last man, and they will march on Faladurn in only a week's time, with or without our assistance. But I am certain His Majesty would much prefer to launch this assault with a mighty divine weapon at the forefront, as promised. Damaria's resilience has surprised him before. And we cannot anticipate how Rienka will respond to such an aggressive move."

"With smug indifference, as usual," Riva snorted as she stomped over to one of the tables and put her hands on the map spread out across it, resting her weight as she studied the tiny inked features. "We've satisfied them with their so-called independence from Damarian rule. They would never rally back to them now, or even see us as a threat."

"And that will be their mistake," I muttered. "Their *final* mistake."

"But ... there is another matter to consider," Riva hissed low, turning around to face the only member of our group who had yet to say a word today. "His Royal Buffoonness was not wrong about *you*."

I turned around just in time to see her walk briskly to our young ward, who stood silently in the middle of the room like an empty shell, staring vacantly ahead. She drew back and slapped the boy hard across the cheek.

I froze, keeping my back to the door and not daring to take a breath.

The young boy, dressed out in gleaming black armor, didn't respond. He didn't move or even blink. He stared back at her, but there was nothing in his expression. Not pain. Not anger. Just an emptiness that still made my stomach turn.

"Useless Maldobarian whelp," she seethed, her face twitching with anger as she grabbed his chin and leaned down to glower right into his face. "That the goddess would ever give such a blessing to a pathetic human child is ridiculous. You were meant to leave none alive —to ensure no one escaped from that library. And yet you let one slip through your fingers. One carrying the very thing we need to ensure success!" She drew back as though she were going to hit him again.

"If I may, Auguress," I interrupted before I could even think to stop myself. "I-I ... believe this may not be entirely a loss."

She stopped, freezing in place, and then slowly turned to me with eyes that practically glowed with wrath. "What do you mean, Edarix? How, by all the gods, could you even dare to imagine this is advantageous to us in any way?"

I couldn't stop my gaze from darting between her hand and the boy, who still hadn't so much as blinked. Anger, dread, and sorrow stirred in my gut like a whirling vortex. But it paled in comparison to the fear that quaked the very foundations of my soul when I met Riva's scorching glare. I barely knew this woman. She'd come into this holy place like a shadow, subtle and silent. Now, she filled it like a sandstorm—blasting, reckless, destructive, and on a path I couldn't predict.

But I had seen what happened to those who tested her.

"You mentioned before that you suspected there were rebel forces stirring," I explained hurriedly, barely managing to keep my tone sharp and even. "Those who would try to subvert our retrieval of the codex or even botch the ritual altogether."

Her dark eyes narrowed, seeming to lose all sense of soul and sense in the process. "Get to the point."

"I am merely suggesting that perhaps letting them run ahead, just far enough to believe they have outsmarted us, would allow us to locate their forces. We could make a more precise attack and remove them from play entirely. It's likely they still don't know what they have, yes? The power of the codex is ancient and extremely fickle. Just reading it alone would be quite dangerous. I doubt any but those schooled extensively in divine magics could even decipher it."

Little by little, the wrath in her eyes began to smolder down. Her brow crinkled with thought and she slowly lowered her hand. "Let the foxes take the hen back to their den, then burn them all at once." A grin curled over her thin lips. "I like your thinking. Perhaps you're not a complete imbecile, after all."

I swallowed and bowed my head. "Yes, Auguress. I do try."

"Other preparations must be made, of course. We will need to mobilize a unit of specialized stealth forces immediately. Then, when the time is right, we will send them *exactly* what they're looking for." Her cold gaze swept back to the boy as her smile widened. "I should also speak to my contacts in Rienka. They need to be on the watch for meddlers."

"I can send the request to General Bazkan immediately," I suggested. "And the Hands of Fate can be mobilized before dawn."

"Yes. Yes, go and do that. I must prepare the Scrying Chamber. I want to know what, exactly, our little foxes are doing."

"If you permit, I will also take the boy to see that he is fed," I offered, attempting to make my tone as indifferent and callous as possible. "He's of no use to us if he dies of hunger or thirst too early."

Fear prickled in my chest as her gaze flickered between us. My heart pounded in deep, hard thuds that seemed to toll like a bell all through my body. I didn't dare move—not to blink, not to breathe.

There could be no weakness. No emotion. No sense of compassion whatsoever.

"Fine," she relented and waved a hand dismissively. "Have him bathe, as well. He still reeks of blood."

The instant the door thudded closed behind me, leaving Riva alone in that chamber, my knees wobbled. I thrust a hand out and caught myself against the wall. My breath came in halting, ragged pants as I put a hand to my chest. Even through the many layers of my black and dark purple silk robes, I could still feel my pulse thumping hard against my palm.

I shut my eyes tightly and focused, trying to slow my rising panic. To control my breathing.

Goddess preserve me. How much longer could this go on? How long until she suspected? How long until she saw my reluctance and had me eliminated the same way she had the others?

I hated this game. I'd been so caught up in the pretending, of doing and saying whatever was needed just to stay alive, I hadn't even realized it was slowly dragging me in closer to her side. I had been sucked in like a beast trapped in a tar pit, unable to save myself from slowly sinking to the murky, oily, burning depths.

My only hope—my only way out—was to keep playing along until the right means of escape presented itself. Once, that hadn't seemed so difficult. I only had to worry about myself. Now, there was *him*. The boy. I couldn't stand the idea of abandoning him to Riva's mercy, especially when she barely seemed to remember he was even alive at all.

I couldn't falter. Riva still trusted me. Otherwise, she wouldn't allow me to speak to the Hands of Fate on her behalf. She wouldn't have let me take the boy from her presence, either.

I just had to hold on. I had to be patient and careful until that moment arrived. Then, perhaps I could get us both out—myself and the boy.

Pushing away from the wall, I glanced down at where he stood nearby, still staring despondently ahead. If he noticed my response at all, it never showed. No emotion ever passed over his features. It had alarmed and disturbed me, at first. Before I knew the reason why. Now, my gaze tracked down to the mark on his hand. Pity like a cold knife twisted in my heart. Whoever he had been before, he couldn't have deserved a fate like this one.

But we were both prisoners now.

The boy followed me from the chamber as obediently as a dog. He didn't say a single word as I walked ahead, leading the way through the Hall of Holies once again. Here, smaller sculptures of all nine gods stood in a semicircle, each one only ten feet tall, and crafted with far more attention to detail. The altars before most were empty, and the candles had long been left to burn down and die. The priests who had attended them were long gone, and so there was no one left to pray at their feet, offer tokens, holy oils, or replenish the incense and candles.

No one apart from me.

I stopped, my feet dragged to a halt as though by some unseen force as I passed before the statue of her—my patroness.

Clysiros, Goddess of Death.

My eyes closed and I bowed my head. Then I held a hand up to the boy. "Wait here."

He stood perfectly still and didn't reply.

Walking to the altar before her, I stopped and gazed up at the beautiful depiction of the goddess. Her many wings carved from obsidian glass shone, wreathing a feminine, alabaster-skinned figure with long hair that fell to her bare feet. She wore a gown of that same black glass studded with diamonds that glittered like stars, and a breastplate of polished silver. One of her hands grasped a small sickle with a bouquet of lilies tied around the hilt.

Drawing a blade from my broad belt of wrapped silk, I cut away the wax drippings off the four golden candles that stood at her feet and added new incense to the censers smoldering on either side of the tall, black stone altar. Then I stood back, pressed my palms together, and bowed my head low.

Once, I had prayed without fear. Without shame. I had been a true shalnii priest serving in Salnis, trained to be one of the finest servants to Clysiros. I had been a guardian of her temple, a teacher of her wisdom, and a diviner of her will. I'd felt truly connected to her, and devoted my energy every day to upholding her charge of guarding the boundary to the afterlife.

Now, I could barely speak her name without my voice trembling and my hands shaking.

"Lady of the Midnight Skies, Guardian of Souls, Keeper of the Final Gate, I beg you hear your humble servant once again," I whispered, keeping my words hushed in hopes that no one else who might be spying nearby would hear. "I know I walk a cursed path, but I plead your pardon and your guidance. My heart has not turned from you. I still bear your oath mark. I still carry your promise and care for the lost spirits. But there are enemies at every turn. I fear I am always one step, one word, away from my own end. If there is some way out, some way to return to your side, I beg that you show it. Guide my steps. Guard my words. Take your revenge with my hands when the time is right."

"She doesn't hear you." Someone spoke suddenly, using the Maldobarian language. Not something I was accustomed to hearing here.

I whirled around, clinging to the altar in shock. Was someone else there? Had they overheard me, or—?

The boy stared up at me with that same empty, slackness to his expression, but his gaze seemed to sharpen and focus for the briefest instant. As though, for only a second, he actually *saw* me.

I took in a deep, steadying breath and pushed away from the altar. Slowly, I stepped closer to him. It had been him speaking, hadn't it? That voice had been so young. I hadn't imagined it.

"The gods always hear those who pray earnestly and truly to them," I countered, poised to flee at the first sudden move that child made. I had, after all, seen him murder ruthlessly. He brandished power unlike anything I had ever seen outside of ancient legend.

A living divine weapon—that is what Riva called him. A gift to aid our cause. And I had come to believe her.

"No," he murmured again. "If that was true ... she would have heard me a long time ago."

My mouth hung open. What? What was he saying?

Before I could ask, the boy blinked owlishly, still staring back at me with that fragment of focus in his cobalt blue eyes. Then his head turned slightly, his soft, boyish features returning to that emptiness he usually wore. Like someone drawing a curtain, a shadow fell over his features and he might as well have been a thousand miles away.

In that state, he only seemed to hear Riva's commands. He only obeyed her, unless she ordered him to do as I asked. Even then, my control over him was limited.

But was it possible ... could her hold on him be weakening? Or was he growing strong enough to throw it off himself?

Riva had told me that this boy's incredible power came from Clysiros, and I knew without any doubt that was the only reason I still stood here, attempting to serve, in hopes that staying close to this boy was somehow part of the goddess's divine plan. I could identify his abilities as they surfaced. I could even teach him some measure of control over them.

It couldn't be coincidence that we had both wound up here, trapped in the same living nightmare. When it came to things divine, there was no such thing. There was only an intent we didn't understand. Perhaps Clysiros meant for me to stay close and watch over him. I didn't know that for sure, and yet the thought of walking away from him always turned my blood to ice. To think of him left alone with Riva ... I couldn't. I had to stay. Someone had to stand watch. He was an instrument of my patroness, and I might very well be the last of her guardians.

We had to stay together, to whatever end.

18

CHAPTER EIGHTEEN

The boy ate like a starving puppy. He shoveled in spoonfuls of stew so fast, I had to wonder how long it had been since Riva let him eat. Days, perhaps? It seemed she had a habit of forgetting that, beneath that power, he was still a living, breathing person that required things like food and sleep.

Then again, she seemed to have a habit of forgetting that about everyone.

Auguress Riva was *not* my friend. She never had been, and she never would be. We were forced into the same environment by chance. Or, rather, astronomical bad luck. I'd always been the sort to sit back and observe others before I made any sort of decision about how I felt about them. When it came to Riva, I had learned very quickly that she was dangerous.

I didn't know where Riva had come from, exactly, or who had trained her. She claimed no home temple, and was very vague about how she'd come into her divination magic. It was far too late to question any of that now, though. She had slithered into the palace like a viper, subtle and silent, claiming to serve Milontos. Riva had proven to have very impressive skills in divination, though. Those talents had quickly earned her the trust and favoritism of the emperor, along with the respect and cautious jealousy of our peers. She was not someone to be toyed with, and I had watched my every move carefully around her from the beginning.

That was becoming much more difficult, however. Especially now that we had this boy tagging along with us. She had never told me his name. We'd had him with us for only a short time, and she had referred to him in many ways. Most frequently she just called him our "ward," but I suspected that was only because of where he had come from.

The old scholars who lived in the Compendium, hoarding their dusty scrolls and tomes, called all the orphans they took in "wardlings." It was my understanding that they educated those children, trained them how to care for the ancient archives, and tutored them extensively in religion and history.

Or at least ... they had.

I shuddered, closing my eyes tightly as the memories flickered through my mind just as the flames had that night. Devouring everything. Leaving only ash behind. Soon, that might be all that remained of my mind, as well.

Looking up again, I watched the boy sitting across from me at the long dining table. A bittersweet sight. It tugged a sad smile over my lips.

"Once, a great many priests and priestesses gathered here for our meals," I recalled aloud, not really expecting any response from him. But that moment in the Hall of Holies made my thoughts turn like spokes on a chariot wheel. Perhaps, somehow, a part of him—of his real self—really was trying to break through Riva's magical influence. At the very least, I now knew he could hear and understand me, even if he couldn't respond.

I sank back in my seat some and rubbed at my chin, watching him carefully for any signs of a change in his blank expression. "They filled this hall with conversation, laughter, and the clanking of dishes. It always reminded me of a holiday feast. Young acolytes about your age would take turns serving the meals. I remember very well when I was first brought here. I was jealous of them, actually. My own training as a shalnii among the Lunostri elves was not so warm and intimate as the comradery they seemed to share. We were isolated when we were young and given strict instruction as soon as we turned six years old."

No reply.

Glancing down the long table, my gaze tracked over all the empty chairs. There were two other tables just like it on either side of ours, each with twenty seats. But we were the only souls here. There were still a handful of acolytes that would prepare meals, clean, and serve, but they had learned to make themselves scarce. They skulked about in the shadows, following orders when given, but avoiding any attention from Riva.

She had no patience for children. Or anyone, really.

That thought drew my gaze back to the boy sitting in front of me. He must have been about fourteen, at most. He ate heartily, but he still stared dejectedly ahead and didn't say a word. His dark hair fell in loose, shaggy locks over his brow and ears. His deeply set eyes were such a dark shade of blue they looked nearly black. He had tanned skin of a medium bronze, and a sturdy build. Knowing he was from Maldobar, it wasn't hard to envision him being some knight's son. The Maldobarians were renowned for their military might and discipline. They were said to be a hardy, resilient, and dangerously stubborn people.

Perhaps that was why ... Hmmm.

I didn't know what manner of spell or enchantment Riva had cast on him. She was very private about that, and insisted it was only to curb his fear and make him more accepting of Clysiros's divine blessing that would otherwise cause him great pain and anguish. I had no trouble believing that. And yet, it was as though his mind was somewhere else entirely—trapped in some other reality altogether. What remained here was just a body brimming with dangerous power. A compliant golem with little to no free will.

Having now seen him in action, and witnessing first-hand the destruction he was capable of, I reasoned it must have been an incredible feat of magic to leash his mind like she had. I'd yet to see him even try to resist it.

That is, until today.

Today he had spoken to me without provocation or command. He had offered an opinion. He wasn't supposed to have those now. That thought put a twinge of unease in my chest like the prick of a needle. Like staring over the edge of a perilous drop, I might have just stolen a glimpse at the chance I'd been waiting so long for—the perfect opportunity to leave all this behind and flee before it was too late.

But it was a long way to fall from the edge of hope to the depths of despair.

If the boy did manage to break free of those magical chains, there was no guarantee he would be pleased to find out where he was or what he had been forced to do. In fact, I had a keen suspicion it would be quite the opposite. He would have no reason whatsoever to trust or want to help me. I had seen firsthand what his wrath could do. He was a child, and yet his hands were already soaked with the blood of the innocent.

Finding out what Riva had forced him to do might be enough to break him completely.

"How are you feeling?" I asked in Maldobarian, since that was the language he had used to speak to me earlier. I didn't know if he spoke anything else, honestly. Riva always addressed him in Maldobarian when she gave him orders, so that seemed the safest bet. "How is the pain?"

"Mild," he monotoned without ever meeting my gaze.

I stiffened, trying not to let my shock show. He was ... answering me.

"Then the healing remedy I gave you has worked. A good sign." I managed to keep my tone calm and composed. "When you stormed the beach like that on your own, I was concerned. Our soldiers have a hard time matching your skill with a blade. They fall behind too easily, and it is dangerous for you to fight alone without reinforcements. You're a very strong young man, but that doesn't mean you shouldn't be careful."

As he went to take another bite, I caught another glimpse of that mark upon his hand. A magical seal bearing the emblem of Enais. I'd heard of such magic, but never actually seen it used. Supposedly, it was an art created by the Avoran elves and lost after the War of the Stones. Riva had given it a thorough investigation, cursing all the while as though it were a huge inconvenience. In the end, however, she hadn't seemed worried that it would conflict with her plans for this child.

"Who was it that put that mark on your hand?" I asked. I held my breath. Would he answer again?

The boy hesitated, going still for a moment. His gaze slowly tracked to the mark on his hand. His dark brows crinkled together slightly. "I-I—" he began and blinked hard, as though trying not to choke.

I didn't dare move or make a sound. Merciful Fates. I'd never seen him make a face like that, or any expression at all besides crazed fury, until this very moment.

"I didn't ... know his name," he managed at last. His brows drew up, crinkling together as he blinked hard a few times. He winced and dropped his spoon. It hit the tabletop with a clatter.

My pulse took off in a rush. I leaned in closer and seized one of his hands. Focused—I had to keep him calm and focused. I was pushing my luck. I knew that. But how could I not? No, I couldn't stop now. This might be my only chance.

"Was this before you came to Nar'Haleen?" I asked in a whisper. "While you were in Maldobar? Did they put that mark on you to try to stall the progression of your power?"

"Yes," the boy answered. I could already see his expression closing up like a door slowly swinging shut. Once it was sealed, it would be over. He wouldn't answer anything else I asked.

I only had seconds.

"What is your name, boy?" I couldn't keep my voice from shaking.

His brow smoothed, jaw going slack as his expression went blank again. He pulled away from my grasp and picked up his spoon to go back to eating. But before he could put another bite in his mouth, his hand halted. One of his eyes twitched.

"Ronan," he murmured in a faint, broken whisper—as though forcing the word through clenched teeth. "My name is Ronan Derrick."

RONAN DERRICK.

That wasn't a name I recognized.

My heart pounded and my ears rang as I left the Hall of Holies with the boy, keeping my head down and my steps slow and steady. I couldn't afford to seem panicked. I didn't know if the acolytes that remained spied for Riva, and I wasn't about to take any chances. Not now.

Thankfully, the long bell sleeves of my robes hid my shaking hands as I held the door ajar and let him back into the archives room. She didn't even look up from where she stood at a table pouring the contents of a large crystal decanter into a series of smaller vials. The red liquid oozed out slowly, but she didn't let a single drop go astray.

"He's fed, washed, and I had him change into fresh clothes. The stench should be far more bearable now," I said as I lingered at the door to watch.

The boy, on the other hand, stepped away from me and went immediately to stand at her side, solemn and still as an empty suit of armor.

Riva didn't comment, but nodded slightly. She never took her eyes off her work as she finished filling the last vial and corked the decanter before putting it back on a shelf.

"Dragon's blood?" I asked, but I already knew the answer. I'd seen her perform her scrying rituals before. She used it as a medium because, unbeknownst to most, the blood of a dragon could act as a powerful conductor for divine magic. If she was using this much, then she must have quite the session planned. A deep scrying that would take a while—maybe even all night.

This was my chance. I just had to choose my words carefully.

"Indeed," she sighed as she began corking all the smaller vials, as well. Her bony brow creased with focus and exasperation, as though the whole process were a bothersome formality that she would rather not fool with.

But if ancient legends were true, only Avoran elves could use scrying, or seeing, magics without any tools or a strong magical source.

"Is the chamber prepared?" I dared to ask.

She stood back, critiquing her work for a moment, and then flicking a fast, piercing glare up at me. "It is. And I'll need you to stand watch outside, as usual. We cannot risk anyone interrupting. Our supply of dragon's blood is running low."

"Shall I make an offering to Clysiros, as well?" I offered.

She rolled her eyes as she breezed past, going swiftly to begin pulling more bottles and jars off another shelf at the other side of the room. "If you can think of no other way to make yourself useful," she muttered.

I frowned. "What about the boy?"

Riva stopped. She turned just enough that our gazes locked over one of her bony shoulders. Suspicion flickered in the depths of her dark eyes like wicked flames. Her lips pressed into a thin, disapproving line.

"He has not been properly sanctified," I reminded her, trying to match the coldness of her tone. Now wasn't the time to show weakness. "He will pollute that holy chamber and that may have an ill effect on your spell."

Her brows rose slightly. Then she panned her steely, cold-eyed stare back to where the boy stood silently at the desk. "True," she relented.

All the wind rushed out of me, and it took everything I had not to let my relief show. "Shall I ask one of the acolytes to attend to him? Or perhaps you would prefer it if we stood watch outside?"

Riva shook her head and carried her wares back to the table. "I don't care what you do," she scoffed. "Just see that I'm not interrupted."

I nodded. "Of course, Auguress. I have every confidence in your success."

19

CHAPTER NINETEEN

I did have every confidence that Auguress Riva would get the results she wanted. When it came to scrying, I'd never met anyone else with talent like hers. Then again, I'd also never met anyone else willing to take the risks she did. There was a reckless confidence in how she performed her rituals, as though she cared nothing about the meaning behind the formalities and treated the entire process as just another means to an end. It was no act of faith or servitude for her.

It was just another rung on the ladder that led to her end goal.

Initially, I'd believed that goal was to be the most favored priestess of the emperor. No doubt that position would grant her permissions and privileges to do nearly anything she wanted. But Riva had long since achieved that goal. She'd made certain of that by slowly edging out all the other priests and priestesses. One by one, they had all been found guilty of heresy or treachery, and were consequently either cast out or executed.

Granted, I had no real physical evidence that she was the one who had ultimately led to their downfall. After the Tibran invasion, there was always a fear of spies in the ranks. The suspicion of enemy eyes spying and conniving from within our own halls was still oppressive. Perhaps Riva was only taking advantage of that atmosphere of fear and using it to her advantage.

But fear only kept people in check for so long.

Now I had to wonder ... what was she really pushing for? Why was obtaining this codex and unleashing this divine weapon so important to her? And what did a boy from Maldobar have to do with it? Was finding him in that library really just a coincidence?

I had no doubts that Riva wasn't sharing everything with me. This wasn't about pleasing the emperor or keeping promises. She had another motive—one she refused to share.

I needed to uncover it.

I needed to find out who Ronan Derrick really was. I needed to know what a young boy from Maldobar was doing living in the Compendium Library in the first place. More than any of that, though, I needed to know why he was of such importance to Auguress

Riva. Was it just because Clysiros had bestowed this terrible power upon him? Or was there something more?

A secret that Riva would never tell.

My list of trustworthy friends was disturbingly short. Even shorter was the number of people from that list that I'd want to risk endangering by asking the wrong questions. But as I lingered outside the grand seeing chamber, waiting for Riva to seal herself inside so she could begin her ritual, there was only one person I could think of who might be able to help me. One person I knew I could trust.

One person who was decidedly outside Riva's ability to accuse. I might not know all of Riva's secrets, but she didn't know all of mine, either.

I just had to play this very carefully.

As soon as the chamber door was closed and the boy and I were left standing alone outside, I began counting. Three minutes. Then I would go.

My voice shook even in my own head, as though my whole head were vibrating with anxiety, as I counted down. One minute. Then two.

On the third, I took in a deep, steadying breath. Time to go.

I turned to Ronan, keeping my focus on the chamber door and my voice low. "Stay here and keep watch. See that no one disturbs her." I cleared my throat, stiffening and giving him what I prayed was a convincing scowl. I'd never been much of an actor, but hopefully the child wouldn't be able to tell the difference.

He didn't respond, even to nod, and I took that as a good sign. No time to hesitate and second guess it now. I had to be swift about this.

Leaving the boy outside the chamber, I started across the Hall of Holies at a brisk pace. My hands shook as I kept my gaze trained forward, stopping only to retrieve a spare acolyte's cloak from a storage closet. My stomach twisted and turned like I might actually be sick as I draped it over me. I pulled the hood down low and hid my arms in the lengths of soft gray silk, doing everything I could to obscure my face, before I stepped outside the temple grounds.

The night outside was eerily calm. No howling, cool desert wind that usually stirred in the huge potted palms and flowering plants that filled the palace halls. Every swish of my cloak or soft pad of my bare feet against the polished marble floor seemed too loud. Too obvious. My heart raced at every corner as I made my way through the looming halls and dark passageways. At this hour, only a few lamps burned low, flickering in blue and green glass bowls set into alcoves on the walls or lining the perimeter of shallow reflecting pools. Any other time, I might have found the tranquility of it beautiful.

But not tonight.

The farther I went, the more intricate and beautiful the palace grounds became. Intricately woven rugs with threads of silver and gold stretched over the floors. The fragrance of jasmine and eucalyptus floated in the air like a sweet perfume. Fine silks of the purest white fluttered from where they were draped along the open ceilings, offering brief glimpses of the starry night sky above.

I passed small companies of palace guards dressed in fine armor. Some stood, silent and still, at their posts in the lavish courtyards. Others walked patrols along the halls, hands resting on the pommels of curved scimitars. Their eyes tracked me as I went by, but they didn't try to stop me.

Members of the temple weren't frequent visitors here, but we weren't forbidden from coming.

A small blessing.

I picked the smaller, less direct halls to take me to the far west wing of the palace. There, between two majestic statues of winged figures leaning against staffs adorned with flowers, a pair of armored guards stood before a large, mahogany door.

I bowed low, then stood and brushed the hood of my cloak back so they could see my face. The markings on my face—silvery runic tattoos that outlined my cheekbones, brow, and chin—would be obvious. They set me apart as a shalnii, a guardian and servant of the temple. I just hoped they would be enough to dispel any suspicion about why I had come.

"An old friend would like to see her, if she would permit," I murmured.

The guards exchanged a look and a silent nod. One stepped back and opened the door, disappearing inside. Minutes passed. Or maybe it was only seconds. I couldn't tell, and my head felt lighter every second. My lungs seemed to squeeze so that every breath was a struggle, and my palms grew slick with sweat. This would work. It had to. I could trust her.

Or so I prayed.

The guard returned and held the door open, motioning for me to come in. He didn't make a sound or say anything at all as I passed by, and returned to his post with the door shut at my back.

Standing in the receiving hall, I hesitated and stared around with my mouth hanging open. My breath caught and my stomach swam as I stared across the wide room. At the far side, one large balcony overlooked the sweeping desert landscape to the west. There, against a backdrop of rocky, dark mountains that gave way to endless golden dunes all bathed in moonlight, the slender silhouette of a woman stood hauntingly still.

Empress Leysa.

"Your Majesty," I kept my tone calm and controlled as I entered the room. My steps were soundless as I crossed the wide, plush red carpets that stretched over the milk white marble floor. "I'm deeply honored that you would see me at such a late hour. And I do apologize for the intrusion."

"Edarix, my dearest friend," her light, airy voice filled the room, as soothing as the babble of a brook. "It's been quite some time since you visited. I hear you've been busy. Scurrying all about the empire. Chasing myths. Burning libraries full of innocent scholars and orphaned children."

I stopped mid-stride. My blood ran cold in a sudden rush that instantly paralyzed me. That edge in her tone, like the prick of a cold needle against the back of my neck, made my pulse skip. She knew? Gods, curse it, of course she knew. She was the empress, after all. She had her own means of finding out what happened, even in the darkest shadows of the palace.

My eyes closed and I bowed my head. "Your Majesty ... I know I need to explain."

"Then please do." Her tone remained so calm, so collected, it made every hair on my body stand on end. I couldn't see her face or tell if she was furious. Hers was a cold sort of fury, like the looming jagged peaks of a frosty mountain.

My thoughts scrambled, trying to think of what to say. Of how to say it. But the truth was all I knew, so that was what I told her.

"It wasn't intended to go that way—not by my understanding. As you may know, Auguress Riva has been fiercely determined to locate a divine codex. We believed it was being stored at the library. It is, or was, a text of great historical significance, dating all the way back to the War of the Stones. The auguress was determined that we should have it, and we had obtained permission from His Majesty to retrieve it."

With her back turned, still gazing out across the horizon, I couldn't see the empress's expression. But her shoulders tensed slightly, betrayed beneath the sheer, billowing gown that spilled over her frame like a river of silvery mist. "Yes," she replied quietly. "I am aware of her ... endeavors."

"I assumed all would go smoothly. We would arrive, meet briefly with High Inquisitor Bellavora, receive the text, and be on our way. But it all went wrong the moment we set foot inside. It was as though .... something came over Auguress Riva. In the time I've been around her, she has always seemed a demanding, impatient, and easily irritated person, but she knows how to act around figures of power. She knows how to hold her tongue when needed. Your Majesty, I've never seen her act the way she did that day. It was as though she was a woman possessed. She went into the Compendium, and the moment she saw that boy—"

"What boy?" Empress Leysa turned, finally meeting my gaze with her vibrant, golden eyes. *Damarian* eyes. They always made my breath catch. I had known her for years, ever since she had first arrived to the palace. She was a beautiful and enchanting young woman—a stark contrast to the much older emperor she had married. Such were the ways of royals.

And her wedding had been quite the explosive ordeal.

Leysa hadn't come here by choice. In fact, I was fairly certain no one had even considered her feelings at all when it came to her marriage. Her father, a powerful Damarian noble, had undoubtedly been paid an incredible amount of money for his cooperation. He had not given her over out of love, but rather to send a message. Her marriage to the Nar'Haleenan emperor was meant to be a symbol of unity and desire for peace between the two kingdoms. It was a farce, though. No one in Damaria had been impressed by that gesture. Having a Damarian bride hadn't won the emperor any trust from the Damarians, and they continued to resist any and all efforts from Nar'Haleen to reunify the two kingdoms.

I knew that had left Leysa in a very dark and isolated place. The people of her homeland saw her as a traitor, and the people of this kingdom suspected she was a spy. Her ladies in waiting kept their distance. She had no friends even among the nobles at court. But Leysa was clever, and I had caught onto that right away.

She had been raised to worship Clysiros, and had come to me early on for assistance in vigils and counsel. We'd grown close since then, even if she was far younger than I was. As a priest, I was sworn to never marry or take a lover, so I had no children or family of my own. Spending time with Leysa had opened my eyes to the realization that, perhaps, I would have liked being a father. We'd become fast friends, and I advised her as best I could when it came to her spiritual struggles and dealing with her social solitude.

We'd grown to trust one another completely, and yet ... she was still the empress. She had the same authority and control over my life the emperor had. I didn't dare take our friendship for granted. I had to remain respectful, subservient, and cautious. If I was going to tell her about Ronan, I had to choose my words very carefully.

Leysa stared at me, a few locks of her brown hair slipping from where it was tied up into a large, intricate knot of braids on the back of her head. "Is this the same boy my husband's servants speak of? The one who can wield flame and summon shadow demons with only the wave of his hand?"

I hesitated, then nodded slightly. "I've never seen anything like it, Empress. And the moment Auguress Riva saw him in that library, it's as though she became obsessed. She insisted on speaking to him alone. It made the High Inquisitor furious. She protested. Things became very tense. And ... I honestly don't know who struck first. It all happened so fast. Suddenly, everything was aflame. I barely managed to escape outside with some of the guards attending us before that whole place became like a kiln."

The empress's long earrings of glittering crystals caught in the light like strands of stars as she held my gaze. Her brow crinkled some, searching my face for an intense second before she asked, "Was it the boy? Did he start the fire?"

My mouth opened, but I couldn't muster a word at first. Telling her this, about what Ronan had done, might seal his fate. She might see fit to simply have him exterminated rather than risk letting him continue serving at Riva's side when his power was so volatile and deadly.

But I couldn't lie to her, even if I wanted to. She would almost certainly be able to tell.

"I think so, Your Majesty. But I can't say with absolute certainty because I didn't see it firsthand. I have seen the boy commit similar acts of violence since then, but always at the auguress's insistence. She ... has done something to him."

One of her eyebrows arched as her golden eyes narrowed slightly. "Done something?"

"Once again, I'm afraid I can't be absolutely sure. She toys with magics I have only read about as theories, not something anyone has ever actually accomplished. I can't say what she did or didn't do to him. I didn't even speak with the boy before Auguress Riva took him from that place, so I don't know what his behavior was like before. I can say with all certainty that he is not like a normal child. It's as though he's sleepwalking. He will stand in total silence, without moving a muscle, for hours until the auguress gives him a command. He won't even eat unless someone insists upon it." I paused, my gaze wandering away from her to the expanse of the desert that stretched out beyond her lofty balcony. "Or at least, he hadn't. Not until today."

A soft hand touched my arm, calling my attention back to where the empress still stared up at me, her expression now riddled with concern. "What's happened? Edarix, you know you can trust me."

I did. She was now the only true friend I had left in this place—the only person here who would give me a chance to explain before jumping to conclusions.

"The boy spoke to me today. It was only briefly, but it was unprovoked and he offered an opinion—something he's never done," I explained, lowering my voice to a barely-audible whisper. "I don't know if whatever spell the auguress might have put him under is weakening, or if he's simply becoming too strong to be subdued by it, but he ... told me his name. This is why I came. I had hoped it might be one you recognize."

"One I recognize?" She blinked confusedly and drew her hand back. "What do you mean?"

I held her gaze, hoping she would be able to read the sincere hope in my face. "Because you have some experience communicating ... with Maldobar."

Her eyes went wide. Her lips parted. But before she could speak or ask what I meant, I continued, "Your Majesty, have you ever heard the name Ronan Derrick before?"

20

CHAPTER TWENTY

The world seemed to stop completely as I waited in breathless silence for her to reply. A thousand thoughts flickered through my mind, passing like shooting stars—too far and fast for me to even consider one of them for more than an instant.

Empress Leysa looked down, her brows drawing together into an intense frown. Then she looked up at me again, and I saw it. Recognition dawned on her beautiful features like a morning sunrise.

"The last name was Derrick?" she pressed, her voice hushing to a cautious whisper. "You're certain?"

I nodded, and the look on her face put emotion like a white-hot spike through my chest. A confused, whirling, painful mixture of worry, fear, dread, and panic took my mind like a sandstorm.

She knew that name.

Merciful gods, what did that mean?

The empress turned away, walking a few steps before pausing and resting her hands on the railing of her balcony. "As you know, my husband has no love for Maldobar or any of the northern kingdoms. Our connection with them has always been full of mistrust. The Tibran War did not improve those relations, although I have been in loose contact with a so-called ambassador who has earned some favor in Maldobar's royal court. She is supposedly a shalnii, like you, and reached out on the behalf of Queen Jenna to establish communication right after I took the throne here."

Those words made my breath catch. Another shalnii? Of what temple? How had she wound up all the way in Maldobar? Before I could ask anything, the empress continued.

"I've been cordial, but brief in my exchanges with her. You know as well as I do that my husband would be very displeased if I were to make any grand effort in forming an alliance with Maldobar—or any other kingdom. But I remember quite clearly her introductions when she first made contact." Empress Leysa's hands gripped the railing harder, making her knuckles go white and her bare back and shoulders flex. "Queen Jenna Farrow, and her newly-wedded husband ... King Phillip Derrick."

All the feeling drained from my body, leaving me numb as I stared at her back. Fates, could it be true? Could this boy be some relation to the Queen of Maldobar? A cousin, perhaps? How in the world had he ended up at the Compendium Library—and without our knowledge?

"They never mentioned any children or extended family members. But I also didn't ask," the empress added quickly. Then she hesitated, seeming to steel herself before she looked back over her shoulder at me. "Is the boy from Maldobar?"

"Yes, Your Majesty. I believe he is." My soul seemed to rattle in my chest like a rock in an old can.

The empress fell silent again. Little by little, her grip on the railing relaxed. Her shoulders dropped, and her head bowed. "You must tell no one you've come here to see me tonight," she murmured. "Does anyone know you're here?"

"No, Your Majesty," I assured her. "No one apart from your own guards."

"Good." She turned back around and stepped closer, reaching up to press a gentle hand to the side of my face. "I will look into this, but it may take time. I must be discreet. And you must be very careful with Auguress Riva. I do not trust her. She has my husband's mind wrapped around her finger now, and I fear that by being at her side, you'll be drawn into something much more serious and dangerous than we now understand."

"I know," I admitted. Putting a hand over hers, I managed a smile that probably looked as painfully forced as it felt. "But I have no choice. There's no one else left to watch her, to monitor what she's doing. And the boy ... I worry what might happen to him if I were to walk away. She seldom remembers even his most basic needs. I don't know what she intends to do with him, but I suspect it is something foul. I can't just—"

She pressed a finger over my mouth to silence me. "Then do what you must, my friend. Watch over him. But if I learn that the boy is of great significance in Maldobar, know that I may call on you to extract him from her. It will be dangerous. You must guard your words more carefully than ever."

I wasn't sure I could manage that—watching my words carefully enough or somehow getting Ronan to leave Riva's side. After all, his power was far greater than mine. I had seen him kill at Riva's command. I had no doubt she could, and would, turn him against me if she thought for an instant that I was working against her in any way. How could I possibly separate them while he was still under her control?

The answer struck me like a stone to the forehead.

It was so simple.

And yet so terrifying it made my breath catch and my eyes squeeze shut.

I couldn't do it. The boy, Ronan, was the only one who could. And based on today, he might already be trying.

I would have to wait. I would have to watch him very carefully from now on, looking for any further signs of him breaking away from Auguress Riva's influence. I would have to act quickly at the first sign of any resistance.

"Please be careful," Empress Leysa said. Her smile looked almost as fractured as I felt when she finally took a step back. She pulled one of the glittering rings from her finger and held it out to me. A shining, golden signet ring with the emblem of a lion's head engraved on it. "Please take this seal so that you may move about the empire without being troubled by any guard or official. Should you find yourself in danger, use it. Flee. Get somewhere safe and send word to me as soon as you can. I will do whatever I can to help you. Promise me that you will, Edarix. I ... cannot lose the last friend I have in this world."

"Thank you, Empress." I murmured, and offered her a deep bow as I took the ring. "If I learn anything else about the boy, or what the auguress is planning, I will make sure you are informed as soon as possible. Until then, may the goddess look upon us both with compassion and guard us from the eyes of our enemies."

She nodded. "Goddess keep you, Edarix. But please, watch your back. I fear my husband's mind is not his own now, and my reach from this gilded prison grows shorter by the day. I am watched at every turn, and I guarantee you are, as well."

"ASSEMBLE THE HANDS OF FATE IMMEDIATELY," AUGURESS RIVA SNAPPED AS SOON AS SHE emerged from the scrying chamber, bursting through the doors like an enraged bull, ready to trample anyone who got in her way. Her face was flushed and her hair was disheveled. Something black ran from her eyes, down over her cheeks and neck like inky tears as she stormed past. "The codex is close by. We must move at once!"

"Close by?" I blurted, stunned as I followed after her toward the archives room. "But how is that possible?"

She whirled on me in a frenzy, her bloodshot eyes wild. "You dare doubt me? The gods have shown it to me! It lies in an ancient temple to the north."

My mind spun, trying to process that information while she rushed about, pulling down maps and scrolls and spreading them out on the tables. She made a delighted crowing sound and thrust a finger down to one of the maps—a particularly old one made of crinkled, yellowed vellum. The inked markings were so faded they were barely legible, and the entire thing was written in a mixture of the ancient Nar'Haleenan language and a dialect of elven that must have been Avoran.

Auguress Riva's expression of twisted, ink-smeared triumph paled some, her too-sharp features going slacker by the second as she stared at the place where the map indicated a very large temple complex had once stood on the northeastern coastline of the empire. Even upside down and several paces away, I knew the symbol pressed in tarnished golden ink to the paper right over the temple complex.

The Dragon's Eye.

My pulse gave a little flourish that sent a chill all the way down my spine. That was a temple of Avgior, the ancient white dragon. Predecessor to the Fates. The All-Seeing One. It was said he had been killed in the War of the Stones, felled by a mortal's arrow that struck his heart and shattered his essence.

Judging by Riva's expression, she knew the legends about him as well as I did. That temple had likely been entombed for a very good reason. No one should ever set foot there. Especially not carrying an artifact of divine magic like the codex.

I swallowed against the rising stiffness in my throat, fighting to collect myself before I spoke. "To tread within those ancient temples after they have been magically sealed is to be cursed for eternity," I reminded her.

"Curses only last as long as the gods who inflict them," she seethed through her teeth as she began roughly rolling up the map again. "Come, we cannot delay. Gather the men we need. We will have the codex before nightfall tomorrow."

"In most cases, I would agree with you," I countered, my gaze flicking quickly to where Ronan stood like a statue by the door, awaiting orders. "But when it comes to dragons ..."

One of his dark blue eyes twitched slightly. But the boy didn't make a noise or even shift his weight.

"Don't be a fool, Edarix," she growled as she thrust the map at me suddenly, nearly knocking me onto my heels. "What can a long-dead god do in a temple that's probably nothing more than moss-covered rubble? Nothing. When the gods die, their power is transferred to something else. Whatever the beast was, it no longer resides there. We have nothing to fear from a dead dragon."

I kept my gaze trained upon the boy, still watching him for any hint of a response as I muttered, "The Dragonriders of Maldobar might beg to differ."

Ronan's whole face twitched. His nostrils flared a little, as though he were taking in a deep breath. Then, for less than a second, his gaze darted across the room and met mine.

And I knew ... he *saw* me.

Adrenaline poured through my veins like molten metal. I was correct. I had to be. Either Auguress Riva's hold on him was weakening, or he was becoming too strong for it to hold him much longer.

It was over in an instant. His expression cooled back to that catatonic emptiness. But it didn't matter. I knew I was right. He could hear us now. Somewhere behind that vacant stare, his soul was trapped in a magical cage and fighting to break free.

I'd have to rattle that cage again.

Until it broke.

Auguress Riva didn't notice our exchange as she went on hastily cramming more of her spell casting wares into a bag she always carried when we left these chambers. When she turned back to me again, her ink-smudged expression still crackled like hellfire. Her dark eyes seemed bottomless, reminding me of a pair of abysmal voids that held nothing but a pure and wicked madness. "Don't be an imbecile. Have you forgotten where you are? There are *no* dragonriders in the southern kingdoms!"

PART SIX

REIGH

21

CHAPTER TWENTY-ONE

I still didn't trust Judan. Not one tiny bit.

Sure, he had been pretty well behaved over the last two days after we had forcibly rearranged the power rankings aboard the ship. One might even say he had been cooperative. But did I trust him not to try something underhanded while I wasn't paying attention? Nope.

I pulled Thatcher and Violet aside long enough to advise them to keep a close eye on our new pseudo-captain. I wasn't taking any chances this time. Maybe with all three of us watching, he would at least be discouraged from getting any reckless ideas.

A guy could hope, anyway.

Thankfully, we didn't have to keep up that charade for long. The storm had actually given us a surprising boost of speed in the right direction, cutting our journey down a bit to make up some of the time we'd already lost, and the crew worked diligently to repair the damage left by the wind and waves. On the dawn of the fourth day, a call from the crow's nest high atop the mainmast announced there was land in sight. We were coming upon Rienka, at last.

And I dared to start hoping again—which for me, was generally when things went wrong.

"Hold still, girl. I need to take a look," I grumbled as I sat in the warm, open air on the main deck, wrestling with my pocket-sized dragoness who was still favoring one of her legs a little. She hissed and fought, squirming around in my grasp. I let out a string of elven curses when she suddenly clamped her jaws down on the meaty part of my hand right between my thumb and pointer finger.

"OW! You little—that was uncalled for! Blast it, Vexi! I'm just trying to help you," I snarled back at her as I scowled down at the fresh half-circle of tiny, needle-point-sized fang marks left on my hand.

"Struggling with your noble mount, I see," Violet snickered as she walked by, the morning wind rippling through her silvery-blonde hair. "You ought to wrap her up in a sock. That's what Arlan's shopkeeper did with her kittens when one of them was injured."

"If I had a sock to spare, I might try it. But she'd probably just burn it to a crisp, and I've already lost a set to Thatcher," I grumbled as I finally managed to pin her wings and neck with one hand. I quickly tested out her injured leg, feeling to see if there was anything off about the range of movement or any glaring evidence of a break in the bones. I couldn't tell if there was any swelling, and with her still kicking and growling, it was hard to be sure.

"I guess if she's fighting me this hard, it must not be too bad," I resolved at last and let her go. "Fine, then. Have it your way."

My angry, tiny green dragoness bounded away to arch up at me, spines flared and wings spread in an indignant display as she spat a tiny plume of fire in my direction. Ridiculous.

"We should discuss our intentions once we reach the harbor. I would advise not lingering there any longer than necessary. We will draw too much attention. I know of a place we can stay the night and get our bearings while I attempt to make contact with an individual Arlan has done business with in the past. He will likely be willing to help us, but it won't come free." Violet sauntered over to the ship's railing and spun around, leaning back against it with her arms crossed.

"And who is this individual, exactly?" I asked. "Don't get all cryptic on me now. Either we are all on the same page, or this isn't going to work."

Violet's expression twitched unhappily, almost like she didn't like having to give up that information so quickly. But she must have taken my point, because she gave a surrendering sigh and answered, "He goes by Sulam. I can't tell you much more than that because people within his organization seldom gather moss, if you catch my meaning. They operate in shadow, much as we do, and know how to move without leaving much of a trail." Her mouth quirked and she cast me a wary, sideways glance. "Talking about leaving trails ... I think we should insist on Judan taking us as far as the port of Sol'Karr. It's one of the largest and busiest. We might find it easier to slip into the background there."

"Worried about someone coming after us?" I really didn't need to ask. I could see the concern and uncertainty written all over her face.

Violet's lips pursed like she'd tasted something sour. "Let's just say, it will be far easier for some of us to pass through a crowd without causing a ruckus than others. We need to be careful. And most importantly, we need to stay together. Rienka has a lovely veneer over a thriving criminal world fed by the volume of coin and raw goods that move through its waters. So keep your wits about you, Lieutenant. We've been careless to lose track of the children before now, but we can't afford that sort of blunder on land."

"Yeah, well, it'd be easier if they actually did what they were told instead of running off every time I turn my back for more than two seconds." I cast her a glare. "Are you ever gonna use my actual name?"

She winked one of her scarlet eyes playfully. "Now where's the fun in that?"

I wasn't sure where the fun in any of this was. Reaching toward my angry dragoness, I tried offering my hand for her to climb back up onto my shoulder. She hissed and recoiled again, her tiny ears pinned back and fangs bared.

"I won't mess with your leg again, I promise," I groaned in defeat. "Come on. You hungry? I've got some jerky left from my rations."

She gave a distrustful little snort, but slowly crawled toward me. Her tiny claws pricked my skin through my tunic all the way up my arm until she settled back on my shoulder with her back turned. She wouldn't even look at me when I gently patted her head with a finger.

Ugh. Tiny dragon drama.

We all looked up as a bell began ringing on the deck of the ship. Excited shouts came down from the sailor posted in the crow's nest. Great. What now?

A radiant smile spread over Violet's face as she rushed past me suddenly, running to the other side of the deck and leaning out over the railing. The wind caught in her silvery-blonde hair and blew it behind her like a satin flag. My heart gave a strange little flutter as she whirled around and waved me over to see.

Gathering my legs under me, I stood up and went over to see what everyone was so worked up about. The sea wind blasted in my face, sending a spray of salty water across my chest as I leaned over to see it rising above the white-capping waves in the distance like hunks of soft jade crystal.

Land.

"Rienka," Violet breathed the name like a sigh of relief.

But I couldn't speak. Staring across the horizon, my chest swelled with a rush of urgent, anxious energy. A confused mixture of relief, dread, and ... awe. I'd seen Maldobar's coast-lines plenty of times. Most of them were jagged, bitter cold, rainy, or swampy. Sometimes they were all of those things at once.

They looked nothing at all like this.

The warm tropical wind blew over my face and through my hair, as soothing as a gentle caress. It made my head tilt back and my eyes want to close lazily. I could get used to that.

From up on the quarterdeck, Judan shouted orders to the sailors as he held firm to the ship's wheel. I guess in these shallow waters, with a reef not far below the crystalline water's surface, they had to be careful. Fortunately, it seemed like this wasn't the first time Judan or the crew had managed it.

Our ship glided through the turquoise waters, passing other boats with vibrantly colored sails of red, blue, green, and purple puffed proudly against a clear blue sky. They all seemed to be coming or going from the massive, crescent-shaped, bay before us that stretched the full length of the horizon.

The ships followed the currents like roadways, using them to navigate through the network of islands all contained inside a huge bay like gleaming gemstones in a basket. The islands themselves jutted up from the reef-covered bottom, their steep limestone cliffs dropping thousands of feet on some sides, or sloping down gently to form pristine white beaches. Some of them were even connected by networks of massive white stone bridges, and nearly all the islands were covered in dense green jungle with tiny, bright blue rooftops peeking through the foliage.

A massive, white limestone statue of the sea goddess, Undae, rose from the ocean floor with a long fishing spear in one hand and a conch shell in the other, held to her lips like she was blowing into it. Gods and Fates, the colossal statue must have been two hundred feet tall. My mouth hung open in awe as we cruised by where it stood, guarding the entrance to the largest cluster of islands straight ahead of us. Beyond it, a network of canals, docks, and waterways led between all the nearby land masses. More statues were carved into the sides of the cliffs, or stood atop the jagged peaks, overshadowing temples with domed roofs plated in gold that shone in the sunlight.

I'd never seen anything more beautiful in my entire life.

"Incredible, isn't it?" Violet said as we stood close together, watching the glittering coastline welcome us in.

I had no words for it. Nothing that would do it justice. Everywhere I looked, it was a world of rich and brilliant color, teeming with life and beauty. There was also something unmistakably ancient about it all, with so many towering temples and statues of divine beings intermingled with the rest of the common buildings all built on fine terraces up and down the steep slopes of the islands.

All I could do was smile back at her so wide it made my face hurt a little.

Violet's expression went blank, holding my gaze and studying me strangely for an instant. Weird. What was wrong with her? Hadn't she ever seen me smile before?

Hmm. Had I done much smiling back in Maldobar? I guess I'd never really paid attention to that sort of thing.

Our reluctant captain guided the ship through the busy canals toward the largest of all the ports I could see. There, the bay was more like a watery fortress, encircled on nearly every side by these steep, mountainous islands. The shoreline was a network of docks, all managed from a central stone complex like a large man-made tower right at the center. There must have been hundreds—even thousands—of ships in all shapes and sizes moving around us, but every single one of them followed the watery pathways without incident. Impressive.

"Welcome to Sol'Karr," Violet murmured, her expression steadily dimming as she eyed the rampways, bridges, canals, and terrace roads all around the huge, circular port. Everywhere I looked, there were hundreds of people thronging around ships and merchant booths, or waiting to board ships and small transportation vessels that moved from island to island. Some were pulled behind horse-like creatures that swam quickly—the same ones we had seen carrying pirates around in the ocean during our battle. These, however, were fastened to fancy little barges like floating chariots. I'd never seen anything like it.

"Crowds getting to you?" I dared to ask, watching her reaction carefully.

Her lips thinned and she snapped her gaze away. "They ought to get to you, too. We will have to be careful now. Come, we should get everyone below deck and discuss our moves once we dock," she urged. "You may want to have a word with our captain, as well."

Right. Probably a good idea. I nodded, pushing away from the railing and making my way to the quarterdeck where Judan was still calling orders to the crew. He didn't even look my way as I stopped and stood beside him, watching with my arms crossed.

"I could do without the smoldering supervision," he muttered bitterly, just loudly enough I could barely hear him over the ambient noise of the port.

"I'm not here to critique your work," I retorted. "We need to talk."

He snatched the wheel to one side, then the other, his brow creased in concentration. "I'm a bit busy at the moment, in case you hadn't noticed."

"Then as soon as you can spare a few minutes. We'll be waiting." I turned away and left him to his work, retreating into the navigation room. I had to gather my things anyway, and find Maylea before she jumped ship and disappeared again.

Luckily, none of them were all that hard to track down. Thatcher was already packing his things when I stepped into the cramped little room, and Lukani had practically glued himself to the lone, small porthole window so he could watch the port pass by. Violet and Maylea talked in hushed voices as they sat, working to get something situated over Violet's head.

I stopped and stared. Was that ... a wig?

It was. Violet had taken all of her long white hair and tied it into a tight bun on the back of her head, then pulled a wig of long, wavy black hair down over it. Maylea was helping her to get the hairline aligned just right, and they both glanced up at me when I wandered over to get a better look.

"I told you, not all of us are going to be a welcomed sight in this part of the world," Violet said, her tone tight and prickly. Almost like she was afraid I might push the issue too far in front of everyone.

But I wasn't as stupid as she must have thought I was. I remembered very clearly our discussion about her being a Viperi—even if I still didn't fully understand what that meant. I could appreciate it was something she might need to be discreet about here, though.

"Okay." I tried to sound as casual and uninterested as possible. "Anyone else we need to worry about?"

"Lukani will also need to cover himself and keep his tail obscured. Rajinna are not considered individuals of equal standing here. They're regarded more as animals than people, and he runs the risk of being arrested if he's caught alone out in the open. It's better for him to pass himself off as someone else entirely," she explained.

"I can do this very easily," Lukani announced proudly. He spun around and took a few confident steps into the middle of the room. Then his form shimmered and warped, shrinking down until he was hardly more than a foot tall.

With his black feathers ruffled and his yellow eyes twinkling in the dim light, he gave a shrill *CAW* and fluttered over to land on Maylea's shoulder ... as a crow.

Violet's scowl, with her nose wrinkled and her mouth all pinched up, made me think she would have preferred a different tactic. I could only assume that's because Lukani could only hold these shapes for so long. But, then again, he had always claimed that smaller, simpler shapes were easier for him. Hopefully he could get by with this until we found an inn or someplace safe to lie low while we worked on the next phase of our plan.

Or rather, the tattered remains of what had once been our plan.

Gods help me.

22

CHAPTER TWENTY-TWO

"I've secured a good spot for the ship at the end of the main public thoroughfare dock," Judan announced when he finally came into the room. He took a quick glance around the room at our group and his broad shoulders rose and fell with a heavy sigh. I could have sworn there was a touch of sympathy in his voice when he turned to me and asked, "What is it you wanted to talk about?"

I nodded back behind him, toward the door. "Let's take this to your new office."

His brows went up. There was something unmistakably suspicious in his expression as he walked beside me out of the navigation room, back into the captain's quarters. Judging by all the stuff that was now piled on the floor, emptied out of drawers, and scattered across the desk—he had been busily going through all of Malina's things. Searching for valuables, probably.

"How's the nose?" I asked as I shut the door behind us.

He patted at it gingerly, cringing up as he probed at the swollen, black-and-blue mess that sat where his nose should have been. "Still broken."

"Want me to set it?"

He flicked me another distrustful look. Then rolled his eyes and nodded. "If you think you can manage it without killing me."

I grinned to myself. "I'll do what I can."

It only took a second, and he was a lot more composed about it than Jondar had been. One good crack and I at least got it pointing in the right direction again. No screaming or whimpering. Minimal flinching. Judan was a former spy trained by his father—who also happened to be a defected Ulfrangar assassin, so I doubted any form of whimpering had been acceptable when he was going through training.

"Here, try not to touch it for a few days, at least," I advised as I handed him some clean bandaging, since it had begun to bleed again. "I'd wrap it up for you, but I doubt that will complement the pirate aesthetic you're going for."

"Indeed, it would not," he chuckled in agreement.

For a moment, the tension between us seemed to ease. It felt normal again, like it had before he'd gotten hurt and lost his hand at Dayrise. It didn't last long, though.

"So, am I correct in assuming you still intend to give me this ship?" he asked, avoiding all eye contact as he went on dabbing at his nose.

"I gave you my word, didn't I?" I muttered. "That still means something to some people."

Judan's thin, frowning mouth scrunched and he went on avoiding my gaze. "It's not personal, Reigh. Not between us, anyway. I didn't choose this or do anything out of spite toward you."

"I know," I replied evenly. "But as your friend, it's my duty to tell you when I think you're doing something astronomically stupid that you're going to regret for the rest of your life. I'd hope you would extend me the same courtesy."

"I did," he countered. "By trying to talk you out of pursuing this mission any further. And yet, here we are." He groaned and shook his head, like he was holding back the urge to let his temper run loose again.

I knew that struggle all too well.

"Why, Reigh? Answer me that, at least. You've gotten nothing but pain and heartache out of these so-called missions for justice. Why go through this again? What's the point?"

I couldn't resist a nostalgic smile. "I wish I had a deep, profound answer for you. But it's simple, really. It's never been about me or my happiness or what I stand to gain from it. I've never gone into one of these situations looking for a payout. I'm doing this for them—for my sister, my brother, my nephew, and the other people who are counting on me to do the right thing. I'm doing it because they need me to. Yes, it's gonna hurt. It might even get me killed. But I won't turn my back on my family. They're the only thing that matters, and I'll do whatever I can to take the pain for them ... because that's what you do when you love someone. It becomes about what you can give, not what you can get."

Judan's dark hazel-green eyes drifted up to hold my gaze, and for the first time since I'd crossed paths with him again, I saw him—the *real* him—bright and clear. Not just a momentary glimpse or a tiny flicker of memory. It was the man I'd known in Dayrise. The one who had nearly given his life to save Phillip and the rest of us.

The friend I'd lost that day that I wasn't sure I would ever see again.

"I'm sorry if you felt like the rest of us turned our backs on you after what happened," I said. "Trust me, that was never our intention."

"I know," he answered quietly.

I rubbed at the back of my neck, trying to find the right words. I'd never been all that good at talking out feelings. But for his sake, I'd blunder through it the best I could. "I do owe Arlan a favor. That's what got me on this ship. But make no mistake, it's not what's keeping me here now. Ronan is my only nephew. There's no distance I won't go to get him back home safely. And I know without any doubt that if it were me that had been taken, Jenna and the others would do the same thing. They'd be right where I'm standing, chasing me down to the ends of the world."

He gave a snort and nodded. "You're probably right about that."

I knew I was. "It's not just my family tied up in this now, Judan. It's yours, too. Maylea is your cousin. She's blood. And she's caught up in this, too."

His gaze turned colder, more serious, as he stared me down again. There was grim acknowledgment in the way his stern, sharp features creased in a scowl. "She's using divine power."

"Paligno's divine power," I clarified.

His eyes went a little wide.

I couldn't hold back a faint, ironic smile. "Looks like the God of Life isn't quite done with your family yet. She might not be a lapiloque, but she's slinging power around just like Jaevid did back when we fought the Tibrans. I trust you know what that means."

His lips parted and his gaze became distant. Quiet mortification crept over his features like a curling fog bank easing in over the marshes of Southwatch. He blinked slowly, then refocused on me with a twinge of terror in his voice. "A war."

"Arlan warned that this is exactly what his sister, Sadeera wants. She's choosing her weapons already. And it would seem the gods are choosing theirs." I leaned in closer, lowering my voice so anyone who might be lurking around outside eavesdropping wouldn't be able to overhear. "It's time to pick a side, my friend. This may be the last fight for all of us."

"EVERYONE, STAY CLOSE. WE'RE GOING TO HEAD SOUTH, UP INTO THE RESIDENTIAL terrace, and make our way to the far side of the island. There, I know of an inn where we can settle for the evening," Violet explained hastily, sticking abnormally close to my side as we all shuffled back out onto the deck. "Reigh, you take lead and I'll guide you. Walk fast and stay in the flow of traffic. We're going to get stared at, so brace yourselves. We're not exactly dressed to blend in, but we can fix that soon enough."

She wasn't wrong about that. One glance along the nearest shoreline, where throngs of people moved along the network of boardwalks, and I had a feeling we were going to need a wardrobe change—quickly. No one else was wearing heavy wool, thick fur-trimmed leathers, or layers of padded clothing like we were. In fact, the styles were a little similar to Luntharda, with lots of thin, brightly colored silks, leather-strapped sandals or light canvas-woven shoes, and broad-brimmed hats of woven reeds or veils to keep the sun at bay.

This was going to be a big change from Maldobar.

Boy, was this a bad time to be redheaded and fair-skinned. The ship had been bad enough, and I'd spent a considerable amount of time below deck. Now, I would definitely need some sun protection as soon as humanly possible, even if it meant I had to wear one of those funny-looking hats. Great.

The sailors on deck of the *Fog Dancer* were still tying the ship down to the extremely crowded harbor as we started down the gangplank onto the network of piers that led back to the boardwalk. Gulls and other sea birds fluttered and squawked overhead, making the tiny dragon on my shoulder hiss some and hide closer against my neck. I guess to them she might look snack-sized.

Judan stood at the base of the gangplank, the wind fluttering in his long coat and the feather on his hat. He watched us deboard, giving Thatcher a nod and awkward handshake before finally settling his steely-eyed gaze on Maylea. She, on the other hand, glared back up at him like a bristled alley cat—fearless and ready to attack at the first wrong move.

They stared one another down for a few seconds, and I couldn't stop my hands from slowly curling into fists as Judan's eyes narrowed. Then he reached back, taking a long parcel wrapped in old burlap from where it was leaned up against a nearby mooring post. I hadn't even noticed it until then, but as he handed it to her wordlessly, I recognized the shape an instant before she unwrapped it.

Maylea's expression went slack in surprise and she stared down, mouth agape, at the beautiful longbow and matching quiver now resting in her hands. I recognized those weapons immediately. That level of craftsmanship, complete with a greevwood blade affixed into the design on the bow's lower limb, was one I'd seen only in Luntharda—in the hands of royals.

That was Judan's old bow and quiver, the one he'd used before he lost his hand. Had he brought that over to our ship at some point? Or ... was that something Malina had of his? Why was she stashing his belongings if she hated him so much. Unless, she hadn't always hated him ... Ugh. Gods. I could not start chasing that rabbit right now.

"Your parents trained you how to fight?" Judan asked her sternly.

She flicked him a guarded, still-suspicious glance. "Yes. And a few others helped."

His lips pursed and he gave one, stiff nod. "Good. Then I trust you'll know how to use that properly."

Maylea stared back down at it, running her fingers over the beautiful engravings on the grip and limbs. Her mouth mashed together and twisted to one side thoughtfully before she answered. "It's my weapon of choice, actually. I can use daggers well enough, but I'm better with a bow—like my mother was."

Something sparked in Judan's expression, cracking that veneer of cold indifference as he watched her gingerly handling that fine weapon. I had to blink a few hard times just to make sure I wasn't imagining it. Was that ... a proud little smile?

Had something I said to him actually made it through that thick skull of his?

No. No way. I had to be imagining it.

"You have a great many family members who also possessed that skill," he said and nodded to the longbow. "See that you take care of it. Practice. It's likely got a heavier draw than you're used to."

"I'll manage," Maylea replied. She cast him another, only slightly wary glance before she stood up straighter and squared her shoulders proudly. "Thank you."

"Shall we call it a truce, then?" He stretched out a hand toward her.

Maylea studied him hard for a moment before she finally took his hand and gave it one, hard shake. Gods and Fates. I couldn't remember a time when she'd looked more like Beckah than she did right then.

"Fine," she agreed at last. Putting the bow and quiver over her shoulder, her sea green eyes darted over him one last time. Then she nodded and stepped around him, passing by close enough that her shoulder barely brushed his.

I had to smile. I couldn't help it. Neither of her parents would have liked that she was here, but I was fairly sure they both could have appreciated the irony of that fearless, stubborn streak. Especially her mother.

Poor Jaevid.

I made my way toward Judan at the end of our group with Violet only a few steps ahead of me. While she waited with the others, I turned to him and sighed heavily. "I don't suppose you've had a change of heart and would like to sail us up to that library, after all, eh?"

Judan's expression dimmed. "Even if I had, it wouldn't be possible. Not with the Nar'Haleenan warships patrolling so often. The *Squall Queen* could take them in a skirmish, if she had to. But this ship wouldn't stand a chance. I'd be doing you more harm than good by even trying."

"Right," I groaned and rubbed the back of my neck. "Well, thanks anyway."

"I wish I had more to offer in the way of help, but my resources are limited. I'll be here for the next few weeks, most likely, while we try to get this ship repaired and seaworthy again. If you happen to make it back here with your precious cargo, I'll happily ferry you back to Maldobar."

"I appreciate the sentiment," I sighed. "We're all working with limitations now. Just try to stay out of trouble, would you? No going after Malina out of spite? That ship has literally sailed."

His smirk was cryptic and a little unnerving. "Ah, yes. It sailed once before, too. But I'll keep that in mind. And you watch your back," he warned before offering me a handshake, as well. "I mean it. This place ... it isn't like home. The same rules don't apply. Take care of yourself, and guard your identities well."

"Doesn't sound that different from home," I managed a hoarse, weary laugh as I shook his hand. After all, he was the one that used to run around our kingdoms, passing himself off as a commoner, all so he could spy and run covert missions for King Jace.

Ahh. Simpler times for us all.

Then again, maybe that should have been an indication to me that he knew what he was talking about. Regardless, all I could do now was take the next step, keep my eyes open, and trust that Violet knew what she was doing. Without her, we didn't stand a chance.

I said my final farewells and our group began to move away from the ship into the flow of traffic on the boardwalk. With her head down and face obscured by the hood of a light gray, linen cloak, Violet couldn't have looked any more uncomfortable if she'd been standing barefoot on pinecones. But having her touch me like that, her much smaller hand reaching up to grip the sleeve of my tunic right above my elbow, didn't feel strange. She kept her side pressed against mine like a frightened child as we passed a company of men dressed in colorful matching armor. Weird. They must have been city guards or something.

I couldn't dwell on who they were for long, though, and I knew gawking at them would only make them more suspicious of the flock of weather-beaten foreigners who had just staggered ashore in their port. Instead, my mind was tangled up in how having Violet's side pressed against mine was so oddly comfortable. Usually, that sort of contact made me cringe and feel sick, like it was just an excuse for someone to get close enough to attack me when I let my guard down. Hmmm.

I shook my head. Nope—stop it. I couldn't go there. Not again. Now wasn't the time or place, and I'd already strolled that avenue enough to know that, for me, it always ended in disaster. No need to repeat that performance.

Even if, deep down, that aching, gnawing, agonizing feeling was already pulling at my heart like someone wringing out a washrag.

Hope—back again like a weed sprouting through the cracks in a stone. And there was nothing I could do to stop it.

23

CHAPTER TWENTY-THREE

Leaving the ship behind felt like abandoning the safety of a fortress in the throes of battle. Not that I was in any way enamored with sailing, but at least it was familiar ground. I'd take that over walking blindly into hostile territory any day.

Now, we were at the mercy of Violet's knowledge and her ability to get us to our next safe point—which was supposedly an inn somewhere farther inland. Or, I should say, *up*land.

"Follow this south until you reach the first terrace road to the left. We need to climb up the island to the fourth tier," she whispered without looking up. I guess the wig wasn't enough to make her feel secure here. It didn't do much to obscure the color of her eyes.

"Right. Okay, then." I reached forward and gave Thatcher a nudge on the shoulder. "Fall to the back, would you? We need to keep a watch in case anyone follows us or tries to get too close."

"On it," he replied, a hand already resting on the pommel of his xiphos blade as he took up a post at the rear of our group. "Expecting problems already?"

I snorted and shook my head. "With the way things have gone so far? I'm not ruling anything out."

Now wasn't the time to get sloppy. We were here, yes. But Rienka was still a long way from our destination, and every second we wasted put Ronan that much farther out of our reach. Our next objective had to be finding some way across the scorching expanse of desert that lay between Rienka and Nar'Haleen.

Gods, I hoped Violet really did have a plan for this.

The road system on the island of Sol'Karr was unique, to say the least. We trekked uphill, following the wide, white-stone road cut into the steep mountainside like a switchback. It zig-zagged for a while, then turned into a spiral that wound around the central peak of the island. That peak was broken up into terraces, or tiers, all the way to the top.

We passed rows upon rows of tightly smashed together buildings that crowded the roadsides to the left, while the right offered a staggering view of the drop down the mountainside to the port. Now and then, we passed a steep stairway that led between the terraces like a shortcut, and white stone lanterns stood along the roadside on the edge of the wide sidewalk.

The farther up we went, the lighter the crowds became. There were fewer sailors and dockworkers, apart from a handful that looked like they were heading home after a shift. More and more, they seemed to be commoners just going about their business. Some pushed hand carts filled with goods from the market along the steep road, and children ran along in groups chasing flocks of brightly colored birds that looked sort of like fancy-painted chickens. Women in vibrant silk clothes balanced large baskets on their heads as they walked with effortless grace. They chatted merrily and paid no attention to us at all. I guess they were used to seeing disheveled, exhausted strangers come staggering out of the port.

What struck me was the sheer broadness in the variety of races I saw intermingling here. We had a decent mix of humans and Gray elves in Maldobar. We even saw the occasional Damarian. But here ... it was a true melting pot of people unlike anything I'd seen. Some people we passed were human, others were Rienkan or even Lunostri elves, and even more had features I didn't recognize at all. I guess the ports brought in people from all over the world. Maybe that was why no one gave us a second glance as we made our way up to the fourth terrace.

From that high up, I got a much better view of the sheer size of the circular port below. Ships all sailed in a circle around the bay, moving with the current around that single, manmade stone tower that stood right in the center like the hub of a wagon wheel. From so far away, all the vivid colors of the ships' sails made them look like hundreds of pond koi all swimming in a circle. Beautiful ... but strange.

I wondered if Isandri had ever been here before. Had she seen this? She wasn't Rienkan, but maybe she had traveled through here on her way to Maldobar all those years ago.

Violet kept giving muttered directions as we turned off the main road to follow a much narrower one that passed between the tall, slim buildings. They seemed to be primarily homes, and the road was barely wide enough for a handcart to pass through. Or, rather, there were many homes all smashed into the various floors of each building. Apartments, I guess. Regardless, each one had at least a dozen windows facing the street. Some of them even had small balconies covered with potted flowers or strings of drying laundry that stretched over the street from one window to another.

We walked until the street took a sharp right turn. There, right on the corner, a building painted a sun-bleached shade of sky blue towered over us. The chipping paint on the wooden sign posted right over the door read The Whale's End. The sign itself was cut in the shape of a whale's tail, and it rattled every time a stiff sea wind howled through the narrow street.

"Here," Violet announced as she tugged my arm to get me to stop. "Let me go in first. The owner is an old friend, but he is wary of strangers."

I nodded, and her hand slid away from me as she stepped to the front door of the inn and gingerly pushed it open to let us all inside. The space within was dark and cramped. The smell of something herbal I didn't recognize hung thick in the air, seeming to come from behind the counter on the right. Embers glowed in a sunken fire pit in the middle of a seating area with a few, well-worn cushions arranged around it. On the far wall, a narrow staircase led up into the rest of the building. There wasn't a soul in sight.

At least, not until Violet made her way over to the counter and reached up to tug on a string of bells hanging from the ceiling. They tinkled musically, and someone made a rasping, coughing, grumbling sound. A figure I hadn't even noticed, leaning up against a corner in the gloom, suddenly lurched to life and hobbled over to the counter. A heavyset, human man glowered at us from down the length of the smoking pipe he held between his teeth. He had more hair on his bushy, white eyebrows than he did on the rest of his head, and they wiggled some as he squinted at each of us. Then his gaze halted on Violet and his puffy, wrinkled features pinched up in what might have been a smile. Or maybe a grimace. I honestly couldn't tell.

"Well, well. If it isn't Miss Violet back to cause more trouble." He rasped, his voice scraping in a way that almost sounded painful. "Bringing a lot of friends with you this time, I see. Let me guess. A few rooms, off the books, and no questions, aye?"

Brushing back the hood of her cloak, Violet cast him a sweet grin and shrugged coyly. "You know me so well, Figall. Dashing as ever, I see. If you can manage it, we'd love two rooms on the top floor."

"Aye. Of course. I take it your boss-man is still digging his fingers around in the markets here, eh? Still looking for trouble in all the right places?" He gave another hacking sound that might have been a laugh as he shifted over to a thick ledger and began jotting something down. A room-roster, maybe? "I got your rooms if you got the coin."

She did, and quickly counted out ten golden coins onto the counter before sliding one extra across it and leaving her finger pressed to it. That coin, I noticed, was a little different from the others. It had something etched into the top. A symbol—no, wait. Initials? I couldn't tell, and the old man, Figall, eyed the coin for less than a second before he quickly swiped it off the counter and tucked it into his pocket.

"Hrrrrmm. Shoulda known it was that kind of trouble. Too much strange talk comin' from the east. How soon you wanting to see him, then?" he asked, his voice edged with caution now. There was a strange, dark twinkle in his eyes as he glanced over our company again.

My nerves gave a jolt of silent alarm when he paused on Maylea, seeming to study her a little bit longer than the rest of us. To be fair, though, she was the only one with a giant, yellow-eyed crow sitting on her shoulder. He didn't even seem all that shocked at the sight of the tiny dragoness perched on me, busily preening her scales. Strange ...

"As soon as possible. Let him know time is of the essence," Violet replied, her voice quieter. "Tonight, if he can manage it."

"I'll see what I can do." Figall grunted as he bent down, rummaging around under his counter for a metal box that he raked all the coins into. Then he handed over a pair of old, tarnished brass keys. "Enjoy your stay. No fighting in the rooms, if you can manage it. I just had them all cleaned last week." He glanced over at Maylea, the crow, and then to the tiny dragon sitting on my shoulder. The embers in his long pipe glowed as he took in a deep breath and sighed, puffing smoke through both nostrils. "And see that your ... *pets* don't soil the floor. I'll charge you extra if I have to clean up fodder."

"Perfectly understandable." Violet's voice had all the sweetness of fresh wild honey as she took the keys and handed one to me. "Let me know when he's ready to meet. We'll be upstairs."

"YOU REALLY TRUST THAT GUY?" THATCHER ASKED AS WE MADE OUR WAY UP THE narrow staircase to the fifth floor of the inn. "Not to seem ungrateful, but he seems a little—"

"Shifty?" Violet finished for him. She rolled her eyes as she stopped before a door and opened it with her key. "Welcome to the criminal world, dragonrider. We're all a bit shifty. No one trusts someone who says what they mean and does what they say—not in this business."

"Sooo, you don't trust him?" Thatcher looked like he might start smoking from the ears as he followed our group inside. "Then why are we staying here?"

"Because he is the lesser of many evils, darling. That's the name of our game, currently. Rienka is a beautiful place, yes, but trust me ... that luster wears off quickly. Make no mistake, we are in a kingdom rife with crime, espionage, war, and more desperate people than you can possibly imagine. We cannot afford to trust anyone but one another now, which is precisely why you will be keeping watch on the children right here while Reigh and I fetch us some decent clothes."

"I thought we needed to stay together," I protested, mostly because I did not believe for a single second that Thatcher was capable of babysitting Maylea and keeping her in one place. Nope. Not going to happen.

"We do, but we also need clothes and supplies. Going in to meet Sulam dressed as we are would be very unwise. The more we can blend in, the easier it will be for us to get to work. My hope is to leave this city far behind us by dawn." She threw down her pack and began rummaging through it, taking out two velvet pouches and tossing one to me.

I snagged it out of the air and bounced it in my hand. It made what sounded like coins inside rattle musically. "Packed a lot of pocket change, did you?"

"Arlan gave me enough to get by if we were to run into trouble, but it's all we've got, so we must be frugal. We'll get clothes and some rations. Nothing more."

Maylea raised her hand and then seemed to realize that was completely ridiculous. She flushed and scratched at the back of her head instead, "I-I, um, I need a few arrows for this bow, if you don't mind."

Violet nodded and stood, straightening out her cloak before she pulled the hood back down. "We can do that. Just ... please promise us you'll stay here. This place is incredibly dangerous. Can you give us your word, please?"

Maylea cast Lukani a sideways glance where he still perched on her shoulder. He ruffled his dark feathers and settled down, teasing at her ear with his beak. It made her grin some and squirm away. "Fine, fine. Yes. We'll stay here with Thatcher."

Somehow, I found that extremely hard to believe.

I guess Thatcher could read my suspicion clearly enough because he put a hand on Maylea's other shoulder and met my gaze with a sympathetic smile. "I've got this. Trust me."

I did. It was *her* I didn't trust. As in, the mischievous little girl who had an incredible talent for doing the exact opposite of what I asked every time I turned my back. Ugggh.

"Come along. You can fret about it on the way," Violet teased as she passed me on her way back out the door.

I began to follow, then stopped in the doorway and glanced back at the two—er, well, three of them. Then I took Vexi off my shoulder and planted her on Thatcher's head. "If something goes wrong and we don't return before sundown, take them and go back to the ship with Judan. Got it?"

"Understood," he confirmed with a chuckle, squirming as Vexi circled around in his mop of golden hair before settling in like a roosting hen.

Right. I sucked in a deep, steadying breath and tried to swallow back against the rising swell of absolute horror that made me want to throw up. No big deal. Just leaving Jaevid's daughter in a strange hotel room in a potentially-hostile foreign kingdom. Nothing to worry about, right? I mean, Thatcher was there with her. So was Lukani. What could possibly go wrong?

Gods above ... someone help me.

I muttered a pathetic prayer as I walked alongside Violet back downstairs and out of the inn. She didn't stop or even say a word to Figall as we went by, and he didn't get up from where he was reclining in a rickety chair in the corner, puffing on his pipe again. I guess he knew better than to ask what we were up to. I tried to take that as a good sign.

Violet led the way back down several terraces to the busier streets lined with shops. She'd gone back to sticking close to my side, keeping her head down, but didn't reach out to take my arm this time. I didn't take it personally, though. Not when I could clearly see two daggers belted down the sides of her legs when the wind blew through her cloak just right.

It took us a few minutes and several stops to find a place that sold simple, everyday clothing in the local style. The woman minding the small, second-story boutique seemed all too excited to adorn me in her fashions. She chattered excitedly to Violet in a language I didn't understand—Rienkan, I guessed, since she was quite obviously a Rienkan elf—and handed me armloads of brightly colored fabrics neatly folded into squares. Each one was a garment, as it turned out, but I couldn't make sense of which ones were meant for me until Violet basically shoved me to the back of the shop where a couple of changing stalls were fashioned out of long wool tapestries that hung from the ceiling.

Violet took the first stall and slipped inside with her own stack of clothes, and that left the other one for me. I hedged inside, staring at the thin sheet of tapestry that separated our changing rooms, and wondered if she was cruel enough to do something to embarrass me while I tried putting these clothes on.

Yeah. She definitely would. Time to do this fast.

Unfortunately, there was nothing swift about how long it took me to peel off my extremely filthy, sea-tattered old clothes and cast them into a pile on the floor of my stall. My socks were basically two soggy sausage casings, and they hit the floor with a slapping sound. Yuck. My shirt wasn't much better off, thanks to being held to my body beneath my leather jerkin. Double-yuck.

"I guess it's stupid to ask if there's anywhere we might be able to get a bath at some point," I muttered as I wrestled my way into the light-weight, baggy silk pants that gathered at my ankles. They tied around my hips, and fit pretty well—apart from the fact that they were so light and airy that it basically felt like being naked. I'd worn similar things in Luntharda, yes, but that was decades ago. It would take some getting used to.

"Perhaps, but it will have to be later," Violet answered, her voice sounding so close thanks to that thin tapestry that it startled me a little. I wasn't used to, you know, changing around strange women like this anymore. Not that she was strange. Ehhh, okay, so she was strange-ish. No worse than the rest of us, though. Whatever. I'd gotten used to Maldobar's much more socially modest habits over the years.

Most of the clothing did fit similarly to robes I'd worn in Luntharda when I was a teenager. But it had been quite some time since I'd put any on, and I couldn't figure out what was going on with the sleeves on the light, white linen tunic she'd handed me. Every time I slipped it over my head, I seemed to come out an arm-hole. What the heck? Arrgghh. Was it not the correct size or something? I muttered Lunthardan curses under my breath as I turned in a circle, still trying to wrestle my way into it properly.

Then I heard her laugh.

I turned around to find Violet peering into my changing stall, grinning wolfishly as though she were enjoying my suffering. Great.

"And here I thought you could manage. Not used to having to don your own clothes without royal dressers assisting, Your Highness?" she snickered, her scarlet eyes glittering with delight.

I scowled and yanked the tunic off again. "Something is wrong with this. Or it's the wrong size."

"Or you just don't know what you're doing," she corrected as she slipped into my stall while I was still fighting with the stupid waist sash thing I had assumed went around my hips.

"For crying out loud—and what are all these ribbon tie things on the sleeves supposed to go to?" I growled.

Violet just rolled her eyes. Already dressed in her own ensemble of dark, midnight blue and black silks, she took my tunic and held it up to scrutinize it for a moment. Then she gave it a little shake to get all those ribbon-things untangled.

I took that moment to quickly and subtly examine her outfit, which was a bit more revealing than anything people wore in Maldobar. The billowy top showed her midriff right below her ribs, but the high-waisted belt and silk wrap covered her lower abdomen. The sleeves were gathered at her wrists, and were open on the shoulders. Her pants looked similar to the ones I wore, only she had already wrapped her legs from her knees to her ankles in more of that silk. She'd slipped on her regular, knee-high black boots over those wraps, and fitted her belt of daggers to her waist, too.

I guess that meant I could still wear my kafki—hopefully, anyway.

Violet gave a snickering little sigh as she stepped over and showed me how to slip into my thin linen tunic so it hung open in the front, then tied it in place with a long sash of dark blue silk around my waist like hers. The ribbons on the sleeves did end up being long fabric ties, and they were fixed to the sleeves so I could fasten them up around my shoulders, effectively making my tunic sleeveless when I wanted. Interesting.

She showed me how to fasten my leather doublet and belt, then wrapped my calves so I could put on my boots again. I felt much better with my kafki hanging back at my hips where they belonged, and stooped down to slip one of my daggers into the side of my boot. The other I tucked into my waist wrap, just out of plain sight.

"That will have to do, I'm afraid." Violet stood with her hands on her hips, still looking me over as though searching for imperfections. "We'd do better with proper sandals, but leatherworking costs more, and we're being frugal. Hopefully we aren't here long enough for it to make much difference."

"Any amount of time I don't have to look at Thatcher's hairy toes is a blessing," I grumbled as I rolled my old clothes up into a ball and tucked them under my arm. "What about the others?"

"I've got clothes for them already." She held a hand out expectantly, almost like she wanted me to take it. "Let's be off. We need to get some rations and waterskins, then I've got to think about this meeting with Sulam before I—"

She stopped mid-sentence as I slipped my hand into hers. Her expression went slack as she stared down at it, then up at me. Then that coy, wry grin curled over her lips again. She batted her eyes and pursed her lips a little. "Oh, my dear Lieutenant. Not that I'm not flattered by the offer, but I was actually asking for your *clothes*."

Oh. Oh crap.

I jerked my hand back and stuffed my old clothes in her direction, my face burning like

I'd stuck my head into a bucket of dragon venom. "You were the one hanging onto my arm earlier," I muttered and looked away.

"Yes, true. It seemed like a pleasing alternative to staring around and having someone notice what I am. But how sweet of you to offer it again." She kept on crooning as I stomped away from the changing rooms.

"I am *not* sweet," I grumbled through my teeth as I stood back with my arms crossed, glaring at her back while she went to pay for the new clothes. I noticed her slip the woman a few extra coins and leave our old, ragged ones there. Hmm. What was that about?

"She'll make sure they're destroyed and forget she ever saw us. Can't leave a trail now, can we?" Violet explained as we made our way back down to the street. She paused right before going outside and donned a new cloak, this one made of a much lighter, silvery gray satin. The hood had a red beaded border that hung down like a veil that obscured her eyes from anyone taller that looked down at her. A distraction to keep people from noticing her eyes? Clever.

"Whatever you say." I sank back on my heels, my gaze roaming the crowds that slipped by on the street before us. The sun was beginning to sink, turning the horizon all around us radiant shades of purple, orange, pink, and gold. It made the ocean sparkle like a field of scattered diamonds. And it made her fair skin shine like alabaster.

But she wasn't watching me. Her eyes were on the ships, the streets, and the people. Constantly moving. Always keen and sharp as a razor's edge. That was a kind of focus I had to admire.

"The last time I stood here, this city was under Tibran occupation," she said suddenly, her voice soft and somewhat broken. "Now, everywhere I look, it's all I can see. Their dark ships in the ports. Their soldiers marching the roads, trampling the bodies of the common people underfoot. Their fires in the night burning the temples like forges. It was many years ago. Obviously, much has been rebuilt and the land has healed. And yet ..."

"You still see it, like a ghost in your own mind," I finished for her.

Her scarlet eyes darted up to meet my gaze from beneath that glittering, bead-trimmed hood. "I know you think I'm only here at my employer's insistence. That I'm only doing all of this because he ordered me to. But the idea of seeing that sort of destruction and cruelty happen again at the hands of someone like Sadeera is ... unbearable. I won't stand for it."

"Neither will we," I agreed. "Just keep showing us the path, Violet. We're all in this together now. We've got your back."

Her expression tensed some and her lips pressed into a firm, uncomfortable line, almost like the idea of that kind of pressure made her uneasy. Or maybe it was the prospect of now being a part of our makeshift little disaster of a family. "You truly trust me that much?" she asked as she flicked me a sideways glance. The failing light caught in her eyes like firelit rubies, and I couldn't ignore the way it made my heart skip a beat. She was ... beautiful.

Ugh. No. Ridiculous—I couldn't get caught up thinking things like that. Especially not now.

"Until you give me a reason not to," I replied. I tried to show her a confident, half-grin. Anything to make it seem like I wasn't having an internal mental breakdown.

It must've been convincing enough because she just gave a snorting, bemused little chuckle and shook her head. "I'll keep that in mind."

A sudden, panicked squawking cry made us both look up—just in time for a flurry of lime green scales to smack right into my face. Tiny claws pricked at my skin as I flailed back. What the—?! Was that Vexi?

She went on yowling and hissing like an angry feral cat as I pried her off and held her out at arm's length. That's when I noticed she was covered in something. A thick red liquid was splattered over her green scales and yellow underbelly. There was even some spray on her wings.

My stomach dropped. Every muscle in my body locked up solid.

Oh no. Was that ... blood?

24

CHAPTER TWENTY-FOUR

Violet seemed to notice it the same instant I did. Our eyes locked. My pulse boomed in my ears like the thundering of war drums. Something had happened—something bad. We had to get back to the inn.

Right. Now.

Without a word, Violet and I took off in unison. We ran through the city streets, ducking push-carts, pushing through crowds of people on their way to the market, and sprinting through the narrow alleys that passed through the terraces. I bit down against the rising, scorching heat that burned at the back of my throat. Gods and Fates, we had only been gone an hour, two at most, and something had already gone wrong? Had someone been following us in from the port? Just waiting for us to separate?

Or was this something else? Gods forbid—it couldn't be Sadeera, could it? Had she sent her Hands of Fate after us already?

That idea hit my mind like a white-hot spike and drove my legs to pump faster. By the time we reached the door of the inn, I had left Violet a few paces behind. I hit the door at a dead-sprint, flinging it open and finding ... nothing. Figall was nowhere to be seen. Nothing in the room looked out of place, though.

I bolted for the stairs with Violet right on my heels.

I heard it before we even reached the fifth floor.

Someone groaned loudly, their cries garbled and desperate as they tried to call for help.

Oh Fates, that was Thatcher!

Rushing down the hall, I spotted the door to our room dangling off the hinges before I even got to it. Blood was smeared across the tiled floor in a mixture of footstep and slide marks that led to a neighboring room right across the hall from ours.

I reached down and grasped the soft leather hilts of my kafki blades.

Violet gripped a dagger in each hand and tipped her head across the hall.

I nodded. She would check there first. I'd check our room.

We stepped apart in perfect formation, whirling to the side of the doors without a sound. Then I stormed into our room, blades drawn, and sank into a defensive position—prepared for an assault.

There wasn't one. The room was an absolute wreck, with the bed flipped against the wall, the washstand smashed, and a smear of blood coating the far wall and pooling on the floor. A strange, acrid smell hung in the air. It burned my eyes and made me cough as I stared around at the chaos.

My pulse skipped suddenly, every nerve firing at once in a rush of panic as movement by the window made me flinch. No, it wasn't an enemy. Across the room, just beside the window, Thatcher stood ... pinned to the wall with a longsword through his abdomen.

Oh, gods!

He looked up at me groggily, blood running from the corners of his mouth and his expression skewed in desperation. "Th-They ... t-took ... them!" he groaned through his teeth, hands still reaching futilely for the hilt of the sword that pinned him. But he couldn't reach it to pull it out on his own. His hands dripped red, palms slashed with fresh cuts like he'd tried to grip the sharp blade itself.

I turned quickly, doing a fast scan of the rest of the room to make sure there was no one hiding, waiting to make a surprise assault. There wasn't. The room was empty. Maylea and Lukani were gone.

I immediately sheathed my weapons and rushed to Thatcher, putting a hand on his shoulder to help hold him up as I examined the place where the blade had punched through his leather jerkin and into his abdomen. Dark blood flowed from the puncture, oozing down his leg and the wall where he was pinned to puddle on the floor. Gods and Fates—he couldn't last long like this. I had to get it out. I had to stop the bleeding.

"VIOLET!" I yelled.

She appeared so suddenly, it was as though she'd materialized on the spot. She rushed past, going to help hold Thatcher upright so he didn't fall as I stood back and gripped the hilt of the longsword. Fast and clean. Then I had to get my medical kit, or he might not make it another five minutes. He'd already lost so much blood.

"It's gonna hurt," I warned him as I prepared to yank it free.

Thatcher's head lolled forward, and Violet cast me a desperate, pasty look of panic.

No time to waste.

It took a hard pull to pry the sword out of the wall behind him. Sweet Fates, whoever had rammed it there must have been incredibly strong. It was stuck several inches into the stone and plaster. But as soon as I pried it free, Thatcher let out a groaning cry and crumpled forward. Violet staggered under his weight, barely able to keep him from crashing to the floor.

I threw the blade aside and rushed in to help lie him down on his side. The blade had cut him through-and-through, and we had to get his clothes off so I could see how bad the damage was. I could only pray it hadn't nicked anything vital, but based on how much blood he'd already lost, I knew those chances were slim.

That meant I might only have seconds to save his life.

"Get my medical kit. I need the surgery supplies—now!" I ordered as I began working to take off Thatcher's doublet and tunic, yanking and cutting them away to get a better look at the wound. He shivered as he lay, eyes fixed ahead and brow drawn into a look of focused terror.

"Th-They came in right a-after you left. M-Maybe ... thirty minutes l-later. F-Five of them. All armed," he rasped. "They w-were ready ... for us. Used a ... knockout ... smoke bomb. I-I was t-too far back ... so I d-didn't go down ... r-right away."

"Take it easy, buddy. We can discuss it later. Just try to focus on calming down. Slow breaths, okay? Gotta bring that pulse down for me." I coaxed, applying pressure to the back of the wound as I probed in with my fingers through the front.

His body stiffened, jaw clenching and eyes going wide in pain. But I couldn't stop. I had to know what organs might be damaged.

"Here! I found the kit. What can I do?" Violet knelt down behind him, her expression paler than usual as she watched me work.

"Open it up and spread out the surgical tools. Feels like it's gone through his intestines. Curse it," I muttered as I reached through the wound, probing around slowly and carefully. "There are a few vials of greenish liquid—and remember that paste I gave you when you got stabbed in the leg? Start shoving that down his throat. We've got to get him stabilized."

I had to give her some credit, Violet kept a cool head as she handed me the items I needed. She took globs of the healing remedy and forced them into his mouth, making him gag and choke some until he managed to swallow. Meanwhile, I got to work setting up an emergency surgery kit. If he'd been pinned there long enough to bleed that much, then time was already against us. I couldn't afford to hesitate.

But surgery always seemed to take an eternity. My hands could only work so fast, and I couldn't afford to rush or be reckless. I had to be steady, precise, and certain.

Anything less, and Thatcher wouldn't survive this.

And I'd lose one of the few true friends I'd ever had.

KIRAN HAD WARNED ME ABOUT THE EMOTIONAL RISK OF OPERATING ON SOMEONE I cared about. That I'd be tempted to push things too far, or it would cloud my judgment and ability to think. Even so, I'd seen him break that rule time and time again. He'd even operated on me after I got shot full of Ulfrangar crossbow bolts.

But in that moment, I felt the weight of that warning for the first time in a long time. We were here, so far from home or anyone who might actually want to help us. We had no resources other than what we'd brought with us. We had no idea if whoever had attacked them might come back for us.

Sweat rolled down the sides of my face as I worked, carefully trying to piece together the slashed intestine and repair the damaged veins. Thatcher had fallen silent long ago, but his chest still rose and fell with halting, weak breaths. Not gone yet. But he was hanging by a thread.

My thread.

I had to work faster. I had to keep steady, and get this done before—

His breathing stopped.

My gaze darted up, locking onto Violet as I immediately put a hand to his neck. No pulse.

CURSE IT!

"Breathe for him on my count!" I shouted as I quickly rolled him onto his back and started chest compressions on his sternum. No—by all the gods—I would *not* lose him! Not here! Not now!

Not like this!

"Breathe!" I shouted, pausing long enough for her to hold his nose and tilt his chin back so she could breathe into his mouth and force air back into his lungs.

Then we did it again. And again.

My pulse roared in my ears, drowning out anything else. My eyes welled, but I didn't stop. I pumped my hands against his chest and paused again, commanding her to breathe into him again.

Over and over.

I put a hand to the side of his neck.

A soft, faint thump vibrated against my fingertips.

Back—he was back!

"Keep your hand here and let me know if you feel his heart stop again," I grabbed Violet's hand and showed her how to keep her fingers in the right spot on his neck.

Then I got back to work. But this time, my hands wouldn't quit shaking. My eyes wouldn't stop watering. I-I wasn't going to be able to do this. I was going to lose him.

Something cold prickled on the back of my neck. A chill that struck me straight to the very core of my being. A feeling I knew all too well.

But I hadn't felt it in ... years. Decades.

My gaze darted up, searching the room and every dark corner.

He was standing at the far corner, leaning into the tall, crooked staff with his eerie white eyes glowing softly like two bog fires against the gloom of the dusk. A wide grin stretched over his face—a face that looked exactly like mine.

Noh.

My mouth opened, but nothing would come out. No sound. No cry of alarm. Not even a confused scream of terror.

He raised a hand and put a finger to his lips, then stretched out a hand toward Thatcher.

Panic took me like a whirlwind. What was he doing? Oh, gods, he wasn't trying to take Thatcher's soul, was he? No—he couldn't! I wouldn't let him. I-I—

Thatcher took in a sudden, much deeper breath. His eyes fluttered open, and lively color seemed to rush back into his features as he stared ahead.

What?

I gaped down at Thatcher, watching as he coughed and wheezed, each breath stronger than the last. The wound on his abdomen hadn't changed or healed at all, but he seemed to be fully stable now. He might be able to survive long enough for me to finish the surgery and save him.

"Waste not, want not, brother," Noh's voice chuckled darkly in the back of my mind. *"How nice to finally see you again."*

Every word ran through my mind like the rush of a churning waterfall. My body stiffened, staring back at him as all those memories came flooding back. The last time I'd seen him, the power he and I had shared as the Harbinger of Clysiros. The pain of having that power ripped from me so Argonox could use it for his own wicked plans.

The years I'd spent running from those nightmares.

But Noh wasn't my enemy.

I just didn't understand what this meant. Why was he here again? Hadn't he been commanded to stay in the Vale and work as the shepherd of deceased souls for Clysiros? That was meant to be his eternal duty. So why was I seeing him now?

I should have known better than to think my thoughts were my own with him around. He had always been able to hear my every thought and doubt like we shared a single mind.

His grin widened, showing pointed canine teeth like small fangs, and his eyes flickered with excitement as he tilted his head to one side. "*So many questions, but they will have to wait, dear brother. Now, get to work. Time is running short, and we are already the last to leave the starting line.*"

25

CHAPTER TWENTY-FIVE

Noh was gone before I could blink again. Like a shadow in the night, he came and went without a sound. Violet didn't even seem to notice my response. She was too focused on calming Thatcher as he stared up at her, gaze fixed straight ahead but clearer than ever.

Noh had bought me time. I couldn't afford to waste it.

I finished closing up the wound, repairing all the places where the sword had cut through Thatcher's body, with my hands still trembling some, and a cold sweat prickling over my body. It wasn't until I had thoroughly coated the interior cavity around the wound with every bit of the healing salve I had and stitched it closed, that I could even feel myself breathing at all. My ears still rang as I wrapped bandaging around his middle, making sure it was tight and secured before I did the same with lengths of that silk we'd just gotten for his new outfit. His leather jerkin would help keep his abdomen stabilized, too, and I made sure I laced it up tight enough that he couldn't bend over or jar himself before I finally sat back on my heels and allowed myself a sigh.

"He ... he should be okay. As long as he doesn't get an infection, or reopen it. He needs to rest and heal. Can we get some blankets and pillows from the other rooms? We need to make him a pallet on the floor." I wiped the blood from my hands on a rag from my kit. I would have felt much better moving him somewhere else, or finding a local healing clinic, but right now it would be too risky to move him that much. "It would be good if we could get him drinking water, too. He needs fluids."

Violet nodded somberly and got up, but she hesitated on her way out of the room. Stopping by the door, she bent down to pick up the longsword that had been used to pin Thatcher to the wall. She held it up to the lamplight that ebbed in from the hall, turning it as her scarlet eyes studied it carefully. Then her grip on the hilt tightened. Her throat jumped as she swallowed hard, and her jaw locked solid.

"What's wrong?" I dared to ask.

She licked her teeth behind her lips and brushed a thumb over the round pommel of the weapon, her fingertip tracing over the engraving of a symbol etched there. The shape of a crescent moon with a blade through it.

Wait a second—I had seen that emblem before, hadn't I? My panic-addled brain scrambled at the sight of it. I *had* seen it before. But where? Gods, curse it, I couldn't remember.

Fortunately, there was no mistaking the way Violet's gaze smoldered as she tossed the longsword back to the ground. Her lip curled in disgust and she leveled a furious, wrathful glare upon me. "I know who has the children," she growled through clenched teeth.

My gaze flashed between her and the sword. "Seriously? Who?"

"The weapon bears the mark of the Zenith's Call. It would seem my contact, Sulam, has his own agenda with us. We must find him." Her eyes narrowed, brow crinkling upward as she looked past me to Thatcher with a look of utter anguish. "We will have to leave him here and do this quickly, before it is too late."

I stared back down at Thatcher. Sure, he was doing a little better now. He'd gotten more color back, and was breathing steadily. His heartbeat was still fast, but it was strong. But leaving him here on his own, completely vulnerable, was a bad idea. It went against everything dragonriders stood for. We didn't abandon our own.

"Are you kidding? What if they come back while we're gone and finish him off?" I argued. "He can't even defend himself!"

"They won't." She sounded extremely sure about that. "Sulam already has what he wants from us."

Rage like cinders burned in my chest as I slowly got to my feet. "Maylea and Lukani?" I guessed. "What would some criminal lord want with two kids? He can't possibly know who she is—we didn't even know she was sneaking along with us!"

"No. This isn't about who they are," Violet shook her head as she met my glare. "What Sulam wants is our attention."

Oh, he had that all right. Sulam was about to have more of my attention than he'd ever bargained for.

"Fine. We get them back," I snarled as I stood up and squared my shoulders, already feeling that hum of primal adrenaline coursing through every muscle. "But we do this fast and clean, and we come straight back here. And before we go, we take care of Thatcher. I won't leave until we make sure he's safe."

She was already on her way out of the room, twirling a dagger between her fingers so fast it looked like a silver blur. "Agreed."

I worked on getting Thatcher settled in an adjacent room—one that hadn't been absolutely wrecked and covered in blood—while Violet left the inn in search of extra assistance. I wasn't willing to risk leaving him here, in a room with a door I couldn't close let alone even lock, with no one to watch over him until we returned.

If we returned.

Violet returned a few minutes later with a young human woman dressed in long, sky blue robes. There were tiny white flowers woven into her long dark hair, and she stared at us warily as Violet ushered her in. They exchanged hushed words, speaking a language I recognized only in bits and pieces.

Languages weren't my specialty, but I had picked up a little of it through Isandri. She'd begun teaching me the Nar'Haleenan tongue, which they called Sokraal, which was supposedly the most common in the southern kingdoms. More so than Rienkan or Damarian, anyway. All three languages had borrowed words from one another over the ages, of course, and those were the ones I tended to recognize.

"She is an acolyte of the Temple of Undae," Violet explained as she guided the young woman over to where Thatcher was lying, barely conscious and blinking slowly at all of us. "She has agreed to watch over him until we return."

I nodded, offering a broken word of thanks in her language that probably sounded like baby babble. Pathetic. But it made the young woman smile a little and nod.

"You're sure we can trust her?" I asked Violet, keeping my expression neutral and using the Maldobarian language so maybe the woman wouldn't catch on.

"Yes." Violet sounded certain. "The followers of Undae are pacifists. They reject all forms of violence and even refrain from eating meat as a gesture of their faith."

Good enough for me.

"S-Sorry," Thatcher slurred as I approached his bedside. "I-I should have ... been f-faster."

"Stop that," I grumbled and flashed him a disapproving scowl. "We had no reason to think anyone would hit us this quickly. But Violet thinks she knows who's responsible, and we have to move fast to try to get to the kids before he does something terrible to them, too."

"I-I know," Thatcher said weakly. He stared up at me, expression dejected and riddled with frantic concern. "P-Please .... Get them back. And ... be careful."

"We will. You lie here and rest. No flirting with the pretty priestess, or I'll tell Garnett," I took one of his hands and gave it a reassuring squeeze.

His face turned ten shades of red and he made a few panicked, choking sounds. Good. At least he still had enough blood left to blush like an idiot. A good sign, in my professional medical opinion.

"I'm kidding, idiot. Just rest. I mean it." I tugged Vexi off my shoulder and placed her on the bed next to him. "Keep an eye on him for me, would you, girl?"

My tiny dragoness sat up on her hind legs, chirping and chattering like a little songbird before she finally turned in a few circles and curled up into a little scaly green ball on the pillow next to his head. Her sky-blue eyes followed me all the way to the door as I left, shutting it softly behind me.

I hated this. Leaving him alone right now was a bad idea. He could take a turn for the worse at any moment, and I doubted that an acolyte woman would know what to do to save him. But what choice did I have? I couldn't let Violet go off and try to run this Sulam guy down on her own. They'd taken down Thatcher like it was nothing, leaving him barely alive like some sort of message to us.

A challenge. Or maybe a threat.

Either way, Sulam was going to pay. I'd make sure of it.

Violet was waiting at the base of the stairs on the first floor, spinning that dagger back and forth between her fingers, when I met her. Her gaze flicked around the room, seeming to pick apart every detail of the shoddy little inn's main floor.

"Figall sold us out," she announced as I approached. "He must have turned around and tipped off Sulam's men as soon as we arrived."

I stopped beside her just long enough to pan my gaze around the room, too. She had a good point. He must have been in on it, or at least complicit, because there wasn't a single item out of place down here. No sign of a struggle—or our host.

"Think he'll come back and do something to Thatcher?" I asked.

She started for the exit with purpose in every step. "No."

"Why not?"

"Because he knows if he shows his face here again while I'm still around, I'll gut him like a pig and leave his head on the doorstep."

Right. Well, again, she had a good point. He was probably pretty far down the criminal food chain. If he had any sense at all and wanted to stay alive, he'd do well to make himself scarce until this all blew over and we moved on.

"Where do we go to find Sulam?" I demanded as we left the inn and stepped out into the cool, windy night streets of Sol'Karr.

"Normally, I would do him the courtesy of requesting a meeting through the formal channels, and send a request to meet him at the Zenith Call's headquarters here in the port." Violet's tone was pure venom as she pulled the hood of her cloak down low and slipped her dagger back into her waist wrap. "But he has tried my patience for the last time. We're going to his personal estate in Kua'Tar."

"And he'll be there?"

"Without a doubt." A vicious smile curled over her lips as she led the way through the winding, sloping streets back toward the port. It gave me a little thrill of terror I wasn't expecting, like looking a pit viper right in the eye.

Yikes.

We stalked the nearly-empty city streets all the way to the port. Most of it seemed to be closed for the evening, with only a few lights burning in the occasional portside tavern or inn at this hour. The ships we passed were closed up and tightly guarded, too, with no sign of any crew members still working at this hour.

It didn't take Violet long to find us some transportation, though. Even with the moon now rising over the bay, she flagged down one of the locals driving what looked similar to a sea-chariot drawn by one of those scaly horse-like creatures. We'd seen them before, swimming around while we battled pirates. I'd even ridden one briefly. Not the worst experience in the world, honestly. They moved sort of like a dolphin in the water, fast and nimble.

"Hippocampus. They're a native species here. Very useful," Violet explained, as though she'd noticed me staring at the creature in mystification. Then she turned her focus to the driver, a young elven man who eyed us curiously from beneath the brim of his straw hat. They spoke quickly in Sokraal, and Violet slipped him a few golden coins before waving me over to climb into the back of the chariot with her.

"You really think whoever took the kids managed to get them off this island?" I dared to ask as the driver gave the reins a jostle and clicked his tongue to his swimming steed. We zoomed away from the docks and took a small canal to the south, cutting through the water at a startling speed.

"I know what I would do if I were trying to hide two valuable captives I'd just abducted from an experienced rival." Violet's eyes never left the horizon as she spoke, her expression seeming to slip into something cold and distant. "He'll move them quickly, use their location as leverage, and try to extort us."

"Sounds like you've played this game before." I couldn't help but notice.

She looked down to where she had gone back to fidgeting with one of her daggers again, twirling it through her slender fingers as though it were as easy as breathing. "That's not so surprising, is it? I'm a dirty little spy and a Viperi, after all. And I've known Sulam for a long time. He likes to dabble in trafficking people, when he thinks he can get away with it."

That prospect kindled fresh fury in my chest. I had to look away then, if only to keep my temper in check. "You're saying he might sell them as slaves?"

"I don't know," she admitted. Her voice was barely audible over the rush of the water whooshing past our chariot as we left the bay behind and zipped along the twisting, narrow canals that led away to the neighboring islands. "But believe me when I say, Lieutenant, there are a thousand miserable fates a person can find themselves trapped in here. Being sold as a slave is just one of them, and possibly not the worst."

"And ... what would be the worst, then?" I couldn't imagine anything more terrible than that.

Too late, I realized I probably shouldn't have asked. It was better not to know—not to let myself visualize what might happen to Maylea and Lukani if we didn't find them fast enough.

But Violet answered anyway. "Death in the Caldera."

☙ 26 ❧

CHAPTER TWENTY-SIX

I didn't know what the Caldera was, and right then, there wasn't time to question her about it. Our driver made quick time through the moonlit waters, zipping through the sound and rounding the other islands that stood like dark shapes dotted with hundreds of tiny burning lights. The temples of all sizes stood tall and bright, bathed in silver moonlight atop the highest peaks of the steep mountainsides—a strange sight. There were a few temples in Luntharda, yes. But most were little more than ruins that had been devoured by the jungle long ago. Maldobar wasn't a very religious kingdom, and only a few temples stood in the largest and oldest cities. They weren't used all that much, though.

Worship of the gods seemed to still be very much thriving here in the southern kingdoms, though. Somehow, with Noh's voice still echoing in my head like a whisper I couldn't ignore, that didn't bring me much comfort. If anything, it just added to the confusion. Was I seeing him again because worship was so much more common here? Or did this have something to do with Sadeera? He'd mentioned we were last to leave the starting line. What did that even mean?

My head spun with every dark, terrible memory of my first encounters with him and Clysiros all those years ago. Our relationship had been ... complicated, at best. Nothing at all like Jae's connection to Paligno. I honestly couldn't tell if Clysiros was good or bad. Could deities be something so simple? Was there even a difference in their world?

Some cultures seemed to revere and respect Clysiros like a loving mother who guarded and protected the spirits of the deceased. Others spoke her name like a vicious curse and feared her like a cruel mistress. My own experiences with her had been a mixture of chaos, desperation, violence, and divine vengeance—confusing, to say the least. She wasn't a mother figure. She wasn't a demoness, either. To me, she just *was*.

And I had no idea what her angle was or why she might be sending Noh to me again. It couldn't be a good sign, though. My gut instinct told me that much. If Clysiros was picking a side and choosing her pawn for the war to come, things must be looking more desperate than we had feared.

Especially if *I* was the best choice she could come up with.

Our driver brought us to a small port on the northern tip of a much smaller, somewhat flatter island than Sol'Karr. The landmass of Kua'Tar might have been less mountainous, but it seemed to be far more densely populated because of it. Nearly every square inch of it glittered with the rising towers of buildings all shining with lights like barnacles gripping a rock. Some even jutted out over the ocean.

What stood out above everything else, however, was a structure I couldn't identify. I'd never seen anything like it before. The massive, round building was easily fifteen floors high and more than double that in width. The roof was open like a giant bowl, and even at a distance, I could glimpse hundreds upon hundreds of rows of seating inside through the arched top floor windows. What the heck was that? Some sort of amphitheater?

I didn't get a chance to ask as we pulled up to the dock and quickly climbed out of the chariot-boat. Violet tossed the driver another coin and waved him off, then turned to the port with quiet wrath in her eyes.

We stalked into the streets, moving fast and keeping to the shadows as much as possible. The city seemed to swallow us whole as we passed into the more tightly-packed roads. There were very few broad avenues and even less lighting, no majestic stone braziers or torches to light the twisting path ahead. The snaking alleys wound through the towering buildings like a maze, and I immediately lost all sense of direction with nothing to orient to.

Well, except for that enormous round building. It seemed to sit right at the city's center, and the closer we drew to it, the more it felt like I was shrinking by comparison to its incredible size. The high sand-colored walls were pocked with little open carved holes like windows but with no glass panes, and hundreds of banners hung down from the high walls. Massive torches burning in mirrored structures were lined around it on every side, pointing beams of light up at it so that it practically seemed to glow in the night.

And the farther we went, the more I began to suspect that Violet was taking us right to it.

Yep. That's exactly where we were going.

Or, rather, a majestic-looking building that was built directly adjacent to it. It was cut from the same golden-toned stone and only five floors tall, but obviously had some sort of connection to the main structure. We crouched in the gloom on the opposite side of the street, watching as a company of four armed guards swapped out shifts at the front door of the place. Each was dressed out in matching bronze armor, carried a shield over their back, and a spear in one hand. A crest of white feathers on their helmet matched the one-shouldered cloak fastened to their shoulder pauldrons.

This was bound to be complicated if that was, indeed, where this Sulam person lived. Judging by the ruthlessly hungry way Violet was eyeing it, I decided it probably was. Oh boy.

"I hope you've got a good plan," I murmured.

"I do," she answered quickly. "First, we bypass the guards and get inside. Then we hold Sulam hostage until he gives the children back to us. Once he has, we kill him anyway, just for good measure."

Wow. Okay, a decent start, buuut I was going to need a little more detail than that.

"How well trained are they?" I kept my voice low and nodded to the guards that took their post on either side of the building's large front door.

"Quite well," she purred low. "Which is why I'm going to knock properly while you sneak in through the rooftop garden."

"I'm going to do *what* now?" I balked. That building wasn't as tall as the trees I'd scurried along in Lunthardа when I was a kid—but still. I didn't see any other structures nearby I could even use to access it. "You do realize I can't fly, right?"

She snorted and rolled her eyes. "Now, now, Lieutenant. Don't they train dragonriders to be creative?"

"No. They don't, actually." I frowned. "But I'll be sure to bring that up at the next academy faculty meeting."

"What a bore you lot are," she scolded and gestured to the right side of the building. "Around the back you'll find two balconies—one at the second floor and another at the fourth. There are ample handholds to make the climb, but take care you stay out of sight of the windows and do not try entering through the balconies themselves. They will certainly be guarded, especially tonight when Sulam knows he has provoked us. Keep an eye out for more patrols around the perimeter of the building, too." Violet paused, casting me a slightly worried sideways glance, as though she were wondering if I could actually pull this off or not.

Great.

I glared back at her. "I was a scout before I was a dragonrider, you know."

"Oh, I am aware," she muttered and shook her head slightly. "That's what I'm worried about."

Ugh. Whatever. I guess I'd just have to prove myself in action.

"There's a servant's entrance hidden in the hedges on the rooftop garden. Far eastern-most corner. It'll be locked, but I trust you can manage that."

I took in a deep, steadying breath. "No problem," I muttered.

It might be a problem. But right now, it was a *later* problem.

"Make your way down to the fourth floor. That is where Sulam's meeting chamber is. I'm sure he'll take me there under heavy guard. When you see an opportunity to strike at him, do not hesitate. The guards certainly won't. You'll have the element of surprise, so see that you don't waste it."

"Got it." I reached back to tie up the sleeves to my tunic, fastening them up around my shoulders so they didn't get in the way.

"If you can manage it, try not to get yourself killed, hm?" she jabbed again.

"You really have no faith in me at all, do you?" I grumbled as I checked my weapons and prepared to break off to the alleyway on our right.

"That depends on if you climb better than you dance." Her grin was a delighted mixture of satisfaction and smugness that sort of made me want to do something reckless purely out of spite. So, I did. Right as I stood to begin my stealthy approach to the building, I quickly licked one of my fingers, getting it nice and slobbery, and stuck it right in her ear.

Violet gasped and hissed sharply, flailing back and wiping frantically at her ear. I could feel her glare at my back as I stalked away, smirking to myself. Did she really think I was just going to sit there and take that kind of abuse? Nope. If she wanted to keep playing those childish teasing games, then I was going to reciprocate.

And I had an entire arsenal of immature pranks that I'd accumulated over my student years at the academy just waiting to get used again.

Getting around to the back of the building wasn't much of a challenge. Thanks to the compactness of the city streets, there were plenty of dark corners to hide in as I made my way there. Violet was right, though. More patrols of armed guards marched in timed synchronization around the base, stopping occasionally and then moving on. I had to time my approach just right and make the climb to that first balcony.

Staying low and moving fast, I darted in as the first company of guards passed around the corner to the right, keeping right behind them and using the *clunk, clunk, clunk* of their armor to hide my footsteps. Picking up speed, I dashed straight for the edge of the building and made my first jump, seizing some of the ornately carved, decorative reliefs along the edges of the building and using them to clamber up to that second-floor balcony. It wasn't pretty. Not by a long shot. My feet and hands slipped and scraped, and my heart hit the back of my throat when one of my hands slid off a smooth handhold and I dangled for a second, scrambling to find a different, better grip.

Then I froze, holding perfectly still as the next patrol of guards began to march by. I held my breath, not even daring to blink as they passed. They paused right on the same mark as the last group, staring out at the streets in every direction, but never looking up. Seconds passed. Then they all turned on a heel and began marching away.

Whew. So far, so good.

I used the railing of the balcony to start my next climb, jumping off and angling my body to avoid the windows as I hoisted myself up one movement at a time. My calves jumped and throbbed from standing with all my weight on my toes. My forearms pulsed and ached, making my hands go strangely numb. Gods, it had been too long since I'd climbed like this. I'd never been more glad Murdoc wasn't here to witness this disaster.

By the time I reached the fourth floor, my hands were so fatigued I could barely close them at all. But something had changed down below. The company of guards had quit marching around on their patrols. Hmm. Was that because of Violet going to the door? Maybe she had drawn all their focus.

Whatever the reason, I decided to use that to my advantage for as long as possible. It took everything I had to climb the last floor and finally haul myself over the edge of the railing that lined the rooftop. I hit the tiled floor, crashing through a few small, potted shrubs on my way down with a cracking of branches and heavy *THUD*.

Ouch.

Great. Someone was bound to hear that.

I lay perfectly still, fighting for every breath as my arms and hands trembled from the effort and my calves twisted themselves up into cramping knots. Fates, help me. I was getting too old for this. My body didn't hold up as well as it had during the Tibran war.

Curse it all.

I lay there and suffered silently for a minute or two, waiting to see if my commotion had attracted any attention. But there was no other sound. No approaching footsteps. Nothing.

I rolled over and slowly got up, keeping my posture in a crouch as I darted through the small jungle of manicured fruit trees, flowers, palms, and exotic plants that were arranged in massive pots or manicured beds. The familiar smell of the jungle plant life soothed my panicked brain as I made my way to the spot where Violet had assured me there would be a door.

And there was. I found it hidden between two huge palms, just as she promised.

I went for the golden handle and began to twist—just as someone on the other side suddenly grabbed it and ripped it open.

I stood, totally exposed, standing in the doorway as a young boy in ragged white clothing gaped up at me. His features were sunken and gaunt, and his golden eyes had gone as wide as saucers in horror. He had a pot of something vile in his rail-thin arms. A chamber pot?

I froze where I stood, my mouth hanging open in surprise. Oh no. He was just a kid. He didn't look ten years old. What was I supposed to do? I wasn't about to hurt him.

Then his mouth slowly closed. A grim sense of resolve settled over his face and he looked down. He took one big step to the side, out of my path, and kept his head low.

And I understood.

He was going to pretend he hadn't seen me.

I didn't know why, but judging by his filthy clothes that hung in tatters off his emaciated body, the scars that flecked his skin, and the way he trembled when I walked past—he wasn't just a servant. He was one of Sulam's slaves.

A sense of helplessness overtook me as I moved by, leaving him in the doorway and going quickly down the steps that led into the house. I didn't know what to do for him. I didn't know how to help. I couldn't take him with me into the teeth of a fight.

But I knew who was responsible for his situation.

And I would deal with that piece of scum right now.

27

CHAPTER TWENTY-SEVEN

My pulse boomed in my ears, fueled by rage and adrenaline that scorched my veins like dragon venom, as I made my way through the interior of Sulam's private home. The servant's hidden passages within the walls took me down behind the large hallways until, at last, I found a door hidden behind another large, potted palm where I could exit and duck down to watch for guard patrols.

A few ran by almost right away, but they didn't stop or even give a second glance in my direction as they rushed over the polished marble floors and disappeared around a corner. Hmm. Probably heading to reinforce security now that Violet was here. I needed to follow. But I had to be careful.

I darted from one hiding place to the next, measuring my steps and keeping out of the center of the hall as much as possible. Once I reached the corner, I peered around it and immediately spotted the entrance to what appeared to be a large chamber off to the left. There, two guards stood on either side keeping watch.

Okay, that was problematic. Time to get "creative."

Pulling the dagger from the side of my boot, I took aim behind me, back down the hall I'd just come from, and flung the dagger into one of the oil lamp sconces mounted on the wall.

CRASH!

Glass and burning oil scattered across the floor. I mashed myself against the wall right at the corner, holding perfectly still. The thumping of footsteps and clanking of armor rushed closer. When the two guards rushed by, spears in hand, I held my breath. But they were focused on the fire. They didn't give me a second glance.

Well trained? Maybe. Still idiots, though.

I waited until they had gone past to step from my hiding place, prowling up behind them with both my kafki blades drawn. Neither of them even noticed me sneaking up behind them. They were too busy staring at the flames, which were now spreading over a rug and tapestry, while shouting at one another in Sokraal.

Heh. Perfect. Time to test out just how good their training actually was.

I clenched my teeth and sprang for the closest one, taking him down with one blow to the back of the neck where his breastplate met his helmet. He fell like a freshly cut tree, hitting the floor with a *THUD*.

The sound made the second guard whirl around, shouting at me in alarm as he took a jab with his spear. I ducked to the side, feeling the wind on my cheek as the spearpoint barely grazed my ear. Close one.

I surged in, using the advantage of his committed strike to sweep his legs out from under him. He ducked back in a flash, avoiding my blow and making a wide swing with that spear again. I threw my weight backwards into a backbend, barely managing to dip under that swing. When I came up, he hit me full force with his knee to my gut. It sent me staggering back a few paces.

Right. I guess they were decently trained, after all.

I caught myself and dove to the side, coming in for a feinting swing with my blades. He was onto me, though, and batted my attack away easily, then spun to crack the blunt end of his spear off the wall right next to my head.

Whew. Okay. That one was even closer.

Baring my teeth, I spun my kafki over my hands and dipped forward, kicking into a tight roll and coming up on his left. He thrust his spear up sideways, blocking my downward strike with both my blades—and leaving himself totally open.

Perfect.

I let go of my blades and dropped low, closing the distance and spinning to put my back to him. My hands shot out to catch my falling weapons and whip them around, making a dual, backwards jab into the base of his breastplate, just above his belt. He let out a sharp cry and staggered, crumpling to a knee.

That was all the opportunity I needed.

I finished the job quick and clean, with one strategic slice at the base of his neck. He fell backward not far from his comrade and lay motionless, blood beginning to pool on the marble beneath both of them now.

I wheezed, still catching my breath as I quickly began stripping away the pieces of armor from the first guy and strapping them onto my body. It didn't have to be a perfect fit—just passable. That was all I needed. A quick disguise.

Fortunately, years of dragonrider training had prepared me for this, and it didn't take three minutes to get the armor on. Sheathing my kafki and hiding them under the white, one-shouldered cape, I picked up my dagger and one of the spears and started for the door to that meeting room. So far, so good.

The door was at least eight feet tall and a lot heavier than I had expected as I began to push it open. I hesitated after I had cracked it only an inch or two, pausing to listen. Voices echoed from inside. A man's deep, gravelly tone spoke with a strong Damarian accent. Then I heard Violet. Her tone snapped sharply, as though she were spitting venom with every word.

Negotiations were going as expected, then.

Gripping the spear harder, I pushed the door open just far enough to side step into the room. I kept my movements smooth and certain as I turned back to close it. Keeping my head down was safest. I had to blend in and act like I belonged here. I could find a formation of other guards posted in the room and take up a post with them, then bide my time until—

Something sharp poked at the back of my neck.

I turned very slowly, and found myself staring straight into the point of a spear aimed right between my eyes.

"Ah, there he is. And here I had begun to worry that he might miss our meeting," the deep, gruff voice of a man cackled from the front of the room. "Please, do come in. Welcome to my home, Your Highness."

Well ... Crap.

HONESTLY, I SHOULDN'T HAVE BEEN SURPRISED. THIS WAS GOING EXACTLY THE SAME way the rest of our mission had so far. Add this lovely little pearl of epic failure to the string we'd already collected along the way. After all, why would anything change now?

No one could say we weren't consistent.

Staring past the end of that weapon, I found a dozen angry guards glaring at me, weapons at the ready. Standing at the other end of their company, Violet stood with her own hands raised in surrender, giving me the world's most exasperated and yet totally unsurprised glare.

I dropped my own spear and raised my hands, too. The best I could do was give her a shrug. Hey, I'd gotten here, hadn't I? No one had said anything about this guy expecting me to come sneaking in dressed like one of his own guards. And to be fair, plan-wise, she hadn't given me all that much to work with.

"My beautiful Lady Violet, I am so pleased you've come to call on me once again. It's been quite some time, hasn't it?" The heavyset human man sitting at the end of a long dining table grinned like a happy toad from over the frilled lace collar of his fine shirt and vest. With his thin, shoulder-length gray hair slicked straight back and his heavily sun-aged skin creasing deeply around his wide mouth, he watched his guards walk both of us to the other end of the table and force us to sit down.

"Varri'dasha, Sulam," Violet seethed quietly, her expression a chilling smile as beautifully dangerous as a poisonous flower. I recognized the customary Sokraal greeting ... as well as that ruthless glint in her eyes. "It seems you've been very busy this evening. I'm so pleased you could work us into your schedule."

He gave a throaty cackle that made his belly bounce as he sank back in his chair. The bejeweled rings on all his hands glittered in the light as he drummed his fingers on the tabletop. "Coy as ever, I see. But you should know better than to think you can outsmart me. I created you, after all. I will always know you better than anyone ever will. Remember that. You may work for someone else now, but I'll always be in that pretty little head. If not for me, you'd still be eating sand in the gods-forsaken desert alongside your mother's corpse."

Violet's throat jumped, even if nothing else about her expression changed. Her knuckles blanched as her hands clenched into fists in her lap.

"But I didn't bring you here to reminisce about our past. You're here because your employer has overstepped his bounds once again," Sulam shifted in his seat and rubbed at his short, neatly trimmed gray beard. "Hiring smugglers out of my port. Bringing dangerous foreign nobles to my shores. Dabbling in my communication networks. And now he's even meddling with the Hands of Fate. All without my permission or blessing. You can imagine how offended I was when he did not even send a friendly greeting. I really had no choice, girl. I had to remind him and you whose ground you walk on here. No one and nothing comes or goes out of this kingdom without me knowing it—especially not *you*."

"We didn't intend to come here at all," I spoke up, sitting straighter in my chair and staring him down from across the table. Criminal boss or not, I wasn't about to let this guy see me sweat. "Our ship was on course elsewhere, but we came under attack during the journey and were forced here while it's being repaired."

His bushy eyebrows rose, seeming genuinely surprised. "I see. So, you intended to go where, then?"

Violet kicked me in the leg under the table. My eyes welled some and I had to bite my own tongue to keep from whimpering. Curse it, didn't she know I'd just gotten done writhing around with cramps before this?

"We had business elsewhere down the coast," she answered cryptically. "That's all you need to know."

He laughed again, seeming to enjoy the spite that danced in her eyes as he glanced between us. "Ahhh. It wouldn't have anything to do with that library being destroyed, would it? They say it's nothing but a heap of cinders and charred bone now. No survivors to be found. If you've come hoping to rescue someone from the ash, I'm afraid you're far too late."

My stomach clenched hard, wrenching itself into a painful knot. He was lying. He had to be. I wouldn't believe Ronan was dead. Not until I saw the evidence myself.

"Where are the children, Sulam?" Violet demanded, somehow managing to keep her composure and completely ignore everything else he'd said. "The two you took from the inn? They had better be in one piece. You've no idea who you are meddling with now."

"NO!" He roared suddenly, standing and slamming an open hand down on the table with a *BAM*. "It is you who has no idea, pitathi mutt. You think you can sidestep around me? Traipse through my territory without consequence? You should know better. You *do* know. And now, you'll remember. Every crooked alley and dark corner in Rienka is my kingdom. Here, I am the Shadow King!"

"Where are they, you spineless swine!" Violet stood, too. Immediately, the guards seized her by the arms and slammed her back down into her chair, pinning her there with a spear-point to her neck.

Sulam stepped away from the table, hobbling along with his wide, burly frame testing the seams of that fine velvet vest. "Why don't you come and see, dear Violet?" he snickered as he threw open a pair of long, dark purple drapes, revealing a set of double doors.

All the color drained from Violet's face as he pulled them open, simultaneously letting bright rays of dawn sunlight and the cheers of a thousand excited voices pour in with a rush. He held the doors open and stood, eyes closing as a blissful smile curled across his lips.

"You hear that? Do you remember it? The thrill of anticipation. The rush of shared adrenaline. The primal hunger for blood. I never grow tired of it," he gloated as he sucked in a long, deep breath as though he were savoring every second of it. "It is a feast for all the senses. And today, your little children will be the first to dine. Now, why don't you come make yourselves comfortable? This promises to be the show of a lifetime, and I'm certain you won't want to miss it."

PART SEVEN
MAYLEA

❧ 28 ❧

CHAPTER TWENTY-EIGHT

Everything hurt. Every heartbeat. Every breath. It felt like someone had poured sand into all my joints, and my head swam even before I opened my eyes. There was nothing but darkness and a rocking, swaying sensation like a rowboat on water.

What happened? Where was I? Where was Uncle Reigh, Thatcher, and the others? Was this a dream?

It felt more like a nightmare.

I blinked hard, trying to clear my thoughts and see. But there was still nothing except for darkness everywhere I looked. That's when I realized something was tied over my head. A bag? Whatever it was, it blocked out everything and made the air around my face hot and uncomfortable.

I twisted and squirmed, struggling when I realized my arms and legs were stuck. Someone had tied me up with my wrists at my back and my ankles together. I couldn't even sit up.

Immediately, my heart began to pound hard and fast. My body trembled as panic prickled at the insides of my lungs. Oh no. Where was I? How did I get here? Think—oh gods, I had to think. Calm down. No panicking.

Memory flickered in my mind like a candle in the wind. Flashes of moments in that inn with Thatcher and Lukani. We were waiting for Uncle Reigh and Violet to come back. Everything was quiet. Lukani had shifted back to his normal, human-looking form and was stretched out on the floor to rest. I was doing the same. It was getting late, and Thatcher was talking about food. We were all hoping they'd bring back something decent to eat.

Then ... chaos.

A crashing sound like the door was being blown apart. Smoke that choked the room like a stinking black cloud. It had stung my eyes, nose, and made every breath agony.

Thatcher yelled. I heard blades clashing.

My legs had gone numb. I'd fallen.

Then there was nothing. Just endless darkness like a featureless abyss. And I was lost in the middle of it. Alone. I didn't even know who had attacked us.

It didn't matter, though. I wasn't going down without a fight.

Now, as I lay perfectly still, I tried to remember everything Uncle Murdoc had taught me about moments like this. I had to be patient. I had to take in my surroundings and plan my escape carefully. I needed information about where I was, who had me, and what they intended to do. I needed an escape route and the right moment to strike.

Patient—I had to be patient.

The more I concentrated, the more I could figure out about where I might be. The rocking motion came with a faint sound of sloshing. I must be on a boat. Probably a small one judging by how much motion I could feel. Was someone taking me off the island? Ugh. Not good.

Voices spoke over me, barking orders in a foreign language. They sounded deep and masculine. The boat's rocking slowed and finally stopped. It bumped against something with a few hard thuds. A dock, maybe?

Someone much larger and stronger grabbed me up like a spring lamb and carried me over their shoulder. I hung limp, doing my best to play dead—or unconscious, rather—and not give any resistance as they hauled me along. Nearby, I could have sworn I heard the sound of muffled groaning, growling, and gasping. Lukani? It sort of sounded like him, but it was too far away and muffled to really be sure.

There was nothing I could do for him right now, though.

I played limp and lifeless as they carried me off, walking for what felt like miles before *THUD*—they dumped me down onto something hard. Not the ground, though. This had a little give to it. A wagon, maybe?

THUD!

Someone or something else was tossed down right next to me, making everything lurch again. Definitely a wagon of some sort. But headed for where? As it rattled into motion, I dared to squirm a little. I inched my way backward, moving only a little at a time until I felt my body bump up against whatever or whoever had been tossed into the wagon with me.

"H-Hello?" a familiar, masculine voice quavered faintly. "Is someone there?"

"Lukani," I whispered. "Keep your voice down. Stay calm. We're going to be okay."

"What's happening?" he whispered back, his voice halting and shaking in terror. "I can't transform. My magic—it isn't working!"

"Shh. It's going to be fine. Just take some breaths for me, all right? We have to try to stay calm," I consoled. "If they wanted us dead, they'd have killed us already. Something else is going on. We just have to wait and bide our time. Stick with me, okay? We can handle this. We'll make it."

"O-Okay," he said, not sounding the least bit reassured. But at least he wasn't whimpering anymore.

Good enough.

Now, I had to work the problem. Step one—I had to get my hands untied. From what little I could feel, it seemed like they'd just used ropes. A good sign. Ropes would flex and stretch easily. Slowly pulling my knees in toward my chest, I waited a few seconds to see if anyone noticed I was conscious and moving around.

Nothing. No sound. No angry words. Maybe my captors weren't watching us, then.

Good.

I slipped my legs through my arms, bringing my wrists to the front and beginning to work the bag off my head just far enough that I could get to the ropes with my teeth. I didn't need to bite through them. I just needed a little bit of slack to writhe one hand loose, then I was as good as free.

Or ... so I hoped.

THE WAGON LURCHED TO A HALT SUDDENLY, AND I FROZE. OH NO. BEFORE I COULD pull the bag down over my head again, someone shouted in Sokraal. "AYE! Look there, she's moving!"

My handle on the common language of this part of the world was actually pretty decent. Er, well, it had been. My parents were strict about our education, and wanted to make sure my brothers and I were well versed in many cultures and languages. We'd learned the Gray elven language right alongside Maldobar's common tongue. Auntie Isa had tutored me in Sokraal some, and I caught on quickly because it had some similarities to Lunthardan. Granted, it had been a while since I'd actually used any of those. I didn't get to practice much on account of being confined to the children's room during every ball and party.

I could understand these idiots well enough, though. They spoke slowly and used slang words, which actually helped since they were shorter than the real ones. More basic and almost child-like.

"Crafty little rat," another voice cackled as someone jerked me off the back of the wagon and threw me against the ground. "Thought you were gonna slip off, did ya?"

My head swam and I wheezed, all the wind knocked out of me at once. I tried to push myself up, but someone grabbed the back of my neck and ripped the bag off my head. A man's sunburned face sneered at me, his crooked yellow teeth right in my face. "And here I thought Lord Sulam was just wanting some feeding fodder for the beasties. But you've got a bit'o venom in you, don't you, girlie?"

"You have *no* idea." I spat right in his ugly, grinning face.

It made the other two men standing nearby laugh as he dropped me back onto my rear in the dirt and wiped at his face, hissing curses before he reared back and kicked me right in the ribs. I doubled over as pain exploded in my side, knocking the wind out of me again. I coughed and wheezed, eyes tearing up as I lay on my side.

"Easy does it, Cal. We'll see how much fight she has left in her tomorrow, aye? Lord Sulam wants them both fresh as spring flowers for the arena." Another of the men growled. "Get them up and let's move. We've got more work to do."

No one argued apart from muttering a few bitter curses. The guy who'd just planted his boot in my ribs reached down to seize me by one arm and drag me to my feet. They did the same with Lukani, snatching the bag off his head and laughing when he cringed away and bared his fang-like incisors at them.

They chained us together with heavy iron shackles fixed around our ankles, then cut the ropes so we could stagger forward. But with only a few short feet of chain between us, it wasn't easy. They kept a guard in front and two behind, watching us carefully with their swords already drawn in case we got any ideas about trying to break free and run again.

Lukani and I stumbled along, our shoulders bumping, through a dark alleyway that followed along the rounded exterior of a massive, circular building. It reminded me a little of the deck, if only because of the shape and sheer size of it. But I had a feeling there weren't any dragons snoozing away inside it. The men led us down a flight of steps to what looked like some sort of underground entrance beneath the building. The door was huge and heavy, crafted of solid steel and heavy iron.

What was this place? Some sort of prison? With two fully armored guards standing on either side of the door, glowering at us through their helmet visors, that was the only answer that seemed to make sense. There were more guards inside, armed with spears and swords, and they stood eerily still as we were marched past into the dark halls beneath that building. The smell from within hit me like another kick to the ribs. A sour, reeking, putrid smell like the mixture of rotting meat and old vomit. It made my stomach clench up. It took everything I had not to gag as they forced us onward into the dark.

We went down more flights of stairs, tunneling farther under the ground, until we came to a long hall. Other, shorter hallways branched off on either side, and each contained a row of cells lit by only a few flickering torches.

Oh gods. It really was a prison.

"These two are for the second round tomorrow at dawn," one of the men still holding a sword at my back barked when we approached one of the armored guards standing at the end of the hall. "Lord Sulam's orders."

The guard didn't even look at us. He muttered a gruff word of agreement and took out a ring of keys before leading the way down the first hall to the right. We staggered after him, our chains rattling with every step as we passed cell after cell. It was so dark I couldn't tell much about whoever might be inside. But shadowed figures moved, seeming to watch us pass, and every now and then I caught the glimmer of torchlight off eyes. It made chills of unease quiver through my stomach.

The guard unlocked the very last cell door. The old rusted hinges squealed and groaned in protest as he yanked it open, then he waited until Lukani and I were both standing inside before he slammed it shut and locked it again.

Not good. That was it. Our only way out now was closed off by a wall of rusted iron bars only a few inches apart. The stone floor was covered in rotted hay and filth. There wasn't even a window, and the only light came from the single torch burning ten or so feet down that hall. The walls between the cells were stone, so we couldn't see who might be next to us.

We were alone, cut off from the world, in this awful place where Uncle Reigh and the others might never find us.

And for the first time, I felt it—fear like the stinging prick of a thousand needles in my chest.

This wasn't supposed to happen. I wasn't supposed to get kidnapped like this! I'd been trained all my life for scenarios exactly like this one. I should know what to do next, how to get us out of here. But my mind was blank. I stared up at Lukani, and he looked back down at me with an utterly lost expression. What was going to happen to us? What if we couldn't get out? What were they talking about when they said we were for the second round tomorrow?

My throat went tight, and I looked down as my eyes welled up again. No. I wouldn't cry. Not now. Not when I had to find some way to get us out of here before—

Lukani bent down long enough to step through his arms like I'd done, bringing his hands in front of him. It was a little more complicated, though, now that our feet were chained together. Took some wriggling around and me stepping through his arms once he got them in front. But then he raised them up and looped them around me, drawing me in close against him in a tight hug.

"It's going to be okay," he whispered.

I shut my eyes and buried my face against his chest. It wasn't okay. He knew that as well as I did. But hearing him say it like he truly believed it ... it made me want to believe it, too.

"I keep getting you into trouble," I realized aloud. "I'm so sorry, Lukani."

"You always say that, like everything that happens is somehow your fault. I think *we* tend to get each other in trouble. It is a joint-effort, at least. Would you agree?" he laughed weakly and then let out a heavy breath that made his chest rise and fall against my cheek.

Something about it made me smile. Or maybe that was just the fact that he still felt like cracking jokes when we were chained together in the bottom of some prison's dungeon. And in that moment, I realized ... I didn't know what I would ever do without him. Not just as a friend. I hadn't grown up with a lot of close friends my age. A few, sure, but it was hard to be close with anyone when your parents were super famous war heroes that made everyone nervous. Ronan had been the exception. And now Lukani, too. But this felt different now. I couldn't explain it.

My heart fluttered and raced when I looked up at him again. The idea of losing Lukani like I had Ronan, gods, it made me sick to even think about. I couldn't lose him, too.

"I'm glad you're here," I murmured.

His expression changed, smoothing to something softer and more thoughtful. His yellow-golden eyes darted down to my mouth for an instant. It made my heartbeat skip again and my stomach flip and spin like crazy. I had never—you know. I mean, this was as close as I'd ever been to a boy, even if he was a bit stranger than anyone else I had ever met. He was the first person I'd ever seen with a tail and green skin. Even so, I didn't know what I should do or ... crap, why was my face burning so much?

"Maylea?" He said my name so quietly, like he was asking permission. It made my stomach start flipping all over again as he leaned down some. His lips inched closer, then brushed mine ever so slightly. It was a gentle, careful touch. Almost like he wasn't sure if it was okay or not.

But only at first.

I gripped the front of his shirt and stood on my toes, pulling him down closer so I could kiss him back. He sucked in a sharp breath through his nose and froze for an instant. But then his arms tightened around me, drawing me in closer against him. His lips pressed more firmly to mine.

And for a moment, everything in that dark, awful, reeking place seemed to fade away.

My head was spinning when I pulled back to look into his eyes again, watching soft crimson color flush over his cheeks all the way out to the ends of his pointed ears. He chuckled weakly and cleared his throat, looking away sheepishly as he mumbled, "I-I ... have wanted to do that for a long time."

"I bet you say that to all the girls you get tossed into prison with," I teased gently.

He laughed and shrugged. "It is my first time, actually. On both accounts."

I blushed and looked down. "Yeah. Me too."

We stood in awkward silence for a moment, looking at everything except one another. My gaze lingered on the cuffs that were shackled around his wrists. They hadn't tied him with ropes like mine. In fact, those shackles looked a lot different from the ones around our feet. Their metal was more bluish, clean, and polished. There were strange little marks, like runes, engraved around them, too.

Hmm. I wondered if that was why he couldn't transform. Were they blocking his magic somehow?

Speaking of being tied up, though ... I still needed to get my hands free.

I scrunched my mouth to one side and got back to work twisting and wrenching the ropes on my own wrists. Lukani took his arms off me when he realized what I was doing and stood back to give me some space to work.

I had to use my teeth to pry the ropes a bit looser, but finally I managed to slide one hand free. I tossed the ropes aside and rubbed at my wrists. Well, that was one problem solved.

"We have to figure out how to get out of here," I whispered, more to myself than expecting him to give me any kind of suggestion. "Uncle Reigh and the others probably don't even know where to look for us. I don't know how long you were awake for our trip, but they definitely took us off the island we were on. Sol'Karr, right?"

Lukani nodded. "Yes. But *we* don't even know where we are."

Right. That was also a problem.

The chains around my legs rattled as I shuffled toward the cell door. The bars weren't far enough apart to even try sticking my head through to get a good look down the hall. All I had to work with was a piece of rope. Not good.

I let my forehead rest against the cold iron bars. I couldn't remember ever feeling so lost. I had been trained to escape all kinds of situations. But I guess no one had imagined I might end up locked up in a prison in some foreign kingdom anytime soon.

"I wonder what Dah would have done in this situation," I whispered.

"Was he never captured by his enemies in battle?" Lukani sounded genuinely curious.

I blinked. Wow. Was he really one of the few people in the world that didn't know every single story about my dah? Whoa ... I didn't know people like that even existed.

"He got locked up in a slaver's wagon once," I recalled. "But that time, he—"

I stopped short, my mouth clamping shut suddenly

That—that was it! The answer!

Pulling my father's old necklace out from where it was still safely under the collar of my tunic, I wrapped my hand around it tightly. Dah's power had saved him countless times in all those stories. He had never been given half the specialized training I had, but he still managed to do incredible things. And the reason why was so simple, so obvious. It was a reason we now shared.

My father's connection to Paligno had never failed him. I wasn't a lapiloque like he had been, but hadn't Paligno said I would be able to wield his power now? That had to be the reason why I'd been able to activate that strange orb-thing that imprisoned Judan before. I'd seen Paligno with my own eyes. He'd spoken to me. He'd promised I would be his paladin.

I just had to have faith. I had to trust him. Paligno had never let my father down. He had always kept his promises to my family. I had no reason to think he wouldn't do the same for me, right?

"Paligno, if you're listening, I could use some help," I begged. "I know you're there. I know you can hear me. So, please, do something. Help us."

No answer.

Lukani watched me carefully for a second or two before he shuffled over to stand right next to me at the cell door. He flashed me a broad, confident smile. "He will help us," he said.

I arched an eyebrow. "You believe in Paligno?"

He gave a small, sideways tip of his head and quirked his mouth. "Mmm. I don't know yet," he said. "But I do believe in *you*."

29

CHAPTER TWENTY-NINE

I didn't get an answer from Paligno.

The doors didn't suddenly pop open to let us out. Our chains didn't magically melt away. There was nothing for hours except silence and the faint wavering of torchlight through the cell bars.

I worked for a while on trying to pick the locks on the shackles around Lukani's wrists. But with only bits of old straw and a few splinters of wood to work with, I didn't make any progress. The lock was a lot more complex than any I had been taught to pick. I decided that probably meant they really were the reason he couldn't use his magic to change shapes like before.

Whoever had captured us knew exactly what he was and how to hold him at bay. Not a good sign.

Lukani and I sat up suddenly as a commotion from beyond our hall echoed through the gloom. We swapped a quick, wary glance, and got to our feet. Something was happening. Scuffles and shifting sounds came from the cells around us, followed by muffled whimpering. I bit down hard to keep my teeth from chattering as nerves made my body go cold. Somewhere in the distance, armor clanked. Cell doors creaked open. Voices shouted out orders. Chains clinked.

"What's happening?" I whispered, stepping in closer to Lukani's side.

"I don't know," he murmured low, his voice tinged with a nervous growl.

Then the clatter and clunk of armor grew closer. Footsteps approached and two big guards stepped in front of our cell.

"This is them?" one of them leaned down to peer at us through the bars. "They're just kids."

"Orders from the top. Get them ready." The other threw down a line of thick iron chain onto the floor in front of our cell. "We don't have much time before it starts. I'll get the others."

They didn't say anything else, and the one still standing at our cell door leaned in to give us another, almost pitying look before he reached into his belt and took out a small, fist-sized bag. He pulled a scarf over his nose and mouth before reaching through the bars and shaking the contents of it into the air. A puff of silvery white dust filled the air, spreading around us so quickly we didn't have time to even hold our breath.

Immediately, my eyes watered and I couldn't breathe. My head swam and my vision blurred, becoming just a moving smear of color. My throat burned with every breath. I-I couldn't even cough!

Next to me, Lukani let out a desperate growl as he hit the ground only a few seconds before I did. My knees buckled as everything seemed to go numb. My arms and legs were too heavy to move. I landed beside him in a heap, staring at the cell door with my cheek smooshed on the cold stone floor.

I could barely make out the shapes of the guard's legs coming toward me, but I couldn't blink or move my head to be sure. He grabbed my legs first and dragged me out into the hall beyond our cell, fastening the shackles on my legs to the big, heavy iron chain the other guard had left in the walkway. Then he did the same with Lukani.

Minutes passed, and I heard the tell-tale sounds of that same process happening to other people up and down the row of cells next to ours. Sometimes there were shouts and struggling, like the people locked inside might be resisting. But it didn't last. And after a few minutes, when I was finally able to see and breathe again, I managed to lift my head groggily and look down the long length of chain where ten other people were fastened just like we were.

They all looked a lot older than we were. Some were so skinny you could see the bones showing through their skin. Others were muscular and covered in battle scars. There were men and women. Elves and humans. But none of them seemed able to shake off the effects of that knockout powder. It took everyone at least five minutes to finally be able to stand, and even then, I had to steady myself against the wall to keep from swooning over and tripping. The heavy chains on my feet didn't help, though.

Especially when they started making us walk.

"You'll keep walking forward until you're told to stop! Then you'll turn right to face the cages. You'll go straight in, no questions, and keep two per cage! Anyone puts a toe out of line, and you'll have my spear in the back of your skull," the guard growled as he stalked by, eyeing us all down one by one. "Now—MOVE!"

And we did. Step-by-step, our line of prisoners moved along the hallway, dragging the chains with us. All the while, more guards seemed to materialize out of the dark halls, joining the patrols that walked down our lines, watching our every move. They marched us to a longer, wider passage that had strange metal cages down one side, the doors were open and ready for us to go in.

The guards gave the order to stop and turn. Lukani and I faced a cage. No—wait. We were being shuffled apart, arranged so that we were going into two different cages.

Panic throttled the breath from my lungs as I stared at him, unable to stop myself from reaching out for his arm.

CRACK!

A guard behind me hit the back of my head with the dull end of his spear, barking for me to move forward.

No ... No, no, no! I couldn't go without him! We couldn't get separated! I cried out for him, but the guard hit me again, this time bashing his spear across my cheek.

My vision scrambled and I staggered, nearly falling to my knees.

"It's okay, Maylea," Lukani shouted back at me. "Just go. We will be fine. Just do as they say!"

B-But ... But what would I do without him? What if I never saw him again? Gods and Fates, what was happening?

The guard shoved me forward into the cage next to his, along with another prisoner—an older elven man with a deep scar over one side of his face. He didn't say anything as the guards began walking down the line of cages, slamming the doors shut one by one. Once all the doors were locked and we were secured inside, they walked back down our row, barking for us to stand close to the side so they could unfasten all the chains around our legs. They had this down to a system, running with a military-like efficiency. Something about that chilled me right to the marrow.

"Lukani," I cried out as soon as they had taken mine off, and I ran to the side of my cage that faced his. "What is this? What's happening?"

He reached through the bars and grabbed my hand, squeezing it as he forced a smile. Before he could get a word out, though, the old man sharing my new prison cell muttered, "It is the end for all of us."

I stared back at him, fighting for every terrified breath. "Wh-What do you mean?"

His eyes rolled back as he slowly looked upward, stretching out a finger to point at the ceiling overhead. "You hear that?"

I listened.

My heart dropped to the soles of my boots. A roar like the rushing rumble of the ocean echoed from somewhere nearby. But it wasn't the ocean. It was sharper, with many different pitches all sounding at once. Screams. Cheering. A massive crowd right above us. And something else—the low booming of impact. The deep thundering bellow of a beast.

Gods ... what was happening up there?

"Make your peace with the gods of your ancestors. It'll be over soon," the old man warned.

"What are you talking about?" Lukani demanded.

The elven man closed his eyes, but kept his head tilted back to listen to the muffled rumble and roar of what sounded like some sort of battle raging right over our heads. "They call it the Caldera."

"The what?" I demanded. "What do you mean? What's going to happen to us?"

He never replied.

But he didn't have to. The more I looked around and took in our surroundings, the easier it was to guess that much. All the cages we had been divided into were built against the side of a smooth stone wall. That wall had the faint outline of hatch doors in front of each and every cage I could see.

That made our situation pretty obvious.

We were going up there. They were sending people, prisoners like us, to fight something—whatever monster I could hear roaring up there. Or maybe feeding us to it. Either way, it sounded horrible. And a crowd was watching it all happen. No, not just watching. They were *enjoying* it.

Oh gods.

I-I had to tell Lukani. He still had those shackles on his wrists that kept him from using his power. We had to get them off somehow! We had to—

CLAAAAANG!

Something mechanical groaned into motion overhead.

I pressed myself back against the bars on the other side of the cage, as far away from that hatch door as possible.

BOOM—BOOM—BOOM—BOOM!

One at a time, each of the hatch doors down our row of cages fell open. Brilliant sunlight poured in, blinding me immediately. My ears rang as the roar of the crowd overtook my senses. I tried to shield my eyes. To squint and adjust so I could see. I blinked hard, and finally saw it.

A massive arena towered around us with stands boiling with crowds clambering by the thousands. I choked on the stench of fresh blood that hung thick in the hot morning air. The relentless glare of the rising sun hit my face and I squinted, shielding my eyes for a moment.

I dared to take a step out, away from the cage. My legs shook with every step as I walked out of the dark and into the glare of the daylight. But everywhere I looked it was carnage. Bodies were strewn across the sandy arena floor, scattered and torn apart like broken toys. I couldn't even tell who they were.

And in the middle of it all, a huge beast crouched, its scales already spattered with blood. I stood frozen, staring at the creature as its big, intelligent eyes fixed squarely on me. Its scaly ears slicked back as it bared rows of jagged fangs. The long spines cresting down its back bristled, and its long tail swished as it lumbered around on two muscular hind legs to face me. It let out a booming roar and shook the arena floor under my feet.

I knew what it was immediately.

Because I'd seen creatures exactly like this every day from the moment I was born.

It was ... a dragon.

THE MASSIVE DRAGON HISSED, BARING ALL ITS DRIPPING TEETH AS IT WATCHED ME. Then its gaze darted away, suddenly noticing all the other prisoners that rushed out into the arena. They began frantically snatching up weapons from the fallen bodies of other people, or prying them off hooks mounted on the wall all the way around the arena floor. Shields, swords, lances, daggers—there was every kind of weapon you could think of.

But I knew none of them were going to help us now.

Some of the other prisoners rushed the beast like a mismatched army. Others tried climbing the perimeter walls, only to have the crowds start throwing things at them—garbage, food, and anything they could get their hands on. Any that made it to the top were immediately struck by one of the many guards stationed there—run through with a blade, or simply kicked back down to the arena floor.

Gods and Fates it was ... mayhem.

And we were trapped right in the middle of it.

"Maylea!" Lukani called out as he rushed toward me, face drawn into a snarl of desperation.

WHOOM!

The dragon's massive tail hit the ground between us, throwing up rubble and dust. I stumbled back, barely managing to stay on my feet as I cried out for Lukani. Oh gods, had he been hit? I-I couldn't see him anywhere!

The dragon rose up onto its hind legs, letting out a furious roar and spreading its wings. Its thick, plated scales of pearly white had a single black blaze down its back, dark stripes on its legs, and black horns that glittered in the morning sun—beautiful but deadly.

One look at the massive dewclaws on its hind legs and I knew it was a male. An older drake. He was every bit as big as my father's mount, Mavrik. That meant his hide would be thick. He would be smart. And judging by the countless slash marks, scars, and blemishes across his muscular body, this wasn't the first time he'd been set loose to hunt people. He was no stranger to combat.

Sweet Fates, we were in trouble.

My heart wrenched in conflict at the sight as the drake dove for a group of prisoners, another sweep of his tail sending them flying like ragdolls as they tried rushing him with spears and swords. Their frantic, dying screams pierced the air, accompanied by the screeching excitement of the crowds all around us.

I looked away, unable to keep myself from cringing. No. I had to focus. I needed a weapon. I looked up, scanning the wall and ground for anything I could find. No, not just any weapon. I needed a bow.

But where could I find—There!

A longbow and quiver lay on the ground near one of the stands of weapons not sixty feet away. It wouldn't be as good as the one Judan had given me, but beggars couldn't be choosers, and neither could prisoners in the fight for their life.

So I started running.

Halfway there, a pair of other prisoners rushed at me, blades drawn and expressions crazed with terror. They both dove in, taking wild swings with a club and sword as they shouted in a language I couldn't understand. Definitely not Sokraal.

"STOP IT!" I yelled back at them, ducking easily under their frantic attacks. Clearly neither of them had any experience fighting because they might as well have been swinging tree branches. "Fight the dragon, not me, you idiots!"

They didn't stop.

I dodged backwards and sank into a crouch, preparing to retaliate full-force, but a dark shape suddenly stepped between us and let out a bellow like a lion's roar.

Lukani bared his teeth, his tail lashing and his strong shoulders flexing as he dove for the two men with his wrists still bound in shackles.

What? No! He couldn't fight them—not with his hands still bound like that. I shouted after him, begging him to stop, but Lukani didn't hesitate. As one of the prisoners made another reckless strike with a sword, he snapped his arms upward and caught the blade against the chain between his wrists, immediately whipping around and wrenching his arms back down to yank the weapon out of the man's grasp.

Whoa ... I-I guess he was a pretty good fighter even without shifting forms.

Now it was my turn. I whirled around, my gaze locking back onto that bow still lying on the ground. My lungs burned and I pumped my legs as fast as possible. Just a bit more. I could get there. I could do this. And then—

"DUCK!" Lukani yelled from behind me.

I immediately dropped into a forward roll.

WHOOOM!

A huge scaly tail as thick as a tree trunk swung over us. I barely managed to hit the dirt before it howled by, smashing into the arena wall and crushing the pair of prisoners who'd been attacking us with a gory crunch.

Oh gods, this wasn't going to work. What was I even thinking? Even if I got a bow, there was no way I could pierce the dragon's thick plated hide. Curse it, I needed a new idea. I needed some way to get Lukani free. He could change forms into that golden dragon again, and then we might have a chance. We could at least get out of here.

I dared to look back, watching as the massive white drake tore into another group of prisoners trying to brandish swords and shields. Strange. I'd never seen a dragon act like this before. Why wasn't he breathing flame? Or flying? Most dragons I had seen, even in the wild, avoided people when they could. They didn't go looking for a fight unless they were trying to defend themselves ...

Hmmm.

One glance at his legs, and I got my answer. The dragon was shackled at both ankles with massive iron chains that bound him to a single, big hook in the arena floor. He probably couldn't get more than twenty feet off the ground, at most. He certainly couldn't get away from the prisoners who kept rushing at him with weapons. But it gave him plenty of range to crawl around and rip people apart with his claws and fangs.

But still ... why wasn't he breathing fire at us? That's what dragons did when they really wanted to kill. Their fire was their greatest weapon—their last real means of defense. Something about this wasn't right at all.

I stumbled to a halt, looking toward the trapped beast as my heartbeat began to skip and stammer. Something warm thrummed right in the center of my chest, seeming to resonate in rhythm with my own pulse. I reached down and closed a fist around my father's pendant. It felt hot to the touch again, just like after I had that dream and first saw Paligno.

Did that mean .... Was Paligno trying to tell me something?

BOOOM!

The dragon beat his wings, surging skyward until the chains went taught and he smashed back to the ground. It threw dust and sand in every direction. The crowd cheered again. More prisoners screamed as they tried to escape the beast's snapping jaws and raking talons.

"He wants to escape," I realized aloud. "H-He just wants to get away. They're making him do this. They're forcing him to fight, just like us!"

"What?" Lukani stared at me, eyes wild with terror. "Maylea, we can't—"

"Find a spear or a halberd, even a longsword will do. We have to break his chains!" I screamed and bolted away, forging across the arena with purpose in every step ... straight for the enraged dragon.

I could hear Lukani calling after me. Protesting. Panicking. I didn't blame him. I knew I looked insane as I ran toward the raging beast with nothing in my hands to defend myself with.

But I trusted that feeling—that warmth against my heart. I trusted every story my father had ever told me. I trusted all the time I'd spent with the dragons at home.

And more than that, I trusted Paligno.

This would work.

It had to.

30

CHAPTER THIRTY

There weren't many prisoners left alive now. Fresh blood pooled everywhere I looked, sloshing under my boots as I ran past the smashed, broken bodies of the others. I couldn't bear to look at their faces. I didn't want to see.

So I kept my gaze trained straight ahead—right at the dragon.

He still hadn't noticed me approaching. He snapped his jaws and hissed, making swipes at a man brandishing a greatsword. Gods, it was the same old man I'd shared a cage with!

He was old and feeble-looking, but he must have had some combat experience, because he fought well. He landed a slash, scoring across the dragon's chest and making the beast recoil and shriek in pain.

I saw it coming an instant before it happened. The way the dragon's chest swelled with a deep breath. The way his nostrils flared and his jaws opened wide, exposing the two jets at the back of his throat.

Oh no.

WHOOOOM!

Fire and the acrid stench of dragon venom filled the air.

With a wave of infernal flame like a rising tide, the old man was instantly consumed. He didn't even get a chance to run. The crowd in the stands all shot to their feet at once, screeching with enthusiasm so loudly my ears throbbed.

Then the dragon's head swung around, burning venom still dripping from his jaws as his eyes fixed on me again. His powerful, plated chest still heaved in rapid, panting breaths, and every dark horn and spine around his head and down his back stood on end. His snout wrinkled, a faint growl thrumming low as his hair-thin pupils watched every move I made.

Or, rather, every move I didn't make.

I stood perfectly still, staring at him from scarcely twenty yards away. Close enough he could have sprayed another plume of burning venom at me and definitely hit. But he didn't. And second by second, the noise of the crowd began to fall silent, as though every soul in that arena were holding their breath. Watching. Waiting.

In the silence, a gust of wind blew through my hair, tangling it around my face and kicking up the sand. And deep down, I knew exactly what I had to do. This was the reason Paligno hadn't done anything to let us out of our cell. This was why he had needed us to stay here.

We weren't the only prisoners in this place crying out to him for help.

I kept my hand squeezed around my pendant as I took a step forward. Then another. And another. With every footfall, I felt the thrumming, radiant warmth in my palm grow stronger. Tingling warm heat spread through me, racing up and down my spine. It made my breath catch as I kept my gaze locked on the dragon.

His growling grew louder. He drew back, strong neck coiling like a serpent about to strike. He bared his teeth and snapped his jaws in warning as I came closer and closer.

Barely ten feet away, I stopped. My whole body trembled as I stretched out a hand toward him. "It's okay. I know you're scared. They've hurt you so much," I said, my voice shaking as tears slipped down the sides of my face. Standing so close to him, I could see all the old scars. Marks from chains on his neck and wing arms. Holes in the leathery membranes of his wings. Broken horns and a missing toe. Even the end of his tail looked like it had been cut short by some weapon.

"I'm so sorry for what they've done to you. But I'm here to stop it. I can help you." I tried to blink back the tears and force a smile, to show him I wasn't afraid. "You just have to trust me a little. I know that's a lot to ask."

The dragon let out a roar like a clap of thunder, lowering his head and snapping his jaws barely two feet from my outstretched hand.

But I didn't flinch. I couldn't. Not now.

If he really wanted to hurt me, there was nothing I could do and nowhere I could run. He could scorch me on the spot just like that old man with the sword and there wasn't anything anyone could do to stop it.

Keeping my gaze fixed on his for one final, earnest second, I took in a deep breath. Then I let my eyes fall closed. "I won't hurt you like they have. I won't make you do anything you don't want to do. I won't treat you like a monster. Neither of us wants to stay in this awful place. But I think we can help each other, if we work together."

The growling stopped.

For what felt like a terrifying eternity, there was no sound. Nothing but the faint brush of the wind and warmth of the sun on my skin. Suddenly, a blast of hot breath hit my face and hand like the gust from an open furnace. It blew my hair back and stung at my nose with a stench I knew all too well. My body trembled so hard my knees nearly buckled, but I forced myself to hold steady. I had to focus. No fear. Calm energy.

I wouldn't falter now.

"Show me," I whispered. "Show me that I can trust you, and let's leave here together."

Seconds passed without a sound.

Then a warm, smooth, scaly snout pushed against my palm so suddenly it made me gasp.

Slowly, I opened my eyes.

The huge dragon sat, hunkered down before me with his head lowered to touch the very tip of his nose to my hand. He loomed right over me like a mountain of white scales and bristling black horns. His piercing green eyes stared directly into mine, so close now I could see my own reflection in them.

Not one of the thousands of people watching all around the arena made a single sound.

"That's it," I whispered. "It's over now. I'm here to help you."

The dragon blinked slowly and drew in a deep breath of my scent. A deep, rhythmic humming came from his throat as he closed his eyes and let his small, scaly ears droop. Every muscle in his massive form seemed to relax at once.

A voice I knew tickled at my ear, whispering in a way I knew only I could hear. *"Well done, my paladin."*

I didn't have to force a smile then. Tears blurred my vision as I gently ran my fingers along his snout, stroking gently over his cheek and down the middle of his head. "Thank you, my friend. Now, what do you say we get out of here?"

"NO!!" A GRUFF, RASPY VOICE FROM SOMEWHERE IN THE AUDIENCE SHOUTED, THEIR furious words echoing all through the arena. "KILL HER! KILL THAT GIRL NOW BEFORE SHE RUINS EVERYTHING!"

I looked up, barely catching a glimpse of a large man standing high upon a balcony that overlooked the arena floor. He gripped the railing and shouted, barking orders to the dozens of guards that stood around the top of the wall. They all drew crossbows and took aim right at me at once.

O-Oh no.

TWANG!

The snap of fifty bowstrings at once cut the air with a sound like the pop of a lightning strike.

Oh gods! I-I didn't have time to duck, hide, or even scream.

Suddenly, everything went dark. I cringed up, shutting my eyes tightly. But nothing happened. There was no pain. No piercing of bolts through my body.

I dared to crack an eye open—just in time to see the big dragon unfurl from where he had wrapped his wings around me. The leathery membranes bristled with arrow bolts, but he didn't even flinch as he curled himself around me and unleashed another blast of flame at the nearest wall.

Oooh no. We had to cut him loose—right now!

Whirling around, I ran for the place where the chains were bound to his hind legs. The shackles were so small that it looked like some of his flesh had actually grown out over them, as though they'd been put on when he was a much younger dragon and left there. The sight stoked rage like hot embers in my soul as I studied the massive hooks that held the chains. I couldn't possibly break them. Not without help.

"Here!" Lukani appeared at my side so suddenly it made me scream and flail backward. He shoved a broadsword into my hands, ignoring my momentary panic, and together we worked on getting it angled with the right leverage to break the chain.

"We push down on three!" he shouted over the thundering roars of the panicked dragon. "One—two—three!"

We pushed with all our strength. The chain groaned, but it was as thick around as my leg. It didn't so much as bend. We ... we weren't strong enough. Gods and Fates, what were we going to do?!

We tried again. The chain creaked and groaned, but still didn't budge. Curse it. Help—we needed help!

A man's scream from overhead made Lukani and I look up just in time to see a pair of guards plummet from the balcony overhead, landing with a grisly crunch.

"You're just as crazy as your father!" Someone shouted over us.

Out of nowhere, Uncle Reigh dropped from the top of the wall right after them, landing in a crouch next to us. He was spattered in blood from head to foot, and dressed in the same sort of armor as the guards who were trying to kill us.

Wh-What? Where did he—? When? How?

Ugh! It didn't matter.

Lukani counted down again, and all three of us threw our weight against the broadsword at once. Maybe it was just dumb luck, or maybe it was Paligno giving us the advantage we needed, but the dragon also pitched his weight against the chain right at that precise moment.

It was just what we needed.

CRACK!

The hook snapped and the chain popped free.

Instantly, the cheering of the crowd turned to panicked screaming as the dragon flared his wings and surged skyward. Every powerful wingbeat sent a swirl of sand through the air, and the shadow of his body circled the arena as he zoomed upward and wheeled around, giving the guards still firing their crossbows at him one final spray of venom.

Then he veered upward, the red light of the dawn shone off his white scales, making them glow orange and scarlet as he let out a trumpeting, victorious roar. I stood in awe, watching him ascend higher and higher until he soared out of sight.

"Time to go!" Uncle Reigh shouted over the pandemonium as he ran back toward the wall. It was too high to climb without help, but I hadn't spent the last fourteen years of my life learning to fight like a Gray elven scout for nothing.

Grabbing up a shortsword left behind by another prisoner, I dashed after him as more crossbow fire zipped all around me. I didn't waste a second, and climbed onto Uncle Reigh's shoulders. I made the jump over the edge of the wall in one leap, landing in a crouch and locking blades with a guard who was already rushing to intercept us. Nice try, buddy.

I whirled in a brutal assault, feinting and striking hard. Then Lukani came up the wall next, and hit the guard with another beastly growl. He looped the chain of his shackles around the guard's neck and bore him to the ground. The guard flailed as Lukani pulled back with all his strength to choke him. They both hit the ground with a thud, rolling and wrestling for control. But Lukani had a firm grip and the advantage of that metal chain that ran between his shackled wrists. It wouldn't take long for him to end that fight.

I ran back for the wall and hung my body halfway over it, watching while Uncle Reigh backed up a few paces to get a running start.

He sprinted for me, managing to bound a few paces up the side before he leapt through the air with his arms outstretched. My body lurched under his much greater weight as I caught his hands in mine. My feet slipped. My body threatened to slide the rest of the way over the wall. But I didn't let go. I braced my feet against the edge and set my jaw, dragging him upward as hard as I could.

Reigh tumbled over the top of the wall and hit the ground next to me, wide-eyed and breathless. "R-Run!" he wheezed.

There was no stopping us, then.

Lukani bounded over, and we disappeared into the tangled, panicked crowds all bolting for the nearest exit point. Lukani reached out to grip my hand so he didn't lose me in the chaos, and I seized the back of Uncle Reigh's weird white cloak. Geez, where had he gotten this outfit? And why was he all bloody?

Violet appeared like a ghost materializing from thin air when we finally reached the street. Her clothes were even bloodier than Uncle Reigh's, and she had a few fresh slash marks across her arms and shoulder. But we were all alive—and we were together again.

We bolted for the nearest alleyway and kept running, letting Violet take the lead as we fled into the city. It was a mad dash, and my heart jumped at every corner and intersection for fear of seeing another group of guards coming straight for us. But the farther we went, the more Violet's pace slowed.

Finally, we stopped right outside what looked like the entrance to some sort of temple. We all ducked inside, under the cover of an archway that was overgrown with climbing, flowering vines. Aaand that was when my legs finally gave out. I dropped to my rear and gasped for breath, leaning my head back against the cool stone.

All around me, the others were doubled over trying to breathe, too. We were a mess. Violet was splattered in blood and she had a lot more slashes, cuts, and bruises than I'd noticed before. Uncle Reigh was definitely wearing the armor of one of those arena guards, and he had a pasty look of horror on his face. Lukani and I were filthy from our night in prison. It would probably take days just to get the knots out of my hair.

But we were okay. We had survived. And that was all that mattered.

Or, at least, most of us were.

"Wh-Where ... is Thatcher?" I managed to gasp between frantic breaths.

"H-He's back ... at the inn. We gotta ... get him," Uncle Reigh answered, still panting as he looked up at Violet. I could have sworn I saw a hint of genuine fear in his eyes as he considered her for a moment. "You don't think that Sulam guy will ... go after him now, do you?"

She doubled over and laughed out loud, gripping her sides like that was the best joke she'd ever heard. "Not unless he can do it from the grave! I got him! All these years, and I finally got him!" she practically screamed amidst breathless laughs. "You hear that, Mother? May the gods curse him to the deepest pits of the abyss!"

No one dared to ask what she meant, but I could have sworn I saw Uncle Reigh's brow crease worriedly. Almost like he was afraid she might actually be having some kind of mental breakdown. We were at capacity for disasters today, though, and it wasn't even midmorning.

He just shook his head and glanced over at Lukani and me, studying us briefly like he was looking for any obvious signs of injury. Ugh, I knew that look. Once a medic, always a medic.

"I'm fine," I told him as I sank back and stretched my legs out in front of me. "But I'd give anything for a bath right now. What about Violet? She's got some injuries."

"I'll live," Violet groaned, seeming to sober up a little. She planted her hands on her hips and looked around, her lips pursing thoughtfully as she took in our surroundings. "Nothing a bath and a glass of decent wine can't fix. Reigh is right, though. We need to get back to Thatcher soon. Even if Sulam is now officially off our list of problems, I don't like leaving vulnerable allies alone any longer than necessary. On your feet, everyone. Let's get to the other side of the island and see if we can't catch one of the ferries back to Sol'Karr. With any luck, we can be back before sunset."

31

CHAPTER THIRTY-ONE

It took several hours to get across the island—mostly because Violet insisted on taking indirect routes that would have less foot traffic. Probably a good idea considering what we'd just done. We stopped only long enough for Uncle Reigh to cast off that armor he'd slapped over his regular clothes, and for him and Violet to wipe as much of the blood off themselves as they could. Violet also took a few minutes to pick the locks on Lukani's shackles, and he quickly changed back into a crow so no one would pay him any unwanted attention. We'd had enough of that for one day.

No one spoke much as we made our way to the nearest port. The tension stayed high, and I couldn't help looking over my shoulder. The farther we got away from this place, the better. I never wanted to see that arena, or the rest of this island, again.

By the time the sun had begun to sink low on the western horizon, we were standing aboard a ferry boat with a few other people, locals mostly, headed for Sol'Karr. The calm seas sparkled as our small vessel set out toward the larger island ahead, and I stood with my elbows leaning on the railing to watch the waves lapping at the hull. The sea wind stirred through my hair and cooled the sweat beading on my forehead. Finally, though, it felt like I didn't have to look over my shoulder anymore.

Er, at least, until Uncle Reigh came striding over and thumped me hard on the back of the head. "You've got a huge bruise on your cheek, you know," he grumbled. "You okay? They hurt you anywhere else?"

I shrugged. "We got kicked around a little, but it's nothing serious. I'd say we were way luckier than a lot of other people today, anyway."

"No argument there," he agreed and stood beside me to lean against the railing, too. "Just a warning, don't do anything to piss Violet off. I've never seen anyone fight like she does. She killed five fully armored guards holding her hostage before I could blink twice." He let out a hollow, somewhat shaky chuckle. Then he cleared his throat, as though trying to collect his frazzled nerves. "I was worried we were going to be too late, that we wouldn't be able to get to you in time. Turns out, you can hold your own just as well as your dad did. Maybe even better—but don't tell him I said that."

I arched an eyebrow, studying his sulky frown extra hard for a moment. "Is that your way of saying I might actually be able to handle being on this mission with you?"

He made a disapproving, snorting sound. "Let's not get carried away."

I rolled my eyes.

"What I am saying is ... you did good today. I think your dad would have been proud, you know, to see you handle that dragon without even raising a blade," he explained. "It was the most Broadfeather thing I've seen in a long time."

I grinned and batted my eyes up at him tauntingly. "It does run in the family, I'm told."

"No, it flows like an avalanche careening down a mountainside, destroying everything in its path, is what it does," he countered. "But regardless, you did a good thing. I didn't know they had dragons this far south."

"I don't think they do," I murmured and fiddled with the pendant around my neck. "That dragon—I think he was brought here when he was small, and they had been making him fight all this time."

"Get all that from Paligno?" he asked.

My mouth scrunched up and I looked away, back out toward the slowly approaching island. "I guess so? Maybe? I don't know. It's just a feeling. And now that he's free, I can't help but worry about where he'll go. It's too far for him to fly back to Maldobar, and he can't possibly be safe here, can he?"

Uncle Reigh's mouth mashed into a thoughtful, crooked line. He rubbed at the back of his neck and scratched at his chin, obviously mulling it over, before he replied, "I don't know, Maylea. But I've got a feeling, too, and it tells me you haven't seen the last of him. I've seen lots of dragons in my time. I've seen them do some pretty incredible and strange things. The way that dragon looked at you—the way he trusted you right away—I think Paligno has more in store than any of us can imagine."

"Are you saying you think that dragon chose me to be his rider?" The idea made my heart skip a few excited beats. I'd always wondered if that path was going to be available to me like it had my parents. But so far, I'd never met a dragon who wanted to choose me.

The idea was as terrifying as it was incredible.

"It's possible," he said. "Time will tell. How do you feel about that? Think you're cut out to join the ranks of the mighty dragonriders?"

I groaned and leaned harder against the railing, letting my head sag forward. "I think it means going to an academy where my dah is the commander and gets to stick his nose in my business all the time."

Uncle Reigh laughed and patted my shoulder sympathetically. "I survived it. You can, too."

Ugggh. The more I thought about it, the more I liked the idea of waiting to go through training until my dah retired. It was bad enough to have my parents being overprotective at home. I seriously did not want that trend to continue when I moved into the next phase of my life.

"I, uh, I want to apologize for what happened," Uncle Reigh muttered quietly. His tone and his expression had gone somber. "That you were taken like that, I mean."

"It wasn't your fault," I reminded him.

"No. But I doubt your dad is going to see it that way," he sighed.

"Well, maybe he doesn't have to know." I let my tone carry the hint without ever looking over to meet his bewildered expression. "He doesn't have to know *everything*, does he?"

"Maylea Broadfeather, are you suggesting I *lie* to your father, Academy Commander and

Dragonrider Champion Jaevid Broadfeather, about you being abducted and forced to participate in gladiatorial combat against a king drake?" he balked.

I pursed my lips. "Maybe ... a little."

He chuckled and thumped the back of my head again. "I appreciate your confidence in my ability to deceive your dad, but I think you've greatly overestimated my skills in that department. Nice try, though."

I grinned and winked at him. "Thanks. I learned from the best."

Uncle Reigh looked like he might faint with relief when we arrived back at the inn to find Thatcher lying in a bed in the room next to ours. He looked awful, more fragile and pale than I'd ever seen him, but he was sleeping soundly while a woman in strange blue robes sat at his bedside.

She looked up with a similarly relieved smile, and quickly got up to speak to Violet in Sokraal. Violet tried giving her a handful of silver coins, but the woman just shook her head and waved her hands in protest. She gave us all a small bow and parting word before she left, disappearing into the city streets like a ghost.

"Don't wake him up," Uncle Reigh said quietly as he shooed us back out into the hall. "He needs to rest. I'll check on him in a few hours and make sure he isn't running a fever. I also need to give him more of that healing paste, providing I still have some left in my kit."

"There isn't any," Violet reminded him grimly. "We used it all during the surgery. But if you wish, I can go out to the market at dawn and see if any of the apothecary shops have some."

"Yeah," Uncle Reigh nodded, his shoulders rising and falling with a heavy sigh. Concern still sat heavy on his brow, creasing his forehead and making the circles under his eyes seem darker than ever. "We'll have to try something, even if they don't have the same remedy. He's in a fragile state. An infection would kill him."

"Is he going to be okay?" I asked once we were back in our room. But one glance around gave me my answer ... and a cold chill scurried up my spine. There was blood everywhere. I grimaced as I stepped past it, going to where my new bow and quiver were still lying on the floor next to my bag. I picked them up and carried them out into the hall to wait while the others gathered their things, too.

"He'll be alright. We just need to give him as much time as possible before we move him," Uncle Reigh assured me. "I'm hoping we can at least find a different place to stay, though. We have no way of knowing who Sulam might have told about our presence here. This place isn't secure."

"I'll see what I can find for us." Violet's tone was heavy as she rummaged around through her own bag like she was making sure all her things were still there. "I swiped a bunch of Sulam's rings on my way out. I can sell them and give us more coin to work with. We're going to need it."

"Do we have enough to at least get something to eat?" I asked and reached up to pet along the soft feathers of Lukani's back. "I'm starving."

"Yes. Actually, there might be something downstairs. Figall is a traitorous pile of dung, but he does have to eat. He might have some food stores we can take," Violet suggested. "I was going to recommend we all spend the night down there on the first floor, anyway. I'd like to keep an eye out in case anyone else decides to give us trouble before we can get out of here."

"Good idea," Uncle Reigh said. "I'm a decent enough cook. Bachelor life, you know. I'll see what I can do. Maylea, grab all the clean blankets and pillows you can find and bring them downstairs. We'll make pallets on the floor and take turns keeping watch."

Everyone snapped into action, not chatting much as we got to work settling in for the night. Only Thatcher stayed upstairs, still asleep in his bed with Vexi curled up on his chest like a lazy housecat. Uncle Reigh didn't want to risk moving him too soon, and judging by the amount of blood on the floor in our old room, I had to agree.

We found enough food to scrape together a meager dinner of rice, small bony fish that tasted okay roasted over the coals, and some sort of spicy pepper paste that was pretty good when you mixed it in with the rice. Violet showed us how to eat roasted kelp, which I couldn't imagine might actually be delicious. But it was. It'd been roasted until it was crispy, and seasoned with salt and something else that made it savory. That—or maybe I was just *really* hungry. It didn't matter, either way. I hadn't eaten in a couple of days, so I took whatever I could get.

After dinner, Uncle Reigh insisted on taking the first watch while Lukani—who had changed back into his normal human form—curled up on our pallets to sleep. Lying side by side, I reached under the blankets and felt around until I found Lukani's hand. I saw one corner of his mouth curl up into a faint, exhausted smile as he wound his fingers through mine. He never even opened his eyes. He didn't have to, though. Just holding his hand and being this close was enough. I could rest knowing he was right there beside me.

Violet sat with Uncle Reigh for a while beside the little fire pit, sipping some wine she had found in Figall's pantry straight from the bottle. For a long time, they didn't say anything. They just sat there while the embers popped and hissed.

My eyes grew heavy. Lying on my side with my back turned to the soothing warmth of the fire pit, I let my body relax into the soft blankets. I hadn't slept in days. And now that I had a belly full of warm food, there was no stopping me.

At least, not until Uncle Reigh cleared his throat some and mumbled, "Not to, uh, stick my nose where it isn't wanted ... but are you okay? Sulam said a lot of things back there. I'm not an idiot. I realize you two had history. I'm not gonna ask about all that. I just want to make sure you're ... you know." He hesitated, stumbling over his words. "I mean, you slit his throat so deep you nearly beheaded him. Not that I'm not impressed, but that was ... kind of intense."

I held still, listening for anything. A gasp. A sigh. Any hint of emotion that might be in her voice when she answered. "I'm fine."

Oh. She was definitely *not* fine. I didn't even need to see her face to be able to tell that much.

Apparently, Uncle Reigh wasn't buying an inch of that excuse either. "You know you can talk to me, right?" he said, his tone much gentler.

"Yes. But that doesn't mean I *should*."

I could hear the frown in his voice. "Don't trust me, then?"

She let out a heavy breath, pausing before she spoke again. "It's not that. Or maybe it is. I don't even trust myself, sometimes. And today, I got sloppy. I sent you off into Sulam's house alone, knowing fully what that man was capable of. I regretted it the instant you left. I knew it was a mistake. My plan was a bad one because I let my hatred for the man get the better of me. I let it make me reckless. But it was too late. And it nearly got us all killed."

"To be fair, this was not even close to the worst situation I've ever gotten tangled up in. Remember my list of dangerous things? You still haven't managed to hit the top ten." He chuckled quietly.

"I'm going to need to hear this list of yours one of these days," she laughed softly, too. "It sounds absolutely fascinating."

"What about physically, then? You got some wounds when the guards rushed you. Need me to stitch you up again?" he asked.

Her tone was softer, almost sounding shy, as she answered, "It's nothing to worry about. Thank you, though."

They were silent again for a moment, and I wondered if the conversation was over. Knowing Uncle Reigh, he was just sitting there silently panicking over what to say next. What an idiot. No wonder he was still single.

"That girl ... did you know about the power Paligno has given her? That she would be capable of things like what happened today?" Violet whispered suddenly.

My pulse skipped. I held my breath, waiting for Uncle Reigh to respond.

"I knew she had awakened some sort of connection to his power on the ship. But, no. I had no idea it was going to be anything of this magnitude. I mean, her family does have strong ties to that god. But I thought Jae and I had sort of cut those ties when we destroyed the stones. I guess I was wrong," he murmured back. "Now I'm afraid for her. She's only ever heard about the good things Paligno did for her family. But all divine power comes with a price. She's so young—I don't think she fully understands what walking this path may cost her."

He paused, and something was off in his tone. I couldn't put my finger on it, but that feeling like there was something more he wasn't saying stuck in the back of my mind like a thorn I couldn't pull out.

And I guess Violet could tell it, too. She sounded truly concerned as she asked, "What's wrong?"

He didn't reply right away. Seconds of tense, uncomfortable silence passed before, at last, he muttered, "When I was trying to save Thatcher ... I saw something today I haven't seen in a long time. Not since before the end of the Tibran War, when I still had my own divine powers."

"What do you mean?" she pressed. "What did you see?"

He sucked in a slow, deep breath. "I saw the spirit that used to haunt me when I was the Harbinger. The one that served me and gave me a lot of my abilities. The spirit of my twin brother, who is now eternally bound to serve Clysiros in the Vale. I used to call him Noh. He was here, back in our world. He helped me save Thatcher. And I ... I don't know why. But knowing he's here again, seeing him like that—Gods and Fates, I don't know what's happening. But it feels like we are getting pushed closer and closer to the edge of something terrible."

For a moment there was nothing to fill the silence but the soft crackle of the flames in the fire pit. I could barely hear it thanks to the pounding of my heart that clashed in my ears. I shut my eyes and squeezed Lukani's hand tighter. Uncle Reigh was getting powers from Clysiros again? Could that really be true?

"It doesn't have to mean anything yet," Violet spoke up suddenly, her tone much steadier than before. "That's why we came here, to get out in front of this before Sadeera can kindle this war. If we get that codex and take it back to Arlan, she won't be able to open that divine gate. There doesn't have to be a war. But we can't hesitate. We can't make any more mistakes. We must get to Nar'Haleen—to the Compendium—and find out what has happened to it."

"I know," he said.

"At first light, I will approach the Zenith's Call for assistance. With any luck, I can arrange safe passage for us soon," Violet went on, seeming to talk more to herself than to him now.

"I have every confidence." Uncle Reigh groaned like he was stretching. "Now, then, if you don't mind keeping watch for a little while, I'm going to take my turn to sleep before anything else attacks, mauls, shoots at, or tries to abduct us."

I could hear a sincere softness, like a gentle smile, in Violet's voice. "Of course. Goodnight then, Lieutenant."

Things fell silent, then. It didn't take long for Uncle Reigh to begin snoring. But even that sound wasn't enough to keep my eyes from drooping closed again and my body from sinking deep into my nest of blankets. My thoughts grew hazy, and kept circling back to that moment when I touched that dragon's nose and he stared into my eyes like he could see all the way down to my soul.

Would I ever see him again? And if I did ... what did that mean? Was I really destined to be a dragonrider like my parents? Or was this the beginning of something else altogether?

Those questions slowly circled in my brain like stars spinning slowly through the clear night sky. So clear, but so far out of reach. All I could do was watch them pass.

Watch—and wait to see what destiny had planned for me next.

PALADIN

THE DRAGONRIDER HERITAGE BOOK SEVEN

PART ONE
JAEVID

I

CHAPTER ONE

"WHERE, BY ALL THINGS DIVINE, IS MY DAUGHTER?!" The words burst out of me like a crack of thunder, echoing through the grand vestibule of the royal castle in Halfax.

Before me, two young dragonriders, a pair of recently graduated lieutenants, flinched and drew back a step. "S-Sir, we've been questioning all the servants and staff that were working the night of the ball, but it's taking longer than expected," one of them stammered. "We've set up a perimeter around the city, as well. No one will come or go without a thorough check. We just need more time to—"

"—to do what?" I interrupted with a snarl. "Continue to be useless? My *child* is missing! My only daughter! Someone took her from this castle and I will not rest until she is found! No one will! If I have to tear this kingdom down brick by brick, I will!"

A heavy, all-too-familiar hand fell on my shoulder and gave a reassuring squeeze. "You need to take a breath, Jae. They're doing everything they can. Jenna has mobilized forces through every street in this city and the villages beyond. We've got dragonriders searching the air and infantry in every surrounding village. Someone will have seen something," Felix Farrow murmured. "Have a little faith."

I flicked him a sideways scowl, but my thoughts tangled in a wild frenzy. Take a breath? How could he even suggest that?

"It's been three days," I shouted back. "They haven't found a single piece of useful information! No one even saw her leave her room! Gods and Fates, what am I going to tell Beckah? How can I go back to her without even a shred of hope? The baby is due any day now, and I—"

"Need to remember who, exactly, we're dealing with here. This isn't some hapless waif of a girl who would be easily duped by a stranger," Felix countered, his tone still calm. "Maylea has been trained by the finest warriors in this kingdom since she could walk. Not to mention she's got twice the rebellious energy and daring spirit you and Beckah ever had. It's very unlikely anyone could sneak up on her let alone kidnap her."

I narrowed my eyes and shrugged his hand off my shoulder. "What are you suggesting?"

His mouth quirked into a half-grin. "Only the obvious, if you'd take a moment to collect yourself and think clearly. You need to consider that perhaps she wasn't taken. Perhaps Maylea left on her own."

My heart seized in my chest at those words, like I'd swallowed a fistful of jagged stones. Felix had known me—had been my best friend and brother in arms—since we were practically children ourselves. But what sort of fool did he take me for? Of course I had considered that! How could I not? Especially when ...

Gods. I-I couldn't bear this. I shut my eyes tightly as guilt twisted through me like someone was turning a knife in my chest. Maylea had been so upset with me that night. I'd left her in her room, stewing in frustration over not being allowed to attend the ball. It was a situation I understood all too well. She'd been like that all her life—frustrated at any boundary we tried to hold for her, even if it was something meant to keep her safe. Maylea had her mother's strong spirit, and my knack for finding trouble wherever it might try to hide.

No one had to tell me how dangerous that combination was.

But to run away? No. I couldn't fathom that. She had been angry with me before for situations much like this, but she had never taken things that far. Yes, she would pout. She might even lock her door or refuse dinner. I couldn't imagine my daughter leaving us without a single word, though. There had to be something else, some other explanation.

Unless ... it was something I had said to her that had driven her away.

I swallowed hard against the rising panic that made my chest constrict and shook my head. I had to compose myself. I couldn't crumble, not when they were all standing there gawking at me.

"Go, then." I growled at the pair of lieutenants, who still stared at me with matching expressions of pasty, wide-eyed anticipation like two goldfish watching someone eat a crust of bread.

They both saluted with a fist over their chests and swift bow before speeding away across the vestibule. Felix and I stood in heavy silence, watching them go. It took everything I had not to bolt out after them. I should be out there searching, too. But I couldn't leave—not when Beckah and the boys were still upstairs. I ... I couldn't stand the idea of leaving them alone. What if something else happened? What if they disappeared, too?

I tried to think, to come up with something else we could do. A new idea. A strategy. But I could hardly concentrate past the way my body ached in all the places where my formal armor had gotten too snug over the years. I hadn't bothered to stop and take any of it off, let alone change clothes or eat anything. I couldn't recall that I had even sat down since Beckah and I returned to our suite to find our daughter gone without a trace. My head swam and I stumbled as my knees threatened to buckle. I barely managed to catch myself against Felix's shoulder.

"Jae?" he grabbed me by the arm and steadied me, his light cognac eyes suddenly sharp and serious. "What's wrong?"

"I-I'm fine," I managed as I straightened. "I'm just tired. Hungry, too, I guess. It doesn't matter."

"It does, actually." I could hear that obnoxious, almost fatherly disapproval in his tone. Not that it was anything new. He'd always fussed after me like an overprotective older brother.

I'm sure that made for an interesting spectacle now, since he was in his seventies and I had only just brushed my mid-thirties. Well, physically, anyway. I had forty years of divinely spelled sleep to thank for that, and a great many other complicated inconsistencies in my life.

"I mean it. You can't keep this up for another day. You need to rest," Felix insisted with a scowl.

"I can't stop. I have to do this, Felix." I sighed shakily, closing my eyes and bowing my head. "If I quit now. I-I ... I can't lose her."

"You won't," he added quickly. "We're not done turning over stones, Jae. Not even close. You know the others love her, too. They won't give up. So you keep your head on straight, yeah?"

I rubbed at my brow and pinched the bridge of my nose, trying to relieve the splitting pain that throbbed in my head. It didn't work. "I know, I know. I just can't shake the feeling that something awful happened. For her to disappear right after our meeting with Arlan the Kinslayer, and knowing there might have been agents from this so-called Hands of Fate faction on the castle grounds? What if they got to her? What if they knew she was my daughter and took her as a hostage? Or worse? Would there even be any evidence to find if that were the case? Wouldn't that explain why no one can find a single trace of her? Gods, if they—" My voice caught and I snapped my mouth shut, biting down hard against that rising swell of panic.

Felix put his hand on my shoulder and gave me another consoling shake. "I know it hurts, Jae. When Jenna left for the battlefront during the Tibran War, I was terrified I would never see her again. Back then, we fought a lot about her roles in the kingdom, and I was so afraid my last words to her would be ones I'd said in anger. I suspect that must be what you're afraid of now, hm?"

My eyes welled and I clenched my teeth, fighting to keep my emotions contained as I stared back at him. How had he known? Was I that obvious? Or was he reading my mind somehow?

"Maylea knows how much you and Beckah love her," he assured. "No matter what was or wasn't said, she knows that."

"I should have told her. I should have said something different. Maybe if I had, then she wouldn't be ..." The words died in my throat before I could even finish that thought. I couldn't. Not when it hurt this much.

I had failed many times in my life, but knowing I had failed to be there when my only daughter needed me the most—Gods. It was more than I could bear.

I turned away, not saying anything else as I began retreating from the vestibule. It wasn't until I was halfway down the long hall of massive oil portraits that led to the grand staircase that I heard Felix's footfalls following. Well, I'd always known him to be more stubborn than an old cow. The years had changed both of us, but they hadn't changed that part of him.

"You do realize the irony of this, don't you?" Felix had that teasing, cunning edge to his tone as he fell in step right beside me.

I frowned and kept my focus straight ahead, not really in the mood for any of his taunting.

"Really? Not a word? Don't tell me you don't remember? Is your memory still spotty after that little divine nap?" he chuckled softly, his pace slowing and finally stopping in the hall.

I stopped, too.

Looking back, I found my now far older-looking best friend standing, gazing up at one of the portraits with a strange, almost sad smile. It deepened the lines on his brow, around the corners of his eyes, and at the corners of his mouth.

I glanced up, following his gaze to the embarrassingly massive painting of myself hanging on the wall. It depicted a much younger, and ridiculously over-muscled version of myself sitting astride my dragon, Mavrik. Just the sight of it made my face flush with embarrassment and I had to look away. Felix had commissioned that absurd thing after ... well, after he thought I had given my life to end the divine curse that was ravaging our world. He claimed it was to memorialize my great sacrifice. I knew better, though. I knew *him*. That portrait was his colorful way of teasing me, even beyond the grave. Gods. There were no words to describe how much I hated that atrocity. Gaudy, tasteless, and mortifying might've been a good start, though. I'd sincerely hoped it might not survive the siege during the Tibran war. No such luck, though.

"If I'm not mistaken, Beckah was the same age as your daughter when we all snuck away from Duke Brinton's estate the night of our very first officer's ball," he recalled. "It feels like an eternity ago. But I still remember it clearly. I already thought you were madder than a rabid ferret, but that night, I was sure you'd lost your mind entirely. And when you jumped off the top of that tower! Gods and Fates, I was already trying to imagine what I'd tell everyone. I didn't understand it then. I didn't know what forces were moving you, or where that path would take us. But I believed in you," he said, finally aiming that familiar grin back at me. "I still do."

My hands curled into fists at my sides. "This isn't like that, Felix."

"Isn't it, though? Ancient powers stirring. Assassins in the shadows. And once again, there's a far-too-young Broadfeather running amok," he chuckled again and shook his head. "Give her some credit, Jae. She might not be a dragonrider yet, but Maylea could wind up being every bit the holy terror you were."

"I know," I murmured, unable to stop my voice from breaking under the weight of the despair. "That's exactly what I'm worried about."

STANDING BEFORE THE DOOR TO THE GUEST SUITE WHERE BECKAH AND OUR OTHER children were still staying, my hand halted before I could even grab the handle. My heart sat like a cold, battered stone in my chest, so heavy that every heartbeat came with a throb of pain. Fates help me, what was I going to say to her? How was I supposed to tell my wife that our child was still missing? It was my duty—my responsibility—to keep our family safe.

And I had failed.

Our sweet little girl was gone and I had no idea how to bring her back.

My shoulders dropped as I let out a heavy breath. Somehow, I had to pull myself together. The rest of my family—my wife and other children—were all depending on me to be their rock. I couldn't crumble. I couldn't falter. Not now.

Opening the door, I stepped into the near-dark of the main sitting room to find nothing but quiet.

For an instant, the stress and fear seemed to ease, as though the curtain of adrenaline had finally been pulled back. Behind it, I could finally feel how every part of me was sore and aching with exhaustion. Even my eyes felt like two overcooked boiled eggs, dry and irritated from going too long without sleep.

Then I heard them.

"DAH!" Both of my boys rushed me at once, bounding from one of the nearby bedrooms like two excited puppies. Calem hit me full force, wrapping his arms around my waist and hugging me tightly. I staggered and nearly lost my balance. Gods, he was getting big. Pretty soon he'd be able to take me right to the floor with a tackle like that.

I put my hand on his head and ruffled his dark brown hair. He blinked up at me and grinned from one slightly pointed ear to the other, displaying his missing two front teeth.

Sile, on the other hand, hesitated a few feet away. Already dressed in his long nightshirt, my oldest son studied my face as though he were trying to read my mind or somehow sense my mood. He wasn't quite eleven yet, but of my three children, he had always been the most cautious. Cautious, and far more attuned to everyone else's emotions and intentions. He also happened to be the one that looked the most like me, with light blue eyes and black hair he wore in a short ponytail. Sometimes, looking at him felt like glimpsing a long-past version of myself, although he was far more certain of himself than I'd ever been at that age. He had a quiet confidence and assurance that, more often than not, led him down paths that got him into trouble.

I was beginning to suspect that was a family trait, though.

Like his elder sister, Sile had already begun to show great skill in combat. Murdoc, Kiran, and Reigh had spent hours teaching him whenever work called me away. But where Maylea had always had an aptitude with a bow, Sile had recently shown preference for a pair of sleek, elven-styled scimitars made of greevwood—a birthday gift from Araxie.

Fates, why did everyone keep giving my children weapons for presents? Couldn't they just manage a simple toy?

"Dah?" Calem asked, tilting his head to one side curiously. "What's wrong?"

I shook my head. "I'm just tired. Has your mother already gone to bed?" I tried to smile, to show both my boys the tiniest hint of hopefulness. I didn't want them to see it—the pain and fear that still twisted in my gut with every breath I took. I had to protect them from that. Calem was still too young to pick up on what was really happening. But I guess it wasn't enough to fool Sile.

His eyes welled as he swallowed hard, holding my gaze for a few seconds with his hands clenched at his sides. Then he bowed his head and looked away.

"Yeah. Mum sang the old song to us, but I still can't sleep. Are we going home soon, Dah?" Calem asked as he immediately grabbed onto one of my hands with both of his. "It's no fun here. I miss my room. And Sile won't even play with me."

"Oh? Well, perhaps that's because he knows you're both supposed to be in bed," I said as I gently shut the door behind me. One glance around the sitting room made that dull throbbing pain twist in my chest again. Beckah had left her stitching on the arm of a big velvet chair close to the fireside. She had embroidered a blanket for each of our children, and it looked like she was nearly finished with this one.

Just in time, too. It wouldn't be long now.

The fire in the hearth had already smoldered down to cinders. She must have already gone to bed after tucking the boys in. Good. She needed all the rest she could manage.

"Come on, boys. Back to bed," I urged. Taking them gently by the shoulder, I guided both my sons back into the bedroom they were sharing.

Two small, child-sized beds with tall canopies draped in blue velvet curtains stood on either side of the room, and a sea of toys littered the fine woven rug between them. Little wooden dragons with pull strings. Dolls in dragonrider armor cut from little pieces of tin. Wooden practice swords and shields. Old helmets.

I spotted a slingshot I was sure I had confiscated after I'd caught them launching grapes at the guards patrolling by our suite. Hmm. I wonder who would have dared to give it back to them after that lecture?

Hah. As if I didn't know.

Curse it, Felix.

After wrestling Calem back into bed and coaxing him through the old elven lullaby my mother had once sung to me, it didn't take even a minute for him to drift off to sleep. I tucked the quilts around him tightly and picked my way carefully across the sea of toys to Sile's bedside.

He was already under his blankets, lying with his back to me, and he didn't say a word. The sight made my heartbeat stammer for an instant. That was exactly how I'd found Maylea the last time I'd seen her.

No—I had to pull myself together. For his sake, I had to be steady. He needed reassurance. He needed me to be his fortress in the storm.

Even if I was terrified, as well.

"I know you're worried about your sister," I whispered as I sat down on the bed beside him. "You want to know something? I'm worried, too."

He rolled over just enough that he could peer at me over his shoulder with one pale blue eye. "Why'd she run away, Dah? Why would she just leave us like that? Does she hate us or something?"

"Hate us? No, Sile. Maylea would never hate us."

"Then why?" He rolled over all the way onto his back, his chin trembling as he bit at each word angrily.

"Son, I ... I don't know why she left," I confessed. "But I will find her. She's going to be okay."

"You promise?"

I reached to take one of his small hands in mine. "Yes. I swear it. But in order to find her, I might have to leave this castle. I might have to fly away to help search. And I need your help with that, Sile. I need you to look after your brother. I need you to make sure he doesn't cause any trouble for your mother. I need you to be a little more grownup than usual and do your best to take care of both of them until I come back. Can you do that for me?"

His chin stopped trembling and he stared back at me, those keen eyes searching me for what felt like an eternity. Reading my thoughts. Looking for any sign of deception. I guess he didn't find any because he nodded sharply and squeezed my hand back hard. "I will."

"Good. I'm proud of you, son." I bent down and kissed his forehead. "Now, get some sleep. I'm going to take care of everything."

Sile seemed to relax back into his bed, giving me a few drowsy blinks before he nodded again.

I'd almost made it all the way to the door when I heard him call out to me again in a faint, sleepy whisper. "Hey, Dah?"

I glanced back. "Yes?"

"Is it okay to pray to Paligno to protect her?"

Once again, my heart gave a lurching jolt in my chest. My breath caught, and adrenaline prickled over my body like a wave of heat. All my children knew the stories of the ancient gods—I'd made sure of that. They also knew I had been the last lapiloque. The last to walk with the God of Life.

But I had never encouraged any of them to actually pray to any of the gods. So where was this coming from?

"I-I suppose so, if you want to. Why?" I tried to keep my voice steady.

"Because ... I think he talks to me sometimes ... when I'm dreaming," Sile slurred groggily as he burrowed down deeper into his blankets. "I hear a voice. He said ... our family is special. He said we're going to change the world."

2

CHAPTER TWO

It ... it couldn't be true.

Paligno was ... talking to my *children?* Why? Fates, what did this mean? Was everything that man, Arlan the Kinslayer, had said true? Was there really a war coming with the realm of the gods?

Was this why Maylea had left? Had Paligno told her to go?

Gods and Fates, what was happening to my family?!

"Jaevid?" Beckah called out as I staggered into our bedroom, barely managing to catch myself against the doorframe. My head whirled and my heart pounded so fast I could hardly breathe. The soft flickers of candlelight in the room seemed to spin around me in a blur.

"What's wrong?" She sat upright in bed, her eyes wide and expression tense with worry.

I nearly tripped over my own feet on my way to the bedside, finally hitting the floor on my knees and gripping the mattress as I wheezed.

"Jae?!" Beckah's soft, cool fingers brushed mine. "What's happened? Please, just talk to me!"

I didn't know. I didn't know how to tell her. How to explain. How to confess that I was no closer to finding our daughter than I had been when we'd first returned to our room and discovered she was gone. Hours of relentless work, and I had nothing. No clues. No evidence that anyone had even seen her that night.

She grasped my chin, turning my face so that I was forced to meet her gaze. That look, with the warm light of the oil lamp on the nightstand shining in her dark green eyes, her dark hair falling to frame her face just right, and all those beautiful freckles on her cheeks and nose like tiny constellations—it was enough to make my whole body go slack. I took in a deep, ragged breath like I'd been holding it for days, swimming frantically for a surface that wasn't there. A surface I might never reach.

At least, not until I looked in her eyes.

"I'm so sorry, Beckah. They're searching everywhere. Every dragonrider in the area is scouring the countryside looking for her. We're interrogating the staff. We're doing everything we can but there's no sign of her anywhere." I bowed my head, too ashamed to hold her gaze any longer. "I lost her. I lost our little girl. And now ..."

I couldn't say it. I couldn't tell her that Paligno might be the reason. Not until I was certain. Not that I thought she wouldn't believe me—I knew she would. But if that were true, if Maylea had been called away by Paligno, then it really was hopeless. My daughter would be beyond anyone's reach. How could I possibly contest the will of the deity who had given me everything I held dear?

"I'm so sorry," I growled through my teeth. "I've failed you. But I won't give up. I'll keep trying. I just need to change clothes, and then I'll get right back to—"

"Oh, my sweet Jae," Beckah whispered as she combed her fingers through my hair. "Nothing is lost. I don't believe that for a second. Just stop for a moment. It won't all fall apart if you stop and look at me." She leaned in, kissing my temple before she scooted over to the edge of the bed and coaxed me up onto it beside her. "I know you're trying your hardest. But it's like you believe I will see you as less of a person if you don't always wind up being the victorious hero in every situation. Like failing would somehow make me love you less."

All the tension in my body gradually began to ease as she spoke gently and brushed my hair behind my pointed ears. I couldn't help but sink into that feeling—of being close to her—as though her presence were a warm blanket wrapping around my weary soul. My eyes fell closed and I leaned into her touch, finally managing a ragged exhale when I felt her fingers begin working at the buckles of my cloak.

"I could never love you less, Jaevid Broadfeather. And if you can't fail in front of me, the woman who loves you most in the world, then what is love?" she whispered as she stacked each piece of my formal, ceremonial armor into a pile beside the bed. "Go and have a bath, and then you need to rest. I have no doubt that you'll find our little girl. But I also know you'll do a much better job of it when you have a clear head."

I opened my mouth to protest. What? She wanted me to stop? To rest? I-I ... I couldn't. Maybe I could change clothes, wash my face, but there wasn't time for anything else. Not if I was chasing the whispers of a god once again. I knew exactly what kind of fight I might be in for.

But, Fates, how could I explain any of that to Beckah? I didn't want to scare her any more than she already was. She was in a fragile state, with only a short time left until our fourth—and quite possibly fifth—child was due to be born, and I had to do what I could to protect her. She wouldn't have said any of this if she had known the gods were involved.

I had to carry this burden alone.

"Go ahead and lie down," I murmured, trying my best to keep my tone steady and more relaxed than before. "I'll be right back."

It wasn't a complete lie. I had every intention of washing my face, changing into more comfortable clothes, and coming back to lie down with her until she fell asleep. Then I'd get back to work, chasing heels and doing whatever it took to bring my daughter home.

I'd barely gotten a foot out of the room when a knock at the suite's main door sent a rush of cold fear through my body. Every muscle locked up solid. My thoughts whirled in a sudden frenzy, spinning out of control even as my pulse slowed to hard, painful thumps.

It was late—far too late for servant staff to be coming by for anything. I hadn't ordered any meals to be brought up.

That ... that could only mean one thing.

Oh, Gods!

I SURGED FOR THE DOOR, WHIPPING IT OPEN SUDDENLY.

Standing directly on the other side, Murdoc flinched back and immediately snapped his hand back to his shoulder, reaching for one of the cross-sheathed longswords belted across his back.

Then our eyes met. He muttered a curse under his breath and dropped his arm, sinking into his heels as he shook his head. "Well, then. Glad to see you're awake."

"I was never asleep," I countered quickly. "What are you doing here? What's happened? Has there been any word? Have they found her?"

Murdoc opened his mouth to answer, but before he could get a word out, his gaze flickered to something behind me. His expression softened, brow drawing up slightly as his mouth mashed into an uncomfortable line. He nodded slowly and dropped his gaze down submissively.

I glanced back over my shoulder to find Beckah standing behind me, dressed in her nightgown and robe, with her long dark hair wound into a loose braid that hung over her shoulder. She flicked a sharp glance between us, her expression as steely as a cat on the hunt. "What's happened?" she asked as she took a step closer and put a hand on my arm.

"I don't know." I looked back at Murdoc. "He was just about to explain."

"Jae—er, I mean, Commander, Sir," he blurted quickly. "I apologize for the intrusion, but you should know, we found a member of the castle staff that remembers seeing your daughter on the night of the ball."

"What?" I took a step closer to him. "Who is it? What did they say?"

Murdoc raised a hand as though to urge me to stay calm. "Just a servant. But he was able to give us a good description of what happened. She ... well, she apparently crashed into him while running through the servants' passages outside the ballrooms. He tried chasing after her, and even alerted some of the castle guards. They assumed she was just causing mischief, nothing serious or malicious, especially since they saw her fleeing through the halls with a boy."

Rage took my brain like a roiling summer storm. "With ... a ... *WHAT?!*" I could practically taste flames licking from my lips as I roared. "Who was he? What did he look like? Where did they go? Fates curse it, didn't that servant know anything useful?"

Murdoc gave a defeated sigh. "Unfortunately, even the castle guards weren't able to catch them. Not that I'm surprised, honestly. We trained her well. But I have a strong lead about where we can find the boy."

I took another aggressive step closer, my hands in shaking fists at my sides. "Tell. Me. Now."

"I spoke to the guards personally. They described the boy as a teenager with black hair, dressed in strange clothing, with greenish-colored skin. One of them swore he saw that the boy had a tail like a lion's, but the other disagreed and called it ridiculous. Seems they've argued about it ever since that night, and they were both were too embarrassed to come forward with this information earlier," Murdoc explained with a knowing smirk. "I don't know about you, but I can only think of one person in all of Maldobar who might fit that description."

I bit down hard against the urge to yell. Curse it all straight to the abyss! Of course I knew who that was. But what did *he* have to do with any of this? Why was he even in the castle at all that night? And why, by all things divine, was he running around with *my* daughter?

"It seems there's someone else we need to interview if we want to get to the bottom of this," Murdoc said cryptically, lowering his voice almost as though he didn't want Beckah to overhear. "I have it from a very reliable source that he's still in Southwatch. We can catch him there before he changes locations, but we would have to leave right now."

"You're talking about Arlan the Kinslayer," Beckah spoke up, fixing him a resolved stare.

Murdoc dipped his head, wincing slightly. "I am."

"I know all about your dealings with him," she said matter-of-factly. Then she glanced up at me.

My stomach clenched hard with a sudden jolt of adrenaline when I saw it—that quiet fire smoldering in her dark evergreen eyes. It was a look that would have moved mountains like building blocks if she wanted. A look I'd never been able to resist.

"So?" She arched an eyebrow expectantly. "What are you waiting for? Go, talk to him, and get our daughter back."

Murdoc made a strange, choking, barking sound that might have been a laugh in disguise. I couldn't pry my eyes away from my wife long enough to be sure—not when I was on the verge of a complete mental breakdown. Was she serious? Leave? I couldn't leave! Not when she was—

"Murdoc, darling, why don't you go and wait in the garden? He'll be down in just a moment, I promise," Beckah assured, still holding me captive with that focused, silently challenging stare. Gods, it was like looking an angry dragoness in the eye and praying she didn't breathe fire and melt my head clean off.

"Uh, right. Of course. I'll just ... go wait." Murdoc cleared his throat and took a step back, rubbing at his mouth like he was still fighting back a smile. I watched him go, barely catching it as he gestured a fast "*good luck*" to me using dragonrider hand-signals.

Great. Well, I suppose I'd probably need it.

Stepping back into our room, I shut the door and scrambled to gather my thoughts. I couldn't go into this discussion half-hearted. Not when she was already throwing those sorts of looks at me. Get it together, man. You fought the primal forces of nature and stood in the presence of angry gods. I could handle reasoning with my wife.

"You should change your clothes and armor to something more suitable," she instructed, tapping her chin thoughtfully. "In fact, you should go ahead and pack a travel bag in case Arlan sends you off immediately."

"Wh-What?" I began to protest, "But, Beckah, I—I can't leave you, not when you're nearly—"

"Silly man, I'm pregnant, not dying," she scolded gently and patted my cheek. "This isn't my first go-round, or even my second, and I've got all the help I can tolerate here. I'll be fine. Go and find our little girl. Do whatever you believe is necessary to bring her back safe." She stood on her toes and stole a quick kiss. "I trust you, Jae—today, tomorrow, and always."

"But, gods, what if something happens? What if you need me and I—"

Her expression softened, becoming calm but serious as she reached to tuck some of my bangs behind one of my pointed ears. "Jaevid, my love. I know you're upset. I know you're worried. But please hear me. I knew from the very first moment I met you that you were someone destiny had immense plans for—the sort of man who would walk with greatness far beyond my understanding. When I say that I trust you, I mean that I trust that you will do everything in your power to fight for what is right and good in this world, and that when it's all over, you'll come back to us. All right?"

A shaky, uncertain breath left my lips as I slowly nodded. "I just worry. I don't want you to regret choosing a dragonrider because I'm never here when you need me the most."

A smile like a spring sunrise over a frost-kissed meadow lit her face as she gave the tip of my ear a playful tug. "I didn't choose a dragonrider, silly man," she laughed softly. "I chose my heart's other half. And I'll keep choosing you every day until we take our last breath together."

I couldn't fight back a smile as I leaned down, gently grasping the back of her head to kiss her. "I'll send word as soon as I've found her," I promised when I pulled back at last.

She nodded approvingly, watching in silence as I gathered my belongings together as quickly as possible. I changed into my battle-ready armor, donned my travel boots, and checked the contents of my go-bag before I buckled my scimitar to my belt.

"You know, I was thinking it's not so different, is it? From the night you and I first met," Beckah said with a wistful smile as she came over with my long blue dragonrider cloak.

"What?" I asked as she worked at buckling it to my shoulder pauldrons one at a time.

"Maylea and running off with this young man. They left in the middle of a ball, called away by some unknown mission," she explained, her smile widening some as she stood back to admire me. "I remember following a dashing boy off into the wide, dangerous world in a very similar way."

My mouth scrunched. "I seem to remember nearly getting ourselves killed several times over, as well."

Beckah tilted her head to the side a little, flashing me another one of those coy, teasing smiles that still made my heartbeat skip. "You're just jealous because I rode a king drake first. Go on. Admit it."

I balked and choked. "That has nothing at all to do with—!"

Before I could finish, she laughed and winked playfully. Then Beckah moved in close again and put her hands on my cheeks, standing on her toes to press her lips to my forehead. "Try to keep those memories in mind, my love. Remember how it felt to have that hand of destiny moving you. If that's what has called our daughter away, you know as well as I do that nothing we do can change it. We can't fight it. And we should do whatever we can to help her."

I closed my eyes and leaned into the warmth of her soft lips against my face, treasuring every second of it. "I will."

❧ 3 ❧

CHAPTER THREE

"You look significantly less furious," Murdoc observed as I walked out into the garden and began making my way toward the Deck where all the dragons staying here at the royal castle were housed.

"Rest assured, I still am," I growled under my breath.

"Saving it all back for Kinslayer?" he asked.

I narrowed my eyes ahead and nodded once, not trusting myself to even talk about it. Just the thought made that heat rise in my throat again. Anything I said might send me erupting into another fit of rage, and I didn't have the time or energy to spare now.

Oh yes, I had more than a few questions for the infamous crime lord. Somehow, I had a difficult time believing he hadn't known about my daughter running off with that boy of his. Nothing seemed to escape that man's notice, after all.

We had quite the fatherly discussion ahead of us.

Murdoc and I split up in the Deck, making our separate ways to where our dragons were housed in their respective stalls. Because of his sheer size, my dragon was in one of the largest available stalls on the top level of the round, honeycomb-like structure. I wasn't up for making that hike twice tonight, so I stopped in the tack room on the first level to fetch his saddle before I started up the long, circling ramp that led to the top floor.

My king drake, Mavrik, lifted his massive horned head as soon as I rolled the door open. He yawned so widely I got a great view of all his jagged teeth. Some of them were as long as my hand. His vivid yellow eyes caught in the moonlight and followed me, nostrils puffing as though trying to detect my mood. His body shifted in the nest of hay like a mountain of deep blue and black scales as he made a few low popping, chirping sounds.

"Up for a flight to Southwatch?" I asked as I set the saddle down beside him and straightened with a groan. Gods, my back was killing me already. I'd definitely feel this tomorrow.

"Is that where he is?" a sharp, feminine voice demanded suddenly.

I flinched and whirled around to find the silhouette of a slender young woman leaning against the doorway. Even with the soft torchlight outside the stall casting her form in sharp relief, I recognized the outline of her pointed ears, long muscular legs, and tall crystal-tipped staff.

I couldn't make out Isandri's face through the gloom, but I didn't need to. That venomous edge to her tone and the way she had one of her hips cocked to the side was more than enough. She hadn't come here for pleasantries.

"I take it you mean Reigh." I sighed and went back to getting my saddle prepped. "He was there, yes. But by now I'm sure he's left for Nar'Haleen."

Her bare feet crunched on the hay-scattered floor as she approached. "He sent me a very ridiculous letter," she muttered. "It said he intends to go to the Southern Kingdoms, and that he did not wish to trouble me by asking me to come with him."

"Sounds about right," I said.

She stopped right before me, leaning her weight into her staff as she watched me work. "I can only assume this is at the request of Arlan the Kinslayer."

"And you'd be correct," I replied. "But I'm afraid he's already left. By now, they've already set sail."

"That fool," she whispered. Isa clicked her tongue in annoyance and muttered something under her breath in her native language. Probably profanity, judging by her bitter tone.

"For the record, it was suggested several times that he should take you, or at the very least, talk to you about it first. Reigh refused. He said he didn't want to trouble you because of your past history with that place," I said as I stood, hefting my saddle up onto Mavrik's back with a grunt. "Thatcher went, as well, so he isn't entirely alone. But I am concerned about what sort of conflict they might be stumbling into. As usual, Arlan hasn't been terribly forthcoming with information. It feels as though we are pawns being shuffled across the board in a grand game all of his making. I don't like it."

"Nor do I," Isa agreed and stepped around to help me fasten the buckles on the other side. I guess she had seen us do this enough times, she knew what came next—the result of spending so many years hanging around a bunch of unruly young dragonriders. "That is why I am going with you to meet with him—Kinslayer, that is. And if necessary, I will find my own way to the Southern Kingdoms."

I arched a brow at her, unable to hide my surprise. How had she known that was the reason we were leaving? Fates, that girl never ceased to amaze me.

"You'd really go all the way back to your homeland for Reigh?" I asked.

She fixed me with an intense stare, resolve as firm as the foundations of the earth flickering in her eerie yellow-green eyes. "Farther, if I must," she said.

Fair enough.

I smiled and stretched out a hand toward her. "Then hand me my helmet, would you? We've got a long flight ahead."

THE HOURS DRAGGED WITH OUR FACES TURNED AGAINST THE WIND AND RAIN AS Murdoc, Isandri, and I made our way southward. Thunder rumbled and lightning flashed in the towering dark clouds around us as we wove around them, trying to avoid the worst of the massive storm front that had settled over the southern tip of the kingdom.

Isa flew on her own for a long while, assuming her alternative form as a sleek, winged feline and drafting off my right wing. But she couldn't match the speed of my king drake for long, especially against the fierce winds. Changing back into her human shape, Isandri slipped into the saddle right behind me with one arm wrapped around my waist and her face pressed against my back.

Then, at last, I saw it—scattered spots of light along the ground far in the distance, barely visible through the clouds and rain. A tangled, prickling mixture of relief and anxiety coiled in my chest like a writhing serpent. We were here. One step closer. But, gods, what was in store for us now? Was Arlan still here? How would we find him? And what about Maylea? Was there any chance at all that she was here, as well?

I had no way of knowing, and the best information I had to go on was Arlan's mention of a tavern called the Speckled Sow. I could only hope that Murdoc knew how to contact Kinslayer's network from there. He had much more experience in that particular line of work, after all. Fortunately, he had also been to the tavern recently. Perhaps that would be enough to give us a decent chance at finding the man before he changed locations again, and with any luck, it would bring me one step closer to finding my child.

Mavrik and Blite began our descent, dropping below the clouds and circling the city with a thundering roar. I led several passes around Southwatch tower, letting the guards patrolling the top know that we intended to land. Then I gave Murdoc the signal to prepare to touch down atop the massive dark metal and stone structure.

Mavrik spread his wings wide, cupping them to catch the strong winds, and stretched out his hind legs to catch the metal grated floor of one of the large platforms at the very top of the tower. He landed like an eagle catching a perch, coiling his tail for balance and puffing heavy snorts at the soldiers who came out to meet us. His massive talons gripped the surface easily and he hunkered low so we could begin to dismount, shaking his head and smacking his jaws.

I lowered Isandri down first, delivering her into the care of one of the three dragonriders manning the landing platform. Then I turned to unbuckle my bag and fling it down to them, as well. As soon as my boots hit the metal grate of the platform, a rush of memories hit me as fiercely as the gusting storm. Memories of Northwatch—my very first duty station after graduating as a young dragonrider. I'd come here to meet Jace when the war between Maldobar and Luntharda still raged. We had flown in the battle at Barrowton, and that was when I'd taken my first steps over that perilous jungle boundary line. Those thoughts chilled me to the marrow even as I turned around to give Mavrik's side a pat.

"Apologies, Commander! We didn't know we would be receiving you tonight. But we can have stalls prepared for your dragons immediately," a young lieutenant called over the roar of the wind.

"Please do, but we likely won't be staying long." I nodded ahead as we followed behind the other dragonriders, who worked at guiding my dragon in through a massive, rounded doorway that led into the tower. Scarcely a minute later, I heard the screeching call and low *boom* of Murdoc's younger drake, Blite, landing right after us.

"Should I inform Colonel Haprick that you're here?" the lieutenant asked. "We can have rooms prepared for you, as well."

I pulled my helmet off and shook my rain-soaked hair free around my shoulders before waving him off. "No, no. That won't be necessary. Send my regards to Colonel Haprick, but we have urgent business in the city. See that our dragons are fed and our gear is dried. Don't unsaddle them, though."

The lieutenant saluted and rushed off, leaving me in my soggy, dripping cloak and armor while I waited for Murdoc to dismount and join up. Isandri prowled over and stood beside right me, her arms crossed and brow tense with a look of impatient unease. Her gaze darted around at all the riders and soldiers in battle armor passing us, seeming to shrink closer and closer to my side while her grip on her staff tightened.

Hmm.

"Everything all right?" I finally dared to ask. "You've been in watch towers before, haven't you?"

She straightened some and flicked me a flustered sideways glance. "I ... yes. But before, they were usually filled with enemies who wanted to kill me, rather than Maldobarian soldiers."

Ahhh. Well, that made sense. According to Reigh, she had spent some time imprisoned in a tower much like this when it was occupied by the Tibran Empire. Since all dragonrider watches tended to look the same, being here probably brought back sour memories for her, as well.

"We won't linger here for long," I assured her.

She gave a small nod but didn't answer, her sharp eyes still panning quickly around at every dragonrider or infantryman that passed. Her scowl softened somewhat when she saw Murdoc approaching, though. He wiped the rain from his eyes and shook his head, grumbling something about how he hated flying through soggy slop as he fell in step on my other side.

I had to agree.

We made our way down through the tower and out into the city, keeping our heads down or hoods pulled up to hopefully give us some small amount of ambiguity. I wasn't all that concerned with keeping a low profile, however. With Southwatch tower so close by, it wasn't uncommon to see dragonriders walking these streets during their downtime. But our faces—particularly mine—tended to be ones that people remembered.

Isandri was a spectacle all her own, though, even if folk from Nar'Haleen were sometimes spotted amidst the sailors and merchants. Her flowing, silken garb and swirling facial tattoos that marked her as a shalnii priestess, however, were truly a rare sight and one that would certainly turn a few heads. There wasn't much we could do about that, though.

Better to be cautious and keep our heads down.

Murdoc took the lead, navigating the rain-drenched streets and back alleys until he brought us to the long, broader avenue that ran along the edge of the docks. Through the gloom and gusting storm, I caught glimpses of the massive dark shapes of the ships rocking and swaying at their moorings just beyond the rickety boardwalk. But in weather like this, there wasn't a single soul in sight to take notice of us making our way to the front steps of a shabby little tavern on the far end of the dock. I glanced up at the sign hanging from the front eaves of the slumped roof—a wooden cutout of a pig's head that creaked as it swung back and forth in the wind. This must be the place.

Somehow, the sight of the windows glowing warm and bright against the chilly gale brought back another faint flash of memory to my road-weary brain. A night, many years ago, when I'd darkened the door of a tavern much like this alongside my dragonrider brothers for the very first time. Fates, that had been so many years ago, and the atmosphere in our company had been much lighter. Happier. Eager to take the next step in a journey and test our strength and courage against any enemy.

A far cry from how I felt tonight.

I bowed my head and tugged my hood down farther to hide my face as we gathered right outside the door. Murdoc turned back just long enough to murmur, "Both of you wait here. I'll see what I can turn up."

Isa and I nodded and huddled off to the side, keeping our backs to the window and staring out across the port while we waited. Minutes passed with nothing to fill the awkward silence but the rushing of the wind and patter of rain off the boardwalk.

"I cannot believe Reigh thought he could do this without me," Isandri muttered suddenly, almost like she was talking to herself and hadn't meant for me to hear. "That imbecile. Did he really assume he could just send me a letter and be done with it? After all this time, have I not earned more trust?"

"While I certainly can't speak for him, I do know Reigh rather well. I don't think he ever intended this to be a slight against you, Isandri," I said. "If anything, I think he meant it as a mercy—considering your past. I'm also sure I don't have to tell you that he is ... a deeply conflicted and complicated man. He has an awful habit of seeing himself as the one to blame in every situation. If anything, him sending you that letter is my fault. I never should have let him go on this venture in my place." I shook my head and shifted where I stood, unable to ignore the flare of dull, throbbing pain that ached in my back.

She turned just enough that one of her vibrant yellow-green eyes peeked out from under her own hood and stared up at me. "Regardless of who is to blame, none of you should have ever considered going to Nar'Haleen or any of the Southern Kingdoms without my help. It is nothing like Maldobar or Luntharda."

I smiled to myself, my hand coming to rest on the pommel of my scimitar, my fingertips tracing over the relief of a stag's head engraved into it. "I do believe you're right about that, but I let Reigh make that choice. Or rather, he insisted on it. You know how he can be once he's made up his mind. Stubborn beyond all reason, just like his father."

"Even to the point of making a *very* stupid mistake," she agreed with a growl. Her full lips scrunched to one side as she seemed to consider me for a few seconds. "I am ... sorry to hear of your daughter's disappearance," she added suddenly. "Murdoc briefly explained the situation. Try not to worry; Maylea is quite clever and resourceful. I'm certain she will be found."

My heart gave another agonizing, wrenching twist in my chest. All I could do was nod slightly.

We both flinched as the door opened again and Murdoc marched out ... with a much shorter figure in a hooded traveling cloak following right behind him.

My heart gave a sudden, frantic jolt and seemed to hit the back of my throat so hard I couldn't speak. I lurched forward, unable to hold back a gasp. Gods and Fates, could it be? Had he found my little girl in there?!

Then the figure turned and looked up at me from under that hood.

It ... it wasn't Maylea.

My shoulders dropped, every breath of hope seeming to leave my body at once as I met Garnett's wide-eyed, startled gaze. The little dwarven woman blinked up at us, seeming at a loss for an instant. Then a forced, uncertain smile spread over her lips. "Sweet stones! You really are here." She laughed weakly and waved, but that smile still hadn't reached her soft lavender-colored eyes. "And Isa, too. You lot certainly have a way of making a timely appearance. Come along, then. We can't dally around."

I arched a brow up at Murdoc, looking for an explanation. Timely for what, exactly?

I guess he could read the bewilderment in my expression because he tipped his chin down some and gave a subtle shake of his head. Ah. So this wasn't something we could talk about here.

"Lead the way," Murdoc offered, gesturing for Garnett to go ahead of us.

Her smile immediately vanished, falling to something like anxiety and anguish as she stepped quickly out into the pouring rain. Isa immediately followed, but I hung back a few paces—waiting for Murdoc to look my way again. When our gazes locked, I gave him a few quick, subtle gestures in the dragonrider hand-code.

"What's going on? Where is she taking us?"

His lips thinned and his eyes narrowed, cutting an intensely focused glare to where Garnett was forging the path ahead, guiding us off into the stormy night. Before he stepped off the tavern's front porch to follow, however, I saw his hands blur through a series of answering gestures.

"Arlan has recalled all his key agents to a safe house here. They're preparing for something big. We have to hurry."

4

CHAPTER FOUR

We moved like shadows through the pouring rain, following Garnett's hasty steps down crooked side streets and twisting alleys to the far north of the city's outskirts. The narrow winding roads broadened, giving way little by little to the more rural country beyond. There, sparse little farms were spread amidst the briny bogs and soggy, rolling flatlands—just a few small homes built upon the highest of the hills where they might not flood. Most of them were easy enough to spot even at a distance, with their windows glowing warmly like faint, floating stars wavering amidst the gale. But the one Garnett brought us to stood much farther back than all the others, miles from the nearest neighbor, and closer to a line of thin pine trees that marched off into the distant, steeper hillsides.

At first glance, I might have thought the place was abandoned. The steep, thatched roof of the two-level, stacked stone cottage was completely covered in moss and the gardens had long been left to run wild. Half of the structure was hidden beneath dense, leafy climbing vines that twisted and snaked all the way to the top of the chimneystack, and the small barn behind it had already collapsed in on one side.

I frowned. Was this really where Arlan the Kinslayer had chosen to hide? Somehow, I expected something ... well, something *more*. He'd always been more daring in his facades—often choosing to hide in plain sight. Granted, I could only assume he had small hideaways tucked in every corner of the kingdom. Perhaps this one was meant to be more discreet?

Or had those others become compromised thanks to this agency he called the Hands of Fate?

My thoughts raced at that idea, and I almost missed it—the faint wisp of smoke curled up from the chimney's opening. It was barely visible, thanks to the rain. But it was enough to give away that someone was inside. As we drew closer, I spotted a faint, golden light shining from a window on the second floor, as well. The rest of the house's narrow windows seemed to be covered with drapes, and I could have sworn I saw the ones on the first-floor rustle as we approached.

We were being watched already.

Hmm.

Garnett didn't hesitate for a moment. She went straight to the front door and knocked, motioning for the rest of us to stand back and keep our distance. Hunched together against the wind and rain, Murdoc, Isandri, and I looked on as the door cracked open only an inch or two. I couldn't see who answered it, but Garnett exchanged a few hushed words with the figure on the other side. After a few seconds, the door finally opened, and she waved for us to follow her into the cottage.

I couldn't resist a deep, weary sigh as I finally stepped out of the rain at last. Swallowed by the dim, cluttered interior of the cottage, I brushed back my hood and tried to shake some of the water from my hair. The smell of musty, stagnant air, dust, old fabric, and something faintly herbal like incense was thick in the near-dark of the cramped entryway. It was a cozy, comfortable smell that called back memories of days spent at Lin's home near Dayrise.

As soon as the door was shut behind us, the faint clicking of a lock followed, and a tall elven man seemed to emerge straight from the shadows to loom before us with a distrustful scowl. His hunter's leathers and sleeveless jerkin revealed sun-bronzed skin covered in faint, darker brown tattoos, and his long black hair was woven into plaited braids down his back. I caught the glimmer of the faint firelight burning in the sitting room nearby off his multihued eyes. He had a bit of Gray elf blood in him, then? Well, we had that in common, at least.

But I had a feeling our similarities most likely ended there.

Without a word, he motioned for us to walk ahead of him into that sitting room, and followed a few paces behind like a lurking specter. His bare feet made no sound on the old wooden floorboards, and his gaze seemed to focus more intently on Isandri than the rest of us. Maybe the sight of her crystal-and-blade-tipped staff was unnerving to him?

Or maybe he knew better than to assume anything she did with that staff would be worse than what she could do with her fangs and claws.

Reclining in a moth-eaten old chair pulled close to the large stone hearth, another human-looking man sat with his legs crossed and a long wooden pipe between his teeth. He glanced at us as we ambled inside, nodding to Garnett before fixing a hard, suspicious glare on me. He sat forward some, his long face framed in a shoulder-length mop of loose brown curls and his thin nose wrinkling as though he'd smelled something foul.

"So much for keeping a low profile," he growled around that pipe still held in his teeth. "It's one thing to be draggin' in soldiers, but *him?* You'll have every eye in a hundred miles trained right on us."

I frowned and crossed my arms. I could only guess that by "him," he meant me. "I'm sorry, I don't believe we've met?"

"Aye. We haven't," the man scoffed. "But I know exactly who *you* are, Broadfeather."

"Oh now, be easy, Roxus. Nobody thinks twice about dragonriders milling about around here," Garnett assured him, although her smile was still as strained and forced as ever. There was the smallest hint of pressure in the way she stared the man down for an instant, as though silently daring him to argue with her or make a scene. "Even the esteemed Academy Commander isn't a sight to blink twice at. And we were careful. Made our way nice and quiet. No one paid any mind."

"You hope," the man—Roxus, apparently—grumbled and sank back down into his chair. He took a long puff from his pipe and blew a few perfect smoke rings into the air.

"Any word from upstairs?" Garnett seemed eager to change the subject.

Roxus made a grunting sound that must have meant no, because Garnett's smile finally drained away and her entire demeanor seemed to wilt and wither like a blossom at first frost.

"I see," she murmured quietly. "Has anyone gone up to check, then?"

"I checked on him several hours ago," the tall elven man murmured, his voice soft and tinged with a strange accent I couldn't place. His gaze darted toward the stairwell in the far corner of the small sitting room, his brow creasing with concern. "He was preparing another ritual and sent me away so he could work."

Murdoc and I exchanged a wary glance. Another ritual? What did that mean?

I had never personally witnessed Arlan casting any sort of magic, but I'd received plenty of accounts of his impressive magical feats from my companions. According to Reigh, Arlan was the sort of sorcerer you only read about in ancient legends and myths. A master of power unlike anything we'd ever seen before.

So, what was he up to now?

"Gods, Howlan, you know better!" Garnett fussed as she muscled her way past him and started up the stairs in a huff. "He's already pushed himself too far. He'll kill himself at this rate, you dolt!"

I started to follow after her, but Howlan immediately planted himself in my path with a forbidding scowl. "No visitors," he warned.

"I'm not here for well-wishing. His boy, Lukani, has my daughter. They've run off somewhere in this gods-forsaken kingdom. I *will* see Arlan, and you'd do well not to get in my way." I glared back, one corner of my mouth tugging at a snarl.

Howlan's hands clenched into fists, and he changed footing to cock a shoulder back slightly. Preparing to draw that bow off his back?

Good luck with that.

I didn't even have to look to know Murdoc and Isandri were right at my back, probably already steeled for a fight.

I liked those odds.

"Let them through," Roxus muttered suddenly without ever looking away from the flames that crackled and popped in the hearth. "I doubt very much the infamous savior of Maldobar has come here to murder the boss."

Well, that all depended on how much he had to do with my daughter's disappearance, really. But I managed to keep that thought to myself.

Howlan gave a snort like an angry young dragon and took a single, slow, calculated step to the side—out of my path. I held his gaze without blinking, waiting for him to look away first before I finally let my own posture relax.

Among these shifty, shadow-dwelling folk, I knew better than to be the one to turn my back first. Maybe they weren't my enemy today, but that was never a guarantee. With Arlan the Kinslayer, you could never be too careful.

"YOU BLOODY IDIOT! YOU'VE GONE AND DONE IT NOW, HAVEN'T YOU?" MURDOC, Isandri and I followed the sound of Garnett's angry growling and sputtering along the narrow, second-floor hallway. "You were supposed to rest!"

At the far end of the hall, I leaned through the doorway of a small room crowded with strange artifacts and objects to find her trying to drag Arlan upright. He lay on the floor amidst a scattered array of tiny candles, strange lines drawn in chalk and speckled with melted wax drippings, and what looked like shattered pieces of glass. A massive, floor-length mirror in a heavy silver frame dominated the far wall directly before him, now mostly covered by a long, black satin drape. The sight of it made my stomach drop and a strange chill prickle up my spine all the way to the back of my neck.

Something about that mirror made every tiny hair on my body stand on end. It put a knot of cold dread in the pit of my stomach and that sense as though I were falling from a height. A feeling I knew all too well...

Because looking at the God Stone had given me that same feeling. Powerless. Small. Like staring into the yawning depths of an eternity I'd never be able to comprehend.

My pulse skipped and I quickly looked away. Was this the mirror Arlan had sent Reigh and the others to find in Northwatch tower? The one they called the Mirror of Truth? What was it doing here? And what, by all the Fates, was he using it for?

Arlan couldn't answer that—not right now, anyway.

Slumped and ashen, he lay with his breathing shallow and fast and his skin drenched in sweat. His head lolled back, nose smeared with blood, and his eyelids fluttering as though he were dreaming. He didn't say a word as Garnett shouted over him, patting his cheeks and trying to wake him.

It didn't work. He groaned something through clenched teeth, but didn't move. Great. I wouldn't get any useful information out of him about where Maylea and Lukani might have gone in this state.

"Go and keep watch at the stairs, just in case," I whispered to Murdoc.

He nodded and strode off to take up a post right at the top of the stairwell, his arms crossed and his expression grim and forbidding.

Good. Now wasn't the time to get clumsy and take any chances. Maybe Arlan trusted the men posted downstairs, but I wasn't turning a blind eye to anyone I wasn't completely certain I could count on.

Brushing aside strings of large, crudely cut crystals that hung from the ceiling, I picked my way across the cluttered floor to help Garnett prop Arlan upright. Pulling one of his arms over my shoulder, I dragged him to his feet and hauled him toward the door. With his weight against me, I looked back at Garnett expectantly. "Where do I put him?"

"A-Ah, thank you. This way. He's got a bedroom—where he *should* have been in the first place," she stammered and scurried past Murdoc, who still watched from the doorway with his narrowed eyes scanning the strangely decorated room.

He leveled a suspicious, disapproving frown on the nearly-unconscious man I carried as we passed. "I'm no expert, but that looks a lot like a dark ritual."

"I know," I murmured back, not wanting Garnett to overhear as she hurried ahead to open another door farther down the hall.

"N-Not ... dark," Arlan suddenly slurred from where he sagged against my side, dragging his feet with every step we took. For an instant, his glowing golden-hued eyes opened to stare at me, as though trying to figure out who I was. Then he groaned, clenching his teeth, as his face seized with a look of pain. "Y-You lowlanders ... know n-nothing of ... magic. You assume e-everything unknown t-to you is ... dark and e-evil."

Stepping into another dimly lit room, I helped him all the way to the edge of a large, canopied bed. Garnett rushed around, lighting oil lamps and stoking the smoldering coals in a small hearth. More books were heaped on nearly every flat surface—hundreds of them were loaded on the nightstands, stacked on the writing desk by the window, and piled on the floor. Garnett even had to shove a few of them out of the way just so Arlan could lie down on the bed.

"I-I see ... the storm w-wasn't enough to deter you. At the v-very least ... I hope you remembered to w-wipe your b-boots at the door," Arlan managed to slur through chattering teeth. Sitting upright in his bed, he shivered as he shrugged out of his sweaty silken robe and let it fall to the floor, leaving him in nothing but a pair of dark, linen breeches. "A-A clean shirt, if y-you don't mind, G-Garnett."

"You need more than a clean tunic, Arlan," Garnett fussed as she began rummaging through an armoire. "A proper bath and something to eat would be a good start."

He chuckled weakly, but didn't reply.

"Would you at least take some tea, then?" she bargained. "Stones, you're as pale as a day-old corpse, man."

He gave a small sigh of defeat and nodded.

Isandri and I kept our distance, looking on without a word while Garnett helped him into a new shirt. With his back turned, I caught a glimpse of something like a discoloration on his skin. No—not a discoloration. Two long, jagged scars that ran along both of his shoulder blades. Each one was gnarled and raised, with angry pink tissue knotted as though they were fresh. The areas around them had small marks from stitching, and a strange purplish webbing like veins that stood out against his pale skin.

I'd seen battle wounds before. I had plenty of them, myself. But this was unlike any injury I had seen before. Something about it seemed more intentional than a mere sword-swipe. Almost surgical.

I must have been staring more obviously than I realized, because Arlan made a coughing, flustered sound when he glanced back at us. He quickly pulled a clean white tunic over his head to cover the scars on his back. "I-I assume you did n-not come here to g-gawk, Commander Broadfeather," he mumbled.

No. I most certainly had not. But the sight of those marks unleashed a new storm of questions in my mind. After all, the way they were positioned on his shoulder blades, not to mention the size, almost made it seem like they might have been—

"Wings," Arlan answered before I'd even mustered the words to ask. His tone was tight and cold as he kept his gaze pointed away, his jawline stiffening as his mouth pinched together as though the word left a bitter taste.

"You had wings?" Isandri asked, seeming confused. I guess she had noticed the scars, too. Granted, they were difficult to miss.

"All Avoran elves have wings, Lady Isandri. We are born with them," Arlan corrected sharply.

"But yours have been cut off," I observed.

"It was a necessity," he clarified, his expression seeming to glaze over into faraway thought, as his tone became steadier. "My homeland is unlike anything you lowlanders can comprehend. Any Avoran elf who leaves it suffers from the severance of the connection we have with the bountiful raw magical power that fills it. It's as though we leave the front steps of heaven itself, and are cut off from the flow of power that ebbs through the doors of that divine realm. That connection cannot be reforged. Once broken, it is broken forever. And without it, our abilities and powers are drastically stunted. The features that mark us as something nearly divine begin to fade. Our wings rot, and must be cut away before they become a source of infection that would otherwise become deadly. But those wounds never fully heal, even hundreds of years later."

"How long ago was it?" I dared to ask. "How long has it been since you left Avora?"

Arlan's eyes closed and he turned his face away. "Come now, Commander. We both know you did not come all this way on a dark and stormy night just to question me about the past."

I stiffened. Well, he was absolutely right about that. Better to get to the point as quickly as possible. "You know why I'm here, then?"

He sighed again, as though he'd been dreading this conversation from the start. "Naturally."

My pulse kicked harder against my chest as I demanded, "What has happened to my daughter? You know where she is, don't you?"

He gave a solemn nod. "More or less, although I doubt very much my answer will be as precise as you want."

I took an aggressive step closer. "Tell me. And by all the gods, she had better be whole and unharmed."

He flicked me an annoyed, sideways glance. "Or what? You're going to hit me?" he scoffed and rolled his eyes. "Lowlanders... you never cease to underwhelm. I assure you, Commander, your daughter's disappearance was not something I orchestrated. In fact, I did not know my own ward had absconded the kingdom until, well, not long before you lot barged in."

Isandri's features sharpened into a disapproving scowl. "What do you mean?"

"I mean, I did not kidnap her. In fact, I have not even met with her." Arlan sat up a little straighter and combed a hand through his sweaty, dark golden hair. "But I know for a fact that she has left Maldobar ... and she's taken Lukani with her."

⁂ 5 ⁂

CHAPTER FIVE

My heart seemed to stop altogether for a few moments. I stood there, staring at him, trying to fathom that. Maylea had left Maldobar? How? And why? Where would she go? Why would she take Lukani with her?

I knew of the boy. I knew he had helped Murdoc, Thatcher, and the others years ago, while they were dealing with Iksoli. But beyond that? He hadn't exactly been a frequent houseguest, and I had only seen him in passing. According to the others, he was an odd young man, but helpful and true to his word. Not someone I would have marked as a credible threat to the kingdom. So I had never given him much thought.

Now, I was wishing I had.

Before I could collect myself long enough to even choke out a sound, Arlan continued, "Lukani has long been my ward, but I don't claim to have any sort of parental relationship with him. I certainly don't claim to be his father—adoptive or otherwise. Rather, I have made efforts to see him raised in such a way that it would be possible for him to rejoin his own kind when he is ready. Rajinna are a complex species. One of the few who can count their origins back to the dawn of time, when the gods themselves first seeded life in this world. And unlike a majority of the other races now living today, they have kept their bloodlines relatively pure and excluded from outside dilution. Because of that, their magic has remained powerful and prevalent, especially in the Southern Kingdoms. Lukani knows this, and had begun to express a desire to return to his homeland in Nar'Haleen to seek out others like himself. That, I can only assume, is the reason he was so eager to facilitate your daughter with a means to ... join your other companions in their mission."

Wait—*WHAT?* I swallowed hard, trying to wrap my mind around everything he'd said. "You're telling me ... Maylea and Lukani left for Nar'Haleen?!"

"Yes," he answered flatly, almost like he knew what was coming next.

I staggered, barely able to catch my breath as the truth hit me like a runaway fruit cart. Gods and Fates, that could only mean one thing—she had left with Reigh. She had gone with him and Thatcher to Nar'Haleen.

A sound somewhere between a growl, a scream, and a sob tore from my throat as I turned away and slammed a fist into the wall behind me. She wouldn't—she couldn't! It wasn't just dangerous. It was deadly. Surely she knew that. Gods, why? Why would she do this? What could have possibly possessed her to want to run straight into the teeth of that nightmare?

"Calm yourself, Commander. As far as I was able to discern, no harm has befallen them thus far." Despite his consoling words, Arlan's tone stayed dry and somber.

"How far have they gotten?" Isandri asked coolly, her expression still sharp and thoughtful as she studied him.

"Far enough that I very much doubt you will be able to catch up with them, even by air," he replied.

"And you're sure about this? That they're still at sea, faring well?" she pressed. "If we intend to go after them, we must know if we are heading into a conflict. We must be prepared."

Arlan's broad, angular shoulders rose and fell as he took a deep breath. Then he turned to level a no-nonsense stare in my direction with those eerie eyes glowing like two golden stars in the gloom. "As I've explained, my powers are waning. Every year I find myself able to do less and less with them, and the cost of performing even simple spells is becoming extreme. But with the help of ritualistic magic and the Mirror of Truth, as you call it, I am able to peer across the expanses of time and space to glimpse fragments of the past. That is, I can see events that have already happened. There are rules and limitations to it, of course. I must have an object or an individual as a focal point. In this case, I intended to find Lukani. I feared perhaps the Hands of Fate had taken him hostage. But it seems the young Miss Broadfeather is the one responsible for leading him away—not that I blame her. I'm sure he didn't need much encouragement. He's always been rather fond of her, and the allure of finally returning to Nar'Haleen likely seemed too good an opportunity for him to pass up. They departed and have been at sea three days now. They should reach Nar'Haleen within the next two days, and from there, the mission should be rather straightforward."

"I'm hearing a lot of 'shoulds'—but I think we can both agree that when it comes to missions like this, what should happen seldom ever does." I growled as I turned to glare at him over my shoulder. My chest still heaved with ragged, angry breaths and my pulse throbbed in my now bruised knuckles.

"Of course. And for that reason, I intend to keep a keen eye upon them for as long as possible. But as I told his highness before their departure, from this distance, my abilities to intervene on his behalf are ... limited." Arlan gave a small grunt of discomfort as he leaned forward and pulled a book from one of the piles on his nightstand. "If you truly intend to go after them, I cannot do much to assist you, either. I can, however, strongly recommend summoning the help of your Queen. The time has come for her to be informed of what's happening."

I balked, blinking and shaking my head some. What? Now he wanted Jenna involved? Why? What had changed?

Unless ...

My stomach hit the soles of my cold, rain-soaked boots as the truth rose up from within me like a swelling, icy tide. I closed my eyes as that feeling seemed to freeze me from the inside out, making my soul go numb with a fear I hadn't felt in years.

Not since the last time I had glimpsed the Goddess of Death.

"Your sister has Ronan." The words left my lips in a broken whisper, seeming to send that chill through the room, as well.

"Yes," he confirmed.

Isandri sucked in a sharp breath of alarm.

"If I go to Queen Jenna ... you know what it will mean," I said, unable to stop my hands from shaking as a new fear grew before my mind's eye, towering and terrible in a way I'd never dared to imagine.

"I do," Arlan said, his voice now much softer and somber, as though he felt the weight of it, too.

"War," I said it—someone had to. The risk was too great, to all-encompassing and destructive, to let it slip by in anonymity.

Arlan looked down at the book in his hand, running his fingers over the battered leather cover as though it were a faithful old friend. And for the first time, I saw real emotion crinkle his usually smooth features. Something like anguish. Regret. Sorrow. "There will be war, Commander, one way or another. The threads of destiny have long been drawn to it, just as they have to each of us. And I'm afraid the only things we get to choose about it is the when ... the how ... and which side we may die on."

ARLAN WAS RIGHT.

I knew that as I stepped back out into the rain, Murdoc and Isandri not far behind. Garnett had pleaded with us to stay in their cottage for the night, and while I despised the idea of trudging back across the city, I needed the space. I had to think. To consider every angle. To come up with some sort of a plan that might actually give us a chance at surviving what was undoubtedly coming next.

It was early morning, only minutes before sunrise, when we made our way back into the Speckled Sow. The kindly bartender showed us to a table in a private nook near the fire and offered to hang our cloaks to dry. She brought a round of warm ales and bowls of lamb stew, small loaves of hearty bread, and a platter of cheese and fruit. Murdoc passed a few gold coins to her and asked that she keep the ale coming. She grinned broadly, revealing a missing tooth right in the center of her smile, and assured us our cups wouldn't run dry.

Isandri explained our situation to Murdoc, recounting every word while we ate. I had to admire her ability to remain calm and composed when talking about what might essentially be the end of the world as we knew it. My hands still shook whenever I tried to lift my fork. But eventually, having a belly full of warm food and drink helped give me back some energy. Too bad it didn't do anything to soothe the fear and panic that tangled in my brain like a growing briar vine.

"Arlan is right," Murdoc concluded as he sat back in his chair. "We have to tell Queen Jenna."

"I know," I whispered, the words bitter on my tongue. "But you know as well as I do what will come after."

"She will take this as an act of war from Nar'Haleen," he mumbled, nodding in agreement. "There's a chance King Phillip can persuade her to try a diplomatic resolution, first. Perhaps merely sending word to the Emperor of Nar'Haleen and letting him know whom the boy belongs to would be enough. I doubt Nar'Haleen wants a war with Maldobar—especially when they are already locked into one with Damaria and Rienka. They certainly aren't in a good position to be making new enemies."

"But if the emperor has become aware of how powerful Ronan is, he may feign ignorance. If that Sadeera woman, Arlan's sister, really has wormed her way into Nar'Haleen's royal court and is pulling strings there, she will want every excuse *not* to give Ronan up. Not alive, anyway. To her, he is likely a powerful pawn. They may use his life as leverage," Isandri reasoned.

"Would Nar'Haleen even consider Maldobar a credible threat? We are a long way away," Murdoc wondered aloud. "Even with dragons, we would still be reliant on naval power to reach them—something we're not exactly known for. Even if Queen Jenna launched every ship at her disposal, it wouldn't be enough to contend with their navy."

I leaned forward, resting my elbows on the table and rubbing at my chin and jaw as I thought. He was right, of course. Maldobar had a navy, but it wasn't on the scale of anything found in the Southern Kingdoms. Our strength had always been in our landed armies. Specifically, in the dragonriders. But it was too far to fly.

"Maybe we're looking at this the wrong way," Murdoc said, flicking a pensive glance up at me from over the rim of his mug.

Isandri arched an eyebrow. "What do you mean?"

"Well, I think Arlan was right. War *is* coming—but not just one between kingdoms and navies. This Sadeera woman is trying to crack open the kingdom of the gods. She's planning to attempt to usurp them. Somehow, now that she has Ronan, I doubt those efforts are going to go unnoticed by those deities. So we don't need to think about what we can do to make Maldobar formidable against Nar'Haleen, we need to think about how to ally ourselves to the right side."

"The divine one," I agreed. My gaze panned over to Isandri, watching the firelight dance in her eerie, yellow-and-green sunburst eyes. She stared right back, her expression remaining as steady and resolved as ever. "You already have the support of one goddess, even if I am confined to a mortal form," she declared, like she knew what I was going to ask next.

I couldn't resist a small smile. "I'm glad to hear it. But what of the others?"

"You really think Thatcher would fight for anyone else?" Murdoc chuckled.

Right. Well, that made two deities on our side—even if they were bound in human bodies. Now wasn't the time to be too choosy. I'd dealt with gods nearly all of my life, in one way or another. I knew most of them, when it came to dealing with the world of mortals, preferred fighting by proxy. They had a habit of finding "champions" in regular people, like Reigh and me, and gifting them with immense magical power rather than actually getting their hands dirty. For one of them to fully manifest here, in the mortal world was ... well, almost unheard of.

Almost.

I had seen that happen only once during our final battle with the invading tyrant, Lord Argonox. Clysiros had crossed beyond the divine realm and come to our world in the flesh ... and the repercussions of that fleeting moment could still be felt today. Nothing grew on the ground where her feet had tread, and the people whose lives and souls she had impacted were left forever scarred.

Reigh was living proof of that. Now, I suspected Ronan would be, as well.

"We're going to have to recruit," Murdoc continued, staring down into his ale horn with a hard frown. "Specifically, we're going to have to recruit the gods to fight or urge them to choose someone to fight in their name. If Sadeera really has the Emperor of Nar'Haleen under her control, then we have to assume his armies are at her disposal, too. She will likely use any means necessary to see her mission succeed. Our best hope for stopping any of this is to cut off the head of the serpent and take her out first. But we've all seen the kind of power that woman is capable of. Without divine help, we will be at a serious disadvantage. Getting as many deities onboard to assist is the only way we walk away from this on the winning side."

"Our thoughts exactly," a cheery, feminine voice agreed suddenly.

We all looked up at once to find Garnett and Roxus making their way toward our table. Garnett grinned from one dimpled cheek to the other as she pulled up a chair right between Murdoc and Isandri and swiped Isandri's mostly untouched drink to down it all in one swig. "Glad to hear we're all on the same page already." She beamed as she wiped her mouth on her sleeve.

Roxus, on the other hand, took his time collecting a chair from a neighboring table and settling into it beside me. With his tall, thin frame dressed in a long brown coat, heavy leather boots, and not a single weapon hanging from his belt, he honestly wasn't much to look at. Like an old scarecrow that had been left out in the elements for too long.

Hmm. I had to wonder what sort of skills a man like him might bring to our little endeavor. As far as I could discern, he was a human somewhere in his thirties, and apparently hadn't bothered to bathe in a few days. Or maybe that was just the lingering fragrance coming from that pipe he pulled out of a pocket and lit up again. It was hard to tell, honestly. But something on him gave off a powerful, almost musky odor that reminded me of wet dog.

Strange.

I wasn't fool enough to think he wasn't a threat, though—even if he did look about as average as any other soggy traveler that might stumble in here tonight.

"You really think leaving Arlan alone in his current state is a good idea?" Murdoc asked, his own steely gaze settling onto Roxus, as well. I knew that look. Jace had stared me down like that many times. It must have been some sort of Ulfrangar interrogation method. Maybe he would be able to sense something about the man I couldn't?

"He's not alone," Garnett replied as she waved a hand, signaling for the barmaid to bring us another round of drinks. "Howlan's worth about ten of us in a fight, and he's jumpy as a jackrabbit already."

"Speak for yourself," Roxus huffed as he sank a lit match into the herbs smoldering from his long, curved wooden pipe and took a few deep breaths.

Garnett just rolled her eyes a little. "Pay no mind to Roxus, he's a bit stuffy, but he's a good'n. And he agrees, as well. We're going to need to recruit as many deities as we can to lend us their power if we're going to come out of this smelling clean and rosy."

"I take it that means you have a plan?" Isandri slid her next drink over to Garnett as soon as the barmaid set it down on the table before her. "Or that Arlan has given you some manner of instructions?"

"Both," Roxus grunted, holding his pipe between his teeth as he slowly panned his gaze around the table at each of us. His guarded, dark brown eyes didn't give anything away. "But first thing's first. It's gonna require some of us to make a deal with a god or two. I think we can all appreciate exactly what that means. Gods and goddesses don't have a long-standing history for cutting fair deals with mortals, eh? But in this case, it's the only shot any of us have got. So, by show of hands, who's ready to sell their soul to save the world?"

PART TWO

REIGH

☙ 6 ❧

CHAPTER SIX

"AUBREN?!"

My voice echoed through the cold stone hallway as I ran, yelling my brother's name to the darkness around me. My heartbeat thundered in my ears, legs aching with every step. I couldn't force myself to move faster, no matter how I fought. My body dragged, every movement so sluggish and strained. Gods, it felt like running through wet sand. What was wrong with me? Was I injured? Bleeding out? Is that why everything seemed so blurred?

I didn't know. But I couldn't stop.

I forced myself to keep running, driving my legs harder and harder with every shred of strength I had. I passed doorways barred with iron. Cells. One after another, endlessly, everywhere, like a twisting maze of stone and metal.

But all of them were dark and empty.

I was ... alone.

"Aubren! Answer me!" I cried out again.

No reply.

Oh gods, I could hear them now. The wild shouts of soldiers and the baying of war hounds grew louder by the second. Thundering footsteps and the clatter of heavy armor followed me, getting closer and closer. They had to be right on my heels! I looked back, trying to get a glimpse of just how close they were, but there was nothing. No light. No figures in the gloom. Just the sound of them gaining on me no matter how hard I ran.

Tibran soldiers.

Faster—I had to go faster. I had to find my brother and get us both out of there right now.

CRACK!

I slammed headlong into something big and solid right in front of me and bounced off like a toy ball. I staggered backward and tripped, landing on my back. All the wind rushed out of me as my head cracked off the stone. Bright spots danced in my vision. Everything seemed to spin.

Boots crunched on the stone, stopping right over me. A huge, looming figure bent over me. Then a face appeared right in front of mine.

A man's vicious, cold smile. Eyes like firelit cobalt. Chiseled features drawn and sunken, like an aged corpse that still resembled a tyrant I knew all too well.

"You thought you could escape me, little prince?" Lord Argonox sneered as he reached down and closed a big fist around my throat.

I couldn't breathe. I couldn't think. Tears filled my eyes as I clawed at his black metal gauntlet—anything to try to get away. Gods, please, no. Not again. Please ... I-I couldn't ... I couldn't do this. I couldn't fight him. Where were my weapons? Where was Jaevid? Help! Someone help me!

I let out a garbled, rasping cry as his grip tightened on my throat. His smile grew wider, stretching and twisting in a way that should have been impossible. It was too wide and warped his features like soft clay. His eyes grew larger with wicked delight. "Cry for them, prince! Cry for them to come save you! No one hears you down here. This kingdom is *mine*." Argonox leaned down, putting his mouth right against my ear as he snarled. "And so are you."

I pitched and flailed in his grip, fighting with all my strength to get free. But it didn't matter. He didn't even flinch. Every blow I landed felt weak and pathetic. I-I couldn't fight back. I couldn't get away. I was trapped. Gods and Fates, I was trapped again.

Help. S-Someone .... Jaevid ... Isandri ... KIRAN!! Please! HELP ME!

"You think they would even *want* to rescue you? The Angel of Death?" Argonox snickered as he snatched me up, holding me off my feet with one massive, powerful hand. "The slaughterer of Barrowton? The one who killed his own father in cold blood? You think they'll ever truly forgive you? You think they'll ever forget? You know they whisper at your back. They can't wait to be rid of you."

Air. Gods, I needed air! Just one breath! I clawed at his arm, still twisting and fighting to breathe. I-I had to. I-I couldn't hang on.

I-I was ... dying.

Alone.

Again.

"No one mourns a monster, boy," Argonox cackled, his voice booming over me as he gave my neck one final, vice-tight squeeze. I choked. Suddenly, my arms and legs wouldn't move at all. I hung limp, helpless, staring straight into the cold light that smoldered in his eyes.

"You belong in the abyss ... right here beside me ... *forever*."

"NO!!"

I bolted upright, throwing the blanket off my chest and yelling into the dark. My whole body shook out of control and my chest heaved with ragged breaths as I sat upright, staring into the black abyss around me.

O-Oh, gods! Wh-Where was I? What was happening? Where was Argonox?! The Tibrans? Th-They had to be here somewhere!

"Shhh. Calm down. You are safe, Reigh. Look at me," a soft, feminine voice cooed gently as something stroked my forehead down to my chin, slowly guiding me to look straight ahead. "Look at me, Reigh, and try to remember."

R-Remember ...?

I blinked slowly as a wave of frigid chills swept over my body from my head all the way down to the tips of my toes. My body shuddered hard and I bit down, shutting my eyes tightly. That's when I finally realized what that feeling was—the touch of warm, gentle hands cradling my face.

I blinked again, and my vision slowly began to clear. I looked down, straight into the face of a beautiful young woman with long, silvery white hair and wide, ruby-colored eyes. She stared back at me, much shorter and more petite, with her brow slightly crinkled with concern.

I ... I knew her. Even if I couldn't remember her name. I-I knew her face. Her fair, flawless skin. Her smooth, almost breathy voice as she said my name again.

"Reigh, can you hear me? You're safe. We're not anywhere near that tower."

She was right. I wasn't in Northwatch. I was ... Gods, where was I?

The young woman holding my face in her hands gave a quick, nervous smile. It made me tense with sudden recognition as a name suddenly broke through my mind like the first clap of thunder from a summer storm.

Her name.

"V-Violet?" My voice came out weak and broken.

She sank down some, relief making her features go slack for an instant. She let out a small sigh and nodded. Then she slowly drew her hands back away from me. "Yes. It's me. You were having a nightmare."

A nightmare?

Oh, Fates. Not again.

Sweat ran down the sides of my face and dripped from the end of my nose as I stared around the room, still shivering so hard it made my neck and back ache. In the weak light of dawn, I could barely make out the shapes of Maylea, Lukani, and Thatcher still sound asleep on their pallets nearby.

Right. We were in Rienka. We'd come here on a mission from Arlan to collect some sacred codex and rescue my nephew.

I sagged forward, burying my face in my hands. But I couldn't get my body to stop trembling. My sweat-soaked clothes stuck to my skin, and my heart pounded so hard it made my ribs ache and my ears ring.

"Are you alright?" Violet whispered, and I could have sworn there was real concern in her tone.

I didn't dare look up to check, though. "F-Fine," I managed through chattering teeth.

"You don't look fine," she countered. "Your eyes were open, but it was as though you were still asleep. You were shouting. Crying for help. Calling out for ... many people."

She had heard all that? Great. My face burned and I rubbed my brow with my fingers, hoping she wouldn't see my face turn red. "I'm fine. Really," I wheezed. "Just give me a minute."

She did—one minute exactly. Then Violet puffed a tight, frustrated breath and got to her feet, moving over to loop an arm under mine and drag me to my feet. "Come on. You need to wash off and get some air."

"S-Stop. I'm fine. I-I don't need—" I started to protest weakly.

"Hush," she said sharply, flicking me one of those no-nonsense glares that made my mouth snap shut on instinct. "Just let me help you. Your tunic is soaked. You're as pale as a peeled banana. If you're going to be sick, you should do it outside, and we can rinse your shirt and hang it to dry."

Ugh. Fine. Whatever.

I wobbled as Violet helped me out the front door of the tiny, first-floor room we had rented for the last few nights. The first blast of salty night air through my hair made my skin prickle. It immediately cleared my senses, though. My vision sharpened and I took in a deep, full breath. Immediately, my pulse slowed, like I was breathing in a soothing balm that soaked down all the way to my soul.

I guess the ocean had that effect.

"Down with you," Violet urged as she led me to the small patio outside our room and sat me down in a chair woven from thin bamboo poles. She disappeared inside for a moment, then returned with a bucket of water. She put it down in front of me, right between my knees, and began untying my tunic and tugging it up over my head.

I didn't have the strength to fight her on it. Not when every muscle in my body throbbed like I'd just finished a sparring match with Murdoc. With my shirt off and bare skin now feeling every slight sea breeze, I leaned forward to rest my elbows on my knees.

"Do you dream of that place often?" Violet asked, her tone quiet and cautious as she dipped a rag into the bucket of water, wrung it out, and began wiping off my back and arms.

"I can do this myself, you know. I just need a minute to catch my breath," I protested, hoping she would take the hint and not push that topic any further.

She didn't.

"It's okay if you'd like to talk to me about it. I realize I'm probably not your first choice of confidant, but ... Thatcher hasn't fully recovered and I do know how to keep a secret. Arlan mentioned you are still tormented by the things that happened to you in Northwatch," she murmured as she wiped at my shoulders. "I admit, I've heard only brief accounts of it."

"There's not much to tell," I muttered. "I was a Tibran hostage during the war. I'm sure I don't have to tell you what they liked to do to their captives. I didn't get special treatment just because I was a royal."

Her tone softened as she stepped around in front of me and started to gingerly wipe at my face. "On the contrary, I've been told that you were given ... *very* special treatment."

My mouth screwed up, and I locked my jaw against the swell of something hot and furious that surged in my blood. It stabbed and stung and twisted inside me like a knot of metal shards. An emotion I didn't have a name for. Shame, maybe? Whatever it was, I didn't want her to see it.

It didn't matter. Violet must have been able to tell because she stopped with the cloth still pressed against my cheek.

Her scarlet eyes searched me, lips pressed into an uncomfortable, uncertain line. "You don't have to lie. You don't have to hide it. Not from me. I'm a Pitathi mercenary turned spy for one of the most dangerous criminal lords in the world. Not exactly someone in a position to judge you for anything in your past, hm?"

"It's not that," I admitted, bowing my head and letting my eyes roll closed.

"Then what is it? Why don't you talk to anyone about what happened there?"

I ... I didn't know. Lots of reasons that had changed and compiled over the years. At first, it was too hard. Then it felt wrong to burden everyone else around me with that sort of thing because they had their own issues to work out. Why should they have to worry about mine? I should have been able to handle my own problems—to control my emotions.

But I couldn't. Not all the time. So, sometimes, it just came out. I lost my temper over stupid things. I ran my mouth. I acted like a jerk. All because I was just so ... tired.

Mentally. Spiritually. I was a patched-up waterskin that had been filled to burst and was leaking from the seams.

Then, years had passed, and there were more important things to do and worry about than some stupid bad thing that had happened to me years ago. I just had to function. To make it through each day. Complaining wouldn't fix it anyway, right? So I might as well forge on. Force it down. Be strong. And maybe, after a while, I'd start to forget.

Only, that wasn't exactly going well.

"Sometimes ... it's like I'm just fighting to survive being in my own head. And ... and I'm losing," I heard myself confess. But that voice didn't sound like mine. It sounded so small, pathetic, and defeated.

I hated it.

And I couldn't do anything to stop it.

The words poured out in a rush as I wrung my hands through my sweat-soaked hair. "Sometimes I could swear I'm still there, chained up in that tower, just waiting to die. Like this, being here or back in Maldobar at the Academy, is the dream and the nightmare is the real world. And I can't escape, so I just keep going in circles. Running. Trying to fight to stay alive. But I'm ... Gods, I'm so tired. I can't run for much longer. And it feels like he knows that. He knows everything—every horrible thing I've done."

"He?" Violet asked.

I snarled his name through my teeth like a curse. "Argonox."

For a moment, neither of us spoke. I scrambled through my own frazzled brain, trying to collect the scattered shards of my sanity and resist the urge to start ripping fistfuls of my hair out. Gods and Fates, why was I saying any of this to her? It was stupid. Beyond stupid. I couldn't trust her. I barely knew her. We weren't friends. We were barely allies.

She didn't care about me.

Strong fingertips touched my chin, lifting my head so I had to look up and meet her gaze again. "You're not alone. Not here. Not there. Never. You know this, don't you? You know the love your friends have for you? You're not a burden they are forced to bear. There's not a single one of them that wouldn't lay down their lives for you, just as you've sacrificed so much of yourself for them. You look at yourself and see only failure, but you don't see the way others regard you when your back is turned. You are a man they respect. A man they know they can count on. A man who tends to the suffering, comforts the dying, and fights for those who cannot fight on their own. You are, and always have been, a good man, Reigh Farrow. A bit rash and mule-headed at times. But good."

I stared at her, unable to keep my mouth from hanging open like the hole on a birdhouse. Little by little, heat crept over my face like a fresh sunburn. I had to swallow a few times before I could even make a sound.

"You don't ... know that," I managed to rasp.

"I *do* know that. It's my job to know things. To notice them. To read people's behaviors and intentions. And I am *very* good at my job," she warned and tapped the end of my nose with her finger. "So take my word over some figment in a nightmare. There is nowhere on earth you might go where your friends would not come to your rescue."

Gods, I hoped she was right about that. We might need their help if things didn't improve on our end here.

Sitting up, I let out a deep, shaking sigh. The tension in my body was gone. The shaking had stopped. I felt grounded—present—again. My thoughts were clear as I looked down at my scar-flecked arms and hands, wondering at all the past injuries that had left them there. Training in Luntharda with Kiran as a kid. The war. Dealing with Iksoli and the Ulfrangar. Training again in the Academy with Thatcher and Murdoc. Teaching my own students there.

I had to wonder what new scars I'd be earning here.

"I should, uh, I mean ... I guess ... thank you. You know, for ... this," I stammered and waved to the space between us. Great. Ugggh. Why did I always say stupid stuff? Honestly, I was a grown man. A prince! And a dragonrider! Get it together already!

Violet had that cattish grin on her lips as she stood back and crossed her arms, cocking her hips to one side. "Can't have you falling apart now, can I? Then there'd only be one adult voice of reason left in our merry band."

Right. Well. Fair point.

"Hopefully we will have Thatcher back on his feet soon, too," I said, half making that a prayer to whatever gods might be listening.

"I have the utmost faith," Violet purred. I could feel her gaze on me as I stood and stretched my arms, trying to work some of the stiffness out before I went to rinse out my shirt in the bucket of water and wring it out.

"I know it frightens you, but it's okay to feel things that hurt sometimes," she said quietly. "The important thing is not to latch onto those feelings. Let them slip by you like wind through the trees. Let them come, but most importantly, let them go."

I stopped and looked back at her. That distant, almost bittersweet expression on her features made my heartbeat skip and stall. Somehow, it almost seemed like she knew that firsthand. Or maybe she was repeating advice someone else had given her? I didn't know, but she bowed her head and began walking back into our room. "Goodnight, Lieutenant. I hope you'll sleep well for the rest of the night."

7

CHAPTER SEVEN

I did manage to sleep better after that.

Unfortunately, that was about the only good news I had to lean on as time dragged on in that cramped room. We were stuck until Thatcher was well enough to get around and handle himself in case we got into another fight. But that didn't look like it was going to happen anytime soon.

"He's getting worse," Violet whispered as she sat down next to me. Cradling two cups of spiced tea. She handed one to me before settling in with her own, blowing over it gently while keeping her gaze trained upon the rest of our group gathered around the firepit.

Across the common area of the small room we'd rented closer to the port, I could see plainly what she was talking about. Thatcher's hands shook so badly, he struggled for each bite of the rice and fish porridge Violet had prepared for us. By the time he got the spoon to his lips, there wasn't much left on it. His coloring was ashen and there were dusky circles under his eyes. Not good signs.

After a few minutes of watching him struggle, Maylea scooted over and offered to help. Our eyes met as she took the bowl and spoon from him and started feeding him small bites. Right. I guess she could see it, too. Curse it. I couldn't afford to sit back and wait for much longer.

After three days, I'd hoped to see Thatcher turn a corner. Sure, he had taken a bad hit. He'd lost a lot of blood. But I'd stitched him up well and I was confident I hadn't missed anything in that department. In any other circumstance, I'd expect him to be up and walking around, being his usually obnoxiously cheery self.

But our current circumstances were less favorable.

When it came to medical miracles, my bag of tricks was pretty empty now. I'd used up all the healing salve I'd brought along—salve that undoubtedly would have prevented infection, sped up the healing process, and helped Thatcher get his strength back.

Instead, he was as ashen as a corpse, and I didn't like the yellow color I saw in the whites of his eyes. That usually meant toxins were building up in his body. He might be going septic. Thatcher couldn't walk more than a few steps without collapsing. He couldn't even stand without help. We could barely get him to eat more than a couple of small bites, and he'd begun running a fever with a cold sweat at night.

All signs pointing to a dangerous infection—which was always a great risk when it came to deep abdominal wounds around the stomach and intestines. If this went on for much longer, he could deteriorate beyond anyone's ability to help him. Not that we hadn't tried. Violet had already gone out a few times to try and purchase local remedies, but none of them proved to be as potent or effective as the salve they could make in Luntharda. No surprise there. Healing practices from Luntharda were renowned as the best in the world.

And we were a long way from Kiran's clinic.

That really only left one choice. Thatcher would continue to get worse. He'd die without more aggressive treatment. That wouldn't happen. No one was dying here. Not on my watch.

"Tonight, I'm going back down to the port. With any luck, the *Fog Dancer* is still there and I can find Judan again. There's a chance he has some of that salve among his own belongings," I murmured, keeping my tone low so that only Violet would hear me.

"And if Judan is nowhere to be found?" Violet studied me, her lips pressed to the rim of her teacup as she took careful sips.

Right. She didn't have to spell it out to me. I could read it all over her face. She didn't like the idea of me going off on my own. Not that I blamed her. I wasn't exactly wild about it, either.

The last time we'd split our group, things hadn't gone well. An old enemy of hers, Sulam, had ambushed Thatcher and abducted the two kids. That's how our resident godling had wound up with a gaping hole in his gut. Violet and I had managed to save him, but only barely, and we couldn't stand around high-fiving about it. We'd been forced to leave him basically right away to rescue Maylea and Lukani from Sulam's personal death arena, known as the Caldera.

Only ... I guess they hadn't needed much help from us, in the end. Maylea had apparently forged some sort of bond with a massive white dragon that had been chained in that arena with them. We had managed to set the dragon free before making a run for our lives, and somehow all returned here, to the island of Sol'Karr, in one piece. I wasn't dumb enough to call it skill. Luck was about all I had to thank for any of us making it out of that place alive.

Well, luck ... and maybe a little Broadfeather-brand divine intervention.

Apparently, the same deity that had once been the source of all Jaevid's power was now showing an interest in his daughter. I could imagine how he might feel about that—probably similar to the way I felt about Clysiros being a presence in Ronan's life. Like I was going to throw up and then run away screaming.

I wanted nothing more than to slam the door on anything else that smacked of the divine. Getting tangled up in the affairs of the gods had brought me nothing but suffering and grief. They'd already torn my life apart over and over. I didn't owe them another second of my time.

But the guy sitting over there, getting spoon fed like a baby because he was too weak to hold his own bowl of porridge, needed my help. He was one of my closest friends. And he was running out of time and options. I couldn't just stand by and watch him suffer. I was a healer. And if I couldn't get the supplies I needed from somewhere in the port, then I'd have to resort to drastic measures, too.

Gods, if it came to that, I just hoped Jaevid would somehow be able to forgive me for it.

Naaah. He was definitely going to murder me on sight. You know, providing someone else didn't beat him to it.

"I'm taking Maylea with me," I said, knowing full well I didn't have to explain to her why. Violet was clever enough to work out what my motives were. "You think you can handle babysitting both of them?" I nodded toward Thatcher and Lukani.

Her lips pursed unhappily, but she gave a small nod and sipped at her tea again. "Take care you stay to the main streets and move with crowds when you can. With Sulam causing such a spectacle, and the Zenith's Call ignoring my requests to meet, I have no doubts we are being watched very carefully."

"By the Hands of Fate or the Zenith's Call?" I asked.

She shrugged slightly. "Both, at least. I'm sure there are others who have taken notice of our presence, by now. They will grow bolder if we linger in one place for long."

"I figured." I sighed and rubbed at the back of my neck as I looked down into the teacup she'd handed me. The spicy aroma stung at my nose with a flavor almost like cinnamon. I took a cautious sip and closed my eyes as that subtle burn of spices left a warm trail down my throat. Hmm. Not bad. "I don't suppose you have any grand ideas about how to get all of us across that desert, eh?"

She turned up her own cup to finish off the contents before putting it aside. "I do, actually. But it's going to be complicated, given the situation Sulam's interference has left us in. I can only assume that is why the Zenith's Call haven't responded to any of my attempts to contact them. They don't like getting tangled up in public conflicts, and we have made ourselves a very indiscreet target. One problem at a time, though. See to your friend."

I shifted some and kept my gaze focused down into my cup as I thought—allowing my brain a few more seconds to chew on what I had to ask her next. Things were ... different between us now. Or, it seemed that way to me. I couldn't quite put my finger on how, though. Relaxed, maybe? Friendly, even? Eh, regardless, there was no good way to bring this up. No amount of fancy phrasing would mask it. Violet would catch on right away.

So, might as well get it over with.

"Is there a temple to Clysiros on this island?"

Violet froze. For a few seconds, I couldn't tell if she was even breathing. Then, slowly, her head turned to focus a wide-eyed stare of alarm right at me like a beacon from a lighthouse. I could see the look of silent horror on her delicate features out of the corner of my eye, like I'd just asked her to ram one of her daggers into my ear. Oh boy.

I swallowed hard and kept my head down, chewing on the inside of my cheek while I waited for her to answer.

"I know things seem rather bleak at the moment, but do you really think that is the answer to our problem? To healing your friend?" she questioned, her tone frosty and sharp with disapproval.

"I don't know," I admitted. "But we're running out of options. And ... I need to know why I'm seeing Noh again. I thought our bond was severed. I thought he couldn't even come back into the mortal world. He was supposed to be contained within the Vale, acting as a shepherd to the souls passing on to the Fates for judgement. But I know what I saw. He's here, using his power to manipulate the threads of life and death, and he called me out face-to-face. I need to know what this means."

Violet was silent for a moment, although her scarlet eyes still studied me like she was searching for some hidden secret in my scrappy, unshaven, sleep-deprived face. Hah. Too bad I was all out of surprises—which was the entire reason I was even willing to entertain speaking to Clysiros again, by the way. Desperation was a cruel master. Or, uh, mistress, in this case.

"I can handle it," I assured her, finally meeting her gaze.

Her lips pursed some, pinching together bitterly like there was something more she wanted to say. Her eyebrows drew up as something like concern passed over her face like a rainstorm slipping into the bay at Southwatch. Wait a second, was that ... *concern?* For me?

No.

No, no, no—I was reading way too much into that. Maybe it was some level of concern, but I did not dare take it personally. She probably just didn't want to be the last sane, fully functional adult in our little group. I mean, she'd said that before, right? Totally understandable.

"There is a hidden grotto in the city of Salnis, east of here. Supposedly, the trail leading to it that starts in the caverns beneath the city's main temple grounds, but I have never been there myself. It is a long way from here, however," she answered quietly, sinking back some with her shoulders drawn in. "I do hope you know what you're doing, Lieutenant."

I managed a weak, tired smile and took my last long sip of that spicy tea. "Nope. Not at all. But it'll take more than a little divine fury to bring me down. I've walked this path of gods and secrets before. I know exactly where it leads."

"Two rules," I grumbled as I fixed Maylea's cloak, pulling the hood down over her head to hide as much of her face as possible.

"Let me guess," she huffed and rolled her eyes. "Stay close and don't talk."

I pursed my lips and glared down at her. "Reading minds, are we?"

"No. But that's what everyone keeps telling me, like I don't know how to handle myself at all," she sulked.

Alright. Fine. I was probably babying her too much. How could I not? I'd been one of the first people to ever put a blade in her hand and teach her to use it. She wasn't my kid, but sometimes it felt like she might as well have been. She called me her uncle, and she was the closest thing to a real niece I'd probably ever have.

But given the antics I'd seen from her lately, I also knew exactly what level of destruction she was capable of. Jaevid-level. I was taking no chances.

"Actually, I was going say stay close and keep your eyes open," I said and handed her the fine, Gray elven bow and quiver she'd acquired from Judan. "This isn't a lecture, it's a warning. Training is over. This is real life with real threats. And now you know exactly what our enemy might try to take. So keep those eyes trained on anything that seems off, and tell me immediately. Murdoc taught you how to watch a crowd, how to feel people out, and what to look for when it comes to suspicious behavior. I'm trusting you to have my back. Understand?"

That look of rebellious exasperation was gone when she looked back at me, her vibrant sea-green eyes now sharp and focused. Maylea nodded and gripped the bow hard, her jawline going tense as she answered, "I won't let you down."

"It's not about letting me down, May. I don't doubt your resolve or your ability. Just trust your instincts and everything we've taught you." I put a hand on her shoulder and gave it a little squeeze, realizing too late that Kiran had done the same thing to me probably a thousand times when I was her age.

Wow. I guess I was going full dad-mode, after all. Sweet Fates, someone send help.

"We'll, uh, we'll be back before dawn." I cleared my throat and turned away, going to the door. I paused with my hand on the knob and flicked one last glance over my shoulder to Violet. Behind her, Lukani had taken over helping change Thatcher's bandages again. My still-tiny dragoness, Vexi, perched on his shoulder like a scaly green parrot, watching and chirping curiously. I had to give that kid some credit. He was a fast learner, and the sight of the angry, red, infected wound didn't seem to faze him at all.

If anxiety had a face, it looked a lot like Violet's as she stepped closer and eclipsed my view. She grasped my other hand and slipped a small object into it, swiftly folding my fingers around it. Hmm. Was that a coin?

"Remember what I said. Keep to the main roads as much as you can. But if anyone from the Zenith's Call approaches you, give them this. It bears Arlan's seal. They'll know what it means," she leaned in closer to whisper, her scarlet gaze holding mine for a single shared second as she squeezed my hand earnestly. A tiny hint of her scent, something like jasmine, wafted past my nose.

Tingling heat crept up my neck and spread over my cheeks. Oh, gods. I-I had to go. Right now. "And they'll let me go about my business without a problem, right?" I forced a cracking, horrible excuse for a laugh as I pulled away and took a step closer to the door.

She gave me a similarly uncomfortable, forced smile back. "That depends on who sent them. But at the very least, they might not kill you outright."

Great. Well, that was something, I guess. I nodded and turned around, nearly crashing right into Maylea who stood close by, grinning wolfishly from under her hood. I didn't like her mischievous, cunning little grin one bit. Like she knew something she shouldn't. What was there to know?

I mean, yes. It was sort of intimate for Violet to act that way toward me. Leaning in all close and whispering like we were, you know, something secret. Ugh. No. Even if she was beautiful, I wasn't that stupid. Violet was like a flowering greevwood tree—beautiful, fragrant, and tempting, but likely to explode violently and blow my head clean off my shoulders if I messed around with her at all.

And I liked having my head on my shoulders, thank you very much.

Unfortunately, I couldn't stop my face from burning with embarrassed heat as I basically shoved Maylea out the door ahead of me. She snickered and waggled her eyebrows at me as she nibbled at her bottom lip.

"You like her, don't you?" she jibed.

"No," I fumed as I stomped forward into the late evening's cool, briny wind.

"Oh, come on, Uncle Reigh. I saw that. And you're still blushing, by the way," she practically skipped along beside me like an excited baby goat.

"Shut up and walk," I growled through my teeth and pulled my own hood down low. "We're on a life and death mission here, remember? Assassins everywhere?"

"It's not like it's a bad thing, you know," Maylea sighed and adjusted the strap to her quiver. She had slung it and her bow across her back, ready to draw at a moment's notice. "So what if you like her? You're always alone. You should have someone that makes you happy."

"I *am* happy," I growled again, trying to sound as resolved and threatening as possible as I walked faster, making my way down the side of the broad, sloped avenue toward the port.

"Oh yeah. You sound *sooo* happy," she taunted, her tone thick with sarcasm.

Augggh. No. I was not about to have this conversation, especially not with her. She wasn't even fifteen. What could she possibly know about love? It wasn't the sappy, doughy feelings she probably had for Lukani now. Sure, it started that way. But that wasn't real. It didn't last.

I knew better than most that love was a battle—one I'd already lost years ago. I wasn't ready to rejoin it again. Maybe I never would be. And that was fine. I could manage alone. I'd been doing it for years, hadn't I? I was content on my own. Content was a lot better than most people could ever hope for, anyway.

Hoping and dreaming of anything else was foolish. I didn't need that door slammed on my nose again.

"Just keep your eyes and ears open," I reminded her sharply as we sped along the roadside, passing the glowing windows of restaurants, taverns, and homes that lined either side of the street. Beyond, the ghostly dark figures of people moved, silhouetted against the old, wavered glass. Strands of shells and sea glass hanging from some of the eaves tinkled musically in the wind.

Here, the lives of the commonfolk seemed slower and simpler than in the port cities of Maldobar. They didn't have to fight the fierce cold in the winter and the near-constant rain in the summer. There was an easiness and sense of calm that seemed to seep into the very stone of the place. Maybe that was what kept my nerves drawn as tight as bowstrings as we moved, fast and silent, toward the port.

Like ripples on the surface of a calm pond, we were a disruption to the usual tranquility here. And it wouldn't be long until someone in the dark noticed our disturbance, and smelled blood in the water.

8

CHAPTER EIGHT

A thick fog curled in from the island's massive bay, slowly seeping into the streets and drifting soundlessly through every alley. It made the lanterns lit along the sidewalks glow like wisps floating in the night.

My pulse thumped hard and heavy, battering against my ribs as I watched every group of people, every dark corner, and every side street we passed. Having a dagger in the side of my boot and my kafki blades belted at my hips didn't make me feel any more relaxed or confident. I was in unfamiliar territory, dancing around an enemy I knew next to nothing about, and hoping I didn't trip and fall right into the point of someone's blade.

Not great odds, even for me.

I just hoped whatever powers were watching us would hold off, spare us another attack, until I found a way to help Thatcher. Otherwise, Maylea might not be the only one dealing out a little divine intervention. Just the thought of dealing with Clysiros again, in any capacity, was enough to snatch all the breath from my lungs and leave my body thrumming with fury and pure terror. But she was calling me out personally, and I might not have any other choice.

Was Clysiros evil? I'd assumed so, at first. She certainly liked to revel in the dark and taboo elements of society. But, no. Death wasn't inherently evil, and neither was she. Death was a natural part of life's cycle. It just wasn't a terribly popular one.

But did that mean I trusted Clysiros to do anything except further her own agenda by any means necessary? No. Absolutely not. I knew exactly what side she was on—her own. And the only pawns she liked moving were the ones decidedly in her favor.

Seeing Noh wasn't a good omen. The gods were stirring, choosing sides, and picking their favorite pieces on the gameboard. That probably meant Arlan's evil sister was, too. Or at the very least, she was doing something bad enough to encourage the gods to act. Rocking the proverbial divine boat. That wasn't good news for anyone.

I stopped at a street corner where the road ahead took a steep downward slope, offering a broad view of Sol'karr's huge, circular port. Ships bobbed in the moonlit fog by the thousands, watched over by the central tower that rose up right in the middle of the bay. Its brilliant beacon turned slowly, panning a wide beam of light all around the docks.

The *Fog Dancer* was somewhere out there. We just had to find it—fast.

"Ready?" I murmured.

Maylea nodded firmly.

Good. Trekking onward, I set my teeth against the swell of adrenaline. The port roads were busier. There would be many prying eyes taking note of our passage. We had to tread lightly and get this done.

Then, I had a date with death herself.

Every step sent a jolt through me, a little rush of apprehension that made my fingertips tingle. Something Noh had said still stuck in my mind like a needle, pricking at my every thought and digging in deeper and deeper. He had mentioned that we were the last to leave the starting line. What did that mean? Were others being chosen just like Maylea had been?

I stole a glance to the left, spotting the rising structure of the grand temple to the sea goddess, Undae, bathed in golden torchlight. It was the largest of all the holy structures on the island, with a domed roof plated in gold and walls of clean white alabaster stone. Even at a distance, I could see the massive pillars that lined the front, and each one was the size of one of the colossal trees in Luntharda.

Sites like that were rare in Luntharda and Maldobar. Not many of them had survived the tests of time. They'd been buffeted by war after war over the centuries, and were now destroyed, buried, or forgotten.

Something about that sight, of beautiful temples gleaming in the night, sent chills up my spine. Should I really go to that grotto? Should I answer Clysiros's call again? It might be my best shot at getting real answers about what was going on with Noh. And if things continued to go poorly for us, I might need her strength and power to ensure our success. I might need it to save Ronan.

But nothing from the gods ever came for free. The price for that kind of power would be steep. The thought made my head spin and a little wave of nausea turn my stomach like I'd taken a sip of sour milk. It wouldn't end well. Encounters with Clysiros never did. But what other choice was there?

Sooner or later, I'd have to decide.

Maylea stuck close at my back as we drew closer and closer to the docks, sweeping through crowds of sailors making their way inland to the taverns and inns for the night. None of them seemed to pay us much attention as we passed. All focused on getting a stiff drink and a warm place to sit, I suppose. Good.

We walked the dockside street for nearly an hour, making our way back to where we'd left Judan and the ship only a few days ago. I honestly had no way of knowing if he would still be there, making repairs to the *Fog Dancer* and preparing it to get underway again, or if he was long gone. If he did leave, I didn't know where he would go. Maybe he'd set off after Malina and the *Squall Queen* again, ready to exact his revenge. I sort of doubted he'd suffer a sudden attack of conscience and go back home—even if that's exactly what he should have done. He was working through some bitterness, clearly. I guess we had that in common, though. We were both princes who were destined to walk in the shadow of older siblings, unsure of our foothold in the world, and exhausted from a lifetime of blood, blades, and battles. Sure, it was selfish of him to just disappear and become a pirate.

But, then again, I'd done something similar.

I shook my head, trying to clear those thoughts. No—I hadn't done anything even remotely close to that. I hadn't bailed on my family; I was out here trying to save them. Ronan, specifically. I wasn't ducking my destiny. I was about to meet it headlong and face down the very worst part of myself that had ever existed ... otherwise known as Noh.

Judan and I were nothing alike.

Right?

"Uncle Reigh, look!" Maylea spoke up suddenly, grabbing my arm and pointing ahead. There, rocking gently amidst the other ships moored along the farthest edge of the dock, I saw it. The lights in the *Fog Dancer's* cabins were lit, glowing brightly in the foggy night. Relief and hope swelled in me, leaving my head throbbing and ears ringing with a sudden rush of heat in my blood. Judan was still here. There was hope, after all. If anyone in this place had any of that healing salve, it was him.

Gods, I just hoped he was willing to barter for it.

"Well, I can honestly say you two are the last people in the world I wanted to see again so soon." Judan cast his deadpan gaze between Maylea and me from where he sat behind his desk. He licked his teeth behind his lips, as though trying to resist spitting angry words my way. Instead, he grabbed the neck of a wine bottle and took a few big gulps straight from it. "What do you want, Reigh? Coming here all cloak and dagger in the middle of the night—it had better not be what I think it is."

Standing in his cabin onboard the *Fog Dancer*, I crossed my arms and waited for him to take another long drink from that bottle before I even tried explaining myself.

"I'm not here to try to recruit you, if that's what you're thinking," I said, casting a quick sideways glance at the pair of armed deckhands that stood on either side of us like his personal bodyguards. "Thatcher's hurt. Badly. He may not make it another day without some medical help."

Judan's dark green eyes narrowed. He slowly put his bottle down on the desk in front of him and gave a dismissing gesture to his pair of cronies. They both huffed, muttering under their breath as they shuffled out of the cabin and shut the door behind them. Only once they were gone did Judan's intense scowl fade some. "Good thing he's got a trained medical professional to help him, then," his tone was as curious as it was careful. "Surely you don't think I've got some skill that you don't in that regard."

"Not skill," I corrected. "Supplies. Look, I know you've probably heard about what happened with Sulam in the Caldera a few nights ago."

His mouth twitched a smirk. "So, that *was* you, after all. I thought it smacked of some Broadfeather nonsense."

"Right. Well, during all that chaos, Thatcher got ambushed by Sulam's men," I continued. "I was barely able to stitch him up, but he's got an infection and I'm all out of salve. You're the only person here I can think of who might have some and might care enough about him to hand it over. You don't like me. I get that. I rub people the wrong way and have all my life. But Thatcher's a good man, and one of the few I've got fighting on my side here. I can't lose him. Not like this."

For a few long, uncomfortable seconds, Judan sat still and didn't say a word. Then he slowly sank back into his chair, making the wood creak a bit under his weight. His lips thinned as he tapped his fingers on his desktop, seeming to think it over before he finally replied, "Reigh, I ... I honestly wish I had a different answer for you. But I don't have any of that healing salve."

My heart sank, sliding like a hunk of ice down the back of my throat all the way to the pit of my stomach. It left a numbing chill that seemed to seep down all the way to the marrow of my bones. "Do you know where I can get some, then?"

"This far from Luntharda? No. A lot of things make their way through this port. Trade goods from all over the world. But medical supplies from the wild jungle aren't something that's in high demand. Not enough to warrant my hearing of it, anyway," he explained, real concern putting a crease in his brow right between his eyes. He licked his lips and tapped on his desktop again, as though mentally scrambling for some alternative idea.

Then I saw his gaze land squarely on Maylea. Or rather, on the pendant around her neck. And I knew exactly what he was thinking.

Because I'd already considered that option ... and now it was the only one we had left.

"I appreciate the honesty," I said and gave a small bow. "I'll see what else I can do to help him. Take care, Judan."

"Reigh," he called out as Maylea and I both turned to leave. "There's something you should know."

We stopped, and I looked back to find him staring daggers at the wine bottle on his desk, almost like he wanted to throw it at the wall in disgust. Or at me. Tough to tell with him.

"Yeah? What is it?" I asked.

"Word around the port is that things in Nar'Haleen's waters are becoming extremely hostile—more so than ever before. Traders are halting their deliveries through those routes. Those who do try to pass are attacked, looted, and sunk without any warning." He reached out for the neck of the bottle at last, swirling it and finally looking up to meet my gaze. "There have been reports of the entire navy amassing for a strike on Rienka. A sort of ... shock and awe campaign. The city officials here are on edge. They're checking vessels coming and going thoroughly, looking for spies. They're fortifying all the garrisons as fast as they can. If you're planning on leaving this city, I'd advise you to do it as soon as you can."

Right. Well, the problem with that was I couldn't go anywhere until I fixed Thatcher. No way was I leaving him behind—especially if this was about to be the site of an all-out naval invasion.

I guess Judan could read that plainly enough in my expression, though, because he gave a hearty chuckle and downed the last of his wine. "Not that you've ever been the sort to leave a man behind," he added quickly. "I suppose I'm living proof of that, eh?"

He had that right, at least. "And what about you? Planning on slipping away from here before the axe drops?" I arched an eyebrow.

His smile broke, fading at the corners until I saw that deep, conflicted look of thought crinkle over his brow again. "Naturally. There's been some word among the other less reputable businessmen docking in his harbor about what we'd do if Nar'Haleen shows up. All of us would rather see the darkest depths than be forced under the emperor's heel. But to fight for Rienka? Or for any rear end sitting on any throne? It goes against the grain of most pirate folk to adopt a royal banner—as most were forced into that lifestyle because they were already social pariahs of some manner. Tough to convince society's unwanteds to rally and save it. My men want to depart as soon as possible, and I don't intend to force them to stay."

Fair point. That logic didn't really apply to Judan, though. He wasn't an unwanted pariah. He was a prince on the run from a family that undoubtedly wanted and needed him at home. He had parents, Queen Araxie and King Jace of Luntharda, brothers, nieces, nephews, and cousins. He had a lot to go back home to, if he wanted. But instead, he was out here playing around like a kid still trying to find himself.

"Of course, you could always take the coward's way out and run away again." I couldn't resist a thin, ironic smile as I waved a hand and turned back to leave. "But it sounds to me like your time to pick a side has finally come. Too bad Malina took the Squall Queen and left, eh? A ship like that might actually do some damage against Nar'Haleen's warships. But I doubt she would ever join a fight like that unless someone asked her to."

Judan's lips thinned, and his expression sharpened like cold steel as he stared me down. "Are you suggesting *I* be the one to extend that invitation to her?"

"Not at all." I smirked and shrugged. "She'd try to kill you on sight, right? I don't know what went down between you two, and honestly, I don't care. But it's not hard to tell that she has no reason in the entire world to want to do any favors for you. All I'm saying is that it's too bad. We could probably use that brand of help, if we can convince her to join our side. We'll all be picking sides before this is over. I hope you choose wisely, my friend. Fates keep you until we meet again."

9

CHAPTER NINE

A warm, restless wind stirred in the port and gusted in my hair as we stepped off the *Fog Dancer* and back out onto the dockside street. Far in the distance, bolts of lightning flickered and flashed, revealing an encroaching storm front looming beyond the port. Crap. We had to make this fast. Rough waves already rocked at the moored ships and a low rumble of thunder echoed like a soft growl.

The smell of the coming storm filled my lungs and seemed to wash over my whole body. Its raw power practically hummed in the air, hitting my blood like a current of crackling power. It put every nerve on edge as my already frazzled brain scrambled for a new plan. No way were we going to get stuck out in the city to ride out a storm. We had to get back to Violet and the others as soon as possible.

"Uncle Reigh?" Maylea's whisper was barely audible as she followed close beside me. Before us, the winds had begun to clear away the fog, giving a better view of the streets and alleys that branched off into the city ahead.

"Thatcher's going to be fine," I assured her, fairly certain I knew what she was worried about. That meeting hadn't exactly ended on a happy note. We'd left without any of the salve Thatcher desperately needed. Discouraging? Oh yeah. But I wasn't out of tricks just yet.

"What can we do? Is there some other medicine that will help him?" she pressed, walking closer at my side and keeping her head down so I couldn't see her face. I guess she didn't want me to see her getting emotional about it.

Too bad there was no easy answer to those questions. Were there other medicines? Yes. But none of the local remedies were meant to treat infections as aggressively as the ones from Luntharda. At least, none that I'd found. Maybe there were—but I was a fish out of water when it came to the intricacies of the medical care available in Rienka.

So what could we do? Something I knew most likely went directly against what Jaevid would have wanted for his daughter. But we were running out of options, and Thatcher was running out of time.

It was time to see just how much power Paligno had given her.

I patted Maylea's shoulder and took in a deep, preparatory breath. "Yes. But fair warning, it may require you to do something you've never done before. Something your father absolutely would *not* approve of."

She turned her head up just enough to peer at me from under the hood of her cloak, giving me that candid perplexed and slightly suspicious look I'd seen her father give me probably a million times. Right. Well, I had to be vague about the details—for now, anyway. Once we got back to the others, I'd feel a lot better about explaining this to her. There, we stood less chance of prying eyes and ears figuring out who we were and what we were up to.

Honestly, the irony of it all made my stomach roll with a wave of nausea that nearly had me running for the nearest alley to throw up. Many years ago, her father had been the one to force my hand and help me channel my own divine power from Clysiros. He had taught me to harness it in a way I'd never dared to before, and together, we had toppled the empire of one of the most notorious tyrants in history. Now, I needed to teach Maylea to attempt that same thing.

Well. Never let it be said the Fates have no sense of humor.

I hated the idea of hanging our every hope on her very young shoulders, though. Yes, healing was sort of Paligno's area of expertise, him being the God of Life and whatnot. He usually provided his chosen candidates with healing abilities. Surely that meant Maylea would be capable of that same sort of power now, too, right?

Only one way to find out.

Time to get back—preferably before the storm hit.

I stopped instantly, my pulse thudding hard against my ribs as Maylea gave a sudden, sharp tug on the sleeve of my tunic. Oh no. Crap. Seriously? Right now?

With every sense and muscle on edge, I panned my gaze around the foggy road where we stood. Nothing. No sound. No movement. Not even any lights burning in the shop windows around us.

Hmmm. If anything, it was *too* quiet.

A familiar little prickle of unease raced up my spine—the same sort of feeling I always got back when I was a scout in the jungles of Luntharda when a predator moved through the area. That sensation of being watched by something bigger and badder that made every hair on my body stand on end.

You know, like when Murdoc glared at me from across the room. Creepy.

"Where?" I whispered, chancing a quick sideways glance down at her.

Maylea stood eerily still, her face now mostly hidden by her hood. "Forty paces back," she whispered, speaking quickly in the Gray elven language. Clever. It was bound to be less commonly spoken in this part of the world, so anyone listening in might not understand.

"You get a count?" I asked.

"Four."

I reached down to the belt at my hips and let my fingers brush the hilts of my kafki blades. "Armed?"

"Yep."

Ugh. Great. This could get messy. But there wasn't time to second-guess. I had to trust that feeling in my gut telling me to brace for the worst.

"Break off and go quiet. You get aerial but hold your fire. Wait for my cue," I murmured. "Might be thugs. Might be someone working for Arlan. Might be worse. Let's see what these guys want."

"Lethal shots?" I caught the tiniest hint of tension in her voice—uneasiness. Hesitation to kill.

Right. As skilled as she was, Maylea was still relatively new to fighting and killing people, even if they did mean us harm. She'd already gotten her hands bloody on the ships, and I hadn't exactly had a chance to talk to her about that.

This was bound to make the fallout worse for her.

"That's your call," I replied as I stepped ahead of her. "Do what you feel is necessary. But if it's all the same to you, and it's obvious that they're trying to kill me, I'd be much obliged if you didn't let that happen."

She made a sarcastic, snorting sound before she cut briskly to the right, vanishing down a small alley like a phantom in the night. No sound. No footsteps. Not a rustle of fabric or click of a boot heel.

Nothing but a quickly fading swirl in the thick white fog.

I smirked as I bowed my head and forged onward, slowing my pace so our pursuers could gain on me. I had to admit, as frustrating as that girl could be, she was handling all this very well so far. She kept a level head even when a battle-hardened dragonrider might buckle. It made me a little proud. Maybe that's because I'd watched her grow up and trained her in some of those combat techniques.

Or maybe just because, once upon a time, I'd been that kid who ran away from home to prove myself, too.

When I heard the scrape of a footstep behind me, I quickened my pace. No doubt about it now. I was definitely being followed. With no idea who it might be—the Zenith's Call, the Hands of Fate, or just a random batch of thugs hoping to rob me—I couldn't afford to take any chances.

My thoughts went silent as I set my teeth against the swell of adrenaline that made every muscle in my body flex and tingle. That rush of heat in my veins kept every sense on edge, made my heartbeat slow, and my breathing deepen.

Time to work.

I cut to the left down a side street and quickened my pace, then ducked to the right along an alleyway that ran back out to the main road. If they were common thieves, I could lose them easily. But trained assassins? Or even mercenaries? They'd be able to follow.

Ducking around a corner, I put my back to the wall and listened, holding still as my fingers found their way to the hilts of my weapons. A second passed. Then two. Nothing. No sound. No voices.

Then I heard it—the faintest splash, as though someone had stepped in a puddle at the other end of the alley.

I smirked.

Assassins or mercenaries it was, then.

Slowly sinking down, I picked up a small rock from the side of the street and waited. Clothing rustled nearby, probably not even ten feet away from me back inside that alley. They were coming. They'd emerge and find me hiding there any second.

I smirked and hurled the pebble off into the dark on the other side of the street, pinging it off a few barrels with a clatter.

Immediately, someone whispered something in the Sokraal language, more fabric rustled, and three figures ran from the alleyway out into the street to investigate. Heh. Well, looks like Maylea's count was off, but still ... too easy.

They sprinted right past my hiding spot, and I held perfectly still with my back to the side of the building. They never even noticed me or took a second glance in my direction.

As soon as they were across the street, I whirled around and started back down that same alley, the way I'd come, and pulled the hood of my cloak up to hide my hair. That tended to be my biggest giveaway, after all. It made me a lot more recognizable in a crowd.

I doubled back the way I'd come, crossing back out into the side street on the other end of the alley. So far, so good. No sign of them. These had to be Zenith's Call. The Hands of Fate had gotten a jump on Violet and wounded her, and these guys were nowhere near that level of skill, apparently. I'd have to ask her about it whenever I got back to the—

Something cold and sharp pricked against the side of my neck.

Oh no. I stopped suddenly, staring straight ahead across the small, heavily shadowed intersection before me. Here, four of those side streets met in the gloom. None of the shops or buildings around had lights burning in the windows. There were no signs of life anywhere. Not even the street lamps were lit.

Curse it.

"You are a clever one, I will grant you that," a heavily accented voice chuckled from behind me. "But not clever enough, it seems. Hands up, if you do not mind, Your Highness."

What? They knew who I was? Fates, this wasn't good.

I licked my teeth behind my lips, tasting the coppery flavor of fury fresh on my tongue. "I do mind, actually," I growled as I slowly turned to see who had a blade to my neck.

The man on the other end of that sleek, glimmering rapier wasn't at all what I'd been expecting. He made no effort to hide his face, wearing a faded blue coat over casual, Rienkan-styled clothes. He stood about my height, maybe a little taller, with his dark brown hair lengthy on top but shaved close to his scalp on one side.

In a swift glance over him, I counted at least two more daggers tucked into the wrap around his waist and what looked suspiciously like one of those exploding metal contraptions Malina had used resting in a leather sheath under his left arm. His chiseled features tugged a half-smile when he spotted me eyeing that weapon. "I see you know what this is," he tapped the weapon fondly with his free hand, "even though no one uses a blunderbuss in Maldobar."

I didn't reply.

His smile faded some, his squared features sobering to a more distrustful, scrutinizing stare. He kept that rapier's point right at the base of my throat as he clicked his tongue thoughtfully. "And where is your companion? Nearby, I'm certain. Call her out."

I narrowed my eyes. "Not a chance." If this guy really meant to kill me, he would have done it already. Clearly this wasn't about robbing, murdering, or even kidnapping. He had a different angle—one he needed me alive for.

I just had to figure out what that was.

He narrowed his eyes, too. Rubbing at the heavy stubble on his squared jawline, he chuckled under his breath. "I see now what they mean by Maldobarian stubbornness. I am curious, Your Highness, how do you see this ending for you?"

"Usually I carve my way out in a path of blood, gore, and corpses. You could say it's my specialty," I muttered, my gaze catching on something tattooed on the top of his hand that held that rapier. It almost looked like the symbol of a sword through a crescent moon. Ahhh, so he was Zenith's Call.

He stared at me for a moment, eyes wide in shock. Then he bent forward and burst out laughing. "May the gods have mercy, you do speak the truth. Well then, if you will not cooperate, I have no choice."

I tensed as he stepped in closer, his grip on that rapier tightening and his bemused smile snapping into a maddened scowl. He opened his mouth, probably to threaten me, but he never got a word out. Something zipped through the air and hit the slender blade of his weapon, knocking it away from me.

Instantly, I stepped in, ramming my fist into his stomach as hard as I could. He barked a wheezing breath and doubled over, and I seized his wrist to try and disarm him.

The man moved faster, though. I spat a curse as he whirled back, hitting me upside the jaw with his elbow and sending me reeling back. He grabbed my arm and twisted it back, ducking down and using me like a human shield from Maylea's aerial assault. With the steel of that blade back against my throat, I stiffened and cursed through my teeth. Fates, he was fast. Maybe even as fast as Murdoc.

"Now then, let us try this again," he snarled right against my ear, gripping me so tight I felt the slow, burning pain of my shoulder starting to dislocate. Gods, he was strong. I couldn't even twist my body to relieve that pressure. "I have not come to kill either of you tonight, but I very well may slip and make a terrible mistake. Call the girl down or I will have my men do it by force. Do we understand one another, Your Highness? Or did you assume I only brought a small force to take you in?"

I growled a few Gray elven profanities as I gave one more desperate pitch against his hold. "If you think I'm calling anyone down right into your hands, you're dreaming. You'll have to kill me, because I can assure you, I've been tortured by the best already. It won't work. I don't compromise. I don't cooperate. I'm a dragonrider of Maldobar, and I'll take you to the abyss right along with me before I betray my companions."

A faint scuffle from another alleyway to my right made me turn, just in time to see the other three individuals who had been chasing me earlier. Two had crossbows drawn and leveled at me. The third held a shortsword in each hand. Crap.

I had no doubts that Maylea could have killed all of them. She was an excellent marksman with a bow. She probably could have even killed the guy holding me. But she'd never dealt with a hostage situation before. I had no idea how she would react to a situation like this, but I absolutely did not want her firing off high-risk shots if she was second-guessing herself.

Not with my head so close to her target.

"What do you want from me?" I demanded, still growling every word through gritted teeth. "No one will ransom me here. You know that."

"I do," he seethed. "I did not come to abduct you. The Mistress of the Call wishes an audience with you."

What? Mistress of the Call? What did that even mean? Was I supposed to know who that was?

"Your little Pitathi friend has tried to contact us many times, but your dealings with Sulam have not gone unnoticed. Tell me, prince, did Kinslayer send you here to eradicate him?" the man questioned. "The Mistress wants to know, and so you will answer to her."

My mind spun, piecing together what, exactly, was happening here. I could only assume that this Mistress of the Call was some sort of leadership figure to the Zenith's Call. She'd obviously heard about what happened with Sulam in his arena. Since he was also a member of this organization, they must want answers. That's why they weren't giving Violet the time of day now, since they knew she worked directly for Arlan.

Great. Now I'd basically become a middleman between international crime factions. Fantastic. Super qualified for that. But maybe, if I played my cards right, I could make this situation work for our benefit. After all, Violet had been trying to contact these people for days without any response. We needed their help to get our mission back on track. We needed resources. A way across the desert. Hopefully, I could negotiate some of that.

Uggh. Gods and Fates, why did stuff like this always happen to me?

"Fine," I agreed. "Let me go, and I'll talk to this Mistress. But I think she's going to be pretty disappointed when she hears what my motives are."

I could hear the sly grin in his voice without having to see it as he suddenly gave me a shove forward and snapped his fingers to his men, ordering them to drop their weapons. "Oh, I very much doubt that, Your Highness. I'm sure she will be extremely interested in whatever has brought a Maldobarian prince and dragonrider to our lovely doorstep. Now, call off your girl. We must move quickly, lest we alert the city guards."

Io

CHAPTER TEN

The rapier-wielding man looked genuinely surprised when a fourteen-year-old girl strode proudly from the shadows, the stormy wind blowing through her hair as she carried her Lunthardan-styled bow and glared at him defiantly. I had to give her credit, Maylea kept a cool head under pressure. She didn't even bat a lash as she prowled through his line of armed mercenaries, each one glaring at her like a pack of ravenous jackals.

The man glanced her up and down, eyebrows raised, and finally spoke. "Well now. Not quite what I was expecting. How old are you, girl?"

"Old enough to know where every one of your major arteries are and ten ways to sever them before you know what's happened," she snapped.

I had to bite back a smile. Murdoc might have even cracked a grin at that—since he was the one who'd taught her all that.

"And my name is Maylea, not girl, thank you very much." She crossed her arms as she stopped right next to me. "Who are you?"

It seemed to take the man a moment to recover after that answer. He blinked a few times like she'd slapped him across the face. Then, with a frustrated sigh, he shook his head and turned away. "Varren, at your service," he muttered sourly and gave another signal to his men. "Come. We must be swift. I do so enjoy standing around in dark alleys in the middle of the night, but I'd prefer not to be caught outside when the storm hits."

I had to agree. Giving Maylea a reassuring nod, I walked ahead right behind Varren as he led the way through the darkened streets. Somewhere along the way, two of his three companions broke off to take separate paths, while the last one kept right at our heels. None of them spoke, however, and I wasn't feeling especially chatty either.

Mentally, I had enough to chew on. This meeting with the so-called Mistress of the Call, might be the ticket we'd been hoping for. I had to keep a cool head and trust that if she really had any ill-will for us, we would be dead already. Then again, maybe she only had dislike for Violet because of who her employer was? Hard to say.

This could get tricky. I'd have to watch my mouth more closely than usual.

And apparently Maylea's, too. Good grief.

Making our way along an indirect route, keeping to alleys and side streets that weren't as well-lit as the main avenues, Varren guided us back toward the docks. There, he finally stopped at the entrance to what looked like an old sailor's tavern and inn that stood only one street back from the dockside. The narrow building seemed to be squished between the ones on either side, like ham mashed into the middle of a sandwich. The clay tiled roof was slumped in the middle, and I couldn't see any signs or insignia anywhere that gave the place a name. Just a big carved statue of a, uh, mostly naked woman with the bottom half of a fish. A siren?

The smell of sour ale, sweat, and stale wine hit me like a hammer as we stepped inside. I cringed, squinting as my eyes watered a little from the thick cloud of pipe smoke that hung in the air like fog over a swamp. The place was packed from front to back with sailors, dockhands, and fishermen. They sat in big crowds at the round tables, playing cards, puffing on long pipes, and swapping stories with loud bursts of laughter. None of them even looked up as we ducked inside.

Varren led us behind the bar, giving a small nod to the bartender—an old man with more hair in his beard than on his head. He didn't seem all that bothered by us, either, and went on filling a round of ale horns without even glancing our way.

"Mark the door," Varren ordered to his one remaining man still following us from a few paces behind. "Just in case that little Pitathi decides to cause more trouble, eh?"

My pulse gave a hard, burning thump at the words. Or, well, one in particular. Now that I actually knew what Pitathi meant, hearing people call Violet that made a sudden spark of anger crackle and catch in my chest. Not that she needed any help defending her own honor, but I didn't like it one bit. It made me wonder what, exactly, her people had done to be referred to with such obvious disgust by everyone else. Even Violet hadn't seemed all that ... proud of her lineage.

I'd have to sort all that out later, though.

Ahead, Varren guided us to the back of the tavern's kitchen and into a storage room. There, under a hatch on the floor, he stepped quickly down a narrow stairwell into a cellar. Huge wooden casks of ale and wine lined the walls from floor to ceiling, kept cool by the natural stone and subterranean air. He walked the line of wine casks, each one so big five people could fit inside, until he came to the last one.

A cask with the symbol of a crescent moon and sword burned into the front of the wooden spigot.

Varren reached for it and gave the spigot a twist, like a door handle, and closed his eyes. He gave a deep, weighty sigh that made his shoulders rise and fall—almost like he was mentally preparing himself for what came next. Then he glanced my way with a worried frown. "You might consider showing a little respect. The Mistress is less forgiving than I when it comes to that endearing Maldobarian stubbornness of yours."

I arched an eyebrow. "Worried I'll embarrass you in front of your boss?"

"Yes, well, you might find this hard to believe, given how we met, but I rather dislike resorting to violence or having any part in it," he quipped. "It happens, of course, in this line of work. One can't always be diplomatic. But based on my keen observations of your little ragtag group, I would hate to see something else unfortunate befall you now. I believe you'll want to entertain what the Mistress has to say."

"Noted," I answered, keeping my voice low as I looked away. So this guy had been watching us? I guess that meant he knew we were in a bad spot with Thatcher. Great. Nothing like having your possible enemy aware of your greatest vulnerabilities, right? I'd have to tread carefully or this could get messy.

Varren turned the cask's spigot a little farther until something on the inside gave a heavy, metallic clunk. The whole front opened like a massive round door, creaking on hidden hinges. Within, instead of a huge barrel of wine, another staircase led down even deeper underground.

Whoa.

Maylea and I swapped a wary sideways glance.

There'd be no speedy retreat or easy escape from this place if things went sour. We were literally stepping into a lion's den.

"Eyes and ears open," I warned her in a whisper before I followed Varren down that staircase. "Let me do the talking, but I need you to make sure they aren't trying to pull a fast one on us while I've got my back turned."

"Uncle Reigh ... I don't think Violet would want us doing this without her," Maylea whispered back.

I flinched and started forward, ducking down in the dark staircase with my heart already pounding in the back of my throat. "Yeah," I mumbled under my breath. "For the record, I don't like it, either."

The soft clinking of glass and gentle plucking of a stringed instrument floated up from the base of the stairs. With every step down from the tavern, the stench of the sour ale and cheap wine faded, giving way to something far sweeter. Was that perfume? Or flowers?

Passing through a beaded curtain strung over the doorway at the base of the stairs, I hesitated as I took in the lavish room. The space was lit by intricate, colored glass oil lamps and flickering candles that hung from the ceiling. The smell of burning incense hung thick in the cool air like a soothing balm. Strange. This wasn't at all what I'd imagined a den of secretive mercenaries might look like. Were we even in the right place?

Portions of the spacious room had been sectioned off into smaller, private areas that were partitioned by beautifully stitched silk screens of gold, green, and purple. The people sitting within them were gathered around low tables, seated on velvet cushions, and sipped from small silver cups as they exchanged hushed conversations. They stared as we passed, their discussions going suddenly silent. I spotted humans, elves, and folk with far stranger features that I couldn't even begin to place. Some held long ivory smoking pipes, or were dealing out hands of gold-foiled cards for some sort of game.

Interesting.

None of them were carrying weapons that I could see. In fact, these didn't even look like mercenaries. More like upper class merchants, wealthy smugglers, or individuals who had made a lot of money in unsavory ways. Arlan's sort, I guess.

Maybe all the actual mercenaries were mixed in the rowdier crowd upstairs? I guess it made sense for this Mistress person not to want to associate too closely with cutthroats and thugs. Arlan only kept a few of his agents close at hand—Garnett, Violet, and Howlan. Well, that I knew of, anyway.

I wondered if Varren had that sort of "inner-circle" contact with the Mistress, too.

He walked ahead of us down the length of the room, past all those sectioned off nooks, and a spot on the end where a beautiful Rienkan elf woman dressed in flowing silk robes and strings of purple gems sat on an intricate woven rug. She cradled a large stringed instrument in her arms, almost like a harp, with her fingertips brushing gingerly over the strings. It filled the room with a light, calming melody. She didn't look up as we passed, though.

The largest sectioned-off area stood at the very back, beyond a hanging curtain and huge partitioned panels of golden thread. Images of the ocean, of fish, corals, crabs, and flowering water reeds were embroidered onto them. Pausing before the curtained entrance, Varren turned back and murmured, "Wait here. I'll announce you."

Uhh. Right. Okay, then.

Maylea and I stood in awkward silence as he ducked through the curtain into the area beyond, and I took that opportunity to examine things more closely. From here, I couldn't see any other exit points from this place. But there might have been a doorway or something hidden behind one of these paneled-off areas. Letting my gaze track along the walls, I picked the shapes of towering figures dressed completely in black—black tunics, pants, and black leather armor—standing every ten paces. Bodyguards. I could spot ten from this vantage point, but that didn't mean there weren't others hiding in the shadows.

If this didn't go well, our chances of getting out of here in one piece ... were not great.

"The Mistress will see you now," Varren stuck his head around the curtain and announced. He waved us in, and I took a slow, preparatory breath. Too bad it didn't stop my hands from shaking. Gods, what I wouldn't give for Jae to be here right now. He'd always been better at these kinds of things. Negotiating. Finding a way out of an impossible situation.

I guess I'd have to learn to pick up the slack.

Ducking beyond the curtain, Maylea and I followed Varren into the spacious chamber. Layers of exotic animal hides and richly woven wool rugs covered the floor, creating a patchwork walkway up to a raised platform where a low, dark wood table crouched on feet carved to look like animal claws. More bodyguards dressed in their black, finely stitched leather armor stood on either side of the door, hoods pulled so low I couldn't see much of their faces. I could see the hand crossbows and weapons secured to their belts clearly enough, though. It sent a little quiver of anxiety through my gut.

But nothing could have prepared me for ... *her*.

The Mistress of the Call.

Seated at the end on a large cushion, an extremely elderly woman with frosty white hair and skin set in a deep bronze from years of the seaside sun sat stiff and straight. Unlike her black-clad bodyguards, she was dressed in fine, high-collared robes of layered, ornately embroidered satin that were all arranged on her tiny frame with extreme precision. There was a large, jewel-encrusted pin tucked into the braided bun on the back of her head, and long earrings made of strings of precious stones hanging down to brush at her shoulders.

"Thank you, Varren. You are dismissed," she said, her tone sharp and direct. She never even looked up from where she was busily scribbling on a sheet of parchment with a purple-feathered quill.

Varren looked like his legs might buckle with relief, but he offered a quick, almost apologetic smile in my direction before he bowed and saw himself out without a word.

Uh oh. This couldn't be a good sign.

For a few tense, painfully awkward moments no one said a word or made a sound. I shifted some, wondering once again what Jae would have done in a situation like this. Interrupting didn't seem like a good idea, but I didn't have all night to stand here waiting for her to—

"Brash and brave. Daring and dangerous. Fierce hearts and tempers like a dragon. They say such things about Maldobarians. But you are the first I have met from their royal house," the Mistress said without even glancing my way. "Somehow ... I had imagined you would be taller."

Wow. Seriously? I wasn't short. Average compared to someone like Thatcher, sure, but I still stood a good five foot and ten inches. *Not* short.

I crossed my arms and looked down, sucking my teeth to keep from firing back at her about how I'd been expecting someone maybe a third her age. Polite—I had to be polite. No mouthing off. I needed this woman's help. Just had to tap into that inner calm. Tranquil thoughts. Nice words.

Whew. I could do this.

I forced a chuckle that probably sounded more like a cough. "Yeah, well, my sister got all the looks and my brother got all the height." Uggh. Gods. I'd definitely need a drink after this was over. "Sorry, you're dealing with the family leftovers, I'm afraid."

Nice—that was nice, right? Casual and friendly? So why was Maylea gaping at me like I'd just sprouted a second head?

"Take heart, young prince, I did not bring you here to play mind games or bait you on. I will be direct, as I'm sure you are also aware that time is against us. I hope we can have a very candid conversation," she said and made a final mark on the paper before finally putting her quill down. Leaning forward on her big silk cushion, she turned and clasped her hands on her knee. The Mistress of the Call studied both of us one at a time, as though silently reading our thoughts. The lines around her eyes and mouth were set deep with age, and yet there was no mistaking that predatory sharpness in her eyes.

I'd seen that look before from a tigrex as it prowled the jungles of Luntharda on the hunt. An apex predator. The top of the food chain.

And I was the faundra fawn caught out in the open.

11

CHAPTER ELEVEN

"I know that Arlan the Kinslayer sent you here," she announced, her tone smooth and calm. "And I know what has become of Sulam. What I must know is whether or not eliminating him was the reason you were sent here."

"No," I answered flatly. She was right—we were out of time, and it didn't make any sense to go dancing around the truth. "He abducted two of our party and nearly killed a third. What happened to him later was ... the result of poking the dragon, if you will. I'm sure you can appreciate that I'm a fish out of water here. I don't claim to know all the intricacies of the social dynamics in this region. But I do know, from Sulam's own mouth, that his motives for attacking us were because he didn't want us, or anyone Arlan the Kinslayer employs, doing business in his territory."

One corner of her mouth curled upward into a wry grin that made her dark eyes twinkle. "I see."

Now, I just had to hope Sulam wasn't her favorite pet or partner. Surely not, right? Otherwise, Violet wouldn't have bothered trying to contact them at all.

"Our intention was to sail to Nar'Haleen, not to harbor here. But a storm damaged our ship and we were forced to make port," I continued, while silently praying Violet wouldn't flay me alive for telling this woman everything I knew. "Sulam made it clear he expected a toll to be paid for being here. I don't know if that's the way business is done here, but my partner—who is a lot more affluent in your culture—didn't seem to think so."

"You speak of the Pitathi woman?" the old woman asked, arching one of her sparse, white eyebrows.

There it was again. That word. My pulse gave that hard kick in my chest again and before I could stop myself, I barked back, "Her name is *Violet*."

Oops. Gods and Fate, my stupid mouth! Arrrgh!

The Mistress's eyes narrowed slightly, the light catching off the lenses of her spectacles as that half-smirk of hers seemed to widen a little. "I am familiar with her."

I took a few, calming breaths and tried to recollect my sanity before I dared to say anything else. "We tried explaining things to Sulam, but he didn't want to hear it. Next thing we knew, it was a bloodbath. Trust me, we did not come here to start a turf war on foreign soil."

"And yet ... you will soon be embroiled in one." The Mistress's tone was quiet and thoughtful. She leaned back in her cushion, seeming to relax. "Sulam has long been a thorn in the side of this organization. He had become a liability. We are not surprised to see that his greed and foolishness led him to such a fate. The Zenith's Call would like to extend its sincerest condolences for what you have suffered at his hand. We do not endorse anything that was done by him in our name, and in the spirit of directness, we are not troubled to see him gone."

Oh. Well. That was good news.

"That said, we are likewise *unsettled* to hear that Arlan the Kinslayer is moving his agents toward Nar'Haleen. Especially given the nature of the tensions between our countries," she added quickly.

I sagged forward slightly, unable to stop my shoulders from drooping. This was definitely a conversation Violet would have wanted to be a part of. He was her boss, after all. This was her area of expertise. "Look, I don't know how much I'm allowed to divulge here. But I do know that Arlan's interest in Nar'Haleen has nothing to do with the war. You probably already know about the attack on the Compendium Library. We were dispatched to retrieve a few items that were being kept there." I decided not to tell her that one of those items in question happened to be my nephew, the crown Prince of Maldobar. That felt a little too personal for a crime lord I'd only just met.

The old woman's mouth pressed into a thin, dissatisfied line. Almost like she knew I was holding out on her. But if she could somehow sense it, she didn't push the issue. "And you still intend to go to Nar'Haleen to see this matter through?"

I nodded. "As soon as I can get my group put back together, we're outta here."

Tilting her chin upward ever so slightly, she looked again at Maylea through the lenses of her spectacles. "You've come well-armed, and with no shortage of talent at your disposal. My agents tell me you travel with Violet, a Rajinna boy, another dragonrider, and this one ..." Another coy smile brushed her sagging features for an instant and she leaned forward again, seeming genuinely curious. "But no one can seem to place who, or what, this young girl is."

Silence.

Maylea cast me a semi-panicked sideways glance, and I motioned for her to speak. After all, she'd already proven she could introduce herself well enough to these people.

Her throat jumped as she swallowed, and her grip on her bow tightened. "I am Maylea Broadfeather, eldest daughter of Jaevid Broadfeather of Maldobar."

The old woman's smile vanished, instantly morphing into something like quiet awe. She sat straight and stared, not making a sound, with her mouth open. Then, at last, the Mistress made a gesture to one of her bodyguards.

Oh ... oh crap. No!

Immediately, every muscle in my body went solid. Every nerve, every reflex, came alive like I'd been struck by lightning.

But the bodyguard didn't draw a weapon. Instead, he stepped forward and pulled something from his belt. I had to squint through the gloom just to be sure. Was that ... a flask?

The bodyguard handed it off to the Mistress without comment, and she sat looking it over for a moment before finally stretching out her hand and offering it to Maylea. "May the God of Life deal kindly with us. You carry his light, do you not?"

Maylea opened her mouth and seemed to hesitate, almost like she wasn't sure what to say or do. Little by little, she hedged closer to the old woman and gingerly took the flask from her. "I-I am his Paladin."

"Then may the Fates guard you and those who walk with you," the Mistress said, catching Maylea's wrist before she could pull away. "Remember well who has helped you. Show them mercy, if you can."

Maylea bobbed her head a little and managed a wincing, uncertain smile. "I'll try." She quickly stepped back to my side, gripping the beautiful silver flask so hard it turned her knuckles white.

"Within that flask, you will find recompense for Sulam's foolishness. I know you have been searching for healing remedies that might aid your wounded companion. The contents are the carefully rendered and purified nectar of the Thornwine flower. It is a highly potent healing draught that might even rival the effects of your Lunthardan remedies. It can counter even the venom of a switchbeast," the Mistress advised. "Take care, for such a thing is worth a hefty sum, and there are many who might even kill for it."

"O-Oh, um, thank you," Maylea stammered, now handling the flask like it might suddenly explode. She carefully tucked it into her own belt and hid it with her cloak, then managed a less-terrified smile back at the woman.

"Now, then. To our next order of business," the old woman said with a pleased smile.

Wait—next order? What was there left to say? Or do?

Unless ...

"Your woman, Violet, has reached out wanting to secure safe passage through the desert to Nar'Haleen. I believe we can accommodate that. However, we would require a favor in return."

Every wheel in my head suddenly locked up solid. My woman? No, she wasn't—I mean, *we* weren't, you know, like that. At all. Why would she even think that? Because I'd asked her not to call her by what was essentially a slur name?

"W-We ... we don't exactly have a lot of resources at our disposal, and, uh ..." Great. Now I was the one stammering. Super professional.

"Do not worry, you have everything you need," she assured, that coy smile tugging at one corner of her mouth again, as though she found me somehow pathetically endearing.

Like I was just a sniveling little kid trying not to wet himself during a wedding ceremony. Gods, spare me.

"I believe, in this instance, we can help one another achieve exactly what we want, Your Highness. We have a means of safe passage across the desert to the library you seek." Her smile became cryptic, and it sent a little thrill of uneasiness through my stomach like I was about to jump off something far too high. "And you ... have a dragon."

"YOU DID WHAT?" VIOLET SPUN ON ME LIKE AN ANGRY RACCOON READY TO CLAW MY eyes out. She stormed at me from across our tiny, rented room with her hands already clenched into fists and wrath like cinders crackling in her eyes. "You made a deal with the Zenith's Call?! Why, by all the gods, would you even consider doing something like that without—!"

"HEY!" I shouted over her, throwing my hands up in surrender. I at least wanted the opportunity to explain myself before she ripped my head off. "Look, there wasn't time to run it by you or anyone else. It's not like I set out to have a secret meeting with them—they practically abducted us! I was in an underground vault staring at a dozen armed guards with no way to even send word to you about what was happening. So yeah, I had to make a choice, and as far as I can tell, this is the best option as opposed to both of us getting shot full of arrows and butchered like spring lambs."

Violet's lips pursed up, her head slowly shaking from side to side as though she were mentally warring with herself over whether she should hit me, choke me, or stab me to death.

"Listen, it's ... it's not a bad deal, okay? They've got a caravan of people they're trying to get out of the area before the Nar'Haleenan navy shows up and tries blowing this place back to the gods' doorstep, and they need hired swords to protect it. Simple. It gets us where we need to go, and gives us the benefit of cover traveling with a group of refugees so maybe we don't stick out like a big fat juicy target in the middle of the sand dunes for Sadeera's people to find."

"*Political* refugees," Violet hissed through her teeth, jabbing a finger at me as her cheeks flushed almost as red as her eyes. "Why else would they specifically want a dragon as a deterrent? We're not talking about simple farmers and city folk just trying to flee to safety. These are people that the Nar'Haleenan military will be looking for and wanting to murder. And last I checked, people like that would make us even more of a target—not less—you thickheaded, impulsive idiot!"

Oh? So now we were calling *names?*

Fine. I didn't have to put up with this.

"*You* were the one who wanted their help to begin with," I growled low and leaned down so that we were nose-to-nose. "I realize I was no one's first choice for this mission. I'm not Jaevid Broadfeather, the great, powerful, wise, and charming. Sorry. But I'm the best you've got. If you don't like this arrangement, then feel free to go back to the Mistress and re-negotiate the terms yourself."

Done. That was it. I didn't have anything else to say to her about it. No way was I about to stand there and have a back-and-forth yelling match with her in front of the rest of our group. Out of the corner of my eye, I could already see Maylea and Lukani looking awkwardly away, like two kids sitting at the dinner table trying not to stare while their parents had a spat.

Ugggh.

Spinning on a heel, I stormed outside and slammed the door behind me. I needed some air. Just a few minutes to cool off. Then I could go back in and look after Thatcher. If that Mistress woman was telling the truth about that potion, we'd be able to get him back on his feet and put this place behind us by tomorrow evening. I could get things pulled together, and maybe salvage this absolute wreck of a mission. Ronan was counting on me. Everyone at home was, too.

I couldn't fail.

Er, well, unless Violet killed me in my sleep tonight. That would certainly qualify as failure.

Dropping down on my rear end at the edge of our room's small front patio, I let my elbows rest on my knees and gave a long, heavy sigh. Rain poured and lashed at the stone street before me and wind howled through the twisting streets. I couldn't tell how close we were to dawn, but it must've nearly been twilight by now. With all those churning, stormy clouds choking out the rising of the sun, however, there was no way to be sure. Thunder cracked and rolled, like heavy stones rumbling down a wooden ramp overhead. For whatever reason, that sound took me straight back to Maldobar. We had storms like this all the time in the spring. I wondered what Jaevid and the others were doing right now. I wondered if Isa had gotten my letter yet, and if anyone had finally told Jenna what was going on with Ronan.

I wondered if she or my brother had even noticed I was gone.

I rubbed at my forehead. Gods and Fates, I couldn't keep doing this to myself. I couldn't keep letting my mind circle to thoughts like that. Even if they hadn't noticed, it was really for the better. The less they knew about this mission, the less likely Jenna was to fly off the handle and send her entire military here and kick off another international war between kingdoms.

Calm thoughts. Happy thoughts. I had to have a few rolling around in my head somewhere, right?

I scratched at the stubble coming in thicker on my chin. I'd have to find a chance to shave soon. Maybe today.

I let out a curse suddenly as the sensation of something like needles pricking up my back and onto my shoulder made me flinch. Vexi perched right next to my head, her tiny wings and tail tucked close to her body, and her side against my neck. She made tiny purring, chittering sounds as she began to lick and groom at my hair. I winced as she nibbled at my ear, and I reached over to pat her head with a fingertip.

"I have a feeling that, given your current state, you aren't exactly what the Zenith's Call is banking on when they want a dragon security guard," I chuckled. "I can't wait to see the looks on their faces."

Vexi turned her attention to preening her scales, still purring happily where she sat on my shoulder like a small, scaly chicken on a roost.

"You won't be small for much longer, though," I murmured. "Arlan said his spell would only last for about fourteen days. If I'm counting right, that doesn't give us much time left, and it'd probably be good to get out of the city before that happens. We don't need that kind of attention, especially if Nar'Haleen is about to drop the hammer on this place."

"Y-You ... always talk to yourself ... wh-when you're upset," Thatcher's thin, halting voice spoke up from behind me.

I looked back to find him leaning in the doorway, sweat soaked and ashen-faced. The circles under his eyes had gotten bigger and darker, and he gripped the doorframe like he was trying not to collapse right where he stood.

Gods. What was he even doing out here? He was supposed to be resting. Maybe my argument with Violet had woken him up. Either way, I needed to get to work fixing him up before he got any worse. "Go lie back down. I've got something that should get you back up to fighting in no time."

"I-I know," he rasped. "Maylea s-said they g-gave you ... some medicine." He hobbled forward, pushing away from the door. He barely managed to limp the distance to where I sat and dropped down right beside me. "Y-You really ... think we're all comparing you to Jaevid?"

Great. This had a heartfelt Thatcher-speech about acceptance written all over it. He'd gotten obnoxiously good at those over the years.

I glared away and worked my jaw to one side without answering.

"I-I think ... *you're* the only one ... comparing y-yourself to him," Thatcher said, his voice catching as he winced and wrapped an arm protectively around his torso. That wound must've been killing him. So why was he doing this? Coming out here to talk to me when he should've had his butt in there resting?

Oh. Right. Because this was Thatcher we were talking about. Big, dumb, overly caring idiot. He was like a living stuffed animal sometimes.

"I've always been compared to him," I grumbled as I kept my face angled away, not wanting him to get the satisfaction of seeing the emotions pull at my expressions. "From the very beginning. When my divine power as the Harbinger first manifested, everyone assumed I was his reincarnation or something. They expected me to walk in his footsteps, but the best I could ever do was just stand in his shadow. Oh, I know he wouldn't agree. He doesn't see himself that way. Never has. But Jaevid Broadfeather, savior of the world and champion of the dragonriders, is a hard act to follow—especially for a third-born son with no prospects beyond burning out my days as an instructor at the academy."

"Wh-What about the guy who defeated Iksoli?" he asked.

"That was you, not me," I reminded him.

"Well ... it was y-your mission."

"You and Murdoc were fighting Iksoli. I was doing inventory in Argonox's treasure plunder—remember?" I sighed and shook my head. "I get what you're trying to say, though. And I appreciate it. But it feels like I've spent my whole life chasing someone else's coattails. Trying to *be* something. To be enough. And I guess ... I'm coming to terms with the fact that there might not be a glorious, it-was-all-worth-it moment for me waiting at the finish line."

A heavy hand fell on my shoulder. I looked over to find Thatcher's sickly pale face grinning at me like he wasn't about to drop dead from an internal infection. "You are enough, Reigh. You've always b-been enough, just as you are. I'll f-follow you to the ends of the e-earth. You know that."

"And when I screw it all up? What then? You know my success record isn't exactly stellar when it comes to missions and things going according to plan."

"Then we'll screw it up t-together," he gave another broken, flinching laugh that made his whole body seize with pain. "That's the best part of doing great things with the people we care about—we're not alone with the victories ... or the mistakes. W-We're in it together, side-by-side, to the bitter end."

I didn't say it, but I was beginning to worry about that bitter end part. My mind whirled back to the thought of that grotto. Of reuniting with Clysiros. Of making another deal with her. Gods and goddesses never gave power away for free. There was always a price.

I just hoped I had enough to pay the tab this time.

"Fine, fine. Whatever," I grumbled and shrugged his hand off. "Enough with the mushy friendship speeches. I'm gonna be really pissed if you sit here and die on this porch because you wouldn't get back inside." With a grunt of effort, I looped an arm under his shoulder and helped him get back on his feet. "Let's go see if this potion works as well as promised."

PART THREE

CLARKE

❧ 12 ❧

CHAPTER TWELVE

"We cannot stay down here forever," Noa said quietly. The flames of our small campfire danced in his turquoise eyes as he sat cross-legged beside me, twisting the bone-carved ring he wore on his thumb.

He was right. It had almost been a full two days since we were abducted by goblins and trapped down here, somewhere in the depths of a long-forgotten temple. At first, I had assumed that finding this place hidden away within the caverns, would mean we would easily be able to find a passage outside. I mean, it was a temple, wasn't it? Temples generally had doors. I'd lived in a secret library built into a cavern system, and even we had multiple doors in and out.

The problem was that this particular temple happened to be enormous, fused with ancient sea caves, and seriously lacking in emergency exits. We had already tried exploring some of the surrounding passages, looking for a way out. Since he could see the best in the pitch darkness, Traegan had even gone off exploring on his own to see what he could find, although he admitted he didn't feel comfortable going too far in case he couldn't find his way back to us. In the end, he hadn't found anything except more tunnels adorned in ancient carvings, statues, and ceremonial rooms.

No doors.

No way out.

"We won't," our new dwarven companion, Traegan, groaned. "We'll starve to death long before forever comes."

Noa shot him an exasperated glare, but didn't reply. I didn't know what issue he had with our most recent friend—if he disliked dwarves in general, or if he just found Traegan particularly annoying. Either way, Noa's patience was getting thinner by the hour, even if Traegan himself didn't seem fazed by it at all.

I sighed and looked up at the massive circular opening far above us in the ceiling of the grand chamber. It wasn't an exit. More like a skylight. And it was far too high for any of us to reach even with the little bit of rope we had. Somehow, sitting there with that clear view of freedom looming right over our heads, it almost felt like the universe was taunting us. So close, and yet so far.

"Why do you suppose they put a big hole up there like that? Wouldn't it let rain in?" I mused, thinking out loud more than anything else.

"Probably for sunlight," Noa guessed. "Or moonlight."

Traegan made a thoughtful noise of agreement. "You know, if I didn't know better, I'd say this place wasn't a temple at all. Seems more like a tomb, eh?"

"We haven't seen any remains or corpses," Noa countered.

"True," Traegan shrugged. "Plenty of altars and sculptures of the gods, though. Hard to imagine a place like this was just lost to time. It's almost like it was intentional. Like someone didn't want it to be found again."

I sat up suddenly, my eyes going wide as I stared up at that massive, circular opening like a window over our heads. What if ... what if they were *both* right? Why would they put an opening like that, right here? What was it meant to shed light on?

I looked down, my gaze following the beam of soft moonlight that ebbed down from the opening all the way to the mosaic on the floor. The one right between the statues of those winged, almost elven-looking figures. The mosaic of Avgior, the first Fate.

Shambling to my feet, I walked slowly toward that mosaic again. I'd uncovered most of it earlier, when I first discovered it in the center of all those statues. But I hadn't thought much about it since. Avgior was sort of an enigmatic figure in the divine lore I'd read. He was largely considered to be an evil god, who had sided against many of the other gods in the War of the Stones. He was known to be a harsh judge, quick to anger, and had no love or compassion for the mortals of the world whose hearts he found afflicted with wickedness. But ultimately, he had been killed. Er, well, as much as a god could be killed, anyway.

There were lots of theories about what had happened to him after. The most common belief, and the one I'd read over and over in the library's many historical texts, said that Avgior's essence had been split into a thousand pieces and scattered to the far corners of the world, so that he might never manifest again.

But was that really true? What did that even mean? Was his essence something tangible or was it purely spiritual?

When it came to the gods, things like that could be so fluid and fickle. Scholars didn't even like to speculate, for fear that speaking his name might somehow draw the gaze of that ominous, all-knowing eye that tended to be his symbol of power. Nonsense, of course. Even if the gods did exist, it was ridiculous to think that just speaking someone's name would conjure them up, wasn't it?

I glanced between the opening and the mosaic. It couldn't be coincidence, could it? That the full moon tonight cast a perfect circle of sterling light down over the mosaic, making all the precious stones and bits of gold glitter. The hidden door we'd used to get into this place had the symbol of Avgior's eye, too. It's as though ... this whole place was dedicated to him.

But who would build a temple to a dead and vengeful god? And why would they hide it away?

I could only think of one reason, and it chilled me straight down to the marrow of my bones.

I swallowed hard. Something cold prickled up my spine, along the back of my neck, and all through my chest. Traegan had said that same symbol had appeared on my forehead before. And then there was ... the book. The voice in my head. All it had said was "*awaken.*"

What did that even mean? Awaken what?

It couldn't just be a coincidence that I had somehow opened that door that let us in here. Something was drawing me to this place. Something that seemed to be able to control me in those moments. Or at the very least, compel me to do things I normally wouldn't do and see things others couldn't.

Could this be what was really wrong with me? The reason I had a ... reading problem? The reason I couldn't forget anything?

"Clarke? What's wrong?" Noa appeared next to me, his expression creased with concern.

"I ... think we've been looking for the wrong thing," I said, bending down to brush my fingers over the mosaic again.

Noa's worried frown deepened. "What do you mean?"

My hand shook as I slowly reached up to slide my glasses off, keeping my eyes closed as my heartbeat raced wildly. I knew what would happen when I opened them. I would see—I'd remember—*everything*.

And here, that might be dangerous.

"We've been looking for a door," I reasoned aloud, the words leaving my lips like a faltering whisper. "But I think ... we already found one."

"What do you mean?" Noa's tone had gone stern with disapproval. He knew what it meant when I didn't wear my glasses. Or rather, he had seen the strange things that happened whenever I took them off.

But if he said anything else, I couldn't tell.

I opened my eyes, and the whispers flooded my mind like a stormy ocean's swell, obliterating all my senses and drowning out everything else.

Lock and Key,
The gate shall hold.
The boundary of Fates
And Souls.
Blood and blade,
And twisting Spark.
To fracture,
Break,
And rend apart.

The words tolled through my head again and again, so loud it rattled my teeth and made my eardrums throb. I tried to pull back—to look away, but all I could do was stagger a few steps until I bumped into Noa. He shouted at me, his mouth moving and his expression frenzied with worry, but I couldn't hear him. Only the voices.

Loud—gods, why were they so loud? Where were they coming from?!

Then I saw it.

Tall, humanoid figures drifted around the room like silent wisps of smoke, transparent and featureless. G-Gods! Were those ... ghosts?!

I had no idea, but the sight of them sent a sharp thrum of chills over my body. The whispers grew louder whenever one of them passed closely by, but none of them seemed to notice or acknowledge us at all. They moved in total silence, the outlines of their misty white forms flickering like smoke in the wind as they floated about, gathering in certain places and then moving like a procession toward the center of the room—right where Noa and I stood.

The figures gathered around the outside of the ring of statues, forming a circle. There must have been dozens of them in all, but only three drifted forward from the group, their arms spread wide and heads bowed in reverence. All at once, the three figures reached into their ghostly robes and drew out an object. One held a long knife that looked like it was made from dark stone with an odd ivory handle. The second cradled a small, teardrop-shaped bottle. And the third ... held what looked like a small metal rod.

One by one, each of the figures took a place before one of the statues. They all bowed in unison, and then the one who held the knife reached up to place it in the outstretched hands of the closest statue. Something shook the floor beneath my feet. It made the little pebbles rattle and shift along the floor, like a deep, concussive boom.

Was that ... thunder?

Overhead, I could see dark clouds gathering beyond the circular opening in the ceiling. Fierce gusts of stormy wind filled the chamber, blowing through my hair and making all those phantomlike figures waver and flicker.

The next figure uncorked the teardrop-shaped bottle and poured the contents over the hands of the second statue.

BOOM!

Another crack of thunder split the sky and echoed through the chamber, so loud it even drowned out the constant rush of whispers in my head.

I staggered back, covering my ears as I watched the last figure stand before the final statue holding that slender metal rod. Lightning sizzled and popped through the sky beyond that circular opening, rattling the foundations of the temple and filling the air with wild, prickling, tingling energy. It made every hair on my body stand on end, and my heartbeat race out of control. My body seemed to flash hot and cold as I stood, frozen in place, and watched while the figure held up the metal rod so that it touched the hands of that statue.

CRACK—BOOOOM!!

A massive bolt of lighting arced down from the sky, hitting the raised end of the metal rod.

Everything went white. My ears rang with a high-pitched squealing sound. And for a moment, I was weightless. Floating. Dead? No. I could barely feel my body like a lead weight, solid and heavy, but alive. The whispers had gone silent. The storm, too.

Gazing up, my mouth fell open in awe as an enormous, winged creature passed over the opening. Its huge form eclipsed the moon with bat-like wings, jagged horns and spines, a lashing tail, and two glowing eyes like bottomless pits of infernal fire.

And somehow, I just knew.

Deep down, in the centermost part of my soul, I knew what I had to do. What I was meant to do. As though destiny itself had leaned down and whispered it into my ear. It wasn't a mistake. Coming here hadn't been just a fluke of bad luck. I was meant to be here —ever since I touched that book. Maybe even before that.

"CLARKE!" A pair of strong hands grabbed my shoulders suddenly, shaking me hard, and forcefully smashing something onto my face.

My glasses?

I gasped for a frantic breath as I blinked. My body shuddered with a chill that raced up my spine and tingled along my scalp. I blinked owlishly up at Noa, who still gripped me like he was afraid I might drop dead on the spot.

"Alright, human. Spill the beans, would you? Something's obviously sticky about you, so fess up!" Traegan barked as he shuffled closer, his beefy arms crossed and his mouth puckered sourly.

"I-I don't ... understand," I stammered.

"Your eyes were glowing again," Noa clarified, still not letting me go. "You went still and wouldn't move or speak. It was like you were having some sort of fit."

Oh. Well, that ... made sense. Sort of.

I shakily adjusted my glasses so they were straight on my nose, wiping at something wet that dripped off my chin. Gods, was that *blood?*

"Your nose is bleeding," Noa confirmed. "What happened, Clarke? What's going on with you? That's the second time this has happened here."

I swallowed hard. Of course, he was right. And now I understood a little better why. I just wasn't sure how to explain it to them without sounding madder than usual. Would they even believe me?

Perhaps it was better to simply try and show them. After all, it might be our only chance.

"Bring the curved blade you found," I said as I steadied myself and gazed back up at the three statues, "I think I know how to get out of here."

NOA AND TRAEGAN KEPT EXCHANGING WARY, CONCERNED GLANCES AS THEY HUMORED my instructions. I didn't know how to explain any of this to them, though. Not when I barely understood it myself. I'd seen a vision of this place, like an echo from an ancient past. A memory locked into the very stones of it that had replayed right before me eyes. It was similar to what had happened on the beach when I saw that young man in the black armor destroying our village. Somehow, my seeing problems were getting worse. Instead of just remembering everything I saw firsthand, I was now seeing things that had happened already.

If there was a word for that condition, I'd never heard it before. I didn't know if this was some sort of manifestation of a divine power, or a curse, or just a horrible stroke of bad luck. Whatever the case, though, I couldn't deny that these visions had been accurate before. Er, well, once anyway. That had to mean something, right? All I could do was stammer and stumble through a terrible excuse of a description of what I'd just experienced to Noa and Traegan and hope they didn't think I was completely insane.

So far, they seemed willing to take it on a little faith. Not like we had a variety of other options, though. We needed a way out, and this might be our only chance.

The curved sword Noa had found in the goblin hoard wasn't anything fine, ornate, or ceremonial. But it was sharp. I just hoped it would do. My stomach swirled and flipped as I took it and made a quick slice over the palm of one of my hands. I handed the blade back to him, and he gave me another one of those lengthy, deeply concerned, almost fatherly stares before he slowly turned to face the statue behind him.

The same one I had seen the misty, ghostly figure place a blade on in my vision.

"Put the blade in its hands," I instructed as I moved quickly to the second statue, holding my hand to try and catch the blood that ran out through my fingers. "And get ready. Traegan, you might want to stand back a little more."

Our new dwarven friend arched an eyebrow like he wasn't buying a single inch of this insanity. "Aye, of course. My pleasure. I'll just stand *way* over here while you two carry out some cursed, ancient blood ritual that'll get us all killed. Happy to be of service."

Noa rolled his eyes, but I saw his jawline go tense as he faced the statue and reached up to carefully place the battered, half-rusted blade into its outstretched hands. He drew back quickly, his broad chest heaving with quick, anxious breaths as he stared around the chamber like he was waiting for the whole room to explode or something.

Silence.

Nothing moved. No rumbles of thunder or gathering storm.

Oh no. What if I was wrong about all of this? What if it had to be a certain blade? Or a specific person's blood? We didn't even have a metal rod. This ... this was stupid, wasn't it?

Noa turned slowly to cast me a confused stare. He nodded once, toward my statue, as though silently coaxing me to get on with it.

Right. We might as well try.

Standing on my toes, I could barely reach to wipe my bloodied hand over those on the statue. I let my fresh dribble for almost a minute before I stood back, next to Noa, and waited.

More silence.

Traegan started clapping slowly. "Well, you certainly had me goin'. You ready to come up with a real plan for how to get outta here, or are we gonna keep—"

I let out what was probably the most horribly undignified scream of my life and flailed backward as something whizzed past my head, grazing my cheek with a sudden sting of pain.

I flailed back, searching for whatever it was that had just hit me in the face.

More objects zipped past, one ripping a hole through my tunic and clattering over the stone behind us. Was that ... an arrow? Oh, Fates, was someone shooting at us?! Had the goblins found us somehow?

Out of nowhere, Noa hit me at full speed, looped an arm around my waist, and basically dragged me down to the floor. "Traegan!" he shouted, as he began dragging me along in a frantic crawl to duck behind the nearest statue.

"I can't see them!" Traegan called back. "We gotta make a run for it! Back left corner! Now!"

Noa seized the back of my head and forced me to look him in the eye. It was only then that I realized he'd been hit, too. The feathered shaft of an arrow stuck out of his shoulder right below his collarbone. O-Oh no. We were going to die!

"Listen to me Clarke, you have to run first. I'll cover you from behind. Make for the passage on the far corner of the chamber. I'll be right behind you," he commanded, somehow managing to sound calm and collected despite the blood that was seeping through his tunic around that arrow. "You do not look back. You keep going. Understand?"

All I could do was nod frantically.

More arrows whizzed past our hiding place as Noa took a few deep, readying breaths. His eyes pinched shut and his expression skewed with pain for an instant. Then he fixed me with a hard, brutally focused glare and counted down on his fingers.

Three ...

Two ...

One.

I scrambled to my feet and ran headlong for the nearest chamber exit without looking back.

13

CHAPTER THIRTEEN

With my heart in my throat and tears welling in my eyes, I pumped my legs as hard as I could. My vision swerved in and out of focus and my lungs seemed to squeeze so that I had to fight for every breath. I ran toward the tunnel opening with my head ducked low, trying to make myself as small as possible. Shouts, like barked orders in a language I didn't understand, echoed through the chamber behind me. More bowstrings snapped, firing off shots that hit the stone all around.

Faster! I had to go faster! Almost there. We could make it! We could find a place to hide, and then—

Noa let out a sharp cry of pain from behind me. Oh gods—no! Was he hit? Had he fallen?

Just as I looked back, my foot snagged on an uneven stone. I tripped and tumbled forward, hitting the ground face-first. My body skidded over the stone and rolled to a halt, finally stopping so that I was lying flat on my back. Stars danced in my vision. I gasped in deep, frantic breaths as I rolled over and pushed myself up onto my hands and knees. I-I couldn't stop now. We had to keep going.

Looking up, I spotted Noa only a few feet away. He lay on his side, blood running from the corners of his mouth. He cursed in the Rienkan language as he bared his teeth and began shakily trying to get to his feet again.

A big boot suddenly planted right on his head, mashing him back down and pinning him against the stone floor. Standing over both of us with a crossbow in one hand and a longsword in the other, a tall figure in black leather armor leered down at us with eyes as red as two fire-lit rubies. I couldn't see if it was a man or a woman—not with most of their face hidden behind a black silken scarf tied over their nose and mouth. But the emblem stitched into it, shining in silvery thread, made my mouth drop open and my eyes widen. Dread like icy fingertips shuddered all the way down my spine. I knew that symbol.

A hand with an eye at the very center.

The Hands of Fate. The Emperor of Nar'Haleen's secret guard. Silent agents of his will that operated only in the darkest shadows.

I'd only read about them, of course. But one glimpse was all it took. I knew. They'd come here ... for me.

Just like they'd come to the library. And to the village.

Now, they'd kill Noa, too, right in front of me.

No.

NO!!

Like a tidal wave smashing a dam to pieces, something inside me broke. And what rushed out of my mouth was a primal, bellowing, piercing cry like the roar of a beast. The lenses of my glasses splintered. My body surged with a rush of primal energy. A power—raw, ancient, and furious—that I didn't understand. It pulsed outward from me and filled the chamber with a shockwave that cracked the stone walls, buckled the floor, and shook massive hunks of the ceiling down all around us.

BOOM—BOOM—BOOM!

Hunks of stone smashed to the ground, shattering the three statues, and punching straight through the floor.

Through the cracked lenses of my glasses, I saw the figure before me stagger back and shakily raise their crossbow right at my head. My body burned with rage like hellfire and I thrust a hand out toward him, snapping it into a fist.

Instantly, the Hand agent flew backward, arms and legs flailing wide and head cracking against the floor.

CRACK—BOOM!

Another massive hunk of stone shook loose from the ceiling and smashed down, burying them and splitting more of the floor wide open. Fissures zigzagged across the floor as it all began to crumble right beneath my feet.

Oh ... Oh no. I-I had to run. Right now.

Where was Traegan? Could Noa even stand?!

I whirled to search the chaos, but before I could even take a step, the floor buckled beneath us. I screamed as I plummeted into the darkness below. The abyss swallowed me down into churning chaos. Massive boulders and pieces of the stone floor and ceiling fell and spun all around me like bashing, smashing meteors.

I'd be crushed to death. Or I'd just die on impact whenever we hit bottom. Either way, I'd never make it out alive. I'd never see Kaili or any of the others again. She'd never know what happened to us.

"The time has come ..." A voice, deep and soft, echoed from somewhere in the depths of my mind. The same one I had heard so many times now. The one I knew I had to trust.

"Awaken."

BAM!

Something slammed into my face like I'd just been smacked with a frying pan.

"Come on, Clarke! Breathe!" A familiar voice shouted over me. "Do it again!"

Someone pinched my nose shut and pushed their mouth over mine, forcing air into my lungs with two deep, long breaths. Instantly, everything seemed to snap into focus. My eyes flew open and I shuddered hard, immediately coughing and wheezing for more air on my own.

"There you go," Noa consoled as he helped me roll over onto my side. "Deep breaths, boy. You're all right."

Was I, though? My head throbbed as I lay there, gasping and sputtering. I tried to blink away the bright spots still dancing before my eyes. But the more I moved, the more everything seemed to hurt.

In the weak light, I could just barely see Noa sitting beside me, wiping at his face with the hem of his tunic. Next to him, Traegan gaped at me with wide, horrified eyes and his face smudged with dirt and fresh scrapes. His little pet rat still perched on his shoulder, sniffing the air and wiggling his whiskers.

I couldn't tell much about our current condition, how wounded they might be, or even how I was. My head still swam and spun, and I coughed as the thick dust in the air burned my throat.

We were alive, though, and that was definitely a good thing.

I just didn't understand *how*.

Looking up, I could still see the remnants of the previous chamber overhead. Moonlight poured down from that circular opening. Er, well, it had been circular before. Now that portions of the ceiling had collapsed, it was more of a mangled crack. It had seemed so far away before, but now gazing up at the sky from down even farther in this new chamber felt like we might as well be sitting at the bottom of the ocean.

"Does anything hurt? Any broken bones?" Noa questioned, leaning in to grab my chin and forcing me to meet his gaze again. "Can you see me clearly? Any pain anywhere?"

I slowly shook my head. I couldn't pinpoint any particular place that hurt worse than any other. My whole body ached like I was a tiny bug who'd been shaken up inside a jar.

"Then you're one lucky human," Traegan huffed. Cradling one of his arms close against his chest, I could tell he'd already wrapped it up in a makeshift sling made from pieces of torn cloth.

I guess he hadn't been so fortunate.

"Wh-Where ...?" I started to rasp.

"We don't know," Noa said quietly. He flinched and clenched his teeth as he stretched out one of his legs. Blood had already soaked through his baggy, sirwal-styled pants around the place where something that looked suspiciously like a snapped-off crossbow bolt stuck out of his calf. He'd apparently already tried to wrap it up with torn-off pieces of his own clothes, but we didn't have anything else to use for medical supplies. He wouldn't be running anywhere with an injury like that. No wonder he had cried out and fallen while we were running from the Hands of Fate.

"It looks like some sort of secondary chamber beneath the one we were in before," Traegan finally spoke, his tone somber as he panned his gaze at the small mountains of debris around where we sat. "Stones, what happened up there? Some sort of earthquake?"

I flinched.

Slowly, Noa and I looked up at the same time. Then we exchanged a long, silent stare. My stomach flipped and spun, leaving me nauseous as I waited for Noa to speak. I didn't want him to tell Traegan. Not yet. Not before I understood what was really happening to me. But if he decided to, there wasn't much I could do to stop him. And after we'd all almost been killed yet again, I really didn't have a good excuse to keep silent.

Noa's mouth scrunched and he finally looked away, glaring down at his wounded leg without saying a word.

"We don't see sign nor speck of anyone else in this gods-forsaken temple, and then out of nowhere there's an army of 'em rainin' arrows down over us?" Traegan went on, looking mournfully down at his arm. I couldn't tell if it was broken or injured in some other way. For his sake, I hoped it wasn't too bad.

"Pitathi, maybe?" Noa guessed. "They've been known to live in this region, and since they prefer the underground cavern systems, we might have stumbled into their territory."

"I didn't get a good look at 'em," Traegan admitted.

"I did." My voice scraped hoarsely, and I coughed again as I pushed myself up into a sitting position. My head still throbbed and pulsed with every heartbeat, like my brain might suddenly burst out my ears or split my skull open like an orange peel at any moment. It was hard to think past that pain, let alone talk.

But I had to try. "One of them did have red eyes. But, um, they were, uh, that is ... they were wearing the symbol of the Hands of Fate. Or at least, the one that tried to kill Noa and me was," I said, wincing with every other word.

"Here." Noa's hand appeared in front of my face, holding what was left of my spectacles. I guess he had noticed my discomfort and figured out what was wrong.

My heart sank as I cradled them. The frames were all bent and the lenses were scratched and cracked. I didn't know if they'd even work now. I sighed and tried to carefully bend them back into the right shape.

"You're sure it was the Hands of Fate?" Traegan's expression had gone dark and ominous, his gaze piercing as he seemed to measure my every word carefully.

"Well, I guess it could have been someone else using their symbol," I mumbled as I gently twisted at the bent metal of my glasses. "It was definitely the hand with the eye in the center, though. They had it stitched onto their face scarf."

"How do you even know what it looks like—wait," Traegan stopped and raised his hand before I could even speak. "Read it in another book?"

I rolled my eyes. "I was raised in a library. Of course it was from a book."

Traegan's throat jumped as he gave a slow, hard swallow. "Well that's unsettling, to say the least. They're supposed to be the emperor's left hand. What, by all the stones, would they want with a place like this?"

"I don't think it's the place they're interested in," Noa said, his tone suggestive as he flicked me a knowing glance.

I flinched and hesitated, going still where I sat. Was he going to tell Traegan about me, after all? If so, I didn't want to hear it. It was better not to know how Noa really felt about having me around because I couldn't imagine he'd have anything positive to say. So far, I'd cost him his home, two members of his family, and gotten us lost and nearly killed down here.

"You think the Hands of Fate are after your little human pet?" Traegan guessed, arching one of his bushy eyebrows. "If you are even human at all."

My stomach gave an uneasy, twisting flutter. Not human? How could I *not* be human? What else could I be? Yes, my hair was a little weird, but I didn't have pointed ears like elves. I certainly wasn't a dwarf. What else was there?

"I've heard tales from far across the seas of young deities cutting their teeth in the realm of mortals. Godlings—that's what they call 'em." He leaned closer, his beady eyes looking a lot like his pet rat's as he studied me. "Is that what you are? Would explain all that weird, eye-glowing nonsense, wouldn't it?"

"I-I ... I don't ..." My voice hung in my throat. I didn't know. I had read some speculation about godlings, yes. Most of it was merely that—pure speculation. There weren't any concrete, historian-confirmed stories about so-called young gods. Most of the texts that even mentioned their existence were from Avora, which meant they were all written in extremely complex allegory that most people couldn't even understand.

Besides, no one had ever said anything like that to *me* at the Compendium when I lived there. Not even High Inquisitor Bellavora. Surely, if that were the case, she would have known about it, wouldn't she? She had been in charge of the library for hundreds of years. She knew the texts held within it better than anyone else.

And she was an Avoran elf.

No. Impossible. There was no way I could be a godling or anything like that. Cursed, more likely. That had always been my most plausible theory.

"Whatever he is, he's a part of our family now. We won't just give him up to the Hands of Fate, or anyone else," Noa growled as he began struggling to get to his feet. He hissed and grimaced, gritting his teeth as he tried putting weight on his injured leg. Not good. He might not even be able to walk without help.

I stared up at him, unable to stop my eyes from welling and my mouth from screwing up. No one had ever said that about me before. Sure, I'd belonged to the library as a ward of the scholars and archivists there. But I wasn't their child. We weren't a family.

I'd never had one before now.

I tried to use sliding my battered glasses back onto my nose as an excuse to wipe my eyes so maybe no one—especially not Traegan—would notice. He'd probably just tease me about that, too.

My shoulders dropped and every muscle in my body relaxed as the constant, pulsing pain in my head finally eased. My glasses were basically wrecked, but the spellwork on them still seemed to be working. For now, anyway. Maybe I'd eventually find someone who could repair them.

You know, if we happened to get out of here alive.

"We should see if there's an exit down here," Noa suggested as he hobbled a few feet away, staring off across the mounts of rubble and broken boulders all around. Beyond them, the shapes of something white rose ominously from the dark. Pillars, maybe? Perhaps they'd been carved from white marble or alabaster. It was hard to tell from here.

"Aye. Those Hands of Fate mongrels had to get in somehow, didn't they? Means there must be an exit somewhere. I spotted a few of their bodies smashed over there," Traegan pointed with his good arm. "Maybe one of them's gotta torch? And I'd like one of those crossbows, if we can find one still intact."

Noa nodded in agreement. "Let's do this quietly, then. Minimal talking, and stay close together. If there are any more Hands of Fate hiding down here, I'd rather not make myself such an easy target a second time."

14

CHAPTER FOURTEEN

For once, we got lucky.

Amidst the rubble and ruin, we found several bodies from the Hands of Fate, and were able to confirm that I was correct. They were, without a doubt, secret agents of the emperor. What they were doing down here, however, was still a mystery. If they were hunting me, then how had they managed to track me all the way down here? It seemed as though this place had been forgotten by civilization centuries ago. So how had they known exactly where I was?

Strange ...

I puzzled over that while Noa and Traegan took their time combing over our fallen enemies' belongings and essentially looting their bodies for whatever we might be able to use. Noa eagerly put on a few pieces of their leather armor that fit him, and took one of their longswords that hadn't been crushed by all the falling boulders.

Traegan found a crossbow with a snapped string, but Noa assured him we could fix it the next time we stopped to take a rest. Armed with that, a couple of daggers, and a quiver of bolts thrown over his back, Traegen seemed a lot cheerier as he held up what I considered to be our finest prize: a freshly lit torch.

Having that spot of light made me feel a little less hopeless as we made our way through the massive chamber and searched for an exit. It didn't take long for that feeling to go away, though.

What I had mistaken for columns and arches of alabaster or marble weren't even stone at all. As the light of our torch filled the massive, ancient cavern, more strange white shapes emerged. They towered over us, seeming to be connected almost like ...

Oh gods, it *was*.

An enormous skeleton.

"Sweet singing stones," Traegor gasped as we slowly approached. "What is that? An underbeast?"

"No." Noa moved closer to us, his tone low and ominous as his turquoise eyes panned over the massive bones. "Look at the wings. The claws. This is no beast of our world."

He was right. As the torchlight fell across the huge, horned skull of a creature as big as a warship resting on the dark stone directly before us, I knew. I recognized its shape, with all those jagged fangs and sloping horns, right away. I had never seen one in person, of course. But they were depicted in drawings and etchings, stories and ballads, and in countless books.

This was a dragon.

A very, *very* big one.

I only knew of one dragon, in all the texts I had ever read, that spoke of one this size. But it couldn't be him, could it? There had to be some other explanation—some other beast who had achieved this colossal size— because otherwise these remains might belong to ... Avgior.

A dead ancient god of Fate and Discernment.

It would have explained a lot, actually. Like why this temple had been lost in the first place. It wasn't somewhere anyone would want to come pay respects. It also explained why all the images of his likeness, or his symbol of the all-knowing eye, were inlaid into the details and decorations here. The mosaic upstairs, the depictions of the three ancient fore-gods, and the deliberate use of ritual blood magic to seal this place off from the rest of the world—it all made sense.

No one wanted Avgior to reawaken.

That thought sent a wave of chills through my entire body, all the way to the tips of my toes. I shivered and hesitated, staring at the massive skull as my pulse began to quicken.

That wasn't correct. Someone *did* want him to awaken.

The voice that kept whispering in my mind.

But why would that have anything to do with me? Why was I the only one hearing that voice, or experiencing anything strange? Before, when I thought that Hand agent was going to kill Noa, I had done something—something I couldn't explain. Traegan had said that Avgior's symbol had appeared on my forehead. Noa had told me my eyes glowed.

What did it all mean? How was it connected?

"This isn't a temple," I realized aloud, my voice a halting, panicked whisper. "It's not a tomb, either."

"What is it, then?" Traegan pressed, squinting suspiciously at me again.

"I think it's a prison." I ducked my head and rubbed the back of my neck. "Think about it—it's been buried and intentionally forgotten. There's very few doors, and the ones we have found are sealed with powerful, ancient magic. It's as though whatever was contained down here was something they didn't want to escape."

Traegan shifted uncomfortably, his hold on our torch tightening. "Such as?"

I flicked one last, terrified look up at Noa before I dared to say it out loud. Afterward, I didn't know what he'd think of me. Maybe he would regret ever calling me family.

Because if my suspicions were correct, then the reason I'd been drawn here—by fate or pure destiny—might mean something terrible for everyone.

I bowed my head and squeezed my eyes shut. I didn't want to see the way either of them looked at me after this. "The essence of Avgior, the dead God of Fate," I answered at last, my voice a shaking, rasping whisper.

A boot crunched over the gravel and bits of grit on the stone floor as someone moved closer. A heavy hand fell on my shoulder and gave a firm squeeze.

I dared to look up, and met Noa's gaze. His brow was furrowed with a look of deep concern as he asked, "Do you hear him, Clarke? In your thoughts? Or your dreams?"

My heartbeat skipped and I couldn't keep my jaw from dropping. H-How did he know that? I'd never told him about the voice in my head. How could he possibly guess that?

I guess my shocked, terrified expression gave me away. Noa sank back some, his posture drooping as his expression softened, becoming more like sympathy and grim understanding. His mouth pressed into a thin, uncomfortable line as he gave one, small nod and let his hand slide off my shoulder.

"I know what it is to be chosen by something you barely understand," he murmured so quietly Traegan probably couldn't hear. "Just know, you do not have to carry this burden alone. Whatever happens, Clarke, your family is with you."

Huh? What was he saying? A thousand questions poured through my mind like sand through a sifter. Did that mean Noa had also heard a voice like this? Or been connected to a deity? Which one? Did he still have that connection? I wanted to ask, but with Traegan bumbling along nearby, I knew it wasn't the right time. Noa didn't completely trust our new friend, and I didn't know him well enough to vouch.

For now, I would have to keep quiet, save all my questions, and trust that the answers would come.

"Well, prison or no, there still has to be a door somewhere," Traegan reasoned as he bumbled over to stand right at the end of the skull's enormous snout. He held his torch up higher, making the shadows shift eerily over all the curves, cracks, and uneven textures of the white bone. Each one of its massive fangs was as big as he was. If the beast had been alive, it could have eaten him whole like a freshly picked grape. "A door big enough for a beastie this size to fit through, yeah?"

Hmmm. Fair point.

"I think we saw that door already," Noa muttered. "Remember the large hole in the ceiling?"

"Oh, I remember. But I don't think even that was big enough," Traegan leaned back some, studying the skull and arching one of his thick eyebrows curiously. "I suppose they wouldn't need a big door, though, if this really is the remains of some old, dead god."

I frowned. "What do you mean?"

Traegan whirled around, making the flames from the torch whip and crackle as he faced me with a broad, wolfish grin. "Aye? What's that? Do I actually know something about gods that *you* don't?"

I frowned harder. "Well, I'm eager to learn."

"Wait, wait, wait. Just let me have this moment. Savor it a little, eh?" He rocked back on his heels, closing his eyes and leaning his head back as he took in a deep, exaggerated breath. Then he smirked at me again. "Is this how you feel all the time, then? All puffy and proud?"

Now Noa was glaring at him, too.

"Whenever you're ready," I grumbled.

Traegan took in a few more deep, theatrical breaths before he finally straightened and started to explain. "I happen to know that there exists certain fables that say the ancient gods used to walk this world disguised as mere mortals," he said, mimicking my voice.

"I know that," I growled.

"Aye, but did you know that in that form, those legends say that the gods were more vulnerable? They could suffer mortal wounds, be trapped or caught, and even have children with real mortals? Supposedly, that's how races like the Pitathi, Rajinna, and Avoran elves all came to be. It's also why they preferred picking mortal champions to fight for their causes, or implanting their essences into magic stones, rather than the risk of walking on mortal ground again."

Oh. Well. No. I hadn't known that, actually. Of course, all those races—and a great many more—attributed their heritage to one deity or another. But I'd never read anything that suggested that they might literally be blood descendants of the gods.

Still, something about this didn't quite fit.

I stared past our new, thickheaded, ridiculous friend at the massive skull looming over us. "Avgior was said to hate mortals," I reasoned aloud. "Why would he turn himself into one?"

"*All* mortals?" Traegan quipped, waggling his eyebrows suggestively. "Maybe one caught his fancy, eh? Lured him down here into a trap?"

"I've never read anything like that," I muttered.

"And you likely wouldn't, would you? A god no one liked, who was supposedly an evil beastie, whose remains have been hidden away down here where no one might ever find them, and sealed with powerful magics. Seems like someone's gone to quite a bit of trouble to make sure the world knew as little as possible about this big boy."

I hated it. It caused me literal, physical internal pain to even think about. But ...

Traegan might actually be right about that.

Noa stepped forward, still favoring his injured leg as he stood next to me, his shoulders back and his jawline clenched with focus. "You know how to find the answer, Clarke," he said, his tone low and ominous.

I tensed.

"If any of this is true, then this god may be trying to make contact. He's been trying to speak to you already. Perhaps it's time to take the glasses off and listen."

"I-I don't know what will happen," I confessed. "What if he takes control of my body? What if he makes me attack you and Traegan? What if—"

"What if you finally get the answers you've been searching for? What if you finally understand why the Hands of Fate have pursued you so ruthlessly?" he countered. "There is always great risk in uncovering great truth. Only you can decide if it's worth it or not, but whatever you decide, know that I will stand at your side."

"I'm not strong like you, Noa. I never have been. I don't know if I can control it if ... if ..." My voice caught, choked out by the rising terror that made my throat go stiff.

A calm, strangely peaceful smile spread over his face as he flicked a sideways glance down at me. "Strength comes in many forms, Clarke. You simply have to embrace that your strength might not look like everyone else's. Now, what do you wish to do? Has your time for truth come at last? Or shall we keep searching? Either way, we will have your back to the bitter end."

15

CHAPTER FIFTEEN

I nearly tripped over my own feet again as I staggered forward, slowly approaching the front of that monstrously huge dragon skull. My heart pounded fast and hard, droning in my ears like the beat of a war drum. It made my chest ache and my head spin as I stopped right at the tip of the white snout bone.

I stole a quick glance back at Traegan and Noa, who stood only a few yards away. They wore mismatched expressions of curiosity, focus, apprehension, and withheld terror. I probably looked more like the latter, though. This was foolish, wasn't it? We should be searching for a way out of here, not worrying about whatever was wrong with my head.

A hard knot lodged in the back of my throat as I stared back up at the huge skull. What if Traegan and Noa were both right, though? What if this ancient being was connected to me somehow? Did it have something to do with reading that strange book? The one that had called out to me in the library?

Or ... had I been meant for this even before that? I'd always had my reading and remembering problem. And I hadn't found that book by chance. It had drawn me to it, maybe the same way I'd been drawn to this place, too.

One way or another, I needed to know. This might be my only chance. I couldn't afford to waste it.

I shut my eyes tightly, my whole body trembling as I slowly slid my bent-up spectacles off my nose and tucked them into my pocket. Immediately, that familiar pain thrummed through my head again. The faint, scattered fragments of whispers flooded through my thoughts like a whirling vortex—tangled and overlapping so that I couldn't even understand what they said.

Then, little by little, I lifted my head and opened my eyes. Before me, the whole chamber seemed to vibrate with a subtle, pulsing power. A presence, like a beacon of raw energy, that ebbed off those massive white bones. It settled over my body like a weight, heavy on my chest and bearing down on my head. I bit down hard against the urge to jerk back. To run. To put my glasses back on to get some relief from the pressure that swelled in my head. The voices—they were so loud. It hurt. I-I just wanted it to stop.

But even more than that I wanted—*needed*—to understand. What was wrong with me? Why was I like this? What was I meant for? Why was I here?

I set my jaw and stretched out a hand toward the skull, pressing my palm to its smooth, cool surface.

Instantly, all those voices in my head went silent. The pulsing, aching pain suddenly stopped. The intense pressure burst, leaving nothing but an airy, floaty feeling behind that made my breath catch like I'd been dropped from a great height. My chest prickled with a strange, tingly heat.

"Five thousand years confined to the dark," a deep, rich voice spoke before me. *"An eternity have I waited for you ... my heir."*

I looked up, my heart already pounding like mad, into the face of a man who looked ... like me. Sort of, anyway. He was much older, and had hard, chiseled features with a longer nose, pointed chin, and high cheekbones. But his hair was white just like mine, and he wore it long in flowing locks and interwoven braids down past his shoulders. His eyes were sky blue like mine, too, and they examined me with an intensity that made a cold sweat shiver over my skin.

"You're the voice I've been hearing," I managed to gasp hoarsely. "Who ... who are you?"

His brilliant eyes narrowed to thin, scrutinizing slits as his head tilted to one side slightly. *"I am you. And you are me. We are fragments of a single essence. The only two that remain."*

"The essence of Avgior," I heard myself wheeze.

A cold, satisfied smile spread over his thin lips. *"You have already fused with the third. The knowledge stripped away has now been reclaimed. All that remains is the reunion of soul and body."*

"What does this mean?" I dared to ask. "What do you want from me?"

"I want what you want—to be whole again. To awaken," he replied.

Was that really what I wanted? I didn't even understand what he meant by all that. What would happen after? Would I still be myself? Or would I be ... him? Would I remember anything about who I was? What about how I felt about Noa, Kaili, and the others? Would I forget them, too?

I hesitated, holding his gaze and taking a single, calculated step backward. "What about my memories? What about who I am now? Will all that go away?"

"You and I are already one in the same. Our minds are not separate. I know what you know. See what you see. But what we lack now lies before you. Our true form," he explained, his chin tilting upward some in a proud, defiant stance. *"We will no longer be confined to a mortal manifestation. We will no longer suffer the indignity of such vulnerability. We will be restored. Awakened once again."*

"And what then? What is it *we* want? Where do we go from here?" I questioned, my hands clenching into fists at my sides. I wasn't foolish enough to go blundering into this without all the details I could get. Even if we were supposedly meant to reunite, even if I was just a missing fragment of some larger, powerful being, I still had a say in this. It was still my choice. My destiny. My fate.

His smile was cryptic, like the silvery surface of the moon. Beautiful and ethereal, but distant and completely unknowable. Avgior extended a hand, offering for me to take it.

An urge, like a gnawing, burning, feral hunger, rose up inside me. A need to take his hand that drug me forward a step. And then another.

I sucked in a sharp breath. What was I doing? What was happening to me? Why did it feel like I should take his hand? Like I could trust him?

I didn't know if accepting that gesture would be enough to seal our bond. I didn't know what would happen to me after. But that feeling, that sense of rightness, jarred me.

I froze up, staring at his hand as he whispered in my thoughts—that smooth, deep voice filling my mind once again.

"To put an end to the one that would destroy all we know."

AVGIOR WAS RIGHT.

I knew exactly whom he was talking about. I'd seen that boy twice now. Er, well, only once in the flesh, but I had witnessed firsthand the carnage, destruction, and death left behind in his wake. I had no doubts that left unchecked, he would hurt more people. He would continue to slaughter, apparently at the command of the Nar'Haleenan Emperor. Whatever power he held couldn't continue to go unchecked.

The boy with the mark on his hand had to be stopped.

But was I really the right choice of candidate to do it? I couldn't fight. I had no idea how to use a sword or spear. What could I possibly do against someone like that?

"Our power is more than sufficient," Avgior said, as though he could read my mind.

Um, er, *our* mind ... I guess.

Looking back at his outstretched hand, I couldn't deny that urge to take it. Maybe he was right. Maybe this was what I was meant to do. I could avenge everyone we had lost. I could stop that boy from hurting anyone else.

One question stuck in my mind like a cold needle, though. Before I agreed to anything, before I dared to take his hand, I had to know.

"I thought you hated mortals?"

Avgior's hand dropped slightly, his narrowed gaze widening in a look of genuine surprise. Then, little by little, his expression closed. His sharp brows drew together into a resigned frown. *"Records recorded by only one perspective often carry the bias of that hand. Our story has never truly been told."*

"What do you mean?" I urged. "I need to understand."

"There were mortals we despised. Mortals who sought the same ends others now pursue—to violate our realm. They seek to pillage and plunder our secrets, to steal our power for selfish gain. Our kin could not see it. They were blinded by their pride. They believed none could breach our realm," he explained. *"It was by those mortal hands that we fell. We—who can see all that a mortal heart contains—were torn asunder and cursed. We were imprisoned, silenced, and forgotten. But our essence, though broken, has endured. It can now be reborn. Awakened anew to stand against those who would see that history repeated."*

My mind churned with that information, trying to make sense of everything he said. Basically, he was insisting that this same scenario had already played out thousands of years ago. Someone—a group of mortals—had tried to siege the kingdom of the gods. They'd killed him in that effort, and found a way to tear his essence apart and scatter it so he wouldn't be able to re-manifest and tell his side of the story. That must have been during the War of the Stones, when man warred against the gods. The result of that conflict had led the gods to decide to remove themselves from the mortal world, interfering only by means of chosen candidates who held certain artifacts that were imbued with their power.

Only, that arrangement had ended not long ago. A man named Jaevid Broadfeather, from the kingdom of Maldobar, had ultimately ended the use of those sacred stones. He had been the spokesperson for Paligno, the God of Life, and had shattered that delicate balance—an act felt around the entire world.

That was fifteen years ago, according the records in the Compendium.

Around the same time I had been brought there.

My heart gave a sudden, frantic jolt in my chest. Could there be a connection between those events? Had something happened to me as a baby when that deal was shattered? Was that why my parents had brought me to the library? What if ... what if that agreement for the gods to tether their essences to those stones had somehow stopped Avgior's essence from being reborn? What if that was what had kept him trapped, unable to manifest, for all these years?

I trembled as I looked up at him again, and got another jolt when I found his expression probably looked a lot like mine. Uncertain. Anxious.

Sad.

"They did not hear our warnings before, but they will hear us now," he promised, his tone firm and resolved. *"We will not fail again."*

With a deep, readying breath, I nodded and stepped forward. I managed a nervous smile as I clasped his hand. Warmth like the soothing heat of a winter campfire spread up my arm, through my chest, down my spine, and all the way out to my fingers and toes.

Before me, Avgior's smile was peaceful as he closed his eyes and bowed his head. The outline of his tall form began to glow ... and gradually dissolve to a fine, shimmering silver mist. Little by little, he faded away, dissolving into nothing but empty air.

And within me, that heat grew. It caught like a wildfire and blazed through my veins. It ignited to the very depths of my soul. I felt it rush to every corner of my body, stretching and molding me from the inside out.

I was the same.

But I was forever changed.

And in an instant, everything went completely dark.

PART FOUR

MAYLEA

16

CHAPTER SIXTEEN

"Heeey. Well, well, look who's eating on his own for a change," Uncle Reigh gave a satisfied snort as he came into our room, lugging along a big sack of provisions for our trip. He'd gone out to get rations, new waterskins, medical materials, and a stockpile of arrows for me.

It was all stuff we needed, sure, but I honestly think he was just looking for an excuse to avoid being around Violet. Ever since their little fight, neither one of them stayed in the same room as the other for long. Ridiculous. How were we supposed to keep working together if they didn't get over this?

Sitting at the small fire pit, Thatcher grinned around a mouthful of rice porridge and raised his spoon in acknowledgement. He was on his third bowl of it, thank the gods. It was so good to see he finally had an appetite again.

Only six or seven hours ago, it had seemed like Thatcher might not be able to recover from his injuries. I couldn't remember a time when I had ever seen Uncle Reigh look more worried than when he mixed up some of that strange Thornwine potion into a cup of tea, and helped him sip it. None of us knew exactly how it would affect him, or if it would make any difference at all. It had instantly made Thatcher drowsy, and he'd fallen into a deep sleep on his pallet. Lukani, Violet, and I took turns watching over him to make sure he kept breathing.

Over the course of the day, with the storm still raging overhead and the tension in the room growing heavier by the second, Thatcher slept. Slowly, the color had returned to his face. His fever broke. The dark circles under his eyes faded away, and he stopped sweating.

By noon, Thatcher began snoring in his sleep, and later in the afternoon, Reigh checked his wounds again to change the bandages. Only, this time, when he removed all the gauze and dressings ... there weren't any wounds. At least, not like before. The two places where the sword had pierced his body were fully scarred over. All the redness, swelling, and inflammation were gone. It looked like an injury that had happened months ago, rather than only a few days.

Even Uncle Reigh seemed shocked, his eyes wide and mouth hanging open in surprise, as he carefully examined them. I had seen him treat people with Lunthardan remedies all my life, but I guess this new potion the Mistress of the Call had given us really was a lot more potent.

Uncle Reigh insisted on being cautious, though. He explained that there had been extensive internal damage to Thatcher's body, not just the open wounds from being stabbed through-and-through with that sword. Those were the injuries that could be far more dangerous. So, just for good measure, we left Thatcher alone to keep sleeping for as long as possible.

The time seemed to drag on like an eternity, each minute leaving me more jittery than the last. I cleaned my bow, checked each arrow, and sat quietly with Lukani while the time passed. Alone in the silence, my thoughts ran wild, flying like dragons on warm summer breezes all the way back to Maldobar. I wondered what my parents were doing right now. My siblings, too. Were they worried about me? Had they figured out where I was? Would they be angry when I came home? Or would rescuing Ronan and bringing him back with me be enough to convince them that I really did have a good reason for coming here in the first place?

Mmm. Probably not.

Closing my eyes, I let my head rest against Lukani's shoulder and sat still, nodding in and out of sleep. Being close to him helped a little. It made things seem grounded, somehow. Wherever he was, that was reality. That was where I needed to be.

But as soon as I closed my eyes and let my body relax, dreams tugged at the edge of my mind, too blurry and distant to remember. But I could have sworn I heard a voice calling my name. Was that ... Ronan?

As soon as I opened my eyes, the voice disappeared like dew in the morning sun. It left my skin chilled and my chest heavy. What if it was him? What if he was trying to reach out to me somehow? Hadn't Dah been given dreams and visions from Paligno when he was the lapiloque? Would the same thing happen to me?

I didn't have much time to think about all that because only a few minutes later, Thatcher finally woke up. His eyes were clear. He wasn't shaking or weak, and all he wanted was water and as much food as we could give him. In true healer fashion, Uncle Reigh insisted on keeping his food options mild and easy to digest—just until we knew that he was fully recovered on the inside, too.

Overall, this had to be a good sign, right? A sign that things were turning around? If Thatcher really was healing that quickly, then we could get moving again. We could find Ronan and bring him home.

"We've only got a little while until sunset," Uncle Reigh warned as he brushed past us and began setting out all the materials he'd gotten at the market. "We need to get ready to move. Lukani, you wanna help me get these rations sorted?"

Lukani's warm, golden eyes flicked down to me, and he gave a faint, apologetic smile before he scooted away to help.

My stomach gave a little flutter as he let one of his hands brush mine on his way past. I nibbled at my bottom lip, hoping my face wouldn't turn red. It was silly, wasn't it? To get worked up over something so small? Even if I was beginning to get a little worried about him.

Out of all of us, Lukani had been the quietest over the last few days. He had stuck dutifully close to my side, even after I'd come back from that unplanned meeting with the Zenith's Call. Never out of arm's length. But he hardly said a word.

Before Reigh and I even left to try and find Judan, I had known he probably wanted to go with me. And honestly, I had wanted him to, as well. But I knew Violet might need help —especially if Thatcher took a turn for the worse. So, I hadn't asked. And he hadn't pushed the issue, either.

Now, I wasn't sure what to say to him. I didn't know what was supposed to happen from here. I cared for Lukani. I wanted to stay close to him. I wanted us to talk, spend time together, and learn more about each other. But how was I supposed to do any of that with Uncle Reigh stomping around like an angry bull? Gods, what if he caught on to what had happened between Lukani and me? What would he say? Obviously, I doubted he would approve. But he wasn't my dah, so it wasn't like I *needed* his approval.

Right?

Ugggh. None of this made any sense. I didn't know what I was doing. I'd never been in love befo—Ah! I mean, if this even was love. Was it? Fates, I didn't know! Lukani and I hadn't exactly had any time alone to talk about ... things. Like, um, the things that had happened while we were being held in that arena.

The, uh, the kiss.

Were we even supposed to talk about it? What was there to say? Did this mean we were a couple now? Or was I assuming too much?

My mouth twisted to one side as I watched Lukani begin sorting through all the packages of rations, putting them into piles for each of us. His dark brows were set in concentration, and his bright golden eyes darted around as he worked. Of course, I thought he was handsome. He had a strong, sharp jawline, beautifully angled features, and a tall, lean, but efficiently muscled frame. His pitch-black hair was thick but impossibly smooth, and I liked how he wore it in a long braid down his back. It reminded me of how the men in Luntharda wore it. He had large, strong hands and a smooth, gentle voice, but I had seen firsthand that he could be fierce when he needed to be.

Like when he was protecting me.

The thought made more embarrassed heat tingle up my neck and over my cheeks. There was a lot to like about him—besides that he was handsome. I liked that he was quiet and thoughtful. He didn't ramble on just to hear himself talk. He didn't brag. He had a calm, steady, reliable presence that was easy to get comfortable with.

But could there really be something between us? Something *real?*

I didn't know. And moreover, I didn't even know who I could talk to about it. Lukani had said it was his first kiss, too. That probably meant he didn't have any experience with these kinds of feelings, either.

I sighed and looked down at the bow resting in my hands. Too bad Auntie Garnett wasn't here. I could have asked her. I guess I could have asked my mother, too, but that was a little embarrassing. Not to mention she would probably be too furious with me when I got back to even think about having a conversation about ... um, boys.

Hmm. I wonder if I could ask Violet? I didn't know her very well, but she seemed pretty experienced about life stuff. She was certainly good at teasing Uncle Reigh. Er, well, when they weren't fighting like a couple of angry chickens, that is.

"Where are we supposed to meet the caravan?" Thatcher asked around another huge mouthful of porridge.

"A port city on the mainland called Esfolar. It's the capital city, so it'll be a lot bigger and more crowded. Because of the warning of incoming attack from Nar'Haleen, I'm also expecting it to be crawling with soldiers and guards on high alert, so I need everyone on their toes," he said, intentionally avoiding even looking Violet's direction as he began arranging the items in his own haversack. Somehow, that seemed like an excuse just so he didn't have to make eye contact with her. "We're supposed to be there at dawn. That gives us the night to travel—but don't get excited. It's a long way to go and we have to move by ferry. As if that's not complicated enough, everyone else in this area who believes an attack is coming will also be trying to evacuate. The sooner we get moving, the better."

"I don't suppose the Mistress offered any sagely words of advice when it comes to the best routes to take?" Violet asked, her tone sharp as she kept her gaze focused down on neatly folding up her own bedroll and cramming it down into her bag.

Uncle Reigh didn't answer right away. He sat down next to Lukani with a grunt and began doing the same thing—packing up our belongings and sorting them out into our bags. "She did," he sighed at last. "Supposedly, she has already secured passage for us on these ferries. I guess we'll find out."

Violet made a huffing, snorting sound and still didn't look up.

Not good. They couldn't go on like this forever, could they? Sooner or later, Uncle Reigh and Violet needed to talk this out. The success of our mission might depend on it. With them still locked in some sort of bizarre, who-is-really-in-charge power struggle, any push in the wrong direction could be a total disaster. It could split up our group for good.

And if it did, I didn't believe for a single second that we stood a chance at getting Ronan or the codex back.

Within the hour, we were on the moonlit streets of Sol'Karr once again. This time, however, we were all together, with Uncle Reigh in the lead and Violet at the very back of our group. I couldn't tell if that was because they wanted as much distance as possible between them, or if they were at least in agreement that we should keep Thatcher in the middle of our group until we were absolutely certain he could hold his own in a fight again.

For the sake of my own sanity, I decided to assume it was the last one.

Moving fast, we kept our hoods pulled down low and made our way down toward the port again, following a lot of the same paths Uncle Reigh and I had used not long ago. Only, this time, there were a lot more people moving around out in the streets than before.

Families with children, young couples, shopkeepers, and groups of elderly city folk gathered around the front doors of buildings and homes. They worked together, moving bags and crates onto wagons or carrying them balanced on their heads and shoulders. The farther we went, the more we passed, and it seemed like they were all beginning to fill the streets and sidewalks leading down to the port.

None of them spoke much, using only hushed voices, and they didn't seem to pay any attention to us at all. I guess to them, we looked like just another group trying to flee the city before it was too late. Maybe that would work to our advantage.

Even so, something about the empty looks of despair and resignation on all their faces gave my blood a chill. I shuddered and looked away. I didn't remember any of the wars that had been fought in Maldobar because I hadn't been born yet. But something deep inside my chest pulled tight, like a cord that might snap at any moment. All these people might lose their homes because of a war they had no control over. It wasn't fair. It wasn't right.

But there was nothing we could do about it.

And a part of me—the one that felt pulled as taut as a bowstring—absolutely hated that.

"Stay close. We're almost there," Uncle Reigh warned as we drew closer to the port. I could already hear the distant sounds of shouts and frustrated voices calling out.

My stomach flipped and my heartbeat quickened. The atmosphere of quiet island tranquility was completely gone now. The sense of frantic urgency, fear, and dread hung thick in the air.

Taking a final turn, my breath caught in my throat as we all stopped for a moment and stared at what lay ahead. Last night, everything here had been quiet and mostly abandoned. Now, the road before us was totally blocked with wagons, carts, and groups of people trying to reach the docks. Throngs of people were all trying to move toward crowded ships at once, where dockhands and sailors were loading cargo and arguing with people trying to make their way onboard.

"What a mess," Violet sighed, her expression creased with worry as her crimson eyes scanned the crowds. "You're certain the Zenith's Call has already secured a way for us to get out of here?"

"That's what the Mistress said." Uncle Reigh rubbed at his chin. He glanced back at all of us, as though counting to make sure no one had gotten left behind yet. "Maybe I should—"

"—Be a bit more patient?" a familiar man's voice spoke up behind us.

A bolt of shock surged up my spine and my body instinctively jerked, reaching for an arrow from the quiver at my back. Uncle Reigh stiffened. Violet already had a dagger out when she spun around to see who had come up behind us. Lukani took a protective step closer to my side.

Only, I knew that voice. And I was ready to swear that Uncle Reigh recognized it, too.

Strolling casually up behind us, the man who called himself Varren still wore that long, scuffed up blue coat draped over his wide shoulders. I recognized that—and his arrogant little smirk—right away. He touched his brow with two fingers and dipped his head slightly, like a small salute to Uncle Reigh, before gesturing to the rest of us. "So glad to finally meet the rest of your merry little band."

"And you are?" Thatcher's expression had gone cold, his eyes narrowed and posture stiffened like he expected a wrong move at any moment.

"Your escort this evening," Varren's grin widened. "How glad I am to see you back on your feet. You held your own against so many of Sulam's thugs and have lived to tell the tale. No small feat, my friend. May you wear your scars with honor."

Riiight.

Thatcher did *not* look honored. Shocked and slightly infuriated seemed closer, if that angry vein pulsing in the side of his neck was any indication. Not that I blamed him. The last members of the Zenith's Call he'd met had run him through the stomach with a sword and left him for dead.

Oh boy.

"I take it you are here to escort us away from this madness?" Violet interrupted, as though she could sense this entire encounter was about to take a sour turn. Something in her eyes when she looked at him was all wrong, though. Not distaste or anger.

No, it was more like ... sorrow.

Varren looked her way, too, his eyes going wide for a moment. Then he glanced her over from head to foot like he was sizing her up. His dark eyes lingered on the black, braided leather whip that was fastened to her belt right at her hip—a weapon I'd never noticed her carry until now. His throat bobbed. His brows furrowed slightly and that smile slipped from his lips. A muscle flickered in his jaw.

But I guess he knew better than to start questioning any of us right now.

"I am," he said at last. He turned on a heel and waved a hand, motioning for us to follow. "We can't tarry here. Come along. We would do well to be as far away from this mess as possible. The port is already in an uproar, but we have our ways."

"Oh, I'm sure you do," Violet murmured as she pulled her hood down lower and flicked Uncle Reigh a meaningful glare. "Let us hope they are enough."

❧ 17 ❧

CHAPTER SEVENTEEN

Varren led the way down backstreets and alleys, circling to the far western end of the port where a small break in the island made for a narrow pass out into deeper waters. Two garrison towers shone with huge braziers already lit for the night. The closer one was perched right on the highest peak of the main island's tip, while the other clung to a tiny spit of rock jutting up from the sea just off the coast. The light from those two beacons sparkled over the inky black water, and revealed the shapes of many small boats bobbing along in the choppy sea. Most of them only had a lantern or two to even mark their position, but all seemed to be loaded down with other people trying to flee this place.

The sight made my stomach churn sourly. I nibbled at my bottom lip. Were we going in a little boat like that? It didn't seem all that safe. But then again, maybe this passage was too narrow or dangerous for the larger ships to use?

"We're not going through Banaris?" Violet protested as Varren began to walk us down the much less crowded dock to where other small dinghy-style boats were moored on rickety piers.

"Not if we can help it. The main flow of refugee traffic is going that way, headed for Malis," he explained, offering me a hand and a playful wink as we stopped before a small, patched-together staircase that led down almost to the water itself. There, hidden by the sheer white rock cliffs and shadows thrown from the garrison's beacon, the entrance to a narrow sea cave led back inland, underneath the island.

I hesitated at that entryway, waiting with Uncle Reigh for the rest of our group to catch up. Leaning in a little, I dared to peek into the utter darkness of that cave. Without any light, though, I couldn't make out any details inside. It stank sort of like old, rotting fish, and the walls felt slimy when I dared to touch them.

Creepy. Why were we going in there?

"Hurry on, no time to waste. This cavern entrance will be back underwater when the tide changes, and I'd rather not swim it, if it's all the same to you," Varren urged as he pulled a small metal lantern from somewhere in his coat. It only took him a few seconds to light it, and he fiddled with an arrangement of small mirrors inside that seemed to make the light more focused and intense. Interesting. I'd never seen one like that before.

We trekked on by the light of Varren's weird lantern, navigating the wobbly, slimy, barnacle-encrusted walkway that twisted and wound through the sea cave. My boots slipped on the slick boards that creaked and groaned under our weight, like they might suddenly give way at any moment. The farther we went, the more that salty, fishy smell intensified, and the more I wondered if this was walking us straight into a trap. Uncle Reigh trusted this guy, sure, but I wasn't quite sold on him. After all, he'd put a knife to the neck of someone I cared about. I owed him at least one arrow for that, didn't I? Not like a deadly one. Just a flesh wound. Maybe in the leg.

"The plan is simple," Varren said as he held his strange lantern higher so the light poured over the slippery walkway ahead. "From here, you go to Kosaar, then onto a larger ship destined for Soman Taal. From there, you can take the Great Bay Road all the way to Esfolar, and meet your caravan on the east side of the city."

"I thought Soman Taal considered itself a Damarian city," Violet asked, stumbling and catching herself against the slimy wall to our left. I noticed Uncle Reigh jerk in her direction, almost like he intended to reach out and catch her if she fell all the way down. Thankfully, she didn't.

Violet spat a few words that must have been curses in Sokraal as she steadied herself and continued on. Hmmm. No one had ever taught me *those*. I decided I'd file them away for later ... just in case.

"In a few hours, it won't matter, I'm afraid. We have good information from our agents stationed along the eastern coast that there is a mighty fleet from Nar'Haleen headed right here, and I doubt very much they've come all this way with so many warships to chat about the weather," Varren said.

Violet faltered, her gaze snapping to him with her scarlet eyes wide.

"Yeah," Reigh murmured. "We heard something similar."

Varren didn't seem surprised and shook his head sadly. "We aren't sure if they will withhold an attack and send in demands for peaceful surrender, or not. One would hope so, of course. But the emperor has become very unpredictable, and the acquisition of *Red Duchess* as his flagship has bolstered his confidence, as well as his reckless disregard for sparing the lives of the common folk who will be caught in the crossfire."

"The *Red Duchess?*" Uncle Reigh stopped him. "Wait—wait. Don't tell me. It's another one of those big pirate ships, isn't it?"

Varren's face lit with a mischievous, knowing smile. "So, you've heard of her?"

"No. Just a had a feeling," Uncle Reigh grumbled as he trudged on. "An awful, nauseating feeling."

"It is the counterpart to the *Squall Queen*. The second ship that sails with a drakkon's bond forged into its hull," Violet explained, her tone hushed and almost reverent. "Does the Zenith's Call truly believe they will use her to attack the cities here?"

"I don't know," Varren admitted, his voice softer as his smile faded. "We pray not, of course. Such a thing has never been done, even under the command of the Skyharts. But as I said before, the emperor has grown unpredictable."

No one else spoke as the atmosphere grew heavy, and I had a feeling we were all probably thinking about the same thing. What, by all the gods, would happen to this place if the Nar'Haleenan military did decide to use a ship like that against regular people? The thought put a pang of cold dread in my stomach, and made all my fingers and toes curl with that deep, jittery urge to get as far away as possible from here.

A warm, strong hand closed around mine. I flinched, then looked up into the worried, golden-hued gaze of Lukani. He tipped his head to one side slightly, wiggling his long, pointed ears a little like a curious puppy. It was as though I could hear him ask, "Are you okay?" without the words ever leaving his lips.

I tried to force a smile, but it probably looked more like I was trying not to gag. I bobbed my head once, just in case he didn't get it. I was fine. But I'd be a *lot* better once we got out of here.

He laced his fingers through mine, and gave my hand a reassuring squeeze. My heart fluttered with a little tingle of anxiety, half because I was terrified someone—Uncle Reigh—would notice, and half because ... well, I wasn't sure. Excitement, maybe?

"There!" Varren called out suddenly, lifting his lantern higher and revealing another narrow gap in the rock ahead. The night sky glittered over foaming surf beyond that opening, and the rickety wooden walkway stopped abruptly. Tethered to the very end of it, a trio of those bizarre, swimming, horse-like creatures watched us approach with their brilliant blue and purple eyes wide and their colorful fins flared. They stirred and blew heavy snorts of salty water from their noses as we drew close.

I couldn't help but gasp at the sight of their brilliant, silvery scales that flashed with vibrant colors, even if I'd already seen others before. Hippocampi were as common as horses here, but I'd never seen one in Maldobar before. Perhaps the water in my homeland was too cold for them? Whatever the case, the thought of getting to ride one again made my heartbeat thrill.

An elderly man in a heavy dark cloak crouched on the flimsy wooden walkway beside them, and stood up as soon as he noticed our approach. He stepped forward, exchanging hushed words and a handshake with Varren—who handed off a small bag of something that I suspected might be coins—before hobbling past us back in the direction we'd come.

"Now, then. You will have to double-up, of course. But that shouldn't be a problem. These will carry you far faster than a boat or ferry," Varren assured. "They're also far more discreet. I take it you all know how to ride?"

"More or less," Uncle Reigh huffed as he reached into the hood of his cloak and peeled his tiny, angry little green dragoness from her cozy hiding spot. She hissed and flapped until he let her go, then fluttered over to land on Thatcher's shoulder instead.

"Traitor," he muttered as he started fastening his bag to the nearest of the hippocampi.

Varren stood by, looking on as we all hedged toward our mounts and handed off our wares. All the while, he shifted his weight and studied us carefully, one at a time, almost like there was something he wanted to say.

"Good. Very good. Seems you know what you're doing," he said quietly. "You'll need to take them to the inlet on the north point of Kosaar. There's someone waiting there to receive you and guide you on from there. Look for the blue lantern."

"You're not coming with us?" Thatcher still sounded suspicious as he handed his bag off to Uncle Reigh to tie onto the next hippocampi in line.

Varren stepped back, watching with a tense, uncertain expression. His lips thinned right before he forced another weak smile that never quite reached his eyes. "Unfortunately, no," he replied with a shrug. "There's work yet to be done, even with demons knocking on our door. But I wish you lot well. Perhaps our paths will cross again someday."

After tying down the rest of our bags, Uncle Reigh finally turned to face him. His expression grew tense, seeming to pick up on that uncomfortable reluctance in Varren's demeanor. And for the briefest instant, I could have sworn I saw sympathy, deep and genuine, in Uncle Reigh's' eyes. I didn't understand it. Was something else going on? Did Uncle Reigh know something about what might happen to this man that I didn't?

I didn't dare to ask.

"Go safely. If you ever find yourself in Maldobar, I'd be more than happy to buy you an ale in thanks for your help," Uncle Reigh offered. "Gods keep you."

"Do they ever?" Varren chuckled weakly. Once again, his smile never reached his dark eyes as his gaze panned to Violet again.

She stared back at him, her own expression a flawless mask of indifference. It might have fooled everyone else, but I spotted the way she clenched her hands so hard her knuckles turned white. There was something like quiet desperation shining in her eyes as they stared at one another for a few seconds, like they were having a secret conversation no one else could hear.

Then Varren nodded stiffly, as though he were having to force himself to leave, and gave a small bow before turning away to leave the same way we'd come in.

We all stood still, not saying a word, watching as Varren's tall figure retreated farther and farther out of sight down the walkway. Somehow, it felt like watching him walk to his own doom. But why? I didn't have any real reason to worry, did I? No. No way. The night beyond the opening of that sea cave seemed so quiet and beautiful, with the dark sky alight with thousands of stars.

Still, I couldn't shake that shivering feeling that trailed up my spine like cold fingertips. A feeling that something wasn't right.

I just didn't know what.

"OKAY, LET'S TRY TO STAY TOGETHER AND KEEP A LOW PROFILE," UNCLE REIGH URGED as we all slipped into place on our hippocampi mounts.

Lukani and I shared one, Thatcher and Violet took the second, and he sat astride the third with the majority of our traveling bags strapped down to the back of his saddle. "Everyone good to go?"

Thatcher gave him a hand signal I recognized—something the dragonriders like my dah used to communicate in the air. Dah and his friends used it sometimes when they wanted to say things in front of the little ones that they wouldn't be able to understand. It'd worked on me too, sadly. But now I knew what they were doing, even if I still didn't understand it fully. Using that code of hand signals was probably habit for Thatcher by now.

Lukani gave a thumb's up as he settled into the saddle behind me, wrapping his arms around me to hold the reins. He sat so close that his chest pressed against my back, and he leaned down to whisper right against my ear, "Hold on tightly."

My stomach gave another frantic little flutter of excitement. Great. I kept my head down when my face started to burn again. Why did that keep happening now? Would it always be that way? Or would I eventually get used to him being so close?

Part of me ... sort of hoped not. That tingling feeling that made my pulse skip, like buzzing under my skin, was weird and embarrassing. But he was the only person who had ever made me feel it. I didn't want it to fade away.

With a flash of colorful fins and splashes of foaming sea spray, we darted out of the tiny hidden sea cave and headed for open water. Apparently, that smelly cavern had taken us underneath and all the way to the back of the island. Here, I could see the massive shadowy shapes of the other small islands, sea arches, and towering columns of rock clustered around. Most of them had at least a few specks of light shining against the dark of the night. Lights from houses and villages? I couldn't tell—not with the sea spray stinging my eyes and the wind blowing my hair into my face as we zipped through the waves.

Uncle Reigh took the lead at first, but quickly motioned for Thatcher and Violet to take over once we turned southward. I guess we were counting on Violet to know where we were actually going. Keeping in close to the rest of our group, we followed along at the very back. I kept my head down as much as possible, shielding my face from the wind as our mounts picked up speed. We skimmed the choppy waves and made our way through the night without a hitch.

At first, it seemed like we might be the first ones to actually leave the large port island of Sol'Karr. But only minutes after we had slipped off across dark water, I spotted others making their way along the wider channels. Ships—dozens and dozens of them. Some were larger vessels, and I noticed several about the size of our former *Fog Dancer*. Others were simple dinghies, little fishing boats, and long barges towed by more hippocampi. The only thing they all had in common, besides heading eastward away from the islands and deeper into the bay, was that each one of those vessels was loaded down with passengers.

Even from a distance, I could see them clustered together on the decks, holding lanterns and torches. We were too far away to see much detail, though. Not that it mattered. I didn't need to see them up close to know who they were.

They were others, like us, just trying to get away to somewhere safe before it was too late.

18

CHAPTER EIGHTEEN

Violet must have known it was better if we steered clear of all the traffic. Nothing good could come from being caught up in a crowd like that.

After what felt like a miserable eternity of battling the strong currents that flowed like an invisible web between all these fragments of islands, our mounts began to tire and their pace slowed. Our hippocampi struggled; their nostrils flared as they heaved for breath and shook their heads, their lithe bodies wriggling like they wanted to be free of our weight. They wouldn't be able to carry us for much longer. We couldn't stop, though.

I shivered, curling back against the warmth of Lukani's chest as the sea spray soaked through my clothes and drenched my cloak. My boots would definitely be sloshing after this. So much for needing to be stealthy.

The island of Kosaar was much smaller than the one we'd left behind. It was also much taller, rising farther above the ocean like an arching mountaintop covered in steep wall faces, thick jungle, and clusters of twinkling lights that must have been villages. The shoreline wasn't nearly as steep as it had been in Sol'Karr, and there were broad, sandy beaches with long piers and manmade jetties made of stacked volcanic boulders.

I could only spot one, chilling similarity to our previous island haven—the stream of ships and people trying to leave it. It put a knot in the pit of my stomach as Violet guided us around the island, just far enough offshore that we didn't get caught up in the traffic leaving from all the small ports along the beach.

Finally, beyond an especially large jetty topped with white stone buildings on the northernmost tip of the island, an inlet opened to what looked like a more residential port filled mostly with fishing vessels. All of them were alight with activity, torches, and people filing aboard. But at the very end, a shadowed figure stood alone in a long dark cloak, holding up a lantern that glowed with an eerie bluish light.

A shaky breath leaked past my lips. Varren hadn't been bluffing. The Zenith's Call really had made arrangements for us to get out of here safely. And so far, it was all going to plan. A rare treat, especially given how things had gone for us on this mission so far.

Maybe we'd get through this without another disaster.

Ehhh. Probably not.

Violet led the way up to the end of the dock, right to where the cloaked figure stood waiting. Only after we'd sidled up to dismount and unload our gear, did the figure move at all. They stepped closer, holding the lantern higher, so the blue glow fell over their features and gave us a better look at what we were doing.

A middle-aged woman's stern face gazed down at us from underneath the heavy hood, her amber-gold eyes keen and critical as she watched. She didn't say a word until we had finished unloading and belting on our packs and gear again, leaving the hippocampi tied to the dock.

"There is not much time. Come quickly and speak to no one," she ordered sharply, her tone thick with a Damarian accent.

We obliged. With Violet still leading our group, and Uncle Reigh bringing up the rear, we followed the woman with the blue lantern away from the docks and into the narrow, twisting streets of the island. Here, the smell of the rich jungle soil and many flowering trees and plants filled the air and reminded me of Luntharda. The roads seemed to bend and move with the land, rather that being cut into it like on Sol'Karr, and we wound a path all the way around the eastern shore until we reached a point where a majestic overlook offered a view off to the south.

My breath caught at the sight of a massive stone bridge that arced over the ocean, bridging the main body of Kosaar and a much smaller island close by. The bridge itself stood so tall ships could easily sail beneath it, and the smooth surface of its pearly white stone shone in the ambient glow of star and torchlight. The sides had been carved in the shape of two hippocampi, their long fishlike tails rippling and finally meeting in the middle of the structure. Crowds of people moved like a stream of winking, bobbing stars across it.

"Take this road to the bridge," the woman commanded, turning abruptly to me and holding something out like she wanted me to take it. "Look for the ship called *Sea Cat*. It's a fishing vessel. Show the captain this, and you will be allowed onboard. But you must hurry. They will depart very soon, with or without you."

Peering into her open palm, I studied the large silver coin she offered. The side I could see had the emblem of the Zenith's Call carved into it—a crescent moon with a sword through it. I managed to nod as I took the coin and tucked it quickly into my pocket.

"Keep that talisman with you, as it may afford you the Call's help in the future," she advised as she licked her fingers and reached swiftly into her lantern to douse the flickering blue-tinted flame. "But I would warn you not to use it lightly."

"Understood," Uncle Reigh said. "Thank you."

The woman flashed him a curious glance out of the corner of her eye, almost like she wasn't sure why he would thank her at all. But she didn't say another word as she turned and left back down the road, departing in much the same the same way Varren had. Strange. These people came and went like the wind, vanishing like shadows into the night, and following orders better than some well-trained soldiers did at home.

Part of me sort of envied that. Their sense of duty, that is. I wondered if that was what had appealed to Auntie Garnett and Violet when it came to working for Arlan the Kinslayer. Was his organization this disciplined, too? Probably, based on what little I had seen. Violet seemed very efficient and calculative in her movements, anyway. Like a lioness on the hunt, she always moved with a cautious purpose. In some ways, she reminded me of Uncle Murdoc, but with *way* better social skills.

Er, well, unless it came to dealing with Uncle Reigh, I guess. Oops. I guess something about him set her off differently. He had that effect on lots of people, though. Sort of like stepping on a pinecone you didn't know was hidden in the grass. Most of us were just used to it. He was basically all bark when it came to that fiery temper of his. Deep down, I knew Uncle Reigh was a huge softy. I'd seen how he baby-talked to that dragon of his when he thought no one was looking.

Embarrassing.

No one spoke as we struck off down the road, walking fast and making our way closer and closer to the massive, white stone bridge. We didn't pass many others on the road, and the uneven cobblestones left the bottoms of my feet sore by the time we finally reached an intersection with a larger avenue. That one seemed to lead right to our destination, and there were more people moving along it with carts, wagons, and heavy packs loaded down with everything from babies and bedrolls to chairs and cages of chickens. One wagon even had a string of goats tied behind it like ducklings in a row.

No one even looked our way as we fell in step with the crowd, clustering together, and keeping our heads down and hoods up. Lukani was the only one I was really worried about when it came to getting negative attention. Several people had warned us about how his people, the Rajinna, were treated here. We had already experienced some of that firsthand on the pirate ships, and I wasn't eager to see that happen again anytime soon. He could have shapeshifted into an animal again, but Violet had urged him to save his magic in case we needed it in an emergency. So, instead of riding on my shoulder as a mouse or a crow, he had opted to tuck his tail down into his pant leg and keep his head down to hide his greenish complexion.

I guess it was working because no one had even given him a second glance. It probably helped that most people—including us—were much more focused on trying to flee the islands than studying anyone's face.

The closer we got to the bridge, the larger it seemed. It wasn't just some simple structure used to bridge these two islands. It was a monument that had probably taken decades to carve and set in place. I couldn't keep my mouth from hanging open as we began to cross, passing by lines of city guards in full regimental armor who must have been posted for crowd control. They looked on with stern expressions, holding torches and spears, but not talking to anyone.

My heartbeat skipped and stammered when one of them locked gazes with me for an instant, and I felt the full weight of my bow and quiver belted across my back. Fortunately, a second later, he looked on and didn't seem interested in who I was at all.

Whew.

The entire bridge spanned probably a half a mile from one end to the other, but crossing it forced all those crowds filtering in from the streets around the island into a bottleneck. It brought traffic to a crawl, and even though we were on foot, we got stuck in the dense group of people right away. With everyone bumping along shoulder-to-shoulder, Uncle Reigh turned and motioned to Thatcher in that hand-code again.

Thatcher answered him, his hands blurring through the gestures, before he whispered back to us. "Keep together in a line, and hold on to each other's packs."

Violet, Lukani, and I nodded and planted our hands on each other's backs, sort of like that string of goats we'd passed earlier. It kept us within arm's length of one another as we snaked through the crowd, dodging and weaving through other groups and past the line of carts and wagons.

I tried not to look at anyone, but my gaze caught on the haunted faces of children and young mothers cradling babies. I'd never seen fear like the kind that shone in their wide eyes. It made that knot in my stomach tighten and twist until I wanted to throw up. My hold on Lukani's bag tightened. These people were being forced to leave everything they knew behind. And for what? An Emperor's pride?

I clenched my teeth and bowed my head lower. Tears welled in my eyes and I tried not to look at them anymore.

Dah had always said that wars were selfish things that often caused the least fortunate to suffer the most. I'd never understood what he meant by that before. Wars seemed so necessary, especially when someone else was in the wrong. Now ... it was all too clear. And it stung at my heart like I'd swallowed a fistful of needles.

I had seen and done a lot of unsavory things since I left my home, but I knew I would remember these faces forever.

By the time we finally reached the midpoint of the bridge, the crowd had come to a complete standstill. I guess there was only so much room on that smaller island, and they could only get people onto the boats there so fast. There was bound to be a delay.

Only, we didn't have time for a delay. Our ship might leave without us, and then we would be stranded here. We might miss the caravan altogether. Somehow, we had to get to our ship—now.

"This isn't going to work," Uncle Reigh grumbled bitterly as he turned back to face us, his jaw tense and brow locked into a frustrated scowl. "We'll never get there in time."

Lukani began to raise his hand like he was volunteering. "I-I could—"

"NO," we all growled at once. No way were we going to risk him exposing his magic right here in front of all these people, who might attack him just for being Rajinna. Nope. Not going to happen.

"You have a better idea, then?" Lukani countered, his voice edged with annoyance as he crossed his arms.

We didn't.

And an instant later ... it didn't matter.

BOOOM!

An explosion burst through the air with a force that hit my body like a punch to the chest. I was instantly thrown forward as the whole bridge shook violently. My vision swerved and spotted as I landed on my hands and knees, my ears ringing with the muffled sounds of screams, shrieks, and shouts all around me.

Wh-What was happening? Was it an earthquake?

CRAAACK!

The solid white stone of the bridge splintered with a web of cracks that spread out beneath me. O-Oh gods. Was the bridge collapsing?!

Up! I had to get up!

Shambling to my feet, I squinted through the tangled, panicking mass of people all scrambling around me. They stepped on my cloak and kicked my side as they ran past, all pushing and panicking. I screamed when someone stepped on my hand and curled back into a ball, trying to cover my head. Trampled—I'd be trampled to death!

"MAYLEA!" A deep familiar voice shouted over me like a crack of thunder. "Get away from her! I said GET OFF!"

People flew away from me, shoved aside like straw practice dummies as they tried running over me. Then a strong hand seized my arm and dragged me upright with one powerful yank. I gasped and wheezed, still trying to get my vision to clear as I stared in numb, paralyzed shock into Thatcher's snarling face.

"Are you alright?" he shouted over the chaos.

I-I didn't know. Fates, what was happening? I managed to nod shakily, and opened my mouth to ask where Lukani and the others were—but I didn't get a single word out.

BOOOM!

The bridge shook again, knocking me into Thatcher's side. He snagged an arm around my shoulders and held me tightly against his chest, holding onto the bridge's stone railing with his other hand so we didn't fall again. "Hang on!" he yelled.

I tried. The crowds battered against us as they ran in all directions. Held tight against Thatcher, I searched all around for faces I recognized. Uncle Reigh? Lukani? Violet? I-I couldn't see them anywhere. With a shriek of panic, Vexi took flight from Thatcher's shoulder and disappeared, flapping away into the dark like a scaly green bat.

A sudden burst of light bloomed in the night, filling the horizon with the scarlet glow of fire. The island—Kosaar—was burning!

My heart immediately dropped to the soles of my boots. My knees threatened to buckle as my gaze caught on a cluster of dark shapes floating in the water less than a thousand yards from shore.

"Look!" I yanked on Thatcher's sleeve as hard as I could.

With all their lamps and cabin lights unlit, the host of black warships were nearly invisible in the night until their second blast of unified cannon fire lit up the dark. Gods and Fates, there must have been twenty of them! Sleek and bristling with gun ports down each side, the Nar'Haleenan warships slipped effortlessly through the dark water, shifting formation as quickly as a flock of blackbirds.

BOOM!

In the distance, another thunderous explosion lit up the night. Another island began to burn.

Then another.

And another.

Tears filled my eyes. I screamed. Then, all at once, the breath was snatched from my lungs. My eyes widened as I stood, utterly paralyzed, staring at the arcing, serpentine body of something enormous breaching the surface of the water right in front of our bridge. I knew what it was—even before I saw its massive head break the surface again just long enough to consider us with one, gigantic, wagon-wheel sized eye.

A drakkon.

It looked almost exactly like the one that we had seen swimming around the *Squall Queen*. But instead of scales of blue and yellow, this one was as red as fresh blood, with stripes of lime green, and frilled fins of rich purple. Its massive body coiled and arced in the water, big enough to sink a ship with a mere flick of its tail.

It wasn't focused on the ships, though.

Everything seemed to stand still, like the whole world had frozen around me, as the drakkon rose up in the water and latched its clawed front legs onto the bridge. The beast's huge talons cracked through the stone bridge, sending huge chunks of it to the ocean floor. It opened its huge jaws and hissed down at the crowds still scrambling to get away like caught mice.

Then its throat began to swell and balloon up as its head coiled back, almost like a dragon preparing to breathe fire. Only ... that wasn't possible, was it? Sea beasts wouldn't breathe fire, would they?

The drakkon's mouth opened wide with a furious screech right before it spat a river of dark purple liquid all over the bridge. The substance spattered across the white stone with an immediate hiss. A sickly, acrid smell filled the air like burning hair. The stone immediately began to bubble and foam as it melted.

Gods and Fates it was ... acid.

Screams and wails filled the night. People ran, crawled, and staggered over one another in every direction to get away. More began jumping off the bridge, their screams fading away as they fell to the churning ocean below.

The drakkon let out deep, rumbling, popping sound and swung its head around, watching everyone flee before it like ants off a log. His huge eyes blinked, fins flaring as it swung its head directly toward us. Its throat began to swell up again, like it was preparing to spit another river of acid.

O-Oh ... Oh gods.

Thatcher squeezed me harder as we both stared, frozen in terror. We ... we had to run. To try to get away before that thing bathed the whole bridge in acid.

But where would we go? The islands were burning. There was no safe place. Nowhere to run. Nowhere to hide.

We were trapped.

"Stay close to me!" Thatcher shouted suddenly, letting me go and thrusting his hand upward to the open sky. The rings of his eyes ignited, burning vibrant gold as the wind whipped up around us.

WHOOSH!

The drakkon spat another avalanche of boiling, sticky purple acid right toward us. It popped and sizzled as it hit Thatcher's shield of crackling golden energy. But not a single drop made it through.

Thatcher groaned through his teeth, widening his stance. His strong shoulders flexed as he leaned into the gesture, standing with his hands outstretched overhead and his palms glowing like molten metal. "I can't hold it for long," he warned. "Get ready to run!"

Run? Run where?!

Tears ran down my face. I wanted to hide, but I couldn't look away. A single word rose up from within me, a cry for help I'd sworn I wouldn't speak out loud.

But I couldn't help it.

I wanted him. I needed him.

I couldn't do this on my own.

I needed ...

"DAH!!" I cried his name at the top of my lungs.

A shrieking call split the sky overhead like the screech of an eagle rising over the rumble, crash, and boom of battle all around us. Thatcher and I looked over at the same time—just in time to spot the glimmer of firelight catching over translucent wings and mirror-like scales. A shrike? At first, I couldn't tell through the wavering energy of Thatcher's shield.

His brilliant yellow eyes were fixed on me with purpose, zooming straight for us through the falling debris and skimming the crowds.

My heart hit the back of my throat.

O-Oh! Oh, gods! I knew that shrike!

"LUKANI!" I screamed.

He gave an answering roar, already flaring his wings and stretching out his clawed front legs.

A sudden wave of determined fury took my mind like a firestorm. This was it. I could feel it like the weight of heavy armor falling over my shoulders. This was the moment I'd been waiting for—the one I had been training for my whole life. I was scared. Terrified, actually. But that didn't matter. My friends needed my help.

And I would fight for them.

"Drop the shield," I shouted to Thatcher as I pushed away.

"What?!" he began to protest.

"DO IT!" I demanded. "I'll meet you at the ship!"

He didn't answer, but his dome-shaped shield of shimmering golden light suddenly burst like a soap bubble. It sent glittering sparks showering through the air around me as I bolted for the edge of the bridge—straight into Lukani's flight path. It was a steep drop. Probably fifty feet or more to nothing but dark water below. But I didn't hesitate. Lukani always had my back.

I jumped into the open air without ever looking back.

PART FIVE

REIGH

19

CHAPTER NINETEEN

BOOOM!!

A sound like thunder split the sky and lit up the night with a fiery explosion. In an instant, it was total chaos.

Attack—we were under attack!

The bridge cracked like a dried-out twig under my boots, shuddering and nearly knocking me to my knees. Gods and Fates, what the heck was happening?

People ran screaming, trampling over one another, clawing, fighting, and flailing to get away. They swept over me like a roaring landslide, pummeling me on every side. Flinging a hand out, I let out a cry as I caught the side of wagon and managed to drag my body against the current of people. I huddled there, searching the terrified faces of the townspeople. But through the floundering, scrambling crowds, I couldn't see any of them. Not Thatcher, Maylea, Lukani, or—

"REIGH!" Violet's voice screamed suddenly off to my left.

I whirled around, spotting a familiar ripple of white hair getting swept away into the rushing mobs that all pushed toward the opposite ends of the bridge all at once.

Curse it! I wasn't going to lose everyone like this!

Letting go of the wagon, I shoved and fought my way through the desperate crowds, flinging a hand out at the last second to catch Violet by the wrist. Her hand immediately clasped onto my forearm, gripping me like a lifeline.

I dragged her in closer, yanking her from the roiling tide of panicked townsfolk. Her wide, terrified scarlet eyes stared up at me with a little blood dribbling from a fresh cut across her forehead. I guess she'd taken more of the impact, or been knocked to the ground.

"Are you alright? Where are the others?!" I yelled over the chaos.

She just stared back at me blankly, eyes wide and face pale, as though she were in shock.

Not good.

Fates, we had to get out of this nightmare. We had to get to shore—preferably to that smaller island where our ship was waiting.

But where was the rest of our group?

"Stay close to me!" I shouted again, keeping my hold on Violet's arm and beginning to drag her behind me through the masses. I shouted for the others, searching the terrified crowds around me for any sign of Thatcher, Maylea, or Lukani.

I winced, snarling a curse as something sharp poked at the back of my shoulder. Reaching back, I grabbed a fistful of scales. Vexi?! My tiny dragoness gave a crowing shriek and hiss of dismay, and I immediately let her go. Well, at least I hadn't lost her, too. Gods, what I wouldn't give for her to be her full size again. That would have solved a whole constellation of problems.

Time to make do. My specialty.

Pulling Violet in closer, I grabbed her by the shoulders and shoved her right in front of me, holding her there and shouting down into her ear so I knew she would hear me, "We're going to the shore! Do whatever you have to—just get there! If we get separated, meet at the ship!"

Violet's haunted, wide-eyed expression suddenly snapped into a smoldering glare of determination. Her eyes narrowed, lips pressing together tightly, and she nodded.

Good girl.

I let her go.

The second her shoulders slipped from my fingers, the bridge shuddered under our feet. I staggered again. Only a few steps ahead of me, a much larger man shoved Violet out of his path as he ran by. She staggered back, hitting my chest and nearly knocking me backward, too. A new chorus of horrified screams pierced the air. We both turned in unison, just in time to see the monstrous head of an all-too-familiar sea monster rise up from the depths behind us.

Oh ... gods.

All the breath rushed out of me at once. I couldn't move. I couldn't think. Every muscle locked up solid as stone as I stared up into the giant eye of a drakkon. Not the same one as before—so that must mean ...

WHOOOOSH!

The gargantuan monster spat a torrent of a dark purple liquid, splashing it over the bridge before us. Immediately, the air was filled with a rancid stench. It reminded me a little of shrike venom. The stone melted away as the purplish ooze turned anything it touched into nothing but goo. It sent large pieces of the bridge and dozens of people plummeting fifty feet to the dark, churning water below.

Was that acid?!

Violet screamed, pitching around wildly all of a sudden. She flung one of her arms around like it was on fire. Gods! Some of it had splashed onto her leather bracer, and was quickly melting through it.

I dove for her, gritting my teeth and snatching a dagger from my belt. I grabbed her arm at the elbow and ran my blade along the seam of her bracer, cutting all the leather straps that held it in place and letting it fall. It hit the ground with a smack and a hiss, melting into a puddle of sludge.

There wasn't time for any words of thanks, though. The drakkon heaved in another breath, as though preparing for a second wave of acid.

"RUN!" I yelled, and dragged Violet forward. We wouldn't make it far. I knew that. But we just had to reach it—the one place I could see to take cover.

WHOOOOSH!

A second wave of acid poured over the bridge, and we dove together under a wagon left abandoned on the bridge. I immediately threw my body over hers, just in case any acid splashed up underneath.

A fresh cacophony of screams tore through the night. People wailed in pain. The smell of burning flesh made my stomach turn. I shut my eyes tightly, and waited for the pain.

CRAAAACK!

The ground under us shifted dangerously. The stone splintered like a broken eggshell. The wagon on top of us began rolling as the area on the bridge where we crouched tilted dangerously. Oh gods, it was breaking off! We were going to fall!

"CRAWL! GO!" I panicked and reached down, grabbing Violet's belt and dragging her up in front of me again. "HURRY!"

As the wagon rolled backward, we scrambled forward on our hands and knees to get out. The stone cracked and groaned, tipping slowly toward the churning sea. We were almost out. We could make it. We'd find a way to shore and then—

Something throttled me from behind, snatching me to a halt. I grabbed at my neck, finding the collar of my cloak pulled tight. Caught. I-It was caught on something! I twisted and gasped, trying to get free as I was dragged backward. I barely caught a glimpse of the other end of my cloak, twisted up in the wagon wheel, as it slowly rolled back.

I tried to call out. To scream for help. But I couldn't get a breath. And Violet didn't see me. She still crawled forward furiously, scrambling to get to solid ground as the bridge around us began to buckle and break apart.

But I couldn't get free.

M-My knife. I'd just had it. I must have dropped it. If I could find it, I could cut my cloak. It had to be on the ground somewhere nearby.

There!

I spotted it lying only a few feet away. Stretching my hand, I tried to grab it. Just a little farther. An inch. I could get it. I had to!

CRAAAACK!

With a violent jolt, the slab of bridge beneath me gave way.

I fell.

The broken edge of the bridge slipped away as I plummeted, my cloak still tangled up in the wagon wheel, down toward the dark depths of the ocean far below.

I WAS NO STRANGER TO VIOLENCE AND GORE. I'D BEEN TANGLED UP IN THE MOST BRUTAL war Maldobar had ever seen when I was only seventeen. I'd been responsible for unspeakable carnage. I'd held the power of death itself in my hands. But as I hit the water, dragged beneath the surface farther and farther into the cold depths, I couldn't remember a time when I had ever been more terrified.

Or sure that I was going to die.

Bodies hung in the dark water around me, falling to the abyss, or kicking and trying to swim away from it. Flashes of fire lit up the sky beyond the surface that slipped farther and farther away. Huge pieces of the bridge splashed down around me, sinking faster like massive stone moons down into the dark.

One plummeted right past, nearly hitting me and smashing into the wagon that was still dragging me down, deeper and deeper. My ears popped. My lungs spasmed. My vision began to grow dim. Where was the surface? I couldn't tell which way was up or down. My arms and legs grew heavy.

I had to do something. I couldn't ... I needed ... I-I ...

"There you are, brother. In trouble once again, I see. Some things never change, do they?" A hissing voice pierced my mind like a white-hot spike. *"Didn't I tell you before? We're running out of time. Now just look at this mess. All because you're still in denial."*

I couldn't see him. But I didn't need to. His voice curled through my head like a poisonous smoke, filling my every thought.

Noh.

"This is the final warning. Your last chance. Complete the rite. There is much work to be done," he snarled, each word as sharp as a dagger's point in my brain. *"Rise and remember our place."*

My eyes flew open as my whole body spasmed again. I coughed a burst of bubbles into the dark as a rush of sudden strength burned through every muscle, drawing my body tense all at once. There wasn't time to question it. I only had seconds now. I kicked downward with all my might, swimming along with the speed of the wagon until I felt the neck of my cloak go slack. I yanked it over my head and swam downward, hanging in the water for a moment as I watched the wagon continue to sink farther and farther away.

Then it was gone—lost to the ocean depths below.

I kicked for the surface, swimming as hard as I could as my lungs began to ache, like a washrag twisted in someone's fist. Far overhead, the rippling red of the surface seemed so far away. My vision tunneled again. My chest shuddered. But I didn't stop.

Curse it all, I was *not* going to die here.

I broke the surface with a desperate, sputtering gasp. My arms and legs still felt heavy and sluggish as I treaded water, trying to figure out where the heck I was. Somewhere under the remains of the bridge, obviously, but I needed to find the shore.

Vexi let out a tiny shriek of alarm as she circled me in the air, puffing tiny plumes of fire as though to warn off anyone from getting too close to me. Heh. Well, it was a nice thought, anyway.

A huge black shape slid past me over the water barely fifty yards away, soundless and almost featureless. But I knew the outline of it against the glow of fire on the islands. A ship—big and bristling with cannons. The sails on all three of its masts puffed full in the night wind, speeding it along as fast and silent as a shadow over the water.

A Nar'Haleenan warship.

It wasn't alone, though. There were more everywhere I looked, moving in perfect synchronization to form firing lines at the islands and line of fleeing boats. They angled themselves broadside, and then with a deep, concussive *BOOOM*—they fired all at once.

Gods and Fates. Those fleeing Rienkan ships were full of innocent civilians, not soldiers. This wasn't war. This was slaughter.

I bit down hard against the anger that burned like cinders on my tongue. I had seen this kind of cruelty before, and I had helped to defeat it.

I could do it again.

I ... *wanted* to.

A screeching roar overhead drew my gaze upward to the glint of red flame catching off mirror-like scales. What the—?

My heart hit my throat like I'd been punched as the graceful silhouette of a leanly-scaled body with six powerful legs, translucent wings, and a long whipping tail zoomed past. Sweet Fates. That was a shrike, wasn't it? It had to be. What was a shrike doing down here? As far as I knew, they only lived in Luntharda. There was no mistaking that piercing cry, though.

Then I caught a glimpse of its face—and bright yellow eyes. Was that Lukani? Oh, gods. It was!

And the petite, dark-haired girl riding on its back with her bow fully drawn looked a lot like ...

Maylea?!

I couldn't decide if I should be relieved or furious as I watched her zoom by, sitting astride Lukani's shrike-form, buzzing low just over the surface of the water. She was alive, at least. But as I watched her zip across the water, darting straight toward the coiling, writhing, acid-breathing behemoth that was still attacking the bridge, I wasn't sure how long that would last.

The monster turned its huge head to consider her as she drew back an arrow. The tip glowed like a brilliant green star in the night, the same color as the pendant that gleamed around her neck. With her dark hair blowing like a black satin flag behind her, she took aim and fired.

The arrow blurred through the night like a comet, glowing brighter and brighter, until it struck the monster in the side of the head with a blinding flash.

What the—? What was that?!

The drakkon bellowed in fury, reeling from the hit. It pushed away from the bridge and dove underwater, the side of its head still smoking from the impact of that magical arrow.

Maylea didn't hesitate. She already had another arrow knocked as her shrike made a wide pass and followed the waves coming from the drakkon's huge body as it swam back toward the warships.

BOOM—BOOM—BOOM—BOOM!

The air shuddered as the warships tried to take aim at her, but they couldn't seem to match the speed of her shrike. No surprise there. Shrikes flew faster than dragons, and were nearly invisible in the night thanks to their mirror-like scales.

I just had to trust that would be enough to give her the edge she needed. I couldn't help her while I was stuck out here treading water like a drowning rat. I didn't know where Thatcher and the others were, either.

But I did know that our ship would be leaving soon, with or without us.

By the scarlet glow of burning homes and belching cannon fire, I spotted the distant shore of that smaller island. Fates help me, it must have been a quarter mile through debris, floating bodies, the occasional Nar'Haleenan warship, and gods only knew what else. I bit down hard and steeled what was left of my already frayed nerves.

I'd never been all that great of a swimmer. But now, I had to swim for my life.

20

CHAPTER TWENTY

I only had to swim, battling the wakes of ships and dodging chunks of debris, for about the first half of the distance. Then I came across a decent-sized piece of wood floating in the water, and used that to hold onto while I kicked the rest of the way to the shore. A small blessing, considering I still had my haversack on my back and my boots on. They filled with water instantly and weighed me down considerably. But kicking? I could manage that.

With Vexi perched on my head like the captain of her own little ship, I made it all the way to the shoreline of the smaller island before I realized that actually getting ashore was going to be its own challenge. Unlike the larger island we'd just come from, this one had steep, craggy, sheer cliffs all the way around. It was only an island in the technical sense. Honestly, it was more like a broad seastack with a few trees and rickety little houses on top.

No wonder they needed a tall bridge to access it.

I paddled around with my makeshift raft, looking for anywhere that seemed accessible that wouldn't require me to go around the whole island. Even if it was small, I wasn't sure I could make it that far without getting swept off into the currents. Then I'd be a dead man for sure.

The best I could find was a large, obviously manmade, circular opening about ten feet above the foaming, roiling waves. With the rocks around it jagged and bristling with barnacles, I was sure I could get enough grip to crawl up in there. Maybe it was the opening of some tunnel that would lead me inland? A guy could hope, anyway.

Turns out, it was a tunnel. Fantastic. The downside? It was a *sewer* tunnel.

And yes, it was absolutely as bad as it sounds.

Violet had bragged briefly about the advancements Rienkans had made in their plumbing engineering, using aqueducts and whatnot to bring water to inland homes and villages and to run sewage out to the ocean. I now had an up close and extremely personal appreciation for it.

Disgusting.

Every step sloshed and slurped, my boots sticking in the muck. Vexi hissed in dismay and hunkered closer to my neck, her tail coiling around her legs. She chittered unhappily like an angry little chipmunk. I tried not to breathe through my nose, but the fear of the vile sludge beneath my feet splashing into my open mouth was more than I could stand. The smell hit me like a brick to the face. I gagged, wretched, and finally threw up after about twenty minutes of slogging farther and farther into the dark tunnel.

At last, I spotted light in the distance. A way out? Oh, thank the gods.

I trudged faster, cringing every time some of the filth on the ground spattered onto my pants and up my back. I'd reek for weeks. Violet had shrugged off my previous requests for a bath, but I sort of doubted she'd be willing to stand in the same room with me after this unless I got one now.

I staggered to a halt directly beneath a beam of light that poured down from a circular opening overhead. Or at least, it looked like it might be an opening. A hatch, possibly. There was a round plate of metal with a few holes cut into it in a pattern, and a hinge on one side. A handle of wrought iron was built into the bottom of it. I had no idea what lay beyond it or where I might come out. It might've been in the middle of the street or the middle of someone's bathroom. Whatever the case, it had to be better than where I was now.

I grabbed the handle and gave a few wrenching shoves. The ironwork hinge groaned and creaked, probably giving me away immediately to anyone on the other side. It didn't matter. I was coming out of this gods-forsaken nightmare if it was the last thing I ever did.

Orange light poured over me as I climbed up through the opening, using my elbows to haul myself out into the middle of a small square. Fire glowed in the night on every side as I shambled to my feet and turned slowly, trying to figure out where I was. All the shops and homes around me were fully engulfed in flame. I didn't see anyone in the streets nearby.

And I had no idea which way to go to reach the docks where our ship was supposed to be waiting. I left a slime trail of rancid muddy footprints like the world's most disgusting slug as I picked a street that looked like it wasn't *all* on fire yet, and started for it.

Ash and cinders floated in the air. Smoke boiled up to choke out the night sky. The roar of the flames droned in my ears, and I could feel the heat of it against my body even through my clothes as I jogged down the street. There was no one around—which was a blessing, honestly—but it also meant I had no one to ask or follow to get to the docks. I needed to see where I was and get my bearings. I needed a vantage point, the higher the better.

In the distance, I saw it. A tower rose up over the other buildings like a monument dead ahead. It wasn't as big as a garrison, but it would do. And as a cheery bonus, it didn't look like it was on fire yet. Perfect.

I ran for it, choking on the smoke and ash in the air, and trying to shield my eyes from the flashes of heat. At the base of the tower, I stared up at all three levels. The fire was coming this way. I wouldn't have long, and the last thing I needed was to get stuck at the top of this building when it did catch fire.

The door at the base was closed but unlocked, and I barged in without knocking. It only took one look around to realize it was, in fact, a temple. I didn't recognize the sculpture of the deity that sat enthroned upon a raised altar at the back of the first floor, though. I didn't stop to figure it out.

Breaking to the left, I took a flight of stairs all the way up to the third level without stopping. From there, I found a long hall with a floor-length window overlooking the entire island. The whole place was probably only a mile across, and I could see off to the north where crowds of people were crammed into the streets along the coast. That must be where the docks were.

I could make it.

Whirling around, I started for the stairs. I'd barely made it halfway down the hall when I heard it—the muffled sound of voices beyond one of the closed doors. I nearly tripped face-first as I came to a screeching halt. What? Seriously? Was someone still in here?

I ran to the door, whipped it open, and was immediately met with a chorus of horrified screams right in my face. There were two small women and a young man wearing long, pale blue robes all mashed into a closet. They stared at me with faces blanched in fear, like they assumed I was an enemy soldier who'd come to slaughter them or something.

Priests? Or, I guess, one priest and a pair of priestesses. Arggh. Whatever. What the heck were they still doing here?

"Are you insane? You can't stay here!" I shouted as I seized the young man's arm and yanked him out of the broom closet. The girls came tumbling out after, wailing and clinging to one another. "This whole place is going to burn with you in it! You have to get out of here *now!*"

Towing them along behind me in a sobbing line, I started for the stairs again. We scrambled down, but didn't make it to the first floor before I heard the roar and crackle of flames. Curse it. Were we too late?

Thick black smoke boiled up from below as I staggered to a halt halfway down the stairwell between the first and second floor. That exit was no good. I whipped around and shouted for them to go back. We had to find another way out.

Too bad the only exit point I found was a window on the second floor. Outside, the rooftop of a neighboring building was only maybe five feet away. We'd have to jump for it.

I used my elbow to break out the glass and stuck my head out, checking as best I could to see if that neighboring building—a house, by the looks of it—wasn't on fire. I didn't spot any smoke coming up from its chimney, and I couldn't see any signs of fire leaking through the reed-thatched roof.

Good enough.

Turning back to my new, appropriately horrified wards, I grabbed the closest one and dragged her to the edge of the window. "You have to jump! Find a place to climb back down to the street! Go!"

She wailed and clung to me, shaking with terror as I basically tossed her up into the windowsill. It took a few seconds of yelling to finally get her to make a wild, flailing leap out into the open air. She hit the rooftop with a thud, rolled a little, but caught herself and managed to get back on her feet. The second girl was braver, and she jumped right away. The young man, with his eyes red and tearing from the smoke, gaped in shock at the tiny green dragoness on my shoulder for a second before he finally managed a shaking word of thanks. Then he followed them, springing the gap and landing close to the other two.

So far, so good.

I waited for the three of them to begin working their way over the thatching toward the next rooftop.

Now, it was my turn.

I climbed up into the windowsill just as the heat of the spreading flames licked at the doorway behind me. No time to hesitate or second-guess it. This was the only way out.

I sprang out into the open air, aiming for a spot where I knew I'd be able to get a good handhold of the roof's thatching. My boots hit first, hands outstretched, and breath held for landing.

And that was when I fell.
Again.

CRACK—CRASH!

The beam holding up the bundles of reeds that thatched the rooftop broke as soon as I hit, and I fell straight through. Vexi squawked in alarm. All the wind rushed out of me at once when I hit the ground. I lay flat on my back right in the middle of a giant mud puddle, with my furious little dragoness sitting on my chest. No, it wasn't just mud.

Oh, gods, what now?

I blinked away the stars dancing in my vision as I shakily sat up, finding myself nose-to-nose with an enormous pig. The big pink sow stared at me, her snout wiggling as she made curious snorting sounds and waddled over closer to investigate.

Vexi immediately fluttered to my rescue, landing between me and the pig and trying to puff herself up like an angry housecat. She hissed and flared her wings, spitting a little plume of flame that didn't seem to discourage the sow at all. I'd give her credit for trying, though. Glad to know that, despite our recent tiffs, she still cared enough not to let a pig maul me to death. How touching.

"Easy there, killer. I think I can handle this one," I said as I hauled myself back to my feet and picked up my dragon. Putting her back onto my shoulder, I climbed over the railing and out of the pigpen. One look around the interior of the barn revealed that most of the pens had been left open, including the one with the pig, and I spotted a doorway on the far right. Perfect. I started for it with sigh of relief. Maybe I could find my way back out to the street. At least now I knew which direction to go in order to find the ship. Things were looking up.

Gods, when had I become an optimist?

Rolling open the barn door, I stared into the interior of a modest farmhouse that was, as far as I could tell, abandoned. Furniture lay overturned, cabinets stood open and emptied, and the front door still stood open to the street outside. I guess whoever had lived here had left in a hurry. They'd even left their pigs behind. In the interest of pig-safety, I left the barn door and front door open, too. At least any animals left in there could flee when this place inevitably caught fire, too.

But that was all I could do for them right now.

The street to my left was already aglow as the tower I'd just jumped out of went up like a torch. Fates, this whole island might burn because there was no one here to try and fight the spread of the blaze. I guess everyone had already fled to the docks—which was exactly where I needed to be, too.

I took to the street in a run, making my way north as best I could. Without knowing the layout of the small city, I was counting on the fact that it wasn't all that big to get me there. Or, at least close enough that I'd be able to spot the crowded docks and reach them in time.

Vexi clung to my shoulder, her tiny talons digging into my skin again as I dashed along avenues and skidded around corners, ducking away from the flickering flames that belched out of first floor windows and dropped heaps of burning debris into the streets around me. I yelped and floundered back as an entire, two-level home caved in right as I darted past it, sending out a shower of sparks, cinders, and ash that stung at my skin and singed my clothes. The crackling, smoldering debris blocked the street ahead of me, and I stared around for another way forward. Down an alley to my right, I saw the back door of another building. Not ideal—but there wasn't time to search for an alternative.

I ran over and flung it open. Staring into the wavering heat of the interior was like looking into an oven. The top floor of this building, which looked like a tailor's shop, was also burning. I could see the flames beginning to eat through the ceiling beams and boards overhead. But ... maybe I could get through. I just had to be fast.

There was no other way around that blocked street.

Sucking in a deep breath, I put my head down and ran inside. I floundered around the front counter; knocking aside mannequins dressed in half-finished gowns, and hit the front door with a wheezing cough. My eyes watered from the smoke, and my throat burned from the heat that rippled in the air.

I had to get out! Right now!

I grabbed the door handled and immediately let out a yell of shock. It was hot—too hot to hold onto with my bare hands. Curse it!

CREAAAK!

I didn't dare look back as I heard the ceiling beams begin to crack and groan, threatening to snap and cave in on top of my head at any moment.

Only one option.

I ripped off one of the still-soggy sleeves of my tunic, wrapped it around my hand, and seized the door. The wet cloth hissed when it touched the metal knob, but I managed to pry it open. I stumbled out into the street again, just as that groaning and cracking grew louder.

Run. Time to run!

I sprinted headlong away from the tailor's shop as a loud *BOOM* and *CRASH* threw more cinders at my back. The burst from the collapsing building sent me sprawling forward. I hit the ground hard and rolled like a log until I lay, on my back again, staring up at the dark sky that was barely visible through all the boiling plumes of smoke.

I tried to remember if, in all my years, I'd ever had a worse night than this. Hmm. Nope. This was definitely in the top three.

My arms and legs shook as I dragged myself upright once again. I staggered, setting my jaw against a new shooting pain in my back, as I shambled forward. It throbbed with every step, so I couldn't run. But I could make it. I had to.

Then I saw it. There, between two narrow shops on the other end of another little town square, the gleam of the fire sparkling off the ocean caught my eye for the briefest instant. A crowd of desperate voices shouted and wailed over the ambient roar of the flames.

The docks.

I was almost there.

A desperate, gasping growl leaked through my clenched teeth as I started limping faster. I was so close. I was going to make it.

By all the Gods, Fates, and anything divine that might be watching, I would get to that ship if it cost me my very last breath.

21

CHAPTER TWENTY-ONE

I found it.

Our ship, the *Sea Cat*, sat still moored amidst all the pandemonium at the docks. Hoards of people rushed the larger ships, trying to beg and barter their way aboard. But our ship was ... well, easy to overlook. It was tiny, by comparison, and looked one good gust of wind away from winding up at the bottom of the ocean. Not ideal for trying to outrun warships.

Beggars couldn't be choosers, though, and I knew it probably wouldn't take long for those desperate townsfolk to try forcing their way aboard any ship or vessel they could find. I kept my head down as I shoved my way through the crowds, keeping to the back until I reached the place where the Sea Cat had her lines tied. Or, rather, her only remaining line. The others had already been taken in, and I spotted an older, balding man in a ragged cloak arguing with his deckhands as they rushed around, trying to take in the gangplank and unfurl the sails.

At least, I assumed it was his own crew he was shouting at. But as I drew closer, I got a much better look at what was happening. And, sweet Fates, something about it made me smile.

Violet's eyes were wide and crazed as she stood stiff, her shoulders squared and stance firm. She bared her teeth like a furious lioness as she planted herself between the older man and the last mooring line, a dagger already in her hand. "NO! He *will* be here!" she roared furiously. "He is not dead! By all the gods, we will wait five more min—"

"N-Not ... necessary..." I wheezed hoarsely as I staggered down the dock, nearly tripping over my own feet. My boots sloshed with every step, and I could still taste ash, grit, and blood in my mouth.

Uggggh. I was getting too old for this nonsense.

I hobbled up the gangplank and only made it a few steps onto the ship's deck before my legs buckled. I hit the wooden floor on my knees and sank back on my heels. Maybe if I just curled up right here, I could sleep and no one would bother me.

Hah. Yeah. Sure.

"REIGH!" Thatcher ran over ahead of the others, trying to take my arm and help me back up. "Gods and Fates! We thought you were ..." he stopped short and made a face, his lip curling some as he covered his nose. "Good grief, what is that *smell?*"

"Well, after almost drowning, I had to crawl through a sewer," I groaned.

"What?" Maylea balked as she rushed toward me, then came to a screeching halt as soon as she caught a whiff, too. "Ew! Why would you—?"

"Then I fell through a roof into a pig pen," I continued. "And then I almost got trapped in a burning house." I cast them all a haggard, put-me-out-of-my-misery glare. I really wasn't up to fielding any follow-up questions about all this right now. "My back hurts, I think I singed one of my eyebrows off, I can't feel my arms, and there's a gallon of water in my shoes. Please just drag me somewhere so I can sleep."

They all stared at me—including the old man who must have been the captain of the ship—for a few awkwardly silent minutes. Then Thatcher burst out laughing. Lukani chuckled and Maylea started snickering, too. Even the captain gave a bemused snort before he hobbled away to continue barking orders at his men to get us underway.

The only one not laughing was Violet. She stared at me with her mouth hanging open and her face pale, as though she were seeing a ghost. I guess, despite that stubborn little speech she'd just made, a part of her had believed I was already dead. Too bad. I'd come close a few times, but it would take more than a drakkon, warships, falling through a roof, and burning alive to bring me down.

"Get him below deck, then," the captain ordered as he snapped his fingers to his small crew of sailors. "No more passengers, and be sure you keep our flags down and our deck quiet. With any luck, we sail for Soman Taal with those warships none the wiser!"

I didn't have the heart to tell the old man that, when it came to ships being sneaky in these waters, he was already at a severe disadvantage. But it must have helped that this tiny fishing vessel had dark sails, a black-painted hull, and absolutely no lights burning. We slipped away from the docks with nothing to guide us but the light of burning homes on the islands and the distant thump, rumble, and flash of cannon fire.

I stood on the deck next to Thatcher and the others, watching it all slip into the distance. Even from here, gazing at the glow of the fire in the night that was now more than a mile away, it still didn't feel safe.

Or ... real.

I knew I shouldn't be alive. Violet wasn't wrong to be shocked and slightly horrified that I'd staggered onto that boat in one piece. I should have died in the depths when I fell from that bridge. Anyone else would be a cold corpse at the bottom of the ocean right now.

But I wasn't just anyone. Noh had made that abundantly clear. Clysiros had plans for me again. That thought put dread like a cold knot in the pit of my stomach. I shut my eyes and turned away, leaning into Thatcher's side as he helped me limp below deck.

The cabin was tiny, but there was enough room for me to shrug off my soggy haversack and stretch out on the floor. I lay there, feeling the roll and vibration of the waves against the ship's hull beneath my back. Every bump and rattle made my heartbeat race again and the fear that we were being attacked wash over me like a splash of icy water.

If something did attack this little boat, it wouldn't survive. We could try defending it, but one decent hit with a cannonball is all it would take to send this rickety bucket straight to the bottom.

I tried not to dwell on that as I lay there, my head rolling slightly with the motion of the waves that rocked us back and forth. Thatcher didn't hang around, and muttered a few words about me trying to rest some before he skulked away. At first, I thought he was just anxious about what might be happening above deck and wanted to go back up to keep watch.

Nope. Turns out, he had a completely different motive for leaving me there. He was setting me up—the jerk.

I didn't hear her enter or say a word to Thatcher. But as soon as the cabin door shut, I caught a glimpse of her long, silvery white hair rippling as she stepped closer to where I lay.

"You smell absolutely terrible," Violet scolded, although her tone was strangely gentle. She sat down right next to me with her legs crossed.

Great. What was this about? More name-calling? I really wasn't up for another argument about my inability to lead this mission. Not until I'd at least had a nap. Or a bath. I'd take whatever I could get.

"I know," I managed to slur drowsily. "Go ahead and call me whatever names you want so I can sleep. I don't care. I'm just glad I didn't die."

I could have sworn I heard her murmur, "I am, too."

Hmmm. I couldn't be sure, though. Not when Violet had angled herself away so I couldn't see her face. And I wasn't about to take anything on a guess when it came to her.

She kept on fidgeting with my soggy haversack as though inspecting it for damage—which was stupid because, like me, it was very obviously a wreck. I wondered if any of my letters had even survived. I had them and my medical kits secured in a pouch that was meant to be waterproof. I guess we would see how well it actually held up to being fully immersed in the ocean.

I wasn't holding out much hope, though.

Sprawled out unceremoniously on my back, I watched her sifting through my personal effects. Any other time, I might've thrown a fit about it. But it wasn't like I had anything embarrassing in there. At least, not that she likely didn't already know about thanks to being Arlan's spy.

Violet's eyes seemed a little puffy when she finally looked my way. Her mouth was all pinched up, too, as though she was trying to keep her expressions in check. It didn't work. Her chin trembled ever so slightly before she could quickly turn away again.

Strange. I hadn't expected her to care so much about what happened to me. We weren't close. I wasn't even sure we were friends. Coworkers, more or less.

Then again, maybe it wasn't my nearly dying that had upset her.

We had just witnessed and barely survived something awful. As someone with a lot of experience in dealing with awful things, I didn't dare assume anyone in our party would be fine after what we'd just seen. Senseless slaughter. Cruelty in its purest form. Destruction that bordered on the unimaginable.

This was far worse than the battles I'd fought in the Tibran War. That had been resistance to a mad tyrant's conquest. Tonight had felt more like ... revenge. Violence for the sake of violence. And if Noh was right about what was coming next, it might only be the beginning.

"Hey, look at me," I managed to rasp weakly, and reached out to put a hand on her arm.

She flinched and snapped her gaze back to meet mine, tears welling in her deep scarlet eyes.

"Are you okay?" I asked, fully expecting the same answer I'd gotten the last time I asked her that. The usual, vague excuse.

Her mouth opened, but she hesitated and blinked a few times. "I-I am so sorry, Reigh," she finally gasped in a broken whisper. "You fell and ... and all I could think about was how I never got to tell you that. I didn't know how. But the last thing you would have heard from me was unkindness and I—" her voice caught and she looked down, her long curtain of smooth white hair falling like a veil to hide her expression.

Oh. Sooo this *was* about me? Hmm. I guess seeing me fall like that might have been traumatizing, too. Watching a ... well, not a friend, per say. Ally? Was that the right word? Anyway, watching someone you know plummet to a gruesome death would scar anyone, right?

And I knew *exactly* what that felt like.

I slid my hand down to gently and carefully take hers. I didn't expect it to make much difference, but sometimes it helped to know you weren't alone. "I get it. It's fine. We're fine. Okay?" I tried to sound reassuring and less hoarse and pathetic. It didn't work.

Violet turned her head to peer at me past her curtain of pale blond hair and went still, her expression completely blank. Little by little, tears welled in her eyes again and ran down her face. She flinched, suddenly seeming to notice, and quickly pulled her hand away to frantically wipe her face.

"I-I am not accustomed to this—to working with others." She gestured to the empty space between us, talking faster and faster as she struggled to explain. "Arlan has always had me working alone before this. Given the nature of my skills and training, I usually perform better that way. I'm used to carrying out my own plans without any outside input, so this has been quite an adjustment. I wish I could say I am handling it well, but it is somewhat frightening to relinquish control and trust someone else to make the right decisions."

I couldn't hold back a weak, exhausted smirk. "Yeah? How am I doing with that part so far?"

A faint smile curved at her full lips for an instant. She sighed, like some of the pressure she'd been bottling up had finally been released. "Better than expected. Even given the company you're stuck with."

I choked and coughed some as I tried to laugh. "Eh. It's not all bad. Thatcher's back on his feet, after all."

She gave a snort and sat forward, resting her elbows on her knees. "Very funny, Lieutenant."

I frowned. Really? Now she was calling me that again? I knew I had heard her use my actual name before. Why did she keep calling me by titles and ranks rather than using my name? Was this some bizarre way of trying to keep things professional?

Or was this just her way of holding me at a distance? And why did that bother me so much? Why did I even care at all?

Urgggh. It didn't matter if she did, right? It wasn't like I felt any certain way about her. She was nice-ish. Beautiful? Sure. Dangerous? Absolutely. Violet was a potent mixture of alluring lethality. The kind of woman that would wreck my entire world with a kiss and a smile. I knew better than to stick my big meaty hand into that hornet's nest.

So ... why did I sort of ... want to?

Wait—what? No. Was I losing my mind? Or had I hit my head when I fell through that roof? I was not getting involved with anyone else. I'd made that mistake once. Never again.

"Were you injured anywhere?" Violet asked quietly.

"No worse than usual," I grunted and shifted, trying to get comfortable despite how nearly every inch of me throbbed. I couldn't keep my face from seizing up when I moved my head, though. That was a deeper, stiffer sort of pain that I couldn't hide as easily.

And I guess she noticed.

"Let me see," she insisted, and started reaching to pull down the collar of my tunic to inspect my neck.

"It's fine," I protested. "Probably just whiplash. My cloak got hung in the wagon wheel. I couldn't get it loose until I was in the water. It's sore, but it's nothing worth writing home about."

Her expression softened as her gaze traveled over my neck, jaw, and finally paused on my nose. "You are used to pain, yes?" she asked as she lightly traced a fingertip over the old scar that cut across the bridge of my nose. A souvenir from a run-in with an angry faundra back when I was a kid.

I didn't dare move or meet her gaze—not with her petting me like that. It sent uneasy chills through me like I was about to plummet off that bridge again. "Comes with the dragonrider territory," I deflected and tried to shrug away.

"You are so diligent to take care of everyone around you," she murmured as she probed at my neck. "But it is a mistake to disregard your own pain. Be a good boy and lie still."

I winced and twitched every time she prodded at my throat. But none of it was sharp pain. I'd have a nasty bruise. Maybe some soft tissue damage. I doubted anything was broken, though. Nothing a few drops of that fancy new healing potion probably couldn't fix.

"What's the verdict? Am I doomed?" I tried to laugh it off as she took my jaw in her hands and slowly turned my head left and right. My whole face twitched as the throbbing intensified, sending waves of dull pain through my shoulders, too. Gods, that was going to hurt tomorrow.

She stopped and flicked the end of my nose. "I cannot feel anything damaged. But you are lucky you didn't break your neck."

No argument there.

"I didn't realize you knew anything about healing." I tried changing the subject.

"I don't. I just wanted an excuse to touch that dashing face of yours," she quipped, clicking her tongue teasingly as she sat back.

My mouth snapped into a tight frown. What? Was she taunting me again? Gods, I couldn't even tell if she was teasing or not anymore. Her expressions were so difficult to read, and my current haze of exhausted pain wasn't making things any easier.

"I learned a little, here and there," she explained quietly. "Enough to keep myself alive."

Ahh. So that was it. Somehow, hearing that was a little disappointing, I just couldn't figure out why.

"Careful," I countered as I let my body relax into the floor and my eyes roll closed. "Or else I'll start to think you actually like having me around."

"I never said I didn't." Her voice was so quiet, I barely heard her.

My heart gave a slow, aching twist in my chest and I swallowed hard. My stomach started flipping and spinning frantically. Gods, what was wrong with me?

Stupid. This was stupid. I knew that. I was a prince. She was a spy. I was too old for ridiculous, childish thoughts of a relationship. I had enough baggage and responsibilities to choke a dragon. I barely knew anything about her. We had absolutely nothing in common.

It would never work.

I should just lay there and keep my stupid mouth shut. I'd just end up regretting anything else I said. I always did.

Fortunately, staying silent wasn't hard to do right then. My aching body relaxed into the floor and my breathing slowed. I knew it wouldn't last. In an hour or so, we would reach the shore and start our trek toward the city of Esfolar so we could meet up with our caravan. Er, well, providing nothing else terrible happened to us before then. I wasn't sure I could handle another all-out crisis, though. I'd reached my limit on near-death experiences for one day.

Drifting in the silence, my thoughts circled back to that familiar, cutting voice that had found me once again. There was no mistaking it now. Noh was back. A certain goddess was definitely calling me out. And I had no alternative but to answer. I had needed that power twice now, and we hadn't even reached Nar'Haleen or picked up Ronan's trail yet.

I didn't have a choice.

I'd have to make a deal with the devil, and pray it didn't cost me everything this time.

PART SIX

MURDOC

22

CHAPTER TWENTY-TWO

Over the last decade, I'd had the privilege of getting to know the man that the rest of the world called the Champion of Maldobar or the Hero of the Gray War personally. I knew him as Jaevid Broadfeather, Academy Commander of Blybrig. He preferred that we just call him Jae, though, even if that felt a little informal.

Whatever the name or title, I had served under Jae as an instructor after graduating as a dragonrider myself. We had worked together extensively to refine and perfect the hand-to-hand and weapon-based combat training that was part of every dragonrider's education. We had also spent a lot of time together as friends alongside Thatcher, Reigh, Garnett, Jenna, and the others.

In all that time, I'd gotten to know Jaevid fairly well. He was usually very stoic, calm, and patient. He kept that reserved, contemplative demeanor even among close friends. It made him difficult to read at times, even for me. He was not the sort of person you expected to fly off the handle quickly at the first sign of trouble. He had a few small tells whenever something really bothered him—subtle traits I doubted he was even aware of that gave him away. But even in those moments, he was always rational.

So, witnessing him come completely unraveled over the loss of his daughter was ... difficult to watch, to say the least. I couldn't recall ever seeing our esteemed commander so reckless and on edge. He had scowled into the distance, standing firm with his helmet under his arm and saying nothing, while the rest of us finished packing our gear and checking our saddles for departure from Southwatch.

Thanks to Jaevid's prestigious reputation and rank within the Dragonriders of Maldobar, he had no trouble securing transportation for Garnett and Roxus. Not dragons, of course, but he had acquired two shrikes for us to borrow long enough to make our journey.

Our plan was simple. Faced with the inevitable necessity of dealing with deities once again, we were left with few options. We had to tread lightly, since Jaevid's young daughter and Jenna's only son were now caught up in the mix. One wrong move could put them both in lethal danger.

Unfortunately, our moves going forward from this point were extremely limited. We could either join the fight and arm ourselves appropriately, knowing full well what it might cost—or we could sit back, wait, and hope Reigh and the others would be able to handle it without our assistance. Neither option appealed to me, and I despised the notion that I had to choose between the lesser of two evils.

I did have the utmost confidence in Reigh's ability to get the job done—that same stubbornness that often got him into trouble also usually made him a formidable opponent to anyone who crossed him. A family trait, according to Jaevid. But it was possible that he didn't know what he was fully up against if Sadeera came after him.

We all knew she was a powerful sorceress—a counterpart to Arlan's own magical prowess. Previously, she had managed to manipulate her way to the center of power in the Ulfrangar using a magical golem Arlan had called an aspect. The idea that she may be doing the same thing now in order to pull at an emperor's strings and make him dance like a puppet, chilled me straight down to the marrow. She meant to crack open the kingdom of the gods, and if she had Ronan heeling like a muzzled dog, she might very well achieve that goal.

Reigh needed help, even if he didn't know it yet. He'd been determined to go at this on his own, displacing as few of us as possible from our normal lives. But the more we learned —the more the true nature of the situation unfolded—the more obvious it became that Reigh was in over his head.

That left only one, terrifying option: we had to join the fight any way we could.

My young dragon, Blite, greeted me at the stall door with exciting grunting, chirping calls. He rubbed his scaly head all over me, nearly knocking me backward as he snuffled through my hair and nipped at the back of my tunic. I scratched his bony brow and under his chin until he gave a deep, satisfied purr.

He wriggled around, intentionally slapping my legs with the tip of his tail and nuzzling around my boots—which were still his favorite thing to steal if he ever got an opportunity when I wasn't paying attention. I had to give one of his scaly ears a yank to get him to hold still long enough to buckle my bag and weaponry back into place on his saddle. He grumbled sulkily the whole time, huffing deep, pouting snorts that blew up the hay in front of his nose.

Ridiculous. And mostly Phoebe's fault. My extremely enthusiastic wife had gone to great lengths to spoil my dragon until he acted more like a housecat than a battle mount.

It didn't take long for us to be ready to leave. With Roxus and Garnett astride the borrowed shrikes, and Isandri on the back of Jaevid's saddle, we struck out before dawn and flew straight for Luntharda. Against the wind and veering around the big rolling storm fronts that moved in from the eastern coast, it was hard flying for our mounts. Jaevid's king drake, Mavrik, managed it better, so Roxus, Garnett, and I tried drafting off his tail as much as possible.

Even with that aid, I felt Blite's sides heaving harder with every wingbeat. If he was tired, I could only imagine the much-smaller shrike was reaching exhaustion. We had pushed all our mounts hard for nearly six hours, and passed Solhelm not long ago. If we could get to Eastwatch, we could let them rest. We could draw up our final plans for when we reached the edge of the wild jungle of Luntharda.

I could ask Jaevid about making an extra stop, just for a moment, as we passed over Dayrise where my family lived.

Blite let out a bellow of excitement when we dipped below a low bank of dark clouds and the dragonrider tower of Eastwatch finally came into view. I sighed, feeling every muscle in my body relax some. One obstacle down.

Several more, much larger ones, to go.

We touched down at Eastwatch tower and handed off our mounts to the young lieutenants manning the stables and landing platform. Jaevid left orders for them to be given food, water, and a place to rest for the next few hours. But we wouldn't be staying for long.

Roxus and Garnett drew a few curious looks from the dragonriders and infantry soldiers as we prowled along through the tower. Probably because Roxus looked like a drunken bum we'd scraped off the side of the road somewhere, and dwarven women like Garnett weren't a common sight anywhere. It didn't seem to bother either of them as we made our way to the tower's dining hall to grab a quick meal for ourselves as well. No point in showing up to barter with deities for the fate of the world on an empty stomach.

Over plates of roasted lamb, creamed potatoes, and dark bread, we kept our conversation low and to the point. Jaevid was the only one who didn't seem to have much to say. His glacier blue eyes were glazed and distant, as though he were already having private, internal conversations with gods.

Or maybe he was just worrying about his child being caught up in this mess and too far away for him to help her if she needed it.

Speaking of which ...

I leaned forward and put my elbows on the table, nudging Jaevid's arm in the process to get his attention. I angled myself so I could send him hand signals in the dragonrider code without the others—namely Roxus, who I didn't completely trust—noticing.

"I want to leave ahead of you and make another stop in Dayrise. If you do a low city pass, I'll catch up."

Jaevid's brows snapped together, his expression sharpening with concern. He held my gaze for a few seconds before he signaled back, *"I can't do this without you."*

"I know," I answered quickly. *"But I have to tell her what's happening. It won't take long. I'll be ready to move as soon as you arrive in the city. Is that okay?"*

Jaevid's demeanor immediately softened. His disapproving frown went slack, and he gave a slow, approving nod before looking away. There was no mistaking that fractured look of heartbreak in his eyes. He hadn't wanted to leave Beckah behind, either. But neither of us had a choice about this now.

Not unless we wanted our families surviving in a world ruled by Sadeera.

I waited a few more minutes, finishing what was on my plate, before I stood up and excused myself. Garnett stared after me, her lavender-hued eyes sparkling with curiosity, almost like she knew I was up to something. There was no point in trying to hide anything from her. Garnett had a mind as sharp and fast as a steel bear trap. Nothing got past her notice.

Not even me.

I gave her a wink, just to let her know she was right, and turned to leave. With any luck, it would only take another two and a half hours to get to Dayrise. Maybe less, if Blite was feeling frisky after his own meal.

We could both be home before sundown.

THE HORIZON HAD JUST BEGUN TO TURN WARM SHADES OF EVENING PINK AS I GAVE Blite the cue to land in the street right outside the Porter family home in Dayrise. My family's home. A few local townsfolk gave yelps of surprise and scrambled to get out of the way, shielding their eyes from the wind as we touched down.

Sliding off my helmet, I clipped it on the back of my saddle before I gave my young drake a nudge to crouch down so I could dismount. I hadn't even finished sliding off my gauntlets before the front door of the Porter home flew open with a bang, and she appeared.

My wife.

"MURDOC!" Phoebe cried out as she struggled along, barely managing an awkward waddle-run out the front door of my parents' home. With her coppery curls and lengths of her flowing light blue gown flying, she started for me with her arms outstretched and her lightly freckled cheeks flushed and rosy.

I stopped as soon as I climbed down from Blite's back and stood frozen, staring at her. I couldn't help it. The sight of her left my head spinning and all my worries scrambled. Fates, she was beautiful. Whenever she called my name like that, it still made my heartbeat race and skip like the very first time, even after all these years.

A smile spread over my face, as I ran out to meet her, leaving Blite crouching in the street. She laughed as I grabbed her face in my hands and kissed her deeply. I savored the smell of her skin and the way her fingers combed through my hair as she stood on her toes to kiss me back.

Home. I was *home* again—after months of being separated while I worked at the academy. One touch, one kiss and sweet laugh from her, and all that stress and worry felt far away. As though nothing else truly mattered.

Phoebe gave my chin a teasing rub and giggled, then tapped playfully at the end of my nose. "You didn't tell me you were coming so soon. You've committed fully to that beard, I see."

"You don't like it?" I asked as I leaned down, stole another kiss, and ran my hand over her round, swollen belly. I could have sworn I felt the smallest thump against my hand. It made my breath catch and I froze, looking up to see her knowing little grin.

"I-I felt a kick," I wheezed breathlessly.

"It happens a lot more often now," she replied, biting at her bottom lip as her light blue eyes shone with all the warmth and light I'd missed so much over the last few months.

Time-wise, I knew Phoebe didn't have much longer. Our first baby was due before the end of the month, and I hadn't been able to stay at her side as much as I wanted because of my job. Being the head instructor overseeing all combat training at Blybrig inevitably required that I spend most of the time at the academy across the kingdom.

I despised the separation. The not knowing if she was all right or needed my help. That was the entire reason I'd requested that Phoebe move in with my parents here in Dayrise, so they could help look after her. Not that my mother and father minded at all. They lavished over Phoebe and gushed at the prospect of getting to help with our first baby.

It was a long way from our home in Halfax, though. And at first, Phoebe didn't like the idea of leaving all her work behind. I had eventually convinced her that, for safety's sake, she would need someone to help her once the pregnancy put more of strain on her very petite body.

I had taken a few days off to move her here only three months ago, but there hadn't been time to visit as we worked with avian students trying to graduate. I had initially worried I might miss the birth altogether. Fortunately, my commander was extremely understanding about my desire to come home and remain there as long as I could manage after the baby arrived—at least until Phoebe felt comfortable with me leaving again. Jaevid had insisted I take all the time I needed.

Now, with this new, incredibly dangerous and slapped-together mission looming before me like a rising dark tide, I had to wonder ... would I actually get to be there for the birth of my first child? Or would I be on a ship somewhere in the ocean? Or fighting for my life somewhere in the desert of the Southern Kingdoms?

I didn't know. And worse, I didn't know how I was going to tell Phoebe any of this.

"I've never cared much for beards, but I admit, it does look very distinguished," she laughed and put her hand over mine. "It's so funny! Just a few minutes ago the baby was kicking around so much, like she was dancing inside me. She must have known you were coming to—" She stopped suddenly, staring at me with those raindrop blue eyes studying me carefully. "Murdoc? What's wrong?"

Fates, I should have known. I'd lost a little of my Ulfrangar edge over the years, but even in my prime, Phoebe could spot my emotions as clearly as a dawn sunrise. There was no keeping secrets from her.

I drew back a little, tucking some of her wild red hair behind her ear, and forced a smile I knew she wouldn't buy for instant. "We'll talk inside. Now, what's this with calling our baby a *'she'* already?" I tried changing the subject.

Phoebe still stared at me as she took my arm for balance and shrugged. "It's just a feeling."

"What if *I* feel that it's a boy?" I countered.

A soft, uncertain smile brushed her lips as she hobbled along beside me. Together, we made our way back to the front steps of the house. "I suppose in a few weeks, we'll know who's right, won't we?"

"I suppose we will," I agreed, but as hard as I tried, I couldn't keep my tone as firm and even as before. Not with that sense of dread welling up in me, spreading like an icy chill through every inch of my body.

At the door, I turned back and gave Blite a signal to take off but remain close to the area. We wouldn't be able to stay here long. An hour or two, at most. In that very limited time, I had to figure how to tell my wife what was happening with Arlan, Sadeera, Reigh, and the others. I had to tell her that I might be leaving Maldobar altogether.

And I had to confess to her that I wasn't sure when, or if, I would be able to return.

❧ 23 ❧

CHAPTER TWENTY-THREE

The conversation went about as well as you would expect.

Phoebe and my parents sat in mute horror as I described to them everything we had learned about Sadeera, Ronan, and what was happening in Nar'Haleen that might threaten the entire known world. For Phoebe's sake, I tried to phrase it as gently as I knew how. But there wasn't a good way to sugarcoat an insane sorceress trying to wage a war against the ancient gods using dark magic and the armies of a powerful emperor whose court she already seemed to control. I'd never been good at sugarcoating to begin with. Chalk that up to being raised by a league of deadly assassins.

Regardless, I didn't want to keep anything from them. What we were doing—what I was about to do—was dangerous. I didn't want to set any unrealistic expectations or leave any mystery behind as to what we were really up to. These were the people I cherished most in the world. I wanted, more than anything, to be honest with them.

Phoebe sat close to me on the couch, gripping my hand like I might disappear at any moment. "If all of this is happening in Nar'Haleen, then why are you going to Luntharda?" she asked quietly.

"According to Arlan's agents, that's the best place to go shopping for a potential divine candidate that might be willing to join our side," I explained as best I could. In all honesty, this was the part that still wound my brain into knots. I'd never fully understood all this divine power nonsense, even when Thatcher was dealing with it years ago. Sometimes, it was still hard to believe any of it was real at all.

But I had witnessed firsthand that it was.

"Isandri's been helping with the excavation and restoration of an ancient temple to the northeast of Aular. It's remote, and until very recently, no one knew it existed at all," I said. "Arlan seems to think that site is our best chance at making contact. We plan to go there, hopefully enlist some divine assistance, and then make our way south. Our intent is to intercept Reigh and the others. Knowing Sadeera has Ronan under her heel now changes things. It puts our friends at a distinct disadvantage. He won't say it aloud, but I think

Arlan is worried she may already have the codex, too. If so, they are already fighting a losing battle, and we won't stand by and do nothing."

"This will be dangerous," Phoebe murmured, her grip on my hand tightening. "More dangerous than before."

I didn't answer. She was right, of course. No need to make that ugly truth any worse.

"What do you need from us, son?" my father asked, sitting forward in his chair to fix me with an intensely focused stare.

"Please continue to look after Phoebe," I asked, bowing my head. Somehow, this felt like begging. Like raw desperation. I hated it. But I had no choice. I wouldn't walk away without making sure my family knew what was happening. I wouldn't abandon my wife—the person I loved most in the world—without telling her the truth about what I was about to do. "I ... don't know how long I'll be gone. I don't know what will happen."

A second passed. Then another. No one spoke, and I could feel myself shaking like a frightened child. I shut my eyes tightly. Phoebe would be upset. She might even be angry. And she had every right to be.

"It's okay, Murdoc." Her gentle voice filled my ears like the soothing pattering of spring rain. "I know you have to do this. Jaevid can't do it alone, and I believe he wouldn't ask anyone unless it really was a problem too big and dangerous for him to handle on his own. Thatcher, Maylea, Reigh, and Ronan—they're our family, too. And they need your help. So, please, go help them. Just promise me you'll come back."

I opened my eyes to stare at her, unable to hide my disbelief.

Her smile was enough to make any goddess jealous as she gave me a small, approving nod. She would be okay. She wouldn't hate me for going.

And that was all that mattered in my world.

"We will do whatever we can to support you, honey," my mother agreed, although I could still see traces of fear in her eyes. "Just try to be safe. We all need you to come back home, dear."

"I know," I replied.

"And don't worry about Phoebe," my father chimed in. "She is more than welcome here for as long as she wants. We're happy to have her."

Once again, I sat speechless, staring at my parents—two people I had never expected to have in my life. Their consistent efforts to be there for me, in spite of all that I did and had done in the past, left my chest feeling heavy and my heart twisting painfully like someone was trying to rip it right out of my chest. I didn't deserve love like theirs. But I had it now, and I would never take it for granted.

The distant, booming sound of a dragon's roar rattled the windows of my family home. It made Phoebe jump some and my parents stiffen.

That was my signal. It was time to go.

"Awww. Not again," Phoebe sighed as she stood on the steps to my family's broad courtyard, staring sadly down at the little pile of white cloth on the ground at her feet with her hands resting on her round belly.

I had to bite back a smile as I walked over, still putting on my riding gauntlets as I prepared to leave. She had no idea how cute it was when she did that. "What's the matter?"

"My balance is terrible, that's what's the matter. I can't bend over to pick things up, but it seems like I drop everything I touch now," she huffed. "I can't even put on my own shoes anymore."

"I'll rescue you, then," I chuckled as I bent down to retrieve her lost handkerchief. "You should go inside and rest."

"Resting is all I'm fit for these days," she groaned. "And it's terribly boring. I miss the workshop at the castle. Jenna had such a nice place for me to work. At least there, I had something to distract me while you were off saving the world one student at a time."

I leaned down to kiss her forehead, offering the handkerchief back to her. "When I get back, and as soon as you and the baby are able to travel, we'll go back home," I promised.

"I made this for you," she protested, pushing my hand back and closing my fingers around the handkerchief. "Your mother's been teaching me embroidery. We've made lots of things for the baby. But I wanted you to have this. It's a token, like the ladies give dragonriders before battle."

A hard, painful knot formed in my throat as I studied it, noting the tiny stitched blue initials below a shield with my family's crest above it in gold. The letters P and R. Our initials. I still didn't use my real name, Rylen, all that much. It was hard to change to that after eighteen years of being called Murdoc.

But I liked it, nonetheless.

Tucking the handkerchief into my pocket, I cradled her chin to tilt her head back and bent down to kiss her again. Then I knelt, putting my hands on either side of her belly, and kissed that place where our child still slept safely inside her. With my heart still in my throat, I stood back and slid my helmet on quickly so maybe she wouldn't see the way my eyes welled. I didn't like it—showing emotion like that. It still felt wrong, like something I might be punished for.

Old habits.

"Please be careful, Murdoc," Phoebe whispered.

"I will." I managed to keep my voice steady.

Her throat jumped as she swallowed hard, her own eyes welling as the late evening wind rustled through her long red curls. "I love you."

Under my helmet, my mouth screwed up. I couldn't stop my voice from catching when I finally managed to tell her, "I love you, too."

Every step I took away from her, toward where Blite crouched in the middle of the courtyard, hurt more than the one before it. I hated this. I didn't want to leave her. She needed me. The baby would need me, too. I shouldn't be going.

But what choice did I have? What if my blade and my strength were all that might tip the scales in our favor? We needed every ounce of power and advantage we could muster for this fight. There could be no bystanders.

So, taking one last look at my wife, standing in the doorway to my family's home, I climbed up into my dragon's saddle. I slipped my feet down into the boot-pockets on either side of his strong, thick neck, and adjusted the saddle handles with my resin-palmed riding gauntlets. Then, with a sweeping rush of wind off his powerful wings, Blite sprang skyward and carried me away.

24

CHAPTER TWENTY-FOUR

I rejoined with Jaevid and the others as they made a slow, arcing pass over the city of Dayrise. The massive blue king drake was difficult to miss, and Blite zoomed in fast to catch up to him, Isandri's sleek winged form, and the shrikes. Just in time.

From his saddle, Jaevid gave me a few hand signals as we fell back into formation off his wingtip. *"Everything okay at home?"*

"Yes," I signaled back.

"Good. We're heading for the boundary line. Landing there and following Isandri to the temple site." He motioned for me to keep in formation, and poured on a little more speed as we veered to the north.

From Dayrise, the boundary line between Maldobar and Luntharda wasn't far. Less than an hour, by air. As the sun began to sink, the ominous dark line of massive trees loomed ahead of us like a giant fence, marking the edge of the dense, dangerous jungle. Beyond that boundary, the canopy spread like a floating green carpet, hundreds of feet above the jungle floor. The branches of the trees wove together so densely that it was difficult to break through, even on a dragon. We wouldn't be able to fly there with Blite and Mavrik. And unless we were lucky enough to secure more shrikes, which were small enough to zip through the colossal trees at speed, we would be making the rest of the journey on foot.

Not ideal.

The moon rose up over the towering tree line as our dragons made a final circle, descending and cupping their wings to land. Blite touched down on the grassy plain and gave a snort and a stretch. I'd pushed him hard today. He was well overdue for some downtime.

Patting his strong, scaly neck, I unbuckled from the saddle and climbed down. I shivered as the cool night air hit my sweat-dampened hair. Then again, maybe that was just a side effect of standing so close to the gaping, earthy maw of that jungle. Even from a hundred yards away, the strange echoes and calls of the creatures lurking within made the hairs on the back of my neck stand on end. I'd heard tales since I was a child, even amongst the Ulfrangar, of the horrors that lurked there. Until now, however, I'd never had much of a reason to go and see them for myself. I didn't get sent on diplomatic meetings to the Lunthardan court, thank the gods, so I had never set foot beyond its border before now.

"Take only what we need," Jaevid advised as he dismounted, too. Sliding his own helmet off, he shook his ash gray hair free and raked some of his bangs away from his eyes before peering up at the looming jungle before us. I could have sworn I saw a hint of a smile tug at his lips. I guess, for him, this was more of a homecoming. Even if he was only half Gray elf, he still had strong ties to this place and relatives that still lived there.

Namely, the Queen of Luntharda herself, who happened to be his cousin.

"We need to travel light," he urged as he turned to face the rest of us. "Passing through Luntharda at night is less than ideal, but time is of the essence. We can't afford to wait for sunrise. Mavrik and Blite can stay in the area until we return. With any luck, we'll back within a day or two."

Heh. Yeah. Because luck was *always* on our side.

"What about the shrikes?" Garnett asked as she came over to stand beside me, her hands on her hips where she kept two small, double-headed axes strung through her belt. "I don't mean to be a downer, but I'm not sure how effective I'll be running through those big trees. I'm not as sprightly at a run as the elfy folk. Shorter legs'n all."

"We can take the shrikes," Jaevid assured her. "They can carry two passengers, if necessary. Roxus and Garnett will be on one. Murdoc, you and I will take the other. Isandri, if you're up to it, we need you to take point and lead us to the temple."

Standing in her elven form, her weight leaning casually against her tall, crystal-tipped staff, Isa glanced my way before nodding. "I can."

"Good. Let's get moving." Jaevid didn't waste a second unloading his bag from the back of the saddle and slipping his scimitar back into his belt.

Leaving behind the bulk of my gear—bedroll, personal effects, and cloak—on my saddle, I took only what was absolutely necessary. Well, apart from the handkerchief. That item I kept folded neatly in the secret pocket of my leather vambrace, where I knew it would be safe. Then I saddled up behind Jaevid on the shrike, hanging on to the back of his belt as we took to the air.

We broke through the timberline of Luntharda's wild jungle like we'd been swallowed whole. Instantly, the moonlight was gone—blocked out by the dense canopy overhead. The cool rush of the open prairie wind immediately gave way to the humid, earthy scent of the heavy jungle air. Even moving at speed, it didn't take long for me to start sweating under my leather armor and breastplate. A few hours in, and my tunic and pants were soaked through. My hair managed to stay somewhat dry, thanks to the wind rushing past as we zipped through the huge tree trunks.

I'd heard tales of the giant trees that grew here, but seeing them this close left me gaping like a child at a parade. Each one must have been twenty feet or more in diameter, and the branches were so wide you could run on them like sidewalks. No wonder the Gray elves preferred to use them to navigate this place, rather than trying to hike on the jungle floor below.

There, where fern fronds and flowering plants as big as wagons grew in soft, squishy soil, there were said to be a whole host of predators thriving in this environment—especially at night. Some of them had even made it into Ulfrangar tales, like the powerful tigrex, a legendary apex predator that was supposedly similar to a king-sized lion or tiger. Stories told of herds of wild faundra, which happened to be the Gray elves' resident species of elk. They had been taming them and using them for mounts for thousands of years, although I had never seen one in person. Supposedly, they could run much faster than a horse and were nearly silent even when charging through the jungle foliage.

There was so much more that hadn't made it into those stories, though. Some of the plant life was bioluminescent, and glowed like a sea of faint blue and green stars around the base of the trees. The eerie calls of the birds echoed for miles, and massive spider webs the size of quilts hung between some of the branches. Thankfully, I didn't see any of the spiders responsible for them—but I had a decent idea that they would be larger than normal, Maldobarian spiders I occasionally had to rescue Phoebe from with a squish of my boot.

The hours slipped by and we never lost pace, darting ahead as fast as the humming, translucent wings of the shrikes could carry us. Isandri, now sporting her black, winged feline form, glided ahead soundlessly with hardly a sound. It wasn't hard to imagine that she would find a place like this perfectly in line with her skillset. Isa was as stealthy as she was powerful, even without the added boost of being the mortal manifestation of Adiana, the moon goddess. She, like Thatcher, was a godling. But where he had modest beginnings as a farrier's son, she had been raised in Nar'Haleen as a shalnii priestess and trained to fight from a young age.

To call her formidable was an understatement. I felt a lot better about braving this place in the dead of night with minimal gear since she was the one leading the way. Now, we just had to reach the temple, broker a divine deal or two, and get back in one piece.

THE SHRIKES TIRED ABOUT THE SAME TIME ISANDRI BEGAN TO SLOW HER PACE, AND after about four hours of zigzagging through the jungle, we were forced to stop and take a breather. Aloft in the massive trees, we found an open spot on a branch with more than enough space for us to stretch our legs while the shrikes and Isandri lay down to rest.

"No campfires," Isa warned as she sank down into an empty spot beside me and let out a loud, heavy sigh. "The light draws things from the jungle, and we certainly don't want that kind of attention now."

"Agreed," Jaevid murmured as he sat on my other side.

Roxus and Garnett settled in, too, and despite not having a fire, we found ourselves sitting in a circle with nothing to look at in the middle but the few bags of gear we'd brought along. In the tense silence, my mind raced back through the twisting jungle all the way to where Phoebe and my parents were sitting, waiting for me to return. Would it be weeks until I saw them again? Or months? What if I missed the birth of my child?

What if I didn't make it back at all?

"Isa, if you're up for it, we should discuss what you know about the temple," Jaevid spoke up suddenly, jarring me from those agonizing questions.

"Very little, I'm afraid," she replied, her vivid green-and-yellow hued eyes staying focused ahead as she seemed to ponder that. "It is very old, predating any of the other structures found in Luntharda—even the temple of Paligno you are already familiar with. For that reason, the king and queen asked for my insight, as my people are far more accustomed to researching and preserving ancient ruins in Nar'Haleen. But what I have found is most mysterious. As best I can tell, it appears to pay homage to Proleus, the God of War, but the architecture isn't Lunthardan craftsmanship. I'm honestly not quite sure what culture created it."

"Arlan would likely know," Garnett said as she leaned back on her hands and looked up into the darkness of the interwoven canopy above. "He's always been on edge about going into Luntharda, though. I suspect because it's a bit close to Avora."

"Could that be the answer, then?" Jaevid guessed. "Could the temple be Avoran?"

"I doubt it," Roxus muttered. He sat hunched forward, legs and arms crossed, and his gaze fixed down on the ground before him. "Avorans never thought much of Proleus. He was more favored by the Holvradix elves and the Tibrans."

"Tibrans?" Jaevid sat a little straighter at the name. "Why would they have ruins that old here?"

Roxus's wide, bony shoulders shrugged under his ragged coat. "Their empire once spanned a lot of this area," he grumbled, his voice hard and rough like he'd spent too long puffing on that beloved pipe of his. "They were one of the first human kingdoms to openly war with the Avoran elves eons ago. If there was anything left of them in this part of the world, it's probably been buried and long forgotten."

"And who is Proleus, exactly?" I pressed, not really interested in ancient history. But gods? Well, I wanted to learn whatever I could about someone we were about to potentially ask for help. "You said he was a god of war. I take it he's not the warm and fuzzy, Thatcher-esque brand of deity, then?"

Roxus gave a bemused snort and finally lifted his chin enough that our eyes met from underneath his unruly mop of shoulder-length curly hair. "No. Not exactly. I'm no priest, but the folk in my homeland like to pay lip service to him when it suits them. Supposedly, he only respects the strong—and not just in body. Mental fortitude, absolute emotional control, relentless force of will, and endurance under pressure are traits that are said to please him. He favors the heart of a true warrior." Roxus chuckled hoarsely as he glanced around at all of us and then bowed his head again. "Any of you think you've got those kinds of marbles rattling around in your can?"

Garnett's mouth scrunched to one side as she looked around at our group, too. Of us all, she was probably the strongest physically. Jaevid had proven many times that he had a relentless force of will. Isandri had the mental fortitude of a sage twice her age. And I'd had emotional control beaten into me by the Ulfrangar since I was old enough to walk. But all of that in just one person? I wasn't sure who among us fit that bill, and I didn't know Roxus well enough to even make a guess at whether or not he could.

Isandri studied Roxus more carefully, almost like she suspected he might know a lot more than he was divulging right now. Or, maybe she was just surprised he knew as much as he did about the gods. "Proleus is not a wrathful god, by what I know of him. He is only glorified by noble victory, and holds personal honor as his greatest virtue," she said. "I did not see any of his symbols within the ruins, but our excavation had only just begun."

"What made you think the ruins might be his, then?" I asked.

Her lips pursed thoughtfully. "Some of the decorum featured items like bronze shields, spears, javelins, and statues wearing helmets with long war headdresses or wreaths of victory. I would expect to see such things in a temple dedicated to Proleus, but again, his insignia was missing."

"And what would that be?" Jaevid pressed, seeming to hang on her every word. "What are his symbols?"

"The wolf," she replied matter-of-factly. "More distinctly, a black wolf."

A cold shiver crawled under my skin, chilling me all the way to my fingers and toes as I sat and listened. I'd worn the emblem of a wolf myself, years ago. The Ulfrangar used a silver one with three eyes as their emblem. I had to wonder ... could they somehow be connected to Proleus?

No. Surely not. The Ulfrangar were an ancient organization, sure. But they weren't known for their upstanding moral virtues in battle. The opposite, actually.

Whatever symbol they chose to wear, they acted more like jackals than wolves.

"I suppose we'll just have to hope one of us suits his fancy, then." Garnett sighed and fidgeted with the end of one of her braided ginger ponytails.

"Or that he's even willing to manifest and grant us an audience at all," Jaevid agreed.

Isa arched her back and stretched her arms above her head, as though trying to shake off the stiffness of flying so far for so long. "Regardless, we should reach the temple by dawn," she said with a yawn. "I think I'll lie down for a moment and rest."

"We all should," Jaevid suggested. "No need to reach the temple already dead on our feet, especially since we don't really know what we might be up against when we get there. I'll take first watch."

"I'll join you," I volunteered. Might as well. Sleep never came easy to me, even years after leaving the Ulfrangar far behind me. I could go for days before I needed to rest, and even then, it was always a fight to get my mind and senses to calm enough that I could actually drift off.

I doubted I'd win that battle here, anyway. Not with so many strange sounds and animal calls echoing through the dark of this wild, forbidding jungle. Something about this place, with its constant dimness, dense undergrowth, and thick, humid air made my skin crawl. It was that sense of being watched, as though something unknown was lurking just beyond my field of vision.

Like a predator just waiting for me to take one wrong step.

25

CHAPTER TWENTY-FIVE

Dawn brought the relief of beams of warm sunlight that broke through the canopy like streams of radiant gold that shone upon the jungle floor and lit the way ahead of us. There wasn't time to sit around and savor a Lunthardan sunrise, however. We had work to do and ground to cover.

With her strength renewed, Isandri led us swiftly to the northeast, deeper into the jungle. It was strange to go so far without seeing any signs of settlement or civilization. Even with the Ulfrangar, we'd always stuck within a few miles of a city. Here, you could go for days on end, lost and hopeless, and never come close enough to a city for anyone to even hear you scream. It gave me a new appreciation for the Lunthardan scouts, like Reigh, who had been trained to survive here.

Hm. I might even tell him that—providing we both survived to see one another again.

As we drew close to the temple grounds, we ran into a group of young scouts running patrols a few miles outside a temporary camp they had built for the researchers and workers still excavating the site. They chatted excitedly with Isandri, who apparently had become quite fluent with the Gray elven language. I suppose Reigh had probably taught her some of that.

Isandri and the young scouts swapped greetings and information, then they stood there and gaped at Jaevid with amazement while we prepared to set off again. It made Garnett burst into a fit of giggling as soon as we started moving again, and Jaevid's whole head flushed with embarrassment.

"You'd think after so many years, they'd be less impressed," I taunted him a little, unable to hold back a smirk. "You've become old news in Maldobar, after all."

His mouth scrunched bitterly and he flicked me an irritated, sideways glare.

Too easy.

After less than an hour, Isandri slowed her pace and began moving more cautiously through the tree boughs. Her ears stayed perked as she leapt soundlessly from one limb to another, swishing her tail and listening to the ground below. The shrikes shivered and twitched, making nervous growling, humming sounds as they sank low into their powerful shoulders and snapped their bony jaws. Something had them on edge.

Shimmering in a radiant beam of sunlight that poured down from a hole in the canopy —I finally saw what.

Bathed in the golden light, the bust of a muscular male form standing tall and straight leaned slightly to one side, as though the vines and roots that snaked up its legs had begun to pull it down. The shining white stone beneath peaked through the foliage, as though half-dressing the towering structure in drapes of leafy green cloth. With its face covered by a helmet with a sweeping feathered crest, the robust figure also held a massive sword in one hand and a round shield in the other.

Hmm. No wonder Isa had assumed this might be some sort of homage to Proleus. It certainly smacked of "war god" to me.

The more I studied the area around the bust, the more I picked out the outlines of a broad courtyard and low, rectangular buildings that had been nearly buried under the plantlife. Toppled stone columns lay in heaps, overgrown with moss and vines. Invading tree roots buckled the ground of the once-paved square, leaving hunks of white stone heaped into cracked hills.

To their credit, the workers had obviously been very busy carefully unearthing the ruins from the jungle entanglement. They had built temporary shelters and spiraling staircases in the trees around it, and there were portions of the jungle floor that were cleared away for larger artifacts to be spread out, cleaned and examined. More areas of the dark soil had also been dug away to reveal stone roadways leading away from that central square.

"We believed this temple might have been the center of a much larger settlement. But we have only just begun to learn the secrets of this place," Isandri explained as she gracefully shifted back into her elven form and beckoned for us to follow. "This way. The entrance is not far."

Jaevid and I swapped a wary look. I knew he had a history with ancient jungle temples —not all of them positive. I had to wonder if he also had that same, eerie feeling I did. That sense of being watched by something.

It didn't seem like the right time to ask, though.

With my nerves drawn as taut as lute-strings, I dismounted and checked the strapping of the cross-sheath I wore to carry my two longswords strapped onto my back. I wasn't about to take a step through this jungle without some manner of weapon. Fortunately, I'd brought along plenty.

I followed the rest of our group as we dismounted and began our descent to the jungle floor. Workers greeted Isandri and stared curiously at us as we made our way down the nearest spiraling staircase, around and around, until we reached the ground.

Standing with my boots sinking into the soft, damp soil, I stared up at the looming fern fronds, colossal trees, and flowers that were bigger than my head. The air was slightly cooler, but heavier with moisture, and water droplets sparkled on the broad leaves and curling fern fronds like scattered diamonds. Dense moss carpeted the earth between a network of tree roots as big around as my leg that snaked through the undergrowth.

"A long way from the tavern, aren't we?" Roxus chuckled as he ambled over to stand beside me. "You know they've got carnivorous trees here? Trees that eat people! Can't swing a cat in here without hitting something that wants to squeeze the life out of you like a cream-filled pastry and swallow you whole."

I flicked him an exasperated glare. "Thank you for that mental image."

He laughed dryly. "I'll be glad when we get our feet on civilized ground."

Well, no argument there.

We followed Isandri in a single-file line, navigating the cut paths through the foliage, into the ruins. Even Isa stopped for a moment to stare up at the huge, leaning bust in the middle of the courtyard. It towered at around twenty feet to the top of its crested helmet, and the style of the engraving was sharp, angular, and almost primitive with very few fine features cut into the stone. Interesting. No wonder Isa believed it wasn't Lunthardan in make.

Navigating the uneven stones and rubble, Isandri brought us to a place where a grove of willow-like trees with long, blossoming fronds veiled an even larger structure. A large, square stone building stood at the top of a broad, steep staircase that led nearly straight up. There must have been more than two hundred steps, and it appeared that the excavation workers had already cleared a path up them through the overgrowth of dirt, moss, plants, and fallen leaves.

At the very top, where the building perched on a wide, solid stone base, the workers had also erected tents and temporary shacks on either side of the single, dark entryway that led into the structure.

The ominous doorway stood open, like the entrance to a cave, and just the sight of it made my stomach drop and every muscle in my body tense. Something about it felt ... off. I couldn't put my finger on why. Caves and caverns had never bothered me before, and saying anything about it felt stupid. It was an old ruin. Not a trap.

Even if every instinct in my brain screamed that it felt exactly like one.

"Lady Isandri, you've returned! And just in time!" A Gray elven man in long, deep purple scholar's robes rushed out of a nearby tent. He tripped all over himself as he ran out to meet us, breathless and grinning from one pointed ear to the other. "It's marvelous—we've just made the most spectacular discovery!"

"What is it?" she faced him with a calm, almost relieved smile.

"Oh, well, we're not altogether sure, my lady. But—but we have theories, of course! I was hoping you would come and see for yourself. Perhaps you can offer some of that expert insight?" He laughed nervously, his multihued eyes darting to the rest of us like he'd just realized we were there. "Oh! I-I do apologize. I did not realize you had brought guests. I am Filoran, lead historian for the queen's court. And you are?"

"In a hurry," Roxus grumbled.

We all glared at him—except for Filoran, who just blinked in confused surprise.

"They are my friends," Isa assured him, and then motioned to where Jaevid stood near the back of our group. "I thought they might provide some additional insight. I believe you may have heard of some of them."

Leaning in closer, the historian squinted at Jae for an instant. Then he jerked back, eyes going wide, and face flooding with embarrassed rosy color. "I-I see! I had no idea! Welcome, esteemed Lord Jaevid. We are honored by your presence! If there's anything we can do to—"

Jaevid waved a hand and bowed his head, as though to dismiss any notion that he wanted special treatment. "Not at all. Please, carry on with your work as before. We will do our best not to get in your way."

The historian rambled on, as frantic and flustered as a wet hen, before he finally seemed to remember himself and got back on topic. He explained that while they had been exploring the interior of the temple before us, they had found many mysterious chambers. Most, he described, were living quarters, baths, and even what seemed to be a kitchen for preparing food. Others had held stockpiles of ancient weapons—namely shields and curved blades much like the Gray elven kafki that Reigh used.

"Initially, we assumed this was simply a temple," Filoran said excitedly. "But based on this most recent discovery, I think it is far more than that. I believe this was, in fact, a monastery of sorts. A place where a few chosen individuals who served this god not only worshipped, but lived and trained."

I arched an eyebrow. "Trained for what?"

"Battle? Potential invaders? Who knows! That's the beauty of discovery, my friend! One great mystery begets another!" Filoran was practically vibrating with excitement, and something about it sort of made me want to hit him. Maybe he'd calm down a little before he gave himself a heart attack. "But I think this most recent chamber has the potential to be the answer to so many of our questions. It is truly an enigma all its own. You must come see it firsthand!"

"Lead on, then," Isandri said, somehow managing to maintain that calm, patient smile. Admirable. But, then again, she was used to putting up with Reigh. Perhaps saintly patience was her finest virtue.

Filoran didn't need any more encouragement. He jabbered like a sparrow that had just found a bread crust, and practically skipped all the way to the huge opening that led into the temple.

Gazing up at the building, there was nothing elaborate or decorated about it. No engravings in the stonework or exterior of the building. It was sleek, perfectly squared, and efficient. Built strictly for function rather than beautiful aesthetic.

And beyond that massive doorway? Nothing but pitch darkness, as far as I could see.

Filoran wasted no time handing a torch to Isandri while he lit another one for himself. He demonstrated their system of tying the ends of long spools of colored rope to our belts before entering—an easy way to keep from getting lost as you explored the tunnels and chambers below. Clever. A scholar sitting by the ends of the spools scribbled our names onto each respective color, to keep track of who came back and who didn't.

"Now then, follow me, and do be sure to stay close together," he said after fixing the end of a yellow rope to the back of his own belt. "We wouldn't want anyone to get lost in a maze of ancient ruins now, would we?"

Once again, Jaevid and I exchanged a knowing stare from across our group. Lost in there? No. But we had come to potentially awaken the ancient god residing there to barter with it for power. No big deal. Not even worth mentioning.

Our chatty tour guide babbled all the way to the edge of that doorway. There, however, he seemed to sober up some at the sight of the inky darkness beyond it. One by one, we followed him through it.

Or—the others did.

I hesitated at the threshold, staring into the dark, as cool air flowed from within. It rustled in my hair and rekindled that prickly sense of unease that still swam in the pit of my stomach. Nothing about this felt right. Something in the aura of the entire temple made my pulse kick harder in my chest. That oppressive sense of being watched, as though some unseen presence was leaning right over my shoulder, intensified. I just wasn't sure how I could express that to the others without sounding paranoid and irrational.

Arrrrgh. I had to pull myself together. I shut my eyes tightly and bit a curse through my teeth. We might only be a few steps away from a solution to helping Reigh and the others.

So why did it feel like I was only a few steps away from hell, instead?

26

CHAPTER TWENTY-SIX

Nearly a mile beneath the surface, lost amidst a network of tunnels and chambers I knew I'd never be able to reverse-navigate on my own, apprehension started to turn my stomach sour. I didn't have a great history when it came to traveling underground, but at least this place didn't seem to have switchbeast infestation. A small blessing.

During our subterranean hike, I'd come to fully appreciate the scholars' rope tether system that kept us linked to the outside world. Our colored ropes had run out of length long ago, stopping at another station manned by another young elven man, with more giant spools. We tied off our current tethers to the new spools, then attached the new ropes to our belts, and kept going. We had repeated that process twice before we finally stopped, and Filoran announced, "Here it is."

Holding his torch aloft, our jittery guide revealed another passage directly before us. This one, however, was the first doorway we had encountered that had some detail work engraved around the outside of it. Sharp, angular designs led up to the top of the doorway, where a shield had been carved into the rock.

A shield ... with the head of a wolf on it.

"Proleus," Isandri whispered in quiet reverence.

"Precisely," Filoran agreed. "It is the first time we have found any sort of defining mark of whom this temple might be dedicated to. We suspected, of course. Now, we can be certain."

"But why here? Why this door?" Garnett asked. "If the whole complex was his, why not have his emblem elsewhere?"

Filoran took a step back out of the way, motioning for the rest of us to come in closer to take a look. "It's just a theory, of course, but we suspect it is because the rest of the settlement here might have been open to visitors and members outside the sacred order that dwelled here. This, however, is a barrier. Beyond this point, we are on holy ground. Perhaps, in order to pass through, one was required to complete some sacred rite? We may never know. But the real treat lies just inside. Our tethers won't reach to the far edge of the chamber, but it is safe to untie them. Just be careful to leave the ropes well organized and remember the color of yours."

No one dared to say a word as we quickly untied the ropes from our belts and walked through that doorway. My breath caught as I passed into the chamber beyond. Every rustle and footstep echoed through the vast space like the interior of a cave. But true to the historian's word—this was anything but a common cavern. Every surface of the wide, circular room had been meticulously carved from the rock. The ceiling stood, tall and domed, more than forty feet overhead, overshadowing a room that must have been nearly a hundred feet across. A series of huge, square-cut columns stood around the perimeter of the room, each one holding a bronze brazier affixed to the side in the shape of a bronze wolf's head holding a lamp in its teeth.

And the floor ... Gods and Fates.

In the very center of the room, roughly sixty feet in diameter, a massive circular relief had been cut straight into the stone floor like a medallion. It depicted rings upon rings of symbols of boars, tigrex, bears, serpents, and men locked in combat with swords and shields—all surrounding the central figure of a wolf's head made from pure obsidian glass. The black wolf. They symbol of Proleus.

As soon as I saw it, a knot of heat sparked to life in the middle of my chest—a heat I knew all too well. It sent energy like a shiver through my body, making my hands clench into fists at my side. My heartbeat slowed. My mind went quiet. I couldn't tear my eyes away from it.

"This is as far as we have dared to go," Filoran explained as he stepped cautiously to the edge of that massive, round engraving. "We need to do a great deal more research, first."

"Why?" Jaevid asked as he hedged over to join him, staring out across the room.

"Ah, well, you see ..." Filoran scooted one of his feet, shifting a few tiny pebbles on the floor to the edge of the engraved medallion. The pebbles rattled and clinked across the ground until, right on the outermost ring, they plummeted down into a crack about an inch wide.

We waited in tense silence, listening to see if they ever hit the bottom of a chamber or tunnel below.

Nothing.

"We suspect that this entire structure is built to move independently of the rest of the room. It is not simply a decorative engraving; it is some sort of device. We just aren't sure what it's for, or what might happen if someone were to put their whole weight on it," Filoran continued. "I have my theories, of course, but until someone actually—"

"We'll do it," Jaevid spoke up suddenly, fixing me with one of his signature steely, determined glares. "It's what we came here for."

I set my jaw and nodded.

"One at a time," Isandri agreed.

"Wh-What? No! It's too dangerous!" Filoran squawked in protest. "We have no idea what this device is even for! It could be dangerous!"

"Absolutely," Roxus snorted.

"O-Or deadly!" Filoran whimpered.

"Most likely," I muttered.

Our frazzled historian gripped his torch so tight it shook in his hands. "And you're still going to do it?!"

"Dangerous and deadly is what we do best," Garnett giggled with a wink. "You just go wait by the door there, love. Take some notes if you like. We'll take care of the rest."

"I'll go first," Jaevid said as we all gathered in a line, right on the edge of the huge circular medallion.

"Oooh, no you don't," Garnett protested. "No one's going at anything alone down here. We all go together. On three, yeah?"

Everyone nodded.

Well, except Jaevid. He just sighed, muttered something under his breath, and shook his head.

"One," Garnett started counting.

"Two," Isandri continued, already holding her foot up in preparation.

"Three," Jaevid finished.

All of us stepped onto the medallion at once.

A second passed. Then another. Everyone stood frozen, staring around in tense preparation for something—anything—to happen.

Nothing did.

I relaxed, letting my arms drop back to my sides where I'd been ready to take my blades out at a moment's notice. Jaevid let out a heavy, ragged sigh. Garnett scowled at the ground as though she were genuinely disappointed.

From the doorway, still shaking like a leaf in autumn while he held that torch, Filoran shouted angrily, "You are the most reckless, thoughtless, irresponsible lot I have ever—"

Darkness swallowed the room as the torches he and Isandri held suddenly snuffed out. The sound of something grinding, like stone upon stone, rumbled under our feet as the medallion flinched and slowly began to turn.

I clenched my teeth, slapping my hands over my ears and nearly falling to my knees as a deep, thunderous voice suddenly boomed in my head like a tolling tower bell.

"FIVE HAVE COME TO THE PROVING GROUND, BUT ONLY ONE STANDS WORTHY."

I forced my eyes open, still reeling as a shriek, yell and scream from the others filled the chamber. One by one, they all flew backward, shoved by some unseen force, until they smacked against the wall on the outer perimeter of the room.

I braced myself, waiting to get tossed, as well.

Instead, the medallion shifted again beneath my feet, and the eyes of the black wolf in the center began to glow red like two campfire cinders.

VOOOM!

A wall of translucent, radiant red light spread between all the pillars around the room, ensnaring me in the center on the medallion with all my companions on the outside. One by one, around the room, the braziers burst to life with flickering flame.

Gods—what was happening? Was this some kind of trap? Why hadn't I been tossed out like the others?

I staggered forward as the medallion spun again, almost falling to my knees as it suddenly locked into place again, aligning some of those stone rings so that the symbols of the boar all lined up. Before me, at the center of the medallion, a column of that blood red light shot upward from the obsidian wolf's head.

The bellow of a beast shook the chamber and rattled the stone an instant before the creature stepped from the light, materializing out of thin air. Bathed in the red glow of that translucent wall, a massive boar charged forward and faced me. Its eyes gleamed like bottomless red pits, and its coal-black fur shone in the firelight. It must have been twenty feet long, twice the size of the largest bull I had ever seen, with tusks as long as my leg.

Holy. Gods.

The voice thundered in my ears again, as deep and powerful as the roll of summer thunder over the mountains. It made my spine curl and sent a bolt of fresh adrenaline surging through my veins like I'd been struck by lightning.

"YOUR VICTORY AWAITS, CHALLENGER. TAKE UP ARMS AND PROVE YOUR WORTHINESS."

WITH A PIERCING BELLOW, THE MONSTROUS BOAR CHARGED STRAIGHT FOR ME.

There wasn't time to think.

I ducked into a side-roll, flinging my body with all my strength to the side and skidding out of the way as the huge creature rumbled past me like a runaway war machine. One stamp from its hoof could crush my skull like an egg. I didn't even want to imagine what those tusks might do.

It didn't matter, though. I was *not* going to die here. Not like this.

Reaching back, I drew my longswords and darted forward, keeping my path arced around the perimeter of our arena. That creature was huge. It would have a hard time maneuvering, even with sixty-or-so feet to charge through. I had to be a moving target, find the right time, and strike.

"Murdoc!" Jaevid shouted in panic, his features barely discernible through the wavering barrier of red light. He reached out to touch it, and immediately let out a cry of pain and stumbled back like he'd been burned.

Right. These must have been some of the rules of this proving ground. No outside help. No escape.

I'd have to get creative.

The massive boar wheeled around with a squeal of frustration, stamped, and started to charge after me again. I couldn't outrun him. But I didn't need to.

I ran straight for that wall, the beast charging right behind me, and sprang at the last second, kicking off the wall and into a backflip as high as I could. Pain shot through my leg, instantly leaving my foot numb. It didn't matter. I whipped my body into a tight spin just as the boar charged beneath me, and landed on its back. The creature pitched and began to tip, like it was going to go into a death roll to try and crush me instead.

I whipped my swords over my hand and immediately plunged them down into the back of the boar's neck—right into the soft place I knew would be lethal.

The flawless points of my weapons cut through the boar's thick, wiry hide like soft cheese. It pitched and bucked, squealing and trying to fling me off. I gave my blades another brutal twist, then ripped them free and sprang off.

BOOOM!

The boar's body hit the ground with a thud that made me stagger. My chest heaved and sweat ran down the sides of my face as I stood back, gripping my weapons in preparation—just in case that monster made another false move.

It didn't. The massive boar lay still, not making a sound, as a pool of dark blood flowed out from the wound I'd left. One strike. One kill. At least, over the years, my own skillset hadn't suffered much.

Slowly, I dared to turn around, looking back out through the rippling wall of red light to where the rest of my companions stood watching. Their faces were a mixture of horror and relief. Not that I didn't understand why. I just had to wonder ... was that it?

Was it over?

Then, as the medallion shifted under my boots again, I got my answer.

I whirled around to find the body of the huge boar gone, like it had disappeared into thin air. The head of the obsidian wolf glowed again, sending up another beam of that brilliant red light. A dark shape moved within it—something slightly smaller and far leaner than the boar. Another opponent? What was it now?

Two leathery black wings stretched out of the light suddenly, unfurling to the radiant red light as the creature rose up and let out a booming roar of fury. The flames sent rippling shadows over its muscular body, glittering off black and red scales, horns, and long curled claws. It landed before me, long tail lashing and jaws snapping as venom dribbled off its chin and ignited into a pool of liquid flame on the floor.

Gods and Fates, that was ... Blite?!

27

CHAPTER TWENTY-SEVEN

My heart gave a frantic lurch, seeming to stop altogether, as I stared up into the face of a beast I knew all too well. Blite was my companion. I trusted that dragon with my life. He would never betray me.

No—no, this couldn't be him. Not really. This was a trick. A cruel ploy to try to get inside my head.

It wouldn't work.

Not when I knew with every fiber of my being that Blite would *never* betray me.

My dragon rushed me, fangs bared and spines bristled down his back, jaws open for the kill. Panic rushed through my body and I drew back, barely managing to feint to the side and dodge as his jaws snapped barely an inch off my shoulder.

Curse it! Didn't he know it was me?

"Blite! Stop!" I shouted as I ran to the side, barely dodging a sweeping lash of his tail. "It's me!"

WHOOOSH!

A plume of burning venom shot past me so close the heat singed my cheek and scorched my leg. I let out a yell of frustrated pain and staggered to a halt. My dragon hissed and crawled closer, his massive black claws scraping over the medallion beneath us. What was I supposed to do? I couldn't fight him! I didn't want to hurt him, but he was leaving me no choice!

Dodging and zigzagging, I tried to sprint around wide so maybe I could get in close enough to make a tactical strike like I had with the boar. I knew every one of Blite's weaknesses. He was my mount, and we'd been flying together for fourteen years. I knew he was slower on the left side. Not by a lot, but enough that I might be able to get in to land a crippling hit. I'd have to be fast. No hesitating.

Kill or be killed.

The Ulfrangar way.

That thought sent a jolt through my brain like a punch to the nose. It rattled me down to the very marrow of my bones.

No. I wasn't an Ulfrangar anymore. I had left that life behind me. I was free now.

I could choose a different way.

BAM!

I screamed as pain exploded through my body and I was snatched off the ground. My blades slipped from my grasp as my body flew through the air and landed with a *thud* that knocked the breath from my lungs. I rolled and skipped over the stone floor, finally landing on my side with my vision spinning in and out of focus.

He'd hit me. I wasn't sure how. Maybe with his tail or a swipe of his claws. But I could feel the blood running from the corners of my mouth as I shakily tried to sit up.

"B-Blite," I slurred as I dragged myself up to my feet again. "I-I know this isn't you. You wouldn't hurt me."

My black dragon roared, crawling forward and drawing in that deep, signature breath that came before the deadly spray of burning venom. From this close, there was no way to avoid it. He would hit me, and I'd die in pure agony.

But I'd rather burn alive than hurt my dragon.

"It's okay. This isn't your fault. I don't blame you," I gasped, my voice catching as a white-hot pain surged through my side with every step. "But I ... w-will ... not ... fight you!"

Blite snarled, showing every one of his jagged fangs, as his nostrils gave one final flare. I caught a glimpse of myself in his brilliant blue eyes an instant before it hit.

I shut my eyes as the rush of heat scorched over me, swallowing me whole. Every inch of my body burned with agony. I opened my mouth to cry out, to beg any god that might be listening to make it end, but there was nothing—no breath or sound. Just endless, raw, searing pain.

And suddenly, in an instant, there wasn't.

The fire vanished.

Wh-What?

I staggered forward, barely catching myself as I gripped my chest and heaved for breath. Looking up, I gaped as my dragon's form slowly dissolved away into curling black smoke.

Then I was alone. I stood motionless on the medallion again, gasping for breath with blood still dribbling from my chin. My side thrummed with wave after wave of stabbing pain that was probably a broken rib or two. It made my vision swerve every time I took in a frantic, ragged breath.

What was happening? Was it over? I'd lost, hadn't I?

Staring around the medallion, I waited for something else to happen. Another monster to appear. Another enemy to fight. Or for all of this to end.

But it didn't.

I turned back, searching beyond that rippling red shield of light for my companions. They all stood clumped together, still watching. Even through the haze of that barrier, I could see the frenzied look of rage and frustration on Jaevid's face. I suppose, if he could have, he would have jumped right into this arena with me.

"They cannot help you," a familiar, deep voice spoke to me in a heavy Damarian accent. "That is the way of the Proving Ground."

Every muscle in my body locked up solid. My blood rushed like an icy river, freezing everything. My thoughts. My breathing. My heartbeat.

O-Oh gods. No. Please, no.

Spinning around, I stared into the face of a man I thought I would never see again. He wore the same black and silver leather armor, the matching silver cuffs bearing the three-eyed wolf's head on his forearms. His lengthy black hair was slicked back, revealing angular features, deeply set golden eyes, sun-bronzed skin, and a neatly groomed beard.

My voice shook, coming out as nothing but a broken, desperate gasp as I dared to speak his name.

"Rook."

It was him. Rook. My handler. The man who had raised me in the order of the Ulfrangar when I was a child. He had chosen me, and spent years molding me into a monster fit for the hunt.

But ... how? How was he here now?!

I'd fought him—killed him! He looked exactly the same as the last time I'd seen him on that stormy night outside of Dayrise. The night we had fought for the very last time. The night I had cut him down.

Rook stared back at me, already holding his xiphos blade in one hand as he gestured to the medallion around us. It shifted and spun again, locking into place with all the carved men in armor facing one another.

"I am impressed that you made it this far, pup," he said as he took a few calculated steps to the side. I knew that movement—that look in his eyes. This was a dance we'd done a thousand times.

And on pure instinct, I began moving, too. It was as though all the pain from the hits I'd taken just slipped away. Pushed down. Irrelevant as my mind fell into the numb silence of the duel like a stone to the bottom of a lake.

I stepped the same way, mirroring his movements, and only stopping long enough to pick up my longswords. My sweaty fingers squeaked on the leather grips of the hilts, and my heart pumped in slow, steady beats.

"You've grown," he said, his golden eyes narrowing as we slowly stepped around one another, like two wolves circling before a brawl. "And I hear you have a new name. Ridiculous, isn't it? Especially when we both know what you truly are."

I bit down hard as anger flared through my chest like a burst of dragon fire. "You know *nothing* about who I am," I snarled.

"Don't I?" He roared suddenly, stepping in with his blade already spinning over his hand like a silver blur.

I kicked off, rushing in to meet him with my longswords swung wide.

CLAANG!

Sparks flashed in the dim red light as our blades locked and clashed, swiping and whirling in a deadly dance until we both drew back.

"I know everything there is to know about you, pup." He gave a sarcastic laugh and shook his head, as though this were all a bad joke. "Even the things you try to forget. I know what you see in your nightmares, what you scream to the dark as you shake in fear. I know what destroys you every time you look into her eyes!"

"NO!" I shouted as I rushed him again. It wasn't real. He wasn't real. This was just another sick, twisted trick! "YOU DON'T KNOW ANYTHING!"

Rook whipped his xiphos as he dipped and dodged, evading my blur of attacks. He ducked back and swung in, as fast as a striking viper. His blade sunk deep into my thigh, and I let out a shout of pain as he ripped it free and immediately struck again.

With a primal growl, I threw up a frantic cross-parry, and barely managed to catch his blade before it sailed down again. With a violent shove, I sent him stumbling backward. That was it. The opening I needed.

I lunged in, relentless as I whipped my swords downward toward his chest.

I missed it—the way his body was angled at the last second. He dipped easily under my swings and drove his elbow into my gut. My vision went white, and I rocked back onto my heels.

Rook came around with a leg sweep, dropping me onto my back. My blades clattered across the stone, far out of reach.

"You will always be Ulfrangar, pup," Rook seethed as he drove the point of his sword down toward my head. "You lived as one of us, and now you will die like one! Like a dog! Like a MURDERER!"

With a desperate cry, I managed to twist my body so his sword hit the ground less than an inch from my ear. Rook drew back, preparing for another strike.

Up. Gods and Fates, I had to get up!

As his second swing came down, I set my teeth against the pain and kicked into a backward roll.

CLAAANG!

His xiphos sparked off the stone, missing me again.

I leapt to my feet, and immediately staggered as the agony from the wound in my leg nearly made me collapse. My pant leg was already drenched in blood. I couldn't keep this up much longer.

Rook laughed as he strolled slowly toward me with his arms spread wide and a twisted grin on his lips. "What did you think, pup? That you'd get yourself a new name, a wife, and a dragon and it would all just go away?"

I bared my teeth and growled, emotions boiling in my blood like molten rock. All the rage. The fear. The dread. The years of pain and regret. Seeing him—hearing his voice again—brought it all erupting to the surface.

Something clicked in my head so suddenly, it snatched the breath from my chest again. I stared at him, the man I'd painted as my own personal demon in every one of those warped nightmares. And I knew.

Rook was not the monster. He called down my dragon on that night. He begged Jaevid to spare me. He tried to throw the Ulfrangar off my trail so I could escape.

Rook hadn't been the one who destroyed me. He was the one ... who saved me. I didn't hate him. I never had.

I hated ... myself.

That realization washed over me like a cool spring rain, dousing all my infernal rage, and making my arms drop slack at my sides. I didn't want to fight him. He wasn't my enemy.

No, I wanted something else. Something no blade or battle could ever give me. The thing that woke me in the night, sweating and shaking with fear. The thing that soured in my heart like a rot that would never heal.

"Rook." My voice cracked as I watched him draw back his blade again, as though preparing to cut my head off in one, effortless stroke. "I ... am so sorry ... that I couldn't save you, too."

Everything around me suddenly went white, as though the room had been engulfed in blinding light.

I shut my eyes and tried to shield my face, cringing back. But there was no escaping it. No hiding from that blinding light. Something warm and soft, like the brush of a summer wind, prickled up from my feet, through my legs, along my spine, and all the way out through my fingers. The pain in my side and leg ebbed away, as though my whole body had suddenly gone weightless. I was floating in that light, drifting in the endless silence. Completely at peace.

"Well done. Anyone can be taught to fight and kill. That alone does not make a warrior," a deep male voice said suddenly, seeming to come from everywhere at once. *"But only a rare few can claim control over the strength of their own mind. That is true power. You are worthy."*

"Who are you?" I heard myself ask, but I couldn't feel my mouth moving. Everything had gone numb, bathed and weightless in that brilliant light.

"I am the one who goes ahead of armies. I am the kingmaker who sharpens destiny's sword and carries the banner of final victory. I am the caller of storms, the vengeance of the just, and the fortress of the honorable," the voice boomed, growing louder and seeming to vibrate through the light like a tolling cathedral bell. *"I am Proleus, and you are worthy in my sight."*

Worthy? What did that mean? I wanted to ask, but I couldn't muster a single sound.

"I know what stirs in the south. I know what covets our power," the voice continued, seeming to grow nearer as a strange prickling heat stirred in my right hand.

My face twitched, and I could feel it—buzzing warmth that spread through my palm and fingers. It grew more intense, becoming hotter and hotter. Gods, what was happening? Was my hand on fire? I had to make it stop somehow before—

"The last war is coming, and you will carry my strength as your own. Know that when you fight, it will be in my name. You alone are worthy ... to be named my paladin."

"MURDOC!" I RECOGNIZED JAEVID'S VOICE CALLING MY NAME EVEN BEFORE I OPENED my eyes to find him standing over me, his expression creased with worry. "Fates, what happened? Are you all right?"

Lying sprawled on my back, I honestly didn't know. I tried to sit up, but my whole body ached and throbbed in protest. I cursed through my teeth and fell back again. "Wh-Where?"

"We're in the temple of Proleus," Isandri said as she and Jaevid helped me sit up. "We triggered some sort of trap. It separated us. We could see you fighting, but we couldn't tell what it was."

I blinked, trying to wrap my mind around everything that had just happened. I'd been trapped in that divinely powered arena. I'd fought a monstrous boar, my own dragon, and ...

Wait a minute—did she just say they hadn't seen any of that?

I frowned at all of them, trying to piece together what was real and what wasn't. Had any of it been real? Or was it all just a nightmare. I didn't know.

Not until I looked down at my right hand. My fingers grasped tightly around a weapon I'd never seen before. The beautiful bronze longsword was simple, but flawless. Its double-edged blade shone like a mirror, polished to perfection, and the hilt was padded with finely oiled black leather. The pommel was made to resemble the head of a wolf crafted from black obsidian glass.

"Incredible," I breathed as I held it up, my arm still shaking some.

"Where did you find that?" Garnett eyed the weapon curiously.

There was no easy way to answer that question. I wasn't sure how it had gotten there. But as I turned the blade over, I realized there was now something branded on the top of my hand: the same symbol of the wolf's head that was carved into the middle of that medallion.

The symbol of Proleus.

"Murdoc?" Jaevid asked, as though trying to jar me out of my daze. Or, maybe he'd just noticed the freshly branded mark on my hand, too.

"It's done," I said at last, meeting his gaze with every ounce of resolve I could muster. "We have the war god's blessing."

Garnett gasped. "You mean ...?"

I held up my hand to show the rest of them the mark. Then I leveled a meaningful stare at Jaevid. "Proleus knows the war is coming. He's on our side now. We need to get to Nar'Haleen as soon as possible."

A determined smile slowly curved over Jaevid's lips. He stretched out a hand to take mine and helped pull me back to my feet. "Well, then, we shouldn't waste another minute. Let's go and help our friends, shall we?"

PART SEVEN

CLARKE

28

CHAPTER TWENTY-EIGHT

"Clarke? Clarke, can you hear me? You've got to wake up," someone called out through the darkness.

Was that ... Noa?

Oh no, had I passed out again? What was happening?

I tried to move, to open my eyes, but my body refused to respond. Curse it, what was wrong? Why did every part of me feel so heavy and numb?

Was I ... dying?

"Come on, Clarke!" Noa called again. "You can pull through this. Concentrate!"

"He hasn't moved in a while," Traegan pointed out, as though he were standing somewhere close by. "Maybe he hit his head when we all fell, eh? Had some bleeding in his brain that finally caught up to him? Look, I know you're fond of him, but I don't think he's gonna make it."

"Just give him a minute," Noa growled back. "Something's been happening with Clarke practically since the day we found him washed up. He's not a normal boy—I saw that much right away. He wouldn't speak about it, and I haven't pushed him to until now. Something about this place has triggered a response in him. "

"Not normal? What, you mean all humans don't have glowin' eyes?" Traegan gasped sarcastically and then chuckled. "You're the strangest lot I've ever met, I'll grant you that."

He really had no idea.

With a groan through clenched teeth, I finally managed to will my eyes open. Everything swerved in and out of focus, like I was looking at the world through the fogged lenses of my spectacles. Er, well, turns out ... I was. Someone must have put them back on my face. Probably Noa. Maybe he thought they would help.

Noa let out a deep sigh of relief as soon as our gazes locked. His shoulders dropped and he slumped forward some, bowing his head as he muttered something in Rienkan I didn't catch. "Welcome back again," he murmured as he bent to help me sit up. "How do you feel?"

How did I feel? I-I wasn't sure yet. Sitting up, my head lolled to the side as everything around me seemed to spin. My stomach rolled dangerously. Throw up. O-Oh gods, I was gonna—

I barely made it onto my hands and knees before I wretched. Thankfully, I didn't have much in my stomach, and all that came up was bile and water. It didn't make me feel any better, but at least it didn't smell so bad.

"What happened?" Traegan asked, coming closer to lean over me. He handed down one of the waterskins we had, er, borrowed off one of the dead members of the Hands of Fate. "Swish your mouth first, and then take a drink, yeah?"

I obliged. With every small sip of cool, fresh water, my head seemed to clear. My hand shook some as I reached up to carefully slide my spectacles off again. I just had to know. I needed to see for myself if anything was different now.

I blinked around, watching Noa and Traegan's haunted expressions morph from worry to surprise. After a few slow, deep breaths, I smiled back at them. No pain. No headaches or crushing pressure. No storm of whispering voices that threatened to drive me mad.

Just calm, blissful silence.

I-I ... didn't need my un-reading glasses anymore.

"What happened, Clarke? There was a strange wind, and all the bones of that monster turned to gray mist. Your eyes were glowing again, and you began to float in the air. It looked like you were talking to someone, and then you suddenly collapsed," Noa explained.

Wow. I hadn't really considered how things must have looked from the other side of my encounter with Avgior. No wonder they assumed I was dead or dying.

Looking down at my hands, I flexed my fingers in and out. I had shaken Avgior's hand. But I didn't feel any different now. Well, apart from not having that awful headache. Had anything changed? I couldn't tell.

Regardless, I needed to be honest with Noa. Going forward, if this changed me in a negative way, I needed him to know about it. I needed him to keep an eye on me in case I did anything strange or bad.

So I did. I told Noa and Traegan everything I could remember about meeting Avgior, what he had revealed when it came to our past, and what I supposedly was. A missing piece of his essence. The last one, in fact.

"And this book—the codex—was the first piece?" Noa asked, his brow crinkled in bewilderment.

"I think so," I replied. "It explains why I was so drawn to it before. I heard it calling to me in my dreams every night when I lived at the library, I just never understood why."

"So, let me get this straight." Traegan sat, scratching at his bearded chin with his good hand as he studied me through narrowed eyes. "You're now the embodiment of an ancient dragon-god?"

Uhh, well, when he put it like that, it did sound pretty unbelievable.

"No offense, boy, but you don't look very godlike to me," he chuckled again, as though he found all of this completely ridiculous.

I deflated.

Noa shot him a scorching glare. "Seen many gods in mortal form, have you?" he fired back.

Traegan just shrugged his brawny shoulders. "No. But I doubt one would ever show up looking like a scrawny human boy."

"I think you'd be surprised." Noa snorted and looked away, as though the argument weren't even worth it.

Maybe he was right.

I didn't look like a god. Honestly, I didn't feel like one, either. But I couldn't deny everything that had happened. Something inside me had definitely changed.

I just hoped it was a change for the better.

"We need to figure out how to get out of here. With you and me already injured and not much good in a fight, we'll have to be extra careful." Traegan muttered and thumbed to Noa and himself. "Hopefully there's no more of those Hands of Fate prowling around."

Right. I didn't know if I should say anything—but I had a feeling there probably were more of them. Something in the back of my mind told me they hadn't found us by accident. We couldn't assume they wouldn't try to hunt us down again."

"We go quietly then," Noa agreed. "I would say we could go without a torch, since you can see just as well in the dark, but if there are Pitathi in their ranks, it won't matter. Dark or not, they'll spot us just the same."

"Makes me nervous as a rabbit in a fox den knowing those red-eyed mongrels are working in the Hands of Fate. Honestly, what's the emperor doing? That lot is naught but poison and hatred. Why, by all the stacked stones of the elders, would he enlist them into his service?"

A cold pang of dread cut through my stomach as I stared out across the rubble-strewn chamber before us. Without the bones, there was nothing left but empty space as far as my pathetic human eyes could see—which wasn't all that far, even with the help of the torch.

If we got attacked again, we wouldn't stand a chance. We needed help. We needed someone to find us. But no one knew where we were. Not even Kaili or any of the other villagers. We had no allies that could fight enemies like that.

We might as well have been on the surface of the moon.

Closing my eyes, I gripped my glasses tightly as I tried to focus all my concentration on a solution. An answer to this problem.

We need help, I thought as hard as I could. *Someone, please ... find us.*

WITH TRAEGAN IN THE FRONT OF OUR GROUP AND NOA HOBBLING ALONG AT THE BACK with the torch held aloft, we trekked around the perimeter of the chamber until we found a small exit. Thanks to the damage to entire room after I had, um, accidentally caused an earthquake, it was hard to tell if it was originally part of the temple or not. But we didn't have much of a choice. We had to press on.

After several hours, the crooked tunnel twisted around and stopped abruptly at a pile of rubble that had caved in from overhead. I couldn't tell if it was a recent tunnel collapse, or something that had happened centuries ago, but Traegan insisted we could dig a way through.

"As something of an expert in rocks, I know an intentional cave-in when I see one," he declared. "The stones are stacked too neatly. It's been sealed off. The ceiling should be sound. We just have to make a way through."

Noa flicked a sideways look at Traegan's wounded arm and mumbled, "You plan on moving a lot of rocks with only one arm?"

"Fortunately, the gods thought to bless me with *two*," Traegan bared back as he stomped toward the stack of rocks blocking our path forward. "I'll manage."

He did more than manage. Even with one arm incapacitated, Traegan rolled and hauled rocks like a stubborn ox. I couldn't help but be impressed. He was half my height, but his shoulders and arms were thick with more hardened muscle than I'd ever had my entire life. He wasted no time getting a top layer of the stones moved out of the way.

Noa helped, too, and I tried rolling some of the smaller ones aside. But after several hours, we all had to stop. Drenched in sweat and weak with hunger, there was only so much we could do at a time—especially given their injuries.

"We could go back the way we came," Noa suggested as he stared mournfully at the still head-high heap of large stones blocking our path.

"And do what? We didn't pass any other tunnels or passages. This is the only way forward," Traegan argued.

Good point. Even backtracking wouldn't help us now.

We needed a different angle. A new solution.

Hmmm.

The idea hit me so suddenly, I almost fell over—as though it had been chucked at me like someone hurling apples at my head. No, not an idea. A memory.

I snapped to my feet and started for the heap of rocks.

I'd shaken them loose before. I could do it again.

"Clarke?" Noa said, his tone uneasy.

Standing before the blocked passage, I widened my stance and closed my eyes. Then I stretched out my hands ahead. Focus. I just had to focus. It was there, buried deep, just waiting to awaken again—power like a muscle that had atrophied over the eons.

I just had to trust that feeling.

I had to trust *myself*.

It started deep, like a tiny seed in the center of my mind. A little shiver of energy. But as soon as I felt it, and focused on it, that feeling grew. It swelled and exploded, blooming through every corner of my brain and surged out through all my extremities. I bit down hard as that sensation stretched me from the inside out, yawning to life and making my hands shake.

The tiny pebbles around my feet began to shift and rattle ... and then slowly levitate.

More—I had to try harder. It wasn't enough.

My chest heaved in deep breaths, my feet beginning to slide as the palms of my hands ebbed a brilliant golden light that lit up the tunnel. Wind stirred around me, snatching through my hair and billowing in my clothes.

And that feeling grew. It rushed through me like a roaring river, bursting through my chest and setting every nerve ablaze. My pulse thundered in my ears. My arms shook as something sprouted along my forearms. Spines? My fingernails grew longer and curled like claws. I could feel my incisors doing the same as a strange sensation spread along my scalp just over my ears.

Before me, the massive stones groaned, shifted, and lifted into the air. A jerk of one hand and five of them sailed off to the left. Working—it was working!

I bore down harder, digging into that feeling. With a twist of my wrists and a shoving step forward, the rest burst outward with a concussive *BOOM!*

I-I had done it! I'd cleared the tunnel!

My arms dropped to my sides like two overcooked noodles. I rocked back on my heels, almost falling until Noa rushed in to catch me and hold me upright. Neither he nor Traegan said a word at first. They stared back and forth between me and the freshly cleared pathway ahead.

"Are you kidding me?" Traegan crowed suddenly. "You couldn't have done that sooner?! We just blew five hours moving rocks around like idiots!"

Before I could stop it, a laugh burst past my lips as I stared at him drowsily, my ears ringing and my vision spotting. "Wh-Who's ... not godlike ... now?" I wheezed.

Traegan's mouth hung open, one eye twitching like he might suddenly take a swing at me. Then, out of nowhere, he threw his head back and started laughing, too.

Noa just stared between us like we'd both lost our minds.

"That'll show me, eh?" Traegan was still chuckling as he bent over to pick up our torch and start toward the empty passage ahead. He stopped in the entryway I'd just cleared and gave a little bow, motioning for the two of us to go on ahead of him. "Gods before beauty, and may the stones forever sing your praises. Remember this humble mortal when you ascend to your divine throne."

Steadying myself against Noa, I tested the strength in my legs before I dared to take a step away. So far, so good. My ears still felt like they were stuffed full of cotton, and my knees felt a little wobbly, but I could manage it. The strangeness in my arms—claws and spines—had all disappeared. I was myself again.

And I could do this. I could get us out of here. I just had to keep trusting that power.

And more than that, I had to keep trusting myself.

THE MUCH LARGER TUNNEL BEYOND THE CAVE-IN WAS DEFINITELY NOT SOMETHING made by accident. With engraved arches along the walls, glittering mosaics tiling the ceiling, a smoothly sculpted floor, and intricate scrollwork bordering the floor—there really was no doubt that this was a part of the rest of the temple complex. Every twenty-or-so yards, little alcoves held statues in jade, onyx, or alabaster that resembled figures of the gods. I could easily identify every one of them, and Traegan teased me about whether or not we should stop so I could properly greet my relatives.

I couldn't decide if he was right or wrong about that. It was strange to think that I might have any relation whatsoever to them. Beyond strange, really. Absolutely bizarre.

No denying the evidence now, though.

"Look there!" Traegan called as he jogged forward a little, waving for us to catch up. "Mountains have mercy, tell me I'm not imagining that there's a bit'o sunlight coming through that doorway!"

He wasn't.

Straight ahead of us, the tunnel broadened again, ascending up a set of carved stone stairs where golden shafts of daylight poured down, creating a shimmering, misty effect thanks to all the dust in the air. A cool breeze blew through, stirring up more of that dirt and rustling through my hair. I could have fainted with relief as I closed my eyes and took in a deep breath of it, savoring the sweet aroma of jungle plants and moist soil.

We were so close. Sure, we had smelled something similar in the room with the big hole in the ceiling. But this was different. I just knew it.

Even Noa had started smiling as he limped along at the back of our group, steadily making his way with one arm on the wall to keep his balance.

Not much farther. We were going to make it. Once we were finally out of this wretched place, we could find Kaili and the others, get our wounds properly treated, and make it to Uru'Nai.

My feet crunched over a fine layer of dead, dried leaves and twigs that began to appear the higher we climbed on those steps. And, at last, I saw it. A wide, arched doorway flanked by two angelic statues with their wings spread high and their hands cupped together in front, like they were meant to be holding something. Incense, maybe? Or candles?

Whatever the case, I practically sprinted the last few steps and dashed out into the warmth of the midday sun, passing Traegan on my way up. The sunlight hit my face, warming my skin as I spread my arms wide and turned in a circle, staring up into the arms of the trees. Sweet freedom. Fates, I'd never go into another cave again.

Something deep in my soul, that tiny quiet place that had kindled all that power, thrummed and buzzed with a joy that brought tears to my eyes. It was more than just freedom for that part of me—the part that was Avgior. It was vindication. It was a second birth.

But that feeling ... didn't last.

29

CHAPTER TWENTY-NINE

TWAAANG!

A burst of cracking bowstrings snapped in the air as a chorus of shouts resounded around me.

Too late, I looked around at the moss-covered rubble and ruins where a small army of people moved. They pointed, shouted, and fired at me with crossbows. Arrows hummed through the air, whizzing past my head and body.

O-Oh no.

Run! We had to—

My body jolted forward as something hit me in the back. Pain exploded through my shoulder. I yelled, and immediately someone tackled me to the ground from behind, grabbing the back of my head and pinning me as more arrows zipped past.

"Stay down!" Traegan shouted over me, still pinning me down. "Curse it, it's those blasted Hands again!"

What? Oh gods! Had they been lying in wait for us out here?

What about Noa? Where was he? He couldn't run with his injured leg! What were we going to do? Where could we go to hide?

"Noa!" I tried calling for him.

No answer. Nothing but chaos as more voices shouted around us, seeming to come from all sides.

"You're shot, but it's just a flesh wound. You can still run, boy. On my go," Traegan growled low, his body tense like a leopard about to spring. "Ready ... NOW!"

We both scrambled up at the same time, stumbling and tripping before we sprinted headlong through the jungle undergrowth. Palm fronds and tree branches slapped against my face as I bolted, running right behind Traegan. My shoulder throbbed, but I didn't dare to stop or look back.

Ahead, a half-toppled stone column covered in moss and vines might give us some cover. We could make it. Just a little farther!

Twenty yards.

Then ten.

I screamed in panic as something snagged around my legs, tying them together. I fell face-first, gasping and trying to breathe, as I rolled onto my side to see what had happened. A contraption, like a snare line made of thick wire and four metal balls, was wrapped so tightly around my ankles. I reached down, trying to untie it, but my shoulder howled with pain every time I tried to move.

"There you are," a voice hissed over me suddenly.

I looked up, my whole body going cold with terror as I met the scarlet-eyed stare of another Hands of Fate agent. He leered at me over the edge of the scarf that covered his nose and mouth, eyes narrowing as he drew a long, curved dagger from his belt.

The air shattered with the sound of a familiar voice crying out in pain. Even from a distance, I knew it was Noa. His voice caught and shook as he cursed in Rienkan. Th-They … they were hurting him. Maybe even killing him. And he couldn't even run or try to defend himself.

Rage took my mind like a molten, infernal storm. That soft seed of energy exploded with force that ripped a scream from my throat as I threw a hand up toward the agent in front of me.

Golden light burst from my palm, hitting him square in the chest, and blowing him backwards. He hit the side of a crumbling heap of stone with a *crunch* and hung there, suspended by my power. My whole body shook with rage as I snatched my feet apart, snapping the thick wire around my legs as though it were nothing but rotten thread.

"YOU!" My voice vibrated, echoing with a second tone that sounded like Avgior. I kept my hand outstretched, watching the agent's body twitch and tremble until I snapped my fist closed.

CRUNCH!

The agent hit the ground with a *thud* and didn't move again.

"Take him down! He must not escape!" A second agent howled as he charged me, swinging another set of those wire-and-ball snares over his head like he was about to throw it at me.

No. Not again.

BOOOM!

I thrust another hand toward him, sending out a second wave of power that knocked over trees, sent boulders rolling, and toppled a column that had been barely standing. Two Hands agents flew back, hitting the ground and rolling away.

I could feel it again, rising within me and spreading out through every corner of my body. Wave after molten wave of power. Spines pressed through my skin, growing from my forearms all the way to my elbows, as a sheen of pearlescent scales formed over my skin. My nails became curled black claws, and my teeth grew into dripping fangs.

VOOOM!

Something hit me again from behind. But this time, it wasn't a friend trying to save my life. I fell to a knee, gritting my teeth against sweltering pain that singed over my back.

"You little wretch," a feminine voice hissed. "Well, at least you've saved me the trouble of digging up that putrid corpse myself. That's one less errand, and one step closer."

Gritting my teeth, I forced my shaking legs to stand again and turned to face her—a woman I didn't know. The woman stood, her gaunt form draped in robes of black and gold silk and her face smeared with designs painted in black oil. Her shock white hair resembled mine, but blew around her wildly as she pointed a bony finger at me and sneered. "You play with power beyond your understanding, boy. Now, you'll learn to heel, like the mutt you are!"

What? Who was this woman? And what did she want with me?

Her eyes glowed white with power as her lips curled back in a feral snarl. She made a gesture with her hand and a sparking, crackling ball of energy formed over her open palm.

Oh gods! She was a sorceress?!

O-Oh no. I couldn't—I couldn't do this! I-I didn't know what I was doing! I barely understood what I was. How could I fight someone like her and ever hope to win?

Then, behind her I saw two Hands of Fate agents drag Traegan from the jungle. He hung limp in their grasp, his clothes stained with blood.

A new wave of raw fury split through my chest and I let out a thundering growl in response. As the sorceress gave a wrenching, twisting jerk of her wrist that sent the ball of crackling energy hurtling toward me like a comet.

I broadened my stance and stretched my arms out wide. I wouldn't surrender. Not that easily. If she wanted to throw fire around ... then two could play at that game.

I was not going down without a fight.

BOOOM!

Her big orb of crackling power met my wave of scorching heat, colliding between us with force that blew down more columns and ripped up trees by the roots. It left a scorched crater around us, breaching the dense jungle canopy so that sunlight poured down over us.

My hands shook. Something warm and wet ran from my nose and dribbled down my chin. My ears rang with a high-pitched, squeal. But I didn't dare drop my guard. Not when I could still see her there through the clearing smoke.

Her smile was venom as she took another step toward me, curling her fingers again as her eyes flashed with eerie, milky light. "You dare to dream that you can match me, child? You know nothing of divine power. You will serve me with your blood—down to the very last drop!"

I stumbled. That feeling that still flared through my body, pulling and stretching me from the inside, began to hurt. I-I didn't know how much longer I could do this. My knees shook and my lungs constricted. My spines and claws had begun to disappear, and I bit down hard, forcing myself to keep standing. I couldn't give up. I couldn't fail. Traegan and Noa needed me.

A sickly green bolt of power lashed out from her open hand. I tried to deflect it, shouting as I pressed outward with all my strength to resist it with my own power again.

It wasn't enough.

That beam of wicked green energy hit me square in the chest. I flew backward, hitting the ground hard on my side. Something in my shoulder cracked. I cried out, digging my fingers into the dirt. Get up—I had to get up! I wouldn't let it end this way!

A shadow fell over me, and I squinted up into the woman's glowing golden eyes as her thin, sunken features pulled into a grimacing smile. She planted a foot squarely on my ribs, digging her heel in and pinning me there as she reached into her robes and drew out a black stone dagger with an ivory hilt.

I sucked in a frantic breath. I-I knew that blade with every fiber of my being. I had seen it before in a vision, yes. But the essence within me, Avgior, knew it, too. And it set terror like cold fire rushing through my veins.

Because that was the same blade that had killed him thousands of years ago.

"You know this weapon, yes? You remember it. I can see it in your eyes, wyrm," she seethed gleefully. "Now, you'll feel its bite again. After all, I only need your blood. The wild dogs can feast on the rest of you and your little friends."

Shutting my eyes tightly, I held my breath. I waited for the end. For more pain. Gods, I wanted to apologize to Traegan and Noa. I wasn't strong enough. I barely knew this power, and I couldn't sustain it long enough to help them.

We would all die ... because I was too weak.

Help me, I thought, begging with every shred of energy left in my brain. *I can't do this on my own. Please—someone help!*

A faint noise rolled overhead like the distant roll of thunder. No, wait. Not thunder. Was that a roar?

I dared to open my eyes, just in time to see a massive shape zoom overhead above the trees. An instant later, a second zoomed past, eclipsing the sunlight. It wheeled into a sharp turn on broad, leathery wings, arcing gracefully through the air like a giant, armored eagle. It let out an ear-splitting roar that made the sorceress reel back and nearly drop that wicked knife.

"No ... no, no, NOOO!" she screeched, her eyes wide and crazed. "I will not let you interfere! Not again!"

Whirling on me, she lunged for one of my arms and drew back that knife, slicing it across my forearm. I yelled, trying to wrench away as she squeezed my arm tighter. Shoving the knife back into her robes, she took out a vial from another pocket and held it against my wound, catching the flow of fresh blood before she let me go.

The sorceress cast me one last, scalding glare before turning to march furiously away. She only made it a few steps before something enormous dropped from the sky and landed before her with a *BOOM!*

G-Gods, it was ... a dragon!

The massive blue-scaled monster prowled closer, the earth flinching under his clawed feet, as his snout wrinkled in a snarl. Vivid yellow eyes searched the rubble and finally landed on her. The dragon's pupils narrowed, nostrils flaring, and spines bristling as it let out a rumbling growl. Burning venom dripped from its jagged teeth as its long tail lashed slowly from side to side.

"You miserable worm," the sorceress spat. "You think I fear you?"

The dragon's lips curled back in a snarl, its growl deepening as a booming voice filled my mind. *"You will."*

Her eyes widened and she stumbled some, staggering back a step as the dragon rose up and gave another shattering cry. It drew in a mighty breath, plated chest heaving deeply. White-hot flame erupted from the dragon's jaws, aimed right at her.

The sorceress paled in horror, frantically throwing up her hands at the last second. One gesture was all it took. She sent a ripple of darkness, like tongues of shadow, bursting from the ground at her feet. It engulfed her form an instant before the flames could touch her.

With a soundless wisp of darkness, she was gone without a trace.

Then the dragon's massive, horned head swung around to stare straight at me.

Oh no.

I couldn't move. I couldn't even sit up. Lying on my side, every inch of me wracked with pain, all I could do was stare as the creature lumbered closer and gave a low, chattering sound in its throat. Then I heard it—that deep voice again, as the dragon's vibrant yellow eyes studied me.

"You still live. Good. We heard your cry for help. We are few, but strong enough. Be still. My rider will come."

His what? Wait a second, was I actually hearing that dragon speak?!

I choked as I tried to say something, to answer him. But nothing would come out. My throat had gone raw, and I shook with pain every time I took in a breath.

"Mavrik!" A new voice called out as a crunching, crashing sound came from somewhere out of my view. "There you are! What happened? I leave you for five seconds and you've burnt down half the jungle. We have to find—" The voice stopped, and footsteps crunched quickly over the ground, coming closer. "Gods and Fates!"

A man in polished silver battle armor and a long blue cloak appeared over me, dropping quickly to his knees and pulling off his helmet. With his sharply featured face framed in shoulder-length, silvery gray hair, his keen eyes darted over me as his mouth set into a tight, worried line. Something about him seemed familiar, although I couldn't imagine why. I didn't know anyone who rode on a dragon. But still ... something about that scar over one of his eyes, and his slightly pointed ears struck a chord in my mind.

It felt like I *should* know him. But why?

"You're safe now. I've got you," he said, speaking to me in the common language as he bent over to check my battered body like he was trying to decide which injuries were the most severe.

I didn't care about my condition, though.

"M-My friends," I rasped weakly. "P-Please help them."

"We'll do everything we can," he said, his smile steady and calm as he reached down to loop his arms under my back and knees. He picked me up in one smooth motion, like I didn't weigh anything at all.

The sudden motion made my head swim and my vision tunnel. My head lolled against his shoulder as he started carrying me toward that huge blue dragon.

"How many others are there?" he asked, his pale blue eyes fixing me with a determined stare.

"Two," I groaned through my teeth. "P-Please. They're ... hurt, too. Traegan and ... N-Noa."

"We'll find them," he promised, and paused to look up as a another, smaller dragon with glossy black scales and a red stripe down its back swooped in for a low pass over us. The wind rushed off its powerful wings, and it let out a trumpeting call that the blue dragon answered with a growl. I could have sworn I saw someone sitting on that dragon's back.

My mind spun. No. Not possible. It couldn't be.

Dragonriders?

"We found another one!" A sing-song female voice called out. She had a thick accent that sort of reminded me of Traegan's. "We're still searching the thickets, but it looks like Isa's also got a prisoner pinned. One of their ranks didn't flee fast enough. He looks like a priest of some sort."

Another one? Oh gods, was it Traegan or Noa? And a priest, too? I winced as I tried to sit up higher in the man's arms so I could see. But my head swam dangerously, and I flopped uselessly against his shoulder again.

"Easy there. You're going to be all right," the man said as he carefully set me down right next to the blue dragon's side. "Mavrik, keep watch in case they try to come for him again."

The huge, scaly beast curled around me protectively, crouching low with its scaly ears slicked back and eyes wide and watchful.

"Wh-Who are you?" I had to know. I didn't understand what was happening or who these people were. Were they someone I should trust? Or was I just trading one enemy for another?

"My name is Jaevid Broadfeather," the man said as he stood back, his regal blue cape billowing in the breeze as he smiled down at me. "I am a Dragonrider of Maldobar, and we've come to rescue you."

PART EIGHT

REIGH

30

CHAPTER THIRTY

A red sun, wrapped in smoky purple and orange clouds, rose early over the city of Esfolar. Battered, bruised, and filthy, we made our way through the streets that were already filled with hundreds of other people who were in similar shape. Refugees from the attack.

The haunting, desperate calls of families searching for one another in the crowds made my soul go numb. Groups mobbed around healers in white and blue robes, waiting for treatment. I could tell just at a glance that some of them wouldn't survive the wait, and it took everything I had not to stop and try to help, too. I was supposed to. I was a healer, too. I should be helping.

But we had to keep moving. Time was running out.

"They didn't stand a chance," Thatcher seethed quietly as he walked beside me. "They had almost no warning. The garrisons didn't even get an opportunity to fight back, let alone barricade the ports."

"It wouldn't have mattered with a drakkon swimming around, destroying everything in its path," I muttered back. "Even with warships to defend the port, they didn't stand any more of a chance than we did when we crossed one in that pirate ship. You can't use cannons and harpoons against a monster like that."

He didn't answer for a long time. Then, I saw his jawline stiffen as he flashed me a sideways glare. "You could use dragons, though. Maylea injured it with Lukani as a shrike."

Hmm. Yeah, he was probably right. Dragons were effective, and a battle-ready flight of them might stand a chance of bringing a monster like that down if they worked together. But this far away from Maldobarian soil? Yeah, not going to happen. The only dragon we had on hand was ... well, literally about the size of my hand.

Vexi nibbled at my ear, gnawing and growling playfully as she tugged at my earlobe and wrapped her long tail around my neck. Maybe she was hungry and my ear looked tasty. I winced and squirmed as her tiny teeth pricked at my skin.

If Arlan was right about his spell, she wouldn't be this size for much longer. He had shrunken her in the evening, and if this spell really was time-sensitive, that only gave us a few hours before she was big again. No one was more thrilled about that than I was. I'd have tiny bite-marks all over my neck and ears for weeks.

Following Violet, we tried avoiding the more crowded main streets where throngs of refugees were standing in lines for supplies and treatment. Many were scouring big wooden signboards that were papered in layers of hastily scrawled notes left by families still trying to find one another. The air hung thick with unsettled murmuring, as though everyone were on edge and just waiting for the next awful thing to happen.

My nerves were already pretty fried. As horrible as it was to think about, I was already used to this sort of situation. I had seen it play out during the Tibran war many times. The aftermath of battles, when the local citizens were left with the task of picking up the pieces of their shattered lives and trying to carry on, wasn't for the faint of heart. Usually, there were some members of local government to help. Soldiers for the heavy lifting. Medical aid.

But here?

Well, I couldn't see anything like that. I didn't even know if Rienka had an army to speak of. They had declared their independence after the fall of the Tibran Empire, when Nar'Haleen was too weak and broken to do anything about it.

Now, Rienka would have to deal with their former ruling power if they wanted to keep that independence. And from where I was standing, it didn't look like it was going well.

"Here," Violet said suddenly, ushering us over to the front of a building with two stone pillars holding up a low awning at the front. With no windows, and a door made from an intricately woven blue and green tapestry, it didn't look like a tavern or inn. At least, not like one I'd ever been to.

The fragrance of oils and minerals hung thick in the air as we all shuffled inside the dim front room. Behind a tall wooden counter, an elderly woman startled where she had been busily cutting towels into long strips. Making bandages?

"I do apologize, but we aren't taking customers for the bath today," the old woman said, visibly flustered as she looked over our group.

"We just need a place to rest and catch our breath for a little while," Violet said. She motioned to Maylea, who took out our Zenith's Call coin and quickly held it out for the old woman to see.

"O-Oh. Yes. Okay, then. There's a room at the back you are welcome to use," the woman stammered and nodded, seeming even more uncomfortable now. "I'm afraid we don't have any of the usual commodities prepared, however. But the baths are always hot, and I will make sure no one disturbs you."

"We appreciate it," Violet murmured, and led the way deeper into the building.

I squinted through the dim light ebbing from wavered glass globes that hung from the ceiling. The hot, humid air filled the rooms with steam that curled from the surface of beautifully tiled soaking pools. Fountains gurgled and gently stirred the water, and pots and vases filled with bath oils and salts sat nearby. There were brushes and towels, robes for sitting in rooms filled with hot steam, and a nearly dark area with heated wooden floors. Pallets filled with what felt like rice were stacked against the wall—probably for dozing on that warm floor.

Any other time, I'd have spent all day at a place like this, and indulged in every creature comfort it had to offer. Maybe had a glass of wine and soaked in a bath, then taken a nap on that heated floor. But now … Fates, I just wanted to get the filth out of my hair and catch my breath.

I threw down my bag, which hit the floor with a soggy slap, and immediately started unlacing my boots. No one questioned as I stripped off my tunic and socks, and then started back for one of those baths. I'd be doing everyone a favor by not starting our desert excursion caked with pig flop.

Before I could get out of the room, Violet seized my arm and tugged me to a halt. "I'm going to see if I can connect with our caravan," she whispered. "There is a chance that, given what's happened, they are delayed or may change the meeting point. I'll find them, and try to restock anything we have lost before we depart."

I nodded, glancing past her where Maylea, Thatcher, and Lukani were already settling down into a circle on the heated floor. They all looked about as miserable as I felt. No one had walked away from this clean—mentally or physically.

"Watch your back out there," I warned as Violet released my arm and started past me. "Caravan or not, we need to be out of the city before dusk. Vexi is due to not be so portable anymore. She'll definitely draw attention, and that's the last thing we need right now."

Violet nodded, but didn't look back as she continued out of the bathhouse.

I watched her go, silvery-blonde hair swishing in a braid that hung down to her waistline. I didn't say anything—mostly because I knew she'd tease me for it—but I hated the idea of her going out alone. We should be staying together, now more than ever. It was dangerous out there. People were desperate and bound to be looking for someone to blame for what was happening. Her being Viperi obviously put her at a greater risk than the rest of us.

I was sure she already knew that. She would try to be careful. But I couldn't shake the fear that it might not be enough. She might get backed into a corner and need help.

And I'd be too far away to do anything about it.

"If only I had a spare pair of *socks*," I groaned and shot Thatcher a hard stare from across the room as I tried to wring my wet ones out before I put them back on. Ugh. Disgusting.

He just rolled his eyes and shook his head. "It wouldn't matter. Everything in your bag is drenched anyway."

He had a point—but still.

"*Almost* everything," I corrected as I did the same with my tunic. I'd rinsed everything and scrubbed it by hand as best I could while I was in the tub, but there wasn't time to hang it to dry. Not much point in that, though. In a place this humid, nothing would ever get fully dry anyway. "My waterproof bag worked, as it turns out. The medical kits are still intact. Thank the gods for tiny miracles, I suppose."

Thatcher didn't say anything else as I went on getting redressed, trying to be as quiet about it as possible since Maylea and Lukani had curled up on the warm floor to sleep. Good thing, too. Who knew how long it would be before we found a quiet, safe place like this to rest again.

I'd almost finished lacing my vambraces when Maylea bolted upright with a sudden, frantic gasp. She stared around the room, her bleary eyes wide and her expression skewed with a mixture of panic and confusion, as though she weren't sure where she was. I waited, holding still and not making a sound, until her gaze finally locked with mine.

She blinked once, hard, and then her mouth screwed up. Her eyes welled and her shoulders shook as her chin began to tremble. Oh no. Was everything that happened finally catching up to her?

"Hey, it's alright." I kept my voice soft and calm as I scooted over close to her and started to put an arm around her shoulders. "We're safe here. It's over. We—"

She flung her arms around my middle and buried her face in my chest. Her whole body trembled as she sobbed and gasped for breath. "Uncle Reigh! I-I ... I think I saw Ronan!"

Huh? What was she talking about?

"What do you mean?" I asked as I put a hand on the back of her head. "You were asleep. It was probably just a dream."

"N-No! No, it wasn't! I was ... I was in this strange castle. Or maybe a cave. It was so dark, and it didn't have any windows. But there were books everywhere. I heard someone calling out for help. A boy. It sounded like he was in trouble. He was scared," she sniffled against me, gripping fistfuls of my soggy tunic. "I-I tried to find him, but this barrier like foggy glass blocked the tunnel. I could see shadows like someone moving on the other side. But as soon as I reached out to touch it, it all disappeared. I could still hear him screaming."

Thatcher and I swapped a wary glance. His mouth set into a hard, bitter line. I probably had a similar expression. We had both been knee-deep in this divine power crap long enough to know exactly what a dream like that felt like. Hell, to be precise. But this must have been Maylea's first real taste of it.

"You're sure it was Ronan?" I asked, still trying to keep my tone as gentle as possible as I rubbed her back and petted her hair. "Did you see his face?"

She hesitated, pulling back some and staring up at me with her cheeks flushed and eyes teary. "I-I ... No. I didn't. But it has to be him, right? Who else would be calling out for help from me like that?"

I didn't want to answer that. I didn't know, and any guess I made might lead her in the wrong direction. Taking in a deep, steadying breath, I pulled her into a tight hug and held her there. "Being connected to Paligno is going to mean you have visions like this sometimes. It's like that for anyone who is god-touched. But they're not always literal. Sometimes, they're just like echoes. So don't let yourself get worked up. Try to calm down and think through it," I said. "Everything's going to be fine. We're going to get Ronan back."

"You promise?" she whimpered, still shaking some as she curled her legs in and relaxed into my arms like a tiny frightened child.

Because, all divine power aside, she still was.

The words stung at my heart and I closed my eyes as I let my chin rest on top of her head. "I promise," I answered, knowing full well that it might be a lie.

31

CHAPTER THIRTY-ONE

Hours passed, and Maylea nodded off to sleep again sitting right beside me. I kept an arm around her shoulders, drawing her in close so her head rested against my chest like a scared little kid. It felt better to have her close, just in case she had another nightmare. Or vision. Sometimes, with divine dreams, it was hard to tell which was which.

My thoughts ran like wild dogs, snarling and snapping at my last few strands of sanity. That moment on the bridge, watching the massive drakkon rise out of the water like a colossal demon, replayed over and over in my mind. I wondered if Judan had stayed to fight, or if he and the rest of his scoundrel crew had fled. Had he been killed? And that Varren fellow—he must have still been on the island when the attack started, right? Unless he had another way to make a swift escape. What about those priests I'd found in the tower? Had they made it somewhere safe, too? There was no way to know any of that now.

After a while of trying to chase down those worries, sitting with the heated floor sending waves of soothing warmth up through my legs and rear, my eyelids began to grow heavy. I must've nodded off completely, because I flailed and nearly dropped Maylea when Violet returned and plopped a satchel on the floor nearby.

Ugggh. Gods. Sitting like that, with my head bent down, made every muscle in the back of my neck howl in protest. I was still reeling after getting dragged around by my throat. This wasn't going to do me any favors in that department. Maybe I really was getting too old for this. I certainly didn't bounce back as fast as I had when I was Maylea's age.

"I've got something for us to eat, but we have to be quick. The caravan is nearly ready. We should eat, and then move to the edge of the city as fast as possible," Violet whispered, her scarlet gaze halting on Maylea and me for an instant. I could have sworn I saw a quick, faint smile brush her lips before she turned her focus back to unpacking the food she'd brought.

It wasn't much—just some flat bread with herbs and figs baked into it and some hard cheese—but a few mouthfuls made my stomach sing with relief. We ate everything in record time and gathered up our belongings. In less than ten minutes, we were all moving again.

The sun hung low in the sky as we trekked through the city. Even more refugees had arrived and filled the streets with carts, wagons, and groups that shambled slowly by with hollow expressions. Bigger crowds swarmed the healers and food lines. Children cried. Women wailed. Men argued.

And once again, my soul went numb.

I put a hand on Maylea's shoulder, keeping her close at my side as we wound through the masses and made our way to the eastern edge of the city. She hadn't said much else after waking up from that dream, and that foggy look of despair on her face put a pang of uneasiness in the pit of my stomach. Maybe she had seen Ronan. Maybe he was calling for help.

Maybe we were already too late.

"Look there!" Lukani exclaimed, dashing a little ahead of us as we crested a small hill at the very edge of the city.

My steps slowed and finally stopped. I stood alongside Maylea and the others, mouth hanging open at the sight that spread out before us. The buildings of Esfolar grew sparse, giving way to rolling swells of bleached white sand that towered like frozen ocean waves. The sparkling dunes shone in the evening sun like heaps of diamond, stretching out as far as I could see to the base of craggy mountains miles in the distance.

"It's salt, not sand," Violet explained as she paused beside me, the setting sun making her red eyes gleam like fire-lit rubies. "They call it the Deadlands because nothing will grow."

"Sounds inviting," I smirked.

"Beyond it, the Dei'Lurn Mountains form a natural boundary between Damaria and Nar'Haleen. They are tall and treacherous to pass, filled with thieves and monsters alike. Not a place a caravan would want to venture unguarded," she advised. "Hence our employment."

"You had me at treacherous." I tipped my head to the side in a shrug and winked—which I immediately regretted. Gah! My stupid neck ...

With the desert wind teasing through a few runaway locks of her hair that had escaped her braid, Violet grinned and started onward again. "I know how much you dragonriders love fighting things, but do try to contain your excitement. We don't want our temporary employers to assume we intend to go looking for trouble."

"Us? Look for trouble? Never," I gasped sarcastically, feigning an offended glare.

Beside me, Maylea finally cracked a little grin of her own. "That's not what Dah says about you."

"Your Dah is responsible for more than half of the near-death situations I've been in, thank you very much," I scolded and flicked her ear before I started after Violet. "And Thatcher's responsible for the rest."

"Hey! That's not true," he protested as he jogged to catch up.

I shook my head and narrowed my eyes at him. "Do I really need to remind you that the whole reason we're here right now is because some crazy goddess tried to kill you a few years ago?"

Thatcher balked angrily, "That has nothing to do with—"

"There they are," Violet interrupted, not seeming interested in our squabbling. She motioned ahead to where a group of large, strangely made wagons sat on big, wide wheels just beyond the last cluster of buildings at the edge of the city.

I'd never seen anything like these wagons before, with their colorful sails on masts that spread out from the sides and center like fins on a fish, and a set of wide, curved beams under the center like runners on a sled. The tops were covered in more colorful tapestries, offering shade from the sun and shelter from the wind.

Each one was hitched to a team of beasts that looked something like a cross between a bison and lizard. Their gray, leathery hides were studded with short horns, and their thick, muscular bodies had short legs with wide feet. Bizarre.

I couldn't help but stare as we made our way up to meet the rest of the caravan, all clustered together like we were a herd of nervous goats. That probably didn't instill much confidence in our new traveling companions, who eyed us through head-wraps and face-shawls like we were a burden none of them wanted to bear.

The leader of the caravan, a middle-aged Lunostri elf dressed in loose green robes, came out to meet us with a tall, wooden staff in his hand. His yellow-green eyes examined each of us thoroughly, then settled on the tiny dragoness still perched on my shoulder like a curious squirrel.

"We were promised a dragon, not this," he spat bitterly, motioning to Vexi. "Is this the Mistress's idea of a joke?"

No one was laughing.

"Her condition is temporary," Violet assured in fluent Sokraal, "And it was necessary to move through the city without raising any alarm or attracting any unwanted attention."

The man regarded her with his lip curled like he'd just found a dead mouse in his shoe. "I did not ask you, Pitathi," he spat. Then he looked squarely at me and tilted his chin upward in a challenging gesture. "If there is no dragon, then there is no deal."

Oh boy. We were going to be best buddies, I could tell already.

Crossing my arms, I leveled a steely glare back at him. "Last I checked, you needed our help a lot more than we need yours. You're about to go rattling into hostile territory with those wagons packed full of soft-handed nobles who are ditching their own people to flee to safety. I doubt any of them even know which end to grip a sword by," I fumed back in Sokraal, as well. "I, on the other hand, am pretty sure I can figure out how to fly to the east on my own. So why don't you try that again—and use her name this time. It's Violet, by the way."

The man blinked like I'd just slapped him across the face. Then his brow furrowed deeply and his lips pulled into a snarl, mouth opening like he was ready to tell me to take my crew and march right off the nearest cliff.

He didn't get the chance, though.

Vexi made a strange, throaty chittering sound on my shoulder—which was my only warning.

And it was all I needed.

"GET BACK!" I yelled as I grabbed Vexi's tiny body off my shoulder and dropped her on the ground. I barely got a chance to hook my arms around Maylea and Violet, dragging them along with me, as I threw myself out of the way just as a burst of light flashed in the air.

With a trumpeting roar, Vexi unfurled before us and spread her powerful wings to the sky, landing in the gritty sand on her muscular hind legs back at her regular size. Now a monster of considerable size, she loomed over the caravan leader and hissed. Her long, whip-like tail swished, and her fangs flashed as she slicked her ears back and let out a low, challenging growl.

I had to give the guy some credit—even with a huge, angry dragoness leering down at him like she might suddenly snap his whole head off in one bite, he didn't scream. Or cry. Or wet himself.

He did spit a stream of curses and stagger back, though, almost tripping over his own feet in the process. Priceless.

The presence of my now large dragon made the beasts tethered to the wagons bellow in alarm and shift. Workers rushed around, trying to calm them, while the people inside the wagons peered out with mixed expressions of shock and awe.

Dusting myself off, I strolled casually over and put a hand on Vexi's strong neck. "Big enough for you?" I asked, chuckling under my breath.

The caravan leader cursed again, and had to straighten the wrap around his head before he could manage a flustered, bitter, "It will do, I suppose. Just make sure it remembers which side it is meant to be on."

"Oh, trust me. I will," I assured him, letting my tone carry a promising edge as he stormed off back toward the wagons.

"Nice guy," Thatcher laughed as he came stumbling across the sand, shaking the grit from his hair and dusting it off his clothes.

"Right? I think this is the start of another beautiful friendship," I snickered, and reached up to give my dragoness a good scratch under her chin.

A deep, satisfied purr rumbled in Vexi's throat as she rubbed her bony brow along my palm, almost bowling me over backward. She was still my queen, no matter what size she came in.

"Well, then, if you don't mind, we should find a place to put our belongings and discuss shifts for keeping watch," Violet insisted, her tone a little stiff as she marched off toward the caravan. I could have sworn her cheeks were flushed.

Hmm. What was that about? Surely it wasn't because of anything I'd done or said, right? Isandri had explained to me countless times that when it came to dealing with her people—the Lunostri—you didn't want to come off as being shy or timid. You couldn't show any signs of weakness or uncertainty. Basically, you couldn't back down for the sake of politeness. Lunostri elves viewed that as being weak, indecisive, and unreliable—none of which this guy probably wanted from his potential guards during a life-threatening journey.

Surely Violet knew that, too, right?

Just as the sun finally began to sink behind us, our caravan rolled out toward the eastern Dei'Lurn Mountains. The gritty earth crunched under the rolling wheels, and the wind whipped wild and unchecked over the barren landscape. Thatcher and I took first watch, letting Violet and the others load into the very last wagon. The kids needed rest. Violet, too. Unlike us, she hadn't gotten any downtime in that bathhouse. Maylea still looked pale after that dream, and Lukani was determined to stick right at her side. Best to let them take advantage of a safe place to rest while we had it.

But that didn't mean I had any intention of walking along the sides of the caravan like the rest of the hired guards.

I didn't have a saddle, but I didn't care. I used a borrowed rope to make myself an emergency line around Vexi's neck, climbed up onto her powerful shoulders, and gave her strong neck a pat. She chittered and chirped with delight, snapping her jaws as her nostrils puffed in deep breaths of the desert wind. After two grueling weeks, my heartbeat raced with a rush of primal adrenaline as she kicked off the ground and surged skyward.

We soared higher, catching the rising updrafts and veering around the caravan that was nothing more than a speck down below. I let my eyes roll closed, feeling every swell of my dragon's scaly sides as she breathed, and every flex of her shoulders as she beat her wings. Her spine rippled with the motion of flight, flowing like a wave. Her wingbeats thumped deeply with every flap. Her warm, smooth scales were like worn leather under my hands.

This feeling—with the wind in my hair and her strength to carry us on—Gods and Fates, I had missed it. My spirit had ached for it. All the dull, throbbing pain in my body seemed to fade away. I was free again.

And now, with nothing before us but open sky, golden dunes, and the first brush of twilight on the horizon, I finally felt it. That rush of certainty, of purpose, flooding back into my soul and setting it ablaze. Hope.

We would make it. We would reach the library in Nar'Haleen, even if it took every bit of strength we had. We would find Ronan and set him free. We would stop Sadeera, whatever the cost, and make sure she never tried anything like this ever again. She was an enemy unlike any other we'd crossed. I knew that. Facing her would undoubtedly be the most dangerous thing I had ever done—but I felt no fear.

Because despite all that, I was Dragonriders of Maldobar, first and always.

And no matter the odds, we did *not* fail.

ETERNAL

THE DRAGONRIDER HERITAGE BOOK EIGHT

PART ONE

REIGH

❧ I ❧

CHAPTER ONE

"VIOLET—INCOMING!"

I dove forward into a front roll, landing right beside her in a crouch with one of my kafki blades swung wide. Grabbing her arm with my free hand, I yanked her down toward me.

VOOOM!

A massive, crab-like claw sailed over us so close I could feel the wind tickle my ears. Gods and Fates, that was close.

The earth rocked and shuddered under my boots as the monster crawled over us on long, spindly legs—headed straight for our caravan. Arrows hummed through the air, pinging off its shell-covered body like pebbles off a breastplate. People screamed and scattered like scared mice. Not good.

Curse it!

"What the heck is this thing?!" I shouted to Violet.

She flashed me an irritated sideways glare as she spun her daggers over her hands. "Do you always talk so much while you fight?"

I did, actually. It took some of the focus off almost dying. "We gotta draw it away from the wagons," I snarled as I stood and drew my second blade.

She took off over the sand like a silver-haired blur. "Less talking—more fighting!"

To be fair, this was the first real battle we'd had since the whole mess in the Rienkan ports with the drakkon. We had been traveling for two long, quiet, normal days without any signs of impending danger. But Violet had been insistent on constant diligence. And, when this creature erupted from the sand like a furious crustacean god, I could suddenly appreciate why.

The beast looked something like a crab, I guess. Six legs, big meaty claws, small eyes on the end of long stalks, and a body plated in natural sand-colored armor. The size was what really threw me, honestly. I'd never seen anything crab-like grow to be thirty feet tall.

Something told me this was one of the less common desert nuisances. Maybe it was that look of unreserved panic in our caravan master's eyes when he shouted for all his wagons to circle up close together so we could "handle the issue."

Right.

Well, we'd handle it one way or another.

The monster gave an ear-splitting shriek as it swung one of those huge, meaty claws, only to have it clash against an all-too-familiar golden shield. Thatcher stood with his hands outstretched and palms glowing with radiant light. Even from this distance, I could tell by that pasty, wide-eyed look on his face that he wouldn't be able to sustain a shield that size for long. He had all the wagons covered—but it wouldn't last. We had to make this quick.

I set my jaw and took off after Violet, giving a shrill whistle and hand gesture to the caravan. An answering roar from overhead hit my chest like a clap of thunder. A smirk tugged at my lips as another blur of motion zipped past me, loping toward the monster on six powerful legs.

Lukani took the form of a switchbeast as he galloped into battle, Maylea perched on his back with her bow at the ready. She fired one arrow right after another, aiming for the joints of its legs and giant eye stalks—places that should have been vulnerable.

Unfortunately, it seemed this particular monster had evolved its defenses, especially with sharp, poky things in mind. All her arrows glanced off, not managing to stick anything crucial. As Lukani dashed off to the left, barely managing to avoid another one of its huge legs, I could have sworn I heard her scream a curse in Sokraal.

Great. Who the heck had taught her that?

Ugggh. Well, that was one more thing Jaevid could punch me for later. Just add it to the growing list.

Violet didn't seem to be having much luck, either. Her daggers were lethally sharp, but dancing around the monster's legs and making swipes at it didn't seem to be phasing it in the slightest.

Time for a new tactic.

Whipping my blades back into the sheaths at my hips, I made steam straight for the nearest big, freestanding object: a boulder. Only a few of them jutted up from the white, salt-encrusted sand nearby. I chose the largest, closest one and ran straight up it, using it as a springboard to jump out into the open air.

WHOOOM!

A big, scaly green body zoomed right underneath me and I landed on Vexi's back, scrambling to get a grip on her smooth scales and spines as she veered upward into the sky. Her powerful shoulders pumped, sides flexing against my legs as she angled her body for a steep turn and circled over the caravan below.

"Good girl," I panted as I patted her neck. "Now, let's pick up Violet before things get toasty, yeah?"

My green dragoness gave a snort and snarl of approval and snapped her wings in closer. I pressed my body down against her neck and got ready as she dropped into a steep dive straight toward the crab monster. The ground rushed up, wind howling past my head. I could barely make out the dark shape of Violet scaling the monster's back using her daggers like climbing hooks. I had to give her credit. Even if those daggers probably wouldn't do much against a beast that size, she had absolutely no fear.

Points for effort.

But I was ready to make this *really* easy on everyone.

Vexi gave another roar as we blurred through the air, heading straight for Violet's position. She stopped her climbing and looked back, scarlet eyes focusing right on me for an instant.

I snapped a hand out.

At the last second, she let go of her blades and sprang upward, arms outstretched.

I grunted, suddenly taking her weight as I caught her hand in mine. We snatched her off the monster's back and I reeled her in, dragging her closer until she could climb the rest of the way onto Vexi's back. She sat down right behind me and snaked her arms around my waist.

"You cannot risk fire!" Violet shouted against my ear, her voice tangled in the constant rush of the wind. "The wagons could burn, too!"

"No, they won't." I rolled my eyes. "This isn't my first ride, you know. I do this for a living."

This was my *entire* job back home, after all. Dragonrider and all that? So would it kill her to have a little faith?

I gave my heels a tap into Vexi's side, pushing against the scales of her back to give her cues. She wasn't wearing her saddle, so we would have to make do with crude signals to communicate. My dragoness seemed to get the point, though.

Her scaly ears flicked back. Her lips curled back over her long, jagged fangs, and her sky-blue eyes narrowed with concentration. Her plated chest and sides swelled as she took in a deep breath.

One of the crab creature's eyestalks swiveled, focusing a giant eyeball right at us as Vexi swooped in, showering its back with a torrent of burning, acidic venom. It screeched and flailed, pitching back and scrambling away from the wagons. It swung huge claws at us as we surged skyward again with a victorious roar.

"Is it following?" I called back to Violet as I kept my focus ahead, guiding Vexi back around in a wide sweep so we could make another pass.

"Yes!" she called.

Excellent.

I didn't know if Vexi's fire would hurt it or even penetrate that thick armored shell. But it was distracting enough to draw the monster's attention away from the caravan. I'd take that as a win.

"All right, girl, let's do it again." I gave Vexi the same signals. Another pass. Another burst of flaming venom. We could do this.

I couldn't resist a grin when Violet let out a scream of alarm as Vexi abruptly snapped her wings in close again and dove, spiraling like a spear toward the monster again. Her arms squeezed around me tighter, hands gripping fistfuls of my tunic. I guess Arlan's spies didn't get many rides on dragons.

Hopefully she didn't throw up or pass out. I'd seen rookie students do both on their first real flights.

My dragon's sides swelled as she took in another deep breath, preparing to spit another plume of burning venom. Leaning down into her speed, I kept my body aligned with her spine and waited. Any second would bring that sudden pitch upward again as we zoomed away.

A horrible noise ripped through the air as the creature's body moved like a traceless blur, snapping up one of its huge claws right as we passed.

Oh—Oh gods!

Vexi howled in panic and pain as its pincer closed on one of her wings. Something cracked. I shouted. Violet screamed.

We pitched wildly through the air, thrown end over end, until—*BAM*—we hit the dunes in a heap. Vexi had managed to angle her body so she took the brunt of the hit, protecting Violet and me from the impact.

I sat up, my body shaking as I spat out sand and squinted into the glare of the sun. Wh-What had just happened? Had it thrown us? Or had Vexi crashed after it crunched her wing? Fates, how had it even moved that fast?

I didn't know. But there wasn't time to sort it out right then.

Violet seized my arm and gasped, mashing herself against my back as something huge and distinctly crab-shaped eclipsed the sun and loomed right over us.

Oh no...

"R ... RUN!" I WHEEZED TO VIOLET. SHE COULD STILL GET AWAY BEFORE THAT THING killed us. One of us had to. The mission ... someone had to see it through.

And I would *not* leave my dragon behind.

"No," Violet hissed shakily. "I won't leave you here to die."

As the monstrous crustacean lunged for us again, with both claws ready to dice us like spring vegetables, Vexi shifted in the sand. She surged up to her hind legs and spat another long spray of burning venom straight at the monster. One of her wings flopped uselessly as she sprang forward and latched onto it, her claws and teeth sparking over its armored shell.

"VEXI!" Her name tore out of my throat as a desperate cry. What was she thinking? She was no match for that beast on the ground!

VOOOOM!

A low, concussive sound rippled through the air with a shockwave of power that blew me down onto my back again. Violet landed on my chest, knocking the wind out of me, and I instinctively wrapped my arms around her and rolled onto my side, trying to shield her from whatever was happening now.

Wind howled around us, blowing sand and debris everywhere.

Vexi's huge, green scaly body rolled past me, landing in a heap in the sand. The monster—had it done something else? What was going on?

Holding up a hand to try shielding my eyes, I squinted through the gusting, stinging sprays of sand.

Maylea stood before the giant monster, tiny by comparison. Her dark hair whipped around her as she held one hand out to the creature. Her eyes glowed like vibrant green infernos, and streams of clean, white light rippled in the air around her, suspended like ribbons of pure energy.

Gods and Fates—that wind was coming from *her*.

Her expression seized, blood oozing from her nose as her lips moved and her eyes narrowed dangerously. Whatever she said, it was lost to the howl of the wind and screech of the beast as she twisted her hand and gave a single snap of her fingers.

CRAAACK!

Another shockwave ripped over us, kicking up a sandstorm that blotted out everything. All I could do was curl myself around Violet, shut my eyes tightly, and wait for it to be over.

The wind slowly calmed, dying away to a low hiss and then a gentle breeze that barely stirred the sand. Half-buried in the dunes, I dared to lift my head and look back to where Maylea had been standing only seconds before.

The monster—giant crab—whatever it was, had *disappeared.*

In its place, a huge mass of pale green vines, as thick around as tree-trunks, protruded from the ground and formed an entangled ball. They stood like an oversized ball of yarn, bristling with red-tipped thorns the length of swords, in the middle of the arid landscape.

Whoa ...

Where, by all the gods, had that come from?

"What happened?" Violet gasped as she stared around with me, her face slowly draining of color. "Where is she? Reigh, where is Maylea?"

Oh no. I didn't see her anywhere.

I shambled up, tripping and stumbling as I dragged myself free of the sand. I-I couldn't see her. Or the monster. Just the tree and—

"REIGH!" Thatcher's voice called out my name in pure panic. "HELP!"

There! I saw him sprinting away from the caravans toward the base of the tree.

I took off running over the dunes, too. My heart pounded, lodged in my throat so tight I couldn't breathe. Gods, no. Please, no!

A few yards away, I saw Thatcher on the ground already, cradling the figure of a young girl who lay motionless in his arms. No glowing eyes.

"MAYLEA!" I shouted her name, but she didn't move.

I fell to my knees at Thatcher's side and immediately reached over to take her body into my arms. O-Oh gods. She was so pale. Her lips were blue and blood oozed from her nose and the corners of her mouth. I couldn't stop my medically trained brain from whirling through every awful scenario. A head injury? What if she was bleeding into her brain? What could I do to stop it? How could I help her?!

All my thoughts, all my training, seemed to dissolve away into nothingness as I stared down at her. It was as though every strategy, every life-saving technique I had ever learned, had all been erased from my mind completely. I didn't know what to do. I didn't know how to help her. She'd overdone it with her power, hadn't she? Curse it all. She wasn't ready for a fight like this. She'd pushed things too far, and now I couldn't do anything to—

Her eyes fluttered open, staring groggily up at me.

I sucked in a sharp breath.

"Uncle Reigh?" she asked hoarsely.

Tears flooded my eyes and I bowed my head, unable to speak. All I could do was bob my head once.

I flinched when Thatcher put his hand on my shoulder, almost like he was trying to share some of that mental burden. "It's okay, Maylea. We're here."

"I-I'm okay," she rasped again.

"No, you're not," I gasped sharply, unable to hide the broken panic in my voice as I carefully cradled her head. "You ... you could have died. Do you even understand what you just did? If you push it too far, I can't ... I can't do anything to ..." Fear clamped down hard on my throat again and I had to look away.

Maylea squirmed in my gasp and made a face, coughing and wiping clumsily at her nose. She made a disgusted face when she noticed all the blood and blinked hard a few times. "I-I'm really okay, Uncle Reigh. I just had to do something. That thing was going to kill you. I had to stop it."

I sank back some, practically falling onto my rear in the shady reprieve under the tree. She had stopped it. She'd turned that monster into a giant tree with a single snap of her fingers. Even if it had left her unconscious, I'd never seen anyone wield power like that. Not even Jaevid.

I didn't even know if Arlan the Kinslayer was capable of something like that.

For a few minutes, all I could do was gape at her while my head threatened to explode with a tangled, spinning mixture of anger, awe, and all-consuming terror. Whatever this girl was becoming, she was a lot stronger than any of us had ever been. And I honestly didn't know how to advise her when it came to using this power. I didn't know what the risks would be. I didn't know if it would eventually kill her.

I didn't know how to help her.

But I knew someone who did.

2

CHAPTER TWO

We played things off to the rest of the caravan with much more confidence than we actually had. Giant monsters exploding out of the sand to kill us all? Meh. Almost dying? Boring. Divine power being wielded by a teenager? Mundane.

I didn't have to fake disinterest when it came to discussing our next move with the caravan's leader, though. Violet took over that debate while I went to look after my dragoness, who had shaken herself free of the sand and lay licking gingerly at her wing.

I couldn't exactly try holding her down to examine it now like I had when she was tiny. That was a great way to get my face singed off. But she did let me take a look at the swollen, angry looking joint that served as her elbow. Based on my understanding of dragon anatomy, it didn't seem like anything was broken. Sprained or possibly over-extended. She needed to rest it. Too bad a single night was probably all she would be able to get.

"Maybe some of that healing remedy you got from the Mistress of the Call would help her, too?" Thatcher suggested as he stood next to me, hands on his hips, studying Vexi's injury.

"Worth a shot," I agreed. "Otherwise, she'll have to crawl along on the ground, and I'm not sure who would hate that more—her or me."

I could feel his worried, sympathetic, quietly caring stare on my back as I turned away to start making my way back to the wagons. Ugh. I knew what came after that look, and I did not want to stick around for it. If he wanted to start making speeches about feelings, then he'd have to catch me first.

"You know you can't save everyone, Reigh," he said suddenly.

I stopped. Slowly, I turned back to stare at him. "What?"

"I know you would if you could. You want to because you're a good man. You love helping people. That's why you make such a good healer and medic. That's also why you made a good teacher at the academy," he said, fixing me with a strangely calm and contemplative stare. Not a look I'd ever seen him wear before. "But you can't save everyone. Sooner or later, something will happen that's beyond your control. Someone isn't going to make it. And when that day comes, you need to understand that doesn't make it your fault."

I had no idea what to say to that. I just stood there, gaping at him and blinking owlishly like an idiot.

"I don't doubt your skill or determination. And I'm not trying to be fatalistic. I'm just saying ... people die. And this is a war, even if it's not necessarily ours," he amended quickly, raising his hands like he suspected I might be on the verge of an angry explosion.

Good call.

"Some would argue it is our war," I countered. "You being a godling and all. I'd say that means you have a pretty big stake in it."

He dropped his hands back to his sides and sighed. "I guess. I just ... Reigh, you're my friend. One of my very best friends. And I just don't want to see it destroy you if one of us doesn't walk away from this."

I crossed my arms. Something in his tone, or maybe that sheepish way he wasn't meeting my gaze, felt off. Like there was more he wanted to say. "Planning on dying or something?"

"No. Of course not." He chuckled and shook his head, beginning to stroll my way so we could walk together toward the caravan. "You know Murdoc would never allow me to die before him."

Fair enough.

I waited a few minutes, letting the silence clear the awkward air between us, to finally ask, "How is she? Maylea, I mean." After all, he'd been sitting in one of the wagons with her until he came waddling over to gift me with that little speech.

"Tired, but that's not surprising, is it? She's been asking about you and Vexi. I promised her I'd check on both of you," he replied.

Ah, so that was it.

"I'm worried about her, Reigh," he continued, lowering his voice as though he were concerned someone else might overhear. "She's been using that power a lot. First at the bridge, and now this? It's getting stronger every time, too. A lot stronger than anything I've ever seen before. Did, uh, did Jaevid do these sorts of things back during the Tibran War?"

"He did some pretty incredible things, but nothing on this scale. Not that I witnessed. I don't know, though. I always heard he did amazing feats of magic during the Gray War. Maybe it was something like this? Who knows," I admitted, running a hand through my grit and filth-caked hair. Two long days in the desert, swimming in my own sweat, and I was already dying for another bath.

"Your father?" Thatcher guessed.

Huh. Yeah, he was probably right about that. My father, Felix, had been his best friend and comrade during all that. He likely knew better than any of us how much power Jaevid had slung around back then. Too bad I had no way of asking about any of that now. I'd heard stories and fables, of course. But over time, it was hard to tell how much of that was the truth and what had been embellished for entertainment value.

"Let's just keep a close eye on her," I suggested, keeping my tone low and cautious now, too. "I'll see if I can pull her aside for a little reality-check chat about the dangers of using too much divine power. But if she's anything like her father, she won't just come out and admit that she's having issues. He was always one to keep his own suffering bottled up."

Thatcher cast me a cattish, sideways grin. "Gee, that sounds familiar. I wonder why?"

"I'll hit you, you know," I grumbled.

"I'm not scared of your punches, mortal," he laughed again.

I flapped a hand at him dismissively. Gods, I was beyond ready to find something that resembled a bed to fall face-first into it. After the potion for my dragon, though. Potion first. Sleep later. Maybe food somewhere in between.

I'd take what I could get at this point, so long as it didn't involve anything else trying to kill me today.

"When we get to Salnis, I need to find Clysiros's temple," I murmured quietly, knowing Violet would hear every word even at a whisper.

Sitting around a campfire underneath the new, gigantic briar patch, I stared around at all the other members of our caravan group. They talked as they gathered around the six or seven small fires surrounding the base of it. Their soft conversations filled the cool night air as they cooked dinner and warmed themselves in the glow of the flames.

"Do you expect her to be helpful?" Violet's voice was tinged with sarcasm. Not that I disagreed with her suspicion of the mysterious and usually conniving goddess of death, but I was standing at a crossroads now, whether I liked it or not. I had to choose a path. A side, according to Noh. And Maylea's future might just depend on which one I took.

All of our futures might.

"No," I muttered, "I expect her to be extremely interested in furthering her own agenda, as usual. But there might be a point where her agenda matches up with ours. If that's the case, then I'm willing to hear her out," I explained as I reached for the nearest waterskin and uncorked it. "Besides, I just got shown up in a fight by a fourteen-year-old. I need to step up my game, don't you think?"

Violet gave a snort and swiped the waterskin from my hand before I could even take a sip. She took three long swigs from it and then passed it back, smirking proudly. "Lucky that wonderful potion from the Mistress of the Call works on dragons, as well, or you might even be forced to walk, like the rest of us poor peasants. How shameful."

Riiight. I guess a few near-death experiences had her in a teasing mood this evening. Fine. Two could play that game, and I was better at it than she seemed to want to give me credit for.

I swirled the waterskin, eyeing the opening she'd just used and wiping it off before I took my own drink from it. "That reminds me, I seem to recall a lot of terrified screaming coming from your general direction during our flight."

Her smile faded a little at the corners.

"Don't tell me a few aerial maneuvers actually cracked that steely spy resolve of yours? Those weren't even difficult ones. We put fledgling students through much worse than that their first year of training," I quipped.

Her eyes narrowed a little, mouth beginning to pinch up sourly.

"You should have told me you were afraid of flying. I would have been *gentler.*" I grinned and turned to take a long, satisfying drink from the waterskin.

Water hit my face in a cold rush as she reached over and squeezed the waterskin with both hands, making it all gush out at once. I choked and sputtered as I wiped my eyes.

"You're an idiot," she fumed quietly.

I couldn't help it. I laughed. Still shaking water out of my hair, I leaned in closer and gave her my most smug, satisfied grin, even waggled my eyebrows. "At least *I'm* not scared of flying."

She opened her mouth to protest. "I am not scared of—!"

She didn't get a chance to finish.

"Aye, there are the noble heroes! Reveling in their mighty victory! Just kiss her and be done with it, already!" An older man, probably one of the merchants transporting goods in our caravan, gave my back a hard pat and shoved me directly into Violet.

Our foreheads cracked together with a *thud* that made my vision swim. And, er, well ... my mouth mashed right into hers.

It didn't last more than a second. But that single, horrifying moment—staring directly into her wide, mortified eyes with my mouth smashed unceremoniously against hers—felt like an eternity. A terrible eternity that probably shaved ten years off my life.

I snatched back immediately, sputtering and stammering as I tried to speak. "I-I ... that ... uh, I'm ... I-I'm so ... I didn't mean to!"

Violet pulled back, too, and immediately looked away. She covered her mouth with her hand and turned so I couldn't see her face at all.

Oh Gods, was she furious? It wasn't intentional! She knew that, right? It wasn't my fault! Someone pushed me! Gods and Fates, I-I would never just—

Violet suddenly snapped to her feet and whirled around, keeping her face angled away as she walked briskly toward the wagons. Her other hand stayed straight at her side, rigid and clenched so hard her knuckles turned white.

My shoulders dropped. My stomach plummeted, twisting into a thousand throbbing knots as I watched her storm off without a single word. Great. Fantastic. How could I even apologize for something like this?

Turning back to the fire, I wiped my mouth and rubbed at my jaw. What a mess. Thatcher could say whatever he wanted about my leadership skills, but Jaevid had never done anything this stupid. At least, not that I'd ever heard about.

While my mind whirled with every possible terrible outcome—Violet slitting my throat in my sleep or abandoning us at the next city—my gaze drifted upward to where Thatcher, Maylea, and Lukani sat on the other side of the campfire. I guess they were oblivious to what had just happened. Thank the gods for small miracles, I guess.

Reaching Salnis promised to be its own special bundle of problems and challenges already. This certainly wasn't going to help. Now that Nar'Haleen was on the offensive and actively attacking cities in Rienka, things would only get more complicated for us going forward. Monsters I could handle. But another invading emperor backed by thousands upon thousands of soldiers and war machines? Yeah. That sat on my mind like a red-hot coal, sizzling away at all my sanity with each passing minute.

And if that wasn't fun enough on its own, Salnis was right on the border between the two squabbling kingdoms but had apparently sworn itself to Rienka's side years ago. No doubt, they had heard what was happening in the bay islands and were already bristled for the first sign of any trouble. I wondered if that would pose a problem when it came to bringing my dragon into the city proper. Most of the cities and villages in Maldobar were used to enormous, scaly, fire-breathing visitors. That wasn't the case here, and I wasn't sure how we would be received. A foreign war beast randomly appearing in the city on the heels of a Nar'Haleenan invasion on their neighbors? Yeah. That was bound to raise some eyebrows. Best not to anger the locals in a city already bracing for a potential invasion. It certainly wouldn't serve to make our efforts discreet.

But what other choice was there? Camping outside the city? Having Vexi keep her distance? I didn't like either of those options, and now I couldn't even discuss them with Violet, who probably knew better than anyone what the best choice was.

I sighed and hung my head. My temples throbbed, and my hair still dripped with water.

I stared at the scuffed-up toes of my boots, chasing those thoughts and worries like smoke in my brain. Before I worked any of this out, I needed to see to another problem. Something more important.

Sitting more than ten feet away on the other side of the fire, her fair face blank of any expression and her green-blue eyes as wide as moons, Maylea looked like she might faint at any moment.

She'd been awfully quiet these last few days, even before that showdown with the crab monster, and it was hard to miss the circles under her eyes that seemed to be growing darker by the day. Obviously, what had happened in that fight hadn't helped. I hadn't seen her eat much more than a few cups of soup. She didn't even seem to be all snuggled up to Lukani anymore. She was pulling away. Diving deep into herself. That was a path I knew all too well—just like that haunted, empty, and quietly mortified expression on her face.

Not a good sign.

I couldn't afford to put this off. And not just because I needed everyone in this group working at maximum capacity. That girl was my responsibility. She had to make it home from this, even if the rest of us didn't. I owed her father that much, at least.

Yes, she had made a deal with Paligno and agreed to become his champion. I knew that of all the gods, he might be the least likely to take advantage of her in a negative way. But divine power was still divine power. It never came easy, and it never came free. The same deity had made a lesser deal with her father and it had nearly killed him and left him trapped in a magical slumber for forty years.

So what would the cost be for Maylea? For Ronan? For me? For any of us?

The gods were growing desperate. The end was near. All I could do now was make sure we stayed together, standing shoulder-to-shoulder, braced for the storm.

⁂ 3 ⁂

CHAPTER THREE

Violet never came back to the campfire.

The longer I sat, the more I wondered if I should go search for her. Would that seem weird? Was it too soon? Would it help? Or would it make the situation worse? Maybe she just needed some space to cool off. I didn't want to give her the impression I was looking to, you know, do *that* again. Or justify it at all. She wouldn't just leave us in the middle of the night, would she? I mean, yes, that incident had been embarrassing. But was it worth abandoning our group and putting the fate of the world in jeopardy because we couldn't bear to sit in the same wagon together?

I didn't know. I didn't know *her*. And that realization stuck in my chest like a white-hot spike. I should know her by now. We had almost died together, how many times now? I should have been able to talk to her about, well, most anything.

But I didn't know where to begin. So, I sat there. Like an idiot. As usual.

Ugggh. This was exactly why I hadn't tried courting anyone else after things with Enyo had fallen apart. Clearly, I had no skills, comprehension, or potential as a romantic partner for anyone. Violet and I weren't even like that, and I still had no idea what to say to her.

I was better off keeping my stupidity to myself for now.

As the evening wound down, the crowds around the campfires thinned. The other members of our caravan either stayed by the campfires to talk quietly, often gesturing up to the massive white tree that now stretched out over us like a protective shield, or they slowly wandered off to find beds in and around the wagons.

Thatcher volunteered to take first watch and lingered by the fire to clean his sword and armor while he chatted with some of the other travelers. They seemed *extra* curious about us now that we'd proven ourselves to be ... slightly above average when it came to combat. And since Thatcher was by far the least intimidating of our group, I guess I could see why they felt more comfortable approaching him with all their questions.

I probably looked like I was on the verge of throwing up, anyway.

I waited in silence, watching Maylea and Lukani walk hand-in-hand back to our wagon where all our belongings and bedrolls were kept, before I finally stood up and stretched.

My back cracked like someone in heavy boots walking over acorns. Everything was stiff and sore from my neck down. I didn't bounce back from being flung around by giant monsters like I had years ago. But that didn't mean I was ready to call it quits just yet. I had to sort some kids out first. Then, if nothing else exploded or tried to kill us for a few hours, I could manage a little sleep.

Pulling back the canvas flap at the back of our wagon, I found Lukani and Maylea sitting together near the entrance. They flinched apart when they spotted me, like I'd caught them doing something embarrassing. Lukani dipped his head, his long, pointed ears drooping some and his lion-like tail swishing nervously. His cheeks flushed and he couldn't seem to look me in the eye as I cleared my throat.

"All right, lover boy, scram," I growled low. "Go help Thatcher keep watch, and don't think for a second I don't know exactly what you're up to. I may be old, but I'm not blind."

I followed his every move with a scorching glare as he scurried past me out of the wagon. He only made it a few steps before he dared to take one last, long, mournful look back in Maylea's direction.

"I mean it!" I snarled, just for good measure.

He tripped all over himself and hurried away back to the ring of campfires. Good riddance. As much as I would have liked to wring his neck for shamelessly flirting with Jaevid's only daughter, I wasn't really within my right to do so. Besides, it was bound to be far more amusing to watch Jae beat the ever-living crap out of him. That was too good to pass up.

"He's not doing anything bad," Maylea mumbled, her cheeks flushed and her expression all squinty and sour as I shut the canvas door and sat down across from her. "He's just worried about me. Why are you being so mean to him?"

"Mean would have been dragging him out of here by that tail of his," I corrected. "I'm not going to chase you two around and make sure you stay an arm's length apart, but at least give me the gift of being discreet with your little romance, would you? That way, I have plausible deniability when your father realizes what's going on. I'd like a good, legitimate excuse for letting it happen under my watch. Or, at the very least, a solid chance to flee while he beats your little boyfriend to death first."

Her mouth scrunched up bitterly and she drew her legs close to her chest, wrapping her arms around her knees. "You make it sound like I'll actually see Dah again."

Whoa. Okay, then. That was a lot broodier and more negative than I was expecting—and not like her at all. Things weren't looking fantastic for us, especially after what we'd all been through trying to get out of Rienka, but she was usually a happy kid. Mischievous, sure, but still happy.

"Why wouldn't you see him again?" I decided to ask, hoping she wouldn't shut down the entire conversation right off.

She flicked me a look, doing a superb job of projecting exhausted sarcasm, as though the answer should have been obvious.

Fair enough.

"I had the goddess of death building sandcastles in my brain for seventeen years," I reminded her. "If something weird is happening to you, you can talk to me about it. I might not know as much about Paligno as your father, but I know plenty about divine power and the toll it can take."

She looked away quickly, her shoulders drawing up slightly at the mention of his name. After nearly a minute of what I could only assume was deep soul-searching, asking herself if she really could trust me or not, I heard her mumble, "I ... I can't sleep."

"Why not?"

Maylea took in a deep breath, as though she were steadying herself before she said any of this out loud. "My dreams aren't dreams. Not anymore. Not normal ones, anyway. They're something else. It feels ... dangerous."

I scooted in closer to her. "Dangerous how?"

"As soon as I fall asleep, that other place pulls me down. It's like falling into the depths of an endless nothingness. Not sleep. Something deeper—closer to the realm of the gods. Fates, sometimes it feels like I'm standing right outside their door listening through the keyhole."

Oooh boy. That sounded unpleasantly familiar. Divine dreams seemed to be fairly common among those of us whose lives they'd touched directly. I knew Jaevid had suffered from them, too. But this sounded a little more serious, like there was more going on that she didn't want to divulge.

I reached out to take one of her hands and squeeze it gently. "I'm right here, May. Whatever it is, you can tell me. I've got you."

She blinked quickly, her eyes welling some when she finally stared back at me. And I saw it—that look of utter terror in her eyes. Fates, how long had this been going on? She had mentioned dreams before. She'd even had some nightmares. I had no idea it was this bad, though.

"At first, there's nothing but darkness everywhere I look," she began shakily, gripping my hand like she was afraid that dream might suddenly suck her down again. "Then I hear them. Thousands of whispers and voices coming from everywhere at once. It's so loud. And they don't stop. It's too much and I feel like my head is going to explode, but I'm stuck there."

"Spirits?" I suggested. "Or the voices of the gods?"

Maylea shook her head slightly. "I don't know. It's too hard to focus on anything they're saying. Sometimes I wake up and I'm soaked with sweat. My body hurts all over like I've been fighting all night long. I just wish it would stop. I'm so tired, Uncle Reigh."

She leaned into my side, and I put an arm around her shoulders. "I know, kid. Believe me, I understand."

"What does it all mean? What am I supposed to do?" she whimpered, her voice muffled as she hid her face against my side. "I thought Paligno would help me. I thought he'd guide me. But I can't find him. Why has he abandoned me? Did I do something wrong?"

I didn't know. Now wasn't the time to seem unsure, though. She needed to feel safe. To feel grounded.

That I could handle.

"I don't think he's abandoned you at all. Just look at what you did today. You saved Violet and me. Vexi, too. You did that with the power *he* gave you," I said and poked my finger against the bone-carved talisman she wore on a resin cord around her neck. The same one her father had worn. "You really think he'd give you abilities like that if you were doing anything wrong?"

"No," she mumbled. "I guess not. I'm just ... so tired, Uncle Reigh."

"Yeah. Me, too." I leaned back against the side of the wagon, letting my weight fall into the tautly fastened canvas. "I don't know what that dream means. But if I were taking a wild guess, I'd say there's something there—something in those voices—that Paligno wants you to hear. Something about it is important. And if he isn't telling you outright what that is, then it must be something that he knows you can figure out on your own. You just need to have some confidence. A little faith probably wouldn't hurt, either."

She let out a deep breath and nodded, pushing away to sit up on her own again. "I'll try." Her tone still sounded defeated.

"Hey, you've got this, okay? You're tough. And you're smart. And you're a Broadfeather, so you're half-crazy. That last bit should be more than enough to get you through this." I couldn't resist a grin.

"Yeah, well, at least I didn't accidentally kiss the person I'm so obviously in love with," she jabbed. "Nice going, by the way. You practically headbutted her."

My eyes popped open. Crap, she had seen that? Ugghh.

Before I could stop it, panicked words spilled out of me in an uncontrollable rush. "I-I —! That is not what happened! It was not a kiss! And it wasn't my fault! Some guy pushed me!" I rambled frantically. "And I am *not* in love with her!"

Her devious little grin was pure venom. "Suuure."

"I mean it!"

"Whatever you say." Maylea rolled her eyes, still smirking wickedly. "What's so wrong with liking her, anyway?"

"N-Nothing," I stammered, acutely aware that this was some sort of mental trap I was staggering headlong into like a wounded fawn. "But that doesn't mean I—"

"She's nice to you, isn't she?"

"Well, yes, but—"

"Don't you think she's pretty?"

"Th-That's ... it isn't ... I mean, yes, she is, but that doesn't mean ... *ACK*—" I choked on my own spit and wound up making a hacking, wheezing sound instead. Fates, why was I sweating? And why did my face feel like it was on fire?

"You know she's in love with you, right?"

My mind went completely blank. All I could do was sit there with my mouth open, my ears ringing, and my eyes fixed on Maylea in mute horror. She ... she was?

No. Not possible. No way. I would have noticed. I would have suspected.

This little game had gone far enough.

"Don't say things like that." I scowled and started to get to my feet, casting her a glare of warning. She could tease me if she wanted, but not about this. That wasn't something you joked about.

I guess Maylea could tell she crossed a line. Her gleeful smirk vanished and she seized the back of my shirt to keep me from leaving. "Wait! I'm not kidding, Uncle Reigh! I really do think she is! I'm sorry, I didn't mean to—"

"Just stop it," I snapped, probably far more harshly than I should have. I couldn't help it, though. I couldn't hold that back.

Not when it hurt ... to even think about.

"I'm not interested in starting a relationship with anyone," I said, forcing my tone to soften. It didn't do anything to mask the pain, though. That was harder to force down and impossible to forget. Just the thought of it set a deep, rotting ache in the center of my chest and I had to turn away again.

Maylea let go of my shirt, and I could feel that awkward weight in the air that made it difficult to breathe.

I didn't like being this way. I didn't like how the pain made me act or the things I said whenever it resurfaced. The safest thing had always been to avoid those topics—love, relationships, and romance—whenever I could. How Violet might have felt about me wasn't something I could dwell on. It didn't matter. I couldn't do that again.

It wasn't worth the agony of the end.

Forcing a brief, apologetic glance in Maylea's direction, I licked my lips before I dared to speak again. Softer. I had to be softer with her. She hadn't meant any harm, I knew that. Shutting my eyes tightly, I pulled back the wagon's door flap and hesitated.

"Try to get some rest. We'll reach Salnis tomorrow, and I might need your help with something important," I said quietly.

"What is it?" Her voice quavered with worry.

My head bowed lower. "I've got my own issues with gods to work out, and if anything should go wrong, I might need some backup."

"You're talking about Clysiros, right?" Her tone steadied, becoming tight with a sense of determined urgency. "Is she choosing you to be her paladin?"

"I don't know for sure," I confessed. Gods, I hated the honesty in those words. It left a bitter taste on my tongue as I stepped out of the back of the wagon and back onto the sand. "But if becoming her servant again is what it takes to get Ronan back, I don't intend to hesitate."

⸙ 4 ⸙

CHAPTER FOUR

Gods and Fates, I had missed this view.

Nothing compared to seeing the world from the back of a dragon. Even here, so far from Maldobar, I wouldn't have traded it for anything. The rising desert sun bloomed on the far horizon like a radiant scarlet flower, unfolding with ribbons of purple cloud. The heat of it made the landscape seem to ripple like reflections in a pond and hit my face with sizzling force. Somehow, it was more intense here than it had been even on the wide-open ocean. Here, it was as though if you flew far enough, you might be able to chase down that huge, swollen red orb and find the place where it touched the ground and set everything ablaze like a world of molten flame.

My head lolled back to the touch of the racing morning wind. That sweet mixture of hot and cool made my skin prickle and my breath catch in my chest. Soaring high up here, far above the salt-crusted dunes between Esfolar and Salnis, the wind was a constant factor as the sunrise made the temperatures spike and the hot air rise in powerful updrafts. Vexi's strong wings pumped hard to catch every mighty upward gust, and I leaned in close to her body as we rode those whirling updrafts and circled wide around the caravan far below. I guess a drink of the Mistress's potion had done the trick. I couldn't feel a shudder or unsteadiness in her flight today.

From so far up, our line of travelers looked like a tiny troupe of ants making their way among the white boulders and jagged canyons. I eyed our group of large wagons that rattled and crunched slowly over the dunes, keeping a close watch for anything that looked out of place. So far, so good.

In the distance, the dark silhouette of the city of Salnis rose up against the backdrop of lofty, snow-capped mountains. We were making good time. In a few hours, we would reach the city's outer limits. Even our grouchy caravan leader seemed satisfied with the progress, even if we had lost a few hours dealing with that crab monster and swapping the wheels on the wagons over to the sled-style runners.

Here, the briny grit was too deep for the wheels to roll without getting stuck, so the drivers had paused our progress just long enough to crank them up and out of the way so each wagon now slid along easily on their wide metal runners. It worked well enough, but they still dragged along as slow as slugs, even leaving a trail of tracks in their wake.

The Lunthardan scout in me didn't like leaving behind that kind of evidence. Tracks like that would be easy for a predator to track and a smart thief to read as a group heavily weighed down and slow to escape if they decided to pursue. But so far, we hadn't seen any signs of bandits or thieves. Giant, man-eating crab monster aside, everything had gone according to plan. The ordeal with the crab beast, which was apparently called a brachyurid, had stirred up more stories among our fellow travelers about past horrors they'd stumbled across in the desert. Even Violet was full of tales of switchbeasts, dunestriders, and something she called a pterodox that sounded absolutely horrifying.

Thankfully, we hadn't spotted anything else that wanted to kill us. Bizarre, I know. Just the thought made my eye twitch and my palms start to sweat. Nothing ever went this well for us. But then again, maybe the sight of a massive, fire-breathing dragon circling overhead was enough to keep most of the danger away. Either way, we were quickly approaching the end of this trip and so far, there were no signs of danger. Nothing exploding. No cannons trying to shoot me out of the sky or giant monsters erupting from the sand.

I dared to dream that luck would hold. Stupid. I should have known better than that by now, eh?

Too bad there wouldn't be time to take in the sights or dally with the local mercenary guild once we got to the city. We couldn't afford to linger in Salnis for long. Time—what little of it we actually had left—was already against us. We had to get to the library, and that meant crossing the desert. But not just any desert. A very large, treacherous desert that was undoubtedly riddled with more dangerous things that wanted to maim, kill, or eat us.

Honestly, nothing we hadn't been up against a hundred times before.

None of that worried me—not nearly as much as knowing that Nar'Haleen was now on the offensive and actively attacking cities in Rienka. Considering the rising pressure in Salnis, I wondered if that would pose a problem when it came to bringing my dragon into the city proper. I could have asked Violet about that. I probably should have. But approaching her still felt ... weird. No, worse than that. Awkward in the most extreme sense of the word. Like trying to swallow a wad of dry cotton.

I hadn't seen any sign of her until early this morning when it was my turn to take over keeping watch. Violet had taken the shift right after Thatcher, and when we crossed paths, she seemed to act like nothing had ever happened between us. Somehow, that made the idea of bringing it up again just to apologize even more uncomfortable. Maybe it was better to just let it go, say nothing, and forget it ever happened in the first place. As far as I could tell, that seemed to be the angle she was taking to deal with it.

Yeah. That I could handle.

Vexi made slow, arcing passes around the caravan as we crept along, getting steadily closer to the city. More and more detail came into view, revealed by the glare of the rising sun. And the sight made my breath catch in my chest.

We had large cities in Maldobar. Halfax, the royal city, was a large and sprawling place I'd grown used to seeing loom below me whenever Vexi and I returned from training at the academy.

But Maldobar had nothing on the scale of this city.

Built into a steep canyon that must have stretched on for fifty miles, Salnis was a tangled, glittering nest of arched bridges and terraces that spanned the treacherous drop from the sheer, black stone cliffs. Many of the buildings seemed to be built from that same slate black stone, and they shone like spires of obsidian in the rising sun. With domed roofs leafed in bronze and gold, a million lights sparkled like a field of golden stars.

Gods and Fates. It was ... I had no words. My stomach flipped and spun at the sight of the seemingly bottomless canyon that plunged down into the dark, completely covered in buildings, walkways, and wide terraced courtyards that clung to the sides of the stone like barnacles. A colossal sculpture of a beautiful, angelic woman holding a staff was built from solid gold atop one central column of rock in the very center of the city. The sight made all my nerves draw as tight as bowstrings. I swallowed hard. That staff—with a large crystal at one end and a tri-tipped blade at the other—was one I recognized immediately.

Because Isandri carried one just like it.

Isa had never talked much about her weapon of choice, and I had never bothered to ask. The only time she'd mentioned it at all was when she spoke of her homeland. Apparently, the priests at her home temple had given it to her and trained her to channel her divine magic through it.

Now ... I finally understood why that was so significant. And I knew exactly who that angelic statue must be.

Adiana, Goddess of the Moon.

The one whose spirit supposedly resided in Isandri's body.

THATCHER MUST HAVE NOTICED THE HUGE SCULPTURE AND RECOGNIZED ITS IDENTITY, too, because he started acting a lot more squirrelly than usual as we finally stopped outside the city's outer limits. He stuck close to my side and fidgeted, his gaze occasionally darting in the direction of the golden statue as he shifted his weight restlessly. His emotions weren't difficult to read. He wore a deep crease of anxiety and thought in his brow like a giant sign that read: *I'M OVERTHINKING EVERYTHING RIGHT NOW.*

I guess I couldn't blame him. If there was a whole city devoted to Adiana, who happened to be a godling like him, then was there also a city somewhere with a huge statue of Ishaleon? If so, where? Would he ever see it?

This godling stuff was still bizarre, even to me. I couldn't fathom what it must have been like for him. Stressful, obviously, but probably intimidating, too. I was only friends with Isa, but seeing that massive golden statue of her spirit's true form still made a strange, uncomfortable, prickling sort of energy hum in my chest. The face didn't look anything like her. Her wings were a different shape, too—more swallow-tipped and sleek than these. But maybe she'd been born into a body that looked more like this one long ago? Back when this undoubtedly ancient city was first constructed?

It was weird to even think about.

I couldn't do much to soothe Thatcher's mental breakdown, so I tried to keep him focused on something else—like finishing the job at hand. As the wagons ground to a halt before the city's massive arched gates, joining the tail-end of a long line of other wagons and carts that waited to make their way inside, I got a good look at the situation. I guess with the pressure mounting from Nar'Haleen, their city guard was checking everyone. Probably looking for spies or enemy soldiers who might try to sneak their way inside.

It wouldn't work, of course. It never did. Spies tended to specialize in subverting city officials. That was just part of the job. But that didn't mean those guards wouldn't give us—

a bunch of weird-looking foreigners armed to the teeth and moving through their territory—a hard time.

I urged Vexi to take off and circle the city but stay out of trouble. She grumbled and snapped her jaws, not liking the separation, but took off with a rush of sand and a glimmer of lime-green scales. I couldn't risk having her too close here, not when I knew nothing about how we would be received in this city.

The last thing we needed was a bunch of guards trying to put chains or shackles on my very sensitive, strong, and temperamental dragoness. That ended badly for everyone.

"I suppose this means you intend to part ways with us here?" our Lunostri caravan leader mumbled as he ambled over to stand beside me, his greenish-yellow eyes tracking my dragon's flight far over the city. I could've sworn I saw a touch of envy in them.

"You're here in one piece, with all your ducklings happily in a row. I'd call that a successful mission by Maldobarian standards," I replied.

He made an approving, grunting sound and started rummaging through the pockets of his robes. "Then here is your payment," he said as he dropped a big purse of coins into my hand. "Where do you intend to go from here, dragonrider? The war will come here quickly. It would not be wise to linger unless you intend to join the fray."

I snorted and shook my head. "I absolutely do *not* intend to do that. I like a good brawl as much as the next guy, but this is one stew I won't be sticking my finger in, even for a taste test. We'll be moving on as soon as possible."

"I see." Something in his tone was dissatisfied. His lips pursed and he gave me a slow, once-over stare from head to foot. "If I may ask, what brings a dragonrider so far from Maldobar? It could not have been an easy journey for you to come this far."

I almost laughed out loud. Gods and Fates, he had no idea.

Slapping a hand on the back of his shoulder in a far-too-friendly gesture I knew he would hate, I gave him a little shake and chuckled. "Haven't you heard? It's the end of the world. Why not come get front row seats?"

I knew he wouldn't get the joke, and I didn't stick around to explain. He'd figure it out on his own soon, anyway. Strolling over to where the rest of my group stood close around Violet, watching me with mixed expressions of curiosity and concern, I tossed the bag of coins at Violet.

She snatched it out of the air and tossed it a few times, as though testing the weight to see if it was enough, then tucked it into her blouse. "Very well. We must go quickly. Come, and stay close." Her tone was all business, sharp and direct. She cast a meaningful look to me and nodded. "Mind your pockets and keep your heads down."

"What about the guards?" Thatcher's gaze was still trained on the security measures at the gate. It looked like they were checking every wagon and person passing through.

Violet wafted a hand as though that wouldn't be a problem, but I could see a slight furrow in her brow as she turned away and began walking. "We will be fine. But Lukani, darling, you might want to be a bit more discreet."

His shoulders dropped and his expression fell some. He nodded reluctantly and changed his shape, transforming into a crow and perching on Maylea's shoulder again. I guess he didn't like having to hide his identity. He had been free to look like himself through our journey with the caravan. If Violet was insisting on it, though, then there must have been a reason.

I dropped to the back of our group, wanting to keep an eye on anyone suspicious that paid a little too much attention as we passed along the line of wagons. No one seemed to care that we were cutting in line, although it made a lot more sense once we actually reached the huge gateway that led into the city proper. There were *two* lines, actually. One was for wagons and merchants with cargo, and the other was for foot travelers. Naturally, the one with the wagons was moving a lot slower since it took longer to check each one.

We shambled along amidst other travelers, most of whom looked as exhausted, dirty, and ragged as we did. Probably more refugees from the island cities. They didn't seem to pay us much mind as we made our way to the front of the line.

As our turn grew near, I got a better look at the structure of the huge gate and all the guards patrolling it. And, Fates, this place made the dragonrider watches look like public parks. The wall surrounding the city marched off across the horizon, spanning more than eighty feet tall with sides bristling with black metal spikes and tarred with crushed glass. The ramparts at the top had fully armored guards and bowmen every twenty paces, all of them watching the procession of travelers through the narrow eye-slits of polished bronze helmets.

The gate itself was about five feet thick and made of strands of iron that were woven together almost like a basket. Going by the trench dug out of the ground directly beneath it, the gate could be dropped via the massive cranks on either side and would go several feet underground. It would be difficult for even Tibran war machines to breach it.

A recent update they made after the Tibran invasion? Hmm. Probably. Every kingdom Argonox had conquered had gone on to make upgrades and modifications to their military forces after they were set free. No one was anxious to see history repeated.

A company of twelve guards worked each of the lines moving slowly through the gate. They searched every single person for weapons—even the children, injured, and elderly—and questioned them on where they'd come from and why they wanted to come into Salnis.

The closer we got to the front of the line, the more my nerves grew tense. My hands twitched and my palms grew sweaty. Thatcher, Violet, Maylea, and I all had numerous weapons strapped all over our bodies. My kafki blades hung at my hips, and I had daggers tucked into the sides of both my boots. Was that going to be an issue? Would they arrest us? I was ready to do whatever was necessary in order to save Ronan, but fighting all these guards, just to die like a dog right here in the gateway, did not sound like fun. Would it even come to that?

I had no idea.

But when our turn finally came up, Violet stepped in close to the first guard that approached us and pulled up the sleeve of her tunic, flashing him a glimpse at something on her forearm, just below the crook of her elbow. Was that ... a tattoo? I only caught a fleeting look, but it resembled the same symbol the Zenith's Call used—a crescent moon with a sword through it.

I frowned. How had I not noticed that before now? Granted, I'd cut off one of her vambraces when we got hit by the drakkon's acid, so maybe it had been hidden under there and I just hadn't noticed it. After all, it wasn't that large. But still ... What did that mean? She worked for Arlan the Kinslayer, right? So why would she have the mark of the Zenith's Call tattooed on her skin like that? Had she been a member of their organization, as well?

The guard took one look at that mark and immediately waved us off, motioning for our group to come through the gate.

Whoa. The Zenith's Call must have a strong presence here, too, then. Interesting. Despite that, the guard who waved us through had a steely edge to his glare as he looked each of us over one at a time. His gaze met mine for an instant, and I caught the glint of something like suspicion as he eyed the blades that hung at my hips. I guess greevwood wasn't common here.

He didn't stop me, though, and I let out a shaky exhale when we finally crossed into the city streets of Salnis. One obstacle down. Now, we just had to find somewhere safe to spend a few hours, regroup, and come up with a plan for crossing the entire Nar'Haleenan desert. They called that desolate landscape the Valley of the Gods, due in part to the ancient battle that had reduced it to nothing but a seemingly endless stretch of barren sand and crumbling granite ruins. It was also said to be home to some of the oldest temples to the gods still standing in the world. That, I knew, was where Isandri had been raised. Her temple home was known as Calo'Luna—or the Temple of Adiana, in the common language. According to her, most of it had been destroyed during the Tibran War, and Isa hadn't been sure how much of it was still standing.

Regardless, she had never been interested in journeying all the way here to find out. Too many bitter memories.

Violet led the way out onto an open concourse that offered a staggering view to that massive pillar of black stone where the statue of Adiana stood front and center. Cool wind swept up from the dark depths far below, and the murmur and rush of the crowds making their way along the walkways, stairways, terraces, and bridges that served as the city's streets echoed through the canyon. Everything about the place seemed intentionally crafted with beauty in mind, carved with extremely detailed scrollwork and embellished with golden paint that stood out against the dark natural color of the stone. Up close, I realized it wasn't black at all. The stone was a very deep slate blue with swirls of cobalt, veins of glittering black crystal, and even deep greens running through it.

The breeze caught in Violet's long, silvery-blonde hair and she closed her eyes, tipping her head back into it slightly as she stopped just before the railing. A strange, soft look ghosted over her features as she let her fingertips graze over it. She took in a deep, weighted breath and then turned to face us.

"Now, then, we can't afford to rest just yet. I know of a place where we can lie low and sort out passage across the desert. It will likely involve another deal with merchants, but considering our special *asset*, that shouldn't be difficult." She nodded toward me as she referred to Vexi.

"Sooo, you like his assets?" Maylea asked, her tone the picture of innocence.

Too bad I knew her better than that, and I absolutely did ***not*** miss that mischievous little twinkle in her beady eyes ... or the way she was sucking her teeth to keep from grinning.

I noticed her tuck a hand behind her back and discreetly bump her fist against Thatcher's. That big idiot was doing a far worse job of hiding his own smirk.

Fates curse it, I would strangle both of them with my bare hands.

Violet hesitated, blinking a few hard times as though she wasn't sure she'd heard that right. Then her mouth mashed into an unimpressed, flat line and she rolled her eyes. "Yes, well, let's hope potential employers find them as enticing, hm?"

"I'm standing right here, you know!" I flailed my arms angrily.

"Yes, Lieutenant, we know. Just stand there and look pretty, would you?" Violet said, somehow managing to sound insulting. "Now, everyone, we must try to stay close. It looks like there is a lot of refugee traffic moving through, and that means pickpockets and thieves will be thick in the crowds. Watch your wares and keep your heads up. We have quite a ways to go, yet, and it would be best if we reach the inn before the sun gets any higher."

5

CHAPTER FIVE

I waited until my head stopped burning and we'd been walking for nearly an hour before I dared to approach Violet. As we wound a twisted route through the city's strange streets and stairways, I managed to move to the front of the group and walk right beside her. Not an easy feat since she was forging onward at a fiercely driven pace, like she was concerned someone else might be trying to follow us.

"You really think it's safe to stay here with Nar'Haleen practically knocking on the door?" I leaned down closer to her so I could whisper.

Her expression hardened with focus. "Of course not, Lieutenant. But there is no other choice. I think we would find any city in Rienka in a similar situation at present."

"Do you intend to try contacting the Zenith's Call again?" I asked, watching her reaction carefully when I mentioned that name.

She puffed a tight, frustrated sigh. "Why would I? They only seem to want to talk to you."

Ugh. Great. This again.

I seized her arm just below her elbow, right where I knew that tattoo was once again hidden under her sleeve. "Come with me this time, then."

Her crimson eyes flickered up to me, wide in surprise. Then her mouth scrunched bitterly and she looked straight ahead with a scowl that made her nose wrinkle. "My involvement with them is ... complicated."

"Yeah, sorta figured that," I mumbled. "Care to share?"

Her tone was sharp with warning. "Not right now, no."

"Later, then?" If she had issues with the secret organization that was responsible for our safety and travel, I sort of needed to know what was going on there.

Violet stopped suddenly and whirled to face me. "Do you mind? I am trying to navigate this very large city that, mind you, I have not been in since I was a child," she snapped, fixing me with a frenzied glare. "We can discuss your many insecurities later. Thank you."

What the—?

All I could do was stare back at her with my mouth hanging open. For a few wildly uncomfortable seconds, we just stood that way. Glaring at one another—me in total bewilderment and her practically snorting steam like an angry dragoness. Her chest heaved with tight, quick, angry breaths and her face flushed pink along her cheekbones as she glowered at me.

"Fine." I shook my head slowly and raised my hands as I backed away, not saying anything else. Why should I? She clearly didn't want to talk to me ... That, or the teasing from the others was getting to her far worse than I'd anticipated. Regardless, that was uncalled for. We were supposed to be the adults here.

And I was all out of patience to deal with anyone's drama today.

All eyes in our ragged little group were on me as I made my way back to the back of the line and kept my mouth shut.

Violet pinched the bridge of her nose, muttering to herself in Sokraal as she turned to start walking again. She spoke so quietly and quickly, I didn't catch any of it, though. Probably profanity aimed at me. Whatever.

I didn't care.

It's not like I liked her. Thatcher and the others could tease and point fingers if they wanted. It didn't matter. Violet was just ... well, I wasn't sure what, but she wasn't someone I wanted a romantic relationship with. Ever. We couldn't even have a normal conversation now without it being an awkward sort of fight. How was that romantic?

Simple—it wasn't.

Violet didn't glance back or say anything else until we had reached one of the lower tiers of the city, farther down the cliffside into the gloom of the shadows there. Every step down was like easing slowly into cool stream waters where the air was tinged with the smell of minerals and the kiss of a crisp breeze. The farther down we went, the more I came to appreciate why she had been so worried about beating the rising sun. The higher it went, the hotter the upper levels became. Fewer people walked the streets, shops closed up, and the whole city seemed to slip into an almost night-like routine.

Almost as though they treated the scorching daylight hours like night here. Strange.

The inn where Violet finally stopped was one of the larger structures on its, er, well, sort of street. If you could call the narrow winding road that was carved into the stone a street. The doorway had been cut directly into the stone, and I noted that many of the other buildings were styled the same way—with a mixture of man-made caverns and balconies fused with the sides of the canyon.

She opened the door to a cozy, dim interior where a lavish spread of fine woven rugs stretched over the stone floor and the aroma of incense hung thick in the air. An elderly woman in neatly arranged silken robes greeted us with a stiff bow and exchanged a greeting with Violet in Sokraal. They spoke back and forth, and Violet showed her tattoo again before handing the woman ten of the golden coins we'd just been paid for working with the caravan. The woman took them, bowed again, and led the way through the inn.

"We have two rooms on the third floor. She will open up the private bath for us and bring food and water," Violet began explaining as we followed along like a line of ducklings. "If you leave your clothes outside the bath, she will bring sleeping robes and launder what we have. It will be ready by dusk. By then, gods willing, we will have secured safe passage on into Nar'Haleen."

I bit back the urge to ask if this innkeeper intended on selling us out to the local thugs like the last one had. Ugh. Not good. My old temper was trying to rear its head again.

Some food and wine would have probably been more than enough to put that to rest. Too bad I couldn't afford to get lazy. Not when this might be my last chance. I stopped at the base of the steep, narrow staircase that led up into the rest of the inn, my hands resting on the pommels of my blades.

"What is it?" Thatcher asked, his frown tight with worry when he noticed I wasn't following.

"Go on and look after the others. I've got some business to attend to here first," I said.

His frown deepened. "Business with who?"

I arched an eyebrow. "I think you know who."

His expression broke into a look of pure sympathy. "Oh, Reigh. That's ... that's not ..."

"I don't have a choice anymore and you know it," I said, already backing away toward the door. "I'll be fine. Just keep an eye on Maylea. Don't let her out of your sight."

He nodded slowly, his brow crinkled upward in a fractured look of concern. "I will. Try to be safe, okay?"

"Always," I snorted and started back out into the scorching midday sun.

I DIDN'T KNOW THIS CITY.

Any other time, that might have been a huge problem. But it wasn't a challenge to figure out where I probably needed to go in order to find this so-called grotto that held a hidden temple to the goddess of death. At the bottom of the deepest, darkest hole, of course. Seemed logical, given how most of society felt about her. And, well, dying in general.

Not that she didn't like to revel in that atmosphere of delicious danger. She always loved to pour on the theatrics.

Staring down into the depths of the canyon outside the inn's door, I kept a firm grip on the stairwell's tall railing and shuddered as a familiar unease prickled at the back of my neck. It came with that sense of swirling, spinning nausea—like I was about to fall off the edge of the world into an endless abyss. I swallowed hard against the rising tension in my throat. My hands went clammy, and my heartbeat kicked fiercely as I started making my way down farther and farther along the city's steep canyon walkways.

Gods and Fates, I was *not* looking forward to this.

Sure, I'd had plenty of time to think about my approach and how I was going to handle seeing Clysiros again. But that didn't make the actual plunge into certain disaster any easier. I couldn't shove the responsibility off any longer, though. It was now or never.

I just ... really wished I didn't have to do this alone. For what must have been the ten-thousandth time, I found myself wishing Jaevid were here. He'd always been better at navigating these situations with the gods. He didn't fear them the way most people did. He didn't walk before them with shame or apprehension. When it came to brokering divine deals, he was the leading expert.

I was just a shoddy stand-in.

For Ronan's sake, though, I had to try.

A sharp shiver raced up my spine as I finally glimpsed the bottom of the canyon—more than two thousand feet from the topside gate where we had first entered the city. But that was just my best guess. It could have been deeper, but the glare of the sun made it hard to look skyward for too long.

I expected to find more city down here, where the crags and looming cliffs offered more protection from the heat. Instead, the base of the canyon didn't have any standing permanent structures apart from a few big, windowless stone buildings built right alongside a swiftly-flowing river. Those buildings were base structures affixed to massive metal cords that ran along wheels up and down the height of the canyon. It sort of reminded me of the elevator system we used in the dragonrider watchtowers to move goods up and down the various floors. Only this much larger system was built to move huge buckets of water from the river up into the city, dumping them into huge stone cisterns that fed aqueducts and fountains all through it.

This, I realized, was how the city got water from all the way down here. Incredible. I'd never seen anything like it. Violet hadn't been kidding about how the Southern Kingdoms, and Rienka in particular, had mastered their plumbing engineering ages ago.

The river itself wasn't all that deep, and I could see the smooth, fist-sized stones on the bottom all the way across. The water moved swiftly, however, and it was crystal clear with a sort of greenish hue. A dip of my hand into the rushing currents quickly made my hand go numb. Fates, it was freezing! Spring water, then? Or snowmelt from the surrounding mountains?

The constant rush of it was nearly musical as I made my way along the uneven road that hugged the shore only a foot or so above the water's surface. At first, I wasn't sure where to go from here. The road was slick with moisture and seemed to go on for miles.

Then I saw it in the distance—the base of that huge natural obelisk where the statue of Adiana perched far overhead, bathed in the radiant sunlight. The water rushed around it on both sides, but there was an extremely precarious-looking rope bridge that led from one side of the canyon to a narrow doorway cut straight into the base of the colossal stone column.

Anyone else might have gone right past it without a second look. After all, that bridge looked like a death wish—with the raging waters of the river so close beneath and nothing but a few soggy ropes and slippery wooden planks to stop you from being swept away. But a pair of statues sat at the cliffside end of the bridge directly before me. I stopped dead in my tracks, my heart thumping like mad as I stared into the white-jeweled eyes of two identical obsidian jackals.

I stood frozen for a moment, staring up at the black glass dogs, with my thoughts racing and memories tearing at my brain like hurricane winds. Fear like a fistful of ice sat right in the center of my chest, making everything ache. The wind currents made eerie howling sounds as they twisted and curled through the canyon around me, stirring in my hair.

What ... what was I doing? Why was I here? I-I couldn't ... I couldn't do this again. It would hurt. Gods and Fates, it would hurt *so much*.

"REIGH!" A woman's voice cried out my name over the lonely howl of the wind.

I turned, utterly speechless, as I spotted Violet sprinting down the riverside path toward me. The wind blew wildly through her hair and she glared at me, scarlet eyes ablaze with a mixture of panic and fury. My body tensed up on reflex, and my hands curled into fists at my sides.

Great. What now?

"What are you doing?" she demanded, panting and gasping for breath when she finally staggered to a stop before me. "You stupid, *stupid* man! Why would you try to do this on your own? Why would you not even tell me where you were going? Do you not trust me at all?!"

I looked away and gave her my shoulder. "Trust has nothing to do with it. It isn't your problem, and evidently, we don't humor one another's many *insecurities*."

Her expression fell, all that fury seeming to melt away as she studied my face. "That isn't ... Gods, you're so stubborn, you know that? It's infuriating!"

"Oh yeah? Why didn't you tell me you were a member of the Zenith's Call?" I cut straight to the point. If she really wanted to clear the air, then there was no point in dragging this out. "That's a pretty big secret you've been sitting on this entire time. Were you ever going to tell me? Or was the plan to just keep stringing me along and hope I didn't figure it out?"

Her mouth opened and closed a few times as though she were struggling to come up with the right words. Then, at last, she made an angry, growling, huffing sound and glared at the ground between us. "I didn't think it was important! And ... that is a part of my life I had hoped I would not have to revisit."

"And yet you agreed to come here?" I arched an eyebrow, not buying an inch of that pathetic excuse. She'd have to do better. "Come on, Violet. You had to have known it would come up sooner or later."

She bobbed her head but still wouldn't look up to meet my eyes as she answered. "Yes, I ... considered that possibility."

Possibility? Oh, for crying out—*of course* it was going to come up! She was waving that symbol around on her arm now like it was a free pass to a minstrel's show! I wasn't sure how she'd managed to keep it concealed until now—makeup, tactically placed clothing, or even some sort of magic—she probably had plenty of tricks at her disposal. But the how didn't matter. Not to me.

I made a wide, sweeping gesture to the area around us. "So you knew it would come up. You knew it might cause issues with people like Sulam. And yet, here you are! Look, I don't know what's going on with you, but as soon as we started getting involved with these people, your moods have been all over the place. You've either snapped at me like a cranky old lapdog, or avoided me outright, and I can't decide which is worse! Because either way, our communication is breaking down in record time, and I already suck at talking to people in the first place," I fumed. "I know some weird, totally accidental things have happened between us—I am sorry about that, by the way—but this was already going on before that happened."

She made another huffing, angry sound in her throat. Her mouth screwed up and she didn't reply.

"Do you hear me, Violet? Am I talking to myself right now?" I pressed, taking a step closer to her and waving a hand in front of her face.

"YES! I HEAR YOU!" she shouted suddenly. Her scarlet eyes finally met mine, teary and filled with a wrath I didn't understand. No, not just wrath. Pain. Confusion. And something else ... Was that sorrow? I wasn't sure.

My heart skipped and gave a painful twist in my chest. I held perfectly still, watching her breathe hard as she began frantically trying to blink away the fresh tears welling in her eyes. "I-I don't expect you or anyone else to understand. It was a long time ago, even for me. I was just a child then. But this place, being back here after everything that happened, it is ... a *lot*. I-I thought I could handle it. I thought I would be fine. But I'm not, and—and you wouldn't understand!"

Her expression seized with pain and she covered her face with her hands.

I stepped in closer, moving swiftly to put my arms around her and drag her in close against me. I didn't know how she would react to it. We weren't, you know, close or anything. Were we? Urgggh. Whatever. I wasn't about to just stand there and watch her break down.

"You decided that already, huh? Without even giving me a chance to try?" I murmured against her hair. "Curse it, woman, stop shutting me out and then chasing after me. I don't know what to do with mixed messages like that. I don't play those games. Either you're with me, or you're not."

Violet buried her face against my chest, her body trembling some as she murmured through ragged, broken breaths. "I-I am ... with you."

Those words crushed ruthlessly at my heart like the teeth of a vice, leaving me shaking. I shut my eyes and squeezed her tighter against me. "Then stop hiding things from me," I growled softly. "I mean it."

When she didn't answer, I put a hand on the back of her head. One heavy sigh seemed to release all the anger, frustration, and heat that had been roiling through my head like a hurricane for days. All gone in a single, slow breath.

"Why come all the way down here after me? You do realize you left Thatcher in charge again, right? That's practically an open invitation to disaster."

"I w-was ... afraid you ... w-would get lost ..." she sniffled.

I couldn't resist a smile. "I'm probably the only guy in this kingdom with red hair. You'd have found me sooner or later."

"D-Dead in some gods-forsaken alley," she grumbled.

"You do realize I'm a dragonrider, right? I can handle myself. You don't have to babysit me." I chuckled.

"Yes, I do. Your Sokraal sounds like baby-babble." Her voice was still a little muffled as she kept her face hidden in my tunic, but I could feel her breathing becoming slow and steady, as though she were trying to collect herself again. "It's so terrible."

I gasped in feigned offense. "Hey, I did practice."

"You need to practice more."

"And you need to trust me more," I said. Grasping the sides of her head, I gently pulled her back some so she was forced to look me in the eye. "I want to know you, Violet. So, for the love of all things divine, just talk to me. You ought to know better than anyone I'm in no position to judge you for whatever happened in your past. But I can't read your mind, and right now, I don't even know you well enough to try."

She blinked a few times, tears still dripping from her long, dark eyelashes as she stared up at me. Pink color crept into her cheeks, and her full lips parted slightly.

Fates, something about that doe-eyed look was so ... beautiful.

And really inviting.

Something about that foggy expression, and the way her long lashes brushed her cheeks as she closed her eyes, drew me in. My heartbeat kicked like an angry mule in my chest. My stomach spun, and I could feel every place where her breath puffed across my cheeks.

I started to lean down closer, as though pulled in toward her by some invisible force I didn't even understand.

Then it hit me.

Oh, Sweet Fates, what was I thinking? Had I completely lost my mind?!

I immediately let her go and dropped my hands back to my sides. "Sorry, I, uh ... I need to figure out where this grotto-temple-thing is. The sooner the better. And, um, you're welcome to come with me. I don't know how you feel about Clysiros, but I'm sort of late to a meeting with her. Very late, actually." I cleared my throat and scratched at the back of my neck.

"I am amazed you found this place on your own." Violet's voice was stiff and uncomfortable, too. "How did you manage it so quickly?"

All I could do was shrug and cast a long, weary stare up at the obsidian jackal statues that guarded the way forward. "Eh, well, you know what they say about old dogs."

"They cannot learn new tricks?" she guessed.

"No," I replied. "They always find their way back to their masters."

6

CHAPTER SIX

Violet stuck close to my back as we made our way across the rickety bridge to the base of the massive stone obelisk. The wind picked up, making the old ropes swing some under our added weight, and I bit back a curse when one of my boots slipped on the slick, soggy wooden planks. I got to the other side first and turned around to offer her a helping hand when she got to the last few steps.

Then, we both stood before the narrow, yawning doorway in the column of stone. A hard knot of anxiety sat like a lead weight in my chest as I stared into it, unable to see anything even a few feet within. There was no light. No sound other than the wind and rushing of the river. Gods, it might have dropped off into an eternal pit of death ten feet inside and I wouldn't be able to see it coming.

Typical.

"I didn't bring a torch," I confessed when Violet leaned around to peer at my face, as though she was concerned I might be having second thoughts.

I was, of course. Running away screaming was still an option. Not a good one, granted, but still an option.

"I did," she announced and brushed back her cloak to reveal one tucked haphazardly into the back of her belt. "I grabbed it from our things when Thatcher told me you were trying to find this place."

"I can always count on him to have the biggest mouth." I sighed as I took it. "Ready?"

"Are you?" she countered.

"No. Of course not," I said in the spirit of full honesty. Slipping my flintstone from my belt, I lit the torch and took in a steadying breath.

No turning back now.

I stepped over the threshold, and my face met the cold, stagnant air within. The heavy scent of minerals saturated my nose as I held the torch aloft, shedding light over a small, circular chamber with a spiral staircase right in the center that led straight down into more utter darkness. Something about it reminded me of the royal catacombs back home. I'd only gone in there once, years ago, to pay my respects at my late mother's tomb. I'd never known her, and that glimpse of her face etched into the stone cover over her vault flickered through my memories like a wisp of smoke.

Sometimes I wondered what she would have thought of her youngest, reckless waste of a son. Not much, probably.

"I had heard that a great number of priests and acolytes once kept this place," Violet whispered as she picked her way carefully down the steps right behind me. "But most of them were put to the sword during the Tibran War. Very few remain. I don't know how many would still dwell here."

"I guess we'll find out." I put my free hand against the damp stone wall to steady myself as we descended deeper and deeper. "You wouldn't happen to know why they'd stick a big statue of Adiana on the top of this place, do you? If it's a temple to Clysiros, it seems a little odd that they'd put a different goddess up there."

"Not at all," she replied. "The two are often depicted together. Adiana is goddess of the moon, and Clysiros is associated with the stars. They are sometimes called the Night Sisters, and it's fairly common to find images of them close together."

"Ahh. Makes sense, then."

"Do they really not teach such things in Maldobar?" She sounded genuinely surprised.

"Not usually," I admitted. "I'm not sure why, except that maybe worship of the ancient gods got lost somewhere in all the wars Maldobar has fought in recent history. Jaevid said the use of the stones to be the focus of the gods' divine power sort of removed them from common knowledge, and the upkeep of worship and tradition fell to whichever individual had been selected to speak for them. The only ones specifically tied to Maldobar were Paligno and Clysiros—and that was only because of Jaevid's ancestors and my unfortunate birthright as the harbinger."

"I see." She clicked her tongue thoughtfully. "The gods have always been sewn into the very fabric of life in the Southern Kingdoms. Most people show loyalty to at least one, if not many. It has been that way for thousands of years."

"The Southern Kingdoms are a lot older than Maldobar," I thought aloud, reasoning more with myself than her. "Makes sense they would have more of a cultural significance here." I made it a few more steps before a new idea, something I hadn't considered before, made me pause and glance back at her. "Were there people here who were also tied to the god stones? People with the powers of the gods like the lapiloque and harbinger?"

Violet nodded, making a face like that should have been obvious. "Of course."

Whoa. I hadn't considered that before now. But it begged another question. "Who were they? Do they still have family members around?"

Her smile was coy as she arched an eyebrow. "They do. In fact, you've met one of them already."

What? I had? "Who is it?" I pressed.

"The esteemed Captain Malina Skyhart," she laughed softly.

My mouth fell open. Wait—*seriously?* She was a stonespeaker like Jaevid and me? "You're kidding. She ... she didn't say anything about ..." I stammered.

"No, no. Malina herself was not god-chosen. But it did run in her family. The Skyharts were of great esteem and power on the sea, as they were chosen by Undae. The goddess herself taught them to craft the ships that control the drakkons." Violet tapped her chin thoughtfully. "I think it was her older brother who was the last to be born with Undae's blessing, but he died during the Tibran War, along with most of his family. He was very young and had not yet fully come into his power. Malina is the only member of the Skyhart family that survived."

Oh. Hmm. That explained her blatant dislike of wars and royals, as well as her fixation on the *Squall Queen*. But it made me wonder, and I had to ask, "Did he have powers over the ocean? Like Jaevid did over plants and animals?"

Violet gave a small shrug. "That was what I heard, but I never met him myself. They say he wore a bone-carved ring—not unlike the necklace Maylea wears that came from Paligno. It was the symbol of his heritage; a powerful gift from Undae herself. With it, it was said he could control both drakkons at once. But the ring was lost with him many years ago, and no one ever found any trace of either of them after the Tibran scourge."

"That's too bad," I muttered as I went back to descending the stairs.

Fates knew we could have used a helping hand like that a few days ago. The drakkon that now served Nar'Haleen was a serious problem. I'd never seen a monster with destructive force like that. And to be able to control not one—but *two* of them?

Considering what we might be going up against, I would have felt a whole lot better about fighting an insane ancient Avoran sorceress if we had some power like that at our disposal. Wishful thinking.

But maybe after this, I'd be able to deal out a little divine wrath of my own. That was my hope, anyway, as I reached the last step and paused, letting my gaze roam through the wide-open chamber before us.

The Temple of Clysiros welcomed us in like the frigid arms of a ghost.

The sound of trickling water filled the utter stillness. My breath turned to a curling white fog in the air as I held the torch higher. Its golden light rippled and shimmered off a grand hall cut from polished black glass, lined with smooth onyx columns, and stretching off into the distant darkness before us. Overhead, the domed ceiling arced gracefully at more than sixty feet, flecked with something like chips of crystal or silver that mimicked the stars in the light of my torch.

Another eerie, familiar cold shiver prickled up my spine. A presence I knew all too well. Every hair on my body stood on end and I bit down hard, steeling myself against that sinking sense of despair that followed.

A small hand closed around mine suddenly, warm and strong. I glanced down, finding Violet standing right next to me with her scarlet eyes trained keenly forward. Her mouth was set in a focused, determined line, and her other hand gripped one of her daggers.

"Someone is coming," she whispered, her lips barely moving.

What? I looked ahead again, but there was nothing there. Not that I could see even with my torch casting light out about thirty feet ahead of us. What was she talking about? There was no one else here. This place was totally abandoned and probably had been for a—

Then I *did* see him.

A bent, willowy figure emerged from the gloom and hobbled into the golden glow of my torch. An old man wrapped in a black hooded robe leaned heavily forward, his back bowed and his features sunken with age. He peered at me with pale, milky blue eyes, not saying anything. Then he considered Violet the same way.

"You're late," he griped, his voice thin and scratchy.

Violet and I exchanged a sideways glance.

"I'm ... sorry?" I wasn't sure what else to say.

"I'm not the one you ought to apologize to," the old man huffed. It took him a solid thirty seconds just to get turned back around, but then the old man was off again, moving ahead like the world's speediest snail back down the grand hall.

"Well? What are you waiting for?" he barked back at us. "Come. You've wasted enough time already, boy. The lady awaits."

"I guess there is one priest left here, after all," Violet said, keeping her tone hushed. As we moved forward, she slipped her dagger back into one of the sheaths belted to her thighs and began to pull her hand away from mine.

Panic seized in my throat and I quickly squeezed her hand harder. I-I didn't want her to let go. Not yet. Just a little longer.

Then I could handle it.

Violet didn't protest. She didn't even look up and kept her fingers wound through mine as we walked together after the old priest. She was just there, with me in that moment. No signs of judgment, or fear, or even apprehension. She walked with me into the dark, into the den of all my personal demons, with her head held high. Not because she had to, and not because I'd asked her to.

Because she wanted to. She had chosen to be here with me in this nightmare.

And for the first time in over fourteen years, I didn't feel alone.

"Well, well, well," a sharp voice cut through my mind like the crack of a whip in my ear. *"Look who finally came to visit."*

I flinched and nearly tripped over my own feet. Noh. He was here somewhere, probably lurking in the dark and watching my every move. I could sense his presence like a cold pressure in the room, and it set every one of my nerves on edge.

I shut my eyes tightly, and tried to focus past the rising tide of dread that made my throat want to close up. I must have started shaking, because I felt Violet's grip on my hand tighten.

Right. I just had to stay calm. Deep breaths. I was in control. Yes, Noh was here. But I had known that was going to be a factor. I couldn't let it rattle me.

I wasn't a kid anymore. I knew all his tricks.

The cavernous hallway ended abruptly at the top of a grand staircase that sloped gradually down into more inky darkness. The old priest didn't hesitate and began his slow descent until he disappeared beyond the glow of my torchlight. But at the top of the stairs, my knees locked up. My stomach turned. That freezing pressure grew more intense, crushing down over my back and shoulders like a yoke of solid ice.

Breathe—I had to breathe. Stay calm. Stay in control. Don't let the memories drag me under again.

"Are you all right?" Violet asked softly, giving my hand a tug. "You're trembling."

"F-Fine," I lied.

"The old man isn't waiting. We should hurry," she coaxed gently.

I stole a glance down at her and couldn't hold back a squeaky, anxious laugh at the irony. "You can see in the dark, can't you?" I guessed.

She made a strange, somewhat uncomfortable face and shrugged. "It is a common Viperi trait. We can see body and light heat quite well."

Right. That was ... bizarre. I'd never heard of anyone *seeing* heat. She was just full of surprises today.

"Spend a lot of time in dark caves, do they?" I asked as I started shambling down the stairs.

"More than anywhere else, actually," she replied, a reluctant stiffness in her tone. She had acted that way before, too, when I asked about her heritage. Yet another page in the book of mysteries that was Violet.

"I'm counting on you to spot anyone sneaking up on us from the dark, then," I said, trying to pick up my pace to catch up with our seemingly indifferent tour guide.

Geez, that old priest had gone a lot farther ahead than I'd anticipated. I didn't spot him again until we'd nearly come to the base of the staircase. He stood there, arms still folded into the lengths of his heavy dark robes, and watched us descend with a grimace of disapproval on his raw-boned features.

"Fates," Violet whispered beside me, her scarlet eyes panning out across to something beyond the reach of my torch's light. "This place is ..."

"Older than time itself, girl," the old man huffed. He dipped his head some, gesturing to the light in my hand. "Douse your torch. Your test begins now."

Test? No one had said anything about a test.

"You know I won't be able to see anything without it, right?" I just had to be sure this old guy was aware that, unlike Violet, I did not possess the ability to see in perfect darkness.

"If the lady has truly chosen you, then you don't need to see. Not with mortal eyes." That unwavering scowl on his deeply creased face didn't budge an inch, like it might as well have been chiseled from stone, too.

Great. This just kept getting better and better.

Dousing the torch, I handed it back to Violet and tried not to panic as the complete and total darkness of the temple swallowed me whole.

I stood still, my eyes open but seeing absolutely nothing. I doubted I'd be able to spot my own hand in front of my face.

"Those who are called by the lady feel her pull even in the greatest depths of despair," the old man's voice spoke nearby, his tone strangely ominous. "You've been brought this far, but you must finish the journey on your own. If you find your way into her embrace ... her blessing will be yours."

I swallowed hard. Right. Okay. Nothing new here, right? I totally had this.

Gods and Fates, what was I doing?!

Letting my eyes fall closed, I let out a slow, steady exhale as I tried not to think. To trust my senses. If Clysiros really wanted me here, now was the time to reach out.

That prickle of unease still shivered deep in my chest, making my breath catch like the first touch of frost over the Farchase Plains back home. I focused on it—the way it seemed to spread like stretching, grasping cold fingers through my lungs, down my spine, and across the back of my head. Every tiny hair on my body stood on end and my heartbeat gave a fluttering skip.

"Come, brother," Noh's voice hissed through my thoughts. *"There is not much time."*

I opened my eyes again, still seeing nothing but darkness in all directions. If Violet and that old priest were still standing nearby, I couldn't see, hear, or sense them at all. I was ... alone.

Alone with my fate, once again.

I took a step forward. Then another. A cold wind stirred through my hair and rustled my clothes, carrying the sweet aroma of incense as I walked slowly forward. My heart pounded in fast, hard thumps that made my ribs ache and my hands and feet go numb.

"Can you tell me why you left?" a familiar voice asked suddenly.

I cringed and froze mid-step. Wh-What? Kiran? Why was he here? *How* was he here? I whirled around, searching the dark for the Gray elven man who had always been like a father to me.

But there was nothing. No one. Only darkness.

"Reigh," Kiran's voice urged gently. *"Talk to me."*

"Kiran?" I called out his name.

No answer.

"I know you think this power you have is evil and that you're not a good person because of it," another voice carried through the dark—softer, feminine, and with a tone that cut me straight to the core. It had been so long since I heard her voice.

Enyo.

"This isn't a choice either of us get to make," Jaevid's voice boomed in my mind, so loud and clear it made every muscle in my body go tense. *"I'm giving you a reason—for being what you are. This is what you were born to do."*

I-I didn't understand. What was happening? Where were they? I couldn't see anyone!

Staggering forward, I nearly tripped as my boots suddenly sloshed in something wet. Water? I couldn't see to be sure. It came to my calves and soaked through all the way to my socks.

"Pushed it right to the brink, didn't you, boy? A pity no one in this kingdom seems to know anything about divine power." A deeper, far more menacing voice snickered, his tone one that resonated deep in my mind like a hammer against a bronze tower bell. It made my spine lock up solid and I stood, gasping and paralyzed.

A ... Argonox.

"Bind him and take him to the experimental wing. Phoebe will have much work to keep her occupied."

No. No.

NO!!

They weren't here. It wasn't real. It couldn't be!

"I wonder, how many people have cursed and condemned you for all the good men you slaughtered at Barrowton?" Murdoc's sharp, venomous tone sliced through the dark and I staggered forward again. *"You killed thousands of Tibrans, yes. But you killed just as many Maldobarian soldiers. You didn't even leave corpses behind for their families to bury. What have you done to atone for those deaths? Or does being the chosen one of a goddess justify murder?"*

"NO!" I shouted, my hands clenched into fists as I forged forward, trying to find the source. "I-I didn't mean to! I was young, and stupid, and it was an accident! I—"

The toe of my boot caught on something, maybe an uneven stone, and I fell forward into the water. It hit my face like an icy slap, immediately shocking my system. I'd been walking in the water only a second before. I should have felt a bottom, or landed on my hands and knees, but I didn't. Dark current roared around me, sucking me down deeper and deeper into the swirling depths of the freezing water.

My lungs spasmed. My arms and legs flailed. I searched in vain for something, any point of reference to tell me where the surface was.

Then I remembered. I knew this. I'd been here before, many years ago.

Oh, gods. Those weren't voices, or ghosts, or even real people.

They were memories—*my* memories.

I shut my eyes tightly, drawing my arms and legs in close to my body as that spinning, whirling sensation all around me intensified. There was no direction in it. No sense of up or down. No sound. No light. No time.

Just eternal chaos.

My personal hell.

7

CHAPTER SEVEN

In an instant, everything stopped.

I sucked in a frantic gasp and opened my eyes, finding myself standing on a small island somewhere in the middle of inky black waters. My clothes and hair were dry, but I was still breathing hard as I stared up at the only feature visible on that tiny spit of land. A large statue carved from black stone loomed before me, bathed in the weak light of seven smoldering braziers. It was the image of a woman draped in flowing robes, her arms outstretched and her head bowed so that her features were hidden in the heavy shadows. Her six angelic wings spread to the faint glow of the embers, each feather crafted from opaque black glass that glittered and sparkled.

I knew her even if I couldn't see her face.

Clysiros.

"Mmm. Not aging very well, are we?" Noh's voice chuckled nearby. *"Best find yourself a wife before those wrinkles really set in."*

I glanced to my left and found him standing there beside me, leaning against his tall staff that looked a great deal like a shepherd's crook. Overall, Noh looked exactly how I expected—exactly like me, only with skin of a chalky deep gray, black hair, and eyes like firelit rubies. He'd always resembled a darker reflection of myself, and not just because he had once been my twin brother. In some ways, it felt like we were the same person, only split in two. That, supposedly, was part of our shared birthright as servants to Clysiros. Two souls. One body. He could walk beyond the Sivanth—the boundary line between the world of the living and realm of the dead. I could, too, in a way. But he was forever tethered to that realm and charged with guarding it.

Once, his presence had confused and terrified me. I hadn't understood who or what he was. Now, I almost felt relieved to see him manifest in that human-looking form. The last time we'd met like this, it had been to say goodbye after the defeat of the Tibran Empire. I hadn't known then if I would ever see him again. Horrifying and unpredictable as he was, Noh had never left my side when I truly needed his help.

I wondered if this was going to be another one of those occasions.

"Good to actually see you again," I muttered as I raked some of my bangs away from my face.

"Likewise," he mumbled back.

"Gonna give me any hints about what I'm doing here?"

He pursed his lips, as though trying to decide. Then tipped his head to the statue slightly. "As much fun as it is to watch you blunder around, guessing blindly, we are rather short on time. This is your final test. A trust fall, if you will."

Trust fall? What the heck was that supposed to mean?

Hmmm.

I narrowed my eyes at him suspiciously, then shifted my gaze to study the statue again. Draped in thick shadows, I hadn't noticed the structure that stood immediately before it, half ensnared by the lengths of her billowing robes and glass-feathered wings. It wasn't an altar. I felt pretty confident about that—even if the base of it was littered with very human-looking bones and skulls. Sweet Fates, what was this?

The structure looked like a slab of black stone in the shape of a person's silhouette, positioned at an angle like a table leaning against a wall. Its surface was studded with jagged glass like dagger points, and I noticed many of them were speckled in something dark. Old blood.

Faaaantastic. It looked like a torture device.

And it wasn't hard to work out what I was supposed to do now. But the sight of all those long-decayed corpses scattered around was not comforting in the slightest. Was I going to end up like that? Just a heap of bones on the floor of this miserable cave?

I stole a look back at Noh, just to be sure this was really what he had been gesturing to. His broad smile was as cold as it was disturbing. Crap, I really hoped I didn't look like that when I smiled too.

Standing right before the table of death, I had to ask myself that all-too-important question: did I really trust Clysiros?

No. Of course not. I didn't trust any of the gods, honestly. But the one thing I did trust—the one thing I knew for sure—was that I had been called here for a reason. The end was coming, and Clysiros needed a champion. She needed a dog in the upcoming fight.

And I happened to be one of her favorite mutts.

Clysiros might not be trustworthy in her own right, but I knew I could trust her desperation to keep her godly throne.

And that was exactly what was at stake now.

She *needed* me.

I bowed my head some, letting those thoughts wash over me until there was nothing but silence left in my mind. All the whispers, all the memories, faded to nothing. I was there, present and ready, to take death's cold hand and walk this path again.

It would be different this time—I could feel it all the way down to my marrow. I wasn't a scared little child anymore. I couldn't be. I had passed through fire and brimstone just to find myself. I had learned to wear my scars with pride. I'd been baptized in the blood of my past mistakes to become the person I was now.

A person who could carry this burden with dignity.

Spreading my arms wide, I let my eyes roll closed and leaned forward until I began to fall ...

Straight down onto that bed of deadly daggers.

I BRACED FOR PAIN. FOR SUFFERING. FOR DEATH'S SMOTHERING EMBRACE.

But there was nothing.

When I dared to look, I found myself standing in an all-too-familiar field. Everything—the sky, the grass, the dirt—was varying shades of silver and gray, like a world completely drained of all color. Before me, on a small rise, the crumbling ruins of seven stone arches stood around a central platform. There, the remains of four thrones made of black glass stood lonely and forgotten.

Three of them had been shattered and broken until they were barely recognizable, but the fourth still towered, strong and imposing, before me with a halo of spines protruding from the back like a dark sunburst.

That was where she sat, legs crossed, and chin resting on her palm as she smiled at me like a wolf admiring a lamb that had wandered into her den.

Not far from the truth, I guess.

The way her black robes hung off her shoulders revealed pearly white skin as smooth and flawless as alabaster as she beckoned me forward. She wore a much more human appearance than the last time I'd seen her in person. No wings. No horns. Even her size was normal.

When Clysiros had entered the battlefield at Halfax to slay Argonox, all those years ago, she had stricken fear into the hearts of every soul who saw her—me included. Now, though, she seemed far more approachable. Maybe this was her attempt at not scaring the poor, sad human idiot? I did appreciate the gesture if that was the case.

"If it isn't my favorite little mortal," she crooned in an alluring, breathy tone. Her dark eyes shimmered like the depths of that bottomless black water as she stared straight at me, seeming to measure my every move. *"How long has it been, my love? Eons, it seems. My, the years have been cruel, haven't they? You look so weary."*

Really? Was it that bad? I'd have to check later. I didn't exactly spend much time critiquing my appearance. Sure, I probably needed a haircut and a good shave. But that wasn't exactly a big priority at the moment. What with the end of the world looming on the horizon and all.

"Yeah, yeah," I waved a hand as I came to stand before her, "I doubt you called me here for beauty tips."

"Indeed not." Her smile was venom as she stood, the lengths of her robes pooling around her bare feet as she stepped toward me. I held perfectly still, not even daring to breathe, as she combed her ice-cold fingers through my hair. She traced a fingernail along my jawline and stopped at my chin, tilting her head to the side as she studied my mouth for an instant. *"I have something much more fun planned for you, my darling."*

"I'm sure you do," I snorted when she finally pulled her hand away.

"You know what's coming, do you not?' she asked, her coy smile fading a little.

"A war," I answered. "An Avoran sorceress seeks the realm of the gods to steal your power and thrones."

Clysiros's expression cooled, becoming as ominous and treacherous as a swelling stormfront. *"She draws nearer by the hour, pulling threads that span kingdoms and realms far beyond your understanding. Already her efforts have begun a chain reaction. Wheels are in motion that cannot be stopped. Avgior has been awakened. She may yet find the gate."*

"A chain reaction?' I questioned, my mind spinning. "Wait a second, who is Avgior? And what gate?"

"Some call it the Gate of Proleus, because it was his mighty hand that sealed it and his chosen guard who once protected it," she explained, beginning to pace a slow circle around me. *"Avgior is the*

Fallen One. He is all that sees and knows. The holder of all secrets. Once he stood at the boundary that the Viepol now keep. They are his offspring and possess fragments of his knowing." She motioned down the line of shattered thrones before us, *"We sat here, upon the thrones of old, and watched over the mortal realm. Giaus, Astaris, Avgior, and myself. I am their firstborn, charged with keeping the only gate that led to Pareilos, our eternal realm. My dear brother, Paligno, might have joined us, as well, had he not already fallen smitten with filling the mortal world with all manner of new life."*

Whoa. This ... this wasn't anything I'd ever heard anyone talk about. Not even Arlan. There was *another* god? A god that had been slain? It must've happened during the War of the Stones. But still—why hadn't I heard of this before?

"His name was struck from all history, and his essence shattered to prevent his rebirth, lest the knowledge he had proven so careless with be given into the wrong hands again," Clysiros hissed, apparently able to read my mind. Somehow, that didn't surprise me at all. *"It was his weakness that compromised us. He shared many things with the Avoran elves, things no mortal should have known. You must remember, darling, that ages ago, the world looked quite different. Avora ruled much of the mortal realm, only to be defied by Tibrus and Nar'Haleen. They quarreled endlessly, and we tried time and again to intervene. But Avgior had already told them far too much. The mortals sought to break our thrones and steal our power, and they might have succeeded had we not enacted the Law of the Stones. That decree closed the Gate of Proleus forever and created the boundary that you now know as the Sivanth."*

"So ... so you're saying there's an actual, physical gate that leads here to the divine realm?" I just had to be sure I was hearing all this right. "And that this crazy Avoran sorceress actually knows where it is and how to open it now?"

Clysiros stopped before me again, her dark eyes glittering with a primal ferocity that sent a chill of terror up my spine. *"Yes."*

Oh. Oh crap.

"She must still assemble all three elements of the ritual, but she already holds the Blood of Fate, taken from Avgior himself, as well as the Blade of Souls."

Blade of Souls? Wow. That didn't sound good.

"It was my own blade, the very one that felled Avgior in the mortal realm in ages past," she said, reading my thoughts again. *"It will kill anything whose heart is pierced by it, be they mortal or divine. I'm quite fond of it, and it seems my little sister has stolen it. If it isn't too much trouble, darling, I should very much like you to bring it back to me."*

"Right. Sure. Just add that to the list," I grumbled. Like I didn't have enough to worry about already—now there was a crazy powerful Avoran sorceress running around with a kill-anything-it-touches weapon. Amazing.

I almost didn't want to ask, but I had to. "What's the one thing she's still missing, then? You said she already has the blood and the blade, so what's left?"

Clysiros leaned in closer, whispering her answer right against my ear like a lover's secret, *"That which all creatures guard most dearly, and you carry in your merry band right this moment. The Spark of Life."*

8

CHAPTER EIGHT

I knew.

Clysiros didn't have to say another word. My pulse thundered in my ears as I stood before her, eyes wide and mouth hanging open, while all the pieces of the grand, mad puzzle finally slipped into place. The destruction of the library. Ronan's disappearance. Even the sudden acts of aggression from Nar'Haleen that had forced us out into the open. None of it was by chance. It was all *her* doing.

Sadeera.

I could see it—how this had all been building from the very beginning. There was only one thing standing between Arlan's sister and her final goal of bringing down the realm of the gods.

And it now hung around the neck of Maylea Broadfeather.

Gods, Fates, and all things holy ...

That was why Sadeera had taken Ronan from the Compendium Library. She didn't need his power. She needed bait. She was luring us straight to her, letting us ferry the last thing she needed straight to her doorstep. And we were falling for it.

But what other choice was there? She had my only nephew as her prisoner! I couldn't just turn back now. I couldn't abandon him. Going forward, closer to Sadeera, would be a mistake. And the idea of leaving Ronan in that woman's grasp was more than I could stand.

I didn't know what to do.

There was no right choice.

"Don't despair, my darling," Clysiros crooned, her alarmingly cold hand brushing my cheek again, like someone stroking their favorite lap dog. *"Already, my dear brothers and sisters have been busily choosing their champions. The sorceress is mighty, yes. But you will be, as well. I'm going to give you everything you need to dispense with her. You'll bring her soul to me personally, and she will pay dearly for all she's done."*

I set my jaw, steeling every single one of my worn-out, frayed nerves before I dared to speak. "No."

Her hand paused, lightly gripping my chin.

I held my breath.

"You are refusing me?"

I leveled my gaze upon hers, doing my very best to channel my inner Jaevid-level of confidence. "I didn't come here to beg for your help," I reminded her. "You were the one who called me here because you wanted *my* help. I'm willing to give it, but not for free. Not this time."

Clysiros withdrew some, seeming to consider me more intensely as her expression became pensive and cryptic. *"I see. Just when I think you can't possibly get more interesting ..."* She made a sweeping gesture, one corner of her mouth twisting upward into a conniving smirk. *"By all means, don't hold me in suspense. What does my favorite little mortal desire?"*

I straightened, squaring my shoulders and keeping my voice as steady as possible. "You cursed Ronan before he was ever born for something that wasn't his fault. He can't help who his father was. It's cruel and unfair for him to have to live this way, and now it's put his life in danger. If you want my help, then you'll have to agree to break his curse."

Her eyes widened as that smile spread fully across her face—a disturbing mixture of delight and surprise. Her melodic laugh ran like bells in the air as she swept in close to me again. *"How noble you are! It's so ... desperately sad. And somewhat disappointing, I must say. You could ask for anything in the world. Immortality. Power. A throne and kingdom of your own. Good fortune for the rest of your days. Even the heart and undying affection of that woman who betrayed you so bitterly. But instead, you barter for a silly little curse."*

"Sorry to disappoint." I crossed my arms, holding my ground. "Should I succeed, then by all means, sprinkle any of that other stuff on our bargain if you find yourself feeling especially generous. Except Enyo. She can keep her heart and undying affections, as far as I'm concerned."

Clysiros gave a small, feigned gasp and put her hand over her chest. *"What? So many long years spent wallowing in grief for a love lost—all for nothing! Does this mean you've finally stopped pining for her?"*

I arched an eyebrow. "I haven't pined for her in years, not that it's got anything to do with, well, anything. Can we get back to the point? I realize my pathetic attempts at romance are endlessly entertaining for everyone, but there is an actual crisis at hand I would really like to deal with."

She tapped the end of my nose with a finger, nibbling gleefully at her bottom lip. *"You really are my favorite, you know. So direct and brash. So defiant and daring. You've grown so much, and yet not at all."*

I smirked back at her. "Thanks, I think."

"Very well, then. If these are your terms, I will agree," she giggled and looped her arms around my neck, pressing her weight against my chest so that her face was directly in front of mine. She licked her lips like a wolf preparing for a feast, her bottomless dark eyes glittering with wicked delight. All the lengths of her long, jet-black hair floated in the air around us, curling and swirling like ribbons of dark silk.

I sucked in a sharp breath, feeling the swell of cold pressure around us as everything began to grow dim. My toes went numb in my boots. Then my legs. I lost the feeling to my hands as that bitter, biting cold climbed my body and spread through me inch by inch.

But her voice only seemed to cut through deeper, delving down through flesh into my soul like a worm into an apple.

"And I will give you such power, unlike anything the world has ever seen. Your name will resonate through all of mortal history, and they will fear it. You will not be my harbinger, nor will you be my mere paladin." She leaned in as everything went dark, her lips brushing mine with every

softly spoken word. *"They will show you the respect befitting of my favorite servant. They will call you my chosen king. The King of the Grave."*

My eyes flew open and I sucked in a frantic, ragged breath. Floundering back, I pushed away from the dagger-studded altar and immediately doubled over. I searched for punctures, bleeding, any signs of trauma or pain. G-Gods, I must have been impaled over a dozen times.

Help—I needed help! Someone, please ... Violet!

But there was nothing. No signs of injury or even tears in my clothes. Gods and Fates. I was ... all right.

Slowly, I stood straight and stared in total mystification at my completely untouched torso. These clothes were *not* the ones I had arrived in. My sweaty, grim-encrusted, travel-tattered robes were gone. In their place, I wore a mantle of shimmering silver depicting spirals of sculpted runes that spanned across my shoulders and down my chest almost like a breastplate. It led to a broad belt with a long panel in the front almost like a tabard, and more of those gleaming designs formed the shapes of tendrils surrounding points like stars—all on a black field of fine silk.

"Wh-Whoa," I managed to wheeze shakily, marveling at how the ensemble glittered in the weak light of the braziers whenever I moved. Every rune, every swirl and interlocking design shone like diamond. Incredible.

"Welcome back, my esteemed brother. Or should I say, Your Majesty?" Noh said, still standing exactly where he'd been before. He put a fist over his chest and bent in a low bow. "I am honored to be at your service once again."

I stared at him, my brain still trying to process everything that had happened. I was alive. I wasn't hurt. And ... I'd made a deal with Clysiros. Again. She had agreed to my terms and promised me the power it would take to really join this fight.

But had it actually worked? The new clothes were a definite statement piece, but what else had she given me?

Then I noticed my hands, and my heart gave a twisting, panicked lurch deep in my chest. They were stained. No—covered in markings. My heart began pumping wildly, making my head spin and my vision spot as I stared in awe. I bit back a curse of alarm, turning my hands over to look at my palms. I quickly brushed up the sleeves of my tunic and found even more.

The marks on my hands and arms appeared like swirling, spiraling veins of black ink that ran from my fingertips all the way to my elbows. My fingertips themselves were solid black, as though the tiny runes that comprised each spiral were so close together that they finally all meshed into one.

Oh, gods. What did this mean? Were there more on the rest of my body? Dressed in my shining new ensemble, I couldn't tell. Stripping down right here didn't seem like the best idea, though. I'd have to check on that later.

A slow, rattling exhale slipped past my lips as I faced Noh again, hoping for an explanation, or at least a hint about what these marks meant.

He stood straight and met me with a broad, arrogant grin that made my skin crawl. It was hard to look at him without feeling like I was standing before a twisted, cursed mirror. A mirror that showed me a far darker, more dangerous version of myself.

He tipped his head to the side slightly, off toward the seemingly endless expanse of black water that stretched out from the island off into eternity. "I believe it's time to go. Age before beauty," he jabbed.

"We're twins," I reminded him sharply as I stepped to the water's edge. "I'm not sure that phrase applies."

"Technically, you are the elder between the two of us."

I scoffed. "By what? Like a minute?"

"Hmm. Maybe two. Although, technically, I was never alive. So any amount of time you live would far exceed mine," he retorted.

Fair point.

"Regardless, I will be here should you need me," Noh said, giving another bow. "I am once again at your disposal."

I nodded. "Any tips on getting out of here?"

His smirk was as impish as it was patronizing. "Oh, I'm sure the King of the Grave can work it out all on his own." With a glimmer like silvery mist and a puff of black smoke, he vanished into thin air without another sound.

Great. So much for being at my disposal. Not that I expected any less from him.

I paused at the water's edge, still sloshing in my boots after the last little dive I'd taken into it. I was a decent swimmer. I'd survived the attack on Rienka, after all. But this—striking out into the gloom with no idea where I was going and no destination in sight—was a lot more daunting than dodging warships and drakkons. At least then, I had been able to see exactly where the danger was.

Right. Time for yet another leap of faith, then.

I started into the water, taking one step forward.

But my boot didn't sink.

The dark water crystalized under my foot suddenly, freezing completely, so I stepped onto the solid surface.

I stopped and stared down. What the—?

I slowly put my other foot into the water. It froze, too.

Whoaaa.

I took another step. Then another. And each time, the water froze under my feet, leaving a path of ice in my wake.

A grin stretched across my lips. Okay, fine. This was pretty outstanding. Nothing at all like before, when I was the harbinger, and I'd blundered through using every one of my powers only to have them nearly kill me.

Still, though, the feel of that tingling, frosty shiver on my skin made my adrenaline run hot through my blood. That contrast, like running training drills in the winter wind, sent wild, primal energy buzzing through my body.

It wouldn't be like last time. I would be no one's captive. I could control this power and bend it to my will. And I would use it to break Sadeera, body and soul, and set my nephew free.

Striding swiftly over the surface of the water, I stretched out my arms to the dark, pushing my will and focus there.

Light. I wanted light. Even with this new power, I still had very human eyes that couldn't see through this all-consuming darkness.

Almost instantly, a dozen or so small, floating orbs of pale white light drifted up from the depths of the water at my command. They hovered around me, shedding silvery light across the waves and my path ahead.

Another thrill of excitement shivered over my skin. Incredible.

I stood, the lengths of my new cloak billowing around me like tongues of shadow, as I watched the wisps dance at my command. This new power—I knew better than to think it would come without consequence or cost. But maybe it was the edge we desperately needed to see this mission done. That would make any pain or suffering worth it. I had to believe that.

And then ... a frantic woman's scream pierced through the darkness.

9

CHAPTER NINE

Violet.

I knew her voice right away. My pulse took off like a bucking mule in my chest, and I clenched my teeth against the sudden spike of panic and adrenaline that made my thoughts scramble in a haze of anger. She was in trouble. She needed me. Right now.

I hadn't used these powers in over a decade, but raw instinct moved my body before my mind could even catch up. My hands snapped forward; all my focus directed to a point between my outstretched fingers. Bitter cold rushed through the air, making my heartbeat skip and my arms shake as the pull of power drew every muscle tense at once.

Valestepping had been the most dangerous use of my power I could attempt back when I was the harbinger. Even now, it might be risky. But I wouldn't stop. Not until I got to her.

A small point of pure darkness opened up between my hands, rippling and growing as I slowly raked my hands outward like I was parting an invisible curtain. My bones creaked. My temples throbbed. My vision began to tunnel. But I didn't let up. The portal grew, like a hovering whirlpool of churning dark shadow, as I tore through the fabric of our reality and punched a hole straight through to another place.

Back to where I had left Violet and that priest standing on the shore.

I had to visualize it—holding that place in my mind—as I stepped into the swirling vortex of cold oblivion.

My stomach immediately dropped to the soles of my boots as the pull of the real world vanished, leaving me floating weightless in the void for a few seconds. In that place, the space between reality and the realm of the gods, there was nothing. No sound. No direction. No time. Fear crept in like frost climbing a windowpane. What if I couldn't get out? What if I got stuck here, where no one would ever be able to reach me? Would I drift on forever, lost in the in-between?

Then light bloomed before me like the first rays of dawn sunlight breaking the horizon.

It pulled me in like a fish on an angler's line, yanking me from the darkness and tossing me back out into the real world again. I staggered as my boots hit solid ground. My stomach rolled dangerously and I wheezed, trying not to throw up. My vision spotted and my ears rang as I looked up—straight into the steel of an incoming sword.

Curse it!

I kicked away and threw myself into a sideways roll just as the blade hummed past my head. Snapping up to my feet, I drew my kafki blades and stole a look around. The familiar chaos of battle raged everywhere I looked. Figures in dark armor and face scarves dashed from shadow to shadow, wielding swords, daggers, and crossbows. They all had the same symbol on their breastplates: a golden hand with an eye in the center. Hands of Fate? I wasn't sure. But most of them seemed preoccupied with the skittering horde of squatty, green-skinned creatures that converged from every side. With oversized heads, big fishlike eyes, scrawny bodies clad in patchwork furs and leathers, and wide mouths bristling with jagged yellow teeth, I had no idea what those things were. But they screeched like feral cats and swung bone clubs, spears, and rusted blades of their own.

What, by all the gods, had I stepped in now?

"VIOLET?" I shouted. I couldn't see her anywhere in the fray.

"Don't just stand there—*kill something!*" I heard her yell back at me.

I whirled around, finally spotting her at the far end of the shoal that led out into the water. With her daggers locked in a cross-block, she shoved her weight into the Hands of Fate agent that bore into her with a long, curved scimitar. She let out a growling scream of rage and planted a boot right in the center of his chest, kicking him backward. The agent only stumbled for an instant, but that was all it took.

Violet sprang at him with a primal scream, plunging both of her daggers into the base of his neck from either side and bearing him all the way to the ground. She bounded back, as fast and nimble as a tongue of flame. Spinning her daggers over her hands, she locked gazes with me from across the chamber. Her scarlet eyes practically crackled with desperate rage. With her face spattered in a spray of fresh blood, she spun to make another deflecting strike as one of those little green creatures lunged at her from behind.

Right. Sooo ... everything in here was bad. Got it.

"Would you like for me to take care of it, brother?" Noh's voice hissed in my brain, making my eardrums throb. Crap, I'd have to get used to that again.

"No. I could use a little practice anyway, eh?" I muttered as I swung my twin, sickle-shaped blades wide and prowled for the nearest group of agents.

He gave a deep chuckle of agreement.

Drawing on that new well of power deep in my soul, I immediately felt its surge hit my veins like a freezing tide. The muscles up and down my spine locked up, making my jaw clench and my toes curl up in my boots. The black marks on my hands thrummed, practically vibrating as I waded into the battle. My mind went silent as I surrendered all my senses to the ebb and flow of each swing of my blades. Every calculated duck, dodge, lunge, and strike moved with that deadly rhythm I had honed over the years, sparring against Jaevid, Murdoc, Thatcher, and Kiran.

And with Clysiros's power humming through my body, I could move faster. I could smell the fear on my enemies and peer over the horizon of their thoughts to anticipate what they would do next. Ribbons of dark power rippled off the ends of my curved kafki blades as I whipped and spun, cutting down Hands of Fate agents two and three at a time.

I felt ... untouchable.

Right up until one of those stumpy green creatures latched onto my leg and bit into my calf like a rabid raccoon. Thankfully, the thick leather of my boots kept it from doing any real damage. A small blessing.

I snarled a curse through my teeth and took a wild swing at it, sending the creature flying across the room, pitching and squealing like a piglet till it hit the ground with a crunch. It was satisfying for about two seconds—then five more of them rushed for me, swinging crude weapons and screeching angry gibberish.

Great. How many more were there?

Time to change tactics.

I slung my kafki blades back in their sheaths and widened my stance, sinking low and drawing on that dark well of power simmering in my soul. The temperature plummeted in less than a second, turning my breath to puffs of white fog, as I stretched my hands out toward the incoming horde. The swirling black sigils on my hand began to glow with an eerie purple light.

I bit back a yell of shock as an arcing bolt of crackling purple energy suddenly burst from my palm. It blew my hair back and sent me rocking onto my heels, hitting the rushing mob of little green monsters with a blinding flash and *CRAAACK* that left my ears ringing.

My fingertips were still smoking and my arm shook as I stared at the ash pile where the creatures had once been.

W ... Wow.

I locked gazes with another agent from the Hands of Fate who had been rushing for me right behind those stumpy monsters. He stood, red-hued eyes wide, and took a single calculated step backward.

A wicked grin curled over my lips as I curled my fingers in slowly, cracking my knuckles and tasting the sizzle of power on my tongue. Oh no, no, no—there would be no fleeing from this fight. I was just getting warmed up.

My back smacked up against Violet's as we fought, cutting down wave after wave of enemies that thronged around us like a swarm of angry hornets. It took every ounce of focus I had to keep up with them all, watching for the next wave of attackers, and plan ahead. Behind me, Violet spat curses in Sokraal, dipping and lunging with her daggers in perfect synchronization to my movements. We fought as one, our assaults a duo of flawless, albeit drastically different, techniques. She was the striking viper. I was the roaring lion. And together, we left a trail of gore that filled the air with the thick, heavy odor of blood.

"Where's the priest?" I shouted back at her, lunging forward to send another arcing beam of purple energy at another cluster of the green monsters.

"The goblins got to him before I could," Violet called back, reaching a hand back to grasp my thigh as leverage for a two-footed kick straight into the chest of a Hand of Fate fighter.

Wait—did she just say *goblins?* Gods and Fates, I'd only heard of them in children's fairy tales back home. We certainly didn't have creatures like this Maldobar.

"We can't keep this up forever!" I reminded her with a grunt, shoving forward to hold my focus on that beam of power, dragging it across the battlefield before me like a tornado of scorching energy.

"Then carve us a path, and we will make a run for it. I've got your back!" she snarled.

Fine. I didn't have a better idea.

Eyeing the stairs of the passage that led out of the chamber, I set my teeth against the rising tension in my chest. Like cold water rising around me, that aching pull made my pulse roar like thunder in my ears. I was pushing myself already. I knew that. It didn't matter how much power Clysiros gave me—my body was still mortal. It could only take so much.

Maybe I could pull off another valestep and take her with me without totally draining myself. Hey, I'd gotten lucky once, right? Might as well go for broke.

I thrust my hands forward, focusing every shred of my will to that space between them where the portal would form.

The whole chamber shook around us. The ground flinched, and I stumbled. Violet caught herself against me to keep from falling. At once, all the swarming goblins around us went silent. The only two Hands of Fate agents left standing stared around, too, as though mystified.

Was that an earthquake?

The temple chamber shook ahead, harder this time.

The huge mob of goblins all crowded around us started to shriek and make panicked, squeaking calls to one another. They bolted past us, climbing over one another and scaling the stairs, fleeing like cockroaches.

What the—?

Violet let out a frantic scream of horror as something massive shot out of the dark water and hit the Hands of Fate agent standing right before her. It must have been sticky, because it snatched him under the water in the blink of an eye. The guy didn't even have time to yell.

Not far offshore, the dark water rippled and sloshed. Something *huge* was moving around just beneath the surface.

Oh no.

"RUN!" Violet seized my hand and darted past me, dragging me along without any explanation.

Whatever that new monster was, I didn't see it. But, Gods and Fates, I heard it. A piercing cry like the squeal of metal on metal, so loud it rattled my bones and made my teeth ache. The ground flinched and shook, making the stone staircase split and start to crumble right at my heels.

Faster—must go faster! Sooo fast!

I pumped my legs harder, gripping Violet's hand tight and doing my best not to trip over goblins that still fled all around us. They scaled the wall and scrambled along the ground, apparently not caring if they trampled their comrades . No honor among goblins, I guess.

"Where do we go?!" I yelled when we reached the top of the stairs, more to myself than anyone else. I didn't expect Violet to have any better clue about how to get out of here than I did.

But she didn't even hesitate, and immediately yanked me down the left passageway toward another flight of stairs.

Okay, then.

Behind us, the rumbling grew louder. Hunks of stone broke away from the ceiling and smashed down around us, squishing clusters of goblins and sending the others squealing and scattering. My heart pumped wildly, throbbing in my throat as my feet flew over the ground. Whatever that huge monster was—it wasn't far behind. Definitely chasing us.

And getting closer by the second.

"Noh! You wanna buy us some time?!" I wheezed as we scrambled around another corner, taking a corridor through what looked almost like a vestibule.

"It is immune to magic," Violet warned as she kept her scarlet gaze focused straight ahead. "Your companion spirit will not be able to stop it!"

Well, crap. This place was just a treasure trove of good times.

"Then what will?" I growled back.

She flashed me a quick, wide-eyed glance.

Fear pierced my heart like a poison-tipped arrow, spreading chills all over my body. She didn't have to answer. I knew what that look meant.

We didn't have anything that might stop that monster.

Running was our only choice.

PART TWO

MURDOC

10

CHAPTER TEN

Reigh Farrow—third-born prince of Maldobar and accomplished dragonrider—was the most obnoxious, shortsighted, hotheaded idiot I had ever met. I had been forced into proximity—friendship—whatever you wanted to call it—with him for years now. We'd met shortly after I had gotten involved with Thatcher, and the three of us had spent years training and working together at the dragonrider academy. Reigh was a loudmouth. He had an astounding impulse control problem. Every one of his emotions simmered right under the paper-thin surface of his extremely fragile ego. But he was also the most talented healer I had ever known. And right then, at that very second, I would have given anything to see his stupid face rushing over to help.

This guy wasn't going to make it. I knew that the instant I saw the short, stoutly-framed man lying amidst the jungle undergrowth, the dust of battle still settling around us. I wasn't a healer, but I had stood over many fallen comrades and enemies when I walked with the Ulfrangar years ago. I had seen more than my share of battle injuries. I knew which of them were survivable.

His weren't.

Running through the low limbs and palm fronds, I stopped over him and hesitated. Was that ... a dwarf? No. It couldn't be. It wasn't possible.

I blinked hard and shook my head, wondering if the jungle heat was playing tricks with my head. I had never seen a dwarf other than Garnett. There weren't all that many left in the world, and yet, there he was. Even lying on his side, I could easily pick out his large, rounded ears, big hands and feet, and extremely stocky frame with wide shoulders. There was no mistaking it.

He really was a dwarf.

Blood spattered the ground all around him. Too much blood. His expression was fixed and distant. He was already gone.

I'd barely had time to process that before I heard the crunch of footsteps following me through the foliage. "Aye, where did you go, grumpy? You best not be back here having all the fun without me!" Garnett crowed cheerily. She loved a good brawl more than anyone. Blood and gore didn't bother her at all.

But, Gods and Fates, she did *not* need to see this.

Too late, I spun around and shouted, "Wait! Stop! There's—"

Staggering, I barely managed to catch myself before crashing right into her.

Garnett stood right behind me, her expression eerily blank, still gripping her double-headed axes in each hand. Her brawny shoulders went slack, lavender-colored eyes going wide as she stared down at the man on the ground. Both her weapons slipped from her grasp and landed with a soft *thud* on the ground beside her.

"I-Is ... is that?" she stammered brokenly.

I stepped closer, trying to eclipse her view of the body. "Garnett, please, go back to the others. You don't need to see this."

She blinked owlishly, then slowly turned her head up to look back at me with something strange and faraway settling over her soft features. "I do, Murdoc. I need to see."

What? Why? This would only cause her more pain, wouldn't it? Why would she possibly want to do this to herself—to implant this memory in her mind forever?

Garnett had spoken before about witnessing the slaughter of her people by the Tibran Empire when she was just a child. She'd told us herself that she didn't think there were any others of her people left now. Wouldn't this reopen those old wounds?

"We're so far from there. I-I never thought I would see another," she murmured, every word falling like bitter cold rain from her trembling lips. "All this time ... I thought I was alone."

It hit me like the final tile clicking into place in a grand mosaic. Suddenly, I understood why she needed to see him—what it really meant to her.

I stepped aside and bowed my head.

This wasn't about opening old wounds. It was about finally closing them.

I shadowed her steps, keeping watch on the jungle around us as she went to the fallen dwarf's side. Kneeling down, she rolled him carefully onto his back with a little gasp of surprise.

"He's so young," she whispered, almost like she was afraid of somehow waking him. "A lot younger than me. He doesn't even have much of a beard yet. Stones, he must've been only an infant when the Shale Halls fell. That's probably why he has no clan marks—he was too young to receive them." Her hand drifted up, brushing at the blue runes tattooed under her left eye.

My mind boggled at that revelation, wondering silently how an infant had managed to survive the scourge of the Tibran Empire's brutal armies. How had he gotten all the way here to Nar'Haleen? And what was he doing getting caught up in the fray of a fight with Sadeera?

Whatever this fellow's story was, we would never know. It had ended here amidst the silent, waving jungle palms.

"Zenith's Call," Garnett gasped again. She had taken off one of the bracers on his forearms and held up his bare arm, revealing a tattooed symbol on the inside of his wrist in black ink. I recognized the crescent moon with a sword through it, too.

So, then, he had been a member of the mercenary guild? Maybe that explained how he had survived. I had only learned a little about the Zenith's Call from the Ulfrangar—which basically amounted to them not being much of a credible threat when it came to our missions. They were skilled in gathering information, yes. They even made decent smugglers. But like

Arlan's organization, they didn't dance much in the circles of assassination, although they seemed to enjoy being confused for that type of agency. Most common folk assumed they really were assassins in disguise. We hadn't considered them an obstacle worth noting, though.

They did, however, have a habit of recruiting the young and vulnerable. They liked scraping orphans and urchins out of the gutter, luring them in with the promise of food and safety, and training them in the fine arts of stealth and deception. It worked wonderfully for them, and they were far kinder than the Ulfrangar. It made for fiercely loyal members, who viewed their comrades more as a family than fellow employees.

But what was this one doing here all by himself? They didn't usually travel alone, as a rule. And for him to be so young—he should have been in the company of an elder mentor.

Hmm. We'd have to check the other three and see if any of them also bore the Zenith's mark.

"We need to go back," I urged, trying to keep my tone as gentle as possible. "The others are going to need our help."

"I know," she said quietly, her tone still halting and thick with despair. "But we can't just leave him here."

"We'll get him cleaned up and give him a proper burial," I assured her. "First, though, we attend to the living. The dead will wait. One of the others might even know more about him."

"All right," she agreed at last and stood, keeping her head down so that I couldn't see her face as she went to pick up her axes again. "I'm sorry, Murdoc. I didn't mean for this to get in the way. It's silly, I know. I didn't know him. I shouldn't feel ... anything."

My heart gave an uncomfortable, twisting thump—like someone trying to wrench their foot into a shoe that was too small. I knew that feeling, that emptiness in her eyes as she gazed ahead. Grief was a strange and ever-changing monster. It looked different depending on who glimpsed it, like reflections in a broken mirror, always changing and never quite making sense. Its wounds cut deep, and they healed slowly.

Or, sometimes, not at all.

I knew that better than most.

"It isn't silly," I replied, walking beside her back through the undergrowth. "And don't apologize. Not to me."

"I miss him," she whimpered, sniffling some and wiping her eyes on her forearm.

She didn't have to explain who. I felt his absence far more sharply in moments like this. Thatcher was better at being soft, at saying the right things at the right time. Whether that was because he was a godling of mercy, or because he just had a natural knack for comforting people, I didn't know. But he always seemed to know what to say and do when it came to the brokenhearted.

And I knew he would have been able to tell her exactly what she needed to hear right then.

"I do, too," I admitted. "But we're going to find them. Soon."

"I hope you're right," she murmured. "But I'm worried, Murdoc. I'm *so* worried we might be too late to help them."

My head bowed lower as I stole one more look down at the dead young dwarf lying still amidst the jungle ferns. "I know, Garnett," I replied quietly. "So am I."

"We found three alive. Could be more. They're still checking the area," Roxus announced as we emerged from the foliage. He stood off to the side, observing as the rest of our comrades dragged corpses from the ruins and lined them up for inspection. We didn't know who or what we were up against, exactly, so now was not the time for half-measures.

Jaevid, Isandri, Garnett, Roxus, and I had all come here with a mission, pulling no punches and calling on everyone we knew who might be able to aid us in stopping Sadeera. But I don't think any of us expected Arlan himself to come along. The prospect hadn't sat well with me. It still didn't. His emotional proximity to the problem—his relentless grudge against his sister—was bound to make him unpredictable should we find ourselves battling another one of her aspects. He would get reckless. He'd take risks that might put us all in danger.

But that wasn't what worried me the most.

Arlan's physical condition seemed to deteriorate rapidly the more magic he used. That would certainly pose a problem if we found ourselves backed into a corner. If he fought, he risked death. And if he died, we would be without his knowledge and expertise moving forward.

I couldn't do anything to stop him from coming along with us, though. He was the mastermind of all our plans. Leaving him out or objecting to the choices he made went against all the training I'd ever had in my life—both Ulfrangar and dragonrider. You didn't buck or question your superiors. You followed orders.

Even reckless, stupid, dangerous ones.

"There's another one back that way. A young dwarven boy. I think he might be Zenith's Call," I informed Roxus, sighing as I shook some of my sweaty hair from my eyes.

The corners of Roxus's eyes pinched up a little, and his mouth pressed into a tight line, almost as though he were holding something back. An emotional response, maybe? He was good at that—guarding his reactions and expressions well—and after several days of traveling with him, I had my suspicions as to why.

"What about the others?" I pressed, gazing past him to where Arlan was slowly walking the line of dead, examining each body one at a time. "Any sign of the sorceress?"

Roxus slowly shook his head. "She fled when the tide turned. No surprise. She's a slippery one."

"Then what is Arlan hoping to find?" I crossed my arms.

"I think it's more about what he hopes he doesn't find," Roxus grunted and rubbed at the lengthy stubble coming in on his pointed chin.

"The codex?" I guessed.

He nodded once.

I frowned. "What about the three live ones?"

"Now, that is a puzzle," Roxus chuckled under his breath. "Come, we should go lend a hand. Otherwise, that Shalnii priestess may see fit to bring that count down to two."

Oh? Hmm. Garnett and I exchanged a sideways look and stepped lightly to follow him through the overgrown temple ruins. It wasn't all that hard to find Isandri, though, even through all the dense greenery. All you had to do was listen for the sounds of angry yelling in Sokraal.

Lined up on the ground in the shade of a half-crumbled ancient pillar, our three living detainees sat side-by-side. I noticed straight away that the first two were injured. Probably the victims of the attack from the Hands of Fate. One, a teenage, human-looking boy with a mop of white hair and big spectacles, stared dejectedly down at the toes of his shoes. He had blood smeared all over his face, mostly coming from his nose and a gash across his forehead. The second one, a young man with an injured leg, was clearly a Rienkan elf. He stared straight ahead, his eyes wide and mystified at the sight of Isandri.

No doubt, she was quite the spectacle to behold, even in her own homeland.

Looming over the third figure, she spun her staff over her hand and leveled the dagger-pointed end at his throat. Her lips curled back in a snarl, and she hissed a curse through her teeth and spat on the ground before him. "You shame yourself and our people to serve such evil," she seethed bitterly.

The man sat, head bowed and expression utterly fractured, with his hands tied behind his back and his ankles bound so he couldn't even stand. I had never seen another Lunostri elf besides Isandri, but he certainly fit the bill. His ebony skin bore the runic marks of a priest, and his fine golden collar and billowing robes of deep purple marked him as someone of status. A court priest, perhaps? What was he doing out here with the Hands of Fate?

"Miwos dahn lei," the man begged, groaning through his teeth as though he were in pain. "Forgive me. Please, holy one, I beg of you—I want only to help. I have no love or loyalty for the one who has wronged you."

Isandri leaned into her staff some, letting that lethal point press against the hollow of his throat as she snapped bitterly, "We shall soon see. You best watch that forked tongue, shalnii, or I will rip it from your mouth."

The priest paled but didn't move an inch as he stared up at her, trembling in horror.

"Isandri? Care for a word?" I sighed and curled a finger to call her over. Better to get out in front of this before it devolved into torture or a death sentence.

She hissed another furious curse at the man before whirling on a heel and stomping over to stand before us. Isandri stood, still working her jaw angrily from one side to the other, as she glared off into the distance as though she were trying to find her inner peace again.

"Friend of yours, I take it?" Roxus wore that roguish, lazy half-smirk as he watched her.

"NO!" Isa snapped, her eyes flickering with wrath as she glared at him. "He is Lunostri, yes, and he is a shalnii—a high priest. But he claims to follow Clysiros. By his attire, I believe he must serve in the emperor's own temple."

Ahh. So, I was right, after all. This wasn't your average temple priest blundering around in the jungle. Interesting.

"What's he doing out here fighting with the Hands of Fate?" Garnett asked. "We're quite a long way from the palace."

"He claims he has been forced into servitude to the chief advisor to the emperor," Isa grumbled, her tone thick with sarcasm. "He said *she* is the one who ordered this attack—the one searching for the codex."

"Sounds promising," Roxus mused.

I had to agree. "Let's get the others and question him further," I suggested. "But, perhaps we should let Arlan do the talking, eh? You seem a bit ... close to the issue."

She flashed me a scorching glare and pursed her lips like she'd bitten into something sour. "Close," she scoffed at the word, jabbing an accusing finger back toward the priest. "If he is indeed serving Sadeera or the Hands of Fate, then he is a blasphemer and a traitor to his holy oaths. He deserves a shameful death for such treachery! And he would dare beg me for a favor? BAH!!" Isa threw her hands up and turned away, her chest heaving with angry, panting breaths.

"If that turns out to be the case, I'm happy to let you deliver it," I said and put a hand on her shoulder briefly as I walked past on my way to inspect our captives more closely. "But until then, let's try to keep a cool head."

Isandri's leanly muscled shoulder tensed under my hand, but she didn't jerk away. Her head dipped some, mouth still screwed up and brows knitted deeply with a look of intense frustration. Her throat jumped some, and her grip on her staff tightened until her knuckles blanched.

I couldn't blame her for losing her temper—not when these were the people who were undoubtedly also hunting Reigh and Thatcher. Not knowing where our friends were, and whether or not we were already too late, was enough to have everyone at their breaking point, not just Isa. Her frustration was likely compounded by the return here to a place she apparently despised.

I just hoped, for all our sakes, that Arlan knew how to twist the right information out of this priest before she finally snapped.

11

CHAPTER ELEVEN

In the interest of keeping the priest alive long enough to question him, Arlan insisted that Isandri take Roxus and Garnett and see to the injuries of the other two survivors.

A good decision, but not one she accepted easily. Fates, she was as stubborn as Reigh sometimes.

Eventually, Jaevid managed to persuade her that her energy was better spent helping the other two since Reigh had trained her in some medical treatments over the years. That aside, she was also the best suited for figuring out who these people really were, especially since it didn't seem like the young elven man spoke anything other than Sokraal and Rienkan.

I could speak Sokraal reasonably well, thanks to my Ulfrangar upbringing. But the Rienkan language was far more difficult. I wasn't sure I could keep up in that tongue, especially since the locals here tended to blend several languages if they'd spent any length of time living throughout the different Southern Kingdoms. This part of the world was considered the cradle of civilization, so there was a wide variety of cultures, peoples, and traditions fused into every city and village.

Fortunately, when it came to the Lunostri priest, he spoke only in Sokraal. His careful phrasing suggested he was highly educated—not unlike Isandri. Not surprising, given their similar occupations. No doubt, they'd had a lot of the same training.

Since Arlan was going to lead the interrogation, I decided to put my focus into watching his expressions for any traces of deception or reluctance.

That, and exacting any amount of pain necessary to ... encourage his full cooperation.

I hoisted him off his feet and lugged him over my shoulder, marching off a distance from the other two before I flung him back down to the ground and shoved him back against another slab of cracked, moss-covered stone that had once been a part of the temple grounds. Clamping a hand around his neck, I pinned him back against the stone and forced him to look me in the eye.

Then I gave him the full force of what Reigh had lovingly dubbed to be my "murder stare."

His pupils narrowed to pinpoints. Beads of sweat rolled down the sides of his face. His pulse hammered like mad under the grip of my palm. There was no faking that response. He was terrified.

Good. He better be.

"Now then, I suggest you sit very still and choose your next words wisely, priest," I warned in Sokraal. "Whether intentionally or not, you have meddled in the wrong affairs and found yourself in dangerous company."

He stared up at me, choking on his words as his sharp, angular features drew into a frantic look of horror. He squirmed against my grasp, gasping like he couldn't breathe, his gaze darting between the rest of us as Jae and Arlan stepped into view. Like a pack of wolves surrounding a snared hare, we stood before him and waited, considering his every move.

"I-I speak the truth. I swear it. P-Please," he gasped, curling back against the stone and cringing as though he expected one or all of us to start beating him.

I did like that idea. Nothing wrong with softening him up a little. But I knew better than to try. Jaevid would never allow it.

Not yet.

"Let us begin with your name," Arlan said, standing right in front of the bound-up priest with his hands clasped calmly at his back. "And what brought you and the Hands of Fate to this place."

"I-I ... I am Edarix. I am a priest of Clysiros. I serve in the emperor's temple in Lahn'Siir," he stammered, stopping to swallow hard. "Please, I ... I don't know the details. She did not divulge such things to me. But I know she has been searching for the Codex of Avgior. First at the Compendium Library, and now here."

"She?" Jaevid stepped forward. "Who are you referring to?"

"Auguress Riva," he answered quickly. "She is the chief holy advisor to the emperor himself and claims to serve Milontos."

"What does she want with the codex?" Arlan pressed, his eyes narrowing ominously.

"She ... she has promised many things to the emperor," he said, his voice halting as he breathed fast and hard, likely struggling to keep his composure. "That she could give him a holy weapon that would ensure his success in reunifying the Southern Kingdoms under his ruling hand again. B-But ... I ..."

"You what?" Arlan took a step closer and bent down, his glowing golden eyes boring into the priest's with cold, relentless fury.

For a few seconds, all Edarix could do was choke and sputter. His chin trembled and he bowed his head, as though some internal fortification had finally broken. "I believe she means to destroy us all! Fates strike me down, but that woman is evil in ways you cannot fathom! If you only knew the things she's done, the people who have been slaughtered at her command—m-my friends. My brothers and sisters of the Hall of Holies. I have watched her dismantle and destroy the place that I loved, that I was trained and charged to care for until I draw my final breath in this realm." His shoulders shook as he began to sob, tears rolling down his face as he looked between us pleadingly. "If you must kill me, so be it. But I beg of you—you must stop her. She must not find the codex! She must not open the gate!"

His words hung in the air like a poisonous vapor as we all stood around, staring down at him, in complete silence.

Gods and Fates, it really was true. Whatever lingering doubts I'd held about Arlan's stories of world-ending disaster all dissolved at once, and I felt the weight of the world shift under my feet. This was it—the fight Proleus had chosen me for.

All of our fates, our destinies, converged here.

"If all this is true, then why serve her?" Jaevid questioned. "Why go along with her campaign?"

"At first, it was survival. Defying her was the same as asking for death, as she holds powerful sway over the emperor's mind. But then, after the library, there was ... the boy." He sniffled, trying unsuccessfully to wipe his nose on his shoulder. "I-I could not just leave him. He was another innocent ensnared in her scheme. I could not bear the thought of abandoning him to a fate at her hands."

I saw Jaevid's hands curl into fists. "What boy?"

"H-He came from the library. We found him there," he explained, his voice still shaking some. "He was young and ... Goddess, I have never seen such destructive force like the power that boy holds. I'm not sure how, but Riva gained control of his mind. She commands him like a sentinel, and he does her bidding without question or hesitation."

"What does he look like?" Jaevid demanded. "How old is he?"

"I-I'm not sure how old," Edarix panicked. "Fourteen or fifteen at the most? His hair is black and—"

"Does he have a mark on his hand?" Arlan asked, still somehow able to sound as calm and composed as ever.

"Yes! The seal of Enais." Edarix's eyes widened with recognition. "Do you know him?"

"Fates, it's him," Jae gasped. "It's Ronan. He's still alive."

"Ronan Derrick!" Edarix blurted, suddenly sitting up straighter. "He told me that is his name!"

Oh. Oh gods. She did have Ronan. And she was using him as her personal executioner because of his curse.

I swallowed against the burning of bile rising in my throat. He was an innocent child. Reigh's nephew. Our queen's only child.

Gods and Fates, we had to get him away from her as soon as physically possible. The more that boy used his power, the stronger it became, and the less able he was to control it. As Arlan had explained to us at great length, the curse was slowly consuming his mind already. Having an evil sorceress impairing his thoughts and forcing his hand would absolutely make it worse.

Ronan was running out of time. The longer he stayed that way, under her control, the less likely it would be that we could actually help him at all. Even if we did manage to rescue him and take him back to Maldobar, his mind might be broken beyond all repair.

But I wasn't ready to accept that just yet. And I guess Arlan wasn't, either.

"I want you to listen to me very carefully." He leaned down farther, his tone becoming eerily quiet and soft as he stared unblinkingly into the priest's eyes. "You are either very lucky or very unlucky. Time will tell which. The woman you have served, the one you call Auguress Riva, is far more dangerous than you can appreciate now. You must tell me everything you know about her, her plans, and where she might be right this second. Lives far more important than our own now depend on it."

"Do you think he's telling the truth?" Jaevid whispered as he and I went to begin searching the bodies of the dead for more evidence.

I stole one last look at Edarix over my shoulder as we left him to continue filling Arlan in on every single detail he could about this so-called Auguress Riva and what she might be planning next. "It doesn't matter what I think," I muttered. "Arlan believes him, and we are at his disposal. The real question is do we trust Arlan?"

Jaevid didn't reply aloud, but his expression darkened as he stopped over the line of bodies spread out before us on the mossy earth. Twelve in all. Most of them were men, but there were three women. Four looked like regular human soldiers with Nar'Haleenan armor and weaponry. But the other eight were far stranger. They all had the same pasty, pale complexions and vibrant red eyes.

Viperi.

I bent down to check each of them, searching for any more marks or tattoos like I'd found on the dwarf. But there was nothing. Hired muscle, then? Or more victims of Auguress Riva's brainwashing? The former seemed more likely. If legend proved true, then it wouldn't take much in the way of convincing to get the Viperi to do something violent in exchange for coin or power. Their subterranean society was built upon a constant, bloodthirsty struggle for dominance, and they had absolutely no love for those who lived on the surface. They also happened to be highly efficient warriors, with reflexes that were unrivaled even by the finest Ulfrangar.

They didn't often associate with people of the surface world, however. Violet was an enigma in that way. I had never questioned her about leaving her people behind, but as I understood it, the Viperi held similar sentiments as the Ulfrangar for those who dared to abandon their society.

To defect was to become a target. A fate I understood all too well, and one that very well might have driven her from the Southern Kingdoms and into Maldobar.

All of the now-dead members of the scouting party, as Edarix had explained, were dressed in similar ensembles of dark silks and well-oiled leather armor. They carried light weapons befitting of scouts and spies. Hands of Fate, no doubt. Apart from the dwarf, of course.

He wore no fine armor and had many old injuries—bruises, cuts, and gashes that had already begun healing. The deep purple bruises around his wrists suggested that his hands had been bound at some point. That, paired with his marking that identified him as a bladesworn of the Zenith's Call, made me scratch at the back of my neck. Had he been their prisoner, then?

"TRAEGAN!" a voice cried out behind me suddenly.

Jaevid and I whirled around to find the white-haired boy standing right behind us, his face still smeared with blood and his eyes welling with tears. His expression collapsed into a look of anguish as he shoved past us and fell to his knees beside the fallen dwarf.

What the—he wasn't a member of Auguress Riva's forces?

For a moment, Jaevid and I stood in silent shock, watching as the boy buried his face in his hands and sobbed. Doubled over, with his blood-spattered robes hanging off his bony frame, it was difficult to imagine this boy was any sort of warrior. He couldn't have been more than sixteen, and there was nothing about him that even hinted at combat proficiency.

Then I heard Jaevid mutter quietly, "The boy mentioned he was traveling with two friends when I first found him. He called them Traegan and Noa."

"If this is one of them, then where is—?" I didn't get a chance to finish that thought.

"I'm here," another, deeper voice spoke up in the common tongue. This time, it was the older Rienkan elf who came hobbling over, still favoring his freshly bandaged leg. Apparently, he did speak something other than Sokraal and Rienkan. Curious.

Isandri and Roxus followed only a few paces behind him, their expressions a similar mixture of somber concern. Isa walked quietly over to crouch down next to the white-haired boy, speaking to him in a hushed whisper I couldn't discern.

"You're Noa?" Jaevid asked, giving him a quick glance over.

"I am," he answered. "And that is Clarke."

"They were ambushed by the Hands of Fate when they came out of the old temple," Roxus announced as he wandered over to stand with us, still watching Clarke and Isa with a hint of unease putting a deep crease in his brow. "It seems the mad sorceress was set upon capturing or killing the boy, they aren't sure which."

"What were you doing down in the temple in the first place?" Jaevid asked.

Noa's chest puffed some as he took in a deep, steadying breath. There was weary resignation in his features as he kept his gaze trained on Clarke, almost like he was afraid to let the kid out of his sight. "It was an accident. We were kidnapped by goblins and taken underground. The rest is ... sort of a long story."

"It's a good thing we love long stories," Roxus mumbled. "Especially ones that explain why you caught Sadeera's special attention."

Noa's broad shoulders sagged some, and his expression seized with pain as he tried to rebalance himself on his one good leg. "I'll be happy to tell you anything you like so long as we can find a place to rest and get something to eat. We've been down there several days without any food. He won't complain or ask for it, but I know Clarke must be starving, too."

"We can manage that," Jaevid assured him. "And we'll take time to bury your dead. The Hands of Fate, however, we'll have to burn."

"Not before we take whatever good weapons'n armor they're carrying. Waste not," Roxus huffed, and ambled off to start outfitting himself.

"We should make camp, but not here," Jaevid said as he glanced at the ruins all around us. "Not where Sadeera knows exactly where we are."

"Hard to be discreet when we've got dragons with us," I pointed out. "And with so many in our company, most of us will be moving on foot."

He sighed heavily. "True. We'll have to be careful. Perhaps the dragons can transport the injured if they're not able to go on foot."

"I'll get him up." Noa hobbled forward, making his way one wobbly step at a time until he stood at Clarke's side. He bent over and put a hand on the boy's back, speaking to him quietly.

"NO!" Clarke shouted suddenly, throwing off Noa's hand and shambling up to his feet. He staggered back, nearly tripping over himself in the process. "Stay away from me! D-Don't you get it? Don't you understand? All of this is *my* fault! It happened again! *AGAIN*—because of me!" he yelled, his voice breaking and halting as he fought back sobs. "First, the library. Then the village. A-And now this! Anyone who gets close to me is going to *DIE!*"

"That's not true, Clarke," Noa protested.

"*YES!* Yes, it is!" he cried, his expression wild and desperate as he stared around at all of us. "A-All this time, it's been me. I'm the one she wants—what's inside *my* head. The codex. I-I read it. A-And now ... now she knows who I ..."

Isandri rushed him, throwing her arms around the boy and hugging him tightly. With a hand on the back of his head, she cooed gently as she held him tightly against her. "I know it hurts. I know you feel like this was your fault. But please, believe me, this was not your doing."

"I-I couldn't stop them. I couldn't save a-any of them," Clarke whimpered against her, gripping her back just as tightly. "Even though I'm supposed t-to be … Avgior."

I froze. My pulse skipped a beat and seemed to halt completely. Did he just say he *was* Avgior? This mysterious, draconic God of Fate was a scrawny, white-haired boy with spectacles? No, that couldn't be.

Could it?

Taking his face in her hands, Isandri gave him an earnest smile and wiped at his tears with her thumbs. "Then you are my brother. Your soul knows mine. Do you not see me?"

He blinked owlishly, still sucking in shallow, fast breaths as he stared back at her. A slow blink and his eyes flashed with a flicker of silvery light. Then, a twitchy, broken smile brushed his lips. His eyes closed and he leaned down to press his forehead to hers, and the voice that left his lips was different. Deeper. Smoother. But no less tearful and desperate.

"There are no words in the mortal tongue … for how I have missed you, Adiana."

❧ 12 ❧

CHAPTER TWELVE

We couldn't afford to linger in one place for long, not when Sadeera knew exactly where we were and that we now possessed something she wanted: Clarke.

Or Avgior, rather. Ugh. Whatever name he was going by—it didn't matter. I wasn't sure what the actual dynamic between that boy and the deity was, and frankly, there wasn't time to sort it out right then. We had to get moving.

There was just one loose end to tie up, first.

No one felt good about leaving Clarke and Noa's fallen comrade, Traegan, unburied or burning him with the rest of the dead Hands of Fate agents. Unfortunately, we could only spare a few minutes to lay him to rest. We found a decent place at the feet of one of the mostly intact statues within the temple grounds and dug a grave. Then we all gathered around in solemn silence while Edarix performed a brief ritual and prayer over the gravesite. I suppose that was his area of specialty, being a priest of Clysiros. And while it was a nice gesture, it wasn't sufficient to win him enough of our trust to let him roam freely.

Jaevid still insisted on keeping Edarix's hands bound and forcing him to walk between Garnett, Roxus, and me—just in case he decided to try anything especially stupid. So far, the priest had kept his mouth shut and his head down, looking appropriately downtrodden and worried. He probably assumed we would kill him eventually.

Depending on how truthful and cooperative he was, he might not be wrong about that. Especially now that we knew Ronan's life was hanging by a thread.

It took time to move everyone through the jungle on foot, and every minute made my nerves draw tense. But with a group as large as ours, and the knowledge that our enemy was likely still somewhere in the vicinity, using the dragons to speed things along would certainly give away our position. We had to be careful, quiet, and cover our tracks well. Even having the dragons circle too closely was a risk, so we sent them off to hold in patterns in the area.

I didn't like that one bit. Judging by his deeply set frown, Jaevid didn't care for it, either. The dragons were usually our primary defense, and if the Hands of Fate did attack us, we would certainly need their help. But the risk that our scaly comrades might give away our position was too great.

We had no choice but to manage on foot.

Therein lay the challenge ... at least for *some* of us.

Clarke's injuries were minor, and yet he moved about as gracefully as a three-legged goat through the jungle undergrowth. Something about him reminded me a lot of Thatcher when we'd first met all those years ago. I could have sworn I caught him talking to himself as he trundled along, tripping over roots and wheezing for breath like he might faint at any moment. Then I spotted a little ball of fur perched on one of his shoulders.

Was that a *rat?*

Just when I thought that boy couldn't get any more bizarre ...

Noa, on the other hand, seemed far more capable when it came to stepping carefully through the jungle, although his injured leg seemed to make it far more difficult for him. He limped and faltered, catching himself against trees and muttering pained Rienkan curses under his breath until Jaevid insisted on helping him.

At first, Noa didn't seem to like that idea one bit. Maybe it was a blow to his pride. Or maybe he just didn't trust us, yet. But after nearly falling face-first into the damp, jungle dirt a few times, he didn't have much of a choice. Noa muttered a stiff, reluctant word of thanks as he looped an arm over Jaevid's shoulders so he could hobble along more easily.

We pressed on for miles, keeping as stiff a pace as we could, and tracking a path southward, down through the steep hillsides. The terrain was rugged, and the air hung thick with moisture from the low-banking clouds. It made every breath a fight, and sweat rolled down the sides of my face and into my eyes.

But as we crested an open, rocky cliff that overlooked the valley below, a gust of cool sea air hit my face with surprising force. It filled my lungs and blew back my hair, making every muscle in my body relax at once. Thank the gods for that.

Standing atop the steep cliff, we could finally see it far below—a large city tucked into a wide, crescent-shaped bay. Before us, the steep, green jungle hills gave way abruptly to a tightly packed network of streets and buildings that spanned for at least thirty miles. Hundreds of ships were docked along the shoreline, bobbing gently in the glittering turquoise water.

I stared in awe at the staggering number of huge ruins that jutted up from within the city, towering over everything else like sea stacks. Dozens of ancient pillars and crumbling archways loomed over the patchwork of red, clay-tile rooftops. It was strange, but intensely beautiful.

It was Uru'Nai, the jewel of the Elondran Ocean.

"We should camp here," Jaevid suggested as he helped Noa sit down on a large rock nearby. "We have a good vantage point in all directions, and it looks like we're less than five miles from the city itself. A safe enough distance."

"I agree." Arlan stepped forward, scrutinizing our view with his eerie glowing, golden eyes. "But we should still be cautious. No campfires. And we must be diligent at keeping watch."

Riiight. *We.* What he really meant was "you."

"You're certain this is where Auguress Riva's forces would retreat to?" Isandri questioned sharply, her gaze cutting distrustfully to where Edarix sat, looking as sweaty and miserable as the rest of us in his heavy, priestly robes.

He bobbed his head in confirmation, but couldn't seem to catch his breath long enough to actually say anything.

"Here," I muttered in Sokraal, unfastening my waterskin from my belt and putting it in front of his face. "Drink. You're no good to us dead."

He blinked up at me, hesitating as though wondering whether or not I was offering him something poisoned. Then he leaned in, drinking several long gulps before he sat back, eyes closed and expression slack in relief. "Thank you," he murmured.

"Don't thank me yet," I growled as I put my waterskin away. "Should we encounter your friends tonight, I fully intend on using you as a living shield."

"I would expect nothing less." He bowed his head again, but I watched his gaze track curiously across the rest of our group. "You are all from Maldobar, yes? Your accents are strange. Apart from the esteemed Miwos, of course."

I couldn't resist a smirk. "You really have no idea how big of a mess you've stepped in, do you?"

He just stared at me blankly. Fates, he was either an excellent actor or the most ignorant person in the world.

Leaning down, I rested an elbow on a knee and motioned toward Jaevid. "You see that guy? The one who doesn't trust you to even walk on your own without three guards watching your every move? His name is Jaevid Broadfeather. As someone versed in the divine, I expect that's a name you'll recognize."

Edarix's eyes went wide and his mouth fell open. He sat up straighter, staring across the clearing at Jae with a newfound horror. "Lapiloque," he gasped faintly.

Jaevid stopped, glaring down at him with his pale blue eyes as frosty as ever. "Not anymore. I surrendered that title years ago. Murdoc, don't encourage him. I need you to—"

"*YOU!*" A cry broke through the air.

Everyone stopped and stared at Noa.

His whole face twitched with fury as he limped toward Jaevid, hands balled into shaking fists at his sides. "It was you—*you* are the one who ended the Law of the Stones?!" he demanded, his voice trembling and halting with blind rage.

Jaevid gaped back at him, brow furrowed in bewilderment. "Yes, I did."

"You had no right!" Noa roared, thrusting an accusing finger at him as he continued to stagger forward. "You took everything from me—my power, my dignity, my livelihood, my family! All of it without a thought! And now you have the audacity to come here painted like some sort of hero! HOW DARE YOU?!"

He let out an agonized groan of pain as he took a wild swing, trying to punch Jaevid across the face.

"What are you talking about?" Jaevid demanded, easily dodging the blow and sidestepping. "I don't even know you!"

"EXACTLY!" Noa snarled, barely managing to catch himself when his blow sailed wide. "You took my choice and you did not even know me! What did you imagine would happen to the others, all around the world, who also carried the power of the stones? What would happen to our lives? Our people? Our kingdoms? You stripped away my only hope of saving them, and now ... now they are all DEAD!"

"Noa! Stop! Please," Clarke begged as he tried to get between them.

But his friend seemed to be in no mood to negotiate. He shoved Clarke aside and started for Jaevid again, a fist already cocked to take another swing.

"Hold your temper and speak sense. Who are you? What connection did you have to the god stones?" Isandri hissed suddenly, seizing him by the back of the neck. She must have sent a small bolt of her power through him, because Noa let out a sharp scream of pain and went up on his toes, back curling and arms flailing wide. He dropped to his knees as soon as she let him go.

Noa's chest heaved with deep, furious breaths as he sat there, head bowed and shoulders hunched forward. Then, slowly, he raised a shaking hand to show all of us the ring he wore. A simple, bone-carved band.

"I was the chosen of Undae, goddess of the sea," he said, his tone low and utterly broken. "And because of you, I was forced to flee and watch my home and people burn under the fists of the Tibran Empire ... and Nar'Haleen. You robbed me of my power, and I ... I could not protect them. My home. My parents. My sister. I lost it all."

"Who are you," Jaevid repeated the question, daring to take a step closer to Noa with his expression drawn into a look of deep concern.

"My name is Noa Skyhart," he murmured brokenly. "The one they once called Wavewalker."

"Do not be so quick to dismiss the strength of your family line," Arlan spoke suddenly, striding forward to stand before Noa. He leveled a no-nonsense stare upon the man, his tone sharp and direct. "Your beloved sister yet lives."

Noa's expression went eerily blank. He gaped up at Arlan and didn't even seem to be breathing. At last, he managed to rasp out two frantic words. "Sh-She's ... alive?"

"Malina Skyhart still sails the ocean, now at the command of one of your family's flagships," Arlan confirmed. "The *Squall Queen*."

"That's ... That's not possible. I-I searched everywhere. I couldn't find any of them!" Noa protested. "Nar'Haleen took our ships. I haven't seen—"

"Nar'Haleen took *a* ship," Arlan corrected. "But the Skyhart family line still endures, as do you. So, I suggest you get to your feet and regain your composure. Now is not the time to bicker over the past. You may yet find yourself in the graces of your goddess again, as have many among you. We have come here with a great purpose, and you now have the chance to regain your family's honor, if you can find the strength."

AWKWARD TENSION HUNG THICK IN THE AIR AS WE ALL SETTLED IN FOR THE NIGHT. Noa and Clarke sat off by themselves, and from what I could tell, neither one of them seemed particularly chatty. If our intent was to recruit them into our band as reliable allies, we weren't off to a great start. Arlan's little speech might help, but there was still bitter resentment in Noa's expression as he let Isandri play doctor on his injured leg again.

The only person who might have been more upset was also sitting off on his own, perched on top of a large boulder that overlooked the view of the glittering city lights far below. Jaevid hadn't said much for the rest of the evening as we took inventory of our weaponry, medical needs, and distributed the food rations to everyone. I could tell, even from a distance, that he wore the same intense, inwardly focused scowl of deep thought he always did whenever issues with the gods arose.

Hmm. We couldn't have him lose his focus now. Whatever issues he and Noa had, we were all fighting for the same cause now. They just needed to swallow their pride long enough to remember that.

"Here," I said as I wandered over to stand beside his pouting rock and handed him a piece of the hard, flat bread we'd packed for the journey. "You need to eat something."

"Thank you," he mumbled as he took it.

"We need to start thinking about our next steps," I reminded him. "By dawn, we need a plan of action. We can't stay here on this hilltop and wait for the world to end. Reigh and the others are still out there, likely headed straight for us. According to our priest, Auguress Riva is likely somewhere in the city. A decent tactic, since she probably also knows we don't want open battle in the streets of Nar'Haleen. There would be civilian casualties. Extensive damage. It would be an act of war, and that is not why we came. Riva—Sadeera—or whatever she's calling herself, is not a fool. She knows what's at stake for us. I believe this is a ploy to keep us at a distance while she moves on to the next phase of her plan."

"You have a suggestion?" Jaevid asked, his head bowing some as he stared at the bread in his hands.

"Arlan does." I crossed my arms, my gaze tracking over the cityscape where the huge, nearly full moon cast eerie shadows from those towering ruins. "Since she was able to take some of Clarke's blood during the fight, he believes his sister has now obtained *most* of what she needs to open the gate. But she's still missing one key element—one she's counting on us providing for her."

His head turned slightly, just enough that I caught the glimmer of the moonlight off one of his sterling eyes as he waited for me to continue.

"The Spark of Life," I explained. "Something only the chosen of Paligno can provide. After Arlan's last peek into our friends' circumstances, he believes it now hangs around your daughter's neck. Thatcher must have passed it on to her at some point, probably after Paligno chose her."

His pupils constricted, jaw going slack as his whole face went pale. "Sadeera is going after Maylea," he realized aloud.

"More accurately, she's likely hoping your daughter finds her way to the site of the Gate of Proleus all on her own, delivering exactly what she needs for the ritual right into her hands," I corrected.

Jaevid dropped his piece of bread and leaned forward, putting his face in his hands. I didn't need to see his face to sense the despair that wafted off him like smoke from a wildfire. "Gods and Fates," he whispered. "My child ..."

"Let's not count our losses just yet," I said. "Edarix has been especially chatty this evening. He may be more useful than we first assumed. I suppose he hopes being helpful will keep me from ramming a blade through his neck. And if he is telling the truth, then he might be right. You see those large ruins down there towering over the city?"

Jaevid's head rose again, and he stared dejectedly down at the city before us. "What of them?"

"According to our captive, they are surface evidence of a much larger ruin hidden beneath. It is the remnants of an ancient city that was part of the Avoran Empire, and is composed of an extensive network of passages and tunnels that lead deep underground." I motioned to an area where several of those huge arches formed a sort of pentagon at one corner of the valley. "He claims that these ruins predate the Law of the Stones and contain relics of power from that era. Things most of modern society has forgotten entirely. Most importantly, he believes these ruins contain hidden gateways that can be activated using vast amounts of magical power. He said the Empire of Nar'Haleen was once connected by these ancient passageways, long before it was split and the war began. Given the magical prowess of our resident Avoran sorcerer, and our recent addition of an actual deity, we might be able to activate one of them long enough to take us to the Gate of Proleus itself."

"Is that really possible?" Jaevid sat up a little straighter, flicking me a worried sideways glance. "Dabbling in ancient relics and magic is dangerous, as you now know."

"I do," I agreed. "But I think this is our best shot. We can send the dragons and our reinforcements ahead of us, and they can offer backup should Reigh and the others reach the Gate of Proleus before we do. The trick will be entering the city covertly and making our way down to the sublevel, where we can find an entrance to the ruins. Oh, and locating one of these magical portals that can actually still function."

I could practically hear the wind rushing out of him as he deflated. "That doesn't sound especially promising, Murdoc."

"No. It doesn't." I snorted and cast him a challenging smirk. "But I'd say it's right on the mark for our usual level of madness, wouldn't you?"

"I suppose you're right about that. And we've no other choice. The longer we sit and wait, the greater the chance Reigh and the others reach the Gate of Proleus first—without us there to tip the odds of battle in their favor." He sighed deeply and shook his head. "Go and tell the others. We'll start moving toward the city soon. With any luck, we can reach it before dawn and use the dark of the night to hide our movements."

"Take heart. We're not out of bad ideas and insane plans just yet." I gave his arm a solid punch as I turned to go back and inform the rest of our merry band of idiots. "Let's not forget, we've got the gods on our side. If it does come to a fight—which I expect it will—we aren't in this alone. And I would bet my blade against any enemy's, so long as I'm fighting shoulder to shoulder with you lot."

A faint smile brushed his features. "Thank you, Murdoc."

I nodded and strode away. "All in the name of duty, Commander, all in the name of duty."

13

CHAPTER THIRTEEN

"Fast and silent. No torches or light. Weapons sheathed. Murdoc is taking point with Edarix since we are counting on him to show us the way to the entrance of the ruins," Jaevid instructed as we all gathered in, assembling our gear and outfitting for the last part of the journey.

It was just over three miles to reach the city's outskirts, and from there, we needed to keep a low profile until we were able to make it down into the sublevels where we could access the ancient passages. Risky with a group this size, it was bound to be a challenge. The eight of us made for quite the gaggle of misfits and foreigners, but we couldn't afford to leave anyone behind.

Not even Noa, who despite his leg injury, seemed to be getting around a little better now. Isa must have given him a hefty amount of that Gray elven remedy she'd brought along—something Reigh had taught her to use, no doubt.

"Garnett, you and I will stay toward the back and keep a distance. We can observe from there in case it seems as though we're being followed," Jaevid went on, his steely gaze tracking skyward as the low, rhythmic thumping of dragon wingbeats filled the night and faded into the distance.

It left a hollow, chilling silence in the air.

Our best offense was now flying west, toward the Gate of Proleus, and leaving us to sort this out on our own. Normally, I'd have insisted on flying on Blite rather than having him go alone. Not to mention, Fornax wouldn't get very far without Blite to guide him on. But we were counting on these magical gates to get us hundreds of miles in a matter of seconds, so it was likely we would beat all the dragons there. Providing it all worked according to plan, anyway.

Heh. As if that ever happened.

Granted, it would take a brave fool to try to cross us. We did have three divinely touched people and an Avoran sorcerer in our group. The objective, however, was not to cause a scene or have an all-out magical battle in the streets of a foreign city where we were, at best, unwanted guests. No need to start an international incident.

Fates help us.

"Murdoc, cut him loose, and let's get going," Jaevid ordered, fixing me with a hard look.

I nodded and immediately went over to cut Edarix's bonds. With his hands now free, he rubbed at his wrists and eyed us cautiously, almost like he wanted to run.

Gods and Fates, I hoped he did. Then I'd have an excuse to put a blade in his back.

For whatever reason—fear or survival—the elven priest held his ground and swallowed hard, managing to meet my gaze when he murmured, "Thank you."

"For what?" I arched an eyebrow.

"Believing me," he replied. "I know I have shamed myself before Clysiros. No doubt, she will punish me eternally for having any part of Auguress Riva's campaign. Or, um, Sadeera, as you call her. But I will do all I can to be of help to you now."

I narrowed my eyes and didn't reply. No point. He could paint things up with pretty words. It didn't matter. We would see exactly whose side he was really on soon enough.

We made quick time to the outer limits of Uru'Nai, able to manage a much better pace once we found a well-traveled road that led in from the north. A few hours before dawn, we were making headway without another soul in sight. So far, so good.

"Do you think Kaili and the others made it here?" I overheard Clarke whispering to Noa as we passed a place where the road ran alongside a wide, fast-moving river.

Noa didn't answer, and his expression stayed grimly focused. Maybe they hadn't been traveling alone initially? No one had questioned him much about what they were doing in this area to start with. That was better saved for another time, I suppose.

Right now, we had to focus on keeping our heads down and our steps silent as we finally crossed through one of those massive, ancient archways and into the city of Uru'Nai. The moon had already set, and the first soft glow of dawn bloomed beyond the huge bay. In less than an hour, the sun would rise, and the port city would stir with people and activity. We needed to be long underground by then. We had to go faster.

"This way. Hurry now," Edarix urged as he guided us through the twisted rat's nest of narrow roads, crowded side streets, and crooked alleys. He seemed awfully familiar with how to get around here for someone who supposedly had been living in the royal palace. Then again, I didn't know much of anything about his life before that. Maybe he'd been more well-traveled than most priests.

Whatever the case, he brought us quickly to a wide, main thoroughfare that was likely an open-air market during the daylight hours. Now, though, the long lines of merchant booths were closed up with their sides covered by long tapestries. Tall globe lamps along the sides of the street flickered with light that cast dancing shadows over the red and white cobblestones. Any other time, I would have marveled at how different it was from any other place I'd ever been. The Ulfrangar had taken me far from my home, but never to the southern kingdoms.

There wasn't time to be a tourist now, though.

The market street emptied abruptly into a large, open forum surrounded on all sides by those massive, looming arches. Five of them stood around, towering well over two hundred feet, in varying states of decay. Hunks of the stone that had broken off still lay where they'd fallen decades ago, and remnants of huge alabaster columns and sculptures stood right at the center of the square. Incredible.

But what stood out above all else was the temple—a huge, dome-roofed structure made from solid black stone that had been polished until it resembled dark mirrors. The dome-shaped ceiling was leafed in gold, and the wide, yawning entrance stood open like the mouth of a cave. Obsidian statues of tall-eared jackals and bronze braziers stood every twenty feet around the entire structure, sending up fragrant plumes of smoke from burning incense.

A temple of Clysiros. Well, that explained how Edarix knew where it was.

"Here. Quiet, now. There may be acolytes tending the temple grounds, but I will speak to them. They will let us pass," Edarix assured us, waving frantically as we made our way across the forum and into the dark reprieve of the temple. "There should be an entrance to the sublevel ruins within the catacombs beneath the temple. The acolytes will know better."

"And they won't rat us out to the city guard or your Auguress Riva?" Isandri questioned, still eyeing him with distrust.

Edarix shook his head emphatically. "No, no. They fear her as much as I do," he assured. "If there is some way to subvert and remove her, I am certain they will be happy to help us. She has done much to manipulate the emperor over the years, but she has won no friends or allies within the holy brethren."

"Is there anyone else you can count as an ally against her?" Jaevid asked as we paused just inside. "Someone you can contact who could send aid to the Gate of Proleus, should we find ourselves outmatched there?"

Edarix turned to face him, seeming shocked at first. I guess he hadn't expected that we would trust him with anything like that. It was a leap of faith, and not one I necessarily approved of. Letting him send word out beyond our group to someone we didn't know? Nope. Bad idea.

But no one had asked for my opinion.

"I-I, um, yes, actually," he stammered, still shaking off his surprise. "I have been close friends with Empress Leysa for a great many years. She already knows about the boy—Ronan—and his connection to your homeland. She has also been in communication with you already, I think." He dared a quick, anxious glance in Isandri's direction while fidgeting with a golden ring around one of his fingers. "She mentioned she has written to the court several times, establishing some amicable contact."

"Yes," she confirmed, her tone still tight and unhappy. "I've exchanged words with her in the past. She seemed ... reasonable."

"I think you would find her very sympathetic to your cause. She despises Auguress Riva's actions, and she is aware of her husband's growing madness," Edarix said quickly, beginning to walk forward again farther into the temple. "I believe she would help you in any way she can. I will have word sent to her as soon as possible. Ah, well, with your permission, of course."

I frowned. Something about this felt off. Involving more people that we didn't know in our mission was adding variables beyond our control to an already highly dangerous situation. It was reckless. And Arlan must have agreed, because his expression had turned cold and thoughtful as he strode along in our midst, saying little as his golden eyes flickered in the dark like two lit candles.

Neither of us spoke, though.

Because at that moment, two figures in long dark robes approached from the oppressive gloom of the dimly lit temple.

A young man and woman, each covered from head to foot in dark silks, with bare feet and simple gold circlets around their foreheads, hurried toward us with matching expressions of surprise, panic, and complete wonder. No surprise there. This place didn't exactly resonate the warmth that would attract many visitors.

As if on cue, Isandri and Edarix stepped ahead, obscuring their view of the rest of us and immediately capturing their complete attention.

I guess it wasn't often a high priest and a goddess visited.

"*Varri'dasha*, we offer you humble greetings and every honor and respect. We are blessed at your presence," the female acolyte said, and they both bowed low, kissed their fingertips, and stretched out their hands toward Edarix and Isa. "How may we serve?"

I didn't catch much more of the conversation. Isa stood, overseeing the conversation like an angry mother hen, while Edarix exchanged hushed words with them. It didn't take long. Two minutes, at most. But I did notice him slide the golden ring off his hand and handed it to the boy. Then he was waving us over while the two young acolytes split off in different directions. The boy rushed away, disappearing into the shadows altogether with that ring still in his hand, but the girl began to lead us deeper inside, past rows of massive, intricately carved columns.

Stepping through that place felt like the darkness had devoured us whole. Something about it set my nerves on edge. Chills raced up my spine, out to all my fingers and toes, and my chest seemed to tighten with every breath. All that kept me grounded was a knot of thrumming heat right in the center of my chest. I felt the weight of my new sword against my back like the reassuring hand of Proleus himself. I wasn't alone in this. I could handle it. I had to keep my eyes open. Senses sharp. Reflexes ready.

I couldn't fathom how the acolytes navigated the interior of this place without so much as a candle in hand, though. With no windows and only the occasional smoldering brazier or glass oil lamp to mark passages that branched off the central hall, it was far too easy to get disoriented. After what felt like an eternity, pale golden light finally bloomed through the onyx hall, coming from a large circular atrium. A huge opening in the ceiling let in a single shaft of sparkling, early morning light. The sun would be up soon.

We had to go—now.

But what stood in the center of that atrium, bathed in the pale light of dawn, stopped me dead in my tracks. My breath hung in my throat, and my pulse gave a flinching twist in my chest. I stared up, every concerned thought in my mind seeming to fall silent, as I met the ruby-eyed gazes of two huge statues.

Statues ... of dragons.

They stood, their wings spread and tails and necks intertwined, in the center of the atrium. The incredible effort that had been put into their construction, carving each scale and horn with extreme detail, made it seem like they might stir and snarl at us at any moment. But they stood, motionless and silent, like two massive fiends of black glass.

"The Viepol," the female acolyte explained as she led the way toward them, motioning to a place right in the center where their clawed forelegs flanked both sides of a narrow doorway. The steps within it led straight down and disappeared into total darkness. "You will find the crypt within."

Of course, we *had* to go down into the dark, scary hole. Faaantastic.

"And there's a passage into the ruins there?" Jaevid asked, eying the two monstrous sculptures with a strange, almost haunted expression. Almost as though they were something he had seen before.

"Yes," the girl replied, moving quickly over to one of the braziers long enough to unhook something from the side. She used a pair of long tongs to take some of the embers, placing them carefully inside a tear-drop-shaped glass censer. Carrying it by a handle affixed to a golden chain, she brought it over and handed it to Edarix with a nervous smile. "To light your path and cleanse the air of restless auras."

"Of course." He took it and nodded to the rest of us. His gaze halted on Jaevid for an instant, seeming to notice how our resident war hero was still staring apprehensively up at the draconic statues. "If everyone is ready, let's be swift."

Jaevid blinked hard, shaking his head some. His chest rose and fell with a deep breath, as though he were trying to clear his thoughts. Our gazes locked from across our merry band, and his mouth snapped into a hard, straight line.

Maybe this was calling back bad memories for him. Or perhaps he had the same sinking, bad feeling about this that I did. It could have been both.

But neither of us had a choice now.

The only other person who seemed at all impacted by the sight of the statues was Clarke. But rather than seeming unnerved or anxious, his gaze was distant and almost sad as he studied them. He almost looked confused, like he was looking at a family portrait where the faces were all wrong.

Hmm.

"Creepy place," Garnett muttered as she drifted closer to my side. "And that's coming from someone who spent years in Tibran tunnels."

I couldn't resist a smirk. "I'm not sure anyone constructs a temple to a goddess of death with comfort and coziness in mind."

"Well, if they did, they might get more visitors," she mumbled, her light violet eyes darting around the gloomy stairwell like a nervous cat. Leaning in closer, she whispered quietly up to me. "I've got a bad feeling, Murdoc. Something's not right here. I just can't put my finger on it."

"I know," I whispered back, stealing a glance over my shoulder at Jaevid's wary expression. "I don't think we're the only ones who feel that way. Just keep your eyes open and your axes at the ready."

She nodded slightly, drawing her bottom lip into her mouth as she kept a brisk pace right next to me.

I knew that look. That focus. I felt it like a quiet tension simmering in my blood, too.

Venturing down into the depths of the crypt, the air grew cooler until it made my skin prickle with a shiver. Our breathing, rustling of clothes, and shuffling footsteps filled the total silence. It felt like descending into a completely different world—one of perfect stillness like a deep winter's night.

The staircase ended in a long room lined with stone burial vaults on either side. Busts and reliefs were carved into the lids, depicting warriors in ancient armor clutching blades, shields, or talismans to their chests. Some were humans. Others were elves. But all of them looked like they might be hundreds of years old.

Hurrying down the length of the room, we passed from one burial chamber into another, each one seeming older than the last. The styles of the burial vaults changed with the eras. Some were leafed in gold, others were encrusted with dusty jewels, and the oldest seemed to be painted with intricate designs. I wondered if any of them were figures from history we might recognize—heroes from legends past.

Would we join them in their eternal slumber someday?

That thought stuck in my mind like a splinter, tiny but sharp, as we approached another archway carved straight into the stone wall. More stairs led downward, disappearing into the gloom, and frigid air wafted up from within. One glance at the engraved doorway betrayed its age—far more ancient than anything we'd seen already. Intricate lettering spiraled and swirled around it, following the contours of carved ribbons and surrounded by a field of stars.

I recognized the styling of the language, even if I couldn't read it. There were few in the world that could read Avoran outside of their own citizens. Fortunately, one of those people walked among us.

Arlan stepped forward, his glowing eyes perusing the script before he read aloud, *"The starry gate welcomes all who would join their voices with the music of the spheres."*

"What does that mean?" Garnett asked, standing on her toes to get a better look.

"This is the entrance to a welcoming hall," Arlan explained, something tender and distinctly sad in his tone as he reached out to brush his fingers over the lettering. "Lost and buried many years ago, likely predating even the War of the Stones. The Avoran Empire spanned a large portion of this very region, and the cities that now stand are built upon the bones and ashes of its dwellings."

"Like the archways and ruins outside?" Jaevid guessed.

Arlan nodded. "What endures now is only the skeletal remains of our once-great society. Ashes and cinders, nothing more."

"But hopefully a few gates still work," I muttered as I leaned through the doorway and peered down the stairwell. "How will we find one once we are inside? I assume the ruins are vast and there's likely been a lot of cave-ins over the years."

"Most assuredly," Arlan agreed. "But I should be able to navigate fairly easily. There is a pattern to such places—one that still exists in Avora today. Our blueprints for residences, temples, and educational structures have not changed much."

"Here's hoping," Garnett sighed, her hands on her hips as she stared up at him with a crinkle of worry in her brow. "Just see that you don't start slinging magic around, aye? You've pushed yourself too far already, and we've more than enough folk here now that can provide a bit of magical power, too."

Arlan's head bowed slightly, eyes closing as a soft, faint smile brushed over his lips. "As you command, Miss Garnett."

⸙ 14 ⸙

CHAPTER FOURTEEN

Walking amidst the fallen cities of Avora felt like stepping off the edge of reality and into a forgotten, fractured dream. Tombs of cold stone gave way to ancient halls of glass, mica, and opal. Columns and sweeping archways of fire opal and floors of polished labradorite shone and shimmered in the light of our censer. Toppled statues of angelic figures lay smashed upon the floors, forgotten and left to collect dust. Overhead, the ceiling glittered with pinpricks of light that mimicked the stars. Enchantments, maybe? It was too far up to be certain, and we didn't stick around for any explanations from our resident Avoran tour guide.

Not that he seemed all that eager to talk.

Arlan forged on at the lead of our group, followed immediately by Edarix, and stopped only when we came to places where the airy, dark halls met. Some had long-dry fountains in the center, featuring intricate mosaics of tiny gold, pearl, and gemstone tiles that spanned more than fifty feet across. My skin tingled and shivered with wave after wave of strange energy that seemed to drift through the place like air currents. My hand instinctively flexed, and I rubbed my fingers together as those subtle breezes seemed to tickle at my ears like whispers from long ago that still echoed here, repeating forever in the darkness.

Our group held a reverent silence as we all stared around, eyes wide and mouths open in amazement. There was nothing anywhere in Maldobar or Luntharda that could compare to the grandeur, beauty, and sheer majesty of this place. And I couldn't help but wonder what the current, thriving cities of Avora must look like by comparison. If this was merely a ruin, then what did those floating palaces, wreathed in cloud and radiant sunlight, truly look like?

Beautiful beyond description, probably.

I was so busy gaping up at the ceiling I nearly crashed into Isandri's back when we all suddenly stopped behind Arlan at another place where six halls intersected in a lavish square. The flickering light of our censer fell across the mosaic that covered the floor like scattered jewels—a depiction of an angelic figure in billowing robes, wings outstretched, and flowing black hair running like rivers of obsidian down to her feet. With a sunburst crown on her head and arms wrapped lovingly around a bunch of scrolls, the figure looked wistfully into the distance.

"High Inquisitor Bellavora?!" Clarke gasped suddenly, his voice shattering the silence. His eyes had gone as wide as moons behind his round spectacles as he stared down at the image.

"Indeed," Arlan confirmed. "I believe this was once her home."

"But ... but ... that's," Clarke choked, as though he couldn't wrap his mind around that idea. Interesting, especially since he was the embodiment of a god. I guess there were some aspects of him that were still mortal.

"Impossible? Hardly." Arlan waved a hand dismissively. "She was one of the high scholars who dwelled here before the Battle of Falling Stars. She always carried an immense love for knowledge and history and could not bring herself to leave it, and instead moved much of what she was able to save to what became the Compendium Library." His smile was wistful and a little patronizing as he eyed the young man. "Or did you assume that place was built by human hands?"

"N-No, I ... I honestly never thought to ask," Clarke said quickly. "I just assumed it had always been there."

"Everything comes from something else," Arlan murmured as he looked away. "It is the greatest detriment of any society to forget that truth—without what came before, there could be no now, and preserving the knowledge of what once was for future posterity may be all that might save it from similar evils."

"You knew her, didn't you?" I asked, daring to take a step closer. "If this was her home, then do you know if she had a gateway in it?"

"I believe so," Arlan replied coolly. "She traveled often to give educational lessons, so a gate would have been necessary for swift travel. I was quite young when I last came here, but I do believe it was this way." He took off at a brisk walk to the left, not even looking back to see if we were still following.

Right. Well, at least this sounded promising.

We walked on through the twisting halls, and after a while, I gave up all hope of memorizing the route back to the surface. Maybe it wouldn't matter. Maybe we would find this gate and leave that way rather than trying to reverse-navigate this path.

Ehh. Crap. My mind really was slipping these days. Jace had warned me that normal life would have that effect—that being around the people I loved would start to dull my Ulfrangar edge. A more than worthy sacrifice, but an inconvenient one given our current situation.

I suppose I'd just have to take this on faith. That seemed to be a trend in my life these days.

After what felt like hours, Arlan finally stopped at another arched doorway. Outlined by a carved relief of moon phases wreathed in ivy and swirling runes, the passage was smaller, closer to the size of a regular door, but no less ornate than all the ones before it. A satisfied smile touched Arlan's sharp features as he beckoned to it, as though expecting the rest of us to have some clue about what any of those runes said.

Only Clarke seemed equally pleased. "We found it!" he announced excitedly.

Jaevid and I exchanged another wary, sideways glance and nod. No time to let our guard down. What came next was a giant unknown, so we had to be prepared for the worst.

Our footfalls thumped softly on the polished labradorite floor as we followed Arlan inside, the light from our censer making it shine in hues of blue, green, and greenish gold. The circular room was unlike any other we had passed through so far, resembling a wide rotunda with a raised platform in the very center. There, an eight-foot-tall structure like a framed dressing mirror stood alone in the silence. Its slender shape arced to a point at the top, and the edges of its framework were covered in lines of runework etched into tarnished gold. Only ... it had no glass center. It was only an empty frame, and I could see clear through it to the other side of the room without interruption.

Hmmm.

Something about it standing there, aloft and alone on that platform, put a knot of cold dread in my stomach. The subtle whispers of breezes still floating past my ears intensified, sending fresh chills up my spine.

This place was ageless in a way I couldn't even begin to fathom, but I could feel it like a pressure soaking into bones.

At the sight of the mirror, that cold veneer of composure broke on Arlan's features like a bursting soap bubble. He stared at it, not even blinking, with his expression a twisted, almost frantic mixture of grief and dread. Almost as though he couldn't believe the gateway was still here. His broad shoulders drooped as he stepped toward it ahead of us, lips parted, but not saying a word.

"Beautiful," Isandri whispered faintly from behind me.

"I ... I've seen one of these before," Clarke seemed to realize aloud, his brow knitting with thought as he tilted his head to one side. "I think there was one in the library, too."

"That would make sense if High Inquisitor Bellavora built it long ago. She would want a means of travel, wouldn't she?" Edarix asked, his tone trembling with eager excitement. Or perhaps just nervous energy. He was not an easy man to read.

"I wish I had asked her about it," Clarke murmured. "I wish I had asked her about a lot of things."

Noa put a hand on his shoulder, giving him a reassuring smile that didn't quite reach his eyes. He hadn't said much at all since his emotional outburst at Jaevid, and I had my own suspicions about where his true loyalties lay. Not with Sadeera, of course, but if things went sideways for us, he might decide to just take Clarke and make a run for it.

A very slow, hobbling run, but still ...

"How do we activate it?" Jaevid asked as he moved ahead, going to stand beside Arlan right before the towering empty frame. "We need magical power, correct?"

"Indeed, and a great deal of it," Arlan confirmed. "Fortunately, we've now two godlings and a paladin in our midst. I believe we can manage."

"I hope you're right." Jaevid rubbed at his jaw, not looking altogether convinced that the dusty, empty frame in front of him was going to be of much help. "Otherwise, we don't really have a backup plan."

"I'm *so* pleased to hear it," a sing-song, female voice suddenly giggled from behind us—back in the direction of the doorway.

Fear ripped through my chest like the jagged point of a spear, striking me right to the core. Oh gods. I ... I knew that voice!

Everyone whirled around at once, our focus snapping to the host of armed warriors now blocking our only way out.

Hands of Fate agents. Highly trained Imperial sentinels. And right at the center, a woman dressed in fine black and gold robes, her eyes as dark as pitch, and a cruel smile twisted over her ebony-painted lips.

"Auguress Riva," Edarix gasped in horror, nearly dropping the censer he still carried.

"Hello, Edarix. It seems you've had a change of heart. You mortals are *so* predictable," Riva snickered, reaching out to plant a hand on the shoulder of the armored young man who stood right beside her. He didn't so much as flinch as she grabbed his helmet and ripped it off, tossing it to the ground at our feet.

Isandri gasped. Jaevid let out a snarling curse. All I could do was stand in soundless horror, staring into the deadpan face of a young human boy I knew all too well.

Merciful Fates. It was Ronan.

For a few terrifying seconds, no one moved. No one spoke. No one even seemed to breathe.

Then, in one smooth motion, all the warriors flanking Auguress Riva drew their weapons. Some leveled crossbows. Others brandished curved swords and sickle-styled blades that reminded me somewhat of Reigh's kafki.

Riva's smile widened viciously, her chin tilting up in proud delight as she ran her hand through Ronan's dark hair like someone petting a lapdog. "You've no idea how difficult it is to find gateways that can still function, and trapped in this miserable prison of mortal meat, my power is only a shade of what it once was—a just punishment, according to Mother and Father. I'm reduced to this disgusting, pathetic *thing*, because of you." Her expression went frosty as she fixed me with a hard, unblinking stare.

My stomach hit the soles of my boots. I drew the sword Proleus had gifted me, the flawless metal blade practically singing as it left the sheath at my back.

One corner of Riva's mouth curled upward in a half-smirk. "But now you've gone and done all the work for me. I'm ever so grateful. You'll have to excuse our rush, though. We've a very important appointment to keep. I'm afraid your services are no longer needed. I trust you'll understand."

At my side, Jaevid drew his scimitar. Isandri cracked her staff off the ground, sending a bolt of crackling power through the gem affixed to the top. Garnett drew both her hand axes and sank into a defensive stance.

But I couldn't move. That voice ... with that face. It was all wrong. Something about it was familiar and I couldn't decide why! Every word from her lips made my blood run cold and adrenaline surge through every muscle in my body like wild panic.

Then it hit me. I remembered. I knew it. I knew *her*. The face and body were different. Even the voice seemed older. But the malice in those eyes and the cadence to her speech were all too familiar. It had echoed in my own head while I was trapped, watching her use my body as a vessel for her own wicked intent.

On pure instinct, my gaze snapped to Arlan. He stood as motionless as a corpse, his sharp features frozen in a look of complete, horrified bewilderment.

Because he saw it, too.

Gods and Fates, she ... she wasn't ... Sadeera.

She was Iksoli, Goddess of Mischief.

It made no sense. There had to be some kind of mistake. Auguress Riva had to be Sadeera! Why was Iksoli here? Hadn't Thatcher banished her back to the divine realm?! Why, by all the gods, was she back?

My mind whirled with questions as the truth sank into my chest like the steel point of a dagger. We were wrong. We didn't know where Sadeera was. And now we were cornered.

A few of us against a company of highly-trained warriors, Ronan, ... and an insane goddess who had nearly destroyed us once already.

Fates have mercy.

"Arlan, you and Clarke must do whatever you can to get the gateway open," Jaevid growled through his teeth. "We will get as many of our people through it as possible, and I will stay behind to see that it is destroyed before they can follow."

"Not alone, you won't." I stepped in closer to his side, taking up dragonrider battle formation with my sword at the ready. Reaching down deep into the depths of my mind, I let my eyes roll closed as the heat of Proleus's power stirred to life like someone stoking a furnace in my soul. The runes down the length of the blade began to glow an infernal red, and I could practically taste the raw power crackling in the air around me as I settled my glare upon the biggest threat before us:

Iksoli.

Even if she truly was bound in mortal form with only stunted divine power to work with, she was the linchpin. The base of the house of cards. Take her down and the rest would crumble. Once she was taken out of play, Ronan should have control of his mind again. He would be neutralized, and we might gain the upper hand.

"Isa, hold Ronan off as long as you can. Jae, we're going after Riva. Garnett, think you and Roxus can handle the rest?" I muttered quickly. We only had seconds, maybe less, before it began.

Garnett cackled as she spun her axes over her hands and sank into a defensive pose. "Hah! You Maldobarian boys just give me some space, eh? I need room to work *my* magic."

Roxus didn't answer—at least, not in words. Out of the corner of my eye, I saw his expression flash with blind fury an instant before the wind kicked up around him, tossing his messy mop of brown hair and the lengths of his ragged coat around him. His whole form swelled, twisting and warping into the shape of a ten-foot-tall grizzly bear that hit the earth beside us with a *BOOM* that made the earth shake under our boots.

So, he really was an Ursinaar. Interesting.

Roxus rose up onto his hind legs and bellowed a thundering roar at our line of enemies. A few of the Hands of Fate drew back in surprise, looking to Iksoli as though this hadn't been part of their grand master plan.

I smirked. Heh. We were just getting started.

"You will not interfere again," Iksoli seethed through her teeth as she snapped her fingers right in front of Ronan's nose. He immediately snapped to attention, eyes suddenly glowing like two red coals in the gloom. Flames sparked to life in his palms and licked through his fingers, casting an eerie crimson glow over Iksoli's pallid features as she leaned in closer to him and hissed, "Kill them all."

PART THREE

MAYLEA

15

CHAPTER FIFTEEN

"Maylea? Maylea, is that you?"

My heart gave a frantic twist in my chest. I knew Ronan's voice right away. It echoed through my head, so loud and clear it was as though he could be standing right in front of me. But trapped in that suffocating darkness, I couldn't see anything. I still couldn't find him, not even in my dreams.

I didn't know much about magic or divine power. All of this—being chosen by Paligno and feeling the presence of his divine power hiding like a secret in my soul—was completely new. Using that power was getting easier, and yet, the more I used it, the more exhausted I got. My arms and legs were heavy. My head was foggy, like I couldn't force myself to focus for long. I just wanted to sleep.

But when I did, I found myself in that dark place again. I could have sworn I felt something like a barrier all around me, blocking me from finding Ronan, like someone had their hands locked over my eyes. All I could do was stumble blindly through the blackness, reaching out for anything to latch onto. I had tried so many times to stop, think, and focus my energy. To control my emotions and push through that blockade. Uncle Reigh seemed to think I could do it. I just had to keep working at it. Ronan was right there, so close, I could feel his presence. I couldn't give up on him.

But nothing was working. And now, it was as though he had begun to fade.

He was running out of time.

"Maylea, p-please ..." His voice grew weaker, like he was exhausted or trying not to pass out. *"Please ... help me. I-I can't ...."*

"I'm coming, Ronan. I promise, we are coming for you. Just hang on a little longer!" I cried out in my thoughts, pouring every ounce of my will into that plea.

Ronan didn't answer.

Then something warm touched my cheek. I sucked in a frantic gasp as my eyes flew open. I jolted, my arms and legs locking up in terror, as I lay on my bedroll staring up into a face directly over mine. A face I knew.

"Maylea, are you all right?" Lukani whispered, cradling my cheeks in his hands. He sat on the floor, right next to my bedroll, his expression tight with concern.

"I-I felt him again. He was s-so close, but I couldn't find him. I—" My arms shook as I tried to push myself upright. Immediately, my head spun and everything seemed to swerve in and out of focus. My heart pounded out of control, and I started to fall sideways.

Lukani's strong arms closed around me suddenly, holding me upright and letting me lean against his chest. "Shhh. It's all right, I'm here," he murmured as he stroked my hair. "Try to slow your breaths. It's going to be all right."

I let my eyes roll closed, relaxing my weight against him. With my ear pressed against his chest, all I could hear was the sound of his voice and steady heartbeat. It sent waves of warmth through my body, relaxing every tense, shaking muscle. Maybe Uncle Reigh didn't approve of how close Lukani and I had become, but I knew I couldn't keep going like this without him. Lukani was always right there when I needed him most, ready to fight at my side or catch me when I fell. He was solid ground beneath my feet when the rest of my world spun out of control. I would have been so utterly lost without him.

I just wished I knew how to tell him that.

"I know you want to find your friend, but you must allow yourself time to rest," Lukani urged.

"I'm so close to reaching him, Lukani. It's like he's right there, within arm's reach, but I can't find him." I swallowed hard against the rising knot of heat that lodged in the back of my throat. It made my eyes water and my breathing hitch. "I don't even know if he can hear me."

"Why don't I help you out onto the balcony? We can have some fresh air," he suggested. "There is still tea, as well."

I nodded a little. "Okay."

It took me a few steps to get stable on my feet, but we picked our way carefully across the room, around the other empty bedrolls, and out onto the small balcony area. It was open to the rest of the room, with a few velveteen pouf cushions and a low table where we could sit and enjoy the cooler night wind. Easing down into one of the cushions, I let my elbows rest on the table as the sounds of the streets above and below washed over me. People chatting. Merchants calling their wares. Music from street performers.

This whole city was bizarre. It was as though it only came alive once the sun had set. I guess it made sense, though. The sun was so oppressive during the day, so it was probably better for everyone living here to avoid it, stay indoors, and wait out the daylight hours. I'd just never heard of a whole city being nocturnal before. Something about it made me smile to myself as Lukani slid a cup of warm, herbal tea toward me across the tabletop. No one back home in Maldobar would ever believe this.

"Is Thatcher okay?" I asked as I took a small sip.

Lukani sighed and ran his fingers through his dark bangs, tucking a few locks behind his long, pointed ears. "He went to take a bath after you fell asleep."

"And Uncle Reigh and Violet?"

He shrugged. "They have not yet returned."

I wondered if Violet had managed to find him. She left in such a flurry, it was beyond easy to see how worried she was about Uncle Reigh going out on his own. I still didn't understand what was going on between them. I mean, clearly, there *were* feelings. So obvious. But it was like neither of them knew what to actually do with those emotions except silently freak out and occasionally argue.

The sooner they finally cleared the air, the better.

Ugh. Old people could be so excruciating sometimes.

"I wonder where we will go from here," Lukani said, as though he were thinking aloud.

"Violet said it's a really long way across the desert," I recalled. "Too far to go in one stretch. She mentioned stopping in someplace called Dumathis?"

He just shrugged again. "I don't know. I have no memories of living here when I was young—before I was taken."

My mouth scrunched some, wondering far too late if that lack of memory was painful for him. He still didn't talk about himself much and brushed off most of my questions by saying his life with Arlan the Kinslayer had been uneventful. I sort of doubted that, but I didn't want to push the issue. Not yet, anyway.

"It must be strange to be back here," I guessed. "Is it how you imagined it would be?"

Lukani looked down and fiddled with his teacup. "I don't know. It is all very surreal to even be here at all. Arlan always promised he would eventually see me return to my people, and I had hoped ..." He hesitated, dark brows furrowing a little. "I had hoped I would see another Rajinna. At least one, even if it was from afar. I would have liked to know I am not the only one left."

"Well, you know how careful we've had to be about keeping you safe and disguised in public," I reasoned. "It's probably the same way for other Rajinna, too, right? Maybe we have seen some, and we just didn't know it."

His throat jumped and his mouth flattened into a stiff, uncomfortable line. "I think I would have known if we had. I can't explain why. It is just a feeling."

I reached across the table to put my hand over his. "When this is over, if you want to go looking for them, I'll help you any way I can."

He stared at me, his eerie yellow-gold eyes reflecting the city lights like two bronze discs. "You would stay here with me for that?"

"Of course," I promised. "I care about you, too, you know? You've been there for me in so many ways. I would love the chance to be there for you, too."

His smile was thin and uncertain. "It scares me some. I am worried if I do find other Rajinna, they will not accept me. Arlan was concerned about this, too. He said my people are not trusting of outsiders."

"But you're not an outsider," I reminded him. "You didn't leave them by choice. Surely, they'll understand that."

He bowed his head some, already looking defeated. "I really hope so."

When Thatcher came back, his hair still wet from his bath and his eyes drooping with exhaustion, we all settled back into our bedrolls for the night. Lukani was right. I had to sleep. At any moment, Violet and Uncle Reigh might come back and say we had to start moving again. They needed me to be ready and able to fight if something went wrong.

And, based on my limited experience when it came to traveling anywhere with them, something *always* went wrong. With astounding consistency. It's like Uncle Reigh was a magnet for every terrible thing in a fifty-mile radius.

No wonder he was always so moody and on edge.

Lukani pulled a thin, sheer curtain over the balcony doorway before he came and sat down on his bedroll next to mine. Through the dim light, I could see the tired lines in his forehead as he rubbed at his eyes and sighed deeply. Even if he didn't want to admit it, he had been pushing himself hard, too. His shape-changing magic was strong, but the bigger and more complex the shapes he took, or the longer he stayed in the smaller ones, the greater the toll on his physical body became. I wasn't sure what would happen if he pushed things too far, and I didn't want to find out.

We all needed this rest.

I just ... didn't think I could. Not when that dark, whisper-filled place always pulled me under the second I closed my eyes and let my mind relax.

Lying on my back, I watched the night shadows move over the walls and listened to the sound of the city beyond our balcony. My thoughts wandered, taking me far across the ocean back to my family's home. I had been trying hard not to think of them too much, mostly because it filled my chest with dread like a roaring tide.

Tonight, though, I thought about my mother. I wondered if she was okay and if the babies had come yet. Would I ever get to see them? Or would they only hear tales of me—the wayward daughter who'd run off and gotten herself killed in some faraway land. I thought about Dah, and how the last things I'd said to him were so whiny and immature. I couldn't remember the last time I had told him that I loved him. I wondered what my brothers were doing. Sile and I had a lot in common, and I knew he looked up to me. He always wanted my approval. I hadn't even spoken to him the whole day of the ball.

Tears welled in my eyes and I wrapped my fingers around the pendant around my neck. I didn't know if Paligno heard prayers, or if he would do me any favors, but I wished more than anything he would let them know I was okay.

And that I was so, *so* sorry.

I hadn't meant to hurt them. The thought of my actions having any impact on them hadn't really crossed my mind until it was far too late. I knew my parents would be angry, of course. But I hadn't expected that to hurt this much.

Now, all I wanted, more than anything, was a chance to make it right. That hope consumed me like the flames of a furnace, and my heart wrenched and twisted with frantic hope as I lay there, silently trying to decide how I was going to apologize to them if I ever saw my family again.

I almost didn't notice.

The floorboards under my back rumbled slightly. It only lasted for a second or two. Then nothing. Had I imagined that? Was it normal for that to happen here? Maybe a heavy wagon outside, or—

It happened again. The floor shuddered, and a glass bottle toppled off a nearby shelf and shattered on the floor. Thatcher bolted upright immediately and floundered for his sword, blinking groggily around for what made the noise.

I sat up, too.

Nope. I definitely hadn't imagined that.

"What's going on?" Lukani slurred drowsily as he rubbed his eyes and lifted his head to see what we were doing.

"I don't know. Stay here." Thatcher was already getting to his feet, blade in hand, and picking his way carefully over to where the bottle had smashed on the floor. He studied it, scowling suspiciously, then glanced up at me as though silently asking if I had seen what happened.

I opened my mouth, but I didn't get a single word out.

VOOOOOM!

Another wave of rumbling shook the room, more violently this time. The small chandelier on the ceiling swung on its golden chain and a stack of teacups and books on another shelf toppled down to scatter across the floor.

Then the screams started.

Outside our balcony, the cheery night sounds I'd gotten used to had twisted into something frantic, terrifying, and awful. Men shouted and screamed. Women cried out. Crashes, bangs, and clattering filled the night air.

Thatcher ran to the balcony and threw back the curtain, his tall frame cast in stark silhouette as a huge fireball soared right past us like a miniature sun. My pulse lurched to a halt in my chest as I sat paralyzed, gaping in mortification. Gods and Fates, what was happening out there?!

Thatcher staggered back immediately, snarling a curse under his breath before he whirled around and ran for his boots and gear. "GET UP AND GET YOUR THINGS! WE HAVE TO MOVE—RIGHT NOW!" he shouted.

"What's happening?" Lukani panicked as he helped throw all our belongings into our bags and crammed his foot into his leather-woven sandals. "What was that thing?"

"Catapult fire! The city is under attack!" Thatcher stood, shouldering his bag and tossing me my quiver and bow. "We need to get away from the outer walls and take cover!"

Adrenaline scorched through my body, making my hands shake and my vision spot as I scrambled to lace up my boots and dash to the doorway. "What about Uncle Reigh and Violet?"

"We can't worry about them right now! Let's go—faster! Go, go, go!" Thatcher boomed over us, holding the door ajar so Lukani and I could dash through first.

With Lukani in the front and Thatcher right on my heels, we scrambled for the stairwell outside our room. Another tooth-rattling boom shook the building and nearly sent us all tumbling down the steps. I coughed and choked as dust rained down from the level above and filled the air. Steadying myself against the wall, I dashed down the steps and jumped the last four, hitting the first landing in a crouch. I whirled on a heel and charged on, focused on my balance as the building shuddered around us again.

THUD!

I smashed right into Lukani's back and rocked back on my heels, barely staying upright.

He stood frozen, as solid as a stone pillar, staring straight ahead down the next flight of stairs. All the color seemed to drain away from his green-hued complexion, making him look ashen and gray. His golden eyes went round and his mouth hung wide open, gaze transfixed on the bottom of the steps before us.

A figure crouched there, staring straight back at him with eyes of the exact same, warm golden color. With most of their features obscured by the hood of a heavy cloak, I couldn't see much else until the figure stood straight. Muscular arms with vibrant red skin emerged from beneath the cloak, brushing back the hood and revealing a beaming, masculine face framed in shaggy black hair.

A gasp tore past my lips. H-He was ... he was just like Lukani!

Okay, so he wasn't *exactly* like him. His skin was a bright red hue, not green. He also had large, curled red horns that swept back from just above his pointed ears and arced upward. Lukani only had tiny green nubs that were basically invisible thanks to his thick, wavy hair. But still, the resemblance was undeniable.

This guy was another Rajinna.

The young man seemed a good bit older, maybe in his mid-twenties, with hard-chiseled features and the same long, pointed ears that had several different piercings on either side. His long, lion-like tail was tipped in coal black fur and flicked back and forth curiously as he stared up the steps at us, tilting his head to one side. His nostrils flared a little as he sniffed the air, then chuckled proudly. "Hah! I was correct, after all!"

A low, uncertain growl rumbled in Lukani's throat as the red-skinned Rajinna prowled up a few steps closer to us. His body tensed, and he shied back, putting himself protectively in front of me and curling his hands into fists. One corner of his mouth twitched, lip drawing up in a half-snarl of warning that showed his pointed incisors.

The young Rajinna man stopped, his collection of golden anklets, necklaces, and arm cuffs clinking musically as he straightened. His smile faded some, dark brows knitting in confusion as he glanced between Lukani and the rest of our group. "I have come to free you at last, my brother. You do not need to serve them any longer. They cannot outmatch both of us, I assure you," he said and motioned for Lukani to follow. "Let's be off swiftly! This human pigsty won't last the night!"

Free him? What was this guy talking about? Lukani wasn't our slave or servant. What the heck was going on?

"These are my *friends*," Lukani declared. "Not my masters. Who are you? Are you the ones attacking the city? Why should we even trust you at all?"

The Rajinna man drew back like he'd been slapped across the face. Blinking hard, he looked at Thatcher and me again, his eyes narrowing suspiciously. Almost like he thought we were manipulating the situation somehow. "Because I came here just to find you, brother! You have been lost to us for far too long, and the Avoran man warned you might be in danger. We have safe passage out of the city, but we must hurry."

Avoran man? Wait a minute, was he talking about Arlan the Kinslayer? Had Arlan somehow told the Rajinna about Lukani? My head spun, trying to make sense of how anyone could send a message from kingdoms away that quickly. I mean, it was some sort of magic, obviously, but what kind? Was it something only Avoran elves could do? Or could I do something like that, too?

"The humans and elves squabble yet again, as they have for ages and will forevermore. They are the ones destroying their city, not us." The strange man's golden gaze fixed on me and he made a disgusted face. "But you must leave these behind. They are useless. Let them perish with their kin—we must be off!"

"I will *not* leave them," Lukani warned. "If ... if you want me to go with you, then you will have to take us all to safety."

The Rajinna man frowned harder, his expression an ominous mixture of anger, confusion, and suspicion as his golden eyes darted between each of us. At last, his wide shoulders rose and fell with a defeated sigh. He rolled his eyes as he motioned for all of us to follow. "As you wish, then, my brother. But if they fall behind, they are left behind. *We* do not waste effort tending to humans."

16

CHAPTER SIXTEEN

Nar'Haleen was launching another brutal attack against Rienka. I knew it the instant we stepped out of the inn and into the fray. Catapult fire rained down like flaming meteors, smashing into the bridges and walkways. Soldiers ran in groups, shouting orders as they rushed to defend the city walls and put out the fires. Citizens fled like herds of panicked sheep, wailing and calling for one another in the chaos. The air reeked of smoke and burning tar from the fireballs being launched over the city walls.

It was just like before, when they attacked the islands.

And once again, we were running for our lives.

With our new Rajinna guide dashing on in the lead, we scrambled along the cliffside streets and walkways, dodging other groups of people trying to flee the battle. Portions of the scaffolding-styled paths had already been blown to rubble or set ablaze, so we had to double back, find new routes, and take our chances that this guy wasn't leading us straight into the blades of our enemies. He obviously had an issue with Thatcher and me—the *humans*—but maybe his interest in Lukani would be enough to avoid leading us straight to our doom.

A girl could hope.

My legs burned as I pumped them faster, sprinting headlong after Lukani. My lungs ached and my throat stung from taking in gulp after gulp of the smoke-filled air. The fumes of burning tar stung my eyes and made my vision foggy. But I didn't dare slow down. I couldn't afford to trip or stumble. It was life or death, and every second counted.

We skidded around a sharp corner and darted down more steep stairs to the next level—right into the path of a dozen Nar'Haleenan soldiers. We all lurched to a halt, smacking into each other's backs. Then instinct took over.

I immediately dropped to a crouch and Lukani did the same, yanking on the older Rajinna's tail so he was forced to join us.

VOOOM!

Thatcher dropped his shimmering golden forcefield over us an instant before the soldiers fired their crossbows. Their arrows pinged off his shield or stuck into it, suspended in the rippling current of energy. I took that second's opportunity to draw my own bow and fit an arrow to the string, already feeling the rising swell of tingling heat rushing through my veins. Paligno's power coursed through my body and roared in my ears as I stood, reaching to draw my bow just as Thatcher dropped his shield.

TWANG!

I let the arrow fly, aiming right for the wooded boardwalk in front of the soldiers. It hit with a small *thunk*, and instantly, the wooden boards burst to life beneath the soldiers' boots. A flash of brilliant green light made them stagger and shout as my arrow's shaft exploded into thick, writhing, thorn-studded vines that snaked through the ranks of armored men like big green serpents. The vines wrapped around their legs and bodies, squeezing, cracking, crushing, and breaking. The men screamed. They tried hacking at the vines. But for every one they severed, four more grew back.

In less than a minute for them, their shouts went silent, and the only thing that blocked our path was a massive bramble patch.

Lukani sprang up again with a growl of satisfaction and offered a hand down to our new sort of ally. The Rajinna man stared at Thatcher and me with what I could only guess was utter bewilderment. "N-Not just normal humans, then?" he wheezed shakily.

Lukani just grinned and slowly shook his head.

"Right, then. That's ... unexpected. And quite useful, I must say." He glanced us over again, as though inspecting us for some obvious signs of strangeness. On the surface, we didn't look like anything especially odd, though. Not by human standards, anyway. He'd have to try a bit harder than that.

I gave him a smirk and a wink, just for good measure.

The Rajinna man arched an eyebrow, but didn't respond. I could have sworn I saw one corner of his mouth quirk upward into a small grin, though.

"There's more soldiers coming toward us," Thatcher shouted suddenly, motioning to the level above us where another group of armed men were heading for the stairs that led straight to where we were standing. "Anyone else got a bright idea?"

I swapped a knowing sideways glance with Lukani. He nodded. Right. Time to work and hold nothing back.

"We are going down, yes?" Lukani asked our new Rajinna ally as he seized my hand.

"Ah, well, yes. There is a passage through the old temple. The entrance is hidden in the ravine below," he verified, still gawking at us like we were out of our minds. "It is much too far for your human pets to ju—"

"Just try to keep up," Lukani jabbed with a chuckle as he sprang headlong over the edge of the railing and into the open air, carrying me along with him.

W-Wait a second—what about Thatcher? Were we leaving him behind? How was he going to get down? Would that Rajinna guy help him, or would he get left behind?

There wasn't time to ask.

Wrapping my legs around Lukani's waist, I set my jaw and fought to focus past the wind howling in my ears as my stomach flipped and spun as we plummeted. Whatever happened, I couldn't lose it. I couldn't panic. He would protect me. He had a plan.

I trusted him completely.

My heartbeat skipped and raced as Lukani's body twisted and warped beneath me, swelling to a monstrous size and sprouting a hard shell, big snapping claws, and six long spidery legs. In a matter of seconds, he took on the shape of a brachyurid—the giant crab-like monster we had fought only days before. I bit back a scream and clung to his shell with all my strength as he suddenly latched onto one of the bridges and crawled along the underside of it. One of his eyestalks kept a watch on me while the other panned around, using his many legs and claws to climb nimbly from the bridge to the side of the canyon and down toward the ground.

Sweet Fates—I'd never seen him transform into something this big. Was he getting stronger, or ...?

People cried out in panic at the sight of us and soldiers fired off more rounds of arrows and crossbow bolts. But just like when we'd fought one of these monsters in the desert, every shot pinged harmlessly off his shell. It didn't slow him down for a second.

BOOOM!

We hit the ground at the bottom of the ravine, splashing into the water of a fast-moving, shallow river that snaked through the base of the steep canyon. Lukani immediately shifted back to his more human form, holding me in his arms and grinning from one pointed ear to the other. I managed a nervous, only slightly breathless smile back. He really was getting more powerful. More amazing. More incredible than anyone I'd ever known.

And now, more than ever, I wanted to kiss him again. To put my arms around his neck and let him know how much he meant to me. But there wasn't time.

Overhead, the burning city sent down a shower of ash and embers like snowfall. Bodies of fallen soldiers and townspeople lay stacked and sprawled in the river everywhere I looked, making the water run scarlet. I cringed and looked away, just in time to see a big glowing orb of sizzling energy strike down right behind us with a splash. No—not an orb.

Thatcher landed in the middle of the river, encased in his shimmering gold shield. He hit like a cannonball, bent on one knee, and then slowly stood. His shimmering shield dissipated around him as his eyes flashed like golden tongues of fire. He gave me a nod, and then his gaze snapped skyward—past us. His expression hardened, becoming a fierce scowl.

I whirled around, and my heart stopped cold in my chest. Everything went numb at once as my blood ran like arctic water. I couldn't blink. I couldn't scream. I couldn't even breathe.

A massive fireball—probably launched from a catapult—grew larger and larger as it sailed straight toward us like a scorching sun.

We only had seconds.

There was nowhere to run. There was nowhere to hide. Nowhere to go. We couldn't get out of the way. It would hit, and the impact would destroy everything in a two-hundred-yard radius, leaving nothing but ash and cinders behind.

Oh gods, we ... we were going to die.

Thatcher stepped past us and straight into the path of the incoming fireball without a single word. His powerful shoulders were flexed and squared, his hard jawline tensed, and his brow was locked into a look of focus as the golden rings of his eyes gleamed like heated metal. The wind blew through his shaggy blond hair as he forged forward and widened his stance, boots sloshing in the water. He bowed his head, preparing for something. His lips moved, as though whispering a final prayer.

I held my breath.

All the water began to rush away from his feet, leaving him on the smooth stones of the riverbed. One by one, all the pebbles and river rocks around him began to rise and levitate. Veins stood out against the skin of his arms and the side of his neck as he thrust both of his hands forward at once. Power hummed and sizzled through the air, arcing off his body and from the palms of his hands like white-hot bolts of lightning.

I could have sworn I heard him shout.

Blinding light burst outward from where Thatcher stood. I winced back, shielding myself against Lukani's side, but I could have sworn I saw two huge feathered wings unfold from his back—so bright and beautiful I couldn't manage more than a glimpse before my head throbbed in sharp pain and my eyes welled.

I squinted, barely able to make out the shape of an enormous hand of pure, brilliant energy stretching out toward the incoming fireball.

VOOOOM!

The hand caught the huge mass of wood, metal, and burning tar in mid-air like someone catching a ball. With a concussive *CRAACK,* the hand squeezed into a fist. It shattered the fiery orb, rocking the air with an explosion and showering burning debris that hissed and splashed into the river below.

Thatcher had—h-he had destroyed it ... without even touching it!

My whole body trembled, tangled up somewhere between awe and terror, as he turned around to face us again. Bright—gods it was so bright. My eyes burned and my head throbbed with a sharp pulse of pain, like I was trying to stare straight into the sun. I could barely see it as he spread his gleaming golden wings over us, shielding Lukani and me from the showering of fire, embers, and flaming globs of tar.

Then the world seemed to grow dim again. The air filled with the acrid stench of burned tar, scorched metal, and cinders. The sound of rushing water filled the eerie silence.

I dared to crack an eye open and peer at Thatcher again. He stood, his wings gone. And for a moment, he didn't move. He just stood there with his head bowed and his chest heaving in deep, slow breaths.

I let out a yelp of surprise when he suddenly staggered forward, trying to catch himself as his legs buckled. He hit the water on his hands and knees, and his whole body shook like he was having some sort of fit.

I ran to him, grasping his shoulder to try and get him back up. No—no, no, no! We couldn't lose him. Not now!

Pain seared through my hand and I jerked back. H-Hot! Fates, his body felt like it was on fire! Steam rose from his back and curled off his head and shoulders as he stayed down, wheezing and gasping like he couldn't get a full breath.

"Thatcher," I managed to gasp as I crouched down beside him, trying to splash him with the water to cool him off. "Oh gods, Thatcher! It's okay. You're all right. You—"

His head lifted slowly, staring up at me with his eyes still glowing a white-hot gold hue. Streams of that same molten color ran down his cheeks like tears as he stared at me, brow crinkled in a faint, confused frown. He blinked slowly, seeming to consider me like a complete stranger.

The voice that left his lips was all wrong. It was deeper, breathy, and strangely ethereal.

"Who is Thatcher?"

SOMETHING WAS WRONG—SO, *SO* WRONG. THATCHER, HE ... HE DIDN'T RECOGNIZE HIS own name? And judging by the way he was studying me with eerie mystification, he didn't seem to recognize me, either.

Oh, Fates, what was happening? What had he done? Had he pushed things too far? Used too much of his divine power? I knew he was a godling, sure. He was supposed to be the mortal host for the spirit of Ishaleon, God of Mercy. But ...

Was that who was staring back at me through his eyes right now?

I choked and sputtered, trying to think of something—anything—to say. What could I do? How could I get him to remember who he was? Gods, what was happening?!

Before I could even stammer out words, Thatcher's expression suddenly went slack. His eyes rolled back and he fell against me, toppling us both into the rushing cold water. His much larger body crushed down onto me, holding me under for a few seconds, until I felt his weight shift and someone dragged him off. Strong arms scooped under my back and hauled me upright.

I broke the surface with a choking gasp, wiping water from my eyes and trying to catch my breath. Lukani gripped me tight, his clothes drenched and his face and arms smudged with ash. Only a few feet away, our Rajinna friend had apparently caught up. Better late than never, I guess. He was busy hauling Thatcher back to his feet and regarding all of us with a look of barely controlled horror, almost like he might take the first chance he got and bolt. Maybe he was rethinking coming to find us in the first place. Hah. Well, if he really wanted a chance to make a run for it, now was the time. I certainly wasn't going to waste my time chasing him down.

Thatcher, on the other hand, seemed to be coming around. He shook his head, blinking hard and rubbing at his forehead and eyes. His legs and arms still trembled, but he appeared more or less normal again—no wings or anything glowing. Nothing out of the ordinary except where those lines had run from his eyes like molten tears. They had left red marks behind on his cheeks.

Burn marks.

Something raw and fractured, like fear tangled with recognition, skewed his rugged features as Thatcher finally looked up at me. His mouth opened like he wanted to say something, or ask me a question, but he didn't. His expression closed, eyes darkening as he looked down and away.

My stomach gave a twist of anxiety. What was that look? What was going on with him?

"I stand corrected, little brother," our Rajinna ally murmured in quiet reverence as he held Thatcher steady, then took a *big* step away from the three of us. "You do not walk with mere humans. You walk with gods."

"Not quite," I corrected. "But we can discuss it later. You mentioned a temple?"

He nodded quickly and took off for the edge of the river, beckoning frantically to a rough trail that twisted alongside the edge of the water farther down the ravine. "Come, come. I'm sure by now they've found the rest of your companions. They may require our assistance," he warned, his tone stiff and guarded as he stole glances at Thatcher out of the corner of his eye.

"Who?" I pressed. Was he talking about Violet and Uncle Reigh? Were they down here somewhere, too? He had mentioned a temple, and I knew Uncle Reigh was looking for someplace affiliated with Clysiros, the goddess of death.

"The rest of my clan," he replied, tilting his chin up proudly as he strode on ahead, tail swishing with every step.

Clan? What the heck was that supposed to mean?

I frowned and walked faster until I was walking side by side with him. He could prance on as fast as he liked; I wasn't going to take any more dancing around the truth from this guy. Not after we'd just saved him from being eviscerated by soldiers and squashed to jelly by catapult fire. "Just who are you, anyway?"

"I am called Neiko." He flicked me a quick, bemused grin and winked—mimicking my earlier gesture. "The rest, my little goddess, you'll likely need to see to believe."

⁂ 17 ⁂

CHAPTER SEVENTEEN

I wondered how our new sort-of friend, Neiko, had made it all the way down the sides of the canyon safely—right up until I saw him vanish with a swirl of dark smoke and reappear a little farther ahead. He did this over and over, blinking in and out of existence like a mirage, crossing over treacherous points in the path or heaps of burning debris that had fallen from the battle far above. As best I could tell, he could only go a relatively short distance, maybe twenty or thirty feet at most. Still, that was a useful trick.

Hmm. Could Lukani could do that, too? Was it an ability all Rajinna had? I made a mental note to ask about that later when we weren't busy running for our lives.

The earth tremored and shook with the low, thunderous booms and rumbles of battle. It rattled hunks of stone and dust free from the canyon walls. They hit the ground all around us like falling meteors, as though the sky itself were caving in. Ash and smoke choked the sky, and I coughed and wheezed with every stinging breath.

Neiko didn't slack off his pace, though, and forged onward through the maelstrom until we reached a crook in the river where the water swirled like a churning whirlpool before continuing on. The path around it was dangerously narrow, and centuries of rushing water had carved away at the stone and left it treacherously smooth. There were no handholds on the stone walls to the left, so I clung to the back of Lukani's belt as we moved cautiously along one at a time.

The wind snagged in my hair, blowing it around my face, but I still caught a glimpse of Neiko pausing at a spot right at the far end of the curved path. He put a hand on the smooth surface of the canyon wall, just below a faint mark etched into the rock. It was so corroded and weather-worn, I couldn't make out what the symbol actually was. But as soon as he touched it, the rock all around it gave a sudden lurch.

My breath caught as a narrow door swung inward, so well hidden in the features of the stone it might as well have been invisible except for that single marking. Fates, how had he known that was there?

Neiko didn't stop to explain himself. He squirmed through the tight doorway and beckoned for us to follow. No time to argue. We hurried after him, leaving the dull roar of battle and the constant *whoosh* of the river behind as we stepped into the cool darkness beyond. Our footsteps and heavy breathing echoed everywhere, and my boots slipped a little on the damp stone floor. The weak light from the soot-gray sky cast eerie shadows along a slim corridor that led straight ahead, flanked on either side by engraved buttresses that met at a sloping point overhead.

"What is this place?" Thatcher asked, his voice hushed and reverent as we passed through the crumbling remains of another arched doorway into a much larger vestibule.

At the front of our group, Neiko stopped. His golden eyes shone in the near-dark, reflecting the weak light from outside like a cat's. With a snap of his fingers, a little burst of flame sparked to life and hovered just above his fingertips. It illuminated the area around us and revealed the sad, almost lonely smile that brushed over his sharp features like the echo of a long-lost memory.

"The back entrance," he replied as he glanced upward to the lofty, vaulted ceilings where objects that resembled massive chandeliers hung still and silent, like stalactites of raw, flawless crystal.

"To what?" I whispered, too. Somehow, it just felt wrong to speak loudly here—as though something unseen slept nearby and didn't want to be disturbed.

"A fortress, castle, shop, or merely a meeting house? Who can say? Its original purpose has long been lost," Neiko explained, his deep voice wistful as it carried through the open space. "While the short-lived races quarrel and war on the surface, the memory of our ancient past still lies in sleep, buried and forgotten by most. But here we will find a safer route to the temple, and to the rest of the clan. Take care where you step and try to be silent—we are not the only ones hoping to use such passages. You have many enemies, it seems, both above and here below."

A chill of unease prickled along the back of my neck at the thought. The people that hunted us on the surface were easy enough to spot, although I didn't think the siege of the entire city was necessarily our fault. Er, well, hopefully not. Nar'Haleen had been at war with Damaria and Rienka for a long time, right? That didn't have anything to do with us.

But here below? He had to be referring to the Hands of Fate. Or maybe another enemy from Violet's past she hadn't mentioned to us yet? Another Sulam sort of figure. Of course, at the very least, it could just be more people working for this Sadeera-sorceress person who had taken Ronan and the codex and was now bent on total world destruction. Or possibly all of them. It was sort of a toss-up.

No wonder Dah seemed so tired. I'd only been at this world-saving business for a few weeks now, and I was already looking forward to a long, restful boat ride home.

Providing nothing here killed me first.

Moving swiftly and quietly, we followed Neiko deeper into the hidden ruins, delving farther along cavernous corridors and through wide-open chambers like ballrooms. Columns of solid jade stood in silence, and we left footprints in the thick layer of dust that had settled across the flawless marble floors. A faint, fragrant smell hung like a whisper in the still air—something like the lingering aroma of incense or herbs.

Every step and rustle of fabric seemed to echo on forever, lost to the endless labyrinth. My stomach fluttered and spun, wave after wave of chills still tingling along my skin and over my scalp as I stared around at every marvel Neiko's flicker of flame revealed. Somehow, it felt like this place was peering back at me, curious but frozen in time and unable to shake off all that dust. It kindled something deep in my chest—a tiny spark that made my teeth chatter and my fingers twitchy on my bow.

"Did the Rajinna build this place?" Lukani paused as we passed a large mosaic set into one of the walls depicting a highly detailed diagram of the moon phases against a field of carefully outlined stars.

Neiko cringed and shot him a look like he couldn't decide if that was an insult or if Lukani really was that ignorant. "No. We built no palaces or grand halls in this region. Our clans all came from the south, in the Endsoldan Wilds. Those of us who reside here were brought here against our will long ago, as has been the struggle of our kind for eons. Has no one taught you your own people's history?"

Lukani's head dipped low and his shoulders drew up, face flushing as he frowned back down at the floor. "Arlan taught me what he could, but he said the Rajinna are very secretive."

With the end of his tail flicking back and forth anxiously, Neiko's pace slowed until he walked right alongside Lukani. He didn't say anything and went on studying Lukani carefully, his expression softening little by little. His mouth quirked from one side to the other like he was chewing on the inside of his cheeks.

"I am the first you have ever seen?" Neiko guessed at last. "Other than yourself, of course."

Lukani nodded slightly.

"Ah. I see. Then ... I owe you an apology, little brother," he said with an awkward pat on the back. "You've much to learn. But your power is already impressive. I'm sure Father will be greatly pleased to see how strong you have become."

"I only know how to shapeshift." Lukani motioned to the flickering ball of flame that still hovered over Neiko's hand. "I can't do anything like that."

"Have you ever tried?" The red-skinned Rajinna grinned broadly. "We will teach this and more, little brother. But your magic is extraordinary. I have never seen such a thing in my lifetime. I suspect you have only just begun to come to know your true power."

Lukani's brow creased with an uncertain frown as he finally looked up to meet Neiko's confident smile. "Why do you keep calling me that? We aren't really family ... are we?"

Once again, Neiko's expression faltered somewhere between surprise and uncertainty. Like maybe he wasn't quite sure how to explain. Maybe he'd never had to before. Overall, Neiko was a fair bit taller than Lukani and looked much more mature. Somehow, it really did make them seem like they might be brothers.

And for Lukani's sake, a part of me hoped that might be true.

"We are all brothers—all family—within the clan. Father leads us, and we take care of one another," Neiko replied and rubbed at the back of his neck. "We do not keep track of family bloodlines as the humans and elves do."

"O-Oh." Lukani looked down again, disappointment plain on his features. It made my heart twist painfully. I knew that probably wasn't the answer he had wanted. He had hoped to find his real family. His parents. But the Southern Kingdoms were vast, and his people were few. The odds that Neiko had even found us at all were astronomical—although, I guess we had a certain Avoran sorcerer to thank for that.

Neiko put a hand on his shoulder, a little less awkwardly this time. "Take heart, young one. The others will be overjoyed to see you. Our clan lingers here in these human-infested lands in the hopes of finding others still trapped and enslaved here. We do whatever we can to liberate them so that we can gather what remains of our kin and teach them our ways. To have found you—so young and powerful—will be a cause for great celebration."

Lukani didn't reply, and we forged on in a tense, uncomfortable silence. Every step made my chest ache as I watched him from a few paces back. I didn't even need to see his face to be able to tell he wasn't happy. His shoulders and arms hung slack, and his tail only slowly swished back and forth. It put a hard knot of emotion in the back of my throat that throbbed every time I swallowed. He was right there—only a few feet away—but it felt like he might as well be on the surface of the moon. I wanted to go to him. To talk about this. To reassure him that everything would be okay.

But what could I say? Especially with Neiko still keeping pace right there beside him. I didn't want to get between them and make Lukani even more uncomfortable than he already was. He had waited so long to finally meet other Rajinna. He had come all this way with only fragments of hope that this moment might actually happen, and now that it had, I could practically feel the conflicted emotions wafting off him like heat from smoldering coals.

And there was nothing I could do to help him right now. Not without risking driving a wedge between him and Neiko—who clearly had serious issues when it came to having Thatcher and me along. Godling status and divine powers aside, he obviously had no love for humans or elves, and I was a mix of both. Butting into their business right now, while things still seemed so shaky, might ruin Lukani's only chance at getting to know more about his people. I wouldn't dare jeopardize that.

For now, I'd have to wait. I'd have to be patient and pray things didn't fall apart before I got a chance to talk to Lukani about any of it.

Squeezing my bow tightly in my hand, I shook my head a little and tried to clear all my frazzled, tangled thoughts. I had to focus and keep my mind on one battle at a time. We had to find Uncle Reigh and Violet, and then we had to get out of the area before—

Sluuurp.

I stopped suddenly as one of my boots stuck in something thick and sticky. What the —? I kicked and twisted, nearly tripping backward as I wrenched my foot free of a pile of something like black slime.

Thatcher caught me by the shoulders and held me steady, eyeing the heap of damp ooze with a lip curled. "Hey, any idea what this is?" he called up to Neiko.

Our Rajinna tour guide stopped and glanced back, already rolling his eyes as though we were wasting his time. Then he spotted the pile of goo, too. Neiko's features went slack and his face seemed to pale a little as he held his hand up higher. The flames dancing above his fingertips brightened, revealing more of the chamber around us, and even more piles of that strange, bluish slime. Heaps of it were caked along the walls and even slowly drizzling down from the ceiling.

Whoa. What the heck was that? Some sort of fungus? Or saliva?

"Th-That is a *slight* problem," Neiko rasped, his voice catching in a panicked squeak. His throat jumped as he swallowed hard, already taking slow, careful steps backward.

Thatcher and I swapped a worried sideways glance, and I got the sneaking suspicion we were both thinking the same thing: Great, what now?

"Man-made or monster?" Thatcher demanded, his tone low and ominous as he dipped two fingers into the slime and rubbed them together, as though trying to figure out what it was.

Ew.

"Monster," Neiko answered in a panicked whisper. "Very much monster."

"Outstanding," Thatcher growled. He wiped his hand on his pants and reached to draw his sword.

I took that as my cue and immediately slipped an arrow from my quiver to fit my bowstring. Curse it, I only had roughly a dozen or so arrows left, and no way to get more. I had sort of been counting on the hope that we might cross a market on our way out of the city so I could buy another bundle of them.

I'd just have to pick my shots more carefully from now on.

"Not, ah, not the word I would choose for it," Neiko whispered haltingly as he waved us on with renewed urgency. "Perhaps the commotion on the surface has already drawn its attention elsewhere. We, um, we should go. Right now, preferably. And, uh, see that you don't disturb anything. Or speak. Or breathe too loudly."

18

CHAPTER EIGHTEEN

The dull roar of running water filled the gloom of the cavernous ruins as we rushed onward for what felt like hours. My legs and feet began to ache, and the strap from my quiver and pack of supplies rubbed my shoulder raw. But Neiko only slowed his brisk pace whenever we passed a crossroads where the huge halls would intersect. He stopped for an instant, glancing around like he was trying to figure out which way to go, then took off down another passage. The farther we went, the more my stomach twisted up into knots. We were trusting this guy with our lives. Maybe Uncle Reigh and Violet's, too, if they were counting on us for help. Was this really the right choice? Or was this guy leading us to our doom?

I didn't know. And it didn't seem like a good idea to question his intentions where he would definitely overhear it.

The minutes dragged, and the noise of the rushing water grew louder. The air also became colder and heavier, with a damp, mineral smell.

Down a tall, narrow corridor riddled with cracked and crumbling stone steps, we finally emerged in a massive chamber split by a wide, rushing river. The sheer drop from our side of the chasm led straight down to the churning black water far below. The only way across that I could see was a long bridge made of polished black stone that stretched over the expanse, arching gracefully from one side to the other. A pair of obsidian statues carved in the shape of jackals stood at each end of the bridge, the light from Neiko's flame making their ruby eyes sparkle.

Something about them made my chest feel tight and cold, like a frosty hand was squeezing at my heart.

Neiko coughed a relieved chuckle as he turned to face us. "Ah, yes! Here it is! It's been so many centuries; I was beginning to worry I had taken a wrong turn."

Thatcher's eyes narrowed suspiciously. "Centuries?"

"Yes, yes. One forgets after so much time," Neiko said, flapping a hand nonchalantly. "But I still found it—the entrance to Clysiros's temple. We should find the others already inside. Father directed me to rescue you, and we will make our escape to Dumathis through the gateway in the temple."

"No, I mean ... you're *centuries* old?" Thatcher still didn't look convinced.

Neiko made a strange face, like that question didn't make any sense to him. "Of course I am. Why is this surprising to you? Don't you know Rajinna live for many centuries?" He motioned to Lukani with his free, non-fiery hand. "He is young, but surely you know he must at least be nearing his one-hundredth year for his powers to be so well developed, yes?"

Lukani cringed and shrugged slightly, avoiding eye contact with all of us as his mouth skewed to one side sheepishly. "I-I don't know exactly how old I am. Arlan could only guess. But I have been living under his care for around fifty years, I think."

My mouth fell open. Lukani had been living in Maldobar for *fifty years?!* No. That couldn't be right. It had to be a misunderstanding. Lukani looked like he was close to my age, no older than seventeen at the most! How could he possibly be a hundred years old?

I wanted to ask, but every word seemed to hang in my throat. My face burned and I couldn't force my lungs to even take in a full breath. The whole world seemed to spin out of control around me until my gaze finally locked with his. Lukani stared back at me, his sharp features skewed in a look of silent, frantic worry and his hands clenched tight at his sides.

All I could do was stand there and stare straight back at him.

"I suppose you're like the Avoran elves in that way?" Thatcher reasoned, seeming a lot less shocked by this news. "Is that a common trait among the ancient races? Magical power and incredibly long lifespans?"

Neiko smirked approvingly and he nodded. "Indeed. Those whose ancestry first stemmed from the gods eons ago share many such qualities."

O-Oh. Well, that ... sort of made sense. In a weird way.

It didn't make Lukani's actual age any easier for me to process, though. Uncle Reigh was absolutely right. The chances had been slim before, but there was no way my dah would ever approve of Lukani and me being together now.

And really ... how could we?

My heart steadily began to sink as those thoughts washed over me. Lukani and I were so different. And deep down, I knew he was meant to be here, in the Southern Kingdoms, with his people. That's what was best for him, right?

My gaze fell from his as a strange numbness settled over me like the autumn's first frost. My throat suddenly felt tight, stiff, and dry. Blinking made my eyes want to tear up. I bit down hard, trying to keep it from showing, but my heartbeat pounded so hard it was like someone punching me in the chest. I had to turn away.

I couldn't explain it. I didn't understand this feeling at all. It was as though a giant rift had opened up between Lukani and me—a distance I had no idea how to cross. I didn't even know if I should try. He'd never want to go back to Maldobar, and I certainly wasn't going to ask him to choose me over his people.

Maybe our being together had been doomed from the start.

A low rumble in the distance made the cavern around us shudder faintly. The ground vibrated under my boots, just enough that dust and pebbles showered down from overhead. Thatcher took a step closer to me, his blade still clenched in his hand. I readied my fingers on my bowstring, staring all around for some sign of what was happening. Was it a monster? Or just another echo from the battle going on somewhere on the surface?

A sudden, intensely cold pressure crushed down over my chest, making my spine go stiff and my lungs constrict with a sharp gasp. It hit me like an icy dagger straight to the heart.

Thatcher stiffened, too. His jawline went rigid and his shoulders flexed as he sank down into a preparatory stance with his sword raised. With his steely gaze focused straight ahead down the opposite end of the bridge, toward the entrance to the temple, I heard him mutter, "Here we go again."

Oh no.

SOMETHING WHIZZED PAST MY HEAD SO CLOSELY I FELT THE BREEZE AS IT PASSED MY cheek. Crap! That was too close.

I instantly dropped to a knee and drew my bow back, taking aim down the length of the bridge. With my eye trained down the shaft of my arrow, I held my breath and waited for a target. There! A figure was moving in the dark tunnel on the other end of the bridge. No. Two figures.

I recognized the ripple of red and white hair bobbing amidst the shadows. Was that ... Uncle Reigh and Violet? Gods and Fates, it was!

They sprinted toward us, hand in hand, expressions blanched in primal fear as small black arrows zipped by them and pinged off the stone bridge. Strange screeching and yowling noises filled the chamber, but I couldn't tell where they were coming from.

Until I saw the squatty, almost froglike creatures climbing the walls like a swarm of demon toads. They crawled along the walls and skittered across the floor, occasionally stopping to fire tiny, crudely made bows in our direction. Some lobbed spears, and others waved bone clubs as they shrieked in fury.

"Goblins!" Neiko hissed in dismay, staggering back with his wisp of fire still crackling in his hand. With his other, he slipped two fingers into his mouth and blew a shrill, whistling note. It echoed strangely in the air, seeming to resonate much longer than it should have. Something about it made chills tingle over my skin. Was that some sort of magic?

There wasn't time to ask.

"There's too many!" I shouted over the screeches of the incoming horde. I didn't have enough arrows to make much of a dent this time. At least, not without risking hurting Uncle Reigh and Violet, too.

"Then we will have to be creative," Neiko growled.

BOOOM!

The chamber shuddered around us again, shaking bigger chunks of stone free from the cavern ceiling. They hit the water like pounding fists and choked the air with dust.

Okay, I had no experience dealing with goblins. We didn't have those in Maldobar, as far as I knew. But I didn't need anyone to tell me that whatever was making that sound was not a slimy little toad-like creature—or even a hundred of them, for that matter.

Neiko's face paled and he drew back, pupils narrowing to pinpoints as a huge, slimy arm suddenly burst from the tunnel behind Uncle Reigh and Violet, taking a swing at them. Its huge curled talons missed them by inches and sparked against the stone floor, flaying a few goblins that weren't quick enough to get out of the way.

My muscles locked up solid as the realization hit me like a smack to the face. Those goblins weren't chasing them. They were running for their lives.

"DON'T JUST STAND THERE! RUN!!" Uncle Reigh waved his arms like a maniac, still sprinting for his life straight toward us.

R-Run? Right. We should—

A screaming, squealing cry broke through the air, so loud and shrill it made my vision swerve and everything seemed to spin. I stumbled, almost falling. Beside me, Lukani hissed in dismay and seized me around the waist, dragging me back a few steps.

The creature emerged, writhing free of the tunnel entrance with a swarm of goblins fleeing all around it like rats from a sinking ship. Its bulbous body was dragged along by eight long, bony legs almost like an insect. But its huge head and wide jaws bristled with rows upon rows of fangs. I couldn't see any eyes, but familiar-looking ribbons of gooey bluish slime leaked from its mouth and smeared over the floor. More of the scrambling goblins got stuck in the goo and floundered helplessly.

The colossal monster burst into the chamber, finally twisting free of the tunnel opening, and immediately opened its jaws wide. A long tongue shot out from the back of its throat, almost like a chameleon or a frog, and hit the ground right at Violet's heels with a *BAM* and splatter of blue slime.

Oh, gods, what was that thing?!

Another rush of strange, cold pressure squeezed at my chest as Uncle Reigh flung a hand back toward the creature, slinging an arcing beam of crackling purple energy at its gaping mouth. It hit with a crack and sizzle, like a bolt of lightning, but the monster just snapped its huge jaws and kept coming.

"Your magic will not help you!" Neiko shouted. "Not unless you've some fire at your disposal!"

"Don't you?" Thatcher snarled back at him.

Neiko shot him a crazed glare. "It is not my specialty!"

Fire? I scrambled to think—to come up with some sort of idea of what to try. I didn't know if I could do anything like that!

"Get behind me," Lukani commanded, suddenly shoving his way to the front of our group. His tail swished slowly back and forth as he prowled forward, pointed canine teeth bared in a snarl. A shimmer of golden scales formed on his cheeks and forearms an instant before he began to change.

His shoulders hunched forward, rippling with corded muscle that grew and warped. Two wings burst from his back as his form unfolded into a large, golden-scaled dragon. He stood every bit as large as my father's king drake, Mavrik, filling the chamber with a thunderous growl as he faced the incoming monster. With one beat of his wings, he sprang from the bridge, over Uncle Reigh and Violet, and landed right in the creature's path.

Neiko froze up, staring up at Lukani with his eyes wide and his expression totally blank.

"We have to go! We have to get out of here, *right now!*" Uncle Reigh was still shouting as he and Violet finally met us on the bridge.

"No!" Neiko hissed defiantly, pointing back down the tunnel they'd just come from. Yeah. The one dripping with blue slime and infested with goblins—all on the other side of two brawling giant creatures. "There is only one gateway in this place that still functions, and it lies in the temple. *That* is our way out!"

Uncle Reigh blinked in shock, looking Neiko over from head to foot like he thought he might be hallucinating. Then he snapped an infuriated glare back to Thatcher and me. "Who the heck is this guy?"

No one got a chance to answer. We all cringed back as Lukani spat a plume of fire at the giant, eight-legged monster. It lit up the whole cavern and filled the air with the acrid smell of dragon venom. The slimy creature recoiled and screeched again, pitching and flailing as it tried to get away from the flames.

But that's the thing about dragon venom—it's as sticky as it is explosive.

"We can chat later, let's get to work," Thatcher yelled over the chaos, rushing in to cleave a group of goblins that had finally reached us on the bridge. "Pick a direction and kill something in it!"

PART FOUR

CLARKE

19

CHAPTER NINETEEN

Everything was chaos.

Magic sparked and sizzled with blinding flashes of light and waves of scalding heat. Arrows zipped through the air in every direction. Swords clashed. Blood spattered the stone floor.

And for a few seconds, I was paralyzed.

How had this happened? What was I doing here? I-I couldn't do this. I wasn't a fighter! My mind raced, thoughts blurring together as I watched the room around me explode into warfare.

Something crashed into me from behind and I fell forward, hitting the ground face-first. Someone pinned me to the ground with a hand on the back of my head just as a column of white-hot flame roared over me. G-Gods, was that from Ronan? Whoever had saved me quickly jumped back and seized the back of my tunic. They yanked me to the side, and I flailed, managing to get a glimpse of that scary dark-headed man with the glowing sword. Murdoc, I think?

"You're supposed to be a god, right?" He growled as he yanked me closer and gave me a hard, wild-eyed stare. "Then either fight or get over there and open that gateway!"

I gasped in a sharp breath, and suddenly everything around me seemed to get clearer—like breaking the surface of water after holding my breath far too long. R-Right. Yes. I had to do something!

Murdoc dove back into combat, surging forward with impossible speed and blurring through strikes and slashes with the Hands of Fate agents that rushed him from every side. His sword hummed with power, cutting through enemy blades and armor like they were nothing but warm butter. His eyes flashed with wrath, reflecting the spells that burst in the air all around us.

I had never seen anyone fight like that.

Something about it put an urgent fire in my gut, and I started for the gate at a sprint. Explosions shook the chamber all around me, lighting up the gloom with strobing bursts of light as Isandri and Ronan dueled like two avenging angels. His teeth bared and features drawn into a crazed snarl, Ronan sent waves of scorching heat lashing through the air with every wave of his hands. His eyes blazed like rings of molten metal, and he didn't seem to care at all when his assaults caught his own comrades in the crossfire.

Isandri darted as fast as a shadow, evading every one of his assaults and sending back a burst of silvery power from the crystal at the end of her staff. The runes on her ebony skin shone, and her body almost seemed to contort in and out of a feline shape when she moved. "You must stop this now, Ronan!" she called out to him. "Your mother sent us here to see you back home! She waits for you, right now!"

Ronan's expression tightened, eyes narrowing and jaw clenching as he made a swirling gesture with both of his hands. On command, a wall of flame closed around her, spinning into the shape of a huge orb that engulfed her like a fiery prison. He staggered back when the sphere of fire suddenly burst outward with a radiant flash of light. Isandri stood, her staff firmly in hand, glowering at him through the curling smoke that rose from the ground all around her.

"You may be fiend-blooded, but you cannot contend with me," she warned. "I do not wish to harm you, but if that is what it takes to bring you back to your senses—so be it!"

Ronan let out a cry of crazed rage in reply, and the two clashed again. He lashed out with a whip made of pure flame, and she deftly dodged each strike. From somewhere nearby, I could barely make out Edarix's pleading shouts as he begged Ronan to stop, too.

But nothing seemed to be working. And I didn't know how long they could keep him at bay.

I nearly tripped over my own feet as I scrambled through the frenzy, reaching for the place in my tunic's breast pocket where a tiny little ball of fur shivered in fear. I'd promised Trick I wouldn't let anything happen to him. Now, I just had to keep that promise. Pulling him out of his hiding place, I staggered to a halt and set him on the ground. "Go find a place to hide!" I urged.

Trick didn't hesitate, and scurried off across the chamber. Good. He would be okay. He was clever.

Now I had to do my part and get that gateway open.

I just hoped my divine power would be enough.

The Avoran man, Arlan, already stood next to it with his hands pressed against the rune-carved frame. With his sharply featured face drawn in a look of desperation, veins standing out against his neck and forehead and body trembling like he might collapse at any second. The runes on the frame around his hands only flickered slightly. Whatever power he had; it wasn't going to be enough.

He needed help—*my* help.

The woman, Auguress Riva, howled in rage as she lingered in the doorway, using her Hands of Fate minions to keep Jaevid and the others at bay. Her eyes glowed white, hands outstretched as she summoned an all-too-familiar orb of crackling energy that began to form between her palms. It lit up the chamber like a small sun, making the air vibrate with incredible force.

Our gazes locked from across the chamber, and I glared at her with every ounce of defiance I had. She had beaten me once. It wouldn't happen again.

Auguress Riva let out a screech of frustration as she launched that sparking, sizzling orb of power straight at me. It sailed like a comet, blowing my companions and the Hands of Fate fighters backward as it passed them—heading straight for me.

Isandri cried out in alarm, raising her staff like she was going to try deflecting it.

"CLARKE!" Noa yelled my name as he scrambled back to his feet.

Garnett whirled on a heel, her expression steely with determination like she meant to try to shield me however she could.

None of them had the time.

VOOOM!

It hit me full force, but I didn't resist. I didn't wince away. I set my jaw and thrust out a hand, letting that power overtake me like a tidal wave. It scorched my skin and sizzled through my veins. My joints ached under the strain. Every muscle drew tighter and tighter until my arms and legs shook. My focus splintered like cracked glass. I couldn't hold on much longer. Regardless of what spirit might be caged within me, my body was still just a human. Flesh and bone that could easily break.

Something snapped deep within me—a divine presence that cracked through all the boundaries of my soul like an eggshell.

Avgior.

His presence burst from the depths of my soul, igniting strength and long-suffered fury in every fiber of my being. His strength surged through my body, forming a shield of rippling light around me like a second skin. I stood steady, holding Riva's orb of energy in my hand like she'd just tossed me a ball. Our gazes met again, and her expression flickered between shock and blind anger.

With one squeeze, I shattered that orb into a shimmering mist in my palm.

"You have troubled me long enough," Avgior's voice rumbled from my throat, deep and menacing like the low growl of a lion. *"You will not interfere again."*

"You dare to challenge me?" Riva seethed. "I will break every part of you, boy!"

"You can certainly try," I growled.

I don't think any of us expected to glance up at that moment and see a furious dwarven woman riding a one-thousand-pound grizzly bear with the arm of a fallen enemy dangling from its jaws barreling past. Garnett howled a manic laugh as she hurled one of her double-headed hand axes ahead, cleaving through another enemy. Wow. These people really were insane.

I'd never been happier that we were on the same side.

"You think just because I'm bound in this mortal prison I cannot end you?" Riva hissed as she drew that long, wicked black dagger from within her robes. "I will do what should have been done long ago."

The sight of that weapon made my heartbeat stammer and freeze in my chest. A cold shiver prickled at the back of my neck. An ancient memory, long lost to the depths of time, echoed through my brain like the distant toll of a bell. Betrayal. Pain. Eons of waiting in crushing silence.

All because of that blade. A dagger that killed anything it pierced in the heart—be they mortal or divine.

The Blade of Souls.

She started to move, to take a step in my direction. I braced myself, ready for whatever she threw at me. I wouldn't back down this time.

A glimmer of silvery light in the doorway behind her caught my attention. It wavered and grew, forming into the outline of something tall and humanoid. Was that ... a woman?

It happened so fast. One moment, Riva stood there with that blade clenched tightly in her fist. The next, a slender, human-looking woman with long, rippling brown hair and eyes of blazing gold materialized directly behind her. The woman moved with a smooth and effortless grace, seizing Riva's wrist and swiping the blade from her hand.

Then she stabbed Riva straight through the back with it.

Riva's body jerked. Her eyes went wide and her back arched. She sputtered a spray of blood that ran from her lips, down her chin, and spattered on the ground.

G-Gods. What was ... what was happening?!

The woman reached around, a strange smile playing over her lips as she placed a hand over Riva's chest, right at her heart. Her palm began to glow, and a sickly green light flashed in the mysterious woman's eyes. She drew her hand slowly back with an exaggerated grasping motion, and a strange tendril of curling golden mist ebbed from Riva's chest. It followed the woman's hand like a ribbon of light, hovering around her hand until she snapped her fist closed.

Riva dropped to the floor, her expression empty and lifeless.

The woman slowly straightened, rolling her head back and closing her eyes, as though she were relishing the feeling of that energy now coursing through her veins. Her shoulders rose and fell with a deep, sighing breath.

"E-Empress Leysa!" Edarix gasped nearby, his face blanched in shock.

What? Did he recognize her?

At the sound of that name, the woman's eyes opened. She stared at him wordlessly as a frigid, disturbingly wide smile spread over her face. "Oh, Edarix, my dearest friend. You have been so helpful," she cooed. "First, providing me with all the information I could ever want, and now leading me straight here."

The longer she stared at him, the more her features seemed to change like a rippling mirage over the scorching desert sands. Her ears became long and pointed. The dark color leaked from her hair like paint being washed from a silken banner, leaving it a silvery pale gold. Beautiful feathered wings of shimmering silver unfolded from her back, as graceful and elegant as a swan's.

"Just look at all the prizes you've brought me. You have more than surpassed my expectations," she praised as her golden eyes considered all of us with a chilling indifference that made my blood run like ice water. Her chin dipped, smile widening to show her teeth, when her gaze finally halted on Arlan. "Hello again, Zarvan. How lovely to see you again so soon."

ACROSS THE CHAMBER, HIS HANDS STILL GRIPPING THE FRAME OF THE GATEWAY, ARLAN stared back at the angelic elven woman without making a sound. His chest heaved in shallow, uneven breaths, and his face twitched and spasmed. His mouth hung open, jaw moving as though he were trying to summon words.

He only managed one.

"Sadeera ..."

All around the chamber, the battle steadily went silent.

The few remaining Hands of Fate agents had frozen in place, focused on the elven woman like they weren't sure what to do next. Likewise, all my companions stood eerily still, staring at her with mixed expressions of terror and fury.

The only one who seemed able to move was Ronan. Weaving on his feet, he blinked owlishly around at everyone, like he didn't know where he was or what had happened. When he spotted Jaevid and Arlan, his expression collapsed in anguish and he hit the ground on his knees with a frantic sob.

If Sadeera noticed, it didn't show. She stepped over Riva's motionless corpse, the lengths of her sheer, silvery gown flowing around her and that metal blade still held tight in her hand. With a snap of her fingers, all the agents snapped to attention as their eyes flickered with a spark of that greenish light. They immediately began to move, converging on us with renewed energy and what seemed like far more strength than ever before.

O-Oh, gods. She had them under some sort of mind control spell—like the one Riva had been using on Ronan!

The roar of battle and clashing of blades boomed throughout the chamber, drowning out everything else. Sadeera stepped lightly through the frenzy as though it were entirely invisible to her, her gaze still fixed on Arlan. Jaevid made a wild dive for her as she passed, swinging his scimitar in a lightning-fast strike aimed right at her neck.

Sadeera's hand snapped up so fast I couldn't even see her move. She caught the blade in her hand, eyes narrowing slightly in annoyance. Jaevid shouted, bearing down with all his strength. Sweat drizzled down the sides of his face, his arms shaking under the force. Sadeera cast the scimitar a brief, sideways glance, and gave it a flippant shove away. Jaevid flew backward, hitting the ground with a *crunch* and rolling several times before he lay motionless right at Murdoc's feet.

"So much for the Hero of Maldobar," she snickered and turned her focus back to Arlan. "Now, brother dear, why don't we finally settle our score? I wouldn't want to pass into divinity with any old grudges still nipping at my heels. And it seems you've all but spent your power on this pathetic lot. What a waste. Well, at least this matter will be resolved quickly."

Arlan pushed away from the gateway, stepping forward to meet her with his golden eyes ablaze and his expression twisted with wrath. "I will die before I see you take even one step beyond this chamber," he seethed in a deep growl.

Her lips bowed with another wry, satisfied smile. "Yes," she agreed. "You will."

20

CHAPTER TWENTY

"Fall back! Retreat!" Murdoc shouted over the battle, barely holding off the hailstorm of strikes from the Hands of Fate agents that had him cornered at the back of the chamber.

But there was no retreating. Not from this.

Arlan was the first to fling a blistering beam of energy at Sadeera, but she knocked it aside with another wave of her hand without even blinking.

BOOOM!

It hit the stone wall and left a big, smoking crater.

He released a second bolt with a frantic shout, wobbling like his knees were about to buckle underneath him.

Her smile vanished, and she held out a hand, easily deflecting the beam of power and sending it blitzing right back toward him.

BOOOM!

The second impact shook the room and blew Arlan backward. His body flew like a ragdoll, skidding over the ground and smacking up against the frame of the gateway.

Sadeera moved, fast and soundless like a phantom, blurring the distance between them. She loomed over him, nose wrinkled in disgust. Her lip twitched, tugging at a sneer. Arlan let out a whimper of pain as she suddenly surged down, snatching him up by the front of his tunic, and holding him upright so he was forced to meet her gaze.

"Did you really think you could stand in my way?" she taunted. "Did you believe that Zarvan, our family's greatest disappointment, would truly be able to stop what has always been an inevitably? I am the future, brother. I am the one true goddess this wretched mortal world deserves."

No.

No, I wouldn't allow it.

Avgior's strength and rage blazed through me, rising like a tide from the depths of my soul. Pearlescent scales of white rose on my skin. My nails hardened and curled into long black talons. Spined horns jutted from my forearms and calves, and curved horns grew from my temples and arced around my ears. Leathery draconic wings burst from my back and filled the chamber with a blinding flash of light.

It must have caught Sadeera's attention, because she stopped and looked back over her shoulder at me. Her expression hardened, brow locking to a furious grimace. She dropped Arlan to the ground and turned to face me, spreading her own wings wide like an invitation.

Fine. If she wanted a fight—she'd found one.

I would teach her the real meaning of divine wrath.

We met in the middle of the chamber, our auras blazing like the sun and sending currents of raw divine power crackling and bursting outward like prominences from the surface of a star. Murdoc and Edarix dove for cover. Noa cried my name, shielding his face and struggling to stay on his feet until Garnett and Roxus rushed to seize him by the shoulders and drag him back. Isandri threw herself over Jaevid in her feline form, trying to shield him beneath her shimmering wings.

There was nothing I could do for them. I couldn't afford to be careful—not with so much at stake. This woman had to be stopped. She could not be allowed to live. So, I would drag her to the very steps of the Sivanth myself.

"I HAVE FELLED GODS BEFORE YOU, BOY!" Sadeera screeched as she struck out with that dark blade. "AND MANY MORE WILL FOLLOW YOU! YOUR ESSENCES WILL ALL BE MINE!"

White tongues of fire leaked from between my fang-like teeth as I snarled, knocking her attacks aside and lunging for her throat with my claw-tipped fingers. I'd crush the life out of her. Right here. Right now.

My hand closed around her throat, and I started to *squeeze*.

Pouring on every shred of power I could summon, the temperature in the chamber rose like a furnace. I heard familiar shouts of alarm around me—my companions trying to fall back and get out of the way. A few Hands of Fate agents who were standing too close screamed as they caught fire. The rest had enough sense to flee, running for the chamber's only functioning exit.

Only a few of them actually made it.

With a primal yell, Murdoc hurled his blade across the room. It spun end over end with blinding speed and hit the last agent right in the back with a *TWAAANG*. It pinned him to the stone wall like an insect on display.

Impressive.

There was a wild light in his hazel eyes as Murdoc stared up at us—and in an instant, I saw it. That look. A mutual understanding. This was their chance to escape. To see this done. I was the only one who could hold Sadeera at bay long enough.

I was the one who had to stay behind.

Murdoc spun on a heel, holding his hand out wide as he sprinted the length of the room toward the gateway. The runes on his sword glowed brightly, crackling with power. It flew out of the wall and zipped across the chamber to land firmly back in his grasp. He seized Noa by the arm, dragging him kicking and flailing toward the gateway while using his own body to block the raging heat of my divine power. Garnett and the massive bear followed not far behind, grabbing Arlan on their way. Isandri carried Jaevid's limp body on her back as she shifted effortlessly into her winged feline form, crossing the room in two bounds. Edarix hurried after her while keeping a guiding hand on Ronan's back. He steered the boy toward the gateway, running like the hounds of doomsday were right on their heels.

They would make it.

I just had to open the door.

"How long do you dream you can restrain me?" Sadeera hissed, every word pure venom as she leaned into the grip of my hand. "You are one essence trapped in a sack of mortal meat. I am a divine-touched ancient with the essences of two of your kind already inside me! I will break you, and then I will snuff out every one of your pathetic friends before your corpse has even cooled!"

I snarled back, my vision swerving in and out of focus. Everything seemed to go red, and my chest spasmed with a sudden ripping sensation like someone was slowly tearing my body open like a banana peel.

I couldn't do this. Not for much longer.

With a desperate shout, I flung Sadeera to the side with all my strength. She flew, smashing down into the ground with a *BOOOM* that buckled the stone floor.

I sped forward immediately—straight toward the gateway. Every muscle in my body screamed in agony. My skin split and burned away, revealing more of those pearlescent scales. There was no turning back. No other options. She would get back up. She would come after me.

I had to make it in time.

I stretched out a hand, flinging every ounce of power I could muster directly at the top of the gateway. The bolt of power left my fingertips like a ray of pure sunlight, gold and gleaming. It hit with a blinding flash, igniting all the runes on the tall, slender frame like trails of molten gold down both sides. The center of it suddenly went dark as a bluish-black energy swirled and spun as though it were mirroring a reflection straight into the abyss.

"GO!" I thundered.

Isandri sprang through first, still carrying Jaevid. Her body disappeared into the vortex, gone without a trace. Edarix, however, stopped right before the portal and began waving the others through it frantically.

Ronan, Arlan, Garnett, and the bear followed.

Murdoc fought Noa, wrestling him toward the gateway and finally giving him a violent shove backward through the portal. He lunged for Edarix next, snatching him by the front of his robes and flinging him through the portal next.

Then Murdoc hesitated. His gaze caught mine again, eyes suddenly going wide and mouth opening like he was going to call out to me.

Pain exploded through my side. It made my wings crumple and I fell, hitting the ground face-down. Stars danced in my vision as I shakily lifted my head up. I stared through the cracked lenses of my spectacles at where Sadeera still had her wicked black blade plunged deep into my side. Blood oozed from it, and my thoughts seemed to all blur together into a hazy fog. M-My power was ... fading. My scales and wings were already gone.

I couldn't hang on much longer.

She stood over me, her whole face red and twitching with fury. She ripped the blade free with one jerk and raised it again, my blood running through her fingers and down her arm. "Now your power will be mine!" Sadeera screeched, aiming that dagger straight at my heart.

I held my breath. Everything around me seemed to slow down, as though the seconds had stretched to minutes. I couldn't move. I couldn't defend myself. Pain surged through every muscle and bone, stemming from that place where she had already stabbed me once.

I barely caught a glimpse of movement out of the corner of my eye as Murdoc plunged through the shimmering vortex. And it was as though my entire being sighed in relief. They were all gone. They were safe, for now. My work was finished.

I could die in peace.

CRAAACK!

An explosion rocked the chamber, splintering the ceiling and floor with a web of cracks and making Sadeera stumble and falter halfway through her killing strike. We both stared up in mute shock as the gateway crumbled. I winced as it suddenly exploded outward, bursting and flinging chunks of golden stone in every direction.

Wh ... What?

"NO!" Sadeera screamed, stepping over me. She rushed to the raised pedestal where the gateway had been, intact and functioning, only a moment before. The foul blade clattered to the ground as she came to her knees, gathering up a few shards of the golden frame and staring at them in pure horror.

Then, Sadeera's crazed glare slowly lifted—fixing on a slender, feminine figure that stood in the doorway.

"*Tch*—that does smart a bit after so long," the figure spoke in a familiar, breathy voice. My heartbeat stammered and lurched, grinding to a painful halt as I watched a beautiful elven woman stride smoothly into the room. The lengths of her sky-blue gown and deep purple scholar's robe billowed around her, and her long black hair was woven into a complex plaited braid all the way down to her knees.

She looked down at me with a smile as calm as a still winter's morning. "There you are, Clarke, darling. We've been waiting for you."

Tears welled in my eyes as her name leaked past my lips like a desperate prayer. "High Inquisitor Bellavora."

"YOU!" Sadeera still crouched low, now gripping the blade in one hand and a chunk of the shattered portal in the other. "You dare defy me?!"

A cold prickle of primal fear skittered up my spine as Bellavora's gaze went as cold as the deepest depths of the sea. She stared back at Sadeera, not blinking or showing any sign of emotion. As she calmly walked forward, Bellavora let the dark purple robe slip from her shoulders and fall to the floor, revealing two angelic wings of sweeping black feathers. "You forget whose house you stand in, heretic," she said, her tone as sharp as a dragon's talon. "Within these walls, my word is law. Begone. I'll not warn you again."

Sadeera's whole body flexed, puffing up like an angry cat as she sucked in tight, manic breaths. The look of crazed rage on her face made veins stand out in the whites of her eyes as she slowly stood up again. Her wings unfurled, currents of energy whipping up winds around the chamber like she meant to face Bellavora head-on.

The High Inquisitor's eyes narrowed. Her mouth set into a firm, reproachful line. Before Sadeera could make a move or say another word, she raised a hand and muttered something under her breath.

CRACK—VOOOOM!

The snap of her fingers split the stone floor before her, opening up a zig-zagging crevice that sliced across the ground straight for Sadeera.

Sadeera staggered, her expression paling as she recoiled. She spat furious words between her teeth—ancient curses I barely understood. With a beat of her wings and a flourish of her hand, Sadeera's form suddenly vanished in a burst of whirling silver dust.

G-Gone ... she was gone.

"And thus, the House of Cirithal threatens the harmony of the spheres once again," Bellavora sighed, her slender brows drawn up in a look of distress as she stared at the shower of silvery dust that still drifted soundlessly down to the ground. Her eyes fell closed, and for a few seconds, she stood in reverent silence.

Then, she finally looked back over at me. Her lips bowed into another gentle smile as she approached and bent down over me, combing her fingers through my hair like someone consoling a child. "I am so pleased you made it this far, Clarke. You've done so well. But I'm afraid we cannot rest now. You must stand and find your strength. Your friends will need you again very soon."

I couldn't stop my chin from trembling as I blinked up at her. Was this even real? Or had I already died and this was some vision of heaven? How could she be alive? There had been no other survivors from the attack on the Compendium Library. At least, not any that Noa's village had been able to find.

But here she was, alive and well.

"H-How?" I managed to croak. "How did you find us? How did you know we were—?"

"Clarke!" I recognized another feminine voice right away as it echoed across the chamber.

Propping myself up on an elbow, I stared in total bewilderment as Kaili ran across the debris-strewn room with her arms open and her cheeks already flushed and wet with tears. "Oh, thank the gods! You're alive!"

She hit me at full speed, wrapping her arms around my neck and sobbing against my shoulder. I could barely move, though. Still staring at High Inquisitor Bellavora, I tried frantically to piece together how any of this was even possible.

"Your darling friend here tracked me down as soon as she arrived in Uru'Nai. She's quite the determined sort," Bellavora laughed softly. Her expression quickly dimmed, though, becoming almost grief-stricken as she looked down at my less-than-ideal state. "I was so relieved to hear that you had been found safe. I know this must have been so difficult for you to manage all on your own. I can only offer you my greatest apology for that, dear one. You were meant for this fight, but I have not done enough to prepare you for it. I had hoped to spare you the pain as long as possible."

"Can you help him?" Kaili panicked, noticing the gaping wound in my side. "There's so much blood—we need to get you to a healer!"

Bellavora reached out to place a hand over my wound. Her expression tensed, lips thinning and brow creasing with focus, as the palm of her hand glowed with a faint, silvery light. The rush of energy scurried under my skin, making my pulse quicken and my muscles twitch. Itching heat tingled around the wound until, at last, she drew her hand back.

My wound was gone. There was nothing left but a blood-stained hole in my tunic. Kaili and I both gaped in awe, looking at my unmarked skin and then back up at Bellavora.

Her smile was thinner, more strained, but no less sincere as she slowly stood and offered a hand to help me up. "I'm afraid we can't linger here any longer. This gateway is forever closed, and we've only a short time to find another before Sadeera does."

"You mean there are more gateways like that down here?" I asked, shambling to my feet and wobbling some as my head spun. Every part of my body felt rubbery and strange, like I might collapse into a heap again at any second.

"Of course." Bellavora's smile was cryptic and confident as she picked up her purple robe and carefully draped it back around her shoulders, hiding her beautiful wings beneath it. "If one knows how and where to look."

Somehow, seeing her do that put a strange knot of unease in my gut. She had worn those robes as long as I'd known her. In fact, I had never seen her without them until this whole mess. Now I knew why. She had been hiding those wings for years, maybe centuries. I had to wonder why.

And ... how? It was my understanding that Avoran elves slowly lost their power after they left their homeland. That meant they couldn't perform big or powerful spells like I'd just witnessed. That also usually meant that they had to remove their wings, which began to rot in the absence of the radiant divine power that filled their lofty kingdom.

Somehow, though, both she and Sadeera still had theirs.

How?

It didn't seem like the right time to ask. Not with the fate of the world now hanging on the next few minutes—hours—days—honestly, I wasn't sure how much time we had left.

I just knew we couldn't afford to waste a single moment of it.

21

CHAPTER TWENTY-ONE

Ancient elves and wings aside, I had a lot of questions and no idea where to begin.

My head still swam and my legs wobbled as I followed High Inquisitor Bellavora through the many halls, staircases, corridors, and courtyards of her ancient home. Every now and then, I had to stop and catch my breath. There wasn't a single part of me that didn't hurt. My head pounded like someone was beating the back of my skull with a hammer. I couldn't afford to stop for long, though.

I fidgeted with my now cracked glasses and tried to think, to walk straight, and to keep my breathing steady as the questions raced through my brain like a wildfire. How had Bellavora survived the attack on the Compendium Library? How long had she known I was essentially the sleeping essence of an ancient, nearly-forgotten god? Was she ever going to share that information with me, or was this doomed to be the world's most terrible surprise of my life from the outset? How did she know Sadeera? Did she know that Arlan man, as well? Were they all related somehow? Why were they even here, in the lowlands, instead of in Avora with the rest of their kin? How did that other boy, Ronan, fit into any of this?

I had no idea. And that was, by far, the worst feeling ever.

The best feeling, I decided quickly, was Kaili walking next to me and holding my hand again. It wasn't until that moment, when her warm fingers wove through mine, that I realized I hadn't expected to ever see her again. I didn't know how she had found Bellavora in the first place, but Gods, I was so thankful she had. It must have seemed to her like Noa and I just vanished into thin air. I wondered how long she and the other members of their village had searched for us. Had they held funeral rites for us like they had the others they had lost? The idea stuck in my brain and replayed over and over. Guilt soured my stomach until I felt like I might throw up.

Or maybe that was just from using too much power at once. I shuddered and rubbed at my arms, feeling nothing but my own human skin there now. But before ... I had almost lost control. I could feel Avgior's presence breaking through my mortal body like an eaglet hatching from an egg. I didn't know what would happen if I lost myself completely to his power. Would I ever be able to go back to this form?

I shut my eyes tightly and squeezed Kaili's hand a little harder. I didn't want to lose this—being with people I cared about. Maybe I would have to in the end, but for now, I just wanted to be myself.

"I'm so glad you're here," I confessed, managing an exhausted smile down at her. "Noa and I got captured by goblins in the jungle and ... well, it's sort of a long story, but we wound up with a bunch of dragonriders from Maldobar."

Kaili nodded, her sea-glass-colored eyes catching the light from the small glass lantern Bellavora carried. "Is ... Is Noa okay, too?" she asked quietly.

I nodded. "He escaped with the others. They're—well, to be honest, I'm not sure *where* they are, exactly. Not here, though, which is a good thing. In my limited experience, being trapped underground in various ruins for the last several days, nothing good goes on down here."

"That particular gateway led to a place we called a Quadrivium. It is a sort of magical crossroads just south of the Gate of Proleus, and it used to be a great intersection point of many such portals," Bellavora corrected without ever looking back at us. "Naturally, not many of the remaining gateways still function, even there. But I do believe we can manage well enough if we put our minds to it."

"High Inquisitor, I-I don't understand what's happening here. Who is Sadeera? What is she doing in Nar'Haleen in the first place?" I tried to keep my voice steady as the storm of questions raged in my mind again.

She must have been able to detect the subtle tones of absolute, soul-crushing panic in my voice because Bellavora stopped and turned to face me. Her glowing golden eyes smoldered like embers in the gloom of the hall as she gazed down with another knowing, gentle smile. "That story would take centuries to tell, my dear. But I can tell you that Sadeera is what becomes of children held to the terrible pressure of impossible standards for far too long. Those children always break—it's merely a matter of whether that fracture occurs externally or internally. Their frustration becomes rage. Their need to earn the respect and love of their parents becomes an obsession with superiority. To them, love is a privilege that must be earned through obedience and success. Anything less is failure, and failure is unacceptable."

I swallowed hard, trying my best to process all of that. I had never known my family, so I couldn't really relate to being held to a standard or feeling the love of parents in any capacity. But I could imagine that, for others, it must have been painful to be held under that kind of pressure.

"For Sadeera, power and control are her only means of feeling worthy. And at some point in her life's journey, she must have found kinship in Iksoli, Goddess of Mischief and most troublesome of the youngest gods. So began her plans, or so I can only assume. I was a mentor and teacher to both her and her elder brother, Zarvan—the man you know as Arlan," she continued. "The two responded quite differently to the familial pressure they endured. While Zarvan's magical talents were less impressive, his social aptitude was extraordinary. I foresaw a great future for him in the Hall of Elders as a High Counselor. Sadeera was much more reserved, and while her magical ability far surpassed my other students, her explosive temper made her unpredictable, volatile, and dangerous. I cautioned her parents about the effects their expectations were having on her, but my warnings were ignored."

Bellavora's gaze drifted as her expression dimmed, as though she'd been carried off by the currents of memory. "Sadeera began dabbling in forbidden magics, likely at the urging of Iksoli. I don't know precisely when she first aspired to godhood, but I do know that it was Zarvan who discovered her attempting to open the divine gate that lies in our homeland. I suspect it was Iksoli who saw to it that he would be blamed for that crime and thereafter exiled to the lowlands. She bends the minds of the weak so easily."

"But Sadeera is here, in Nar'Haleen, now. Why would she come here if she let her brother take the fall? Coming here is ... ultimately painful and deadly for your people, isn't it?" I asked, watching her expression carefully. Not because I thought she might lie to me, though. Rather, I was searching for some idea of how much time she had left here. She had been using a lot of magical power over the years, and I didn't know what that meant for her lifespan.

Surely she wasn't, you know, killing herself just to help me. Er, well, us, I guess. This wasn't about just me anymore.

"Yes," Bellavora answered quietly, her lips thinning some as her brows rose slightly. There was a cryptic hint of uncertainty in her expression when she finally looked back down at me again. "But I could not bear to see Zarvan cast down on his own. Even more so, I could not bear the thought that Sadeera might continue her campaign here, in the lowland realms, where the only other gateway to the divine realm lies."

"The Gate of Proleus," I realized aloud.

She nodded and motioned for us to continue on through the hallways beside her. "I imagine she is feeling the pain and strain of being here in the lowlands. But she has only been here a short time—not even an entire human lifetime—so she has likely only begun to experience the effects of being cut off from our homeland. I also suspect that, now that she has apparently slain two young gods and absorbed their essences and power, she is able to stave off those effects."

"*Two* young gods?" I echoed, unable to mask my horror. Of course, I knew about Iksoli. I had seen it happen right in front of me. But ... who was the other?

"Indeed." Bellavora's tone softened again, as though the words were painful. "It is my understanding that, upon leaving Avora, she was able to summon and slay the Tykeron, God of Luck and Good Fortune. No doubt Iksoli helped her in that endeavor, as well."

I had to let that information sink in, like a stone slowly sinking to the depths of the ocean floor. I didn't know much about Tykeron. He was another largely unknown deity in most of the world. No wonder no one had noticed he was missing.

"If they have worked together this long, why would Sadeera betray Iksoli now?" I wondered aloud.

"Perhaps her usefulness had come to an end," Bellavora sighed. "Or, perhaps she now requires full use of Iksoli's power and essence to complete the next step of her plan."

"But you were able to outmatch her," Kaili spoke up, her voice hopeful. "Can't you stop her?"

I had to admit, seeing Bellavora cast her out of this place so quickly had me wondering the same thing. More specifically, I wanted to know how Bellavora had kept so much of her power at her disposal if she had been here in the lowlands a lot longer. Arlan was obviously struggling, and by the sound of it, they had both been here about the same amount of time.

A hint of wry confidence glimmered in Bellavora's secretive smile. "My dear, I am *far* older than either of them. They are still merely children by the standards of our people, where I have enjoyed ages of time to absorb the divine power that showers our kingdom," she said. "But it was not mere magic that drove Sadeera from this place. This was my home, and the protective runes that surround it are still mine to control. All magic, even that of the divine, is governed by laws and strict parameters. Sadeera might have remembered that the rite of banishment was covered early on in our lessons, had she not been so preoccupied with her own aspirations."

O-Oh. That sort of made sense, I guess. Almost like a magical security fence.

That still left one question tumbling around in my brain, though, and it was the one that scared me the most. I couldn't even look at the High Inquisitor as I muttered, "So, if I'm supposed to be a full god, why couldn't I defeat her? Why couldn't I just incinerate her?"

Bellavora didn't answer right away. The sound of echoing footfalls filled the gloom for nearly a minute before she finally stopped at the end of a long hall. A pair of double doors more than twenty feet tall loomed before us, carved straight from the bedrock and covered in the engravings of willows, deer, ivy vines, and butterflies.

"Because, my dear, you are still clinging to the mortal mind you've known for so long," she replied at last, pressing her fingers to the center line where the two doors met. Light bloomed under her fingertips, spreading across the stone and every chiseled outline, as though the engravings themselves were coming to life.

Kaili gasped and stepped closer to my side as we stood in awe, watching the clean silver light bathe over the beautiful, intricate images. The deer seemed to move to graze. The fronds of the willows seemed to sway in a gentle breeze. Clouds floated over a starry sky, eclipsing a crescent moon.

"You now stand at the precipice of your own destiny, Clarke. The way forward is split. Either you will embrace the rite of your divine power and become Avgior fully once more —or you will remain mortal and that essence will fade. It has been dormant for so long, and it now hangs by a fragile thread that only you can sever. Before the end, you will have to choose," Bellavora clarified and stood back, holding her glass lamp higher as the two doors shuddered and slowly swung inward with a low *boom*.

I SQUINTED INTO THE GLOOM, BARELY ABLE TO MAKE OUT THE GHOSTLY SILHOUETTE OF something tall and white. A tree. A large white tree that glowed like moonlight stood in the center of the dark of the chamber. The thick trunk stood like a pillar of alabaster with a skirting of raised roots snaking out across the floor. Its wide branches stretched upward, covered in hundreds of small, silvery leaves.

Placing her glass lamp down at the doorway, Bellavora led the way inside. The door slid closed again behind us, and I stared in total bewilderment as those glowing lines of light continued to spread along the walls, revealing more engravings of an entire enchanted forest on all sides of the chamber. Incredible.

"What is this place?" Kaili whispered to me, like I had any clue.

With her gaze now fixed on the tree, her fair features drawn into a look of strained emotion I didn't understand, Bellavora began walking slowly toward it. "The only thing I brought with me from Avora," she said. "A seed of eternum, the very first seeds of life. This one has already matured."

"What does it do?" I managed through chattering teeth. Every step we took closer to the tree made flurries of tingling energy buzz through my body. My stomach flipped and spun, and a cold, anxious sweat made my skin go clammy.

Bellavora grinned like she was silently cherishing my ignorance. I knew that look all too well. It still made my ears burn and my face flush with heat. Yes, I'm sure that sounded like a stupid question—but in my defense, there wasn't a lot written about the specifics and inner workings of the Avoran kingdoms. I had no idea what they were truly capable of, and Avgior didn't seem eager to share any insight with me, either.

"It's not what it *does*, my dear, it's what it *is*," she corrected. "The seeds of life contain creation's purest essence. The very spark of it, some might say. They are a wish not yet spoken, but can only be used once."

Every alarm bell in my head rang at once, leaving me frozen and speechless. This tree ... had come from a seed. A seed that contained a pure *spark of life?*

Sweet Fates. Was this what Sadeera was looking for? The last missing piece needed to open the Gate of Proleus? I-I didn't understand. This was a tree, not a seed.

Once again, Bellavora seemed to be able to read my thoughts. Or, at the very least, she could see the confusion twisting at my expression. "Once planted, it cannot be undone. The wish must be fulfilled and the tree will die." She stepped closer to me, putting a hand on my shoulder. "Initially, there were many such seeds given from the hands of Paligno himself. Now, only one remains unplanted, and it is carried by his chosen."

"Jaevid's daughter," I recalled. "Her name is Maylea, I think. I heard them talking about her some."

"She comes from a long family line of those who have spoken for Paligno. It is not surprising she would be entrusted with it, just as her ancestors were," Bellavora confirmed. "It is the only seed that still contains the spark. That is why Sadeera is so desperate for it, and why we must all do whatever we can to keep it from falling into her hands."

"But ... what should I wish for?" I still didn't quite understand what all this was meant to do. "Can I just wish for Sadeera to die?"

Bellavora's expression dimmed, becoming distant as she panned her gaze from me up to the outstretched limbs of the beautiful tree. "This is where the wisdom of Avgior is required, dear one. To find the root of the problem. To stop it from ever growing again. You must find that wisdom in yourself, Clarke. Find it and choose the right path. The fate of many now hangs in the balance."

PART FIVE

REIGH

22

CHAPTER TWENTY-TWO

Nothing good ever happened when we split up our group. I really should have learned that lesson several caves, monsters, and battles ago. Buuut I'd always been stubborn—a family trait, apparently. The idea of getting things done faster on my own, or in any degree of privacy, always lured me back to that pathetic, futile hope that surely nothing bad would happen *this time*.

Heh.

Now I was staring up at a disgusting, giant snot monster, watching in horror as it bashed around the cavern, screeching like a banshee, and taking wild swings at Lukani's dragon form. Thank the gods we had found them, or rather, that they had found us. I wasn't sure how all of that had come to pass, but we could hash out the details later.

Right now, we had goblins to kill.

Thatcher rushed in, sword drawn and jaw clenched as he stepped through one flawless maneuver after another, hacking through the squealing green creatures two and three at a time. I had to hand it to him, his skill at swordsmanship was impressive now. He had Murdoc to thank for that, of course, but I'd never been happier to see that big, dumb kid moving like a lethal machine of war into the teeth of our enemy.

Violet kept close at my side for her first few assaults, carving a path through the onslaught until she had enough room to work. Then she flipped her daggers into a reverse grip, widened her stance, and bared her teeth. Her pupils went as small as pin-pricks. She moved like a blur, bending and twisting in ways that, in my medical opinion, shouldn't have been physically possible. Was, uh, was that a Viperi thing?

She executed a mid-air spinning kick and nearly did the splits when she landed in a low crouch. But the back-bending leap she made after that was really what made me stop and stare. I forgot all about the rest of the goblin hoard around me for a second.

Whoa ...

A whack of a bone club against the side of my head jarred me back to reality, and I had to turn away. Crap! Head in the game, old man. Now wasn't the time to gawk.

We kept the upper hand, using the bridge like a funnel for almost two full minutes as the goblins rushed us like a slimy, panicked, angry river of green filth and rusty weapons. But when I spotted Maylea drawing her very last arrow from her quiver, I knew we couldn't do this much longer. Thatcher staggered, catching himself against the bridge's railing and heaving for breath. His face was blanched and covered in a sheen of sweat. He had strange, gruesome-looking wounds under his eyes. I didn't know that red-skinned, fiend-looking guy well enough to tell how much fight he had left in him, but clearly, they had all been through a lot before finding Violet and me down here.

"How long can Lukani hold that shape?" I shouted as I sent another arcing beam of crackling purple energy sizzling through the thickest crowd of goblins I could spot.

No one got a chance to answer.

The huge goo-spitting monster floundered into the bridge suddenly, nearly engulfed in burning dragon venom with all its legs slamming into the stonework. The bridge shuddered underneath our feet, knocking me backward and sending the goblins fleeing in every direction. Violet screamed something that I couldn't make out over the roars, shrieks, and cracking of stone. Too late, I knew.

The bridge couldn't take that much weight.

Oh gods, not again.

I crawled forward, desperately trying to reach Violet as I felt the stone beneath me lurch sharply. I seized her hand and immediately looked around for Maylea and Thatcher. He had just started running toward me when the bridge buckled. The stone beneath us gave way, and we fell toward the rushing dark water below.

SPLASH!

The surge of cold water rushing all around me sent a shock through my system. I didn't dare let go of Violet. I'd never find her again. Holding my breath, I kicked and clawed with my free hand toward what I could only hope was the surface. The water raged, moving with incredible force. I couldn't see anything in the pitch darkness, even after my head broke the surface and I sucked in a desperate gulp of air.

"Reigh!" Violet cried, still holding onto my hand tightly. She coughed and sputtered, and I heard her start to gasp out something else. A warning. "Th-There ... is ... a—!"

The earth fell away again, so suddenly, I didn't even have time to yell or hold my breath. Gods and Fates, it was a waterfall. My body pitched end over end as I plummeted through the dark. Violet's hand slipped out of mine. Her scream was lost to the roar of the water around us.

And all I could do was beg the gods not to let me hit a rock, the edge of a chasm, or the bottom of a pool somewhere far below.

SPLAAASH!

I hit the surface of a body of water, and immediately, the pounding of the waterfall shoved me under the surface. I paddled and kicked, fighting to get far enough away that I could come up for breath without getting a mouthful of water. With nothing—no light or point of reference—to orient toward, all I could do was paddle blindly until my boots struck a rocky bottom. I staggered out of the cold water, drenched and shivering, with my arms stretched out in front of me to feel for anything I might run into.

"Vi ... Violet!" I called out hoarsely.

No answer.

Gods, what if I was the only one who—no. No, I couldn't start thinking like that. The others were here somewhere. They had to be.

"Thatcher!" I shouted, louder this time.

"Reigh," he called back immediately, his voice sounding closer than I expected. "I-I can't see anything. Where are you?"

"Just stay still. I'll come to you. Are you hurt?" I started slowly shuffling toward the sound of his voice.

"I-I don't know." He coughed and sputtered, like he was still trying to work water out of his lungs. "I don't think so."

A wave of relief washed over me when my hand finally hit his shoulder. He reached over to grasp mine back, and I let out a ragged, heavy sigh. One down. But where were the others?

"I think I have a torch in my bag still," he managed through chattering teeth. "But I'm sure everything in there is soaked now."

I cringed back, spitting a furious elven curse as a flame sparked to life in the dark right beside me. The red-skinned guy stood, dripping a puddle immediately on my left, and holding a wisp of flickering fire over his palm. For crying out loud. Who was this guy? And what kind of magic was that?

"It's okay," Thatcher assured me, his face seeming much paler and more exhausted in the light of that single flame. "He's been helping us."

I arched an eyebrow. "And you are ... who, exactly?"

"Neiko." The strange man gave me a hard, suspicious look and flicked his long, lion-like tail. That and the eerie yellow eyes made me wonder if he was some relation to Lukani. Hmmm.

Whatever. I couldn't think about that right now.

I turned away and squinted out across the dark, churning water. I couldn't see much beyond ten feet—not with such a small source of light. I could do better, once I caught my breath.

We stood on a narrow rocky beach leading out of the dark pool. Only fifty or so feet away, the waterfall crashed down and filled the chamber with a constant rumble like thunder and thick mist that made the air seem heavy and difficult to breathe. I couldn't see the waterfall, of course. But I could feel the vibrations and the gusts of cold mist rushing away from it.

"VIOLET!" I tried calling out again. "MAYLEA!"

Nothing. No reply.

Curse it, maybe they couldn't hear me over the noise of the falls. Yeah, that's the hope I had to cling to. The alternative was ... not acceptable.

"MAYLEA!" Thatcher stepped forward to join me, cupping his hands around his mouth.

My pulse kicked like a wild mule in my chest, going faster and faster as my whole body shivered with dread. Gods, I couldn't accept this. They couldn't be gone. I ... I was responsible for—

"Reigh!" a panicked female voice called back.

My heart hit the back of my throat so hard it made my eyes tear up and my voice cracked as I staggered forward into the water a few steps, drawn to the sound. "Violet! I'm right here! Are you all right? Can you see us?"

"I'm okay," she cried out over the rush of the falls. "Maylea is here. We found Lukani! He is unconscious! I cannot swim with him that far!"

"How far is it?" I shouted.

"I don't—I'm not sure," she answered haltingly, her voice shaking as though she were on the verge of total panic. "Maybe a hundred feet!"

I bit down hard. Gods, what was happening over there? I needed to see.

"What are we going to do?" Thatcher murmured, staring with me out into the darkness.

"I'm going to them," I decided aloud. "Wait here. If Lukani is injured, I'll need my medical kit out of my bag. Did you bring it?"

Thatcher nodded.

Good.

I closed my eyes, keeping my jaw locked as I fought to force down all those worried, frenzied thoughts. I had to drift in silence to feel the pull of Clysiros's power. It climbed out from the center of my soul and spread through my body like a creeping winter's frost. I stopped shivering. My pulse roared in my ears, slow and steady, like the toll of a tower bell.

Opening my eyes again, I steeled my nerve. I'd done this before. I could do it again.

"Fates," Thatcher gasped beside me. "Reigh, your eyes are all black."

Were they? Eh, well, too bad that didn't make my vision in the dark any better. I could fix that now, though.

"Violet, I'm coming to you," I called. "Stay put!"

"Okay!" She agreed.

I bowed my head some. Then, with my hands clenched into fists, I took a step out onto the water. Just like before, the cold of Clysiros's power swirled around me. The surface of the water solidified, and I stepped off onto a solid layer of ice.

Perfect.

I raised my hands, calling forth orbs of light that rose from the depths of the water and floated around me like glowing paper lanterns. I bade several of them to remain at the shore, drifting soundlessly around Thatcher and Neiko. The rest followed me as I walked across the surface of the water, leaving a melting pathway of ice behind. The pull of that power was a lot sharper now. A metallic taste in my mouth and a twinge of sharp pain in the back of my mind made me wonder just how far I would be able to push myself. I'd used a lot of power today already—above and beyond anything I had ever been able to do before. But where was my breaking point now?

I didn't know. I just hoped it wasn't somewhere over the water in the middle of this gods-forsaken pool. Fates preserve me.

Every tense muscle in my body went slack in relief when my feet finally struck solid ground on the other side of the pool. Crunching my way across the pebbles, I looked around for any sign of the others. They couldn't be far. Especially if Lukani was—

Maylea hit me like a charging buck and nearly knocked me over. With her arms around my waist, she squeezed me hard and started to sob. She trembled and gasped, almost like she couldn't get a full breath, as she frantically tried to spit out words. "Uncle Reigh! I thought you were ... oh gods, you have to help Lukani! He's not moving and—h-he saw the bridge collapse and he tried to save me but we b-both went over the falls a-and ..."

I grabbed the sides of her face, bending down so she could look me in the eye. "I need you to try to calm down for me, okay? Deep, slow breaths. In through the nose, out through the mouth," I coaxed. "That's it. Take a few more."

Maylea's eyes were rimmed with tears and her soggy dark hair stuck to her forehead and cheeks as she tried to follow my instructions. Little by little, she started to calm, but her shivering never went away. That was a problem all of us were about to share. We were drenched and it was cold down here. The wind and mist coming off the falls didn't help.

Hopefully, Thatcher and Neiko could work out some way to use that little bit of fire magic to fix this problem. The last thing we needed was to all die from hypothermia down here.

"Take me to them," I said, keeping my tone calm and even. No need to scare her any more than she already was.

Maylea bobbed her head and took off along the shore. I sent one of my orbs of pale light bobbing along after her. Not far away, they both stopped over the huddled forms of Violet and Lukani. With his upper body cradled against her, his head against her shoulder, Violet patted his cheeks as though she were trying to rouse him.

As far as I could tell, it wasn't working. His face was dangerously pale when I jogged over and crouched down beside them. Not good. Blue veins stood out against the sides of his neck, and when I tested for a pulse, it was fast and light. His breathing was shallow, too. But I couldn't find any obvious signs of injury. No discoloration or evidence of internal bleeding. No wounds or trauma anywhere. That really only left one option that I felt confident was the culprit.

Because we'd seen this happen once before.

"He's pushed himself too far and used too much magic," I concluded, reaching down to take him from Violet's arms and carry him bride-style against my chest. "Not much we can do except let him rest as long as possible."

"I-Is he going to be okay?" Maylea sniffled, staring at him with her pale, sea-foam green eyes wide and chin trembling.

"I don't know," I admitted, the words bitter on my tongue. "But unless we find a way to get warm and dry off, none of us will be. Thatcher and that Neiko guy are waiting on the other side."

"I can see a stairwell over there," Violet revealed, staring past me to the opposite shore of the pool. "Perhaps it leads back up to the temple."

I wasn't ready to hope for that kind of luck. Not after the day I'd had so far. "Come on, we have to get back across together. You'll have to stay close and walk right next to me. We'll take this one step at a time."

23

CHAPTER TWENTY-THREE

I had really been hoping that by the time I finally got the rest of our group back across the water, Thatcher and Neiko would have worked out how to start a fire and maybe lay some of our things out to start drying. But no. In fact, they were still standing exactly where I'd left them, doing a great job of looking surprised and concerned when we came striding over the water toward them. Ugggh.

As soon as my feet were back on solid ground, I passed Lukani off to Thatcher. Then I made sure Maylea and Violet made it to shore right behind me. Well, at least we were all back in one place. A small victory.

It wouldn't mean much if we all died of hypothermia, though.

"We've got to find a way to get warm." I gave Violet a sideways glance. "Or a way out of here, at least."

She nodded. "I can go scout the stairs."

I quickly stretched out an arm to block her path. "No, no, no, no. Not again. We all stay together. No more splitting up."

Her lips pinched up, and she narrowed her eyes a little. I guess she still didn't like me getting in the way of her plans.

Too bad.

"I've almost been drowned, eaten, and mauled by a hoard of goblins—all in one day." I shot her a challenging glare right back, trying to add a little bit of that stubbornness she seemed to find so amusing as I repeated, "We stay together."

"Fine," she groaned and rolled her eyes.

I almost missed it. Before Violet turned away, she huffed a deep breath and then winced, her expression skewing with pain for the briefest second. She reached a hand toward her right shoulder, but stopped and kept herself angled away from me. I could see it, then, even in the weak light of my floating wisps—she had a few holes in the wide neck of her tunic, along the back of her shoulder and collar bone.

A bite from one of the goblins, maybe? I couldn't tell without getting closer. With her dark tunic drenched, I couldn't tell if it was bleeding or not.

My mouth mashed up as a bitter taste rose in my throat. I'd have to insist on looking at it later. Great.

"How can you trust this Pitathi woman?" Neiko hissed suddenly. I'd been too distracted to notice the way he was glaring at her, tail flicking slowly back and forth and lip twitching at a snarl. "Her blood runs thick with deceit. She will surely lead us straight to the Hands of Fate."

Violet froze. She stared back at him wordlessly, her expression blank, as though she were holding back her own emotions. She couldn't hide them that easily from me now, though. I saw the light dim in her scarlet eyes. It was that same unspoken defeat and embarrassment she kept carefully hidden away beneath a mask of indifference.

I don't know what happened. I was tired, cold, hungry, and soaking wet. My head was pounding from using so much of my divine power. I was sick of wearing the same disgusting socks every day. Whatever the reason, hearing Neiko say that word—Pitathi—and seeing that look in her eyes snapped the final, frazzled thread that was barely holding my sanity together.

Everything went red, and I couldn't hold it in.

I stepped in between them and got right in his face. I jabbed a finger right into the center of his chest, leaning down so my nose was less than an inch from his. "You *do not* talk to her like that," I seethed. "I don't know where you came from, or who you think you are, but if you use that word again in my presence, I'll introduce you to Clysiros personally. Do we understand one another?"

Neiko drew back slowly, blinking at me in complete shock. His golden eyes darted back and forth between Violet and me, his brow crinkled in confusion. "But she is—!"

"NONE OF YOUR CONCERN," I growled louder, taking another threatening step toward him. "Test me again, *stranger*, and see what happens. Go on. Do it."

A hand grabbed my forearm suddenly, giving me an urgent tug. "That's enough, Reigh," Violet said, her voice tense and quiet.

I stood there for a few seconds more, keeping my steady, smoldering glare on him as an unspoken promise, before I finally let her pull me away. My pulse thumped furiously, adrenaline making my hands shake and my vision swerve some as I followed her toward the hidden staircase at the far end of the shore. The others followed close behind, but Neiko kept a few paces of distance between himself and the rest of us.

I snorted and licked my teeth. Good riddance.

It took a few minutes of walking for my blood pressure to get back down to where it didn't feel like my head was about to explode. Only then could my pea-sized brain begin to fully process what I'd just done. Fates, I was such an idiot. I'd probably embarrassed her. Even if he was out of line, there were better ways of handling it. I was supposed to be the leader here, wasn't I? I had to do better.

I rubbed the back of my neck, trying desperately to read her mood by the back of her head and the way she walked right ahead of me. Impossible. I could barely read her when she was staring right at me. Augggh.

What was I supposed to do now?

EVERY STEP UP THE LONG, TWISTING STAIRWELL TOOK US FARTHER FROM THE NOISE OF the falls. After twenty minutes, my calves were screaming for a break and my toes were numb. Thatcher huffed with every movement, and I had to take over carrying Lukani for a little while. Clearly, however they had wound up meeting us at that bridge, he had been forced to use a substantial amount of his own power.

I was feeling the drain, too. Dismissing my floating orbs of light left us in near darkness again, but Neiko seemed able to maintain that little tongue of flame on his hand much more easily. Maybe he was useful for something, after all.

About as useful as a small torch, to be precise.

"Oh, thank the gods," Violet breathed suddenly. She stopped before us, leaning out through what appeared to be a narrow doorway at the top of the stairs. "It appears we are in the temple archives. There is a door here that should lead to the outside."

Finally. I sagged against the wall, fighting for breath and wiping my sweaty hair out of my eyes. Thank the gods, indeed.

"With your permission, Lieutenant, I will do a quick survey of the room and make sure it is unoccupied. Is that allowed?" she asked, casting me a quick, patronizing little smirk over her shoulder.

I smacked my lips, tasting every sarcastic word that would have been so sweet on my tongue in that moment. "Go on," I muttered.

She gave me one of those once-over glances that I still didn't understand, then dashed away into the dark as fast as a shadow. Seeing her disappear like that put a sharp knot of worry in my chest. I didn't like it. Not one tiny bit. But what else could we do? She was the only one who could see in the dark. I knew she could handle herself in a fight, and she knew a lot more about the dangers that lurked down here than I did. She was the obvious choice for something like this.

I just ... didn't like the idea of not being there if she, you know, needed help. My help.

"You need to tell her," Maylea whispered from right behind me.

I flinched, doing everything in my power to keep my expression neutral as I stared out the doorway. "Tell who what?"

"Tell Violet how you feel, dummy," she scolded. "It's *so* obvious."

"Yeah, it kind of is," Thatcher added. "You and Murdoc always say I'm bad with flirting, but this is just painful to watch."

I gave him my best crazed glare. "I'm sorry, do you see me trying to keep all of us alive? And I don't remember inviting any of you to give opinions on my personal life."

"All clear." I nearly jumped straight out of my filthy boots when Violet suddenly appeared at the doorway again. Gods and Fates, she was as quiet as a cat. "And there is a door! It requires magic to unseal it, but I believe you can open it."

Fantastic. Conversation over.

I whipped around and followed as Violet led the way through another large chamber lined with row after row of floor-to-ceiling bookshelves. They were stocked full of tomes left to rot in their own dust and cubbies crammed tight with scrolls wrapped around ornate golden sticks. The smell of old, mildewing paper hung thick in the still air, and dust sparkled through shafts of light that poured down from huge bronze chandeliers that hung along the central aisle.

I was about to ask Violet how she had managed to light them, but then I realized it wasn't flame that glowed from the dozens of golden glass spheres on each of those chandeliers. The glass itself was shining—or rather, the small lines of runes etched along the outside of the glass globes were. Strange. Had they been glowing all this time, alone down here for hundreds of years? My mind boggled at the amount of magic required to do something like that. Incredible.

"You said there's a door to the outside?" I asked, just for clarification, as Violet guided us down another aisle and stopped at the end, where a large shelf dominated the entire wall.

She nodded and gestured to the shelf.

Ummm. Okay. "It was likely placed here as an emergency exit for the scholars keeping the temple archives."

I leaned around, looking up and down and studying all the dust-laden spines of the books. Nope. Not a door in sight. "I'm gonna need a hint here."

Violet snapped her fingers and grinned. "Oh, that's right! I nearly forgot. You dragonriders aren't taught to be creative."

"Rude." I crossed my arms. If she felt good enough to tease me, then maybe she wasn't *that* injured.

Or ... hmm. She laughed again, but her voice hitched slightly and she winced into her wounded shoulder again. Her mouth mashed into a tight, uncomfortable line, but she collected her composure almost immediately. Nope. She was definitely in need of some medical treatment.

Standing on her toes, Violet reached up to tap her fingers on the spine of a short, dark leather-bound tome, swiping away the layer of dust to reveal a small symbol leafed in gold. The sight of it, faded with age and nearly worn away, sent a bolt of alarm through me. I knew that symbol. I'd seen it before—when Arlan the Kinslayer magically branded it onto my nephew's hand as a seal against his curse.

The symbol of Enais, the foregod of all that is.

"Ahhh, yes. I have seen this before. It is a simple enough magical lock," Neiko piped up suddenly, striding forward and squinting at the book. He made a gesture with his hands, flourishing his fingers in a swirling motion. A tiny spot of brilliant, glittering light formed between his hands and he quickly caught it, snapping a fist around it. Pressing his fist to his lips, he slowly uncurled his fingers and blew through his hands. A shower of shimmering dust came out the other side and drifted through the air, gravitating toward the spine of the book and clinging to it.

As the symbol on the spine began to glow, Neiko reached for it and slowly pressed the book deeper into the shelf. The whole bookcase shifted, sending out a shower of thick dust. Rusted metal hinges groaned and creaked.

I squinted, holding a hand up to shield my eyes as radiant sunlight poured into the room. A narrow, four-by-five-foot section of the shelf opened up like a hidden door, revealing the bottom of a steep canyon of sun-bleached stone. The shock of the heat outside hit my face like a blast from a blacksmith's forge. It made the air ripple, as though everything beyond that threshold was liquid.

"How far are we from the city?" Thatcher asked, seeming just as bewildered to find nothing that even resembled Salnis outside that door.

"Without scouting, it's difficult to say," Violet surmised. "But I would guess perhaps five miles. Maybe more."

"I don't hear the battle anymore," Maylea murmured, her expression still fraught with apprehension as she stayed close to Thatcher's side. Probably because he was still carrying Lukani.

"What battle?" I demanded.

"Nar'Haleen is attacking Salnis now," Thatcher clarified. "We barely managed to get out."

Violet's shoulders rose and fell with a resigned sigh. "Then it's likely the fighting stopped as soon as the sun began to rise. The heat here is far too intense. Even the

Nar'Haleenan soldiers would perish in heavy armor with no way to cool themselves." She took a few steps out the door and looked both ways, then quickly came back in. "We might suffer a similar fate if we try to venture out now. The land here, between Salnis and Dumathis, is a scorching wasteland of pitch pits, brine, and brittle stone. They call it the Pitch Graves."

"Then we have to stay here until nightfall?" I guessed.

The uncertain grimace on Violet's face didn't give me any confidence. Clearly, this wasn't part of her master plan, and I could understand fairly easily why. If we went on foot, we would die in the heat. There were too many of us for my dragon to carry, and Lukani couldn't use any of his magical shapeshifting to assist with that, either. We only had two options now—either we had to go back into the ruins, navigate the caves, and try to find the so-called gateway that might get us to Dumathis ...

Or I could try something *really* stupid.

I sighed heavily, already knowing full well what I had to do. It would be messy. Dangerous, too. But Clysiros had named me her King of the Grave, and I already knew that title came with considerably more power than I'd ever had at my disposal before.

Time to find out just how much more.

"We're in no shape to go anywhere right now," I said, making a point to look at Thatcher. He still stood, holding Lukani's unconscious body in his arms, but I'd known him long enough to be able to tell that he wasn't in good shape, either. "Let's take the rest of the day, rest, and regroup inside."

I glanced around at the rest of our ragged, bloodied group. No one protested. Thank the gods for that. I hadn't gotten a second to sit down, let alone have something to eat or even a swig of water, since we had arrived. It was more than overdue.

I just hoped, for all our sakes, we could manage a few hours of undisturbed rest and recuperation before the next disaster hit.

24

CHAPTER TWENTY-FOUR

We left the hidden bookshelf door open a crack, just enough to let some light inside, and settled into the archives chamber. We still had a few waterskins and rations to pass around, and Thatcher had already stretched out on the floor with his eyes closed.

No rest for the healer, though. Not yet, anyway. I immediately focused on getting Lukani laid out on the floor on his side, putting him in the recovery position with a rolled-up cloak under his head and another spread over him. His color looked a little better, but I still didn't like that shallow, gasping way he breathed. There wasn't much more I could do for him at the moment, though. Overuse of inborn magic wasn't exactly something we'd covered in my many years of medical training under Kiran. In Maldobar, those sorts of afflictions were extremely rare.

Fortunately, our newest special *friend*, Neiko, was apparently also a Rajinna. He was familiar with Lukani's condition and assured us that while our young shapeshifting hero had pushed himself too far, he was not beyond help. The fancy potion the Mistress of the Call had given us wouldn't help him in this state, but Lukani would recover. He just needed to be left alone to rest as long as possible.

Maylea was not willing to entertain the idea of sitting anywhere else in the chamber except at Lukani's side, however. Neiko clearly didn't like that she insisted on being so close to him, as he scowled at her suspiciously when she sat down at Lukani's side and gently took his hand. He kept his mouth shut, though. Smart move.

He didn't have to like me—but I'd already given him one warning about his behavior toward my friends. He wouldn't get a second. Not when I knew absolutely nothing about who he was, how he'd found us, and what his intentions really were.

Neiko was obviously mostly concerned with Lukani and had a healthy fear of the rest of us. Me, in particular. But as for his end goal? I could only guess.

I didn't know much about Rajinna. Even Lukani was still a walking mystery, as far as I was concerned. I hadn't been around the kid long enough to form an opinion on his character. Maylea clearly liked him, though, and he'd been reliably loyal. He had fought for us again and again, so I wouldn't turn my back on the kid now. Whatever Neiko wanted with him, it would have to wait until Lukani was awake, lucid, and able to decide for himself.

With everyone more or less settled, I looked around for Violet next. She was injured, too. I needed to check on her and make sure it wasn't serious. Based on past history, I knew she would hide an injury for as long as she could—even if it was life-threatening.

But I didn't see her anywhere.

My pulse quickened, a little prickle of fear in the pit of my gut beginning to make my stomach turn. Where did she go? Was she all right? Had something taken her when I wasn't looking?

Armed with my medical kit, I paced down the length of the archives chamber, searching every row of shelves. A glimmer of white caught my eye off to the left, and I stopped suddenly. Down a wider aisle of dust-covered bookcases, Violet sat on the floor in front of a large, white stone fireplace. Moth-eaten low couches and cushions were arranged around it, and several low tables were piled with more slowly decaying heaps of books and scrolls. A tarnished, long-forgotten bronze teapot sat on a tray with an assortment of cups, and a large feathered quill stuck out of an ornate silver inkbottle in the shape of a peacock.

I stood perfectly still, watching in silence as she struck a piece of flintstone over a large candelabra in the middle of one of the tables. She lit the skinny candles one by one, then slowly sank down to sit next to the table with a hissing curse. Her expression screwed up, and she gingerly touched her right shoulder again.

Ahh. There it was. I'd been right all along. She really was hurt worse than she was letting on.

"And here you thought you could sneak off and avoid all my medical expertise," I scolded as I made my way toward her. "Nice try."

Violet flinched and cast a startled glance in my direction before quickly turning away, her lips pursed like a pouting child who'd just been caught in the act.

"Is there a specific reason you decided to settle down here so far from the rest of us?" I asked as I dropped my medical kit onto the table beside her and picked up the old teapot. Opening the lid and peering inside, I didn't find anything. Not even the remnants of old tea leaves. It smelled clean enough, so I took my waterskin from my kit and began to fill it.

When she didn't answer, I decided to push my luck. "Is it because Neiko has a problem with you being here? Because you know I'll happily toss his butt outside and slam the door, if that makes you happy."

Violet snorted, fighting back a smile as she shook her head. "No, it's not that. I just ... needed a moment to think."

"This place is getting to you again, eh?" I guessed again.

Her mouth twisted to one side, but she didn't reply. She didn't have to. That fidgety, almost ashamed look on her face said it all. Whatever had happened to her in this city, or maybe even in these ruins, being here was bringing it back to the surface. It was eating away at her.

Gods, I just wished she'd tell me why.

Plucking one of the candles out of that fancy candelabra, I carried it and some of the old scrolls over to the fireplace. I pretended not to notice her look of absolute horror as I tossed them, and a few of the old books, into the fireplace and lit it.

"Th-Those are ancient texts! You cannot just—!" she began to protest.

"What? Use some old, rotten, and completely illegible paper to make a fire so I can sterilize my medical equipment?" I interrupted.

Violet's expression scrunched sourly. "Those texts likely date back to before the War of the Stones."

"And that would be extremely interesting if they weren't also covered in mold, rot, and probably written in a language no one's used in a thousand years." I hung the pot on the hook over the fire and sat down on the raised outer hearth. "If it makes you feel better, I'll only burn what I need for this. But I'm betting that wound on your shoulder needs to be cleaned out, too. I need sterile water for that."

Violet flinched back, turning her injured shoulder away almost like she was still trying to hide it. Rosy color flushed over her smooth, pale cheeks as she fixed me with a hard look.

I held her gaze and didn't even blink. We both knew she needed this. I'd helped her once already, and whether it was just pride or lingering distrust, she would have to get over it and let me help her again.

She didn't say another word while I waited for the water to boil, then used it to sterilize my stitching needle, some of my cutting implements, and a washcloth. I washed my hands off as best I could, too, and brought all my tools and the remaining water still in the pot over to the table next to her. Violet stiffened as I sat down behind her and made a diligent effort not to let me see her face.

Fine. We'd just do this the awkward way, then.

"Gods, Fates, and all things divine, if I ever set foot in another cave, it'll be too soon. Nobody said a word about goblins or anything like that slimy monstrosity," I groaned as I began running clean thread through my needle.

No reply.

Arrrgh. Why was she being like this again? What did I do wrong this time?

"You want to give me some clue about why you're angry at me now?" I fumed under my breath. "Because whatever it was, I can't apologize if I'm not even aware of what I did wrong."

"I'm not angry at you," she said, her tone much softer than I expected.

"Really? It sure seems like it," I huffed and scooted around to face her back, slowly rinsing the rag in the hot water. "Slide that sleeve off for me, would you?"

Violet carefully pulled one arm out of her tunic, leaving her beautifully slender shoulder bare. I hadn't expected it to, you know, have any kind of effect on me. She was my patient. You didn't ogle patients.

But it was nearly impossible not to admire her, and my heartbeat skipped stupidly as I brushed my fingers through some of her long, silky, light hair to comb it over her other shoulder and out of the way. Gods and Fates. Why did something so simple make my chest feel so tight? Like I couldn't even take a real breath?

"I'm not angry at anyone," Violet admitted quietly, her neck arching as she bowed her head slightly. "I am ... worried. We have taken so long just to leave Rienka. What if we are too late?"

I'd considered that, too. Unfortunately, there was nothing we could do except keep trying. We had to forge forward, even if we wound up being too little too late for Ronan and the codex.

"I'm not ready to give up yet," I murmured as I readied the rag and began to slowly wipe away the layers of smeared and dried blood caked around the top of her shoulder, just beside her collarbone.

"I'm not either," she agreed. "I'm just concerned. Everything about this mission has seemed to go wrong. I am so sorry about that. I know you must be worried about your nephew."

Her whole body tensed again as I began cleaning away the blood and grime. Little by little, numerous small punctures came into view. Teeth marks. It was a bite, after all. By the look of it and how the wounds were torn into her skin, the goblin had managed to get ahold of her and hang on while she tried to fling or pull it off.

No wonder it was causing her so much pain.

"Yes, I'm worried about Ronan. This whole mission has been a mess nearly from day one. But I don't blame you for that, Violet. If I've learned anything over the years of dealing with insane, dangerous, and impossible situations like this, it's that things never go according to plan. You just have to solve one problem at a time, take the next step, and hope it's enough." I kept my tone even and steady, half because I was focused now on checking each puncture for any foreign material inside, and half because I could feel her trembling slightly as I touched each puncture. Her pulse was pounding in the side of her neck, and I didn't know if that was from pain or nerves.

"Whatever happens, rest assured that my primary concern is making sure we *all* get there in one piece. I won't let anyone or anything get in our way. Not even this new guy who has apparently decided to tag along—Neiko, or whatever his name is. Obviously, he wants to take Lukani and skip off into the sunset and leave the rest of us to rot down here. He's lucky I don't put a blade between his eyes."

"You don't have to keep doing that, you know," Violet murmured, her tone strangely tense.

"Do what?"

"Defending my honor every time someone calls me by that word. I realize chivalry is practically ingrained in the very marrow of your very Maldobarian bones—but, truly, it isn't necessary. I'm quite used to it by now."

Wait, was she serious? I stared at the back of her head for a minute, trying to process that. "It doesn't matter if you're used to it or not. You're a member of my team. And I'm going to demand that he shows you the same respect he shows to the rest of us. That's not me being chivalrous. It's asking for common decency."

Violet's head turned slightly, and I caught her stealing a swift peek at me with her expression skewed uncomfortably and her cheeks now flushed deeply. I couldn't tell if it was with embarrassment or frustration, though. "Yes, but it's a bit ... strange to have it done by a man of your social standing."

My what now? Social standing? Ugggh. This was about me being a prince, wasn't it? Great.

I scowled back down at the wounds on her shoulder and got back to work carefully stitching each one of the openings. I finished the last one quickly and wiped everything clean again. No need for a bandage this time, although I still wished I had some of that medicinal salve.

Oh well. Better to get this done so I could escape the rest of this conversation as quickly as possible.

"Being the third-born doesn't count for much," I grumbled at last. "I'll never rule over anything. And I don't want to. So, it's worthless. It's just a stupid empty title. It doesn't mean crap."

Violet was still peering at me, and I could practically feel her gaze like a tingling heat on my skin. "I was not trying to tease you about it. No need to be prickly, Lieutenant."

"I'm not being prickly," I muttered.

"You are," she countered. "Why? Why does talking about your birthright always make you so angry? Anyone else would be—"

"Anyone else *isn't* me," I snapped, flashing her a glare that I sincerely hoped would get her to finally drop the topic. "That title has never done anything good for me. Ever."

Violet didn't reply, and we sat in tense, uncomfortable silence. Minutes passed, and I finally let myself begin to relax again.

"This is about the elven woman, isn't it?" she asked suddenly. "About the reason you two went your separate ways many years ago? Is that the reason she ended your relationship? Because of your title as prince?"

My heart wrenched violently and I stopped working. A bolt of panic ripped through my chest like I'd been run through with a pike. Heat scorched my throat and for a moment, I couldn't even blink. Everything from my neck down went completely numb. My ears rang. How, by all the Fates, did she know about that? Had Arlan's people been snooping through my personal letters?! Had she read them when I wasn't looking?

No. She wouldn't do that. Violet was a spy, assassin, and a lot of other things. But I couldn't imagine her intentionally prying into my personal life like that. She did seem to have at least some sense of boundaries.

Calm. I had to stay calm.

"Reigh," she said my name slowly and carefully, like a gentle warning. "You want me to trust you. To talk about difficult things from my past. I need you to do the same."

She wanted me to *talk* about it?

I sat, barely able to breathe, and tried frantically to think. To see a way out. The urge to drop everything and run was enough to make my hands shake and I sank back, not trusting myself to touch her with anything sharp until I got this under control. I didn't want to hurt her, even by accident.

I took in a deep breath and slowly let it out.

"Reigh?" When I didn't answer, Violet started to turn where she sat like she was going to face me.

Without even thinking, I put a hand on the back of her neck and held her firmly in place. Violet held still and didn't say another word.

I couldn't do this ... I could not talk about this and look her in the eye at the same time.

"Yes," I heard myself answer, but the voice sounded all wrong. Broken. Defeated. Pathetic. I bit down hard, but I couldn't stop it. The words crawled out of me like bugs from a rotten log. "Enyo ... she didn't want ... that. She said it was too much for her. I tried to explain, to tell her it wouldn't make a difference. I'd never be king. She would never have to be queen. We didn't have to live at the castle or even in Halfax. We could make it work. I could even renounce my title completely, if that's what it took. But she didn't want it. She didn't want to live in Maldobar. She didn't want me to leave for Blybrig Academy to work with the other dragonriders. And I couldn't just drop everything and run off to Luntharda. My family needed me, and I'd waited a lifetime to finally see them. I thought she understood. I thought I was doing a good job of going to see her as often as I could. Everything seemed fine. But I guess ... there was a lot more going on than I realized."

I shut my eyes tightly, fighting with every shred of strength I had left to keep my emotions in check. I wouldn't break down. Not now. Not in front of her. "Enyo said I wasn't the same after the war ended. Apparently, I wasn't the person she'd known before. And this person I am now ... she didn't want."

With my hand still lightly holding the back of her neck, Violet didn't move. She didn't try to turn or look at my pathetic, twitching face or my watering eyes. And when she spoke, her voice was as smooth, even, and sure as wind under my dragon's wings.

"I do."

25

CHAPTER TWENTY-FIVE

My hand slid off the back of Violet's neck as those two simple words hit me full force, lodging in the center of my heart like a well-aimed crossbow bolt. Pain shattered through every part of my brain. Dread and terror stole the last bit of breath from my lungs.

I couldn't move—not even when she turned around to face me at last. I stared at her, trying to figure out some way that she could mean something else. She didn't mean it that way. Impossible. No.

My jaw clenched as I looked down at my blood-smeared hands. I had been an utter disappointment to everyone in my life for as long as I could remember. I let people down again and again. I would never be enough. I would always fail. I'd always have to rely on other, better people to carry my dead weight because, in the end, I was never strong enough.

She couldn't possibly *want* that.

And even if she did, how could I ever justify putting another person through it? It would hurt. Gods and Fates, it would hurt both of us. It might even destroy me. It was better to not even go there, to never feel that way ever again. I wouldn't dare hope for it. I wouldn't look for it. I-I wouldn't—

"Reigh," Violet breathed my name gently, like the softest wish whispered into candlelight. Her hands touched my cheeks, cradling my face so she could look me in the eye. I could see it in the depths of her ruby-colored eyes. There was more she wanted to say. Emotions simmering right beneath the surface.

Then, all at once, those walls began to come up again. And an instant before that mask of indifference sealed itself over her face, I saw the fear in her eyes. A fear I knew all too well.

Because it was the same fear I felt whenever she touched me, said my name, or teased me like we'd known each other all our lives. It was an all-consuming, crippling, soul-crushing fear that grew and festered.

It was the fear of getting hurt again by someone you trust.

Violet's hands slid away. She started to get up.

I ... Gods and Fates, I couldn't ... I couldn't take it anymore. How could she just stop? How could she throw up those defenses after insisting I trust her and talk about these things?

She was so—ARGH!

Her gaze met mine for one tiny, fleeting instant. And I saw it: the truth I'd been running from practically since the moment we met.

I was no different.

How many times had I done that *exact* same thing to the people I cared for? How many times had I held them all at a distance out of fear? How many times had I ran away from feeling something important because of how bad the pain might be?

All my life.

I didn't know the details of Violet's past, but I could see an echo of the same kind of person I'd become reflected in those beautiful scarlet eyes so clearly. Whatever or whoever she had been before, I knew who Violet was now.

And that was all that mattered.

My heartbeat thundered in my ears as I snapped to my feet and stormed straight for her, fury in every step. My hands clenched into shaking fists. My vision tunneled. My head swam. My knees threatened to buckle with every step.

But, by all things divine, I was going to do it. I was going to make the biggest mistake of my life, and there wasn't a force in the entire universe that could stop me.

I caught up to Violet in four paces, right in front of the smoldering fireplace, and seized her around the waist with one arm. Grasping the back of her head with the other, I dragged her in close enough to press my mouth against hers.

I kissed her fiercely, holding her body against mine with all my strength.

Violet gasped sharply. She went stiff, her hands pressed against my chest.

Then her arms wrapped around my neck. She kissed me back like the world might crumble beneath our feet at any moment. Her lips were soft, but the kiss was rough and ruthless. Something about it lit a fire in my soul. Her fingers scraped over my scalp and twisted into my hair, and I couldn't hold back.

I grabbed her thighs and snatched her off the ground, backing her right up against the nearest bookshelf, and pinned her there.

This was stupid. Beyond stupid. Fates, what was I even thinking? Had I finally lost my mind? Violet and I were completely wrong for each other. I had already been down this road once. I'd waded neck-deep into reckless love and nearly drowned in the depths. I shouldn't have wanted more. I shouldn't have wanted her.

But I did.

Gods and Fates, I wanted all of her—and not just to hold her and kiss her like this. I wanted her to stay at my side. I wanted her to keep driving me insane, teasing and taunting me like a cat batting at a caught mouse. I wanted to keep having those quiet fireside talks, and walking together through the crowded markets. I wanted to keep learning about her. I wanted to hear her laugh again. To feel her hand in mine. To see her smile.

I didn't want to live without it. Not for a single second.

I needed her. Gods, I had never needed anything more. I would spend my very last breath protecting her. I would pry open the gates of the divine realm with my bare hands if it meant she could stay right here in my arms. I couldn't imagine a future without her right at the center of it.

And before I could stop it—before I could even think about it at all—the words spilled out past all my better judgment.

"I-I ... I love you."

It hurt. Gods, those words scorched through every part of me like burning oil. I'd regret it. I knew that. It was reckless to even think that, let alone say it to her face. She would reject me. One word from those beautiful, impossibly soft lips would seal my fate.

Violet pulled back slightly. Still gasping for quick, frenzied breaths, she studied me with those eerie scarlet eyes. I knew she was seeing me—all of me. The ugly, scarred, misshapen depths of my heart that I'd never intended to show anyone.

With my arms still around her and my body pressing hers against the bookshelf, I bowed my head so maybe she wouldn't see my mouth screw up. I wanted to take it back. To catch those words in midair and cram them back into my mouth. But it was too late.

I was already burning.

Violet's smooth, cool palms slid along my jaw, thumbs caressing my cheeks as she tilted my head back up to meet her gaze. Her legs squeezed at my waist harder, lips brushing mine, as she leaned in to whisper, "I have loved you longer than you will ever know, Reigh Farrow."

My pulse skipped. Every muscle tensed, like someone had just dumped a bucket of icy water over my head. She ... she did? Gods and Fates, she *loved* me? I couldn't speak. I could only stand there, staring into those stunning scarlet eyes, while every brick of shame, doubt, fear, anger, and pain I had stacked around myself over the years crumbled away.

Violet loved me.

She wanted me, even knowing what and who I was.

And I wanted her—more than anything.

Adrenaline surged through my body, and my skin buzzed with wild, savage energy as she dragged a finger down the bridge of my nose and teased at my bottom lip. "Now, shut up and kiss me again."

"My sister is going to kill me," I murmured as I lay with my eyes closed, sprawled on my back in front of the hearth. With one of her lovely, strong legs draped over me, and my arm around her, Violet had her head nestled into my shoulder and one hand on my chest. We lay so close I could feel every breath she took as if it were my own.

"And why would she do something like that?" She laughed softly.

"I think she had another meeting lined up with yet another potential bride next month." I winced a little. "Oops."

"Is that so? And who was it this time?"

"Some duchess out of Ethalan, I think. I don't remember. I wasn't paying much attention, to be honest," I confessed. Sure, so it was probably rude to brush off those young noblewomen before I'd even met them. But I couldn't help it. Jenna had started doing this a few years ago—sneakily arranging meetings between myself and a conveniently single noble girl under the guise of some political crap that *required my presence*. Whatever that was supposed to mean.

"For shame," Violet scolded playfully. "Such a naughty prince."

"You'd think after the last few she forced me into, Jenna would have figured out that trying to set me up with anyone like that was doomed to be a disaster. I'm not interested in being sold like a sow at market." I sighed and stared up at the ceiling, enjoying the ambient warmth of Violet on one side of me, and the hearth on the other. If I stayed here like this much longer, I might actually fall asleep. Heh.

"And what a handsome sow you are," Violet teased. "How did I ever get so lucky?"

I couldn't resist a drowsy grin. "Luck is a strong word. You may decide it's something else after the luster wears off."

Violet laughed again and flicked the end of my nose. Rolling over onto her stomach, she propped herself up on her elbows and stared down at me. With her face framed in flowing locks of nearly-white hair and those dazzling red eyes sparkling like polished gemstones in the firelight, I couldn't resist the urge to brush my hand along her cheek again. Gods and Fates, I was the lucky one. How could someone so beautiful really want anything to do with me?

Her expression changed some as she held my gaze, that playful smile fading, as though a veil of worry had fallen over her features. But I didn't ask. I didn't push her. Whatever she was about to say, I could see she was still wrestling with it. I had to wait until she was ready.

At last, Violet looked down, nibbling at her bottom lip before she finally spoke in a quiet, cautious voice. "You spoke your truth to me. Now ... I must do the same."

Whoa. Okay, then. I nodded and kept silent, watching her carefully.

Her throat jumped as she swallowed, flicking me a quick, worried glance before she began. "You already know I was with the Zenith's Call before I came to Maldobar to work for Arlan. I was very young then, and my life here was quite complicated. It was good, mostly. Fast-paced. Often dangerous. Not at all what I had envisioned for myself. But I grew to love it, and the people I worked with." She paused, her face seeming to glaze over with a faraway expression, as though the memories had carried her off to some distant past. "The last mission I ever worked for the Call was ... the reason I had to leave them. I lost someone important to me. Someone I loved. And without him, I couldn't see a future anywhere until Arlan approached me about going to Maldobar. I must have been about eighteen or so?"

"You don't remember how old you were?" Somehow, that struck me as odd.

"Before I was with the Zenith's Call, my life was much more chaotic," she replied, lips pressing together into a thin, uncomfortable line. "I'm not proud of the person I had to become in order to survive. I lost track of things that didn't seem to matter—like my age."

Oh. Wow. Sooo, she really had no idea how old she was. I wondered if Viperi had the same lifespan as other human races, or if they were like the Avoran elves and lived for centuries. Now didn't seem like a great time to ask, though.

Better to let her finish first.

"That person I loved ... he and I first began to trust one another here, in these very ruins. We had a mission together that brought us here, and I realized he was someone I could actually count on," she murmured, fiddling with a lock of her hair. "I never thought I would feel that way about anyone else. And to be honest, I didn't want to. It hurt too much to lose someone I cared for like that—someone I assumed would always be in my life. I went to Maldobar for the purpose of working for Arlan, but I wanted to go because ... I wanted distance from this place and everything that had happened here. I wanted a place without memories of *him*." She paused, her gaze darting up to meet mine again with a cautious vulnerability I wasn't expecting. "And then I saw you."

"Me?" I couldn't help but sound surprised. Gods, if she came to Maldobar right after the Tibran war, that meant she'd first seen me as a very angry, very confused, very traumatized young man with absolutely no idea what to do with himself or anything he felt.

Fine. So not much had changed on that front. But hey, I was working on it. I'd definitely made some progress.

"Arlan wanted eyes on the divinely blessed people in the immediate area. He assigned several agents to each and insisted we take note of your movements or any changes in your habits—always from afar, of course. We were never permitted to engage with you directly," she continued. "I was assigned to watch over you from a distance. And I did, for a while."

I leaned in a little closer, squinting my eyes and scrunching my mouth up disapprovingly. "You spied on me in the bath, didn't you?"

Violet put a hand over my face and pushed me back. "No!" she laughed.

"Watched me change clothes?" I guessed again.

"No!"

"Followed me through the street?"

She pulled a thinking face with one eye shut and her mouth mashed to one side. "Mmmm, now *that* I probably did."

"Impossible," I scoffed and flopped back down on my back beside her. "I would have noticed you immediately."

Violet scooted closer, resting her chin on my chest with a roguish little grin. "Apparently not. This may come as a surprise to you, but I am actually quite good at my job."

I rolled my eyes. "To slip by under a dragonrider's nose? Not likely."

"Oh? Like how it was *such* a struggle for me to make my way into your little academy under so many dragonriders' noses?" she quipped.

Ugggh. I'd almost forgotten about that. I wondered how many lieutenants Jaevid had yelled at about it after we left.

"All right, fine, so maybe you did spy on me and follow me around with all your fancy, former assassin skills," I surrendered with a smirk. "But I remember very clearly what I was like at that age, and I find it very hard to believe anyone would have fallen for me at first sight. I was angry a lot back then. I did and said a lot of stupid things, even to people I cared about, because of that anger."

Violet smiled—a real, genuine, affectionate smile that made her eyes shine and her whole face seem to glow. "That's not what I saw," she countered. "I saw a young man who was struggling, yes. But even from the depths of your despair, you were always the first to reach out in compassion to the sick and injured. You take care of people; even ones you don't necessarily like. Your own needs always come second if there is someone to be helped. I saw that." She reached out to stroke her fingers through my hair again. "I still do. And just like then, I wonder who looks after you? Who is there when you wake up shaking from your nightmares? Who notices the pain that still lingers from your past injuries? Who can you be honest with about the things you have experienced?"

I held still, watching that smile fade gradually away to a look of sorrow. She was *worried* about me? I, well, I hadn't thought anyone really noticed any of those things. I was a dragonrider and a prince. I wasn't supposed to show anything except steady, constant strength.

But now I knew. I knew why she had been the one who found me after my most recent nightmare. I knew why she had come to watch over me after the attack on Rienka. I knew why she ran after me every time I wandered off on my own.

She was worried about me.

She ... really did love me.

Reaching for her wrist, I tugged the sleeve of her tunic down to reveal the hidden branded mark on her forearm, just below her elbow. The emblem of the Zenith's Call. I pressed my lips against it. Her porcelain pale cheeks went rosy again, and I could have sworn I heard her gasp faintly, a sound that made my toes curl up in my boots.

Gods, I adored that sound.

"Stay with me. Don't leave my side. Ever. And when we get back to Maldobar, I'll court you properly," I ventured, not sure how she would respond to an offer like that. Maybe it was too sudden?

She wiggled her way up so that her face stared directly down into mine, her long hair falling like a sterling curtain around us. "You'd parade a Viperi assassin and spy through Maldobar's royal court as your partner?"

I grinned. "To the horror of all the stuffy nobles and uptight officers? Absolutely. Without hesitation. In fact, I'll probably hire someone to follow us with a bell just to make sure no one misses it."

She laughed and leaned down, kissing my lips again. "Very well, Lieutenant. Court me, if you dare."

26

CHAPTER TWENTY-SIX

Gathered in the failing light that still ebbed in from the open hidden door, it didn't take any special insight to sense that everyone—including myself—was on edge. Thatcher had filled me in on everything that had happened on the surface, in Salnis, while Violet and I were down here in the temple. Knowing there was at least a legion of Nar'Haleenan soldiers camped all around the area did not make me feel all warm and fuzzy inside. We couldn't risk going back to the city for any reason. But the way forward didn't seem any safer.

"We basically have two choices here," I said as I stood in the middle of our group. "Fair warning, neither of these options are great, but at this point, we have to make a decision and get moving as soon as possible."

After quite a few hours of rest, food, water, and basking in the warmth of the heat from outside to dry our things, we couldn't afford to dawdle for even one second longer. Lukani was back on his feet, still a little pale-faced, but mostly coherent. Thatcher still had those burns under his eyes, but he seemed a lot steadier on his feet now that he'd had some rest and food. Maylea was out of arrows, but she had a steely look of resolve as she gripped her bow firmly. I'd seen that look in her father's eyes many times. No one would be holding her back from whatever fight came next—with or without arrows.

Neiko was, er, still tagging along. Ugh. He stood right in our midst like he was now a part of the group, listening and nodding intently. I tried not to let that annoy me.

I did not succeed.

"First option: we go back into the ruins, hope we can find our way to the gateway, that it still functions, and that nothing else terrible tries to eat us in the process." I hesitated, feeling the full force of Violet's suspicious frown from where she stood beside me. "Or, uh, option two would be ... um, I can try something a little risky but potentially far more direct to get us there."

"Risky how?" Violet questioned, her eyes narrowing suspiciously.

I winced a little. Crap. I'd forgotten about this little relationship snag—primarily because I had not been in one since I was a teenager. Old dog, new tricks. I had, however, been around Jaevid and Murdoc and their wives enough to realize that the decision to put my life in jeopardy for the greater good was now no longer mine to make. Not solely, anyway. I had to take her feelings into account when it came to my usually-almost-deadly stunts.

Ohhh boy. She was *not* going to like this.

"Um, okay, you see ... since I have been granted Clysiros's blessings and power again, I have certain abilities. It's sort of like before, when I was the harbinger, although my powers seem a lot stronger now. So far, anyway. And one of those abilities is—well, it's called valestepping, but it's actually more like teleporting," I rambled, already sweating bullets as I kept my gaze locked on Thatcher's forehead like my life depended on it. Anything to keep from meeting that now scorching glare coming from the small, angry, white-haired woman standing beside me.

Fates preserve me.

"And it is dangerous?" she asked sharply.

"Yeeeeah, uh, sorta? It was very dangerous for me before. Almost killed me a few times, actually," I said with a nervous chuckle. "But I've already tried it once and it doesn't seem to be nearly as draining as it used to be."

"You already tried it?" she fumed. "Even though it could have killed you?!"

Great.

I turned to face her and flailed my arms. "You were in *danger*! Gods, woman, I didn't have any other way to reach you in time!"

"Not that we're not enjoying your little lovers' quarrel, but can we refocus here?" Thatcher chimed in, his expression every bit as shocked and dismayed as Violet's as he crossed his arms over his chest. "You're saying you can valestep us all the way to the Compendium Library?"

I winced again, giving him that forced, toothy, grimacing look that probably wasn't going to win me any more of their confidence. "Uhhh, I'm not exactly sure how far I can do it. I've never tested that since, you know, it was so dangerous before."

"What's the farthest distance you were able to cross with it before?" Maylea asked.

I shrugged. "A mile? Maybe two?"

Violet's mouth scrunched up bitterly as she glared at me. "And you want to try to cross thousands of miles and arrive in a location you've never even seen before?"

"Hey, I'm open to suggestions here!" I threw my hands up again in surrender. "If anyone has a better plan, I'm all ears!"

"I believe I do," a deep, heavily accented masculine voice interrupted.

We all turned in unison, whirling to face the source with weapons already drawn. My jaw dropped and I took a protective step toward Violet as I stared across the small crowd of men gathered not even ten feet away from us. No, not just men. They were all *Rajinna* men.

Sweet Fates, where had they come from?!

I counted twelve in all, dressed in a wide spectrum of colorful robes, long strings of jewels, and golden bands. Every one of them had the same features as Neiko and Lukani—lion-like tails, horns, pointed incisors, and eerie yellow eyes. They also had varying shades of oddly colored skin. I saw several shades of blue, purple, and even pink and gray.

The one at the very front of the group appeared to be the oldest. He was also the largest, with thick, brawny, bare arms exposed by his sleeveless open vest. His dark cobalt skin was mottled with scars and swirling tattoos of red and black that spanned across his chest and down his arms all the way to his wrists. His curled dark horns were sheathed in gold at the tips, and his thick black hair hung down to the middle of his back like a mane.

He loomed over us, standing a few inches taller than Thatcher, and slowly scanned our group with his deeply set yellow eyes. His expression stayed stony and guarded, not betraying anything about what his real intentions were—friendly or hostile.

I had a pretty good idea what he wanted from us, though.

Lukani seemed to shrink as he stared across the crowd, his long, pointed ears drooping and his shoulders drawing up. He didn't say a word, even when Neiko let out an excited shout and went trotting over to stand right in front of the huge man like an excited terrier.

"Father! You received my distress call!" Neiko exclaimed. "I was beginning to worry we were too far apart."

The big Rajinna man put a hand on his shoulder, giving Neiko an approving nod before he looked back at the rest of us again. "And these must be the ones Arlan spoke of."

"Yes, indeed," Neiko confirmed, quickly stepping aside and making a sweeping gesture to the rest of us. "I have found the young one, but he travels with many humans. It seems many of them are god-touched."

The man nodded, then strode proudly toward me. It was only then that I noticed the massive, double-headed great axe he wore in a leather harness across his back. Gods and Fates, it was bigger than I was, and appeared to be crafted from solid bronze. It must have weighed a hundred pounds, at least.

It took every bit of my nerve to hold steady and keep my expression neutral as he stopped only a few paces away and stretched out a hand like he wanted me to shake it. "I am Ziryan. Arlan the Kinslayer sent word that you might be in need of aid, and that one of our own was also in your midst. We were on our way to find you in the temple but were delayed. It seems the Hands of Fate are not far behind you. We discovered them after they had already destroyed the gateway in this temple."

My shoulders dropped and I resisted the urge to scream up at the ceiling. The Hands of Fate had already destroyed that gateway? So much for that option.

Ziryan's huge hand all but swallowed mine when I returned the gesture. My attempt at a strong shake probably felt pathetic to him. "Yeah, we ran into a few," I replied. "You can call me Reigh. This is Thatcher, Maylea, Violet, and ... Lukani." I hesitated on the last name, not sure if I should have let the kid introduce himself or not. He looked ready to pass out again as Ziryan's gaze finally landed right on him.

But the big Rajinna man's expression softened immediately, looking down at Lukani with the same expression I'd seen on Jaevid's face when he first held his infant sons. He stepped past me, moving through our group and finally crouching on one knee in front of Lukani. "Arlan told me much about you, young one," he said, his deep voice much gentler now. "You truly have no memory of your capture?"

Lukani slowly shook his head. Even from several paces away, I could see his shoulders and arms tense like he might bolt at any moment.

Ziryan's expression fell some, his strange yellow eyes panning over the boy as though he were examining every tiny detail. "I see," he murmured. "Perhaps that is for the best. Your mother defended you bravely, and I will forever carry the shame that I could not save her."

"Y-You knew my mother?" Lukani's voice shook with desperation as his entire body seemed to go slack in shock.

A faint, agonized smile tugged at the corners of Ziryan's sharp features. "I did. She was my mate," he answered quietly. "And you ... were our greatest treasure."

You could have heard a mouse sneeze in the silence that hung in the chamber. Lukani didn't seem to be breathing. He didn't blink. He just stared at the big Rajinna man, his eyes as wide as two yellow saucers and his mouth hanging open.

So, Ziryan was his *actual* father? Not just some term the Rajinna used for their elders? Even Neiko seemed shocked at that revelation. I guess Ziryan had kept that little tidbit to himself. Heh. Interesting.

"I know this must be difficult for you to hear," Ziyran said, bowing his head some. "You see, all Rajinna are born male. We take partners only from royal bloodlines of Lunostri elves, as we have since the dawn of our species. Once that bond is forged, it can never be broken, and children born of those unions are even more rare, but are always Rajinna. They grow far slower than most other children, and that is when we are most vulnerable—before our power truly manifests and we cannot defend ourselves. That is why you and your mother were targeted. And I was too late." His wide, sharply angled jawline went rigid. His densely muscled frame seemed to stiffen in quiet wrath at the memory as his eyes smoldered ominously. He reached out, slowly and cautiously, for one of Lukani's much smaller hands. "I am sorry that I failed you, my son."

Lukani sprang toward him suddenly, crossing the small distance in a heartbeat and flinging his arms around the big man's neck. He hugged him fiercely, gripping the back of his silken vest and burying his face against Ziryan's thick mane of hair. I could have sworn I saw tears in Ziryan's eyes as he hugged Lukani back tightly.

A small sniffle was my only warning before I felt someone's weight lean into my side, too. Maylea hid under my arm, her chin trembling and fresh tears rolling down her cheeks as she watched them.

Right—this was bound to be awkward and painful for her. A strange mixture of joy and sorrow for a young girl who'd only just dipped her toes into the ocean of love. Lukani might continue with us for a short time, if he wanted. But ultimately ... he would stay here in the Southern Kingdoms. And he *should* stay here. He'd been robbed of an entire childhood that should have been spent with his family. This was his chance to reclaim some of it.

We had no right to stand in the way of that.

Pulling back, Ziryan held Lukani's head in his large hands and kissed his forehead. Then he finally looked back up to the rest of us. "You have brought my only blood child back to me. What can the Korvaal Clan do to repay such a debt?"

"You did mention you had an idea about how we could get out of here," I reminded him. "That would certainly be welcomed at this point. We need to get to The Compendium Library as soon as possible."

Ziryan stood, his hand still resting on Lukani's shoulder as he faced me with a look of proud resolve. "No," he corrected. "According to your man, Arlan, you do not."

Oh? I flicked a sideways glance to Thatcher, who already wore a skeptical frown. I wasn't feeling all that trusting, either. Even if Arlan had somehow managed to contact this guy—which was plausible, considering the strength of the magic I'd seen him use before—what connection did he actually have with Ziryan? Were they allies? Acquaintances? Or was I standing in front of yet another one of Arlan's old enemies who would turn on us the first chance he got?

I didn't know.

Fortunately, it wasn't up to me whether we should trust him or not. Violet was the expert, here. She didn't waste a second and immediately spoke up. "And what did he say, exactly?"

Unlike Neiko, Ziryan didn't seem the least bit thrown by the fact that she was a Viperi. He considered her with the same guarded yet intensely focused stare he did the rest of us as he answered. "The codex you seek has already been removed from play. Avgior has been awakened. The game has officially changed, and your first and only order of business should be reaching the port of Uru'Nai as soon as possible."

My stomach dropped to the soles of my boots. My heartbeat slowed, and a shuddering breath left my lips like a death rattle. The codex was out of play? What did that even mean? Were we too late? Gods and Fates, what was happening? Was Ronan all right? Who the heck was Avgior?

"Avgior," Violet gasped in horror. "Then ... it's really happening. Sadeera is going to try to open the gate to the divine realm. Is that what he suggested?"

"It would seem so," Ziryan confirmed. "Arlan made mention that he is moving more formidable forces to the Gate of Proleus, I assume to make a final stand against her."

I frowned. "Formidable forces?"

"Dragonriders," he said matter-of-factly. "But I would advise against venturing there. We have a powerful seer among us who has already glimpsed the size of the forces gathering there, most likely to prevent outsiders from interfering with the ritual. At least ten thousand men with war machines, cavalry, and arcane cannons."

"Gods ..." Thatcher whispered hoarsely. "It must be Jaevid and the others."

I spat a string of Gray elven curses and spun on a heel, pacing a few feet away and wringing my fingers through my hair. Gods, Fates, and all things divine! *Of course* it was Jaevid. Who the heck else would be that stupid? That idiot didn't know how to keep his nose out of a world-ending disaster. And if he was going there with Arlan, then I had to believe Murdoc, Garnett, and maybe even my sister would be skipping along right behind them.

"You mean my dah is here? In Nar'Haleen? But that—that can't be! H-How would they even get here that fast?" Maylea stammered, her face paling as she glanced back and forth between us frantically. "It took us so long to get here by ship, and dragons can't fly that far all at once, can they? It's impossible, isn't it?"

"No," Violet announced. "It isn't."

I snapped around, pacing slowly toward her with my head tilted to the side as I eyed her suspiciously. "What do you mean?" I demanded. "What haven't you told us?"

Violet glanced skyward, as though trying to collect her thoughts, before she gave a heavy, defeated sigh. "Let's just say that ... Arlan has been planning this confrontation for a very long time. He had no interest in leaving margins for errors and missteps. And with Miss Phoebe's brilliant engineering mind now readily at his disposal, he has not been idle over the last fourteen years."

"He's had Phoebe building something for him?" Thatcher guessed.

"There really is no name for it in any language I can speak, simply because something like it has never existed before now," she said, still avoiding eye contact with me. She shifted her weight from one foot to the other, tucking some of her hair behind her ear as her mouth scrunched to one side and then the other. "But suffice it to say, it could move a decent number of dragons, riders, and even soldiers here in relatively short order. That said, I don't believe he would actually risk bringing it into Nar'Haleenan territory until the conflict was underway. He would probably try to keep it out of sight for as long as possible. It's not exactly subtle—at least, not from the few schematics and diagrams I've seen."

I started pacing again, rubbing at my forehead with the heel of my hand as my temples throbbed. "And how long would it take this whatever-it-is to reach Nar'Haleen from Maldobar?"

She finally met my gaze, her expression fractured with worry as she replied, "At most? Two days."

☙ 27 ❧

CHAPTER TWENTY-SEVEN

Two. Days.

Arlan had the means of getting us here in *two* days? And instead, he'd just slapped us on a boat with Malina? What the—?!

There weren't enough profane curses in the world for me to scream right then. Curse that Avoran slime-ball. He always had secrets—things tucked away in his back pocket that he kept hidden until it benefited him.

One look at Maylea made my temper fizzle, though. She stared around at all of us, her eyes rimmed with tears and her chest heaving in quick, terrified breaths. "My dah is headed straight for those armies," she seemed to realize aloud. "H-He can't fight against that many people on his own. We have to help him!"

I rushed over to her the instant I saw her expression start to go foggy. Fates, she was going to pass out if she didn't calm down. Taking her hands in mine, I kept my voice as calm as possible. "May, look at me. Take some deep breaths, okay? Try to calm down. We will do everything we can to help your dad," I promised.

She blinked owlishly at me, her chin trembling and her brow skewing as she fought back a sob. "How? How can we get there in time? I-I don't have any arrows, and—"

"It would be unwise for you to enter this fight," Ziryan insisted. "You would be fighting against the very best of the emperor's forces. With such small numbers, you will stand no chance of survival, and you will be bringing the sorceress the very last element she needs to open the gate."

"What are you talking about?" I snapped. I'd about had it with everyone holding back these vital tidbits of information.

"He means Maylea." Violet stepped forward, reaching down to stroke her fingers over the bone-carved pendant that hung around her neck on an old resin cord. I'd seen that necklace many times before. Jaevid had worn it first during the Gray and Tibran Wars, and then Thatcher during our confrontation with Iksoli. It was just a family heirloom. A trinket.

Right?

Maylea frowned, her voice still shaking some. "I-I don't understand."

"Lock and key, the gate shall hold. The boundary of Fates and souls. Blood and blade and twisting spark. To fracture, break, and rend apart," Violet recited. "It is an ancient curse that speaks of the Gate of Proleus that was sealed thousands of years ago. To break that gate open again, you need three things: the Blood of Fate—Avgior's blood, the Blade of Souls—forged by Clysiros in the pits of pandemonium, and the Spark of Life." She paused, her expression falling to something like grim acceptance as she ran a thumb over the pendant again. "The spark contained in this, the last Seed of Life. The energy of creation in its purest form."

"The ... the what?" Thatcher wheezed, rubbing at his own neck where that very trinket had hung only a week or so ago. "I thought it was just bone!"

"Its true identity was hidden away ages ago, likely to protect it for this very reason," Violet explained, her voice still hushed. "Placed around the neck of those charged by Paligno to speak in his place. The lapiloques. Your ancestors, Maylea."

"And if that sorceress, Sadeera, gets her hands on it?" I dared to ask.

"Then she will have the last thing she needs to complete the ritual and open the Gate of Proleus," Violet confirmed.

Great. Just ... fantastic. Our friends were headed straight into the heart of the hornets' nest and, what, we were just supposed to wave as we passed and head on our merry way?

No. Absolutely not.

I was a dragonrider. I did not betray my own. Win or lose, futile or not, I would rather die side by side with them in battle than face the rest of my life knowing I had abandoned them in their hour of need.

One look at Thatcher, and I knew beyond any doubt that he felt the same way. His wide, squared jaw clenched. He nodded once.

Fine. Let's do this, then.

Straightening, I let my arms drop to my sides as all my thoughts seemed to snap into focus. That mental state, the dragonrider state of mind, came over me so easily now. I could be objective in that cold silence, far removed from doubts and fears that paled in comparison to failure.

"Violet, you need to take Maylea and go to Uru'Nai. Mr. Ziryan, I appreciate the delivery of this ... update on the situation. If you really wish to repay our efforts in bringing your son here, I'd ask that you make sure these two make it there safely, since you seem more than capable of navigating this region discreetly." I bent down, beginning to gather up my bag and sling it onto my back.

Thatcher did the same without saying a single word.

Violet had plenty to say, though. She dashed over and grabbed my upper arm, pulling me around so she could glare up into my face. "What are you talking about, Reigh? You can't be serious! There's no way you can just—"

"I won't abandon Jaevid and the others to fight this alone," I cut her off quickly. "I am a dragonrider, and they are my *family*."

"THEY'RE MY FAMILY, TOO!" Maylea shouted suddenly. Gripping her bow in a shaking fist, she stormed toward me. "I have been trained by the finest warriors in our kingdom. I came here to help Ronan. I was chosen by one of the gods and given their power. That is my father you're talking about! I have just as much right to fight for my family as you do!"

"Not with that thing around your neck, you don't," I fired back. "This is not up for debate. Are you seriously suggesting we go marching into a fight carrying the one object that would help Sadeera bring the world and the divine realm to its knees?"

Maylea opened her mouth like she was going to keep arguing, but Violet swiftly put a hand on her shoulder and shook her head slightly. When she looked up at me again, my heartbeat skipped and stammered erratically. I'd never seen that profound, all-consuming anguish flickering in her scarlet eyes before. "This isn't a choice we get to make, Reigh," she said quietly. "I know it doesn't seem right. I know you want to do everything you can to protect us. But Paligno didn't select Maylea to be his paladin just so she could stand on the sidelines. He knew she was carrying this artifact when he chose her. He knew the risks of having her face Sadeera in battle. We cannot get in the way of that, even if it doesn't make sense to us now."

Little by little, I felt all the anger slowly drain from my mind. The adrenaline seeped away, leaving me breathless and lightheaded. My vision spotted some as I slowly panned my gaze from Violet to Maylea ... and that pendant hanging around her very young, very inexperienced, very innocent neck.

I knew Violet was right. This wasn't up to me. We could cut our losses and run, but what then? We were just supposed to sit around and wait for Sadeera to slither back into our lives and start this cycle all over again? She wasn't going to just decide to mark this up as a loss and back down after plotting for centuries. Not when she had two of the three components she needed already. This wouldn't end just because we decided to bow out and run. We couldn't hide from her—not for long, anyway.

Maylea's destiny had been sealed the instant she accepted becoming Paligno's paladin. Regardless of how I felt about it, she was meant for this.

And so was I.

"We started this together. That's how we'll finish it," I murmured, hating every word. Even if it was right, I couldn't celebrate this moment. I was taking her into the lion's den armed only with faith and an empty quiver. Jaevid would curse my name till the day he died.

Which might also be the same day I did.

"We still need a way to get there," Thatcher pointed out, seeming a little more at ease as he ambled over to stand beside me. "It's still all the way across the desert, isn't it?"

"If your ability to valestep is sufficient enough to take us to Dumathis, then I believe we can help get you the rest of the way to the Gate of Proleus," Ziryan offered with a broad, knowing grin as he patted Lukani's shoulder roughly.

"Yeah. I think I can handle that." I smirked back and arched one eyebrow in Thatcher's direction.

He was grinning, too. "Now this is beginning to feel like one of those suicidal Jaevid plans you always talk about."

I laughed and punched him on the arm as I started for the door in the bookshelves. "Yep. That's how you know it's totally going to work."

I COULDN'T DO THIS INSIDE THE RUINS. NOT BECAUSE OF ANYTHING DESTRUCTIVE opening a portal into the extra-dimensional unknown might do—no, I was more concerned about the sheer size I would have to make in order to cram my cranky green dragoness's butt through it.

Vexi was already in a snit, thanks to circling the battle and probably getting all sorts of arrows, spears, and catapult fodder fired at her while she searched for me. She never liked it when we were separated in the first place, and I could empathize that she had probably seen all that playing out below and feared the worst for me.

But she didn't have to hold me down and lick the back of my head because of it. Gods, my hair would never look right again. I could already feel the dragon spit drying and basically cementing it into place. Ugh. Once it dried, it took weeks of washing to get it out. Longer to get rid of the smell.

Now wasn't the time to focus on that, though. I had work to do, portals to open, and legions of angry Nar'Haleenan soldiers to butcher.

Everyone, including the group of Rajinna, gathered in the canyon outside the hidden door of the ancient archives. Bathed in the clean, sterling light of the newly risen moon, I stepped away from the rest of my audience. My boots crunched over the gritty earth, and a light wind licked the lengths of my new robes. I flexed my hands, cracking my knuckles one at a time, as I chose a nice flat spot on the ground and stopped there.

I had a vague idea of which direction we had to go. According to Ziryan, Dumathis was due east from our current location. I had an idea of the distance, too—roughly a hundred miles. Unfortunately, I had absolutely no idea if knowing any of that would help me accurately pinpoint a place I had never seen in my life and valestep to it. Before, all I had to do was visualize the place in my mind. But I had no idea what Dumathis looked like.

Ziryan had tried to help with this. According to him, we needed to arrive at a place that was a sort of crossroads where many of these ancient magical gateways met. He described it as a circular courtyard surrounded by petrified trees where a great many of these large, empty frame-like structures stood.

Hopefully, that mental image would be sufficient.

"No offense, brother, but this feels a tad desperate," Noh's voice hissed through my thoughts.

I shuddered, not even bothering to look over as a bitter cold puff of wind blew against my cheek. I could spot the flickering outline of his dark silhouette out of the corner of my eye just as clearly as I could feel his presence, like a sudden drop in pressure that made my ears pop.

"Desperate plans are about all I've got left at this point." I sighed and stole a glance back over my shoulder, just to make sure no one was standing too close. Nope. Although they did all appear appropriately terrified.

"Some things never change," he snickered.

"Do you mind? I'm trying to tear a hole through time and space here," I grumbled. "Unless you'd care to lend a hand?"

"I can attempt to guide you to your destination, but I'm not certain if it will be very effective," he replied dryly.

"Right. Well, can you at least tell me if this is going to kill me or not?"

He made a thoughtful, clicking noise with his tongue. *"You are the first to ever carry the title King of the Grave, so in all truth, it's difficult to guess. The well of power within you runs far deeper now, so perhaps there is a greater chance of—"*

"Noh," I growled. "Am. I. Going. To. Die?"

He shrugged. *"Possibly."*

Fabulous.

"Will they make it, at least?" I asked, lowering my voice just in case any of my audience was feeling especially nosy.

I could feel Noh's stare like a prickling chill on my skin. For a few, uncomfortable seconds, he didn't answer. Then I heard him murmur, *"Yes."*

Good enough for me.

Widening my stance, I let the world around me fade into the background as I turned my focus inward. I could feel it—that well of power Noh had referenced—simmering and swirling just beneath the surface of my conscious mind. Finding it sent waves of cold chills through every part of my body. My hands went numb. My breath caught.

This was it. No holding back.

I stretched my arms out in front of me, palms facing forward, and every fragment of my focus fixed on a point right between my fingers. My legs clenched as the temperature around me plummeted and frigid wind rushed around me and blew through my hair. The drain was instant, like a hook had snagged in my heart and someone was slowly pulling it from my chest. My arms shook. My teeth chattered.

But I didn't let up.

As soon as I saw that tiny speck of darkness appear between my hands, I set my jaw and pressed harder. My bones ached all the way to the marrow, and my chest seized with a sharp stab of pain. It made my vision begin to tunnel. My knees trembled.

No—I had to get it together. Focus. Control. I could do this.

I had to.

That small point of pure darkness began to swell, growing wider and wider as I slowly pushed my hands outward like I had before. It probably looked ridiculous to the crowd behind me, but it felt like I was trying to pry open stone vault doors with my bare hands. Sweat ran down the sides of my face and dripped from the end of my nose. My whole body shuddered and trembled, muscles twisting and cramping as I held my footing. Wider; this portal had to be wider.

Something warm and wet drizzled from my nose. I could taste it on my lips. Blood. My ears rang with a piercing shrill note. My back seized suddenly, and I let out a shout of pain as I fought to keep my footing. No! I couldn't slip up now. Just a little longer. I had to hold on.

The portal swelled, growing larger and larger. It hung like a window straight into the abyss, floating in the air before me. The icy wind gusting from it blew my hair back and stung my eyes. It snatched all the breath from my lungs. I screamed again as something cracked in my chest and blood filled my mouth.

Then everything went dark. My eyes—gods, I couldn't see! But I didn't dare let up. This was it. Almost there.

I gasped as the portal suddenly stabilized, whirling silently before me like the gaping maw of oblivion, and I could feel the presence of something on the other side. Was it Dumathis? I-I couldn't see to be sure. I just had to trust it. To trust Noh.

"GO!" I yelled with every ounce of strength I had left. "GO NOW!!"

Footsteps thudded over the ground as someone ran past me. Then another. And another. I couldn't see who it was, and it didn't matter. I was standing in the gap, holding back the fabric of reality while they dashed through. Gods, I just hoped they all made it. I couldn't ... I couldn't do this much longer.

My knees gave way first. I crumpled forward as the last bit of my strength went out like a candle in the night. The portal! It was collapsing. I had to get up. I had to get through. But I couldn't move. I was falling. I—

Strong, scaly toes suddenly curled around me. They snatched me up before I even hit the earth, carrying me forward at a blistering speed. The rush of the bitter wind inside the portal raced past me as the low *boom—boom—boom* of strong wingbeats filled my ringing ears.

Vexi. My dragon. She had me, just like always.

Even as everything around me faded to empty silence, I could still feel the warmth and strength of her big toes wrapped securely around my limp body. She would carry me as far as she had to and protect me with her last breath. No matter what lay on the other side of this portal, I would never doubt that.

Not even with my last breath.

PART SIX
MURDOC

28

CHAPTER TWENTY-EIGHT

I hit solid ground on the other side of the gateway, the toe of my boot snagging on an uneven stone and sending me pitching forward. I dropped my sword and managed to throw my arms up in time to protect my face, landing on my elbows and forearms instead. A fierce gust of wind blasted at my back, hot and arid like a blast of heat from a blistering furnace. Fine golden dust swirled around me, shooting up my nose and stinging my eyes. I coughed and sputtered. My breathing scraped in ragged, shallow gasps. Every muscle tremored.

Alive. Gods and Fates, I was alive.

But where ... where was I? Where was everyone else?

I shakily lifted my head, coughing again. I had to get up. I had to find Arlan and the others before—

"Murdoc!" Garnett called, rushing over to me with her blood-spattered face the picture of relief. She took my arm at the shoulder and began hauling me back onto my feet. "Blessed stones, man, we were worried you hadn't made it."

"What is this place?" I rasped as I seized my sword and looked back at the gateway I'd just tumbled out of. It stood as it had before, hidden deep in those ruins. Just a tall, empty golden frame.

But unlike before, it wasn't alone.

Dozens more exactly like it stood all around us on a wide, raised stone platform arranged in circular rows like the rings on a tree. Some were fractured and lay in shattered pieces. Others still appeared to be whole, although obviously dormant and tarnished from exposure to the merciless desert sun. Sand blew in ripples over the bleached stone, gathering around the bases of the frames and piles of rubble.

"This is a Quadrivium," Isandri said, appearing seemingly out of nowhere on my other side. Her long hair blew around her as she stared out across the endless rolling sand dunes that stretched out before us to the west. To the east, the dawn's brilliant light had just begun to turn the steep, mountainous horizon a deep crimson. "It is a place where many gateways once met, and it is not far from the Gate of Proleus."

I swallowed against the dryness in my throat. That meant ... we had made it. We were really here. Now, we just had to see this finished. I had no doubts that Sadeera would not be far behind. She would be more determined than ever knowing that we were already at least one small step ahead of her.

We couldn't afford to stand idle or let our guard down.

"Let's go. We need to get out of sight," Garnett urged. Then she hesitated, glancing between me and the gateway I'd just tumbled out of with her brow crinkled in concern. "Where's the boy? Where's Clarke?"

Every muscle in my body locked up solid. I stared at the gateway's now empty frame as my last glimpse at that chamber in the Avoran ruins replayed over and over in my mind. I didn't know how to tell them. Clarke was gone. I hadn't been able to save him.

I guess the look on my face was telling enough. Garnett's brawny shoulders went slack as her expression dissolved to sorrow. She stared up at the gateway, too. Without another word, she turned to start winding a path through the other rows of encircled frames. Isandri followed, keeping a low profile and moving fast, and I quickly sheathed my weapon before I took off after them.

No time to waste, and the last thing we needed was to get caught out in the open by Sadeera's spies or the Hands of Fate. We couldn't afford to be so careless and shortsighted again. Losing Clarke was a significant blow to the strength of our group. We were down one god.

We could *not* lose anyone else.

WE RETREATED TOWARD THE MOUNTAINS, FOLLOWING GARNETT DOWN A ROUGH AND narrow path that cut around the jagged dark stone boulders. It offered decent cover from anyone who might come searching for us, and the wind quickly covered any footprints we left in the sand.

Less than a mile from the Quadrivium, Garnett left the path and ducked through some prickly, bare-limbed scrub. There, in a small clearing hidden away between the looming mounds of black rock, the rest of our group sat huddled close together. They all stared up at us with battered, blood-smeared faces, tense and wary, as though they were looking for some indication that we needed to flee again.

Well, all except for one.

Noa staggered to his feet, his eyes wild with panic as he glanced between the three of us. "Wh-Where is he? Where is Clarke?" he demanded.

I dropped my gaze.

But that wasn't enough of an answer for him.

Noa stormed toward me, his voice cracking as he yelled, "Where is Clarke? Tell me! Did you leave him behind?!"

I bit down hard, steeling myself before I finally managed to look him squarely in the eye. "Clarke made a choice. That choice was to save the rest of us, and it's the only reason any of us are still breathing right now."

Noa gaped back at me and went completely still. His eyes darted back and forth, side to side, as though he were trying to process that. To understand. His face went deathly pale. Then ... he screamed.

Noa fell to his knees before me, clutching at the sides of his head and yelling at the top of his lungs. The sound cut through my mind like a freshly sharpened blade. It was one I knew all too well.

Grief, no matter the cause, always sounded the same.

Roxus—now back in his human form—was on him in a second, pinning his arms to his sides and slapping a hand over his mouth to stifle the noise. Noa didn't even struggle. His muffled cries broke into sobs as Roxus lugged him away to the edge of the clearing. Garnett followed after them, tears welling in her lavender eyes and her mouth screwing up as though she were struggling to hold back her own sobs.

The air hung heavy with despair as I finally sank down onto my rear end at the edge of our pitiful campsite. Jaevid sat nearby, staring ahead blankly as though he'd gone completely catatonic. With dried blood smeared around his nose and mouth, the red, blistered beginnings of a burn developing on the right side of his face along his cheek, forehead, and neck, I couldn't imagine he wasn't in pain. Sadeera had hit him straight on with a blast of her power. He was lucky to still be alive.

Then again, I guess we all were.

Following Jaevid's hollow stare across the clearing, I spotted Arlan and Edarix sitting on either side of Ronan. They spoke to him in hushed voices, and the boy occasionally nodded or shook his head. His red eyes and flushed, puffy cheeks made it clear he'd spent some time crying, too. It must have been a lot for him to come to terms with being under Iksoli's mind control for so long.

I knew exactly what kind of hell that was.

I'd only endured that torment for a short time, but the scars from it were lasting and my memory of it hadn't faded in the slightest. There were no pretty words to describe what it felt like for someone else to climb into your head and take full control while you had no choice but to look on. It left you feeling filthy, inside and out.

"I would like to scout the area. We know Sadeera has been amassing forces here, and we need to plan our movements accordingly," Isandri announced. She was apparently the only one who still had her head on straight after everything we'd just been through. Good. Better one than none.

"You need me to go with you?" I offered, even if I clearly wasn't in a state to go tromping through the mountains. Unlike many of our other divinely blessed friends, I was still adjusting to the feel of the drain after using so much of that power. I needed a minute or two to collect myself.

Isa shook her head. "We are very vulnerable now. You and I are perhaps the only ones still fit for battle if something happens suddenly, and I am much faster on my own. Stay here and watch over them. I will return before the sun rises."

No argument there.

Isandri dashed off, shifting into her winged feline form and all but disappearing into the twilight without even the rustle of a feather.

Sitting in silence, I looked down at my hands. A few cuts and bruises. Nothing serious. I checked myself over for any more indications of injuries. But for the most part, I was whole. A few of those Hands of Fate warriors had gotten a lucky swipe here and there, but they were all minor.

"We have to stop her," Jaevid murmured suddenly, so low and soft I could barely make out the words. He still hadn't moved an inch, and his stare remained fixed on Ronan. But rather than hollow emptiness, there was a new wrath smoldering in the depths of his pale blue eyes. A gathering fury that made my heart skip a beat.

"That's why we came here, isn't it?" I replied, wondering if I should be concerned about him doing something especially reckless. I guess something about taking that blast from Sadeera had really rattled his cage. Hmm.

Jaevid's chin slowly dipped down, his jawline hardening and brows drawing into a furrowed scowl. His hands curled into fists where they rested on his knees. His lip twitched, as though he were fighting a snarl. "Whatever it takes, that sorceress must not see tomorrow's dawn. I will not allow her to touch my daughter or threaten my family. She dies here, by our hands. Swear it to me, Murdoc."

A little rush of adrenaline made my skin prickle. I straightened as my pulse gave a racing flourish. "On your orders, Commander. We came here to finish this, once and for all. I don't intend to leave until it's done."

He nodded firmly. "Neither do I."

"We have to consider our next move carefully," I reminded him. "Arlan is all but useless now. His magic appears to be spent. I don't know what other power he holds that might be useful to us, but given the fact that he couldn't even open the gateway to come here on his own, I doubt we will see him be very effective in battle. Ronan might be able to fight. He's young, but we all know he's a considerable force. The issue, naturally, is that he's already been ensnared by Iksoli's power once. Now that Sadeera holds that ability, he might be likely to fall victim to it again. We'll have to watch him carefully."

"What are you saying?" Jaevid cut straight to the point.

"Well, if you want an Ulfrangar's opinion, I say we are at an extreme disadvantage in our current state. The best choice would be to send word to our reinforcements that we plan to strike at sundown. Without them, failure is certain. Then, we let our company here rest out the day and take that time to scout the area to see exactly what we are up against. We keep an eye on the enemy forces, decide on an entry point into the Gate of Proleus, and wait for nightfall. At sundown, we carve a path of least resistance straight to the gate and make our stand there. Perhaps we can hold off whatever forces Sadeera brings along with her there in a bottleneck while a few of us see that the gate is destroyed, once and for all."

Jaevid finally glanced my way, his expression sharp and severe. "Tell me, Murdoc. I want the truth. Do you believe we stand any chance of success?"

I hesitated, my mind blurring through scenarios, backup plans, potential enemy strategies, and what powers we had at our disposal. Without knowing exactly what Sadeera was bringing to this fight, it was hard to say with any degree of certainty. But I could make a solid, Ulfrangar-based guess, and maybe that was all he wanted.

"It depends on what you define as success," I answered at last. "Can we destroy the gate? Yes, I believe so. We might even be able to kill Sadeera. But committing all our energy to those goals is going to make withstanding any other onslaught difficult—maybe even impossible. If she brings a number of Hands of Fate, or even soldiers with her, it will be a bloodbath. We didn't come here with a whole army to back this cause. I think it's very likely we will have casualties."

Jaevid looked away again, his expression tightening as though he were processing that information. "We may not make it back from this," he concluded aloud.

I couldn't decide if he was just talking out loud to himself or looking for consolation. Curse it, all these years and talking to people, even people I knew well, still felt like I was trying to cram both my legs into the same pantleg sometimes. "I believe that is a reality we all accepted when we agreed to come here in the first place," I said, with absolutely no idea if that was the response he'd been hoping for.

I guess it was, because he bowed his head lower and clasped his hands, fiddling with the wedding band around his left ring finger. "Should you survive, and I ... do not, I would ask you to see that my family is taken care of," he said, his voice quieter, but no less resolute. "I know Felix will want to help, but he has his own children and grandchildren to think of. Gods only know what attention they might need at the end of all this."

Everything from my neck down steadily went numb as I sat, listening and wondering what my own family would do if I didn't return. I had considered that, of course. But maybe I hadn't been as deliberate with my planning as I should have been. It was far too late now, though. I'd have to trust that my mother and father would help Phoebe.

"You won't need to provide for them," he assured. "I've made those sorts of preparations already. But they will need someone to oversee the final arrangements and make sure the assets are successfully passed over to them. Beckah won't like accepting help, but between the boys, Maylea, and a new baby or two, she'll certainly need it."

"Of course. Without question," I agreed. "And I would ask the same of you. I don't have any assets set aside. But maybe you could look in on them now and again."

Jaevid didn't hesitate. "I will."

I had hoped hearing him say that would do something to ease the growing tension in my chest. The worry that I'd agreed to this too hastily. The fear that I might not ever get to hold my own child.

I didn't like the way those thoughts cracked away at the foundations of all my resolve. Fates, I couldn't afford to let my concentration fracture. Not now. Hesitance in battle was a death sentence. I had to keep my mind here, in the moment.

I had to focus on staying alive.

29

CHAPTER TWENTY-NINE

By the time the sun finally slipped free of the horizon, the temperature had shot up to a smothering, paralyzing heat that drove us into whatever shade we could find amidst the craggy hills and massive boulders. I'd never sat in a kiln before, but I had to imagine it felt a lot like this. Every breath was a struggle, and sweat soaked through all my clothes. Those of us in armor were forced to shed it, and we rationed out what water we had—which wasn't much.

Yet another reason we couldn't stay out here for one more day. Tonight, everything had to come to an end, one way or another.

The only members of our group who appeared entirely unfazed by this hellish, scorching nightmare were Isandri and Edarix. It must have been some sort of shared Lunostri elf genetic trait that made them especially tolerant of the heat. Whatever the case, that left two of us who weren't reduced to heaping piles of sweat and agony while we tried to rest and wait out the daylight.

Edarix seemed especially chatty and was intent on telling us absolutely everything he could think of in relation to what he had heard and seen from Auguress Riva. Sadly, there wasn't much he could share that we couldn't guess by now—especially given our most recent revelation about who Empress Leysa really was and how she had been deceiving and manipulating everything, including Edarix. Maybe he felt guilty about that. Arlan didn't seem to fault him for it, though. Deception and manipulation were Sadeera's specialties, according to him. Any one of us might have fallen for that ruse.

Speaking of Arlan, after his extensive chat with Ronan, he had elected to sit off by himself. He stared into the distance, wind catching through his long golden hair, and eyes narrowed. He'd demonstrated he had at least some power left, and used his abilities to send a message back to our reinforcements. A small spark of hope.

Apart from that, Arlan hadn't said much at all. With his legs crossed and his elbows on his knees, he surveyed our surroundings like an eagle on a perch. I couldn't begin to fathom what he must be thinking. Given what Isandri had reported seeing in the manner of forces that now stood between us and the Gate of Proleus, I had to imagine it wasn't anything happy.

More like contemplating his final fate.

After Isandri returned from her long scouting venture, I felt confident that we were all having thoughts along those lines.

She had been gone for hours, taking time to see everything she could about our enemy's position. Overall, it wasn't good. Not for us, anyway. By her count, there were two full legions encamped around the entrance to the gate. That meant ten thousand men, at least. A fourth of Nar'Haleen's entire army. And they hadn't come armed with shovels and pitchforks.

Isa described trebuchets and catapults, cavalry on big scaly dog-like creatures known as dunestriders, and net throwers similar to what the Tibran armies had used to take down dragonriders. That last part sent a clear signal to me that Sadeera was fully aware, even before she found us down in that Avoran ruin, that there were dragonriders coming to the Southern Kingdoms.

Specifically, dragonriders that intended to interfere with her plans.

That was troubling in more ways than I cared to entertain. Gods only knew what else she had planned if she was already aware that we would be coming for her. The whole situation put my nerves on edge. My Ulfrangar instincts demanded that I withdraw, re-evaluate, and come at this from a different angle because the odds of success were devastatingly low.

But I wasn't an Ulfrangar anymore. I was a dragonrider, and retreat was not an acceptable option. We would have to be extremely careful about this.

"I think it is possible for a few of us to reach the entrance, but the rest will need to focus on drawing the enemy's focus," Isa suggested. "They are very mindful of our intent, and the ranks positioned around the entrance are aligned to form a shield wall at a moment's notice. It will be difficult to get anyone through unseen."

"But you think we can?" Jaevid frowned. "How?"

"No. Not *we*," she corrected with a proud, cunning grin. "*I* can. Tomorrow is a full moon. I am able to become invisible."

Jaevid's expression went blank in surprise.

Oh. That's right. I'd never actually seen her do it before, but Isandri had mentioned having that ability before. Hmmm. That might be just the advantage we needed.

Garnett slapped her knee and crowed with delight. "HAH! I'd forgotten about that little perk of yours. Excellent timing, too, isn't it?"

I wasn't ready to get that excited about it just yet. "But that's just you alone," I pointed out. "It's unwise for you to go in by yourself. If Sadeera is already in there—"

"Then what do you suggest?" Isa interrupted sharply.

I paused, holding her gaze long enough to make sure she knew I didn't appreciate being cut off like that. This wasn't an argument. I wasn't here to pick sides or bicker over whose attack plan was best. I was here to give facts, plain and simple.

"I suggest no one going deep behind enemy lines without someone to watch their back. I suggest trying to keep our group together as much as possible," I growled and leaned back against the side of the boulder behind me with my arms crossed. "I don't know much about Nar'Haleenan war techniques, but I know plenty about stealth operations and murder. If we want to get past all those lines of soldiers undetected, then we need to all be invisible."

Isandri scoffed and rolled her eyes. "I suppose you can manage that, then? Because it is not within my power."

"I can, actually. I've done it before," I said, casting Jaevid a sideways smirk. He undoubtedly remembered that particular event. "And if I can pass Thatcher Renley off as a Tibran soldier, I'm pretty sure I can pass the rest of us off as Nar'Haleenan ones. We just need a few sets of armor—simple, common infantry and one officer, to be precise. You can keep an invisible aerial watch, and we'll make our way to the gate."

Garnett shifted uncomfortably in her seat. "That's ... incredibly risky."

"It is," I agreed. "But I guarantee you one thing: every soldier standing out there under the Nar'Haleenan banner is poised for a fight with dragonriders and gods. The tools of war they've brought along suggest just that. They're watching the skies, not their own ranks. So the best way for us to be invisible, is to be all too visible."

"It's just mad enough to work," Roxus chuckled. He sat nearby, rubbing his thickly stubbled chin. "It would be even better if we gave them exactly the enemy they're looking for. It would make it even less likely that they noticed our movements."

My smirk widened. "Yes. And at nightfall, we'll have just that. Our dragons and reinforcements will arrive, and that is when we need to make our move."

"It's insane," Jaevid sighed, rubbing his forehead with his fingers.

"Agreed. No one in their right mind would ever try something like this," Isandri muttered.

"Yeah," I agreed. "And that's *exactly* why it will work."

Not all of us would go on this mission. That was a given. Edarix was a priest, not a soldier, and he didn't have any magical abilities. He would be a liability in any kind of conflict. On the complete opposite end of the spectrum, Ronan was a potential threat to us and anyone standing in a fifty-foot radius if Sadeera got control of his mind. As I understood it, he was a literal divine weapon cursed into a human body. That boy had already endured that torture once, and judging by the empty, catatonic stare he wore as he sat silently next to Jaevid, he wouldn't survive it a second time. Not mentally, anyway.

It wouldn't be a wise choice to bring him along with us, either.

I figured Edarix would be more than willing to sit here, in the safety of our makeshift camp, and wait out the battle with the boy. And when I posed the question to him, Edarix heartily agreed. He apologized profusely for our initial meeting, and thanked me again and again for showing Ronan mercy. I don't know if he fully grasped the depth of the connection we all had with that kid, but I guess it made him feel less like a burden if we gave him something to do, even a menial task like babysitting.

Ronan, himself, didn't protest when he heard he would be sitting out of the battle, per my suggestion. In fact, he didn't say anything. At least, not until the sun began to set and we finally started to gear up for battle.

Dressed out in a sleek, fitted ensemble of elaborate black armor, Ronan picked up his own vambraces and began buckling them on. He scowled under that unruly mop of shaggy black hair, his mouth set in an uncomfortable, mashed-up line. Every move he made was sharp and jerking, tinged with suppressed anger that put my nerves on edge. That kid was a barrel of black powder, just waiting for someone to light the fuse.

Best to handle this with extreme caution.

Walking over to him, I gave Ronan a nudge with my elbow and tipped my head to the side, gesturing for him to follow me. He blinked those big, cobalt blue eyes up at me in surprise, then his whole face scrunched with frustration. His cheeks flushed deep red and he bowed his head. He trundled along as I led him a few yards away from where the rest of the group was still making preparations.

I could feel the sizzle of Jaevid's worried glare the entire way. Ugggh.

Once I was sure we were well out of earshot, I stopped and faced Ronan. No point in dragging this out. He was just a kid, sure, but we didn't have time for sugar-coating. "You're not going with us," I said firmly.

Ronan sucked in a sharp breath and stood straighter, bowing up like a startled alley cat. "I've just as much reason to fight," he protested. "I've been trained ever since I—"

"No one's arguing that," I stopped him quickly. "You probably have more cause than most of us to want to see Sadeera dead. But this is the part where you learn what it means to be a soldier. If you go with us, you and I both know you'll be putting all the people you care about here in danger. This is what we call sacrifice for the greater good, and it's the hardest lesson you'll ever learn in life, boy."

Ronan's mouth screwed up bitterly and he held my gaze, probably trying to look determined. "B-But ... I did... such horrible things. If I don't try to make it right ... I-I ..."

Ahh. So, that's what this was about.

I leaned down some, looking him straight in the eye. "You know what I was before I became a dragonrider, don't you?"

He swallowed hard. "You were an assassin."

"No," I corrected. "I was an *Ulfrangar* assassin—which is worse than anything you can possibly imagine. I didn't just kill people, I butchered them like animals. I tortured innocent people. I snuck into their homes and murdered them in their sleep. And the worst part is, there were times when I even enjoyed it. I wanted to do it because it made the other assassins respect and fear me. It made me feel powerful and secure in my status within their order."

With every word, Ronan's eyes went wider and he leaned back a little, as though wanting to put more space between us. I didn't blame him one bit for that. I'm sure the dragonriders talked and swapped rumors about me, especially the young students. No doubt Queen Jenna had also told him stories about mine and Thatcher's adventures. But I was willing to bet good coin she had left those details out.

"I did all of those things when I was your age. Some of them when I was even younger. And you know what?" I pointed back to our group. "Those people standing over there believed they saw something good in me. They forgave me for all those awful things I did. They helped me find a better life I know I will never truly deserve—and I was a complete stranger to them. But these people have helped raise you. So, believe me when I tell you, there's absolutely nothing that vile woman made you do that can't be forgiven, Ronan. Whatever lies she told while she was in your head, you have to find a way to let that go. You have to remember who you really are. You have to make hard choices to keep your friends safe."

Ronan's head bowed low as his shoulders drew up to his ears. He cowered before me, shaking as he whispered, "I know who I really am now. And ... it's not anything good. I'm evil, Uncle Murdoc. I ... I shouldn't even exist!"

I frowned. "What do you mean?"

"She ... she told me everything. That's why my mother sent me away. That's why they hid me from the world. It wasn't just because of my curse. It's because of who my real father was! Because I never should have existed!" He started to break down, his whole face twitching as he fought to keep the emotions controlled. It didn't work. Tears slid down his cheeks, and he squeezed his eyes shut. "You know, too, don't you? Everyone does! But they pretend like they don't or that it doesn't matter. But it does! IT MATTERS! Because now ... I-I'm just like him. I'm a murderer, just like he was. The son of Argonox could never be anything good!"

The sound of his sobbing filled the awkward silence. Now everyone from the rest of the group was staring at us. Er, staring at *me*, specifically. I could read their tense, accusatory expressions plainly; they were all wondering what I'd said to upset him like this.

Yeah. This was not going as planned.

But, Gods and Fates, I hadn't expected a response like this. I thought he just wanted to atone for the things Iksoli had forced him to do. Apparently, this ran much deeper. Ronan seemed to think he had to atone for even existing in the first place. Sadeera had planted those sick ideas in his head, and I didn't believe for a single second that Queen Jenna had sent him to the Compendium Library or kept him out of the public eye for any reason other than to protect him.

But I was probably the last guy in the world who should be trying to talk through this with him. I didn't have any real parenting experience—not when it came to situations like this. For his sake, however, I had to try. Fates, I just prayed I didn't make it worse. Jenna might actually decide to revoke that royal pardon she'd given me.

With a deep breath, I leaned down close again and put a hand on his shoulder. "Listen to me, Ronan. I don't know what Sadeera told you. But you need to take a breath and think about what's real and what's a bunch of made-up garbage she fed you just to get into your head."

"But it's true, isn't it?" he whimpered. "Argonox was my father, wasn't he?"

I sighed and pinched the bridge of my nose between my eyes. Gods help me. "Yes, he was. No one can change how they're born or where they come from, Ronan. We don't get to choose our origins. But we do get to choose our future. We get to choose every step we take on our journey. And yeah, not all of them are going to be good. You'll screw up. You'll make mistakes. You might even hurt people. But that doesn't have to be your ending. You can choose something different."

"Then I choose to fight," he argued, tears still fresh in his eyes as he curled his hands into fists. "I have to. I need to. Don't you understand that?"

Yeah. I did. He needed to fight Sadeera for the same reason I'd needed to fight Rook. Closure. Retribution. Atonement. Gods, he was so young, though. And the risk of him turning on us made my stomach sour. There was no good choice here.

Then again, maybe that was the whole point. It wasn't my choice to make.

"All right. You want to fight. I know you have the skill, and no small amount of magical power. But let me ask you something—Can you control it? Because one second of losing control could get us all killed."

His jaw and his shoulders tensed. "Yes. I can."

"I hope so," I warned. "Now tell me, what's your name?"

He looked up at me again, obviously confused. "Wh-What?"

"What is *your* name?" I repeated.

"Ronan," he answered uncertainly, like he still didn't understand what I meant.

I pressed a finger to the middle of that fancy black breastplate. "No. Your name is Ronan *Derrick*, Crowned Prince of Maldobar. Not Argonox. Not Argonox's son. Not Iksoli's puppet. Not Sadeera's toy. You think you can remember that when she's trying to get her claws back in your brain?"

He blinked a few times, seeming to mull that over with fresh worry crinkling his brow. Then his eyes went steely. His expression cooled to a look of pure, relentless focus. Heh. I knew that face all too well.

He might have been a relation to Argonox, but he was Jenna's son. No doubt about it. That was a Farrow look if I'd ever seen one.

"Yes," he answered confidently. "I can do this."

"All right, kid. I'm worried about you. I've had that woman play around in my head, too. I know what that feels like. But I guess that means you're no more susceptible to her tricks than I am." I held out a hand toward him. "Let's make her pay for it, shall we?"

Wiping his eyes on his forearm, he gave a deep, steadying exhale before he grasped my hand and shook it firmly. "Thank you, Mr. Porter."

"That's Murdoc to you," I scolded as I walked away. "And fix your left pauldron. It's crooked. I know your mother's taught you better than that."

PART SEVEN

MAYLEA

30

CHAPTER THIRTY

"REIGH!"

Violet's scream tore through the air as Vexi's huge, scaly green head emerged from the spinning dark vortex.

The dragoness barely managed to wriggle through before the portal collapsed behind her. In the blink of an eye, it shrank down to a marble-sized ball of pure darkness and then exploded with a deafening *POW!* The shockwave sent me rocking back onto my heels, and I threw up a hand to shield my face as cold wind surged past, leaving my nose and cheeks numb.

BOOOM!

Vexi landed before us, shaking the frost from her scales and snapping her jaws. Through the frigid blast of wind, I caught a glimpse of something dark dangling from one of her hind legs. Oh, Fates—it was him! It was Uncle Reigh!

Violet must have spotted him, too, because she broke away at a sprint straight for Vexi, screaming his name over and over. Vexi recoiled, curling her tail and wings in close like a protective barrier and hissing a warning. Oh no. This wasn't good.

"Curse it," Thatcher muttered beside me before he took off running, too.

I followed right on his heels, seizing Violet by the arm as soon as she got within reach. "Stop! You have to calm down. You're frightening her, and she doesn't understand," I warned. Dragons always got extra protective when they knew their rider was injured, and Vexi and Uncle Reigh had been a bonded pair for longer than I'd been alive. She might spit flame at us just on principle.

Luckily, Thatcher understood this. He approached the dragoness much more slowly, with his arms raised in surrender. "Easy, girl, it's okay," he cooed to her in a calm, steady voice. "I know he's hurt. We just want to help. It's all right."

Vexi's sky blue eyes focused on him, pupils narrowed to hair-thin slits and lip still twitching at a snarl. A deep growl rumbled in her throat, but her ears perked forward. She was listening. Her nostrils puffed wide, taking in Thatcher's scent as he moved slowly and carefully toward her. One step at a time.

I couldn't help but be amazed. I had seen Thatcher work with dragons my whole life. He had a natural way with them, as though he could connect with their energy and relate in a way no one else could. Dah had put him to work many times helping to train young or difficult dragons that had past trauma or trust issues. It was hard not to envy that skill.

When Thatcher finally put a hand on the end of Vexi's snout, my body sagged in relief. She sniffed him over, still growling softly, and finally gave him a blasting snort straight to the face that blew his hair back. He smiled, but it never reached his eyes.

"That's a good girl," he crooned. "Now, then. Let me take a look at Reigh. We'll be gentle, I promise."

Slowly but surely, Vexi unfurled her wings to reveal where Uncle Reigh lay on the ground, sprawled out on his side. My breath caught in my throat, snagging like I'd tried to swallow a briar branch. Violet covered her mouth with her free hand, probably trying to stifle another scream.

There was blood ... *everywhere*.

Uncle Reigh's clothes were soaked with it, and more was puddled on the ground around him. With his back to us, I couldn't see if he was awake or not. I couldn't even tell if he was breathing.

Thatcher somehow managed to keep his emotions in check. He kept his movements as calm and slow as ever, stepping over and gathering Uncle Reigh into his arms with a grunt of effort. Then he turned and walked back toward us, and ... I saw it. That look of withheld panic in his face. As though it were taking every single shred of his self-control to keep his composure right then.

"Maylea, get the medical kit from Uncle Reigh's bag," Thatcher murmured, every word tight and commanding. "Violet, find the rest of that healing potion from the Zenith's Call."

Lukani and Ziryan hurried over as Thatcher carefully laid Reigh on the ground. It wasn't until that moment that I'd even noticed where we were. Some sort of old temple? I couldn't tell. And it didn't matter right then.

Thatcher had offered to carry Uncle Reigh's things through the portal while he focused on using his power, but he'd dropped everything when he dashed over to help. I seized the medical bag and quickly made my way back—just in time to see Thatcher start forcing breath into Uncle Reigh's lungs. He pinched his nose shut and tilted his head back, blowing in several deep gulps of air.

O-Oh gods.

Uncle Reigh's eyes were open, but his expression was completely empty. His pupils were so wide you couldn't see the light cognac color of his irises, and his skin was so pale he looked ... gods, he looked ...

Tears filled my eyes as I knelt beside him, squeezing his medical kit tightly. I didn't know what to do. I didn't know how to help him. This wasn't like before, when one of us had been cut or stabbed. On the outside, Reigh didn't have any obvious injuries. It was all inside his body.

Like he'd been ripped apart from within.

Blood still ran from his ears, nose, and corners of his mouth. Something dark, like veins of ink or fine, curling tattoos, covered the sides of his neck all the way to his jaw. I didn't understand it. Those definitely hadn't been there a few minutes ago.

What was happening to him?

Violet gripped one of Uncle Reigh's hands, clutching it tightly against her chest as she gasped in frantic sobs. "Not like this. Come on, you fool. Breathe," she begged. "You can't leave me like this. Not now. Please ... please, just breathe!"

Thatcher held out a hand without looking away. "The potion," he demanded.

Violet passed it over shakily, her brow skewed with desperate concern. "There isn't much of it left. Will it be enough?"

He didn't answer. I doubted he knew. I certainly didn't. Yes, it was a strong remedy. It had worked wonders for us already. But would it help an injury like this? Something that stemmed from divine power?

"Oh, my dear little sprout," a smooth, luxuriously deep voice brushed across my mind like a sheet of fine silk. It sent a warm shiver racing up my spine. *"Have you already lost faith in the gift I have given you. I would not deny my paladin any of that power once carried by your ancestors. Come now, show me what you can do."*

I held my breath, feeling each word like the chord of a love song—as though Paligno himself had reached in and plucked the strings of my heart as beautifully as a harpist. And he was right. It was him. He was here, with me, in this moment. And he was absolutely right; I'd barely used any divine power. I didn't understand it or what it truly meant. I didn't know what I could do.

But I did remember what my dah had done. I'd heard his stories so many times. Paligno had given him incredible abilities as the lapiloque. He had healed people with a single touch.

Now, I had to try it. I hadn't come this far, fought through so much, just to hesitate and falter at the very end. I was here for a reason—the same reason Paligno had chosen me to be his paladin to begin with. I had a role to play.

And it was long past time to swallow all my insecurities and finally embrace it.

As Thatcher started to uncork the bottle of potion, I snapped a hand out to stop him. He flashed me a wild, befuddled glance like he might start yelling. But he didn't. That frenzied look of panic slowly dissolved to something like acceptance. He leaned away and nodded without a word.

Settling on my knees, I leaned over Uncle Reigh's motionless body and placed my hands on his chest. I closed my eyes and bowed my head, beginning to turn all my focus inward to that subtle flicker of warmth that simmered quietly in my soul. That sacred place that only Paligno could reach, where he'd planted that seed of power within me.

All it took was a moment, a breath, and a rush of warm, tingling heat all over my skin to feel that power beginning to grow. It bloomed bright, spreading through me, down to all my fingers and toes. My palms grew hot. My heartbeat raced like the tempo of a minstrel's drums. Flashes of color danced through my mind's eye, following that rhythm and chasing sparks of energy through my mind like falling stars. The whispers filled my ears like the hiss and roar of the surf. They came and went, calling out to me. But I didn't focus on them.

I could feel him there—Uncle Reigh. His presence seemed to hover before me like a column of invisible cold. Something about it felt so scattered and erratic, like a part of his soul was broken or lost. He couldn't find his way back. Not without help.

My help.

"It's not time for you to go yet," I whispered as I stretched out every ounce of will I could toward that presence. "We need you. Please ... I can fix it. Please come back."

My pulse gave a thundering studder as that battered, ragged essence of Uncle Reigh's soul suddenly latched onto me. I could feel it, as though his hand were gripping mine with a fierce determination. He didn't want to go. He wanted to live.

Good. We could do this together.

Feeling that solid contact, I fed his broken essence all the energy I could. All that energy that welled up in my soul poured into his soul like a life-giving stream. The broken fragments shivered and moved, sliding back into place like puzzle pieces.

My heartbeat began to thump slower and harder. I flinched as a twinge of discomfort pricked like a needle in the back of my mind. I struggled to draw a breath, as though someone had stacked heavy sacks of grain on my chest. I couldn't do this for much longer. I needed to stop.

But what if it wasn't enough? What if he needed more power? What if—

"STOP!" a voice cried out suddenly.

I jolted, my eyes flying open as someone snatched me backward. I flailed, rasping out a scream as pain shot through me like I'd been struck by lightning. My hands burned. My body shook out of control. All I could do was flop back against someone's chest and fight for air.

"It's all right, I've got you," Lukani's voice murmured in my ear. Just that sound sent a wave of relief through me. I went slack in his grasp, sagging into the warmth of his body. My head lolled against his shoulder as everything around me seemed to spin.

But he was here. Lukani was still with me. I was always safe with him.

"Reigh!" Violet gasped nearby, her voice still shaking with sniffling sobs.

What was happening? Had it worked? Had I helped him? I couldn't lift my head to see.

"Wh ... Wh-Where ...?" Uncle Reigh's voice slurred weakly.

Tears welled in my eyes and I squeezed them shut. A whimper of relief leaked past my lips. Gods, he was alive. Uncle Reigh was alive. I didn't know if anything I had done was the reason, but I didn't care. It didn't matter, as long as he would be okay.

"Hey, now, take it easy," Thatcher coaxed. "You were just at death's door. Lay there for a few minutes and try to relax."

Warm lips pressed against my forehead, and I breathed in the familiar scent of Lukani's skin. It reminded me of vanilla, clove, and cinnamon—like the spiced wine my parents liked to make in the winter. It was the kind of smell that made you feel warm inside and out. I loved it.

And at the same time, feeling him wrap himself around me again like a fearless guardian put a sharp, fresh pang of agony through my heart. I wanted to push away. To run. Hide. Get away from everyone and everything.

Because I didn't know how many more times I would get to be with him like this. It felt wrong—like calculated torture—for him to treat me this way when we both knew he wouldn't be going back to Maldobar with us. He wouldn't want to leave his family. And I wouldn't dare ask him to.

"How is she doing?" Thatcher called over. "Is she okay?"

"Yes, I think so. She's conscious, and I don't see any injuries," Lukani confirmed.

"Sweet Fates, let's never do that again," Thatcher groaned.

Uncle Reigh's voice scraped and hitched hoarsely. "D-Did ... we make it?"

"You did, indeed." Ziryan actually sounded impressed. "Now, it would be wise for you to rest while you can. My clan will assemble what tools and supplies we can to assist you. We do not have much, but we are happy to share."

"W-Water ... would be nice," Uncle Reigh croaked.

Ziryan's laugh rumbled deeply. "That, we can certainly accommodate."

31

CHAPTER THIRTY-ONE

It took an hour for my head to stop pounding. After that, I could sit up on my own and sip at the waterskin Lukani brought me. If I moved too suddenly, everything began spinning again. I'd have to take it slow.

My palms still ached like I'd slapped them onto a hot stove, although I couldn't see any obvious signs of burns or damage. Maybe I'd still be able to use my bow after all.

Whatever discomfort using that much power had given me, it was more than worth it to see Uncle Reigh walking around again—albeit stiffly—checking on the rest of us and talking to Ziryan about supplies. He had lively color back in his face, and had cleaned off all the blood from around his nose, ears, and mouth. I couldn't hold back a smile when he finally came my way carrying a bundle of new arrows.

"And how's our little miracle worker feeling?" he asked as he put two fingers against the side of my neck to check my pulse.

I scrunched my nose at him playfully. "Better now that you are okay, old man."

He flicked my forehead. "You must be if you're already mouthing off like that. Good. We'll give it another hour or two, then we need to get going. Destiny calls."

I took a deep breath and let it out slowly. Right. We had no time to spare.

"Thank you, Maylea," Uncle Reigh murmured quietly, his gaze catching mine with a much softer, earnest look. "You took a big risk. But I'm grateful for it."

I forced a smile. "I can't let you guys keep showing me up with all these divine tricks, now, can I?"

I knew he'd see right through it. Lying to him was pointless. I could get by with fibbing to my parents easily enough, but Uncle Reigh must have had some sort of sixth sense when it came to lying.

He frowned and arched one of his eyebrows, like he was offering me a chance to try again.

Ugggh. Fine!

"Paligno spoke to me again," I confessed, fiddling with the cork to the waterskin so I didn't have to look him in the eye. "He wanted to know why I had already lost faith in the power he'd given me. He reminded me of how Dah healed people before. Soooo I tried it."

Reigh puffed a heavy sigh and scratched at the back of his head. "I don't know if that makes me feel better or worse. Clearly, we were right in assuming he had given you this power and position for a reason. He wants you to use it. But knowing that we're just getting wound up for what is most likely going to be a bloodbath also makes me want to throw up."

Somehow, hearing him say all of that out loud made me feel strangely ... better. Like my own fears and apprehensions weren't just a symptom of being too young or inexperienced for this. If Uncle Reigh was nervous, then I could be, too. I didn't need to feel ashamed or inadequate because of it.

It almost made me want to smile for real—until he jabbed a thumb toward Lukani and said, "I think it's time you had a chat with your little suitor here about what he plans to do."

My whole head burned like someone had just lit my hair on fire. What? Seriously? He was just going to say that out loud while Lukani was sitting right there beside me? Gods and Fates, why?! I drew back, wanting nothing more in the entire world than to climb into a hole and bury myself in it.

Lukani, on the other hand, did not miss a beat. "I am going with you."

Nearby, I saw Ziryan's gaze snap over to us. He'd obviously overheard that. And judging by the tight, disapproving, and slightly terrifying frown on his lips, he did not like it at all. Oh no. I could see this disaster coming from miles away.

"You sure about that, kid?" Uncle Reigh pressed, like he had consciously decided to pretend like I wasn't sitting right there. Gods, kill me now. "This is your family. Your real, actual *family* that very much wants you back. That's not something to just toss aside lightly."

"I'm not," Lukani argued. "I've already made my choice. Where she goes, I go."

I ducked my head some, trying desperately to hide behind my hair so no one could see my face turning red. Would anyone notice if I started slowly crawling away?

"I think you might want to talk that over with your father first," Reigh insisted. "The sort of fight we are headed into isn't the kind everyone gets to walk away from."

Lukani didn't even blink. "I know that."

Reigh's whole face skewed with frustrated bewilderment. "Then why are you—?"

"Because I love her."

I froze. My heart dropped to the pit of my stomach.

Uncle Reigh's eyes went as wide as dinner plates. His mouth hung open, like he'd already been preparing a retort for whatever excuse Lukani came up with. I guess he hadn't been prepared for that one, though. Uncle Reigh blinked a few times and shook his head a little, like he couldn't decide if he'd actually heard that or if he might just be hallucinating.

Nope. This was real. Mortifying and completely real.

"I ... am going to walk away and pretend I didn't just hear any of this," Uncle Reigh decided aloud. "Because, believe me, you have not seen wrath like her father's if you expect to go trotting around spouting stuff like that. He will literally strangle you to death with your own tail. You've been warned."

Spinning on a heel, Uncle Reigh strolled off back toward where Thatcher and Violet were still taking inventory of all the items the rest of Lukani's clan had brought for us. Daggers, grappling hooks, crossbows—that sort of thing.

None of it interested me at all right then. I was still trying to figure out how to breathe and blink at the same time. I couldn't even force myself to look at Lukani as I sat beside him, silently panicking.

"I mean it," he murmured at last. "I know you have been ... worried about that. About what I would do. But my loyalty is to you, first and foremost. I intend to remain at your side for as long as you will allow." His hand slid over to gently take mine.

But what could I say? How was it not selfish and wrong for me to want him to stay? Especially when this fight could very well take his life? I didn't know. My thoughts whirled and spun, as scattered as autumn leaves, and I didn't know how to talk about any of them. This was all too much.

"Maylea?" Lukani's voice had gone quiet, as though he could sense that all my sanity was hanging by a thread. "Please know that you don't have to answer or offer any reply. I know this is very sudden. But I want the truth to be known. I want them to understand, and I don't want to hide my motives from you."

I squeezed his hand, finally managing to stare up at him. With my heart in my throat, I searched his face for what felt like an eternity. But there was no reluctance anywhere—no traces of hesitance or uncertainty. He meant it. Nothing I could say would ever change his mind.

"He's right, you know," I whispered. "My dah is going to be furious."

One corner of his mouth quirked into a roguish grin. "Mine already is, so I suppose that's only fair."

Leaning in, I let my forehead bump against his. Feeling him so close, his breath on my cheeks and his warm, strong fingers laced through mine, was all it took. I could breathe again. I could think. I was safe here, close to him.

"I don't think I can do this without you," I confessed.

"You don't have to. Whatever happens, we will face it together," he said, his other hand reaching up to gently grasp the side of my neck. His thumb stroked at my jaw, and I couldn't remember a time when I'd ever wanted to kiss him more.

I couldn't though—not with so many stupid adults standing around glaring daggers at us.

Later. Somehow, somewhere, I'd find a chance to be alone with him. Then I could tell him everything I felt. Everything I wanted.

Before the end came.

THE TENSION IN THE AIR WAS SO THICK I COULD PRACTICALLY TASTE IT. IT WAS A SOUR, bitter sort of flavor that made my insides twist and bind up every time I made a move. As much as I would have preferred to blame it all on the situation between Lukani and me, I knew that wasn't the root of the problem. I could see it on everyone's faces, like it had been painted right onto their foreheads.

What came next would be the most dangerous thing any of us had ever done. Somewhere across the desert, our friends were in danger. They might even be fighting already. And every second we spent here could mean another life lost.

Standing before an array of weird, tall, empty golden frames, I tried to keep my hands from shaking as I held my bow and an arrow at the ready. There was a subtle, humming ancient energy that suffused into the very heart of this place. I could feel tiny vibrations, and it made every little hair on my arms and neck prickle. I had to wonder if it was coming from those frames, although it looked like they were all empty. Something about them reminded me of oversized dressing mirrors with the insides already smashed out. They stood in neat lines, one right after another, and appeared to be identical.

Something in the back of my mind told me that wasn't true, though.

"You're sure this is the one that leads to the Gate of Proleus?" Uncle Reigh asked as we all gathered around one of the frames.

Ziryan nodded. "Without a doubt. You will arrive at a place much like this one, but without the cover of the acropolis." He motioned to the tall, dome-shaped ceiling overhead. It was held up by a row of white stone pillars, and one circular opening in the center that let in a single shaft of radiant moonlight, almost as though it had been specifically cut and placed to frame tonight's full moon.

"Great." Uncle Reigh rubbed his hands together as he walked around the frame, studying it from top to bottom. "And you're sure my dragon will be able to get through it?"

"The portal is not constrained to size. The magic can flex and contract. Your beast will pass through without a problem," Ziryan assured.

Uncle Reigh licked his lips, his gaze darting over to where Vexi crouched nearby, sniffing the air curiously. Maybe she could tell this place was odd, too.

"You said magical power activates it? How much is required?" Thatcher spoke up.

"It depends on the source. For us, it is quite draining. But for those drawing directly from divine power, I assume it will be far easier. Between the three of you, I'm sure you will manage well enough." Ziryan motioned to Thatcher, Uncle Reigh, and me.

"Okay, then. Here's hoping." Uncle Reigh sighed deeply, then turned back to face Ziryan and the rest of the Rajinna clan gathered behind him.

Well, all except for Lukani.

"On behalf of my group, Maldobar, and the rest of the world, I offer my deepest thanks for your help," Uncle Reigh said and gave a deep, formal bow. "We're the ones in your debt now. If you need anything—anything at all—reach out to me or any member of the Farrow family. We won't hesitate to help you with whatever you need."

I understood exactly why Ziryan didn't look all that satisfied even as he shook Uncle Reigh's hand again. His son was still determined to come with us. It probably made everything he'd been through to find and help us feel pointless. For whatever reason, however, I hadn't noticed him trying to pull Lukani aside to discuss it. Maybe there was a cultural reason for the Rajinna not to impose their will on their children like that. Whatever the case, I absolutely hated the idea that they might part ways with any bitter feelings between them. I had to believe that wasn't what Lukani wanted, either. But it wasn't my place to try forcing them to talk. This was a family matter, and I wasn't family. I had to respect that boundary.

Gods, I just hoped Lukani didn't regret this someday.

With a few more solemn, muttered farewells, we turned to face the gateway's empty frame. Thatcher put a hand on one side. I did the same on the other. Uncle Reigh came to stand right beside me, his hand right next to mine. His brow was locked in a deeply furrowed frown, sweat already beading on his forehead. I could see his pulse throbbing in the side of his neck, where all those new swirling, dark marks mottled his skin.

This was it. No turning back.

I took a final, deep breath and reached down into that quiet place in my soul for Paligno's power again. Uncle Reigh and Thatcher must have done the same, because a flash of blinding golden light lit up the entire frame before us. The vibrations in the air intensified, so strong they made my temples throb and my teeth ache. We all drew back, staring into the center of the frame. It wasn't empty anymore. Strange hues of light rippled inside it, twisting and curling like currents of smoke. Sometimes, I could have sworn I saw figures or objects forming, like faint shadows. But they didn't last for more than a second.

Vexi gave a low, disapproving growl. Her scaly ears slicked back and she crouched down lower, her massive head now right next to me.

I had to agree; this thing was bizarre. I'd never felt energy like that before. It wasn't divine, like mine. But it wasn't mortal, like Lukani's. It was something else entirely—something I'd never felt before.

And we had no choice but to trust it.

PART EIGHT

CLARKE

32

CHAPTER THIRTY-TWO

"Clarke?" Kaili called my name softly.

Sitting on a raised hunk of stone before the magnificent white tree, I glanced over to find her cautiously walking toward me, her expression tense and unsure. She nibbled at her bottom lip, brows drawn together as she looked me over as though trying to tell if I was angry or upset.

I gave a smile that probably looked as thin and forced as it felt. "It's okay. I'm just thinking," I said.

She smiled weakly and sat down on the hunk of stone right beside me. "You're good at that."

"It doesn't feel like it," I admitted, letting my head hang low as I sighed deeply. It didn't do anything to stop the way my head still pounded. "I only get one shot at this. One wish to make sure everyone is safe and nothing like this ever happens again. I don't understand the rules or parameters, and I don't know what will happen once my wish is made. The easiest solution would be to just wish Sadeera away—but I'm not sure that's the right one. High Inquisitor Bellavora is right. Even if Sadeera is gone, someone else might try this again in the future. And they might be successful. I mean, Jaevid already tried once to remove the powers of the gods from the hands and devices of mortals when he dissolved the Law of the Stones. A lot of good that's done, right? We're right back where we started."

"I see," Kaili mused. "Perhaps taking the gods and their powers out of play isn't the answer, then."

I rubbed at the back of my neck. "I don't think it is. I just don't know what is."

Kaili didn't answer, and for a long time, we just sat there together in silence. She stared at the tree, the light reflecting in her beautiful turquoise eyes. I couldn't help but stare. Gods, I thought I would never see her again. But here she was, right beside me. I would have given anything to be able to send word to Noa, just to let him know we were both okay. He must've been so worried.

Out of nowhere, a tiny squeak made both of us startle and look over. A little ball of black and white fur scurried over the floor, dashing straight toward me.

Kaili drew back with a shriek. "A rat!"

Jumping spirits, it ... it was Trick!

I laughed and bent over, scooping the tiny creature up and putting him on my knee. He sat up on his hind legs, whiskered nose wriggling and little pink ears perked. I carefully stroked his head with a fingertip, unable to keep my eyes from welling up some. I couldn't fathom how he had survived that battle, let alone found me here. But, gods, I was so glad he had.

"He's not just any rat," I explained as I gave him a little chin scratch. "His name is Trick. He's really clever. He saved my life, actually."

Kaili's gaze flicked between the little rat and me a few times before she gave a reluctant, "O-Okay. If you say so."

I relaxed some, resting my elbows on my knees as Trick climbed up my arm and settled onto my shoulder. He perched there and preened himself, sniffed at my ear, and watched Kaili with his curious dark eyes. "He belonged to a friend of mine. A friend who gave his life for us only a day ago."

A cautious smile tugged at the corners of her mouth as Kaili leaned in closer, finally daring to stroke him. "I suppose he is sort of cute," she said. "I've never seen a rat this color. He looks a bit like a teeny cow with those black spots."

Trick squeaked at her, sniffing her hand before finally venturing to climb along her arm and perch on her shoulder, as well. She flinched and went stiff, but only at first. When Trick curled himself against her neck, hiding in her long dark hair, she giggled and petted him again.

I didn't have to force a smile then. Seeing her that way, happy for even a second, was all I needed. The answer I'd been searching for crystalized in my mind, and I glanced back over my shoulder to where High Inquisitor Bellavora stood waiting, gazing up at the tree as though she were lost in her own thoughts.

I didn't know if she could read my thoughts. Sometimes, it certainly seemed that way. But the second I looked her way, Bellavora's gaze shifted and met mine with a soft earnest gaze. Time was running out. If I was going to do this, it had to be now.

"Maybe Trick should stay with you," I suggested, facing Kaili again. He couldn't very well stay with me—not with what I had planned.

Kaili had moved on to making kissy sounds at the little rat as she petted his head. "I'm happy to look after him, if you like."

"Yeah, I think that would be best." I cleared my throat and sat straighter. "I ... I know what I have to do. How I can fix this and make sure it doesn't happen again."

She went still, her eyes going wide and her expression twisting with concern. Maybe she could sense it or somehow hear it in my voice. The goodbye that was coming next.

Because I didn't know how much of me would survive this.

"Clarke?" she breathed my name with a tremor of worry.

"It's okay, Kaili. I have to do this. It's the only way." I tried to sound comforting and like I wasn't completely scared out of my mind.

She didn't look convinced at all and opened her mouth like she was going to protest. I didn't give her the chance.

Leaning in, I cradled one of her cheeks in my hand and pressed my lips lightly against her forehead. "Thank you ... for everything," I whispered. Then I stood, dusting off my knees and combing some of my gritty, sweaty hair away from my face.

"I'm ready," I said, more to myself than anyone else. I needed to believe that. It was the only way I could go through with it.

"I cannot go with you," Bellavora said, appearing at my side as I began to walk toward that softly glowing tree.

"I know."

"You will not be received warmly as a mortal," she warned.

I nodded. "I don't intend to go there as one."

She blinked, pausing some as I walked on ahead of her. "Clarke, my dear, are you certain about this? Once you make your wish, there will be no turning back."

I bit down hard against the swell of nerves, anxiety, and fear that made my stomach turn. "I know. But this is the only way. They've watched in silence for far too long."

"Then I wish you every success. I wish, more than anything, I could go with you. But my re-entering the city would very likely end my life." Bellavora's voice had gone quiet, her tone much more reserved and maybe even the slightest bit anxious. That didn't bode well.

But I couldn't afford to start doubting myself now.

"It's okay," I assured her. "I can handle this. I think ... I was born to."

Stopping before the huge trunk of the tree, I tilted my head back to stare into its broad, outstretched limbs one last time. Then I sucked in a deep, steadying breath, closed my eyes, and stretched a hand out toward the tree trunk.

My heartbeat pounded so fast it made my vision spot. It could be a mistake. It could be the wrong choice. But one way or another, their time standing on the sidelines while the world churned in turmoil had to end. This was their battle, with an enemy of their own making, and it was long past time they finally joined it.

If that meant I had to shed my mortal shell for the last time and knock on their door personally, I would. I would surrender fully to Avgior and become something they couldn't just brush off—a god of the old world.

So, I would walk the streets of Avora and demand more of its people.

Their indifference to the crimes of one of their own, while she was systematically dismantling the very foundations of the rest of the world, could not continue. Not for one more minute. Sadeera was a problem they had created and left unchecked, and now they remained silent and indifferent while everyone else was left to suffer for it. However, High Inquisitor Bellavora was right—the Avoran elves would never take a mortal's word seriously. I couldn't go there as Clarke and expect to be heard.

But they couldn't ignore Avgior.

Closing my eyes, I tried to focus, to call upon the ancient god's presence within me. I'd already pushed my luck once today. I'd nearly crossed the point of no return and lost myself. Now, I had to surrender fully ... and hope that some tiny fragment of myself, of Clarke, survived. I didn't know if that was even possible. I didn't know if I would remember anything about Kaili, Noa, or any of the others after this.

Still, I had to try.

And as my fingers brushed the shining silver bark of the tree, I let the last of my doubts and reservations slip away like sand through my fingers. Ready or not, it was time to end this once and for all. And in order to do that ... I had to get to the root of the problem.

I had to force Avora's involvement before it was too late.

PART NINE

MURDOC

⸙ 33 ⸙

CHAPTER THIRTY-THREE

During my years of Ulfrangar training, I had been educated fairly thoroughly on what I could expect when it came to the level of ability from the warriors and soldiers of other kingdoms. Maldobarian forces were considered worldwide to have far superior training and capabilities compared to most. But I had always been told that Nar'Haleen was not far behind us in skill.

As I dragged the remains of the last enemy soldier we had, er, quietly abducted and stripped of his armor, I now had to question that fact. I tossed him into the pile with the rest of his fallen comrades and wiped my hands on my pants. Only nine thousand, nine hundred, and ninety-three more to go. These fellows hadn't put up much of a fight. So, either the ability of Nar'Haleenan's military had been greatly exaggerated, or we'd gotten incredibly lucky and found the one group of soldiers that were entirely incompetent, or our own skillset was vastly superior. It was a toss-up, honestly, and any of those reasons satisfied my peace of mind. We could use any advantage we could get.

Jaevid had not approved of any means of torture when it came to dealing with these fellows, so we hadn't questioned any of them very thoroughly about their battle plans. Only two out of the seven were willing to give up any information. Nothing they said was shocking, however. These two legions provided by the Emperor of Nar'Haleen himself were at the command of his wife, Empress Leysa—the woman we now knew was actually Sadeera. They knew they had been brought here to fight dragonriders whom they believed were offering secret assistance to Rienka and Damaria.

Nothing earth-shattering there.

With all the armor we needed, everyone quickly began donning our new disguises. So far, so good.

We had just one, smaller than average, problem.

None of the armor we had retrieved was made to fit Garnett's dwarven frame. It made every piece of Nar'Haleenan gear we put on her look ridiculous, like a child trying on her father's armor. No one was going to buy that she was really a soldier. It would raise suspicion as soon as we walked into their camp.

"You can ride piggyback under my cloak," Roxus snickered.

Garnett scowled and made a rude gesture. "Do you like havin' kneecaps?"

"We need a real solution," Jaevid grumbled, adjusting the fit of his own Nar'Haleenan bronze breastplate. "And fast."

"I spotted some cavalry horses, they're a bit far from our current location, but it appeared that they were unattended," Isandri spoke up, lurking nearby with her weight leaning onto her staff. "We may be able to swipe one and put her in the officer's armor. No one will question an officer on horseback. It'll make her size difference less obvious, especially if we can fashion longer false legs out of the armor we have left here."

"That could work," I agreed.

Garnett clapped her hands and snatched up the officer's much more intricate breastplate and helmet from the pile. "Excellent—I get to be in charge of you lot, then. Roxus, dearie, you'll be walking behind my horse in case he decides to drop a nice warm pile."

He smirked, but didn't retort.

At least everyone seemed to be in good spirits. That was something. Morale was half the battle.

"All of you get to work on these false legs, then. Isa, you and I can fetch the horse. Let's hurry," I said. Given our skill sets, if we did have to trek to fetch the horse, we would be able to manage it faster than the others.

She nodded and followed, holding her staff at the ready while I got up and adjusted the last piece of my own Nar'Haleenan disguise. At least if we were spotted, the enemy might not realize I was a threat straight away. But I wouldn't be able to keep up a ruse like that for long. My Sokraal was decent, but my accent would never pass as authentic.

We had to do this fast, clean, and quiet before the last of our dumb luck ran out.

ISANDRI AND I MADE OUR WAY AS SPEEDILY AS POSSIBLE THROUGH THE ROUGH TERRAIN back to the border where the enemy forces were encamped. Even from a distance, the sound of thousands of men moving, talking, and readying themselves for battle was thunderous. I felt it like a lead weight crushing down over my back, making sweat bead on my brow and my pulse thump heavily and slowly in my chest. I'd been through a battle before, years ago. I'd never been through it as a soldier on the frontlines, though. This shift in perspective had my nerves on a knife's edge.

I didn't like being this far from the rest of our group. Not one tiny bit.

Gods and Fates, this *had* to work. If it didn't, we would be slaughtered in seconds—even with the individuals among us who had access to magical and divine power. The odds were more than against us.

"Wait," Isa hissed suddenly, stopping and throwing up a hand. She dropped into a low crouch, peering through the gloom ahead of us with her yellow eyes reflecting the moonlight like a cat's.

I immediately dropped into a crouch beside her, watching for any sign of movement. My pulse thudded hard and steady against my ribs. I held my breath, tensed and ready with my hand already on the hilt of my blade. I should have been expecting this. Of course, they would have scouts patrolling the area. Gods, I really was starting to go soft.

Footsteps crunched in the dry, gritty soil dead ahead. Heavy. Wide gait, judging by the sound of the pace. Probably masculine. Solider? Or a scout?

I bit down hard and slowly curled my fingers around the padded leather hilt of my blade.

Then, more rustling crunched in the dry brush off to my left. Voices whispered faintly. I caught the glimmer of something white catching in the moonlight. Multiple targets, then. A whole scouting party?

I sucked my teeth and held steady, senses attuned to that place. Beside me, Isandri's slender form blinked out of sight with the faintest shimmer of silver light. In an instant, she was gone. Invisible without a single sign or trace.

Incredible. Too bad I couldn't do that. It would've made this entire mission a lot simpler.

Knowing full well Isa would advance to make first contact, I prowled through the shadows, staying low and making a wide arc around the enemy soldiers. I couldn't rush this. I had to wait for her to take them by surprise. Then I would come in from behind and—

"YOU!" Isandri yowled.

The sudden noise sent a surge of pure adrenaline through my system like someone had stuck a hot branding iron to my rear end. I rushed forward, lunging from the thickets with my blade drawn ... just in time to see Isandri re-materialize and smack a medium heighted man across the face with an open-handed slap.

A man with a head full of messy dark red hair.

Freezing in place, I stared at the back of the man's head. I didn't recognize his strange, dark, silken clothes, but I knew his posture—just as I knew those two distinctly Gray elven-styled blades that were belted to his hips.

Holy. Gods.

"Murdoc!" a familiar voice wheezed hoarsely in surprise.

Tha ... that voice ... it was ...

I turned, my heart pounding like it might launch right out of my chest. I almost dropped my sword. It couldn't be. It wasn't possible.

Thatcher hit me so hard it knocked the wind out of me and I rocked back onto my heels. He threw his arms around my shoulders and shook me like a kid squeezing a teddy bear. "You're here! Gods and Fates, we were so afraid we would be too late!"

"Th-Thatcher? H-How?" I managed to rasp when he finally let me go. With his hands gripping my shoulders tightly, he held me out at arm's length.

Thatcher shook his head, his eyes teary as he gave me another shake. "What do you mean? I should be asking *you* that! How in the world did you guys get here so fast? Wait—where are the others?" He did a terrible job of keeping his voice down, his brow creased in concern as he glanced around, searching for anyone else still hiding in the brush.

I didn't get a chance to answer.

"REIGH FARROW! How *dare* you come here without telling me," Isandri yelled suddenly, her face twitching with fury. She paced back and forth in front of him like an angry lioness, spinning her staff over her hand as though she were fighting back the urge to crack him over the head with it. "You send me that utterly *ridiculous* letter and just assume I will find peace with that? You stupid, mule headed—!"

I winced, waiting for the crack of impact.

There wasn't one.

Isandri lunged at him suddenly, the exact same way Thatcher had at me. She flung her arms around his neck and gripped him so hard his face turned almost as red as his hair. Reigh stood stiff, hands thrown up in surprise for a few seconds. I guess he had been expecting to get smacked again.

Gradually, his shoulders relaxed and he lowered his arms to gingerly hug her back. "Yeah. I'm an idiot. I know," Reigh chuckled weakly. "I'm really sorry about this, Isa. I just ... didn't want to cause you any more pain by asking you to come here."

"And you didn't think me learning that you'd come out here and *died*—because you know absolutely nothing about the culture of my homeland—would somehow be less painful for me?" She snatched away from him, her mouth pinching and her yellow-green eyes sparking with wild fury again. She grabbed the sides of his face, mashing his cheeks. "Are there any thoughts in this head at all?"

He cringed. "Weeell, when you put it like that ..."

"*Never* do this again, Reigh Farrow," she snapped. "Or the dangers of some wicked sorceress will be the least of your worries, I promise you that."

"Oh, I think he's learned his lesson quite thoroughly," another much smoother and heavily accented female voice snickered softly. "At any rate, I might suggest you keep your voices down. We wouldn't want to invite any unwelcome guests to this little reunion, hm?"

Isandri's head snapped up to stare past Reigh with a startled scowl.

One look and all the threads of tension and worry that had been pulled to their breaking point in my mind suddenly went slack.

Violet stood between Maylea and Lukani with her arms crossed and hip cocked to the side in a pose of pure confidence. A fond, amused smile played over her painted red lips as she glanced between us, not seeming the least bit surprised to see us here. Then again, she was likely far more skilled in disguising her emotions than most. She couldn't do anything to hide the fresh blood spatter on her clothes, however.

In fact, all of them looked like they'd just walked away from a brawl. Mottled in bruises, cuts, and dirt, every single one of them had heavy circles under their eyes. Thatcher, however, had something more. Red and swollen, they looked a lot like burn marks in the shape of tear streaks that ran from his eyes halfway down his cheeks.

Fates, what had happened to them?

"Uncle Murdoc," Maylea whimpered shakily as she stumbled a few steps toward me and stopped. Her face paled as she glanced around—the same way Thatcher had—undoubtedly searching for anyone else she knew nearby.

I didn't even need to guess whom.

When her wide, teal-green eyes landed back on me with her brow crinkled up in distress, I managed a faint smile that I sincerely hoped came off as reassuring and not, you know, sympathetic. I couldn't tell if it worked. She appeared every bit as ragged, exhausted, and road-weary as the rest of them.

But she did still have that pendant—the Spark of Life—hanging around her neck.

The sight of it made me want to drop to my knees and start thanking whatever god had protected them so far. No doubt, Sadeera had been pulling out all the stops as her persona of Empress Leysa to find them and take it.

"It's ... really good to see you all whole and alive, but Violet is right, we need to keep the noise down. We also need to move," I murmured, keeping my voice as low and steady as I could given the way adrenaline was still scorching through my veins. It made it hard enough just to breathe and think at the same time. "Do you have any injuries that need immediate attention?"

Reigh shook his head. "We may not look it, but we're as fit as we've been this entire time."

Wow. That did not fill my heart with confidence at *all*.

I tried not to let that show and nodded, motioning for them to follow. "It's a long way back and we have to cut fairly close to the enemy lines, so stay low and try to keep the talking to a minimum. We've been fortunate enough not to run into any enemy scouts so far, but I think we can all agree every reckless chance we take might be our last."

34

CHAPTER THIRTY-FOUR

There was no simple or easy way to do this. Emotions were already running high. Everyone was hanging by a thread, watching the last few grains of sand drop through the proverbial hourglass. But this, I suspected, would push everyone over the edge—either for better or worse. I just had absolutely no idea which.

Part of me—the Ulfrangar side—wanted to put off all the tearful reunions and lengthy discussions about what manner of hell we had all been through over the last several days. We simply didn't have time for that. But another part of me knew that keeping one group from seeing the other would send everyone into an uproar of anger and anxiety. If this battle went the way I feared, this might very well be their last chance to see one another. It would be cruel to keep them apart.

Especially a certain pair that I knew was desperate to see one another.

Jaevid shot to his feet the instant we entered the makeshift hiding spot where the rest of my group was still waiting for us to reappear with a stolen cavalry horse. All the color drained from his face when he saw Isa and Reigh following right behind me. He took a single step and faltered, as though his legs might give out at any second. His mouth opened, but no sound came out.

Not until he saw *her*.

"MAYLEA!" Jaevid yelled, the sound leaving his mouth like the despairing cry of a wounded animal.

The girl stopped cold in her tracks, her whole body cringing as she stared back at him. She didn't blink. Gods, I couldn't even tell if she was breathing or not. She gaped back at him like a phantom had just appeared before her. She made an unintelligible, choking sound.

Then the dam broke.

Maylea dropped her little travel bag and elven-styled bow and ran toward him, tears pouring down her cheeks as she screamed back, "DAH!"

Jaevid met her halfway, locking his arms around his little girl and immediately sinking to his knees as he gripped her tight against his chest. Maylea sank down with him, her arms around his neck and her face buried against his shoulder as her whole body shook with ragged sobs. With a hand on the back of her head, Jaevid kissed the top of her head again and again, gasping frantic prayers of thanks to Paligno.

The rest of us stood around, watching and not making a sound. Not for lack of feeling or empathy. Rather, it just felt wrong to say anything that might disturb them in that moment. I knew Jaevid had been living in a constant nightmare since the second he'd lost his child. Having her back in one piece must have truly felt like a miracle.

Quite frankly, given the circumstances, it was.

After a few minutes, I guess Garnett couldn't stand it anymore. She sprinted past Jaevid and Maylea to embrace Thatcher, who hugged her back and spun her around. They talked in hushed voices, exchanging a few hasty kisses as they kept their foreheads pressed together.

Envy writhed in my gut like a live eel and I had to look away. Gods and Fates, what I wouldn't give to hold Phoebe like that. To kiss her just once.

One by one, the members of our two groups converged, becoming one family again under the pale moonlight in that gods-forsaken desert. Violet greeted Arlan, then dashed over to hug Roxus. He smirked at her playfully, and I had to wonder how, exactly, those two knew each other. The way the roguish-looking older man considered her wasn't like someone looking at a coworker, even if they did both work for Arlan. More like a parent and child. Hmm.

The only individuals who didn't jump right into the merry reunion were Edarix, Noa, and Ronan.

Edarix and Noa, I could understand. They didn't know these people. They barely knew us. But Ronan?

He knew Reigh, of course. That was his uncle, who had doted on him since birth. Reigh didn't fancy himself any sort of family man, and yet no one would ever question whether or not he loved his nephew.

And then there was Maylea. Heh. Those two had been thick as thieves since they were old enough to waddle off and find trouble. I could see the quiet desperation in the boy's face as he stared at her from afar, looking as confused as he did overwhelmed. His throat jumped as he swallowed hard, blinking fast and shifting his weight from one foot to another—right up until Reigh approached him.

Grabbing the boy up in his arms, Reigh hugged him and tousled his hair. Ronan's expression didn't change much, however. He still looked confused, uncomfortable, and didn't say much except a few mumbled words I couldn't make out.

Eventually, everyone seemed to collect themselves. With a lot of sniffling, our company of tear-streaked faces and bloodshot eyes all turned back to focus on Arlan and me. Somehow, it felt like the two of us had become the default leaders. Gods and Fates, that was disturbing. I mean, yes, it made sense for Arlan. He was the reason we were all standing here right now.

But *me?* What in the world made them think I was the one calling the shots here?

Oh. Right. Because ... I sort of had been so far.

Ugggh.

"Obviously, this changes things," I muttered, more to myself than to anyone else. We had more people fighting for our cause now, but not much time to plan out anything. Half of us were already outfitted with Nar'Haleenan armor, ready for a stealth mission that would take us right into the heart of the enemy's camp.

And the rest?

Isandri could go invisible, so she was taken care of. But that left most of our newly acquired comrades and one nagging question that I hadn't gotten around to asking.

"How, exactly, were you planning on launching any kind of attack against two legions of Nar'Haleenan soldiers?" I asked, looking directly at Reigh.

He shrugged. "To be honest, we thought you lot would already be locked in combat by the time we got here. We were expecting to come in as support. A group of Rajinna came to us with word from you," he said, motioning to Arlan. "They said you were going to engage with the enemy soldiers, so our intent was to come in and back you up however we could. Vexi's circling the area, waiting for my signal, but we hadn't come up with a plan yet. You caught us before we even got a look at the enemy forces."

Jaevid's eyebrows rose, but he didn't say anything. He didn't have to.

That was it? They were just going to go for it and see what happened? Somehow, that didn't surprise me nearly as much as it should have. Gods and Fates.

I looked down and rubbed my forehead for a moment, trying to collect my sanity. Fortunately, I had already arrived at the only solution I could think of that made any sense whatsoever. Hopefully, they would agree.

"I think we should move forward with our plan as intended," I suggested, glancing over to Arlan to try and gauge his response. He just nodded without offering any comment. "When our reinforcements appear, those of us who are hidden in the ranks will act and disable as many of the war machines as possible so the dragonriders will be more effective."

"How many did you bring?" Reigh asked suddenly, his expression sharpening with that calculating focus I'd been counting on. Even if he was a little late to the game, he did have a mind for war strategy.

"Counting your Vexi, we have seven dragons fit to fight," I replied.

Lukani raised his hand. "Make that eight."

Standing beside him, Maylea shifted uncomfortably and shot him a frosty sideways look. She didn't say anything, though.

"Okay, then. That we can work with," Reigh said. "As soon as they arrive, we need to relay to them to carve a path in flame straight to those temple steps. Thatcher can get us through, but the Nar'Haleenan soldiers won't be able to touch us."

"We're literally going to walk through fire." Jaevid sighed, slowly shaking his head. I guess we had finally surpassed his level of comfort when it came to insane plans. "So, who is going into the temple to destroy the gate and potentially confront Sadeera? As much as I would enjoy the idea of converging on her with a unified front, some of us will have to remain outside and make sure none of the enemy soldiers interfere."

Hmm. A good point. Some of us would have to stay behind to hold the line.

"I will." Garnett raised her hand confidently. "I'm not much use in a magical fight, but I can slice through soldiers well enough."

"The same goes for me," Roxus spoke up next.

A few more hands went up. All told, Garnett, Roxus, Noa, Lukani, Violet, and Jae volunteered to remain outside the temple to hold the enemy forces at bay. They all scowled at once, like a flock of angry vultures, when I raised my hand, as well.

"You've got the blessing of Proleus," Isandri objected. "You carry his power. Why would you not fight Sadeera with us?"

"Because between Reigh, Thatcher, Isandri, Maylea, and Ronan, you ought to have plenty of divine power fighting for you in the temple. And while we will have plenty of dragons outside, we will need considerable strength on the ground, as well, to make sure we keep our casualties to a minimum." I frowned back and crossed my arms. "Let me be clear here, we may succeed in stopping Sadeera. We may destroy the gate. But make no mistake, we're talking about sending six people to fight an army of nearly *ten thousand* armed men. I know we've all proven ourselves in battle ten times over, but we won't hold out for long—even if I'm there to help. This is a race against time. And once it's done, we need to retreat immediately."

No one spoke. There wasn't so much as a pensive hum from the group of people now gathered around me. The heaviness in the air intensified, and I could see the faintest traces of fear seeping into Jaevid's pale eyes when I met his gaze. Not for himself, of course—for the fourteen-year-old child standing next to him with a bow in her hand.

"I'm not trying to scare you," I added at last, my voice halting and sweat beginning to run down my neck. I wasn't cut out for this sort of thing. For leadership. I wasn't the one who should be giving this kind of talk "I'm not running from a fight with Sadeera, or avoiding that conflict in any way. I'm not even trying to be the one in charge of this mission. I just think it's important that we all keep our expectations firmly in mind here. I-I ... I'm sorry, I know I'm not doing this right. I should be delivering some inspiring speech, but I'm not ... I don't know what to ..." My voice died in my throat as I stared out across the faces of almost all the people in the world I cared about.

Was I failing them?

"We know, Murdoc," Thatcher spoke up suddenly, stepping forward and putting a hand on my shoulder. "And we couldn't do this without you. You're right, we need to be careful. We—"

The ground rumbled under our feet, shuddering with a low, groaning roar like an earthquake. It lasted nearly thirty seconds before silence resumed, and we all stared at one another in mute horror.

"What was that?" Maylea whispered, gripping her father's arm tightly.

After hours of saying next to nothing and hardly showing any emotion, Arlan the Kinslayer stepped forward with a fearsome scowl making his golden eyes glow like lit torches. "That," he seethed in a low, vicious tone, "was the opening of the temple door."

PART TEN

REIGH

35

CHAPTER THIRTY-FIVE

Time was up.

Everyone huddled together, exchanging a few hushed words, parting kisses, and quick embraces before moving into position. Jae hugged Maylea again, his expression a twisted mixture of fractured grief and terror. They couldn't be in the same group. Jae wasn't the one slinging divine power around this time. He was still a good swordsman, though, and the group holding the line outside would need his expertise.

So they had no choice but to say their goodbyes.

Jae stared down at his daughter, tenderly tucking some of her dark hair behind one of her slightly pointed ears. "You know, I was not much older than you when I set off on my own, trying to save your grandfather. And I remember how it felt to go to the officers who were supposed to be looking out for everyone's safety and be brushed off as a nuisance. I'd never been more frustrated, or more determined to prove myself. I hope ... that is not how I've made you feel. Like you can't talk to me about the things that trouble you."

She shook her head quickly. "No, Dah. No, it's not that at all. I ... I wanted to help everyone. And I wanted to find Ronan. I thought those were the only reasons I came here. But now, it's like I can see how this is so much bigger than just Ronan or me. And ... it scares me." She sniffled some, her chin trembling as she looked down to the toes of her boots. "I've always been so afraid of living my life in your shadow. But following in your footsteps is much more intimidating and difficult than you made it seem in all those stories."

His smile was hollow, like the very soul was being cut straight out of him as he listened. "If it's any consolation, I was scared out of my mind during all of those so-called adventures."

"Yeah," she laughed weakly. "I guess that's just part of it, huh?"

"Without a doubt, little flower," he assured her and bent down to kiss the top of her head again.

Maylea's mouth mashed up, eyes shutting tightly as she wrung her hands on the grip of her bow. "I'm scared now, Dah. I-I know Paligno chose me for this, but I don't know if I can. I'm so sorry, Dah. I shouldn't have just run away like that. I should have said something when—"

Jaevid grasped her chin, tilting her head back up so she had to look him right in the eye. "Listen to me, Maylea. I'm scared, too. But Paligno has put his trust in you. He believes in you, and so do I. You can do this. And whatever happens, remember that your mother and I are so proud of you and the young woman you've become."

I had to turn away then. Watching them in that moment felt like someone was twisting a blade in my chest. It was too much.

But that's when I noticed Ronan standing not ten paces away from them. With her back turned, Maylea likely had no idea he was staring at her, his expression the picture of earnest concern. With his brow knitted and his mouth slightly open, he watched her as though he were looking for some sort of opening—a chance to interrupt so he could speak with her. Whether he lost his nerve or simply realized now wasn't the time, Ronan ducked his head low and retreated a few steps, finally turning away and striding toward me instead. He puffed a heavy sigh that made his cheeks flap when he stopped beside me.

"Got something you want to say to her?" I asked and gave his armor a quick, once-over glance, just in case he'd overlooked anything. "She came all the way here for you, you know."

"Y-Yeah ..." He faltered, his voice hushed and somewhat embarrassed. "I know. I never meant to cause her any pain. She's always been there for me, and now, I don't even know what to say to her."

I snorted. "Well, a simple thank you is probably a good place to start."

He didn't reply, and I didn't push it any further. Ronan had always been a more reserved, contemplative kid. He was a lot like Jenna in that way.

We stood together in silence, watching as the rest of our companions hurriedly made their final preparations. Arlan swiftly passed his stolen armor off to Violet, and she dressed in it in record time. Something told me she'd done a pre-battle armor swap a few times before. I'd have to ask her about that later.

Er, well, providing we didn't both die.

Those charged with infiltrating the Nar'Haleenan forces gathered around Garnett and Lukani—who easily shifted into the shape of a horse. With a little help, Garnett climbed onto his back and slipped her feet into the false legs the others had put together from greaves and sabatons stuffed with clothing. It wasn't a perfect disguise, but it would do. Maybe the rest of the Nar'Haleenan forces would be too preoccupied to give her a second glance.

We left, moving together as quickly and silently as we could toward the enemy's encampment. Once we were within sight, we split into our groups and went completely silent, communicating only with dragonrider hand signals. The first group continued on, and we followed at a distance. Since we had no disguises, we had to remain out of sight for as long as possible. Soon, it wouldn't matter if we were disguised or not. We just had to wait for the chaos to begin—for our friends in the first group and the dragonriders to make a path—and then we would move, too.

We would head straight for the temple's front door.

The thunderous rumble of the armies moving rattled the loose stones and stirred up dust like a sandstorm over the seemingly endless field of black armored figures. My steps slowed, heart hammering in my throat so hard I couldn't swallow without my eyes watering. I stared out across the churning, roiling sea of dark armor, war machines, and war beasts I had no name for.

Gods, Fates, and all things holy. I hadn't seen anything like this since the Tibran War. It gave me that exact same horrible, sick, sinking feeling like I might throw up.

Murdoc was right—we would be lucky if any of us walked away from this fight.

Ducking and hiding where we could, I motioned for everyone to stay silent and still as we watched our friends make their way closer and closer to the enemy's ranks. Isandri was somewhere overhead, watching but completely invisible to the naked eye. It gave me a strange sense of comfort, despite the way my cheek still burned where she'd slapped me. I guess I'd earned that, though.

The lay of the land wasn't ideal for any sort of battle. With a forbidding wall of jagged, dark stone mountains to the east, all the enemy ranks fanned out in squared clumps to the west. Those clumps must have been individual units, or cohorts, of soldiers each under the command of a separate officer. They were far more structured than the Tibran forces had been, I'd grant them that.

With all their muscle positioned to the west, my gaze tracked along the ridge of steep mountains until I spotted it—the Gate of Proleus. It stood like a man-made dam of bronze and black stone, towering well over two hundred feet, with only one large, arched doorway in the very center. That massive doorway led out onto a wide forward courtyard in a half-circle shape that overlooked the sprawling desert. But there were no other features about the place. No windows. No battlements. No ramparts or towers. Clearly, this place had been built right into the mountains to act like a cork in a wine bottle, stoppering up whatever lay beyond.

Just a dormant gateway straight into the divine realm of the gods apparently. No big deal.

By my crude mental calculations, we were roughly a mile from the door to the temple. Only one wide stone staircase led up to that rounded courtyard and the doorway beyond. One way in, one way out.

Fates, this would be risky.

My gaze tracked the sky in every direction, looking for anything out of place. Any sign of movement. A glimmer of green scales that might be Vexi, or a sign of these so-called reinforcements Murdoc and the others kept talking about. For our sakes, I hoped they weren't tossing around that term lightly. We needed all the help we could get.

My lungs squeezed and shuddered with every breath as I watched the last of our group finally merge with the rest of the Nar'Haleenan ranks. They were careful about it. They took their time, moving casually at first, and then with a purpose that matched the energy of the other soldiers around them. It was seamless and absolutely terrifying at the same time. With helmets disguising their features, it didn't take ten seconds for me to lose track of them amidst the chaos of the enemy lines all forming up and taking a defensive position around the gate. Deep down, I knew that was a good sign. They were blending in beautifully. But, curse it, I hated not knowing where they were.

All we could do now was wait. Wait—and pray.

Every second that passed made my pulse boom in my ears louder. I gnashed my teeth, gnawing on the inside of my cheeks until I could taste blood. How much longer would this take? Where were those reinforcements? How long ago had they sent for them? What if something happened and they didn't come at all?

A shattering cry boomed through the night like a distant clap of thunder. Immediately, every nerve in my brain fired at once. I knew that sound like I knew the beating of my own heart.

A dragon's mighty battle roar.

"Sweet merciful Fates," Thatcher whispered. "Wh ... What is that?"

I had absolutely no idea. But it might as well have Phoebe's name written all over it in big, bold letters.

Sailing through the sky on broad, fin-like wings, the contraption looked almost like a ship if not for its massive size. It dwarfed the dragons that flew all around it, with a long hull bristling with two rows of twenty gun ports down either side and one that ran directly across the bottom. I counted six of those huge, fin-shaped wings and one enormous balloon-like fixture on top held on by a complex series of netted ropes and cords. That seemed to be what was keeping it aloft, as best I could tell.

"We have been calling it an airship," Arlan announced, a hint of pride in his voice as he watched the machine cruise toward the battlefield with a renewed, satisfied smile. "Though the official name is the *Dawn Chaser.* It has taken all of fourteen years to build, and it is the first and only of its kind."

I tried to speak, but it came out more as an excited, choking wheeze.

This was it. This was the edge we needed. The thing that might actually give us a real fighting chance.

And in that moment, watching the *Dawn Chaser* align itself for the first volley of roaring cannon fire at the Nar'Haleenan forces below ... I finally dared to hope.

BOOOOM!

The shockwave from the *Dawn Chaser's* first round of cannon fire rocked the battlefield, leaving my vision swerving and my eardrums throbbing. The result? Instant chaos.

The Nar'Haleenan forces scrambled below, positioning their war machines and beginning to fire volleys of arrows up at the huge airship. That was when the dragons descended. I recognized four of the beasts straightaway. The big purple and teal green drake was my sister's, Phevos—although from this distance, I couldn't tell if she was in his saddle or not. Blite and Fornax flew right off his wingtips, assuming a V-shaped battle formation for an aerial assault.

"Fornax," Thatcher blurted, unable to contain himself at the sight of the big, orange and black striped dragon.

The sight of the fourth dragon made my chest swell with a sense of reckless defiance. Or maybe that was courage? Whatever it was, seeing Jaevid's blue king drake zooming into view from underneath the airship with one beat of his black leathery wings, set my teeth on edge. Mavrik unleashed a shattering war cry to the enemy ranks below, and my hands instinctively found their way to the hilts of my kafki blades.

The sound of so many of her kin must have been too much for my girl, Vexi, to resist. I whipped around as I heard her give an answering screech, spotting the flash of her vibrant green scales against the moonlit sky as she flew toward them, joining up behind Mavrik like we had done in dragonrider training a thousand times.

Gods, what I wouldn't give to be on her back, anchored to my saddle, with the wind from her strong wings in my face right then.

"Time to move in closer. Prepare yourselves. This'll be a sprint to the finish line," I warned, stealing a sideways look at Thatcher. "You ready with that shield?"

He nodded firmly, the colored rings of his eyes already sparking with little streaks of golden light.

As Phevos, Fornax, and Blite lined up to make their first fiery pass over the ranks of

Nar'Haleenan soldiers below, we hurried down closer to the edge of the enemy ranks. I still couldn't see any of our friends or tell where in the fray they might be. I'd just have to trust they could hold up their end.

"Go, go, go!" I called down the line of my own group. "Once you see fire, start running straight for it!"

BOOOM!

Another shockwave burst through the air, making me stagger. The impact hit my chest like the blow of a war hammer, and I stared up in awe as the *Dawn Chaser* fired another volley at the lines of troops below. Cannonballs rained down, hammering the ground with another rolling *BOOM!*

On the ground, the Nar'Haleenan forces began to respond. I guess their initial shock at the sight of the huge airship had worn off. Their catapults and trebuchets fired back, sending huge projectiles sailing through the air like flaming meteors. So many arrows flew it looked like plumes of smoke rising from the lines of soldiers.

Dragons roared. Men shouted. And then, with one sweeping low pass, Phevos, Blite, and Fornax bathed the ground in their burning venom. They laid a path of fire straight to the heart of the enemy's forces—right to the steps of the temple.

Right where we had to go.

36

CHAPTER THIRTY-SIX

It was a mad race through pure pandemonium.

With our only path now burning in the night, we ran straight for the roaring inferno with blades and bows drawn. Thatcher took the lead with his hands outstretched, calling forth that shimmering shield that closed around us like a globe of golden light. We kept in close and didn't slow down, stepping directly into the flames. They hissed and crackled, licking at the outside of the shield, but never making it through. Arrows pinged off it, mere inches away from our faces. But every enemy soldier insane enough to try to rush at us was immediately consumed by dragonfire.

Even with Thatcher's shield keeping the flames from ever reaching us, the intense, acrid smell of the burning venom still stung my eyes and left my throat raw. The heat made my forehead bead with sweat. My pulse boomed, clashing hard against my ribs. My ears roared with the dark symphony of battle that raged all around us. I wasn't sure how long Thatcher could maintain that shield while running at full speed. This wasn't exactly something we'd practiced in training.

Halfway there, I caught glimpses through the dancing flames of the towering temple looming before us. The flames of war made all of its polished dark stone walls shine an eerie orange. It might as well have been the gates to the abyss.

In a way, it basically was.

CRAAACK!

Something huge slammed into the ground off to the left, throwing up dirt and stones. Soldiers screamed. I lost my footing, the toe of my boot snagging on an uneven stone. *WHAM!* I hit the ground face first, my vision swerving in and out of focus.

Oh ... oh, gods, no.

The rest of the group kept running. They hadn't seen me fall—or so I thought.

I braced for the scorching hell of dragonfire to overtake me. I wouldn't survive. I'd be burned alive. Curling my arms and legs in close, I waited.

"GET UP!" someone shouted over me suddenly.

Wh-What?

I looked up, spots still dancing before my eyes.

Ronan stood over me, his expression drawn into a snarl of focus with his teeth bared and his eyes glowing deep red. Sparks flew like fireflies and the lengths of his dark cloak billowed behind him as he kept his arms outstretched to the side. The roaring fire swirled around us, but parted like a crackling curtain as I pushed off the ground and began staggering forward again.

Ronan followed, and we ran after the others at full speed. Without the protection of Thatcher's shield, however, the smoke and heat assaulted all my senses. My eyes watered until I could barely see. My lungs burned. I choked, gasping for air. But each breath came with fresh agony from the intense heat.

Then I saw them. Through the wavering flames, the glow of Thatcher's magical shield shone even brighter. I bowed my head and forged on, forcing my legs to go faster. Almost there. I would make it. Gods and Fates, I would not die like this.

I hit the ground on my knees, my head spinning and my body shaking from the pain. The relief of Thatcher's shield closed around me, bathing me in somewhat cooler air without smoke. I gasped and wheezed, spitting black ash and wiping my eyes before I finally managed to get back on my feet.

Then I looked back for Ronan.

He stood on the other side of the shield, the inferno still raging around him like he was standing in the middle of a furnace. His eyes still shone like red molten metal, and he didn't so much as flinch or cringe away as the flames licked up his legs and fanned across his shoulders. Not a single part of him looked burnt. Fates, he wasn't even singed. Without a word, Ronan just pointed onward, straight ahead of us.

Right. We had to keep going.

Sprinting forward again, we closed the gap to the base of the wide stone staircase that led up to the front of the temple. There, the line of dragonfire ended. We would be exposed. And we would be primary targets.

Thatcher's jaw clenched hard, veins standing out against his neck and forehead as he held that shield around us. I drew my blades. Maylea nocked an arrow and took aim. When we emerged from the fire, the soldiers would be on us like flies on crap. I couldn't see our other group nearby, but the fire obstructed most of my view of what was going on around us. Gods, I just prayed they had made it this far. We couldn't do this—not without their help.

As we stepped from the flames, arrows immediately pinged off Thatcher's shield. Enemy soldiers rushed us, bouncing off the exterior like birds flying full speed into windowpanes.

WHOOOSH!

A wall of fire surged upward, catching a group of soldiers before they even managed to reach us. With his hand clenched into a shaking fist, Ronan stood firm—still snarling like a furious wolf. He jerked backward, yelling in anger and pain as an arrow caught him in the shoulder. It didn't slow him down much, though. With a shoving gesture, he sent another plume of fire arcing around all the soldiers still advancing toward us. They screamed in panic but couldn't get away.

Not when they were already burning.

"Keep moving!" I shouted, not sure if he would even hear me over the roar of battle.

Whirling to face me, Ronan didn't hesitate to follow as we all started up the steps. We wove a path around the charred bodies of soldiers that lay scattered, still smoldering where they'd fallen. More followed, rushing after us in hot pursuit. Arrows fell like rain.

BOOOM!

I staggered again, barely managing to stay on my feet as another huge projectile hit the stairs to my right. It landed and smashed through the stone steps, missing us by only a few feet. Curse it, were they firing at us with catapults now?!

A dark shadow suddenly eclipsed all that wonderful, sterling moonlight ... and I got my answer.

Looking up, I stared in slack-jawed horror at the enormous block of stone coming straight at us.

Yep. They were definitely firing catapults at us.

THERE WASN'T TIME TO RUN, OR SCREAM, OR EVEN PRAY. I BARELY GOT IN A STARTLED gasp of horror.

WHAM!

A gigantic clawed paw appeared out of nowhere, slamming into the flying boulder and slapping it away like a kitten batting away a ball of yarn. Covered in gleaming golden scales, Lukani's dragon form appeared over us like a towering god. He thundered a shattering roar, and breathed a column of flame behind us, cutting off the approach of any more soldiers trying to chase us up the stairs.

Oh, thank the gods. They were here. Our other group had made it!

Thatcher dropped his shield as we all turned, running under Lukani's dragon legs and scurrying the rest of the way up the stairs to the temple courtyard. There, the rest of our friends met us, their eyes wild with battle fever. Many of them were already spattered with blood, and we all startled when Isandri suddenly appeared in our midst like she had just materialized out of thin air.

"You must hurry. They are bringing the dunestriders this way," she warned, spinning her staff over her hand restlessly.

"The path into the temple is clear," Murdoc rumbled ominously, his gaze cutting skyward as Phevos led the dragons on another pass. "We'll hold them off here as long as we can."

I grabbed his shoulder and squeezed it roughly as I walked past. "Try to stay alive, you broody jerk."

He didn't reply.

While they forged on, following Lukani down the stairs to make their stand, I turned to face the open temple doorway. All the bent metal and scattered bits of smoking rubble lying around must have been the remains of whatever door had been breached when Sadeera went inside. The sight sent a pang of cold dread down my throat all the way to the pit of my stomach.

"She broke through all the ancient seals," Arlan breathed in startled surprise.

"And that's difficult?" I guessed.

"They were set down by Avoran knights of the Eternal Circle," he explained, his voice still hushed and tinged with uncertainty. Obviously, the title meant nothing to me. But I could guess this didn't bode well for us.

"Let's keep moving," I muttered. "This place is too quiet for my comfort." I turned and fixed my gaze on the tall, narrow doorway before us, seeing nothing but darkness beyond.

"We have to be careful," Thatcher warned, appearing beside me with his face already looking disturbingly pale. He'd pushed himself hard already, but this was where it all had to count the most.

"Agreed. Eyes open, everyone. We don't know what kind of nightmare is waiting for us in there." I motioned for the others to follow as I started toward the busted-open doorway.

Cold sweat prickled on the back of my neck as I stepped over the rubble-strewn floor and into the darkness. Every move, every breath, seemed too loud. She would hear us. She probably already knew we were here. She might even be watching us right now.

Not thirty yards into the temple, we found our first batch of victims.

Around twenty bodies lay scattered in pools of fresh blood, twisted and broken like they'd been hit with incredible force. The pink burns on their skin reminded me of the wound left behind on Jaevid after he had taken a direct blow of Sadeera's power.

She must have done this, too.

"Zenith's Call," Arlan murmured, leaning down to inspect one of the bodies more closely.

I frowned. How could he tell that? And if he was right, then what, by all the gods, were they doing here? Violet might have known, but she was still outside.

I cut my gaze down the cavernous passage ahead. Unlike the other temples I'd ventured through, this one had a completely different feel. There were no decorative elements. No fine carvings, windows, arches, braziers, sculptures, or polished floors. Everything about it seemed crude, unrefined, like it had been crafted more as a vault than a place of worship.

And the heaviness in the atmosphere was oppressive.

This place had a presence that sat like an anchor on my chest, making every breath feel like a fight. It was a bitter cold sort of pressure, and the farther we went, the more intense it grew. I could feel something like a dull rhythm pulsing under my feet with every step. The ground vibrated, as though I were standing in front of an orchestra and feeling the hum of the instruments reverberating through the floor.

"I see something," Isandri whispered suddenly.

I saw it, too.

A faint glow of bluish light ebbed from the far end of the corridor. Immediately, my pulse took off like a wild stallion. My hands squeezed at the leather grips of my kafki blades. Every nerve in my body drew tense and taut, waiting for something—anything—to happen.

Step by step, we moved toward the light.

Twenty feet.

Ten.

Five.

I threw up a hand with a closed fist, gesturing for the others behind me to stop right at the edge of the corridor's end. Holding my breath, I slowly peeked one eye around the corner. Just one look. That's all I needed to get the lay of the room and—

The sight of the huge stone ring on the far side of the chamber turned my blood to icy slush in my veins. My heartbeat seemed to stop completely. All I could do was stare in paralyzed wonder. Never, out of all the strangeness I had witnessed over my many years, had I ever seen anything like this.

It must have been twenty feet tall, at least. Cut from the same black rock as the rest of the temple, the stone ring acted as a sort of frame for a giant golden disc fixed in the center like a mirror. The layers upon layers of runes engraved into the stone shone with an eerie blue glow, connecting to more rings that formed an identical circle on the floor directly in front of it. Another disc of gold was inlaid in the center of those runes, as well, although this one had a feature sort of like a sundial directly atop it.

It wasn't hard to imagine that the dial and golden disk it was attached to were meant to move. To spin, probably, almost like a vault lock. But what for? Did it have something to do with all those runes? From where I was standing, I could see a slot at the top that looked like it might be for a key.

Or a blade.

But you'd need a considerable amount of power to move a device that size, even if it wasn't magically warded against mortal hands. You'd need something greater. Something beyond this world.

Something divine.

I took a step into the room to get a better look, careful not to make a sound.

The minute my boot struck the stone of that chamber, I felt that energy that vibrated so heavily in the air now buzzing through my entire body. Every single one of the tiny hairs on my arms and along the back of my neck stood on end. That crushing pressure in my chest made every heartbeat painful.

But where was Sadeera?

A glance around the room didn't give me any clues. She wasn't anywhere in sight. Hmmm. A queasy sense of dread made my stomach flip as I glanced back over to the rest of my comrades.

"What is it?" Thatcher signaled, using the dragonrider hand code.

I didn't know how to even begin describing this to him, so instead, I waved the rest of them into the room behind me. I didn't want to venture one step farther into this place on my own. Staying together was safer.

One by one, they moved into the long chamber, staring in similar amazement at the structure glowing and thrumming with power at the far end. A portal straight to the divine realm.

The Gate of Proleus.

"Where is she? Something about this feels very wrong," Isandri whispered, gripping her staff in both hands as though she were ready to deal out some divine punishment at the first hint of trouble. The silky sleeves of her robes brushed against my arm as she stepped in closer to our group, her yellow-green eyes reflecting the creepy pale light coming from the portal.

"Maybe she gave up when she couldn't get the gate open?" Thatcher suggested. While that relentless, childish hope in his voice was endearing, I seriously doubted we would ever be that lucky.

I opened my mouth to remind him that no one called two legions of soldiers out into the middle of the desert just to throw their hands up and walk away. But a sudden glimmer of light sent a swell of chills over my body.

Maylea noticed it, too. The smooth, thumb-sized pendant around her neck glowed with a pulsing white light that matched the dull rhythm of the vibrations in the floor. Fates, it was true. That really wasn't just a bone trinket.

"I can hear them," Maylea whispered as she closed her hand around the pendant, the light still beaming between the cracks in her fingers as she stared up at the portal before us. "Do you hear the whispers? There's ... so many."

I didn't. But something about that faraway look on her face made me lurch toward her, seizing one of her arms and drawing her closer to my side. I cast Thatcher a worried glance, but before I could even get a word out, something behind him made every muscle in my body lock up solid.

Movement along the wall, like a shadow creeping past, faint, fast, and utterly silent.

My expression must have given it away, because Thatcher's hold on his xiphos blade tightened. He sank slowly into a defensive stance, lowering his chin and widening his footing. His features drew into a fierce, cold glare of focus and he gave me a slow, affirming nod.

I nodded back. Whether or not it was Sadeera, I wasn't sure. But we weren't alone in here.

"She is here," Arlan announced suddenly. Standing in our midst with his head bowed, eyes closed, and expression strangely calm, he finally looked up and fixed a smoldering glare upon the portal. "Prepare yourselves."

Wait—*prepare ourselves?* What did he mean by that?

I got my answer as he stepped away from where we stood, clumped together like a herd of panicked goats. With both hands outstretched, his golden eyes flickered like torches in the gloom. After a few steps, he stopped and bent down, pressing two fingers to the ground in front of him. Rippling rings of strange silver light arced out from that point like a stone dropped into the center of a pond. They spread out through the chamber, leaving behind faint, misty trails.

With my heart in my throat, I turned in a slow circle, searching for what the lighted ripples might reveal. Some sign of Sadeera, or anything that seemed out of place.

I jerked to a sudden halt. Instantly, my entire body went cold as the ring of light passed over our group and revealed the wavering outline of a ghostly figure ...

Directly behind Ronan.

The sorceress appeared like a phantom of shining silvery mist, her eyes of brilliant gold focused squarely on me. Her sharp laughter echoed through the chamber, seeming to come from everywhere at once.

I ripped my blades free of their sheaths and started toward Ronan, drawing in a breath to shout a warning.

I wasn't fast enough.

Her long, pale fingers closed around the back of Ronan's neck, and he immediately went stiff, drawing up onto his toes like he'd just been stabbed in the back. Then his eyes began to smolder that deep, molten red again.

Oh ... Oh gods, no.

NO!

Everyone stiffened, snapping into defensive stances as they spotted her, too. But it was too late.

As Ronan's expression darkened with empty, uncontrolled wrath, Sadeera's smile widened. Her laughter rattled through the chamber again, shrieking and maliciously joyful as flames began to dance from Ronan's clenched fists. His smoldering gaze fixed right on Maylea with lethal intent.

"Now then, my pet, let's finish what we started," Sadeera snickered into his ear. "Burn the soul from her and take what is rightfully ours!"

PART ELEVEN

MURDOC

⸙ 37 ⸙

CHAPTER THIRTY-SEVEN

Things were ... going. Not well, mind you, but decently enough considering the impossible odds we had been set up against.

Positioned in the center of the raised courtyard, directly outside the yawning open doorway that led into the temple, we had set ourselves up in an arc shape to hold our enemies at bay. First, they only came up the tall, sloping staircase that led from the lower desert up into the courtyard itself. The staircase was roughly fifty or sixty feet tall, without any railings, and maybe thirty feet wide. It formed something of a funnel for all the lines of soldiers that managed to reach the top to engage with us.

But they must have already factored this into their battle plans, because it didn't take long for them to start bringing out siege ladders with hooks affixed to the ends. We knocked down as many as we could, but with ten and twenty being put up at a time, I knew it wouldn't be long before we were completely overrun here.

I moved with a lethal speed and precision I hadn't felt in over a decade. It was one thing to train fledglings and avians at the academy. It was another to step onto the field of battle carrying the blessing and power of the war god himself.

Every slice of my sword was effortless. Its long, perfectly balanced blade glowed like it had just been pulled from the forge, cutting through armor like wet paper. The night wind hummed a deadly melody with every swing. Men screamed. They fell before me like wheat to the threshing floor.

Ripping through another whirling strike, I sank back onto my heels and glanced around for the rest of my comrades. So far, they seemed to be holding out the best anyone could expect. We had been at this for only a few minutes, and already my tunic was soaked through with sweat and I'd already flung off that ridiculously heavy Nar'Haleenan helmet.

To my right, Roxus had taken on his giant bear-form again and rose up on his hind legs, bellowing in fury. His massive paws crushed through shields and his jaws closed around enemy soldiers, wrenching and ripping them apart one by one. I'd never seen an Ursinaar in battle before, but he certainly lived up to all the fearsome tales I'd heard.

Garnett and Violet had joined forces on his other side, whirling through joint-combat tactics and keeping their movements perfectly attuned. Garnett was the brawn, hacking away with a double-headed axe in each hand. Violet was the speed and had a range of incredible flexibility and battle-sense any Ulfrangar would have admired. It was almost as though she could see things before they happened, reacting and positioning herself perfectly for each flawless kill. She'd taken a long, braided leather whip from her belt and used it to trip up enemies that approached, making them all the easier for Garnett to deal with.

On my other side, Noa held his own a lot better than I'd expected he might. I couldn't quite make out where his fighting style had come from, but he brandished a halberd swiped off a fallen soldier with impressive skill. His formerly injured leg must have been feeling the benefits of all those Gray elven healing remedies, because it didn't slow him down in the slightest.

Jaevid fought as well as every story I'd ever heard. That Gray elven blood gave him a speed only someone like Violet might rival, and his human blood matched that with impressive strength. He spun his scimitar over his hand, dipping and feinting through strikes and parries I recognized from my own training. Ulfrangar fighting tactics that Jace had likely taught him years ago. He executed them decently, and didn't hesitate to land a killing blow. I guess his capacity for mercy and sympathy with these folk had officially run out. Good. We had no time for either.

Lukani, of course, was no less impressive than he'd ever been. In fact, he seemed to have greatly improved in his fighting and magic-using ability since the last time I saw him. He blurred between shapes, shifting first into that dragon and then shrinking to a smaller but no less lethal form of a shrike. His mirror-like scales rippled like a mirage as he tore through the encroaching enemy lines, bony jaws punching straight through their armor and zooming around faster than their archers could take aim.

We were holding our own. No one had taken more than a minor cut here or there. It was all going according to plan.

But the cold, unrelenting truth still hung like a suspended dagger, waiting to fall in my mind: we couldn't last forever, and we were vastly outnumbered. More soldiers were storming the stairs and ladders by the second. For every one we cut down, three more took his place. Meanwhile, enemy catapults fired over and over, hurling boulders and massive iron payloads at us. They smashed against the outer walls of the temple and left the courtyard around us pocked with craters. It took everything I had to keep a watch on the sky as well as the soldiers around me. It split my focus—a dangerous gamble for any warrior.

"INCOMING!" I shouted as another massive hunk of stone came sailing in, hitting the ground less than ten yards behind me.

BOOOM!

The impact threw me and all the Nar'Haleenan soldiers I'd been dueling off balance. Dust and shards of stone choked the air. Curse it—how long could we possibly keep up the fight like this?

Overhead, hope soared with the wings of a mighty blue dragon as Mavrik zoomed past, bathing the staircase and edge of the courtyard in another plume of fire. Men screamed. Some of them bailed over the edge of the stairs, falling around fifty feet to perish on the ground below.

It was a welcome break, but I knew it wouldn't last. With nothing but bodies and armor to burn, the venom would use up all of its own fuel and smolder down. Then the soldiers would return, marching over the corpses of their fallen comrades, and attack again.

"Form up! Form up!" I shouted over the chaos, giving the order for everyone to close ranks so we could evaluate our status. Anyone injured would be rotated to the back, closer to the temple doorway. "Check in!"

"Still alive," Garnett spat, wiping blood from her freshly split lip on her sleeve. "So's Roxus!"

Somewhere nearby, a bear's answering roar sounded off. Heh.

"I'm fine," Violet called next.

Noa stepped in closer to my side, closing ranks. He was beginning to favor that leg again, although apparently doing everything in his power to hide it. "Fine," he growled through clenched teeth, as though he could somehow sense my concern.

When the esteemed commander didn't sound off, I stole a glance in his direction and shouted, "Jaevid?"

"I'm still up," he grunted, appearing from the curling plumes of dust with fresh cuts sliced across his forehead and on his cheek. Neither looked like a wound from a blade, though. More like he'd taken hits from some of the debris flying around after the impact of the catapult fire.

"Where's Lukani?" Garnett called. "I don't see him!"

"There!" Noa pointed the end of his halberd to a blur like a streak of silver lightning that arced through the sky.

Lukani landed, shifting back to his more human-looking form as soon as his feet touched the ground before us. "Incoming!" he gasped as he came scrambling toward me. His chest heaved with manic, ragged breaths and his face and hair were drenched with sweat. Ash and blood were smeared over nearly every inch of him, and his eyes were wide and petrified as he tried to wheeze out words again. "Th-There's ... a line of war beasts ... a-and catapults coming ... th-this way! Too many for me to stop!"

Curse it. They knew we were here, of course. And now they were coming in to make their final assault. We would be cornered. Out manned. Faced with weapons of war we stood no chance of overpowering.

Time to change tactics.

"Commander, I think it's past time you got in the saddle," I muttered. "We need our aerial forces to start backing us up in a big way, because we're going to get overwhelmed soon."

He gave me a hard look. "And you?"

I shook my head. "Blite's the only one trained to fly tandem with Fornax and guide him, and they need my power here on the ground."

His smoldering, dissatisfied glare said it all. He didn't like the idea of leaving me behind.

Fine. He didn't have to like it. But he knew I was right.

"Once the catapult fire intensifies, we fall back to the doorway," I snarled loudly enough they would all hear it. "We don't have to outlast them! We don't even have to win this fight! We just have to hold on long enough for the others to finish the job inside!"

No one argued.

"I'll work on thinning out the incoming projectiles," Jaevid promised before he ran off, blasting shrill whistles through his fingers. With a flourish of his long, royal blue cloak, his tall frame vanished into the rolling clouds of dust and smoke. It didn't take even a minute for the low *whoom—whoom—whoom* of dragon wing beats to thunder past, accompanied by the bellowing roar that rattled the splintered stone beneath my feet.

A gust of wind, likely from Mavrik's takeoff, cleared the floating clouds of dust from the courtyard, and I got my first good look at what Lukani had been talking about when he warned of an encroaching force. My mouth fell open. All the feeling seemed to drain away from my hands as I stared at the lines of war machines grinding their way toward us.

Holy. Gods.

These weren't the usual catapults and trebuchets the enemy had been using so far. No, these were ... something else. They were smaller, more mobile, and accompanied by a mounted cavalry that protected them from all sides. There must have been more than twenty in all, coming in fast.

"They fire orbs of burning tar," Violet hissed, her expression drawn tense in a look of complete horror. "They're going to try to force us out of the courtyard."

"Fighting fire with fire," I realized aloud. Curse it. I should have known this was a possibility. They hadn't spent centuries warring with all their neighboring kingdoms and not picked up a few tricks.

"We need to pull back. Even if they don't hit us, the fumes will be toxic," she warned. "We will suffocate."

I knew that probably better than she realized. The Ulfrangar used the same tactics sometimes, albeit on a much smaller scale. But a full retreat? Risk bringing this fight in closer to Reigh and the others, who undoubtedly already had their hands full? We couldn't risk that. We had a job to do. We had to see it through.

The others were counting on us.

But, Gods and Fates, we needed some reinforcements—*now.* Having Jaevid back in the saddle would help. He could coordinate aerial efforts with Jenna and the *Dawn Chaser*. But would it be enough?

I didn't know.

And there wasn't time to work it out.

"I MUST GO HELP," LUKANI GROWLED, HIS HANDS BALLED INTO FISTS AS HE PROWLED forward. "If the soldiers are able to fire those tar bombs, it will impair the dragons, as well. Their fire will only make it worse. The war machines must be disabled before they can begin firing."

Really? He thought he could do all that at once? By himself?

I started to protest, but Violet beat me to it.

"You're doing it again!" She lunged forward and seized him by the elbow. Dragging him to a halt, her expression was frantic as she shouted over the ambient roar of battle. "If you use too much magic, you won't be a help to anyone! And we might not be able to get to you before—"

His smile was strangely distant as he put a hand over hers and slowly pulled away. "I will be careful. I promise."

"You're never careful! You're reckless! You always push things too far!" she yelled.

But Lukani wasn't listening. Striding away with his shoulders back and head held high, the outline of his leanly muscled frame had already begun warping and changing. He crouched, legs coiling beneath him, and lept skyward. His form shifted mid-jump, like a butterfly bursting from a cocoon. He took on a shape I had never seen him use before.

Gods and Fates, was that ... a gigantic crab?

It certainly looked like it. I had never even heard of a creature like that before. Crawling on long, spindly legs, he loomed over the battlefield like a colossus, wringing meaty armored claws and beginning to crunch his way through the enemy lines. Whoa ...

That kid really was full of tricks today.

"INCOMING!" Noa shouted suddenly, drawing my focus ahead again to where the enemy soldiers were beginning to throw down their shields and use them as a makeshift walkway to get past the swamp of burning dragon venom.

CRACK—BOOM! CRACK— BOOM!

Two of those lighter catapults fired, hurling orbs of burning tar through the air. The shots sailed over our heads and smashed into the ground behind us, cutting off our only exit point into the temple. Black smoke immediately boiled into the air. My eyes teared up. My lungs burned and spasmed as the toxic fumes engulfed us.

Oh gods ... we ... we weren't going to make it.

"Murdoc!" Garnett's panicked cry broke my focus. It was only for an instant—just long enough to see her flailing and trying to get her cloak off. That and the back of her armor had been hit with a splatter of the tar. She was on fire.

She needed my help.

White-hot pain surged through me so suddenly, everything went white. I gasped, staggering sideways as my ears began to ring. The world swerved back into focus, blurry and dim. Something was hurting. Something in my chest.

I blinked down to see the end of a sword rammed all the way to the hilt through my abdomen, right below my ribs. The soldier on the other side of that blade stared at me through the visor-slit in his helmet, eyes wide and almost as shocked as I was that he had actually landed that blow.

Oh no ...

The warm, coppery thickness of blood filled my mouth as my thoughts began to race and spiral. Was I dying? Was this really the end? I-I didn't want to die. Not like this. Not so far away from my family and ... Phoebe.

Her name hit my brain like a lightning strike. My spine curled. My mouth opened in a primal shout as something poured into my veins like molten metal into a mold. My fingers stretched. My arms and legs flexed. A voice like the drums of war boomed in my head, setting my pulse ablaze with a fury I didn't understand.

"You will carry my strength ... as your own."

Strength. I felt it like the current of a raging river rushing through me. My vision snapped into focus. The pain faded. Overhead, something cracked across the sky with a blinding flash. Lightning?

BOOOM! CRACK! CRACK! CRACK!

Thunder shook the earth and the very foundations of my soul. Lightning popped off the ground around me. I felt each strike like an extension of myself, like a thread pulled through the fabric of my own consciousness.

Something I could manipulate.

The soldier before me released his blade and stumbled back as all the Nar'Haleenan troops around me froze, their expressions a panicked mixture of awe and terror.

Reaching down, I grasped the hilt of the blade still buried in my gut and ripped it free, tossing it aside. It clattered across the stone. I could see glimpses of my reflection in the polished dark armor and shields that surrounded me now on every side. My eyes shone with radiant yellow light. Even the veins under my skin gave off a dull glow along my neck, brow, and hands. My hair and cloak seemed to float in the air around me as though they were weightless.

In that moment, I wasn't Murdoc. I wasn't Rylen Porter. I was the embodiment of a god's will.

I was Proleus, God of War.

In one fluid motion, I widened my stance and raised my sword skyward. An arcing bolt of lightning raced downward, slicing through the air with a deafening *CRAAACK* and hitting it with another white-hot flash of power. My body burned, caught in the crossfire of the blazing shockwave that spread out around me like a ring of sizzling, popping electricity.

The first five lines of enemy soldiers instantly exploded into plumes of black dust, incinerated on the spot. They didn't even have time to scream. The following ranks were blown backward, tossed like ragdolls, and left to scream and convulse as electrical current snapped off their metal armor.

Again. I had to do it again. Over and over—as many times as I could stand.

Until this was over.

"Fall back!" I heard Roxus shouting somewhere in the chaos. He had Garnett dangling from his now human arms as he ran past, but he moved so fast I couldn't tell if she was alive or not.

CRACK—BOOOM!

Another light catapult fired one of those tar bombs. It smashed into the ground before me, exploding in a wall of molten tar like a burning black wave. There wasn't time to run or try dodging out of the way. I had no idea if my power would be enough to allow me to survive a hit like this, as well.

Out of nowhere, the ground before me erupted. A massive wall of rock and stone jutted upward and arced over me, maybe fifteen feet tall. What the—?

I didn't question it.

Running forward, I ducked against it for cover as the infernal burning wave sloshed over. The acrid reek of the toxic smoke engulfed me, and I held my breath. Out, I had to get out of here. But everywhere I looked, the ground was a swamp of burning tar.

Curse it—what now?

Thud—thud—thud—thud!

The ground flinched, almost as though something massive was running nearby. No, not something. *Someone*.

"Hang on!" a deep voice bellowed as a hulking, masculine figure lumbered through the burning mulch straight toward me. With an enormous, bronze great axe resting over one of his huge shoulders, a creature I had no name for thundered to a halt before me. His bluish-toned body looked like it was made from solid stone. Some kind of golem? Where the heck had it even come from?

Before I could decide if I should try to run or fight back, he reached out his other hand and seized me like someone picking a carrot.

I gaped at him, trying to find words somewhere in the scrambled shock that swirled in my brain. I wasn't successful, and he tossed me over his shoulder like a caught lamb and started lumbering off across the battlefield again.

That's when I saw the others.

There must have been around a dozen strange folk striding through the courtyard, seeming to come from nowhere and envoking all manner of magical strangeness. One fellow's entire body ignited like a walking torch, and he sent out blasts of fire from his hands upon the encroaching Nar'Haleenan soldiers. Another did something similar, only with ice. His whole body gleamed and bristled with pale blue crystals, wearing ice like an armor around himself.

They all had something in common, though. Something I hadn't noticed the first time I saw that monstrous, rock-skinned man lumbering at me.

Tails.

Gods and Fates, they were Rajinna!

I didn't know who they were, where they'd come from, or why they were fighting alongside us now—but it didn't matter. They were successfully pressing back the enemy forces and beginning to douse the pools of burning tar with their magic.

And that was just the sort of help we needed.

"I can fight!" I shouted down to the huge Rajinna still carrying me like a sack of flour.

He stopped, not protesting as I squirmed out of his grasp and hit the ground with my sword still in my hand. Standing before me like a tower of living stone, I had to tilt my head all the way back to see his face. Whoa.

"Where is my son?" his deep voice boomed.

Son? What was he talking abou—ohhh. Okay. That made sense. Sort of.

I pointed at the giant crab monster still stomping through the lines of infantry at the base of the stairwell like a kid jumping through piles of dead leaves.

He looked up, rocky brow raising in surprise. Yeah. Today was one of those days for both of us, I guess.

"We've got to hold out as long as possible," I shouted over the noise as the dragonriders made another low, zooming pass nearby. "See if he needs some backup!"

He nodded in agreement and hefted that huge axe as he began lumbering off to join Lukani in the fight.

Right. Back to work. And the odds now skewed more in our favor, I dared to hope that we might actually make it. Reigh and the others could handle Sadeera. They had her outnumbered six-to-one.

What could possibly go wrong?

PART TWELVE

MAYLEA

38

CHAPTER THIRTY-EIGHT

"GET BACK!" Uncle Reigh yelled, grabbing for the back of my tunic and dragging me out of the way as a column of white-hot fire shot past me.

The heat singed my cheek, filling my nose with the putrid scent of burning hair. I winced, throwing up a hand to try and shield my eyes as I squinted through the sudden rush of fire.

Was that ... Ronan?

Oh gods! No!

Our reunion hadn't been anything at all like I had hoped. I had wanted to run to him, to hug him and apologize for not coming to rescue him sooner. I'd wanted to let him know everything was going to be okay. We were here now, and we would make sure he got back home safely.

But that wasn't how things had gone.

Ronan wasn't himself. I had been able to see that from the beginning. He stood off on his own, watching everyone else with an uncomfortable frown almost like he was looking for the first opportunity to run. He seemed so scared and unsure. He didn't even try to come close or talk to me, and I didn't know how to approach him. All the things I'd wanted to say seemed to tangle up in my throat.

Now, I realized I should have tried harder. I should have gone to him anyway. I should have made sure he was okay.

Because it was far too late now.

Ronan lunged for us like a rabid animal, hurling fire spells while his eyes burned like two rings of red-hot metal. His vengeful scowl stayed fixed on me, as though I had suddenly become his primary target. No—not me. The pendant around my neck was what Sadeera really wanted, wasn't it? And now she had control over his mind again. I could see it like an emptiness in his expression. The Ronan I knew, my best friend for so many years, wasn't in there anymore. Or at least, he wasn't the one in control of his movements. It was that woman, that wicked sorceress making him do terrible things again.

She was using him as an instrument for her own gain.

Fates, I had to find some way to help him break free.

"SPREAD OUT!" Uncle Reigh shouted again, motioning for us all to fan out to put some distance between ourselves and our attacker.

But there was only so far we could go. The chamber wasn't huge. This would be a close-quarters fight.

I'd have to be extra careful.

As explosions of magical power began to shake and shudder the chamber around me, I kept my focus on Ronan. I drew back an arrow, taking aim, but I-I ... I didn't want to hurt him. Gods, what if I killed him?

Tears blurred my vision as I let my first arrow fly, screaming at the top of my lungs. "Stop this! Ronan, you have to stop!"

My arrow zipped through the air, lodging into the stone wall behind him, mere inches from his ear.

He didn't even flinch and stormed toward me with fire wreathing his shoulders and rippling down his arms. With a flourish of his hands, he summoned forth a long, coiled whip made of pure, rippling flame. He looped it around his forearm, gathering it in as though in preparation.

I staggered back, already reaching for another arrow. "Ronan, please! You have to remember! I'm not your enemy! We're friends," I begged. "We're *best* friends!"

He didn't react, his expression remaining furiously detached as he prowled toward me.

TWANG!

I fired another shot, this one so close it nicked his cheek and left a line of fresh blood right along his cheekbone.

Ronan didn't so much as blink.

I clenched my teeth, already nocking another arrow and drawing the string to my cheek. Tears ran in cool streams down my face as I glared at him down the barbed point of my arrow's tip. I didn't want to kill him. Gods, I didn't even want to hurt him! But ... what if he didn't give me a choice?

The pendant around my neck thrummed with a pulsing, buzzing heat I could feel like a heartbeat. A gentle reminder. I couldn't give up. Not yet.

Narrowing my eyes, I called forth Paligno's power, sending it down the length of the arrow's wooden staff. It trembled and shook in my grasp, the metal point glowing brilliant green. I fired the next arrow and hit the ground right in front of him as he took a step. Just like before, in Salnis, massive thorned vines burst from the arrow. They grew and snaked across the floor, wrapping around his legs and waist. He snarled and fought, grabbing a fistful and trying to tear them away. But my vines grew fast, becoming as thick around as my forearm and squeezing at him like green, thorny pythons.

This was my chance.

I backed away, putting a bit more distance between us as I ducked around a pillar and readied another arrow. The room shuddered and shook all around me, flashes of spells firing off in every direction as Uncle Reigh and the others fought. Hunks of the stone ceiling fell with a smash. Sadeera crowed with wicked laughter. It must have taken all of them to hold her off.

CRACK!

A wave of fire hit the pillar and I tucked myself tight against it, braced against the surge of heat. Crap, he must have already gotten free of the vines. I'd have to try something else.

Shutting my eyes tightly, I tried to think.

A flash of color darted past as soon as I opened my eyes. What the—? Was that a bird? What was it doing down here in the middle of this chaos?

The glimmer of those brilliantly colored feathers struck a chord in my mind as it hovered in front of me for a second and then began flying in a wide pass around the room, straight for Ronan.

Wait a second, I knew that bird!

My heartbeat skipped, lips parting as I leaned out from behind the pillar long enough to glimpse the towering inferno that was Ronan. He was already coiling that whip again, coming for me with purpose in every step. I only had seconds.

I had done this once before, hadn't I? I could do it again.

Because this wasn't about Ronan. It wasn't about me. It was about the gate. That's what we'd come to do—first and foremost. It had to be destroyed.

When the bird flitted past Ronan, zipping right behind him, I sprang from my hiding place and took aim. My bowstring cracked, releasing an arrow that sailed across the room, its metal point glowing like a green shooting star. It hit the bird dead-on.

VOOOM!

A blinding flash of colorful light bloomed through the entire chamber with all the radiance of the first light of dawn, followed by a screeching roar. The monster unfurled behind Ronan with a long, serpentine body covered in vibrant red and purple scales. With its dragon-like head frilled with yellow, green, and blue fins, it unfolded feathered wings and immediately lunged for him. The creature coiled around him, ensnaring Ronan in its serpentine body with a defiant hiss.

There. That ought to keep him occupied for a few minutes.

With another arrow already in my hand, I turned my focus to the target that mattered. The portal still thrummed with energy that made my chest feel heavy and my skin shiver. But not for much longer.

I narrowed my eyes, murmuring a frantic prayer to Paligno as I drew my bowstring to my cheek. I didn't know if this would work. Would my power be enough to even make a dent in that thing? I was wearing the final piece that would even make it work at all. So maybe, right?

I had no idea.

But I had to try.

Drawing in a steadying breath, I took aim straight for the center of it and poured every ounce of divine power I could into the tip of my arrow. It glowed brighter and brighter, just as the pendant around my neck seemed to grow hotter and hotter.

Then I shut my eyes and let the arrow fly.

KAAA—VOOOOOM!

The entire room rippled like a mirage, first bowing in from the point where my arrow hit right at the center of that big golden disc. Then, with a rocking explosion, the world around us seemed to spring back outward, blowing everything apart in its path. Rubble flew. Pillars cracked and crumbled. My friends cried out in alarm. Sadeera screamed with rage.

I flew backward, tossed end over end until I hit the back wall of the chamber. My head swam and bright spots danced in my vision as I shakily got up on my elbows. I couldn't see them. Uncle Reigh, Isandri, Thatcher, Arlan ... where were they? Oh no—oh gods, I hadn't hurt them, had I?

My body shook, throbbing with pain as I tried to gather my legs back under me. I had to get up. I had to find them.

There!

"YOU!" Sadeera's crazed scream shattered the eerie silence that still hung over the chamber as the dust settled.

I squinted up, barely able to make out the silhouette of her standing right before the portal's haunting bluish light. She had someone by the neck, holding them up off their feet. With her angelic wings spread wide, her other hand drew back with a blade gripped tightly in her fist.

The Blade of Souls.

My mouth went dry. My heart stopped, frozen in horror. G-Gods—it was *Uncle Reigh!*

He kicked and fought, clawing at her arm as she held him up with a triumphant sneer. But it was as though all his dark power melted away in her aura, dissolving like fog at sunrise.

"You lot thought you could outsmart me. You thought you could stand in my way. You are nothing! You've always been nothing! And now, you will all perish just like the insects you are!"

She struck as fast as a viper.

But he was faster.

Arlan burst from the curling clouds of settling dust, springing for her like a tiger. He knocked Reigh from her grasp and seized her arms, trying to wrestle the blade away from her. Sadeera screeched in Avoran. Arlan's eyes blazed with golden light, face twisted into a vengeful snarl of pure hatred. He bared his teeth, finally yelling back in a language I understood as he sent a blast of power through his hands like an electric shock.

"THEIR LIVES ARE NOT YOURS TO TAKE!"

Her face twitching with pain, Sadeera recoiled. With one beat of her wings, she flung Arlan to the ground at her feet. He hit the ground hard, head cracking off the stone.

Before he could get up or even try moving, she planted a foot on his stomach, pinning him down, and drove that cursed blade deep into his chest. Arlan's body tensed, spine curling and mouth gaping wide for an instant. His eyes went wide. Then ... that radiant light in his eyes began to dim. His face went completely slack.

He lay motionless.

Sadeera stepped off him with another screeching, maniacal laugh. She licked his blood from her blade and then slowly turned to face the rest of the chamber, her gaze now focusing squarely on me.

I couldn't move. I couldn't scream or even make a sound. Paralyzed with shock, I lay on my side where I'd still been fighting to get on my feet again. No matter how hard I tried, I couldn't look away from the motionless body of the man who now lay lifeless at her feet.

Arlan the Kinslayer ... was dead.

❧ 39 ❧

CHAPTER THIRTY-NINE

Uncle Reigh made a sound—something between a furious yell and a desperate scream. The temperature in the chamber plummeted, crystals of frost fanning out across the floor and climbing the walls in a matter of seconds. My whole body shuddered, feeling the sudden swell of pressure and power that thrummed outward, not from the portal, but from where Uncle Reigh stood.

All around the room, the shadows seemed to come alive, moving and spreading like tongues of dark fire. Pairs of white, ghostly eyes flickered, fading in and out of view like bog fires in the dark. Squeals and screams echoed, like the wails of spirits.

They converged on Sadeera at once like a swelling dark tide. Uncle Reigh rushed in, too, the curved points of his kafki blades leaving ribbons of black smoke curling and twisting the air with every spin and strike. Writhing tentacles of pure darkness erupted from the ground around Sadeera, wrapping around her wings and trying to drag her to her knees. Thatcher moved in from the other side, emerging from the shadows with his xiphos sword in one hand and a shield of pure golden power in the other. Isandri materialized right behind him, brandishing her staff with its crystalline end shining like a caught star.

I started to get up again, to reach for my bow. They needed my help. We had to do this together or—

All of a sudden, I couldn't breathe.

Pain burst through my body as something—no, *someone*—sprang on top of me and pinned me to the floor with their hands squeezing my throat. I kicked and fought, gasping for air as my vision blurred in and out of focus.

Then I saw him.

Ronan bore down, throttling me with all his strength. With his expression drawn into a crazed grimace, his eyes still burned like smoldering coals as he crushed my throat. I wheezed and struggled, grabbing his forearms and trying to pry him off. Just a little, then I could get a breath.

"P-Please," I managed to rasp out hoarsely.

Ronan's brow and mouth twitched. Tears welled in his eyes and began rolling down his cheeks, hissing and turning to steam as they touched his skin. It was as though he were warring with himself, fighting and trying to break Sadeera's hold over his mind.

The Ronan I knew, the one I had grown up with, was still in there. He was still fighting. I had to believe that.

I had to set him free.

It took every shred of strength I had left to thrust my hands out and grasp the sides of his face. As my vision began to tunnel, the last of my consciousness fading to darkness, I stretched all my focus in deep to the farthest reaches of my heart. To that place where Paligno had tucked away that kernel of his light.

The place in my soul where his power flowed like a spring river, cool, clear, and cleansing.

I poured every drop of that power into Ronan, letting it run freely out through my fingers and into the sides of his head. My bones ached as though they were bending from the inside. My muscles quivered, and I could feel every beat of my heart like a smashing of cymbals in my ears. The pendant around my neck, the Spark of Life, burned like someone had pressed a branding iron to my chest.

But I didn't stop. Gods, I just hoped it was enough.

"Let ... him ... go!" I prayed through gritted teeth. I barely caught a glimpse of my own palms shining with brilliant green light, and Ronan's features suddenly seizing in shock.

He kicked backward off me suddenly, screaming and gripping his head as he pitched wildly. Everything spun in a dizzying haze as I sucked in a deep, frantic gulp of air. As my vision cleared, I squinted groggily to where Ronan crouched on his knees, yelling and grabbing fistfuls of his hair.

With a final, hysterical shout he threw his head back as his body arched. Green light flowed under his skin like shimmering streams, spreading down his neck, over his arms, and blasting outward from his eyes and mouth.

I drew back, snatching up my bow and shakily fitting an arrow to the string. What was happening? Gods and Fates, what had I done to him?

The light blazing from within Ronan's body faded. His eyes rolled back and he slumped sideways onto the floor in a heap.

Oh gods!

"Ronan!" I cried out. Dropping my arrow, I flung my bow over my back and scrambled toward him on my hands and knees.

He didn't resist or move as I grabbed him by the shoulders. His face was slack and his eyes were closed when I rolled him over onto his back. Oh ... oh no. Had I killed him? My hands shook as I tried to check for a pulse—for anything that might tell me he was alive. I-I couldn't. My hands wouldn't stay steady. Tears filled my eyes and blurred everything.

"Ronan, please," I begged as I gathered his upper body into my arms and hugged him tight. I couldn't hold it back then. The sobs broke free, cracking through every bit of strength I'd been clinging to since I first set foot on that ship, determined to find him. "I-I should have talked to you. I should have told you why I came here. I should have made sure you were okay. I've wanted to find you for so long. I've wanted to know why you left. I'm so sorry, Ronan. P-Please, you have to wake up. You have to because ... I'm going to save you."

"You already did," a hoarse voice answered.

I gasped as his warm, strong arms closed around me, hugging me back with startling strength. He was alive?

Oh, Fates, he was alive!

Pulling back, I found exactly what I'd been hoping for shining in his deep, cobalt blue eyes as he smiled back at me: the Ronan I'd known all my life. My best friend. My favorite, and only, first cousin. The person I had always been able to trust to keep all my secrets since we were children.

He was back.

And together, I knew there was no enemy we couldn't overcome.

Not even Sadeera.

ANOTHER EXPLOSION OF RAW, DIVINE POWER SHOOK THE CHAMBER. RONAN THREW AN arm up to shield both our faces, then leveled a harrowing glare in Sadeera's direction. His dark brows knitted together and his nose wrinkled in a disgusted, vengeful scowl. There was no mistaking the wrath that burned in his eyes as he slowly got to his feet, hauling me up with him, but keeping himself positioned between the fight and me.

"Their power won't be enough to hold her for long," he warned in a low, ominous growl. "She's absorbed the essences of two gods."

I could tell that much. For every desperate strike and parry my friends made, Sadeera evaded so easily it was as though she were only toying with them. She moved like a radiant blur, so fast I couldn't keep track. It took all three of them just to keep her distracted enough that she didn't land any attacks of her own. They were barely holding on, and one misstep, one hit with that cursed weapon, would seal another person's fate. We had to stop this. We had to get rid of her.

But how?

My bird-turned monster was already gone. I guess the blast had been enough to break that spell, and I didn't even see the bird anywhere. Was there anything more I could try?

Reaching down for the arrow I'd dropped, I stared at the point and back at the shimmering golden disc at the center of the portal. I hadn't been able to destroy it. Not on my own. But it had caused a decent explosion. If we all attacked her together, combining our divine power, maybe that would tip the scale.

I had to try. I was all out of ideas, and nearly out of arrows. Gods only knew how long our friends outside could hold off the invasion of enemy soldiers.

"You have to get closer," I declared, flicking a determined glare at Ronan with that arrow still gripped firmly in my fist. "Tell the others to get ready! We hit all at once!"

Ronan's expression flashed between confusion and uncertainty. But when I slid my arrow into place, fitted against my bowstring, his jaw went solid. He nodded once, turned on a heel, and ran into the fight.

I darted for the shadows, ducking and leaping over debris until I found a good vantage point. Now I just had to wait. To look for the opening. The perfect shot.

That tiny spark of power kindled deep in my chest, blazing brighter and brighter with every steady heartbeat. My senses sharpened. My hands became steady. Before me, my friends raged against Sadeera like the clash of angels. Dark fog rolled off Uncle Reigh's form as he dueled, his curved blades spinning and whirling impossibly fast.

Isandri moved like a living mirage, using that ability to go invisible to encircle and strike at Sadeera with her staff. White beams of pure sterling light sizzled from the end of her staff, slamming against Sadeera's aura and sometimes even bouncing right back at her. Isa yowled and hissed, slipping into her feline form and springing like a tigress on the hunt.

It was no use, though. She managed to sink her fangs into Sadeera's arm, but the sorceress immediately flung her aside. She raised a hand, her face twisted in rage as she prepared to take a swipe at Isa with that wicked blade.

Thatcher wasn't having that, though. Darting in from behind, he drove the point of his xiphos sword through Sadeera's back. Golden blood like shining ichor sprayed through the air, but Sadeera didn't so much as whimper. Ripping herself free of his weapon, she whirled on him with a blast of power that sent him flying. He hit the nearest wall with a thud, but didn't fall. With a stagger, he managed to keep on his feet with his sword raised, the end still dripping with her strange blood.

CRACK!

Sadeera was on him in an instant, stabbing down with that cursed blade. It hit the wall with a shower of sparks mere inches from his head. As she drew back for a second swing, Thatcher's whole demeanor changed. The usually green colored rings of his eyes blazed to life with radiant gold light. Currents of power arced and curled off his tall, broad-shouldered frame like tongues of white fire. He bared his teeth, powerful shoulders hunching as wings of pure light unfurled from his back, sending out a flash like the glare of the sun.

My stomach dropped to the soles of my boots like a stone to the depths of a riverbed. Oh no. I had seen this happen once before in Salnis. Thatcher was using too much power. He was pushing himself to the brink. He was ... becoming Ishaleon.

"Know your place, pretender," his voice boomed, accompanied with a chorus of whispers as he surged for Sadeera again.

I ducked back behind the half-shattered pillar beside me just before their impact sent out another blast of radiant power through the room. Even with my eyes shut tight, I still felt the stinging burn of it. Fates, what was happening out there? How was I ever going to get a good shot in if I couldn't even see?

Something landed on my shoulder. The soft twitter of a bird filled my ear. I didn't need to be able to see to know what it was.

Paligno was still sending me signs. He was with me, right here, in this storm. He believed in me.

I just had to believe in myself.

"Show me the way," I murmured with one final, steadying breath.

The little pendant around my neck seemed to pulse in answer. I stared down at it, and something tugged at the back of my mind. This wasn't just a necklace or talisman. It was a tool. It was a piece of Paligno's own essence.

Oh gods, I knew what I had to do.

It only took a few seconds—long enough for me to snatch it from around my neck. Its shape was something like an elongated oval with a point on one end, and it was just the right size. Almost as though it had been meant for just this.

I pried the tip off my arrow and replaced it with the pendant, my hands shaking with anxiety as I used its own resin cord to tie it there as securely as possible. It didn't have to be perfect; it just had to work once.

One final shot to finally end this.

Stepping out from my hiding spot, I drew my bowstring to my cheek. I pulled from that power again, and the force of Paligno's divine presence that blazed through my body like holy fire. Everything seemed to go quiet, as though time itself had frozen in that moment.

The newly crafted point of my arrow shone like a shard of green starlight, and just past it ... I saw what I needed.

My opening.

Uncle Reigh's tentacles of darkness had ensnared her by one wing and arm. Ronan's fiery whip had her other wing pinned, as well. Thatcher bore in with his sword drawn back, springing through the air to land another swing. Isandri had her feline jaws clamped around one of her legs.

They all looked up at me at once.

And I let the string slip from my fingers.

That fraction of a second seemed to stretch on for an eternity as the crack of my bowstring barked in the air with an echoing report. Streams of clean green light followed it like a shooting star as it flew, straight and true.

It hit Sadeera right in the heart and pinned her against the golden disc of the portal behind her.

She lurched as my arrow burrowed in deep, blinking a few times as though in shock. Then her expression went strangely blank. Her eyes widened.

Her chest around my arrow's shaft began to splinter and crack, almost like a porcelain doll. Vibrant green light exploded from those fractures as veins of it began to glow under her skin, spreading through every part. Across her chest. Down her arms. Up her neck. Even over her face.

Sadeera let out a howling, panicked scream as she began to convulse. Her wings pitched wildly as she struggled against the others, who still held her firmly in place. Reigh was the first to reach out, gripping the arrow shaft and sending a bolt of his own dark power through it. Thatcher did the same, his golden wings spread like a vengeful angel around them. Then Ronan slapped his hand over theirs. Isandri appeared in the blink of an eye, so fast I hadn't even seen her shift forms. She put her hands on top of theirs.

VOOOOOM!

The incredible rush of pure divine power that overtook the chamber sent me rocking back onto my heels so suddenly, I didn't even have time to brace myself. I fell onto my rear, dropping my bow and covering my face and eyes with my hands as I curled into a ball. My ears rang. My body burned. But all I could do was wait—wait and hope I wasn't incinerated alive.

Something dark suddenly closed around me, wrapping me in a cool release and the sharp smell of evergreen, rich soil, and old decaying leaves. That deep, earthy smell filled my lungs like a healing balm, and I instinctively wriggled closer to it, hiding my face against something soft and warm. It almost made me forget about the sounds exploding, cracking, and booming through the air around me. Something like the creaking bending of wood, the splinter of stone, and a frenzy of sizzling pops.

Gods and Fates, what was happening out there?

When I tried to look, I realized who was crouching right before me, his arms wrapped protectively around me like my father's own embrace. But it wasn't Dah. It was ...

My pulse skipped as I stared up into the shadows of a cloak's heavy, oversized hood. Two green eyes sparkled like emeralds as they stared back down at me, set into the impossibly handsome face of a man with long, angular features and a thin, smiling mouth. His white hair hung like bolts of clean satin, interwoven with feathers, clay beads, raw gems, and leaves. His flawless skin was a deep, sun-kissed bronze, and something about his countenance shone with an ageless beauty.

Paligno.

"Well done," he whispered, that secretive smile bowing his thin lips.

Before I could even wrap my mind around the fact that he—the god of all living things—was kneeling right there with his arms around me, he was gone. His tall, angular form dissolved to shimmering mist and fell around me, leaving me sitting in dumbstruck awe.

He ... he had saved me.

"Maylea!" Uncle Reigh shouted, staggering and stumbling over the huge roots that had buckled the floor. The pasty look of shock and desperate concern on his face was a dead giveaway. He had seen Paligno, too. He staggered to a halt right over me, the others not far behind him.

But I couldn't stop gaping upward.

The roots of a huge, white tree had burst upward, punching straight through the top of the chamber and growing like a column of platinum straight toward the night sky beyond. Moonlight fell in sterling streams through its outstretched branches, and wind rustled its thousands of golden leaves. The trunk must have been a hundred feet wide, at least, and stood right where the portal had once been.

Gods and Fates, was it really over? Was Sadeera gone? Had the Gate of Proleus been destroyed, too?

I could hardly breathe—even before Ronan hit the ground on his knees before me and hugged me tight. He sobbed against me, and behind him, Uncle Reigh, Thatcher, and Isandri gathered around to stare down at us with tears in their eyes, as well.

We ... we had done it.

Sadeera was dead.

The gate was destroyed.

I gasped and wheezed, hyperventilating as those truths sank into my mind like ice into boiling water. Oh gods, we had actually done it!

"No rest for the weary," Uncle Reigh said, ruffling Ronan's hair and then offering a hand to help me up. "Come on, kids. We still have a battle to win. There's a lot of people outside still counting on us to even up the fight. Think you're up for it?"

As Ronan pulled back, releasing me from his vice-tight hug, I seized Uncle Reigh's hand and sprang back to my feet. I snatched my bow up and checked my quiver. Only three arrows left.

But I did enjoy a challenge.

"Absolutely," I said as I met the smoldering determination that still blazed in all my friends' faces. "Let's go work."

40

CHAPTER FORTY

There wasn't time to pay respects or even move Arlan's body. Not now. We had no choice but to leave him where he had fallen with the hope that we would be able to come back for him once this was over. Something about that left a dull ache in my chest. Even if I hadn't known him, I had seen all the results of his careful planning. He had been looking out for us from the beginning, even from miles away in Maldobar. He had paved the way for our success, partnering us with Malina and contacting the Rajinna.

We owed him a lot—probably a lot more than I could even appreciate right now.

Surely someone like that deserved a proper funeral.

Thatcher held out that white glass orb, using a pulse of his power and touching it to Arlan's head. With a soft shimmer of light, he vanished into it. That was all we could manage before we all ran out, heading for the doorway of the temple in a mad dash. We armed ourselves as best we could as we headed for the only way out, steeling ourselves for the next phase of our plan. I was almost out of arrows, yes, but I still had Uncle Murdoc's daggers. Not ideal in a fight like this, but I could make do until I managed to loot a better weapon off someone else. A sword or scimitar—whatever I could get my hands on first.

Regardless, this would be messy. Even so far from the entrance, the roar and rumble of battle shook the temple around us. It vibrated under my feet and made the walls shudder with repeating, booming impacts. The stench of something sharp and alchemical stung my eyes and made me choke. Was that sulfur? Or pitch?

"Tar bombs," Uncle Reigh growled under his breath. "Curse it, I hope we're not too late."

My heart trembled at the thought—the fear that we had taken too long. What if our friends were hurt? Or even dead?

Where was my dah? Was he okay?

"GARNETT!" Thatcher yelled, suddenly taking off ahead of us at a sprint.

Not far down the hallway, two figures sat with their backs to the wall, one much larger than the other. I recognized one of them as Auntie Garnett right away. But the tall, scruffy-looking older man sitting beside her was still a stranger to me. I had only met him briefly, just long enough to determine that he was someone traveling with Dah's group, but I didn't even know his name.

He blinked up at us groggily, face ashen and one arm clutched around his middle, seeming almost confused at first. "Y-You're ... late," he groaned weakly, then he let his head rest back against the wall with a deep, relieved sigh.

Garnett didn't respond, even when Thatcher fell to his knees before her and cried out her name again. Sitting with her head slumped to the side to rest on his shoulder, I noticed that the underpadding and clothing on one whole side of her body had been burned away. Beneath it, her skin was riddled with burns that had already become blisters ... and far worse. A pile of charred, reeking Nar'Haleenan armor lay scattered all around her, slathered in burned tar.

Oh gods. Had she been hit with it?

"Garnett," Thatcher rasped, his hands shaking as badly as his voice as he reached to cradle her cheeks in his hands. "H-Hey, it's me. I'm here. I'm right here. You're okay. E-Everything's going to be just fine. We're together now ... p-please wake up for me. G-Garnett? GARNETT!"

Her eyelids fluttered and she groaned, expression screwing up with pain. Her light lavender eyes opened slightly. The faintest smile brushed her lips. Her mouth opened, like she was going to say something. Then her gaze became distant, fixing straight ahead.

"G-Gods—no! NO!" Thatcher shouted, sitting with his hands hovering over her like he didn't know what to do. "S-Someone, please! Do something! Help her!"

No one moved. Uncle Reigh stood back with Isandri, still gripping his kafki blades, watching, his expression locked into a mashed-up, anguished frown. Why wasn't he helping? He was a healer wasn't he? Did ... did that mean she was ... too far gone?

I guess Uncle Reigh could tell what I must be thinking by the way I was staring at him. He shut his eyes and bowed his head, throat jumping as he swallowed hard.

Thatcher curled himself around her, gathering Garnett into his arms and closing his shining wings around them as he let out a primal, horrible screaming sob. It tore at my heart like the claws of a beast. Tears filled my vision, blurring out everything.

And I knew I had to try.

Taking all that remained of the Thornwine potion that the Mistress of the Call had given to me, I pressed the flask into Uncle Reigh's hand and nodded toward the other fellow. There wasn't much left in it now. Maybe enough for two people with minor injuries, or one that was severe.

But I didn't need any potion for what I wanted to try next.

I had done it once before, and yes, it was dangerous. I'd used so much power already. My body already ached and my thoughts were sluggish. I didn't know if it would work, or if it would push me too far beyond my limit.

I just knew I needed to help.

"Let me see her," I whispered, putting a hand on Thatcher's shoulder gently.

He flinched, closing his wings tighter around them as though I were a potential threat.

"Thatcher," I pleaded. "Please. You know what I can do. I'll be careful, I promise. Please, let me try."

Little by little, Thatcher unfurled from where he sat, his arms and wings still around her. Cradled against his chest, Auntie Garnett looked so small and fragile. But I knew the instant I saw her face that she was hanging by a thread. Fates, I had to hurry.

Swallowing against the rising panic that made my throat go stiff, I got down on my knees right beside him. I took her hands in mine and let my eyes fall closed, turning my every thought and shred of focus inward. It wasn't like before—I could tell that much right away. Paligno's power had always been so quick to respond. But whether because the core of our mission had been accomplished, or because of how much of that power I had used, I didn't feel it like I had before. What had once been a lively spark was now just a small ember, barely burning.

Fatigue gripped me like a hand at my throat as I tried to fan that quiet little flame. It made my head feel heavy and everything seemed to spin around me. My arms and legs grew heavy, and something hot and wet dripped from my nose and dribbled down my chin.

Blood.

"You said you wouldn't deny any of the power you gave my ancestors," I prayed in a quiet, broken whisper. "Please don't abandon me. Not yet. I ... still need you."

I didn't know if Paligno would hear me. I didn't know if he was even here anymore. But he had saved me once before. I had to believe there was a purpose for it. A reason I was still here.

His presence filled the air around me like rays of sunlight. Warmth spread over my skin as his voice whispered softly in my ear, *"Oh, little sprout, how beautifully you bloom. I would never abandon you."*

My eyes were still closed, but I didn't need to see. I could feel the gentle flow of power from my soul to hers, knitting every broken place and strengthening that fragile thread that gleamed so beautifully in my mind's eye. Her thread of life.

Thatcher sucked in a sudden, halting gasp. I heard him sob again, and when I opened my eyes, I found Garnett still lying in his arms, staring back at me. She blinked slowly, a faint smile putting those familiar dimples in the corners of her rosy, freckled cheeks. All the severe burns along the side of her neck, arm, shoulder, side, and even down her leg were closed and healing, but the white discoloration of scars was still there. It probably would be for the rest of her life.

Fortunately, it didn't seem like Thatcher was worried about that. He hugged her again, pressing his lips to her forehead as he held her close. This time, she hugged him back, managing a weak, hitching laugh.

"Ya almost ... lost me there," she managed brokenly. "Sorry, love."

Healed or not, it was easy to see she wouldn't be rejoining this fight. The scruffy older man, either, for that matter. Uncle Reigh spoke quietly to him, offering a swig of that powerful healing potion, and taking a quick look at what looked suspiciously like an arrow wound to the gut—if the snapped-off bolt sticking out of him was any indication.

"I gotta take it out before that potion starts working," Uncle Reigh warned. "On my count. One ... two ..."

On three, he yanked the bolt out in one stiff jerk.

The older man gave a low, growling groan through his teeth and keeled backward, resting against the wall again. "They teach you that ... in Luntharda?" he asked, his voice still tired and scraping.

"Nope. That one's fresh out of the dragonrider academy," Uncle Reigh quipped.

The man snorted. "Figures."

Standing up, Uncle Reigh pocketed the flask and looked back to the rest of us. "We need to get moving. Who knows what state the others are in," he urged, then pointed at Garnett and the older man. "You two stay put. I mean it. The name of the game is Run Away Bravely. So just sit tight, and we'll be back to get you as soon as we can signal the *Dawn Chaser* in low enough to pick us all up."

It wouldn't be that simple.

I knew that the instant I tried to stand and my legs nearly collapsed out from under me. Stars danced in my vision as Thatcher caught me under the arm, keeping me on my feet and letting me lean into his side. Breathe—I just had to breathe. My hand shook out of control as I tried to wipe at the blood on my chin. It still hadn't stopped.

I was pushing things too far. If I had to do something like that again, it might be more than my mortal body could take.

"You all right?" Thatcher asked, his brow creased with worry as he reluctantly let me stagger forward on my own.

"F-Fine," I said, turning my face away so maybe he wouldn't see my expression screw up with pain. My legs tingled like they'd fallen asleep, feeling heavy and strange until I'd managed a few more shaky, limping paces. It got a little easier with each step. But not much. My joints ached like someone had poured hot sand into them, and my fingertips were almost completely numb.

Curse it all, I had to pull myself together. We still had a battle to fight. I could not go down this easily.

By the time we reached the doorway, the feeling was beginning to return to my extremities. But as we stumbled to a halt there, staring out at the absolute pandemonium raging in the night, fear hit me like a punch to the chest and knocked the breath from my lungs all over again. Fire flashed in the night. Men screamed and wailed. Black toxic smoke, arrows, and flying chunks of stone filled the air. Explosions of magic flashed in the night. I searched in vain for anyone standing nearby that I recognized. But there was no one.

Gods and Fates, what were we going to do?

"Noh," Uncle Reigh growled suddenly. "Find Violet and make sure she gets out."

A wisp of shadow darted around us, moving like a flying banshee before it finally landed on the ground before him and took the shape of a canine with tall, pointed ears, and an emaciated body. With white eyes glowing in the night, its too-wide mouth grinned, revealing countless jagged fangs.

"As you wish, dear brother," the creature's hissing voice replied and it surged forward into the chaos without hesitation.

"I see Murdoc!" Thatcher pointed off to the far right. There, a glowing sword whirled through the haze of battle, giving him away.

"Go give him a hand, then," Uncle Reigh ordered. "Isa, you look for Noa. That leg of his wasn't fully healed, so he may need some help getting out of there. Ronan, you and I are gonna start clearing this courtyard as best we can for the ship to arrive. Keep your eyes open—Violet, Jae, and Lukani are somewhere out there, too. Anyone you find, you send them here to this doorway!"

"And me?" I asked, already suspecting I knew exactly what kind of orders I would be getting.

"You stay here and guard the doorway," he said. "Don't let anyone in there to hurt our friends, got it?"

Uggh. Great. After all that, he was back to sitting me in a corner like a little kid again? No. Absolutely not. Yes, I was not at my best, but if he thought I was going to just stand here and twiddle my thumbs while everyone else fought for their lives, he was out of his mind. I could still fight.

I shot him a glare, which he didn't even seem to notice, as he forged onward into battle along with all the rest of my companions.

I waited, giving it a good minute before I reached back into my quiver for one of my remaining arrows, and deliberately disobeyed to the very best of my ability. I ran to the left, searching for anyone familiar in the mayhem. Dah—I had to find my dah.

Yelling his name, my heart pumped wildly as I bounded over pools of burning tar and ducked around huge boulders that had apparently been flung into the courtyard by enemy siege machines. He had to be here somewhere. I wouldn't believe anything else.

Two Nar'Haleenan soldiers ran past me, appearing through the smoke and not seeming to notice me. That is, until I let my arrow fly and struck the first one right at the base of the skull. He fell instantly, and his comrade whirled around to face me. Ripping a sword free from his belt, he stormed straight at me with murder blazing in his eyes.

Two arrows left. I'd have to do this up close and personal.

Reaching into the sides of my boots, I drew out my borrowed daggers and whirled them over my hands, already examining the soldier's every movement for weakness. His armor had gaps at the neck line, just above the pauldrons. I'd aim for that, and—

Five more soldiers stepped from the curling plumes of dark smoke behind him, emerging like demons in their polished black armor. One of them held a crossbow already aimed for my head.

Oh no. This ... might be a problem. Curse it!

I took a step back, trying to decide if I could run. There wasn't anywhere nearby to hide, though. No boulders to duck behind to avoid crossbow fire. No pools of molten tar I could use as a deterrent for them to run me down.

I was alone and completely exposed.

A sound over the constant roar and boom of battle drew my gaze up, behind the advancing soldiers, an instant before I saw it: something massive flying toward me on huge wings. I knew that sound. I knew it like the beating of my own heart.

A dragon's battle cry.

Scales as white as sunbleached bone. Horns, spines, and claws as black as onyx. Eyes as blue as the spring sky.

It wasn't just any dragon.

It was *my* dragon.

PART THIRTEEN

MURDOC

41

CHAPTER FORTY-ONE

KABOOOM!

A sound like the sky itself was cracking open made everyone around the courtyard stop and look up, just in time to see a colossal tree punch straight up out of the temple compound and spread branches out in every direction. It shone like a statue of pure pewter, gleaming in the moonlight and dwarfing everything in the surrounding area. Sweet gods, it must have been eight hundred feet tall! Where the heck had that come from?

There wasn't time to sort it out or even determine if it was a good thing or bad thing. Our enemies were only amazed for about ten seconds before they seemed to remember why we were all here and started attacking again.

And things were beginning to get dire.

With several fresh slashes bleeding down her chest and legs, Violet hung closer to my side. Her movements were slowing. Her fighting style wasn't ideal for this situation, and I could tell she was getting tired.

Garnett was already out of the fight—or so I assumed since I hadn't seen her after Roxus had carried her off. She'd been hit pretty hard by that wave of burning tar. I just hoped he had found somewhere safe to put her down.

Noa was probably the worst off, however. That already weakened leg of his had him on the defensive now, barely able to keep up and deflect the constant hailstorm of enemy strikes. Even with the Rajinna still fighting around us, and the dragonriders and *Dawn Chaser* making tactical passes to try to control the influx of enemies in the courtyard, we were awash in the dark tide of Nar'Haleenan forces—outnumbered and out of time.

We couldn't hold on much longer.

Not without taking some serious losses.

As another wave of soldiers advanced into the courtyard, I stood with my arms hanging limp, heaving for breath, watching them sprint toward me through the flames. "Come on, Reigh," I growled through my teeth as I whirled through another set of maneuvers, cutting down two more soldiers and locking blades with a third. Every muscle in my body burned. My back and shoulders ached. My calves throbbed, and the constant ebb and flow of adrenaline left my grip shaky and my mind a hazy wreck. I was losing strength.

Fates, we needed help—right now.

"DUCK!" someone yelled behind me suddenly.

I didn't even question, immediately dropping to a low crouch just as something sailed right over my head like a massive fireball. An orb of golden light like a miniature star hit the front line of the incoming soldiers and burst, rocking the sky with a flash of radiant power and sending bodies flying in every direction ... including my own.

I hit the ground flat on my back so hard it knocked the wind out of me. Holy gods, what was that? Everything seemed to spin and tilt, like I'd had too much wine, as I started trying to stand again.

Then a hand appeared in front of my face.

Thatcher grinned down at me, his eyes glowing sort of like Arlan's and a halo of golden light ebbing off his entire body. Two huge feathered wings spread from his back, making him look more like something celestial than human.

A godling.

I gripped his hand and he immediately kicked skyward with one beat of those gleaming wings. "What are you doing?!" I kicked and yelled in protest, watching the earth fall away beneath me.

A flash of red and black scales gave me my answer.

Blite zoomed right underneath us, and with a sheepish grin, Thatcher let me go. Uggh. That idiot. He could've warned me.

I hit the center of Blite's saddle with my blade still gripped in one hand. Thank the gods for that. Er, one god in particular, I guess. Working my feet down into the deep leather pockets on either side of my dragon's strong neck, I slipped my sword back into its sheath and reached for the saddle handles. Fates, I'd never felt anything so right in my entire life.

Ahead, Jaevid and Mavrik still flew in the lead, and when I glanced over to where Fornax was holding position off his left wingtip, I couldn't resist a grin as I watched Thatcher take his own spot in his dragon's saddle. It was a strange sight—an angelic figure riding a dragon—but this entire day had been outside my normal expectation of strangeness.

My heart beat like thunder in my chest as we veered in perfect formation over the sea of dark armor and war machines still churning below. Lines of dragonfire still burned high, but even as hard as we had fought so far, it didn't look like we had made much of a dent in our enemy's ranks. Curse it. No time to let up now.

I spotted Jenna's big drake, Phevos, approaching with Vexi close off one wing and a familiar golden dragon on the other. Heh. Well that made two full formations. Good odds for any dragonrider.

And we had trained nonstop for years for this very moment.

"We are going to carve a path for the Dawn Chaser to descend and pick up our allies in the courtyard," Jaevid communicated back, using the dragonrider code of hand signals. *"Primary targets are ground war machines. Make it hurt."*

Thatcher and I signaled our agreement.

Squeezing my legs tighter to Blite's side, I twisted the saddle handles to send him signals, steering in perfect synchronization with Mavrik to begin our assault run. Jaevid and Jenna must have had some sort of exchange about this already—maybe when he'd taken over leadership of our two dragons—because she immediately led her two wingends on a similar pass coming in the opposite direction so we would cross midway over the battlefield.

Excellent.

Blite snapped his wings in tight as we dove down, falling like a flock of speeding falcons, and zoomed over the advancing line of enemy war machines. Catapults burned. Trebuchets toppled as their ropes and cables snapped. Men ran like scared cockroaches. War beasts bucked and tried to flee, their saddles and armor already ablaze. Only a few even dared fire at us, using everything they had. Arrows and crossbow bolts zipped past, a few even pinging off Blite's armored chest. Fortunately, none seemed to pierce his scaly hide, and he slicked his little ears back and hissed in defiance as we broke skyward again.

A smirk curled over my lips as I saw Jaevid give another signal, gesturing for us to do another pass before falling back to offer backup to the *Dawn Chaser* while it made its far slower descent. A good plan considering the airship was much slower and less agile, and it would have to come low enough to drop ropes or ladders down so our allies on the ground could get onboard. It would inevitably become a big juicy target as soon as it came within range of those war machines.

I heard it an instant before I saw it; the sound like something large whipping through the air extremely fast. Almost like a whip or—

Mavrik let out a roar of alarm as a huge net made of thick metal cables whipped through the air, heading straight for us. Fornax and Thatcher immediately veered to the right, evading the incoming net. Mavrik shot upward with one beat of his mighty wings. Blite saw it, too ...

A second too late.

Oh gods, it was going to hit us!

I cringed, bracing for impact.

With a defiant roar, a huge blue-scaled blur flashed between the incoming net and us, so fast I had no time to react. Mavrik screeched in rage as the net wrapped around one of his wings and hind legs, tangling immediately with weighed ends spinning and wrapping around him.

Wh-What? He'd intentionally taken that hit? For *me?!*

The king drake fell, roaring and still beating his one free wing, as he plummeted from the sky straight down toward the roiling mass of enemy soldiers below.

He would hit hard. He'd land right in the middle of a block of enemy soldiers.

Gods—NO!

Slamming my hands against the saddle handles, I yelled a curse and ordered Blite to dive after him. I didn't even check to see if Thatcher followed. It didn't matter. I would not let the commander go down without someone there to back him up. The hit would be ugly, but Mavrik was experienced in battle. I just prayed he would be able to protect Jaevid from the brunt of the impact.

With the wind howling past my ears, I leaned down against Blite's neck. Out of the corner of my eye, I spotted the flash of orange and black scales. Fornax made a veering tight pass around us, beginning to throw down a fiery perimeter around the place where Jaevid was likely to land. It wasn't perfect, but it might help. It would at least keep us from getting swarmed right away.

BOOOOM!

Mavrik hit hard. The impact threw up dust and sand in every direction so that I couldn't tell how he landed or if Jaevid was all right. I only caught obscure glimpses of blue scales and black horns as he writhed and clawed at the net. No sign of his rider anywhere.

Pulling my legs out of the security of the boot pockets on my saddle, I prepared myself for a rough landing of my own. I gave one last command to Blite, ordering him to ascend rapidly and rejoin with Fornax as soon as I left his back. He didn't like it. He hissed and snapped his jaws angrily. But this wasn't up for debate.

I would not leave Jaevid down there to fight on his own. Even though my own strength was nearly spent. Even though we were so far behind enemy lines that none of our other friends could even dream of reaching us in time. Dragonriders never abandoned their own, no matter what the odds.

So, I drew my sword again and jumped, leaping out into the open air to fall the last twenty feet to the desert below.

NO ORDINARY BLADE COULD CUT THROUGH THE THICK CABLES THAT BOUND MAVRIK UP like a salmon in a gillnet. Fortunately, I hadn't brought an ordinary one. Still armed with Proleus's divine sword, I squeezed the hilt in both hands as the blade glowed with power. I ran for the downed king drake and started cutting, slicing through as many of the cables as I could while I yelled Jaevid's name.

Mavrik lay on his side, his back facing away, so I couldn't see the saddle. I didn't know if that's even how the dragon had landed, or if he'd just rolled over. Regardless, I didn't hear an answer. Dread burrowed deep in the pit of my stomach like I'd swallowed a knot of cold iron. I cut a few more of the cables, enough that Mavrik could stand up and use both his hind legs, before I started to run underneath the massive dragon to search for his rider.

That's when the attack began.

Nar'Haleenan soldiers converged from everywhere like we'd just been dropped into the very center of a fire ant hill. Fornax's circle of flame kept the majority at bay, but they wasted no time firing crossbows, longbows, and hurling spears. Pain shot through one of my legs as I caught a bolt to the thigh. I tripped, but managed to stay on my feet. Jaevid—where was he?! We had to get off the ground right now!

WHOOOM!

Mavrik breathed another blast of venom, scorching an encroaching group of soldiers who'd been caught in Fornax's fiery circle.

"JAEVID!" I yelled at the top of my lungs.

No answer.

I spat and cursed, hobbling as fast as I could as the heat from the dragonfire scorched my throat with every breath. Fates, what if I couldn't find him? What if the soldiers already had?

"JAEVID!"I tried again

"Mur ... doc ..." a voice called my name weakly.

I spun, finally spotting that royal blue cloak splayed on the ground. There!

Jaevid lay on his back, jaw set and expression tight with pain. With arrows still whizzing past my head, I bolted for him, ignoring the shooting pain from my thigh with every step.

"You have to get up! Come on, your dragon's nearly free!" I urged as I slid to a halt, seizing him by the arm to drag him to his feet.

He let out a desperate scream of pain and didn't even try to stand.

What? What was wrong? I-I didn't see any blood on him or—

"It hurts," he groaned, chest heaving for every breath. "I think ... I think something's broken. I-I can't move my legs."

Oh gods.

"Y-You're going to have to ... leave me," he said, his voice catching as he stared up at me with a determined scowl I knew all too well. "You can't carry me. Get Mavrik ... and g-go."

I couldn't speak. Wh ... What? No. How could I ...? This wasn't ... *NO!*

"After you nearly get yourself killed for me? Absolutely not! We leave no one behind. You taught me that, Commander," I seethed, grabbing the front of his breastplate and heaving him up over my shoulders. "You don't need your legs when you've got wings!"

Every step was fresh agony as I shambled across the sand with Jaevid on my back. Sweat ran down my back and face, drenching my hair as my arms shook with fatigue. Too late, I realized I couldn't do it. I couldn't make it. My injured leg buckled and we both dropped to the sand. Arrows hit the sand around us, and another bolt of pain shot up through my shoulder.

Gods, we ... we couldn't move. Mavrik was still caught, snarling and bellowing with fury as he whirled around. He lashed his spine-tipped tail and breathed flame, pitching wildly to get his wing free. He wouldn't leave us, even if he did.

Even the Ulfrangar knew that a dragon would die before he ever abandoned his chosen rider.

But I couldn't walk. I couldn't even get up. The best I could do was drag myself over so my body partially covered his, protecting him from the incoming hailstorm of arrows. It was futile. We'd be overrun, and not even Mavrik would be able to stop it. They would butcher us all like cattle.

A frustrated shout leaked through my clenched teeth as I slammed a fist into the sand. All I could think of in that moment was the handkerchief still tucked into my vambrace. Phoebe—Fates, I had promised her I would come back. I had given her my word.

I was going to fail her. I was going to fail everyone.

My whole body tensed as a deafening *BOOOOM* shook the ground beneath me. I squinted up, just in time to glimpse a flurry of brilliant white scales appear directly in front of us. G-Gods, what was that?

A huge paw landed right in front of me, each one of his white-scaled toes tipped in a massive black talon. No, not a paw. An enormous *dragon's* foot with what looked a lot like an old shackle's metal ring still around its ankle.

The creature rose up before us like a pale demon king—the biggest dragon I had ever seen in my life. He dwarfed even Mavrik, with a crest of black horns curling back from his wide head and bristling spines as big as spears that ran all the way to the tip of his tail. The creature's roar boomed like a volcanic eruption, its plated chest heaving deeply before it shot a column of blue flame at the enemy soldiers that made our attempts look like children's play.

With tattered wings and its brawny body striped with old scars, the white dragon swung its tail like a flail, smashing through more soldiers and cracking another one of those net-throwing devices into splinter. Then its huge, viper-shaped head turned to us. The dark pupils of its vibrant blue eyes narrowed to slits, snout twitching in a snarl as burning venom drizzled from its toothy jaws. The huge dragon's nostrils flared, taking in our scents.

Behind us, Mavrik had finally stopped struggling and lay still, his throat vibrating with a low, uncertain growl of warning. Whoever this dragon was, I had never even heard of him. And the way he was staring us down did not fill me with warm feelings of hope.

"Easy, there, big boy," a feminine voice cooed suddenly. "Be easy now. It's okay. They're with us, remember? I know they're strangers, but they're just like us."

I looked up in absolute disbelief at the petite young woman sitting just behind the dragon's head, holding onto his horns and peering down at us with a worried expression.

Holy. Reigning. Gods.

"Dah! Uncle Murdoc!" Maylea Broadfeather cried out, leaning over her dragon's bony brow and hanging on to his massive, curved black horns. "Don't worry! Help is on the way! Just hang on!"

Another symphony of roars sounded overhead, and I didn't even have to look to see who they were. Jenna, Thatcher, and all the other dragonriders were coming. They hadn't left us.

They never would.

"Is ... m-my daughter ... riding a d-dragon?" Jaevid asked, his voice weaker than before, as though he had to fight for every gasping word.

I couldn't hold back a crazed, hoarse laugh. "Like she was born for it, Commander."

"Sh ... she was." I could have sworn he laughed, too. "T-Tell her ... I-I was glad. Tell her ... I was ... p-proud."

What? What did he mean by that?

Oh. Oh, Fates. No ...

Jerking back, I looked down at where Jaevid lay partially shielded beneath me. One look was all it took. One look and I knew.

H-He wasn't breathing anymore.

Panic stole everything in that moment. My thoughts. My breath. My everything.

I stared down into his pale, arctic-blue eyes and felt the world stop. The sounds of battle faded, becoming muffled and faraway. I barely heard it when the other dragons landed around us, and the others ran over to find us. Maylea's frantic, horrified screams might as well have been a thousand miles away.

I hung limp, awake but not altogether conscious, as someone dragged me the rest of the way off him and started carrying me away. I couldn't tell who. It didn't matter. They threw me onto the back of an orange and black-scaled beast, buckling me down and prepared for takeoff.

And in that moment, the only sound that pierced the crushing, frigid silence in my mind was the wild, agonized cry of a great blue dragon ... still protecting his fallen rider.

42

CHAPTER FORTY-TWO

"DAH!"

I could still hear Maylea sobbing as they took Jaevid's motionless body off of Fornax and carried both of us to the cover of the temple. Somewhere nearby, the booming of dragon wingbeats and trumpeting roars still echoed, making the whole structure shudder as they laid me out on the ground.

"I've still got a pulse," Reigh's voice growled low, every word tight with extreme focus. I knew that voice. He had switched over to that war medic state of mind, leaving all other emotion at the door. "Maylea, I need you to sit right here with your fingers on his neck. You let me know if his heart stops. Thatcher, get over here and get ready to breathe for him on my count."

My body shook with agony, teeth grinding, as I willed my body to move. I had to see. I needed to. With a rasping groan, I managed to roll over halfway onto my side—just enough that I could see them now.

Not ten paces away, Reigh, Thatcher, and Maylea crowded around Jaevid's motionless body. Noa and Violet stood a little farther back and watched with quietly terrified expressions. Neither of them dared to say a word.

Reigh snatched a silver flask from his belt and uncorked it, immediately pouring all the contents down Jaevid's throat. He flung the empty flask aside and began stripping away all the pieces of Jae's battle armor, chucking them away just as fast as he could get them unbuckled. Cutting through all the layers of protective padding and clothing beneath the armor, Reigh stripped Jae all the way down to his small clothes.

"Now!" he ordered and gestured for Thatcher to start forcing breath into Jae's mouth. "Pulse?"

"I-I can still feel it," Maylea whimpered, her whole body trembling as she watched with her face completely blanched in terror.

With his brow locked into a forbidding, utterly focused scowl, Reigh checked Jaevid's body over inch by inch. He tested joints in his arms, neck, shoulders, chest, ribs, and probed around his abdomen with his fingers. It wasn't until he reached Jaevid's hips and legs that his eyes widened and his jawline went stiff, as though he were fighting to keep his emotions in check.

"Broken pelvis, likely damage to the lower spine, mid-shaft fractures of the left femur, and the knee is completely shattered—curse it all, he's bleeding out internally," Reigh seethed and cursed under his breath, almost like he was thinking out loud.

"W-Will the potion help?" Maylea's voice hitched, catching as she choked back a sob. "Is he going to be okay?"

Reigh worked his jaw from one side to the other, staring at Jaevid's expressionless face as Thatcher went on forcing air into his lungs. Finally, he looked up and fixed her with a hard, uncompromising stare. "I can't do a surgery like this here. I can't save him," he said. "But *you* can."

Maylea's eyes went wide with an all-consuming fear.

"I know what I'm asking," he continued, his voice lowering but never breaking that relentless gaze. "It's a risk. But a few drops of potion won't be enough. Not for injuries like these. He doesn't have time to wait for it to take effect. I'm a healer, not a miracle worker. That's *your* birthright."

For a few seconds, no one made a sound. No one moved.

Sitting at his side, Maylea's gaze panned over her father's bruised and broken body. His face had begun to turn ashen, lips going an unsettling shade of blue. Then her eyes closed. She bowed her head, lengths of dark hair spilling over her shoulders as she slid her hand away from Jaevid's neck and placed it gently on his chest, right over his heart.

"I know you're still there," she whispered brokenly, her chin quivering and mouth screwing up. "I can feel you. Don't leave me. Please, Dah, I can't do this without you."

I winced and nearly fell back as a blinding white light filled the air. What was happening? I couldn't see. Gods, that light burned. It seemed to pierce through my eyes straight into my brain, scorching through every thought and searing over every nerve. But ... I had to look. I needed to see. Just one glimpse.

Covering my eyes with a hand, I bit down hard against the stinging, scalding pain and squinted through my fingers.

And I saw her.

With her hair floating weightless around her, Maylea's whole being glowed like a living, breathing star. Tendrils of power arced and wavered around her, flowing ribbons of radiant light that wreathed her like the petals of a blooming flower. A pair of white, elk-like horns sloped back from her head, and three sets of slender, feathered wings unfurled from her back to stretch out over her father's motionless body. Her lips moved, breathing words I couldn't hear, but each one seemed to send out a soft current into the air.

My pulse seemed to come to a scattered, frantic halt as a figure rose up behind her, tall and imposing, draped in a deep green cloak covered in moss, lichens, and tiny flowers. It descended in one smooth motion, putting a much larger hand over hers.

I had to turn away, my head threatening to split open like a cracked eggshell at the sudden tolling of a deep, rich voice that whispered four words.

"Live well, my children."

MY CONSCIOUSNESS SLIPPED, COMING AND GOING IN FOGGY, DELIRIOUS WAVES OF SOUND and motion that didn't make any sense. With my eyes still burning like I'd just poured dragon venom into them, I couldn't see much. Just the occasional dark shapes of people around me and the muffled sounds of their voices. I could have sworn I heard Jaevid, but I wasn't sure enough to bet my life on it.

The next thing I knew, I was being carried by Thatcher again. With my head lolled against his shoulder, I caught a hazy view of the dragons circling overhead, their wings stretched out against the shower of silver moonlight. Where were we going? Was everyone here? Were we going to be all right?

I groaned, trying to work up the strength to ask, but my body sagged limply. I was only vaguely aware of being tied down to a dragon's saddle like cargo. Blite? No. This one was orange. Fornax.

"Isandri! Gods and Fates, I thought we were going to have to come find you. Did you manage to get Edarix?" Reigh's voice shouted from very close by, so suddenly it made me jolt and I got a little surge of adrenaline—just enough to make everything suddenly snap into focus for a few seconds.

That's all it took, though. One quick glance and I knew we were now in full retreat. Reigh was calling out orders. The dragons were descending long enough to pick up their riders.

We were going to make it.

I was ... going home.

PART FOURTEEN

REIGH

❧ 43 ☙

CHAPTER FORTY-THREE

"GO, GO, GO!" I yelled as loudly as I could as the last few stragglers came scrambling out of the doorway to the temple. I could already see it coming—the *Dawn Chaser* slowly approaching like a great, finned beast. With its broad hull already scarred and pocked with punctures, craters, and countless arrows, the airship flew low enough that I could already spot Maldobarian soldiers scrambling around within the open gun ports.

Not long now. Seconds. We had to be ready.

Those of us not leaving in a dragon's saddle had to be onboard this ship. There would be no second passes to pick up stragglers. This was our only chance to get out of here fast and clean.

"Sweet Fates, what is that?" Violet gasped beside me, gripping my arm like she was afraid to let me out of her sight. She pointed to the far horizon, beyond the end of our enemy's ranks.

I narrowed my eyes. What *was* that? It almost looked like a field of diamonds zipping through the air toward us. I set my jaw and cut my eyes back toward the airship. Whatever it was, be it more Nar'Haleenan military forces or the gods themselves riding into battle, I didn't intend to stick around and find out. We had everyone. It was time to get the heck out of here.

"Get ready!" I called over our group.

As the hull grew closer, rope ladders poured down from over the deck railings to brush the ground of the courtyard. I made sure Garnett, Roxus, Noa, Edarix, and Violet all made it onto one before I even dared to grab one myself. The Rajinna also scrambled aboard, and I spotted Lukani making his own way right alongside them.

Good. That took care of my end. The rest were either riding dragons, or strapped to them because they were too injured to manage on their own.

I hauled myself over the railing of the airship and hit the deck with a thud. Immediately, Maldobarian soldiers rushed to help me, asking if I needed medical attention, and trying to usher me below deck. I waved them off, staggering to the other side of the ship's broad deck to peer out over the horizon again. From this far up, I got a much better view.

And I finally recognized what those thousands of diamond-like objects were.

Gods and Fates, they almost looked like ... *people*.

Not just any people, though. They crossed an incredible distance at a speed I couldn't even begin to fathom, and the closer they came, the more detail I could make out. Garbed in flowing robes of purest white and gleaming silver armor, they flew with wings like angels. They soared for us in a group that must have been two or three thousand strong.

I drew back slightly, body already tensed and braced for the worst when I realized, no—wait, they weren't coming for us. They were headed for the legions of Nar'Haleenan soldiers down below.

What the ...?

"Avoran elves," Violet whispered in breathless awe as she dashed to the railing beside me. "Gods have mercy."

Those were *Avoran* elves? Whoa. Immediately, my mind spun with an endless flurry of questions. Had Arlan sent for them? He must have, right? Nothing else made sense right then. But how had he contacted them? What had he said to convince them to fight like this? Or had the gods compelled them to do it? Fates, none of this made any sense!

My eyes threatened to pop right out of their sockets as I watched a cavalry of Avoran elves clash with the Nar'Haleenan lines and slice into them like a knife through soft cheese. I had never witnessed anything like it. But just the sight, even as we slipped away through the sky at full sail, made my eyes well up. I bit down hard to keep it in, but my chin still trembled. It was like watching the divine hand of justice finally smash through the darkness that had been devouring everything in this region.

I didn't know why they had come. I didn't know if it was even really happening or if I was just hallucinating, but that image stayed burned into my brain long after we had left the battlefield far behind.

Drifting over the jagged mountain peaks under the soft glow of the full moon, I felt the last strand of worry snap loose in my brain. The cool wind teased through my sweaty hair. My shoulders sagged as every muscle in my body seemed to turn to mush. I turned around and sank down onto the deck of the ship, realizing only once I had my elbows on my knees that I was still panting for breath. There wasn't a single part of me that didn't hurt.

But I was alive. Somehow, we had all made it through this.

It was finally over.

"Reigh?" Violet spoke my name softly as she sat down beside me, tucking herself close against my side.

"Yeah?"

"I overheard some of the crew talking. They said there's a fleet of Maldobarian ships coming, too. They're going to meet us at the coast. They should be there by the time we reach it to give us an escort back to Maldobar, just in case the emperor attempts to intercept with his navy."

I had to laugh. "Is that so?"

"Although, if the Avoran elves are indeed now intervening and fighting against his campaign, I doubt very much he will have the soldiers to spare for that effort," she added, smiling as though she found the idea hilarious, too. "I suppose it all depends on how much damage Sadeera and Iksoli have done to his mind. Time will tell."

Yeah. Time would tell. And for once, I was in no hurry whatsoever.

"Well, if they can't sort out their differences without outside assistance, they're going to have to look elsewhere, because I'm officially retiring from it." I sighed and let my head rest back against the deck railing.

"Had your fill of the hero's life, then, hmm?" She gave my shoulder a playful nudge with hers.

"Several times over," I replied.

"And what do you intend to do with all your spare time now?"

I didn't even have to stop and think about that. "Take a long, hot bath, have a nap, and drive you crazy till the end of our days."

A COMMOTION FARTHER DOWN THE DECK DREW OUR ATTENTION AS SOLDIERS BEGAN rushing by, shouting orders, and gathering on the bow end. Hmm. What was this about?

Making our way toward the gathering crowd, Violet and I muscled our way to the front ... just in time to see my sister helping a much taller man hobble down from her dragon's back. Wrapped up in his dragonrider cloak, most likely to hide the fact that I'd basically cut his clothes to shreds trying to save his life, Jaevid Broadfeather looped an arm over Thatcher's shoulder to steady himself as he limped forward.

"Dah!" Maylea burst past us, shoving her way through the crowd and running to meet him. With tears streaming down her face, she threw her arms around him, nearly taking him all the way to the ground in a wild embrace.

Jae just laughed, his expression twitching a little in pain as he used his one free arm to hug her back. The sight made a soft round of applause go up from the crowd that gathered in closer. Fates, it was just good to see him upright and breathing on his own. That idiot had already died once. I didn't need to bring him back from the dead a second time.

"REIGH FARROW! You idiot! You ran off without telling me," Jenna bellowed suddenly. She stomped for me with wrath flickering in her eyes like lightning snapping in a thunderstorm.

Oh no. Run. I should probably run, before—

She hugged me so tight I thought my head might pop off like a cork from a wine bottle. "How *dare* you? You've got some nerve! Of all the reckless, foolish things to do. I am your sister—don't you trust me at all! And now I hear you didn't even tell Isandri!" she went on, leaving my ears ringing as she squeezed me hard enough that I began to suspect this was her subtle way of making her point. She could crush the life out of me if she wanted to. And she would, if I ever pulled a stunt like this again.

"I'm sorry," I managed to wheeze.

"I know you are, just not nearly enough. We've got some business to tie up here, and then we are *all* going straight back home to Maldobar, and I don't want to hear any protesting!" She scowled down at me, her eyes teary as she combed her fingers through my hair like she was searching me for more signs of damage.

I caught a glimpse of Violet grinning cattishly, watching this humiliating display as though she were cherishing every second of it. Gods. Why did Jenna insist on treating me like a child? Yes, I was her little brother. But for crying out loud, I was in my thirties now.

Ugggh. Some things never changed, I guess.

Thank the gods for that.

Finally prying myself free of my sister's iron grasp, I straightened my robes and glanced back at where Jaevid and the others were gathering together in the middle of the deck. Murdoc was in need of medical treatment. But, then, most of us were. I'd get to that next. First, however, I found myself standing there, watching them all rally around Jaevid and Maylea with tearful smiles and relieved laughs.

That's when I finally saw it: a truth that had been staring me in the face for so long. What this all meant. What Jaevid Broadfeather had really done.

Yes, he was the Hero of Maldobar. He had fought against impossible odds again and again. He had faced down gods and forever changed the face of our world.

And yet, that wasn't what made tears well in my eyes as I watched him talking to Thatcher, Murdoc, Maylea, Lukani, and all the other people we had collected on this mad journey.

The heritage of honor, compassion, loyalty, and love that one man had fostered in every single person standing around him now—that was his greatest accomplishment. It was his legacy that had brought everyone here, scraping us together from every corner of the world, and making us into something more. Not just soldiers, dragonriders, assassins, would-be princes, queens, or godlings.

We were family.

His family.

Whether Jaevid had known this would happen or not, he had certainly made sure that no matter what, no one in this group would ever feel alone again. And I knew I would do everything in my power to make sure that never faded, no matter where in this wide, strange world we went next.

✠ 44 ✠

CHAPTER FORTY-FOUR

The sea shone so bright in the morning sun, the glare of it hit my eyes with a stinging force and heat that tingled over my face as I sat on the bow of the airship. With the salty wind in my hair and fresh bandaging on nearly every inch of my body, I watched as we soared the last few miles to the coast. Our dragons followed close, soaring together with Mavrik in the lead, the first rays of sunlight dancing off his deep blue scales.

It had taken the rest of the night to get there. Hours, I guess. And in that time, I'd spent most of it helping the other medics onboard the vessel treat our many wounded. Murdoc was probably the worst off, but as usual, he insisted he was fine—even with four arrows sticking out of various parts of his body. Stubborn idiot. He really had no idea when to quit.

Not that I'd prefer him any other way.

I could tell just by the look on his face as I worked on him that he was taking Jaevid's near-death-experience extremely hard. It wasn't difficult to guess why, though. I'd gotten an account of it from Thatcher and learned that Jaevid had willingly thrown himself in the line of an attack that probably would have killed Murdoc and Blite. No doubt, Murdoc felt responsible for everything that had happened as a result.

But that wasn't how being a dragonrider worked. No one who had ever sat in the saddle would ever point at him with blame for that. Dragonriders protected their own—first and always. Jaevid had done exactly what any one of us would have done in his place. Deep down, I had to believe Murdoc understood that as well. He just needed to remember it.

He did seem a little better after Jaevid finally pulled him aside and spoke to him. Jae had always been better with words when it came to things like that. Murdoc still seemed to have a hard time looking him in the eye, though—right up until Maylea cornered him below deck and hugged him like her life depended on it.

It was almost like I could see the gravity of his world shifting in that moment, as though he was realizing that he wasn't just another expendable soldier on our frontlines. He was our brother, too. His life mattered. And we were just as relieved to have him here, alive and breathing, as we were Jaevid.

Maybe, eventually, he'd learn to see that for himself.

As the rocky coastline came into view, I could feel the rumbling rhythm of the mechanisms that controlled the airship change slightly. We began to slowly and gracefully descend toward the water, those fin-like sails on the sides flaring like a swan about to land on a pond. Incredible. Phoebe really had outdone herself this time.

Six ships had gathered to greet us, anchored not far off shore, when we finally touched down. With a flock of dragons wheeling around, skimming the water and sunning themselves in the sand, I didn't think we'd have any issues with enemy forces trying anything funny.

But I got a real thrill of panic and dread when I recognized not one, but two of those anchored ships as pirate vessels.

Specifically, *drakkon-summoning* pirate vessels.

The sight made me bolt to my feet and run over to lean out, just to get a better look. It really was them! The *Squall Queen* and the *Red Duchess* sat, anchored side-by-side, their sails fluttering proudly in the morning breeze. I had absolutely no idea how they'd done it, but seeing both ships together put a smile on my face I couldn't hold in.

Right on cue, Noa hit the railing right next to me, his eyes so wide they looked like they might go rolling overboard at any moment. The look on his face, like a man seeing his very first dawn after a lifetime trapped in a prison's dark depths, was absolutely priceless. He climbed up on the railing and threw his fists to the sky, yelling at the top of his lungs in Rienkan.

On the deck of the *Squall Queen*, an answering call rose up like a victory cry. I spotted Malina high on the very back of the poop deck, the wind snagging through her long dark curls as she waved like a madwoman.

I almost missed it. But the ridiculous fluttering of a big feather made me take a second look. No way—was I hallucinating? Nope. That was definitely him, stupid hat and all. Judan stood beside her, hands on his hips, and a broad, roguish grin stretching from one pointed ear to the other. That crafty devil. He'd been busy, too, apparently.

I couldn't help it. I laughed out loud and leaned against the railing, shaking my head in disbelief when our ship passed close enough by the *Squall Queen* that Noa dove overboard and started swimming for it.

Heh. Well, I guess he had his own story to share. Good. Everyone needed a few of those; stories with good endings and happily-ever-afters. There weren't enough of them in the world.

And somehow, this felt like one of those a long time in the making.

Speaking of which ... hmmm.

I should probably get to work on my own. It was long overdue, wasn't it?

As eager as I was to set sail for Maldobar and leave this place, with all its many nightmares, as far behind as possible. Buuut there were a few remaining stones we couldn't afford to leave unturned. I had every intention of spending the day tending our wounded in the medical bay below deck. But Jenna had spared no effort or resources in outfitting this ship with supplies and personnel to run it like, er, well, a well-oiled machine, I guess. She'd brought along three healers—some of Kiran's veteran apprentices—to look after everyone. A good thing, too. While some of us were decidedly worse off than others, we had all taken hits and needed stitching, salve, and bandaging.

Jaevid and Murdoc were, by far, the worst off. But thanks to Maylea's efforts, her father was at least on his feet again. Er, well, one foot, anyway. He wasn't fully recovered, but he wasn't on the verge of taking his last breath anymore. Time would tell how he continued to recover. I had seen Paligno's power do some incredible things many times over, and Maylea had really pushed herself. She had been unconscious and bleeding from the nose and ears when we took her out of that temple. That Broadfeather stubbornness knew no bounds, however, and she had been back on her feet trying to act like she hadn't just nearly killed herself using that much power.

Until her father commanded her to lie down and let the healers check her, however. A few sips of chaserroot tea and she was out like a candle in the wind. Good thing, too, because Lukani had come in not long after, ashen-faced and weaving on his feet again from using so much of his own power. If she had seen him like that, I had no doubt she would have insisted on fretting at his bedside rather than getting actual rest.

In a similar fashion, I was ordered to sit down and be a good patient.

I ... was not.

Fiiine, maybe I did have a small problem letting go of control when it came to things like this. But I wanted to know my friends and allies were getting the best care possible. And since several of us had practically been at death's door less than an hour ago, I wasn't taking any chances.

Eventually, the atmosphere aboard the ship began to calm—likely due to the offer of the first hot meal any of us had eaten in days. Hard to argue with a good meal and some decent sleep. Not even I could resist that. The instant my body sank into the cot, my stomach full and a hefty dose of pain remedies soothing every aching muscle, I didn't stand a chance. I slept like the dead, and didn't stir until late that night—and that was only because of Violet.

When I tried to roll over, I found a petite white-haired woman had successfully snuck her way into my bed and curled up right beside me. I smiled and leaned down, pressing my lips against her cheek as she breathed slowly in her sleep. It made her nose twitch a little, but she didn't wake up. I guess they'd given her some of that medicinal tea as well. Her injuries had been less worrisome, but she had one of her arms wrapped in gauze from her forearm to her bicep. She had small cuts and nicks all over her body, and dark bruises forming along her collarbone and around one of her cheeks.

It didn't matter, though. She was still the most beautiful thing I'd ever seen.

I did my best not to jostle her or shake the cot too much as I sat up on the other side and put my bare feet on the smooth wooden floor. Leaning forward, I let my elbows rest on my knees as I stared around the ship's medical bay. The long room was lined with ten cots on each side, and most of them were occupied. Jae, Maylea, Lukani, Noa, Roxus, Garnett, and several Rajinna I didn't know were sleeping soundly. One bed, off to itself, had a body lying in it that was completely covered by a clean white sheet.

Arlan the Kinslayer's body.

The question of what to do with him still hung in the air. Did we bury him in Maldobar? Did we have a funeral? What about his numerous residences and sprawling business?

All questions no one had any answers to right now.

At the far end of the room, a young healer in long gray robes sat, nodding off at his desk that was now crowded with injury reports and records. The lantern hanging over his head rocked gently back and forth, making the shadows in the room shift.

Save for one.

He stood on the far wall, his arms crossed inside the bell-sleeves of his baggy black robes, and stared right at me with those ghostly white eyes. Noh tipped his head to the side, motioning toward the door like he wanted me to go outside.

I frowned. Great. I knew exactly what this was about.

Biting hard against a pained groan, I managed to get up and make my way there without making much noise. I snagged my cloak off the row of hooks at the door and wrapped it around my shoulders, since I was only wearing light cotton breeches and a nightshirt. My teeth chattered as the cool ocean breeze hit my face and tousled through my hair.

Noh was already waiting outside, now holding his tall shepherd's staff in one hand, and watching my every move with a grim, appraising frown on his face. I wondered if that's how I normally looked when I stared at people—like I was on the verge of throwing punches. We did share the same face after all. Hmm. I'd have to work on that.

Neither of us spoke as I paced slowly around the bow area, feeling the weight of a certain item tucked away in my cloak's pocket like a block of solid ice. I'd known from the moment my fingers touched it, eventually, I had to do something with it. I had made a deal after all. So far, no one seemed the wiser about my having picked it up. That was probably for the best.

I didn't trust anyone else to carry the Blade of Souls.

Once we were far enough away from all the soldiers keeping watch that I was sure no one would overhear, I stopped right at the ship's forecastle deck. There, I could lean against its higher railing. Noh stood directly across from me, still watching me silently. Around us, the dark ocean seemed calm. Gentle waves rocked the huge vessel slightly, and a veil of clouds offered enough cover to the waning moon.

"I appreciate your help," I said finally, not liking that heavy silence between us.

"It was interesting to be at your side once again, brother," he replied, and I couldn't tell if that was a compliment or an insult. At least, not until he clarified. *"You have changed much over the years. You are more cautious. More conscious of those around you."*

"You could say I finally grew up," I chuckled dryly.

He smirked and looked away, out across the ocean. *"You did not need my help as much as before. It is a bittersweet thing, to no longer be needed. I had never considered I might actually miss that boyish ignorance of yours."*

Ahhh. So that's why he was being weird. It must've been strange for him—especially given how often I had borrowed his strength the last time we had walked this earth together.

I shrugged, trying to play it off like I hadn't noticed that hint of sorrow in his tone. "Eh, what can I say? You save the world a few times and you're bound to pick up a few tricks."

He nodded slightly. *"And more than a few friends."*

I narrowed my eyes a little. Was that ... a tinge of jealousy I heard now? Nooo. Surely not. Noh was now an immortal spirit, a guardian of a whole divine realm. He couldn't possibly envy my scrambling, bumbling mortal existence, right?

"Regardless, you know what must be done now," he said, standing a little straighter as he changed the subject.

Right.

Reaching into my cloak, I took out the heavy black metal dagger and held it up to the faint glow of the moonlight seeping through the veil of clouds. At twelve inches from hilt to tip, the weapon shimmered with a wicked beauty. The hilt and blade were incredibly intricate, engraved with spiraling scrollwork and the shapes of skulls, bones, and runes like the ones that still covered my hands. The pommel was the strangest, however. It featured a void, like a keyhole, in an oval shape I knew right away. That was the same shape as the pendant Jaevid and Maylea had worn. The lapiloque's pendant.

Was that how it was meant to work, then? Had Sadeera intended to lock that pendant into place and insert it into that sundial-shaped mechanism on the Gate of Proleus in order to open it? I didn't know, and I'd never been more pleased that no one would ever find out.

"I take it this will seal our bargain?" I asked as I turned the weapon over, inspecting the other side.

"It will," Noh verified. *"Upon its return, she will lift the mantle of your power and relieve your nephew of his curse. All will be as it should be."*

"Just like that, huh?" I arched an eyebrow dubiously.

His expression stayed grim as he held out a hand for it. *"Just like that,"* he repeated.

I took in a deep breath and slowly let it out. No point in putting this off for one more second, then. Holding his eerie, silver-eyed stare, I placed the Blade of Souls into Noh's palm and took a step back to lean against the railing again.

His straight, tense posture relaxed some, almost like he'd been braced for the worst. Had he expected me to refuse? To want to keep that thing for myself? Gods, I'd rather jump off this ship and take my chances with the drakkons.

A strange, resigned smile curved over his lips as he slowly closed his hand around the weapon and it began to dissolve away into a fine black mist. In a matter of seconds, it was gone—apparently straight back to the possession of the one who had created it.

A queasy chill raced up my spine, making my pulse skip. I looked down at the strange, runic black markings on my hands and forearms—the last traces of Clysiros's dark blessing. A relieved smile spread over my face. I'd never been so happy to see them steadily fading away. They could take every bit of pain, regret, shame, and uncertainty I'd carried right along with them.

It really was over.

"I am ... very proud of you, brother," Noh said suddenly, still watching me as though quietly mystified. *"I wish you all the best."*

I stretched a hand toward him to shake. "Don't say it like that, idiot," I teased. "Good-byes for us are always temporary, right?"

He smirked and gripped my hand with his bitter-cold palm. *"Naturally."*

"Then let's just call this 'until next time.' Sound good?"

His snicker was devious, even if the outline of his shadowy form was already beginning to fade away like fog at sunrise. *"Until then, dear brother. Try to stay out of trouble, if you can."*

45

CHAPTER FORTY-FIVE

I stayed on the forecastle deck, watching the sun begin to rise over the far horizon, as my thoughts circled back over everything that had happened. I must have stood that way for hours, lost in my own head. I didn't even hear Jaevid approaching until he spoke right behind me and nearly made me jump overboard in surprise.

"I figured I would find you out here," he said.

I gripped the rail and did some panicked wheezing for a few seconds, then finally turned to find him standing there, leaning against a wooden crutch. His injured leg was wrapped entirely in gauze and a thin layer of clay-plaster from his ankle all the way to his thigh, and he wobbled some whenever the ship rocked in the waves.

Ugh. Idiot. If he fell out here he wouldn't be able to get back up on his own. He'd just have to lay there until a deck hand or soldier found him and propped him back up—like a toppled mannequin. Ridiculous.

"You look tired." His lips pursed thoughtfully, like he was trying to figure out why I'd come out here on my own.

"I'm not," I sighed. "This is just my face now."

That got a chuckle out of him as he hobbled the rest of the way over to stand next to me. With a small grunt of discomfort, he eased his weight off that crutch and hung onto the railing for balance instead.

"What's the verdict on that leg?" I dared to ask.

He stared down at it, a small scowl of concern making that scar over one of his eyes crinkle. "Maylea was able to heal the internal injuries to my hips, pelvis, and organs. But one doesn't take the hit from a crash at that height and expect to walk away completely unscathed. They believe the fracture to my femur is in the advanced stages of healing, but my knee ... may never be the same."

Oh. Well, based on what I had seen of his injuries before Maylea tried healing him, that was understandable. Knee injuries were always complicated, painful, and slow healing. I guess that was why they were letting him get up and move around—he needed to keep the blood flowing.

"She feels bad about it." Jae laughed, like that was a terrible joke. "Maylea thinks she should have been able to heal me completely. Fates, that girl ..."

"She gets it honest," I reminded him.

He made a face with his lips pursed and his eyes squinted up and shrugged. "Yes. I suppose she does. But I'm not altogether sad about it—the leg, I mean."

I arched an eyebrow. "Oh? What's there to be sad about?"

"If I'm unable to take the saddle again, that would mean it's finally time to retire," he replied, something softly pleased in his tone.

My jaw dropped. Seriously? Jae was considering *retirement?* From dragonriding?

"And who'd take your place as Academy Commander?" I asked, almost not wanting to know the answer. Surely, he wouldn't pass that burden over to me. I mean, yes, I might be one of the logical choices for it. I had no family or kids of my own to distract me from my duties.

But I did *not* want that.

"Fortunately, that's not a decision I get to make. I can submit my suggestions, of course, but your sister will be the one to choose," he said. "And it's not something anyone has to worry about right now."

True. "I need to thank you, Jae," I murmured, unable to pry my gaze away from the water far below. "If you guys hadn't come, I ... I know we wouldn't have been able to pull this off. I would have failed and put the entire world in danger."

"I don't believe that for a single second," he countered. "We didn't come here because we assumed you would fail, we came because when one part of our family is threatened, we all rise to meet that threat together. This was never meant to be your responsibility alone, Reigh. It concerned all of us. It *required* all of us. And the gods knew that when they chose each of us to fight in their names."

Crap. I hated when he gave speeches like that—usually because he was right. Hanging my head some, I rubbed at my jaw while I mulled it over. He made a good point. I just hated feeling like I had let everyone down. I had volunteered because I wanted to keep him from being the one to shoulder the burdens of a world on fire once again. But here we were, standing in the ashes, just like the good 'ole days.

A hand clapped on my shoulder, squeezing firmly and giving me a little shake. "You did well. You kept my daughter safe. I know for a fact that's no small feat. I'll forever be grateful for it."

I winced and pinched my eyes shut, half expecting him to follow that up with a swift right-hook to my jaw. "Gods, Jae, I swear that by the time I knew she was even on that ship, we were already—"

He just laughed and shook his head. "I know, I know. Save your breath, I know how my daughter can be. Trust me."

I slumped down, basically hanging over the rail like a soggy towel in relief. He wasn't going to kill me. Thank the gods for that. "I think she's aged me twenty years," I groaned.

"Kids have that effect," he agreed. "But ... they have a strange way of making you feel young again, too. It's a mad mix. You'll see."

I'd see? What was that supposed to mean? I wasn't on the verge of parenthood, and probably wouldn't be any time soon. Fates, if this little venture was any indication, I was *not* cut out for actual fatherhood.

I stayed that way, choking and sputtering on my own shock for several minutes, until Jae tapped on my shoulder again—this time like he wanted to get my attention.

"What's that?" He pointed southward, back over the rising dark mountains that stood along the coast. Back in the direction we had come from our battle.

My stomach dropped. All the feeling drained out of my body in one shivering rush. Even if they only looked like a cluster of thousands of shining diamonds in the first light of the dawn, I knew what they were.

The Avoran knights were headed straight for us.

WE DIDN'T HAVE TIME TO PREPARE FOR THEIR ARRIVAL. THEY FLEW LIKE A LIVING meteor shower, so fast and completely silent. We barely had time to raise the alarm aboard our own ship, let alone alert the others anchored nearby, before they were upon us.

Jenna burst out of her chambers in a long, silken nightgown and fur-trimmed cloak, sword in hand and long golden hair utterly wild. She shouted to her men to be at the ready, and marched straight up onto the quarterdeck without hesitation.

Soldiers scrambled in every direction, racing to arms and heading below deck to bring the airship's engines back to life. Pumps blasted air heated with burning dragon venom into that big, round balloon-shaped container that stretched the length of the whole ship, making us steadily begin to rise away from the water.

There would be no fleeing, though. We couldn't possibly outrun them, even in the air. But we could at least be ready to stand our ground, if it came to that.

Fear hung thick in the air as the Avoran knights encircled us, soaring effortlessly on powerful, swan-like wings, but keeping a cautious distance. Jenna called down orders, demanding everyone hold their positions and not fire upon them. If this was going to be a fight, it would be a short one, and we weren't going to be the ones provoking it.

Jae and I made our way to the quarterdeck, as well, joining Jenna, Ronan, Isandri, and Ziryan as three of those angelic beings finally swooped down low to land in the middle of our ship's main deck. Our soldiers scrambled away from them, staring in slack jawed awe as the figures stood tall and silent, their hair like flawless bolts of silk and their eyes as bright as molten gold. All three wore circlets on their heads of the same silver as the beautifully ornate armor they wore.

The one in the center, however, was obviously a leader of some sort. His circlet was encrusted with glittering slivers of diamond, and he wore a one-shouldered cape of deep red. The curved scimitar at his hip had an eagle's head on the pommel with a huge ruby, and his breastplate was emblazoned with the symbol of a winged lion.

He moved with a smooth, effortless grace as he strode forward, making his way toward the quarterdeck to meet us. His two followers weren't far behind, and they kept one hand on the swords belted to their hips. With his ancient gaze crackling with power, and his tall, muscular frame standing well over six feet, the leader of the Avoran knights gave a subtle gesture to his men, leaving them at the bottom of the stairs to approach our group alone. He ascended slowly, the tips of his large, graceful wings brushing the ground behind him.

I had to give my sister credit. When that man stopped before her, looming like a young god with every inch of him flawless and shining with radiant power, she didn't even flinch. Still gripping her sword in one hand, she stood straight and firm, staring up at him with her expression locked into a look of expectation.

"You are Queen of Maldobar?" the Avoran knight asked, his deep, rich tone and accent reminding me a lot of Arlan.

"I am," she verified. "And you are?"

"Levauran of House Cirithal. I come on order from the High King, who has seen the plight caused by our kinsmen in your lowland realm. His order brought us to correct this mistake, and to return the remains of Zarvan to be suitably entombed in the halls of his ancestors, for his exile was unjust and his name must be restored." He panned that otherworldly gaze over all of us, pausing on Ziryan for an instant and almost seeming surprised. Then again, I supposed of us all, the Rajinna were the closest to being some sort of relation to the Avorans. They were both ancient species. Maybe he hadn't expected to see them here, fighting in the dirt right along with us mere mortals.

"I see," Jenna replied quickly and handed her blade off to Ronan. "We welcome you, then. And we are grateful for your assistance. The man you seek is indeed here, although we have known him by a different name. In the lowlands, he called himself Arlan. If you wish, we can have his body prepared for transport."

"That would be acceptable," Levauran agreed.

"Give us a moment, then." Jenna gave her first mate a nod, and the man left the ship's wheel and sped past us on his way down below deck.

"I beg your pardon, but how is it you came to hear of our situation here?" Isandri asked suddenly, her expression no more intimidated than when she'd first met the rest of us. I guess she didn't find these angelic elves all that impressive.

Levauran considered her, his brow furrowing some as though something about her confused him. Maybe he was having a hard time placing what, exactly, she was. Godlings—what can you do?

"Avgior descended from on high and imparted this information to us," he explained, his tone as calm and even as though he might as well be talking about the fine weather we were having this morning.

"Avgior?" Isandri frowned, blinking in confusion. "You mean ... Clarke?"

He nodded once.

Huh? What were they talking about? Who the heck was Clarke?

"He is well, then?" Isandri questioned.

"He has been returned to the lowland city of Lahn'Sirr. He claimed to have further business with the Emperor of Nar'Haleen."

You could have knocked every single one of us over with a hard look. I didn't even know who this Clarke guy was, but the mere idea of going to face down the Emperor of Nar'Haleen personally was ... unfathomable. Gods, help him, Clarke was either insanely brave or bravely insane.

"I believe I will go and assist him, then," Isandri decided aloud. "It has come to my attention that the Hall of Holies lacks proper management and is in dire need of sanctification."

Levauran seemed to approve, although it was honestly hard to tell. He didn't seem to have much range of expression and stared straight back at her without even blinking. "A worthy cause," he commented.

The stir of commotion on the main deck below made everyone turn. We watched in collective silence as the other two Avoran knights carried a body wrapped in several clean white sheets out of the medical bay below deck. A few of our other friends followed a few paces behind them, staring in awe at our unexpected guests.

Violet, in particular, looked a breath away from fainting as she snapped a wide-eyed stare up at me and mouthed the words, "What is happening?"

Yeeeah, we'd have to wait and discuss that a little later.

"The High King sends his thanks for your service," Levauran said as though it were farewell. He bent in a swift, smooth bow to my sister before turning to begin walking back down toward the rest of his men.

"Sir, one ... one last question," Jaevid blurted suddenly.

We all stared at him, half in mortification and half in awe that he'd actually dared to interrupt this whole procession. Typical Jae.

Levauran paused, turning just enough to glance at Jae over one of his shoulders. "Yes?"

"We were told that Avorans who depart their homeland are unable to return. That leaving would mean eternal severance from its divine power and that, for you, is essentially a death sentence." Jae frowned, his pale eyes flicking between the Avoran knights on the deck below.

"It is," Levauran replied.

"Then ... all of the men you've brought with you ..." Jae's voice faded to silence, as though he was having a difficult time wrapping his mind around that.

Levauran must have been able to sense his confusion. He bowed his head slightly, his flawlessly handsome features finally crinkling with the slightest look of sorrow. "We will perish as mortals and never see the halls of our kin again," he confirmed in a solemn tone.

"And yet you came?" Jenna gasped in disbelief.

He turned away again, looking toward the two knights who took to the air carrying Arlan's body between them. "This was a misjustice caused by House Cirithal, so it falls to us to correct it, no matter what the cost. We will gladly perish to restore our house to honor."

No one said another word as he left, taking flight and rejoining all the other Avoran knights still circling in the air. They flew up higher, streaking across the dawn skyline and heading to the north. In a few short minutes, every trace of them was gone, leaving us all standing there frozen in awed silence.

Gods and Fates. I definitely hadn't seen that coming.

"I meant what I said." Isandri was the first to speak again. "I must go to Lahn'Siir and assist Clarke however I can. And you must let Noa know he is still alive. There is still much work to be done here, much to repair that has been badly broken."

"We will definitely let him know," Jaevid agreed. "You should take Edarix with you. I'm certain he would like to assist. He did mention he had been living there for quite some time."

Isandri bobbed her head, finally glancing my way with a soft, apologetic smile. "I will return to Maldobar as soon as I can, my friends."

I stepped closer, pulling her into a hug with an arm around her neck. "Do what you have to do, Isa. And let us know if there's anything we can do to help."

She squeezed me back and puffed a deep sigh. "Take care of yourselves."

"Same to you." I pulled away and smirked, knowing full well that no matter what face I tried to make, she would still be able to tell that watching her go wasn't something I enjoyed. I did understand, though. This was her chance to truly shine and do something to redeem her homeland. I wouldn't dare send her off with anything less than all my faith that she could do this.

Destiny certainly worked in funny ways, and hers had finally come to call.

46

CHAPTER FORTY-SIX

"So, what happens now?" Violet asked as she strolled over to join me standing at the ship's bow.

Over the last day and a half, I'd made a habit of sitting here and watching the sea roll by as we soared several hundred feet above it. I liked the smell of the ocean wind and the occasional taste of that salty spray in my mouth almost as much as I liked watching the dragons play around the airship like a flock of mischievous, giant, scaly gulls.

We were crossing the distance much faster than expected. If we kept up this pace, I had no doubts we would be arriving in Maldobar in a day, two at most. But, Gods, that still felt like an eternity. Sometimes, I could have sworn I could already see it like a mirage on the far horizon.

Hopefully, by tomorrow, it wouldn't just be a figment of my hopeful imagination.

"I believe we all get down on our knees around Phoebe and kiss her feet while singing praises to her for this masterful piece of engineering." I chuckled and patted the ship's wooden railing.

Violet giggled and gave me a poke with her elbow.

I knew that wasn't the answer she was looking for. She wanted to know what my personal plans were once we got back. I had been thinking about it, yes. But I wasn't sure. Not yet. There were still some things to be settled once we got home, and I had no illusions about getting to flop down on my rear and relax. I doubted she did, either. Violet, Garnett, and Roxus would have to figure out what happened with Arlan's very well-established business as an international crime lord. Between the three of them, though, I was sure they'd figure it out.

She leaned over to rest her head against my arm, taking one of my hands and lacing her fingers through mine. It still made my heart skip a few beats when she did that. I moved, drawing her in closer so my arm was around her and I could lean down against her back with my head resting on top of hers.

"Look at you two, chirping about up here like a couple of lovebirds, eh?" Garnett teased as she and Thatcher strolled over to join.

"You should have seen them before they finally confessed their feelings," Thatcher added, grinning wolfishly.

"I really am gonna hit you," I promised.

He just waggled his eyebrows suggestively. That jerk.

"I have every intention of going straight home and locking all my doors. None of you had better dare to visit until *after* the baby is born," Murdoc muttered, scowling like a cranky old dog as he shuffled stiffly to the railing as well. I guess his injuries still had him a little slow on the move. "I will let Blite chew on you for as long as he wants."

"You'll be glad for the visitors afterward," Jaevid added, wobbling along not far behind him with that crutch ."It's the only time you'll get any rest."

Murdoc's mouth pinched up, looking slightly concerned for a moment. It made Jae laugh and give a little, consoling punch in the arm.

"And what about you, eh?" I countered. "You won't be getting much rest, either. Fates, it's like a parade of babies around here now."

"Guess that means you'll have to get straight to work on your contribution when we get back, hm?" Jae fired back, his steel-blue eyes catching mine with a look that made my whole head burn like my hair was on fire.

I couldn't speak. Looking at Violet, she had her head bowed and her hair brushed deliberately forward over her shoulders so her own face was hidden. It didn't do anything to hide how red her ears were, though. Ugggh. Someone just throw me overboard already.

Standing all together at the bow of the airship, we watched as our flock of dragons circled and soared all around us. It was obvious that Phoebe had planned everything about this ship with dragonriders in mind. The main deck had ample space for two of them to rest from flying, and there was plenty of food stored to supplement their diet. They could definitely manage the journey a lot more comfortably than if we were trying to cram them below deck in a sea-bound ship.

Vexi seemed to be especially fixated on Maylea's new companion, and followed the much larger white dragon like a puppy toddling along after a much older dog that was completely disinterested in her existence. There was no doubt that he had chosen Maylea as his rider, and while he seemed to accept his lot as a member of our ragtag flock, there was no mistaking his tense reluctance to fly alongside the rest of the dragons. Ah, well, maybe he would in time. It was a big change for him from the state we had found him in. He had a lot to look forward to, even if that old white dragon didn't know it yet.

Mavrik kept his position of dominance at the front of their group, but chattered musically to the rest of them all the way. He led the older dragons through graceful arcing passes around us, his trumpeting cry setting off a chorus of answering roars from all the others. I couldn't hold back a smile as I watched them spiral upward, dipping through clouds before they zoomed back down and skimmed the waves with their strong wings stretched out wide to the brilliant sun.

The sight made my chest swell with a pride I'd never felt before. A sense of belonging that carried me all the way back to the shores of my home. We would be there soon, back where we belonged.

And, Gods and Fates, there was nowhere else in the world I'd rather be.

It didn't take long for all the playful dragon sounds to bring Maylea and Lukani over to see what we were all looking at. Despite the rest of his family remaining in Nar'Haleen, Lukani had kept his word and elected to stay with us. He'd promised to return to them to visit, but made no mention of when that might be. Somehow, I got the impression he wouldn't do it for ... approximately however long it took for Maylea to grow old and pass on.

But that was just a guess.

They held hands and exchanged hushed words as they stood nearby. Up to no good, as usual. Probably plotting their next daring act of mischief.

To my surprise, their obvious affection didn't seem to bother Jaevid all that much. I'd sort of been hoping for a little fatherly fury, but he hadn't even spoken to them about it. Not that I had witnessed. I decided to hold onto hope that he was just biding his time, waiting until he could get Lukani alone before he exacted his paternal wrath on him. Every now and then, I saw him glance at her with a quiet, knowing smile tugging at the corners of his mouth. Something about it seemed dim and shaded with sorrow, as though he were privately grieving that distance between him and his daughter.

I could understand why. Maylea had proven herself to be a lot more capable than any of us anticipated. She was growing up. Soon, she would leave him and the safety of their home completely behind her. That reality was probably bittersweet for any parent. But for all that subtle grief deepening the lines in the corners of his eyes, there was something else shining in them that gave me pause—because it was something I recognized.

Hope.

It was faint, but it was there. And in time, I knew it would grow—just like it had for all of us. That feeble hope for a better future would become something bigger, braver, and stronger with every passing day. Courage would embolden it. Patience would refine it. Love would guide it. That hope would become a fierce and mighty thing that rode with wings like a dragon, fearless, free, and ready to chase every star across the far horizon.

Because that's how all great stories in Maldobar began. With a little bit of hope ... and a dragon.

WOLF OF THE WASTES

A DRAGONRIDER SHORT STORY

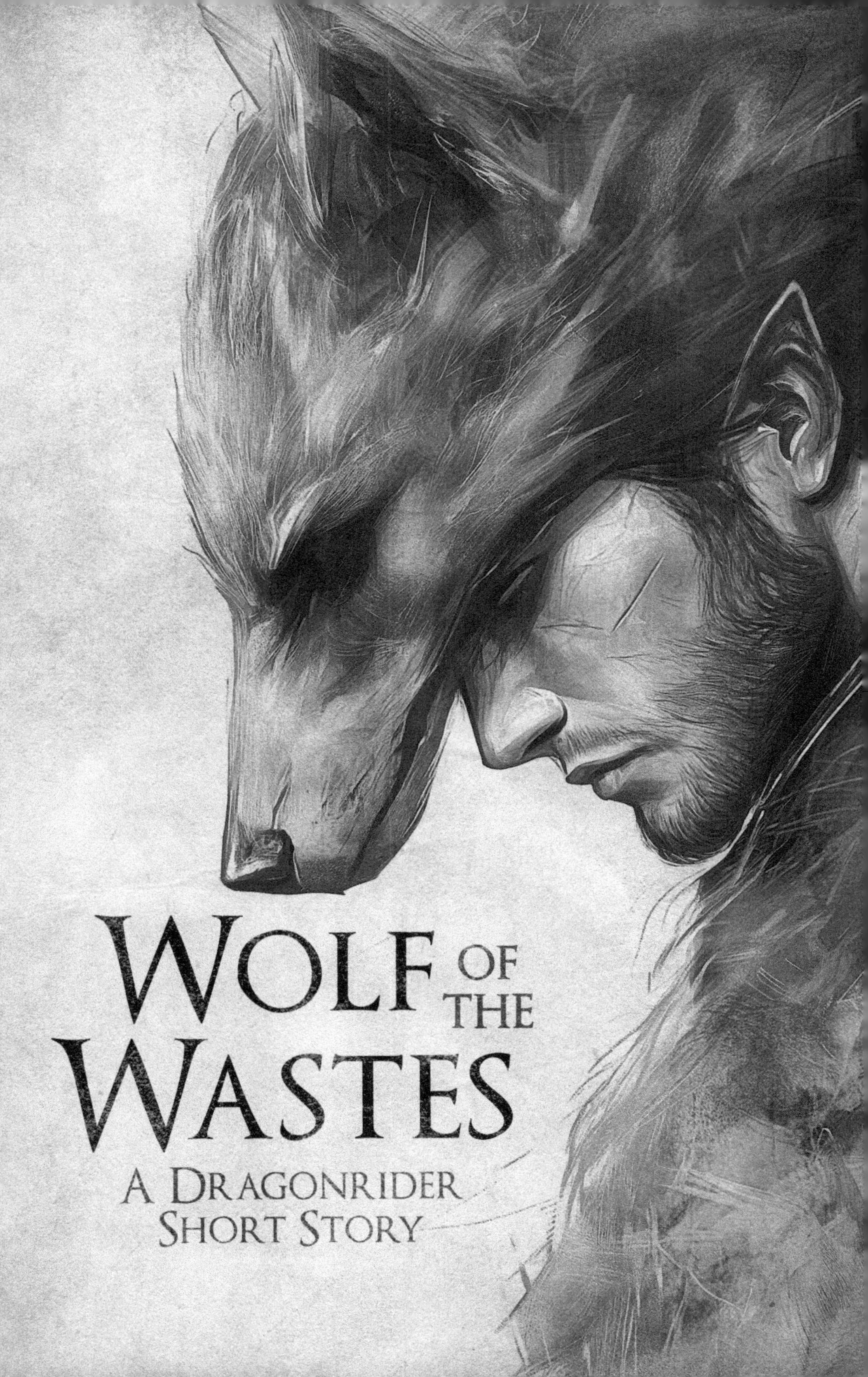
WOLF OF THE WASTES
A DRAGONRIDER SHORT STORY

I

THATCHER

BANG—BANG—BANG!

I bolted upright in bed, cold sweat already prickling on my skin. All the muscles in my body tensed as the pounding sound echoed through my suite again, coming from the main door in the next room. Sweet Fates, what was happening?

Was that coming from downstairs?

No. Closer.

The main door.

Someone was trying to get into my chambers.

My heart hammered as I flung the blankets off my legs and floundered for the shortsword I kept tucked under the edge of the bed.

"Urhm ... Thatch? What's going on?" Garnett asked groggily, sitting up on the other side of the bed and rubbing her face. Her eyes went wide as I prowled past, ripping the sword free of the sheath and starting out of the bedroom.

"Stay here," I whispered low.

She did—for about two seconds.

As I crossed the sitting area in my suite's main room, picking my way quietly through the furniture by the glow of the embers still smoldering in the hearth, she suddenly gripped my arm. My heart nearly jolted straight out of my chest as the pounding on the door sounded again, rattling it so hard the knob rattled.

We exchanged a wide-eyed glance, huddled close, wearing nothing but our nightclothes. Slowly, Garnett shook her head in silent warning. This wasn't right.

My mind whirled. It had only been a few weeks since we'd returned from the Southern Kingdoms. Hardly a month. Had something else happened?

Gods, I hadn't even been back at the Cromwell estate for two days. Those of us who had worked the mission in the Southern Kingdoms had all wanted to keep a low profile for a while after everything that happened in Nar'Haleen. Give ourselves time to rest. To process. To decompress. So, only a few people even knew I was here at all.

Murdoc knew, of course. Phoebe, Queen Jenna, Jaevid, Maylea, Ronan, Roxus, Violet, and ...

"OPEN UP, THATCHER!" Reigh's voice roared from the other side of the door.

I rushed to unlock it.

Disheveled and breathless, Reigh stood on the other side of the door with his long blue dragonrider cloak thrown over what looked a lot like his nightshirt and breeches. Well, we had that in common, I guess. Neither one of us had planned to be up at this gods-forsaken hour.

But what was he doing here? How had he even gotten into the Cromwell house in the first place?

One glance past him, to where the pasty, flustered housekeeper who managed Ezran Cromwell's estate was storming toward us down the hall, made it easy to guess.

Dressed in a long robe with her hair still tied up in a silk bonnet, the housekeeper's eyes were wild with a mixture of worry and rage. She glared at the back of Reigh's sleep-tousled hair like she might like to start ripping fistfuls of it out. He must have barreled right past her when she opened the front door.

Typical.

"What's wrong? It's the middle of the night. Did you ride all the way here from Halfax?" I asked as I stepped aside, making way for him to enter. I gave the housekeeper a weary smile, mouthing an apology as I shut the door again.

"She's gone," he blurted as soon as the door was closed.

"What?" I swapped another dubious, confused glance with Garnett. "Who?"

Reigh lurched for the nearest sofa and poured himself onto it, sitting with his head in his hands as he mumbled, "Violet. She disappeared. I can't find her anywhere. I ... I didn't know what else to do. I-I thought Garnett might ..."

His voice trailed off, halting as though he were fighting back sobs.

"Oh, darlin'," Garnett crooned as she went over to sit next to him. "She didn't say anything? No strange behavior beforehand?"

Reigh looked up through his fingers, still rubbing at his face as he spoke. "No. I mean, sort of. We were both rattled after everything that happened in Nar'Haleen. I'm sure all of us are. But things were good. We were good. Or, at least, I thought we were."

"You've been staying in that townhouse together, right? The one in Halfax? When did she go missing?" I asked. I slipped my sword back into its sheath and set it on the coffee table before I sank down into a chair across from him.

Reigh nodded. "I thought she'd like it—having our own place. And she was still getting acquainted with her new role. You know, taking over Arlan's affairs. It was a lot, but she seemed to be on top of things. She wrote letters constantly. She was stressed, but I thought everything was fine. Then day before yesterday, I came home from a meeting with Jenna at the castle, and she was just ... gone."

Garnett and I swapped another wary look. She'd been gone that long already? Fates, she could be anywhere by now.

"I've looked everywhere. Asked everyone we know. She disappeared and ... gods." He slumped forward again, hiding his face in his palms as he let out a faint, agonized groan through his teeth. "Was it something I did? Gods, did I say something wrong?"

Garnett put a hand on his back, petting him soothingly. "Now, now. I've seen you lot together. She's smitten with you. And she's nothing if not capable. I'm sure wherever she is, she's more than safe."

She said that, and I had no trouble believing it ... but there was no mistaking the flicker of unease in Garnett's expression as she looked to me again. She was worried, too.

Yes, Violet was capable. Yes, she could hold her own as well as any seasoned dragonrider. But Arlan the Kinslayer had been a criminal lord. It was possible she'd been called away to handle something from his past that she might not be able to take on by herself. And if she hadn't even bothered letting Garnett know?

It didn't exactly fill me with fluttering reassurance.

"Have you tried reaching out to anyone else from Arlan's network? Roxus knows her far better than I do," Garnett hinted, her tone careful. She probably didn't want to let on to how concerned she really was.

"I tried," Reigh answered. "But he's every bit as slippery as Arlan was when it comes to giving a straight answer. I tracked him down to a tavern in Southwatch yesterday, but he brushed me off. He said to let her take care of her own business. That she'd come back when she was ready. Gods... what does that even mean?"

I gnawed at the inside of my cheek. Fates, I couldn't blame him for being so frustrated ... or desperate. Their relationship was still new. I'd watched it develop while we were forging our path through the Southern Kingdoms—her homeland.

I had to wonder if that might have something to do with it. If being there, back in her home country, had dredged up some things from her past. Something worse than what seemed like a long-stale feud with the Zenith's Call—whoever or whatever they actually were.

I still didn't quite understand what the Zenith's Call did. Clearly, she had a history with them, though, and not all of it was good.

Could that have followed her all the way back here?

"What if she's hurt? What if things got out of hand and someone kidnapped her? Holding her hostage somewhere? Or blackmailing her into doing something? She's supposed to be in charge of Arlan's entire network, but even he never moved or acted alone. He *always* took backup. He *always* had reinforcements waiting in case something went wrong. Gods ... I-I don't know what to do," Reigh said, his voice tight and seething with what looked like anger.

I knew better, though. He wasn't angry with Violet.

He was terrified and angry with himself. For not seeing the signs. For not realizing things weren't right with her. For not being there now, when she might need his help.

I swallowed hard. "We find her—that's what we do."

Reigh looked up again, his expression drawn in anguish. "How?"

"By looking." I shrugged. "We have our own resources. If Roxus won't help, then we will."

Garnett gave his shoulder a squeeze and gentle shake. "He's right, love. This can't have come from nowhere. There'll be signs somewhere. We'll find them. And we'll find her, I promise you that. Give me some time. I have access to a lot of the same connections she does. Someone will know something. And if they don't, I'll beat Roxus black and blue until he spills what he knows. Curse him, he ought to know better than to play such a game."

"In the meantime, you should go back to Halfax, just in case she returns. We'll come to you when we learn something," I promised. "Stay the night here, and fly back in the morning, yeah?"

Reigh nodded, his chest heaving with a deep breath of resignation. Maybe the first he'd taken since he discovered she was gone.

"I'll go see that Vexi gets settled into one of the barns." I stood and went to retrieve my boots and cloak from the bedroom.

"Thank you," he murmured, his voice thin with exhaustion and his expression utterly broken.

I paused in the doorway. "You don't have to thank us, Reigh. We're all family now. And we look after our own, right?"

His throat bobbed, and he nodded again.

"We'll sort this out, one way or another. You're not alone." I hesitated, meeting Garnett's gaze again.

She still looked uneasy, her mouth twisted to one side, as she quickly looked away and her brow furrowed slightly. Whatever had happened to Violet, it couldn't be good. Now, we just had to pray we could track her down before it was too late.

2

REIGH

My world was utterly broken.

Standing in the doorway of our modest townhome in Halfax the next morning, all I could do was stare straight ahead, through the entryway foyer into the dim hall beyond. There was no sound. No movement except for the dust sparkling in the early dawn's glow through the windows.

She wasn't here. And it's like she had taken every trace of light and life with her.

Without Violet, this place might as well have been a tomb.

And I might as well be a shambling corpse.

I couldn't tear my eyes away from the empty peg on the wall where her cloak usually hung ... right next to mine. She'd taken it with her. She'd also taken her old haversack, packed with some of her clothes, and her weapons. She'd taken the time to prepare—did that mean she'd left willingly? I didn't know.

But that was all I'd been able to find missing.

It was enough.

Wherever she had gone, she had felt the need to arm herself. So it wasn't safe—at least, not entirely. And taking so many changes of her clothes meant she planned to be gone for a while.

She hadn't taken all of her toiletries, though. Violet had left her favorite perfume on our dresser and her rouge and kohl at her dressing table. She hadn't taken any food or even one of my emergency healer's kits. That meant she intended to come back, right?

I didn't know.

Gods and Fates, I didn't know *anything*.

My legs buckled. I hit the floor on my knees, wheezing and grasping at my chest. My lungs seemed to close up entirely. My vision spotted.

Why?

Why had she left me?

Had I done something wrong? Said something I shouldn't? Put too much pressure on her to settle down here, with me? Or had my title gotten to her the same way it had Enyo? Had she realized she didn't want any of this? That she didn't want me?

Or was something else wrong and she just didn't trust me enough to confide in me about it? Was this all just some kind of sick game? Or was it something worse?

Was someone after her? Was she caught up in a bad situation because of Arlan's criminal network and felt she had no choice but to flee? That would explain why she didn't say anything to me—because she had to know that I would follow her to the very bottom of the abyss if it meant we stayed together. For her, no risk was too great. No favor was too much to ask. No secret was so terrible that I wouldn't stay at her side.

Leaning against the wall, I fought to control my breathing. In and out. Deep and slow.

Now wasn't the time to lose it.

Violet needed me. I would find her, even if it meant searching every single household throughout this entire kingdom.

My ears rang as I forced myself to stand. Garnett had promised to do her own digging. I trusted her. She had known Violet a lot longer—had worked with her a lot in the past. If anyone could find her, it was Garnett. That's the whole reason I'd gone to them in the first place.

Now, I just had to wait.

And not go completely insane.

NOTHING.

I had turned over every inch of our house. I'd been through every drawer. Every bag. Every pocket. The pages of my medical books. The stacks of letters she'd been receiving from various informants. I'd even gone through Vexi's saddlebags in case Violet had decided to tuck a letter into them for me to discover later.

But after two more days of relentless searching, there was absolutely nothing that would have suggested she was on the verge of abandoning me and our entire life together.

I couldn't decide if that was better or worse.

I'd bought her a shrike for her own personal use right after we returned. Nothing too high-spirited, but it would get her around swiftly if she needed it while I was away with Vexi. The silvery-scaled beast was housed at the royal stable, and I'd found it still snoozing away in its stall when I went to check. No one at the stable had seen Violet come by, either.

Wherever she had gone, she hadn't flown there.

I tried to tell myself that wasn't surprising. Violet wasn't as fond of flying. She had ridden shrikes in the past, yes, but only out of necessity. She preferred to keep her feet on the ground.

But tracking her over land, when she knew exactly how to disappear into cities like mist at sunrise, would be nearly impossible. If she didn't want to be found ... she wouldn't be.

Sitting in the middle of the floor in our shared study, I stared at the sea of her papers spread out on every flat surface. Both desks. The floor. A lot of it was written in languages I couldn't understand. That, or what seemed to be a complex code I couldn't even begin to unravel.

I had nothing. No clues. No hope.

No idea if she would ever come back.

I'd sworn to myself I would never meddle in her affairs. Violet had taken on the mantle of Arlan's network, and I had decided right then and there that I wouldn't stand in her way. She'd been very obviously honored by that responsibility, and I would never ask her to give up something important to her.

But I also couldn't get too involved. I was a recognizable figure even without the stupid prince thing. You didn't work alongside Jaevid Broadfeather and not get recognized. I would draw unwanted attention if I injected myself into her business.

Now ... I sort of wished I had.

Just a little, so that maybe I might notice if something was going horribly wrong. Wrong enough that she felt like she had to disappear.

"Reigh?"

My heart nearly launched straight out of my chest as a soft, feminine voice called from downstairs.

I floundered to my feet, sprinting from the office and barely managing to scramble around the corner to the stairwell. I bounced off the walls as I went, finally grabbing onto the railing and taking the steps two and three at a time on my way down.

"VIOLET?" I yelled at the top of my lungs.

It wasn't her.

Standing in the front foyer, bathed in the midmorning sun, Garnett and Thatcher gaped at me with shared expressions of horrified surprise.

"Sorry, we ... you didn't answer, so we let ourselves in," Thatcher rambled, his gaze tracking over me from head to foot. Drinking in every ragged detail. "You, uh, you're still in your bedclothes, I see. Are those the same ones from before?"

I glared at him. "What do you think?"

"Going by the smell, I'd say yes," Garnett quipped. "Stones, man. Pull yourself together. Go and have a bath, a shave, and put on some proper clothes. I'll put some supper on—providing you've got anything decent in your larder—and we'll have a chat about what I've found."

What she had *found?*

"You ... you have information?" I could hardly draw in a breath.

"I do. But it's complicated. Hurry on, now. You look like a proper wreck," she scolded gently as she brushed past me on her way inside. "Nice place here, by the way. I can see why you prefer it to the castle. Quieter, I imagine. Much more private."

"We'll just, uh, wait in the kitchen," Thatcher mumbled as he followed her, casting me a long-suffering look of apology on his way by.

I glared after them, my temper already at its boiling point.

They had information on where Violet was ... and they expected me to give a flying crap about how I looked?!

Anger rattled in my chest like a dragon's deep growl. My eyes stung as I swallowed all the furious words I wanted to snarl at them. It wouldn't help. Thatcher might cave if I threw a fit. But Garnett wouldn't. She didn't scare easy.

But this was Violet. *My* Violet.

"Just ... please," I begged, taking a lurching step after them and catching myself against the wall as all the strength seemed to drain from my body at once. "Please tell me if she's alive or not. I-I can't ..."

My voice caught, tangling in my throat.

They both stopped. Thatcher turned back, his expression drawn with empathy. He gave me a weak smile and nodded slightly. "She is."

A sound broke past my lips—something like a sob, a wheezing gasp, and a broken wail.

Alive. She was alive.

That was something.

No—it was everything.

"Go and get cleaned up," Thatcher coaxed, bowing his head slightly. "We'll talk over dinner. I promise, this is something you'll want to consider carefully. And regardless of what you decide, Garnett and I will have your back."

MY STOMACH LET OUT A FIERCE, ANGRY GROWL—GIVING ME AWAY IMMEDIATELY AS I hedged into the kitchen.

The smell of toasted bread and some sort of meat and vegetable stew was enough to make my knees go weak and my vision swerve. Garnett stood on a stool at my stove, stirring a pot that sent up curling plumes of delicious steam into the air.

They both turned and stared at me. Thatcher's shoulders relaxed some, and his mouth tugged at a weary smile. Garnett gave an approving nod and went back to stirring the pot.

"Now, then. You look less like a drunken street bum," she said as she spooned a portion of the stew into a bowl. "Have a seat. I found some potatoes, carrots, onions, and a bit of dried ham. It won't be a feast, but it'll put some color back in your cheeks."

I eased down into the chair next to Thatch, adjusting the collar of my tunic. I'd opted for my dragonrider's uniform, not knowing where we might be going or what we might be doing. If this meant delving into nefarious territory, better to flex a little. Let them know who they're dealing with.

"Now, then," Garnett puffed as she sat down across from me with two more bowls—one for her and one for Thatcher. "Let's have a chat, shall we?"

I nodded, spooning some of the stew into my mouth. The rich flavors warmed my throat all the way down to the center of my chest. Fates, she was a good cook. It was a miracle Thatcher could still fit in any of his uniforms, especially given how much he loved food.

"I sent out word through some of my old contacts," she began to explain. "Folks we used to work with who have since scattered to the four winds. They were hesitant to speak up. Not surprising, given our line of work. But a few of them were sympathetic. They claimed to have seen her passing through Mithangol, heading west through the mountain trails."

I almost dropped my spoon.

What? She was going westward? Why?

"She's made stops in a few villages along the way, probably tossed a few farmers some coin to put her up for the night. We used to travel that way when we worked for Arlan. It keeps things discreet," she went on. "After putting a little pressure on Roxus, I managed to wring some truth out of him. He's stubborn and protective of her, you see. Stones, the man practically raised her."

I frowned. That crusty old bear had given me the brush-off. He'd flat-out refused to help me or tell me anything except that I needed to mind my own business.

But Violet *was* my business, now.

Curse him. I'd suspected he was holding out. I should have pushed him harder. I should have made him—

"Easy now." Garnett reached across the table to pat my hand soothingly. Only then did

I notice I was gripping my spoon like a weapon, squeezing it so tightly my knuckles went white and my whole arm shook.

"He has his reasons," Thatcher added, his tone quiet and careful. "Not good ones, in my opinion, but we can deal with him later."

I let out a shuddering exhale. Right. Later. Gods preserve me.

"He believes she is heading to Westwatch," Garnett said. "There are some folks there she has history with. One fellow in particular. They call him the Wolf of the Wastes. I couldn't find much else about him, but Roxus seemed to think that's who she was going to see."

She'd left to find another man?

Who? And why?

Knowing it was someone from her past—the same past that had haunted her all through the southern kingdoms—made my chest constrict with tight, prickling heat. My throat went dry, and I couldn't eat another bite.

Was this someone she'd been romantically involved with? Was that why she hadn't said anything to me about it? If it was just a former coworker with the Zenith's Call, surely she'd have told me about it, right? I wouldn't have cared if she wanted to touch base with some of those people, especially given what we'd just gone through.

"It's been four days. By now, she's less than a day from Westwatch. If we're smart about it, we can find her. We could even follow her, if you really want to see what she's up to," Garnett suggested. "The choice is yours, of course. But if we're going to do this, then we need to leave fairly soon."

Everything in my brain seemed to freeze solid as my thoughts whirled like I was caught in the middle of a blizzard. My pulse boomed in my ears, the only thing I could feel other than the faint scrape of my own breath.

We could go. We could leave right now for Westwatch. The flight would take Vexi roughly six hours—maybe a little longer since we'd be heading into the wind. But we could make it there by nightfall. We just had to leave.

Right. Now.

My heart gave a desperate lurch and seemed to drop to the pit of my stomach. I swallowed hard.

If we did follow her, what would I see? What would I discover that Violet apparently didn't want me to know about? Was this a violation of her trust?

I didn't know.

She hadn't said anything—had given me no clue she was leaving beforehand. She'd just disappeared like dew at sunrise. So it was only natural that I'd worry, right? That I'd be ready to tear the kingdom apart brick by brick to find her? Surely she realized that.

Gods, *I didn't know.*

And I needed to.

"Reigh?" Thatcher put a hand on my back.

I sucked in a sharp breath, like I'd just been grounded. The sounds of the room, the crackle of the flames in the stove, and the scrape of Garnett's spoon stirring her own bowl of stew hit me with sudden force.

"I don't know what to do," I confessed, my voice shaking. "I don't know what's right."

He held my gaze as I looked to him, searching every corner of his expression for some indication of approval or disappointment. There wasn't any. Only sympathy. Only understanding.

"Sometimes there are no right choices," he replied quietly. "There's just ... taking steps and seeing where it leads."

"Ask yourself—if she comes back tomorrow, will not knowing the truth haunt you?" Garnett asked.

I had to sit on that question for a few minutes, listening to the ringing in my ears and the ragged scrape of my breathing. Would I ever be able to look at her without wondering? Without picturing her with someone else doing ... whatever they planned on doing?

No. No—I trusted Violet. She wouldn't run to the arms of another man like that. She'd taken weapons, and you didn't take blades to visit a long-lost lover, right? This was something else.

"I need to know," I said at last.

"Then finish your stew." She motioned to my bowl with her spoon. "We'll leave for Westwatch as soon as we get this place tidied up. You don't need to bring her back to this place with it looking like thieves have turned it over."

I sat back in my chair, blinking owlishly at both of them. "You're ... coming with me?"

Thatcher gave my shoulder a reassuring shake. "Of course. I've got Fornax and the tandem saddle for us, so you just worry about your dragon. We're here for you, Reigh. As long as you want us, we're here."

I stared back down into my bowl of stew, my pulse already quickening. We would go to Westwatch. We'd find Violet. One way or another, I would figure out what was really happening here.

Even if it was something dangerous and deadly.

Gods, if it was, I just hoped I wasn't already too late.

3

VIOLET

I always ended up on the wrong side of town.

Er, well, the wrong side of everything, honestly.

That was generally where all my business had been done for as long as I could remember. Back alleys and sketchy side streets littered with crates, barrels, and drunks were my home turf. Run-down taverns packed full of vagrants and mercenaries. All familiar territory.

But, Fates, I *had* to see him.

I needed to.

I couldn't do anything else until I did.

"Close one door before you open another, Vi."

Those words stung at my heart as I walked my horse along the muddy road leading in from the south. I'd bought the old gelding off a farrier outside of Halfax, who seemed wildly confused at why I'd be willing to pay five gold for him. Now, I better understood why. The poor beast couldn't handle anything faster than an ambling stroll after I'd pushed him so hard through the mountain roads, but I wasn't in a rush. I needed to go slow, to feel every step, to drink in the smell of the wet, dark earth and the brine of the cold western ocean.

Maldobar had several lovely coastal regions. Many I had visited over the years while I worked for Arlan. But nothing about this place was beautiful. It was rugged and fierce, brutal and blunt.

I loved it.

The skies were choked with thick gray clouds, and the rugged, bare mountains to my right seemed to jut straight upward like an impenetrable wall of dark gray stone. The land that spilled off into the sea to my right was barren—nothing but drab prairie grass that was riddled with briars.

Here, the winters were long and ruthless. The summers, I'd heard, were a brief reprieve from the constant blast of the sea wind that only lasted a few weeks. The farther north you went, the colder it grew.

Thankfully, I was almost there.

My cheeks and nose were numb from the icy wind that had turned the mud into half-frozen sludge. I looked up through my tousled hair to see the city rising in the distance, perched in this narrow strip of land between the mountains and sea. The crowded buildings seemed to huddle against one another, bunched up like barnacles and made of the same dull gray stone as the mountains. Their thatched roofs were crusted with years of sea salt, and their chimney stacks spat plumes of dark smoke.

But Westwatch tower was the largest of them all. It rose above the landscape like a black spike, visible for miles in every direction. That was the dragonriders' tower—one of their four great strongholds.

The thought made my breath catch and my pulse skip.

My dragonrider ...

I squeezed my eyes shut. My mouth screwed up. Gods, Reigh must be going out of his mind. He'd be furious. Hurt. Sad. Confused. He'd start doubting himself because of what that wretched elven girl had done to him. He'd think I had abandoned him just like she had.

I'd have to find some way to make it up to him, to convince him he could still trust me. That I was still worthy of his time. I should have said something. Gods, I wanted to.

But then he would have wanted to come with me.

And I had to do this alone. It was my penance. When it was over, I would go back. I'd beg his forgiveness. I'd explain everything.

Just ... not yet.

I squeezed the reins harder, my jaw tightening. I should have left him some sort of message. A note or a letter telling him I'd be back. But the news of what had happened to Sulam would spread quickly, even here. I needed to get to them first. There was no time to hesitate.

It was done. I had left days ago, and I couldn't afford to turn back. Reigh might come after me, but it would take him time.

Hopefully, enough time to see this finished.

My stomach fluttered. Every nerve in my body hummed with tension, drawn far too tight for far too long. I had to find them. Whatever the cost, I had to do this. Reigh would forgive me. He had to.

Otherwise ... everything in my life had been a lie.

The biggest lie I'd ever been told.

I LEFT MY HORSE WITH A FARMER OUTSIDE THE CITY WALLS.

A few gold coins bought his silence and a helping of good grain and hay for my noble steed. The elderly farmer must have known better than to ask too many questions. He took my coin and left it at that. Smart man.

I ran my hands along the animal's strong neck, unfastened my haversack and weapons from the saddle, and left.

The hike into the city was only a few miles, and I kept to the road with my hood pulled low. With my hair now bound into a tight braided bun, no one would see it. I needed to keep a lower profile here. Maybe I should have dyed it?

I'd done that before, when I first came to Maldobar. Viperi were unheard of in this part of the world, so my features made me even more of a spectacle. White hair, red eyes, and skin as pale as milk—all viperi had those features. I couldn't do much about my complexion or eyes, but I had dyed my hair darker gold and even black a few times. It helped keep people from staring.

Well, most people.

My hair had been dyed gold when I'd first met Reigh, but he had stared anyway. It was impossible not to feel a little tingle of pride at that memory. That poor man was awful at guarding his emotions. His face betrayed his every thought.

And when he looked at me, I could see the awe and affection written all over him.

It made my chest constrict with another sharp jab of guilt. I was hurting him. Right now, I was causing him pain.

I had to do this fast. I had to get back to him.

The muddy streets carried me through the yawning south gate of the city, past the high ramparts and towers where guards patrolled. The great stone walls were still scarred from the Tibran war, with sections obviously recently repaired, scorched black, or pocked with holes left from catapult fire.

Banners of blue and gold hung along the entrance, their ends frayed from being whipped around in the constant sea wind. The skies were grim and dark, still thick with clouds, but every now and then, I heard the rhythmic thunder of dragon wingbeats.

The dragonriders were flying patrols, too.

My eyes welled, and a smile twisted over my lips, half agony ... half a deep, incredible feeling I never thought I'd feel for someone again.

Before him, I'd been terrified of flying. Before him, I had been determined to prove that any love for me would be a short-lived farce. I hadn't dreamt of a home, or a family, or quiet evenings by the fire, curled up together reading and sipping sweet Lunthardan wine.

But now, Reigh was everything. My heart. My safe place. My wings.

My fire.

I couldn't lose him.

I had to close this door.

Tonight, I would.

Nightfall drew closer, the heavy clouds smothering the last rays of sunlight like a blanket thrown over the land. I made my way through Westwatch's portside streets, passing fishermen and dockhands tightly bundled in their clothes, weathered faces to the wind. They didn't even glance my way, likely used to seeing folk come and go through this place.

It wasn't one of Maldobar's busier ports, but I'd learned it was one of the oldest. Maybe that was why a sense of grim stoicism seemed to grip it like a knight's steel gauntlet. Proud. Stiff. Stern. Resolute in the face of time.

I walked until I found the place—a dumpy little tavern right off the docks. Light glowed from the old, cracked windows, and the plucking of a lute carried through the half-open door. A wind-battered sign swung from a rusted hook over the eaves, the painted face of a one-eyed cat all but worn away.

This far away from the tower, I doubted I'd see a dragonrider. As much as they liked to go out, take a break from their cramped quarters, and drink away their pay, they wouldn't stray far from the center of the city. Certainly not this, toward the docks.

I peered through the partly open door, taking a quick inventory. No fine blue cloaks trimmed in fox fur. No armor. Just sun-baked sailors, grimy fishermen, and a few burly dockhands turning up tankards and muttering.

Overall, the place was fairly busy, despite how empty the streets were outside. A few especially loud sailors were playing a card game in the corner and crowing with laughter. A bit closer to the small stone hearth, a young gray elf minstrel picked away on her lute and hummed sweetly. More figures crowded tables, heads down and voices low, although it was difficult to get a solid read on any of them from so far away.

I smirked. Perfect.

No one looked up when I finally stepped inside—not even when I took a seat at the bar and ordered a glass of whatever passed for wine.

The barkeep, a tall, middle-aged man as thin as a reed and red-faced as a schoolboy, fumbled clumsily as he hurriedly rushed to the cellar. He was gone for a while, long enough that I wondered if he'd fallen down the stairs and injured himself. Odd.

When he finally reappeared, bottle in hand, he poured me a glass with shaking hands. His mouth twitched and mashed from one side to the other as he set the full glass down on the bar and slid it slowly toward me. His throat bobbed with a hard swallow.

Hmm.

"Not used to a lady darkening your door, I'd wager?" I asked, honeying my words as I took up the glass and swirled it lazily.

A strange shimmering hue on the surface of the liquid made my pulse skip.

Poison? Or something else?

He could hardly choke out words, and sweat was beading on his forehead as he hacked a nervous cough. "Y-yes, well, mostly we see sailors, ma'am. Ruffians from the ships and locals. Not many travelers through this part of town."

"I see." I held the glass up, pretending to admire the color.

A glimmer of motion behind me glinted in the glass's reflection. Someone sat alone at a table in the corner, right by the window—a slim, tall figure with a hood pulled low, nearly invisible in the deep shadows.

I frowned.

Turning slightly, I angled my glass again, spotting a similar pair of figures seated on the other side of the room, just behind the minstrel. The glint of their eyes caught in the weak firelight, but their faces were too deep in shadow to make out unless I turned around for a better look.

I traced my teeth with my tongue, weighing my options. There were any number of reasons I might be targeted. Being viperi, of course, was first and foremost. My kin were despised in nearly every corner of the world. Being Arlan's heir was another. He had many enemies hungry for his influence and resources—all of which had been passed to me now.

This felt different, somehow. These individuals had been posted in the room before I even came inside. They were lying in wait and counting on the barkeeper to soften up their prey with either poison or something to make me woozy. Hard to tell which without tasting it.

Hoping to abduct lone women traveling through, then?

But why did the barkeeper seem so rattled? His hands shook as he fumbled around, wiping down the bar and putting away tankards—all while his gaze darted between the cloaked thugs lurking in the corners of the room and me. Sweat rolled down the sides of his face. And he dabbed at it with his washcloth.

I smirked. Fine, then. Only one way to find out what this was *really* all about.

I turned the glass up, letting the liquid touch my lips to feign taking a sip. Then I waited. The barkeep moved further away, his fidgety demeanor intensifying. I pretended to take two more sips before touching my brow, blinking hard, and making a show of squinting.

Without a word, I put a silver on the bartop and stood, leaving the glass of wine untouched. I started for the back door, ducking around the crowded tables and pretending to stagger. I held onto the wall, the backs of chairs, and even stumbled into one of the other patrons. I slurred an apology and quickly ducked out the back door.

The dark of the moonless night swallowed me whole. This side of the tavern, facing away from the docks, was angled into a narrow, dead-end alley. The reek of old seawater, rotting garbage, and vomit made my stomach turn. No lamps burned. But I didn't need them.

Sidestepping, I dropped my haversack and pressed my back to the cold stone wall of the tavern just beside the door. Then I slipped one of my daggers from the side of my boot.

With a hard blink, my vision changed. I saw shades of gray instead of pitch-black and could easily pick out the shapes of trash and debris strewn about the alleyway. A few small spots of warm body heat appeared—rats crawling around the piles of garbage.

I held my breath, letting my senses open.

The soft thud of footsteps approached, reverberating over the wooden floors in the tavern nearby. Voices murmured on the other side of the door. Deep. Two men.

I squeezed the small dagger tighter. My lips pulled back in a snarl, and my pulse quickened as adrenaline flooded my veins like molten metal.

The doorhandle creaked. The hinges groaned. A cloaked head emerged.

Every muscle in my body clenched hard, coiled to strike.

Wait—I had to wait.

I couldn't make a move without seeing some evidence that this person was, in fact, coming back here to pursue me. It could just be a drunken patron staggering back here to vomit or take a piss.

The man stepped forward, his cloak obscuring his face. It didn't matter. I spotted a hand emerging from the cloak, armed with a small crossbow. His head turned, looking down the alley toward the exit that dumped into another side street. Searching.

I didn't know what they wanted. To murder me. To kidnap, rob, or violate me. Maybe all of that and worse. It didn't matter, though.

He'd picked the wrong woman tonight.

The man's head turned again, to glance in my direction.

And I struck like a coiled serpent.

Snatching an arm around the man's neck, I dragged him downward and jabbed my knife into the side of his neck, right at his shoulder. He cried out, and I twisted my arm, slinging him aside. He hit the putrid mud and rolled, gasping and gripping his neck.

His accomplice wasn't far behind—and apparently a lot more experienced in combat.

I barely had time to spring back out of the way as he rushed me, shortsword drawn and eyes wild. He pressed in, forcing close combat, and I ripped my twin blades from their sheaths at my hips. My spelldrinkers.

The two long, much larger daggers hummed through the air as I parried, each with a ten-inch blade molded in the shape of a sloping bird's wing. Pure dwarven vidrathian steel. Ruthless, light, and elegant.

The man leaned in, hitting with brutal force. Probably hoping to overpower me. I dipped each swing, whirling and feinting around the swing of his sword. Sparks flew as our blades locked, and I drove a knee into his gut.

He barked a cry and staggered back a step. I lunged in immediately, going for his neck.

BAM!

My vision swerved as something slammed into the side of my head, making spots dance in my vision. Another crushing blow hit me right in the gut, and I wheezed, barely managing a glimpse of a second, much larger man with bare, burly arms. He clamped a large hand over my windpipe and slammed me against the nearest wall, squeezing so hard I thought my neck might snap.

I couldn't stop it, then. The surge of rage that lit up my spine like a cannon fuze exploded in my brain. Everything went red.

I snarled and dropped both my daggers. His puffy face wrinkled with a smile ... right before I twisted my body, snatching the second small knife hidden in the side of my other boot and ramming it into his forearm all the way to the hilt.

Then I gave it a brutal twist.

The massive man howled in pain and released his hold on my neck.

I dropped to the ground in a crouch and kicked forward, grabbing my daggers where I'd dropped them, and swinging wide.

It was a deadly dance. The bigger guy was now working with only one arm, but he moved fast for a man his size. The second still swung with that blade, performing clean strikes and parries like a well-trained soldier. Definitely Maldobarian. A former infantryman?

With both of them looming over me, raining blows in a constant barrage, I didn't notice the third until a crossbow bolt hit me square in the bicep.

Pain exploded in my arm. I screamed—half in agony, half in fury.

It took everything I had not to drop my dagger.

Another crossbow bolt howled through the night, and I barely managed to dip to the side as it blurred past my head.

Curse it. I wasn't prepared for this.

Or for the fourth man who came barreling out the tavern's door, axe in hand, to join the fight.

I darted back, faltering as my arm throbbed. My hand was already going numb as blood left warm trails under my clothes. All four men prowled toward me, cutting off the only path out of the alley. I was cornered. Injured. Under-armed for a fight like this.

Fear settled in the pit of my stomach like a stone at the bottom of a frozen lake.

Think. I had to think.

WHAM!

The biggest of the men jolted strangely, his expression suddenly going blank. He coughed a mouthful of blood before he fell forward like a cut tree. The remaining three men hesitated, watching in slack-jawed surprise as their giant comrade hit the ground in front of me, face down, with a short-staffed morningstar mace sticking out of the back of his skull.

We all looked at once to the other end of the alley that emptied into the street, sharing a few seconds of shock and awe. A tall figure stood, stance wide and still gripping another one of those spine-studded morningstars.

My lips parted, heartbeat skipping as I glimpsed a slender jaw and long, coppery-red braid peeking out from beneath a ragged hood. Then she looked up, her face visible thanks to my viperi vision, and her lips slanted in a cruel smirk.

Gods ... that was—

The men scrambled. They shouted at one another like they couldn't decide who was in charge. Two rushed for the mace-wielding figure. The one with the shortsword came for me.

I liked these odds much better.

Dropping the dagger in my wounded arm, I met him blade-to-blade again. We blurred through maneuvers, stepping and whirling as our weapons hummed a deadly melody against the roaring chaos going on at the other end of the narrow alley.

I saw it—an opening. A hitch in his gait. He left his right guard slightly open. That was all I needed.

I dropped into a roll, kicking to the side and surging in as fast as a whip's snap. Hooking a heel around his ankle, I slammed my shoulder into his. He faltered. Fell. His blade clattered across the stones, too far out of reach.

I drew back to end it.

"NONLETHAL!" A feminine voice shouted from the fray down the alley.

I flinched and froze, blade poised less than an inch over the hollow of his throat. Lying on his back beneath me, his hood now thrown back, I got a good look at the man's utterly horrified expression. He was middle-aged, maybe in his early forties, and his face was a wreck of old battle scars.

His throat jumped as he swallowed, not daring to even breathe.

I held his gaze a second longer, my lips bowing into a vicious, hungry smile. "You're lucky tonight, soldier," I hissed before slamming the blunt end of my dagger into the side of his head.

One stern, solid blow, and he flopped back, unconscious.

I stayed crouched, studying him a few seconds longer. I didn't even notice the rumble of combat had gone silent until the crunch of footsteps approached and stopped right next to me.

"Well, well. You always did know how to get in way over your head," the woman's voice murmured, tone tinged with smug amusement.

I stood, spitting on my fallen enemy's chest, before I glanced at her. "I had it sorted."

She snorted, her deep green eyes flicking over me with an appraising arch to her brow before she finally met my stare.

I couldn't help it. I did the same.

She stood nearly a foot taller than me—which wasn't a great feat, honestly. I was barely an inch over five feet. And Chrysa ... she had always been taller. Even when we were children.

But now she rivaled Reigh in stature.

She had thrown off her cloak, revealing shoulders that were wide and taut with lean, hard muscle and tattoos of swirling runes down both of her corded bare arms. While her waist was narrow, her hips were wide and shapely in her fitted fighting leathers. All her rugged clothes were trimmed in fur, and her face still bore the faint pale lines of scars across her forehead and cheek just beside her nose.

Chrysa still gripped one of her short-staffed morningstars, the spiked bulb at the end dripping fresh blood. She'd always preferred abrupt weapons, and these seemed to have been crafted especially for her. Appropriate and not at all surprising.

"Friends of yours?" I asked as I reached for the crossbow bolt still sticking out of my bicep. Just a flesh wound, thank the gods, but it sent pangs of agony down my arm and through my shoulder.

Chrysa crossed her arms and cocked her hips, watching me crack the bolt off and leave the tip still embedded in my muscle. I'd have to deal with it later.

"Hardly. There's still a lot of tension here from the Tibran war," she said dryly. "This area was invaded and practically razed to the ground. The locals have endured much. Many of the population are former Tibrans, stranded or displaced from their homeland. They're trying to carve out new lives here, but the locals haven't exactly welcomed them with open arms."

I nodded, listening as I stalked toward my haversack and pulled out a length of gauze to wrap and stabilize the wound until I could see a healer for it.

"The local Maldobarians are none too pleased to have Tibrans of any sort lingering where they were once burning homes, even if it was at the command of a tyrant," Chrysa went on. "Some of them have begun assembling in secret, calling themselves the Threshers, and stalking the streets and taverns."

"They're just roaming around in packs looking for former Tibrans?" I turned in time to see her wander over and rip her other mace out of the back of the dead man's head with a gory crunch.

"That's what they'd claim—but their tastes have become less discerning. They go after anyone who looks like an outsider," she replied.

Fantastic. That was a problem. Not one that I could solve, though.

Jaevid Broadfeather and his gaggle of do-gooders would be better suited to looking into it.

"Do they give you problems?" I had to ask, given her ... history. She clearly wasn't a local, either.

Not with that Tibran slave mark branded into the side of her neck.

"They've tried." Chrysa's hungry smile crinkled that scar beside her nose. Beneath that, she was staggeringly beautiful. Her gingery-red hair was thick and long, woven into a heavy braid she wore slung over one shoulder.

"I'm surprised you wanted me to spare him, then," I mused as I slung my bag over my shoulder and resheathed my weapons.

She tipped her chin to the one I'd left unconscious. "He was infantry, but his injuries forced him from the ranks. He scrapes by as a tanner now. He's got a wife and four children. They'd starve without him."

My brows rose.

"Shocked that I care?" she called me on it.

I shrugged. "And that you know."

"I keep an ear to the ground." Chrysa bent to rifle through the big man's pockets, seizing a pouch that jingled with coins. She didn't meet my gaze as she stuffed it into her own belt. "I assume you didn't come all this way just to beat up the village idiots in a back alley together for old times' sake."

Fair enough.

I straightened, facing her with my expression as controlled as I could manage as the words left my lips numb. "I need to see him."

She stood, not even glancing in my direction, as she worked her jaw from one side to the other. Thinking. Choosing her words carefully.

When she finally met my gaze again, something different shone in her eyes. It was fractured and tired, worn down over years spent battered and bleeding.

My heart seemed to twist in my chest.

"You're sure?" Her voice was quiet. Cautious.

I nodded slightly. "I gave him my word."

"It won't change his mind," she warned.

A faint, broken smile brushed my lips. "I know. He's stubborn that way."

Her smile mirrored mine, dying long before it ever reached her evergreen eyes. "They call him the Wolf of the Wastes here. He hates it."

"Because he's started hunting again?" I guessed.

Her small, indifferent shrug passed for a confirmation.

A beat of tense silence passed before I dared to speak again. "I know it won't change anything. But this is my debt. I have to repay it before things can … go on."

She bobbed her head like she understood. "Come on, then."

I lowered my head and followed her out of the alley, stepping over the fallen thugs. My pulse quickened, thudding hard and fast against my ribs as my lungs seemed to close tighter and tighter with each breath.

Fourteen years—I hadn't seen him in fourteen long years. Not since I'd left the southern kingdoms behind and set myself to work here, in Maldobar. Not since everything had gone wrong and broken both of us so completely.

Now, I'd face him again.

The man I had so cruelly betrayed.

4

REIGH

I couldn't move.

Standing in the front room of a slummy inn on Westwatch's dockside road, all I could do was watch through the cracked glass pane as Violet and another, very tall woman strode away into the night.

Garnett had an iron grip on my arm like she was afraid I might bolt for the door or bash the glass out and run after them. I couldn't even feel my legs, though. I could hardly even breathe.

All the sensation and warmth had drained from my body as I stood, noting how Violet now favored one of her arms. Something had happened to her. She was injured.

But, Gods and Fates, she was alive.

"They're going north," Thatcher observed, his voice hushed.

Garnett's expression was solemn as she slowly released my arm.

"That other woman—is she someone you know?" I stared down at her, the numbness spreading to my face and neck.

Garnett must have noticed the sheer desperation in my eyes because she loosed a heavy sigh and stepped away from the window. "Her name is Chrysa. She's ... an old work acquaintance."

"She's got a Tibran brand on her neck," Thatcher pointed out.

"And nothing but venom in her veins," Garnett added darkly. "But if Chrysa is here, it's not a far leap to work out who this Wolf of the Wastes really is. Stones, curse them. I should have known they'd all come here. Violet must have given them one of Arlan's old safehouses to stay in."

"Who?" I demanded.

Her brawny little shoulders heaved with resignation, and she gave my arm a consoling pat. "It's not my tale to tell, love. This you most certainly need to hear from Violet's mouth, not mine. You ought to follow, but take care—Chrysa is as well trained as your lady. They'll catch on if you get sloppy."

"We aren't going?" Thatcher stepped toward me, his tone defensive.

Garnett ambled to his side, but didn't touch him. All the joyous light that usually danced in her lavender eyes had gone dark. Her forehead was creased with thought. Or maybe concern.

"This isn't for us," she replied at last. "Trust me. He won't want us there. And besides, dragonriders are never truly alone, are they?"

Thatcher's mouth scrunched unhappily. He stared at me like he was waiting for me to object or insist they tag along.

But ... I understood it.

Garnett was right. Whatever was about to happen with Violet, it was personal. Deeply and profoundly personal that she felt she had to endure alone.

If I went after her, then she might be furious. But she had left without telling me anything. What else could I do except find some way to reach her? To make sure she was all right? I had every right to be terrified out of my mind when I found her gone without a trace.

Still, it was one thing to see that she was alive and somewhat safe, and another to march up to her and start demanding answers.

None of this was good.

And I knew I had to face it alone. I had to see what this was all about. I needed to understand why.

"Wait for me here, would you?" I put a hand on Thatcher's shoulder as I walked past him for the door.

He muttered a sour word of agreement, and I could feel the heat of his disapproving glare on my back as I put my cloak on and ducked out into the bitter night wind. Thatcher was nothing if not loyal. He didn't know how to go into any relationship or friendship half-way. It was a good thing.

Most of the time, anyway.

I turned into the howling north wind as the figures of Violet and Chrysa grew small in the distance, all but lost to the moonless night. They kept to the main road, continuing north. I had to follow and keep a low profile.

Gods willing, this wouldn't all end in disaster. Hopefully, she would at least hear me out long enough to explain to her the fresh, unfettered hell I'd been through the last few days trying to find her.

The gods had never cut me much slack, though.

And I had no reason to start expecting miracles tonight.

I HADN'T NEEDED MY LUNTHARDAN SCOUT SKILLSET IN QUITE SOME TIME.

No surprise, I was rusty. Stealth had never been my strong suit. But in the hopes of not betraying myself right away, I followed from a considerable distance and took side streets and cut-throughs when I could. Anything to keep out of sight whenever possible.

I guess it worked, because they never stopped.

The two women were hardly more than specks in the night, making their way farther to the north until they passed through the gate leading out of the city proper and into the open, wind-blasted landscape known as the Salt Wastes. I'd only flown over this side of the kingdom coming to and from the Canrack Islands for dragonrider training, and it looked bleak even from a few hundred miles in the air.

Slogging my way along the slushy, near-frozen, muddy road ... I couldn't say it was any better from the ground. The mud stank of rotten seawater. The wind howled in from the sea like a constant blast of ice against the side of my face. It cut straight through my cloak and dragonrider uniform all the way to the bone.

To my left, the vast, dark ocean expanse loomed in the distance, barely visible under the starlight that managed to break through cracks in the heavy clouds. To my right, there was only open, flatlands leading to the base of the mountains miles away. No farms. No houses. No trees or little scrubby bushes. Nothing except brittle, brown sea grass grew in the marshy soil.

We continued on for hours, hiking miles to the north until the lights of Westwatch shrank behind me. Dawn had just brushed the eastern sky, hitting the white of the snow-crowned mountains with faint pastels of pink and orange, when I saw it in the distance.

The shabby little stone cottage was the only thing standing for miles around far off the road and facing the ocean. Warm light glowed in the windows, and dark smoke curled in a dark wisp from the chimney.

Someone was home.

Suddenly, I realized my mistake. I'd been so distracted, so caught up in the worries and what-ifs, I'd forgotten any need for stealth. The sun was rising, and out here in the open, there was nowhere to hide. No cover to duck behind. They would definitely see me, even from a long way off.

Curse it.

I had no choice, then. I had to keep going. I had to confront this head-on.

My stomach clenched and cramped as I went on, back rigid and fists clenched at my sides.

Up ahead, I watched Violet and Chrysa approach the house. Chrysa stayed back, giving a few yards of space, as Violet stopped before the door. With their backs turned, I couldn't see either of their faces or hear anything they might have said over the wind. I was still too far away. Fates, I couldn't even tell if they had spotted me yet.

But I saw it when that door opened, and the huge silhouette of a man—or maybe a beast—eclipsed the light. Whatever he was, he was massive, and tall pointed ears stood up from his head like a wolf.

And I saw it when Violet fell to her knees before him.

5

VIOLET

Oh gods ... I couldn't do this.

Chills rushed through my body, prickling up my spine and over my scalp. I couldn't move. I couldn't blink. Too much—this was too much.

Everything around me seemed to fade away to smears of color and fuzzy, muffled noise as the cottage door slowly swung open. Light poured out from within.

And there he was.

His massive frame filled the doorway, dressed in rugged leathers and furs. The cloak he wore was made from the pelt of a black wolf, the head of it serving as a hood. It made him look like some sort of shaggy beast. His dark golden hair had grown out and gotten darker at the roots, falling over his wide shoulders and down his chest in messy braids. The points of his ears peeked through that tousled mane, pierced with golden rings, and his deep, moss-green eyes narrowed slightly.

But his face—gods. Every second he held my stare felt like another year rolled back, carrying me farther and farther back in time. Shrinking me back into that wretched little feral beast I had been before. The Violet he had known and trained with. The girl who barely understood herself, let alone how her actions impacted anyone else.

The one who had hurt him so profoundly.

Tears filled my eyes.

My knees buckled, and I hit the ground before him with a desperate sob.

Declan didn't move. He didn't say a word.

It took everything I had, every shred of strength, to reach into my pocket and take out that old signet ring. It was dirty and battered, but I knew Declan would recognize it as I shakily held it up for him to see. My wounded arm throbbed, but I kept my hand stretched out.

Neither of us would ever forget the hand that had worn it.

"It's done," I gasped, my head bowed. "Sulam is dead."

Grit crunched under Declan's boots as he took a step closer. I flinched when I felt his heavy, callused fingers brush my palm as he took the heavy gold signet ring.

I held perfectly still.

"You killed him?" he asked, his voice still that deep, rumbling growl that made my pulse stammer. There was no kindness in it. No warmth.

I clenched my teeth, managing to hiss, "I slit his throat and let him die like a pig, choking on his own blood."

Declan made a grunting noise, but I couldn't tell if it was approval or indifference. His stony expression betrayed nothing when I dared to glance up at his face. He held the ring up, turning it over and studying it.

The years showed on him. He looked a lot older, because we both were, and yet he'd lost none of that savage beauty of a man hardened and made powerful by years of combat. Chalk that up to his elven blood. His sharp features were fiercely handsome, even with deep creases in the corners of his eyes and across his forehead. The tattoos that ran up his neck to his jaw were a bit faded with time, but they still suited that hard glower he wore.

"Why come all the way here? You could have sent this and spared us from having to see your face," he retorted as he stuffed the ring into his pocket.

My heart gave a violent twist. My chin trembled. I couldn't stop it—that feeling that welled up from a dark, forgotten place in my soul. The shame and grief. The last words we'd said to each other all those years ago.

I deserved his hatred. His dismissal.

I knew that.

And yet, a foolish part of me had hoped this might change something. That he would see that our friendship had mattered. That I still cared about him and wanted—needed—to make this right somehow.

"Declan," Chrysa growled his name in warning. "She has submitted. She has atoned. Can we not put this behind us? What more do you want?"

He turned his face away, jaw clenching so hard it made a vein stand out against the side of his neck.

I bowed my head, drowning in the silence filled only by the howl of the wind. There was something else. Something I needed to tell both of them because ... because they understood what it meant. But the words hung in my throat, stinging and pricking like I'd tried to swallow a sea urchin.

"I-I ... I found him," I finally managed to rasp brokenly.

More silence.

I sucked in a sharp breath as Declan's footsteps crunched closer again until he stood right over me.

"I can see that," he muttered low, his tone still stiff. "He followed you here ... and brought reinforcements."

My heart stopped.

Wh-what?!

I nearly fell over as I whipped around, frantically scrambling to my feet. My entire body trembled, going numb in an instant as I gaped at the figure approaching in the distance. Even from so far away, the light of dawn fresh on the horizon, I knew him. His stride, always so stern and confident. His dark red hair blowing around his face.

Reigh. *My* Reigh.

He was here. He'd found me. And ... Declan was right, he hadn't come alone.

Farther behind him, the shapes of two dragons wheeled through the grey skies—one green and the other orange striped in black.

"A dragonrider?" Chrysa asked, arching a brow at me.

I couldn't answer. Not when every step Reigh took toward me made my heart tremble and my blood course with frigid terror. I wanted to shrink. To run. I'd left him without saying a word, and now here he was. He'd want an explanation, but I owed him so much more.

I owed him everything.

Reigh kept his eyes on me as he strode to us, breezing right past Chrysa like she wasn't even there. He stopped a few paces away and just ... stared. His expression was strange, caught somewhere between confusion, anguish, and relief.

The dark, heavy circles under his eyes betrayed that the last several days had been a nightmare for him—one I was undoubtedly responsible for. But he wore one of his fine dragonrider uniforms underneath his old traveling cloak. It was a touch of formality I wasn't expecting.

I held my breath, knowing full well what I must have looked like right then. Disheveled from travel. My hair tousled and fuzzed by the wind. My face streaked with tears.

A mess.

I took a stumbling step toward him. "R-Reigh, I ... I can explain, I just ..."

He hugged me.

I stiffened, choking on my breath, as he threw his arms around me and dragged me into his chest. Immediately, I was encased in his strength, his smell, and the sound of his voice murmuring against my ear. "Gods and Fates, woman."

I couldn't hold in a big sniffling sob as I clung to him, burying my face against his shoulder.

"You can't do this to me," he whispered as he stroked the back of my head. "Never again."

"Never again," I cried, squeezing him tighter. "I-I'm so sorry."

I didn't know why I kept doing this—hurting the people I cared for the most. It had been roughly fifteen years since I set foot in this kingdom, and in all that time, I hadn't changed. Not really. I was still running. Still reckless and stupid.

Reigh pulled back some, holding my face in his hands as his light amber eyes searched me. He ran his thumbs over my cheeks, wiping at my ears.

"You're all right?" he asked.

I bobbed my head a little.

"She lies," Chrysa spoke up. "She took a crossbow bolt to the arm. It needs to be treated soon."

I grimaced.

Reigh's expression darkened. "Someone *shot* you?" His gaze immediately flashed to Declan with an accusing glare.

"It's a long story, my dear," I cooed to him, stroking the side of his neck in a way I knew would diffuse some of that protective temper I'd come to adore. He never failed to take up the fight in my defense.

"You can tell him inside," Chrysa insisted, giving me her own hard, challenging look as she passed us on her way into the cottage. "Come. We'll have breakfast and you can see to her."

6

REIGH

None of this was going the way I'd expected.

Who were these rough-looking people? How did they know Violet? Was this going to devolve into a fight as soon as my back was turned? Why did I keep catching that enormous elven guy glowering at me out of the corner of his eye?

I didn't know, and it put all my nerves on edge as I stalked out into the open grassland beside the cottage, my eyes trained on the sky. Curse it, I'd told them to stay behind. I should have known better than to believe they'd actually listen. Well, Garnett probably would have, but Thatcher must have won that argument.

Ugh. Overprotective idiot. Didn't he have any faith in me at all?

Vexi and Fornax circled low, powerful wings flared and scales flashing in the morning sun. The earth shook with impact as they touched down, and I walked to meet Thatcher and Garnett before they could dismount.

"I distinctly remember telling you to stay at the inn," I growled.

Thatcher scowled down at me, the wind blowing his lengthy golden hair around his face wildly. "Old habits, you'll have to forgive me. The last time we got separated, you—"

I waved a hand, silencing him and shaking my head. He didn't have to remind me. We'd gone through some exquisitely horrible things in the Southern Kingdoms. I didn't blame him for not wanting to see any part of that history repeated.

"We'll go back," he relented, his suspicious glare panning over to where Violet stood before that massive elven man. "If you feel good about this."

I didn't. Not at all. But there wasn't time to explain everything to them, so I kept it brief and promised to meet them back at Westwatch Tower this afternoon. Right now, I had to go in and figure out what the heck was going on and tend to Violet's wound.

"You're sure?" Thatcher's frown was still suspicious.

I sighed as I unfastened my medical pack from Vexi's saddle. "Yeah. I think we'll be fine. Whoever they are, they know Violet, and it doesn't seem like they mean us any harm."

Garnett stared toward the cottage, her expression tense and distant. Almost like she'd just glimpsed a ghost.

"Watch the woman," she warned, her voice quiet.

I paused with my medical bag slung over my shoulder. "Is she a threat? You said she was a Tibran before, right?"

Garnett's brow creased, her brows scrunching together. "I don't know. I haven't seen her in a great many years. I'm sure much has changed, but I don't know where her loyalties truly lie now. Just be careful, love. Mind what you say to them."

I frowned and nodded. "I can manage."

Hopefully.

I stood back, watching as Fornax leapt skyward again and soared back toward Westwatch. Vexi stayed, flattening herself against the grass and eyeing me with her scaly little ears slicked back and her nostrils puffing in defiance. She wouldn't go back with them—not with me still here.

"Keep watch, girl. I'll be back." I patted the end of her snout.

She made a few affectionate, musical clicking sounds and curled up with her tail and wings tucked in tight. She lay, a mountain of green and yellow scales, with her bright blue eyes tracking me all the way to the cottage door.

It helped—knowing that she was there. If it came to a fight of any kind, I wasn't in it alone. If Violet and I needed to run, all we had to do was call for her. I was a dragonrider. I was never truly alone.

Remembering that made me stand a little straighter when I entered the small cottage.

The first floor was mostly a rustic kitchen. Pots and pans hung from hooks on the ceiling, and bundles of drying herbs were hung over the table. A stairwell in the far corner led up to the second level, probably to a bedroom or two.

Two rusted iron and glass lamps hung on chains from the ceiling, leaving the room thick with shadows. The stuffy, warm air smelled of soot from the wood stove, and everything about the place was battered, worn, and old—like maybe they had found this place abandoned and patched it back together well enough to live in. It didn't seem like the right time to ask about any of that, though.

All eyes were on me as I stepped inside and shut the door.

Violet sat at the kitchen table, her hands in her lap, and her expression drawn into a tense look of withheld panic. On the other side, the massive elven man had to sit back since his too-long legs wouldn't fit under the table.

It made me snort, remembering the last time I'd seen Jondar. He had the same problem. I guess not much in Maldobar was made to accommodate the stature of Holvradix elves.

The woman, Chrysa, gave me a cold glance over her shoulder as she stood at the stove, cooking eggs and bacon in a large black skillet. My stomach gave a hopeful growl. It had been far too long since Garnett's stew.

I sat down next to Violet and dropped my pack of medicinal supplies on the table. Scooting my chair around to face her, I began pulling out my tools and setting them on a clean white strip of cloth. I had specialized tongs, slender scissors, needles, thread, gauze, healing salves, and everything else all neatly arranged.

"I'll need some hot water," I said and motioned for Violet to take off her cloak and roll up her sleeve.

"A dragonrider, prince, and a healer," Chrysa observed as she set a bowl down beside me and filled it with steaming water from a big kettle. "You have a lot of titles."

"Let's not forget Harbinger of Clysiros," Violet added with a taunting smile as she presented me with her blood-smeared bare arm.

I rolled my eyes. "That one I *would* like to forget, actually. Just call me Reigh."

Chrysa didn't reply and went back to her cooking. Meanwhile, the giant of an elf—all dressed in his furs and leathers—still didn't say a word. He was watching me much more intently now, though. Almost like he was watching for any sign of foul play as I began gently cleaning Violet's wound with a rag dipped in the hot water.

Awkward.

Violet gave me a tense, apologetic little smile.

"And you are?" I dared to task, still focusing on my work.

"Chrysa," the woman replied flatly. "And he is Declan."

"And you're what? Zenith's Call?" I flicked Violet a questioning glance.

Her brow furrowed slightly, and she immediately looked away.

"No," Chrysa replied.

"Mercenaries?" I guessed again.

Chrysa made an amused, snorting sound. "Something akin to that, yes. But we do not work in Maldobar, if that's your concern, prince."

"Reigh," I reminded her, hating the sound of that title even more when she said it. It sounded like a slight or an insult. It probably was meant to be one. "And Violet is my only concern here. If she doesn't have a problem with you being here, then neither do I."

No reply. Not even from Violet—who was staring away at the floor like she wished she could vanish entirely. Not that I blamed her, really. I doubted any of this was going how she'd planned.

"We heard that Arlan the Kinslayer has died," Chrysa spoke up again after a few long, excruciating minutes of silence filled only by the crackle of the fire in the stove and the sizzle of bacon.

The latter didn't bother me much, though, to be fair.

"Is it true, then? That he was killed in Nar'Haleen? And that he passed his empire to you?" Chrysa's tone had a slightly critical edge, almost like she found that especially hard to believe.

Violet seemed to shrink into herself, the light in her scarlet eyes dimming. "It's true. I don't understand why he did that, to be honest. I'm still trying to sort out what it means ... and what to do with any of it. Some of his key people took the opportunity to retire, and I have no intention of forcing them to stay."

I stole a glance up at her, wondering if she was talking about Garnett and Roxus.

Probably.

"You could dissolve it completely if you wished," Chrysa pointed out as she began slicing a loaf of dark bread.

Violet's sigh was tight and strained—probably because I'd begun gently widening the wound so I could work the barbed arrow tip out of her arm. "That is an option, yes."

"But he has been grooming you for this." Chrysa's tone was impossible to read. I couldn't determine if that was a statement of fact or just an educated guess on her part. "You already speak the necessary languages. You know the divine history. All his secrets. All his connections. And now that Sulam is dead, your name would bear far more weight of influence even in the southern kingdoms."

Violet swallowed hard.

"Why do you hesitate?" Chrysa pressed.

There was a glint of steely defiance in Violet's eyes when she shot her a look, mouth pursed sourly. As though she knew Chrysa already had the answer to that question.

But Chrysa just arched an eyebrow expectantly.

"I'm sorry to have to remind you of this *yet again*, but I am Viperi. Our reputation doesn't carry the same credibility as someone of Avoran blood, now does it?"

The big guy shifted in his seat, but still didn't make a sound. Tension hummed off him like energy, filling the room with subtle pressure like a blackpowder keg primed to explode.

Chrysa's green eyes seemed to smolder, narrowing slightly as she held Violet's gaze. "Credibility? No. But some might argue your reputation carries something just as meaningful in that business."

"Fear," I guessed.

They were both staring at me now.

I cleared my throat and went back to work, gently tugging the arrowhead free before I began cleaning her wound. She didn't so much as flinch the entire time.

"Arlan named you as his heir, so he had faith that you could carry on in his stead." Chrysa went on, beginning to spread out a modest breakfast on the table while she talked. "But just as he hid his true self, his true motivations, behind the mask of being the feared criminal lord—you will also have to adopt such a persona. You are not an ancient Avoran. But you are a Viperi. The reputation of that name alone will give you all the respect and credibility you might need."

She did have a point. Violet likely wouldn't even need to do much of anything to reinforce her claim to his criminal empire. All she had to show up, look scary, and most would cower before the monster they most feared without her having to lift a finger."

Too bad I could see the discontent written all over her beautiful face. She didn't want that—to be viewed as a monster. If half of what she'd told me about her childhood was true, she had spent most of her life trying to throw off that stereotype.

Embracing it would likely feel wrong ... and like a betrayal of herself.

I put a hand on her knee. "You don't have to decide anything right now," I murmured quietly. "Arlan offered you this opportunity, but that doesn't mean you have to take it. He gave you the greatest gift he could—he gave you a choice about your future. But it's your life, and I don't think he'd fault you for choosing your own path, instead."

Her smile was weak and twitchy, but real.

"Frankly, given the complete brush-off he gave me while I was trying to find you, I think you should drop all this responsibility in Roxus's lap. Did he really say he was just going to retire and walk away?"

"He did." Her eyes welled some as she gave a little, sniffling giggle and covered her mouth. "Gods, he would be so furious."

I gave her a wink.

Her smile widened.

"You would support this?" The big guy finally spoke, his voice a deep, gruff growl as he pinned me with a smoldering glare. "You, a prince and dragonrider, would support this woman becoming the leader of a criminal network? You would march her into the castle as your partner?"

I didn't even blink. "I already have. Several times, actually. She gets on quite well with my sister."

His jaw clenched, eyes narrowing as his nostrils flared a little. One of his eyes twitched.

Fine. I'd had enough of soft-stepping around this guy. I didn't know what his problem was, or why Violet had come all this way just to fall at his feet like she was begging for forgiveness, but I didn't owe him a thing.

I finished wrapping up Violet's wound and wiped my hands clean, then turned to face him. "Why? Is that a problem for you? She came all this way and fell at your feet, for reasons I can't even begin to fathom, but you won't even acknowledge her? Just who are you, exactly? And why should anything you say carry any weight with me?"

Declan's eyes widened in surprise. Maybe he had expected his stature and aesthetic to be intimidating to me. Yes, he was hilariously taller than I was. Undoubtedly physically stronger, too. But it would take a lot more than that to rattle my cage.

I had lived through the Tibran war, faced down ancient sorcerers and tyrants, fought monsters straight from the deepest pits of the abyss, and stared the goddess of death straight in the eyes. I wasn't about to tremble in fear in front of any mortal man, no matter how tall he was.

"Who I am wouldn't matter to someone like you," he growled again. "But I expected a prince might have higher standards."

I let all of that anguish and pain, the years of suffering, of fighting through the mire of being chosen by a goddess who really only wanted to use me as a pawn, fill my expression like the creeping cold of a deep winter. "I fail to see how my standards are any of your concern, *outlander*."

I bit at that last word, expecting full well that it would probably touch a nerve.

I didn't know much about Holvradix elves, just what little Jondar had told me about his father, but I knew they didn't look kindly on those who abandoned their people. Jondar's father had done that—had left his clan and life among the Holvradix—and so become what they called an outlander. An exile, basically.

This guy was likely only half Holvradrix, too. But based on the way he dressed, he must have held some sentimentality toward that part of himself—even if, simply by being here, that meant he could never be a part of their culture again.

Declan bristled, massive shoulders tensing and hunching forward slightly. He put a hand on the tabletop between us. Every one of his knuckles was thick with scars, misshapen, and too large—like he had injured them repeatedly over a long period of time.

"You think you know me?" His voice rumbled deeply.

"I've known men like you my entire life." I held his gaze and never blinked once. "Angry at the world. Paralyzed by the unfairness in their lives. Wasting away behind scowls and bitter words, thinking somehow if they stay angry long enough, it might prove something."

One of his eyes twitched again.

I shook my head and scoffed, "It doesn't, by the way. You'll die angry, bitter, and completely alone. No one will mourn you. They'll be relieved by your passing because they no longer have to step softly around you. And when you pass into the Sivanth, where my brother will receive you, you'll realize what a waste it all was. That you didn't prove a thing except that you're an insufferable coward."

Violet went stiff next to me, as though she were holding her breath. Her eyes were as wide as two scarlet moons, and all the color had drained from her face.

Declan's lip curled into a snarl. His nose twitched. But I could see it—the cracks in that mask of scowling fury. The grief and shame behind it. I didn't know him. But I knew what that meant. He'd lost something important. Something he was desperate to blame Violet for.

But beneath it all, he knew who was really to blame. He just hadn't allowed himself to admit that, yet.

"You don't know me. And you don't know her. She will lie," he fumed defiantly. "She will hide things from you."

I smirked. "Well, she already tried that. You can see how well it worked out for her."

Violet's throat jumped. She finally let that tense breath loose, blushed, and looked down into her lap.

"I don't expect her to tell me everything that goes on in her life," I added. "And I don't understand why she does some of the things she does. But I know her heart. I know she fights tooth and nail to keep her word when she gives it, and she carries the burdens of her failures much longer than she should. I also know that whatever she was before, she's mine now. And I don't intend to let her go easily."

Violet put a hand on mine, squeezing it hard. Her scarlet eyes shone, glistening with tears.

Tense silence filled the small, dimly lit cottage. Out of the corner of my eye, I saw Chrysa and Declan exchange a brief glance—his filled with quiet rage and hers with icy warning.

"Interesting," Chrysa said at last as she sank down into the chair next to Declan, sitting back and crossing an ankle over her knee. "It seems in the end ... he was right, after all."

Violet blinked hard, wiping shakily at the tears that spilled down her cheeks.

I frowned. "Who?"

Violet squeezed my hand harder.

Declan's thin mouth pulled into a proud smirk, and he slowly shook his head, never breaking eye contact with me as he sank back in his chair. "Well, you were right about one thing, prince—she has not told you much of anything that happened in her life. Seems she has not changed much, after all."

"Declan," Chrysa barked his name like a warning again.

But this time, he didn't stop. I'd egged him on too much. Now he was looking to retaliate. "You ought to ask her about it now, while we're here, so we can tell you whether or not she lies to your face."

Violet's chair screeched across the floor as she jumped to her feet, her face flushed and her eyes still teary. She glared at him, her whole face twitching with anger. "Shut up—just shut up, you miserable, self-righteous prick! Who do you think you are that you would put me on trial? Like you have any idea what I've been through!"

Declan went still, staring up at her with a look of genuine shock.

As though she'd never stood up to him like this before.

Violet leaned down, jabbing a finger at him with a snarl. "I did not kill your sister—Sulam did that before you even set foot in that gods-forsaken pit. All I did was throw back the curtain and show you the truth, and you chose to believe his lackeys instead. Now I've made him pay, all but brought you his head on a pike, and you dare speak about me that way?!"

I didn't dare to move. Not unless I saw Chrysa or Declan make a move, first. My heart thundered in my chest, and I watched Violet seethe hissing breaths through her teeth as she glowered at him.

"I have atoned for my part in what happened," she snapped. "You may keep this house, but consider it a parting gift. Reigh is right. I will no longer carry the burden of your regret, Declan. We are finished."

He opened his mouth like he might shout something back, but Chrysa slammed a hand down on the table in front of him so hard it made all the dishes and my medical tools rattle.

He shut his mouth, licking his teeth behind his lips and keeping that heated glare on Violet. I had to admit, the fact that Chrysa could reprimand someone like him without even saying a word spoke volumes about who was really the one to fear in this room.

I made a mental note never to cross that woman unless I had absolutely no other choice.

Violet turned to me, and I could see right away that she was fighting to keep her composure. Her mouth was pressed into a tight, crooked line and her chin trembled. "I'd like to leave, please."

Fates, I couldn't agree more.

Nodding, I packed up my gear quickly while Violet crossed the room and slipped out the door. Then I was alone with the two of them while I crammed my supplies back into my bag as fast as I could without breaking anything.

After what felt like a frantic, uncomfortable eternity, Declan stood and went upstairs. I heard a door slam somewhere on the upper level.

Good riddance.

"It was not always this way between them," Chrysa murmured quietly, looking at the breakfast she'd made and sighing. "It is as you say—that he is paralyzed by guilt and anger. He likely knows this, too. But he is stubborn."

The understatement of the year.

"Why do you stay here with him?" I dared to ask as I slung my bag over my shoulder. "Are you ... involved?"

It seemed only fair to assume that they might be romantically intertwined, given the hold she had on him. They obviously weren't siblings. They might just be *very* dedicated comrades.

"In a way." Her lips pursed thoughtfully. She picked up a fork and began dishing some of the eggs and bacon onto a plate. "It isn't that simple. And I suppose I am stubborn, too. I remember how he was. I keep hoping I'll see that man return. Maybe it's foolish, but I won't leave him to face the future alone, even if he never thanks me for it."

"And Violet?" I couldn't help myself. I needed to know.

"She was always a better person than the rest of us—an inconvenient trait for a Viperi. Take care of her, if you can. She's had very few people in her life she could truly count on. Perhaps that's why she still keeps things about her past secret. It will take patience and time."

"Good thing I've got plenty of both." I grinned and swiped a piece of bacon off the plate, cramming it into my mouth. "If you need anything, send a letter. I'll do what I can."

It seemed only right, given the history between Violet and this woman. Whatever had gone wrong with Declan—something about the death of his sister—it apparently hadn't bled over into the connection they had. Chrysa still defended her. That meant something.

I'd be a fool not to honor that.

Chrysa nodded, her expression as solemn and indifferent as ever. There was no hope of reading her thoughts or feelings just by looking at her. If Declan wore a mask, this woman wore armor.

Still, I had to respect that anyone wearing that Tibran brand had undoubtedly lived through pure hell. Whatever else Chrysa was, she was a survivor. Declan was too, I guess, although I hadn't noticed any Tibran brand on him. The scars on his hands were telling enough, though.

We all had a past. He just needed to work out how to deal with his and move on.

Because I wouldn't tolerate Violet graveling before him ever again. Whatever she had been before, she was my partner now. In life. In love.

To whatever end might come.

7

VIOLET

It was ruined—everything was an unfathomable mess now.

Of course there were things in my past I still hadn't shared with Reigh. Not that I didn't intend to, but it wasn't that simple. The time hadn't felt right. I ... I didn't know how he would react.

I didn't want to lose him.

I left the cottage and walked to Vexi, my legs still shaking as waves of heat rolled down my spine. I knew it wouldn't matter. Declan would never let it go. But part of me had hoped that, after all these years, he might have come to terms with what happened. That he might have realized that I wasn't his enemy—I never had been. I'd made stupid mistakes, yes. I had been a child. Gods, we both were.

Time hadn't changed anything, though. It had only served to harden him further. He would never choose to see the truth. He would never choose to heal.

And there was nothing I could do about that.

"There you are, you beautiful queen," I cooed as I approached Reigh's dragon, stretching out a hand for her to sniff.

Her warm snout pressed into my hand, puffing deep, humid breaths through my fingers. She made a rumbling, purring sound like thunder in her chest as I ran my hands along her scaly chin. She was proud as a mother hen, this one. I'd never been around dragons long enough to get to know any of them until very recently, and I could see the appeal.

They were large and dangerous, yes. But they were also wickedly clever and had a wide range of personalities. Vexi was used to being spoiled and had no issues making her opinions known. She was fiercely protective of Reigh—a trait we now shared.

"How shall I reward you for coming so far to find me, hmm?" I scratched behind her small, scaly, cat-like ears.

"I'm thinking a hot bath and a glass of good wine would be an excellent start," Reigh chuckled nearby. "For me, anyway. I'm sure she'd settle for some salmon."

I flinched, my shoulders tensing at the sound of his footsteps approaching over the dry prairie grass.

I didn't dare turn around to see him. Not yet. Not while I couldn't get my eyes to quit tearing or my face from going all twitchy. I swallowed again and again, trying to will it to stop. To regain control.

It didn't help.

Then his warm, strong hand settled onto my shoulder. He gently turned me around until I had to face him. Red-faced. Teary-eyed. Trembling like a caught fawn. Gods, just strike me down.

"Hey," he coaxed, his tone unbearably soft as he lifted my chin until I had to meet his gaze. "I'm going to take you home now, all right?"

Home.

Our home.

He still wanted me there.

"I-I'm so sorry, Reigh," I gasped in a ragged sob. "I was going to tell you ... I just ... I didn't know how or ... or when ... I-I should have—"

He pulled me closer, putting his arms around me again and holding me against his chest. His warmth was everywhere. His smell filled my nose with every sobbing breath.

And I was safe.

"I know you have a history. Fates know I do, as well. But the last thing I want is for our relationship to be built on trying to make amends or trying to prove ourselves to one another. So you don't have to explain anything to me about what happened in your past unless you want to," he said. "It's your future I want, Violet. Will you give me that?"

"Y-Yes," I managed hoarsely.

He pulled back some, brushing my windswept hair away from my face, and leaned down to press his mouth against mine.

Everything in my mind—the frenzy of fear, shame, and dread that had all but consumed me ever since I'd left Halfax—went quiet. And in the stillness, one thought crystallized. A truth I'd hold myself to forever.

"I love you," I whispered, my lips still brushing his.

He smiled faintly. "You're just saying that because I taste like bacon," he teased.

I smiled back. "Oh yes. It has nothing at all to do with you coming all this way to rescue me from what might be the worst day I've had in years."

"Might be?" He gasped in feigned offense, putting a hand over his chest as we walked to Vexi's back. "I'd like to remind you that I nearly died tearing portals in time and space a few weeks ago."

I elbowed him as he helped me up into the saddle. "*Nearly* doesn't count, darling."

Reigh threw his head back and laughed. "Noted! I'll try harder next time."

"Please don't. I'm not trying to set a record," I quipped.

He gave me a playful wink and climbed into the saddle in front of me, waiting until I had my arms tight around his middle before he gave Vexi the signal to rise and take off. She shook herself off and spread her wings to the gusting sea air. Her fangs flashed as she gave a trumpeting cry and sprang skyward.

As we soared toward Westwatch, I let my chin rest on one of Reigh's shoulders, talking directly into his ear so he would hear me over the howl of the wind.

"I do want to tell you about everything," I said. "About who I was before. About how I came to Maldobar to work with Arlan. All of it. When we get home, I promise I'll try."

"Then I'll listen," he replied.

"Some of it is going to sound terrible. I was not always a good person then. But there was someone who believed in me." The words burned from my face all the way down to the deepest core of my chest. "He was the one ... who told me to find you."

Reigh turned his head far enough to give me a confused look over his shoulder.

I winced. "I know. It's all going to sound very strange."

"Stranger than battling ancient Avoran sorcerers alongside godlings?"

Oh dear. He really had no idea. My life before this had been a bizarre tapestry of intrigue, divine secrets, betrayal, and murder. I hadn't joined the Zenith's Call entirely by choice, and I'd left them not knowing where I truly stood with them.

Part of me had always known that life would eventually bleed over into this one. Some things you couldn't outrun, no matter how far or fast you went. Perhaps Arlan had known that, too, and that's why he'd made me his heir—because I was probably the only one of his agents who understood what sort of power his criminal empire possessed.

And what could happen if it wasn't carefully attended.

"Whatever it is, we'll get through it," he added when I didn't answer. "I've got you."

I closed my eyes and let my head rest against his back. I did want to tell him. I wanted to trust him fully, to share everything and leave no hint of mystery about myself in his mind. I wanted him to know me fully in a way no one else had.

It would be uncomfortable. It might even hurt to reveal those things.

But I'd begun my life in darkest shadow. Now, sitting astride Reigh's beautiful green dragon with my body pressed against him as we sailed through the skies, I knew exactly how I wanted to spend the rest of it.

With both of us like this—together—soaring into the radiant light of the sunrise. Seeing everything. Fearing nothing.

And knowing we both had found real peace at last.

www.ingramcontent.com/pod-product-compliance
Lightning Source LLC
Chambersburg PA
CBHW070339030726
47504CB00001B/6
9781952554278